TALES IN CONTEXT

TALES IN CONTEXT

Sefer ha-ma'asim in Medieval Northern France

(Bodleian Library, University of Oxford, Ms. Bodl. Or. 135)

Rella Kushelevsky

Translations by Ruchie Avital and Chaya Naor

With a Historical Epilogue by Elisheva Baumgarten

Wayne State University Press | Detroit

ISBN 978-0-8143-4271-8 (hardback) ISBN 978-0-8143-4272-5 (ebook)

Library of Congress Cataloging Number: 2017951958

Published with support from the fund for the Raphael Patai Series in Jewish Folklore and Anthropology.

All facsimile pages are courtesy of the Bodleian Library, University of Oxford, Ms. Bodl. Or. 135, ff. 300a–339b.

Wayne State University Press
Leonard N. Simons Building
4809 Woodward Avenue
Detroit, Michigan 48201-1309
Visit us online at wsupress.wayne.edu

Dedicated to my late father of blessed memory,
Rabbi Yitzhak Eliyahu Geffen, with love

Contents

Abbreviations

Manuscripts

Bodl. Heb. d. 21 (2676)	Oxford, Ms. Bodleian Library Heb. d. 21 (2676)
Bodl. Or. 135	Oxford, Bodleian Library, Ms. Bodl. Or. 135 (1466)
Bodl. Opp. 27	Oxford, Bodleian Library, MS Opp. 27
Cambridge-Harvard 39	Cambridge (Mass.), Harvard University Heb. 39
Cambridge Add. 663	Cambridge, University Library Add. 663
Cincinnati 61a	Cincinnati, Hebrew Union College, Ms. Cincinnati 61a
Darmstadt, cod. Or. 25	Darmstadt, Hessisches Landes- und Hochschulbibliothek, Ms. Cod. Or. 25
Darmstadt, cod. Or. 26	Darmstadt, Hessisches Landes- und Hochschulbibliothek, Ms. Cod. Or. 26 (DARM Cod. Or. 26)
Jerusalem 1970	Jerusalem, National and University Library, Ms. Heb. 1970
Jerusalem 5245	Jerusalem, National and University Library, Ms. Heb. Jerusalem 5245 (Innsbruck)

Jerusalem 3182	Jerusalem, National and University Library, Ms. Jerusalem Heb. 3182
JTS 2374	New York, Jewish Theological Seminary, Ms. JTS 2374
London, Beth-Din 28	London, Beth Din and Beth Hamidrash, Ms. Lon Beth-Din 28
London-Montefiore 431	Ms. London, Montefiore Library 431
Manchester-Gaster 82	Manchester, John Rylands University Library, Ms. Manchester-Gaster 82
Moscow-Günzburg 111	Moscow, Russian State Library, Ms. Günzburg 111
Munich 95	München-Bayerische Staatsbibliothek, Cod. hebr. 95
Munich 100	München-Bayerische Staatsbibliothek, Cod. hebr. 100
Munich 140–141	München-Bayerische Staatsbibliothek, Cod. hebr. 140–141
Munich 207	München-Bayerische Staatsbibliothek, Cod. hebr. 207
Munich 222	Muenchen-Bayerische Staatsbibliothek, Cod. hebr. 222
Munich 495	Muenchen-Bayerische Staatsbibliothek, Cod. hebr. 495
Paris 716	Paris, Bibliothèque Nationale, Hébreu 716
Parma 2269	Parma, Biblioteca Palatina, Cod. Parm. 2269 (De Rossi 473)
Parma 2295	Parma, Biblioteca Palatina, Cod. Parm. 2295 (De Rossi 563)
Parma 2342	Parma, Biblioteca Palatina, Cod. Parm. 2342 (De Rossi 541)
Vatican 107	Vatican, Biblioteca Apostolica, ebr. 107
Vatican 249	Vatican, Biblioteca Apostolica, 249

Warsaw 374	Warszaw, Zydowski Instytut Historyczny 374
Wolfenbuettel 36.25	Wolfenbuettel, Herzog August Bibliothek Cod. Guelf. Aug., Wolfen Herz. Aug. fol. 36.25
Zurich 192	Zurich, Zentralbibliothek Heid, Heid Zurich 192

Printed Publications, Websites, and Archives

AJS	Association for Jewish Studies
AT	Antti Aarne and Stith Thompson
ATU	Hans-Jörg Uther, *The Types of International Folktales*, based on the system of Antti Aarne and Stith Thompson
Ben-Amos, *Mimekor Yisrael*	*Mimekor Yisrael, Classical Jewish Folktales* . . . , with an introduction and Headnotes, by Dan Ben-Amos
The Cambridge Companion to Medieval French Literature	Simon Gaunt and Sarah Kay, eds., *The Cambridge Companion to Medieval French Literature*
E.D.N.A.	IFA search engine: http://ifa.haifa.ac.il
EM	*Enzyklopädie des Märchens*
EedB	Étienne de Bourbon, *Anecdotes historiques, Légendes et Apologues*
Encyclopedia of the Jewish Story	Yoav Elstein et al., *Encyclopedia of the Jewish Story*
Gesta I	*Die Gesta Romanorum, Nach der Innsbrucker Handschrift*
Gesta M	[The] *Gesta Romanorum*, ed. F. Madden
Gesta Ö	*Gesta Romanorum*, ed., H. Österley
Gesta, Swan	*Gesta Romanorum*, translated by Charles Swan

Harmony of Form and Content	Jonah Fraenkel, *Harmony of Form and Content*
Ḥibbur yafeh mehayeshu'a, ed. Hirschberg	R. Nissim, *Ḥibbur yafeh mehayeshu'a*
IFA	Israel Folktale Archives
JAF	*Journal of American Folklore*
JQR	*Jewish Quarterly Review*
JSQ	*Jewish Studies Quarterly*
JSIJ	*Jewish Studies: An Internet Journal*: www.biu.ac.il/JS/JSIJ/
Midrash rabbah	2 vols. Vilna: Romm, 1887, and reprinted editions
Oqimta: Studies in Talmudic and Rabbinic Literature	ancientworldonline.blogspot.co.il/2013/04/new-open-access-journal-oqimta-studies.html
Pesikta zutarta	R. Tobias b. Eliezer, [*Midrash*] *Lekah tov (Pesikta zutarta)*, ed. S. Buber
PUSHD	Princeton University Sefer Hasidim Database
Talmud bavli	Vilna: Romm, 1880–1886. Reprint.
Th.	Stith Thompson, *Motif Index of Folk-Literature*
Tubach	Frederic Tubach, *Index Exemplorum*

Preface

The discovery—which I found surprising—that the thirteenth-century *Sefer ha-ma'asim* shares some quite extensive intertextual affinities with contemporary French literature first took shape during my work on the text. I had my first inkling when I noted a particular oddity in the compilation, combined with a certain sense of familiarity or even intimacy. In my efforts to make sense of these incongruent features, I attributed them to a number of factors: the fairly arbitrary sequence of the tales in the compilation, which for the most part do not correspond to a a specific editorial organizing principle; their episodic structure and the often schematic plot lines that run counter to modern expectations of narrative redundancy; idiosyncratic motifs borrowed from medieval French romances that are not typical of traditional Jewish contexts—all these gave me the impression of a certain distance, of a buffer between past and present. This process involved, to a certain extent, my adapting to a different horizon of expectations—that of a medieval audience. This made the compilation especially challenging, and the curiosity and interest that it piqued in me because of these distinctive features captured and retained my attention.

Throughout the reading, a balanced, tolerable level of tension is maintained between distance and intimacy. This is primarily so because everyone, whether during the Middle Ages or today, enjoys stories. What are love, family, community, courage? Contending with each of these spheres differs among different cultures in accordance with social and personal contexts, but human experiences are fundamentally universal and do not belong exclusively to one period or another.

Each story is impressively introduced with the phrase "*Ma'aseh be-*"—"A tale of" or "Once upon a time"—graphically designed in meticulous detail, offering a joyous promise to satisfy the expectations of everything stories can offer. Values such as prayer, Torah study, charity, as well as marital and family life come up frequently in the compilation. Religious and social values represent faith in the possibility of a better world, and this basic faith is also what leads us to view these tales in a favorable light, even if in the Western reality of today, cynicism seems to dominate almost every aspect of our lives. The experience of an encounter with a world that is familiar despite being so dissimilar is what generates the fluctuating impressions throughout the compilation; the intimate experience of reading that varies in response to a certain remoteness, sometimes both in the same story. The fusion of an aesthetic sensibility—which today we can identify as medieval—with modern notions that we tend to apply through our own reading processes is what makes these texts so stimulating for us today.

The literary-historic perspective in this book is manifested in an awareness of cultural symbols that serve as interpretive keys to an artistic product imbued with significance. Based on my comparative study, I suggest that the very fact of the intertextuality between narratives of two different cultures—Jews probably became acquainted with French narratives by way of oral performances and written texts—implies their participation in the great upsurge in literature and culture that occurred in France and Western Europe as a whole during the Middle Ages. Jews however, responded to it in terms of their own Jewish values and identities. Furthermore, intertextual links to Jewish sources imply a relative level of erudition on the part of the book's editor, possibly the scribe himself, and a readership that was quite conversant with the sources of the stories. Thus *Sefer ha-ma'asim* refutes the dichotomy, accepted in the past, that was seen as a result of the romantic orientation between belletristic literature geared to the elite, on the one hand, and folklore aimed at the broader and lower levels of society, on the other. The intertextuality in *Sefer ha-ma'asim* makes it impossible to draw simplistic conclusions regarding how this compilation of tales was conceived and received.

The edition of *Sefer ha-ma'asim* and the analytic chapters and discussions in this book are based on a comprehensive study supported by the Israel Science Foundation (grant 693/08), and conducted in conjunction with Elisheva Baumgarten. I am grateful to Elisheva, a longtime colleague and friend, for her conscientious and constructive reading of the manuscript *Tales in Context*: *Sefer ha-ma'asim in Medieval Northern France*.

The publication of the diplomatic edition of *Sefer ha-ma'asim* and the facsimile pages are courtesy of the Bodleian Library, University of Oxford, Ms. Bodl. Or. 135, ff. 300a–339b. I appreciate the kind assistance of Dr. César Merchan-Hamann, the Hebrew and Jewish curator at the Bodleian Library, and Dr. Rahel Fronda, the deputy curator.

Making *Sefer ha-ma'asim* accessible to readers of English was possible thanks to the work of Ruchie Avital and Chaya Naor, the translators of my manuscript. Ruchie Avital translated the compilation of stories in the second part of the book with a sensitive awareness of the medieval style of the text. Chaya Naor translated the first and third parts of the book. I appreciate her help in conveying my ideas into English.

The trigger for comparisons to French literature was my encounter with Simon Gaunt and Sarah Kay's *Cambridge Companion to Medieval French Literature*, especially its introduction. I can still feel the excitement I experienced while reading it, when I realized its relevance to my own research on *Sefer ha-ma'asim*. This enterprise was made possible thanks to Tovi Bibring, who devoted her time to translate relevant excerpts from Old French for me.

My gratitude to Nurit Shoval, an expert in Latin, for locating the Latin parallels of the *Sefer ha-ma'asim* tales in the exempla collections from the Middle Ages, and for translating and paraphrasing them. Special thanks to my research assistants Orit Kandel, Udi Sat, and Galit Brin. Galit, my longtime research assistant and dear student, prepared the initial drafts for the Hebrew notes included in this edition of *Sefer ha-ma'asim*, as well as the bibliography and appendices. Itamar Drori, who assisted me with an earlier research project of mine, prepared a first draft of the transcription of *Sefer ha-ma'asim*.

Eli Yassif and I share a common and deep interest in the Hebrew story in the Middle Ages. His pioneering article on *Sefer ha-ma'asim*, published more than thirty years ago, motivated me to engage in this study of *Sefer ha-ma'asim*. My thanks also to Idit Pinţel-Ginsberg and Prof. Haya Bar-Itzhak for oral parallels to tales in *Sefer ha-ma'asim* in the Israel Folktale Archives (IFA).

A complex study of this nature requires skill and knowledge in numerous and sundry areas. Due to the ramified nature of this research, I was helped by the suggestions, comments, and expertise of additional researchers and friends. These include Malachi Beit-Arié, Dan Ben-Amos, Edna Engel, Yehuda Galinsky, Avraham Grossman, Yaakov Guggenheim, Ephraim Kanarfogel, Benjamin Kedar, Ilana Klutstein, Rebecca Kneller, Nili Landsberger, Zohar Livnat, Sara Offenberg, Micha Perry, Adina Portowitz, David Rotman, Rivka Shemesh, Moshe Shoshan, Sandra Stow, Vered Tohar, Sarah Tsfatman, Dan Yaffe, and Israel Yuval. Special thanks to both lectors on behalf of Wayne State University Press—Ephraim Kanarfogel, as I later learned, and the anonymous reader—whose comments and suggestions contributed to the manuscript of my book. I would also like to express my warm gratitude to Revital Refael-Vivante, my colleague and friend in the Department of Literature of the Jewish People, for her wholehearted support.

I have learned a great deal from my teachers and colleagues, but most of all from my students. The recent years of teaching the stories of *Sefer ha-ma'asim* in the context of a course on the medieval Hebrew story, and the dialogue with the students that ensued, have given me great pleasure, and I thank them for the opportunity given me to hone, expand, and enrich my insights on *Sefer ha-ma'asim* and the medieval Hebrew story.

Bar-Ilan University, the Faculty of Jewish Studies, and the Department of Literature of the Jewish People provided me with a pleasant and genial work environment. Special thanks to the librarians at the Wurzweiler Central Library and the internal loan library, which I used extensively. I am also indebted to Chedva Agmon (Hebrew and comparative seminar library), Smadar Weisper (English seminar library), and Rona Tausinger (*Encyclopedia of the Jewish Story*). I spent many hours at the Institute of Microfilmed Hebrew Manuscripts (IMHM) in the Jewish National and University Library in Jerusalem, and would like to thank its staff, especially Yael Okun and Ezra Chwat, for offering their professional advice whenever needed.

Dan Ben-Amos is far more than the editor of the Raphael Patai Series in Jewish Folklore and Anthropology, which is hosting my book. I am honored by the interest he has shown in my research. His broad folkloristic perspective, along with his generous collegiality, encouraged me to ask that he consider publishing my book as part of his series. I would also like to thank Kathryn Peterson Wildfong, the director and editor-in-chief of Wayne State University Press; Kristin M. Harpster, the editorial, design, and production manager and Kristina Stonehill, the promotion manager. Special thanks to Mindy Brown, who edited my book's manuscript efficiently, attentively, and professionally, to Shlomo Liberman for his professional proofreading of the final text and to Kate Mertes for her meticulous indexing of the book.

There are no words to express my appreciation and thanks to my husband, Moshe, whose friendship, willingness, and love are the fuel that feeds my work. Our four children, their spouses, and our grandchildren are an immeasurable source of strength, power, encouragement, enjoyment, and love. Last but not least, I would like to express my gratitude to Yael Tendler, my only sister, for her constant love and generosity of spirit concerning my work.

This book is dedicated to my late father, Rabbi Yitzhak Eliyahu Geffen, whose passing at a ripe age I will apparently never cease to mourn. He was a role model for me and for our whole family. The writing of this book took many years, and his interest and regard for my work gave me great joy.

❧

The brief description of the structure of the book provided here may help guide the reader in making sense of the stories, their overview, and the individual analyses that follow.

The first part of the book consists of three chapters, in which I present my thesis that *Sefer ha-ma'asim* is a product of its time and place, and should therefore be studied within its medieval, Jewish, and European settings, particularly that of northern France. An investigation of the scribe's techniques in reworking his sources, Jewish and non-Jewish, into a medieval discourse supports this claim.

The second part of the book consists of a diplomatic edition of *Sefer ha-ma'asim*, and includes both the original Hebrew and the English translation of the tales. This is the first publication of a Hebrew-English diplomatic edition, accompanied with brief comparative comments, citations, and explanations. The publication of this edition will serve scholars from a wide range of disciplines, as well as a broader readership.

The third part of the book, "An Analytical and Comparative Overview: *Sefer ha-ma'asim*, Its Tales, and Its Parallels" (hereafter "Tales and Parallels"), offers an analysis of each tale as an individual unit, contextualized within its medieval framework and against the background of its parallels. While they are neither brief comments nor full-length articles, the studies in this section serve as the backbone for the introductory section and support generalizations put forward there. These short essays on each story offer potential directions for further elaboration in future forums. Some of the tales have indeed already been the subjects of full-scale articles—"A Slave for Seven Years," "The Poor Bachelor and His Maiden Cousin," and "One of Ten."

The four appendices in the book include facsimile images of the tale collection; a list of the tales, which follows their order in *Sefer ha-ma'asim*; a list of texts in

Ms. Bodl. Or. 135; and indexes of tale types and motifs (Tubach, ATU, Thompson, and IFA). The facsimile images reproduced in the volume are from the Bodleian Library, University of Oxford. While the entire Ms. Bodl. Or. 135 was recently digitized and retrieved into the Bodleian Library website, it is my hope that including the facsimile here will serve the convenience of the reader. Elisheva Baumgarten's epilogue adds social and historical background to *Sefer ha-ma'asim*, and discusses new ways in which *Sefer ha-ma'asim* and other story compilations may be used by historians to inquire into the everyday lives of medieval Jews. The bibliographical list includes manuscripts, primary sources, and studies. An alphabetical index of the tales precedes the general index. Transcriptions in this book follow the *Encyclopedia Judaica* rules and those of the Littman Library of Jewish Civilization.

Cultural, Literary, and Comparative Perspectives in *Sefer ha-ma'asim*

Sefer ha-ma'asim

A Compilation of Medieval Hebrew Tales in Northern France

> Once it was decreed that Aliḥaraf and Aḥiya, two of Solomon's scribes, would die at the gates of Lod. And the Angel of Death regretted that he was unable to vanquish them. And anyone who was within the city of Lod, the Angel of Death had no control over. And because Solomon was fond of them, he made Asmodeus swear that he would take them there.

This anecdote, which later ends with the deaths of Solomon's scribes, despite the king's efforts to deceive the Angel of Death, appears in a compilation of tales known in the scholarship as *Sefer ha-ma'asim*, one of the most impressive of its kind from the Middle Ages. The tale has its sources in the Babylonian Talmud (*Succa* 53a). In this version, however, the scribe omitted certain parts of the talmudic narrative, emphasizing instead Solomon's special affection for his scribes, the reason he helped them escape far from his palace to "Lod" (i.e., Luz), the city over which the Angel of Death has no control.[1] The motif of Solomon's special affection for his scribes, the changes made in the text compared to the original, and the very choice of this anecdote about Solomon's scribes—all these are significant when contextualized within the tale's new environment in *Sefer ha-ma'asim*. In the cultural consciousness represented in *Sefer ha-ma'asim*, the scribe, as a medieval topos, joins his patron in preserving collective treasures, and the story he included and adapted in the compilation can be seen as an *ars poetica* declaration about the nature of copying as a form of creative writing. The fondness

1. See more on Luz, where no one dies and where those who wish to die exited its gates: *Sotah* 46b.

of Solomon for his scribes, a motif that is first introduced in *Sefer ha-ma'asim*, is what seems to be important in this specific version of the tale. Scribes in the Middle Ages, both Jews and non-Jews, greatly interfered with the text, even with those attributed to a specific author. They adapted and changed the texts, added comments in the margins, and forcefully expressed their opinions of the text by means of their interpolations.[2] They presented their readers—and us, hundreds of years later—with stories that are familiar in some respects and new and surprising in others, with fascinating intertextual affinities.

The two definitions of the Hebrew word *sofer* are fused in the persona of the medieval scribe, in the range between preservation and innovation: a scrivener, skilled in the writing of documents, contracts and letters, bills and memoirs, according to the medieval meaning of the word; and in a certain sense also a creative writer according to the modern meaning of the word.[3] Although the division of these tasks is not unequivocal, and a number of scribes, narrators, and redactors were probably involved in fashioning the stories during their oral and written transmission up to the compilation's final consolidation, *Sefer ha-ma'asim* will be discussed in this book as a literary product of its time and place, in the thirteenth century in northern France, against the background of the culture of the society in which it was created, which is represented by the figure of the anonymous scribe.

Sefer ha-ma'asim in the Bodleian Library, University of Oxford, Ms. Bodl. Or. 135

Sefer ha-ma'asim includes sixty-nine tales copied in Ms. Bodl. Or. 135 (1466 in Neubauer's *Catalogue*), which is archived in the Bodleian Library in the Oxford Library.[4] Its boundaries are marked by a grandiloquent rhymed introduction and a closing verse. The first is a kind of prayer for the success of the task: "*Be'ezrat*

2. See Ta-Shma, "*Sifriyatam shel ḥakhmei Ashkenaz*" ("The Library of the Sages of Ashkenaz"), 21–39; Huot, *The Romance of the Rose*, 34–40.

3. See Abraham Even Shoshan, *The New Dictionary*, vol. 3 (Jerusalem: Kiryat Sefer, 1983 [Hebrew]), for the meaning of the word *sofer*.

4. Hereinafter Ms. Bodl. Or. 135, marked in the National Library of Israel 16385 (F). For a description of the manuscript, see Neubauer, *Catalogue* no. 1466, cols. 519–521; and for supplements and corrections, see Beit-Arié, *Catalogue, Supplement*, no. 1466. The total of 69 tales includes two tales each in two different versions ("The Loan" [nos. 2 and 34], as well as "Ukva" [nos. 15 and 61]), and tales that are attached to others and which therefore lack the typical title of "*Ma'ase be-*" (i.e., "a tale of . . . ," or "Once . . ."). Hereafter, references indicate tale numbers. Originally the manuscript did not contain the headings and titles, which I have added to facilitate the discussion. The tale titles are conventional in the study of folklore and in some cases are mine, due to various considerations.

ha-e'[l] oseh nisim, aḥel likhtov ma'asim" ("With the help of God who works miracles / I shall embark on writing these tales"). The latter expresses contentment and gratification: "All is done with no fault or disgrace."[5] Among them are tales involving the justification of God's verdict, sanctification of God's name, justice and wisdom, war and valor, demonology, adventures, travels, love and eroticism, as well as asceticism. There is a medieval flavor to the descriptions of herbs that cure leprosy; a fairy princess with golden tresses using magic charms to heal her lover's wounds and restore him to life; a fire-breathing dragon ("*tanin*"); a two-headed creature; and a giant's daughter for whom the rind of a watermelon containing twelve spies is no more than a speck of dust. Jewish, Christian, and Celtic motifs, which were readapted to the narrating community, are interwoven among the tales. The familiar and foreign intermingle. The rational and the miraculous are juxtaposed, creating an intriguing and challenging narrative.

The manuscript was apparently copied in its entirety by a single hand.[6] The time and place of the manuscript have been discussed at length. Eli Yassif, in his pioneering study of *Sefer ha-ma'asim* more than thirty years ago, assessed them based on a comparison of the sources and the time notations in the manuscript.[7] Malachi Beit-Arié dates and situates the compilation—based on a codicological examination and a linguistic consultation with Menachem Banit—in mid-thirteenth-century France, northern Champagne, and in any case from 1215 to the early 1260s.[8] Following Beit-Arié's criteria for the approximate date of the manuscript (mid-thirteenth century), the Bodleian's internet site gives the span of dates as 1226 to1275, leaving

5. Cf. the parallel phrase in use today: "All is done without error or omission." However, this phrase also suggests the scribe's affirmation of the legitimacy of his adapted or edited tales, especially in light of the many affinities in *Sefer ha-ma'asim* to contemporary non-Jewish literature, particularly French legends and romances, which will become evident throughout the chapters of this book.

6. Edna Engel cautiously makes this assumption on the basis of a paleographic examination of the manuscript. I would like to thank her for this and other paleographic data about *Sefer ha-ma'asim* in the following pages. Samuel, the scribe's name, is marked on pages 33b, 62a, and 99a.

7. Yassif, *Kemargalit bemishbeẓet*, 136–139 (first published in *Tarbiẓ* 53, no. 3 [1984]: 428). See also Yassif, "'Leisure' and 'Generosity,'" 891. Yassif points to 1215, which is mentioned in the manuscript (as the Hebrew year 4975), and the mention of R. Berakhiah Hanakdan after his death, *z"l* (of blessed memory), as reference points. There is some dispute over when R. Berakhiah lived, but the accepted view today is that he died before 1215. See Golb, *The Jews in Medieval Normandy*, 324–327. I am grateful to Tamás Visi for pointing this out to me.

8. On this decision and the reasons for it, see Beit-Arié, *Catalogue, Supplement*, no. 1466, 244–245; Beit-Arié, "Ms Oxford Bodl Or. 135: In the Margins of Yassif's Article," 631–634.

twenty-five years of leeway at each end of the century.[9] A sample paleographic analysis carried out by Edna Engel ascribes the manuscript to the late thirteenth century in France, with all the necessary caveats regarding verification by additional means. In light of the findings of the paleographic analysis, we can narrow the aforementioned time frame accordingly and adopt the *terminus ad quem* determined as the time of the manuscript: that is, between the early 1260s and 1275. This dating also seems reasonable in terms of the compilation of tales in itself and its sources, as will be explained in the following discussion. The manuscript made its way to England already in the late thirteenth or the early fourteenth century, according to the ownership signatures of the Bishop of Exeter (John Grandisson, 1327–1369), and this is yet another later touchstone for the dating of the manuscript.[10] The Bodleian Library received the manuscript in 1603 from the collection of Sir Robert Cotton Conningtonensis, together with other manuscripts that were transferred to the library in 1602–1603.[11]

The manuscript's 363 pages include quite a large number of works, not a single one of which is halakhic. Among them are two grammatical works and a dictionary by Abraham Habavli and Solomon b. Abraham ibn Pirḥon; lists of Hebrew homonyms, one of which is translated into Old French (transcribed in Hebrew); *Ben Sira*; the *Fox Fables* of R. Berakhiah Hanakdan; *Tales of Sendebar* (*Mishlei*); the pseudo-historiographical treatise *The Chronicles of Moses* (*Divrei hayamim shel Moshe rabbenu*); and *Midrash aseret hadibrot*.[12] *Sefer ha-ma'asim* is copied between *Tales of Sendebar* and *Divrei hayamim shel Moshe rabbenu* (300a–339b). This rich assortment represents narratives of different genres—fables, travel literature, historiography, and tales—that attest to the cultural milieu of the narrating community and the owner who commissioned the manuscript.[13] In its literary

9. Based on e-mail exchange with Dr. César Merchan-Hamann, the Hebrew and Jewish curator at the Bodleian Library, June 6, 2016.

10. His partially erased signatures can be found on pages 1b and 363a. Bible references that appear between the lines in Latin were apparently added by the owner, Bishop John Grandisson.

11. For more on the collection, which was founded in 1580, and how it reached the Bodleian Library, see Tite, "Lost or Stolen or Strayed," www.bl.uk/eblj/1992articles/pdf/article8.pdf, especially 108 (accessed July 5, 2016).

12. *Midrash aseret hadibrot* (346b–352a) is a compilation of tales and homilies about the commandments, originated most probably in tenth-century Persia, that was disseminated in many various manuscript versions throughout the Middle Ages. The version copied in Ms. Bodl. Or. 135 is different from the one edited by Shapira, *Midrash aseret hadibrot*. See Appendix B for further details of the manuscripts' contents.

13. For a portrait of the owner who commissioned the manuscript, as well as a description of the manuscript, see Yassif, "Theory and Practice," 888–889.

diversity the manuscript resembles works in French vernacular literature from the twelfth and thirteenth centuries. These included various writings in rhyme and prose, with a flexible definition of genres: romances, legends of the saints, rhymed stories (*lais*), and *fabliaux*.[14] The manuscript of *Sefer ha-ma'asim*, like its counterparts in French from the same period, is indicative of the great interest in literary writings in both the Jewish and non-Jewish societies. Because what we have here is an expensive copy on parchment rather than a print edition, the inclusion of the compilation of tales in the manuscript as well as the various prose works is fascinating and attests to an interest in prose writings, which is far from obvious.

The scribe was apparently commissioned by a wealthy patron for whom he produced the manuscript.[15] The writing is clear, Ashkenazic, and semi-cursive. The boundaries between the compositions in the manuscript are generally marked by introductory and closing verses written by the scribe, some of them in rhyme: "Alphabet of Ben Sira," "*Nishlemu hameshalim tehilah lemoshel—le Berakhiah meshalav memashel*" ("The parables have been completed, praise to the Maker [i.e., God]—to Berakhiah, crafter of the parables"). These verses are marked by quotation marks above the words to distinguish them from the texts themselves.

Each story begins with the large, graphically accentuated heading "*Ma'aseh be-*" (lit., "A tale of"), and the spaces around it render it even more prominent. While no illustrations accompany the tales (or any part of the manuscript), its aesthetics lie in a carefully crafted script (there are relatively few erasures, and the arrangement of the words on the page is pleasing to the eye), the accentuated headings in *Sefer ha-ma'asim*, and the scribe's rhymed poetic phrases. Yet the compilation's beauty, the effort of its copying, and the implied justification for its high cost reflect more than this. As Yassif puts it: "The fact that such a magnificent codex as the Oxford manuscript from the first half of the thirteenth century is entirely dedicated to tales is a clear indication of these cultural changes."[16] Yassif is referring to the intensified literary activity in Europe from the second half of the twelfth century, and he situates the growing interest in narratives manifested in *Sefer ha-ma'asim* within this process.

Sefer ha-ma'asim indeed played a role in the great cultural flourishing in France, and responded in various creative ways to the literary processes that occurred around

14. For the contents of the manuscripts of the period as a source for the perception of genres, see Busby, *Narrative Genres*, 147–151.
15. However, the absence of colophons throughout the entire manuscript might indicate that the scribe copied the manuscript for his own use.
16. Yassif, *Kemargalit bemishbeẓet*, 164.

it. At the same time, embedded in its stories are typical Jewish values with nuances and emphases that represent the narrating community during the time of the Tosafists and the Pietists of Ashkenaz. A consistent investigation of each tale on its own, within its context in Western Europe, where it was adapted and created, as well as its various affinities to earlier and later versions produces a comprehensive and detailed portrait of *Sefer ha-ma'asim* as a literary work that has features in common with other works in the same cultural context. At the same time it is a compilation with unique features, in that it is composed of stories that have their own individual histories in the Jewish sources.

Time and Place of *Sefer ha-ma'asim*: A Reassessment

Yassif presented a hypothesis dating *Sefer ha-ma'asim* to the second half of the twelfth century or the early thirteenth century.[17] In light of the findings of the current study, I suggest that this assessment be updated, determining the late thirteenth century as the time of the compilation and its location as northern Champagne, approximately in accordance with the time and place of the manuscript.

Yassif's considerations are based on a study of sources. He believed *Ḥibbur yafeh mehayeshu'a* by R. Nissim of Kairouan, which had already been translated in the Middle Ages from Judeo-Arabic, was one of its sources. He implicitly attributes differences in style between *Sefer ha-ma'asim* and the translations of *Ḥibbur yafeh mehayeshu'a* to translation versions that no longer exist. Assuming that the translations of *Ḥibbur yafeh mehayeshu'a* arrived in Europe at the start of the twelfth century at the earliest, and that a length of time is required for their integration into Europe, Yassif dates *Sefer ha-ma'asim* to the second half of the twelfth century or early thirteenth century.[18] However, the stylistic differences between the two works are not minor; they are substantial and cannot be overlooked—which brings me to conclude that *Ḥibbur yafeh mehayeshu'a* was not one of the sources of *Sefer ha-ma'asim*.[19] Yassif also referred to "The Weasel and the Pit" (no. 43) as indicating the date of *Sefer ha-ma'asim*, based on its similarity to a version of the *Arukh* by Nathan b. Jeḥiel of Rome of the late eleventh century. Since the Tosafists relied

17. Ibid., 139.

18. Ibid., 138–139.

19. Cf. "The Bizarre Deeds of Elijah the Prophet" (no. 1). The comparison in this story is based on Medieval Hebrew renditions of *Ḥibbur yafeh mehayeshu'a* in manuscripts from the fourteenth and fifteenth centuries, compared to the original Judeo-Arabic version in *Ḥibbur yafeh mehayeshu'a*, as translated by Hirschberg into Hebrew. Other tales in the *Sefer ha-ma'asim* which have parallels in *Ḥibbur yafeh mehayeshu'a* also represent different narrative traditions.

greatly on the *Arukh* dictionary in the first half of the twelfth century, Yassif assumed that the tale entered *Sefer ha-ma'asim* through them. "The Weasel and the Pit" is indeed indicative of the origin of *Sefer ha-ma'asim* in Ashkenaz during the time of the Tosafists, although the Tosafists lived and wrote during the twelfth century too, and there is no need to limit the time of *Sefer ha-ma'asim* to the late twelfth or the early thirteenth century.

I have several reasons to believe that *Sefer ha-ma'asim* in the format before us should be dated later, to the second half of the thirteenth century—presumably the late thirteenth century, close to the time of the manuscript or even simultaneous with it.[20] I based my hypothesis mainly on (1) the figure of the scribe, his creativity, and his involvement in *Sefer ha-ma'asim* beyond the technical act of copying, and especially the associations he created between tales in *Sefer ha-ma'asim* and other works included in the manuscript; (2) a study of its sources: The scribe played a major role in shaping *Sefer ha-ma'asim* in its affinity to other texts in the manuscript, and certainly in the compilation itself. He lent it its character, whether he copied groups of tales from previous manuscripts and combined them or produced new groups or created certain stories himself. His repeated comment in *Midrash aseret hadibrot* in the manuscript—"*katavti le-ma'ala*" ("I wrote above")—is particularly striking, referring to *Sefer ha-ma'asim* in order to avoid the need to copy the shared stories a second time. However, the versions of the stories in *Midrash aseret hadibrot* and *Sefer ha-ma'asim* are not necessarily identical, and in many cases, the differences are substantial.[21] This is an expression of the license taken by the scribe, which does not necessarily correspond to the norms of verbal precision. The comment "I wrote above" diverges from technical data to a type of intertextuality, although the version of the stories he had no longer exists. More explicit intertextual affinities can be found in the manuscript in two stories in *Sefer ha-ma'asim* which, as we shall see in the coming chapters, maintain a dialogue with Berakhiah Hanakdan's *Fox Fables* and *Mishlei Sendebar*, in the same manuscript. Consequently it seems reasonable to identify the time of the compilation with that of the manuscript, or at least not to distance them too much, thus attributing to the scribe or his predecessor the creative skills of a writer involved in reworking the tales he has copied.

Intertextual links within *Sefer ha-ma'asim* are a further consideration in deciding on the dating of the book and the role of the scribe in shaping it. The book

20. Perhaps a previous scribe of the entire manuscript is involved, but this does not significantly affect the dating of the manuscript.

21. Ms. Bodl. Or. 135 is early among the extant manuscripts of *Midrash aseret hadibrot*.

contains repeatedly used idioms, such as "*Kol hamekaḥeshet leba'alah mekaheshet leborah*" ("She who betrays her husband betrays her Creator" in two different tales); and repeats the expression "*neki'ut*" (lit., "cleanliness" in the sense of purity in family life) in two tales.[22] It contains repeated introductory formulations which, although familiar from other compilations, are conspicuous in *Sefer ha-ma'asim*: the testament of a father to his son on his deathbed; childless parents who have a son in their old age; and praise for the norms of prayer and time spent in the synagogue. Certain motifs are repeated more than once in *Sefer ha-ma'asim*, such as that of the deposit: A trustee is given a deposit for safekeeping and betrays his trust (or is accused of doing so). The name Saul ("Shaul") appears twice, in different tales, as a name given to a son born in old age. It appears feasible to me that Shmuel, the scribe who copied Ms. Bodl. Or. 135, or a previous scribe who was active near the same time—and from whom Samuel ("Shmuel") copied *Sefer ha-ma'asim*—is the one who created these links.

It is also possible to estimate *Sefer ha-ma'asim*'s date by way of its affinities with the writings of the Tosafists in that period. Although the commentary of the Tosafists extended over the twelfth and thirteenth centuries which, as mentioned, makes it difficult to determine an exact date, some of the book's sources in the Tosafists' commentary on the Torah and on tractate *Succa* might narrow this span of time for *Sefer ha-ma'asim*. These include R. Samson b. Abraham of Sens (d. 1214), R. Moses b. Jacob of Coucy (*Semag*; first half of 13th c.), R. Nathaniel, the student of R. Jeḥiel of Paris (d. c. 1265), the Tosafot of R. Asher b. Yeḥiel (Rosh, 1250–1327), and R. Ḥaim Paltiel (d. 1300). It would appear that *Sefer ha-ma'asim* was consolidated in the mid-thirteenth century.[23] From the aggregate of all the data, and not necessarily from each datum individually, the second half of the thirteenth century emerges as the time of the story compilation.

Further source criticism also suggests that *Sefer ha-ma'asim* was consolidated in the late thirteenth century. Five tales are common to *Sefer ha-ma'asim* and the compilation of stories in Ms. Parma 2295, whose *terminus ad quem* is the late thirteenth century in northern France.[24] Based on differences among the versions, they

22. Cf. a *baraita* cited in tractate *Avodah Zarah* 20, 2: "cleanliness leads to purity, purity leads to abstinence, abstinence leads to holiness."

23. See my discussion of "The Spies and the Giants in Canaan" (no. 44).

24. The shared tales are "Who Is the Thief?" (no. 16), "Ben Sever and Shefifon Ben Layish" (no. 27), "Saved from Drowning by Charity" (no. 31), "R. Joshua b. Levi and the Angel of Death" (no. 46), "Ukva" (no. 61). See the parallels in Ms. Parma (Kushelevsky, *Penalty and Temptation*, 25–28; 142–145; 199–200; 216–217). A further shared story, "Joab's Valor" (no. 4), appears in Ms. Parma with only the introductory sentence (*Penalty and Temptation*, 78).

were apparently not copied from one another but represent prevalent narrative traditions in northern France during the thirteenth century.

Similarly, a comparative study of the non-Jewish sources in *Sefer ha-ma'asim* and the relative profusion of associations with contemporary French works point to a marked familiarity with writings in vernacular French, most likely in the second half of the thirteenth century, when they became more popular (as attested to by the number of manuscripts from this period). These topics will be discussed at length in the following chapters. However, here I would like to point to a unique linguistic affinity of *Sefer ha-ma'asim* with one of the most well-known French works of the period—Béroul's romance about Tristan and Iseult—as a more specific clue for dating our compilation later in the thirteenth century.[25] The tale of "The Poor Bachelor and His Rich Maiden Cousin" (no. 55) in *Sefer ha-ma'asim* shares with Béroul's romance an episode of two young lovers who are discovered by the girl's uncle while they are in the same bed, a sword separating them. The boy's uncle, who in the French romance is also the girl's husband and in the Jewish story opposes the couple's marriage (but changes his mind later on), reacts in a sort of apologetic monologue:

> Bien puis croire, se je ai sens / Se il s'amasent folement / Ja n'i eüsent vestement/ entrè eus deus n'eüst espee / Autrement fust cest' asenblee.[26]
>
> (It is reasonable to conclude that / if they loved each other sinfully / they would not be dressed / and there would not be a sword between them / They would be together in quite a different way!)

And in *Sefer ha-ma'asim*:

> He said [the uncle to his wife]: If he intended to spoil her, he would not have placed a sword between them. But he acted solely out of their love. (no. 55)

The similar linguistic expressions in both narratives might serve as a clue to *Sefer ha-ma'asim*'s date, despite the differences in language. Both monologues share the syntax of the conditional sentence—"If . . . then,"—and are uttered in a similar situation. This is a level of internalization that allows us to hypothesize that the episode of the two lovers was adapted in *Sefer ha-ma'asim* some time during

25. For the dating of Béroul's version, see Béroul, *The Romance of Tristan*, ix.

26. Ibid., v. 2001–2006, 94, and the translation that follows, 95.

the thirteenth century, when the text of Béroul's romance—which was written only in the late twelfth century (1191)—became accessible to broader audiences, particularly Jewish communities.[27]

The affinity of another of the *Sefer ha-ma'asim* stories with *The Tales of Sendebar*, which was also copied in Ms. Bodl. Or. 135 (292a–300a), is yet a further indication of its date. There are two branches of this work: the Eastern branch known as *The Book of Sindebad* and the Western branch known as *The Seven Sages of Rome*. *The Tales of Sendebar* belongs mainly to the Eastern branch of the work, although it also has affinities with *The Seven Sages of Rome*. It would be expected for *Sefer ha-ma'asim*, in the tale entitled "The Prophecy of the Ravens" (no. 66), to rely on the Hebrew *Tales of Sendebar*, but this is only partially accurate. The tale has clear affinities with the Western branch as well—that is, to *The Seven Sages of Rome*. It parallels a tale unique only to the Western branch, known as *Vaticinium* (meaning prophecy).[28] This position in *Sefer ha-ma'asim* has implications for its date. Because the Western branch was known in Old French starting from only the second half of the twelfth century (1155–1190),[29] becoming more widespread in the thirteenth century, and because literary and cultural processes are gradual—in this case the adaptation of a European tradition of the work by a Jewish narrating community—I tend to date its integration into *Sefer ha-ma'asim* to a time during the thirteenth century, presumably its second half.

We can also draw further conclusions regarding the location of *Sefer ha-ma'asim* in northern France, where it was written, based on the penetration of calques from French on which I will elaborate later, and in light of the list of lexicographical words in the manuscript in French transliteration. As I noted earlier, *Sefer ha-ma'asim* was copied by a single hand. It is also likely that the compilation was located specifically in Champagne, where the manuscript was created. Champagne was an influential literary center in medieval France.[30] Chrétien de Troyes wrote in the twelfth century under the authority and patronage of Marie, wife of King Henri and countess of Champagne (1145–1198). The numerous affinities with the vernacular French literature in *Sefer ha-ma'asim* can be explained by the dominance of the literary climate that was created in this region.

27. "Text" in this context does not necessarily refer to written text; it may also refer to an oral performance.

28. For further elaboration and references, see part 3 of this volume.

29. See Speer, *Le Roman des Sept Sages de Rome*, 67–71.

30. See Benton, "The Court of Champagne."

In this book I refer to "northern France" particularly when referencing the intertextual connections between *Sefer ha-ma'asim* and French vernacular literature: for example, the works of Chrétien de Troyes and the ethos of courtly love which they represent, and Béroul's version of the *Tristan and Iseult* narrative compared to that of Thomas in Normandy. Romance literature also spread outside of France, to Germany and other countries of Europe, but its primary origin and inspiration was northern France. Its traces in *Sefer ha-ma'asim* indicate the role of French medieval literature during the twelfth and thirteenth centuries in the formation of *Sefer ha-ma'asim* as the first significant Western European tale collection in Hebrew. This implies also the effect of medieval French literature on the development of Hebrew tale collections in the Middle Ages by way of *Sefer ha-ma'asim*. I also use the term "northern France" rather than Germany to signify affinities in certain stories with the commentaries of the Tosafists on the Torah and the Talmud. Although the Tosafists wrote in Germany as well, the center of their *yeshivot* (study halls) and their dialectic method of study were in France. The more general term "Ashkenaz" in this book denotes a distinction between modes of adaptation and reworking of tales in the Judeo-Christian territory in Europe in comparison to their parallels in Arab countries. While in Ashkenaz they took on a different mode, one whose nature I attempt to explore, there is often no need in this context for a distinction between Germany and northern France. This is illustrated in a number of tales which I chose to read in view of values that were shared by Ashkenazi society as a whole.

The Narrating Community

The familiarity of the narrating community with rabbinic literature and with the linguistic stratum that typifies it is implicit in a reference to a variety of sources, the way they are used in *Sefer ha-ma'asim*, and the linguistic register of the Hebrew. About a third of *Sefer ha-ma'asim* (i.e., 22 tales) is from the Babylonian Talmud and earlier and later *midrashim* (with the exception of one story from the Palestinian Talmud).[31] Twelve of them are borrowed from the Talmud without the mediation of

31. Stories that belong to this category are "The Loan" (no. 2); "The Heir's Test" (no. 3); "The Drunkard and His Sons" (no. 6); "R. Meir and Kiddor" (no. 26); "The Seven Good Years" (no. 29); "Saved from Drowning by Charity" (no. 31); "R. Akiva's Daughter and the Snake" (no. 32); "A Valley Filled with Gold" (no. 35); "A Precious Stone from Heaven" (no. 36); "From Rejoicing to Mourning" (no. 37); "Hadrian and the Old Man" (no. 38); "The *Ḥasid* and the Ruler" (no. 39); "R. Ḥanina b. Dosa and the Snake" (no. 40); "Solomon's Scribes" (no. 42); "Soft-Shelled Walnuts" (no. 45); "R. Pinḥas b. Yair" (nos. 56–59); "A Meal of Herbs" (no. 62); "The Tribulations of Naḥum Ish Gamzo" (no. 63); "Naḥum Ish Gamzo and His Mission to the Emperor" (no. 64).

other sources, and a certain degree of literacy in the Talmud may be assumed.[32] In some cases, the scribe preserved the Aramaic of the Talmud either partially, in combination with Hebrew as the more dominant language,[33] or entirely.[34] More frequently the story was presented only in the Hebrew, either in translation and adapted to some extent[35] or based on later midrashic sources in the various versions of the *Tanḥuma*.[36] A basic familiarity with the Talmud is also evident in the epilogue from links among various talmudic sources in a manner unique to the *Sefer ha ma'asim*, compared to the other versions of the tale,[37] as well as references to exegetic and halakhic contexts that are neither mentioned nor emphasized in earlier versions of the story.[38] The compilation contains numerous citations and paraphrases of biblical verses that attest to proficiency in the Bible, as well as talmudic aphorisms in the original Aramaic or paraphrased in Hebrew.[39] Influences of the French are also discernible, such as certain mistakes in verb conjugation as well as the erroneous use of masculine and feminine pronouns.[40] Its style ranges from rabbinic Hebrew (manifesting a familiarity with midrashic and talmudic sources) to a lower register (for example, the use of the word *naḥash* for snake instead of the original *arod* in the source).[41]

The scribe was also familiar with the commentaries of Rashi and the Tosafists to the Talmud and Torah, at least to some extent, as evinced first and foremost in

32. "Pinḥas b. Yair" (nos. 56–59); "One of Ten" (no. 17); "Joshua b. Levi and the Angel of Death" (no. 46); "R. Akiva's Daughter and the Snake" (no. 32); "The Mother and Her Sons" (no. 12); "Hadrian and the Old Man" (no. 38); "Saved from Drowning by Charity" (no. 31); "Joseph-Who-Reveres-the-Sabbath" (no. 21); and "R. Meir and Kiddor" (no. 26). The tales that directly originated from the *Tanḥuma* are "A Precious Stone from Heaven" (no. 26); "R. Pinḥas b. Yair" (nos. 56–59; a combined influence of the Babylonian Talmud and the *Tanḥuma*); and "The Commandment of *Ẓiẓit*" (no. 18).

33. "Solomon's Scribes" (no. 42); "Joseph-Who-Reveres-the-Sabbath" (no. 21).

34. "Naḥum Ish Gamzo and His Mission to the Emperor" (no. 64).

35. "One of Ten" (no. 17); "R. Meir and Kiddor" (no. 26); "R. Akiva's Daughter and the Snake" (no. 32).

36. "R. Pinḥas b. Yair" (nos. 56–59).

37. "Slander Kills Three" (no. 30).

38. "Joshua b. Levi and the Angel of Death," in the epilogue (no. 46); "The Cow That Observed the Sabbath," in the story itself (no. 20).

39. E.g., "A person's legs are responsible for him. They take him to the place where he is wanted" (in Aramaic), in "Solomon's Scribes" (no. 42); "Come and see that it is not the snake that kills but rather the sin that kills," in "R. Ḥanina b. Dosa and the Snake" (no. 40).

40. Thus, for example, in "Joḥanan and the Scorpion" (no. 28), the word for "ring" is used in the masculine instead of in the feminine, as a result of French influence.

41. In "R Ḥanina b. Dosa and the Snake" (no. 40).

his selection of tales but also from his comments in the epilogues.[42] Four of the tales, in addition to the better-known "The Weasel and the Pit," are common to *Sefer ha-ma'asim* and the commentary by the Tosafists from the twelfth and thirteenth centuries. Three are less well known, and it is apparent that their choice was influenced by an ongoing discourse at the time rather than by previous versions in existing story compilations.[43] Numerous tales are retrieved from the more popular *Midrash aseret hadibrot*, which was adapted to a wide audience and was prevalent throughout Europe in various versions.

In light of the combination of scholarly and popular features, and of divergent sources from the Talmud, Midrash, Tosafot, and *Midrash aseret hadibrot*, *Sefer ha-ma'asim* would appear to have been geared to a broad yet educated audience. It becomes evident in recent studies that, alongside the elite of the Tosafists in France and their students, who were entirely submerged in the study of the Talmud and devoted to it all their free time, there were other individuals who studied Talmud and Tosafot but "chose to focus attention on varied areas of Jewish religious culture, such as religious poetry (piyyut), exegesis of piyyut and/or Bible and religious-ethical thought, Christian-Jewish polemics, and more."[44] Galinsky refers, in this quotation, to the different readerships of *Semag* by R. Moses of Coucy in northern France, but this is apparently true also for the potential audiences of *Sefer ha-ma'asim*, or particularly for its scribe and his milieu in France. The appearance of the Tosafist Torah commentaries in the thirteenth century is yet another aspect of the variety of readerships in France for the study of Torah and Talmud. Kanarfogel points to a scholarly class in northern France from among the Tosafists who engaged in Torah commentary and other Torah subjects, but not in the Tosafot on the Talmud. The study halls of these secondary elite scholars, unlike those of the more elitist circles among the Tosafists, appealed to a broader public, as opposed to the select group of scholars who studied the Tosafot with their rabbis using dialectic methods.[45] In Germany as well, there were different levels of literacy rather than a distinct and elite group of rabbis contrasting with an illiterate and uneducated majority. Kanarfogel demonstrates this, for example, with Ashkenazi practices at the synagogue services. Congregants were reciting by heart the daily prayers and the verses of the

42. These will be discussed in the next chapter, "The Reworking of Jewish Sources."

43. "Joab's Valor" (no. 4); "The Two-Headed Man" (no. 5); and "The Spies and the Giants in Canaan" (no. 44) are the three lesser-known tales, in addition to "Ukva" (no. 61).

44. Galinsky, "The Significance of Form," 311, and the broader context of this statement, 311–318.

45. Kanarfogel, *Intellectual History*, 289–373; 359–361.

Torah portion, thus manifesting a high level of "liturgical memory" among the laymen.[46] At the backdrop of this social portrait, the literacy of the scribe of *Sefer ha-ma'asim* and his readership in the talmudic and midrashic sources, as well as the exegesis of the Tosafists, come as no surprise. While tale collections are neither Torah commentaries nor liturgical texts for religious practice, the present study of *Sefer ha-ma'asim*, as compared to other popular tale compilations such as *Midrash aseret hadibrot* from the East, does confirm recent notions of literacy in Jewish societies in northern France and Germany.

The depiction of Christians is a further characteristic of *Sefer ha-ma'asim*. The work contains no explicit mention of Christians, since these are stories of early rabbinical sources. However, sometimes the figure of the Christian is implied between the lines, in the manner in which the tales were readapted in Ashkenaz. The Christian in one of the tales is referred to as a *min*, a heretic who does not merit the world to come. The Christian represents the pleasures of this world, in contrast to the Jew, whose pleasures are spiritual; see, for example, the concept of *Oneg Shabbat*—the delight of the Sabbath—in one of the tales.[47] Against the background of persecutions and forced conversions, *Sefer ha-ma'asim* warns its Jewish audience to resist the temptations of Christianity, or as the text puts it: "Bow not to the dead but to He who puts to death and revives the dead."[48]

Despite the clear definitions of identity and the distinctions between Jews and Christians, *Sefer ha-ma'asim* implies that Jews were familiar with the lifestyle of the Christians living around them and with issues related to Christianity. Two tales relate indirectly to the prevalent Christian discourse in the Middle Ages regarding the Seven Deadly Sins, which focused on the constant presence of evil that governs the world.[49] They are well known from the Babylonian Talmud and the Midrash, but the very fact of their being chosen and included in *Sefer ha-ma'asim*, along with their unique nuances in the epilogues, attributes these tales to a medieval discourse, representing a Jewish response to the Christian discourse regarding greed and gluttony, two of the Seven Deadly Sins.

As noted, one of the interesting findings of the current research is the strong affinity between *Sefer ha-ma'asim* and the literature of the period, especially in France and Western Europe as a whole. This is in line with various studies of the

46. Kanarfogel, "Prayer, Literacy, and Literary Memory," 252–260.

47. See Isaiah 58:13: "You shall call the Sabbath a delight."

48. "The Mother and Her Sons" (no. 12).

49. "A Valley Filled with Gold" (no. 35); and "Soft-Shelled Walnuts" (no. 45).

last decade, such as those by Susan Einbinder,[50] Sarah Japhet,[51] Kirsten Fudeman,[52] Hanna Liss,[53] and Ivan Marcus.[54] Unlike some of the examples in these studies, *Sefer ha-ma'asim* has no direct quotes from vernacular literature but rather demonstrates their adaptation into Hebrew and integration into Jewish stories, as will be elaborated in chapter 3. Its scribe presented to his readership stories familiar to them from their surroundings which were reworked to the point of being almost unrecognizable and modeled after stories in Jewish sources, as well as stories that originated in Jewish sources that were reworked to include motifs that were prevalent in Europe. Acquaintance with the vernacular literature is evinced mainly in thematic affinities, the selection of tales that represent aesthetic tastes of both the Jewish and non-Jewish societies in France, and the references to the short-story genre, examples of which were numerous and varied in the twelfth and thirteenth centuries: the *Lais of Marie de France*, which found its way into one of the tales in *Sefer ha-ma'asim*, through the mediation of R. Berakhiah Hanakdan;[55] tales embedded within a frame story, such as "The Seven Sages of Rome";[56] *fabliaux*, which left their mark on one of the tales in *Sefer ha-ma'asim*;[57] exempla;[58] and legends of saints, such as "St. Alexis."[59] The high concentration of very short anecdotal tales in *Sefer ha-ma'asim*, in some cases as many as three to a page, and the redaction that joined tales without any connecting interim homilies, underscore its status as a compilation of tales against the background of the popularity of the various genres of the short story in northern France.

In some cases we can find traces of romances of chivalry, such as that about Tristan and Iseult; *Yvain, or the Knight of the Lion* by Chrétien de Troyes; and

50. Einbinder, *Beautiful Death*, 139.

51. See Sarah Japhet, ed., *The Commentary of Rabbi Samuel b. Meir*, 250, as well as the conclusion drawn by the author in the introduction to her book (68–69) that this comparison to "love songs in the manner of the world" is indicative of Rashbam's familiarity with the general culture and spirit of his time.

52. Fudeman, *Vernacular Voices*, 120–121.

53. Liss, *Creating Fictional Worlds*, 148–193.

54. Marcus, "Why Is This Knight Different?"

55. "R. Meir and Judah of Anatot" (no. 25).

56. "The Prophecy of the Ravens" (no. 66).

57. "Hadrian and the Old Man" (no. 38).

58. On the formal acceptance of the exempla of Jacques de Vitry into *Sefer ha-ma'asim*, see chapter 2, "Genre."

59. "A Slave for Seven Years" (no. 52).

Aucassin and Nicolette by an unknown writer.[60] We can also discern traces of the quest motif typical of the romance, such as Chrétien's *The Story of the Grail*;[61] and of the French heroic epics, which is expressed by the inclusion of narratives of Jewish valor in the compilation.[62] It would appear that the narrator or scribe and his Jewish audience were well-versed in the local vernacular literature and were familiar with written versions or oral performances, or at least were aware of the oral traditions on which this literature was based. The adaptation techniques were varied, as will be discussed here later, but beyond their description and classification, they create and represent an existing literary and cultural discourse in Jewish society with a close affinity to a parallel discourse in the non-Jewish society in France, albeit with religious differences.

The stories emerge as junctures where a wide variety of Jewish and French vernacular sources meet and create a rich and dynamic textual fabric. The combination of these sources, the familiarity with French literature of diverse genres, as well as with talmudic and rabbinic literature, and their mutual integration into the compilation display a fascinating portrait of the society in which the compilation was created and the complex, varied ways in which it contended with the majority culture. Regardless of whether the various affinities with the literature of the surrounding society reflect cultural images and a common historical horizon or express an internal and external polemic for the purpose of stressing differences between Jewish and Christian values, the subdued tension between the internal cultural sources and those from the surrounding culture is a very interesting component in the definition of Jewish identity which the compilation represents.

Sefer ha-ma'asim and the Ms. Parma 2295 Tales: Distinctions Between Two Story Compilations in Northern France

The unique nature of the compilation of stories in Ms Bodl. Or. 135 also becomes apparent in light of another compilation of tales from the same period in northern France, at the end of the thirteenth century, which was copied in Ms. Parma 2295.[63] There is no way of knowing for certain which of the compilations came first, but it

60. "The Poor Bachelor and His Maiden Cousin" (no. 55); "Joḥanan and the Scorpion" (no. 28); "The Sabbath Observer and the Bear" (no. 14); "The Maiden in the Tower" (no. 67).

61. "Joḥanan and the Scorpion" (no. 28).

62. "Joab's Valor" (no. 4) and "The Maiden in the Tower" (no. 67), also known as *Midrash vayissa'u*.

63. Published in Kushelevsky, *Penalty and Temptation*, accompanied by an extensive study of the tales.

is evident that they drew on a shared repository of tales, in particular in view of the talmudic story about the man who was "Saved from Drowning by Charity" (no. 31), which was included in both compilations but not in other medieval collections of tales. The Parma compilation is much smaller and contains thirteen stories that are not necessarily adjacent but appear in the same textual environment in the manuscript. This is not the place to draw a detailed comparison of the shared stories but rather to make a general observation about the different nature of the compilations and their separate purposes, although they were more or less created at one place and time. Does this teach us anything about the diversity of the narrating communities and the various audiences of the two compilations in northern France in the thirteenth century? What can we infer particularly about *Sefer ha-ma'asim*?

The value of Torah study and the figure of the talmudic scholar, the images of heaven and hell, the context of "distinguished women" possessed of influence and status, and life within a Christian majority—all these and other concepts are aspects that emerge in the two compilations. Other common characteristics are, as mentioned, certain features of Ashkenazic piety (*Ḥasidut Ashkenaz*), in particular their penitential theory, which apparently spread throughout Jewish society in the region. But here too there is a marked difference between the compilations. The salient characteristic of the compilation in the Ms. Parma is its strong affinity with the world of the Pietists of Ashkenaz, the major touchstone in comparisons between the compilations. The study of *sodot hatefila* (lit., "mysteries of prayer") and its links to the theological principle of *bekerasim ubelula'ot* ("with clips and loops," referring to Exodus 26:11); the devotion of the worshipper's thoughts to *reẓon habore* (the will of the Creator) and the virtue of *ormah beyir'ah* (resourcefulness in fearing God) that characterize the Pietist in his worship; the symbolism of the "holy community" and its roots in the emigration narrative of the Kalonymos family to Mainz; the role of the liturgical poem and its exegesis in Ashkenaz; the doctrine of repentance in its various forms in a manner that is not found in *Sefer ha-ma'asim*, including *teshuvat hakatuv* (the penance [equivalent to] Scripture), *teshuvat hamishkal* (the penance of weighed [suffering]), *teshuvat haba'ah* (the penance that involuntarily confronts [the sinner]), and *teshuvat hagader* (the penance of [making] a safeguard); demonology as evidence of the wonders of the Creator—all of these are aspects that create the context of Ashkenazic Pietism which is dominant in the Parma compilation but of minor significance in *Sefer ha-ma'asim*.[64]

64. For contextualizing the Parma compilation with regard to Ashkenazi Pietism, see ibid. For the repentance doctrine in Ashkenazi Pietism, see Marcus, *Piety and Society*.

Compared to the Parma compilation, with its strong affinity to Ashkenazic Pietism, the unique nature of *Sefer ha-ma'asim* in its two combined aspects is striking—a reasonable literacy in the Talmud and the commentary of the Tosafists and, in parallel, a familiarity with vernacular literature in Europe, at least in its oral performance and often also in writing. The coexistence of both compilations in northern France does imply the existence of Ashkenazic Pietism beyond the boundaries of the initial circle in the region of the Rhine, indicated primarily in the Parma compilation;[65] but the response, particularly in *Sefer ha-ma'asim*, to the literary and cultural developments in twelfth-century France—the common spheres of interest and aesthetic taste while at the same time engaging in polemics and rejection—is what denotes it as a northern French compilation of Jewish tales, unlike the Parma compilation and its dominant Ashkenazi flavor.

Between Pleasure and Didactics

The compilation was probably intended to serve the purposes of both pleasure and didactics, in the same way other literature in the Middle Ages combined the two. The purpose of entertainment is evident from the fact that the stories are consecutively arranged without any connecting words of exegesis and edifying homilies; from the diversity and scope of the compilation in a thirty-nine-page format; and from the very legitimacy given to the copying of such a large compilation of stories which is neither law nor exegesis. In comparison to story compilations in the East the didactic purpose of which was particularly emphasized, and certainly in comparison to midrashic literature the purpose of which was homiletic and exegetical, *Sefer ha-ma'asim* is a unique compilation. The *Midrash aseret hadibrot*, for example, contains stories and linking homilies about the Ten Commandments, the scope and length of which vary.[66] In the eleventh-century work *Ḥibbur yafeh mehayeshu'a* by R. Nissim of Kairouan, the stories are embedded in a framework of homilies that were intended to hearten their audiences in times of distress.[67] That is not the case with *Sefer ha-ma'asim*, which is first and foremost a compilation of tales, replete with stories that lack any linking homilies. The aesthetic impact is created by a combination of a magnificent design, a plenitude of stories, a rich diversity in theme and genre, and sharp, rapid transitions between short, didactic tales and extended,

65. Cf. Kanarfogel, *Peering through the Lattices*, 251–258; idem, "R. Judah he-Ḥasid."

66. See *Midrash aseret hadibrot*, ed. Shapira.

67. See the author's prologue in Brinner, ed., *An Elegant Composition Concerning Relief after Adversity*, 3–4.

episodic narratives capable of gratifying curiosity and a desire for adventure in the Middle Ages. The scope of the stories ranges from two or three to a page to those that take up several pages. The longest and most convoluted, "Joḥanan and the Scorpion" (no. 28), extends over about nine pages in the manuscript (313b–317b), and is full of the adventures experienced by Joḥanan, a sort of Jewish knight who strives to gain an unattainable princess for his king and to fulfill the tasks she allots him.

At the same time the tales, many of them exempla told as true stories, were intended to instill the values of the Jewish ethos, such as those of the Sabbath, Torah study, prayer, and charity. The moral is engraved in the tale and stems from the structure of the plot, which advances from a sin to its punishment, and from the fulfillment of a commandment to its reward; it is also explicit in the epilogue that accompanies the story.[68] The exemplum is a prominent genre in *Sefer ha-ma'asim*, in fact a dominant one, which takes up about a third of the compilation. In these exempla unequivocal messages are clearly preferred to twisting plots.

At times the desire to give pleasure and appeal to the aesthetic taste of the period is not entirely compatible with the didactic aim. In "The Poor Bachelor and His Maiden Cousin" (no. 55), the scene mentioned earlier that alludes to Béroul's *Romance of Tristan* is scarcely within the boundary lines of Jewish law, yet it is tame in keeping with the scribe's polemical purposes against the latter's courtly norms while didactically addressing his Jewish audience. Tension is created between the two poles: the aesthetic for the purpose of giving pleasure and the didactic for the purposes of instructing and imbuing meaning. In any case, the very dialogue with the romance, a very popular genre at the time, and the use of a story as a sort of Jewish substitute for its non-Jewish parallel in France, are means for providing pleasure and interest within the narrating community.

Textuality and Orality

The stories in *Sefer ha-ma'asim* were apparently transmitted both orally and in writing, a frequent occurrence in the Middle Ages prior to the invention of printing. In writing their existence is first of all on the linear continuum of the manuscript, which renders it a "text." The large scope of the compilation and its beautiful design—as well as para-textual aspects such as well-maintained, balanced margins; headings such as "*Ma'aseh be-* in bold at the top of every story, endowing the opening with a

68. On the exemplum in medieval Jewish literature, see Yassif, *The Hebrew Folktale*, 310–324. See also, on the medieval Christian exemplum in the introduction to an exemplum of Jacques de Vitry, *Exempla* (xv–cxvi), in particular in relation to de Vitry's influence on later collections of exempla (liii–lxx).

high hierarchical status; and opening and ending formulae that separate *Sefer ha-ma'asim* from the works that precede and follow it—all reflect the purpose of a written compilation of tales that is competing with vernacular literary works that flourished in France in the twelfth and thirteenth centuries, and which were copied into beautifully embellished manuscripts.[69]

Other signs, such as the epilogues attached to several of the stories of *Sefer ha-ma'asim*, indicate that they were performed—that is, read orally before an audience, not necessarily dramatized. While the story itself is fashioned more or less on the basis of its sources, the epilogue enabled the scribe to address his audience directly and to relate the story to events of his own time. The verbal gesture "come and see" as an appeal to a collective audience appears in several excerpts of epilogues in *Sefer ha-ma'asim*. Another example of a performance situation is the narrator's warning against religious conversion as a result of the persecution of the Jews by the Christians: "You may not exchange me for idols. . . . Bow not to the dead [=Jesus] but to He who puts to death and revives the dead." The narrator's moral of "cleanliness" in intimate relations, as mentioned in some of the tales' epilogues, might express an awareness of a possible influence of the courtly romances and their ethos of love on the minds of his Jewish audience.

One can also assume the existence of recitation and performance events from the numerous rhetorical questions in the stories, particularly from the consistent tendency in *Sefer ha-ma'asim* to leave out words that are clear from the context, and often those whose purpose was to clarify the pragmatic function of the expression ("request," "question," "declaration," etc.), as well as details that create an effect of redundancy.[70] The plot is preserved, the events of the story are told, but in a more condensed manner. The reason may have been financial—due to the great expense of writing in the preprint period. It does not seem, however, that the scribe tried to save on space. In Eli Yassif's words, there is an air of "leisure and broad spirit" in the work, as the resources apparently allotted to the writing of the compilation by a professional scribe would suggest.[71] It is more reasonable to assume that it was the seemingly banal schematic scaffolding of the story that enabled the narrator to add

69. For an example of a culture of illustration and iconography in medieval manuscripts, see the opening page of the *Roman de la Rose* (Ms. Bibl. Nat. fr.) in Huot, *The Romance of the Rose*, 276, and the author's discussion, 273–322. In *Sefer ha-ma'asim*, however, there is no internal division into paragraphs within the story.

70. See, throughout the present edition of *Sefer ha-ma'asim*, ample examples of this stylistic tendency to condense the plot, leaving out redundant descriptions.

71. Yassif, "Theory and Practice."

details of color and volume on the occasion of a recitation, in a context common to him and his listeners. By providing a scheme rather than a redundant plot, "chapter headings" rather than rich and full descriptions, the narrator was left with a broad space for acting and maneuvering during the performance. Nonetheless, although the scribe may have condensed the text for pragmatic considerations of context and performance, as well as to conform to a specific aesthetic taste, his language is no less rich or anchored in Jewish sources.

In a certain sense, this rhetoric of foregoing narrative redundancy can be likened to *The Golden Legend* by Jacobus de Voragine.[72] The compilation was composed in the 1260s and was an enormous success. It was circulated in the Middle Ages in about a thousand manuscripts and was translated from Latin into all the West European languages. A contemporary reader seeking the reason for its success in the texts themselves, in the written narratives, would be disappointed. The legends are written in the most banal fashion, eschewing any opportunity to include any psychological or historical depth. It seems that is actually the reason for its success, as Kleinberg suggests.[73] The shallow description left the local priest ample opportunity to augment the story and bring it closer to his listeners. In the Jewish context of *Sefer ha-ma'asim*, the stories that were familiar from the rabbinic literature were probably supplemented and reworked when they were performed before an audience in the Middle Ages, in order to draw them closer to the reality of their own lives. In their "multiple existence" as tales that were told and retold time and again in various versions—taken out of their context in the compilation as a whole and treated as distinctive units to be performed and copied on different occasions and in different places—their brevity and sparse style left enough room for individual improvisation.[74]

Where and in what circumstances were the tales read aloud, and what was the place of Hebrew in these performances in comparison to French, the spoken language? The transitions between the written and oral media are not unique to the Middle Ages—those stories were widespread in oral form throughout all the generations since the rabbinical period of the Mishnah and the Talmud, in parallel with their written form.[75] Many of them can also be classified as international tale types,

72. Jacobi a Voragine, *Legenda Aurea*; Jacobus de Voragine, *The Golden Legend*, vols. 1–2.

73. Kleinberg, *Fra Ginepro's Leg of Pork*, 321–327.

74. For the term "multiple existence," see Dundes and Pagter, *Urban Folklore*, xix; for its application to Jewish narratives, see Yassif, *The Hebrew Folktale*, 5.

75. See Shinan, "The Aggadic Literature."

despite their Jewish character.[76] The feature that renders them special in the Middle Ages is the discourse the stories represent; the aggregate of contexts that accompany them, which the researcher has to reconstruct from the written text; and the connotations they probably evoked among their audiences in performance situations. The tales may have been recited within the family and circles of friends as a kind of leisure entertainment. The owner of the manuscript commissioned it in the thirteenth century from a very professional scribe, so we can assume he was wealthy. One can see that—taking into account his financial status, literacy skills, and grasp of cultural and religious resources, which become apparent in a study of this compilation—it is likely *Sefer ha-ma'asim* was commissioned so the stories could be recited at family, social, and cultural events.

We can also assume that stories from *Sefer ha-ma'asim*, particularly the short, didactic exempla, were recited or orally transmitted in the framework of sermons in the synagogue or at other public occasions, as rabbinic legends were previously done. Stories from the Talmud and the Midrash occupy a prominent section in the compilation, and owing to their adaptation and the nuances that enabled their reception as texts relevant to their medieval audience, they were particularly suited to being integrated into various sermons on religious occasions, especially in the synagogue. Those tales, brought into the compilation from the non-Jewish society in France, were also adapted to *Sefer ha-ma'asim* according to familiar patterns from rabbinic literature, as a Jewish response to foreign ideas, and as a no-less-attractive and enjoyable substitute.

The tales were recited in Hebrew in a bilingual Jewish society, even though they may also have been told in the vernacular. Hebrew was used even when it was not a daily spoken language. Lists of homonymic words in the manuscript are translated into French (in Hebrew letters). Two books of grammar and lexical clarifications by Abraham Habavli and Solomon ben Abraham ibn Pirchon attest to the relevance of the Hebrew language to the Jewish society in northern France. It would have been reasonable to expect the use of Hebraico-French in writing and reciting the stories, since French was the daily spoken language, but, like the development of poetry and liturgy in France, which is largely in Hebrew and not in Hebraico-French, the prose in *Sefer ha-ma'asim* is in Hebrew. Very few literary texts in Hebraico-French—namely Old French in Hebrew script (Judeo-French did not develop during that period)—are extant. There are several wedding songs and one

76. See references to international indices of tale types (ATU) throughout the book and in Appendix C.

lament. This is not actually because manuscripts were lost but because the Jews preferred Hebrew as a language for writing, parallel in status to Latin in the society at large.[77] French was the spoken language, but Hebrew was the language of writing and of the study of both sacred and secular works, the language of communicating among Jews from afar as they came together for social or business activities. No distinction was made between exegetical and halakhic writings and poetry and prose. The recitation of tales from a Hebrew manuscript was part of this activity.

French and Hebrew existed side by side among Jews, and mutual influences between the two are evident in the manuscript. Two interesting examples from the stories are the word *taba*, meaning a ring, in the story "Joḥanan and the Scorpion" (no. 28), and the word *nekhed* in "The Poor Bachelor and His Maiden Cousin" (no. 55), which Yassif commented on, to denote the family relationship of a nephew.[78] The word for "ring" in Old French as well as in modern French is masculine: *anneua* or *annel.*[79] The grammatical pattern of the masculine voice was copied into Hebrew and also translated into Hebrew. In the manuscript the Hebrew word *taba'at* became *taba.*[80] Along with the word *taba* in "Joḥanan and the Scorpion," there are errors in the masculine and the feminine in the third person singular, since the distinction between the two was not yet clear-cut in Old French. One example is "*samaḥ hamalka simḥa gedola.*"[81] "Joḥanan and the Scorpion" is not known from the Jewish sources and was apparently created within the narrating community represented in *Sefer ha-ma'asim* on the basis of contemporary non-Jewish models. For this very reason it contains irregular expressions that reveal its source in French.

The Poetics of Hybridism

Notions of pleasure and interest are, of course, culture-dependent. The aesthetic taste of the scribe and his audiences in the Middle Ages is not necessarily the taste of modern, contemporary readers. One would expect a well-thought-out redaction based on certain fixed principles, and indeed in *Sefer ha-ma'asim* there are several clusters of two to four tales that share a common motif, as well as other local,

77. Fudeman, *Vernacular Voices*, 118–123.
78. The word *nekhed*, influenced by the French *neveu*, appears in this sense in Rashbam's and Rabbenu Tam's commentary: Yassif, *Kemargalit bemishbeẓet*, 139n14.
79. See the entry *Anel* (n.m.), in A. J. Greimas, *Le Dictionnaire de l'ancien français* (Paris: Larousse, 2012), 28.
80. A different hand has completed the word *taba* in the manuscript, making it *taba'at.*
81. Literally, "the queen was very happy"; but while the Hebrew word for "queen" is feminine, the verb here is in the masculine ("Joḥanan and the Scorpion" [no. 28]). I am grateful to Tovi Bibring for this information.

unifying elements that were mentioned earlier—idioms and similar opening formulae in a number of stories. Nonetheless, they are inadequate for organizing the compilation as a whole. We have here a poetics that I call "poetics of hybridism," the kind that joins various types without any order or logic dictated in advance.

Nearly forty years ago, Joseph Dan noted the eclectic nature of the stories in Jewish compilations from the late Middle Ages in comparison to compilations edited according to a guiding theme or overall framework.[82] Eli Yassif dated the phenomenon earlier, to the thirteenth century, based on the eclectic nature of *Sefer ha-ma'asim* as a whole.[83] Eclecticism is a distinct attribute of non-Jewish medieval literature as well, in contrast to the unitary book in the classical Greco-Latin world.[84] Eclecticism in *Sefer ha-ma'asim* is particularly striking in the stories themselves, because they are brief and condensed. The basic unit of the stories in *Sefer ha-ma'asim* is the episode. The story often brings together a number of episodes from different sources which are related to one another only chronologically. The events occur in a sequential order of some kind, but without being dependent on cause and effect. In these stories it is easy to change the order without influencing the plots. The final product is a narrative made up of episodic subunits, each of which stands on its own. A distinct example of this in *Sefer ha-ma'asim* is "The Grateful Dead" (no. 65). It is composed of three episodes, joined together in coordinated syntax, which are based on separate sources: the Book of Tobias in the Apocrypha, the Talmud, and the thirteenth-century German verse tales the *Rittertreue.* Recurrent motifs create links among the episodes, but the story, probably created by the scribe, is not integrative, in keeping with the taste of the target audience in the Middle Ages.

The term "poetics of hybridism" suggested here is an extreme manifestation of this eclecticism. In addition to being a random corpus of gathered tales with no guiding thematic principle, *Sefer ha-ma'asim* combines tales of different sources, genres, and themes, which create the hybridic aggregate of the compilation as a whole. Metaphorically this can be likened to the figure of the dragon typical of medieval iconography, which combines different animals yet is identified as a creature in itself. Stories clearly originating from rabbinic literature and others based on the vernacular literature of the period are intermixed in *Sefer ha-ma'asim*, and thus lack a unifying theme. Stories from *Midrash aseret hadibrot* are not necessarily grouped according to their thematic affinity with a specific commandment but are copied

82. Dan, "'Ma'aseh Yerushalmi' and Ms. Heb 8⁰3182," 492–498.

83. Yassif, *Kemargalit bemishbeẓet*, 139–140.

84. Petrucci, *Writers and Readers*, 1–18.

alternately between the commandments, returning time and again to the same commandment in different spots of the compilation. A similar split occurs in different versions of the same story, and there are two such examples in *Sefer ha-ma'asim*. The versions are not in consecutive order, thus the shared plot was not a consideration in the decision regarding where they are placed in the compilation.

A similar hybridism characterizes the classification by genre in the compilation. From the ethnic standpoint of the narrating community, each of the tales is a *ma'aseh*, an event perceived as reliable and meriting emulation, regardless of whether it actually occurred or is possible, whether it is realistic or touches on the "wondrous" and the supernatural.[85] From the analytical perspective of the scholar, the exempla, heroic epics, *mirabilis* tales, legends, popular novellas, romances, and fabliaux in *Sefer ha-ma'asim* lack any centralized principles of compilation. The boundaries are not clear-cut even within a single story. A story which in rabbinic literature is an exemplum par excellence takes on characteristics of fabliaux in *Sefer ha-ma'asim*.[86] A story of war and valor, a sort of versed epic, also turns into an exemplum.[87] Attributes of the romance are also incorporated into a folk novella.[88] Borders are crossed and analytic categories are not fully applied. The "different" in *Sefer ha-ma'asim* seems to be more dominant than the "similar," and that invests the compilation with a hybridic nature. Compared with parallel tales in rabbinical literature, these are not revolutionary changes but rather a change in focus, a broadening of the reader's horizon of expectations while maintaining a certain balance between the new and the old.[89]

What emerges in *Sefer ha-ma'asim* is quite consistent with the findings of the research on genres in the French literature of the period—namely the breakdown of works of poetry, drama, and prose into subgenres according to certain formal characteristics.[90] Various terms coined in the Middle Ages in the field of lyrical poetry, which are also relevant in the modern era, indicate the existence of a

85. This is opposed, for example, to tall tales in rabbinic literature. On native taxonomy as "a qualitative, subjective system of order," and for a methodological discussion of different folkloristic systems of taxonomy, see Ben-Amos, "Analytical Categories and Ethnic Genres," 275–297 (quote p. 285).

86. "Hadrian and the Old Man" (no. 38).

87. "Joab's Valor" (no. 4).

88. "The Poor Bachelor and His Maiden Cousin" (no. 55).

89. On "horizon of expectations" as an alternative criterion for rigid definitions of genres and their types, and which is appropriate for the Middle Ages, see Jauss, *Toward an Aesthetic of Reception*, 87–90, and the broader context in the chapter "Theory of Genres and Medieval Literature," 76–109.

90. For a discussion on this topic, see Busby, "Narrative Genres," 139–152.

well-defined concept of genre in relation to poetry[91] and drama, which was given the general name of *jeu* ("play").[92] In prose, on the other hand—and *Sefer ha-ma'asim* is a narrative in prose—the distinctions in genre were more diffuse. In the Middle Ages, the hero epics and poems were known as *chansons de geste* but also by the very general term *romans*, which applied to every vernacular narrative, including chronicles, legends of saints, and animal fables. Similarly, the distinction among fabliaux, proverbs, or short courtly narratives was not always clear-cut. One example is *Aucassin and Nicolette*, a text that is so hybrid in its genres (romance, prose, poetry, music) and so ambiguous in its purposes (representative or satiric) that interpretations of the work range between two opposite extremes. It transpires that hybridism is a poetic characteristic that typified a broad range of works in the Middle Ages, and *Sefer ha-ma'asim* is one of them.[93]

The Boundaries of *Sefer ha-ma'asim* and Its Status as a Compilation of Stories in the Middle Ages

Although the compilation was assigned the title *Sefer ha-ma'asim* in the research for reasons of convenience, it is not actually a book with fixed boundaries but rather an open, nondefinitive compilation from which tales can be added or subtracted, based on need and choice. If *Sefer ha-ma'asim* is a representative medieval compilation, which it seems to be in light of its scope and attractive appearance, then its study has implications for additional medieval compilations of tales, which were far more numerous than scholars of the period's literature—who focused on poetry and liturgy—had assumed.

In the previous section, I discussed the eclectic and hybridic nature of *Sefer ha-ma'asim*, and I now will relate to its definition as a compilation of tales, based on its boundaries and not only on its contents. At the opening of the compilation, the scribe declares his intention to copy "*ma'asim*," tales, and ends it with a comment about his satisfaction at having completed the task, but he does not define the compilation as a "book," as a closed corpus. Unlike other treatises in the manuscript which he does define this way—*Sefer Pirḥon, Sefer ben Sira, Mishlei Sendebar, Divrei hayamim shel Moshe*—*Sefer ha-ma'asim* is assigned the general title "Tales"

91. Such as the *grand chant courtois*, which denotes a long love poem; *aube*, to denote a "dawn poem"; and the ballad, characterized by the refrain.

92. There is a distinction in the Middle Ages between subgenres of religious and secular dramas.

93. Kay, "Genre, Parody and Spectacle," 167–174.

in the manuscript.[94] The decentralized concept of the compilation is also evident from a number of tales copied outside the boundaries of *Sefer ha-ma'asim*, between other treatises: two between *Sefer ben Sira* and *Mishlei R. Berakhiah Hanakdan*, and one tale between *Mishlei R. Berakhiah Hanakdan* and *Mishlei Sendebar.* This can be compared to the "copying strategy" of *Midrash aseret hadibrot.* After *Midrash aseret hadibrot* and the following *Midrash vayosha*, the scribe apparently came upon some more excerpts from *Midrash aseret hadibrot* (homilies in particular) and copied them randomly where he happened to be in the manuscript. As he declares: "The *agadot* [narratives] of *Vayosha* were completed and I found some more narratives [of commandments]." As mentioned, within *Midrash aseret hadibrot* itself, the scribe often refers to *Sefer ha-ma'asim* with the wording "I wrote above" to save himself the trouble of copying stories that he has already copied. From his point of view, the basic unit is the story, in which alterations can be made and which can be moved from its location, rather than the compilation as a whole. Apparently the opening and ending points of the compilation were arbitrarily chosen.

This does not mean that the scribe created the compilation from thin air. It is likely that large sections of it were copied from earlier compilations, like *Midrash aseret hadibrot* and others that are no longer extant. Certainly individual tales were copied from earlier sources with some changes. It is possible to distinctly discern the practice of copying in one of the tales, where specific words were copied in the wrong place because they were skipped over and then recopied in the proper place.[95] The attractive script in *Sefer ha-ma'asim* and its arrangement on the page may be indications that it was copied from an early source.[96] It is likely that the compilation was produced on the basis of an existing inventory along with stories that we encounter for the first time. And despite the likelihood of a gradual process of development, or actually because of it, *Sefer ha-ma'asim* in the format we have before us—in its scope, its selection of stories, and the boundaries of the compilation—is a one-time phenomenon, not a consolidated, closed corpus fixed in the form of a "book."

94. Similarly, in the manuscript "*Agadot shel vayosha*" and "*Agadot shel dibrot*" are not named as "books" with clear-cut boundaries.

95. "Once R. Shimon b. Ḥalafta had nothing to eat for the Sabbath and he gave it to the moneychanger." The last words are out of place here and belong later, after R. Shimon b. Ḥalafta receives a precious stone from heaven: "God gave him a precious stone from heaven, and he returned [to the town] and gave it to the moneychanger."

96. I thank Edna Engel for this comment.

This hypothesis may explain the "disappearance" of any evidence of the original version of *Sefer ha-ma'asim*, which was preserved in only one manuscript, as well as of other eclectic story compilations in medieval Europe, for which there is also no such evidence.[97] It is at least partly reasonable to assume that manuscripts were lost. A relatively small proportion of medieval manuscripts are extant. Manuscripts were destroyed in fires—for example, the Paris fire of 1242—in persecutions, and during other incidents suffered by Jewish communities, to which one can apply the saying "Even a Torah scroll in the Temple is in need of good fortune." Consequently, the manuscript is not a conclusive indication of the date of the compilation, but at the most it attests to the latest date of its formation. Nonetheless, the scope and consistency of the phenomenon—namely the survival of *Sefer ha-ma'asim* and other story compilations in a single manuscript—suggest that there is a need to reconsider this hypothesis. Along with the assumption about the loss of manuscripts, it is also feasible that stories or sections of stories from *Sefer ha-ma'asim* and other compilations carried on their lives in new contexts, just as *Sefer ha-ma'asim* itself is based in part on *Midrash aseret hadibrot.* If that is the case, then *Sefer ha-ma'asim*, like other eclectic medieval story compilations, is a reservoir of tales that underwent partial copying, deletions, additions, changes in order, and adaptation. Its ability to survive stems from its openness, flexibility, and dynamism, in contrast to a closed work that merits the definition of a "book."

This hypothesis is affirmed when one follows the influence of *Sefer ha-ma'asim* on later story compilations. *Sefer ha-ma'asim* continued its life in later periods as a direct source, and even more likely, as an indirect source, of the story compilations in the manuscripts Ms. JTS 2374 (14th–15th centuries), which shares eleven stories with it, four of them sequentially and in nearly the same wording; Ms. Jerusalem 3182, which shares twenty-four stories with *Sefer ha-ma'asim*, some nearly identical in style;[98] and the manuscript editions of *Mayse bukh* in Yiddish, from the sixteenth century, which share four to five tales with *Sefer ha-ma'asim*.[99] The

97. Eclectic medieval story compilations for which there is no evidence of original sources are Ms. Parma 2295, Ms. JTS 2374, and Ms. Jerusalem 3182.

98. On the affinity to *Sefer ha-ma'asim*, see Yassif, *Ninety-nine Tales*, 20–21, 296–297.

99. The shared stories (although they are not identical in wording) with *Sefer ha-ma'asim* and the Innsbruck (Ms. Jerusalem 5245) and Rovere (Munich 495) in the *Mayse bukh* are: "R. Pinḥas b. Yair" (nos. 56–59); "The Tribulations of Naḥum Ish Gamzo" (no. 63); "Ben Sever and Shefifon Ben Layish" (no. 27); and "The Defamed Woman" (no. 24). "The Man Who Never Took an Oath" (no. 13) and "The *Ḥasid* and the Tax Collector's Son" (no. 60) were

compilation was an important source of influence and at the same time was perceived as a reservoir of tales that did not dictate their selection and linear order. Stories probably moved from it to these and other compilations by means of mediating links both oral and written. From there, as well as through the channels of *Midrash aseret hadibrot* in Europe, the stories moved to printed story compilations like *Ḥibbur hama'asiyot vehamidrashot vehahagadot*, Joseph Shabbtai Farḥi's *Oseh pele*, and the 1602 edition of the *Mayse bukh* in Yiddish. At the same time they were orally recited throughout the Jewish Diaspora, a fact that is documented in the Israel Folktale Archives in Haifa. The ongoing influence of *Sefer ha-ma'asim*, both direct and indirect, through intermediate oral and written links, does not depend, then, on defined boundaries of the tales within the compilation, its consolidation, or its definition as a book. In it the story, or more so the episode, is the dominant unit, as it is as well in other eclectic story compilations from the thirteenth century and thereafter.

This status of *Sefer ha-ma'asim* can be compared once again to that of French vernacular works, even to those with an identified author. These works were dynamic and changed frequently in a process of transmission and copying. Particularly striking in the Middle Ages is the transmission of literary works in many numerous versions, a type of intertexuality that renders it impossible to reconstruct one authoritative, "original" text. The fact that they were repeatedly copied influenced the status and boundaries of the "text." The differences among the versions are sometimes so great that they can be viewed as different works rather than adapted versions of one work. At times, as a result of adaptations for very different purposes, which create excessive gaps within the text, tensions may occur that destabilize the text. *Romance of the Rose* is an example par excellence, not only because its two parts are attributed to different authors. Didactic, philosophical, entertainment, and popular approaches compete with one another in each part, and its messages are so contradictory that it is impossible to relate to one authoritative text. As it was transmitted and copied in many scores of manuscripts, it was the object of deletions and interpretations that greatly changed its character. The question of the work's reception becomes more relevant than a reconstruction of the "original" work.[100]

---

included only in Ms. Innsbruck. See a comparative index of tales in the *Mayse bukh* in manuscripts and the printed Basel 1602 edition: Kotlerman, "*Mafte'ach haMayse bukh*" ("The Complete Index of Stories in the 'Mayse-bukh,'" 294–325.

100. Huot, *The Romance of the Rose*, and her reference in n. 6 to Kennedy.

Initial Publications from *Sefer ha-ma'asim*: Israel Lévi and Moses Gaster

The publication of ten stories from *Sefer ha-ma'asim* and their translation into French by Israel Lévi (1856–1939), in two issues of the quarterly *Revue des etudes juives*, was not a coincidence.[101] Israel Lévi, the editor of *REJ* several years after its establishment in 1880, had a well-defined world view. He epitomized a blend of an Orthodox lifestyle and a scientific research-oriented approach to Jewish studies. He was awarded the prestigious chair in Jewish studies at the Sorbonne (Ecole Pratique des Hautes Etudes). He conducted research and published articles on talmudic legends, the history of the Talmud, messianism, and ties between Jews and Christians, as well as about popular culture in Jewish sources. At the height of his career, he served as the chief rabbi of France. The publication of a selection of tales from the Ms. Bodl. Or. 135 in *REJ* was part of an effort to acquaint the non-Jewish society in France with the treasures of Jewish culture, as an expression of the Jewish contribution to French culture. Lévi represented the intellectual Jewry in France of that period who aspired to integrate into the French culture but at the same time to preserve their Jewish identity. This trend in France was influenced, in its own particular way, by the German *Wissenschaft des Judentums* in the nineteenth century, as well as by internal processes in France that had begun with the French Revolution and the Emancipation in 1791, which granted powers and equal rights to the Jews.

The backgrounds for the copying of the stories in the thirteenth century and the translation and publication of a selection of them hundreds of years later, at the end of the nineteenth century, were of course totally different. Whether we are considering the processes of borrowing and adaptation of non-Jewish narratives in the thirteenth century at times of persecutions or we are in the nineteenth century, looking at a translation of Jewish tales into French as part of French culture and the national and religious approach of a scholar and rabbi in a time of putative equal rights, *Sefer ha-ma'asim* was an arena in which Jewish societies in France, at different periods, grappled with the need to sharpen the definitions of their identities as minority societies.

101. The following discussion of Israel Lévi is based on Dan Jaffé, "La *Wissenschaft des Judentums* à la Française." I am grateful to him for introducing me to his article before its publication. The tales published in issues 33 (1896) and 35 (1897) of *Revue des etudes juives* are "The Loan" (nos. 2, 34); "The Drunkard and His Sons" (no. 6); "The Three Treasures" (no. 7); "One of Ten" (no. 17); "The Defamed Woman" (no. 24); "Joḥanan and the Scorpion" (no. 28); "Do Not Fail to Attend Public Prayers" (no. 41); "The Hard-Boiled Egg" (no. 54); "The Portal to Gehenna" (no. 69).

Moses Gaster (1856–1939), a contemporary of Israel Lévi, was born in Romania and engaged in research in England. He was a public figure and a *ḥakham* (rabbi) of the Sephardic community in London.[102] He, like Lévi, was influenced by *Wissenschaft des Judentums* in his comparative and philological approaches, as well as in his drive to uncover and publish old Jewish texts. Many of his publications are in the field of Jewish folklore, and these include several tales from *Sefer ha-ma'asim*.

Seven tales from *Sefer ha-ma'asim* (or eight, since one was printed in two versions), were published by Gaster in his bilingual *Sefer hama'asiyot*, or *Exempla of the Rabbis*.[103] In addition to publishing the full Hebrew text of these seven stories, his book includes thirty-seven short summaries in English of tales from *Sefer ha-ma'asim*, along with a rich apparatus of comparative references to parallels.[104]

The interest in *Sefer ha-ma'asim* taken by Israel Lévi and Moses Gaster, both of the same period and cultural mentality, is intriguing in the present context. It reflects their recognition of this compilation of tales as a precise, rare cultural treasure that deserves to be presented as a national asset, studied, and published. Now, a century later, the vantage point from which I choose to look at *Sefer ha-ma'asim* is naturally different. My purpose is not a philological-historical study, although my conclusions are based on source studies, and the contribution of scholars of *Wissenschaft des Judentums* to this book are definitely considerable. Nonetheless, I am primarily interested in the nature of *Sefer ha-ma'asim* as an eclectic and hybridic literary work of the Middle Ages, and in its role within the culture in which it was created: thirteenth-century France, a time of momentous, intensive literary flourishing.

The richness and diversity of the sources in *Sefer ha-ma'asim* and the mode of their adaptation, its distinct medieval character, the interactions between the spoken and written languages, the channels through which the stories were transmitted, its status as a compilation and its genre definition, its affinity to the surrounding vernacular literature and to various aspects of the non-Jewish narrating community, the thematics so familiar to and yet very different from what we are

102. For the following discussion, see Yassif, "Moses Gaster."

103. See in *Exempla of the Rabbis*: "The Loan" (no. 307, pp. 206–207); "The Sabbath Observer and the Bear" (no. 303, pp. 194–195); "R. Akiva's Daughter and the Snake" (no. 306, p. 206); "The Three Treasures" (no. 302, pp. 193–194); "The Defamed Woman" (no. 304, pp. 195–197); "Joḥanan and the Scorpion" (no. 305, pp. 197–206); and "Do Not Fail to Attend Public Prayers" (no. 308, pp. 207–208).

104. *Exempla of the Rabbis* (English), 113–122, and comparative references, 185–270. The abstracts specify general plot lines, leaving out their particular characteristics in *Sefer ha-ma'asim*.

accustomed to—all of these, and the annotated edition of the sixty-nine tales in the compilation, provide endless opportunities for further study of Hebrew medieval prose. In an era that heralds a new impetus for research on the medieval Hebrew story, in contrast to the previous focus on liturgy and poetry, this book offers a diversity of paths of study on Hebrew prose. In its uncommon structure and framework, and its inclusion of lengthy chapters of discussion as well as an edition, this book is an invitation of sorts to continue the dialogue conducted between its pages and among the lovers of the medieval Hebrew story wherever they may be.

Several comments on the structure and principles of the book are in order. The present introductory chapter describes the contours of *Sefer ha-ma'asim* as a medieval Hebrew compilation of tales in northern France. The following two chapters focus on the sources of the compilation, the modes of their adaptation, and their integration into *Sefer ha-ma'asim*. They also address the topoi of the scribe as a creative writer, and suggest, rather implicitly, issues of identity that the compilation represents, in contrast to its sources, in the historical circumstances of a Jewish minority in northern France. One chapter is devoted to the Jewish sources and the other to non-Jewish sources mainly in France and in Western Europe in general. Together they represent the arena of the narrative strategies behind the scenes: the techniques that turn tales from earlier Jewish sources and non-Jewish sources into a narrative of its own time and place in thirteenth-century northern France, a discourse of the narrating community. The two chapters in combination provide a bidirectional view of *Sefer ha-ma'asim*: the modes of adaptation and integration of non-Jewish narrative materials into Jewish narratives, as well as the reworking of non-Jewish narratives that render them as Jewish stories.

Particular studies of the tales follow the diplomatic edition of *Sefer ha-ma'asim*, creating an extensive section of its own. In contrast to the three introductory chapters that precede the edition and provide a panoramic survey of *Sefer ha-ma'asim*, the point of departure for and focus in Part III, "Tales and Parallels," is the tale as a distinctive unit in *Sefer ha-ma'asim*, and its unique characteristics as a medieval narrative and cultural product in northern France, against the background of an aggregate of versions in the Jewish literature and its parallels in Western Europe.[105]

105. Tale no. 10 ("Ḥananiah, Mishael, and Azaria") is briefly commented on together with tale no. 9 ("Abraham in the Furnace"). Tale no. 11 ("The Generation of Dispersion of the Tower of Babel") is left for future study. Parallel versions of the same story in *Sefer ha-ma'asim*,

In my discussions of the tales and their parallels, I have also included references to sources later than *Sefer ha-ma'asim*, up to the edition of the *Mayse bukh* printed in Basel in 1602 (in order to learn about the impact of *Sefer ha-ma'asim* after its time), as well as references to a selection of some later sources that might interest scholars of literature and folklore. Comments and additional references to sources that are beyond the purview of this book are noted in the rich research literature and indices of Micha Joseph Bin Gorion, Moses Gaster, Ḥaim Schwarzbaum, Dan Ben-Amos, and Eli Yassif, all of whose contributions to the present study and research are paramount.[106]

General conclusions in the three introductory chapters rely on the detailed studies in Part III ("Tales and Parallels"). The particular analysis of each tale on its own and the overview of the compilation as a whole enabled me to determine *Sefer ha-ma'asim* as a product of both the cultural flourishing in medieval France and the milieu of the Tosafists there. At the same time the compilation also represents shared cultural codes in Ashkenaz and northern France, such as the esteem of Torah study, certain aspects of abstinence, and the penitential system of Ashkenazi Pietists. This book progresses therefore, from the general to the particular, from the introductory chapters to detailed studies, which together form the outer structure of the edition itself.

As an editor I added, in square brackets, minimal additions and corrections or citations to the Bible or the rabbinic literature. Punctuation marks—on the level of commas and periods—are scattered throughout the manuscript, not always consistently or in a manner compatible with the end of the sentence. I did not always take the punctuation marks in the manuscript into account, because they were not always consistent and often interfered with the continuity of the text (for example, a period in the middle of a sentence).[107] Round parentheses in the edition signify the deletion of distorted or repeated words. Letters intended to fill the ends of rows were not documented.

Angular brackets< >signify a correction, addition, or erasure by the scribe (as is obvious from an analysis of his handwriting and his habit of erasing the first and

namely "The Loan" (nos. 2, 34) and "Ukva" (nos. 15, 61), are discussed together rather than separately.

106. Gaster, *Exempla*; Schwarzbaum, *Studies*; Ben-Amos, *Mimekor Yisrael*; Bin Gorion, *Mimekor Yisrael*; Yassif, *The Hebrew Folktale*.

107. Gaster partially and inconsistently preserved these marks in the stories he published in *Exempla of the Rabbis*, even when the sentence was truncated in the middle.

last letters of the word to indicate an erasure of the entire word).[108] It is not always possible to ascertain the source of an erasure—whether it was the scribe or someone at a later time—and in such cases the erasure is signified by a line through the word, as it appears in the manuscript.[109] The erasure of the beginning of a word, after which the word is copied correctly in its entirety, is signified in this edition by angular brackets as an erasure by the scribe. Above quotations of verses in the manuscript, a reference in Latin is recorded by a later hand, and in one of the stories a reference is cited to a parallel in Gaster's *Exempla.* These are not documented in this edition.

Curly braces {} signify the addition of words by a hand other than the scribe and at a later time, which is evident from the different handwriting and later technical markings: a caret^under the line indicates the insertion of an addition that appears above the line, in the corresponding location;[110] the insertion of the symbol **—O** above a line directs the reader to an addition that appears in the adjacent margins (at times with vocalization marks).[111]

The apparatus of this edition includes quotations from a selection of story versions in earlier and later sources, as well as paraphrases of parallel excerpts and comparisons. Although my editorial decision is to integrate in the apparatus citations and paraphrases of mainly similar versions of a tale, I include, at times, comparisons and references to other parallels, whenever they enable fruitful discussions to be presented in Part III ("Tales and Parallels"). In such cases, I prefer paraphrases to exact citations. The manuscript of the Ms. Bodl. Or. 135 collection is the only textual witness for *Sefer ha-ma'asim* in its entirety. It is also legible and of high quality, so the present edition is not a critical apparatus of variant readings of *Sefer ha-ma'asim*. The purpose of the apparatus is not to provide a reliable version of *Sefer ha-ma'asim* as a whole, or a reliable version of each of its tales, but rather to focus on each tale separately, in comparison to selected sources, as an infrastructure for the studies offered in Part III, as well as in the introductory chapters in Part I, which summarize general aspects of the compilation as a whole. My assumption is that the findings from the individual comparisons of each story and from the data

108. The addition of words in the margins is marked in the manuscript by a double apostrophe ('') in the text, wherever an addition is required. A double apostrophe also signifies the end of a sentence or a paragraph in the manuscript, but not consistently. In these cases, the double apostrophe sign '' is documented in this edition, too.

109. In the English translation of this edition, these additions, erasures, and corrections made by a later hand are not transcribed.

110. See the example on facsimile Appendix A, p. 598, 606.

111. See the examples on facsimile Appendix A, p. 597, 606.

that accumulate throughout the compilation will make it possible to draw general conclusions about the purposes of editing and adaptation in *Sefer ha-ma'asim*, and to pinpoint stylistic and thematic characteristics that go beyond the boundaries of the individual tale. Other than the comparisons to sources and parallels, whether these are especially similar or disparate, the apparatus also includes explanations of difficult expressions and occasionally necessary comments, such as those regarding biblical allusions. Citations and paraphrases from the same source throughout the edition are quoted without repeated reference to it, and its specific details can be found in the first footnote to each of the tales.

The affinities between the stories in *Sefer ha-ma'asim* and their parallels are examined in Part III on two levels: the stylistic and the thematic.[112] On the stylistic level, the consistent trend in *Sefer ha-ma'asim* to delete details that are obvious from the context, and to compress the text but not necessarily shorten the plot, is evident only from a consistent comparison to similar parallels. On the thematic level, choices in *Sefer ha-ma'asim* render it possible to draw further conclusions about its role within the narrating community. A careful comparison between similar versions of a tale should reveal consistent adaptation trends of motifs in *Sefer ha-ma'asim*, as a tool for deciphering its cultural-historical discourse against the background of its time and place in medieval northern France. Particularly telling are the numerous exempla it contains.

Appendices to the book include a facsimile of the entire *Sefer ha-ma'asim* (Appendix A); a list of the tales in *Sefer ha-ma'asim* (Appendix B); a list of the texts in the Ms. Bodleian Or. 135 (Appendix C); and a classification of the tales according to the several indices of tale types and motifs (Tubach,[113] Uther,[114] and IFA oikotypes; Appendix D).[115]

My colleague Prof. Elisheva Baumgarten adds, in her epilogue to this book, the social and historical background to *Sefer ha-ma'asim*, and discusses new ways in which *Sefer ha-ma'asim* and other story compilations can be used by historians for an enquiry into the everyday lives of medieval Jews.

---

112. Although most of the tales are discussed in Part III, two that require further analysis (nos. 10–11) are not included in the discussion. Parallel tale versions in *Sefer ha-ma'asim*—namely "The Loan" (nos. 2, 34) and "Ukva" (nos. 15, 61)—are combined for discussion in Part III.

113. Tubach, *Index Exemplorum*.

114. Uther, *The Types of International Folktales*.

115. See ifa.haifa.ac.il/index.php?option=com_content&view=article&id=199&Itemid=114 (accessed June 20, 2016).

The guiding approach of this book—that tales are always anchored in a specific culture and express aesthetic tastes, values, and images of the narrating society—is not obvious, since the tales have numerous versions, some of which were transmitted in an ongoing tradition over thousands of years. They seem to have nothing in common with a defined time period, a specific culture, and an identified society. However, stylistic and structural changes in the stories, when compared to earlier versions, provide an approach to their unique aspects, the product of the culture in which the *Sefer ha-ma'asim* was created. What today seems deviant and odd was not necessarily so in the Middle Ages, and the encounter with a compilation made by adapting and reworking its diverse sources inspires us to rethink the nature of the medieval Hebrew story in Western Europe.

The Reworking of Jewish Sources and Their Integration into *Sefer ha-ma'asim*

The previous chapter provided an overview of the rich diversity of sources in *Sefer ha-ma'asim*. The most prominent of these is *Midrash aseret hadibrot*, which takes up about a third of *Sefer ha-ma'asim*. Its impact on the compilation is evident not merely in the proportion of shared stories but due to the nature of *Midrash aseret hadibrot* as a distinct collection edited around the unifying framework of the commandments. A no less sizeable section is from the Talmud and the Midrash, the ultimate sources for any Jewish story compilation during the Middle Ages. Other tales, as mentioned, have contemporary parallels in the Tosafists' exegesis. In this chapter, examples will be cited in order to follow trends of editing and adaptation, to survey the distinct discourse of *Sefer ha-ma'asim* in its affinities with its sources, and to propose interpretive options, often relevant to questions of identity, that represent the narrating community. I will consider a number of categories: the selection of the tales, their order in *Sefer ha-ma'asim*, and the thematic adaptations of their sources. This analysis will uncover the role of these tales in medieval northern France, as well as the dialogue they carry out with French vernacular literature contemporary with *Sefer ha-ma'asim*.

The stylistic attributes of *Sefer ha-ma'asim* will also be addressed. Three stylistic attributes will be demonstrated in comparison to earlier and contemporary sources in rabbinic literature and *Midrash aseret hadibrot*: (1) condensation of the text by omission of details given in parallel versions, where they could be filled in on the basis of textual, oral, and cultural contexts; (2) affinities and allusions to biblical verses and talmudic terms or aphorisms (along with the use, at times, of French grammatical patterns, as mentioned in the previous chapter); (3) the use of simple sentences combined by the conjunction "and" (in Hebrew: *vav ha-ḥibbur*), which creates dynamic situations and a narrating rhythm. These different stylistic aspects will be noted in the course of introducing the integration of various sources in *Sefer ha-ma'asim—Midrash aseret hadibrot*, rabbinic literature in the Talmud and Midrash, and contemporary commentaries of the Tosafists—as well as thematic aspects, such as the tales' affinities with contemporary non-Jewish literature.

Midrash aseret hadibrot

Twenty-two tales out of sixty-nine—nearly a third of *Sefer ha-ma'asim*—are from *Midrash aseret hadibrot*, which presumably originated in tenth-century Persia.[1] *Sefer ha-ma'asim* was a prominent medium for transferring its tales from East to West, both as independent units and within the frame of *Midrash aseret hadibrot*.[2] Nonetheless, *Midrash aseret hadibrot* was not copied into *Sefer ha-ma'asim* as one continuous section. The order of stories is arbitrary and often deviates from the sequence of the commandments.[3] Other tales from *Midrash aseret hadibrot* are inserted later in the compilation but not in sequence: the Ninth Commandment (one story),[4] the Third Commandment (one story),[5] the Fifth Commandment (one story),[6] and the Eighth Commandment (one story).[7] The original sequence of the commandments was disrupted, and the choice of stories from *Midrash aseret hadibrot* is eclectic. Accordingly, the basic unit of *Sefer ha-ma'asim* is the single story, not the *Midrash aseret hadibrot* as a whole, nor does it present a group of tales around a commandment, and the synchronic sequence that creates the texture of *Sefer ha-ma'asim* is loose. Its loose sequence is particularly striking, because *Midrash aseret hadibrot* is also copied in the manuscript as a work in itself (346b–352a),

1. Numerous and varied versions of *Midrash aseret hadibrot* were created throughout their transmission over the centuries. See the discussion based on Ms. Paris 716 and references to earlier studies: *Midrash aseret hadibrot*, ed. Shapira, 99–117.
2. See Yassif, "Hebrew Prose in the East," 61–62.
3. The tales in their textual order are Second (no. 8), First (nos. 9, 10, 11), Second (no. 12), Third (no. 13), Fourth (no. 14), Seventh (15), Eighth (no. 16), Seventh (nos. 17, 18), Fifth (no. 19), Fourth (nos. 20, 21, 22), and Ninth Commandments (no. 24). Tale no. 25 is linked only indirectly to the Tenth Commandment.
4. "Slander Kills Three" (no. 30), which, in different versions of *Midrash aseret hadibrot*, illustrates the commandment "Thou shalt not bear false witness."
5. "R. Joshua b. Levi and the Angel of Death" (no. 46).
6. "R. Joshua b. Elem and Ninus the Butcher" (no. 47), which illustrates the commandment about honoring one's parents.
7. "That Which Was Stolen Is Returned by Guile" (no. 48), which illustrates the commandment "Thou shalt not steal."

and there, the order of the commandments is retained.[8] *Midrash aseret hadibrot* was therefore a source for *Sefer ha-ma'asim*, but one that was not binding insofar as the selection and order of the stories were concerned.

The epilogue, which in *Midrash aseret hadibrot* links individual stories to a commandment, is also not necessarily copied verbatim in *Sefer ha-ma'asim*. Thus, for example, the epilogue to the well-known story about the mother and her sons who refused to prostrate themselves to a statue of a Roman emperor and sanctified the holy name is expanded in *Sefer ha-ma'asim* in comparison to *Midrash aseret hadibrot*. This was probably done in view of the persecution of Jews during the Crusades and of their status as a minority in the Middle Ages, with the purpose of heartening the readers and listeners.[9] Another tale, "Who Is the Thief?" (no. 16), which I will discuss shortly, is also based on *Midrash aseret hadibrot*, but an epilogue is added, composed of excerpts from homilies and aphorisms from the Talmud, as well as a quotation from the Bible, which is unique to *Sefer ha-ma'asim*. Sometimes an epilogue that does not originate in *Midrash aseret hadibrot* is added, and hence was probably composed in *Sefer ha-ma'asim* itself. At other times the affinity with a commandment is only implied; for example, in "Slander Kills Three" (no. 30), which illustrates the Ninth Commandment, "Thou shalt not bear false witness." Yet at times there is an original epilogue that is not copied from *Midrash aseret hadibrot*, as in the story "R. Joshua b. Levi and the Angel of Death" (no. 46, 321b–322a); R. Joshua never took an oath, which illustrates the commandment "Thou shalt not take the name of the Lord in vain." Yet other tales in *Sefer ha-ma'asim* have no epilogue at all, unlike their parallels in *Midrash aseret hadibrot*.[10] I would therefore conclude that also from the standpoint of the different types of epilogues, *Midrash aseret hadibrot* was not a binding source of *Sefer ha-ma'asim*.

Changes were also made in the stories themselves, not only in the epilogues, which indicates that *Midrash aseret hadibrot* was perceived as a nonbinding source also as far as their wording was concerned. The tales primarily represent story traditions that were received in the East, but when they came into *Sefer ha-ma'asim* in the West, motifs were inserted into them from parallels widespread throughout

8. A third instance of *Midrash aseret hadibrot* toward the end of the manuscript, in a different version, is accompanied by the scribe's comment, "And I found this too among the legends of the commandments."

9. Baumgarten and Kushelevsky, "From 'The Mother and Her Sons' to 'The Mother of the Sons' in Medieval Ashkenaz."

10. That is the case with "Joseph-Who-Reveres-the-Sabbath" (no. 21) and "Mattiah b. Ḥarash" (no. 33).

Europe, and these were adapted to norms of Jewish culture. From this vantage point, *Sefer ha-ma'asim* mediated between Christian and Jewish story traditions, and not only between East and West.

It is quite difficult to reconstruct these thematic and stylistic processes, since Ms. Bodl. Or. 135 is the earliest extant manuscript of the *Midrash aseret hadibrot*. Other manuscripts of *Midrash aseret hadibrot* accessible to us are later than *Sefer ha-ma'asim*, from the fourteenth century in Provence and thereafter. The numerous versions of *Midrash aseret hadibrot* were created in different periods and cannot be treated as a single entity. And yet we have only these manuscripts, and even based on them it is possible to discern traces of reworking in *Sefer ha-ma'asim*—that is, marked thematic and stylistic changes—from which conclusions can be drawn.

"The Man Who Never Took an Oath" (no. 13) in *Sefer ha-ma'asim* is an example of a fusion of various narrative traditions: Jewish and Christian, Eastern and Western. It originated in *Midrash aseret hadibrot* as an illustration of the Third Commandment ("Thou shalt not take the name of the Lord in vain"), and it has non-Jewish parallels in both East and West.[11] The tale opens as the father orders his son never to take an oath, not even a true one, and then relates the tribulations of the hero as a result of his steadfast faithfulness to his promise. First, he lost his inheritance because he refused to swear to his father's creditors that his father died clear of any debt. Later, his wife and then his children were abducted and taken on ships to unknown destinations. After several twists and turns, the family is united at the very happy end of the tale.

The bulk of the story is based on *Midrash aseret hadibrot* but also has affinities with its thirteenth-century parallel, the legend of Saint Eustace (previously "Placidus") in *The Golden Legend* by Jacobus de Voragine.[12] These affinities are evident in several motifs that are typical in Western Europe: In its content and syntax, it is reminiscent of the Book of Job; the beauty of the hero's wife is particularly emphasized; and she is not a member of a royal house (unlike her counterpart in *Midrash aseret hadibrot*, where her royal lineage is mentioned), in line with its non-Jewish source in the East. The emphasized affinity with the Book of Job in *Sefer ha-ma'asim*, rather than in *Midrash aseret hadibrot*, is especially significant, and it imbues the tale with a somewhat martyrological tone. The man devotedly adheres to his father's will despite his misfortunes and calamities, which, as in the case of Job,

11. *Midrash aseret hadibrot*, ed. Shapira, 54–59.

12. Jacobi a Voragine, *Legenda Aurea*, no. 161, 712–718; Jacobus de Voragine, *The Golden Legend*, vol. 2, 266–271.

strike him repeatedly and rapidly. In *The Golden Legend*, Eustace indeed becomes a martyr. He is tortured, and after his death he is declared a saint. *Sefer ha-ma'asim* realizes the martyrological potential of the Jewish tale, somewhere between *Midrash aseret hadibrot* and *The Golden Legend*. It adds a martyrological tone to the former yet avoids the option of actually becoming a martyr and a saint given in the latter.

On the stylistic level, there are numerous examples of condensing the text. Two will suffice here to demonstrate this. In *Sefer ha-ma'asim* the father says: "My son, beware never to take an oath, even if it is the truth." *Midrash aseret hadibrot* has: "My son, beware never to take an oath at all," and later, "And even a true oath I never swore, hence."[13] The father's legacy to his son is condensed in *Sefer ha-ma'asim* into one sentence that contains the information given in two sentences in *Midrash aseret hadibrot*. Also, in response to the mendacious demand of creditors for payment of a fabricated debt of his father, the man replies: "I would rather pay them and not swear." The more detailed description in *Midrash aseret hadibrot* is: "I would rather pay them the money, all that they ask of me, and not swear."[14] Apparently, narrative redundancy, which is appreciated by modern readers, is not the approach adopted by the scribe in *Sefer ha-ma'asim*, nor by his audience.

"The Defamed Woman" (no. 24), like "The Man Who Never Took an Oath" (no. 13), is another arena of encounter between East and West and between Jewish and Christian literary traditions. Here too it is evident that the Jewish narrator and scribe relied on a mutual cultural context, familiar to his audience in northern France. The story originated in the East, and already there it was introduced into *Midrash aseret hadibrot* as an illustration of the Ninth Commandment: "Thou shalt not bear false witness."[15] In her husband's absence, a woman is left in the care of her brother-in-law. He tries to seduce her, and she refuses. He reacts by falsely accusing her of having betrayed her husband, and she is sentenced to death by stoning, as an adulteress. She is saved, but defamed time and again in various situations and on numerous occasions. Later on she becomes a well-known healer, and her brother-in-law and others who slandered her come to her to find a cure for their illnesses. She forces them to confess their actions. Thus her husband learns of her innocence, and they reunite.

13. *Midrash aseret* hadibrot, ed. Shapira, 54.

14. Ibid., 54.

15. Ibid., 217–221.

Here, as in the "The Man Who Never Took an Oath" (no. 13), the tale's affinity with *Midrash aseret hadibrot* is manifested by the lack of an episode generally found in the European parallels, in which the woman jails her brother-in-law until her husband returns in order to stop his attempts to seduce her. Nor does the tale have the European episode wherein the slandered woman is banished to the forest and hanged by her hair.[16] In *Midrash aseret hadibrot*, as in the non-Jewish parallels in the East, she is stoned.

Nonetheless, in *Sefer ha-ma'asim* there are also distinctly Western characteristics. The European parallels are shorter than those from the East, and that is also true of the version in *Sefer ha-ma'asim*. The European tales generally do not include, similarly to *Sefer ha-ma'asim*, an episode found in the Eastern parallels, and consequently also in *Midrash aseret hadibrot*, about an ungrateful thief whom the slandered woman saves from the gallows. In return he sells her as a servant. An implied dialogue between *Sefer ha-ma'asim* and the non-Jewish parallels, against the backdrop of the cult of the Virgin Mary in twelfth-century Europe, is particularly interesting. Mary reveals herself to the persecuted woman and gives her a healing herb with which she cures the ill, especially lepers, and is saved from her predicament. In *Sefer ha-ma'asim*, in the spirit of Jewish culture, the figure of the Virgin Mary is not introduced, but the "miracle" motif prevalent in the Christian legend is implied: "God provided her with all kinds of herbs, and she healed lepers and every [kind of] disease." This becomes obvious when compared with *Midrash aseret hadibrot*, where her characterization as a healer is rational, without implying a miracle: "And God gave her intelligence and understanding and she knew all manner of remedies in the world and she sold all kinds of balms and herbs, many of which were able to heal all the illnesses of the body."[17] It seems that *Sefer ha-ma'asim* joins in the discourse of saint legends, particularly those about the Virgin Mary, that flourished then in Europe, but from the Jewish position of monotheistic faith.

The discourse that we noted in "The Man Who Never Took an Oath" (no. 13) also emerges in the present tale, and as we shall soon see, in other tales as well. *Sefer ha-ma'asim* absorbed narratives that took shape in the East in *Midrash aseret hadibrot*, embedded in them motifs characteristic of non-Jewish parallels in Europe, and adapted them as Jewish. Thus the compilation represents a medieval discourse in Europe, yet one that is distinctive in its Jewish attributes.

16. For references to the tale in Europe, see the Oxford Library site: csm.mml.ox.ac.uk/index.php?p=poemdata_view&rec=5 (accessed June 20, 2016).

17. *Midrash aseret hadibrot*, ed. Shapira, 219.

The comparison of these two versions, the detailed and redundant description in the one versus its more condensed parallel in the other ("God provided her with all kinds of herbs, and she healed lepers and every [kind of] disease), also attests to a stylistic choice in *Sefer ha-ma'asim*, as mentioned earlier. The compressed, succinct rhetoric in "The Man Who Never Took an Oath" is also palpable in "The Defamed Woman" (no. 24). It should be emphasized, however, that its language is not sparse but rather anchored in the sources. The expression "Egyptian rope"—"They immediately took her and placed an Egyptian rope on her neck"—is charged, and alludes to a broader context in the Talmud (*Sotah* 7:2). It is a rope made of palm fibers intended to tie the clothing of the stoned woman so her nudity would not be exposed. In *Midrash aseret hadibrot*, at least in the parallel version in Ms. Vatican 107, there is no such mention. Another expression inspired by the sources is in the assertive response of the woman as she rejects the advances of her brother-in-law: "for she who betrays her husband betrays her Creator."[18] This phrase, rich with biblical and exegetical resonances and cited in *Sefer ha-ma'asim* more than once, does not appear in *Midrash aseret hadibrot*. It would seem that *Sefer ha-ma'asim* draws quite heavily on Hebrew classical sources, while condensing its text. The textual surrounding of the quoted phrase is: "Heaven forbid that I should do so, for she who betrays her husband betrays her Creator. And furthermore, her soul will be doomed to Gehenna. And what's more, my husband is your brother and he entrusted me to you to safeguard me and not to corrupt my spirit and yours." This conjunct syntax of simple and combined sentences produces a rapid dynamics, appropriate for conveying the woman's emotional state.

There are similar processes, thematic and stylistic, in some other tales as well. "The Bizarre Deeds of Elijah the Prophet" (no. 1), transmits the *Midrash aseret hadibrot* version but has affinities also with its Christian parallels in the exempla of Jacques de Vitry and Étienne de Bourbon. Similarly, "Who Is the Thief?" (no. 16), based on *Midrash aseret hadibrot*, is also based on oral folklore traditions in Europe documented in Boccaccio's *Decameron*, from the fourteenth century. "Joseph-Who-Reveres-the-Sabbath" (no. 21) combines in *Sefer ha-ma'asim* the talmudic and the *Midrash aseret hadibrot* versions, but contains a nuance that resonates with the *Golden Legend*. In all these, which I will shortly illustrate, *Sefer ha-ma'asim* follows the basic versions of *Midrash aseret hadibrot*, but stylistic nuances and changes in motif create an intertextual affinity with the European

18. The phrase is based on a verse in Proverbs ("Who forsakes the companion of her youth, and forgets the covenant of her God" [Proverbs 2:17]) and on exegesis of the verse in the rabbinic literature (Num. R. 9b; *Pesikta rabbati*, ed. Meir Friedman [Ish Shalom], ch. 21, 107a–b).

parallels, which slant the stories into a new context. While they are part of a long heritage transmitted within Jewish communities to imbue Jewish values and traditions and enhance Jewish identities, they also conduct a cultural dialogue with their non-Jewish surroundings by means of shared narratives and literary conventions.

In "The Bizarre Deeds of Elijah the Prophet" (no. 1), R. Joshua b. Levi joins Elijah on a journey and observes his manner of behavior as they travel to various places. He is exposed to very strange behavior, scandalous and unjustified in his view, but is forbidden to question it. He is committed to "suffer"—"*lisbol*"—in silence what he witnesses. In *Midrash aseret hadibrot*, the core of the story is Elijah's revelation to R. Joshua b. Levi, for which he yearns. The journey is presented as fulfillment of this deep desire.[19] While the theodicy issue does come up in *Midrash aseret hadibrot*, it is secondary to the revelation itself. *Sefer ha-ma'asim* follows its source in *Midrash aseret hadibrot* in terms of the plot, but changes the ratio between the two poles: "*ẓidduk hadin*" ("vindication of divine judgment") and "Elijah's revelation." Compared to *Midrash aseret hadibrot*, it assigns additional weight to the *ẓidduk hadin*. This can reasonably be explained by the influence of the tale's European parallels, which focus primarily on the theodicy issue rather than on the revelation scene, although definite distinctions between the two are glossed over. Thus *Sefer ha-ma'asim* shares with its European parallels a similar rationale for *ẓidduk hadin*, while it introduces religious disputes regarding the supreme authority one should believe in, as well as distinct identity definitions that are implied in the tale.

As these changes in emphasis are introduced, the scope of the text is reduced by almost a third, in comparison to the parallel version in *Midrash aseret hadibrot*. Thus, for example, in *Sefer ha-ma'asim* one reads: "And R. Joshua said: May I accompany you and observe what you do in the world?" In contrast, the more expanded wording in *Midrash aseret hadibrot* is: "He said to Joshua, 'What do you wish?' He said to him: 'I wish to go with you and see what you do in the world.' "[20] The dialogue is maintained in *Sefer ha-ma'asim*, as is the content, but it lacks the dramatic dimension created by the narrative expansion in *Midrash aseret hadibrot*.

"Who Is the Thief?" (no. 16) is also based on *Midrash aseret hadibrot*.[21] The frame story, in which Solomon is required to reach a verdict in the absence of any witnesses and to identify the thief from among three merchants, illustrates the

19. *Midrash aseret hadibrot*, ed. Shapira, 89–92.

20. Ibid., 90.

21. Ibid., 81–84.

commandment "Thou shalt not steal." The internal story presents a conflict in the figure of a woman who is faithful to her husband but also committed to a childhood boyfriend, whom she promised to marry in due time. How the woman and the two men cope with this situation is interesting in itself, but for now the various types of discourse in *Sefer ha-ma'asim* and in *Midrash aseret hadibrot* are particularly interesting. A significant scene is that in which the girl and the boy make mutual vows in *Sefer ha-ma'asim*, in contrast to the one-sided vow of the girl in *Midrash aseret hadibrot* ("and swore to him she would").[22] This is how it is phrased in *Sefer ha-ma'asim*: "the boy said to the girl that he would take her for his wife and she would take him as her husband. And they both swore on these conditions, if the Almighty should make it possible." Although *Sefer ha-ma'asim* basically follows the tale's version in *Midrash aseret hadibrot*, the nuance noted here enhances the text with a far broader context, that of matchmaking ceremonies in Ashkenaz. At these ceremonies the parents of the betrothed couple shook hands, a gesture that expressed a commitment to protect the woman against annulment of the marriage agreement. In Jewish communities in the Muslim world, the male could far more easily annul the agreement, and that is also manifested in *Midrash aseret hadibrot*, where the girl is required to take an oath while the young man does not have to. This entire context is brought into the fabric of the text by the nuanced deviation of *Sefer ha-ma'asim* from *Midrash aseret hadibrot* regarding the commitment scene between the couple. Indirectly, an affinity is also created with the non-Jewish parallel in the *Decameron*, which was inspired by and responded to the ethos of courtly love.[23] The mode of mutuality in *Sefer ha-ma'asim*, which is manifested in the commitments between the boy and the girl, is expressed in the *Decameron* in the two conflicting relationships of Dianora, the female character: with her husband, Gilberto, and with Ansaldo, the courting knight. In her relations with Ansaldo, it is she who decides on the conditions of the agreement between them and the tasks he must carry out to win her hand; these same conditions define her commitment to him, should he meet her demands. In her relations with her husband, mutuality is expressed in his empathetic attitude toward her predicament—her commitment to their marriage, but also to the promise she made to the knight. The ethos of courtly love was rejected in *Sefer ha-ma'asim*, but the mode of mutuality in relations between the sexes was preserved.

---

22. Ibid., 82.

23. The *Decameron* is from the fourteenth century, later than *Sefer ha-ma'asim*, but based on oral folklore (Lee, *Decameron*, 322–323). For the tale, see Boccaccio, *Decameron*, ed. Cesare Segre, 613–617.

"Joseph-Who-Reveres-the-Sabbath" (no. 21) is, finally, one more example of the different discourse in *Sefer ha-ma'asim* as compared to *Midrash aseret hadibrot. Sefer ha-ma'asim* combines two versions from the Talmud (*Shabbat* 119a) and from *Midrash aseret hadibrot.*[24] Joseph, who made every effort to buy delicacies in honor of the Sabbath, was appropriately rewarded by divine intervention. One Sabbath eve, a fisherman who had been unsuccessful in selling a large, beautiful fish, approached Joseph in the hopes that he would want it. Joseph did indeed purchase the fish, and in it he found a precious gem. It turned out that the gem belonged to a rich gentile who lived nearby. Because the gentile had feared he would lose all of his property to Joseph, he had converted it into one precious stone. It was lost in the river and swallowed by a fish, which finally came into the hands of Joseph, who greatly revered the Sabbath.

In comparison to its sources in the Talmud and in *Midrash aseret hadibrot*, the focus has changed in *Sefer ha-ma'asim*. The metonymic link in these sources between the value of honoring the Sabbath and the person who honored the Sabbath made it possible to introduce a certain nuance in *Sefer ha-ma'asim*. Its new focus is on the label of Joseph, the man "who-reveres-the-Sabbath," rather than on the value of honoring the Sabbath itself.[25] The broader context of this subtle change might be the medieval legends about Gregorius, St. Arnold, and others, in which a gem in the belly of a fish marks the finder as a saint or is a sign of absolution of sin.[26] Although Joseph, who greatly revered the Sabbath, is anonymous in rabbinic literature, he is more delineated and rounded out in *Sefer ha-ma'asim* when compared to its sources. This might indicate some traces of the legendary discourse prevalent in Europe. On the other hand, as a Jewish symbol of sacred time, the Sabbath in *Sefer ha-ma'asim* opposes the Christian concept of the saint as a category grounded in the incarnation of Jesus and his tormented body, and repudiates it.

The Talmud and the Midrashim

As I noted in the previous chapter, a large section of stories are from the rabbinic literature in the Babylonian Talmud (excluding the Palestinian Talmud); in the Jerusalem *midrashim* (*Leviticus rabbah*, *Pesikta de rav Kahana*, and *Lamentations rabbah*); and in the later *midrashim* (*Tanḥuma*, *Pesikta rabbati*, *Ruth zuta*, *Midrash*

24. *Midrash aseret hadibrot*, ed. Shapira, 61.

25. For further elaboration, see tale no. 21, in Part III.

26. See Tubach references 4102; ATU 736A; Loomis, "The Ring of Polycrates," 44–47; Elstein, "The Gregorius Legend," 195–215.

Proverbs, *Avot de Rabbi Natan* version B, and *Yalkut hamakhiri*). The influence of the Babylonian Talmud is especially apparent, and to a certain extent that of the *Tanḥuma* as well. An indirect influence of rabbinic sources is found in tales mediated through *Midrash aseret hadibrot*; for example, the well-known story of the mother and her sons, against the background of Hadrian's edicts.[27] Other tales are introduced into *Sefer ha-ma'asim* in a sequence that more or less follows the order of the commandments, but their direct source is actually the Talmud.[28] Certain tales are based on more than one source. "Joseph-Who-Reveres-the-Sabbath" (no. 21) is made up mainly of the tale version in *Midrash aseret hadibrot* but relies also on the Talmud. Like *Midrash aseret hadibrot*, the talmudic and midrashic sources were adapted to their new contexts in *Sefer ha-ma'asim*, as a work of thirteenth-century northern France. We will now follow these processes on the levels of genre, theme, and style.

Genre

The exemplum as a prominent genre in *Sefer ha-ma'asim* was an obvious choice, being a direct continuation of the exemplum in the Talmud and the Midrash. However there are several instances in *Sefer ha-ma'asim* when the genre is taken to an extreme, and from which I shall draw conclusions about their cultural contexts in the Middle Ages. There are ten exempla that are especially brief (up to approximately 70 words), even in terms of the anecdotal tales in the Talmud and Midrash.[29] One example is the anecdote about the man who was saved from drowning thanks to his custom of giving generously to charity (no. 31), which was cited in the Talmud in connection with the laws regarding the *agunah*.[30] Rabbi Akiva, who witnessed the sinking of a ship, testified that a man's wife was permitted to remarry, but her husband soon turned up alive and well, and the mistake was discovered in good time.[31] Quite a few other anecdotal exempla include those of the scribes of Solomon (no. 42) who wanted to flee from the Angel of Death to the city of Luz, where there is no

27. *Midrash aseret hadibrot*, ed. Shapira, 48–50. For its sources in rabbinic literature, see tale no. 12, in part 3, "Tales and Parallels."

28. "Joshua b. Levi and the Angel of Death" (no. 46); "One of Ten" (no. 17); "The Commandment of Ẓiẓit" (no. 18).

29. They were not mediated to *Sefer ha-ma'asim* by *Midrash aseret hadibrot* in this case.

30. *Yebamot* 121a.

31. The story is also cited in Ms. Parma 2295, from the same region and period—northern France at the end of the thirteenth century. It was not included in other story compilations in the East.

death, but encountered him at its gates;[32] four consecutive anecdotes about R. Pinḥas b. Yair (nos. 56–59);[33] a tale about the gentile host of Rabban Shimon b. Gamliel, who angrily turned over a table heaped with all sorts of good food only because there were no soft-shelled walnuts there to satisfy his lust (no. 45);[34] a tale about a wedding feast that turned into a curative feast when the groom was bitten by a snake and died (no. 37);[35] and another one about the students of R. Shimon b. Yoḥai, who envied their friend for going abroad and becoming rich (no. 35). In this last tale the students were taken to a valley filled with coins of gold so they could collect as much as they wished for themselves, but at the expense of their portion in the world to come.[36] Finally the tale about R. Shimon b. Ḥalafta should also be noted, in which he rejected the gift of a precious gem from heaven so he would not lose its remuneration in the world to come (no. 36).[37] The didactic messages in these exempla—values of charity, justification for a death verdict, piety, the study of Torah, and frugality—are embodied in particularly short narratives that illustrate these values and generally are accompanied by a moral epilogue.[38] Since they are so short, two or three such exempla are all on one page, and they can easily be discerned by the graphically accentuated heading "*Ma'aseh be-*."

In view of the consistent choice of these very short anecdotes from a rich selection of proportionally longer stories in rabbinic literature, and the fact that they were chosen directly from the Talmud and Midrash rather than mediated by medieval story collections, one can assume that they attest to a defined aesthetic taste and horizon of expectations. Specifically because of these features—that is, their emphasized brevity and didactic messages—they were included in *Sefer ha-ma'asim* in preference to other exempla in rabbinic literature.

---

32. *Succa* 53b.

33. B. *Ḥullin*, 7a; *Deuteronomy rabbah, Ekev.*

34. *Pesikta de rav kahana*, ed. Mandelbaum, 115–116.

35. *Leviticus rabbah* 20, 3, ed., Margulieus, 451–452.

36. P. *Berakhot* 9, 2 [13, 4]; *Tanḥuma*, ed. Buber, *Pekudei*, 7.

37. *Tanḥuma*, ed. Buber, *Pekudei*, 7.

38. Some of these epilogues are, respectively: "A person's legs are responsible for him. They take him to the place where he is wanted" ("Solomon's Scribes," no. 42, in translation from Aramaic); "Come and see human faithfulness. From their faithfulness you will know the faithfulness of the Almighty" ("R. Pinḥas b. Yair," no. 56); "And on that matter Solomon noted in his wisdom: 'The righteous eats to his heart's content, but the belly of the wicked shall want' " ("Soft-Shelled Walnuts," no. 45); "Whoever takes will be subtracting from his portion in the world to come, because the Torah's reward is not given in this world, but rather in the world to come, as it says: 'And she shall rejoice in time to come' " ("A Valley Full of Gold," no. 35).

It seems that the exceptions in *Sefer ha-ma'asim*—those ten exempla that stand out for their brevity—prove the rule: the role of the exemplum in *Sefer ha-ma'asim* in correlation to the contemporary exemplum in Europe. Compilations of exempla were prevalent in the second half of the twelfth century and in the thirteenth century in Europe, its golden age.[39] There are the compilations of exempla of Peter Alfonsi as far back as the eleventh century, and of Jacques de Vitry and Étienne de Bourbon in the twelfth century, as well as *The Golden Legend* by Jacob de Voragine and *The Dialogue on Miracles* by Caesarius of Heisterbach in the thirteenth century, among others. In the exempla of Jacques de Vitry, and after him in other compilations of exempla, the concentration of very brief anecdotes is striking: two to four per page, bearing a succinct, clear-cut religious message very similar to the condensation in *Sefer ha-ma'asim*.[40] To sum up, the choice of the exemplum as a genre is striking in *Sefer ha-ma'asim* not only because of the proportion of exempla in the compilation but also in view of the choice of a prevalent genre in Western Europe at a time of Jewish and Christian religious devoutness.

Three other genres that were prevalent in Medieval Europe left their imprints on *Sefer ha-ma'asim*. These were the romance, the fabliau (in one story only), and the parable. The impact of the romance is reflected especially in tales from non-Jewish sources, which will be discussed in the following chapter. In this chapter, which is focused on the Jewish sources of *Sefer ha-ma'asim*, the tale of R. Akiva's daughter, who was saved from death on her wedding day (no. 32), is an indication of the imprint of the romance. The talmudic narrative (*Shabbat* 156b) was extraordinarily reworked in comparison to its source. R. Akiva's daughter marries "a very handsome young man," despite the fact that everyone told her in advance that she was doomed to die on her wedding day. On the night of the ceremony, a poor beggar comes and asks her for food, and she gives him some. On her wedding night, after "she got into bed with her husband," a snake emerged from a hole in the wall to bite her. She leaned away from her husband, took her hairpin, and, placing it in the hole, killed the snake either deliberately or unwittingly—it is ambiguous in *Sefer ha-ma'asim*. The following day, when her father discovers to his great surprise that she is still alive, she tells him about the beggar, and he goes out to teach his pupils about the power of charity. The story ends with an epilogue that is not in the

39. See Le Goff, *The Birth of Purgatory*, 78–80.

40. See the detailed introduction in Jacques de Vitry, *Exempla*, xv–cxvi, in particular regarding de Vitry's influence on later compilations of exempla, on pages liii–lxx. And see detailed descriptions of these exempla compilations in Tubach, *Index Exemplorum*, 517–525.

Talmud: “When a person observes numerous commandments faithfully and out of fear of the Almighty, God preserves him and preserves his body.”

The impact of the romance as a genre that glorifies the ethos of love is probably reflected in *Sefer ha-ma'asim* in the bride’s decision to marry for love and to ignore the danger lying in wait, as well as in the erotic tone that is absent from the talmudic version.[41] The changes in tone and in the portrait of the bride in no way minimize the message of the value and virtue of charity, but they may express aesthetic expectations evoked by the flourishing of the romance in northern France.

The fabliau left hardly any imprint on *Sefer ha-ma'asim*, because the genre is so blatant in its erotic and sexist messages: extreme misogyny and the stereotype of the foolish, betrayed husband vis-à-vis the deceiving, seductive wife. Nonetheless there are some traces of it in one story whose source is the midrash *Leviticus rabbah* (25:5): “Hadrian and the Old Man” (no. 38). When Hadrian, emperor of Rome, and his legions were on their way to war, they came across an old man who was planting a fig tree. Hadrian was surprised. After all, by the time the tree would give fruit, the old man would be dead. But the old man planted the tree not for himself but for his descendants. Sometime later, Hadrian passed there again on his way back from the battlefield, and the old man greeted him with a basket full of figs, the fruit of the tree. The emperor was so amazed that he ordered the basket to be filled with gold in exchange for the fruit. Jealous of the old man, a neighboring woman sent her good-for-nothing husband to the emperor with a basket of figs and other fruit, so she too would receive a large sum of money for them. Instead the husband was severely beaten and sent home sobbing. The narrator’s conclusion is: “This is to teach you that all women are wicked and cause their husbands to fall, and woe is he who listens to them.” This misogynistic statement goes far beyond the original version in *Leviticus rabbah.* There the lesson applies only to those whom the narrator identifies as evil women, without branding the entire female gender as such. The conventions of the fabliau are inferred between the lines, but not necessarily as a reflection of the status of women in Ashkenaz; to the contrary, women held a respected position in the life of the community. Rather, it is an expression of the reception of *Sefer ha-ma'asim* for purposes of pleasure and amusement, along with its didactic aim. As a genre the fabliau is a literary convention, not a reflection of real life.

Finally, “A Meal of Herbs” (no. 62) is one more example of the role of *Sefer ha-ma'asim* within the literary flourishing in northern France, as well as within

41. Another possibility is that she decided to accept the very idea of the marriage, despite the expected fatal outcome, as her father too decided to go ahead with the marriage despite the bad portents of the astrologers.

Jewish narrative traditions. It tells the tale of Solomon during his exile from his kingdom, after he was ousted by Asmodeus, king of the demons. I present it here against the background of the popularity of parables in the Middle Ages and their wide reception in Europe.[42] When Solomon descended from his throne, so it is told, two people invited him to dine with them. One sacrificed a bull for him and served him meat and delicacies, but reminded him during the entire meal of his past days of glory, until Solomon "was sated with his tears." The second one served him a sparse meal of vegetables but never stopped consoling him and assuring him that in the end the Almighty would relent and restore him to his kingdom. The tale ends with an epigram that summarizes Solomon's conclusion: "Better a meal of herbs where love is than a fatted ox and hatred with it" (Proverbs 15:17). The tale functions as a parable on the verse from Proverbs. With the latter functioning as the moral, the tale forms a definite unit. That is probably why it was not included as an episode in a much larger, far more popular tale about Solomon's ouster by Asmodeus, which includes a number of episodes: a conflict between Solomon and Asmodeus, king of the demons; Solomon's banishment from his throne and its takeover by the demon in his image; Solomon's wandering throughout his kingdom, rejected and mocked; as well as other episodes that were added in later versions of this tale.[43] In light of the dynamics of the tale of Solomon and Asmodeus over the generations, the interpolation of the "Meal of Herbs" (no. 62) into it, as an episode in the longer narrative, would be expected. This, however, did not occur. Furthermore, the choice to include the "Meal of Herbs" in *Sefer ha-ma'asim*, and to prefer it over the expanded, accepted, and far more dramatic tale of Solomon and Asmodeus, is odd and quite surprising, unless we take into account the story's genre as a parable, and the widespread reception of parables in medieval Europe.

More concretely, we can compare "A Meal of Herbs" with *Solomon and Marcolf*, which was very popular in the Middle Ages. An earlier, Latin version of the work existed in France in the twelfth century. It survived in many later manuscripts in vernacular versions, and its roots are in oral folk literature.[44] Solomon, the learned, wise king, and Marcolf, a simple, outspoken, devious peasant, verbally spar with each other using various parables, idioms, and witticisms. Solomon parries with proverbs anchored in the Bible, and Marcolf, the popular figure of the village idiot,

42. See Ziolkowski, *Solomon and Marcolf*, 28–44.

43. On the reception of the story, see Kushelevsky, "King Solomon and Asmodeus (Ashmedei)," 85–111.

44. See Ziolkowski's introduction (*Solomon and Marcolf*, 6–12), and Tubach's references to tale type no. 4462.

retorts with brazen, titillating folk parables. "A Meal of Herbs" and *Solomon and Marcolf* are very different, but aside from their use of the parable genre, they also have in common the character of King Solomon, who gains folk wisdom from the simple man: Marcolf, in the non-Jewish story, who competes with him in telling parables and wins; and the poor host, in the Jewish story, who teaches him indirectly that a vegetable meal in which there is love is better than a banquet with a fatted ox where there is hatred. Apparently the choice of "A Meal of Herbs"—a less familiar tale, chosen as a sort of parable over the tale of Solomon and Asmodeus—brings to light trends of reception and aesthetic expectations within the narrating community, against the background of the surrounding non-Jewish population.

Theme

Aside from those aspects of genre discussed above, the choice of stories from rabbinic literature highlights *Sefer ha-ma'asim* as a product of its time and place also in regard to its thematic aspects. Motifs common to *Sefer ha-ma'asim* and European narratives are not necessarily the outcomes of genealogical development. They represent independent Jewish and non-Jewish sources of influence in the East and the West. Nonetheless, the reasons for the unusual choice of one story or another, in light of other choices in other story compilations, as well as editing trends and stylistic choices unique to *Sefer ha-ma'asim*, can often be explained in light of its literary parallels in northern France particularly, and in Europe in general.

In "One of Ten" (no. 17), which originates in the Talmud (*Baba Batra* 58a), a father discovers that only one of his sons is really his, but he does not know which one. He reacts by leaving a will that is obscure regarding inheritance: Only his legal son is entitled to it. When the time comes, a judge is required to arrive at a decision, under difficult circumstances, since there are no witnesses. A paternity test is held to determine the legal son. The boys are required to strike their father's tombstone to make him reveal who should receive the inheritance. They all do so, except for the legal son, who is incapable of desecrating his father's honor and is willing to forgo the inheritance under these conditions. Consequently, he is identified as the son who merits the inheritance according to his father's will. Certain thematic changes in *Sefer ha-ma'asim*, compared to the talmudic source, place an emphasis on the value of honor, loyalty, and unity within the family, in contrast to an emphasis on the legal situation and the figure of the judge in the Talmud. There are various parallels in European exempla from the twelfth to fourteenth centuries.[45] The

45. See, for example, Étienne de Bourbon, *Anecdotes historiques*, no. 160, 136–137.

two major differences between them and the tale in *Sefer ha-ma'asim* are the number of sons (ten in the Jewish tale and three in the Christian parallels) and the paternity test (which is particularly brutish in the Christian parallels—usually a competition in which the sons shoot arrows at the heart of their father's corpse). The symbolic meanings in each parallel are deeply rooted in Judaism and Christianity. In Jewish culture ten men constitute a *minyan* and create a "quorum": a collective to which the individual is committed insofar as certain religious rituals are concerned. In the context of "One of Ten," the "collective" is the family unit, which is more than its parts. In the Christian parallels, the number 3 invokes the symbolism of the Holy Trinity. In the paternity test, the shooting of arrows into the father's body in order to strike his heart, places the story within the Christian discourse on Jesus' suffering in the Passion scene and its imitations, and fits into the ethos of suffering that reached its peak in the High Middle Ages. In these parallels a story about father-son relations becomes an allegory on the relations between the Christian believer and Jesus, and a Christian-ascetic dimension is added which is absent from the Jewish story. This reflects a tension inherent in Christianity, between family life and asceticism.[46] The inclusion of "One in Ten" in *Sefer ha-ma'asim*, as an expression of a widespread interest in its parallels in Europe, and the special emphases in it are therefore part of the cultural and religious discourses that digress from the story itself.

"R. Meir and Kiddor" (no. 26) is another tale whose source is the Talmud (*Yoma* 83b). It is one of five tales in *Sefer ha-ma'asim* about the embezzlement of a deposit left in trust.[47] It tells the story of R. Meir, a disciple of Rabbi Akiva, who was meticulous about the names of people and would refrain from entering the home of anyone who did not have a good name. Once, while on his way with two of his friends, his companions said they wanted to stay at Kiddor's home. R. Meir perceived his name as an acronym for the verse "For they are a perverse generation" ("*ki dor tahapukhot hemah*" [Deuteronomy 32:20]). Unlike his friends, who deposited their money with Kiddor on the eve of the Sabbath, R. Meir hid his money elsewhere. His decision proved to be the right one. After the Sabbath Kiddor denied R. Meir's friends' claims for their deposit, while R. Meir had his money safe at his side. His friends were now forced to trick Kiddor's wife in order to get hold of their purses. They gave her a "sign" to prove they had her husband's approval,

46. See Kushelevsky, "Family Images," 228–240.

47. The others are "Who Is the Thief?" (no. 16); "The Loan" (nos. 2 and 34); "That Which Was Stolen Is Returned by Guile" (no. 48); and "The Pious Pretender" (no. 50).

which made her open the "chest" where their money was hidden and return their purses to them.

Only in *Sefer ha-ma'asim*, in contrast to the talmudic version and others in the Jewish tradition of this tale, does the word "chest" (*teva*) appear, evoking the tale of the "The Ten Chests" in Alfonsi's *Disciplina Clericalis.*[48] This work was translated into Old French in the twelfth century and greatly influenced the popular and didactic literature written thereafter. Although the stylistic choice of the word "chest" might indicate the use of such chests in medieval households, it apparently stems from an acquaintance with Alfonsi's tale and its parallels in Europe.[49] Thus a talmudic tale about the importance of a good name was reworked as a discourse on deposits, depositors, and "bankers," and on cheaters and deceivers. This change of emphasis in the tale posits *Sefer ha-ma'asim* within the larger context of medieval literature in Europe.

The four tales about R. Pinḥas b. Yair (nos. 56–59), one of the late Tannaim (second century), depict a figure of a *ḥasid* who adheres to strict norms of behavior, who is learned in miracles and devoted to public works. Thus, for example, he helps the inhabitants of one city get rid of a plague of mice that were destroying their harvest, and promised them that if they were meticulous about paying their tithes, the mice would disappear and their harvest would be blessed. On another occasion he parted the waters of a river twice: once for himself and then for his fellow Jews, so they could cross it on their way to circumcise a Jew. The epilogue compares him to Moses, who, unlike R. Pinḥas b. Yair, split the Red Sea only once. The first three tales are from *Deuteronomy rabbah*, which is in Hebrew and more appropriate for the target audience of *Sefer ha-ma'asim*. The fourth tale, about the Ginnai river that divided itself for R. Pinḥas, is talmudic (*Ḥullin* 7a). The preference of the Ginnai tale over other tales about R. Pinḥas b. Yair,[50] and the citation of the Babylonian version rather than its parallel in the Palestinian Talmud (tractate *Demai* 1a), point up the special emphases on the choices made in *Sefer ha-ma'asim*. The common feature of all four tales is the figure of R. Pinḥas b. Yair as a *ḥasid* who was devoted to the good of the community and learned in miracles. Regarding the Ginnai tale, it should be noted that only in the Babylonian Talmud is R. Pinḥas referred to as a man "learned in miracles."

48. *The Disciplina Clericalis of Petrus Alfonsi*, ed. Hermes, no. 15, 128–130.

49. For a discussion of thematic changes in the medieval version, see tale no. 26, in Part III.

50. Another tale, for example, is about his ass's piety, also in tractate *Ḥullin* (7b).

Whether or not there is in this unit of tales a deliberate editing trend, as there seems to be, a thematic affinity is created to the Virgilian legends that were very popular in Europe and also known among the Jews.[51] Virgil, the Roman poet of the ancient era, was perceived in medieval literature as the protector and patron of the inhabitants of Naples. He was also thought of as a necromancer; stories are told of how he saved the people of the city from a plague of flies and another of leeches by means of a ruse. The points in common between the stories underscore what is different and unique to each culture. For example, the elimination of the mice is presented as a miracle, not as witchcraft, and it is enacted in exchange for the decision by the people of the city to strictly observe the rule of tithing. Nonetheless, the reception of similar narratives in the same cultural surrounding indicates the existence of shared foci of interest.

The examples given here can point to various affinities in *Sefer ha-ma'asim* with the vernacular literature in France and in Europe as a whole, where it took shape. They are expressed in the choice of stories and their inclusion in the compilation in light of other choices in other compilations; in stylistic changes that function as cultural codes in the *Sefer ha-ma'asim*; and in the editing trends of story cycles, such as the one discussed here about R. Pinḥas b. Yair. The comparative vantage point makes it possible to pinpoint these features and to observe the intercultural dialogue, on the one hand, and differences between the narrating societies, on the other.

Style

The tendency to compress and condense the text is expressed in *Sefer ha-ma'asim* in the abridgement and omission of words that can be understood from the textual context as well as, at times, from a shared performance situation conducted orally. Here I will use only one story to illustrate this function: "R. Joshua b. Levi and the Angel of Death" (no. 46). Its source is the Talmud (*Ketubot* 77b): The Angel of Death comes to R. Joshua b. Levi to take his soul. The latter asks to put off his death for thirty days so that he might revise his study before going to the next world. In due time, on their way to the Garden of Eden, R. Joshua b. Levi persuades the Angel of Death to hand him his knife; he flees to the Garden of Eden and refuses to allow the angel to take his soul. Because he had never sworn an oath, not even a true one, God allows him to remain alive in Paradise. Up to this point *Sefer ha-ma'asim* follows the talmudic version. The charged phrase, however, influenced from various

51. See tale nos. 56–50.

adaptations of the talmudic tale in Ashkenaz is, "Show me Gehenna [hell] and the Garden of Eden," and later on, "He showed him Gehenna and the Garden of Eden."

Other versions in Ashkenaz—for example, in Ms. Parma 2295[52]—contain lengthy descriptions of the Garden of Eden and Gehenna, which are only implied in *Sefer ha-ma'asim*. In these versions R. Joshua b. Levi is asked to tour the Garden of Eden and Gehenna in order to inform Rabban Gamliel, head of the Sanhedrin, whether its inhabitants are Jews or Gentiles: Are there Jews in Gehenna and gentiles in the Garden of Eden? What he sees is described extensively. The Garden of Eden is a magnificent place, with houses made of white glass, silver, and gold, in keeping with the rank of the *ẓaddikim* worthy of living in them. The homes are inlaid with precious stones and furnished with beds of gold and silver, lovely fruits, and food and drink. Rivers of persimmon flow in the garden, and the scent of lavender fills the air. The Patriarchs—Abraham, Isaac, and Jacob—live there, as well as the first generations, including the twelve tribes and the dead of Egypt; Moses and Aaron; converts who have converted out of love; and the Messiah, son of David and Elijah, all waiting for the day of redemption. In contrast, in Gehenna, which has seven names, including "Sheol" and *ẓalmavet* (lit., "the shadow of death" or the netherworld), evil gentiles are punished alternately by snow and burning fire, and are beaten by angels of destruction. Similar descriptions are also embedded in other medieval texts in Ashkenaz (whether created there or transmitted): on the one hand, the abundance in the Garden of Eden, with its rivers of water, oil, wine, and honey, and all manner of trees and spices; on the other hand, four types of fire blazing, alternating with the freezing cold of snow, rivers of fire mixed with hail, tar, and boiling sulfur. In Gehenna there are scorpions that contain the drug of death and thousands of angels of destruction.[53]

Although *Sefer ha-ma'asim* mentions briefly, "He showed him Gehenna and the Garden of Eden," thus omitting the lengthy and concrete descriptions extant in Ashkenaz, a much broader context is implied. Compared to the talmudic phrasing, "Show me my place," the code words in *Sefer ha-ma'asim*—"Gehenna" and the "Garden of Eden"—load the text with their full charge in Ashkenaz. The mere

52. Ms. Parma 2295, 87a–88b; see Kushelevsky, *Penalty and Temptation*, 25–29.

53. See, for example, Yassif, ed., *The Book of Memory*, "*Seder Gan Eden*" ("Tractate Gan Eden"), 103–109, and "*Seder Gehenna*" ("Tractate Gehenna"), 99–103; *Masekhet gehenom* ("Tractate Gehenom Gehenna"), in Jellenik, *Bet hamidrasch*, vol. 1, section 1, 147–149. On the transformation of texts on Paradise and Hell in the Middle Ages, including references to the story about R. Joshua b. Levi, see Perry, *Tradition and Transformation*, 197–217. In the context of "the world of the dead" as part of the phenomenon of the marvelous in the Middle Ages, see Rotman, "The Marvelous in the Medieval Hebrew Narrative," 346–361.

suggestive force of the phrase "Gehenna and the Garden of Eden" inserts into the text a body of medieval images of the world to come as well as story traditions prevalent in Ashkenaz.

Sources in Ashkenaz (Germany and Northern France): Rashi and the Tosafot

A certain selection of tales is based on medieval sources in Ashkenaz and Italy: the commentary of Rashi and the Tosafot on the Talmud; the eleventh-century *Arukh* dictionary of the Roman Nathan b. Jeḥiel, which the Tosafists often used; and a version of the *Maḥzor Vitry*, authored by a disciple of Rashi. The most prominent of these tales is "The Weasel and the Pit" (no. 43), which was accepted in Ashkenaz in relation to engagement ceremonies, as mentioned earlier.

A maiden adorned with jewels was on her way to her mother's home. On the road and outside of any inhabited area, she was thirsty and tried to quench her thirst at a well, but fell into it. A passerby who heard her shouts and sobs helped her get out, but first made her swear she would marry him. He wanted to have his way with her at once, but she convinced him to wait for their engagement and marriage, and they "made a covenant with one another": a contract that they would marry when the time came, as a kind of ceremony at which conditions are set forth. The heavens, a weasel that passed by, and the pit she had fallen into were chosen as witnesses for their covenant. Later on the man forgot her and married another, but she adhered to her commitment and pretended to be insane in order to put off other men. In the course of time, the man's sons died of weird causes. One was choked by a weasel, and another fell into a pit. His wife understood these tragedies may have occurred as a result of something her husband had done, so they divorced, and the man went back to his intended and married her. They were finally blessed with sons and prosperity.

The tale is not known from any sources prior to Rashi, although it is mentioned under its title in the Talmud with no further details. Nor is it included in story compilations from the East that were earlier than *Sefer ha-ma'asim*, such as *Midrash aseret hadibrot*, *Ḥibbur yafeh mehayeshu'a*, and others. Apparently the direct or indirect source for *Sefer ha-ma'asim* was commentary on the Talmud ascribed to Rashi (*Ta'anit* 8a) in the first half of the twelfth century, and a very similar version in the *Arukh*;[54] the tale is cited also in a fourteenth-century commentary of the Tosafists to *Ta'anit* 8a.

54. R. Nathan of Rome, *Arukh*, "*heled*" (weasel), 395.

Another typical tale known from the Tosafists is "The Two-Headed Man" (no. 5), about a creature from another world with two heads and four eyes.[55] Ashmedai (Asmodeus) pulls him out from under the ground to show Solomon an amazing spectacle he has never seen before, thus proving Solomon's limitations. Alarmed by what he sees, Solomon learns that the order of the world in the creature's region is upside down. The sun rises in the West and sets in the East. Solomon asks Asmodeus to put the two-headed man back where he belongs, but that is impossible. The creature remains in Solomon's kingdom, marries, and has children. The tale continues with a quarrel among the creature's seven sons over their inheritance—the only two-headed son demands a double share—and describes Solomon's clever solution.

The tale is cited in the Tosafot in the context of the laws of *tefillin*, but the quarrel over the inheritance is left out. Apparently the source in *Sefer ha-ma'asim* is not the Tosafot but a more expanded version known in Ashkenaz, on which the Tosafists relied in their commentary.

"Ukva" (no. 61) differs from the two previous tales, "The Weasel and the Pit" and "The Two-Headed Man," in that it has earlier parallels in the tradition of the Ga'onim, in Babylonia. Unlike the two other tales, it documents a separate narrative tradition distinct from that of Ashkenaz.[56] It is a tale of repentance about Ukva, who covets a married woman and tries to seduce her, but changes his ways, becomes a talmudic scholar, and marries the daughter of the head of the local yeshiva (study hall). There are prominent differences between the Eastern and Western versions of the tale, and it is evident that *Sefer ha-ma'asim* preserves the Ashkenazi tradition of the story. This is, then, another example of the way *Sefer ha-ma'asim* took shape in Ashkenaz in the Middle Ages.

"The Spies and the Giants in Canaan" (no. 44) recounts the adventure of the twelve spies who, as recounted in the Book of Numbers (13:1–33), were sent to spy on Canaan. They encounter there the giant inhabitants of Canaan, and are terrified. One of the giants' daughters casually throws away a peel of a pomegranate, along with the twelve spies who were hiding in it—a description that illustrates how

55. *Menaḥot* 37a. The Tosafists cite the tale as a *midrash*. We do not know whether its source is a *midrash* or whether the Tosafists relate to a contemporary interpolation in some copy of a midrashic work they had, but the mention of the tale in the commentary by the Tosafists suffices as an indication of its reception in Ashkenaz. On a tendency among Torah students in Ashkenaz to proofread eastern-Sephardic texts according to their own study traditions prevailing in Ashkenaz, see Ta-Shma, "*Sifriyatam shel ḥakhmei Ashkenaz*" ("The Library of the Sages of Ashkenaz"), 21–39.

56. Rashi to the *Sanhedrin* 31b, and in other sources in Ashkenaz.

frightened the spies are by the promised land on which they had been sent to spy. The source of this tale is probably a Palestinian *midrash* that was lost, like other midrashic narratives that were lost and preserved in Ashkenaz, but it apparently came into *Sefer ha-ma'asim* through the mediation of exegeses by the Tosafists of the Torah and the Talmud.[57]

Another tale from medieval Ashkenaz, and apparently from northern France, is "Joab's Valor" (no. 4), which is also copied in one of the manuscripts of the Vitry Maḥzor from the twelfth century.[58] In it Joab is described as a fearless, merciless hero in his war against the enemies of Israel, the Amalekites.

"The Maiden in the Tower" (no. 67) is particularly interesting in its medieval context, because it can be linked to the commentary in the Tosafot, on the one hand, and may even point to a source in the school of the Tosafists and to French literature, on the other hand. This tale, too, like others in *Sefer ha-ma'asim* and in vernacular narratives in general, is made up of independent episodes joined together.

The first episode tells about an alliance between Solomon and Ḥiram, king of Tyre, after the king witnessed the wonders God had done for Solomon. In their commentary on the tractate *Yebamot* (23a), the Tosafists question this alliance (1 Kings 5:26) in light of a prohibition against alliances with gentiles.[59] One of the pretexts they use to reconcile the problem is that Ḥiram was a *ger toshav* (a legal term for the status of gentiles who undertake certain Jewish precepts), and hence the prohibition did not apply to him. The present tale about Ḥiram, who was extremely impressed by Solomon's God, may preserve an unknown tradition from the school of the Tosafists.[60]

The second episode tells about the daughter of Joshua the high priest, whom Solomon locked up under guard in a tower after he learned she was going to marry a bastard.[61] His plan is thwarted, however, and the divine decree is carried out: An

57. *Tosafot Shanz* on *Sotah* 35a, and in other sources of the Tosafists.

58. The story is mentioned in one of the text witnesses of *Maḥzor*, which refers to a version (now lost) in *Midrash tehilim* (*Shoḥer tov*). See this reference in the Horowitz edition of the *Maḥzor Vitry*, 332, and in the Goldschmidt edition, B, 555.

59. The Talmud, *Yebamot* 23a, relates to the verse: "You shall make no covenant with them, nor show mercy to them" (Deuteronomy 7:2).

60. Tosafot, *Yebamot* 23a; Tosafot Rosh, *Kiddushin* 68b.

61. The better-known version of this tale is about Solomon's daughter rather than about the daughter of Joshua the high priest. See *Tanḥuma*, ed. Buber, introduction to part I, 68b, no. 42, and other references; Elstein, "The Theme of 'The King's Daughter Locked in a Tower,'" 80–82.

eagle carries the intended groom into the tower, and later she conceives a child with him. The motif of a girl confined in a tower was common in medieval romances, as, for example, in the anonymous romance *Aucassin and Nicolette*. From this aspect, "The Maiden in the Tower" is within the horizon of expectations of the Jewish audience of *Sefer ha-ma'asim*.[62]

Alongside tales originating in Ashkenaz or particularly in northern France, one can cautiously discern inferred affinities with medieval commentaries as well. These often appear in the epilogue.

"The Cow That Observed the Sabbath" (no. 20) is a tale about a cow sold to a gentile that refuses to plow the field on the Sabbath. Consequently, the gentile converts. The tale is linked to the halakhic prohibition against selling big cattle to a gentile (*Avodah Zarah* 15a), and to a discussion in the Tosafot about the limitations of the prohibition in real life in the Diaspora either in the post-talmudic era or later, in Ashkenaz.[63] This halakhic context is implied in *Sefer ha-ma'asim* rather than *Midrash aseret hadibrot*, which focuses on the sanctity of the Sabbath.[64] It is possible, then, to discern the movement of the story from the house of study to the narrating community, as well as its adaptation, which is influenced by the halakhic discourse being conducted there. This occurs parallel to the reverse dynamic pointed out by Yassif: the Tosafists' employment of contemporary folktales such as "The Weasel and the Pit" in Ashkenaz.[65]

The tale of "The Defamed Woman" (no. 24) has an epilogue that clearly refers to the Tosafists of the period: R. Moses of Coucy in his *Sefer miẓvot gadol* (*Semag*), and R. Ḥaim Paltiel in his commentary to the Torah.[66] Both discuss a link between the prohibitions against spreading slander and "standing on the blood" of one's neighbor (i.e., refraining from standing up for the life of the other when threatened), based on their proximity in Leviticus 19:16. Spreading slander ends up with murder. Accordingly *Sefer ha-ma'asim* says in the tale's epilogue: "'You shall not spread slander among your people, neither shall you stand on the blood of your neighbor' [Leviticus 19:16]. Thus, the slander brings evil." This link is not made in its earlier parallels, such as *Midrash aseret hadibrot*.

62. Mason, *Aucassin and Nicolette*, 13.

63. Tosafot, *Avodah Zarah* 15a.

64. *Midrash aseret hadibrot*, ed. Shapira, 62–63.

65. Yassif, *Kemargalit bemishbeẓet*, 163–164.

66. Moses b. Jacob of Coucy, *Sefer miẓvot gadol*, vol. 1, *Lo-Ta'aseh*, no. 9, 46; R. Paltiel, *Perushei hatorah* (*Commentaries on the Torah*), 19:27, 426.

The story of "R. Joshua b. Levi and the Angel of Death"(no. 46) mentioned earlier ends with a unique epilogue, absent from other versions of the story, that advises its audience, perhaps under the influence of R. Jonah of Gerona, to avoid any casual conversation "that contains neither good nor bad" (in other words, no benefit or harm) but is based on falsehood and fabrications.[67] R. Jonah often relied on the teachings of the French and Ashkenazi Torah scholars, which might be indicated in this tale as well. However, in this way, the epilogue expands the prohibition against the taking of oaths in the epilogue of *Midrash aseret hadibrot*.

If one follows the scribe's choices and adaptations—either those of the scribe of Ms. Bodl. Or. 135 or those of his predecessor—there emerges the figure of a creative, dynamic narrator who makes use of diverse sources, beginning with the Bible, as reflected in quotations embedded in the stories and the epilogue, and continuing up to sources from the rabbinic and contemporary medieval literature. He likely possessed many of the stories in advance, but his hand has left a mark on them, expressing a particular northern French aesthetic taste and a medieval horizon of expectations. The unique discourse in *Sefer ha-ma'asim* was created in the wake of thematic, structural, and stylistic adaptations, and in the compilation's affinity with its sources in the Talmud, the Midrash, and *Midrash aseret hadibrot*. The means employed include a choice of certain versions over its parallels in other sources; a greater emphasis on selected motifs rather than others in the original versions; structural alterations within a given unit of connected stories; expansion of the epilogue on the basis of additional sources and by means of messages intended for the contemporary audiences; and, finally, newly created tales based on existing models. All of these create a new discourse while still sharing a long-standing narrative tradition.

Sefer ha-ma'asim combines literacy in a broad range of Hebrew sources: both scholarly sources, such as the Talmud, and more popular sources, such as those manifested in tales from *Midrash aseret hadibrot*. This blend is also discerned linguistically, by both a tendency to mediate the talmudic Aramaic on the basis of Hebrew translations in the *Tanḥuma* and the use of Hebrew translations with the original Aramaic from the Talmud.

The specific discourse in *Sefer ha-ma'asim* is also reflected in its affinities with the vernacular literature in Europe, even within tales originating in the rabbinical Hebrew sources. Here we are dealing mainly with differences in style, which are implied by the connotations they evoke. Sometimes the change or addition of one

67. R. Jonah, *Sha'arei teshuvah* (*The Gates of Repentance*), part 3, 172.

word compared to the source will suffice; for example, the adjective "all" applied to the female sex as a whole in one of the stories ("all women are wicked") brings into the text a broad context from the French vernacular literature, such as the fabliau.

The cross-cultural dialogue is also expressed by a choice of tales not known from earlier Jewish sources and imported into *Sefer ha-ma'asim* from the vernacular literature. In these cases, which will be demonstrated in the following chapter, the reconstruction of a medieval discourse is possible on the basis of a broad extranarrative context and a comparative study of narrative parallels in Europe. This process is similar to the analysis just completed in this chapter but from an opposite point of view. Instead of focusing on the processes of adaptation of rabbinic tales from the Talmud or Midrash or from Jewish tales in *Midrash aseret hadibrot* as they are transferred into *Sefer ha-ma'asim*, I will follow the processes of adapting non-Jewish narratives and their absorption into *Sefer ha-ma'asim* on the basis of internal Jewish models.

Non-Jewish Sources

Editing, Adaptation, and Hermeneutic Horizons

In the previous chapter we noted a consistent trend in *Sefer ha-ma'asim* to conduct a dialogue with the vernacular literature in the non-Jewish environment. Stories from the rich repository of Jewish sources in the Talmud and thereafter were selected and reworked with an affinity to works in French, and a new discourse, a product of the medieval renaissance, was created. Rather than being explicit, this discourse is implied through editing decisions and stylistic nuances in *Sefer ha-ma'asim* that can be deciphered on the basis of their affinities with non-Jewish parallels in medieval literature and by comparing them to earlier and contemporary Jewish versions. It turns out that Jews in northern France played a role in the great literary flourishing that occurred in the surrounding society, and shared an aesthetic taste and a similar horizon of expectations. At the same time these tales were accepted as part of a cultural heritage and constituted a substantive component in the Jewish identity of the narrating community. While affinities in these stories with the surrounding non-Jewish literature cast a new light on them that calls for a new inquiry, the points of contact are also points of departure for a definition of differences and distinctions. Junctures of otherness are located within the spheres of contact and sharing.

This dynamic grows more intense in stories whose sources are not Jewish but rather stem from the vernacular literature in France and in Europe in general. There are not very many such stories in *Sefer ha-ma'asim*, but they do occupy a relatively large space, since they are longer than the tales from Jewish sources, taking up two to five pages. Here affinities with the vernacular literature in France are already evident on the level of plot and structure, unlike tales from Jewish sources in which the intertextual dialogue takes place mainly on the level of style, while the original plot in the Talmud and the Midrash is preserved. The intercultural dialogue depicted in the previous chapter is also carried on in those tales whose sources are in the vernacular literature, and to an even greater extent. In these tales, however, the point of departure is located in the arena of the "other," which is mediated to the Jewish community through modes of adaptation based on Jewish norms and models.

The non-Jewish subtext, whether a saint's legend or a vernacular romance, does not appear in *Sefer ha-ma'asim* in its original form, and not only owing to the change in language (from French to Hebrew). It is mediated to its Jewish audience through models available in Jewish sources. When the non-Jewish source in European literature is obvious and its reworking for the Jewish audience is sketchy and superficial, the handprint of the scribe as editor and adaptor is easily recognized. At times the adapting processes are so overwhelming that it is nearly impossible to identify the vernacular source, and the tale takes on a Jewish character. In such situations certain deviations from the Jewish source to which the story was adapted, which seem irregular against the background of its original context, are the only leads for the scholar, and they enable him or her to trace the non-Jewish substructure and the modes of its adaptation and reworking. It is not always possible to locate a parallel either in the vernacular literature or in Jewish sources. In these cases, when its plot and motifs seem foreign, it would be logical to assume a non-Jewish source. We remain then within the realm of hypothesis.

In *Sefer ha-ma'asim* the choice of Jewish models to convey vernacular narratives to its Jewish addressees is significant, because it indicates—albeit through my mediation as a modern, contemporary reader and through interpretation based on my own historical horizon (in Gadamer's sense of the term)—points of contact between the narrating societies, and simultaneously trends of detachment. The reception of the vernacular story manifests a common historical horizon that we identify as a medieval culture, and at the same time, modes of explicit and implicit adaptation mark the narrating community as a subgroup within the majority society, as a minority that frequently needs to define its distinct identity in view of its environment.

Let us illustrate some of the claims made here by looking into a choice of tales that share themes and motifs with the surrounding vernacular literature in Western Europe, particularly in France. Thirteen tales in *Sefer ha-ma'asim* are unknown from earlier sources and apparently were circulating in Ashkenaz.[1] Four of them are

1. "The Three Treasures" (no. 7); "The Sabbath Observer and the Bear" (no. 14); "R. Meir and Judah of Anatot" (no. 25); "Ben Sever and Shefifon Ben Layish" (no. 27); "Joḥanan and the Scorpion" (no. 28); "Torah Saves from Death" (no. 49); "The Power of a Single Act of Charity" (no. 51); "A Slave for Seven Years" (no. 52); "The Hard-Boiled Egg" (no. 54); "The Poor

particularly striking in their unequivocal affinities with the literature of the period: "Joḥanan and the Scorpion" (no. 28), in the context of the Arthurian romances in the twelfth and thirteenth centuries with the motif of the quest for the Holy Grail, as well as Béroul's version of the Tristan and Iseult narrative; "A Slave for Seven Years" (no. 52), based on "The Life of St. Alexis"; "The Poor Bachelor and His Maiden Cousin" (no. 55), which alludes to *The Romance of Tristan*; and "The Prophecy of the Ravens" (no. 66), in parallel to the *Seven Sages of Rome.* A detailed discussion of these will illustrate the contribution of the vernacular infrastructure to the significance of the story in its cultural-historical context, and their poetics of adaptation. This chapter is focused, then, on the interaction between the single story and *Sefer ha-ma'asim* as a whole; the third part of this book, "Tales and Parallels," will focus on each story in itself, in light of its versions and parallels.

Joḥanan, the protagonist of "Joḥanan and the Scorpion" (no. 28), which is the longest tale in *Sefer ha-ma'asim*, adheres steadfastly to his father's last wish, on his deathbed, to purchase the first thing he sees in the market and to watch over it. Joḥanan indeed purchases a marvelous chalice after paying a fortune for it; he keeps it carefully at home until the Passover festival, when he decides to decorate the festive table at the *seder* with the chalice. When he opens it, he discovers inside another chalice, which contains a small scorpion. Joḥanan cares for the scorpion and feeds it in keeping with his father's will, but the scorpion grows to enormous proportions and requires huge quantities of food, more than Joḥanan and his wife are able to supply. They are left with nothing to eat and pray to the Almighty to save them. Then the scorpion opens its mouth and grants them the opportunity to make a wish. It turns out that he is the son of Adam, and that he is immortal, a creature that regenerates in cycles of a thousand years. Joḥanan wishes to master all the languages of the world, including those of animals and birds, while his wife asks for wealth so she can provide for her family. The scorpion fulfills their wishes, blesses them, and departs. In the course of time, Joḥanan becomes famous for his wisdom and is called to the royal palace to serve as the king's counselor. One day the king orders him to locate his destined bride wherever she is on earth, and to bring her to him to marry. Joḥanan has one only indication for identifying her: a golden strand of hair that was cast by a crow onto the king's lap. After a long and adventurous journey, Joḥanan manages to find her, but, hoping to avoid the

Bachelor and His Maiden Cousin" (no. 55); "The Grateful Dead" (no. 65); "The Prophecy of the Ravens" (no. 66); "The Portal to Gehenna" (no. 69).

marriage, she conditions her agreement to marry the king on Joḥanan's fulfillment of three particularly arduous tasks. She assumes he will fail, and she will be saved from having to marry the king, whom she thinks of as "evil"; but Joḥanan succeeds in his tasks with the help of three grateful animals and achieves the unattainable. The queen-to-be travels with him to the king. Envious of Joḥanan, the ministers in the royal court murder and dismember him, but the queen, who is apparently also a fairy, joins all his body parts together with water from the Garden of Eden, lies over him, and kisses him to restore him to life. Seeing this, the king goes out to war in confidence that she will do the same for him should he be killed; but when this happens, she pours over him and his ministers the water of hell, and they are burned. Joḥanan, whose wife has died in the meantime, marries the queen and reigns over the kingdom. They have many sons and daughters and live together happily ever after.

The affinity with the Arthurian romances of the search for the Holy Grail—namely the unfinished romance *The Story of the Grail* by Chrétien de Troyes in the twelfth century and its "continuations" in the thirteenth century[2]—is created primarily through the motif of the chalice in "Joḥanan and the Scorpion." It is a covered vessel large enough to hold an additional vessel, in keeping with the image of the grail in Chrétien's romance and in later ones. In *The Story of the Grail*, Perceval, the protagonist, watches a ceremonial procession that passes by him time after time while he dines with his host; he sees a "grail" in a girl's hand, a vessel deep and wide enough to be a serving platter, which holds the consecrated host. Although in Chrétien's work the chalice is not presented as the Holy Grail, the symbolic charge in this episode is implied by its content: namely the consecrated bread and its special appearance. The grail is made of pure gold and adorned with precious gems—the costliest, most exquisite in the world.[3] Perceval falls silent and fails to ask a number of the questions he is supposed to ask. If he had asked the right questions, his paralyzed host, the first in the dynasty of the keepers of the grail, who is known as the "fisher king" (*Roi Pescheori*), would have been healed. Perceval swears he will try again to reach the castle where the grail is kept and succeed in his task this

2. On the four continuations to Chrétien's romance, see Barber, *The Holy Grail*, 30–34.

3. "Le graal, qui aloit devant, / De fin or esmeré estoit; / Pierres precieuses avoit / El graal de maintes menieres, / Des plus riches et des plus chieres / Qui an mer ne an terre soient: / Totes autres pierres passoient / Celes del grail sanz dotance" ("The grail, which preceded / was of fine pure gold; set in the grail were / precious stones of every kind / the best and costliest / to be found in earth or sea: / the grail's stones were finer than any others in the world, beyond any doubt"). Chrétien, *The Story of the Grail*, ed. Pickens, v. 3198–3205, 158 (French); 159 (English).

time, but the romance is unfinished and that episode is lacking.[4] In the continuations from the thirteenth century, the motif of the grail is further expanded, and its sacral meaning is explicit. Its symbolism is linked to the Last Supper—which, according to the New Testament, was held on the eve of Passover—and to the sacrament of eating and drinking Jesus' body and his blood, manifested in the consecrated bread and wine.[5]

In the Jewish context, unlike the Christian one, the chalice in the form of a covered serving platter is unusual; its resemblance, in "Joḥanan and the Scorpion," to the Holy Grail in the medieval romances is implied, more so because of its magnificence, which charges it with additional significance. The chalice is described in "Joḥanan and the Scorpion" as "very beautiful," and it is brought out to adorn the festive table at Passover. The chalice is metonymic with the figure of the father, because it represents Joḥanan's commitment to his father's testament; in contrast, the Christian Holy Grail and the sacred wine and bread it contains embody Jesus, the son. Unlike the case in the romances of the Holy Grail, Joḥanan locates the chalice right at the start, but like Perceval, he has to undergo a trial of initiation rites that prepare him to own it and realize its potential—the challenges of attending to the scorpion and attaining the queen. Joḥanan withstands all this and is rewarded in the first part of the tale with wisdom, wealth, and the knowledge of the animal languages, and in the second half with a high status in the royal court, up to the climactic moment when he marries the fairy-queen and is made king. Only then does his father's command that he buy the first thing he sees in the market make sense. Only then is the riddle of the chalice "bequeathed" him by his father, as well as its purpose, solved. In comparison to the romances of the quest for the Holy Grail, the order of events in both parts of the tale as one whole is topsy-turvy. The quest typical of the genre of the romance—which ends in *The Story of the Grail* with the protagonist's failure to pass the test—takes place in "Joḥanan and the Scorpion" after he has found the chalice at the very beginning of the tale, and its objective is to decipher its riddle and its purpose. These become clear only after a long journey that entails fulfilling the father's will and finding the destined queen. In this manner the quest motif connects the two parts of the story, even though each one stands on its own on the basis of the episode.[6]

4. Ibid., v. 3156–3277, 156–160 (French); 157–161 (English); v. 3513–3577, 172–176 (French); 173–177 (English).
5. Putter, "The Twelfth-Century Arthur," 49–51; Barber, *The Holy Grail*, 135–160.
6. Shapira, "To Make a Short Story Long," 309–312, 317–320. Shapira points to the structure of a diptych in the tale, namely a structure of two sequences that can stand on their own but are connected by certain shared themes.

The father's will is relevant to the present discussion in yet another respect—its parallel to the mother's will in *The Story of the Grail.* On the eve of his departure to become a knight, Perceval's mother instructs him about how to behave, and then she faints and dies in agony out of grave concern for her son.[7] As he proceeds on his journey, and ignorant of his mother's death, Perceval does indeed carry out her instructions, but to an absurd extent. Unfamiliar with chivalric norms, he fulfills his mother's instructions literally, as he understands them, in irksome contradiction to his social environment. Nonetheless he is accepted as a courageous knight, and his strict compliance with his mother's instructions proves itself. Thus the circumstance of his departure from his mother becomes the occasion of a will and testament, parallel to that of Joḥanan's father. And like the case in *The Story of the Grail*, the performance of the command in the Jewish story is total, at any cost and under any condition. An example in *Perceval* is a casual meeting between him and a maiden he meets in her bedroom while her lover is away. This unplanned encounter very quickly turns into a violent incident when the girl objects strongly to his intrusion into her home and to his behavior: He greets her, falls upon her to kiss her, and tears off her ring. He believes he is behaving this way in keeping with his mother's counsel to greet every maiden he meets, without realizing that he is offending good taste and proper etiquette.[8] In parallel, Joḥanan and his wife in the Jewish tale are prepared to devote all of their property and remain destitute in order to meet the scorpion's needs, in keeping with what seems to be an absurd will.

Another parallel between "Joḥanan and the Scorpion" and the French romance is the dual figure of the queen: the virgin queen who rules over "a large, beautiful city," accompanied by her maidservant, in "Joḥanan and the Scorpion"; and the golden-haired queen and the woman with her in *The Story of the Grail*, who live in an enchanted, magnificent castle and rule over the state.[9]

7. His mother's instructions—which later, in view of her death, turn out to be her last will—are to come to the aid of every maiden in distress who asks for his help, to respond to her kiss, to accept her ring if she offers it to him as a sign of love, to remain in the company of gentlemen, and above all, to pray in the church and listen to the mass. Chrétien, *The Story of the Grail*, ed. Pickens, v. 509–580, 26–30 (French); 27–31 (English). Cf. Tubach 1282: "Three counsels given to son."

8. Chrétien, *The Story of the Grail*, ed. Pickens, v. 649–760, 32–38 (French); 33–39 (English). A passage repeated in several variations is: "Pucele, je vos salu / Si con ma mere le m'aprist. / Ma mere m'anseigna et dist / Que les puceles saluasse / An quel que leu que les trovasse"; v. 664–668, 34 ("Maiden, I greet you / just as my mother taught me. / My mother instructed me / to greet maidens / wherever I found them").

9. Ibid., v. 7486–7499, 366 (French), 367 (English).

The scorpion is an additional Christian symbol of what the New Testament describes as Judas Iscariot's treachery at the Last Supper. In Jewish sources the scorpion carries a negative value as well, because of the danger of its sting. Here, in "Joḥanan and the Scorpion," it appropriates the quality of *of ha-ḥol* (lit., the "sand-bird"; phoenix), namely the ability to regenerate in endless cycles of extinction and renewal. In this way the scorpion is invested with a positive value, and the Christian symbolism of the scorpion that assigns a negative image to the Jew is neutralized. Moreover, in contrast to the phoenix as a symbol of Jesus' resurrection in Christian sources, the scorpion in the Jewish tale signifies a revival of the Jewish entity as manifested in several episodes: Joḥanan's death and his restoration to life by the queen; transitions from poverty to wealth; Joḥanan's rise to the status of a king; and on the national level, the symbolism of the Passover festival of redemption after enslavement and exile. These all occur to Joḥanan, in marked contrast to the fate of the king, whom the queen signifies as the "other" and refuses to restore to life. In *The Story of the Grail* there is no scorpion as such, but the symbolism of the scorpion is integrated into the scene of the Last Supper in the figure of Judas, and is imbedded in the romance.

In its second half, "Joḥanan and the Scorpion" is based mainly on Béroul's version of the well-known romance of *Tristan and Iseult* and the story of the couple's irrepressible, forbidden love under the influence of a love potion prepared by Iseult's mother.[10] Two episodes are particularly relevant to the present discussion of "Joḥanan and the Scorpion": the king's counselors' envy of his nephew Tristan, because the king greatly loved him and planned to bequeath the kingdom to him upon his death;[11] and the task assigned to Tristan—to find a wife for King Mark based only on one strand of golden hair carried by a bird in its beak.[12] The king's counselors, who want to get rid of Tristan, repeatedly urge King Mark to marry to ensure an heir to the throne. Aware of their jealousy of his nephew Tristan, the king refuses. To rid himself of their pressure, he poses a condition. He would marry the one woman whose hair matches the golden strand carried by the bird. Tristan, who identifies Iseult, daughter of the king of Ireland, as the one suitable for the king due to her magnificent beauty, tells King Mark about her. But Ireland and Cornwall (Mark's kingdom) are enemies, and the task seems impossible. Tristan's competitors see this

10. Béroul, *The Romance of Tristan*, ed. Lacy.

11. Ibid., v. 581–626, 28–30, and English translation, 29–31.

12. Yassif, *Kemargalit bemishbeẓet*, 151. Cf. the tale type "The Clever Horse" or "The Golden-Haired Maiden" (ATU 531), which is not relevant to Béroul's *Romance of Tristan* nor to Thomas's version of *Tristan and Iseult.*

as an opportunity to get rid of him, and they advise King Mark to send him to Ireland to acquire Iseult for him. These events are embedded in "Joḥanan and the Scorpion," and the affinity between the two narratives is palpable. A stylistic affinity with the Book of Esther—namely allusions to the queen sent to save her people at the cost of giving herself to Aḥashverosh—is intended to Judaize the fairy-queen in the story and mediate the *Tristan and Iseult* narrative for the readers of *Sefer ha-ma'asim*, but they are cursory and not integrated into the plot.

By now, three conclusions can be drawn: (1) The narrator and his Jewish audience were familiar with the surrounding romances, or at least with the narrative traditions embedded in them, and their reception in *Sefer ha-ma'asim* manifests a common aesthetic taste and horizon of expectations. (2) The basic unit of the tale is the episode, and accordingly its narrative amounts to a hybridic combination of episodes rather than an integrative work. Affinities with vernacular narratives are not necessarily consistent throughout the entire plot line, and are more often depicted in specific episodes only. It is this episodic structure that made it possible to reconstruct *The Story of the Grail* and *The Romance of Tristan* as narratives addressed to Jews amid the background of shared areas of interest and aesthetic taste. (3) Largely, "Joḥanan and the Scorpion" is a Jewish story that debates both the courtly ethos of love and the Christian narrative of the Grail, but their use as literary motifs implies a discourse distinct from that of talmudic narratives. The adventures of Joḥanan, who exemplifies the figure of the knight in the story; the charms of the fairy-queen as she restores her lover to life; and the eroticism that cannot be glossed over by a sudden, contrived mention of the death of Joḥanan's wife as an explanation for his second marriage—all of these are integral elements of French literature that apparently also captivated the hearts of the Jews. Narratives like "Joḥanan and the Scorpion," unknown from Jewish sources earlier than *Sefer ha-ma'asim*, are what characterize it more than anything else as a medieval compilation.

"The Poor Bachelor and His Maiden Cousin" (no. 55), mentioned earlier, and on which I will further elaborate now, is about two brothers: the one rich and stingy, while the other so poor that he cannot even afford to buy some wheat to bake the *matzot* he would need for his family for the Passover festival. His brother would not lend him any unless he left his beloved son, Isaac, with him as collateral. Having no other choice, Isaac moves into his uncle's house. Inevitably, his maiden cousin falls in love with him, but her mother opposes the marriage and prefers her own brother, who is not a talmudic scholar like Isaac. Seeing this, the head of the yeshiva instructs his student to show the girl signs of affection, to kiss and embrace her for several days, and then even to sleep with her in one bed—likely a ploy to force the mother to marry them off. Isaac, although extremely shocked, is forced to carry out his rabbi's command, which clearly deviates from the religious commitment. He then places a sword between himself and the maiden in bed, to restrain himself from giving in to his sexual urge. While they are asleep, the girl's father discovers the couple with the sword between them. He covers them with his robe and blesses them so that no fault should be found in them. When he tells all this to his wife, her objection to Isaac grows stronger. When Isaac awakes and realizes his uncle had visited his bedchamber, he flees and tries to take his own life. His mother reports this to the rabbi, who invites the maiden's parents for a talk. Since the mother still refuses to accept Isaac as a son-in-law and prefers her brother, a competition between the two suitors is announced. They must travel afar, take with them no more than the initial sum of one hundred dinars each, and return in a year. At that time the one who had made the most money would win the maiden's hand.

At this point the second part of the tale begins. It recounts Isaac's adventures in foreign lands, beginning with a storm at sea, after which he is washed up on the shore, and then his success in healing the king of a city of lepers with special herbs. When the year is over, Isaac returns to his beloved as the wealthy governor of the city, on the very day when she was to be married to his competitor, her mother's brother. And so she and Isaac marry.

The motif of the "sword between the lovers" has a clear affinity to Béroul's *The Romance of Tristan*.[13] King Mark discovers the lovers in the forest and watches them sleep in an embrace under a bower of branches. Tristan's sword separates the two. The king convinces himself that they are faithful to him, since otherwise they would not be clothed, nor would they have placed a sword between them. He removes Iseult's ring, which he had given her, from her finger and replaces it with his own ring. He then places his gloves on her face to shield it from the sun's rays, replaces Tristan's sword with his own, and leaves while they are still asleep. When they awake, they discover the signs of the king's visit. Tristan doubts the sincerity of the king's intentions; afraid he will return to kill them, they flee.

The rationale behind the king's decision to trust his wife's loyalty, the rhetoric he employs to explain his conclusion, his reaction, and the signs of his visit that he leaves behind—all of these are parallel in their details and rhetoric to "The Poor Bachelor and His Maiden Cousin" (no. 55), when the uncle rationalizes finding his daughter and his nephew together in bed.[14] Especially striking in regard to the

13. Béroul, *The Romance of Tristan*, 87–89.

14. For more details, see Kushelevsky, "Chastity versus Courtly Love," 61–82.

narrator's techniques of reception and adaption is the attitude shared by both narrators in relation to the transgressions they narrate: identification in *Sefer ha-ma'asim* with the figure of the rabbi despite his unconventional instruction to his favored student (the explanation the rabbi gives for his decision is "for the sake of God"), and in Béroul's *The Romance of Tristan* with the love affair which, according to Christian morals, is adulterous. The Jewish narrator could not identify with this forbidden love; hence in *Sefer ha-ma'asim* there is no romantic attachment between a man and a married woman, but rather between a boy and girl who would marry. However, he is clearly in favor of the rabbi, who prefers a love marriage over an arranged marriage (and the Torah scholar over a rich but ignorant suiter) even at the risk of violating a halakhic norm.[15] The love theme in the romance and its transgressive potential exist also in "The Poor Bachelor and His Maiden Cousin," even though they are adapted to establish the sanctity of marriage. Love in the relations between a man and a woman is legitimate and even preferable, but only within the frame of marriage.[16] The affinity of the two tales, "Joḥanan and the Scorpion" (no. 28) and "The Poor Bachelor and His Maiden Cousin" (no. 55), with the romance genre; the role of love in them (whether implicit or explicit); and the sanctity of marriage in contrast to courtly love in the romances indicate a broader phenomenon in *Sefer ha-ma'asim*. Many of its other tales, also exempla from Jewish sources, participate in a discourse of love, marriage, and family relations. Nineteen out of the sixty-nine stories in *Sefer ha-ma'asim* (about 27 percent) have erotic motifs, either implicit or explicit, and represent values of marriage and loyalty in the family.[17] Four of them are adjacent to one another in a cluster that underscores

15. For further elaboration of this matter, see part 3, tale no. 55.

16. Elisheva Baumgarten, "Three Voices of Medieval Jewish Marriage" (lecture, Katz Center for Advanced Judaic Studies, University of Pennsylvania, Philadelphia, December 5, 2012). The tale is one of three types of "voices" in Baumgarten's talk about Jewish marriage arrangements in the thirteenth century: legal writings, moral writings, and the literary genre. See Kushelevsky, "Chastity versus Courtly Love," 77–78, with special emphasis on the high tension in the tale between transgression and legitimacy, due to its affinity with the romance genre.

17. These tales are "The Man Who Never Took an Oath" (no. 13); "Ukva" (no. 15); "Who Is the Thief?" (no. 16); "One of Ten" (no. 17); "The Commandment of *Ẓiẓit*" (no. 18); "The Defamed Woman" (no. 24); "Joḥanan and the Scorpion" (no. 28); "Slander Kills Three" (no. 30); "R. Akiva's Daughter and the Snake" (no. 32); "Mattiah b. Ḥarash" (no. 33); "The Weasel and the Pit" (no. 43); "A Slave for Seven Years" (no. 52); "One Man in a Thousand Have I Found" (no. 53); "The Poor Bachelor and His Maiden Cousin" (no. 55); "Ukva" (no. 61); "The Grateful Dead" (no. 65); "The Prophecy of the Ravens" (no. 66); "The Maiden in the Tower" (no. 67); "The Portal to Gehenna" (no. 69). Other tales that touch on family relations but not in an erotic context are "The Heir's Test" (no. 3); and "The Mother and Her Sons" (no. 12).

this thematic choice.[18] In two of them the value of loyalty is explicit in the epilogue.[19] The other tales are scattered throughout the compilation. Five of them, including the two discussed above, are particularly long in relation to the others in the compilation, a fact already noted by Yassif, and hence they carry a great deal of weight in representing the love motif in its various forms that is so prevalent in *Sefer ha-ma'asim*.[20] Certain phrases and idioms in the epilogue and in the story itself function as code words that recur in the compilation, to emphasize the moral of loyalty between husband and wife.[21] Three additional tales extol the value of abstinence, which is the other side of the coin we are discussing here, and one of them, "A Slave for Seven Years" (no. 52), will be discussed later in this book.[22] A didactic moral censuring adultery is not unusual in Hebrew story compilations, particularly in *Midrash aseret hadibrot*, but in *Sefer ha-ma'asim* it is linked to the value of "family," and its intactness and continuity.[23] The importance of loyal family relations is salient both in the narrator's attitude toward tales borrowed from the non-Jewish environment and reworked in *Sefer ha-ma'asim* and in the attitude toward those tales familiar from the rabbinical literature and reworked in the compilation.[24] It is obvious that *Sefer ha-ma'asim* includes a relatively large number of tales about love, married life, and family loyalty.

The Champagne region, in which *Sefer ha-ma'asim* was copied, circulated, and apparently also created, was one of the most important centers, where writers such as Béroul, Thomas, Marie de France, Andreas Capellanus, and Chrétien de Troyes created literature. They all lived and worked in the twelfth century, and two of them,

18. The cluster includes "Ukva" (no. 15); "Who Is the Thief?" (no. 16); "One of Ten" (no. 17); "The Commandment of *Ẓiẓit*" (no. 18).

19. In "One of Ten" (no. 17), the epilogue says: "Come and see the fulfillment of the verse: 'The eye of the adulterer waits for the twilight, Saying, "No eye will see me." And he disguises his face.' [Job 24:15] He who dwells in secret, his face will be exposed; his deeds will eventually be revealed. May your children be in purity [lit., 'cleanliness']." And in "The Commandment of *Ẓiẓit*" (no. 18), the moral is: "And always make sure that your sons are born in purity. And marry a pure [honest] woman who will not betray you. For this you will be rewarded with righteous sons, who will respect and honor you."

20. These are "The Defamed Woman" (no. 24); "Joḥanan and the Scorpion" (no. 28); "The Poor Bachelor and His Maiden Cousin" (no. 55); "The Grateful Dead" (no. 65); and "The Prophecy of the Ravens" (no. 66). And see Yassif, *Kemargalit bemishbeẓet,* 146.

21. See, for example, tales nos. 15, 18, 24: the word *neki'ut* (lit., "cleanliness," purity) and the phrase, "She who betrays her husband betrays her Creator."

22. The two other tales are "Mattiah b. Ḥarash" (no. 33) and "Torah Saves from Death" (no. 49).

23. Friedman, "The Man Who Was Meticulous about the Commandment of Fringes."

24. See Kushelevsky, "Family Images," 228–239.

Andreas and Chrétien, lived in the Champagne district. As the present discussion shows, the prominence of the discourse of love and eroticism in the context of values of love and loyalty in family life was a reaction to these romances—their reception in *Sefer ha-ma'asim* as part of the repository of Jewish fiction, on the one hand; along with their adaptation and criticism, which brings a distinct Jewish identity sharply to the fore, on the other.

The two tales to which I shall now relate, "A Slave for Seven Years" (no. 52) and "The Prophecy of the Ravens" (no. 66), are based on narratives of other genres: the hagiographic exemplum and the novella. "A Slave for Seven Years" begins with a childless man whose prayers for a son are answered, and who devotes himself to teaching his son Torah. When the man dies, the boy's mother insists that her son must take over his father's trade and engage in commerce. The son, unable to reconcile himself to the norms of cheating and guile, returns to his mother empty-handed. While he is speaking to her, a funeral procession happens to pass by, and he joins it to pay his respects to the dead. Then he meets Elijah, who is plowing a field—a decent occupation that attracts him. Elijah offers the young man an opportunity to make a wish, and he asks for a worthy, God-fearing wife. At once Elijah takes him to the place where one of the three women of valor in the world lives; Elijah asks her if she would marry the young man, and she agrees.

On the seventh day of their nuptial festivities, Elijah finds the young man "sporting with his wife." He rebukes the young man for abandoning the Torah because of his passion for his wife, and informs him that, to offset the seven days of festivities, he will be sold into seven years of slavery. Hearing this, the young man bursts into tears. His bride, who was not present at his meeting with Elijah, assumes he is missing his family, and she suggests she return with him to his mother's home. But their plan fails: On their way, while the young man bathes in the river, Elijah appears, grabs him, and sells him as a slave. When the young man does not return, his wife, who was not present during her husband's abduction, realizes that this event must have been ordained by God. She reconciles herself to her husband's absence and settles there, at the same spot where he had left her. She foresees a period of famine in the land and decides to implement a plan that would bring her husband back. With the help of her slaves and maidservants, she establishes a city and sows a field of wheat. Her plans succeed. She becomes famous, and when the famine arrives, people from all over travel to her to trade for her wheat, among them her husband and his master. She makes herself known to him, and he tells her everything that happened to him since he was sold into slavery five years beforehand. Although they were both emotional about their reunion, the man, with his wife's consent, decides to leave again to complete the remaining two years of his slavery. When the time has come, Elijah brings him back to his wife, and together they travel to visit his mother. The epilogue ends with praise for his wife, of whom it is said: "Who can find a woman of valor?"

The story introduces a conflict between Torah study, which one should "meditate therein by day and by night" (Joshua 1:8), and married life.[25] Between a wife and the Torah, the correct choice is the Torah, and thus the tale establishes "abstinence," albeit temporary abstinence, as an acceptable and even positive value. The narrator does support married life. After all, the young man indeed reunites with his wife, but only after he recognizes the superiority and sublimity of the Almighty, as expressed in his decision to complete his period of slavery.

The motif of abstinence also exists in another tale in *Sefer ha-ma'asim*—"Torah Saves from Death" (no. 49), which is based on a well-known topoi in rabbinical and medieval sources but which deviates from them in the figure of a saintlike and abstinent protagonist.[26] It seems that abstinence in *Sefer ha-ma'asim* is legitimate and sometimes desirable.

The theme of abstinence also exists in the well-known talmudic tale of Rabbi Akiva's early life as an ignorant shepherd and then as a great scholar (*Ketubot* 61b–63a, *Nedarim* 50a).[27] At his wife's initiative, Rabbi Akiva leaves home to study Torah, only to return twenty-four years later as a great Torah scholar with thousands of disciples. His words to them about his wife when she approaches to welcome him have become a well-known idiom: "Mine and yours are hers"—that is, all he has acquired and learned is hers. The broad context of the story in *Ketubot* is indeed the conflict between marriage and Torah study and the attempt to reconcile it through pragmatic solutions.[28]

In view of "A Slave for Seven Years," neither in the talmudic story nor in the entire tractate does abstinence receive a positive value and a status of its own. This also holds true the other way around: In view of the talmudic story and in contrast

25. For elaboration on the historical context in *Sefer ḥasidim*, see Kushelevsky, "Discourse of Abstinence."

26. See tale no. 49.

27. Boyarin, *Carnal Israel*, 150–156.

28. These include maintaining contact with the home during one's absence; limiting the period of absence from home; and conditioning the husband's absence, when deviating from a certain set time, on his wife's agreement.

to it, abstinence stands out as a positive value in "A Slave for Seven Years," as long as it is limited to a specific period. Thus the two narratives when read together emphasize the disparate against the background of the similar—namely the mutual motif of abstinence—and cast light on one another. It would seem that the talmudic tale is not the source of "A Slave for Seven Years," although the narrator relied on it in domesticating and adapting it to its non-Jewish source, as we shall see.

The legend "The Life of St. Alexis" was very widespread from the eleventh to the fourteenth century in Latin versions, such as in the popular *The Golden Legend* by Jacob de Voragine,[29] and in vernacular versions in Old French.[30] "A Slave for Seven Years" is apparently based on French vernacular versions, in view of some nuances that exist only there. Alexis is born to wealthy, childless parents, in answer to their prayers for an heir and as a reward for their piety and their charity to the poor and the needy. After his birth, his parents decide that from then on their marriage would be one of purity and abstinence. They entrust their son to teachers who would teach him the sacraments of the church and other subjects of study, in particular spiritual ones. When he is of marrying age, they choose for him a bride they regard as suitable, and the two are married in an elaborate church ceremony. When night falls, the father encourages his son to approach his bride on the adorned marriage chamber bed, but when the couple is left alone, Alexis lectures her on the main articles of religious faith, gives her his belt buckle, and leaves her to embark on his life of abstinence. He goes directly to the port, boards a ship, and sails to Laodicea, and from there to Edessa in Syria, where he visits the church of St. Mary. He distributes his belongings among the poor and settles in the churchyard, dressed in rags. When his father in Rome learns his son has left, he sends his servants to search for him, but when they arrive in Edessa, they do not recognize him. Throughout these years of his absence, his wife remained in his mother's home, and they mourn their son and husband. For seventeen years Alexis huddles together with the poverty-stricken and beggars in the courtyard of the Virgin Mary, until Mary recognizes him as a saint and orders him brought into the church. But Alexis, resisting honor and admiration, embarks on a sea journey for another destination; due to a storm he ends up in Rome, the city of his parents. Assuming that his parents would not recognize him, and hoping to avoid becoming a burden to strangers, he returns home, where he lives for another seventeen

29. Jacobus, *The Golden Legend*, vol.1, no. 94, 371–374.

30. Versions in Old French: Odenkirchen, *The Life of St. Alexius*, 55–95; Stebbins, *Saint Alexis*, 21–63.

years under his parents' staircase, wretched and humiliated. After his death, Alexis's memoirs, written in his handwriting on a parchment, are found. His parents, who never recognized the beggar under the staircase as their son, are racked by grief, shock, and frustration. Alexis is declared a saint and buried in the Boniface church. In some parallels of the story, the couple is reunited after their deaths, in Paradise.

The main difference between this legend and "A Slave for Seven Years" is the temporary nature of the abstinence in the Jewish story, as expressed in the reunion of the couple in marriage at the end of the predetermined period of time. From this standpoint the story supports marriage. But the commonalities between both tales are striking when compared to the talmudic story of R. Akiva and his wife. In contrast to the narrator's stance in the talmudic story, in "A Slave for Seven Years" a positive value is attributed to abstinence, and the dangers of giving in to temptation and being led astray in marriage are exposed. While the narrator in *Sefer ha-ma'asim* delimits the areas of overlap between "A Slave for Seven Years" and "The Life of St. Alexis," thus distinguishing himself from the non-Jewish narrating community, he also shares with his contemporaries in Europe a historical horizon distinct from that of the talmudic narrator of the legend about Rabbi Akiva.

"The Prophecy of the Ravens" is about the only son of elderly parents who desires to learn the wisdom of the Torah. To his parents' sorrow, the young man parts from them and travels far away, to a city "filled with very wise men who are most knowledgeable in all the wisdom of the world." Three years later, he returns to his parents as he had promised, but then leaves again for another three years of study, and yet again for a third time, until he achieves "the essence of wisdom." By this time he has learned the language of the animals and the birds, and there is no one wiser than he. At the end of his studies, his father arrives to take him back home, and together they make their way on a ship to their country. During the voyage, the son hears the prophecy of a raven on the top of the mast, which foretells a reversal in his father's life: One day he would lose all of his fortune, but then he will regain his previous status and recover his wealth. Upon hearing the raven's prophecy, the young man "was greatly amused," perhaps because of the wealth his father would amass in the end, or perhaps because the prophecy confirmed his view that "at the hour of death one has neither silver nor gold nor precious stones nor pearls, but only the Torah and good deeds." In any case, he refuses to divulge the content of the prophecy to his father or the reason for his laughter. His father rages at what he regards as his son's foolish laughter, despite his many years of study in a foreign land, and he casts him into the sea. As in the case of the prophet Jonah, the son is swallowed by a fish and is then washed up on the shore of a different kingdom.

At this stage the story moves to that kingdom, whose king was very perturbed by a large flock of ravens above his house which no one seemed able to drive away. The king promises anyone who would solve the mystery the hand of his daughter and half his kingdom, but with no result. Even the king's wise counselors could not solve the problem or find why the ravens flocked around him. When the young man arrives, he explains the reason: There is a controversy among the ravens about a female which the king has to resolve. The king indeed pronounces his judgment, and the ravens carry it out and leave at once. As promised, the young man wins the hand of the princess, and at his request all the inhabitants of the kingdom, without exception, are ordered to come to the wedding feast, including his old parents. When they arrive, he learns they have lost all their property and have become impoverished, in keeping with the prophecy of the raven at the top of the mast, which is now fulfilled. At first they do not recognize their son, who is now deputy to the king, but then he reveals himself to his parents in a manner reminiscent of the biblical story of Joseph and his brothers. The tale ends with the son's marriage and the ensured well-being of his parents.

As mentioned earlier, the tale is based on two models: the Eastern frame story of *The Tales of Sendebar* and the embedded tale *Vaticinium* (prophecy), which appears only in *The Seven Sages of Rome*, the Western branch of the Sendebar tales.[31] The scribe's use of the *Vaticinium* in *Sefer ha-ma'asim* attests, once again, to the Jews' familiarity with the vernacular literature of their environment. By combining the two models, the scribe created a new narrative appropriate for his Jewish audience and its values. For example, the commandment "Thou shalt honor thy mother and thy father" and the belief in the Divine Providence are contrasted in "The Prophecy of the Ravens" with the role of fate in the *Vaticinium*, where the parents lose all of their possessions, in keeping with the prophecy of the ravens, and are obliged to serve their son, who has become king. Thus the *Vaticinium* was adapted in "The Prophecy of the Ravens" according to Jewish values.

"R. Meir and Judah of Anatot" (no. 25), unknown from earlier sources, is based on the topoi of "charity saves from death" in rabbinic literature, as well as the parables of Marie de France and her contemporary, R. Berakhiah Hanakdan. Judah of Anatot is doomed to die because he has never done a charitable deed in his life. Rabbi

31. For a note on the tale's versions, see Runte, Wikeley, and Farrell, *The Seven Sages of Rome*, 170.

Meir learns about this in a conversation between two snakes, one of whom was sent to bite Judah and all of his household members. The rabbi rushes to Judah's home to get him to do an act of charity, and thus save him from death. At a certain point Judah remains alone at home; the snake knocks on his door and begs him, in the voices of his wife and children, to allow him into the house because he is cold and thirsty. But R. Meir has warned him in advance, and Judah refuses to open the door. The following day he discovers the snake dead at his threshold, and realizes the danger he has just escaped. Two parallels by Marie de France and Berakhiah Hanakdan include a similar episode, although the story as a whole is different.[32] In Marie de France's parable, a goat strictly warns her kid not to open the door when she goes out to graze. Very soon, a wolf knocks on the door, imitating the voice of the goat to tempt the kid to open the door, but the kid refuses to do so, and is saved. The episode is transferred to the Jewish context with a change that glosses over the opening of the story common to both versions, replacing the secular message, which cautions against trusting strangers, with a religious one about the importance of charity. The adaptation techniques imbue the story with a more emphasized Jewish nature in comparison with the four tales discussed above.

The discussion in the last two chapters evokes the figure of a scribe involved in his creative work, much beyond the technical task of copying. The boundaries between a scribe as an editor who adapts his material slightly—for example, by deleting an original opening homily—and an editor-writer who creates a new story are obvious. In contrast, the transition from an editor who makes extensive changes in the story but leaves the basic plot of his source and a writer who produces different combinations of independent episodes, resulting in a new story, is not clear-cut. The tales in *Sefer ha-ma'asim* move on a rising scale of creativity and intervention by the scribe in his materials, influenced by ideological approaches, a self-image, and an aesthetic taste that is not necessarily identical to that which prevails in the modern age. Accordingly, intertextuality is expressed in *Sefer ha-ma'asim* on all levels of the text, to a varying degree: stylistic nuances whose broad contexts exist in vernacular literature; changes in motif and content; and structural changes such as either expansion or reduction of the plot. The relationship among these trends varies, from stylistic changes mainly in tales from Jewish sources and the use of highly charged words that bring broader contexts into the story, to a new creation mainly in narratives whose

32. Marie de France, *Fables*, "The Wolf and the Kid," no. 90, 229–231; Berakhiah Hanakdan, *Fables*, trans. Hadas, no. 21, 44–45.

sources are in the vernacular, and were adapted on the basis of episodes and materials in a narrative repository available to the scribe. *Sefer ha-ma'asim* illustrates, in diverse ways and in scores of variations, substantive differences in the approach to the text and the anonymous author in the Middle Ages, as compared to the present day.

❧

A Diplomatic Edition of *Sefer ha-ma'asim*

A Hebrew Transcription with Notes and an English Translation

Translators' Note

In translating this edition of *Sefer ha-ma'asim*, every effort was made to maintain the original style of the narrative text from the Middle Ages, along with its unique characteristics, while at the same time creating a text that is consistent with normative, standard English. The narrative nature of the stories, which were apparently read aloud, is expressed in the successions of conjunctive sentences joined by the word *and*, and by dialogues in direct speech, with the different speakers noted by their appropriate pronoun and the verb *said* (e.g., he/she/they said).

A further characteristic is the frequent allusions to the Bible and Talmud as a reservoir of expressions in Hebrew, a language that was not spoken in daily life in medieval France. This is in addition to the use of a lower language register drawn from the later and more popular midrashic compilations, such as the *Tanḥuma*, that were addressed to broader audiences. In some cases, the influence of Old French is evident, especially where masculine and feminine pronouns are concerned, but this is not apparent in the English translation.

A number of words that function as cultural codes are presented both in transliteration and translation, such as *ẓiẓit*, *ẓadeket*, *ẓadik*. The word *ḥasid* is especially salient in the richness of connotations that it evokes in Jewish culture, particularly in Ashkenaz. The word can be translated as a pious or righteous man, although in medieval Ashkenaz the word is especially associated with a well-founded ideology that appears in *Sefer ḥasidim* and with the social group known as the Ashkenazi Pietists. The word *ḥasid* in the stories here does not necessarily refer to this specific context of *ḥasidim* in Ashkenaz, and often the use of this word can be found in an earlier source on which *Sefer ha-ma'asim* is based. However, the range of this word's interpretation is broad, and the decision to use the original appellation *ḥasid*, transliterated from the Hebrew, is aimed at enabling these interpretations, in accordance with the relevant context in each individual case.

The decision to try to maintain the original style as much as possible, but without turning the text into a literal translation, and to refrain from paraphrasing the text or resorting to certain interpretations, often led to a text that in some places may be less elegant and fluent in the English. Ultimately, this was a case of weighing the advantages against the disadvantages—with each such decision having its own repercussions for the text.

With the help of God who works miracles
I shall embark on writing these tales

1. The Bizarre Deeds of Elijah the Prophet (300a–300b)

A. [300a] Once R. Joshua b. Levi yearned to accompany Elijah. He prayed, and Elijah appeared before him. And R. Joshua said: May I accompany you and observe what you do in the world? Elijah said to him: You will not be able to endure what I do. R. Joshua answered: I will.

B. The two walked together. One night, he [they] slept at a poor man's house. When the poor man saw them, he offered them food from his meager supplies. At midnight, Elijah arose and killed the man's cow, which was worth a thousand zuzim. The next night they slept at the home of a rich man. Seeing that the rich man had offered them nothing to eat, Elijah arose in the morning, took hold of a rope, [giving] one end to R. Joshua, and measured one hundred and eighty houses in the rich man's courtyard. And then he built them all. On the third night, they slept in a place where everyone was poor. And they shared their meager sustenance with them. In the morning, Elijah said: May God give you but one leader [lit., head]. The next day, they arrived at a place where everyone was rich and seated in golden chairs, the wealthy in accordance with their riches and the poor [i.e., less rich] in accordance with their poverty. And they did not offer them a thing. Elijah said: "May God make you all leaders."

C. R. Joshua was puzzled and said: Yesterday, you killed the cow of the poor person who served us. Does Elijah kill the cows of the poor? Isn't it Elijah's practice to sustain the poor? If you are Elijah, you must explain your deeds to me. He said: If I explain, we will have to part ways. R. Joshua said: Just the same, explain: Why did you kill the cow of the poor man? Elijah said: Because his wife was dying, so I acted first and killed his cow—to exchange one soul for another. And that rich man who did not offer us anything to eat, why did you build up his courtyard? Elijah said: Because money was buried in that courtyard and in that place which is engraved with God's name. Were he to dig two cubits into the earth, he would find an endless reserve of money. That is why I acted first and built up the courtyard, after which the buildings would fall. And as for those poor people who offered us food, why did you tell them that God would give them but one leader? He said: I thus blessed them to have a single leader, that everyone obey, so this is a blessing. And the rich ones who sat in golden seats, why did you tell them God will make them [you] all leaders? Elijah said: That is a curse. It is a curse for them to

בעזרת הא' עושה ניסים אחל לכתוב מעשים

1. מעשיו התמוהים של אליהו הנביא (300א–300ב)

A. [300א] ***מעשה*** ברבי יהושע בן לוי שהיה מתאוה לילך עם אליהו.[1] ועשה תפלה,[2] ונגלה אליו (אליו).[3] א"ל רבי יהושע: רצונך שאלך עמך ואראה מעשיך בעולם?[4] א"ל אליהו: אין אתה יכול לסבול מעשיי. א"ל: אני אוכל לסבול.[5]

B. הלכו שניהם ביחד. בלילה אחד לן עם אדם עני. כיון שראה אותם כבדם מתוך עניותו.[6] בחצי הלילה עמד אליהו והרג פרתו, שהייתה שווה אלף זוזים"[7] לילה שנייה לנו אצל אדם עשיר.[8] כיון שראה שלא כבדם,[9] עמד אליהו לבקר ולקח כל בידו חבל ור' יהושע בראש החבל, ומדדו בחצירו שמונים ומאה בתים. ובנה אותם כולם.[10] לילה שלישית לנו למקום שכולם עניים,[11] ומתוך עניותם כבדו אותם.[12] לבקר א"ל אליהו: המקום יתן לכם ראש אחד. למחר באו למקום שכולם עשירים. והיו יושבים בקתדראות של זהב העשיר לפי עושרו והעני לפי עניותו. ולא כבדו אותם.[13] א"ל אליהו: המקום יעשה כולכם ראשים.[14]

C. והיה תמיה ר' יהושע. א"ל ר' יהושע: אתמול הרגת פרתו של עני שכבדנו. וכי אליהו הורג פרתן של עניים, והלא אליהו דרכו לפרנס עניים? אין אתה אליהו. אלא פרוש לי מעשיך.[15] א"ל: אם אפרוש לך, אפרוש ממך. א"ל: אמר לו: אף על פי כן פרוש לי. מפני מה הרגת פרתו של

---

1. במדרש עשרת הדברות, שפירא, 89–92: אליהו זכור לטוב. ההשוואות להלן לכ"י זה, שבו הסיפור מפורט יותר, מחדדות את המגמה לתחביר אליפטי ולסיכום בספר המעשים.
2. ישב כמה ימים בתפילה ובתחנונים עד שעלתה תפילתו לשמים לפני הב"ה ונתן לו רשות.
3. מיד נגלה עליו אליהו ז"ל.
4. אמר ליהושע: מה אתה מבקש? אמר לו: מבקש אני לילך עמך ולראות מה אתה עושה בעולם.
5. אמר לו: אין אתה יכול ללך עמי. אמר לו: למה? אמר לו: לפי שתראה דברים הרבה שאין אתה יכול לסבול. אמר לו: אף על פי כן. אמר לו: לך.
6. לילה ראשונה לנו אצל אדם אחד עני עם אשתו, ולא היה להם אלא פרה אחת. כיון שראה אותם האכילם והשקם וכבדם כבוד גדול כראוי להם.
7. במעשה"ד, תגובות ר' יהושע בן לוי כאן ולהלן מתפרטות בשעת מעשה ותוך כדי המסע. בספר המעשים הן מתפרטות רק לאחר מעשה, כסיכום של ההתרחשויות. סימן המרכאות מצביע כנראה על סוף המשפט.
8. הלכו למקום שיני ומצאו שם עשיר גדול אחד שהיה עוסק בבניין.
9. וכשראה אותם לא קם ולא זע מפניהם, לא האכילם ולא השקם.
10. בחצי הלילה עמד אליהו הנביא ז"ל ואמר לר' יהושע: עמוד. ועמד. אמר לו: תפוש בראש החבל ואליהו הנביא ז"ל תפש בראש האחד, ומדדו הכתלים ובנו שם פלטורין גדולים מאה ושמונים בתים.
11. במעשה"ד הסדר שונה – בלילה השלישי הם מתארחים אצל אנשי הקהילה העשירה ובלילה הרביעי אצל אנשי הקהילה הענייה.
12. כיון שראו אותם התחילו להסביר להם פנים והאכילום והשקום וכבדום כבוד גדול מתוך דוחקם ועניותם.
13. והיו כלם עשירים. כיון שראו אותם, ברוב גאותם ובגובה לבם לא רצו לראותם סבר פנים ולא האכילום ולא השקום.
14. בבקר השכים אליהו ואמר: הקב"ה יעשה כולם ראשים.
15. אמר לו ר' יהושע: איני יכול לעמוד על דבריך ואיני יכול לסבול מעשיך, אלא אמור לי מה הדבר הזה אשר אתה עושה.

be likened to a ship that has many sailors [captains], because it will ultimately sink.

D. He said: Do you wish me to accompany you farther? Elijah said: It has already been decided that you will not accompany me farther. And if [300b] you see a wicked man prosper, do not wonder, for it is not to his benefit. And if you see anyone impoverished, it is because of his sins that it is caused to him, or to atone for his soul.

עני?[16] א"ל: לפי שהיתה אשתו נטויה למות לכך הקדמתי והרגתי פרתו, כדי שתעמוד נפש תחת נפש.[17] ואותו עשיר שלא כבדנו, למה בנית חצירו?[18] אמר: מפני שהיה ממונ(י) באותו חצר ובאותו מקום ושם חקוק עליו,[19] שאם היה חופר שתי אמות בקרקע היה מוצא שם ממון שאין לו הפסק לעולם. לכך הקדמתי ובניתי חצירו, ואחר יפול הבנין.[20] ולאותן עניים שכבדו אותנו, מפני מה אמרת להם המקום יתן לכם ראש אחד? א"ל: ברכתי אותם כך. מקום שאין ביניהם אלא ראש אחד הכל שומעין לו, וזו היא ברכה.[21] ולעשירים שהיו יושבין בקתדראות של זהב, מפני מה אמרת להם המקום יעשה כולכם ראשים?[22] א"ל: זו קללה הוא, שקיללתם שהם משולים לספינה שמלחיה מרובים כלומר שסופן ליטבע.[23]

D. א"ל: רצונך שאלך עמך? א"ל: כבר נפסק דבר שלא תלך עמי.[24] ואם [300ב] תראה רשע שהשעה משחקת לו אל תתמה, כי בשביל רעתו בא לו.[25] ואם תראה אדם שבא לידי חסרון כיס, בשבילו רעתו בא לו[26] או בשביל כפרת נפשו.

16. אמר לו: האיש שעשה לנו הכבוד למה הרגת פרתו?
17. אמר לו: אותו הלילה היתה אשתו ראויה למות והיא חביבה עליו מאלף דינרי זהב. לפיכך הקדמתי והרגתי את פרתו כדי שתהא כפרתה ותכנס נפש תחת נפש.
18. אותו עשיר צר עין שלא עשה עמנו חסד למה בנית לו כל הבנין הגדול?
19. במעשה"ד חסר: מפני – חקוק עליו. השוו למוטיב השם המפורש על פתח מי התהום באגדת דוד שכרה את יסודות בית המקדש, סוכה נג, ע"א-ב.
20. במעשה"ד נוסף: וזה הבניין לא הנחתי לו קיימה, כי מעשה נסים הוא ויפול פתאום ולא ימצא הממון לעולם.
21. ואותן עניים שכבדו אותנו אמרתי להם שלא יהיה להם אלא ראש אחד, שכל מקום שאין שם אלא ראש אחד לסוף מתיישב שכך אמר בן סירא (טז, ו): "באחד מבין תתיישב עיר".
22. ואותם עשירים שלא כיבדו אותנו למה ברכת אותם שיהיו כולם ראשים?
23. אמר לו: חרבן התפללתי באותו המקום, שכל מקום שיש שם ראשים הרבה סופו ליחרב, שכן משל בני אדם: ספינה שרבו מלחיה סופה ליטבע.
24. במעשה"ד, שאלה ותשובה זו חסרות.
25. אף אתה, אם ראיתה רשע שהשעה משחקת לו דע שאינה לטובתו.
26. כלומר, מדובר בעונשו של צדיק בעולם הזה, על חטאיו המועטים. במעשה"ד: אינה לרעתו אלא כפרת נפשו.

2. The Loan (version 1) (300b)

A. Once there was a *ḥasid* [a pious man] who used to recite the three prayers every day, and his prayers would rise before the Divine throne like a daily sacrifice placed upon the altar. And the *ḥasid* resolved never to accept a gift from anyone. And every day, he would go to the garbage heap and gather rags, and he put them on his front and back to cover his nakedness. That was his practice.

B. When God saw the man's misery and suffering, He said to Elijah: Go give him four zuzim. Elijah went and found him praying, as was his custom. Elijah waited until the man had finished praying. He said to him: Bless you, Rabbi, and the man responded in kind. Then Elijah wanted to give him the four [coins] as God had commanded him, but he refused to accept the money until Elijah persuaded him to take them. The *ḥasid* went to the market and bought himself a robe. And a man came up to him and coveted the robe he was wearing. He said: Sell me that robe. The *ḥasid* said: For how much? He said: For 24 gold coins. He said: Take it. And he [the *ḥasid*] became rich from those 24 gold coins and used them to buy slaves and maidservants, and became the owner of towns and ships sailing at sea. And after he became rich, he stopped praying, abandoning his previous practice.

C. God said to Elijah: Look at that *ḥasid* upon whom I poured an abundance of wealth, property, and honor, and he has stopped praying. Go and take from him everything I have given him. Elijah found the man sitting in a golden chair in the synagogue. He said to him: Bless you, Rabbi, and the man responded in kind. Elijah said: Do me a kindness and return to me that which I deposited with you. The man asked: What did you deposit with me? Elijah answered: The four zuzim that I gave you. The man said: I don't know you. Elijah responded: This is my name, and I gave you the money when you were praying in the synagogue. The man said: Thank you for reminding me. He immediately wanted to give Elijah back the money, but Elijah said: No, give me back the exact coins I gave you and no others. He said: Who knows which ones they are and how can anyone tell them from among all the other coins? Elijah said: Bring me your purse and I will pick them out. At once a miracle occurred, and Elijah took the very same coins and left. That *ḥasid* at once became destitute, and all his sons and daughters and slaves and handmaidens died, and his ships sank at sea. And he reverted to his previous practice, again gathering rags from the garbage and reciting three prayers a day.

2. ההלוואה [נוסח ראשון] (300ב)

A. מעשה בחסיד אחד שהיה מתפלל בכל יום שלשה תפלות. והיתה תפלתו עולה לפני כסא הכבוד, כתמיד שהיה קרב על גבי המזבח.[1] וקבל עליו אותו חסיד שלא יקבל מתנה משום אדם. והיה מהלך בכל יום באשפות ומלקט סמרטוטין ונותן לפניו ולאחריו, לכסות ערוותו. וכך היה מנהגו.

B. וכשראה הקב"ה עלבונו וענותו אמר לאליהו: לך ותן לו ד' זוזים. הלך אליהו ומצאו מתפלל כמנהגו. המתינו עד שנתפלל. א"ל: שלום עליך רבי, והחזיר לו שלום. ורצה אליהו ליתן לו ד' כמו שציוהו הקב"ה. ולא רצה לקבלם עד שפייס אותו וקבל. הלך לשוק וקנה מהם בגד לצורכו. ובא לו אדם אחד וחמד אותו טלית שעליו. א"ל: מכור לי טלית זה. א"ל: בכמה? א"ל: בעשרים וארבעה זהובים. א"ל: קחהו. ומן אותן כ"ד זהובים נתעשר וקנה מהם עבדים ושפחות, עיירות וספינות היו לו פורשות בים. כיון שנתעשר נמנע מהתפלל, ושכח מנהגו הראשון.

C. אמר הקב"ה לאליהו: ראה מאותו צדיק שהרביתי לו עושר ונכסים וכבוד ומנע תפלתו. לך וקח ממנו מה שנתתי לו. הלך אליהו ומצאו שהיה יושב בקטידרא של זהב, בבית הכנסת. א"ל: שלום עליך רבי, והחזיר לו שלום. א"ל אליהו: עשה לי טובה, וחזור לי מה שהפקדתי <ממך> אצלך. א"ל: מה המעשה שהפקדת אצלי? א"ל: ד' זוזים שנתתי בידך. א"ל: איני מכירך. מיד א"ל אליהו: כך שמי, ונתתי לך כשהיית מתפלל בבית הכנסת. א"ל: יפה הזכרתני. מיד רצה ליתן לו. א"ל אליהו: אותן עצמן תן לי, ולא אחרים. א"ל: ומי מכירן ומי יוכל לפשפש אחריהן? תביא ארנקי שלך, ואברר אותן. מיד נעשה לו נס, ולקח אותן עצמן והלך לו. מיד נתמעט אותו חסיד, ומתו כל בניו וכל בנותיו ועבדיו ושפחותיו, וספינותיו טבעו בים.[2] וחזר אותו חסיד למנהגו הראשון, ומלקט סמרטוטין באשפות ומתפלל ג' תפלות בכל יום.

1. הסיפור מובא פעמיים בספר המעשים, בגרסאות שונות. ראו סיפור 34.
2. השוו איוב א, טו–כ.

D. God had mercy and said: That *ḥasid* is very dear to me, and I cannot bear to see his suffering. Go and lend him ten zuzim, but make him swear in My name that he will never again neglect his customary prayers. At once, Elijah came to the man and found him in prayer, and waited until he had finished his prayers and greeted him. And he said: Take what I am giving you, but you must swear that you will never neglect your prayers.

D. כבש הקב"ה רחמיו ואמר: אותו חסיד חביב עלי ביותר, ואיני יכול לראות צערו. לך והלווה לו עשרה זוזים, והשביעהו בשמי שלא יבטל תפלתו לעולם כמנהגו. מיד בא אליהו אצלו ומצאו מתפלל, והמתינו עד שנתפלל ונתן לו שלום. וא"ל: טול מה שאני נותן לך, ואשביעך בי"י שלא תבטל תפילתך.

3. The Heir's Test (301a)

A. Once there was a very wealthy man who traveled to distant lands, and had but one son. The man fell ill and was on his deathbed. He called his host and said to him: I hereby leave all my money in your hands. If my son comes for it, test and examine him in three ways. Should he prove that he is wise, give him my money, and if not, let it be sanctified to heaven. And the man died.

B. In time, the son received word that his father had died, and he traveled to that land. And the practice in that land was not to show a sojourner where he could go to spend the night. What did the son do? He went to a place where they sold wood, and bought some. And the son told a man: Go bring this wood that I have bought to the place where you put up guests, and I will pay your wages. So the man went and brought the wood to the inn, and the son followed him. The son then stood and called out at the inn door. The innkeeper came out and asked: Who are you? He said: I am the son of so-and-so, your friend. He asked: And who showed you where I live? He said: I did such and such. The man thought to himself: This is one of the three things [tests] that his father instructed me to do.

C. The innkeeper then put the son up for the night. [Later], they sat down to eat, and the innkeeper served the son a cooked chicken. The host said: Divide this chicken up among us. And the innkeeper had two sons and two daughters. He [the son] gave the head of the chicken to the innkeeper and the tail to his wife; he gave the wings to the daughters and the legs to the sons, and kept the breast for himself. The innkeeper asked: Why did you divide up the chicken this way? He answered: You are the head, so I gave you the chicken's head. Your wife remains at home, so I gave her the tail. Your daughters will soon marry husbands and fly off from home, which is why I gave them the wings. The legs I gave to your sons, who are the pillars of your home. I, who came by ship and will return by ship, took the breast, which resembles a ship. The innkeeper said: You divided up the chicken well.

3. מבחן הבן היורש (301א)

A. מעשה באדם אחד שהלך למדינת הים[1] והיה לו ממון גדול. ולא היה לו אלא בן אחד. חלה אותו האיש ונטה למות.[2] קרא לאושפיזו ואמר לו: הרי ממוני מופקד בידיך.[3] אם יבא בני בשבילו, בחנהו ונסהו בשלשה דברים. אם תראה שהוא חכם תן לו ממוני, ואם לאו יהיו הקדש לשמים.[4] והלך האיש לבית עולמו.

B. לימים שמע הבן שמת אביו, והלך לאותה מדינה. וכך היה מנהגם,[5] לא היו מראים מקום לאורח להכניס שם ללון. מה עשה אותו הבן, הלך למקום שהיו מוכרים עצים וקנה מהם.[6] ואמר הבן לאיש אחד: לך והבא העצים האילו שקניתי לבית האושפיזכן, ואני אתן שכרך. והלך האיש והביא העצים לבית האושפיזכן, והבן הלך אחריו. עמד וקרא לפתח הבית. יצא אליו בעל הבית, וא"ל: מי אתה? א"ל: אני בן פלוני אוהבך.[7] א"ל: ומי הראך מקומי? א"ל: כך וכך עשיתי.[8] חשב אותו האיש בלבו: הנה אחד משלשה דברים שציוה לי אביו.

C. הלינו בבית הלילה. ישבו לאכול, הביאו לפניו תרנגולת מבושלת.[9] א"ל האושפיזכן: חלוק אותה תרנגולת בינינו.[10] והיה לבעל שני בנים ושתי בנות. נתן הראש לבעל הבית, ואת האליה נתן לאשתו,[11] והכנפיים נתן לבנותיו, והירכים לבניו והחזה לקח לעצמו. א"ל: מפני מה חלקת כך?[12] א"ל: אתה הראש, ונתתי לך ראשה. אשתך יושבת בבית, על כן נתתי לה האליה. בנותיך למחר ינשאו לבעליהן ויפרחו מביתך, לכך נתתי להן הכנפים. בניך שהם עמודי ביתך, נתתי להם הירכים. אני על ספינה באתי ועליה אני חוזר, על כן לקחתי את החזה שהוא דומה לספינה. א"ל: יפה חילקתה.

---

1. באיכה רבה, וילנה והורדנא, פרשה א, ד, ד"ה: רבתי בגויים: מדינה [=עיר]; במהדורת בובר, 46: אתינס [אתונה]. ההשוואות להלן הן למהדורות אלה של איכה רבה.
2. באיכה רבה וילנה, ללא ציון מחלתו אלא בהכללה [הגיע עתו למות].
3. שם, דיווח עקיף על הפקדת הרכוש.
4. הקדש לשמים – תוספת בספר המעשים.
5. במהדורת בובר: ועשו ביניהם הסכם, ובדומה, במהדורת וילנה.
6. באיכה רבה וילנה ובובר פירוט רב יותר של דרכי הפעולה של הבן: הוא יושב בשער העיר ורואה איש טעון משא עצים.
7. אוהבך – תוספת כאן לעומת איכה רבה, וילנה. במהדורת בובר, בעל האכסניה מכונה: אוהבו. באיכה רבה וילנה פירוט רב יותר של השיחה בינו ובין מוכר העצים, ובינו ובין בעל האכסניה.
8. באיכה רבה וילנה ובובר, בתוספת איזכור של ארוחה שהכין המארח עבורו.
9. באיכה רבה וילנה ובובר, הסדר הפוך: מבחן חמש הפרגיות הוא ראשון ומבחן התרנגולת הוא שני.
10. באיכה רבה וילנה ובובר בתוספת הסתייגות הבן, האורח, מחלוקת המנות מפני שזה תפקיד המארח, והבטחת המארח שהדבר לרצונו ולהנאתו.
11. באיכה רבה, וילנה: בני מעיים.
12. באיכה רבה וילנה, הבן נדרש להסביר את פתרון שתי החידות ברצף, לעומת מהדורת בובר וספר המעשים בהם נדרש הבן להסביר את מעשיו לאחר כל חידה.

D. The next day, five chickens were served. The innkeeper said: You divide them up among us. The son served the man and his wife one chicken to share between them, one to be shared by the two daughters, and one by the two sons, taking two for himself. The innkeeper asked the son: Why did you do it this way? He said: I divided them up well. You and your wife plus one chicken make three; your two daughters plus one chicken make three; your two sons plus one chicken make three, and I plus two chickens make three. The man said: You are certainly worthy of inheriting your father's fortune, and he gave it all to him.

D. למחר הביאו לפניו חמשה תרנגולות.[13] א"ל: חלוק אותן בינינו.[14] נתן תרנגולת אחת בינו ובין אשתו, ואחת בין שתי בנותיו, ואחת לשני בניו, ושנים נטל לעצמו. א"ל: למה עשית כך? א"ל: יפה חילקתי.[15] אתה ואשתך ותרנגולת הרי ג', שתי בנותיך ותרנגולת הרי ג', בניך ותרנגולת הרי ג' ואני ושתי תרנגולות הרי ג'. אמר הבעל ודאי זה ראוי לירש ממון אביו, ונתן לו הכל.[16]

13. באיכה רבה וילנה ובובר: חמש פרגיות.
14. שם, מוזכרת גם הסתייגות האורח מן התפקיד שהוטל עליו (ראו הערה 10 לעיל).
15. באיכה רבה וילנה ובובר, בהרחבה נוספת.
16. באיכה רבה וילנה ובובר, הבן תובע את ירושת אביו.

4. Joab's Valor (301a–302a)

A. [301a] Once in the time of David, David sent Joab, son of Tseruya, to Kisary, the city of the Amalekites, to fight for it. The Amalekites closed the gates of the city, and the Israelites encircled the wall for six months. And Joab had twelve thousand warriors.

B. After six months had passed, the warriors gathered [301b] and all stood around Joab, saying to him as one: We can no longer bear to encircle the wall. After all, it has been a long time since we have left our towns, villages, and children. Joab said to them: So what do you wish to do? They said as one: We wish to return home. He said to them: We will not return in disgrace, and we will not return to the king empty-handed. [If that should happen,] all the nations would hear of it and attack us. Make a catapult and cast me into the city. Joab immediately took a thousand coins and his sword. Then Joab told them: Wait for me for forty days. If you see blood emerging from under the gates of the city, you will know that I am alive, and if you don't, that means that I am dead and you may go home.

C. They catapulted him, and Joab fell into the courtyard of the city onto the roof of a certain widow, who had a married daughter. And the daughter came outside and found Joab in the yard, neither dead nor alive. Then the three of them [mother, daughter, and her husband] went outside and carried him into the house, washed him with water, and anointed him with oil. Joab's spirits were restored, and they asked him: Who are you? He said: I am an Amalekite, I was with the battalion of Israel, and they caught me and brought me to the king and sentenced me and catapulted me into the city. And you, be so kind to me and revive me. He took ten coins and gave them to the girl's husband and said to him: Go and buy us what you wish. And he stayed with them for ten days. He then planned to go into the city to have a look around. They said to Joab: Do not go wearing those clothes. So they dressed him in clothes of theirs and he went to the marketplace.

D. The city had 140 marketplaces, each larger than the other. So he observed how to enter and exit each and then went to a blacksmith and said: Make me a sword like the broken one I am holding. When the blacksmith saw the sword, he was amazed. Joab asked: Why are you amazed? He said: Because I have never seen one like it. Joab said: Make me one like this, and I will pay you well. He made him a sword, and he [Joab] held it in his hand and swung it, and it broke, and the same happened with the second and the third. The blacksmith made yet another sword for him, and Joab swung it and it did not break. Joab asked the blacksmith: Whom

4. גבורת יואב (301–302א)

A. מעשה היה בימי דוד, ששלח יואב בן צרויה[1] לקסרי מדינת עמלק להלחם עליה.[2] וסגרו (וסגרו) העמלקיים דלתות המדינה. והיו בני ישראל מקיפין את החומה ששה חדשים.[3] והיו מגיבורי ישראל עם יואב שנים עשר אלפים.

B. לאחר ששה חדשים נתקבצו [301ב] הגבורים ועמדו כולם על יואב ואמרו פה אחד: לא נוכל לסבול זאת להקיף החומה, הרי כמה זמן עבר שהנחנו עיירות וכפרים שלנו ובנינו. אמר להם יואב: ומה אתם רוצים לעשות? אמרו כולם: נרצה לחזור בבתינו. אמר להם: לא נחזור בפחי נפש ונשוב למלך פנינו ריקם, וישמעו כל העמים וילחמו עמנו. עשו קלע וקלעו אותי בעיר. מיד לקח יואב אלף כסף והסייף שלו. ואמר להם יואב: המתינו לי ארבעים יום. אם תראו הדם יוצא מתחת דלתי המדינה, דעו שאני חי ואם לאו דעו שאני מת ולכו לבתיכם.

C. וקלעוהו ונפל יואב בחצר המדינה על גג אלמנה אחת. והיה לה בת אחת נשואה לבעל. ויצאה הנערה ומצאה יואב מושלך בחצר לא חי ולא מת.[4] ויצאו שלשתן[5] וישאו אותו והכניסוהו לבית, ורחצוהו במים וסכוהו בשמן. ותשב רוחו ושאלו אותו: מי אתה? אמר להם: עמלקי אני,[6] והייתי בגדוד ישראל,[7] ותפשוני והביאוני למלך וגזר עלי וקלעוני במדינה. ואתם עשו טוב עמי והחיוני. לקח עשרה כספים ונתנם לבעל הנערה. ואמר לו: לך קנה מהם לנו מה שתרצה. והיה עמהם עשרה ימים. ובקש לילך בעיר ולעיין. אמרו לו: לא תלך בזה הלבוש, והלבישוהו משלהם ויצא לשוק.[8]

D. והיו במדינה מאה וארבעים שווקים, וכל שוק ושוק גדול מחברו, וראה מוצאה ומובאה והלך אצל נפח אחד וא"ל: עשה לי סייף כמו זה שבור בידי. כשראה הנפח הסייף נזדעזע. א"ל: למה נזדעזעת? א"ל: שלא ראיתי כמוה מימיי. א"ל: עשה לי כזה, ואני אתן לך שכרך. עשה לו ותפשו בידו ונענע ונשבר וכן השנייה וכן השלישית. עשה לו סייף אחד ונענע ולא נשברה. א"ל לנפח:

1. הסיפור פורסם על ידי יסיף, גבורת יואב, 17–20.
2. בחיבור המעשיות והמדרשות, סיפור ט': קינסרי מדינתא דעמלק. ציטוטים מן הסיפור להלן הם ממקור זה.
3. השוו מלכים א, יא, טז: "כי ששת חדשים ישב שם יואב וכל ישראל עד הכרית כל זכר באדום".
4. בחיבור המעשיות מצבו של יואב אינו מתואר.
5. בחיבור המעשיות הנערה מקדימה לקרוא לאמה ולבעלה.
6. השוו שמואל ב, א, ח: "ויאמר לי מי אתה ויאמר אליו עמלקי אנכי"; שמואל ב, א, יג: "אי מזה אתה ויאמר בן איש גר עמלקי אנכי".
7. השוו שמואל ב, א, ד: "ממחנה ישראל נמלטתי".
8. 'שוק' כאן הוא במובן של רחוב או כיכר בעיר שעוסקים שם במקח וממכר. ראו מילון אבן שושן: שוק.

shall we strike with this sword? The blacksmith answered: King Joab. Joab said: O impure one, I am Joab, look behind you. The blacksmith turned his head, and Joab struck him in the stomach. Joab said to him: What is in your stomach? He said to him: Snow.[1] He pushed him, and the blacksmith fell, half here and half there.

E. Joab went outside to the courtyard, where he found eight hundred warriors and killed them, and not one escaped. Afterward he sheathed his sword and returned to the house where he was staying. And the word spread about the dead, [that is] the people of the city were saying: Asmodeus, the king of the demons, killed them. And the people of the house asked Joab: Do you know anything about this news? No, he said. He took out ten more coins and gave them to them. Joab stayed with them a few days more and afterward exited through the gate, and with his unsheathed sword in hand, killed one thousand, five hundred men. And the sword became stuck to his hand, and he placed his other hand on it. And he returned to that house and found the girl there. [He said to her]: Prepare me some warm water, perhaps the sword can be removed. She screamed and said: You eat with us yet kill the people of our city?! And she was pregnant. He plunged the sword into her belly, and his hand was healed, and he returned to the market.

F. He heard a herald announce: Anyone who has a guest in his house must bring him to the king. Joab encountered him and killed him [302a], and went on killing whoever he encountered, thus killing two thousand more, beyond the previous ones, until he arrived at the gates of the city and struck all those who were there and opened the gates of the city. Blood was pouring out beyond the boundaries of the city, and Israelites were weeping for Joab and intending to return home. But when they saw the blood emerging from the city, they rejoiced and said: "Here O Israel, the Lord is our God, the Lord is one" [Deuteronomy 6:4]. When Joab saw this, he climbed to the top of the tower so that the Israelites could see him, and he raised his voice and said "God will not forsake his people" [1 Samuel 12:22]. "The Lord will fight for you while you keep silent" [Exodus 14:14]. They sent a dispatch to the king, and all entered the city, donned their weapons, and unsheathed their swords. And Joab turned his head and saw two verses written on his right leg: "The Lord will hear in times of trouble" [Psalms 20:2], "The Lord will give victory to the king" [Psalms 20:10]. And David came to Joab and asked him: What did you do? You killed all the Amalekites in the city as it says, "You shall blot out the memory of Amalek" [Deuteronomy 25:19]? He responded: That is what I did, and not one was left save

1. "Snow," meaning a sense of coldness.

מה נכה עם זה הסייף?[9] א"ל: מלך יואב. א"ל: אי טמא, הלא יואב אני הבט לאחריך. חזר הנפח ראשו, והכהו בבטנו. א"ל יואב: מה יש בבטנך? א"ל: שלג.[10] דחפו ונפל מת חציו לכאן וחציו לכאן.

E. ויצא לחוץ ונכנס לחצר,[11] ומצא שם שמונה מאות גבורי מלחמה[12] והרגם ולא מלט מהם איש ושם חרבו לתערה. וחזר לבית שהוא שוכן שם. ונשמע קול על ההרוגים שהיו אומרים אנשי העיר: אשמדאי מלכא דשידי הרגם. ושאלו אנשי הבית ליואב: כלום אתה יודע משמועה זו? אמר להם: לאו. הוציא עוד עשרה כספים ונתן להם. המתין עמהם ימים, ואחר כך יצא לשער וחרבו שלופה בידו, והרג אלף וחמש מאות איש. ותדבק [ידו אל החרב], ויצר ידו על זרועו.[13] ובא לאותו הבית ומצא שם הנערה. [א"ל]: עשי לי מי חמין אולי יפטר החרב מידי.[14] צעקה ואמרה: עמנו תאכל ותהרוג אנשי עירינו?! והיא מעוברת.[15] תקע החרב בבטנה, ונתרפא ידו וחזר לשוק.

F. שמע כרוז שמכריזין: כל מי שיש לו אורח יביאנו למלך. פגע בו יואב והרגו [302א], וכל מי שהיה פוגע בו היה הורגו. עד שהרג ב' אלפים חוץ מן הראשונים. עד שבא לשערי המדינה והכה שם כל הנמצא ופתח שערי העיר והיה הדם מתגלגל ויוצא חוץ למדינה, וישראל בוכים על יואב, ורוצים לחזור לבתיהם. וכשראו הדם יוצא מן העיר שמחו ואמרו: שמע ישראל י"י א-להינו י"י אחד [דברים ו, ד]. כשראה יואב כך עלה לגג המגדל שיראוהו ישראל, והרים קולו ואמר: כי לא יטוש י"י את עמו [שמואל א, יב, כב]. י"י ילחם לכם ואתם תחרישון [שמות יד, יד]. שגרו למלך ונכנסו כולם למדינה, ולבשו כלי זיין ושלפו חרבותם מתערה. וחזר יואב ראשו וראה על רגלו הימין פסוקים כתובים: יענך י"י ביום צרה [תהילים כ, ב] י"י הושיעה המלך [תהלים כ, י].
וכשבא דוד אל יואב א"ל: מה עשית, הרגת כל העמלקיים שבעיר כמו שכת' תמחה את זכר עמלק [דברים כה, יט]? א"ל: כך עשיתי, ולא נשתייר מכולם[16] כי אם המלך לבדו. והלך יואב והביא המלך לפני דוד, והרגו דוד בידו[17] ולקח יואב הכתר ונתן על ראש דוד.[18] והיה הכתר מככרים זהב

---

9. למי נאה להרוג עם זה החרב.
10. שם, ללא חילופי דברים ביניהם. 'שלג', כלומר תחושה של קור. השוו לתהילים קמז, יז: "הנתן שלג כצמר".
11. ונכנס ברחוב המדינה.
12. חמש מאות איש שכירים גבורי מלחמה.
13. כלומר, הצר את אחיזת ידו על זרועו. ונצר ידו על זרועו.
14. וקבלי את החרב מידי.
15. בחיבור המעשיות הריונה אינו מוזכר.
16. לא נשתייר משונאי אלא המלך לבדו.
17. השוו שמואל א, טו: לג: "וישסף שמואל את אגג לפני ה' בגלגל".
18. השוו שמואל ב יב, ל: "ויקח את עטרת מלכם מעל ראשו [. . .] ותהי על ראש דוד".

the king alone. And Joab brought the king before David, and David killed him with his [own] hands, and Joab took the crown and placed it on David's head. And the crown was made of pure talents of gold, and a precious stone was mounted on it. And he took all the property that was in the city and burned their idols, to uphold the injunction: "Shatter their altars" [Exodus 34:13]. And all of Israel came to Jerusalem in great joy and praised the eternal Lord, and fear of Israel fell upon all the nations [Esther 9:2], a great fear of David, as it says: "And David had success in all his undertakings" [1 Samuel 18:14].

מזוקק, והיה בה אבן יקרה. והוציא כל הרכוש כל אשר בעיר[19] ושרפו עבודה זרה שלהם, לקיים מה שכת': את מזבחותם תתוצון [שמות לד, יג].[20] ובאו כל ישראל לירושלים בשמחה גדולה ומהללים לא-ל חי עולמים, ונפל פחדם על כל העמים [אסתר ט, ב] מאוד מאימתו של דוד, שנ': ויהי דוד בכל דרכיו משכיל.[21]

19. בחיבור המעשיות נוסף תיאור הביזה וההרס: וכל הטף וכלי כסף וכלי זהב ושללו ובזזו כל אשר במדינה.
20. שם נוסף: ושרפו כל העיירות שבאדום ולא היתה להם תקומה כמו שכתוב יהי אדום עובדים לדוד.
21. השוו שמואל א, יח, יד: "ויהי דוד לכל דרכו משכיל". בחיבור המעשיות תוספת באפילוג: כן יהי ה' א-להינו עמנו ועם כל ישראל.

5. The Two-Headed Man (302a–302b)

A. [302a] Once in the time of Solomon, Asmodeus came to him and said: Are you the one of whom it is written that he is wiser than all men [1 Kings 5:11]? He said: That is what the Lord promised me. Asmodeus said: If you like, I can show you something the likes of which you have never seen before. He immediately stretched out his hand to the earth and took out a man with two heads and four eyes. At once Solomon was amazed and terrified at the sight. He said: Bring him into the room. He called for Benaiahu son of Jehoiada. He said to him: Do you know if there are people beneath us? Benaiahu said: On my life, sir, I don't know, but I once heard from Aḥitophel, your father's general, that there are people beneath us. Solomon said: I will show you one of them. And Benaiahu asked: How can you when this land is five hundred travel years away, and between one land and another is a distance of five hundred years?

B. They immediately brought him [Benaiahu] before the man, and when he saw him he fell on his face and said, "Blessed are You, Lord, our God, Ruler of the Universe, who has granted us life, sustained us and enabled us to reach this time" [cf. bBerakhot 54a]. Solomon asked him: Whose son are you? He said: I am a descendent of Adam and from among the offspring of Cain. He said: Where do you live? He said: In the land of Tuval [Tevel]. He asked: Do you have a sun and moon? He said: Yes. And we plow and sow seeds and are shepherds. And in what place does the sun rise? He said: It rises from the West and sets in the East and we pray. And what is your prayer? He said: "How countless are Your works, O Lord! In wisdom, have You made them all" [Psalms 104:24]. He said: Do you want us to bring you back home? At once he called Asmodeus and said: Take him back home. Asmodeus said: It is impossible.

C. That being the case, the man married a woman who bore him [302b] seven sons. Six resembled the mother, and one resembled the father. The man sowed and plowed and became very wealthy. And after some time the man died and left a large inheritance for his sons. Six sons said: We are seven, but the son with two heads said: We are eight. They went to Solomon to seek justice. When Solomon saw them, he didn't know what to do. He immediately summoned the Sanhedrin and asked them. They [too] fell silent. He said: Wait for me until morning. At midnight he entered the sanctuary and stood in prayer before the Lord and said to Him: Master of the Universe, when you were revealed to me at Givon and told me that I could ask what I wish of you, I did not ask for silver or gold, but for wisdom to judge your people of Israel. God said to him: In the morning, I will give it to you, and you will

5. בעל שני ראשים (302א–302ב)

A. מעשה היה בימי שלמה.[1] יום אחד נכנס עליו אשמדאי.[2] א"ל: אתה הוא שכת' עליו ויחכם מכל האדם [מלכים א ה, יא]. א"ל: כך הבטיחני הקב"ה. א"ל: אשמדאי אם תרצה אראה לך דבר שלא ראית מעולם.[3] מיד הושיט ידו בארץ והוציא משם איש בעל שני ראשים וד' עינים.[4] מיד נזדעזע שלמה ונבהל. אמר {לו ~~להם~~} הכניסוהו לחדר. שלח לקרא לבנייהו בן יהויידע. א"ל ידעת אם יש תחתינו בני אדם? א"ל חי נפשך אדוני[5] לא ידעתי אבל שמעתי מאחיתופל אלוף אביך[6] שיש בני אדם תחתינו. א"ל אראה לך אחד מהם. וא"ל והיאך אתה יכול להראותי והלא עומקה של ארץ זו חמש מאות שנה מהלך, ובין ארץ לארץ מהלך ה' מאות שנה.[7]

B. מיד הביאו אצלו וכיון שראהו נפל על פניו ואמר ברוך אתה י"י א-להינו מלך העולם שהחיינו וקיימנו והגיענו לזמן הזה.[8] א"ל: בן מי אתה? א"ל: מבן אדם מתולדות קין.[9] א"ל: ובאיזה מושבם? א"ל: בארץ תובל.[10] יש לכם שמש וירח? א"ל: כן,[11] ואנו חורשים וזורעים ובעלי צאן. ובאיזה מקום תזרח שמש? א"ל: ממערב ותשקע במזרח[12] ואנו מתפללים. ומה היא תפלתכם? א"ל: מה רבו מעשיך ה' כולם בחכמה עשית [תהלים קד, כד]. א"ל: תרצה שנחזור אותך במקומך?[13] מיד קרא לאשמדאי וא"ל: חזור אותו למקומו.[14] א"ל: איני יכול להחזירו לעולם.[15]

C. כיון שראה כך נשא אשה והוליד ממנה [302ב] שבעה בנים. ששה מהם בדמות האם ואחד בדמות האב.[16] והיה חורש וזורע ונעשה עשיר גדול. ולאחר זמן מת האיש ~~ונעשו י~~ והניח ירושה גדולה לבניו. ששה בנים היו אומרים אנו שבעה, והאיש לשני ראשים אומר אנחנו שמונה.[17] הלכו

---

1. במדרש עשרת הדיברות כ"י ותיקן 285, ובחיבור המעשיות והמדרשות וההגדות: שלמה מלך ישראל. ההשוואות להלן הן למקורות אלה.
2. בחיבור המעשיות, סיפור י"א: אשמדאי מלכא דשידי.
3. במעשה"ד ובחיבור המעשיות: אמר לו: הין.
4. תוספת במעשה"ד: וארבעה אזנים.
5. במעשה"ד ובחיבור המעשיות: אדוני המלך.
6. במעשה"ד: למדתי מאחיתופל אלוף אביך.
7. תוספת בחיבור המעשיות: גם כן מהלך חמש מאות שנה.
8. במעשה"ד: ברוך שהחיינו והגיענו בזה היום עד שהראנו סוד גדול כמו זה: ודבר גדול זה שלא ראה אדם מעולם. בחיבור המעשיות: שהחיינו וקיימנו לזמן הזה. השוו ברכות נד, ע"א.
9. במעשה"ד: בני קין.
10. במעשה"ד וחיבור המעשיות: ארץ תבל.
11. בחיבור המעשיות: יש לכם שמש או ירח? אמר לו: הין, וגם אנו חורשין וקוצרין ובעלי צאן ובהמות. במעשה"ד: א"ל, יש לכם כלום מעשה? א"ל: אנו חורשים וזורעים וקוצרים ובעלי צאן אנו.
12. במעשה"ד: א"ל, תזרח ממערב ותשקע במערב.
13. במעשה"ד: תוספת של מילת פניה 'בני'.
14. במעשה"ד: א"ל, עשה טובתך והחזירני למקומי.
15. במעשה"ד: מיד השיב לו אשמדיי ואמר, אתה הוא שאומרין עליך ויחכם מכל האדם? אתה החזירהו. אמ' לו איני יכול להחזירו לעולם.
16. תוספת בחיבור המעשיות: שהיו לו שני ראשים.
17. במעשה"ד: הששה היו אומ' שבעה אנו, והאחד שהיה דומה לאביו היה אומ' שמֹנה אנו, כי אני במקו' שנים ואטול שני חלקים. בחיבור המעשיות: הששה אומר', אנו שבעה לחלק ממון אבינו, והאחד שיש לו הב' ראשים אומר: אנו שמונה ועלי ליטול מן הירושה שני חלקים.

know that the wisdom is from God, as it says: “The plans of the heart belong to man, but the answer of the tongue is from the Lord” [Proverbs 16:1].

D. The next day he sent for and gathered the entire Sanhedrin and said: Bring me the two-headed man. He told them: Look what I do: If the other head knows what I am doing, then it is clear that he is one. And if not, then he is two. He said: Bring me hot water and aged wine and a linen cloth. Then he placed the cloth on the man’s face and poured the hot water and old wine over him. And both heads cried out and said: We are dying, for we are one and not two. Solomon said: But you said you should get a double portion. When all of Israel saw the verdict of the king, they were amazed and trembled in fear of him.

לפני שלמה לדין.[18] כיון שראה שלמה כך נתעלם ממנו הדבר. מיד קרא לסנהדרין, שאל להם ושתקו. אמר להם: המתינו לי עד הבקר.[19] בחצי הלילה נכנס בהיכל ועמד בתפלה לפני הקב"ה ואמר לפניו: רבונו של עולם כשנגלית לי בגבעון ואמרת לי שאל מה אתן לך, לא שאלתי לא כסף ולא זהב אלא חכמה כדי לשפוט עמך ישראל.[20] א"ל הקב"ה: לבקר אני נותן לך ותדע כי החכמה מי"י, שנ' לאדם מערכי לב ומי"י מענה לשון [משלי טז, א].[21]

D. למחר שלח וקבץ כל סנהדרין ואמר: הביאו לפני אותו האיש בעל שני ראשים. אמר להם: ראו אם זה הראש יודע מה שאני עושה בידוע שהוא אחד, ואם לאו הרי שנים.[22] אמר: הביאו לי מים חמים ויין ישן ובגד של שש והניח הבגד על פניו וזרק בו מים חמים ויין ישן. וצעקו השני ראשים ואמרו: אנו מתים שאנו אחד ולא שנים.[23] א"ל: והלא אמרת ליתן לך פי שנים. כיון שראו ישראל כך משפט המלך, תמהו ורעדו ופחדו ממנו.[24]

18. במעשה"ד ובחיבור המעשיות מובא פירוט של טיעוני הבנים בפני שלמה.

19. מעשה"ד: באותה שעה קרא לסנהדרי' ותיקן הדבר לפניהן, ואמ' להם: מה אתם אומ' בדבר זה? אמרו: אם אנו אומ' שנים מתייראים אנו שמא אחד הוא, ואם אנו אמ' אחד מתייראים אנו שמא שנים הם. באותה שעה כשראה שלמה כך שלא פירשו הסנהדרין את דינם אמ' להם לבקר משפט; חיבור המעשיות: מיד קרא לסנהדרין ואמ' להם: מה אתם אומרים בדבר הזה? אמרו: אם אנו אומרים אחד הוא שמא שנים הם, שתקו. אמר להם שלמה לבקר משפט.

20. חיבור המעשיות: לשפוט בצדק בני אדם.

21. שם: אני נותן לך חכמה בבקר.

22. מעשה"ד: ואמ' לכל ישראל: דעו שאם ידע זה מה שאני עושה לזה דעו שאחד הוא, ואם לאו שנים; בדומה לכך בחיבור המעשיות.

23. במעשה"ד ובחיבור המעשיות בתוספת פנייה: אדוני, אדונינו המלך, אנו מתים שאנו אחד ולא שנים. בחיבור המעשיות, פעמיים: אנו מתים אנו מתים.

24. תוספת אפילוג במעשה"ד ובחיבור המעשיות: לכך נאמר ויחכם מכל האדם.

6. The Drunkard and His Sons (302b–303a)

A. [302b] Once there was an old man who had two sons. And he loved wine and loved to drink, and each day would drink everything his sons had earned [that day]. One evening, one of the sons said to the other: What shall we do about our father who drinks up everything we earn while we cannot even afford to buy shoes for our feet? If you take my advice, we can save up our wages for two or three days and give him enough to drink until he is intoxicated. What did they do? They gave their father wine until he fell into a deep slumber. They called the neighbors and said: Come to our father who has died. They prepared a shroud for him and took him to the cemetery. [At that time], the dead were buried in rock caves that resembled buildings, and were placed on the ground. And because the father was sleeping so deeply due to all the wine he had drunk, he neither woke nor moved, like a dead body, and they buried him and went home.

B. The next day, Ishmaelites came carrying wine, meat, bread, and all kinds of other foodstuffs that they were delivering to a city that had been under siege. And they encountered pursuers. And when the merchants realized that pursuers had come to the city, they hid all the food and wine in a cave and fled on their camels. On the third day, the old man woke up and was confused because he didn't know where he was. So he groped around him and called out, but could find no one there in the cave [to help him]. And he searched with his hands and found the wineskins, meat, bread, and cheese [303a]. He said: My sons have abandoned me here, and blessed is my Creator who has come to my aid. What did he do? He sat down and ate and drank until he again became drunk. And he stood up and laughed and sang songs [accompanying himself with his hand].

C. Three days later, his sons came to visit him, to see if he was dead or alive. They went to the burial chamber and heard their father singing. They said: He's still alive. They approached him and asked: Father, how are you? He said: You are wicked; you intended to do me harm, and God turned it into something good, and kept me alive on this day. Go away; God will help me all the days of my life. I have found many wineskins and much bread and meat and cheese. They told their father: Come home, and we will swear to support you all the days of our lives. They loaded up the food and wine and took it home and fed him all their lives.

6. השיכור ובניו (302ב–303א)

A. מעשה בזקן[1] אחד שהיו לו שני בנים,[2] והיה משוך אחר היין מאד ואוהב לשתות.[3] וכל מה שמרויחים בניו בכל יום שותה אביהם.[4] בערב אמר האחד לחבירו: מה נעשה מאבינו ששותה הכל, ואין אנו יכולים {לקנות}[5] מנעלים לרגלינו?[6] אם תשמע לעצתי נעכב שכירותינו או מב' ימים או מג'[7] וניתן לו לשתות עד שיהא שכור.[8] מה עשו, השקו את אביהם יין עד שחטפתו שינה עזה. קראו לשכיניו, ואמרו: בואו אל אבינו שנפטר.[9] עשו לו תכריכים והוליכוהו לבית הקברות. והנקברים מקברים בסלעים נקוקים שהיו כמו בית, ומניחין אותם על הארץ.[10] ומתוך השינה עזה שחטפתו ומתוך היין ששתה לא קם ולא זע כמת וקברוהו, ונפטרום לבתיהם.

B. למחר באו ישמעאלים[11] טעונים מיין ומבשר צלויה ולחם וכל מיני מאכל, להביא אותו העיר שהיה במצור,[12] ופגעו בהם הרודפים.[13] וכשהבינו הסוחרים שרודפים באו לעיר, החביאו כל המאכל והמשתה במערה, וברחו להם והלכו על גמליהם. ליום שלישי[14] ניגער הזקן ותמה על עצמו, ולא ידע היכן הוא. ומשש אצלו וקרא אצלו ולא מצא שום אדם הולך בתוך הסלע.[15] ומשש בידו, ומצא גרבי יין ובשר ולחם וגבינה [303א]. אמר: בני עזבוני כאן, וברוך בוראי שעזרני.[16] מה עשה, ישב לאכול ולשתות עד שנשתכר ועמד לצחק, והיה מנגן בידו.[17]

C. לאחר ג' ימים הלכו בניו לבקרו, אם מת ואם לאו. הלכו עד הסלע, ושמעו שהיה מנגן אביהם.[18] אמרו: עודינו חי. הלכו אצלו ושאלו לו: מה לך אבינו? אמר להם: רשעים, אתם חשבתם עלי רעה והקב"ה חשבה לטובה למען החיותינו ביום הזה. לכו, בוראי יעזריני כל ימי חיי.[19] ומצא[ו] גרבי יין ולחם ובשר וגבינה לרוב. אמרו לאביהם: בא נא לבתינו ונשבע לך שנפרנס אותך כל ימי חיינו. טענו המאכל והיין לבתיהם, וזנו אותו כל ימיהם.[20]

1. ויקרא רבה, מרגליות, פרשה יב, א, רמ"ה: אדם. ההשוואות להלן מתייחסות למקור זה, שרובו בארמית.
2. בויק"ר אין פירוט של מספר הבנים.
3. שם, פירוט נוסף: שהיה מוכר כל כלי ביתו ושתה בהן יין, קורות ביתו ושותה בהן יין.
4. שם, הערת מספר זו חסרה.
5. המלה מנוקדת בשוליים, בכתב היד.
6. בויק"ר, בלי: מנעלים לרגלינו.
7. פירוש: נחסוך משכורתנו מב' או ג' ימים, כדי להשקותו לשכרה.
8. בויק"ר מפורטת תכניתם לפרסם את דבר מותו.
9. שם, ללא תיאור פנייתם לשכנים.
10. הסבר זה חסר בויק"ר.
11. שם, בתוספת משלח ידם: מוכרי יין.
12. שם, איזכור כללי בלבד של נאדות היין.
13. שם מוזכר חשש הבנים מן המוכסים.
14. אין בויק"ר פירוט של משך שנת השכרות.
15. אין בויק"ר תיאור של מאמצי האב להתמצא בסביבתו. והשוו להערה 10 לעיל.
16. אין בויק"ר איזכור של תלונת האב על בניו.
17. מנגן בידו: אולי בהוראה של משמיע קולות תיפוף או מחיאת כף. בויק"ר מפורט שהוא שר.
18. בויק"ר הבנים מוצאים את אביהם עם נאד יין בפיו, והוא יושב ושותה.
19. שם, בלי תוכחת האב.
20. שם בפירוט נוסף: הבנים מחליטים לקבוע ביניהם תורנות לצורך אספקת יין לאביהם.

7. The Three Treasures (303a)

A. Once there was a *ḥasid* [a pious man] who used to give charity and perform numerous favors and benevolent acts for Torah scholars and ordinary people. His wife, however, was mean-spirited. And he had three treasures: one of gold coins, one of silver, and one of pennies. When he came to his students, he would give them of the gold coins; to orphans and widows, he would give of the silver coins; and he would support orphans who did not study with the pennies. And how would he support them? He would give five gold coins to whomever had five souls in his home. And that was his practice every day.

B. Once he went to a certain place, and widows and orphans and scholars came [to his home] and could not find him. What did his wife do? She entered the treasurehouse to give the scholars gold coins and found scorpions there. She went to the silver treasure and found ants there. She went to the treasure of pennies and found fleas there. After seeing this, she was ashamed to go outside. And they [the people] waited outside, lingering until her husband arrived, and he found them standing there. He said: Sirs, what are you doing here, and why haven't you come inside? They said: It is not proper to enter a home when the owner is not present. The man went inside and found his wife weeping. And she said: Why did you leave me without money? He said: But all my treasures are in your hands. She said: You left me nothing but treasures of ants and scorpions and fleas. He went inside [the treasurehouse], took handfuls of gold coins and gave them to the scholars, handfuls of silver coins and gave them to the orphans and to the widows, and the pennies [to the orphans who did not study]. That is why it says: Eat not the bread of he who is stingy. The Lord said: "He that has a bountiful eye shall be blessed; for he gives of his bread to the poor" [Proverbs 22:9].

7. בעל שלושה אוצרות (303א)

A. מעשה בחסיד אחד[1] שהיה רגיל ליתן צדקה, והיה עושה טובות הרבה וגמילות חסדים עם בעלי תורה וכל אדם.[2] והייתה אשתו צרת עין. והיו לו שלשה אוצרות, אחד של דנרי זהב, ואחד של כספים, ואחד של פרוטות. וכשבאין אצל[3] תלמידיו[4] היה נותן להם מדינרי זהב, וליתומים ולאלמנות משל כספים,[5] וליתומים שאינם הולכים ללמוד[6] היה מתפרנס [!] בפרוטות. ואיך היה מפרנסם? כל אחד שהיה לו חמש נפשות בתוך ביתו, היה נותן לו ה' דינרי זהב לכל אחד ואחד מהם.[7] וכן היה רגיל לעשות בכל יום.

B. פעם אחד הלך למקום אחד,[8] ובאו אלמנות ויתומים וחכמים ולא מצאוהו שם.[9] מה עשתה אשתו? נכנסה לבית האוצרות כדי ליתן לחכמים דנרי זהב, ומצאה שם עקרבים. הלכה לאוצרות של כסף, ומצאה שם נמלים. לאוצר של פרוטות,[10] ומצאה שם פרעושים. כיון שראתה כך, הייתה מתביישת לצאת.[11] והם יושבים בחוץ ומעכב{י}ן עד שבא בעלה,[12] ומצאן כשהן עומדין.[13] אמר להם: רבותיי מה אתם עושים כאן, ומפני מה לא נכנסתם לבית?[14] אמרו לו: לא כך דרך ארץ, שיכנסו בני אדם בבית שאין בעל הבית בתוכו.[15] נכנס הוא לביתו, ומצא אשתו בוכה. ואמרה לו: למה הנחתני בלא כסף?[16] אמר לה: והלא כל אוצרותיי בידיך. אמרה לו: לא מסרת לי אלא אוצרות של נמלים עקרבים ופרעושים.[17] נכנס הוא, מילא חפניו דינרי זהב ונתן לחכמים, ומילא חפניו כסף ונתן ליתומים ולאלמנות,[18] והפרוטות.[19] לפיכך כתיב:[20] אל תלחם לחם רע עין.[21] אמר הקב"ה: טוב עין הוא יבורך כי נתן מלחמו לדל [משלי כב, ט].

---

1. בכ"י ירושלים 3182, דף 105א (יסיף, מאה סיפורים, 182, סיפור י"א): מעשה באדם חסיד. ההשוואות להלן מתייחסות לכתב יד זה.
2. בכ"י ירושלים: ועם כל אדם.
3. על פי ההמשך, ועל פי עד הנוסח בכ"י ירושלים 3182, נראה שהמחיקה מיותרת, וצריך להיות: וכשבאין אצל[ו] תלמידיו.
4. וכשבאו אצלו תלמידי חכמים.
5. היה נותן מן הכספים.
6. ולאותן שאין הולכין ללמוד תורה.
7. כל אדם שהיה לו ה' בנים היה נותן להם דינרי זהב.
8. הלך לשוק.
9. הסדר שם שונה: באו תלמידי חכמים ויתומים ואלמנות ולא מצאוהו בביתו.
10. נכנסה לאוצר של פרוטות.
11. נתביישה לשוב אצלם.
12. והם עומדים בחוץ וממתינים לבעל הבית עד שיבא מן השוק.
13. ומצאן כשהם עמדו בחוץ.
14. מפני מה לא נכנסתם?
15. אמרו לו: אין דרך ארץ ליכנס אצל אשת איש.
16. בכ"י ירושלים, בהרחבה: אמרה לו תן לי גטי. אמר לה: למה אמרת כך? [. . .] מפני שלא הראית לי ממונך.
17. אמר לה והלא כל המפתיחות בידך. אמר[ה] לו: מסרת לי מפתיחות של נמלים ופרעושים ועקרבים.
18. מלא חפניו כסף ונתן ליתומים ולאלמנות.
19. על פי כ"י ירושלים נראה שההמשך חסר: ומן הפרוטים ליתומים שלא היו לומדים תורה.
20. על זה אמר שלמה ע"ה.
21. השוו משלי כג, ו.

8. The Demon in the Carob Tree (303a–303b)

A. Once there was a *ḥasid* who observed all the commandments. He had a field, and in the field was a carob tree. And people would pass by, and the *ḥasid* would lose [303b] all the seeds he sowed in that field, because the passersby used to sit in the shade of that carob tree. And the man said to his wife: Let's cut down the carob tree, so that we won't lose all the seeds. He went to chop down [the tree] and took an axe, and was about to chop it down. And the tree screamed out to him and said: If you do not chop me down, I will give you a gold dinar every day. The man said: No. He [The tree] said: I will give you three dinars every day. He immediately let the tree be and went home.

B. The next day the man returned to the tree and found three gold dinars there. And he did this every day until he became rich, and amassed a fortune [lit., built vaults], and bought slaves and handmaidens. And he did not know where the three dinars had come from. Then, his sons and daughters and slaves began to die. When he saw this, he said: Am I a sinner that my children and slaves should die? What did he do? He and his wife went to the tree and saw people [the passersby] indulging in revelry there. And they did not find what [the gold coins] they had been accustomed to finding there. So he decided to chop the tree down. A demon came out from under the tree and said: [If you chop me down] I will no longer give you any money, but the man set about to chopping it down. The tree responded: If you chop me down, I will kill you. And the *ḥasid* was afraid.

C. What did he do? He went to the *Sanhedrin* and told them the whole story. They instructed him as follows: Go and sell everything you bought with those golden dinars, return them to the tree, and chop it down. He immediately did as they had instructed him and set about chopping the tree down. And called his servants and was about to chop it down. The demon emerged and said: Take twenty golden coins a day, but don't chop me down. The man said: Even if you give me a thousand dinars I will not let you be until I have chopped you down. At once the demon disappeared, and the *ḥasid* chopped the tree down and returned home. He then sowed a measure of seeds in the same field. That year he reaped a thousand measures and sold them for eight hundred golden dinars. One day when he was plowing, he found a golden treasure under a tree and brought it home, to teach you that whoever fulfills a commandment, the Lord

8. השד בחרוב (303א–303ב)

A. מעשה בחסיד אחד שהיה מקיים כל המצוות כולם.[1] והיה לו שדה אחד. והיה שם חרוב אחד.[2] והיו שם עוברים ושבים, והיה מפסיד כל [303ב] הזרעים שהיה זורע אותו חסיד באותו שדה. לפי שהיו עוברים ושבים יושבים בצילו של אותו חרוב.[3] ואמר[4] לאשתו: נלך ונקצץ את החרוב,[5] שלא נפסיד הזרעים. הלך לקצצו ולקח הקורדום ובקש לקצצו.[6] וצוח לו האילן ואמר לו: אל תקצצני,[7] ואני אתן לך דינר זהב בכל יום. א"ל: לאו.[8] א"ל: אתן לך ג' בכל יום.[9] מיד הניחו והלך לו לביתו.

B. ביום השיני חזר אצל האילן, ומצא שם ג' דינרים של זהב.[10] וכן עשה בכל יום עד שנתעשר[11] ובנה אוצרות[12] וקנה עבדים ושפחות. והוא לא היה יודע מהיכן היו ~~ה~~יוצאים אותם ג' דינרים זהב. והתחילו בניו ובנותיו ועבדיו למות. כיון שראה כך אמר: וכי בעל עבירות אני שמתים בניי ועבדיי? מה עשה, הלך הוא ואשתו לאותו אילן והיו משחקים שם.[13] ולא מצא שם כמנהגם,[14] ובקש לקצצו. יצא שעיר אחד מתחת האילן, וא"ל: אין לך עלי שכר.[15] ובקש לקצצו. ענה לו האילן: אם תקצציני אהרוגך. והיה מתיירא אותו צדיק.[16]

C. מה עשה, נכנס אצל סנהדרין וספר להם כל המעשה. אמרו לו: לך ומכור כל מה שקנית מאותם דנרי זהב, וחזור אותם לו וקצצהו[17] מיד. הלך ועשה כן ~~וקראו לעבדיו~~ ורצה לקצצו, וקרא לעבדיו ובקש לקצצו.[18] יצא אותו שעיר כנגדו. וא"ל: טול עשרים[19] זהובים בכל יום, ואל תקצצני. א"ל: אפילו אתה נותן לי אלף דינרים של זהב,[20] איני מניחך עד שאקוץ אותך. מיד

---

1. במעשה"ד, שפירא, 47–46, חסר: 'שהיה מקיים כל המצוות כולם'. להלן השוואות למקור זה.
2. במעשה"ד בתוספת איזכור של פולחן עבודה זרה במקום.
3. שם תוספת: וממפסדים הזרעים.
4. ואמר אותו צדיק.
5. לכי ונקוץ את האילן.
6. הלך הוא לקצוץ את האילן ונטל הקרדום בידו ובקש לקצץ האילן.
7. יצא רוח מן האילן ואמר לו: אל תקצץ אותי.
8. אף על פי כן אקצץ אותו.
9. טול ממני שלשה זהובים בכל יום.
10. שלושה זהובים.
11. בתוספת נושא המשפט: עד שנתעשר אותו חסיד.
12. במקום המלה "אוצרות" – ובנה בתים.
13. ומצאו בה אנשים משחקים תחתו, והוא לא שיחק עמהם.
14. ולא מצא הזהובים כמנהגו.
15. תוספת במעשה"ד: אמר לו: למה? אם היית משמח עם אותן האנשים ששמחו עמי היום היה לך שכר, עכשו לא שמחת עמהם אין לך עוד עלי שכר.
16. במעשה"ד חסר: והיה מתיירא אותו צדיק.
17. מכור כל מה שהיה מאותן דינרי זהב והחזר אותם לו וקצץ את האילן.
18. חסר: וקרא לעבדיו.
19. במעשה"ד הסכום המובטח הוא שלשה זהובים.
20. אם תתן לי אלפים זהובים בכל יום איני מניחך.

doubles his reward. As it says: "God will be with you." When the sages heard about this, they said: "He will fulfill the desire of those who fear him" [Psalms 145:19].

הלך[21] אותו שעיר וקצץ אותו חסיד את האילן וחזר לביתו, וזרע איפה באותו שדה. ומצא באותה שנה אלף איפות,[22] ומכר אותן בח' מאות דינרי זהב. ועוד כשהיה חורש מצא מטמון של זהב תחת האילן והביא לביתו.[23] להודיעך שכל העושה מצוה,[24] הקב"ה מכפיל לו שכרו. שנ': והיה שדי בעזרך.[25] כיון ששמעו חכמים כך קראו עליו: רצון יריאיו יעשה [תהילים קמה, יט].[26]

21. ברח.
22. באותה שנה יצאו ממנו אלף כורין.
23. ועוד מצא באותו שדה, כשהיה חורש אותו, מטמון שהיה טמון באותו מקום שהאילן מונח שם.
24. שם, במקום המלים "עושה מצוה" – העושה דבר לכבודו של הב"ה.
25. השוו שמות יח, יט. במעשה"ד הפסוק אינו מצוטט.
26. במעשה"ד חסר מן המלה כיון–יעשה.

9. Abraham in the Furnace (303b–305a)

A. [303b] How was Abraham born? When Abraham was born, a star rose and swallowed the four stars of the four winds. When Nimrod's astronomers saw this, they approached him and said: A boy was born today. We must kill him and pay his father and mother whatever they ask. Nimrod asked: Who is this boy that you wish to kill? They said: The day that he was born, a star rose and swallowed the four stars of the four winds, and in time, he will inherit both this world and the world to come. [They came to Teraḥ and offered him money in return for his son's death.] Teraḥ[1] said: Fools, I will tell you a story. To what can this be compared? To a mule who is told: We will give you a large measure of barley and cut off your head. The mule said: Fools that you are, if you cut off my head, who will eat the barley you give me? So, if you kill my son, who will inherit the property that you give his father and mother? They said [304a]: We understand that a son was born to you. He said: A son was born, but he died. They said: We are here for a living son, not a dead one.

B. After hearing what they said, Teraḥ hid his son Abraham in a cave for three years. After that, he took him out of the cave. When Abraham saw the sun rising in the East, he said to himself: It is the sun that is the master of the universe. I will pray only to the sun that must have created me and the whole world. He immediately prayed to the sun, all day long. And when the sun set in the West and the sunlight went dark and the moon rose, Abraham said to himself: This one must certainly be the master of the entire universe, since the sun stopped shining and the moon has risen to shine [in its stead]. I will pray only to it, for it must be the master of the entire universe, because it created me and created the entire world. And he prayed to the moon all night until morning. And when the moon set and the sun again rose, he said: Now I know for sure that neither of them is the master of the entire universe, but rather that they both serve yet another master, and that that master created the heavens and earth and the entire universe.

C. He then asked his father, Teraḥ: Who created heaven and earth? Teraḥ answered: Our gods. Abraham said: If so, then I will offer them sacrifices and please them as one pleases people. He immediately went to his mother and asked her: Bake me a cake of fine flour so that I may sacrifice it to the gods of my father. She immediately made him a cake of fine flour. What did Abraham do? He took the cake and placed it before the largest of the idols, since his father, Teraḥ, used to make

1. It may also be inferred from the mention of Teraḥ's name that he was present, with the astrologers, in Nimrod's residence.

9. אברהם בכבשן האש (303ב–305א)

A. מעשה היאך נולד אברהם אבינו.[1] בשעה שנולד אברהם קם כוכב אחד ובלע ד' כוכבים מד' רוחות שבעולם. כשראו איצטגנונים של נמרוד כך, הלכו לפניו ואמרו לו: נולד היום בן אחד. נלך ונהרגינו, ונִתן לאביו ולאמו כל מה שירצה. אמר להם נמרוד: מה זו הבן שאתם רוצים להמיתו? אמרו לו: אותו יום שנולד קם כוכב ובלע ד' כוכבים מד' רוחות השמים, ועתיד לירש העולם הזה והעולם הבא. אמר להם תרח: שוטים, אמשול לכם משל. למה הדבר דומה? לפרד שאמרו לו: ניתן לך כור שעורים ונחתוך ראשך. אמר להם הפרד: שוטים שבעולם, אם תחתכו את ראשי מי יאכל השעורים שתתנו לי? וכך אם תהרגו את הבן, הנכסים שתתנו לאביו ולאמו מי ירשם?[2] אמרו [304א] לו: לדבריך רואים אנו שבן נולד לך. אמר להם: בן נולד לי, והוא מת. אמרו לו: על בן חי אנו, ולא על בן מת.

B. אחר כך כששמע את הדברים, בא תרח והחביא את אברהם בנו במערה ג' שנים. לאחר כן, הוציאו משם. וכשראה אברהם את השמש שזורח במזרח אמר בלבו: זה השמש אדון לכל העולם, ולא אתפלל אלא לאותו שמש שבראני וברא כל העולם כולו. מיד התפלל אליו כל היום. וכששקע השמש במערב ופסק אור השמש, וזרחה הלבנה, אמר בלבו: ודאי זה אדון לכל העולם, שלאחר שפסק זה זרחה זאת ולא אתפלל אלא לה, כי הוא אדון לכל העולם, כי הוא בראני וברא כל העולם. ויתפלל לה כל הלילה עד הבקר. וכששקעה הלבנה וזרחה השמש, אמר: ודאי עתה ידעתי כי לא זה ולא זה אדון לכל העולם, אלא שניהם עובדים לאדון אחד. ואותו אדון ברא שמים וארץ וכל העולם.

C. מיד שאל אברהם את תרח אביו: מי ברא שמים וארץ? א"ל: בני, האלהים שלנו. א"ל אברהם: אם כן הוא, אני מקריב קרבן לפניהם וירצוני כמו שרוצין בני אדם. מיד הלך אל אמו, ואמר לה: עשי לי עוגה אחת של סולת, ואקריב אותו לאלהי אבי. מיד ע{לש}תה [עשתה] לו עוגה אחת של סולת. מה עשה אברהם, לקח העוגה וישם אותה לפני הגדול שבצלמים, כי תרח אביו היה עושה

1. פורסם: טוהר, אברהם בכבשן האש, 161–160. גרסת ספר המעשים מייצגת את נוסח מעשה"ד, אך בשינויים סגנוניים. ההשוואות להלן הן למקור זה.

2. איך ידע תרח את תכני השיחה בין נמרוד לאיצטגניניו? בנוסחים אחרים הפער מתמלא באחד משני אופנים: נמרוד בא אל תרח ומציע לו כסף וזהב אם ימסור לו את בנו למיתה, או שתרח היה אחד משרי נמרוד ושמע את הדברים. ראו הפניות שפירא, מעשה"ד, 41, הערה 57.

idols. And Abraham said to the largest idol: Receive this sacrifice from me. But the idol didn't take it. So Abraham placed the cake in its mouth and said: Eat of it, but it neither ate nor drank. He went to the smallest of the idols and sacrificed to it too, but it too neither ate nor drank. And he did the same to all of them. What did Abraham do? He set the idols on fire and burned them. The Divine spirit immediately came over him, and he said: "They have eyes, but they cannot see; they have ears, but they cannot hear, etc." [Psalms 115:5]. And when Teraḥ came to see his gods and found that they had been reduced to ashes, he said to his son: Who burned my gods? Abraham said: Father, the big idol became angry with the others and burned them. Teraḥ said: But it can neither see nor walk nor hear nor speak. How can you say that it burned them? Abraham said: Father, may your ears hear what your mouth is saying. Why would you abandon a God who created the heavens and the earth to worship one that can neither hear nor speak?

D. Teraḥ went with Abraham to Nimrod. He said to Nimrod: What should be done with he who burned my gods? Nimrod said: Who burned your gods? Nimrod said: My son. Nimrod asked Abraham: Why did you burn them? Abraham said: I didn't burn them. Nimrod said: So who burned them? Abraham said: The biggest idol burned the others because he became angry with them. Nimrod said: Fool, the idol can neither hear nor speak. How could it burn them? Abraham said to him: Why would you abandon a living God who created the heavens and the earth and the entire universe to worship one that can neither hear nor speak? Nimrod said: Who created the heaven and earth if not I myself? Abraham said: This is how I will know that you created [304b] everything if you can make the sun, which rises in the East and sets in the West, rise in the West and set in the East. That is how I will know that indeed you created everything. At once, bewildered at these words, Nimrod placed his hand in his beard.

הצלמים. ואמר אברהם לגדול שבהם: קבל ממני זה הקרבן. לא לקח ממנו. ונתן אברהם העוגה לתוך פיו אמר לו: אכל ממנו. ולא אכל ולא שתה. הלך לפני הקטן שבכולם והקריב לפניו, ולא אכל ולא שתה. וכן עשה לכולם.[3] מה עשה אברהם, נתן בהם אש ושרפם. מיד שרתה עליו רוח הקודש ואמר: עינים להם ולא יראו, אזנים להם ולא ישמעו וגו' [תהלים קטו, ה]. וכשבא תרח אל אלהיו ומצאם שרופים אמר לבנו: מי שרף אלהי? א"ל אברהם: אבא, הגדול כעס על האחרים ושרפם. א"ל: שוטה, אינו רואה ואינו הולך ואינו שומע ואינו מדבר, ואיך תאמר שהוא שרפם. א"ל אברהם: אבא, השמיע לאזניך מה שאתה מוציא מפיך. למה תעזוב א-להים שברא שמים וארץ, ותעבוד זה שאינו שומע ואינו מדבר?

D. הלך תרח אצל נמרוד עם אברהם. אמר לנמרוד: מי ששרף את אלהי מה יעשה לו? א"ל נמרוד: מי הוא ששרף אלהיך? א"ל: בני. א"ל נמרוד לאברהם: למה שרפת אותם? א"ל: לא שרפתים. א"ל: מי שרפם? א"ל: הגדול שבהם שרפם, לפי שכעס בהם. א"ל נמרוד: שוטה, אינו שומע ואינו מדבר היאך שרפם. א"ל אברהם: למה תעזוב א-להים חיים שברא שמים וארץ וכל העולם, ותעבוד למי שאינו שומע ואינו מדבר? א"ל נמרוד: מי ברא שמים וארץ אם לא אני לבד? א"ל אברהם: בזאת אדע שבראתה [304ב] הכל, אם השמש שזורח במזרח ושוקע במערב, אם תעשה כן שיזרח במערב ותשקע במזרח. בזאת אדע שבראת הכל. מיד תמה נמרוד מדבריו, והשים [ושם] ידו בזקנו.

3. במעשה"ד חסר: וכן עשה לכולם, ושם בהרחבה נוספת: אברהם מקריב מנחה לצלם הקטן, זה "מסרב" להקדים את הצלם הגדול, אברהם מבקש מאמו עוגה נוספת ומשובחת מן הקודמת ומקריבה לצלם הגדול, וזה אינו נענה לו. אז מסיק אברהם שאין בהם ממש.

E. When the king's astronomers saw Abraham, they recognized him and said to Nimrod: Our lord the king, this is the baby of whom we said—let us bring wood and burn him and give his father and mother great riches. And now, our king our lord, since he has come here, let us burn him in the fire. Nimrod said to them: Do as you wish with him. What did they do? They fueled a furnace for seven days and seven nights and threw Abraham into the furnace. At once, the angels cried out to God: Let us go and save this righteous one from the furnace. And they argued among themselves, with one saying: I will go down to save him, and another saying: No, I will go down to save him. The angel Michael said: I will go down, and the angel Gabriel said: No, I will go down. God said: I myself will go down, because he was the first to see my oneness in the world, and I am the only one, and it is right that I myself go down. God Himself in all His glory immediately went down and saved him from the furnace's fire.

E. כשראו אותו איצטגנוניו הכירוהו ואמרו אל נמרוד: אי אדונינו המלך, זה התינוק שאמרנו נלך ונביא עצים ונשרפינו, וניתן לאביו ולאמו ממון גדול. ועתה אדונינו המלך הואיל {בא} לידינו, נשרפנו באש. אמר להם נמרוד: עשו חפציכם ממנו. מה עשו, הסיקו כבשן שבעה ימים ושבעה לילות. והשליכו אותו לתוך אותו כבשן. מיד אמרו המלאכים לפני הקב"ה: נלך ונציל צדיק זה מן הכבשן. והיה קטטה ביניהם. זה אומר: אני ארד להצילו, וזה אומר: אני ארד להצילו. אמר מיכאל: אני ארד. אמר גבריאל: אני ארד. אמר הקב"ה: אני ארד שהוא יחיד שייחד שמי בעולם ראשון, ואני יחיד ודין הוא שארד. מיד ירד הקב"ה בכבודו ובעצמו והצילו מכבשן האש.

10. Ḥananiah, Mishael, and Azaria

A. Also, Gabriel, who saved Ḥananiah, Mishael, and Azaria when Nebuchadnezzar cast them into a furnace.[1] And then too, the angels argued over who would go down to save them. And Michael said: I will go down and save them. Gabriel said: That will not display the might of the Lord, because you are made of water, and it is the way of the world for water to extinguish fire. But I am made of fire and I will cool the furnace from within and heat it from without, and in that way, the might and wonders of the Lord will be seen by all. They cast three [lots], and the four drew, and the fourth was Gabriel. And at that time, all the kings and pashas and deputies of the nations gathered to see if the fire would overcome them or not and saw that the fire did not scorch even the hairs on their head [of Ḥananiah, Mishael, and Azaria] and that their garments were untouched, and the fire could not prevail over them. Immediately all the nations praised God, and thrashed and beat the people of Israel, dancing before them saying: With such a God, you bowed down to an idol? Immediately, the face of the people of Israel fell, and they struck their mouths saying: "Lord, you are righteous, and we are covered with shame this day" [Daniel 9:7].

B. God uproots anyone who worships idols both from this world and the next, and he will see all the good that God will do for the righteous ones, and they will be ashamed and say: Woe unto us that we did not merit this honor, because we abandoned a living God to worship a dead one. And then fire will emerge and consume all the apostates who abandoned God and did not repent.

1. This is the comment of the narrator, who is now relating to a later event, at the time of Ḥananiah, Mishael, and Azaria (cf. Daniel 3:12–33).

10. חנניה מישאל ועזריה

A. ואף גבריאל הציל חנניה מישאל ועזריה, כשהפילם נבוכדנצר לכבשן. וגם היו מתקוטטין המלאכים לירד להצילם. ואמר מיכאל: אני ארד ואצילם. א"ל גבריאל: לא גבורותיו של הקב"ה נראין כל כך. לפי שאתה ממים ומנהגו של עולם שהמים מכבין את האש, אבל אני מאש ואצנן את הכבשן מבפנים ואחמם אותו מבחוץ, ובכך נראין נפלאותיו של הקב"ה. והפילן שלשה ונמצאו ארבעה, והרביעי היה גבריאל. ובאותה שעה נתקבצו כל מלכי האומות הפחות והסגנים לראות אם שלטה בהם האש אם לאו. וראו שלא חרך שער ראשם, ומלבושיהם לא נשתנו, וכ֗ו֗ח֗ אש לא שלט בהם. מיד שבחו כל האומים לפני הקב"ה. והיו מכין וחובטין את ישראל ומרקדין לפניהם ואומרים להם: היה לכם א-להים כזה, השתחויתם לצלם?! מיד נפלו פניהם של ישראל, וטפחו פיהם ופתחו ואמרו: לך י"י הצדקה ולנו בושת הפנים כהיום הזה [דניאל ט, ז].

B. וכל העובד ע"ז הקב"ה עוקרו מן העולם הזה והעולם הבא. ויראה הטובות שיעשה הקב"ה לצדיקים ויבושו ויאמרו: אוי לנו שלא זכינו לכבוד זה על שהנחנו אל חי ועבדנו לאל מת. ואז תצא אש ותאכל כל המשומדים שעזבו הקב"ה ולא חזרו בתשובה.[1]

1. במעשה"ד, שפירא, חסר: ויראה הטובות—ולא חזרו בתשובה. והשוו לאפילוג של סיפור האם והבנים בנוסח מעשה"ד שבכתב היד של 'ספר המעשים', 349ב.

11. Generation of Dispersion and the Tower of Babel

A. And this is what we found among the people of the Generation of Dispersion whom God uprooted, because they said, "Come, let us build ourselves a city, with a tower that reaches to the heavens" [Genesis 11:4], and we will strike it with our axes and split the firmament, and the water [that is there] will come down to us below, and God will never do to us what he did to the generation of the flood. And we will cut the heavens in pieces and wage war on the one who is in the heavens and establish idolatry there. And how could they have built the city without stones [305a]? And what did they do with the bricks? They built the city and the tower very high with seventy stairs, and when one ascended, he ascended in the East, and when he descended, he descended in the West. And if someone fell from there, they would pay no note. And Abraham saw that their deeds were wicked, and he cursed them in God's name, and they did not fear his words. And God came down with the seventy angels that surround the throne of glory and confused their languages into seventy languages.

11. דור הפלגה ומגדל בבל

A. וכן מצינו באנשי דור הפלגה שעיקרם הקב"ה שאמרו הבה נבנה לנו עיר ומגדל ונעלה לשמים [בראשית יא, ד], ונכנו בקרדומות ונבקע את הרקיע, ויזובו המים שיהיו כאן עמנו למטה, שלא יעשה לנו כאשר עשה לדור המבול. ונעשה מן השמים חתיכות, ונעשה מלחמה עם אותו שבשמים, ונעמיד שם ע"ז. והיאך היו יכולין לבנות את העיר שלא היה להם [305א] אבנים לשם? אלא מה היו עושים לבינים ובנו העיר והמגדל גבוהים מאד, ושבעים מעלות היו לו וכשעולין, עולין ממזרח וכשיורדין, יורדין במערב. וכשנופל אדם משם, לא היו שמים על לב. וראה אברהם מעשיהם מקולקלים וקיללם בשם י"י, ולא היו חוששין לדבריו. וירד הקב"ה עם שבעים מלאכיו הסובבים את כסא הכבוד, ובילבל את לשונם לשבעים לשון.

12. The Mother and Her Sons (305a)

A. [305a] Once there was a woman who had seven sons, and they were summoned before the emperor. The emperor said to the eldest: Bow down to the idol. The boy answered: I will not deny God, because it says: "I am the Lord your God" [Exodus 20:2]. He was executed. He [the emperor] summoned each one separately and said the same, and each and every one quoted a verse from the Torah to him. He had them all executed. To the seventh son he said: Bow down to the idol. The boy answered: Let me go and ask my mother. The emperor said: Go.

B. The boy went to his mother and asked her: Mother, what should I do? She said: Do you want all your brothers to sit in the presence of the Almighty while you remain outside? Do not listen to this evil man. He returned to the emperor and said: I will not deny God who wrote: "You have today chosen the Lord to be your God, and the Lord has today chosen you to be His people" [Deuteronomy 26:17–18]. We have vowed to our God that we will not replace him with any other god, and He has sworn to us that He will not replace us with any other people. The emperor said: I'll throw down my ring before the idol and you kneel down and pick it up. That way, people will say that you have done my will. The boy said: Woe unto you, O emperor, that you seek your honor in this way. How much greater is the honor of the Almighty. They took him out and executed him.

C. The mother said: I beg of you, let me kiss them. They gave them to her. And she said: My sons, tell Abraham not to be too proud. He sacrificed but one son; I sacrificed seven. She then climbed up to the roof and threw herself down and died. And a voice emerged from heaven, saying: "The mother of sons is joyful" [Psalms 113:9]. And they have a portion in the world to come together with the righteous.

12. האם והבנים (305א)

A. מעשה[1] באשה אחת[2] שהיו לה שבעה בנים, והובאו לפני קיסר.[3] ואמר הקיסר לגדול, עבוד ע"ז.[4] א"ל: לא אני כופר בא-להים,[5] שכך כתוב לנו אנכי י"י א-להיך [שמות כ, ב].[6] והרגוהו. קרא לכל אחד ואחד, ואמר להם כך. וכל אחד ואחד אמרו לו פסוקו.[7] והרג כולם.[8] ולשביעי אמר: עבוד ע"ז.[9] א"ל: אלך ואתייעץ לאמי. א"ל: לך.

B. הלך אצל אמו. אמר לה: אמי,[10] מה אעשה? אמרה (לה) [לו]: וכי תרצה שכל אחיך ישבו במחיצת הקב"ה שבראם, ואתה תשב מחוץ? אל תשמע אל זה הרשע.[11] חזר אצל קיסר ואמר לו: איני כופר בא-להים, שכתוב לנו: את י"י האמרת היום וי"י האמירך [דברים כו, יז], ונשבענו לא-להינו שאין אנו ממירין אותו באל אחר, והוא נשבע לנו שלא ימיר אותנו באומה אחרת. א"ל קיסר:[12] אשליך טבעתי לארץ בפני הצלם, וכרע ולקח אותו, לפי שיאמרו רצוני עשית. א"ל:[13] אוי לך קיסר[14] שלכבודך שאלת כך, ולכבוד הקב"ה על אחת כמה וכמה.[15] הוציאוהו והרגוהו.

C. אמרה להם אמם: בבקשה מכם, תנו אותם לי ואנשקם.[16] נתנו אותם לה,[17] ואמרה להם: בניי, אמרו לאברהם אבינו שלא יגביה לבו,[18] אם עקד הוא בן אחד, אני עקדתי שבעה.[19] ואף היא עלתה לגג ונפלה ומתה. ויצתה בת קול ואמרה: אם הבנים שמחה [תהלים קיג, ט], ויש להם חלק לעולם הבא עם הצדיקים.

---

1. פורסם: באומגרטן וקושלבסקי, אם הבנים, 342. ההשוואות להלן הן למעשה"ד שמועתק גם הוא בכתב היד, וכן הציטוטים הם ממקור זה. ההשוואה היא חלקית בעיקר כדי להצביע על מגמות מעתיק דומות Bodl. Or. 135 בשתי הגרסאות, ועל הבדלים שמקורן בהקשריהן במעשה"ד ובספר המעשים. 349—349ב (להלן: מעשה"ד).
2. מעשה במרים בת תנחום.
3. תוספת במעשה"ד: מה עשה קיסר? חבש כל אחד ואחד בפני עצמו והובא הראשון לפניו.
4. השתחווה לצלם כשם שהשתחוו אחיך.
5. חס ושלום לא השתחוו אחי אף אני לא אשתחוה.
6. במעשה"ד מובא פסוק אחר.
7. במעשה"ד, כמו בגרסה הנוכחית מספר המעשים, אין פירוט של דברי כל אחד מן הבנים ופסוקיהם.
8. במעשה"ד מגמת סיכום דומה: וכן כולם.
9. שם הפנייה לקטן היא בלי: עבוד ע"ז.
10. במעשה"ד חסרה המלה: אמי.
11. שם תוספת: ואל תפרוש מאחיך.
12. במעשה"ד חסר התואר: קיסר.
13. תוספת במעשה"ד: הנער.
14. במעשה"ד בהדגשה נוספת: אוי עליך קיסר, אוי עליך.
15. במעשה"ד בהרחבה נוספת: כי אתה בשר ודם ומתייראו אתה מן בשר ודם שכמותך, אני לא אירא ממלך מלכי המלכים הקב"ה?
16. במעשה"ד: אמרה לו אמו. קיסר שלוף חרבך וחתוך צוארי. מיד צעק אותו רשע, איך אני עושה כתוב בתורתכם אותו ואת בנו לא תשחטו ביום אחד. והיתה האם בוכה עליהם ואמרה להם בני אל ירע לכם שכולכם נוצרתם לקדש שמו של הקב"ה.
17. במעשה"ד חסר: ונתנו אותם לה".
18. במעשה"ד: אמרו לאברהם אביכם שלא יגאה לבך עליך לומר.
19. במעשה"ד: אני בניתי מזבח אחד ולא העלית בנך עליו. אני בניתי שבעה מזבחות והעליתי שבעה בני עליהם. נטלוהו מחיק אמו והרגו.

D. That is why the sages said: "Praise the Lord before the nations, because that is why I have scattered you among the nations who do not know me so that you will tell of my wonders. You may not exchange me for idols, because God is a jealous and eternal God. Bow not to the dead but to He who puts to death and revives the dead, as He said to you when he said the commandment "You shall not have [any other gods before me]." Israel immediately responded and said as one: "Hear O Israel, the Lord is our God, the Lord is one" [Deuteronomy 6:4]. God said to them: You have declared my oneness in this world, and I will make you unique in the next world, as it says: "And who is like your people Israel the one nation on earth!" [1 Chronicles 17:21].

D. על כן אמרו חכמים: שבחו את הקב"ה בפני הגויים כי על כן פיזרתי אתכם בין הגויים אשר לא ידעוני למען תספרו נפלאותי [השוו טוביה יג, ד]. ראו נא אל תמירוני באלילים כי א-ל קנא אני חי עולמים, ואל תשתחוו למתים אלא לממית ומחייה. וכן אמר להם: כשאמר להם הדיבור לא יהיה לך. מיד חזרו ישראל ואמרו בפה אחד: שמע ישראל י"י א-להינו י"י אחד [דברים ו, ד]. אמר להם הקב"ה: אתם מייחדים שמי בעולם הזה אני אייחד אתכם לעולם הבא, שנאמר ומי כעמך ישראל גוי אחד בארץ [דבהי"מ א, יז, כא].[20]

20. שם: אפילוג אחר.

13. The Man Who Never Took an Oath (305a–306b)

A. [305a] Once there was a very rich *ḥasid.* And he never took an oath in his entire life. Before his death [305b], he summoned his son in the presence of the elders of the city and told him: My son, beware never to take an oath, even if it is the truth, and I will give you everything I own, since I earned all my wealth because I guarded my tongue from ever swearing. And the son answered: I will uphold your command to never swear, even if it is the truth.

B. When the *ḥasid* died, the son fulfilled his father's wishes. When swindlers heard that the son refused to swear even to the truth, they came to him and said: We've heard that you now own all your father's property. He owed us a lot of money, but because he was trustworthy, we weren't worried. And now that he has died, you'll have to pay us for him. The man said: I never heard that my father owed any money to anyone in the whole world. They said: Swear to us that you don't know about the debt, and we'll release you from it. The *ḥasid* said to himself: If I swear, I will be desecrating the name of heaven and disobeying my father's will. And moreover, I don't know if they are telling me the truth or not; and what if they are telling the truth? I would rather pay them and not swear. So he paid them everything they asked for. Afterward, other swindlers kept coming until he had nothing left. And this all happened because he refused to disobey his father's command. Then came a cruel man and said: Give me a golden dinar, which your father owed me. He said: I have no money with which to pay you. The man said: Swear that you have nothing with which to pay, and I'll let you go. He [the son] said: I will not swear. They came before a judge, but he refused to swear. He was immediately arrested and taken to jail.

13. האיש שלא נשבע מימיו (305א–306ב)

A. מעשה בחסיד אחד שהיה עשיר מאוד. ולא נשבע (בימיו) מימיו. ובשעה [305ב] פטירתו קרא לבנו לפני זקני העיר.[1] וא"ל: בני, הזהר שלא תשבע כלל אפילו באמת,[2] ואני אתן לך כל נכסיי, שכל העושר שיש לי בשביל ששמרתי את פי משבועה.[3] וענה לו: אקיים ציווייך, ולא אשבע אפילו באמת.[4]

B. וכשנפטר החסיד, היה הבן מקיים מצות אביו.[5] כששמעו רמאים שלא נשבע אפילו באמת, באו לו ואמרו לו: שמענו שכל נכסי אביך יש לך, והוא היה מחוייב לנו ממון רב, ולפי שנאמן היה לא חששנו. וכיון שמת, תשלם לנו עבורו.[6] אמר להם: לא שמעתי מעולם, שאבי היה מחוייב לשום אדם שבעולם.[7] אמרו לו: השבע לנו שלא ידעת, ותיפטר. אמר החסיד[8] בלבו: אם אשבע אחלל שם שמים, ואבטל מצות אבי.[9] ועוד, שאיני יודע אם אמת אמרו אם לאו, ושמא כנים דבריהם.[10] מוטב שאפרע אליהם, ולא אשבע.[11] ופרע להם כל מה שאמרו.[12] ואחרי כן באו רמאים אחרים, עד שלא נשאר לו מאומה.[13] וכל כך, לפי שלא רצה לבטל מצות <מצו> אביו.[14] ואחר כך בא אדם אכזר[15] אחד ואמר לו: תן לי דינר זהב אחד, שהיה מחויב לי אביך.[16] א"ל: אין לי כלום לפרוע.[17] א"ל: השבע לי שאין לך כלום לפרוע, ותיפטר.[18] א"ל: לא אשבע.[19] הוליכוהו לפני הדיין, ולא רצה לישבע.[20] מיד חבשו אותו בבית האיסורין.[21]

---

1. במעשה"ד, שפירא 54–59 בלי: לפני זקני העיר. להלן ההשוואות הן למקור זה.
2. במעשה"ד חסר: אפילו באמת.
3. שם: שכל העושר הזה שאני מניח לך לא קניתיו אלא ששמרתי פי משבועה, ובתוספת: ואפילו שבועת אמת לא נשבעתי, על כן הצליחני הב"ה בכל סחורותי.
4. אני מקיים מצותך ולא אשבע כלל.
5. חסר: והיה הבן מקיים מצות אביו.
6. שם, בדיבור עקיף: באו רמאין על היתום ובקשו ממנו ממון הרבה שהיה להם חייב אביו או יעשה להם שבועה ויפטר.
7. חסר: אמר לו–לעולם.
8. כינויו במעשה"ד הוא: היתום.
9. חסר: ואבטל מצות אבי.
10. חסר: ועוד–דבריהם.
11. מוטב שאפרע להם הממון כל מה שיבקשו ממני ולא אשבע.
12. הלך ופרע לרמאין את כל העושר שהניח לו אביו עד שנותר עני בלא כלום.
13. חסר: ואחרי כן–מאומה.
14. ועל כל זאת היה רודף במצות ומקיים מצות אביו ומכבד את תלמידי חכמים.
15. במעשה"ד הוא מכונה: רמאי.
16. נותר עליך עוד דינר.
17. בבקשה ממך הנח לי שלא נשאר לי מחית רגע. וגלוי לאל יתברך שאם היה בידי כלום הייתי פורע אותך.
18. חסר: ותפטר.
19. חסר: א"ל–אשבע.
20. והוליכו לפני הדיינין אמרו לו פרע לו את דינרו או השבע שאין לך כלום לפרוע. אמרו לו הדיינין לרמאי או יפרע לך או חבשהו בבית האיסורין.
21. תוספת במעשה"ד: באותה שעה היה בוכה ואמר: רבונו של עולם, גלוי וידוע לפניך שלא היה בידי כלום, ואם היה בידי הייתי פורע. ישתבח שמך לעד, שמכסף וזהב שהיה לי לרב מאד נותרתי נעור ורק [על פי נחמיה ה, יג]. ואלמלא היו תובעין ממני באמת לא הייתי מצטער כי ערום יצאתי מבטן אמי ערום אשוב שמה [על פי איוב א, כא].

C. And his righteous wife was very beautiful. And she was ashamed to ask anyone for anything. And she used to launder clothing to support her husband and sons. One day she went to the river to wash clothes. And a ship came by, and when the owner of the ship saw her, he desired her. And he said to her: Wash my clothes, and I will give you a golden dinar. She took the dinar and gave it to her elder son, and he went to free his father from prison, and she washed the [ship owner's] clothes. And when she came to return the clothing, the ship owner abducted her and sailed away. And her sons saw it [the ship] from afar, and they wept and cried out: Our mother, what shall we do? And they went to their father and told him what had happened, about how their mother had been abducted. He immediately raised his eyes to the heavens and cried out and wept, saying: Praised be the name of the Almighty for all the property my father left me, and now I have been left with no testator [father], no money, and no way to support myself, and without my wife. And all this happened because I obeyed my father's injunction [not to swear]. And he walked off alone until he reached the middle of the river. And God made a plank of wood appear, and he sat on the plank and it took him far away, until he found himself in another land. And the boys stood and wept until a ship came along and captured them, taking them away.

D. The people of the city said to the *ḥasid*: Where are you from and what place do you come from? He immediately told them what had happened. They asked him: Is there anything you know how to do? He told them: I know how to learn Torah and write books. They answered: We don't need that, but herd our sheep for us and we will reward you with the best [306a] sheep and the best wool. He went and herded their cattle.

C. ואשתו הצדקת הייתה יפה מאוד.[22] והייתה מתביישת לבקש כלום. והיתה נוטלת בגדים לכבס לפרנס את בעלה[23] ואת בניה.[24] יום אחד הלכה לנהר לכבס בגדים.[25] ובאתה ספינה אחת, וכשראתה בעל הספינה, חמדה בלבו.[26] ואמר לה: כבס[!] לי בגדי, ואתן לך דינר זהב. נטלה את הדינר ונתנה אותו לבנו הגדול, והלך ופדה את אביו מן הסוהר, וכבסה את הבגדים. וכשהלכה להחזירם חטפה בעל הספינה, והלכה לה.[27] ובניה היו רואין אותה מרחוק ובוכין ואומרין,[28] אמינו מה נעשה?[29] הלכו לאביהם וסיפרו לו המעשה,[30] היאך נשבית אמם. מיד נתן עיניו לשמים, ונתן קולו בבכייה גדולה.[31] ואמר: ישתבח שמו של הקב"ה מרוב נכסים שנשאר לי מאבי, ועתה נשארתי בלא מצוה[32] ובלא שום ממון, ובלא שום מחייה שבעולם, ובלא אשתי. וכל כך, לפי שקיימתי מצוות אבי.[33] והלך ביחיד עד שהגיע לחצי הנהר. וזימן לו הקב"ה דף אחד, וישב על אותו דף והלך לו עד שהוליכו רחוק ונפל למדינה אחרת. והנערים בוכים עד שבאתה ספינה אחת, ולקחם והוליכם בשבי.[34]

D. אמרו לו אנשי העיר לאותו חסיד: מאין באתה ומאיזה מקום אתה?[35] מיד סיפר להם כל המעשה.[36] אמרו לו: יודע אתה לעשות כלום?[37] אמר להם: יודע אני ללמוד תורה ולכתוב ספרים. אמרו לו: אין אנו רוצים בכך, אלא רעה נא לנו את צאנינו וניתן לך במיטב [306א] הצאן ובמיטב הגיזה.[38] הלך, ורעה את מקניהם.[39]

---

22. במעשה"ד יופיה הרב אינו מוזכר.
23. לפדות את בעלה מן הרמאי.
24. ולכלכל הוא ובניו.
25. היא ובניה עומדים על שפת הנהר.
26. כשראה אותה בעל הספינה שהיתה יפת תואר חמדה בלבו אמר ודאי ממשפחת מלוכה היא. שאל אותה ואמר לה: למה אתה מכבסת? ספרה לו כל מה שאירע לה ולבעלה.
27. בין כך עשה סחורתו בעל הספינה ותקן את התורן וכשבאת אותה צדקת להשיב לו הבגדים חטפה בעל הספינה וברח עמה.
28. מיללין ובוכין.
29. מה נעשה מעכשיו.
30. חזרו אל אביהם נתנו לו הדינר.
31. קרע את בגדיו ונתאבל על אשתו. פרע את הדינר ויצא מבית האיסורין.
32. למלה "בלא מִצְוָה" אין מובן כאן, ולכן נראה שיש לקרוא ב"לא מְצֻוֶּה" במובן המטונימי, כלומר בלי אביו שציווה לו ירושה וצוואה רוחנית.
33. מה אעשה אם אמות לפתי [אם אחזור לביתי] אמות ברעב, ועוד יבאו רמאין ויעשו לי כמו שעשו האחרים. מוטב שיגלה למקום אחר שלא יכירוני. הרים קולו ובכה בכיה גדולה ומרה ואמר: ראה יי' והביטה, כי נשארתי אני ובני יתומים בלא שום מחיה בעולם. ויבכו יחד עד שתשש כחם, והלכו משם למקום אחר. התיקון בסוגריים מרובעים הוא על פי הערת שפירא במהדורתה, 55, הערה 95.
34. והיו התינוקות בוכים זה עם זה והנהר (בנתם) [בינותם], עד שבאת אניה ושבאום.
35. וכיון שראוהו בני המדינה ערום, שאלוהו מאי זה מקום הוא.
36. אמר להם: איש יהודי עני אני.
37. אמרו לו: מה אומנותך?
38. אם רצונך לרעות את בהמתנו אז תוכל לישב עמנו ונתן לך שכר טוב.
39. תוספת: והיה רועה באמת ובאמונה. אמרו לו: השמר בעצמך פן תקרב אל הנהר הזה כי הוא עמוק ביותר שמא יפול אחד מן הצאן שמה לא תצא לעולם. אמר להם: כן אעשה.

E. One day, as he was sitting by the river, which was filled with snakes and scorpions, he recalled the riches that his father had left him, and he raised his voice and cried out aloud, and said: Master of the Universe, of all the servants and maidservants and of all the good things that my father of blessed memory left me, nothing remained. He wished to throw himself into the river, but when he saw all the bodies of the people that the snakes and scorpions had killed, he wanted to go back. And he saw a man standing on the other side of the river, and the man said to him: Stop going back and forth, because I have a lot of money that I've been keeping for you for many years, for the Almighty has elevated you to greatness for respecting your father's wishes and not desecrating the name of the Lord. Take the money and buy slaves, handmaidens, land, and ships. And he did. The man, who was an angel, told him: Go buy this river from the people of the town. He went to the people of the town and said: Sell me this river. They said: You are a fool. What will you do with it? He answered: Sell it to me anyway, and I will pay you the price. They sold it to him with a contract. He returned to the angel and said: I did as you commanded me. The man became rich, and then became king, and he became famous throughout the world. And he proclaimed that whoever wished to chop down trees should come and take ten gold coins each day. When [people] heard, they came from many different lands to chop down trees, until the ship that held his sons arrived. And when the *ḥasid* saw them, he recognized them and bought them from the owner of the ship for a great deal of money. And he treated them better than all his servants.

F. One day the ship that held his wife arrived. It was the practice of that *ḥasid* to invite the crew of every ship that docked there to share a meal with him. What did he do? He invited the owner of the ship. But, he said: My lord, I must guard my ship; I cannot leave it alone. The *ḥasid* said: Here are my two sons, who will guard it for you. His sons went to guard the ship and the man's wife. And when the boys saw the ship, they recognized it and called out loudly, crying: Woe unto us. This looks like the ship that captured our mother. The woman said to them: Boys, why are you crying? At once, they told her everything that had happened about how their mother had been abducted. At once, the woman recognized the story and realized that these boys were her sons. She wept all night with them but said nothing to them until morning.

E. יום אחד היה יושב על הנהר שהיה מלא נחשים ועקרבים, וזכרו מן העושר שנשתייר לו מאביו,[40] והרים קולו בבכי גדול מאד[41] ואמר: רבונו של עולם, מרוב עבדים ושפחות ומכל טוב שנשארו לי מאבי זכור לטוב, לא נשתייר לי מאומה.[42] ורצה להשליך עצמו בנחל.[43] וכשראה ההרוגים שהרגו הנחשים והעקרבים, ורצה[!] לשוב.[44] וראה איש אחד עומד בצד אחר על שפת הנהר,[45] ואמר לו פלוני: אל תלך אנה ואנה, כי כבר עברו כמה שנים שאני שומר לך ממון גדול, שהקב"ה מעלה אותך לגדולה על ששמרת מצות אביך ולא חיללת שם שמים. וטול את הממון הזה, וקח לך עבדים ושפחות וקרקעות וספינות. וקנה הכל. א"ל האיש, ואותו האיש היה מלאך:[46] לך וקנה הנחל הזה מבני העיר. הלך אצל בני העיר ואמר להם: מכרו לי את הנחל הזה.[47] אמרו לו: שוטה אתה ומה תעשה ממנו? אמר להם: מכל מקום מכרו אותו לי, ואני אתן לכם את הדמים.[48] מכרוהו לו בשטר. הלך אצל המלאך וא"ל: עשיתי כאשר ציויתני.[49] ונתעשר האיש עד שנעשה מלך. ונשמע שמועתו בכל העולם. והכריז שכל מי שרוצה לכרות עצים יבא ויטול עשרה זהובים בכל יום. כששמעו, נתקבצו מכל הארצות לכרות עצים,[50] עד שבאת ספינה ששם היו בניו. וכשראה אותם החסיד הכירם, וקנה אותם מבעל הספינה בממון גדול. ועשה להם טובה מכל עבדיו.[51]

F. יום אחד באתה ספינה ששם אשתו. והיה מנהגו של אותו חסיד, שכל ספינה שבאת לשם מזמן אנשי הספינה לסעודתו. מה עשה, זימן בעל הספינה. וא"ל: אדוני, יש לך לי לשמור ספינתי, ולא אניחנה ביחיד.[52] א"ל החסיד: הרי שני בני שישמרוה.[53] הלכו בניו ושמרו הספינה וגם אשתו.[54] כשראו הנערים את הספינה הכירוה, ובכו בכייה גדולה ואומרים: אוי לנו שהספינה הזאת דומה לאותה ספינה שנשבית אמינו.[55] אמר' להם האשה: בניי, מה לכם שתבכו? מיד סיפרו לה כל המעשה, היאך נשבית אמם. מיד הכירה האשה כל המעשה, וידעה שהם בניה. בכתה כל הלילה עמהם, ולא הודיעם כלום עד הבוקר.

---

40. ונזכר העושר והשדות שהיו לו.
41. בכה כמר נפש.
42. ואמר: מה לי חיים? הואיל ושנשבית אשתי וגלו בני ונותרתי אני לבדי טוב מותי מחיי.
43. השליך עצמו לנהר.
44. והיו שם נחשים ועקרבים מיד נחפז ויסוב ללכת.
45. וכשהפך שכמו ללכת שמע קול הקורא אותו בשמו.
46. ואמר פלוני: חזור לכאן. חזר לאחוריו וראה דמות מלאך. אמר לו המלאך בא הנה שכמה ימים שמור לך זה המקום טול ממון ששמרתי לך שהגיע קצך לעלות לגדולה על ששמרת מצות אביך ולא נשבעת.
47. אמר לו: קנה לך את הנהר מאדון המדינה ואחר כך בנה בכאן עיר גדולה. וכן עשה. הלך לפני אדון המדינה והעיד עליו עדים ואמר לו: מכור לי הנהר עד מקום פלוני.
48. אעפ"כ מכור אותו לי. מכרו בדמים יקרים.
49. חסר: מכרוהו–ציותני. תוספת: ונתן לו מיד וכתב והעיד עליו עדים במכירה עולמית ושכר פועלים ובנה על שפת הנחל עיר גדולה .ופלטרים גדולים עד שנעשה מלך.
50. ומכל מקום באו שם לסחורה והיה עושה טובות לכל עובר ושב ויהי שמעו בכל הארץ ונאספו שם לסחורה.
51. והכניסם לפלטריו ולא גלה עצמו להם אך כי היה מטיב להם יותר מעבדיו.
52. אמר לו בעל הספינה: אדני, איני יכול להניח הספינה שאשתי שם.
53. אמר לו המלך: הרי שני נערי נאמנים שישמרוה.
54. שלח הנערים והלך בעל הספינה אל הסעודה.
55. תוספת במעשה"ד: והיו בוכין כל הלילה.

G. When the owner of the ship saw her, he could see that she was sad. He asked her: What's the matter? She told him: You sent boys here, and they caressed me all night. When the ship owner heard this, he went to the *ḥasid* and said: You sent young men to my ship who abused my wife. The king immediately sent for his sons and asked them: Is it true what this man is saying? They answered: Heaven forbid that we would do such a thing. Call the woman here, and if she says we did that, you may execute us. He immediately called for the woman and said: My daughter, don't be afraid of me and don't hide anything from me. [306b] Tell me what happened. She immediately bowed down to him and weeping, said: Your majesty, I beseech you, they are my sons. She told him the entire story, about how she had given her sons the dinar to free their father, and when she went to return the clothes, she was abducted by the owner of the ship.

H. The righteous man instantly understood what had happened and that she was his wife. He said to the owner of the ship: Where did you find this girl? If you do not tell me, I will behead you. The ship owner immediately told him: Upon my word, your majesty, I abducted her from the river where she was washing clothes, and upon my word, from the day I captured her, I have not been able to touch her. I am here in your hands. Do with me as you will. He immediately gave the ship owner a large sum of money and sent him away, and his sons and wife were restored to him. Blessed is the Lord who does not deprive the righteous who refrain from swearing their reward.

G. כשראה אותה בעל הספינה, ראתה עצובת רוח. אמר לה: מה לך? אמרה לו: שלחת אלי הנערים ששחקו בי כל הלילה.[56] כששמע בעל הספינה כך, הלך אצל החסיד[57] וא"ל: שלחת לספינתי אנשים ליצנים והתעוללו באשתי.[58] מיד שלח אחרי בניו ואמר להם: אמת הדבר שזה אומר?[59] אמרו לו: חלילה לנו מעשות כדבר הזה. תבא האשה, אם היא אומרת כך, תמיתנו. מיד שלח לקרוא לאשה. אמר לה: בתי, אל תפחדי ממני ואל תכחדי ממני,[60] [306ב] ואמור[!] היאך היה המעשה.[61] מיד השתחוה לפניו ובכתה[62] ואמרה: אדוני המלך, בחייך בניי הם.[63] וסיפרה לו כל המעשה, היאך נתנה לבניו הדינר לפדות את אביהם, וכשהלכה להחזיר {הַבְּגָדִים}[64] שחטפה בעל הספינה.[65]

H. מיד הכיר החסיד כל המעשה, וידע שהיתה אשתו.[66] אמר לבעל הספינה: איפה מצאת את הילד{ה} הזאת? אם לא תגיד אחתוך ראשך.[67] מיד א"ל בעל הספינה: בחייך אדוני המלך, אני שביתיה מהנהר שמכבסת בגדים, ובחייך מיום ששביתיה לא יכולתי לנגוע אליה.[68] והרי אני בידך, עשה ממני מה שתרצה. מיד נתן לו לבעל הספינה ממון גדול ושלחו, ועתה נחזרו לו בניו ואשתו.[69] ברוך המקום שאינו מקפח שכר לצדיקים ששומרים את פיהם משבועה.[70]

---

56. אמרה לו: לא היה לי שתניח אצלי אלה פרוצים להתעולל בי?
57. מיד הלך אצל המלך.
58. אמר לו: אדני המלך לא היה לך אלא אלו הפריצים ששלחת לספינתי לשחוק לאשתי כל הלילה?
59. כלום אמת הדבר שאתם עשיתם כך עם אשתו של זה הלילה?
60. ואמר לה: בתי, אל תכחדי ואל תראי מפני.
61. חסר: היאך היה המעשה.
62. מיד נפלה לפניו על פניה ארצה.
63. ואמרה לו: אדני. תן רשות ואדברה לפניך מעט דבר אחד. אמר לה: אמרי.
64. המלה מנוקדת בכתב היד.
65. אמרה לו: בבקשה ממך, שאל להם מאין הם? אמר להם: מאין אתם? ספרו לו כל המאורע. עמדה האשה חבקם ונשקם על ראשם ואמרה: חי נפשך, בני הם. וצועקת ובוכה ספרה לו על המעשה.
66. כששמע המלך את דבריה הכיר שהם בניו והיא אשתו.
67. אמר המלך לבעל הספינה: היאך באת לידך? ואם לא תאמר באמת אחתוך את ראשך.
68. לא נגעתי בה ולא נזקקתי עמה מעולם.
69. מיד צוה המלך ושלחו לשלום. ואומר: ברוך משלם שכר טוב ליראיו ומחזיר אבדה לבעלים. ועמד עם אשתו ובניו בעושר גדול כל ימיו.
70. ואמרו חכמים ז"ל מה זאת שלא שמר אלא מצוה אחת שלם לו הב"ה כך השומר מצות הרבה על אחת כמה וכמה שמשלם שכר טוב לאלפים כמו שכתו' עושה חסד לאלפים לאוהביו ולשומרי מצותי [שמות כ, ו] לכך נאמר לא תשא את שם יי' א-לוהיך לשוא כי לא ינקה יי' את אשר ישא את שמו לשוא [שמות כ, ז].

14. The Sabbath Observer and the Bear (306b–307a)

A. [306b] Once, three merchants were traveling home from a business journey on the eve of the Sabbath. They said to one another: What shall we do? There are robbers and wild animals on this road. Two of them said: It is better to desecrate the Sabbath [and continue traveling] than lose all our money. The third said: I will not move from here, and I will not desecrate the Sabbath. The Almighty who gave us the Sabbath so that we rest and safeguard it can also protect and save me from the wild animals and robbers.

B. So what did the two men do? They continued on their journey and desecrated the Sabbath, and the one who refused to desecrate it put up his tent, set his table, lit his candle, and recited the *Kiddush* to sanctify the Sabbath. And while he was eating, a bear unlike any ever seen before came and stood before him. When the *ḥasid* saw the bear approach, he gave him of his bread and meat and ate, and never did any fear enter his heart. After he ate, he recited the Grace after Meals and lay down and slept, and the bear lay down next to him. The next day, which was the Sabbath, he saw the bear lying next to him. He looked up to the heavens and gave praise and thanks to the Almighty for not allowing the bear to harm him. What did the *ḥasid* do? He got up to say his prayers, sat down to eat, and shared his bread and meat with the bear, and stayed with the bear all day. In the evening, he recited the evening prayers and the *Havdalah* and set out on his way. The bear accompanied him all that night.

14. שומר השבת והדוב (306ב–307א)

A. מעשה בשלושה אנשים שבאו מן הסחורה וקדש עליהם שבת.[1] אמרו זה לזה: מה נעשה? כי זה הדרך דרך ליסטים וחיות רעות. אמרו השניים: מוטב שנחלל את השבת ואל נפסיד ממונינו. אמר השלישי: לא אזוז מכאן, ולא אחלל את השבת. הקב"ה שנתן לנו שבת לנוח ולשמור, הוא יכול לשומריני ולהצילני מן החיות רעות ומן הליסטים.

B. ומה עשו השניים? הלכו לדרכם וחללו את השבת. והאחד שלא רצה לחללו תקע אהלו, וערך שולחנו, והדליק את נרו, וקדש השבת. וכשאכל, בא דוב אחד שלא היה כמוהו ועמד נגדו. כשראה החסיד הדוב אצלו, נתן לו מפתו ומבשרו ואכל.[2] ומעולם לא עלה פחד בלבו. לאחר אכילתו בירך ברכת המזון, ושכב וישן. והדוב שכב אצלו. למחר שהוא שבת, ראה את הדוב שהוא שוכב אצלו, נתן עיניו למרום, ונתן שבח והודיה למקום שלא הזיקו (את) הדוב. מה עשה החסיד? הלך וסידר תפילתו. וישב ואכל, ולקח מפתו ומבשרו ונתן לדוב.[3] ועמד אצל הדוב כל היום. לערב התפלל תפלת ערבית, ועשה הבדלה והלך לדרכו. והלך הדוב עמו כל אותו הלילה.

1. בכ"י פרמא 2269, 62א: מעשה בשלושה אנשי[ם שבאו] מן הירדן וקידש עליהם היום. בכ"י ירושלים 3182, 123א (יסיף, מאה סיפורים, 522, סיפור ס"ג): מעשה בג' אנשים שבאו מן הירדן. ההשוואות להלן הן למקורות אלה.
2. תוספת בכ"י פרמא: [ובירך] ברכת המזון. בכ"י ירושלים מדובר בזאב ולא בדב.
3. כאן מסתיים הסיפור בכ"י ירושלים.

C. Robbers from among the king's servants emerged from the forest and found the two men who had desecrated the Sabbath, attacked them, and stole all their money. Eventually, the *ḥasid* arrived with the bear. When the bear saw the two men who had desecrated the Sabbath, it attacked them furiously and ferociously and killed them. When the man saw that it had killed them, he felt sorry. Meanwhile he encountered the robbers. They said: Who are you? He answered: I am a Jew. They said: Where are you from? He said: From the king's palace. They said to him: Who gave you the bear? He said to him: The king, and the king commanded it to protect me from the robbers. The robbers said to each another: How much the king must love this man! He might report us to the king [307a], and then he [the king] would hang us. They said to him: We will give you a great deal of money but say nothing to the king. What did they do? They gave him a great deal of money and escorted him on the way so that he arrived safely home. When he arrived home, the bear left. And now see how great is the reward of the righteous, those who carry out the commandments and observe the Sabbath. God performs a miracle for he who observes the Sabbath, and he who observes the Sabbath all the days of his life, all the more so. And now, come see how great is the reward of the righteous who perform the commandments and observe the Sabbath!

C. יצאו ליסטים מעבדי המלך מן היער, ומצאו שני האנשים שחיללו את השבת, ושללו אותם וגזלו להם כל ממונם. בין כך ובין כך, בא זה החסיד עם הדוב. כשראה הדוב את שני האנשים שחיללו שבת, בא בחימה ובקצף גדול והרג אותם. כשראה זה האיש שהרגם, היה מצטער בעצמו. בין כך, פגע את הליסטים. אמרו לו: מי אתה? אמר להם: יהודי אני. אמרו לו: מאין אתה? אמר להם: מבית המלך. אמרו לו: מי נתן {לך} את הדוב? אמר להם: המלך, וצוה לו המלך שישמריני מן הליסטים. אמרו הליסטין זה לזה: כמה אוהב המלך אותו האיש. אמרו: שמא ילשין אותנו למלך [307א], ויתלה אותנו. אמרו לו: נתן לך ממון רב, ואל תאמר למלך ממנו מאומה. מה עשו, נתנו לו ממון רב והוליכוהו עד ביתו לשלום. כשבא לביתו, חזר הדוב לדרכו. ועתה בא וראה כמה שכרן של צדיקים, עושי מצות ושומרי שבת. ומה זה ששמר שבת עשה לו הקב"ה נס, השומר שבת כל ימיו על אחת כמה וכמה.[4]

4. בכ"י פרמא: ובא וראה כמה [שכרן] של צדיקים ששומרים את השבת. זה ששימר את השבת [נס] נעשה לו. זה ששומר שבתות הרבה על אחת כמה [וכמה] לפיכך יהא כל אדם [זהיר] בשמירת שבת.

15. Ukva (version 1; 307a–307b)

A. [307a] Once there was a *ḥasid* who had an exceedingly beautiful wife. And the *ḥasid* was destitute. And there was a young man in his town who was very rich. And he desired the wife of the *ḥasid* very much. One day, the *ḥasid* fell ill. The young man sent her messengers who said: Do as I ask and I will give you anything you want. The *ẓaddeket* [righteous woman] said: I will not betray my husband. She who betrays her husband betrays her Creator. They returned to their master and told him: Such and such did the woman say, that she will not do your will. They went to her again, and she said the same. At once the young man himself went to her and said: Madam, submit yourself to me, and I will give you anything you wish. Furthermore, your husband is poor and I am rich, he is ugly and I am handsome and wealthy. The *ẓaddeket* told him: Even if you were as beautiful as the sun and my husband as ugly as can be, I would not betray him, because she who betrays her husband betrays her Creator. He said: Do as I ask, for if you do not, I will die of my love for you. She said: Better die than lose—you and me—our portion in this world and the next. When the young man saw that she would not do his bidding, he went home and fell ill with longing for her.

B. What did the *ẓaddeket* do? She went to see how her husband was doing, and she found that he was neither alive nor dead. The *ḥasid* said to her: You wicked woman. I know what you intend to do. You coveted that young man and planned to kill me and marry him. The Almighty [and not you] will demand my soul from me. And she would support her husband day by day. One day it was raining, and she had no work. Her husband told her: Go to that young man who is very rich and he will lend you money. She said: Woe is me today. For days, he promised me all his riches if I agreed to do his bidding and you suspected me. I swear I will not go.

C. They fasted for three days and neither ate nor drank. After three days, the *ẓaddeket* said to her husband: Give me a divorce for one day, so that if I sin with that young man, it will not be such a great sin. And the *ḥasid* did. And she went to the young man, saying as she was walking: God of Abraham, Isaac, and Jacob, protect me this day so that I do not sin with that young man. [307b] She went to the gate, and the young man said: See who is calling at the gate. They [his servants] went out and saw that it was the *ḥasid*'s wife. They said: It is the woman so-and-so. The young man said: If that is indeed true, you are all freed. They went to her and opened the gate for her. And when the young man saw her, he was cured of his illness. He said to her: My daughter, blessed you are to God, who brought you to me. She said to him: One thing brought me to you. He said to her: Speak. She said: My

15. עוקבא (נוסח ראשון: 307א–307ב)

A. מעשה בחסיד אחד שהיתה אשתו יפה ביותר.[1] והיה החסיד עני גמור.[2] והיה שם בחור אחד בעירו שהיה עשיר ביותר. וחמד אשתו של אותו חסיד מאוד. יום אחד חלה החסיד. שלח לה הבחור שלוחיו לאמר: עשי רצוני, ואני אתן לך כל מה שתרצה.[3] אמרה להם הצדקת: לא אכחש בבעלי, שכל אישה שמכחשת בבעלה מכחשת לבוראה. הלכו לאדוניהם ואמרו לו: כך וכך דברה לנו האשה, שלא תעשה רצונך. הלכו פעם אחרת ואמרה להם כך. מיד הלך הבחור הוא עצמו ואמר(ה) לה: פלוניתא השמיעי לי, ואני אתן לך כל מה שתרצי. ועוד שבעלך עני ואני עשיר, והוא מכוער ביותר ואני יפה ועשיר. אמרה לו הצדקת: אם אתה יפה כחמה ובעלי מכוער ביותר לא אכחש בו, שכל המכחשת לבעלה מכחשת ליוצרה.[4] אמר לה: עשי רצוני, שאם לא תעשי רצוני אמות באהבתך. אמרה לו: מוטב שתמות ולא נאבד אני ואתה, בעולם הזה ובעולם הבא. כשראה הבחור שלא רצתה לעשות רצונו, הלך הבחור לביתו ונפל למטה בשבילה.

B. מה עשתה הצדקת, הלכה לראות בעלה מה היה עושה, ומצאו לא חי ולא מת. אמר לה החסיד: אי אשה רעה ידעתי מה את מבקשת לעשות, נתת עיניך באותו בחור וחשבת להמיתני, וליקח אותו לבעל. הקב"ה יבקש את נפשי ממני. והיא הייתה מפרנסת בעלה בכל יום. יום אחד היו גשמים, ולא היה לה מלאכה לעשות. א"ל בעלה: לכי לאותו בחור שהוא עשיר מאד, וילוה לך מנכסיו. אמרה לו: אוי ל{יה} היום, כמה ימים ביקש ליתן לי כל נכסיו אם אעשה רצונו, ואתה חשדתני ממנו. בשבועה לא אלך.

C. עמדו בצום שלשה ימים שלא אכלו ולא שתו.[5] לאחר ג' ימים אמרה הצדקת לבעלה: תן לי גט ליום אחד, שאם אעשה חטא עם אותו בחור לא יהא חטא גדול כל כך. וכן עשה החסיד.[6] והלכה לבחור ואמרה בהליכתה: א-להי אברהם יצחק ויעקב שומריני היום שלא אחטא עם אותו

---

1. ראו נוסח אחר של הסיפור בספר המעשים, 330ב–331ב. ההשוואות להלן הן לנוסח הנ"ל שבספר המעשים.
2. שם הוא מכונה 'עוקבא', ובהתאם הכותרת כאן.
3. שם, הבעל מושם במאסר עקב חוב שאין בידו לשלם.
4. מכחשת הוא במובן של מעל והתנכרות. ראו אבן שושן: "כיחש". וראו להלן הערה 8.
5. שם, מוטיב הצום חסר.
6. שם חסר: וכן עשה החסיד.

husband is very ill, and I have nothing to support him with. Out of kindness, please lend me money to support him. He said to her: Do my wish, and I will give you anything you want. She said: Sir, I ask you in God's name to be kind for the sake of your Creator and overcome your desire and do not do such a shameful thing to me today. Know that if you overcome your desire, you will have a portion of the world to come together with the righteous.

D. At once the man was filled with compassion for her, and he attended her words and said: God of Abraham, remember this moment when I had the opportunity to commit an act such as this and I overcame my lust. What did the young man do? He gave the *ẓaddeket* a great deal of silver and gold, and she went to her husband and told him everything that had happened, and he did not believe her.

E. In time, the *ḥasid* was healed of his illness, and he went to the market and met the young man who had given his wife the money. He saw a lit candle hovering over his head. The *ḥasid* said: My son, what have you done to deserve this lit candle hovering over your head? The *ḥasid* said: I gave charity. He said: Many Jews give charity but have nothing like this. Swear to tell me the truth. He said: Since you have made me swear, I will tell you. Such and such happened to me, and I overcame my lust. At once the *ḥasid* rejoiced, believing his righteous wife. He said: A good woman is her husband's crown, but a wicked woman consumes her husband like a tree worm. For she who commits adultery betrays her Maker, as it says: "She who forsakes the companion of her youth forgets the covenant of her God" [Proverbs 2: 17], and he who is wise and clever will keep his distance from her.

בחור. [307ב] הלכה לשער. ואמר הבחור: ראו מי קורא לשער. יצאו וראו שאשתו של אותו חסיד הייתה. אמרו: פלוניתא היא. ואמר הבח' [הבחור]: אם אמת הדבר תהיו כולכם משוחררים. והלכו אחריה ופתחו לה.

D. וכשראה אותה הבחור ניצל מחוליו ואמר לה: ברוכה את בתי לה' שבאתה אצלי. אמרה לו: דבר אחד שיגרני אצלך. א"ל: דבר[י]. א"ל: בעלי חולה מאוד, ולא היה לי לפרנס{ו}. למען חסדך לוה לי לפרנסו. אמר לה: עשי רצוני, ואני אתן לך כל מה שתרצה. אמרה לו: אדוני בקשתיך בא-להים שתעשה חסד בשביל בוראך, וכבוש את יצרך ולא תעשה עמי נבלה היום. ותדע שאם תכבוש יצרך, עתיד אתה להיות לך חלק עם הצדיקים לעולם הבא. מיד נתגלגלו רחמיו של אותו בחור ושמע אליה ואמר: י"י א-להי אברהם, תזכור לי שעה זו שבאתי לידי מעשה כזו וכבשתי את יצרי. מה עשה הבחור, נתן לאותה הצדקת כסף וזהב לרוב, והלכה לבעלה וספרה לו כל המעשה. ולא האמין לה.

E. לימים נתרפא החסיד מחוליו והלך לשוק, ופגע הבחור שנתן לאשתו הממון. והיה נר דולק על ראשו. א"ל החסיד: בני, מה מעשיך שנר דולק על ראשך? א"ל: עשיתי צדקות. א"ל: הרבה ישראל עושין צדקות ולא היה להם כך. משביעך אני שתאמר לי האמת. א"ל: הואיל והשבעתני אומר לך. כך וכך מעשה {בא} לידי, וכבשתי ~~ת~~ יצרי. מיד שמח החסיד והאמין לדברי אשתו הצדקת. אמר: אשה טובה עטרת בעלה,[7] אבל אשה רעה אוכלת בעלה כתולעת העץ.[8] שכל המנאפת מכחשת ליוצרה, שנאמר: העוזבת אלוף נעוריה את ברית א-להיה שכחה [משלי ב, יז].[9] וכל חכם ונבון ירחק ממנה.[10]

7. השוו משלי יב, ד: "אשת חיל עטרת בעלה".
8. הדימוי לתולעת המכלה את בעלה הוא על בסיס פירוש רש"י להמשך הפסוק במשלי יב, ד:"וכרקב בעצמותיו "מבישה". רש"י ד"ה: רקב – תולעת הנכנס תוך העצמות וטוחן אותם כן אשה מבישה ורעה שמעשיה בושים.
9. יחסי ישראל והקב"ה מדומים ליחסי בעל לאישה. והשוו לדרשות על הפסוק ממשלי: במדבר רבה, ט, ב; פסיקתא רבתי, פיסקא כא, י' הדיברות, מהדורת איש שלום, קז ע"א–ע"ב.
10. במקבילות האחרות באשכנז הסיפור אינו נקטע כאן, ויש המשך נרחב על קורות עוקבא לאחר מותו של ראש הישיבה.

16. Who Is the Thief? (307b–308b)

A. [307b] Once, in the days of Solomon, there were three merchants who were traveling on the road as the Sabbath was about to begin. And they took all their money and hid it in a certain place, and they all knew the place. After the Sabbath, one of them went and took it all. And when the three came to the place to take their money, they found nothing. There was an argument among them, with one saying, "You stole it," and another said, "You stole it," and thus the third.

B. They went to be judged before Solomon and told him the whole story. Once Solomon heard their words, he thought about the matter and said to himself: If I do not hand down judgment, people will say that I have lost my wisdom. So he said to himself: I will use my wisdom to investigate them by their words. And he said to them: Listen you three to this thing.

C. King of Beivar recently consulted me about something to tell him what to do. Once a boy and a girl lived in the same courtyard, and they made a covenant with one another. [308a] The boy said to the girl that he would take her for his wife and she would take him as her husband. And they both swore on these conditions, if the Almighty should make it possible. And if He should not, he would not be allowed to take a wife without her permission, and she would not be allowed to take a husband without his permission.

16. מיהו הגנב? (307ב–308ב)

A. מעשה היה בימי שלמה בשלושה בני אדם שהיו סוחרים,[1] והלכו בדרך[2] וקדש עליהם השבת.[3] ולקחו כל צרורותם והטמינום במקום אחד, והיו יודעים כולם אותו מקום.[4] ולמוצאי שבת הלך אחד מהם ולקח הכל.[5] וכשבאו שלשתם אל המקום ליקח כיסם, לא מצאו כלום.[6] והיה קטטה ביניהם.[7] זה אומר: אתה לקחתם, וזה אומר: לא כי אתה לקחתם, וכן השלישי.[8]

B. הלכו לדין לפני המלך שלמה וספרו לו כל המעשה.[9] מיד שמע שלמה דבריהם[10] וחישב על הדבר ואמר בלבו: אם לא אדונם באמת עתה יאמרו נסתלקה חכמתו ממני.[11] ואמר בלבו: אחקרם בחכמתי בדבריהם.[12] ויאמר להם:[13] שמעו שלשתכם את הדבר הזה.[14]

C. מלך ביבר שלח דבר אחד לי להודיעו מה טוב.[15] שהיה מעשה בתינוק ובתינוקת שהיו דרים בחצר אחת ויקחו ברית ביניהם.[16] [308א] ואמר האיש לאשה שהוא יקח אותה לאשה והיא אותו לבעל. ועשו שניהם שבועה מזה התנאים, אם יזמין להם הקב"ה. ואם לא יזמין להם, שלא יהא רשות לזה ליקח אשה בלא רשותה, והיא לא תהיה נשאת לאיש אחר בלא רשותו.[17]

---

1. במעשה"ד, שפירא, 81–84 ובכ"י פרמא 2295 (בתוך: קושלבסקי, סיגופים ופיתויים, 182), בלי: שהיו סוחרים. ההשוואות הן לכתבי יד אלה.
2. תוספת במעשה"ד ובכ"י פרמא: בערב שבת.
3. במעשה"ד: וקדש עליהם היום. בכ"י פרמא חסר: וקדש עליהם השבת.
4. במעשה"ד: אמרו זה לזה באו ונטמין במקום אחד הממון שלנו. הלכו והטמינו הממון.
5. במעשה"ד: חסר. בכ"י פרמא: ולמוצאי שבת הלך אחד מהם ולקח הכל.
6. מעשה"ד: במוצאי שבת הלכו לקחת הממון ולא מצאוהו. בכ"י פרמא: במוצאי שבת ביקשו לילך לדרכם. והלכו לאותו מקום שהטמינו שם באותו מקום הממון. לא מצאו שם כלום.
7. במעשה"ד ובכ"י פרמא: חסר.
8. במעשה"ד ובכ"י פרמא: זה אומר אתה גנבתו וזה אומר אתה גנבתו.
9. במעשה"ד: וספרו לו כל טענותיו.
10. תוספת במעשה"ד: אמר להם דינו, לבקר משפט.
11. במעשה"ד: כששמע הדברים היה מצטער ואמר אם אין אני דן דין זה יאמרו היכן חכמתו של שלמה? בכ"י פרמא: כיון ששמע המלך את דבריהם היה מצטער. אמר: אם איני דן להם את הדין יאמרו ישר' חכמה נסתלקה ממנו.
12. במעשה"ד וכ"י פרמא: מה עשה? ישב וחקר בחכמתו להשיב להם תשובה, לתפוש אותם מתוך דבריהם. תוספת בכ"י פרמא: חשב שלמה בעצמו ואמר: כיצד אעשה? אם אני מטיל שבועה ביניהם נמצאו השניים נשבעין באונס והאחר לשקר. אמר: לבקר משפט.
13. במעשה"ד: כיון שחזרו התחיל לומר להם. בכ"י פרמא: כיון שבאו לפניו התחיל ואמר.
14. מעשה"ד וכ"י פרמא: אתם בעלי סחורה ובעלי חכמה ומשפט יש עמכם. במעשה"ד: אבקשה מכם מה. בכ"י פרמא: אמרו לי דבר אחד שאשאל מכם.
15. מעשה"ד: מלך עדסי שלח אלי לחקרני בדבר שאירע במלכותו. בכ"י פרמא: מלך של רומיים שלח אלי לחקריני לחקריני בדבר אחד במעשה אחד שאירע בעירו.
16. במעשה"ד: ונתאהבו זה את זה. בכ"י פרמא: ונאהבו זה את זה.
17. במעשה"ד בדיבור ישיר: אמר התינוק לתינוקת בואי ונעשה תנאי בינינו בשבועה שאם ארשתיך עד יום פלוני מוטב תנשאי לי ולא לאחר תוך הזמן כל מי שירצה לארוש אותך אל תשמעי לו שלא ברשות. נשבעה לו בכך. בכ"י פרמא: אמר התינוק לתינוקת השבעי לי שאם אירסתיך מוטב ואם לאו כל אדם אירש אותך אל תישמעי לו אלא ברשותי. נשבעו זה את זה.

D. In time, the girl's father betrothed her to another man, and she married him. When her husband wanted to lie with her on the first night, she told him: Please sir, do not touch me, for I must tell you something. When I was a young girl, I agreed with a young boy that I would never sleep with another until getting permission from him. The young man heard the girl speak, overcame his desire, and did not touch her. The next day they arose, and they went to the boy. And the girl said to him: Dear sir, I know that in truth we made a condition between us as you know. And now, the Almighty has not made it possible, and I have married this man. And in kindness, accept this money from me and give me permission to lie with him. The boy answered: My dear one, whatever is yours is yours, I will not take anything from you. Since this was not possible from God, you are free to any man. And they left him and bid farewell. They encountered an old man, and he took everything they had and stripped them naked. He wanted to kill the husband and lie with the girl. And the woman said to the old man: Sir, overcome your desire, for you are old and this young man overcame his desire for me. The old man said, what happened? And she told him everything and said to him, if my husband—to whom I am married [lit., who is my husband] and is young and can lie with me sinless—overcame his desire, you who are old can surely do so. What did the old man do? He returned everything he had taken from them and gave them many gifts. And now King of Beivar asks me, Which of them is more praiseworthy? Now [that you know the details], consider it, and I will hear your answer.

D. לימים קדש אותה אביה לאיש אחר, ונשאה.[18] וכשרצה בעלה לשכב אצלה אמרה הנערה: בי אדוני, אל תגע בי ואדברה אליך דבר אחד. בנערותי התניתי עם נער שלא ישכב אדם לעולם עמי עד שאטול רשות ממנו.[19] וישמע <~~הנער~~> הבחור לדברי הנערה, וכבש יצרו ולא נגע אליה. למחר השכימו, והלכו אצל הנער.[20] ואמרה הנערה אליו: אדוני חביבי, ידעתי כי באמת עשינו תנאי בינינו כאשר אתה יודע. ועתה לא הזמין הקב"ה לעשות, ונשאתי הבחור הזה. ובחסד קבל ממני ממון, ותן לי רשות לשכוב עמו.[21] ויען הנער: חביבתי יהי לך אשר לך, שלא אקח כלום ממך. הואיל שלא בא הדבר מאת י"י, הרי את לכל אדם. ויצאו ממנו בשלום.[22] ופגע בהם זקן אחד[23] ולקח כל מה שלהם, ופשטם ערומים.[24] ורצה להרוג בעלה, והנערה הניח הזקן לשכב עמה.[25] ואמרה האשה לזקן: אדוני כבוש יצרך, כי אתה זקן וזה איש בחור וכבש יצרו בשבילי. ויאמר לה הזקן: איך היה המעשה? וספרה לו הכל[26] ואמרה לו: ומה בעלי שהוא בעלי, שהוא בחור, ויכול לעשות חפצו בלא חטא כבש יצרו, ואתה זקן לא כל שכן.[27] מה עשה הזקן, השיב להם כל מה שלקח מהם ונתן להם מתן רב[28] ועתה שלח אלי מלך ביבר, איזה מהם מכל אלה יפה עשה? ועתה הבינו אתם בדבר, ואשמע המענה מכם.[29]

18. במעשה"ד ובכ"י פרמא: לימים נתארסה התינוקת לאדם אחד.

19. במעשה"ד: כיון שרצה החתן לישכב עמה, אמרה לו: איני רוצה לך עד שנלך אצל פלוני ונטול ממנו רשות שכך נשבעתי לו. בכ"י פרמא: כיון שרצה בעלה לישכב עמה לילה ראשונה אמרה לו: איני נשמעת לך עד שתלך אצל פלוני ותטול ממנו רשות שכך נשבעתי לו.

20. במעשה"ד: הלך בעלה ונטל כסף וזהב, והלכו שניהם יחדו לאיש ההוא לפטור אותה משבועתה. בכ"י פרמא: מה עשה הבעל? נטל כסף וזהב לפתות בו את האיש.

21. במעשה"ד ובכ"י פרמא: כיון שבאו אצלו אמרה לו: אני עומדת בשבועתי אשר נשבעתי לך. אם תרצה הרי לך כסף וזהב ופטרני משבועתי.

22. במעשה"ד: אמר לה: אני פטרתיך, ותהי מותרת לבעליך ולא אקח משלך כלום. ואמר לה: לכי לשלום. בכ"י פרמא: אמר לה: הואיל ועמדת בשבועתך תהי מותרת לבעליך. לכי ושמחי בחלקך.

23. במעשה"ד: ויהי הם הולכים בדרך פגע בהם לסטס[ים] אחד זקן. בכ"י פרמא: כשהיו חוזרים לביתם פגע בהם זקן אחד וליסטים.

24. במעשה"ד: נטל לעצמו את הנערה ואת הכסף ואת הזהב והטכשיטין שהיו עליה. בכ"י פרמא: נטל הממון.

25. במעשה"ד ובכ"י פרמא אין איזכור של כוונת השודד להרוג את בעלה של הנערה.

26. במעשה"ד: כיון שרצה לבא עליה, אמרה לו: בבקשה ממך אדוני, המתן לי עד שאספר לך מה שאירע לי. והיא ספרה לו כל המעשה.

27. במעשה"ד: ואמרה לו: ומה אותו בחור עומד על פרקו וכבש יצרו, אתה זקן על אחת כמה וכמה שהוא דין שתשים לפניך יראת שמים ותכבוש יצרך ואל תחטא עמי ואל תקח ממוני. בכ"י פרמא: והנערה אמרה לו: אדוני הניחני. ואלך עם בעלי שכך וכך אירע לי ואותו האיש שהיה בחור לא נגע בי וכבש את יצרו ואתה זקן על אחת כמה וכמה.

28. במעשה"ד: מיד נכמרו רחמיו ולא נגע בה ונפטרו ממנו לשלום ולא לקח מהם כלום והחזיר להם ממונם. בכ"י פרמא: כיון ששמע הזקן כך נשא קל וחומר בעצמו והניחה לבעלה והחזיר לה כל הממון והלכה עם בעלה.

29. במעשה"ד: ואמר המלך, זה שאני שואל מכם אי זה מהם משובח? הבחורה שלא רצתה לאישה עד שקיימה שבועתה ונטלה רשות מאותו התינוק? או אותו התינוק שנתן לה רשות ולא לקח ממנו כלום? או זקן הלסטס שהיה בידו יכולת ליקח כל הממון ולענות התינוקת וכבש את יצרו ולא לקח מהם כלום? ועתה אמרו דעתכם ואחר כך אשיב תשובה לדין שלכם. בכ"י פרמא: ועכשיו שלח לי [מלך של רומיים] איזה מהן משובח מכולם?

E. One said: I praise the young girl for not violating the vow she made to the young boy. The second said: I praise the groom, who could have had his desire without sin and yet overcame his desire. The third, who stole the money, answered: I praise the old man, who paid them back what he stole and refrained from killing the groom and lying with the bride. But I am surprised at this. Is it not enough that he did not kill him and allowed him to go, but that he also returned all their money to them? And moreover, that he added and gave them many gifts of his own. He was certainly a fool. Solomon answered and said to him: You are wicked if you are upset and harbor evil thoughts in your heart about money that you have not seen and did not hold in your hand and did not know, but only heard about; this is all the more so regarding money that you saw and knew and took, that you will not return except by force. They immediately took him and beat him severely until he confessed.

F. And now come and see the greatness of the Almighty who revealed that which was hidden. And so one must be careful not to covet the money of another and not to steal it, because the Almighty will not dwell with him and will bring everything to light, as it says "And he will disguise his face" [Job 24:15]. The sin of stealing causes ugly acts, the dressed become naked. Come and see, for God made ten canopies of pearls in the Garden of Eden for Adam and Eve, and when they stretched out their hands to steal the fruits of the tree [308b], he drove them out of the Garden of Eden. They were as high as the angels, and the Almighty placed His hand on them and they were lowered down. They were dressed in the clouds of glory, and their skin was horny, and they became naked. And why [did they deserve] all this? So that you should not be haughty and consider stretching out your hand to steal.

E. ענה האחד[30] ואמר: משבח {אני} את הנערה שלא עברה הברית שהתנית~~ה~~ עם הנער.[31] והשיני אמר: משבח אני את החתן שהוא יכול <~~חפצו~~> לעשות חפצו בלא חטא וכבש יצרו"[32] ענה השלישי שגנב את הממון: משבח אני את הזקן ששילם להם כל מה שגזל, ומנע עצמו מלהרוג את החתן ולשכב עם הכלה" אבל תמיה אני על זאת, לא דיי שלא הרגו והניחו ללכת, אלא שחזר להם הממון. ועוד שהוסיף להם משלו מתן רב. ודאי שוטה היה"[33] ויען שלמה ויאמר לו: רשע, ומה ממון שלא ראית ולא בא לידך ולא ידעת כי אם לשמע האזן אתה מתחרט וחושב רעות על לבך, ממון שראית וידעת ולקחת על אחת כמה וכמה שלא תחזור אותו כי אם בכח.[34] מיד תפשוהו והלקוהו מכות גדולות עד שהודה.[35]

F. ועתה בא וראה גדולתו של הקב"ה, שהוציא את הסתר לגלוי. לפיכך יהא אדם זהיר שלא יחמוד ממון חבירו ושלא יגנוב אותו, לפי שהקב"ה לא יכנ{י}ס [יכנס] במחיצתו והוא יוציא הכל לאור, שנ': וסתר פנים ישים [איוב כד, טו]. שבעוון גניבה באים מעשים מכוערים, לבושים נעשו ערומים.[36] בא וראה, שהרי אדם וחוה עשה להם {הקב"ה} עשר חופות בגן עדן ממרגליות.[37] וכשפשטו ידיהם בגזל בפירות האילן [308ב] וגרשם מגן עדן. והיו גבוהים כמלאכים והניח הקב"ה ידו עליהם ומעטם, ונעשו שפלים.[38] הם היו לבושים מענני כבוד והיה (ערום) [עורם] כצפורן,[39] ונעשו ערומים. וכל כך למה? שלא תתגאה ושלא תעלה על דעתך לפשוט ידך בגניבה.[40]

---

30. הסדר במעשה"ד שונה – קודם משבחים את התינוק ואח"כ את התינוקת.

31. במעשה"ד: ויען השני ואמר: אני משבח את התינוקת כי מנהגן של נשים שלא לשמור אמונים אפילו לבעלה בעת משכבה ודעתן של נשים קלה. וזו שמרה אמונתה היא המשובחת לפי דעתי. בכ"י פרמא: פתח אחד משבח אני את הנערה שעמדה בשבועתה.

32. במעשה"ד: ענה אחד משלשתם ואמר: משבח אני את התינוק כי נתן רשות לנערה. יען כי אהבתה קשורה בלבו ימים רבים והיה חפצו בה ואהבתו שלמה מאד.

33. במעשה"ד: ענה השלישי ואמר: אני משבח את הלסטס הזקן אשר לקח את הממון והיה יכול לענות את הנערה ואין מוחה בידו, ואף על פי כן שמר את עצמו מחטא ולא ענה וגם החזיר הממון נראה לי שהוא צדיק גמור. בכ"י פרמא: פתח השני ואמר: משבח אני את הבעל והאשה אבל הבחור היה שוטה שלא לקח את הממון שרצו ליתן לו.

34. במעשה"ד: אמר לו המלך שלמה, יפה דנת. מהר לך החזיר הממון לחברך, כי אתה גנבת אותם. אמר לו: לא אדוני, אנכי אשבע. אמר לו המלך: לך החזיר הממון ואם לא אשימך בבית הסוהר עד יום מותך. בכ"י פרמא: כיוון ששמע שלמה כך אמר: מה אתה שלא היית בדבר המעשה הרהרתה כך ואמרתה הבחור היה שוטה, הממון שיש בידך על אחת כמה וכמה.

35. במעשה"ד: מיד הלך והביא הממון שהיו טמונים בארץ והחזירם לחבריו כיון שראה כי נגלה קלונו. ואז חבריו הודו למלך. על כן נאמר: "ויחכם מכל אדם" [מלכים א ה, יא]. בכ"י פרמא: כפתוהו והודו [הסוחרים] לפני המלך.

36. ראו זיקה בין גנבה לגילוי עריות בהקשר לפסוק מאיוב, כד, טו: "וסתר פניו ישים" – בילקוט שמעוני לאיוב, רמז תתקי, מהד' שלוניקי קעג, ע"ב.; ילקו"ש לירמיה, רמז שה, ד"ה: "אם יסתר איש", מהד' שילוני, נביאים אחרונים, 456.

37. ראו בבא בתרא עה ע"א, ד"ה: אמר רבי חמא בר חנינא.

38. השוו סנהדרין לח, ע"ב, ד"ה: אמר רב אלעזר: אדם הראשון מן הארץ עד לרקיע היה [. . .] כיון שסרח הניח הקב"ה ידו עליו ומיעטו, שנאמר: "אחור וקדם צרתני ותשת עלי כפך" (תהילים קלט, ה).

39. השוו רש"י לבראשית ג, כא, ד"ה כתנות עור: שהיו מדובקים על עורן, על פי תנחומא (בובר) לבראשית, סימן כד ד"ה הן האדם.

40. במעשה"ד ובכ"י פרמא חסר האפילוג: ועתה בא וראה–לפשוט ידך בגניבה.

17. One of Ten (308b)

A. [308b] Once there was a woman who would scold her daughter, who was a harlot, and she would say to her: My daughter, if you are promiscuous, do so in secret so that your husband does not know, just as I did; I bore ten sons, and only one of them is from your father. The husband heard what his wife had said while she was talking with her daughter, and kept the matter to himself. And when he was on his deathbed, he willed his inheritance to only one son, but he didn't say which, because he didn't know which of them was really his son.

B. After he died, the ten sons argued among themselves, with one saying: The inheritance is mine, and another saying: It's mine. They came for judgment before R. Bana'ah. He said to them: Do what I tell you to do, for this is a mysterious matter and no human can judge it. Now, go to your father's grave and strike it with stones until he reveals the one to whom he intended to leave the inheritance [lit., the gift]. They heard what he told them to do, and nine went and struck the grave with sticks. And the man who was certainly his son said: Heaven forbid that I should strike my father. Better I should lose the entire inheritance than to dishonor my father. When R. Bana'ah the judge heard this, he gave the entire inheritance to him.

C. Come and see the fulfillment of the verse: "The eye of the adulterer waits for the twilight, saying, 'No eye will see me.' And he disguises his face" [Job 24:15]. He who dwells in secret, his face will be exposed; his deeds will eventually be revealed. May your children be in purity [lit., cleanliness].

17. אחד מעשרה (308ב)

A. מעשה באשה אחת שהייתה מייסרת בתה זונה.[1] והיית[!]אומרת לה: בתי, אם את עושה זנות אל תעשי כי אם בצינעא, כדי שלא יכיר בך בעלך כדרך שעשיתי אני, שעשרה בנים יש לי ואינם מאביך אלא אחד מהם. שמע הבעל דברי האשה[2] שהיתה מדברת עם בתה, ושמר את הדבר בלבו.[3] וצוה בשעת פטירתו שלא יתנו מן הנחלה כי אם לאחד, ולא אמר לאיזה מהן. כי לא היה יודע איזה מהן היה בנו.

B. לאחר שמת התגרו זה בזה כולם עשרה, זה אומר: שלי הנחלה, וזה אומר: שלי.[4] באו לדין לפני רבי בנאה. אמר להם: עשו הדבר שאומר לכם כי הדבר סתומה, ואין יכול לדונה אדם.[5] ועתה לכו אצל קבר אביכם וחבטו עליו באבנים, עד שיגלה לכם לאיזה מכם עלה בדעתו ליתן המתנה. שמעו הדבר והלכו התשעה, וחבטו את הקבר במקלות. ואותו האיש שהיה בנו בוודאי אמר: חלילה לי להכות על אבי, מוטב לי לאבד כל הירושה ולא אבזה את אבי.[6] כשראה ר' בנאה הדיין כך, נתן לו כל הירושה לזה.

C. ובא וראה איך נתקיים זה הפסוק: ועין נו{שא}ף [נואף] שמרה נשף לאמר לא תשורנו עין וסתר פנים ישים [השוו איוב כד, טו]. מי שיושב בסתר, פנים ישים לדבר,[7] לסוף עתידה להגלות.[8] לכך יהיו בניך בנקיות.[9]

1. בבא בתרא נח ע"א: ללא הכינוי 'זונה'. ההשוואות להלן הן לתלמוד, במסכת בבא בתרא.
2. כאן נפתח הסיפור התלמודי: ההוא גברא דשמעה לדביתהו.
3. בתלמוד, אין התייחסות לרושם של הדברים על האיש.
4. שם אין איזכור של התגרות הבנים זה בזה.
5. ההסבר של ר' בנאה להנחיה שנתן לבנים, חסר.
6. חסר פירוט של התלבטות הבן.
7. השוו תנחומא, בובר, פרשת נשא, סימן ו: שם פנים של נואף באותו העובר [. . .] כדי שידעו הבריות ויאמרו בודאי פניו של זה דומין לפני נואף, שצר צורת העובר בדמות הנואף.
8. חסר מוסר ההשכל והפסוק מאיוב. השוו לתנחומא, נשא, סימן ד, ובמהדורת בובר סימן ו, שם הפסוק נדרש על חטא הניאוף.
9. בתלמוד מובאת תוספת ארוכה שהושמטה כאן, על מעצרו של ר' בנאה על ידי השלטון הזר ונסיבות שחרורו בהשפעת אשתו.

18. The Commandment of *Ẓiẓit* (Fringes; 308b–309a)

A. [308b] Once there was a man who was very meticulous about observing the commandment of *ẓiẓit*. He heard about a harlot in one of the towns by the sea who used to take four hundred gold coins, and he set a time for her [i.e., to lie with her]. He came [there] and sat on her doorstep. Her maid went into [her mistress] and told her: The one who sent you four hundred gold coins has come and is sitting on your doorstep. She said to him [her]: Show him in, and he entered.

B. And she prepared seven beds—six of silver and one of gold. And she climbed up and sat herself down naked on the top bed, and he too climbed up and sat at her side. His four fringes came and struck him across the face. He slipped down and sat on the ground, and she too slipped down to the ground. She said to him: On my word, I will not leave you until you tell me what blemish you have found in me. He said: Never have I seen a woman as beautiful as you; but there is one commandment which our God has commanded us, it is called *ẓiẓit*—and in its context it is twice written: "I am the Lord your God." One is to say: I am He who will exact punishment in the future, and the other to say: I am He who will give reward to the righteous who do my will in the future. And now [309a], they appeared to me as four witnesses. She said to him: On my word [lit. by the Roman capital], I will not leave you until you tell me your name, and the name of your town, and the name of your rabbi, the name of the academy where you study. He wrote all this down [lit., he put all this in writing].

18. מצוות ציצית (308ב–309א)

A. מעשה באדם אחד שהיה זהיר במצות ציצית.[1] ושמע שהיתה זונה בכרכי הים שנוטלת ארבע מאות זהובים[2] וקבע לה זמן. בא וישב לה על פתח ביתה.[3] ~~נכנסה~~ נכנסה שפחתה ואמרה לה: אותו[4] ששיגר לך ארבע מאות זהובים בא וישב לו על הפתח. אמרה לו [!]: יכנס. נכנס.

B. והיא היציעה שבע מטות. שש של כסף ואחד של זהב.[5] ועלתה וישבה לה על העליונה ערומה, ואף הוא עלה וישב לה בצדה.[6] באו ארבע ציציות וטפחו לו על פניו. נשמט וישב לו על גבי קרקע, ואף היא נשמטה[7] על גבי קרקע. אמרה לו: גפה של רומי שלא אניחך עד שתאמר לי, מה מום ראית בי.[8] אמר לה: העבודה לא ראיתי אשה יפה כמותך, אלא מצוה אחת ציונו א-להינו וציצית שמה, וכתוב בה שני פעמים אני י"י א-להיכם. האחד לומר: אני הוא העתיד ליפרע, והאחר לומר: אני הוא שעתיד ליתן שכר טוב לצדיקים עושי רצוני. ועכשיו [309א] נזדמנו לי כארבעה עדים.[9] אמרה לו: העבודה[10] שלא אניחך עד שתאמר לי מה שמך, ושם עיר{ך}, ושם רבך, ושם מדרשך[11] שאתה למד בו. (תמה)[12]" כתב לה בכתב כל זה.[13]

1. ההשוואות להלן הן לתלמוד מנחות מד, ע"א, על פי מהדורת הדפוס של האלמנה והאחים ראם, וילנה, המייצגת בדרך כלל את רוב כתבי היד, ופעמים על פי נוסח התלמוד בכ"י מינכן 95.
2. שיגר לה ד' מאות זהובים בשכרה.
3. כשהגיע זמנו בא וישב לו על הפתח.
4. אותו אדם.
5. בתלמוד תוספת: ובין כל אחת ואחת סולם של כסף ועליונה של זהב.
6. שם, תוספת פירוט: ערום כנגדה.
7. תוספת של המלה: וישבה.
8. איני מניחתך עד שתאמר לי איזה מום ראית בי.
9. בתלמוד בהרחבה נוספת: וכתיב בה אני ה' א-להיכם שתי פעמים, אני הוא שעתיד ליפרע ואני הוא שעתיד לשלם שכר, עכשיו נדמו עלי כד' עדים.
10. בלי מילת השבועה: העבודה. בכת"י מינכן 59: העבודה.
11. חזרה על מלת השאלה: מה שמך ומה שם עירך ומה שם רבך ושם מדרשך.
12. מילה לא ברורה.
13. כתב ונתן בידה. כאן, הדגשה נוספת של תעודה כתובה.

C. What did the woman do? She divided her estate into three parts: a third for the government, a third for the poor, and a third she took for herself, except for the bedclothes. She then came to the academy of R. Ḥiyya, and said to him: Rabbi, give instructions so that I may become a Hebrew woman. He said: Perhaps you have set your sights on one of my students? She thereupon took out the paper and handed it to him. He said to her: Go and enjoy your acquisition, and those very bedclothes which she used for a forbidden purpose she now spread out lawfully. This was their reward in this world, and in the next, they will bask in the radiant light of the Divine presence. And always make sure that your sons are born in purity. And marry a pure [honest] woman who will not betray you. For this you will be rewarded with righteous sons, who will respect and honor you.

C. מה עשתה האשה, חילקה כל נכסיה שליש למלכות שליש לעניים ושליש נטלה בידה[14] חוץ מאותן מצעות שהיו לה,[15] ובאתה לפני מדרשו של ר' חייא. אמרה לו: ר' צוה עלי, ויעשוני עברייה.[16] אמר לה: שמא עיניך נתת באחד מן התלמידים.[17] הוציאה כתב מידה, ונתנה לו. א"ל: לך[18] זכי במקחך, ואותן מצעות שהציען באיסור עתה הציעם בהיתר.[19] וזה היה מתן שכרן בעולם הזה, ולעולם הבא יהנו מזיו שכינה.[20] ולעולם {~~שתהא~~ הִזהֵר שְׁיִהְיוּ} בניך נולדים בנקיות. ושא אשה נקייה שלא יבגוד בך, כדי שיהו בניך זריזים במצות~~ך~~ כבודך.[21]

14. בלי השאלה הרטורית: מה עשתה?
15. בלי התוספת: והיו לה.
16. ויעשוני גיורת.
17. תוספת של מילת פנייה: בתי. בכת"י מינכן 95 בלי מילת הפנייה.
18. לכי. בכת"י מינכן 95: לך זכה במקחך.
19. צ"ל: שהציעה לו באיסור, הציעה בהיתר. בכת"י מינכן 95: אותן מצעות שהציעה לך באיסור תציע לך בהיתר.
20. זה מתן שכרו בעולם הזה, ולעולם הבא איני יודע כמה.
21. בתלמוד בלי האפילוג מן המלה: לעולם–כבודך.

19. The Book of Genesis (309a–309b)

A. [309a] Once, there was a *ḥasid* who was seventy years old and had no children. And he thought to himself and said: What do I need my property for? I will give it to Torah scholars so that they do not have to engage in trade and can study Torah, and I will earn a place in the world to come together with them. He would go every day and ask boys their verses, and each would cite him his verses. And he would respond: Happy are your parents who are privileged to have sons who study the Torah. The Almighty's compassion was immediately aroused, and at the age of seventy, He gave him a son. When the son grew, his father carried him to school. He went to his teacher and said to him: Rabbi, with what book shall we start the boy? He said to him: With the book of Leviticus. He said to him: Better he should start with the book of Genesis, which tells of the feats of the Almighty. And he did.

B. And every day, his father would carry him on his shoulders to study in the study hall. One day, the boy said: Father, why should you take such trouble with me every day? I know the way, and I can walk by myself. [So] the boy went to school on his own. As he was walking along the way, a servant of the emperor found him. And when he saw him so handsome and dressed so well, he took him on his horse and carried him off to his land. When evening came, the time when the boys leave school, the *ḥasid* saw that his son had not come home. He went to his teacher and said: Where is my son whom I sent to you? He said to him: I did not see him today. At once he cried out loudly and bitterly and cast himself [lit., his face] into ashes. He went to a crossroads and asked passersby: Have you seen a certain boy of such and such a description? They said to him: We have not seen him. He and his wife immediately cried and wept loudly and bitterly. At once the Almighty's compassion was aroused, and He caused the emperor to become very ill. The book of remedies was brought before him, and a miracle occurred, and it became the book of Genesis. They opened the book, and no one knew how to read it. They said to him: Your majesty, this is a book of the Jews. And he sent out messengers to look for a Jew throughout the land, but they could not find one. One of them answered and said to him: Your majesty, once I went to a city of the Jews and saw a Jewish boy and took him [309b]. Perhaps he knows how to read this book. The king said to him: Bring him to me.

19. ספר בראשית (309א–309ב)

A. מעשה בחסיד אחד שהיה בן שבעים שנה, ולא היה לו בן.[1] וחשב בלבו ואמר: למה לי נכסים, אלא אתן אותן לתלמידי חכמים שלא יעשו סחורה ויעסקו בתורה, כדי שאזכה עמהם לעולם הבא.[2] והיה הולך בכל יום ויום[3] ושואל הנערים מפסוקיהם,[4] ואומר לו כל אחד ואחד פסוקו. והשיב ואמר: אשרי יולדתכם,[5] שזכו לבנים שעוסקים בתורה.[6] מיד נתגלגלו רחמיו של הקב"ה, ונתן לו בן לשבעים שנה. וכשהגדיל, השים[7] אותו [על כתפיו](אפי) לבית הספר.[8] הלך לרבו ואמר לו: רבי, באיזה ספר נתחיל לנער? א"ל: בספר ויקרא. א"ל: ר' מוטב שיתחיל בספר בראשית, שהן גבורותיו של הקב"ה.[9] ועשה כן.

B. ובכל יום מוליכו אביו על כתיפו ללמוד לבית המדרש. יום אחד אמר לו הנער: אבא למה תטרח עלי בכל יום,[10] אני ידעתי הדרך ואני בעצמי אלך. הלך הנער יחיד לבית רבו.[11] וכשהיה הולך בדרך מצא אותו אחד מעבדיו של קיסר.[12] וכשראה אותו יפה ומלובש הרכיבו עמו על הסוס,[13] והוליכו לארצו. כשבא לערב שהנערים נפטרים מבית רבן, ראה אותו חסיד שלא בא בנו. הלך אצל רבו וא"ל: איה הנער ששלחתי אצלך?[14] א"ל: לא ראיתי היום. מיד בכה בכייה גדולה ומרה,[15] והתל [והטיל?] פניו באפר.[16] והלך בפרשת דרכים ושאל לעוברי דרכים: ראיתם נער אחד, כך וכך (בנים?) סימנים היו בו?[17] אמרו (בו): לא ראינו אותו. מיד זעקו ובכו הוא ואשתו, בכייה גדולה ומרה.[18] מיד נתגלגלו רחמיו של הקב"ה, ושלח חולי גדול למלך קיסר. והביאו לפניו ספר רפואות, נעשה נס וחזר ~~ונחזר~~ אותו ספר בראשית.[19] פתחו הספר, ולא היו יודעים לקרות בו. אמרו לו: אדונינו המלך, הספר הזה של יהודים הוא.[20] ושלח בכל ארצו לבקש שם יהודי, ולא מצאו. מיד ענה אחד מהם וא"ל: אדוני המלך, פעם אחת הלכתי לעיר אחת של יהודים וראיתי נער יהודי אחד ולקחתיו [309ב], שמא הוא יודע לקרוא בספר הזה.[21] א"ל המלך: הוליכו אצלי.

---

1. תוספת במעשה"ד, שפירא, 69–67: והיה לו ממון הרבה. ההשוואות להלן הן למקור זה.
2. במעשה"ד חסר: למה לי נכסים–לעולם הבא.
3. תוספת: לבית הכנסת.
4. וכשהיו יוצאין התינוקות היה מחבקן ומנשקן ואומר להם: בני, אמרו לי פסוקתכם.
5. אשריכם ואשרי אביכם.
6. במעשה"ד תוספת: ואומר בלבו: אוי, לא היה לי בן, מה הנאה יש לי בנכסי? עמד ופזר מנכסיו לתלמידי חכמים ואמר: שמא יהא עמהם לעולם הבא.
7. השים: בניין הפעיל של הפועל שם.
8. כיוון שהיה בן חמש שנים היה מרכיבו על כתפו והוליכו לבית המדרש.
9. ששם כתוב שבחו של הקב"ה.
10. עד מתי תטריח להרכיבני על כתיפיך?
11. במעשה"ד תוספת: אמר לו אביו: לך בני כרצונך.
12. שליח המלך ומצאהו יחיד.
13. במעשה"ד: בלי מוטיב הרכיבה על הסוס.
14. בני ששלחתי לך היכן הוא?
15. כששמע כך צעק ובכה.
16. במעשה"ד מוטיב ההתפלשות באפר חסר כאן, ומובא בהמשך.
17. ראיתם נער אחד שהוא יפה ביותר וסימן כך היה לו?
18. במעשה"ד תוספת: ומתפלשים באפר עד שעלה בכייתו למרום.
19. כשהיו מביאין אותו בא גבריאל והפכו לספר בראשית.
20. כמדומין אנו שהוא ספר של יהודים.
21. כשהלכתי בכפר היהודים גנבתי משם תינוק יהודי, אולי הוא יודע לקרות ספר.

C. They immediately brought him. The king said to him: My son, do you know how to read this book? When the boy saw the book, he fell to the ground on the book and began to kiss it and weep. The emperor said to him: My son, do not fear me, and read this book. He said to him: Your majesty, I do not fear you, but your majesty, it was this book that my teacher began to teach me. He said to him: Do you know how to read it? He said to him: Yes. The king said to him: My son, read it. The boy began immediately to read from "In the beginning" until "The heavens and the earth were completed." The king said to him: Can you explain it? The Almighty gave him wisdom and understanding, and he explained from "In the beginning" until "The heavens and the earth were completed" to the king.

D. When the king heard of the feats of the Almighty, he arose from his throne and sat down opposite him on the ground and said to him: My son, you have brought me a great cure. Ask me for anything you want. He said: I ask nothing of you except to be returned to my mother and father. The king immediately went to his treasury and gave him a great deal of silver and gold and returned him to his mother and father. And when they saw him, they gave praise to the Almighty. And the sages said: He who honored his father but one moment in this world received a reward; he who honors him all his life, all the more so that the Almighty will pay him a great reward.

C. מיד הביאוהו. א"ל המלך: בני, יודע אתה לקרוא בספר זה?[22] כיון שראה הנער הספר, נפל מלא קומתו ארצה על הספר ונשקו ובכה.[23] א"ל קיסר: בני, אל תירא ממני וקרא בספר הזה. א"ל: אדוני המלך, אין אני ירא ממך,[24] אבל בחייך אדוני המלך, בזה הספר התחיל לי רבי ללמוד.[25] א"ל: יודע אתה לקרות בו? א"ל: כן. א"ל המלך: בני, קרא בו. מיד קרא הנער מבראשית עד ויכולו. א"ל המלך: יודע אתה לפרש? נתן לו הקב"ה דיעה ובינה, ופירש לו מבראשית עד ויכולו.

D. כששמע המלך גבורותיו של הקב"ה קם מכסאו, וישב לו בארץ כנגדו,[26] וא"ל:[27] בני, רפואה גדולה באה לי על ידך, בקש ממני כל מה שאתה רוצה. א"ל הנער: איני מבקש ממך כלום, אלא שתחזירני לאבי ולאמי.[28] מיד הלך המלך לבית גנזיו ונתן לו כסף וזהב אין מספר,[29] והחזירו לאביו ולאמו. וכשראו אותו נתנו שבח[30] להקב"ה. ואמרו חכמים:[31] ומה זה שלא כיבד אביו אלא שעה אחת בעולם שלם לו הקב"ה שכר; המכבד כל ימיו על אחת כמה וכמה שישלם לו הקב"ה שכר גדול"[32]

22. בני, אם אתה יודע ספר זה אשריך ואשרינו.
23. צעק ובכה וחבט מלוא קומתו ארצה.
24. במעשה"ד תוספת: אבל הייתי בן יחיד לאבי ולאמי ונתנני הב"ה להם לאחר שבעים שנה.
25. וזה הספר שלמדני אבי ולפיכך בכיתי.
26. כששמע המלך את החכמה ואת התבונה היאך ברא הב"ה את עולמו היה מתודה למי שברא העולם מיד נתרפא וישב על מטתו.
27. במעשה"ד תוספת: ברוך ה' ששלחת לי רפואה ביד זה הנער.
28. איני שואל ממך כלום אלא שתשיבני לאבי ולאמי.
29. מיד צוה המלך להכניסו בבית גנזיו ונתן לו כסף וזהב ומרגליות שאין קץ ואין שיעור.
30. שם, תוספת: והודאה.
31. באותה שעה אמרו חכמים: ומה זה שלא למד אלא ספר בראשית, כך המלמד תורה ומשנה על אחת כמה וכמה.
32. ומה זה שלא כיבד אלא לאביו בדבור אחד, שאמר לו אל תרכיבני על כתפיך, נתן לו הב"ה ממון זה, המכבדו כל ימיו על אחת כמה וכמה.

20. The Cow That Observed the Sabbath (309b–310a)

A. [309b] Once there was a man who had a cow, and he would plow with it on the weekdays, and on the Sabbath he would not plow, as it says: "So that it may rest" [Exodus 23:12]. In time, the cow's owner became needy and sold her to a gentile. He [the gentile] said to him [the owner]: I am buying the cow on the condition that you know not of any blemish with it. And the gentile took the cow and plowed with it all week long. And he wanted to do likewise on the Sabbath, and he placed the yoke upon her to plow. What did the cow do? She collapsed and fell to the ground, which is what she was accustomed to doing on the Sabbath. And the gentile struck her a few times, and she refused to get up and plow.

B. And the gentile went to the synagogue and called out to the man who had sold him the cow and said: Why did you cheat me? Well do you know that you guaranteed that the cow you sold me had no blemish. He said: Yes. [The gentile said:] But, she does have a blemish. As long as I plowed with her [she was fine], but today when I wanted to plow, she refused and collapsed in the field. The man understood and went with the gentile to the field, where he found the cow collapsed on the ground, and the gentile wanted to strike her. He said: Don't strike her. And he spoke into the cow's ear: Cow, cow, don't you know that when you lived with me, you rested on the Sabbath, and now because of my sins I had to sell you to a gentile, and neither he nor his beast rests on the Sabbath? Kindly, stand up and do your work, and don't cause me strife with the gentile. When the cow heard [this], she stood up on her legs and did her work.

20. פרה שומרת שבת (309ב–310א)

A. מעשה באדם[1] אחד שהיה לו פרה אחת, והיה חורש בה כל השבוע ובשבת אינו חורש,[2] שנאמר: למען ינוח [שמות כג, יב].[3] לימים נצטרך בעל הפרה,[4] ומכרה לגוי אחד. א"ל: על מנת כן אני קונה את הפרה, שאינך יודע בה מום.[5] ולקח הגוי וחרש בה כל השבוע.[6] וכן רצה לעשות ביום השבת,[7] ונתן עליה עול לחרוש.[8] מה עשתה הפרה, הפילה עצמה לארץ,[9] שהיה מנהגה לנוח בשבת.[10] והכה הגוי כמה פעמים, ולא רצתה לקום ולחרוש.[11]

B. והלך הגוי לבית הכנסת,[12] וקרא לאותו שמכרה לו וא"ל: למה רימיתני, הלא ידעת כי ערבת לי הפרה שמכרת לי שאין מום בה. א"ל: הן. והנה היא בעלת מום, כל מה <שמכרתי> שחרשתי עמה, והיום רציתי לחרוש, ולא רצתה שהיא נופלת בשדה.[13] הבין האיש[14] והלך[15] עם הגוי בשדה, ומצאה שהיא נופלת. ורצה הגוי להכותה.[16] א"ל: אל תכה אותה.[17] ואמר האיש לאזן הפרה:[18] פרה פרה, אין אתה יודעת שכל זמן שהייתה עמי הייתה נחה ביום השבת, ועתה בעוונותיי מכרתיך לגוי, שלא ינוח אותו ולא בהמתו.[19] ובחסדך קומי ועשי מלאכתיך, ואל תגרמי לי להתקוטט עם הגוי.[20] כששמעה הפרה עמדה על רגליה, ועשתה מלאכתה.[21]

---

1. במעשה"ד, שפירא, 62–63 האדם מאופיין בלאומו כיהודי. ההשוואות וחילופי הנוסח להלן הם למקור זה, אלא אם צוין אחרת.
2. וחורשת כל ימי המעשה. במעשה"ד, שביתתה בשבת משתמעת בלבד בשלב זה, ואינה מפורשת.
3. במעשה"ד, ציטוט הפסוק חסר.
4. ונתדלדלה ידו.
5. במעשה"ד חסר תנאי המכירה והקנייה: על מנת כן–שאין מום בה.
6. כל ימי המעשה.
7. וכשבא יום שבת רצה לחרוש בה.
8. במעשה"ד חסר: ונתן עליה עול לחרוש.
9. והיא רבצה תחת העול ותמאן לחרוש.
10. במעשה"ד חסר: שהיה מנהגה לנוח בשבת.
11. ולא רצתה לנוד ממקומה.
12. הלך אצל יהודי.
13. חסר המשא ומתן הארוך ובמקומו בקצרה: טול פרתך שמכרת לי כי מום יש בה שאינה רוצה לחרוש היום. והשוו למסכת עבודה זרה יד ע"ב–טו ע"א.
14. כששמע היהודי כך.
15. במעשה"ד תוספת: הבין שבשביל שבת היא עושה כי כן היתה מנהגה לנוח בשבת. אמר לגוי בא עמי ואני אעמידנה. הלכו שניהם אצל הפרה.
16. במעשה"ד חסר: ורצה הגוי להכותה.
17. חסר: ומצאה נופלת–אל תכה אותה.
18. ודבר באזנה ואמר.
19. השוו יתרו כ, י; דברים ה, טו. במעשה"ד: פרתי פרתי, אתה ידעת כשהיית ברשותי [היית נחה] בשבת, ועכשו גרמו עונותי מכרתיך לגוי ואת ברשותו.
20. במעשה"ד חסר: ואל תגרמי לי להתקוטט עם הגוי.
21. מיד עמדה על רגליה וחרשה.

C. And when the gentile saw her, he said: What did you say in the cow's ear? Will I have to go to you to whisper in her ear each time I want to plow with her? Teach me the spell, and if not, return my money and take your cow back. [310a] The man said: I did not whisper a magic spell, but this is what the Almighty commanded us in our Torah, "So that it should rest on the Sabbath." And he told him everything that had happened. When the gentile heard the story, he was amazed and cried out that it was all the more so for him, saying: Woe is me if even a beast recognizes its Creator and honors Him by not doing any work on the Sabbath. How much more must I?

D. What did the gentile do? He converted to Judaism, he and his wife and all the members of his household, and he studied in school and became a Torah scholar, and was appointed to a high position over the public and carried out many acts of charity among the Jews of Israel. And a divine voice proclaimed that he was entitled to life in the world to come. So come and see how much good is brought about by observing the Sabbath.

C. כשראתה אותה הגוי א"ל: מה דברת לאזן הפרה, וכי כל זמן שאני רוצה לחרוש אלך בשבילך לומר לחש באוזניה? הוריני הלחש, ואם לאו חזור לי מעותי ותקח פרתך.[22] [310א] א"ל[23] האיש: לא לחשתי שום לחש,[24] אלא כך ציונו הקב"ה בתורתינו למען ינוח. וסיפר לו כל המעשה.[25] כששמע הגוי תמה בעצמו, ובכה ונשא קל וחומר בעצמו,[26] ואמר: אוי לי השתא [=עכשיו] הבהמה[27] שהיא מכרת יוצרה ונותנת לו כבוד שלא לעשות שום מלאכה ביום השבת,[28] אני על אחת כמה וכמה.[29]

D. מה עשה הגוי, הלך ונתגייר.[30] הוא ובניו וכל אנשי ביתו,[31] ולמד בבית הסופר ונעשה תלמיד חכם.[32] ומינוהו גדול על הצבור ועשה צדקות רבות בישראל. יצתה בת קול ואמרה שהוא מזומן לחיי העולם הבא.[33] ובא וראה כמה גורמת טובות על ידי שימור שבת.

22. במעהש"ד מוזכרת קודם הטענה השנייה: טול פרתך ותן לי הדמים כי כל פעם שתרבץ אלך ואסבב אחריך להעמידה, ולאחר מכן הטענה הראשונה: ועוד לא תתפרד ממני עד שתאמר לי הכשפים שלחשת באזנה.
23. תוספת: התחיל היהודי לבכות ואמר לו מכשף אני אמר לו הגוי מי יאמינך אני הכיתיה כל היום במלמד ויגעתי עליה ולא עמדה ואתה בלחישת שפתיך תעמידנה אלמלא כשפיך לא תעמידנה.
24. א"ל בשבועה כך וכך שחתי באזנה ועל כן עמדה.
25. במעשה"ד חסר: כך ציונו – כל המעשה.
26. הרהר תשובה בלבו.
27. מה פרה שאין לה לא שיחה ולא דעת, הכירה בוראה.
28. במעשה"ד חסר: ונותנת לו כבוד–ביום השבת
29. שבראני הברוך הוא בצלמו ונתן בי בינה ודעת.
30. מיד הלך ונתגייר. חסרה השאלה הרטורית: מה עשה הגוי?
31. במעשה"ד, התגיירות בניו ושאר בני ביתו אינה מוזכרת.
32. במעשה"ד: וזכה ללמוד תורה הרבה. ותוספת: ונקרא שמו בישראל חנינא בן תורתא ועד עכשיו רבותינו אומרים הלכה על שמו, יהיה חלקו עם הצדיקים בגן עדן.
33. במעשה"ד אין איזכור של בת קול.

21. Joseph-Who-Reveres-the-Sabbath (310a)

A. [310a] A tale of Joseph-Who-Reveres-the-Sabbath, who had a gentile neighbor who was very wealthy. And all those who saw him would say: All your property will Joseph inherit. When the gentile heard this, he hurried to sell all his assets, and with the payment he purchased a precious stone and inserted it into his hat, which he put on his head. And when he was crossing a bridge, a gust of wind came and blew his hat off his head, and it fell into the water and was swallowed by a fish.

B. And God appointed the fish to a certain fisherman on the eve of the Sabbath. The fisherman said: Who will buy my beautiful fish? But he was unable to find anyone to buy it. He thought to himself: I will go to Joseph-Who-Reveres-the-Sabbath, who always buys delicacies for the Sabbath. And he [Joseph] bought it, and when he slit open the fish, he found the precious stone that had belonged to his gentile neighbor and sold it for thirteen roomfuls of gold dinars.

21. יוסף מוקיר שבת (310א)

A. מעשה ביוסף מוקר [!] שבי,[1] שהיה לו גוי בשכונתו עשיר מאד.[2] וכל רואיו[3] אמרו לו: כל נכסיך יוסף ינח״ל [ינחל] אותם.[4] כששמע הגוי, הלך ומכר כל נכסיו,[5] וקנה בהם מרגלית אחת וקבעה במגבעתו,[6] וקבע אותו בראשו. וכשעבר על הגשר[7] בא הרוח והפריח המגבעת[8] מעל ראשו, ונפל במים ובלעו דג.[9]

B. וזימן הקב"ה אותו דג לדייג אחד[10] לערב שבת.[11] ואמר הדייג: מי יקנה דג יפה שלי?[12] ולא מצא שום אדם שרוצה לקנותו.[13] אמר הדייג בלבו: אלך אל יוסף מוקר שבי, שרגיל לקנות תענוגים לכבוד השבת.[14] וקנאו.[15] וכשקרע יוסף הדג מצא המרגלית שהיה לגוי שכינו,[16] ומכרה בשלש עשרה עליות[17] מלאות דינרי זהב"[18]

1. על פי מסכת שבת קיט, ע"א ומעשה"ד, שפירא, 61: ומעשה בחסיד אחד, ושמו יוסף מוקיר שבי.
2. מעשה"ד: שם והיה גוי אחד שכנו והיה עשיר גדול.
3. מעשה"ד: הוברים [חוזים בכוכבים].
4. שבת: יאכל אותם; מעשה"ד: כל ממוניך מוקיר שבי אוכל אותו.
5. מעשה"ד: ככששמע כך הלך ומכר כל אשר לו.
6. שבת: הלך מכר כל נכסיו [בתרגום מארמית]. מעשה"ד: וקנה מהם מרגלית אחת וקבעה במגבעו.
7. מעשה"ד: יום אחד היה עובר על הגשר.
8. שם, הכובע.
9. שם, דג אחד.
10. שם, וזימנו הקב"ה לדייג אחד.
11. תוספת במעשה"ד: בין השמשות.
12. שבת: מי קונה בשעה כזו?; שאלה זו חסרה במעשה"ד.
13. במסכת שבת, הערת מספר זו חסרה. מעשה"ד: ולא מצא אדם שירצה לקנות דג גדול כמוהו.
14. מעשה"ד: אמר הדייג בלבו, אלך אצל יוסף שהוא רגיל לקנות תענוגים לכבוד שבת אולי יקנה אותו.
15. במסכת שבת: קנאו. במעשה"ד: הלך אצלו וקנהו ומיהר לתקנו לכבוד שבת.
16. מעשה"ד: כשקרעו מצאו בו מרגלית שהיתה מהגוי שכינו.
17. עליות, בכינוי רבים של: עלייה, כלומר עליית גג.
18. תוספת במסכת שבת: פגש אותו אדם מבוגר ואמר לו מי שמלווה לשבת השבת פורעת לו. במעשה"ד בלי תוספת זו. אלא: וכל זה אירע לו מפני שהיה מכבד שבתות.

22. The Butcher from Ludkiya (310a)

A. [310] And once I was the guest of a certain Jew in Ludkiya, and they brought before him a golden table carried by sixteen people with sixteen silver chains hanging from it. And on the table were all kinds of food and delicacies. When they put it down, they would say: "The earth is the Lord's, and all it contains" [Psalms 24:1]. And when they removed it, they would say: "The heavens are the heavens of the Lord, but the earth He has given to mankind" [Psalms 115:16].

B. I asked him: My son, what have you done to earn all this? ["*Ma ma'asekha shezakhita le'khakh*?" (lit., What are your deeds that you earned all this?).] He said to him: When I was a butcher, I would buy the finest animals, and I would put aside the best ones for the Sabbath. I said to him: Blessed is the Almighty for giving you the reward you deserve.

22. הקצב מלודקיא (310א)

A. ושוב פעם אחד נתארחתי אצל יהודי אחד בלודקיא,[1] והביאו לפני שולחן זהב משאוי שש עשרה אנשים,[2] ושש עשרה שלשלאות של כסף תלויות בו.[3] ועל אותו שלחן כל מיני מאכל וכל מיני מגדים. וכשמניחים אותו אומרים: לי"י הארץ ומלואה תבל ויושבי בה (תהילים כד, א). וכשמסלקין אותו אומרים: השמים שמים לי"י והארץ נתן לבני אדם (תהילים קטו, טז).

B. שאלתי לו:[4] בני מה מעשיך שזכיתה לכך?[5] א"ל: (כשב) [קצב] הייתי וכשהייתי קונה בהמות טובות, החשובות לעצמי הייתי מניחם לכבוד השבת.[6] אמרתי לו: ברוך המקום ששילם לך שכרך.[7]

1. מובא במעשה"ד, שפירא, 61–62. להלן כל ההשוואות הן למקור זה.
2. מעשה"ד : שש עשרה בני אדם.
3. שלשלאות של כסף היו בו.
4. אמרתי לו.
5. מה עשית שזכית לכך?
6. הייתי בורר הטובה לכבוד שבת.
7. ברוך המקום שישלם לך שכר טוב כזה.

23. Turnus Rufus and R. Akiva (310a–310b)

A. And Turnus Rufus, a heretic, asked R. Akiva: Why is this day special that you honor it? He said to him: Because it is the Sabbath, and that is when God rested from all his labors. Turnus Rufus said: How do you know that it is indeed the Sabbath and not another day? R. Akiva said to him: Go to your father's grave and see that smoke rises from it all week long because his soul is burning in Gehenna. And on the Sabbath it rests, because it is not burning and does not give off smoke. And yet, come and see how the River Sambatyon flows all week long, and on the Sabbath it does not flow. And see the manna that did not fall on the Sabbath and fell double on Friday [310b].

B. And the sages said, one should always set one's table before Sabbath begins, and even if he has food the size of an olive only [which is a small measure in Jewish law], because two angels accompany him home from the synagogue, a good one and a bad one. When he arrives home and finds a candle burning and a table set and a well-made bed, the good angel says: May it be God's will that the next Shabbat will also be like this. And the bad angel reluctantly answers Amen.

C. And R. Shimon b. Pazi said: All those who fulfill the requirement of three meals on the Sabbath are saved from three punishments—from the tribulations of the Messiah, the law of Gehenna, and Gog and Magog. And R. Joḥanan said: He who delights in the Sabbath is granted his heart's desire, as it says: "Delight also in the Lord and he shall give you the desire of your heart" [Psalms 37:8].

23. טורנוסרופוס ורבי עקיבא (310א–310ב)

A. שאל טורנוסרוס [טורנוסרופוס][1] מין אחד היה לר' עקיבא: מה היום מימים שאתם מכבדין אותו? א"ל: מפני ששבת הוא, ובו שבת הקב"ה מכל מעשיו. א"ל: ובמה ידעתם ששבת הוא, שמא לא אינו זה אלא אחר? א"ל רבי עקיבא: לך אל שוחת אביך ותראה שעלה ש עשן כל השבוע כולה בשביל ששורפת נשמתו בגיהנום. ובשבת נוחה שאינה שורפת, ואינו עולה עשן. ועוד בא וראה שנהר סמבטיון מוגר כל השבוע ובשבת אינו מוגר. והמן שאינו יורד בשבת אלא ביום הששי יורד [310ב] כפליים.[2]

B. ואמרו חכמים לעולם יסדר אדם שולחנו בהכנסת שבת,[3] ואפילו לא יש לו לאכול אלא כזית, ששני מלאכים מלוין לו לאדם לביתו מבית הכנסת. אחד טוב ואחד רע. כשבא לביתו ומוצא [ומוצא] נר דלוק ושלחן ערוך ומיטה מוצעת מלא[ך]{ה}[4] טוב, אומר יהי רצון מלפני הקב"ה שיהא לשבת האחרת הבאה כך. ומלאך רע עונה בעל כרחו אמן.[5]

C. ואמר ר' שמעון בן פזי כל המקיים ג' סעודות בשבת ניצול משלש פורעניות מחבולו [מחבלו] של משיח ומדינה של גיהנם ומגוג מגוג.[6] ואמ' ר' יוחנן כל המענג את השבת נותנין לו משאלות לבו שנ' והתענג על י"י ויתן לך משאלות לבך[תהלים לז, ד].[7]"

---

1. טינאוס רופוס היה מושלה הרומי של הפרובינציה יודיאה בתקופת מרד בר כוכבא.
2. ראו פרשת המן בשמות טז, יא–לו.
3. במעשה"ד, שפירא 63, קטע זה מובא בשינויים קלים, לאחר סיפור פרה שומרת שבת.
4. השלמת הכ"ף הסופית היא מעל לשורה.
5. במעשה"ד, שפירא, 63, חסר: ואפילו יש לו לאכל אלא כזית.
6. השוו שבת קיח, ע"א.
7. דרשה זו מובאת בשם ר' יהודה במסכת שבת קיח, ע"ב.

24. The Defamed Woman (310b–311b)

A. [310b] Once there was a man who set out to trade. He left his wife to his brother and instructed him: My brother, keep your eyes and heart on my wife to cultivate and keep her until I return home safely. And his brother answered him: I will do as you say. The man set out on a distant journey to trade [his wares], and the wife remained alone with the husband's brother. What did he do: He went to her and kept visiting her day after day, saying: Heed me and I will do whatever you want, and I will give you whatever you want. But she said: Heaven forbid that I should do so, for she who betrays her husband betrays her Creator. And furthermore, her soul will be doomed to Gehenna. And what's more, my husband is your brother and he entrusted me to you to safeguard me and not to corrupt my spirit and yours. How dare you lay your hand on that which your husband has deposited in your hand [which means], that one does not have the right to enter property that is not his. And all the more so when the wife of your brother is involved, and I am forbidden to you during his lifetime. He who covets his neighbor's wife will lose his money and will ultimately be stricken with leprosy and will be doomed to Gehenna, into which he will descend and never rise.

B. What did that man do? One day he came into her house. He said to the servant, take the bottle and draw water. And after the servant went to draw water, he jumped to attack her and wanted to rape her. He said to her: Do as I ask. And the woman screamed very loudly and bitterly, and no one came to save her, until he left her alone because of her screams. He went out into the street and hired false witnesses to testify against her and told them: Come and testify that you saw that I found her with a servant in her house. What did the wicked men do? They went to the Sanhedrin and led her there before them and testified: This and that is what we saw this woman do with her servant. And the Sanhedrin sentenced her to be stoned to death. They immediately took her and placed an Egyptian rope on her neck.[1] And they took her to the place of stoning outside Jerusalem and stoned her to death, until she was covered by a pile of stones, as is the law regarding one who is stoned.

C. On the third day, a man came from another city who was taking his son to study Torah in Jerusalem [311b]. And when he reached the place of the stoning, it became dark, and they could not continue on the way to Jerusalem, and they spent the night at that place and placed their heads on the pile of stones, and lay down.

1. An Egyptian rope—made of palm fibers. See *Sotah* 7b. The rope was placed above her breasts to tie down her clothes and prevent her from being exposed. Here, in *Sefer ha-ma'asim*, the rope is placed around her neck, unlike in the source.

24. האישה המושמצת (310ב–311ב)

A. מעשה באדם אחד שהלך לסחורה[1] והניח את אשתו לאחיו, וציוה לו: אחי, שים עיניך על אשתי ולבך לעבדה ולשמרה[2] עד שאשוב לשלום.[3] וענה לו אחיו: אעשה כדבריך. הלך האיש לסחורתו בדרך רחוקה, ותשאר האשה לבדה ביד אחי בעלה. מה עשה, היה יוצא ונכנס והולך אצלה יום אחרי יום, ואמר לה: השמיעני ואעשה כל חפצך, ואתן לך כל מה שתרצה.[4] והיא אומרת לו: חלילה לי מעשות זאת, שכל המכחשת לבעלה מכחשת <~~לבעלה~~>[5] לבוראה.[6] ועוד, כי נפשה נידונת בדינה של גהינם. ועוד, כי בעלי אחיך הוא, והפקידני בידך לשמור אותי ולא לחבל נפשי ונפשך. ואיך תעלה בדעתך לשלוח יד בפקדון אחיך, כי בתורת פקדון שמני בידך בלי ליכנס ברשות שאינה שלו. וכל שכן שאשת אחיך אני ואסורה אני עליך בחייו. וכל החומד אשת חבירו יתרחק ממנו ממונו, ולסוף בא לידי צרעת. ועתיד להיות נידון בגהינם יורד ואינו עולה.[7]

B. מה עשה אותו האיש,[8] יום אחד בא ונכנס אצלה בבית. ויאמר אל העבד: קח את הבקבוק ולך לשאוב מים. וכיון שהלך למים קפץ האיש ורצה לאונסה, ואמר לה: עשי רצוני. וצעקה האישה צעקה גדולה ומרה ואין מושיע לה. עד שהניחה מפני שצעקה.[9] ויצא לשוק ושכר עליה עדים שקרים. ואמר להם: בואו והעידו שאתם ראיתם שאני מצאתיה עם עבד ביתה. מה עשו הרשעים, הלכו לפני סנהדרין והוליכוה לפניהם [בפני הסנהדרין], והעידו: כך וכך ראינו שעשתה פלוניתא זאת עם עבדה. ודנוה סנהדרין לסקילה. מיד לקחוה ונתנו על צוארה חבל המצרי.[10] והוציאוה לבית הסקילה מחוץ לירושלים וסקלוה. עד שנעשה גל של אבנים כדין הנסקל.[11]

C. ויהי ביום השלישי,[12] בא אדם אחד מעיר אחרת שמול{י}ך את בנו ללמוד תורה בירושלים [311א]. וכשהגיעו לבית הסקילה חשך עליהם היום ולא יכלו להגיע לירושלים. ולנו הלילה באותו מקום, ושמו ראשיהם על הגל, וישכבו במקום ההוא. וישמעו קול מדבר בתוך האבנים, שהיתה מתאנחת וצווחת ואומרת: אוי לי כי נסקלתי בלשון הרע. וישמע האיש את הקול מדבר בתוך האבנים, ויהפוך את האבנים כל הלילה לצד אחד[13] וירא כי אשה היא. ויאמר לה: מי את בתי? ותאמר לו: אשת פלוני הייתי. ויאמר אליה: מה לך פה? אמרה לו: כך היה מעשה, וסקלוני בלא פשע ובלא חמס בכפיי. אמרה לו: אדוני, לאן אתה הולך? א"ל: לירושלים ללמוד

1. ההשוואות להלן הן למעשה"ד, כ"י וטיקן 107 (180א-181ב), בעיקר השוואה תמטית ולא סגנונית, כי הניסוח שונה. במעשה"ד הבעל מוצג כחסיד העולה לירושלים על מנת להתפלל לבן.
2. השוו בראשית ב, טו.
3. במעשה"ד, יש תחילה פירוט של דברי הבעל לאשתו על כוונתו להפקידה למשמרת בידי אחיו.
4. שם, ההטרדה היא גם במחוות גוף: היה מחבקה ומנשקה ומרוב אהבה שאהבה תבעה.
5. מחיקה בקו אלכסוני של שתי אותיות ראשונות (למ"ד ובי"ת). כנראה כוונה למחיקה של המלה כולה: לבעלה.
6. במעשה"ד חסר: שכל המכחשת–לבוראה.
7. שם בקצרה, וללא מוטיב הצרעת או הגיהנום.
8. במעשה"ד האח מתבייש, וחושש שאחיו יגלה את מזימתו.
9. שם, ללא ניסיון אונס.
10. 'חבל מצרי' – עשוי מסיבי דקל. ראו סוטה ז, ע"ב. החבל נועד לקשור את בגדיה כדי שלא תיחשף במערומיה. במעשה"ד ללא איזכור של חבל המצרי, אך בפירוט נוסף של האירוע: האבנים שנסקלה בהם נעשו לה כמערה על ראשה, ולא מתה.
11. ראו על עונש מוות לנואפת, ועונש מוות לנערה המאורשה (שהיא במעמד של נשואה) דברים כא, כב; שם, כד.
12. במעשה"ד: באותה שעה באותו הלילה.
13. שם, נוסף נימוק: הואיל שרגמוהו ולא מת נראה שאין עליו חטא מוות.

And they heard a voice speaking from among the stones, and it would groan and scream, saying: Woe is me that I was stoned to death because of slander. And the man heard the voice from among the stones and turned over the stones all night to the other side, and he saw that it was a woman. He said: Who are you, my daughter? She said: I was the wife of so-and-so. He said to her: What happened to you here? She said: This is what happened, and I was stoned to death although I committed no crime and did nothing wrong. She said: Sir, where are you going? He said to her: To Jerusalem to teach my son Torah. She said: If you take me to your land, I will teach him Torah, Prophets, and Writings. He said: But do you know how to teach? She said: Yes. He immediately took her to his land, and she taught his son Torah.

D. One day, a house servant noticed her and said to her: Listen to me and do what I ask, and I will give you anything you want. And she refused to lie with him. What did the servant do? He took a knife and wanted to kill her, and struck the boy and killed him [instead]. He then fled, and the news was heard in the home of the boy's father that the boy was dead. He said to the woman: He is dead, so leave my home and go away, because every time I look at you, my heart rages, and I miss my son.

E. What did the woman do? She went on her way, and when she arrived at the seashore, a pirate ship came and abducted her, taking her captive. And God cast a storm wind on the sea, and there was a great storm at sea, and the ship almost sank.[2] And the sailors saw, and each cried out to his gods and said to one another: Let us cast lots and see why this calamity has happened to us. And they cast lots, and the lot fell on the woman. They said to her: Tell us what work you do? And she told them: I am a Hebrew woman, and I fear the God of the heaven who made the seas and the land. She told them everything that had happened to her. What did the people do? They felt compassion for the woman. And God performed a miracle for her, and none of those pirates touched her, and they cast her onto dry land and built her a small house. And the stormy sea grew calm, and the ship continued on its way.

F. The woman remained in the district and became an excellent and distinguished healer, and God provided her with all kinds of herbs, and she healed lepers and every [kind of] disease. And she advanced to a high position and amassed much gold and silver and became known all over the world. One day her husband returned from his business travels to Jerusalem, where he had lived, and he heard that his wife had been stoned to death. What did God do? He caused those people who had

2. From this point forward, cf. Jonah 1:4–15.

תורה לבני. אמרה לו: אם תוליכני לארצך, אני אלמדנו תורה נביאים וכתובים. אמר לה: וכי יודעת את ללמוד? אמרה לו: הן. מיד הוליכה לארצו עמו, ולימדה תורה לבנו.

D. יום אחד נתן עבד הבית עיניו בה, ואמר לה: השמיעי לי ועשי רצוני, ואני אתן לך כל מה שתרצי. ולא אבתה לשכב עמו. מה עשה העבד, לקח סכין אחד ורצה להורגה, והכה את הנער והרגו. ויברח, והקול נשמע בית אבי הנער כי מת העלם. ויאמר לאשה: מאחר שכך הוא לך מביתי וצאי לדרכך. כי בכל עת שאני רואה אותך לבי סוער והומה על בני.[14]

E. מה עשתה האשה, הלכה לדרכה.[15] וכשהגיעה על שפת הים, באה ספינה מליסטים ולקחוה ושבאוה בשבי. וי"י הטיל רוח סערה אל הים,[16] ויהי סער גדול בים והאניה חשבה להשבר. ויראו המלחים ויזעקו איש אל אלהיו ויאמרו איש אל רעהו, לכו ונפילה גורלות ונדעה בשלמי הרעה הזאת לנו. ויפילו גורלות ויפול הגורל על האשה. ויאמרו לה: הגידה לנו מה מלאכתיך? ותאמר להם: עברייה אני ואת א-להי השמים אני יריאה, אשר עשה הים ואת היבשה. וסיפרה להם כל הקורות אותה. מה עשו האנשים, נתגלגלו רחמים על האשה. ועשה הקב"ה לה נס, ולא נגעו כל הליסטים אליה, וישליכוה אל היבשה, ועשו לה דירה קטנה. וישתוק הים מזעפו, ותלך האניה לדרכה.[17] והאשה הזאת נשארה במחוז {והיתה}[18] רופאנית מעולה ובחונה. והזמין לה הקב"ה כל מיני עשבים שבעולם והייתה מתרפאת כל זב ומצורע וכל חולי.[19] ועלתה האשה מעלה מעלה. ותקבוץ זהב וכסף לרוב עד שייצא טבעה בכל העולם.

F. לימים חזר בעלה לירושלים מסחורתו אשר הוא גר שם, ושמע קול בעיר שאשתו נסקלת.[20] מה עשה הקב"ה הביא צרעת גדול על אותן אנשים שהעידו שקר עליה ועל אחי בעלה.[21] שמעו שמטרוניתא אחת רופאנית הייתה בכרכי הים. אמרו איש אל אחיו: נתנה ראש,[22] לילך אל הרופאנית. ויאמר האיש אל אחיו לך עמנו. הלכו כולם ארבעה עד שהגיעו [311ב] למקומה. נכנסו אצלה. מיד הכירם, והם לא הכירוה. אמרו לה: אדונתינו מארץ רחוקה באנו, ושמענו שמעך שאת רופאנית מעולה, ורפאי אותנו מצרעתנו, ותקח[י] ממנו כסף וזהב לרוב. אמרה להם: לא אוכל לעשות רפואה לשום אדם אם לא יגיד לי עוונו הגדול, כי לא יועיל לו. אמרו לו: כזאת וכזאת עשינו. אמרה להם: רואה אני פניכם, שחטאים גדולים אתם ולא גיליתם לי כל עונותיכם. וכל זמן שתכסו על פשעיכם לא יועיל רפואה לכם. מה עשו, ספרו והודו ולא בושו, וספרו כל המעשה לפני בעל האשה. אמרה להם: הרעותם ופיכם ענה בכם. בשבועה לא אעשה לכם רפואה. כי כל רפואות שבעולם לא יועילו לכם. כי לא איש אל ויכזב [במדבר כג: יט], מאשר דבר ביד משה עבדו בחירו וביד עבדיו הנביאים. דכת' לא תלך רכיל בעמך ולא תעמד על דם רעך [ויקרא

14. במעשה"ד העבד מציע לאשה לברוח, ואילו הוא נשאר וטופל עליה את האשמה.

15. שם, נוסף אירוע: היא מצילה גנב מחבל התלייה, והוא מגיב בכפיות טובה, תופס אותה ומוכר אותה לרב חובל.

16. מכאן ולהלן השוו ליונה א, ד–טו.

17. במעשה"ד היא משכנעת את רב החובל להרפות ממנה ולהשליכה ליבשה, תמורת ריפויו מצרעת. בהמשך ריפויו מתואר כנס: וזימן לה הקב"ה נס אחד ושב בשרו מאות החובל שהוא מצורע כבשר נער קטן ויטהר. וכן: הואיל ועשה לי הקב"ה נס במקום הזה. גם בנוסח מעשה"ד שבכ"י וטיקן 701 היא מתפללת לריפויו של המצורע ומרפאה אותו בצמחי מרפא ("סם אחד" בלשון הטקסט), ובהמשך ריפויו בתואר כנס, כנ"ל.

18. תוספת בשולי הדף.

19. במעשה"ד: ונתן לה הקב"ה בינה והשכל והיתה יודעת כל מיני רפואות בעולם ומכרת כל מיני בשמים ועשבים איזה מהם טובים לרפאת כל תחלואי הגוף.

20. במעשה"ד הבעל אינו מאמין לדיבה על אשתו.

21. במעשה"ד, אחי בעלה וכן העבד נענשים בצרעת, והעדים שהעידו עדות שקר נעשים אלמים.

22. השוו במדבר יד, ד.

testified falsely against her, along with the husband's brother, to fall ill with leprosy. They heard that a certain woman was a healer and lived in a town by the sea. They said to one another: Let us go to the woman healer. And the man said to his brother: Come with us. The four traveled until they reached [331b] the place where she was. They went in to see her. At once she recognized them, but they did not recognize her. They said to her: Madam, we have come from very far away, and we have heard that you are an excellent healer, [and pray,] cure us of our leprosy, and take from us much silver and gold. She said to them: I cannot heal anyone unless he tells me what his great sin was, because otherwise the cure will not work. They said to her: We did such and such. They said to her: Your faces tell me that you are great sinners and that you have not revealed all your sins to me. Until you atone for your sins, you cannot be cured. What did they do? They told her and confessed, concealing nothing [lit., and weren't ashamed], telling the entire story before the woman's husband. She said to them: You have done evil, and your mouth has related it. I swear that I will not cure you, for all the cures in the world will not help you. For God is not a man, and He will not break His word, as He spoke to Moses His chosen servant and to His servants, His prophets, as it says: "You shall not spread slander among your people, neither shall you stand on the blood of your neighbor" [Leviticus 19:16]. Thus, the slander brings evil. And you wicked [people], I, the woman standing here before you, am the one against whom you committed all these evil acts and took me out to be stoned to death because of your lying tongues. And the Almighty saved me out of His compassion and great charity. And this is my husband, whom you brought before me. And the Almighty knows all the mysteries of the world and all that is unknown of all creatures and reveals all secrets. As it says: "And he disguises his face" [Job: 24:15]. And those three people who were ill with leprosy died of it.

G. The man immediately understood the entire story and knew that she was his wife. They were happy and joyous and gave praise to their Creator for all these miracles. So come and see how great is the punishment for slander, and the end of those who bring false testimony and defame—they are to be stricken with leprosy. And all those who fear the Lord will guard their tongue from speaking evil. As it says: He who guards his mouth and tongue keeps himself from the calamity of the soul.

יט, טז]. נמצא שהרכילות מביא לידי רע. ואתם רשעים, אני הנ האשה הנצבת עמכם אשר עשיתם כל הרעות האלה, והוצאתם אותי לסקילה בשביל לשונכם שקר. והקב"ה הצילני למען רחמיו וחסדיו הרבים. וזהו בעלי אשר הולכתם לפניכם אלי. והקב"ה יודע רזי עולם ותעלומות סתרי כל חי וכל סתר מביא לגלוי. שנ' וסתר פנים ישים [איוב כד, טו].[23] ואותם שלשה אנשים לקו בצרעת, ומתו בו.

G. מיד הכיר האיש כל המעשה וידע שהיא אשתו.[24] והיו שמיחים וטובי לב, ונתנו שבח לבוראם על כל הנסים האילו.[25] ובא וראה כמה גדול עונש לשון הרע, ומעידי שקר ומוציא דבה – סופו [סופם] ללקות בצרעת. וכל יריאי השם ישמרו לשונם מדבר רע. שנ' שומר פיו ולשונו שומר מצרה נפשו.[26]

23. ציטוט זה ראו גם באפילוג של 'אחד מעשרה' (308ב).
24. במעשה"ד האישה חוזרת ומדגישה בפני בעלה את תומתה.
25. במעשה"ד: מיד נתן שבח והודאה להקב"ה עושה נסים. כמו כן שם, הזוג זוכה לבנים כמענה לתפילת הבעל בבית המקדש בירושלים
26. השוו משלי כא, כג.

25. R. Meir and Judah of Anatot (311b–312a)

A. [311b] A tale of R. Meir, who usually did not leave the study hall before the fourth hour of the day. Once he recited [only] the morning prayers and left early. After leaving, he wondered to himself and said: Why did I rush out to leave today? Will God perhaps perform a miracle through me? While standing [there] a while, he saw two snakes talking to each other: Where are you going? [asked the first snake] He said: The Almighty has sent me to kill Judah of Anatot, his children, his wife, and his whole household. Why? he asked, and he [the other] said: Because he never did [gave] charity in his life. Said R. Meir: I will go [to Judah of Anatot]. Perhaps I can save him. He immediately ordered the snake not to cross [the river]. And R. Meir went to the home of Judah and disguised his face so that Judah would not recognize him. When he [Judah] saw him, he said: This must be a thief who intends to steal our property. When R. Meir heard that, he went and hid among the camels. And when Judah sat down to eat, R. Meir came and sat among them. His sons began quarreling among themselves to drive him [312a] out of there. He said: Even if you kill one another, I will not move from here until I have eaten my fill. After eating and drinking, he took a loaf of bread in his hand and said to Judah: Take this loaf and give it to me, saying: This will be charity unto you. Judah said: Is it not enough that you have eaten your fill but you also want me to give you a loaf of bread? What did R. Meir do? He extinguished the candle and removed the turban from his head, and the house glowed with the light of R. Meir. When they recognized him as R. Meir, they stood up at once in order to appease him. And when he was appeased, Judah took the loaf of bread and said: This will be charity unto you.

B. Now R. Meir said: Listen to my advice and send your wife somewhere and your sons and daughters-in-law and daughters as well, and tell them not to return here until two hours have passed. And he did so. And R. Meir and Judah remained home alone. After the second hour of the night, R. Meir released the snake, and he crossed the river and came to the home of Judah. And R. Meir went outside to attend to his needs, and the snake entered the house and sought to kill. And he [Judah] screamed and said: R. Meir, save me from this snake that seeks to kill me. R. Meir immediately entered the house and found the snake. He said: What are you [doing here]? The snake said: The Lord has sent me to kill Judah and his household. He asked: Why? And the snake said: Because he has never given any charity of his property. R. Meir said: But last night he gave me to eat and drink, and then he gave me a loaf of bread as charity. At once R. Meir decreed and forced the snake out of

25. רבי מאיר ויהודה הענתותי (311ב–312א)

A. מעשה ברבי מאיר, שלא היה רגיל לצאת מבית המדרש עד ארבע שעות ביום.[1] יום אחד התפלל תפלת שחרית, והקדים לצאת. לאחר שיצא תמה בעצמו ואמר: מפני מה יצאתי היום מהרה,[2] שמא הקב"ה יעשה היום נס על ידי? כיון שעמד קימעא, ראה שני נחשים שהיו אומרים אחד לחבירו: לאן אתה הולך? א"ל: הקב"ה שיגרני להרוג יהודה הענתותי, ובניו, ואשתו וכל ביתו.[3] א"ל: למה? א"ל: מפני שלא עשה צדקה מימיו.[4] אמר ר' מאיר: אלך, שמא אוכל להצילו.[5] מיד גזר עליו ר' מאיר שלא לעבור.[6] והלך ר' מאיר לביתו של יהודה, וכסה פניו שלא יכירנו. כיון שראה אותו ואמר: זה בודאי גנב הוא שרוצה לגנוב נכסינו. כיון ששמע כך, הלך ונתחבא בין הגמלים.[7] וכשישב יהודה לסעוד, בא ר' מאיר וישב ביניהם. התחילו בניו מריבין זה עם זה לגרשו [312א] משם.[8] אמר להם: אם אתם הורגים זה עם זה,[9] לא אזוז מכאן עד שאוכל ואשבע.[10] לאחר שאכל ושתה נטל חלת לחם בידו, ואמר ליהודה: טול חלת לחם בידך ותנה לי ואמור: זו יהיה לך לצדקה. א"ל יהודה: לא דייך שאכלת ושבעת אלא שתרצה שאתן לך חלת לחם?![11] מה עשה ר' מאיר, כבה את הנר, והסיר הצניף שעל ראשו,[12] והבהיק הבית לאורו של רבי מאיר. כיון שהכירוהו שהיה ר' מאיר, מיד עמדו על רגליהם לפייסו. וכשנתפייס[13] נטל יהודה החלה ואמר: זו יהיה לך לצדקה.

B. א"ל ר' מאיר: שמע לעצתי, ושגר אשתך במקום אחד ובניך וכלותיך ובנותיך כמו כן, ואמור להם שלא ישובו הנה עד שיעברו ב' שעות ביום.[14] וכן עשה. ונשתיירו בבית ר' מאיר ויהודה[15] לבדיהן. כיון שעברו ב' שעות בלילה התיר ר' מאיר לנחש, ועבר הנהר ובא לבית יהודה. ויצא ר' מאיר לצרכיו, ונכנס הבית אותו נחש וביקש להרוג. והיה צועק ואומר: ר' מאיר הושיעני נא מן הנחש שמבקש להורגיני.[16] מיד נכנס ר' מאיר לבית ומצא הנחש. וא"ל: מה טיבך?[17] א"ל:

---

1. ההשוואות להלן הן למעשה"ד שפירא, 92–94, אלא אם צוין אחרת.
2. מעשה"ד: ואמר מה יום מימים שהקדמתי לצאת מהרה מבית הכנסת?
3. מעשה"ד: אותו ואת אנשי ביתו.
4. שלא עשו צדקה מימיהם.
5. שמא אוכל למלטהו.
6. הלך ר' מאיר בדרך אחד והנחש בדרך אחרת כיון שהגיע ר' מאיר לנחל אחד פגע בנחש שהיה רוצה לעבור וגזר עליו שלא יעבור את הנחל כי אם ברשותו.
7. באבוסי גמלים.
8. ורצו להוציאו מן הבית.
9. חסר: אם אתם הורגים זה את זה.
10. תוספת: כי רעב אנוכי.
11. לא דייך שאכלת לשובע, אלא ששאלת ממני יותר?
12. והסיר הצעיף מעל פניו.
13. חסר: וכשנתפייס.
14. קח נא את אשתך ובניך ובנותיך ושלח אותם במקום אחד. במעשה"ד, כ"י מוסקבה-גינצבורג 111: שגר אשתך במקום אחר ובניך במקום אחר ובנותיך במקום אחר וצוה אותם שלא יבאו בכאן עד שיעברו שתי שעות מן היום למחר.
15. במעשה"ד, ר' יהודה מוזכר בכינויו: הענתותי.
16. בלי איזכור צעקתו ופנייתו של יהודה הענתותי אל ר' מאיר.
17. שם, תוספת: במקום זה?

the house, and shut the door. And he told Judah that he should not open the door until the next day.

C. After waiting awhile, the snake came and took on the voice of his [Judah's] wife, saying: My husband, open the door, for I am cold. And he [Judah] intended to open [the door]. R. Meir told him: Beware not to open the door, because it is not your wife. He [the snake] waited awhile, and came and took on the voice of his eldest son. And he said: Father, open the door for me, for I am dying of thirst. R. Meir said: Beware not to open, because it is not your son. And similarly, he took on the guise of his sons and daughters-in-law. In every case, R. Meir did not let him open the door. And when the snake saw that he was unable to kill Judah, he stood on his belly, screamed and cried, and said: Woe that those on high decree and those on earth annul; woe that the Almighty decrees and R. Meir annuls. It immediately flung itself down to earth, and its belly split open and it died. The next day, two hours later, Judah's wife, sons, and daughters came, and R. Meir said: Come and see who was calling [you] last night. They all gathered [lit., stood] with R. Meir and found the snake lying dead. He said: This is what was calling [you] all night. He immediately applied to him the verse: "Riches won't help on the day of wrath: but charity saves from death" [Proverbs 11:4].

המקום שיגרני להרוג יהודה וביתו.[18] א"ל: למה? א"ל: מפני שלא עשה צדקה מנכסיו מעולם. א"ל ר' מאיר: והלא אמש האכילני[19] והשקני, ואחר כך נתן לי חלת לחם לצדקה.[20] מיד גזר ר' מאיר והוציאו מן הבית בעל כרחו, וסגר הדלת. ואמר ליהודה שלא יפתח הדלת עד למחר.[21]

C. כיון שהמתין שעה בא אותו נחש, ונדמה כקול אשתו. והיה אומרת: בעלי פתח לי הדלת שהרי אני בצינה,[22] ורצה לפתוח. א"ל ר' מאיר: הזהר שלא תפתח, שאינה אשתך.[23] המתין מעט [הנחש],[24] ובא ונדמה בקול בנו הגדול. וא"ל: אבי פתח לי שאני מת בצמא.[25] א"ל ר' מאיר: הזהר שלא תפתח, שאינו בנך.[26] ובאותו דמות דמה לבניו ולכלתיו.[27] מכל מקום לא הניחו ר' מאיר לפתוח. וכשראה הנחש שלא היה יכול להרוג יהודה, עמד על בטנו וצעק ובכה[28] ואמר: אוי שהעליונים גוזרין והתחתונים מבטלים, אוי שהקב"ה גוזר ור' מאיר מבטל.[29] מיד נפל לארץ, ובקע כריסו ומת.[30] ולמחר, כיון שעברו ב' שעות ביום באתה אשתו ובניו ובנותיו[31] ואמר להם: בואו וראו מי היה קורא אמש. מיד עמדו עם רבי מאיר ומצאו הנחש נופל מת. א"ל: זה שקרא כל הלילה.[32] מיד קרא עליו זה הפסוק: לא יועיל הון ביום עברה "{וצדקה תציל ממות} [משלי יא, ד].[33]

18. הקב"ה שלחני להרוג יהודה ובנותיו ואת בני ביתו.
19. שם, תוספת: מלחמו.
20. חלת לחם צדה לדרך. תוספת: צא מן הבית כי אין לך רשות לשלוט בו לשם רע.
21. מעשה"ד: השמר בנפשך על הדלת שלא יפתח עד מחר.
22. שם: שהרי שינה גדולה נופלת עלי כ"י מוסקבה-גינצבורג: שהרי אני מתה מן הצנה.
23. אל תפתח כי אין אשתך לחוץ.
24. שם: עמד עוד שעה אחת.
25. אבי, פתח לי כי ירא אני מן החיות הרעות. כ"י מוסקבה-גינצבורג: אבא פתח לי הדלת שהרי אני כמעט מת מן הצנה.
26. אל תפתח כי זה הקורא אין בנך הוא. לך שכב ואל תפתח להם הדלת.
27. כעוד פעם שלישית ונדמה לו כדמות בניו ובנותיו, וכל זאת התרהו ר' מאיר ואמר לו: אל תשמע לו ואל תפתח להם הדלת.
28. נזדעזע ונבהל ונחבט בקרקע.
29. במעשה"ד חסר: אוי שהקב"ה גוזר ר' מאיר מבטל.
30. הפיל עצמו ומת.
31. תוספת: ואמר להם יהודה: באתם הנה הלילה? ואמרו: לא יצא איש מפתח ביתו.
32. בא עמי ואראך מי בא הנה הלילה. הראה לו הנחש מת ומצער.
33. ומיד נתנו צדקה למי שהצילם מיד מזיק.

26. R. Meir and Kiddor (312a–312b)

A. [312a] Once R. Meir and R. Yossi and R. Judah were walking along the way. And R. Meir was very particular about [people's] names and would never enter a home whose resident had an inauspicious name. They arrived at the home of a man named Kiddor. R. Meir said to them: He is wicked, as it says: "For they are a perverse generation" [Deuteronomy 32:20]. What did R. [312b] Judah and R. Yossi do? They deposited with him [lit., gave him] their purses [at the eve of Sabbath], and R. Meir did not deposit with him his purse. He squeezed his purse into a ball and buried it at the grave of Kiddor's father.

B. Kiddor's father came to him in a dream and said to him: My son, come and take a purse that lies at the head of my grave. The next day, Kiddor came to R. Meir. He said to him: I saw such and such during the night. R. Meir said: A Sabbath dream at twilight has no meaning. What did R. Meir do? He guarded his purse all that day, and after the Sabbath took back his purse. The next day, R. Judah and R. Yossi came and asked for their purses and said to Kiddor: Give us our purses that we left with you on the eve of the Sabbath. He said to them: Nothing of the kind happened. R. Meir said: Why were you not careful about names? They said to him: Why didn't you tell us [warn us]?

C. What did they do? They took him [Kiddor] and brought him to a shop [tavern] to give him wine to drink to get him to agree to give them back their purses. They saw by his beard that he had eaten lentils at home. They went and gave the sign to his wife and said to her: Give us the purses that we deposited with your husband on the Sabbath eve, and this is the sign—that he ate lentils today. She said to herself: They did indeed speak the truth. She went to the box and gave them their purses. When Kiddor came home, he said to her: Where are the purses? She said: But you sent a sign to give the purses to their owners. What did he do? He killed his wife. Come and see that when one covets money, it can lead to murder.

26. רבי מאיר וכידור (312א–312ב)

A. מעשה ברבי מאיר ור' יוסי ור' יהודה שהיו הולכין בדרך. והיה ר' מאיר מדקדק בשם, שלא רצה ליכנס בבית אם לא היה שם טוב לאדם.[1] הגיעו לבית אותו אדם ששמו כידור. אמר להם ר' מאיר: רשע הוא. שנ' כידור תהפוכות המה [דברים לב, כ].[2] מה עשו רבי [312ב] יהודה ור' יוסי, הפקידו לו את כיסיהם, ור' מאיר לא הפקיד לו את כיסו. והלך ושם כיסו ככדור, וקברה בקבר דאבי כידור.[3]

B. בא לו אביו של כידור בחלום א"ל: בני בא וקח כיס אחד שהיא מונחת בראש קברי. למחר {בא} כידור לפני ר' מאיר. א"ל: כך וכך ראיתי הלילה. א"ל: חלום דשבת בין השמשות בטל הוא.[4] מה עשה ר' מאיר, שמר כיסו כל אותו היום, ולמוצאי שבת נטל כיסו.[5] למחר באו ר' יהודה ור' יוסי ושאלו כיסם, ואמרו לכידור: תנה כיסינו שהפקדנו אצלך ערב שבת. א"ל: לא היו דברים מעולם.[6] א"ל: למה לא דקדקתם בשם? אמרו לו: מפני מה לא אמרת לנו?[7]

C. מה עשו, משכוהו והכניסוהו לחנות אחת להשקותו יין, להוציא מפיו שישלם להם כיסם. ראו בזקנו שאכל עדשים בביתו. הלכו ואמרו הסימן לאשתו, ואמרו לה: תני לנו הכיסין שהפקדנו לבעלך ערב שבת וזה לך האות, שאכל עדשים היום. אמרה בלבה: באמת אמרו. הלכה לתיבה, ומסרה להם כיסיהם.[8] כשבא כידור לביתו א"ל: איה הכיסין? אמרה לו: והלא שלחת אלי אות, לשלם הכיסין לבעליהן. מה עשה, הלך והרג את אשתו.[9] ובא וראה כי מפני חימוד ממון באין לידי הרג נפש.[10]

---

1. יומא פג, ע"ב: רבי מאיר ורבי יהודה ורבי יוסף היו הולכים יחד בדרך. רבי מאיר היה מדייק בשמות רבי יהודה ורבי יוסי לא היו מדייקים בשמות [בתרגום מארמית]. להלן כל ההשוואות מתייחסות למסכת יומא אלא אם צוין אחרת.

2. כשבאו למקום אחד ביקשו מקום ללון בו ונתנו להם. אמרו לו לבעל האכסניה: מה שמך? אמר להם: כידור שמו. אמר ר' מאיר בלבו: למד מכאן אדם רשע הוא שנאמר, "כי דור תהפוכות המה" (כאן ובהמשך, בתרגום מארמית).

3. במסכת יומא ר' יהודה ור' יוסי הפקידו בידו את כיסיהם, שבהם מונח כספם, שכן באו ללון אצלו בשבת. ר' מאיר לא נתן את כיס הכסף שלו. הלך והניח אותו ליד קבר של אביו של בעל האכסניה.

4. ונראה לו [אביו של בעל האכסניה] בחלומו. [אמר לו]: בוא וקח כיס [כסף] שמונח על ראשו של אותו אדם. למחר אמר להם [לחכמים]: כך נראה לי בחלומי. אמרו לו: חלומות של ליל שבת אין בהם ממש [בתרגום מארמית, כאן ולהלן].

5. הלך רבי מאיר כל היום [של שבת] ושמר את כיסו והביאו.

6. למחר אמרו לו [חכמים לבעל הבית]: תן לנו כיסנו. אמר להם: לא היו דברים מעולם.

7. אמר להם רבי מאיר: מדוע לא דייקתם בשם [ללמוד שאדם רשע הוא]? אמרו לו: מדוע לא אמרת לנו? אמר להם: נאמר שאומר אני שיש לחשוש מכך, אולם להחזיקו [כרשע] האם אמרתי?

8. משכוהו והכניסוהו לחנות. ראו עדשים על שפמו. הלכו ונתנו סימן זה לאשתו. ולקחו את כיסיהם ובאו. במדבר רבה, כ, כא: מעשה באדם אחד שאכל קטנית ולא נטל ידיו וירד לשוק וידיו מטונפות מן הקטנית. ראה אותו חבירו הלך ואמר לאשתו: אומר ליך בעליך סימן שאכל עכשיו קטנית שגרי לו אותה טבעת. נתנה לו (עברית במקור).

9. הלך הוא והרג את אשתו. במדבר רבה: אחר שעה בא בעלה אמר לה: היכן הטבעת? אמרה לו: בא פלוני בסימנין שלך ונתתיה לו. נתמלא עליה חימה והרגה.

10. הוא ששנויה [ברייתא] מים ראשונים האכילו בשר חזיר, מים אחרונים הרגו את הנפש. ולבסוף היו [אף הם] מדייקים בשם. כשבאו לאותו בית שבעל הבית נקרא בלה לא נכנסו אליו. אמרו בוודאי רשע הוא שנאמר: "ואמר לבלה נאפים" (יחזקאל כג, מג), כמו "אחרי בלותי היתה לי עדנה" (בראשית יח, יב), כלומר זקנה בנאופים. במדבר רבה: לפיכך כל שאינו נוטל ידיו לאחר המזון כהורג נפש.

27. Ben Sever and Shefifon Ben Layish (312b–313a)

A. [312b] Once there was a man who was called Ben Sever because he was a great Torah scholar and a man of charity.[1] He heard about a certain orphan in the Land of Israel who had been betrothed to a woman, and seven years had passed and he was not able to wed her. What did Ben Sever do? He took silver and gold vessels and all kinds of foodstuffs, enough to load five donkeys, and walked fifteen days until he arrived in the town of that orphan, and married him to his wife and celebrated for seven days with them and their guests. And afterward he returned home.

B. He came to a high mountain that was eighteen miles long. And there was a great dragon [*tannin*] there that used to bite and burn all who passed by. But when Ben Sever reached that spot, the dragon turned itself into a bridge, and he crossed over it. And when he came down from the mountain, he was met by an extremely ugly man, and that man was the Angel of Death. And the Angel of Death asked: Who are you? He said: I am so-and-so the son of so-and-so, and I went to that certain orphan and arranged his wedding with his wife. He said: I'm the Angel of Death. Your name [lit., your slip] has already been given from heaven, and tomorrow I shall take your soul. At that moment Ben Sever raised his eyes and hands to the heavens and prayed and cried out and wept before the Almighty and said: Master of the Universe, doesn't it say in your Torah that He who keeps the commandment will meet no evil [Ecclesiastes 8:5]? Am I—who went all this way to perform a commandment—to die on the road without declaring my will to my sons? Then, a divine voice was heard saying: You have just been given fifteen days [more], until you go home and declare your will to your sons.

1. In Hebrew the name "Sever" alludes both to his capability to explain (the Torah) and his bright face, i.e., his kindness.

27. בן סבר ושפיפון בן ליש (312ב–313א)

A. מעשה באדם אחד שהיו קורין לו בן סבר, לפי שהיה {גדול} בתורה ובעל צדקה.[1] פעם אחת שמע שיש יתום אחד בארץ ישראל שארס אשה והיה (בן) ז' שנים שלא היה יכול לכונסה.[2] מה עשה בן סבר,[3] נטל כלי כסף וזהב וכל מיני מאכל משאוי חמשה חמורים,[4] והלך מהלך ט"ו יום עד שבא לעיר של אותו יתום, והכניסו עם אשתו ועשה לו שבעה ימי המשתה ושושבינין.[5] ואחר כך הלך לביתו.

B. הלך להר גבוה,[6] שהיה אורכו שמונה עשר מילין.[7] והיה בו תנין גדול אחד,[8] שהיה נושך ושורף כל עובר ושב. וכשהגיע לאותו מקום עשה התנין עצמו כגשר, ועבר עליו. וכשירד מן ההר פגע בו אדם מכוער ביותר, והיה מלאך המות.[9] וא"ל: מי אתה?[10] א"ל: אני פלוני בן פלוני, והלכתי אצל אותו יתום והכנסתיו עם אשתו.[11] א"ל: אני מלאך המות,[12] כבר נתנו פתקיך מן השמים,[13] ולמחר אני נוטל נשמתך. באותה שעה נשא בן סבר עיניו לשמים וכפיו והתפלל וצעק ובכה לפני הקב"ה, ואמר: רבונו של עולם[14] הלא כתוב בתורתך שומר מצוה לא ידע כל דבר רע [קוהלת ח, ה]. אני הלכתי לדבר מצוה אמות בדרך ולא אצוה את בני?[15] יצתה בת קול ואמרה לו: כבר המתינו[16] לך חמש עשרה ימים[17] עד שתלך לביתך ותצוה את בניך.

---

1. הסברים שונים למשמעות השם 'סבר': בכ"י פרמא 2295, 138א–138ב: שהיה בעל סבריו והיה עין טוב. בכ"י קימברידג'-הווארד 39: 115א–116ב: מפני שהיה בעל סברא.
2. מקבילות הסיפור, בהן אין המלה: בן, עשויות להסביר את התחביר התמוה של המשפט הזה. זהו השיקול למחיקת המלה כאן.
3. בכ"י קימברידג'-הווארד: מה עשה אותו צדיק?
4. בכ"י פרמא ובכ"י קימברידג'-הווארד בלי: 'משאוי חמשה חמורים', ותוספת בכ"י פרמא: בגדים.
5. כ"י פרמא: והכניסו לחופה. בכ"י קימברידג'-הווארד: והלך [לאותו] מדינה והכין לו בית ומצע לו מיטה ושלחן ומנורה ונעשה לו שושבין ועשה לו [חופה] ונתן לו כל צרכו. [כתב היד משובש, וההשלמות הן על פי כ"י ירושלים 3182, דפים 125א–126ב.]
6. כ"י קימברידג'-הווארד: פגע בו נהר אחד.
7. כ"י קימברידג'-הווארד: שנים עשר מיל.
8. שם, תוספת של מידות התנין. בכ"י פרמא: ארכו שנים עשר מיל.
9. בכ"י קימברידג'-הווארד חסר זיהויו כמלאך המות.
10. תוספת בכ"י פרמא: וכן מאיזה עיר אתה ומאיזה מקום ומאין אתה בא? בכ"י קימברידג'-הווארד: ואמר לו שלום עליך רבי. אמר לו שלום עליך רבי ומורי. א"ל מאין תבא ולאן אתה הולך?
11. תוספת בכ"י קימברידג'-הווארד: ועכשיו אני חוזר לביתי.
12. כ"י קימברידג'-הווארד: אמ' לו אין אתה מכירני. תשובת בן סבר בכ"י קימברידג'-הווארד: אמ' לו אני מלאך המות בא ליטול את נפשך.
13. כ"י פרמא: כבר נתנה ה' נשמתך בידי.
14. תוספת בכ"י פרמא: רודף צדקה וחסד ומצא חיים וכבוד.
15. כ"י פרמא: מי שהלך לעסוק בצדקה ימות בדרך ולא יצוה לביתו? כ"י קימברידג'-הווארד: ואני הלכתי לעשות פריה ורביה ועתה אני אמות ולא אצוה על ביתי ועל אשתי ועל בני?
16. כ"י פרמא: כבר הוספתי.
17. בכ"י פרמא ובכ"י קימברידג'-הווארד: חמישה ימים וחצי.

C. And he walked along, weeping, until he reached a big city, and he met a certain man at one of the gates [313a]. And he asked: Is there a Torah scholar in the city? The man said: There are a lot of Torah scholars in the city, and there is a great Torah scholar here, whose name is Shefifon Ben Layish. He has twelve thousand disciples who sit before him. Ben Sever said: Lead me to him. And Ben Sever's face shone with the brightness of the sun. When Shefifon saw him, he realized that he was a great scholar. He stood before him with all his disciples. As Ben Sever stood there for a little while, the appearance of his face changed. Shefifon asked: Why has the color of your face changed? Do you need to eat, or is there something else? He said: No. Tell me what's wrong? Ben Sever told him [his story], and Shefifon said: Fear not this thing. Sit with me and teach me Ecclesiastes and Job, and I guarantee that you are not going to die now. He said: How can you guarantee this? Doesn't it say: "A brother cannot redeem a brother [No one can redeem the life of another] or give God a ransom for him" [Psalms 49:8]? Shefifon said: Stay with me and I shall redeem you. He [Ben Sever] immediately sat down with him, teaching him.

D. When Friday came, the Angel of Death came and brought darkness on Shefifon Ben Layish. And they [the disciples] said: Our rabbi, darkness has fallen on the world. [He said]: Go out and see if the whole world has grown dark. If it is dark only around our courtyard, we may rest assured in the compassion of the heavens and that our prayer will be heard. The Angel of Death came and crouched in front of Shefifon Ben Layish. He said to him: Give me that which I deposited with you. What deposit? asked Shefifon. He said: Give me Ben Sever, whose time has come. At that moment, Shefifon made the Angel of Death swear in the name of the Lord of Hosts, and sent him away.

C. והיה הולך ובוכה עד שבא לעיר אחד גדול,[18] ופגע בשער אחד [313א] אדם אחד.[19] וא"ל: כלום יש תלמיד חכם[20] בעיר? א"ל: הרבה תלמידים יש בעיר, ויש כאן תלמיד חכם גדול ושמו שפיפון בן ליש.[21] יש שנים עשר אלף תלמידים בפניו.[22] א"ל: הוליכני אצלו.[23] והיו פניו של בן סבר מבהיקות כזיו חמה.[24] כיון שראה אותו שפיפון, הכיר בו שהוא חכם גדול.[25] עמד לפניו וכל תלמידיו. כיון שעמד מעט, נשתנו פניו.[26] א"ל: למה נשתנו פניך,[27] שמא צריך אתה לאכול או שמא דבר יש לך?[28] א"ל: לאו. הודיעני מה טיבך. מיד הודיעו,[29] וא"ל: אל תתיירא מדבר זה. שב עמי ולמדיני קהלת ואיוב, ואני ערב לך שלא {ת}מות[30] בפעם הזאת.[31] א"ל: היאך אתה יכול לערב בי? והלא כתיב: אח לא פדה יפדה איש ולא יתן לא-להים כפרו [תהלים מט, ח].[32] א"ל: שב עמי ואני פודה אותך. מיד ישב עמו [בן סבר] והיה מלמד לו.[33]

D. כיון שבא יום שישי, בא מלאך המות וחשך כנגד שפיפון בן ליש. ואמרו לו: רבינו, חשך העולם.[34] [אמר להם] צאו וראו אם כל העולם כולו חשך, ואם סביב חצירנו [בלבד] חשך בטוחים אנו ברחמי שמים שתפילתנו נשמעת.[35] בא מלאך המות,[36] ורבץ כנגד שפיפון בן ליש.

---

18. תוספת בכ"י קימברידג'-הווארד: ושמה לוז.

19. תוספת בכ"י קימברידג'-הווארד: נתן לו שלום.

20. כ"י פרמא: חכם שאקבל את פניו.

21. כ"י פרמא: ר' שפיפון בן ליש.

22. בכ"י קימברידג'-הווארד חסר מספר תלמידיו.

23. כ"י פרמא: בבקשה ממך הכניסוני אצלו ואקבל את פניו. גסטר, ספר המעשיות: הוליכני אצלו. שמא נשא ונתן בתורה ונשמח. שכן כתוב: פקודי ה' ישרים משמחי לב [תהלים יט, ט]. הוליכו אצלו.

24. כ"י קימברידג'-הווארד: [והיו לו שמונה] תלמידים חכמים כיון שראו אותו הכירו אותו שהוא היה אדם [גדול וצדיק] לפי שהיו פניו מבהיקות כזיו החמה.

25. חסר בכ"י קימברידג'-הווארד.

26. כ"י פרמא: נשתנו זיו פניו. כ"י קימברידג'-הווארד: כיון [שראו אותו עמדו מפניו הוא וכל חביריו וכשנכנס וישב נשתנו פניו והפכו מוריקות.]

27. כ"י פרמא: ר' שפיפון בן ליש כשנכנסת כאן פניך מבהיקות כזוהר החמה ועכשיו נשתנו. כ"י קימברידג'-הווארד: רבי מה טיבך כשנכנסת היה פניך כזיו החמה ועכשיו השתנו והיו פניך מוריקות?

28. בשני כתבי היד חסר: או שמא דבר יש לך.

29. כ"י פרמא: יש עמי מכל מעדני שבעולם אלא כך וכך היה לי מעשה. כ"י קימברידג'-הווארד: א"ל לאו מיד סיפר לו כל המעשה כמו שהיה.

30. האות תיו תלויה מעל לשורה.

31. כ"י פרמא: שכבר למדתי תורה ותלמוד ומשנה ואגדה ותוספות ושמועות, ואיוב וקהלת לא למדתי אותם ואגדות שלהם. למד אותם לי ואני אערב לך בדבר. כ"י קימברידג'-הווארד: בן סבר למדתי כל התורה שלא נשתייר אלא קהלת ורות ואגדה של קהלת ואיוב.

32. בכ"י פרמא חסר: היאך אתה יכול לערב לי–כפרו.

33. כ"י פרמא: מיד ישב עמו והיה מלמד אותו והיו שניהם מתענין ומבקשים רחמים ותחנונים לפני הקב"ה שיחשיך. עולם כ"י קימברידג'-הווארד: מיד גזר תענית על כלם והיה יושב עמו הימים ומלמדו קהלת ורות ואגדה של קהלת ואיוב.

34. כ"י פרמא: נכנסו תלמידיו אצל ר' שפיפון בן לייש אמרו לו כבר חשך עולם. כ"י קימברידג'-הווארד: באו תלמידיו ואמרו לו רבינו ואור עינינו. חשך כל העולם.

35. כ"י פרמא: אמר להם צאו וראו, אם כל העולם חשך. מה שהיה היה. ואם על חצירינו הוא, כבר רחמינו נשמעין. בכ"י פרמא תוספת: אמרו לו אין חשך אלא סביב חצירינו. כ"י קימברידג'-הווארד: אמר להם צאו וראו אם כל העולם חשך מה שהיה כבר היה ואם על המדינה הזאת חשך בלבד אנו בטוחים שהקב"ה יעשה רצונינו ויקבל תפילתינו ותחנונינו. א"ל תלמידיו: רבי לא חשך אלא על המדינה זו בלבד.

36. כ"י קימברידג'-הווארד: ירד מלאך המות מיד באותו ענן.

E. The Angel of Death returned and stood before the Almighty and said: Master of the Universe, Ben Layish has refused to give me permission [to take the soul of Ben Sever], to save a single soul from my hands. The Almighty said: Ben Layish is very dear to me. Go and tell him that if the soul of Ben Sever is more precious to him than his own, he may die in his stead, and if not, Ben Sever must die. He went and told Shefifon Ben Layish. Shefifon said: My soul is not dearer than his, and nor is his dearer than mine. Go and tell the Almighty that if He lets him live, He should let us both live, and if He takes Ben Sever's life, He should take both our lives. May this pious man not die before us, while we keep on living.

F. The Angel of Death returned to the Almighty and told [this to] Him, while Shefifon was standing in prayer and supplication before the Almighty, until a divine voice came and said: What am I to do with these righteous men that although I decree, they rescind the decree through their righteousness? Go and add two hundred years to each of their lives. It is said that during those two hundred years, there was no famine in the world, and no man died less than seventy years old, and no son died before his father or the younger before the elder, and no woman miscarried the fruit of her womb.

G. And after their death, there was a great famine in the land. They [the people] fasted four days and took upon themselves to give charity and not to covet the money of others. And they stood in prayer and supplication before the Lord. And they said: Master of the Universe. We are the sons of Abraham whom you loved and the seed of Isaac whom you chose—judge us with mercy. Immediately, rains began to fall and relief came and life was enabled, and as it says: "Then your light will break forth like the dawn" [Isaiah 58:8].

א"ל: תן לי הפקדון שהפקדתי אצלך. א"ל: איזה פיקדון?[37] א"ל בן סבר תניהו לי, שכבר הגיע זמנו ליפטר.[38] באותה שעה השביע שפיפון למלאך המות בשם י"י צבאות, וסילקו.[39]

E. חזר מלאך המות ובא ועמד לפני הקב"ה,[40] וא"ל: רבונו של עולם, מאן בן ליש לתת (לו) [לי] רשות [לקחת את נשמת בן סבר, כדי] להציל נפש אחד מידי.[41] א"ל הקב"ה: חביב הוא עלי מאוד. לך ואמור לו אם נפש בן סבר חביב עליך משלך תמות תחתיו, ואם לאו ימות הוא.[42] הלך ואמר לשפיפון בן ליש. א"ל: לא נפשי חביב עלי מנפשו ולא נפשו חביב עלי מנפשי. אלא לך אמור אל הקב"ה אם יחיינו יחיינו יחד ואם ימיתנו, [ימיתנו] יחד. ואל ימות לפנינו צדיק זה ונחייה אחריו.[43]

F. חזר המלאך ואמר להקב"ה. באותה שעה עמד שפיפון בתפלה ובתחנונים לפני הקב"ה, עד שיצתה בת קול ואמרה: מה אעשה לצדיקים הללו שאני גוזר והם מבטלין אותה בצדקתם.[44] לכו והוסיפו על חייהם מאתים שנה לכל אחד מהם. ואמרו: אותם מאתים שנה לא היה רעב בעולם, ולא מת אדם פחות משבעים שנה, ולא מת הבן בפני האב ולא הקטן לפני הגדול, ולא הפילה אשה פרי בטנה.[45]

G. ולאחר מיתתן היה רעב גדול בעולם. עשו ארבע תעניות וקבלו עליהם ליתן צדקה משלהם ולא יחמדו ממון חביריהם. ועמדו בתפלה ובתחנונים לפני המקום. ואמרו לפניו: רבונו של עולם אנו בני אברהם אוהביך וזרע יצחק בחיריך שב עלינו במדת רחמים. מיד ירדו גשמים ונתרווח והתיר שעת היוקר לקיים מה שנ' אז יבקע כשחר אורך [ישעיהו נח, ח].

---

37. כ"י קימברידג'-הווארד: לא הפקדת אצלי כלום.

38. כ"י פרמא: תן לי הפיקדון שהפקדתי אצלך (בן סבר בידי) שכבר בא (יומך) [יומו] להפטר מן העולם; כ"י קימברידג'-הווארד: תן לי נשמתו של בן סבר למיתה.

39. כ"י פרמא: אמר איני מוסרו בידך כ"י קימברידג'-הווארד: א"ל משביע אני עליך שתלך לפני הקב"ה ותאמר לושפיפון בן ליש לא הניח להשליך נפשו של בן סבר למיתה.

40. כ"י קימברידג'-הווארד: הלך ואמר לו כך.

41. כ"י פרמא: לא רצה שפיפון בן ליש למסור בן סבר בידי. חסר בכ"י קימברידג'-הווארד.

42. כ"י פרמא: אם חייך חביבין עליך מסור אתה בן סבר למיתה שכבר הגיע זמנו להפטר מן העולם כ"י קימברידג'-הווארד: לך אמור לשפיפון בן ליש אם נפשך חביבה עליך מנפשו של בן סבר תשלים נפשו למיתה ואם נפשו חביבה עליך כנפשך תמות תחתיו.

43. כ"י פרמא: בא ואמר לו ר' שפיפון איני מבקש להחיות אחר בן סבר אפילו שעה אחת. תוספת בכ"י קימברידג'-הווארד: וכל כך למה להודיע לכל באי עולם כמה חברים צדיקים לפני הק' וכמה כוחן של צדיקים.

44. חסר בכ"י קימברידג'-הווארד.

45. כ"י פרמא: לכן נאמר כי פועל אדם ישלם לו וכאורח איש ימצאהו [איוב לד, יא]. תוספת בכ"י קימברידג'-הווארד: אלא כשהם נולדים כך הם מתים. ולא שלטה חיה רעה בעולם ולא חרב ולא רעב באו עליהם, ועליהם הכתוב אומר רצון יריא[י]ו יעשה ואת שוועתם ישמע ויושיעם [תהלים קמה, יט].

28. Joḥanan and the Scorpion (313b–317b)

A. [313b] Once there was a righteous man who was very rich and old, and he had but one son, whose name was R. Joḥanan. And that R. Joḥanan had a beautiful wife who was very righteous. In time, the old man fell ill and was dying, and he called his son to him and instructed him to occupy himself with the commandments of the Lord and to always be charitable, and he gave him everything he had. And he also ordered him as follows: My son, when the days of mourning me have ended, go to the market and sit there until you see a man bringing some goods to sell in the market. And buy the first goods that you see and don't desist, and bring it to your home and watch over it.

B. The old man died and was buried. His son mourned him for thirty days, and when the days of mourning were ended, R. Joḥanan arose and recalled what his father had commanded him. He went to the marketplace and sat there until he saw a man bearing a very beautiful chalice in his hands. R. Joḥanan said to him: Do you want to sell me the chalice that you carry? He [the man] said to him: Yes. He [Joḥanan] said: For how much? He said: For a hundred gold coins. He said: Give it to me for sixty gold coins. The man refused and walked away. R. Joḥanan said to himself: What shall I do with my father's command if I do not buy it? He called after him and said: Give it to me and take the one hundred gold coins as you said. He said: If you wish to give me two hundred gold coins, I will give it to you, and if not, let me go on my way. He said: I will give you but one hundred, as you said. He went away. And R. Joḥanan came back and said: Against my will I must buy it in order to fulfill my father's will. He called after him and said to him: Take two hundred as you said. The man said to him: If you wish to give me a thousand gold coins for it, I will give it to you, and if not, leave me be. R. Joḥanan thought to himself that he would continually raise the price and that he must buy it even against his will, because this was what his father had commanded. What did he do? He brought the man to his home and gave him a thousand gold coins for the chalice, and so it was his to safeguard. He tried many times to open the chalice but was unable to do so.

C. And it was [in the days] before Passover. When they sat down to eat on the first night of Passover, he said to his wife: Bring me the chalice that I bought as my father commanded, to place it on the table in honor of the holiday. The righteous woman brought it to him. R. Joḥanan took it and tried again to open it, and it opened immediately. And inside he found a smaller chalice in the larger one. And he opened the smaller one and found a small scorpion inside it. And they were greatly amazed. And R. Joḥanan took the scorpion and fed it, and it ate and it ran about his neck and

28. יוחנן והעקרב (313ב–317ב)

A. [313ב] **מעשה** בחסיד אחד שהיה עשיר מאוד[1] וזקן, ולא היה לו כי אם בן אחד ושמו ר' יוחנן. והיה לאותו ר' יוחנן אשה יפה וצדקת מאוד. לימים חלה אותו זקן למות, וקרא לבנו וציוהו להתעסק במצות הבורא ולעשות צדקה תמיד, ונתן לו כל אשר לו. וגם ציוהו וכך אמר לו: בני, כשיתמו ימי בכי אבלך לך בשוק, ושב שם עד שתראה שום אדם מביא שום סחורה למכור בשוק. ואותה סחורה שתראה ראשונה קנה אותה ואל תניח, ותביא אותה לביתך ותהיה לך למשמרת.

B. נפטר הזקן והלך לבית עולמו. ויבך אותו בנו שלושים יום, ויתמו ימי בכיתו. ויקם ר' יוחנן, ויזכור ממה שציוהו אביו. הלך לשוק וישב שם, וראה איש אחד נושא בידו גביע אחד יפה מאוד. א"ל ר' יוחנן: רוצה אתה למכור לי זה הגביע שאתה נושא? א"ל: הן. א"ל: בכמה? א"ל: במאה זהובים. א"ל: תן אותה לי בששים זהובים. ולא רצה, והלך לו. אמר ר' יוחנן בלבו: מה אעשה ממצות אבי אם לא אקנה אותו. קרא אחריו ואמר לו: תן אותה לי, וקח מאה זהובים כאשר דברת. א"ל: אם תרצה ליתן לי ב' מאות זהובים אתן אותה לך, ואם לאו הניחני לילך לדרכי. א"ל: לא אתן לך כי אם ק', כאשר אמרת. הלך לו. וחזר ר' יוחנן ואמר: בעל כרחי צריך אני לקנותו בשביל מצות אבי. קרא אחריו ואמר לו: קח הב' מאות כאשר דברת. א"ל האיש: אם רצונך ליתן לי אלף זהובים בעבורו אתן לך, ואם לאו הניחני. חשב ר' יוחנן בלבו כי הוא הולך ומייקר אותו תמיד, וצריך הוא לקנותו בעל כורחו משום מצות אביו. מה עשה, הביאו לביתו ונתן לו אלף זהובים בעבורו ויהי לו למשמרת. ופעמים הרבה נסה לפתוח אותו, ולא יכול לפתחו.

C. והיה בפני חג הפסח. וכשישבו לאכול בליל ראשון של פסח אמר לאשתו: הביאי לי הגביע שקניתי במצות אבי, ויהיה על השלחן לכבוד יום טוב. הלך הצדקת והביאה אותו. לקחו ר' יוחנן לנסות לפותחו, ויפתח אותו מיד, וימצא בתוכו גביע קטן בתוך הגדול. ויפתח הקטן וימצא בתוכו עקרב אחד קטן, ויתמהו מאוד. ולקחו ר' יוחנן ונתן לו לאכול, ואכל וירץ סביב צוארו ויחבק לו וינשק לו. וכשהיה שבע הלך לו ונכנס בתוך הגביע קטן, וסגר אותו ר' יוחנן, וישם הקטן תוך הגדול כאשר בתחילה. ויאמר ר' יוחנן אל אשתו: לא בחנם ציוני אבי דבר זה נאכילנו ונגדלנו ונדע מה יהיה בסופו. האכילוהו בכל יום וגדל העקרב ולא היה יכול עוד ליכנס בגביע קטן, והיה

1. אין לסיפור מקבילות קודמות. גרסה מאוחרת מצויה במעשה בוך, #143; מעשה בוך, גסטר, #143, 1, 265–276. הסיפור פורסם על ידי גסטר בספר המעשיות, #305, 197–205.

it embraced and kissed him. And when it was full, it went inside the smaller chalice, and R. Joḥanan sealed it and placed the smaller one inside the larger, as it was from the start. And R. Joḥanan said to his wife: Not for nothing did my father order me to do this thing. We will feed it and raise it and see what happens in the end. They fed it every day, and the scorpion grew until it no longer fit inside the smaller chalice, and they placed it inside [314a] the larger one, and it continued to grow greatly until he had to build it a house to live in. And R. Joḥanan became impoverished, because the scorpion ate everything they had until he grew so big that it could no longer fit inside any house and it lived in the courtyard. And it grew and grew so much that it was like a great mountain, and it continued to eat until R. Joḥanan no longer had any food left to give it to eat. R. Joḥanan wept and said to his wife: What more can we do to give it food, because we no longer have anything because it has eaten everything we had? The righteous woman said: Sell your robe today and buy food for it, and I will sell my mantle tomorrow and give it to him. And that is what they did, and they no longer had anything left at all. And R. Joḥanan came before the scorpion and fell on his face and wept and prayed to God and said: Master of the Universe. You know that I have given everything I had in order to fulfill my father's command, and we have nothing left. I don't know what more I should do, for we no longer have anything. I and my wife and our children are naked and barefoot and hungry and thirsty and have nothing. Support us, O God, for you are merciful and righteous to all your creatures, and tell me, my Lord my savior, the nature of this scorpion that I have grown and raised and what will happen with him.

D. And the scorpion opened its mouth and said: The Lord has heard your prayer and given me permission to speak to you. I know that you have done everything you could and never refrained from doing whatever you could to please me. And now, you may make a wish and I will fulfill it. R. Joḥanan answered: If so, then teach me all the languages in the world. The scorpion taught him, and he learned well and could understand the language of beasts and birds and animals and all the languages in the world. And your righteous wife who would take such trouble for me and served me skillfully may also ask for one thing from me, and I will give it to her. And the woman came and said to him: Sir, give me great riches so that I may support my husband and family decently. It said to her: Follow me and bring wagons and horses and donkeys and any beasts you can bring with you, and I will load them with silver and gold and precious stones and pearls. And they did as it had instructed and followed it until it took them to a forest called Debey Illay, and they entered the thick of the forest and the scorpion began to whistle. And all the

בתוך [314א] הגדול, וגדל לרוב מאוד עד שעשה לו בית להיות בה. ונפל ר' יוחנן מאוד מנכסיו כי זה העקרב אוכל כל מה שיש להם, עד שגדל שלא היה יכול ליכנס בשום בית והיה בחצר. וגדל מאד עד שהיה כהר גדול ואכל, ולא היה לר' יוחנן עוד מה ליתן לו לאכול. בכה ר' יוחנן ואמר לאשתו: מה נעשה עוד לתת לו לאכול כי אין בידינו מאומה, כי הוא אכל כל אשר היה לנו. אמרה לו הצדקת: מכור טליתך היום וקנה לו לאכול, ואני אמכור סרבלי למחר ואתן לו. וכן עשו, ולא היה להם יותר מאומה. ויבא ר' יוחנן בפני העקרב ויפל לפניו ויבך ויתפלל אל י"י ויאמר: רבונו של עולם גלוי וידוע לפניך כי נתתי כל מה שהיה לי בשביל לקיים מצות אבי, ולא נשאר לי מאומה ולא ידעתי מה יש לי לעשות ממנו כי אין לי עוד כלום, ואני ואשתי ובניי ערומים ויחיפים ורעבים וצמאים מכל טוב. פרנסנו א-להי כי אתה רחמן וחסיד על כל מעשיך, והודיעני א-להי ישעי מה טיבו של זה העקרב שגדלתי ורוממתי, ומה יהיה בסופו.

D. ויפתח העקרב את פיו ויאמר: שמע א-להים תפלתך ונתן לי רשות לדבר אליך. ידעתי כי עשית לי כל מה שתוכל ולא מנעת אותך מליהנות לי בכל כחך, ועתה שאל נא לי דבר אחד מה שתרצה ואתן לך. ענה ר' יוחנן: אם כן הוא למדיני <~~שפ~~> כל לשונות שבעולם. למד לו, והיה יודע בטוב להבין לשון בהמות ועופות וחיות וכל לשונות שבעולם. ואשתך הצדקת אשר היתה תדיר מטרחת בעבורי וזריזה לשמשני תשאל ממני דבר אחד ממה שתרצי, ואני אתן לה. ותבא האשה ותאמר לו: אדוני {תֵן} עושר לי גדול כדי שאוכל לפרנס בעלי ובני ביתי בכבוד. אמר לה: בואו אחרי והביאו עגלות וסוסים וחמורים וכל מה שתוכלו מבהמות עמכם, ואעמוס אותם מכסף ומזהב ומאבנים טובות ומרגליות. וכן עשו וילכו אחריו עד שהוליכם אל יער אחד ששמו יער דבי עילאי,[2] ונכנסו בעובי היער והתחיל העקרב לשרוק בפיו. ובאו אליו כל החיות שבעולם נחשים ועקרבים וכל מיני חיות, וכל אחד ואחד היה מביא לו דורון כסף וזהב ואבנים טובות ומרגליות, וישליכו בפניו כשם שמביאין דורון למלך. ויאמר העקרב אל ר' יוחנן ולאשתו: קחו לכם ומלאו אמתחותיכם והעגלות וכל מה שיש לכם מלאו הכל, כדי שיהיה לכם הרבה שלא תצטרכו לשום אדם. ויעשו כן. ויאמר ר' יוחנן אל העקרב: אל נא יחר לאדוני ואדברה אליו, הודיעני מי אתה ומאין באתה. א"ל: בן אדם הראשון אנכי [314ב] שבא אדם הראשון על כל בהמה וחיה ועוף, וכשבא על אמי הוליד אותי.[3] וכן אני הולך ומתמעט ~~ב~~כל אלף שנה עד סוף האלף, ולאחר האלף אני גדל עד סוף האלף שנה אחרות,[4] ולא הייתי בכלל ביום אכלך ממנו מות תמות.[5] א"ל ר'

---

2. ראו חולין נט, ע"ב, ופירוש רש"י שהוא שם יער.

3. על מסורות אגדה על לילית כדמות חוה הראשונה (ראו יסיף, סיפורי בן סירא, 64–67).

4. ראו מוטיב עוף החול בבראשית רבה יט, ה (מהדורת אלבק, 174–175), ופירוש רש"י לאיוב כט, יח: עוף ושמו חול ולא נקנסה עליו מיתה שלא טעם מעץ הדעת ולבסוף אלף שנה מתחדש וחוזר לנערותו.

5. השוו לבראשית ג, ג.

animals in the world came—snakes and scorpions and all sorts of animals—and each brought it [the scorpion] a gift of gold and silver and precious stones and pearls and cast them before it like one brings a gift to a king. The scorpion said to R. Joḥanan and his wife: Take this and fill your sacks and wagons and fill everything you have so that you will have a great deal of treasure and never be in need of any man. And so they did. R. Joḥanan said to the scorpion: Please do not be angry with me if I speak to you, but please tell me who you are and where you come from. It said to him: I am the son of Adam [314b], who before the creation of Eve lay with all the female beasts, animals, and birds, and when he lay with my mother, she bore me. And so every thousand years I diminish until the end of that millennium, and then, after a thousand years, I grow and increase in size until the end of another millennium. And because I was not there on the day they ate from the Tree of Knowledge, I became immortal. R. Joḥanan said to the scorpion: If you are the son of Adam, bless me. It said to him: May God save you from all the bad things that the future holds for you. R. Joḥanan was surprised and said to him: What are the bad things that the future holds for me? And the scorpion did not want to tell him anything. It bid farewell and departed, and R. Joḥanan returned home and was extremely rich and wise.

E. The king heard of R. Joḥanan's wisdom and sent for him and asked him about many matters requiring wisdom and found him to be exceedingly wise and clever in all matters. And the king was more fond of him than of all his other wise men. And that king did not have a wife. One day, his wise men came to him and said: Your majesty, it is unseemly for you to be always without a wife, and you have no son to sit on your throne after you. After your soul rests, your kingdom will remain without an heir, and the kingdom will be left to a stranger, and no memory of you will remain after you are gone. And so, a beautiful young woman should be sought for your majesty throughout all the countries of his kingdom, and he should marry her, and she will be his wife. But the king did not wish to listen to them about taking a wife until they came to him a second and third and fourth time and many more times and compelled him very much. He said to them: If you indeed wish me to take a wife, give me three days, and I will give you an answer if I should indeed take a wife or not. They gave him three days. On the second day, he went to sit out in his courtyard and was completely absorbed in his thoughts. While he was contemplating, a raven flew above him, and in his claws it held a very beautiful strand of hair that looked like gold, and that strand of hair fell on the king. He took it and on the third day brought it to his wise men. He said to them: You wish me to take a

יוחנן: כי בן אדם הראשון אתה, ברכיני. אמר לו: המקום יצילך מן הרעות העתידות לבא עליך. תמה ר' יוחנן ואמר לו: מה הן הרעות העתידות לבא עלי? ולא רצה לומר לו כלום. נפטר ממנו בשלום, והלך לו ור' יוחנן שב לביתו והיה עשיר גדול וחכם אין כמוהו.

E. שמע המלך מן חכמתו ושלח אחריו ושאל לו חכמות ועניינים הרבה, ומצא אותו חכם מחוכם ונבון לכל דבר, והיה המלך אוהב אותו מכל חכמיו. ואותו המלך לא היה לו אשה. ~~ו~~ליום אחד באו לפניו חכמיו ואמרו לו: אדונינו המלך לא נאה לך להיות תמיד בלא אשה, ואין לך בן לישב על כסא מלכותך אחריך. וכשתנוח נפשך תשאר המלכות בלא יורש וישאר המלכות ביד איש נכרי, ולא יהי לך זכר בעולם הזה. לכן יבקשו לאדונינו נערה יפה בכל מדינות מלכותו, וישאנה ותהיה לו לאשה.[6] ולא רצה המלך לשמוע אליהם ליקח אשה, עד שבאו לפניו פעם שנייה ושלישית ורביעית וכמה פעמים, עד שהכריחו אותו מאד. אמר להם: אם כן הוא שאתם רוצים שאקח אשה, תנו לי זמן שלשה ימים ואשיב לכם דבר אם דין הוא שאקח אותה אם לאו. נתנו לו זמן שלשה ימים. יום שיני הלך וישב לו בחצירו נתפס מאד ממחשבות. בתוך המחשבות שהיה פרח עורב אחד עליו, והביא בין רגליו שער אחד יפה מאד ודומה לזהב, ונפל על המלך אותו שער. לקחו והביאו אל חכמיו ביום השלישי. אמר להם: אתם רוצים שאקח אשה, אם תוכלו להביא לי אותה אשה שזה השער היה מראשה מוטב ואשאנה, ואם לא תוכלו אחתוך ראשיכם. אמרו לו: תנה לנו זמן שלשה ימים לידע מה נעשה. נתן להם, ונתייעצו יחד ואמרו אין איש בעולם יכול לעשות דבר זה אלא ר' יוחנן, כי הוא יודע כל הלשונות ואין חכם כמוהו בכל הארץ.[7] באו ביום השלישי אל

6. השוו לאסתר ב, ג.

7. השוו למלכים א, ה, י–יא.

wife. If you can bring me the woman to whom this hair belongs, I will marry her; if you cannot, I will cut off your heads. They said: Give us three days to decide what to do. He gave them the time, and they consulted one another and said there is no one in the world who can do this thing other than R. Joḥanan, because he knows all the languages and there is none wiser than him in the whole world. They came on the third day to the king and said: There is a wise man in your kingdom named R. Joḥanan, and he knows all the languages in the world, and there is no one who can do that which you ask but him. The king sent for him. And as this was happening, a raven flew over R. Joḥanan's study hall and shouted: May God save R. Joḥanan from all the bad things that the future holds for you. R. Joḥanan heard and was very surprised, because those were the very words with which the scorpion had blessed him.

F. Then the king's servants came to him and said: Come now to the king, because he has sent [315a] for you. R. Joḥanan was very afraid. He arose and went to the king and bowed down before him. The king said to him: I have heard that you are wise and clever and know all the languages in the world. I want to take a wife and beget children, because it is not proper for a king not to have a wife. That is why I want you to bring me the woman to whom this hair belongs, because a raven brought it and cast it before me, and I saw that it belonged to a woman, and it is her whom I want. R. Joḥanan answered: No king, minister, governor, or ruler has ever asked to do the thing that you ask, to seek out a certain woman according to a strand of hair that you have in your hand. The king said to him: If you do not bring her to me, I will cut off your head and the heads of all of your coreligionists. R. Joḥanan said to him: If that is the case, give me three years' time to seek her out and bring her to you. He gave him the time. R. Joḥanan went home and made a will for his wife and sons and told them the whole story. His sons and daughters and wife wept for him for the worries of his heart. He bid them farewell and set out to the forest of Debey Illay, saying to himself: Perhaps I will come across the scorpion that I nurtured and raised high. And he took along three loaves of bread and ten gold coins.

G. He entered the thick of the forest and encountered a very large dog, the likes of which he had never seen before, because the beasts in that forest were strange and very large. And the dog shouted and groaned, saying: Master of the Universe, you created me a large and strange dog, and I am unable to find enough food to satisfy myself because a handful cannot satisfy a lion, and if I were small like other dogs, I could be satisfied with a small amount. And you are merciful and compassionate to all your creatures. Did you create me to die of starvation?

המלך ואמרו לו כך: חכם אחד יש במלכותך ושמו ר' יוחנן והוא יודע כל לשונות שבעולם, ואין אדם יכול לעשות דבר זה שאתה שואל כי אם אותו. שלח המלך אחריו. ובין כך ובין כך עבר עורב אחד פורח על בית מדרשו של ר' יוחנן וצועק ואומר: המקום יצילך ר' יוחנן מן הרעות העתידות לבא עליך. שמע ר' יוחנן ותמה מאד, כי בלשון הזה ברכו העקרב.

F. ואז באו עבדי המלך אליו ויאמרו: קום בא אל המלך כי הוא שלח [315א] אחריך. ויחרד לר' יוחנן חרדה גדולה. ויקם {וילך} אל המלך, וישתחו לפני המלך. ויאמר לו המלך: שמעתי עליך שאתה חכם ונבון ויודע כל הלשונות שבעולם. ורוצה אני ליקח אשה, שאין דין מלכות להיות בלא אשה ובלא בנים. לכן לך והביא לי אותה אשה שזה השער יש מראשה, כי עורב אחד הביא אותו והשליך אותו לפני וידעתי כי שער ראש אשה הוא, וחפץ אני בה. ענה ר' יוחנן ואמר: לא כל מלך שר ונגיד ושלטון לא שאל בדבר הזה שאתה שואל, לבקש אשה אחת אחרי שער אחד שיש בידך. א"ל המלך: אם לא תביאנה לי אחתוך ראשך וכל אנשי דתך.[8] א"ל ר' יוחנן: אם כן הוא, תנה לי זמן שלש שנים לבקש אותה ולהביאה אליך. נתן לו זמן. והלך ר' יוחנן לביתו וציוה את אשתו ואת בניו, וסיפר להם כל המעשה. ויבכו אותו בניו ובנותיו ואשתו על דאגת לבו. נטל רשות מהם והלך לו דרך אותו יער דבי עילאי, כי אמר אולי יקרה לפני העקרב שגדלתי ורוממתי. ונשא עמו שלשה חלות לחם ועש{ר}ה זהובים.

8. השוו אסתר ג, ח: "ודתיהם שונות מכל עם ואת דתי המלך אינם עושים."

R. Joḥanan answered him: The Almighty did not create you to die of starvation, because he is merciful toward all his creatures. Take a loaf of bread of mine and eat. The dog took it and ate and said: May God save you from all the bad things that the future holds for you, and may God allow me to return the kindness that you have shown to me. R. Joḥanan continued on his way, when he encountered a very large raven unlike any other, screaming and groaning, speaking as did the dog. And R. Joḥanan gave him the second loaf of bread he had taken with him. And the raven blessed him as did the dog in its tongue. R. Joḥanan continued on his path and left the forest. He then saw a river, and he sat on the banks of the river and ate the remaining loaf and drank from the water. Then he saw a fisherman in the water. And the fisherman said to him: Would you like to buy what I catch in my trap? He answered: Yes. He said: How much will you charge me? He said to him: The ten gold coins you have in your pocket. R. Joḥanan was surprised and said [thought]: Who told him that I have ten gold coins in my pocket? It can only be from God. He took the coins and gave them to him. The fisherman pulled out his trap, and in it was a very large and beautiful fish that was worth [315b] a hundred gold coins. When the fisherman saw the great fish, he was exceedingly vexed at the transaction he had made. The fisherman then cast the fish before him. The fish came and bowed down before R. Joḥanan and said: Sir, you know that I am big, and you are unable to carry me to and fro, and if you wish to eat of me, a small piece will give you much. Do that which is right and good and cast me back into the river where you found me, and with God's help I will pay you your reward, and God will be with you and may He save you from all the bad things that the future holds for you, and may God allow me to return the kindness that you have shown to me. R. Joḥanan threw the fish back into the river, and the fisherman saw this and became very angry. He said to him: Why did you do that? Why did you throw it back into the river? That was a foolish thing to do because it was worth a hundred gold coins. R. Joḥanan said: That is what I decided to do because as it says: "He has compassion on all the creatures He made" [Psalms 145:9].

H. R. Joḥanan arose and walked along the bank of the river, and on the other side saw a large, beautiful city resting on the bank of the river. And in the city were two beautiful women: One was the queen of that city, a very righteous woman and a virgin whom no man had known, and she was the most beautiful woman in the land. The other woman was her maidservant. The queen said to her maidservant: See that righteous man on the other side of the river. He has come for me and seeks to give me to a very evil king. Although that king has never seen me before and has

G. נכנס בתוך עובי היער, ופגע כלב אחד גדול מאד כי לא ראה כמוהו מימיו, כי הבהמות שבאותו יער היו משונות וגדולות מאד. והיה הכלב צועק ומתאנח ואומר: רבונו של עולם, יצרתני כלב גדול ומשונה כי לא יכולתי למצוא לאכול די סיפוקי, כי אין הקומץ משביע את הארי. ואילו הייתי קטן כמו כלבים אחרים הייתי מתפרנס מדבר מועט. ואתה רחום וחנון על כל מעשיך וכי בראתני למות ברעב? ענה ר' יוחנן וא"ל: לא בראך הקב"ה למות ברעב, כי רחמיו על כל מעשיו. טול חלת לחם שיש לי ואכול. לקח הכלב אותה ואכלה, ואמר: המקום יצילך מכל מיני פורעניות העתידות לבא עליך, ויתן לי [ה]מקום שאוכל לגמול לך זה החסד שעשית עמדי. הלך לו ר' יוחנן ופגע בעורב אחד גדול ואין כמותו, צועק וגונח ואומר כאשר אמר הכלב. ונתן לו ר' יוחנן החלה האחרת שהיה לו. וברכו העורב כאשר עשה הכלב בלשונו. הלך ר' יוחנן לדרכו ויצא מן היער, וראה בפניו נהר אחד. הלך וישב על שפת הנהר ואכל שם החלה שנשאר לו ושתה מן המים. וראה כנגדו דייג אחד במים. וא"ל הדייג: רוצה אתה לקנות מה שתעלה מצידתי? א"ל: הן. א"ל: בכמה תתן אותו לי? א"ל: באותן עשרה זהובים שיש בכיסך. תמה ר' יוחנן ואמר: מי סיפר לזה שהיו עשרה זהובים בכיסי, אין זה כי אם מאת הא-להים. לקחם ונתנם לו. עלה מצודתו והיה בה דג גדול ויפה מאד, והיה שווה [315ב] מאה זהובים. כשראה הדייג הדג גדול, חרה לו עד מות על הסחורה טובה שעשה לו. בא הדייג והשליך הדג בפניו. בא הדג ונשתטח לפני ר' יוחנן ואמר לו: אדוני, אתה ידעת כי אני גדול ואין יכולת בידך להביאני אנה ואנה, ואם תרצה לאכול ממני, מחתיכה קטנה יש לך הרבה. עשה הישר והטוב והשליכני אל הנהר אשר יצאתי משם, ובעזרת הצור אני משלם לך משכורתך ויהיה א-להים עמך ויצילך מכל הרעות העתידות לבא עליך, ויתן לי [ה]מקום לגמולך החסד שעשית עמדי. בא ר' יוחנן והשליך אותו אל תוך הנהר, והדייג ראה והטיב חרה לו. וא"ל: מדוע עשית כן להשליכו אל הנהר עתה הסכלת עשה, כי הוא היה שוה מאה זהובים. א"ל ר' יוחנן: כך עלה בדעתי לעשות, משום דכתיב ורחמיו על כל מעשיו [תהילים קמה, ט].

H. קם ר' יוחנן והלך לו על שפת הנהר, וראה מעבר הנהר כרך גדול ויפה ויושב על הנהר. ובפני[ם] הכרך היו שם שתי נשים, האחת היתה מלכה מן אותו כרך וצדקת מאד והיא בתולה ואיש לא ידעה והיא היתה אשה יפה אין כמוה בכל הארץ. והאחרת היתה שפחתה. אמרה המלכה אל שפחתה: ראי זה הצדיק שבעבר הנהר, הוא בא אחרי ורוצה הוא להוליכני עמו ולתתו לי מלך

never heard of me, a certain raven took one of the hairs from my head and brought it to him. And he sent this righteous man after me. And I know that I will go with him if he can fulfill three things that I will ask of him. Go and tell the sailor to bring him to me. The sailor went after him and brought him before the queen.

I. R. Joḥanan stood before her and bowed down and greeted her. She said to him: Welcome, where have you come from, and where are you going? He said: I have come from a distant land to seek a certain woman whose hair resembles this hair that I have brought with me here. She said to him: Stay with us for a month, and we will give you what you are asking for. And he remained with her. And the queen commanded her chief servant to watch over R. Joḥanan. And he took him and washed and anointed him with oils and gave him the finest things to eat and drink. After a month, R. Joḥanan came to the queen and said to her: My lady, tell me if I can find what I seek in your kingdom. She said to him: Yes, I, the woman standing before you, am the woman you are looking for. And this is the sign—that my hair resembles the hair that you carry. Know well that I will go with you, but you must do three things if you wish me to go with you. R. Joḥanan said to her: Do not delay me; God has made my journey successful. Come with me and save all the people of Israel, because the eyes of all the people of Israel are on me. If I do not bring you before the king within four months, know that he is resolved to destroy all Israel's enemies [lit., all of the people of Israel]. She said to him: I have two barrels. I want you to bring me one filled with water from Gehenna and the other with water from the Garden of Eden. R. Joḥanan wept and said: [316a] Who can do such a thing? She said: If you do not do this, I will not go with you. He said to her: If so, then bring me the two barrels, and I will do my best. They brought them to him.

J. He crossed the river until he reached the Debey Illay forest, and he sat there and wept bitterly and prayed to the Almighty and said: Master of the Universe, may it be your will that you send me the raven to whom I gave of my bread and who swore to return my kindness. The raven came and flew above him and said to him: Here sir, I am here to do your bidding. Tell me what to do and I will do it, because God has heard your voice and seen your suffering. R. Joḥanan said to him: Blessed is God, who has not taken His compassion and truth from His servant, I am on the way to the woman I sought. He took the barrels and hung them on the neck of the raven and said to it: Bring one filled with water from the Garden of Eden and the other filled with water from Gehenna. The raven said to him: I will do as you ask. He sent the raven off, and it continued on its journey until it reached the river of Gehenna, in which it immersed to fill one barrel with the water of the river. And the water

אחד רשע אין כמוהו. אמנם לא ראה אותי מימיו ולא שמע ממני, אך עורב אחד לקח אחד משערות ראשי והביאו אליו. והוא שלח זה הצדיק אחרי. וידעתי כי אלך עמו, אם יוכל לעשות לי שלשה דברים שאשאל ממנו. לכי ותאמר אל הספן להביאו אלי. הלך הספן אחריו והביאו לפני המלכה.

I. עמד ר' יוחנן לפניה וישתחו לה, וישאל אליה לשלום. ותאמר לה: ברוך אתה בבואך. מאין באתה ולאן אתה הולך? אמר לה: מארץ רחוקה באתי, ולבקש אשה אחת אשר שער ראשה דומות לשער זה שאני נושא הובאתי הנה. אמרה לו: שב עמנו חדש ימים ונשיב לך דבר ממה שתבקש. וישב עמה. ותציו המלכה לאשר על ביתה לשים עיניו ר' יוחנן. ויקחהו וירחצהו ויסכהו, ויתן לו לאכול ולשתות מכל טוב. ויהי מקץ חדש ימים ויבא ר' יוחנן אל המלכה, ויאמר אליה: אדונתי, הגידי לי אם אוכל למצוא מה שאני מבקש במלכותיך. אמרה לו: הן, אני האשה הנצבת לקראתיך שאתה מבקש, וזה לך האות ששערותיי דומות לשער שאתה נושא. ותדע כי אלך עמך, אך צריך אתה לעשות לי שלשה דברים אם תרצה שאלך עמך. אמר לה ר' יוחנן: אל תאחרי אותי וי"י הצליח דרכי. באי עמי והציל כל ישראל, כי עיני כל ישראל עלי. אם לא אביאך אל המלך בתוך <ארבע>חדשים, דעי כי הוא יאבד שארית שונאיהם של ישראל.[9] אמרה לו: שני דרדורים יש לי, רוצה אני שתביא לי האחד מלא ממים של גהינם והאחר של מים מגן עדן.[10] בכה ר' יוחנן ואמר: [316א] מי יוכל לעשות זאת. אמרה לו: אם לא תעשה כן, לא אלך עמך. אמר לה: אם כן הוא הביאי לי אותן שני דרדורים, ואעשה יכולתי. הביאו לו.

J. ועבר הנהר והלך עד שבא אל יער דבי עילאי, וישב שם ובכה במר נפש והתפלל לפני הקב"ה ואמר לפניו, רבונו של עולם יהי רצון מלפניך שתשלח לי העורב אשר נתתי מלחמי אליו ונדר לי לשלם גמולי. בין כך ובין כך בא העורב פורח עליו ואמר לו: הנני אדוני הנני מוכן למשלחתך, גזור עלי ואקיימה כי שמע י"י את קולך וראה את ענייך. א"ל ר' יוחנן: ברוך י"י אשר לא עזב חסדו ואמתו מעם עבדו, אנכי בדרך נחני בית האשה אשר ~~אני~~ בקשתי. לקח הדרדורים ותלה אותם על צואר העורב וא"ל: תביא לי אחד מלא ממים של גן עדן והאחר של מים מגהינם. א"ל: כך אעשה כאשר דברת. וישלח העורב מ מאתו וילך לדרכו ויבא ויטבול בתוך נהר גהינם וימלא האחד מימי הנהר. והיו המים רותחין מאד וחמים ביותר כי לא יוכל אדם לשים אצבעו בתוך המים מפני חמימותן, ואילמלא רחמי שדי עליו בזכות הצדיק, היה נשרף. ומשם הלך אל נהר ההולך בתוך גן עדן, וימלא האחר מן אותם מים. ויטבול במים וירחץ כל גופו, וישב בשרו וירפא מן החבורות והפצעים אשר היו לו ממי גהינם. נטל דרדוריו והלך לו, ובא אל ר' יוחנן וא"ל: הנני אדוני הנני, עשיתי כאשר ציויתני, ולך לשלום וא-להי ישראל יצילך מכל רע. לקח ר' יוחנן

9. "יאבד שארית שנאיהם של ישראל" – בלשון שגיא נהור, ומושא המשפט הוא ישראל ולא שונאי ישראל. השוו אסתר ד, יג-יד, שם מרדכי מצווה את אסתר לקבל על עצמה אחריות להצלת עמה.

10. דרדור הוא חבית של עץ על גלגלים, או חבית עגולה הניתנת להתגלגל (אבן שושן: "דרדור", והפנייתו למסכת כלים טו, א). וראו הוראה דומה נתן בן יחיאל, ערוך השלם, ג', ערך "דרדור", 145.

boiled furiously and was so hot that no human could put his finger into the water because of the heat, and if not for God's mercy because of that righteous man, it [the raven] would have been burned. And from there, it went to the river that flows inside the Garden of Eden, and there, it filled the other barrel with water. And it immersed itself in that water and bathed its entire body in it, and its flesh was restored and cured of all the bruises and wounds that it had from the waters of Gehenna. It took the two barrels and came to R. Joḥanan and said to him: Here I am, sir, here I am. I have done as you commanded. Go in peace, and may the God of Israel save you from all evil. R. Joḥanan took the barrels and returned to the queen. He said to her: My lady, here are the barrels filled with the water of the Garden of Eden and the water of Gehenna, as you requested. The queen took them from his hand, and she saw the water and saw that the waters of Gehenna were exceedingly hot and foul smelling, and the waters of the Garden of Eden were very cool, and their fragrance was as the fragrance of heaven. The queen was very joyful, and she said to him: "May all who take notice of you be blessed" [Ruth 2:19].

K. There is one more thing I need you to do: It has been twenty-five years since my father died and gave me his ring, and it had one precious stone, the likes of which there was nowhere else in the whole world. One day, I went to sail on the river, and the ring fell from my hand into the river. I asked my servants to build a dam to take the water a different way, but they did not find it. If you could bring it to me, I will go with you without delay. R. Joḥanan said to her: Who can do that? Something that has been lost in the river for twenty-five years—how could anyone find it? She said to him: If you do not bring it to me, I will not go with you. R. Joḥanan went to the bank of the river, up to the place where he had cast in the fish that he had bought in the river. He sat there and wept and prayed to God, saying: May it be your will God the Lord of Israel that you send me the fish that swore to reward me for what I did for it. As he was talking and praying, the fish came and said to him: Sir, God has heard your prayer, and I am here to do your bidding, and I know what it is you ask. And God knows that I do not [316b] have it in my possession, but I know well the fish that took it and who still has it in his possession. I must summon him for judgment before the whale, and I will tell him the whole story and that the lives of the people of Israel depend on that ring, and with the help of the Creator he will give it to me. The fish went and stood before the whale and said to him: Sir, listen to me. There is a righteous man who is standing on the bank of the river, and he related the whole story. The whale said to him: Go after the fish and ask him if he knows where the ring is, and I will ask him to give it to you. So the

הדרדורים, והלך לו ובא אל המלכה. ואמר לה: אדונתי, הנה הדרדורים מלאים ממי גן עדן וממי גהינם כאשר שאלת. לקחם המלכה מידו וירא המים ויכירם, כי אותן מים של גהינם היו חמים ביותר ומוסרחים מאד, ואותן של גן עדן קרים מאד וריחם כריח של בשמים. שמח המלכה שמחה גדולה,[11] ואמרה לו: יהי מכירך ברוך [רות ב, יט].

K. עוד דבר אחד יש לי שצריך אתה לעשות: הנה כבר עבר עשרים וחמש שנים שמת אבי ונתן <לי> טבעתו מעל ידו,[12] והיה בו אבן טובה אחת לא היה כמותה בכל העולם. יום אחד הלכתי לשוט על פני הנהר ונפל הטבע{ת}[13] מידי אל תוך הנהר, ובקשוהו עבדיי ויעשו שֶׁכֶר במים ויוליכו המים דרך אחר ולא מצאוהו. ואם תוכל להביאו אלי, אלך עמך בלא איחור. אמר לה ר' יוחנן: מי יוכל לעשות זאת, דבר הנאבד בנהר כבר עברו עשרים וחמש שנים היאך יוכל אדם למצוא אותו? אמרה לו: אם לא תביאנו אלי, לא אלך עמך. הלך ר' יוחנן על שפת הנהר עד מקום אשר השליך הדג שקנה בתוך הנהר. וישב שם ובכה והתפלל לפני הקב"ה ואמר: יהי רצון מלפניך י"י א-לוהי ישראל שתשלח לי הדג שנדר לי לגמול לי מה שעשיתי לו. עודנו מדבר ומתפלל, והדג בא. וא"ל: אדוני, שמע א-להים תפלתך והנני מוכן לעשות רצונך, וידעתי את אשר אתה מבקש. ויודע הצור כי אין [316ב] אותה ברשותי אבל אני יודע ומכיר אותו דג שלקחו, ועודנה ברשותו וצריך אני להזמינו לדין בפני הלויתן, כי אספר לו כל המעשה ושכל ישראל תלוין באותו טבע{ת} ובעזרת הבורא הוא ישלם לי אותו. הלך לו אותו דג ובא לפני הלויתן ואמר לו: אדוני שמעני, יש צדיק אחד עומד על שפת הנהר, וספר לו כל המעשה. א"ל הלויתן: לך אחריו אותו דג ונשאלה את פיו אם הוא יודע היכן הוא אותו טבע[ת], ואבקש פניו לשלם אותו לך. הלך אחריו והביאו לפני הלויתן וא"ל: יש לך טבע[ת] אחד שלקחת ומצאת באותו זמן, שלם אותו אל זה הדג והוא ישאנו

11. טשטוש זה ואחרים בסיפור בין זכר לנקבה, גוף שלישי יחיד, הוא תרגום שאילה מצרפתית עתיקה.

12. השוו למבנה התחבירי בפסוקים: "ויסר פרעה טבעתו מעל ידו ויתן אותה על יד יוסף" (בראשית, מא, מב), וכן: "ויסר המלך את טבעתו מעל ידו ויתנה להמן" (אסתר, ג, י). נראה שהמעתיק הרכיב את שני אברי המשפט יחד.

13. תוספת של האות תי"ו תלויה מעל לשורה ביד אחרת.

fish sent after it and brought it before the whale, and the whale said: You have a ring that you took and found at the time; pay it [give it] to this fish, and he will bring it to a righteous man who is standing on the riverbank, for all of the people of Israel are suffering because of that ring. The fish went and gave the ring to the other fish, and that fish brought it to R. Joḥanan. And when the fish spat it out, a large pig came and took the ring and swallowed it and went away. R. Joḥanan wept bitterly and cried out and said: Woe is me. The fish was also very angry about the matter and said to R. Joḥanan: I can do no more for you in this matter. Only God can grant the wishes of your heart and take you from calamity to relief. And the fish bid farewell and departed.

L. R. Joḥanan kept praying and said: Master of the Universe, I showed kindness to a dog, and it swore to me to repay me what I did for it. May it be Your will that You bring it to me, and we will go together to seek out that pig and try to find it. As he was speaking, the dog came barking and shouting and said: Sir, God has heard your voice and your prayer and sent me to you, and here I am to do your bidding. I encountered the pig that took the ring, and I killed it. I tore up its innards and guts and removed them from its body, and they are lying on the ground, and the ring is inside the guts. And go with me and I will take you there, and you can open the guts and you will find it there. R. Joḥanan followed him and found the dead pig as the dog had said, and he opened its guts and found the ring inside them. He took the ring and set out on his way and was filled with great joy. And the dog also set out on its way. R. Joḥanan came to the queen and gave her the ring. And when she saw it, she took him and kissed him and made a great celebration. R. Joḥanan said to her: Because God has given me success in my path, let us go together to my place and land, because I did everything that you asked and denied you nothing. So do the right and good thing and do not delay us. She said: Since this is from God, I can speak neither ill nor good to you, and I will go with you to the place you wish to take me.

M. And they arose and went together and arrived in the place of the king who had sent to seek after her. And the king heard that they were coming, and he together with his horsemen went out to meet them, and they brought them to his palace. When they arrived in the palace, R. Joḥanan heard that his wife had died and his children had been taken captive and that everything that they had was lost and nothing remained, because it had been taken and stolen by those wise men who were [317a] jealous of their father and his riches and took them captive. When R. Joḥanan heard about his, he became very angry about his wife and children, and he

אל צדיק אחד העומד על שפת הנהר, וכל ישראל צרורים בצער בשביל אותו טבע[ת]. הלך אותו דג ונתנו לדג אחר, ואותו דג הביאו אל ר' יוחנן, וכשהקיא אותו מפיו בא חזיר אחד גדול ולקח אותו טבע[ת] ובלעו והלך לו. בכה ר' יוחנן במר נפש וצעק ואמר: אוי לי אוי לי. גם הדג היה כעוס מאד בעניינו ואמר אל ר' יוחנן: לא יכולתי עוד לעשות לך שם דבר מזה העניין, אלא המקום יתן לך משאלות לבך ויוציאך מצרה לרווחה. ונפטר הדג והלך לדרכו.

L. ור' יוחנן היה מתפלל ואומר: רבונו של עולם, גמלתי חסד עם כלב אחד והוא נדר לי לשלם לי מה שעשיתי עמו, יהי רצון מלפניך שתביאנו אלי ונלך אני והוא לבקש אותו חזיר אם נוכל למצוא אותו. בין כך ובין כך שהוא מדבר, בא אותו כלב נובח וצועק ואומר: אדוני, שמע א-להים את קולך ואת תפלתך וישלחני א-להים לפניך, והנה עשיתי שאלתך ובקשתך. פגעתי אותו חזיר אשר לקח הטבע[ת] בפניך והרגתיו, וקרעתי את קרבו ובני מעיו {ה}וצאתי חוץ מגופו, והנם שוכבים לארץ והטבע[ת] בתוך הבני מעים. ולך עמי ואוליכך שם ותפתח הבני מעים ותמצאנו בתוכו. הלך ר' יוחנן אחריו ומצאו מת כאשר אמר. ויפתח את בני מעיו וימצא את הטבע[ת] בתוכם. נטל את הטבע[ת] והלך לדרכו ושמח שמחה גדולה. וגם הכלב הלך לדרכו. ובא רבי יוחנן אל המלכה ונתן לה הטבע[ת]. וכשראתה אותו לקחה אותו ונשקה אותו, ועשתה ממנו שמחה גדולה. אמר לה ר' יוחנן: והואיל והצליח י"י את דרכי שלחני ונלכה יחד אל מקומי ולארצי, כי עשיתי לך כל מה שבקשת ממני לא כחדתי ממך. לכן עשי הישר והטוב, ואל תאחר אותנו. אמרה לו הואיל ומי"י יצא הדבר לא אוכל לדבר אליך רע או טוב, אלא עמך אלך לאיזה מקום שתרצה להוליכני.

M. ויקומו וילכו שניהם יחדיו, ויבואו עד מקום המלך אשר שלח אחריה. וישמע המלך כי הם באים ויעל לקראתם הוא ופרשיו עמו, ויביאו אותם אל בית מלכותו. וכשבאו אל בית המלכות שמע ר' יוחנן שאשתו מתה ובניו הלכו בשבי ואבדו כל מה שנשאר להם ולא נשאר להם מאומה, כי לקחו וגזלו אותם חכמים שהיו [317א] מתקנאים באביהם כל ממונם, ונשבו אותם. וכששמע ר' יוחנן כך היה כעוס מאד מאשתו ומבניו, ובכה וצעק עליהם. ויבואו כולם לנחמו וגם המלכה דברה על לבו וינחמו. וישלחו אחרי בניו, אשר היו מחזרים על הפתחים. וכששמעו שבא אביהם שמחו שמחה גדולה ובאו אליו וראה אותם, וספרו לו את כל התלאה אשר מצאתם, וילבישם ויאכילם ויהיו עמו. והיה ר' יוחנן אהוב ונחמד בעיני המלך, כי הביא לו אשה יפה וטובת מראה לא היתה כמוה בכל מלכותו. ורצה המלך לכונסה מיד, ולהכניסה לו לחופה. וענתה ואמרה אותה

wept and cried out because of them. They all came to comfort him, and the queen too encouraged and comforted him. And they sent to search for his sons, who had become beggars. And when they heard that their father had returned, they were overcome with joy, and they came to him and he saw them, and they told him about all the trials and tribulations they had experienced. And he dressed and fed them and they lived with him. And R. Joḥanan was much beloved and cherished by the king, because he had brought him a beautiful wife, fairer than any other in the entire kingdom. And the king wanted to marry her immediately and to place her under a canopy. And that righteous woman responded: That is not the custom where we live to propose to a woman and immediately place her under a marriage canopy. You must give me time—twelve months—for this is the custom among the maidens, to be six months in oil of myrrh and six months in perfumes and cosmetics of women, and this is the suitable way for a maiden to come to the king [cf. Esther 2:12; 5:13]. So the king said to her: All your wishes and requests, I will fulfill. Do as you see fit. And so she did.

N. And R. Joḥanan was very beloved and cherished by the king and queen. The king removed his ring from his hand and gave it to R. Joḥanan and ordered that he be master over his house and governor over all he had. The [other] wise men envied R. Joḥanan and said to one another: If we do not kill R. Joḥanan now, he will repay us for all the evil we did to him and his children. And they arose and lay in wait for him and beat him and cut him up and dismembered him. When the word was heard at the king's palace that R. Joḥanan had been killed and that he had been cut up and dismembered, the king and queen were exceedingly saddened. The queen said: Take me to the place where his limbs lie. They took her, and she took each of the limbs and put them back together as they were at the start, and she took her ring and touched the wounds with the stone, and the bones and tendons were rejoined, thanks to the power of the stone in the ring. And she took the water from the Garden of Eden and washed his flesh, and he was cured and his flesh was restored to that of a young boy. Then she lay atop him and placed her mouth over his mouth and kissed him, and prayed to the Almighty; and God heard her prayer and restored his soul, and he arose and stood on his feet. When people saw that she had revived the dead in this way, they were amazed at her and feared her and were frightened.

O. The king said: If this is so, then let us go out and fight all those around us, and if I am killed in war, she will revive me. What did the king do? He and all his ministers and wise men set out to besiege another king and fought a great war, and the king and all his ministers and servants were killed. And they came to the queen

צדקת: לא כן יעשה במקומינו[14] לדבר אל אשה ולהכניסה מיד לחופה. אלא תן לי זמן שנים עשר חודש, כי כן ימלאו ימי מרוקי הבתולות להיות ששה חדשים בשמן המור וששה חדשים בבשמים בתמרוקי הנשים, ובזה ראויה הבתולה ~~אל~~ לבא אל המלך. ויאמר לה המלך כל שאלתך ובקשתך אמלא עשי הטוב בעינייך, ותעש כן.[15]

N. ויהי ר' יוחנן אהוב ונחמד מאד בעיני <המלך> והמלכה. ויסר המלך את טבעתו מעל ידו ויתנהו לו, ויצוהו לאדון לכל ביתו ומושל בכל אשר לו. ויקנאו בו החכמים ויאמרו איש אל אחיו: אם לא נשים עיצה להרוג את ר' יוחנן עתה, יגמול לנו את כל הרעה אשר גמלנו לו ולבניו. ויקומו ויארבו לו ויכוהו, ויחתכו אותו אבר אבר. וישמע הדבר בית המלך כי נהרג ר' יוחנן, וכי חתכו אותו אבר אבר. ויתעצבו מאד המלך והמלכה. ותאמר המלכה: הוליכוני אל מקום שהאיברים שם. הוליכו אותה, <ולקחה> כל אבר ואבר ונתחברה אותם יחד כאשר ~~היו~~ היו בתחלה, ולקחה הטבע[ת] שלה ונגעה מן האבן הפצעים, ונתחברו העצמות והגידים בשביל כח האבן שהיה בתוך הטבע[ת]. וגם לקחה מן המים של גן עדן ורחצה כל בשרו, ונתרפא וישב בשרו כבשר נער קטן.[16] ואז שכבה עליו ותשם פיה תוך פיו ונשקה אותו, ונתפללה אל הקב"ה וישמע אליה א-להים והחזיר לו את נשמתו, ויחי ויקם וילך על רגליו. וכשראו כך שהיא מחייה מתים במי[ם], תמהו ופחדו ורהו[17] ממנה.

O. ויאמר המלך: אם כן הוא, נלך ונלחם אל כל סביבותינו אם אהרג במלחמה היא תחייה אותי. מה עשה המלך, הלך הוא וכל שריו ועבדיו וחכמיו לצור מלך אחד וערכו אתם מלחמה גדולה, ויהרג המלך וכל שריו ועבדיו. ויבואו אחר המלכה ויאמרו לה: בואי ותחיי את המלך ושריו ועבדיו, כי הם נפלו בחרב. הלכה לשם עם ר' יוחנן, ועשתה להם כאשר עשתה אל ר' יוחנן, ולקחה המים של גהינם והשליכה עליהם ונשרפו כולם. אמרה להם: ראו את נפלאות א-להים כי לא ממני החכמה והדעה להמית ולהחיות, כי הא-להים הוא ממית ומחיה ומוחץ ומרפא ומשפיל ומרומם. ולא נאה לפניו להחיות אילו הרשעים [317ב] כשם שהחיה זה הצדיק. ולא ידעתי

14. השוו בראשית כט, כו: "ויאמר לבן לא יעשה כן במקומנו לתת הצעירה לפני הבכירה".
15. השוו אסתר ב, יב; ה, ג.
16. ראו מלכים ב, ה, יד.
17. פחדו. ראו בישעיה מד, ח: "אל תפחדו ואל תרהו." וראו "רהה" במילון אבן שושן.

and said to her: Come and revive the king and his ministers and servants for they have fallen by the sword. The queen went there with R. Joḥanan and did to them as she had done to R. Joḥanan, but she took the water of Gehenna and poured it on them, and they were all burned. She said to the people: See the wonders of God, for the wisdom and knowledge to master death and life are not mine, for God is the master of death and life, He crushes and heals and casts down and raises up. It would not be proper for Him to revive these evil ones [317b] as He revived this righteous man. I know how to do nothing more. They went home, and the kingdom was left without a king. The people chose R. Joḥanan and crowned him king, for all the people who sought to kill him had died. And they gave him the righteous woman to be his wife, and they lived for many years together in peace and tranquility and had many sons and daughters. And regarding this, it says: "Cast your bread upon the waters for after many days you may find it [Ecclesiastes 11:1].

לעשות עוד מאומה. הלכו לביתם ונשאר המלכות בלא מלך. נתנו עיניהם על ר' יוחנן והמליכו אותו עליהם, כי מתו כל האנשים המבקשים את נפשו. ונתנו לו את הצדקת לאשה. וחיו יחד ימים רבים בשלום ובהשקט ובהנחה והולידו בנים ובנות. ועל זה נאמר: שלח לחמך על פני המים כי ברוב הימים תמצאנו [קהלת יא, א].

29. The Seven Good Years (317b–318a)

A. [317b] Once there was a man who was exceedingly poor. He would sit in the synagogue for many long hours and pray. And every single day, he would hire himself out to toil the earth. Elijah of blessed memory encountered him and said: The Almighty has granted you seven good years, but tell me if you want them in your old age or in your youth. He said to him: [I fear] that you may be a magician or sorcerer, and I have nothing to give you in return. He left him and went away. Elijah came to him a second and then a third time and said to him: If you accept them, fine, but if not, I will not come back. He said to Elijah: Wait until I have spoken to my wife and the members of my household. He went home and told them everything. His wife said: Take them now. He said to her: But now I am a young man and I can work. It is better to receive the seven good years in our old age. She said to him: Blessed is God day by day.

B. He returned to Elijah and said to him: I request the seven good years now. Elijah said: Go. He took one step and said: What should I do now? If I go home, I will have not used the time for work, not even to collect weeds. He said to him: Go and trust your Creator. The man's sons came out to greet him and asked him for weeds. And he was ashamed because he had nothing to give them. He evaded them and entered his home. He found the home filled with good things. He and his wife gave thanks to the Almighty. His wife said to him: You may not benefit at all [from this wealth] until you bring me a scribe who will write down everything I give to the poor. He went and brought her a scribe. She came and sat him down at her door, and said: Any poor man who comes here, if he is accustomed to riding a horse, place him on a horse, and if he is accustomed to wearing wool robes, dress each according to what he is accustomed to. And write everything down, as it says: "He that has pity on the poor lends to the Almighty [and that which he has given he shall be repaid]" [Proverbs 19:17].

29. שבע שנים טובות (317ב–318א)

A. מעשה באדם אחד שהיה עני ביותר. והיה יושב בבית הכנסת ומאריך בתפלתו. ובכל יום ויום היה משכיר עצמו לאדמה.[1] פגע בו אליהו זכור לטוב א"ל: שבע שנים גזר לך הקב"ה לטובה, ותאמר אם אתה רוצה בזקנותיך או בבחרותיך.[2] א"ל: שמא אתה אדם קוסם קסמים, ואין לי בידי ליתן לך כלום.[3] הניח אותו והלך. בא אליו פעם שנייה, ואחרי כן בא אליו פעם שלישית. וא"ל: אם אתה מקבלם מוטב, ואם לאו לא אשוב אליך.[4] א"ל: המתן לי עד שאדבר לאשתי ולבני ביתי. הלך וספר להם כל הדברים.[5] אמרה לו אשתו: קבל מעכשיו. אמר לה: עכשיו אני בחור ויכול אני לטרוח. טוב לקבל לעת זקנה. אמרה לו: ברוך י"י יום יום.[6]

B. חזר אל אליהו אמר לו: אני אקבל עכשיו. א"ל: לך.[7] היה מהלך ברגלו אחת[8] ואמר לו: באיזה צד אעשה ~~להם~~,[9] אם אלך לביתי נתבטלתי ממלאכתי, ואפילו עשבים לא ליקטתי.[10] א"ל: לך וסמוך על בוראך.[11] יצאו בניו לקראתו, והיו מבקשים ממנו עשבים. והיה מתבייש מהם שלא היה בידו ליתן להם כלום. נשמט מהם, ונכנס לבית. מצא הבית מליאה כל טוב.[12] בא הוא ואשתו ונתנו הודאה להקב"ה.[13] אמרה לו אשתו: לא תהנה כלום[14] עד שתביא לי סופר שיכתוב לי כל מה שאתן לעניים.[15] הלך והביא הסופר אצלה.[16] באה, והושיבו אצל פתח הבית. אמרה: כל עני שיבא אצלך[17] אם דרכו לרכוב על הסוס תרכיבהו ואם דרכו ללבוש כלי מילת תלבישהו כל אחד לפי דרכו.[18] וכתוב הכל[19] כמו ~~ה~~שכתוב: מלוה י"י חונן דל [משלי יט, יז].

1. בכ"י ירושלים 3182, דף 132א–132ב (יסיף, מאה סיפורים, 245–247, סיפור ע"ט), בלי מוטיב התפילה בבית הכנסת. ההשוואות להלן הן לכתב יד זה.
2. שבע שנים [טובות] גוזר עליך המקום, אם תרצה אותם עתה או בשיבתך?
3. א"ל: אתה אדם קוסם קסמים ואני אדם עני ואין בידי כלום ליתן לך שכרך.
4. וכן עשה לו ג' פעמים ופעם ג' אמר לו: וכי לא אמרתי אתמול שאתה קוסם קסמים, מפני מה אתה מבטל אותי ממלאכתי? א"ל אליהו ז"ל: אמרתי לך שתקחם ג' פעמים. אם תקחם מוטב ואם לאו לא יבאו לך לעולם, לא עכשיו ולא בזקנותך.
5. בכ"י ירושלים דבריו לאשתו מפורטים.
6. א"ל: עכשיו אני בחור ויש לי כח לעבוד, אך מה רצונך, יהא.
7. כ"י ירושלים: א"ל: לך לביתך.
8. פירוש: הוא התחיל ללכת. עשה צעד.
9. פירוש: "צד" במובן של בחינה – מאיזו בחינה/איך אוכל לעשות זאת?!
10. וא"ל: באיזה צד אעלה לביתי הרי כבר נתבטלתי ממלאכתי ואפילו פשוט [מטבע קטן] לקנות בו עשבים אין לי.
11. א"ל אליהו ז"ל: לך לביתך וסמוך על בוראך שכבר עלה זכרונך לברכה.
12. כיון שבא לביתו יצאו בניו לקראתו ואמרו: תן לנו לאכול. נשמט מהם ובא לבית ומצא הבית מלא כל טוב. בא אצל אשתו ואמר לה: עמדי וראי מה עשה לנו הקב"ה. עתה בא לנו הטובה שאמר לנו אותו האיש.
13. שמחו שמחה גדולה ונתנו שבח והודייה להקב"ה.
14. איני מניחך להינות מטובה זו.
15. שישב על פתח ביתי ויכתב כל מה שתתן לעניים מממון זה.
16. הלך ועשה כל מה שאמרה לו אשתו והשכיר סופר אחד.
17. ראה כל מי שיבא אצלך לבקש ממך דבר.
18. ועשה לכל אדם כפי שאלתו; והשוו כתובות סז, ע"ב.
19. בכ"י ירושלים חסר: וכתב הכל.

C. After seven years, all the good things were gone, and they were left bereft of all the good things, as they had been at the start. They began to weep. Her husband said to her: That is what I said. Now the world believes that we are wealthy, and we and our children will die of starvation. She immediately went to the study hall of R. Ḥanina [should be: R. Ḥiyya] in Tiberias and said: Doesn't it say: "He that has pity on the poor lends to the Almighty" [Proverbs 19:17] and I have done a great deal of charity and lent to the Almighty, and now I and my household are dying of starvation. R. Ḥiyya said to her: How much did you lend? She said to him: Three hundred loaded camels [of documentation] and upon all [these pages], it is written: "He that has pity on the poor lends to the Almighty." He said to her: Go and bring all the written records, and spread [318a] them out on the roof of the study hall. And when the rooster cries, stand on your feet before the Almighty and say to Him: Master of the Universe, You have written: "He that has pity on the poor lends to the Almighty" and I have done much charity and remained bereft of all good things. May it be Your will God Almighty that You should show them to me, so that I and my family do not die. And at that moment, God said to Elijah: Go and support them all their days in this world. Now come and see the power of charity and prayer.

C. לאחר שבע שנים הלכה כל הטובה, ונשארו ערומים מכל טוב כאשר בתחלה.[20] התחילו היו בוכין. אמר לה בעלה: הלא זה שאמרתי, עתה העולם סבורים שאנו עשירים ונמות אנחנו ובנינו ברעב.[21] מיד הלכה לבית המדרש של ר' חנינא בטבריא[22] {ואמרה}: והלא כתיב מלוה י"י חונן דל, והרבה צדקות עשיתי והלויתי להקב"ה, ועכשיו אני וביתי מתים ברעב.[23] אמר לו [!] ר' חייא: כמה הלויתה [!]? אמרה לו: שלש עשרה גמלים טעונים כתבים, ובכולם כתיב מלוה י"י חונן דל.[24] אמר לה: לכי תביאי הכתבים,[25] ופשטי [318א] אותם על הגג מבית המדרש.[26] ובעת קרות הגבר עמדי על רגליך לפני הקב"ה ואמרי לפניו:[27] רבונו של עולם, כתבת מלוה י"י חונן דל והרבה עשיתי צדקות ונשארתי ערומה מכל טוב, יהי רצון מלפניך י"י א-להי שתראם לי ולא אמות אני ובני. ובאותה שעה אמר הקב"ה לאליהו: לך ופרנסם כל ימיהם בעולם הזה.[28] ועתה בא וראה כחה של צדקה ושל תפלה"[29]

---

20. כיון ששלמו השבע שנים השכימו ומצאו עצמם ערומים ואפילו כסות שעל צווארם לא מצאו. כמו שבא להם במהירות כך הלך במהירות.

21. התחיל לבכות ואמר לאשתו: וכי לא אמרתי לך שיהיו ז' שנים בזקנותי טובים יותר עכשיו מה תהא עמנו? כבר שמעו כל העולם שהיינו עשירים גדולים, עכשיו היאך אני הולך לבקש פרנסה מהם? ועוד התפנקתי ואין בי כח לעשות מלאכה, עכשיו נמות אנו ובנינו ברעב.

22. צ"ל: ר' חייא, כבכ"י ירושלים 3182.

23. ואמרה לו: ח"ו שכתוב בתורה דבר שאין בו אמת. א"ל: ח"ו אין בתורה אלא דבר אמת. א"ל: מה טיבך שאמרת לי כך? אמרה לו: שכתוב בתורה: מלוה ה' חונן דל, והלוואה גדולה הלוויתי להקב"ה ועכשיו אני ובני מתים ברעב.

24. בכ"י ירושלים חסר: שלוש עשרה גמלים–דל.

25. הכתבים האילו.

26. חסר: מבית המדרש.

27. בכ"י ירושלים: ואמרי לפניו דבריך, בלי הפירוט שבהמשך: רבונו של עולם–חונן דל, אך בהרחבה אחרת.

28. על משקל הפסוק: מלוה ה' חונן דל, ניתנת לאישה האפשרות לבחור אם לקבל את פרעון ההלוואה בעולם הזה או בעולם הבא, והיא מבקשת רחמים בעולם הזה. היא ובעלה זוכים לפרנסה טובה בעולם הזה ולשכר רב בעולם הבא.

29. האפילוג: לכך נאמר: מלוה ה' חונן דל.

30. Slander Kills Three (318a)

A. Once, a pious man [*ḥasid*] had three daughters, one of whom was a lazy slattern, the second a thief, and the third a gossip. People were concerned about marrying them, and he too was careful not to deceive anyone. A wealthy man who was also good hearted, came over. He said: Behold, your daughters are old. Marry them off. He said: They have many faults. He said: Don't worry. I have three sons for your three daughters. To the lazy one, he gave many slaves and maidservants. He said to them: Beware to do everything she asks. To the one who was a thief, he gave all the keys to his treasure. She said: Why should I steal if everything is mine? To the one who used to gossip all day long, he would come early every morning and tell her: Daughter, anything you need, let me know, and how do you get along with your husband. And he would tempt her with words.

B. One day the *ḥasid* came to visit his daughters. First, he went to the lazy one. She said: Father, may you be blessed, for you have given me to a good man. Then he went to the gossip. As soon as she saw him, she began to cry. She said: You have given me to two husbands, both the son and the father, and if you don't believe me, come to the room and see. So he went into the room. In the morning, her father-in-law came, as was his practice, and kissed her on the head. She said: Don't touch me! When her father saw this, he said: He who lies with his daughter-in-law deserves death. He attacked him [the father-in-law] and killed him. His son-in-law came, saw his father dead, and killed his father-in-law. The girl's brothers came, saw that their father was dead, and killed his [their] sister's husband.

C. Do you realize the disaster brought about by gossip and slander? And so it was with Joseph, the Righteous: "And Joseph slandered them to their father" [Genesis 37:2], telling him: My brothers call the sons of the maidservants slaves. And that is why he was sold into slavery. And he said: They look at the girls of the land, and that is why "His master's wife cast her eyes at Joseph" [Genesis 39:7]. And he said: They eat the flesh of a living animal, and for this "They slaughtered a male goat and dipped the tunic in the blood" [Genesis 37:31]. Slander is worse than idolatry and incest and murder. That is why Solomon said: "He who guards his mouth and his tongue, guards his soul from troubles" [Proverbs 21:23].

30. לשון הרע הורגת שלושה (318א)

A. מעשה בחסיד אחד[1] שהיו לו שלשה בנות, אחת עצילה ואחת גונבת ואחת מספרת לשון הרע. והיו בני אדם יריאים ליקח <~~אותם~~> אותם, וגם הוא בעצמו לא רצה להטעות בני אדם. בא עשיר אחד וטוב היה. א"ל: הנה בנותיך זקינות, תשיא אותם.[2] א"ל: הרבה יש בהן מומין.[3] א"ל: אל תחוש, יש לי שלשה בנים לאותן בנותיך.[4] לאותה עצילה, נתן לה עבדים ושפחות הרבה. אמר להם: השמרו לכם שתעבדו אותה בכל מה שתאמר.[5] לאותה גנבתה, נתן כל מפתיחות שלו מן הממון. אמרה: למה אהיה גונבת, הכל שלי.[6] לאותה שהיתה מספרת לשון הרע בכל יום ויום היה משכים ואומר לה: בתי אם את צריכה לשום דבר תודיעני, והיאך את נוהגת עם בעלך. והיה מפתה אותה בדברים.[7]

B. לימים בא החסיד לראות בנותיו. בתחלה נכנס אצל העצלה. אמרה לו: אבא תבא עליך ברכה כי נתתני לאדם טוב. ואחרי כן נכנס אצל המספרת לשון הרע. מיד שראתה אותו, התחילה לבכות. אמרה לו: אתה נתת לי שני בעלים הבן והאב, ואם לא תאמין לי תבא בחדר ותראה. הלך בחדר. בא אותו חמיה כמנהגו בשחרית, ונשקה על ראשה.[8] אמרה לו: אל תגע בי.[9] כשראה אביה כך אמר: זה שבא על כלתו חייב מיתה. עמד עליו והרגו. בא חתנו וראה אביו הרוג, והרג את חמיו. באו אחי הנערה וראו אביהם הרוג, הרגו את בעל אחותו.[10]

C. ראיתם כמה פורענות גדול באה בשביל לשון הרע.[11] וכן ביוסף הצדיק: ויבא יוסף את דבתם רעה אל אביהם [בראשית לז, ב], שאמר לאביו: אחיי קורין לבני השפחות עבדים. לפיכך נמכר לעבד. ואמר: הם נותנים עיניהם בבנות הארץ לפיכך, ותשא אשת אדוניו [בראשית לט, ז]. ואמר: הם אוכלים אבר מן החי,[12] לפיכך וישחטו שעיר עזים ויטבלו את הכתנת בדם [בראשית לז, לא]. ולשון הרע קשה מע"ז וגילוי עריות ושפיכות דמים. לפיכך אמר שלמה: שומר פיו ולשונו שומר מצרה נפשו [משלי כא, כג].[13]

---

1. במעשה"ד, שפירא, 86–87, ובכ"י ותיקן 107, 178א–178ב: מעשה באדם אחד. ההשוואות להלן הן למעשה"ד, שפירא, אלא אם צוין אחרת.
2. פעם אחת בא אוהבו להתארח בביתו ואמר לו: מפני מה לא תתן בנותיך לאנשים?
3. שתק ולא אמר לו כלום.
4. אמר לו: יש לי שלשה בנים ובכבודך ובאהבתך אם ייטב לך תן בנותיך לבני; כ"י ותיקן: בא אדם אחד שהיו לו שלשה בנים אמ' לו תן בנותיך לבני.
5. מה עשה להן? העצלה הושיבה על המטה והעמיד לפניו עבדיו ושפחותיו ואמר להם: אל תניחו לעשות לה כלום.
6. ולגנבתא הפקיד כל המפתחות ואמר לה: כל מה שיש בידי ובבית יהא בידך וכל מה שתעשי תהא עשוי; כ"י ותיקן: מה עשה? לקחם שלשתם לשלשת בניו. לגנבת נתן בידה המפתחות של כל ממונו לעצלה העמיד עליה עבדים ושפחות עושים מלאכתה.
7. היה משכים בכל יום ונשקה על ראשה והשיבה אצלו.
8. בא חמיה לשאול בשלומה כמנהגו; כ"י ותיקן: הושיבה בחיקו ומחבקה ומנשקה.
9. חמי חזור לך ואל תביישני.
10. במעשה"ד, שפירא נהרגים הבת, אביה וחמיה.
11. במעשה"ד, שפירא, האפילוג הוא: מכאן אנו לומדין שלשון הרע הורג שלש נפשות, האומרו והמקבלו ומי שנאמר עליו. בהמשך האפילוג מתקשר לדיבר התשיעי: ואמרו חכמים: אין דבר קשה בעולם מלשון הרע, לכך צוה הב"ה: לא תענה לרעך עד שקר" (שמות כ, יג").
12. איסור אבר מן החי נגזר מן הפסוק: "אך בשר בנפשו דמו לא תאכלו" (בראשית ט, ה). ראו ירושלמי פאה א, א [טו, ד–טז, ד].
13. במעשה"ד, שפירא חסר: וכן ביהוסף הצדיק–שומר מצרה נפשו.

31. Saved from Drowning by Charity (318a–318b)

A. Once there was a man who was accustomed to giving charity. One day he boarded a ship, and a wind came and it sank. And R. Akiva [318b] had seen him board the ship. He came and testified for his wife that she was permitted to remarry. As R. Akiva was arriving home, he saw the man walking toward him. R. Akiva said to him: Didn't I see you drown at sea? He said to him: Yes. Who raised you up? He said: The Almighty raised me up because of the all the charity I gave. I heard a roaring noise at sea, and they [the waves] were saying to one another: Run and save that man, because he is worthy and is accustomed to giving charity.

31. הצלה מטביעה בזכות צדקה (318א–318ב)

A. מעשה באדם אחד שהיה רגיל ליתן צדקה.[1] פעם אחת נכנס בספינה, בא הרוח וטבעה.[2] ורבי [318ב] עקיבא[3] ראה אותו שנכנס בספינה. בא והעיד על אשתו שמותרת לינשא.[4] עד שלא חזר ר' עקיבא לביתו, בא אותו האיש כנגדו.[5] א"ל רבי עקיבא: וכי לא ראיתי אותך שטבעת בים?[6] א"ל: הן. ומי העלך? אמר: הקב"ה העלני בשביל הצדקות שעשיתי. שמעתי קול רעש בים, ואמר זה לזה: רוצו והעלו את האיש כי הוא ראוי ורגיל בצדקה.[7]

1. מובא בשני נוסחים שונים במסכת יבמות קכא, ע"א. גרסת ספר המעשים שלפנינו היא על פי נוסח שלישי באבדר"נ, מהדורת שכטר (ט נוסחא א), ובעקבותיו בכ"י פרמא 2295. ההשוואות להלן הן לגרסת הסיפור שבכ"י פרמא.
2. תוספת בכ"י פרמא: ורצה לילך למדינת הים.
3. ראהו ר' עקיבא ובא והעיד על אשתו להנשא.
4. עד שלא בא לביתו בא אותו האיש ועמד לפניו.
5. אמר לו ר' עקיבא לא אתה טבעת בים?
6. ומי העלך מן הים? אמר לו צדקה וחסד שעשיתי בעולם הזה העלוני מן הים.
7. אמר לו ר' עקיבא מניין אתה יודע? אמר לו בשעה שירדתי לעמקי תהום שמעתי קול רעש גדול שאומר[ים] זה לזה רוצו והעלוהו זה האיש שהוא רגיל בצדקה כל ימיו. בכ"י פרמא נוסף אפילוג בשבח דברי תורה ודברי חכמים הכולל ציטוט של הפסוק: שלח לחמך על פני המים [קהלת יא, א].

32. R. Akiva's Daughter and the Snake (318b)

A. A tale of R. Akiva's daughter, to whom everyone would say: Take notice, that on the day of your wedding you will die. She married a very handsome young man. On the night of the wedding ceremony, a poor man came to her to ask for food. When she saw him, she gave him to eat and drink. The poor man left, and she went to her marriage canopy until [the end] of the evening.

B. When she got into bed with her husband, a snake emerged from a hole in the wall to bite her. And she leaned away from her husband and took her hairpin and placed it in the hole. The pin became entwined in the snake's head, and it choked and died. When she awoke and took her hairpin, she found the dead snake entwined in the hairpin.

C. R. Akiva said: I thought you would not live until morning. And she told him the story of the poor man, and R. Akiva went and told it to all his disciples. He said: See how great is the power of charity.

D. R. Eliezer says: When a person observes numerous commandments faithfully and out of fear of the Almighty, God preserves him and preserves his body, as it says: "The Lord safeguards your going and coming" [Psalms 121:8] and "The Lord is your shade on your right hand" [Psalms 121:5].

32. בתו של רבי עקיבא והנחש (318ב)

A. מעשה בבתו של ר' עקיבא שהיו אומרים לה כל העולם:[1] ראי ביום שתיכנסי לחופה תמות[י].[2] קדשה בחור אחד נאה ביותר.[3] באותה לילה מן החופה בא עני אחד לבקש לחם. וכשראת אותו, הלכה והאכילתו והשקתו.[4] אותו עני הלך לו,[5] והיא הלכה לחופתה עד הערב.

B. כשנכנסה עם בעלה במיטה[6] בא נחש אחד בחור הכותל לנושכה, והרחיקה מבעלה, ולקחה מכבנת{אה} [מכבנתה] ונתנה אותה בחור. ונתקשר המכבנת בראש הנחש, ונחנק ומת.[7] השכימה ולקחה המכבנת ומצאה הנחש מת במכבנת.[8]

C. אמר לה ר' עקיבא: הייתי סבור שלא תחיי עד הבקר.[9] וסיפרה לו כל העניין מן העני, והלך ר' עקיבא וספר לכל התלמידים. אמר: ראו כמה כחה גדולה של צדקה.[10]

D. תניא רבי אליעזר אומר: כשאדם מרבה במצות באמונה וביראת הקב"ה, הוא (משמרן) משמרו ושומר גופו כדכתיב: י"י ישמור צאתך ובאך [תהילים קכא, ח] וכת' י"י שמרך י"י צלך על יד ימינך [תהילים קכא, ה].[11]

1. במסכת שבת קנו, ע"ב מבשרי הבשורה הם חוזים בכוכבים. ההשוואת להלן הן לגרסת התלמוד, וילנה, הדומה בעיקרה לנוסח כתבי היד של מסכת שבת: מינכן 95; וטיקן 108.
2. במסכת שבת, בתוספת תגובת רבי עקיבא – דאגתו לבתו.
3. אין איזכור של הקידושין, ואין תיאור של חתנה.
4. היא נותנת לעני את מנת האוכל שלה.
5. אירוע הנחש מסופר רק לאחר אירוע הצדקה לעני, כדיווח של הבת לאביה על קורותיה.
6. אין איזכור של מיטת הכלולות.
7. האירוע מדווח עם גילויו בבוקר לאחר מעשה (בהתאם להערה 5 לעיל).
8. תיאור מפורט יותר: בבוקר, כשלקחה את הסיכה מהקיר נמשך אחריה הנחש.
9. במסכת שבת חסר: הייתי סבור שלא תחיי עד הבוקר.
10. מוסר ההשכל נמסר כדרשת פסוק: נפק [יצא] ר"ע ודרש וצדקה תציל ממות ולא ממיתה משונה אלא ממיתה עצמה.
11. מסכת שבת, חסר: תניא ר' אליעזר–ימינך והשוו לתנחומא, משפטים, סימן יט.

33. Mattiah b. Ḥarash (318b)

A. [318b] A tale of R. Mattiah b. Ḥarash, who used to sit and study Torah, and his face was as bright as the sun, and he had never raised his eyes to look at a woman in his life. Once, Satan passed by, saw him, and felt envious. He went to God and said: What is Mattiah b. Ḥarash to you? God answered: A perfectly righteous man. Said Satan: Give me permission to tempt him, and God said: Go then. Satan went and found Mattiah b. Ḥarash sitting and studying Torah. He took on the likeness of a beautiful woman, more beautiful than any ever seen before. When Mattiah saw her, he turned away to the right, and she also turned to the right. He said: I fear the evil inclination. He himself went to bring fire and nails, and thrust them into his eyes and blinded them. When Satan saw this, he was shaken. He went to God and said: Thus and thus happened. God said: Have I not seen that? I told you so.

B. Then God summoned the angel Raphael and told him: Go and heal Mattiah b. Ḥarash. He went to him, and Mattiah b. Ḥarash said: I do not wish it, lest today or tomorrow the evil inclination will do the same. The angel went to God and said: So and so he said to me. God said: Go and tell him that I guarantee him that he will no longer have an evil inclination. The angel returned to Mattiah b. Ḥarash: This and this is what God said. If so, said Mattiah b. Ḥarash, do His will.

33. מתיא בן חרש (318ב)

A. מעשה ברבי מתיא בן חרש שהיה יושב ועוסק בתורה והיו פניו דומין לגלגלי חמה,[1] ולא נשא עיניו לאשה מעולם.[2] עבר שטן וראה אותו ונתקנא בו.[3] הלך לפני הקב"ה. אמר לו: מתיא בן חרש מהו לפניך? א"ל: צדיק גמור.[4] א"ל: תן לי רשות ואפתה אותו.[5] אמר לו: לך.[6] הלך השטן, ומצאו שהיה יושב ועוסק בתורה. ונידמה לו כאשה יפה שלא הייתה כמותה.[7] כיון שראה אותה הפך פניו לצד ימין, והיא הלכה לצד ימין.[8] אמר: מתיירא אני מיצר הרע.[9] הלך והביא אש ומסמרין בידו, ונתנן בעיניו ועיור עיניו.[10] כיון שראה כך שטן, נזדעזע. הלך לפני הקב"ה, א"ל: כך וכך היה. א"ל: וכי לא ראיתי, אמרתי לך כך.[11]

B. באותה שעה קרא הקב"ה לרפאל. א"ל: לך רפא את מתיא בן חרש.[12] הלך אצלו. אמר לו: איני רוצה שמא היום או למחר כמו כן יעשה לי יצר הרע.[13] הלך אצל הקב"ה, א"ל: כך וכך אמר לי. אמר לו: לך ותאמר לו כי אני ערב שלא יהיה לו עדיין יצר הרע.[14] חזר אצלו, א"ל: כך אומר הקב"ה. א"ל: אם כן עשה רצונו"[15]

1. מעשה"ד, שפירא, 74–75: והיה זיויה פניו דומות לחמה וקלסתר פניו דומות למלאכי השרת ביראת שמים. ההשוואות להלן למקור זה.
2. שמימיו לא נשא עיניו באשת איש.
3. ראהו שטן אחד ונתקנא בו אמ' אפשר לאדם נאה כמו זה שלא חטא?
4. השוו לאיוב א, ה.
5. תן לי רשות ואני אסית בו.
6. אמ' לו הב"ה: אין אתה יכול לו. אמ' לו: אעפ' כן תן לי רשות. אמר לו: לך.
7. נדמה לו כאשה יפה שלא היתה כמותה בעולם.
8. כיון שראה הפך עיניו לצד אחד.
9. וכשראה שהיא מתהפכת לכל צד אמ' מתירא אני שלא ישלוט בי יצר הרע.
10. במעשה"ד תלמיד מביא לו מסמרים ואש.
11. כיון שראה השטן כך נזדעזע מפניו ועלה למרום וחזר ובא לפני הב"ה. אמ' לפניו: רבונו של עולם כך וכך היה מעשה אמ' לו: לא אמרתי לך שאין אתה יכול לו.
12. במעשה"ד מובא דיאלוג נרחב בין השטן למתיא בן חרש.
13. הניחני כי מתירא אני שמא ישלוט בי יצר הרע.
14. מיד ריפא את עיניו.
15. במעשה"ד בתוספת אפילוג, שכל מי שאינו נושא עיניו לנשים אחרות אין יצר הרע שולט בו.

34. The Loan (version 2) (318b–319a)

A. [318b] A tale of about R. Abraham, who lived in Ashkelon. And he was [319a] very poor. And he would always close and open the synagogue, as he was always the first [to arrive] and the last [to leave]. Elijah the Prophet saw him and wished to show him compassion. He said to God: Give me permission and I will provide him with a livelihood. God said to him: Do as you wish, and do not drive him away from me. Elijah went and gave him a sela.[1]

B. He [Abraham] went to the market to buy tools. Elijah appeared before him in the form of a young man. He was carrying a robe worth a gold coin. Elijah said: Take the robe. Abraham said: I have but a sela, and he gave it to him. Then Elijah came to him in the form of an old man. He said to him: Sell me the garment. He said: How much will you pay me? The man said: Ten gold coins and a sela. Abraham said: Willingly. Then, Abraham became very rich and a great merchant, and all the other merchants would come to him. And he no longer went to the house of prayer.

C. God said to Elijah: I had one beloved, and you drove him away. Elijah went to the man and said to him: Give me the sela that I gave to you. He said: Take a hundred gold dinars from me, because I cannot find that sela. He went and searched until he found it and returned it to him. All his money was immediately lost, and he became even poorer than he had been to start with. He began to go back to the synagogue as he had before, and cried and wept. Elijah said to God: I cannot bear his cries. Let me go and give him his livelihood. God said to him: Do as you wish, but

1. Sela—in Hebrew, a coin used in the mishnaic and talmudic periods.

34. ההלוואה [נוסח שני] (318ב–319א)

A. מעשה ברבי אברהם[1] שהיה שרוי באשקלון.[2] והיה [319א] עני מאוד.[3] והיה סוגר בית הכנסת ופותח,[4] כי היה ראשון ואחרון. ראה אותו אליהו הנביא[5] ובקש לרחמו.[6] אמר לפני הקב"ה: תן לי רשות ואתן לו כדי לפרנסו.[7] אמר לו הקב"ה: עשה כרצונך ואל תרחיקהו מעלי. הלך אליהו נתן לו סלע.[8]

B. הלך [אברהם] בשוק לקנות כלים. נזדמן לו[9] אליהו בדמות בחור אחד. והיה נושא בידו בגד שוה זהב.[10] א"ל: קח זה הבגד.[11] א"ל: אין לי כי אם הסלע. לקח הסלע ונתן לו. אחר כך בא אליהו בדמות זקן.[12] א"ל: מכור לי את הבגד. אמר לו: מה תתן לי?[13] א"ל: עשרה זהובים והסלע.[14] וא"ל: ברצון.[15] עד שנעשה עשיר גדול ונעשה סוחר גדול, והיו כל הסוחרים באים אצלו.[16] ולא הלך לבית התפלה.[17]

C. א"ל הקב"ה: היה לי אהוב אחד והרחיקתו מעלי.[18] והלך אליהו אצל האיש,[19] אמר לו: תן לי הסלע שנתתי לך. אמר לו: קח ממני מאה דנרי זהב,[20] כי לא מצאתי הסלע.[21] הלך ופשפש עד שמצאו והחזיר לו. מיד הלך כל ממונו לתוהו ובהו,[22] ונעשה עני יותר ממה שהיה בתחילה. התחיל לילך לבית הכנסת כבתחילה,[23] והתחיל לצעוק ולבכות.[24] אמר אליהו לפני הקב"ה: איני יכול לסבול צעקתו, הנח לי ואתן לו כדי לפרנסו.[25] אמר לו הקב"ה: עשה כרצונך ואל תרחיקהו

1. כ"י ניו-יורק, בהמ"ל 4732, דף 118א–118ב: מעשה בחסיד אחד ושמו אברהם. ההשוואות להלן הן לכתב יד זה.
2. במדינת אשקלון.
3. תוספת בכ"י בהמ"ל: והיה ירא שמים.
4. ולעולם היה מקדים לבית הכנסת.
5. אליהו הזכור לטוב.
6. בכ"י בהמ"ל חסר: ובקש לרחמו.
7. רבונו של עולם תן לי רשות שאתן לצדיק זה דבר שיחיה.
8. תוספת בכ"י בהמ"ל: לקחו ר' אברהם.
9. פגע בו.
10. יש להשלים כנראה: זהוב.
11. אמר לו: זקן, קנה בגד זה.
12. הלך אליהו ופגע בדרך אחרת כדמות זקן.
13. אמר לו: היאך?
14. בערך י' זהובים והסלע ותן לי הבגד.
15. חסר.
16. ונעשה תגר גדול שמעו כל התגרים שמועתו ובאו לישא וליתן עמו.
17. התחיל לעסוק בסחורה ומאחר התפלה.
18. כששמע הקב"ה כך אמר לאליהו: אוהב אחד היה לי ומרחקתו עלי.
19. בכ"י בהמ"ל תוספת: אמר לו: אברהם, אין אתה מכירני. אמר לו: לאו.
20. אמר לו: רבי ומורי קח ממני מאה דינרים.
21. שאיני יודע היכן הוא.
22. אמר לו: לך ופשפש. כל מ' יום הללו בדק ומצאו והחזירו לו. מיד נעשה כל ממונו לתהו ובהו.
23. כשראה כך התחיל לילך לבית הכנסת להשכים ולהעריב כמנהג הראשון.
24. מלים אלה חסרות בכ"י בהמ"ל.
25. רבונו של עולם תן לי רשות שאתן לזה הצדיק כלום שיחיה.

do not drive him away from me. Elijah said: I assure it. God said to him: Do as you wish. Elijah went to him and said: I am the one who gave you the sela and then again took it away from you because you stopped going to prayers. If you like, swear to me that you will not absent yourself from prayers, and I will reward you. He said to him: Willingly. And he blessed him as he had the first time.

D. Once the merchants heard about him. Five merchants went to him to test his riches. They said to him: Take all our merchandise and give us pepper for it all. He said: With pleasure. Then they said to him: We want nothing but oil and take all our merchandise. He said: With pleasure. Then they said to him: We want nothing but gold and silver. He said to them: Willingly. Then he took them to his treasury and gave them what they wanted, and they left.

מעלי.[26] אמר אליהו אני ערב בדבר.[27] א"ל הקב"ה: עשה רצונך. הלך אליהו אליו, אמ' לו: אני הוא שנתתי לך הסלע, וחזרתי ולקחתי ממך בשביל שהייתה מפסיד תפלה.[28] ואם תרצה תשבע לי שלא תפסיד תפלה, ואני אשלם לך.[29] א"ל: ברצון.[30] ובירכו יותר מבתחילה.[31]

D. פעם אחת שמעו סוחרים את שמועתו. הלכו אליו חמשה סוחרים לנסות את עושרו.[32] אמרו לו: קח כל סחורתינו ותן לנו פלפלין מן הכל.[33] אמר להם: ברצון.[34] אחרי כן אמרו לו: אין אנו רוצים כי אם שמן, ותקח כל סחורתינו. אמר להם: ברצון.[35] אחרי כן אמרו לו: אין אנו רוצים כי אם כסף וזהב.[36] הביאם לאוצרותיו ונתן להם כרצונם, והלכו להם"[37]

26. אמר לו הקב"ה: הנח לו, אל תרחיקהו מעלי.
27. ולא היה סובל אנקתו. אמר לפניו: רבונו של עולם אני ערב בו.
28. אמר לו: שלום עליך ר' אברהם. אמר לו: אינך מכירני? אמר לו: לאו. אמר לו: אני הוא שנתתיך הסלע ואני הוא שלקחתיו ממך.
29. ועכשו בא והשבע לי שלא תניח התפלה לעולם ואתנהו לך.
30. מיד נשבע וברכו.
31. ונתן לו שבעתים ממה שנתן תחלה.
32. פעם אחת שמעו התגרים, שמעו ובאו אצלו ב' תגרים.
33. ואמרו לו: קח ממנו סחורה ותן לנו פלפלין, תן לנו כמון, תן לנו שמן.
34. בכ"י בהמ"ל: קחו.
35. היו מנסים אותו עד עשרה מינים. אמר להם: קחו.
36. כשראו כך אמרו אין אנו צריכין אלא ממון.
37. מיד פתח מ' חביות שהיו מלאים כסף וזהב ונתן להם ממון והלכו. ועל כן נאמר: מי הקדימני ואשלם [איוב מא, ג].

35. A Valley Filled with Gold (319a)

A. Once R. Shimon b. Yoḥai had a student who went abroad and became rich. The other students saw he had become rich, and they too desired to go abroad like him. When R. Shimon noticed this, he took them all outside the city, into a valley, and prayed. The entire valley filled up with golden coins. He told them, whoever wishes to take [coins] may do so, but you should know: Whoever takes will be subtracting from his portion in the world to come, because the Torah's reward is not given in this world, but rather in the world to come, as it says: "And she shall rejoice in time to come" [Proverbs 31:25].

35. בקעה מלאה זהב (319א)

A. מעשה בתלמיד אחד של רבי שמעון בן יוחי[1] שיצא לחוצה לארץ,[2] ונעשה עשיר.[3] והיו התלמידים רואים אותו עשיר,[4] והיו הם מבקשים לצאת לחוצה לארץ כמותו.[5] כיון שהרגיש[6] ר' שמעון בדבר, הוציאם כולם[7] מחוץ לעיר בבקעה[8] ונתפלל.[9] נתמלא כל[10] הבקעה דנרי זהב. אמר להם: מי שרוצה ליטול יטול,[11] אלא היו יודעין שכל[12] הנוטל, הוא נוטל מחלקו של העולם הבא, כי מתן שכרה של תורה אינה לעולם הזה[13] אלא לעולם הבא, שנ' ותשחק ליום אחרון [משלי לא, כה].

1. ההשוואות להלן הן לתנחומא, פקודי, סימן ז (מהדורת בובר, דף סו, 131–132) ולשמו"ר נב, ג, המייצג נוסח קרוב לגרסת בספר המעשים (נוסח א), ולילקו"ש תהלים, רמז תתמג, ולמדרש תהלים [שוחר טוב], מזמור צב, סימן ח, דף רד, 407 – המייצגים נוסח אחר (נוסח ב).
2. כך גם בתנחומא פקודי: שיצא לחוצה לארץ. בנוסח ב, ילקו"ש תהלים, רמז תתמג (מהדורת שלוניקי רפ"ז): שיצא לסחורה. מדרש תהלים: שיצא להדנקי [להודו].
3. תנחומא פקודי: ובא עשיר; בנוסח ב, ילקו"ש תהלים: והרויח והעשיר, ובמדרש תהלים: ואתא טעין [וחזר טעון], "ופירוש בובר שם: "ובא עמוס בממון.
4. כך גם בתנחומא פקודי: והיו התלמידים רואין אותו, ובשמו"ר נב, ג: והיו התלמידים רואין אותו ומתקנאין בו. בנוסח ב, ילקו"ש תהלים ומדרש תהלים: והיו התלמידים רואים את הרויח שהרויח.
5. בתנחומא פקודי: היו רוצין לצאת לחוצה לארץ. בשמו"ר: והיו מבקשים הן לצאת לחוצה לארץ. בנוסח ב, ילקו"ש תהלים ומדרש תהלים: והיו מצירין עצמן.
6. תנחומא פקודי: וידע ר' שמעון.
7. והוציאם כולם: חסר בכל הגרסאות.
8. תנחומא פקודי: והוציאם לבקעה שעל פני מרון עירו. ראו הערות בובר, מדרש תהלים, שם, על חילופי הנוסח בשמה של העיר.
9. תנחומא פקודי: ונתפלל לפני הקב"ה.
10. שם: ונתמלאת הבקעה דינרי זהב.
11. שם: מי שמבקש ליטול יטול.
12. שם: כל מי שהוא נוטל עכשיו, מתוך חלקו של עולם הבא הוא נוטל.
13. שם: שאין מתן שכרה בעולם הזה.

36. A Precious Stone from Heaven (319a–319b)

A. [319a] Once R. Shimon b. Ḥalafta had nothing to eat for the Sabbath [and he gave it to the moneychanger]. He went out of town and prayed. God gave him a precious stone [319b] from heaven, and he returned [to the town] and gave it to the moneychanger and had enough for Sabbath expenses.

B. On Sabbath eve he was sitting and dining. His wife said: Where is all this from? He said: From what God has supplied his creatures. She said: If you do not tell me, I will taste nothing. He told her the whole story. She said: Give everything back. Why? he said. She said: Tomorrow you will be in paradise with your companions, and they will receive more than you, because the Torah's reward is not given in this world but rather in the world to come, as it says: "And she shall rejoice in time to come" [Proverbs 31:25]. After the Sabbath was over, he returned it all.

36. אבן טובה משמים (319א–319ב)

A. מעשה ברבי שמעון בן חלפתא שלא היה לו מה לאכול לשבת[1] (ונתנה לשולחני). יצא חוץ לעיר ונתפלל.[2] נתן לו הקב"ה אבן [319ב] טובה מן השמים,[3] ונכנס ונתנה לשולחני ופירנס את השבת.

B. והיה אוכל ויושב בליל(י) שבת. אמרה לו אשתו: מהיכן אילו? אמר לה: ממה שפירנס הקב"ה בריותיו.[4] אמרה לו: אם אין אתה אומר לי, לא אטעום כלום. אמר לה כל העניין. אמרה לו: החזר הכל.[5] אמר לה: למה? אמרה לו: למחר אתה בא בגן עדן עם חביריך והם יטלו יותר ממך,[6] לפי שאין מתן שכרה של תורה אלא לעתיד לבא,[7] שנ': ותשחק ליום אחרון [משלי לא, כה]. לאחר שבת החזיר(ה) הכל"[8]

1. תנחומא, בובר, שמות, פקודי, דף סו: מעשה בר' שמעון בן חלפתא, שבא ערב שבת ולא היה לו מאין לאכול. ההשוואות להלן הן לתנחומא, מהדורת בובר.
2. ערב שבת עם חשיכה יצא לו חוץ מן העיר ונתפלל לפני הקב"ה.
3. מיד נתנה לו אבן טובה מן השמים.
4. אמר לה כך וכך היה מעשה ונתפללתי וניתנה לי אבן טובה מן השמים ואלו ממנה.
5. אמרה לו איני טועמת כלום עד שתאמר לי שאתה מחזירה למוצאי שבת.
6. מחר אתה בא וחביריך עמך והם נוטלים יותר ואתה נוטל פחות מהם.
7. לעולם הבא.
8. כיון שהלך השבת עמד והחזירה, מיד ניטלה ממנו.

37. From Rejoicing to Mourning (319b)

[319b] Once, one of the most important men of Kabul was anointing his son in preparation for his wedding, and he made a great banquet for the sages. He said to his son: Bring me such and such a wine, from the barrel that is in the attic. His son went, and a snake came and bit him and he died. His father waited with the guests. He said: I will go and see what my son is doing. He went and found him dead. What did the father do? He waited until they had finished eating and drinking. When they had finished their feast, he said to them: You came here to bless the groom, bless the mourners. You have come to place him under the bridal canopy, place him in his grave.

37. משמחה לאבל (319ב)

A. מעשה באחד מגדולי כבול[1] שהיה מושח בנו להכניסו לחופה,[2] ועשה סעודה גדולה לחכמים. אמר לבנו: הבא לי מן יין פלוני, מן חבית שבעלייה.[3] הלך בנו, בא נחש ונשכו ומת.[4] המתין אביו עם המסובין.[5] אמר: אלך ואראה מה עושה בני.[6] הלך, ומצאו מת.[7] מה עשה אביו,[8] המתין עד שאכלו ושתו.[9] כיון שגמרו סעודתם[10] אמר להם: באתם לברך ברכת חתנים, ברכו ברכת אבילים.[11] באתם להכניס בני לחופה, הכניסו אותו לקבורה"[12]

1. תנחומא, בובר, פרשת שמיני סימן ג, 24: בבל. ההשוואות להלן הן לתנחומא, מהדורת בובר, הזהה כמעט לגרסת התנחומא הנדפס, סימן ב, ד"ה: ויהי ביום השמיני.
2. שהיה משיא את בנו.
3. חבית יין פלוני מן העלייה.
4. עלה לעלייה הכישו נחש בין החביות ומת.
5. המתין אביו עם המסובין ושהה ולא בא.
6. אעלה ואראה מה בני עושה.
7. עלה אביו ומצאו מושלך בין החביות מת.
8. מה עשה אותו חסיד.
9. המתין בעצמו עד שאכלו האורחין ושתו כל צורכן.
10. כיוון שגמרו.
11. לברך ברכת חתנים באתם על בני, ברכו עליו ברכת אבלים.
12. להכניסו באתם, הכניסוהו לקבורה. וכן תוספת אפילוג: עלה ר' זכאי דכבול ואמר לשחוק אמרתי מהולל [קהלת ב:ב].

38. Hadrian and the Old Man (319b)

A. [319b] Once King Hadrian went out to war accompanied by his legions. He found an old man planting figs. The king said to him: You are old and yet you plant? He said to him: I may eat from them, and if not, my children will eat from them.

B. He returned three years later and found the old man in the same spot. The old man went and filled a basket with the figs. He said to him: I am the old man whom you saw planting, and here are some of the fruits that I planted, the best of my figs and fruits. When the king heard [this], he was shaken. He said [to his servants]: Fill up the basket with golden dinars instead of the figs.

C. And a neighboring woman was standing, and she said to her husband: You sit all day at home and never do anything like so-and-so, and see how he has become rich. He went and took a basket. He said [to the king]: I heard that you like fruit. I have come to bring you the most beautiful figs and fruits. A soldier came and beat him, and he was covered with bruises. Finally he returned home, weeping, and his wife thought that he was bringing a basket filled with gold. He said: Woe is me that I listened to you. This is to teach you that all women are wicked and cause their husbands to fall, and woe is he who listens to them.

38. אדריינוס והנוטע הזקן (319ב)

A. מעשה באדריינוס המלך שהיה יוצא למלחמה וגייסות עמו.[1] מצא זקן אחד נוטע תאינים.[2] אמר לו המלך: אתה זקן ואתה נוטע?[3] אמר לו: שמא אוכל מהם, ואם לאו בני יאכלו מהם.[4]

B. חזר לאחר שלש שנים,[5] מצא הזקן באותו מקום.[6] הלך הזקן, ומלא כלכלה מן התאינים.[7] אמר לו: אני הוא הזקן שראיתני נוטע, והילך מן הפירות שנטעתי מן היפות שבהן. כששמע המלך נבהל מאד.[8] אמר לו: מלאו הכלכלה מדינרי זהב תחת התאינים.[9]

C. והיתה שכינתו עומדת[10] ואמרה לבעלה: לעולם אתה יושב בביתך ואין אתה עושה כמו פלוני, כי עתה נעשה עשיר.[11] הלך ולקח סל אחד.[12] א"ל: שמעתי עליך כי אתה אוהב הפירות, הבאתי לך מן היפות שלי מן התאינים והפירות.[13] הלך סרדיוט אחד והכה אותו, ונתמלא כולו חבורות.[14] עד שחזר והיה בוכה,[15] ואשתו הייתה סבורה שהיה מביא הסל מלא זהב.[16] אמר: אוי לי ששמעתי לדבריך.[17] ללמדך שכל הנשים רעות ומפילות את בעליהן ואוי לו למי ששומע להם.[18]

---

1. תנחומא, בובר, ויקרא, קדושים, סימן ח' בובר, 76: מעשה באדרינוס המלך שהיה עובר למלחמה, והיה הולך עם גייסות שלו להלחם עם מדינה אחרת שמרדה בו. ההשוואות להלן הן למקור זה.
2. ומצא זקן אחד שהיה נוטע.
3. א"ל אדריאנוס: אתה זקן עומד וטורח ומתייגע לאחרים.
4. א"ל לאדריאנוס: אדוני המלך, הריני נוטע אם אזכה אוכל מפירות נטיעתי, ואם לאו יאכלו בני.
5. עשה שלוש שנים במלחמה, וחזר לאחר שלוש שנים.
6. בתנחומא בובר: חסר.
7. כלכלה היא טנא. ראו אבן שושן: כלכלה.
8. המלה "נבהל" מבטאת כאן כנראה פליאה מן הפגישה עם הזקן המופלג פעם נוספת, ובניגוד לכל ציפיותיו. בתנחומא תגובת ה"בהלה" אינה מוזכרת.
9. אמר אדריאנוס לעבדיו: טלו אותה ממנו ומלאוהו אותה זהובים, ועשו כך.
10. נטל הזקן את הכלכלה מלאה זהובים, והתחיל הולך ומשתבח בביתו לאשתו ולבניו, וסח להם את מעשה. היתה שכינתו עומדת שם שמעה מה אמר הזקן.
11. אמרה לבעלה כל בני אדם הולכים, והקב"ה נותן להם, ומזמן להם טובה, ואתה יושב בביתך חשוך באופל, הרי [שכן] שלנו כיבד את המלך בכלכלה של תאנים, ומילא אותה לו זהובים, ואתה עמוד וטול סל גדול ומילא אותו מיני מגדים מן תפוחים ותאנים, ושאר מיני פירות יפים, שהוא אוהב אותן הרבה, לך וכיבדו בהן, אולי ימלא אותו לך זהובים, כמו שעשה לשכננו הזקן.
12. הלך ושמע לאשתו ונטל סל גדול ומילא אותו תפוחים ותאנים, וטען על כתיפו והלך ועמד לפניו.
13. וקירב לפני המלך בקופנדר, ואמר לו: אדוני המלך שמעתי שאתה אוהב את הפירות, ובאתי לכבדך בתאנים ותפוחים.
14. אמר המלך לסרדיוטין, טלו הסל וטפחו לו על פניו, וכן עשו וטפחו אותו על פניו, עד שנפחו פניו, ושברו את עיניו, ועשאוהו דוגמא.
15. והלך לביתו כשהוא עשוי דוגמא ובוכה.
16. והיא סבורה שהוא בא בסל מלא זהובים, וראתה אותו פניו נפוחות, וגופו מושבר ומוכה, אמרה לו: מה לך?
17. אמר לה: ששמעתי לך והלכתי וכבדתי אותו באותו דורון, וטפחו אותי על פני, אילולא שמעתי לך והיטלתי בסל מיני פירות קשין, כבר היו מרגמין את פני ואת כל גופי בהן.
18. וכל כך למה, ללמדך שהנשים הרעות מפילות את בעליהן, לפיכך לא יבטל אדם מן הנטיעות, אלא כשם שמצא עוד יוסיף ויטע, אפילו זקן, אמר הקב"ה לישראל למדו ממני, כביכול אמר ויטע ה' א-להים גן בעדן מקדם.

39. The *Ḥasid* and the Ruler (319b–320a)

A. [319b] Once there was a *ḥasid* who was walking on the road. A ruler encountered him. He greeted him, and the man did not respond. He [the ruler] waited for him until he had finished praying. He said to him: Doesn't it say in your Torah: "Only take heed to yourself, and keep your soul diligently [320a]" [Deuteronomy 4:9]? And it also says: "So watch yourselves carefully" [Deuteronomy 4:15]. If I were to cut off your head with this sword, what then? He said: Wait until I tell you something. If you were standing before the king, pleading with him, and a man greeted you, would you respond to him? He said: No. So, if this is the case before a king of flesh and blood, who is here today and in his grave tomorrow, how much more so is it with the King of Kings, God Almighty, before whom I was standing! The ruler was mollified, and the *ḥasid* bid him farewell.

39. החסיד וההגמון (319ב–320א)

A. מעשה בחסיד אחד שהיה מהלך בדרך. פגע בו הגמון אחד.[1] נתן לו שלום {ולא} החזיר לו. המתין לו עד שסיים תפלתו. א"ל: והלא כתיב בתורתכם רק השמר לך ושמור את נפשך [320א] מאד [דברים ד, ט]. וכת' ונשמרתם מאד לנפשותיכם [דברים ד, טו].[2] אילו הייתי מתיז ראשך בסייף מה היה?[3] א"ל: תמתין לי עד שאומר לך דבר.[4] אילו היית עומד לפני המלך לחנן לו, ואדם אחד היה נותן לך שלום הייתה משיבו? אמר לו: לאו.[5] ומה לפני <~~לפ~~> מלך בשר ודם שהיום כאן ולמחר בקבר כך, לפני מלך מלכי המלכים הקב"ה שהייתי עומד ומתפלל לפניו, על אחד כמה וכמה. נתפייס ההגמון, ואחרי כן נפטר החסיד ממנו.[6]

---

1. ברכות לג ע"ב: בא הגמון אחד ההשוואות להלן הם למסכת ברכות.
2. לאחר שסיים תפלתו א"ל: ריקא והלא כתוב בתורתכם רק השמר לך ושמור נפשך [דברים ד, ט] וכתיב: "ונשמרתם מאד לנפשותיכם" [דברים ד, טו].
3. כשנתתי לך שלום למה לא החזרת לי שלום? אם הייתי חותך ראשך בסייף מי היה תובע את דמך מידי?
4. א"ל: המתן לי עד שאפייסך בדברים.
5. א"ל: אילו היית עומד לפני מלך בשר ודם ובא חברך ונתן לך שלום היית מחזיר לו? א"ל: לאו. ואם היית מחזיר לו מה היו עושים לך? א"ל: היו חותכים את ראשי בסייף. א"ל: והלא דברים ק"ו.
6. ומה אתה שהיית עומד לפני מלך בשר ודם שהיום כאן ומחר בקבר, כך אני שהייתי עומד לפני מלך מלכי המלכים הקב"ה שהוא חי וקיים לעד ולעולמי עולמים על אחת כמה וכמה. מיד נתפייס אותו ההגמון ונפטר אותו חסיד לביתו לשלום.

40. R. Ḥanina b. Dosa and the Snake (320a)

A. [320a] Once there was a snake that used to harm people. They came to R. Ḥanina b. Dosa to inform him. He said to them: Come and show me his hole. They looked for it and found it. He went and placed his heel on the opening of the hole. The snake came out and bit him, and it died. R. Ḥanina took it on his shoulder and brought it to the study hall. He told them [his students]: Come and see that it is not the snake that kills but rather the sin that kills. They said: Woe to the man who encounters a snake, and woe to the snake that encounters R. Ḥanina b. Dosa.

40. רבי חנינא בן דוסא והנחש (320א)

A. מעשה בנחש אחד שהיה מזיק את הבריות. באו והודיעו לר' חנינא בן דוסא.[1] אמר להם: בואו והודיעו לי את חורו. בדקו ומצאו אותו.[2] הלך והניח עקיבו על פתח חורו. יצא ונשכו ומת הנחש.[3] נטלו ר' חנינא על כתיפו והביאו לבית המדרש. אמר להם: בואו ראו שאין נחש ממית אלא החטא ממית.[4] אמרו: אוי לו לאדם שפגע בו נחש ואוי לו לנחש שפגע ברבי חנינא בן דוסא"[5]

1. ברכות, לג ע"א: מעשה במקום אחד שהיה ערוד והיה מזיק את הבריות. באו והודיעו לו לר' חנינא בן דוסא. ההשוואות להלן הן למסכת ברכות.
2. אמר להם: הראו לי את חורו. הראוהו את חורו.
3. נתן עקבו על פי החור יצא ונשכו ומת אותו ערוד.
4. נטלו על כתפו והביאו לבית המדרש. אמר להם: ראו בני אין ערוד ממית אלא החטא ממית.
5. באותה שעה אמרו: אוי לו לאדם שפגע בו ערוד ואוי לו לערוד שפגע בו ר' חנינא בן דוסא.

41. Do Not Fail to Attend Public Prayers (320a–320b)

A. [320a] Once there was a *ḥasid* who was wealthy and had close ties to the king. He had an only son who was handsome and good-looking and wise. And before this *ḥasid* passed away, he instructed his son not to leave the synagogue from the moment that the prayer leader arose to pray and recite the *Kaddish* prayer [for the dead] until he had completed all of his prayers. And even if someone who did not hear the prayer should rise to recite the [introductory] *Barkhu* prayer, you should wait with him until he completes reciting his prayers. And that is what I did all my life, and I was successful in everything I did. And should you pass through a city that has a synagogue and you hear a prayer leader, go inside and do not leave until the prayer leader has completed his prayers. And the *ḥasid* passed away.

B. And the son won the favor of everyone who saw him, and he served the king and poured the wine in the goblet of the king and queen and cut their bread and meat. And they loved him very much, and his heart was dedicated to heaven. The viceroy saw him and was envious of him. He came to the king and said to him: Your majesty, you have eyes but you do not see that this young man loves the queen, and they are committing adultery together. The king rebuked him and did not believe him, but he continued to tell him day after day until he managed to make him feel jealous.

C. One day, the king went to observe workers who were preparing a bonfire of wood and stones to make lime for him. He said to the foreman: The man who comes first tomorrow morning, take him and cast him into the furnace forthwith. And if you do not do so, your life will be taken instead. He answered: Your majesty, I will do as you wish. And the king went home. And night came, and the young man was serving the king. He summoned him and commanded him: Early tomorrow morning, go to the place where they are making lime and tell the foreman to light the fire well. And the young man answered: I will do as you wish.

D. In the morning, the young man arose and mounted his horse. He passed by the synagogue, and when he heard [320b] the prayer leader, he dismounted his horse and entered the synagogue to pray. After the prayer leader had finished, one who had not heard the prayers stood up and recited the *Barkhu* prayer, and he [the young man] waited until he had finished, and he was delayed until the sun was high in the sky.

41. אל תחמיץ תפילה בציבור (320א–320ב)

A. מעשה בחסיד אחד שהיה עשיר וקרוב למלכות, והיה לו בן אחד יפה תואר ויפה מראה וחכם.[1] ובעת פטירתו של אותו חסיד צוה לבנו, שלא יצא מבית הכנסת משעה שיקום החזן להתפלל ויתחיל קדיש, עד שיגמור כל תפלתו. וגם אם יקום אחד לומר ברכו שלא שמע תפלה, המתן אותו עד שיגמור תפלתו.[2] וכן עשיתי כל ימי, והצלחתי במעשי. וגם אם תעבור בעיר שיש בו בית הכנסת ותשמע החזן, תכנס ואל תצא עד שיגמור החזן תפלתו. והלך אותו חסיד לבית עולמו.

B. והבן היה מאד נחמד לכל רואיו, והיה משרת לפני המלך ומוזג יין בכוס המלך והמלכה, וחותך לחם ובשר לפניהם. והיו אוהבים אותו ביותר, ולבו לשמים. וירא אותו משנה המלך, ויקנא בו. ויבא אל המלך ויאמר לו: אדוני המלך, עינים לך ואין אתה רואה כי זה הבחור אוהב את המלכה, ומנאפים יחד. ויגער בו המלך ולא האמין לו עד כי אמר לו היום ומחר, עד שהכניס קנאה בלבו.

C. ויהי היום, וילך המלך לראות פועלים שהיו עושין לו מדורת עצים ואבנים לעשות סיד. ויאמר לרב הפועלים: אותו האיש אשר יבא הנה למחר ראשון, קח אותו והשליכהו לתוך כבשן האש בלא איחור. ואם לא תעשה זאת, נפשך תחת נפשו. ויען לו:<אדוני>המלך, אעשה כמצותך. וישב לו המלך לביתו. ויהי הלילה, וישרת הבחור לפני המלך ויקרא הבחור ויצו לו: השכם בבקר למחר ולך למקום שעושין הסיד, ואמור לרב הפועלים שידליק האש היטב. ויען הבחור: אני אעשה כמצותך.

D. ויהי בבקר, ויקם הבחור וירכב על הסוס, ויעבר לפני בית הכנסת ושמע [320ב] החזן, וירד מעל הסוס ונכנס לבית הכנסת ויתפלל. אחר שסיים החזן, עמד אחר שלא שמע תפלה ואמר ברכו, והמתין עד שגמר ואיחר עד שהיה היום גדול.

---

1. מועתק בגסטר, ספר המעשיות (#308, 207–208).
2. 'ברכו' היא ברכת: "ברכו את ה' המבורך" הנאמרת לאחר התפילה, והקהל עונה: "ברוך ה' המבורך לעולם ועד".

E. The king called to his viceroy and commanded him: Go to the place where they are making lime, and ask the foreman if he did as I commanded. The viceroy hurried off, riding his horse, and he said to the foreman: Have you done as the king commanded? They took the viceroy and cast him into the furnace. When the young man arrived there, he saw that the viceroy had been cast into the furnace. He said to the foreman: The king will kill you when he finds out about this. The foreman responded and said: Yesterday, the king commanded me to do this: Cast the first man I send you first thing in the morning into the furnace, and he was the first to come.

F. The young man returned to the king and said to him: Your majesty, why did you command that the viceroy be burned? The king was greatly horrified and amazed, and he said to the young man: Now I realize that you are a God-fearing man and that your Creator loves you, because the viceroy said such and such about you and the queen, and I commanded that the first man whom I sent to the foreman making the lime should be cast into the fire. And I commanded you to be the first. Then I asked my viceroy to go and see if my command had been fulfilled, and you were delayed, and he was cast into the fire in your stead. Now I know that you are innocent. In other words, as it says: "The righteous is delivered out of trouble, and the wicked comes in his stead" [Proverbs 11:8]. That is why one must wait in the synagogue until the prayer leader has finished praying, even if there is just one who rises because he has not heard the rest of the prayers.

E. ויקרא המלך אל המשנה ויצו לו: לך למקום שעושין הסיד ושאל לרב הפועלים אם עשה מצותי. וימהר המשנה וירכב על סוסו, ויאמר לרב הפועלים: עשית מצות המלך? ויקחו המשנה ויאסרו אותו, וישליכו אותו בכבשן. ויבא הבחור לשם, וירא כי השליכו המשנה בכבשן. ויאמר לרב הפועלים: המלך יהרוג אתכם אם ידע זה. ויען רב הפועלים ויאמר לו: המלך ציוני אתמול: האיש אשר אשלח לך למחר בבקר ראשון, השליכהו בכבשן האש. והנה הוא בא ראשון.

F. וישב הבחור אל {~~הבחור~~ המלך}[3] ” ויאמר לו: אדוני המלך, מדוע ציוית לשרוף המשנה? ויחרד המלך חרדה גדולה ויתמה מאוד, ויאמר אל הבחור: עתה ידעתי כי ירא אל-הים אתה ובוראך אוהב אותך, כי כך וכך הלשין המשנה אותך מן המלכה, וציויתי להשליך <~~אותך~~> באש האיש אשר אשלח ראשון אל רב הפועלים אשר עושה הסיד. ואותך ציויתי לילך ראשון. ואחר כך אמרתי למשנה: לך וראה אם עשו מצותי, ואתה איחרת והשליכו אותו במקומך. עתה ידעתי שאתה נקי. היינו: הכי דכתיב צדיק מצרה נחלץ ויבא רשע תחתיו [משלי יא, ח]. ולכך יש להמתין בבית הכנסת עד שיגמור החזן להתפלל, ואפילו קם אחד שלא שמע עם הצבור.

3. תוספת עילית בכתב היד.

42. Solomon's Scribes (320b)

A. [320b] Once it was decreed that Aliḥaraf and Aḥiya, two of Solomon's scribes, would die at the gates of Lod. And the Angel of Death regretted that he was unable to vanquish them. And anyone who was within the city of Lod, the Angel of Death had no control over. And because Solomon was fond of them, he made Asmodeus swear that he would take them there. And when they were at the gates of Lod, the Angel of Death came and killed them. Solomon said: A person's legs are responsible for him. They take him to the place where he is wanted.

42. סופרי שלמה (320ב)

A. מעשה באליחרף ואחיה שני סופרי שלמה המלך,[1] שהיה עליהם גזירה מן המקום שלא ימותו כי אם בשער לוד.[2] והיה מלאך המות מצטער עליהם שלא היה יכול להם. וכל מי שהיה בתוך העיר של לוד,[3] לא היה לֹ שולט בהם מלאך המות.[4] ומתוך שהיה שלמה מחבבן השביע אשמדאי לנושאם לשם.[5] כשהיו בשער לוד בא מלאך המות והרגם.[6] אמר שלמה: ריגלוהי דאיניש אינון ערבין ביה. לאתר דמתבעי תמן מובילין יתיה [רגליו של אדם ערבים לו. למקום שהוא מתבקש שם מובילים אותו]"[7]

1. השוו למלכים א ד, ג: "אליחרף ואחיה בני שישא ספרים". סוכה נג, ע"א [בתרגום מארמית]: אותם שני כושים שהיו עומדים לפני שלמה אליחרף ואחיה בני שישא סופרי שלמה היו. ההשוואות להלן הן למסכת סוכה (וילנא, האחים ראם; כ"י מינכן 95).
2. במסכת סוכה, וילנא קביעה זו אינה מוזכרת כעובדה אלא משתמעת מדין ודברים בין שלמה למלאך המוות: יום אחד ראה (שלמה) למלאך המות שהוא עצוב אמר לו מדוע אתה עצוב. אמר לו [מלאך המוות] אני צריך את שני הכושים [שני סופרי המלאך] שיושבים כאן.
3. במסכת סוכה, וילנא: לוז. סוכה, כ"י מינכן 59: לוד.
4. במסכת סוכה, וילנא, בלי התוספת, שמי שיושב בלוז אין מלאך המוות שולט בו. והשוו לפירוש רש"י על אתר, סוכה נג ע"א: ולא היה יכול ליטול נשמתם כיון שלא נגזר עליהם למות, כי אם בשער לוז.
5. בלי איזכור אשמדאי: מסרם [שלמה] לשני שעירים [שדים] ושלחם למחוז העיר לוז.
6. כאשר הגיעו למחוז העיר לוז – מתו. בכ"י מינכן 140: כאשר הגיעו לשער של לוז. בדפוס וילנא תוספת: למחרת ראה את מלאך המוות צוחק. אמר לו: למה צחקת? אמר לו: למקום בו נתבקשו ממני, לשם שלחת אותם [בתרגום מארמית].
7. מיד פתח שלמה ואמר.

43. The Weasel and the Pit (320b–321a)

A. [320b] Once there was a girl who was walking to her mother's home, and she was adorned with silver and gold, and she lost her way and walked on a secluded path. When noon came, she was thirsty, but there was no water. She saw a well with a rope and bucket hanging from it. She took hold of the rope and climbed down into the well to drink. She wanted to climb back up, but could not. She screamed and cried until a man passed by and heard her voice. So he looked inside, but he could not see her. He said to her: Are you a human or demon? She said to him: I am a human. He said: What if you are a spirit and you overcome me? She said: No, I am a human. [321a] Swear to me. And she swore to him. He said: If I pull you up, will you marry me? She said: Yes.

B. He pulled her up. Once he had brought her up, he wished to have his way with her immediately. She said to him: Of which people are you? He said: I am from Israel, from such and such a place, and I am from a priestly family. [She said:] I am from such and such a place, descended from well-known and respected people. She said to him: You who are from such a holy people, whom the Almighty chose and sanctified from among all the nations, yet you wish to act like a beast without a marriage ceremony or marriage contract? Follow me to my father and mother, and I will become engaged to you. They made a covenant with one another. He said to her: Who will be the witness between you and me? And a weasel happened to pass by before them. He said to her: The heavens and the weasel and the pit will be witnesses. And each went on their own way.

43. חולדה ובור (320ב–321א)

A. מעשה בנערה[1] אחת שהייתה הולכת לבית אמה[2] והייתה מקושטת בכסף[3] וזהב[4] ותעה בדרך והלכה בלא יישוב. כיון שהגיע חצי היום צמאה ולא היה לה מים.[5] ראתה באר וחבל דלי תלוי עליו. אחזה בחבל[6] וירדה בתוך הבאר ושתתה. בקשה לעלות ולא יכלה. והייתה צועקת ובוכה עד שעבר עליה אדם אחד ושמע קולה, והביט בה[7] ולא היה יכול להבחין. אמר לה:[8] מבני אדם את או מן המזיקין? אמרה לו: מבני אדם אני. אמר לה שמא מן הרוחות את ומתגברת[9] עלי? אמרה לו: לאו, מבני אדם אני.[10] [321א] השבע לי.[11] ונשבעה לו.[12] אמר לה: אם אני אעלך תינשאי לי? אמרה לו: הן. העלה אותה.

B. כיון שהעלה אותה, ביקש להיזקק עליה מיד. אמרה לו: מאיזה עם אתה? אמר לה: מישראל אני, ממקום פלוני וכהן. [אמרה לו:] אף אני ממקום פלוני,[13] מבני אדם ידועים ונקובי שם. אמרה לו: עם קדוש כמותך שבחר בך הקב"ה מכל ישראל וקידש אותך,[14] ואתה מבקש לעשות כבהמה בלא קידושין ובלא כתובה? בא אחרי אצל אבי ואמי, ואני מתארסת לך. נתנו ברית זה לזה.[15] אמר לה: מי יהיה עד ביני ובינך? והיתה חולדה אחת עוברת לפניהם.[16] אמר לה:[17] השמים וחולדה ובור יהיו עדים.[18] הלכו כל אחד לדרכו.

---

1. תוספת אפילוג בערוך השלם, מהדורת קוהוט (כרך שלישי, ערך 'חלד', 395): א"ר חנינא בא וראה כמה גדולים בעל אמנה מנא לן מחולדה ובור. ומה המאמין בחולדה ובור כך המאמין בקב"ה ההשוואות להלן הן לנוסח ערוך השלם, 395–396.
2. בערוך: לבית אביה.
3. כלי כסף.
4. תוספת בערוך: יפת תואר.
5. ולא היתה לה לויה.
6. תוספת בערוך: ונשתלשלה.
7. ועמד על הבאר והציץ בה.
8. תוספת בערוך: מי את?
9. בערוך: ומתנכרת.
10. בערוך, בלי: מבני אדם אני.
11. אמר לה: השבעי לי שמבני אדם את.
12. תוספת בערוך: אמר לה: מה טיבך? סיפרה לו כל המעשה.
13. שם, תוספת: ממשפחה פלוני.
14. שבחר בך הקב"ה וקידשך מכל ישראל.
15. זה לזו וזו לזה.
16. עוברת כנגדן.
17. אמרה לו.
18. השמים וחולדה זו ובאר זו יהיו עדים שאין אנו מכזבים זה בזה.

C. The girl kept her word, and whoever wanted her, she refused him. When they [her family] put pressure on her, she behaved as if she were mad and possessed, tearing her own clothes and the clothes of anyone who touched her, until people kept their distance from her. And as for him, once he had gone away from her, his lust overtook him, and he forgot her and went to his hometown. And he married another woman, and she became pregnant and bore a son. When the son reached the age of three months, he was choked to death by a weasel. And the woman became pregnant again and bore a son, and he fell into a pit. His wife said to him: If your sons had died a natural death, I would accept the verdict. But seeing that they have died an unnatural death, it cannot be for no reason. Tell me what you have done. He told her what he had done, and he divorced her, and she said to him: Go to the one whom God has fated you to be with.

D. He went and looked for the girl. He was told: She is possessed, and she does such and such to anyone who seeks her hand. He went to her father and told him the entire story and said to him: I accept her with all her blemishes. He summoned witnesses. He came to her, and she began acting as she was accustomed. He told her the story of the weasel and the pit. She said to him: I kept my part of the covenant. At once she came to her senses, and they were fruitful and multiplied both in offspring and property. Of her the Bible says that the eyes of God will be upon the faithful of the land [cf. Psalms 101:6].

C. אותה נערה עמדה באמונתה וכל מי שהיה תובעה היתה ממאנת עליו. כיון שהחזיקו בה[19] התחילה לנהג עצמה כשוטה ונכפת[20] ומקרעת בגדיה ובגדי כל מי שהיה נוגע בה, עד שנמנעו ממנה בני אדם.[21] והוא, כיון שעבר מנגד פניה תקפו יצרו, ושכחה והלך לעירו.[22] ונשא אשה אחרת ונתעברה, וילדה בן.[23] כשהגיע שלשה חדשים[24] חנקתו חולדה. ועוד נתעברה וילדה בן,[25] ונפל לבור. אמרה לו אשתו: אם בדרך בני[26] אדם מתים בניך הייתי מצדקת הדין.[27] עכשיו שמתו מיתה משונה, אין זה בלא שום דבר.[28] ספר לי מה מעשיך. גילה לה כל המעשה, ונתגרשה ממנו. ואמרה לו: לך אצל חלקך שנתן לך הקב"ה.

D. הלך ושאל אותה הנערה.[29] אמרו לו: נכפית היא, וכל מי שתובעה, כך וכך עושה לו. הלך אצל אביה, סיפר לו כל המעשה. אמר לו: אני מקבל כל המומין שבה עלי.[30] העמיד עליו עדים. בא אצלה, התחילה לעשות כמנהגה. ספר לה כל המעשה דחולדה ובור. אמרה לו: אף אני בבריתי עמדתי. מיד נתיישבה דעתה, ופרו ורבו בבנים ובנכסים. ועליה אמר הכתוב עיני י"י בנאמני ארץ"[31]

---

19. כלומר, כיוון שלחצו עליה.
20. ונכפה.
21. תוספת: והיא היתה משמרת בריתה לאותו האיש.
22. ונפנה למלאכתו.
23. תוספת: זכר.
24. כשהגיע לג' חדשים.
25. זכר.
26. כל.
27. הייתי אומרת צידוק הדין.
28. חסר: שום.
29. הלך ושאל בעירה.
30. אני מקבל כל מום שבה.
31. השוו לתהילים קא, ו.

44. The Spies and the Giants in Canaan (321a–321b)

A. [321a] Once the daughter of a giant entered an orchard and ate a pomegranate and discarded its peel. When the spies saw that peel, they thought it was a cave. The twelve spies went and entered it and hid there. A while later, the giant's daughter remembered that she had eaten a pomegranate. She said: I will go and throw away the peel so that my father doesn't see it. She went and cast the peel together with the twelve spies inside it outside the orchard, and she did not notice them. When they emerged they said: See the strength of the women. The men must be even stronger. R. Joḥanan said: Each of the giants was sixty cubits high. And since Caleb recounted the praise of the land, they were ashamed and said to Caleb: Were you not together with us as part of the same plan?

B. This may be likened to a *margelitos*, a merchant of precious stones and pearls who used to travel along the way and carry his merchandise. Robbers attacked him and said to him: Give us everything you have. He said: I have nothing with me, only glass. They let him go, and he entered the city and set up a table upon which he placed precious stones and pearls. And each of them was of inestimable value. One of the robbers came and asked to touch one of them. He said: It is not fitting for someone like you to touch them. The robber was frightened and said: Aren't these the same ones you said were only glass? So it was with Caleb, who when he was with the spies made his peace with them because he feared them. But when he came before the Israelites, he said: "It is a land of milk and honey" [Deuteronomy 14:8], "Let us go up at once, and possess it; for we are well able to overcome it" [Numbers 13:30].

44. המרגלים והענקים בכנען (321א–321ב)

A. מעשה בבתו של ענק שנכנסה לפרדס ואכלה רמון אחד והשליכה קליפתו.[1] כיון שראו המרגלים אותה קליפה היו סבורים שמערה היתה. הלכו השנים עשר מרגלים ונכנסו בתוכה ונטמנו שם.[2] לאחר שעה נזכרה בת הענק שאכלה רמון. אמרה: אלך ואשליך הקליפה שלא יראה אותה אבי. הלכה והשליכה הקליפה עם השנים עשר איש אשר בתוכה חוץ לפרדס, ולא הרגישה מהם. כשיצאו אמרו: ראו הגבורה שיש בנשים, באנשים על אחת כמה וכמה.[3] אמר ר' יוחנן: כל אחד מן המרגלים גובהן ששים אמה.[4] וכיון שסיפר כלב שבחה של הארץ נתביישו ואמרו לכלב: לא עמנו היית באותה עיצה?

B. משל למרגליטוס[5] הוא סוחר [321ב] נושא אבנים טובות ומרגליות שהיה הולך בדרך ונושא סחורתו. פגעו בו ליסטים, אמרו לו: תן לנו כל מה אשר בידך. אמר להם: אין עמי, רק כלי זכוכית. הניחוהו ונכנס למדינה, ושם שלחן לפניו ונתן עליו האבנים ומרגליות. וכל אחת ואחת אין שיעור לדמיה. בא אחד מן הליסטים לפניו ובקש ליגע באחת מהן. א"ל: הנח שאין לאדם כמוך ליגע בהן. נבהל אותו ליסטים. אמר: וכי אין אילו מאותן שאמרת לנו של זכוכית הן? אף כלב כשהיה עם המרגלים השלים עמהם, שהיה מתיירא מהם. וכיון שבא אצל ישראל אמר להם: ארץ זבת חלב ודבש [במדבר יד, ח], עלה נעלה וירשנו אותה [במדבר יג, ל]"

1. תוספת בפתרון תורה, פרשת שלח לך (מהדורת אורבך, 155): והיו מרגלים מתחבאים שם.
2. בכ"י פרמא 2342 (דה רוסי 541), 89ב–90א (בתוך: שכטר, ספר קוהוט, 492): נכנסו לעירו של ענק ראוהו ונפחדו וכשראו המרגלים את הענק הלכו להטמין עצמן תחת אותה קליפה שהיו סבורין שהוא פי מערה אחת [. . .].
3. פתרון תורה: אמרו זה לזה ראה גבורתה מה שהיתה סבורה שאנו חגבין, וכיון שבאו אצל ישראל אמרו להן ונהי בעינינו כחג' וג'; כ"י פרמא 2342: וכיון שיצאו אמרו זה לזה ראו גבורה שיש בנשים. באנשים על אחת כמה וכמה.
4. בפתרון תורה הסיפור מסתיים בתיאור הענקים: אר' יוחנן קולית שברגלו של אחד מהן חמישים וארבע אמות חוץ מראשו, ואת צוארו וראשו במידה מעוטה שש אמות הרי ששים אמה.
5. משל זה אינו מצוי בגרסאות האחרות של הסיפור.

45. Soft-Shelled Walnuts (321b)

A. [321b] Once there was a non-Jew who invited Rabban Shimon b. Gamliel and set a table made of thirty talents of gold. He ordered his servants to bring every variety of food in the world, and they brought him everything except soft-shelled walnuts. When they came to eat, the gentile noticed that there were no soft-shelled walnuts. He took the table and smashed it in anger. Rabban Shimon b. Gamliel said: Why did you break this very valuable table because of a small species that your servants overlooked? He answered: My heart and yours know that I have no portion in the world to come. That is why I pleasure my spirit with all my strength, and why I am unhappy if I have all the species in the world before me except one. And on that matter Solomon noted in his wisdom: "The righteous eats to his heart's content, but the belly of the wicked shall want" [Proverbs 13:25].

45. אגוזי פרך (321ב)

A. מעשה היה בגוי אחד שזימן את רבן גמליאל,[1] ועשה שלחן אחד משלשים כיכרי זהב.[2] וצוה למשרתיו להביא מכל מיני מאכל שבעולם, והביאו לו לבד מאגוזי פרך.[3] כשבאו לאכול ראה שאין שם אגוזי פרך.[4] נטל השלחן ושברה בכעס.[5] א"ל רבן גמליאל: למה שברת את השולחן ששוה ממון גדול מפני מין קטן שחיסרו עבדיך?[6] השיב לו: לבי ולבך יודעין שאין לי חלק לעולם הבא.[7] לכן אתענג נפשי בכל כחי,[8] ולכן אני עצב כי {אין} אין לפני כל מינין[9] שבעולם לבד ממין אחד. ועל זה אמר שלמה בחכמתו: צדיק אוכל לשובע נפשו ובטן רשעים תחסר [משלי יג, כה]"

1. רבן גמליאל דיבנה היה נשיא הסנהדרין בשלהי המאה הראשונה ותחילת המאה השנייה. היה צאצא של הלל הזקן, וסבו של רבי יהודה הנשיא. בפסיקתא דרב כהנא (מנדלבוים, א, 115–116), ובפסיקתא רבתי (איש שלום, פיסקא טז, דף פב, ע"ב) הסיפור הוא ממורט בגוף ראשון מפי רבי מאיר, המספר על האירוע לרבי דוסתאי מהיישוב כוכבא. ההשוואות להלן הן לפסיקתא דרב כהנא ולפסיקתא רבתי, שבדרך כלל זהים.
2. ועשה סעודה לכל זקני העיר וזימנני [או זימני] עמהם.
3. והביא לפנינו מכל מה שברא [או ברה] הקב"ה בששה ימי בראשית ולא היה שולחנו חסר אלא אגוזי פרך בלבד. אגוז פרך הוא בעל קליפה דקה שנקל לפרכה, להבדיל מסוגי אגוזים אחרים (ראו: פרך, מילון אבן שושן, והפנייתו לשיר השירים רבה ד, יא: "מה האגוז הזה יש בו אגוזי פרך, אגוזים בינוניים ואגוזים קנטרנין").
4. חסר בפסיקתא דרב כהנא ובפסיקתא רבתי.
5. בפסיקתא דרב כהנא: מה עשה, נטל את הטבלה מלפנינו שהיתה יפה בששה ככר כסף ושברה. בכתבי יד מסוימים של פסיקתא רבתי שווי השולחן הוא כשישים ככרי כסף.
6. אמרתי לו: מפני מה עשית כן?
7. אמר לי רבי, אתם אומרים העולם הזה שלנו והעולם הבא שלכם, אם אין אנו אוכלין עכשיו אימתי אנו אוכלין.
8. חסר בפסיקתא דרב כהנא ובפסיקתא רבתי.
9. 'מין' בהוראה של 'סוג' ובמובלע גם בהוראה של 'כופר'.

46. R. Joshua b. Levi and the Angel of Death (321b–322a)

A. [321b] A tale of R. Joshua b. Levi, who had never taken an oath in his life—not even for the truth. Once, when the time came for him to pass from this world, God said to the Angel of Death: Go to Joshua b. Levi and do whatever he wishes and then take his soul. The Angel of Death went to R. Joshua and found him busy studying Torah. The Angel of Death said to him: I am an envoy of God, and He has sent me to take your soul. He said to him: Give me some time—give me thirty days until I can review my studies, as it says: Happy is he who comes here with his studies in hand. He gave him the time.

B. When the thirty days were up, he returned to him. The Angel of Death said to him: God has sent me to you to do whatever you ask, after which I will take your soul. He said to him: Show me Gehenna and the Garden of Eden. He said to him: All right. As they were walking along the way, R. Joshua said to the Angel of Death: Show me your knife that kills people. He did. He showed him Gehenna and the Garden of Eden. He said to him: Show me my place. He showed him his place. He departed from him and fled to his place. And the Angel of Death took him under his cloak, and R. Joshua left his robe in his hand. He said to him: Come out, and I will take your soul. He said to him: I swear in God's name that I will not come out.

46. יהושע בן לוי ומלאך המוות (321ב–322א)

A. מעשה היה ברבי יהושע בן לוי שלא נשבע מימיו אפילו באמת.[1] וכשהגיע זמנו ליפטר מן העולם א"ל הקב"ה למלאך המות: לך לר' יהושע בן לוי ועשה לו כל רצונו, ואחר כך טול נשמתו.[2] הלך מלאך המות אצל ר' יהושע, ומצאו שהיה עוסק בתורה. א"ל מלאך המות: אני שלוחו של הקב"ה והוא שלחני ליטול נשמתך.[3] א"ל: הב לי זמן עד שלשים יום עד שאחזור תלמודי. שכך אומרים לשם: אשרי מי שבא לכאן ותלמודו בידו.[4] הב ליה [נתן לו].

B. לסוף תלתין יומין הדר לו [בסוף שלושים יום חזר אליו]. א"ל: הקב"ה שלחני אליך שאעשה כל מה שתשאל, ואחר כך אטול נשמתך. א"ל: הראיני גהינם וגן עדן.[5] א"ל: הן. כד הוו קאזלי באורחא [כאשר היו הולכים בדרך] א"ל ר' יהושע למלאך המות: הב לי סכינך דקא מעכבת לבני אינשא [שהיא מעכבת לבני האדם]. הב ליה.[6] הראה לו גהינם וגן עדן. א"ל: הראה מקומי. הראה לו מקומו.[7] פרש ממנו וברח למקומו.[8] ומלאך המות נטלו בכנף מעילו, והניח ר' יהושע טליתו בידו.[9] א"ל: צא משם ואטול נשמתך. א"ל: חי י"י לא אצא.

---

1. מעשה"ד, שפירא, 53–51: בא וראה כמה שכרן של צדיקים ששומרים פיהם משבועה. ולמוד מר' יהושע בן לוי שלא נשבע לשקר [=לשווא] מימיו והיה צדיק גמור השוו לספר חסידים (תתתפה) המזכיר את הסיפור כדוגמה לזהירות משבועות ומנדרים מעיקרם. ההשוואות להלן הן למעשה"ד, שפירא, אלא אם צוין אחרת.
2. מעשה"ד: לך ועשה לר' יהושע כל רצונו.
3. מעשה"ד: הלך מיד ומצאו יושב ועוסק בתורה. אמר לו מלאך המות: הקב"ה שלחני ליטול נשמתך וצוני לעשות לך כל רצונך.
4. שם: המתן לי עד שלשים יום שאחזור תלמודי, וכן עשה. וראו ממרה זו: פסחים נ, ע"א; מועד קטן כח, ע"א; כתובות עז, ע"ב; בבא בתרא י, ע"ב.
5. רוצה אני שתוליכני לגן עדן.
6. תן לי סכינך כי מתירא אני ממך. מיד נתנו לו. ושם תיאור הסכין, שאין בספר המעשים.
7. באו לגן עדן. אמר לו ר' יהושע: העלה לי מקדם לגן והראה לי מקומי. וכן עשה.
8. מיד הפיל עצמו ר' יהושע בגן עדן.
9. השוו לבראשית לט, יב בעניין יוסף ואשת פוטיפר; במעשה"ד ללא רמיזה זו: תפסו מלאך המות בטליתו ואמר לו.

C. The angel went to God and said to Him: This is [322a] what R. Joshua did. He said to him: Go to all the places where R. Joshua has been, and see if he has ever sworn, even for the truth. He went and found that he had never taken an oath in his life. The Angel of Death returned to R. Joshua. He said to him: Since you have done this [escaped into the Garden of Eden], give me back my knife. He said: I will not, unless you return to God [and ask Him to release you from your task]. He went, and a divine voice called out and said: Give it to him, because it is needed for mankind. He returned it to him. And R. Joshua still lives in the Garden of Eden, because he guarded his mouth from taking an oath. And even a [casual] conversation [of lies] that contains neither good nor bad, is forbidden, because it says: "He who tells lies shall not remain in my presence" [Psalms 101:7].

C. הלך המלאך אצל הקב"ה. א"ל: כך [322א] וכך עשה לי ר' יהושע.[10] א"ל: לך בכל מקומות שהיה שם ר' יהושע, אם נשבע מימיו שום שבועה אפילו באמת.[11] הלך ומצא שלא נשבע מימיו.[12] חזר מלאך המות אל ר' יהושע. א"ל: מאחר שכך עשית חזור לי סכיני. א"ל: לא אעשה, אלא עד שתחזור להקב"ה.[13] הלך ויצא בת קול ואמרה: הב ליה משום דצריך לברייתא.[14] הדר ליה [החזיר לו].[15] ועדיין ר' יהושע חי בגן עדן על ששמר פיו משבועה.[16] ואפילו סיחה [שיחה] שאין בה לא טוב ולא רע אין אדם רשאי לאומרה משום שנ': דובר שקרים לא יכון לנגד עיני (תהלים קא, ז)[17]

10. רבונו של עולם, כך וכך עשה לי ר' יהושע בן לוי.
11. לך בכל שעמד בו ואם תמצא שנשבע לשקר או שנשאל לחכם על השבועה, תהא שבועתו בטלה. ולא - תניחנו לשם.
12. מיד הלך מלאך המות וסבב בכל המקומות שהיה שם ר' יהושע בימיו, ולא נשבע לשקר. מיד הניחוהו לשם ועדין הוא חי בגן עדן.
13. כתובות: לא הוה קא יהיב ליה [לא החזיר לו]. במדעשה"ד: לא אשיבנו עד שתשבע לי שלא תקח נשמתו של בני אדם בפרהסיא. מיד נשבע לו.
14. כתובות: הב ניהליה דמתבעא לברייתא [תן אותה לו שצריכה לבריות]; במעשה"ד ללא הנמקה: השב לו הסכין.
15. במעשה"ד מתואר עימות בין ריב"ל לבתיה בת פרעה.
16. ועדין הוא חי בגן עדן. ראו הערה 12 לעיל.
17. במעשה"ד חסר: ואפילו–עיני.

47. R. Joshua b. Elem and Ninus the Butcher (322a–322b)

A. [322a] Once R. Joshua b. Elem had a vision of God in a dream, and He [God] said to him: Rejoice, for you and Ninus, the butcher of Kfar Kitor, have equal seats in Eden. When he awoke, he thought to himself: Woe to the man who from the day of his birth was in perfect awe of his Creator, and toiled at nothing other than the Torah and did not walk four cubits without his fringes or phylacteries, and who had two [thousand] disciples—yet now my deeds and learning are equal to some butcher. By faith, I will not rest until I have seen my companion.

B. So what did he do? He went from town to town and from region to region until he arrived in his [Ninus's] town. He asked them [the townsfolk]: Where is Ninus? They said: Your lordship, who is a great and important man, the person that you seek is a common fellow, and what would you need him for? He said: By God, I will eat nothing until I see that man. They sent for Ninus at once, went there, and told him: R. Joshua has sent for you. He said: Who am I and who are my ancestors that R. Joshua should send for me? They said: Get up and come with us. He said: I will not go with you. They returned to R. Joshua and said: Sir, he would not come. He said: By God, I will not seat myself until I have seen him. He immediately arose together with all his disciples and the elders who were sitting before him, and they all walked along. At once Ninus approached R. Joshua, and said: My lord, Should the Light of Israel come to his servant? And R. Joshua said: I have something to say to you. Say it, my lord, said Ninus. What is your occupation? ["*Ma melakhtekha*?"] asked R. Joshua, and he said I am a butcher and I have an aged father and mother who can neither stand nor sit, and I dress and feed and wash them. At this R. Joshua rose and kissed him on his head and said: Happy are you and happy am I to be your companion in Eden.

47. ר' יהושע בן אלם ונינוס הקצב (322א–322ב)

A. מעשה היה ברבי יהושע בן אלם שראה בחלום א-להים, וא"ל: שמח בלבך שאתה ונינוס בן כפר קיטור קצב, ראה מושבך ומושבו בגן עדן שוין.[1] כשניעור משנתו חשב בלבו ואמר: ווי לאותו איש שמיום שנולד (תמיד) [תמים] היה ביראת קונו, ולא היה עמל אלא בתורה, ולא הלך ארבע אמות בלא טלית ובלא תפילין,[2] והיו לו שני [אלפים] תלמידים, עכשיו שקולים מעשי ותורתי עם קצב אחד. באמונה לא אשב עד שאראה חבירי.[3]

B. מה עשה, הלך מעיר לעיר וממדינה למדינה עד שבא לעירו.[4] אמר להם: היכן נינוס? אמרו לו: אדונינו, אותו האיש אתה מבקש, שאתה גדול ושר והוא הדיוט, ומה אתה צריך לו?[5] אמר להם: העבודה, שלא אוכל עד שאראה אותו האיש.[6] מיד שיגרו בשבילו הלכו ואמרו לו: ר' יהושע משגר בשבילך. אמר להם: מה אני ומה אבותי שר' יהושע משגר בשבילי? אמרו לו: עמוד ולך עמנו. אמר להם: לא אלך עמכם.[7] חזרו ואמרו לר' יהושע: אדונינו, אינו רוצה לבוא.[8] אמר להם: העבודה שלא אשב עד שאראנו.[9] מיד עמד הוא וכל תלמידיו והזקינים שהיו יושבים אצלו, והיו כולם הולכים עמו. מיד בא לפני ר' יהושע. א"ל: אדוני מה היה זה שאור ישראל בא אצל עבדו? א"ל: דבר לי. א"ל: אדוני אמור. א"ל: מה מלאכתך? א"ל: אני קצב ויש לי אב ואם זקינים ואינם יכולים לעמוד ולא לישב, ואני מלבישן ומאכילן ומרחיצן.[10] מיד עמד ר' יהושע ונשקו על ראשו, וא"ל: אשריך ואשריני שזכיתי להיות חבירך בגן עדן.[11]

---

1. מעשה"ד, שפירא, 71–72: ומעשה בר' יהושע בן אילם שאמרו לו בחלומו: שמח בלבך שאתה וננס קצב מושבך ומושבו שרויין בגן עדן וחלקם שוין כאחד. ההשוואות להלן הן למקור זה.
2. שניעור משנתו חשב בלבו אוי לי שמיום שנולדתי הייתי תמים ביראת קוני ולא היה לי עמל אלא בתורה ולא הלכתי ארבע אמות בלא ציצית וללא תפילין.
3. והיו לי שמונים תלמידים ועכשו שקולין מעשי ותורתי עם קצב אחד? אמר לתלמידיו: תדעו שלא אכנס לבית המדרש עד שאראה מי זה האיש שחברי בגן עדן.
4. מיד הלך הוא ותלמידיו מעיר לעיר ושאל בשם האיש ובשם עירו ובשם אביו, עד שבא לעירו.
5. כשנכנס בעיר מיד שאל היכן ננס קצב עומד. אמרו לו כל בני העיר: אדננו למה אתה מבקש אותו האיש ואתה חסיד ותשאל לאיש כמותו?
6. אמר להם: ומה מעשיו? ואמרו: לא תשאל ממנו כלום, אבל שב וסעוד אתה ותלמידך, שאתם עייפים מן הדרך. אמר להם: לא נאכל כלום עד שתראו לי האיש.
7. מיד שגרו בשבילו ואמרו לו: ר' יהושע שואל אותך. אמר להם: מי אנכי ומי ביתי בישראל שר' יהושע שואל אותי? אמרו לו: עמוד ולך עמנו. חשב בלבו שכל מה שאמרו לו שקר הוא. אמר להם: לא אלך, שאתם משחקים בי.
8. מיד חזרו אל ר' יהושע ואמרו: אי, אור ענינו עטרת ראשנו, איך תשגרנו בשבילו? לא רצה לבא עמנו.
9. אמר להם: לא אשב עד שאראהו ננס קצב. מיד הלך הוא ותלמידיו וכל הזקנים שהיו עמו והלכו כלם אצלו.
10. כשראהו ננס קצב את ר' יהושע אמר לו: אדני, מה היום מימים שעטרת ישראל טרח לבא אצלי? אמר לו: דבר יש לי לדבר עמך. אמר לו: אדני, אמור. אמר לו: מה מעשך ומה מלאכתך? אמר לו: אדני, קצב הייתי ויש לי אב ואם זקנים ואינם יכולים לעמוד על רגליהם ולא לישב, ואני מלבישן ומרחיצן ואני מאכילן בידי.
11. מיד עמד ר' יהושע ונשקו על ראשו, אמר לו: בני, אשריך ואשרי חלקי שזכיתי להיות חבירך בגן עדן.

C. This is to teach you how important it is to honor one's father and mother. And Jacob feared his brother [Esau] only because he [Esau] was quick to fulfill the commandment of honoring his father. And he who honors his father and mother, it is as if he honors the Almighty, because there are three partners to the creation of a child: the Almighty and his father and mother. From the father are created the brain and bones and tendons and nails and the white of the eye. And from the mother are created the hair and skin and flesh and the black of the eyes. And the Almighty provides the spirit and a wise soul and intellect [322b]. And when he passes from this world, the Almighty takes His part and places the part of the father and mother before them. And anyone who puts his father and mother to shame and mocks them is not given a proper burial, and the birds of the skies eat his flesh. As it says: The eye that mocks a father will be pecked out by the ravens [of the valley], will be eaten by the vultures. And he who honors his father and mother, the Almighty rewards him well both in this world and in the world to come.

C. הא למדת כמה גדול כבוד אב ואם. ואף יעקב לא היה ירא מאחיו אלא בשביל שהיה זריז בכבוד אביו. וכל המכבד אב ואם כאילו מכבד הקב"ה, ששלשה שותפין יש באדם ביצירת הוולד: הקב"ה ואב ואם.[12] מן האב נוצרים מוח ועצמות וגידים וצפורנים ולובן שבעינים. ומן האם נוצרים שער עור ובשר ושחור שבעינים. והקב"ה נותן בו רוח ונשמה חכמה ובינה [322ב] וכשנפטר מן העולם הקב"ה נוטל חלקו וחלק אביו ואמו מניח לפניהם. וכל המבזה אביו ואמו ולועג מהם ואינו זוכה לקבורה ואוכלים בשרו עוף השמים. שנ' עין תלעג לאב יקרוה עורבי נהל [נחל] וי{א}כלוה בני נשר[13] וכל המכבד אביו ואמו הקב"ה נותן לו שכר טוב בעולם הזה ולעולם הבא.[14]

---

12. השוו לנידה לא, ע"א. וראו הפניות שפירא במהדורתה למדרש עשרת הדיברות, 71, הערה 138.
13. השוו משלי ל, יז.
14. במעשה"ד, שפירא, 171–172, האפילוג מורחב יותר.

48. That Which Was Stolen Is Returned by Guile (322b)

A. Once, a merchant went somewhere to trade. And he took five hundred gold coins with him. The merchant said to himself: What shall I do? If I take them with me, perhaps robbers will steal them from me. So I will hide them until the day comes when I have business. What did he do? He went to a secluded place and looked this way and that, and seeing that there was no one [Exodus 2:12], he dug a hole and hid the money. The hole he dug was near a wall, and at that spot there was a hole in the wall that he did not know about, and the owner of the house saw him. After the merchant left, the man came at once and stole the money.

B. In time, the merchant came to take his money but could not find it. He began to grieve: What will I do? Who can I get my money from? Wasn't it so, that when I hid the money, there was no one there? He looked up and searched and saw the hole. He thought to himself and said: Perhaps the owner of this house saw me. And he asked around who he was, and they pointed him out to him. He came to him and said: Sir, I have seen and heard about you that you are a good advisor. I would like to ask your advice. He said to him: Speak. He said: Sir, I came here to trade, and I brought with me two purses, one with five hundred gold coins and the other with a thousand gold coins. And when I came here, I did not know anyone in this town with whom I could leave my money. What did I do? I went to a secluded place and put my purse with the five hundred gold coins in it, and it is still there, and the purse with the thousand coins with me I carry with me. That is why I am asking you what to do: Should I hide this purse in the same place or deposit it with a trustworthy person? He said to him: If you take my advice, do not deposit it with anyone, because you don't know the people and they will betray you. Go hide it together with the other purse. He said to him: I will do as you say. The thief immediately thought to himself: When he goes to hide the other purse and doesn't find this one, he will not put anything there. He went home and put the purse back. The merchant said to himself: Perhaps he will return the money if he plans to take both [purses]. He went there and found it [his purse]. He said: Blessed is He who returns that which was lost to its owner. So no man should stretch his hand out to steal.

48. גניבה שהושבה בתחבולה (322ב)

A. מעשה שהיה בסוחר אחד והלך לסחורה במקום אחד.[1] והיו עמו חמש מאות[2] זהובים. אמר אותו סוחר בלבו: היאך אעשה? אם אני מוליכם עמי אולי רמאים יגנבו אותם לי,[3] אלא אטמינים [אטמינם] עד שיבא יום שיזמן לי סחורה. מה עשה, הלך למקום צנוע ויפן כה וכה וירא כי אין איש [שמות ב, יב] ועשה חפורה[4] וגנז שם הממון. והחפורה היתה אצל קיר. ובאותו מקום היה חור בקיר <~~ולא~~> והוא לא ידע וראהו בעל הבית.[5] לאחר שהלך הסוחר משם מיד בא אותו האיש וגנב הממון.

B. לימים בא הסוחר ליטול ממונו ולא <מצא>. התחיל לצער עצמו. אמר: מה אעשה, למי אבקש הממון, והלא כשגנזתי הממון לא היה בזה שום אדם? נשא עיניו וחיפש בה, וראה אותו חור. חשב בלבו ואמר: שמא בעל הבית הזה ראני.[6] ושאל עליו מי הוא, והראוהו לו.[7] בא אצלו ואמר לו: אדוני הנה ראיתי ושמעתי עליך שאתה יועץ טוב,[8] מבקש אני ממך עצה. א"ל: אמור. א"ל: אדוני <באתי> בכאן לסחורה, והבאתי עמי שני ארנקות האחד של חמש מאות[9] זהובים והאחד של אלף זהובים.[10] ואני, כשבאתי לכאן לא הייתי מכיר שום אדם בזאת העיר להפקיד ממוני. מה עשיתי, הלכתי למקום צנוע ושמתי שם הארנקי של חמש מאות[11] זהובים והיא עדיין שם שמורה,[12] ואותה של אלף אני נושא עמי. ולכן אני שואל ממך מה אעשה: או אטמינה באותו מקום או אפקידנה <~~באותו מקום~~> לאדם[13] נאמן. א"ל: אם אתה שומע לעצתי אל תפקידנה,[14] לפי שאין אתה מכירם ו{י}כפרו בך.[15] לך טמון אותה עם האחרת.[16] א"ל: אעשה כדבריך. מיד חשב אותו גנב כשילך לטמון האחרת ולא ימצא זו, לא ישים שם כלום. הלך והחזירה.[17] אמר הסוחר בליבו: אולי החזיר הממון שהוא סבור ליטול את שתיהן. הלך לשם ומצאה. אמר: ברוך המחזיר אבידה לבעלים.[18] לכך לא יפשוט אדם את ידו בגניבה"[19]

---

1. מעשה"ד, שפירא, 84–85: והלך למקום אחד רחוק לעשות סחורה; ההשוואות להלן הן למעשה"ד.
2. שש מאות זהובים בארנקי אחד.
3. יראו אותי בני אדם ויגנבו אותה ממני.
4. תוספת: בארץ.
5. ובקיר הסמוך לאותו מקום היה שם חור, וראהו אדם משם כשהטמין הממון.
6. שמא בעל הבית השכן הזה ראה אותו מאותו החור כשגנזתי אותו והוא לקח הממון.
7. כל עיקר, לא היה מכירו, הלך ושאל מי הוא.
8. במעשה"ד, תוספת: וחכם.
9. שם: שש מאות.
10. אלף דינר.
11. שש מאות.
12. שם, חסר: והיא עדיין שם שמורה.
13. לאדם אחד נאמן.
14. לא תפקדנה לאדם.
15. שם, חסר: לפי–ויכפרו בך.
16. אלא תשימנה באותו מקום ששמת האחרת, וטמון שם הארנקי אשר עמך.
17. אלא אחזיר הארנקי במקומה והוא יניח שם האחרת ואטול את שתיהן. הלך לביתו והחזירו לשם.
18. שם, תוספת: ואתה אנוש שאחריתך רמה, למה תתגאה ותפשוט ידך בגניבה? לכך ציונו הקב"ה: לא תגנוב [שמות כ, יג].
19. חסר: לפיכך–בגניבה.

49. Torah Saves from Death (322b–323b)

A. [322b] Once there was a man who asked God for a son and said: Lord of the Universe, give me a son so that I can teach him Torah. God heard his prayer and gave him a son, and he called him Saul. Saul grew up and turned five years old, and studied [323a] much Torah and became very wise. And his father would go out every day, and any poor orphan or beggar he saw, he would take him in and bring him to his son and say: My son, teach them, and he would sit and teach them. That was the father's custom every day. He would sit at the door of the school, and if a passerby wished to greet his son, he would answer him, so that he [his son] would not interrupt his Torah study. He did this until he [the son] was seventy years old.

B. Then, God sent the Angel of Death to take his soul. He disguised himself as a human. When he wanted to go through the door, his [Saul's] father met him, as was his practice. He said to him: Where do you wish to go? He said to him: I have a matter that is between your son and me. He said: What is it? I will attend to it [lit. answer you]. He said to him: On my life, it is a secret between your son and me, and I will not tell you what it is. He grabbed him and said: On my life, you will not go in there until you tell me the secret. He said to him: I gave him something seventy years ago, and now I wish to take it [his soul] from him. The old man said: On my life, my son's life is only seventy years, and is there anyone who trusts a newborn infant with something? The Angel of Death said: I do not know if he is seventy or eighty years old, but it is now seventy years since the debt he owes me. He said: Since my son did not inform me of that, enter. He entered and said: Good day to you, Rabbi. He answered: Good day, come [with me], for God is calling you. He said to him: Welcome, to where shall we ascend? I see neither a cloud nor a ladder. The Angel of Death said to him: Rabbi, you have read the Torah, and [yet] do you not understand? That which God gave you is what He seeks. He said to him: What is it? He said to him: You have read, "Then shall the dust return to the earth as it was: and the spirit shall return to God who gave it" [Ecclesiastes 12:7], for it is your soul that He seeks. He said: Heaven forbid. How can I leave these orphans? Go in peace.

C. The Angel of Death went and said: Lord of the Universe, he refuses. He said to him: Go and decorate yourself with tokens of death. It was said of the Angel of Death that he had three hundred heads, sixty-five mouths, three hundred and five eyes, and an unsheathed sword in his hand. He went and decorated himself and wanted to go through the door. When the old man saw him, he fell down. The Angel of Death caught him and said: Fear not. He said to him: I have never seen a person like you enter the synagogue. He said to him: Get up. He said to him: Why?

49. תורה מצילה ממוות (322ב–323ב)

A. מעשה באדם אחד ששאל בן מהקב"ה ואמר: רבונו של עולם תן לי בן על מנת שאלמד{נ}ו תורה.[1] שמע הקב"ה תפלתו ונתן לו בן. וקרא שמו שאול.[2] ונתגדל ונעשה בן חמש שנים, ולמד [323א] תורה הרבה ונתחכם ביותר. והיה אביו יוצא בכל יום, וכל עני ויתום שהיה רואה {מ}קבצן והביאן לבנו ואמר לו: בני למוד את אילו. והיה יושב ומלמדן. וכך היה מנהגו של אביו. בכל יום היה יושב בדלת של בית הספר, ואם היה אדם עובר ושב ומבקש לומר שלום לבנו עונה ומשיב לו, כדי שלא יענה הוא ויבטל מן התורה.[3] כך היה עושה עד שנעשה בן שבעים שנה.

B. ואז שלח הקב"ה מלאך המות ליטול את נפשו. ועשה עצמו כבשר ודם. בא ליכנס בדלת, פגע בו אביו כמנהגו. א"ל: להיכן אתה רוצה לילך? א"ל: יש לי דבר ביני ובין בנך. א"ל: מה הוא, ואני משיב לך. א"ל: בחיי, סוד הוא ביני ובן בנך ואיני אומרו לך. תפש בו ואמר: בחיי, לא תיכנס לשם עד שתאמר לי הסוד. א"ל: יש לו שבעים שנה שנתתי לו דבר, ואני רוצה ליטול אותו הימנו.[4] אמר הזקן: בחיי כל שנותיו של בני אינן אלא שבעים שנה, ויש אדם שמאמין דבר לתינוק בן יומו?[5] א"ל מלאך המות: איני יודע אם הוא בן שבעים או בן שמונים, אלא ביום הזה יש שבעים שנה שהוא חייב לי. אמר: הואיל ולא הודיעני בני, הכנס. נכנס ואמר: שלום עליך רבי. השיב לו: שלום, בוא שקראך הקב"ה.[6] א"ל: ברוך בואך, לאיזה מקום נעלה? ענן איני רואה, סולם איני רואה. א"ל מלאך המות: ר' התורה קריתה ואין אתה מבין? בדבר שניתן לך ממנו, אותו הוא מבקש.[7] א"ל: איזה דבר?[8] א"ל: קריתה וישוב העפר אל הארץ כשהיה והרוח תשוב למעלה אל המקום אשר נתנה בך [קהלת יב, ז], כי את נפשך הוא מבקש.[9] א"ל: חס ושלום, היאך אעזוב את היתומים הללו? לך לשלום.[10]

C. הלך מלאך המות ואמר: רבונו של עולם, אינו רוצה. א"ל: לך קשט עצמך סימני מיתה. אמרו עליו על מלאך ~~על~~ המות שיש לו שלוש מאות ראשים, וששים וחמשה פיות, ושלש מאות וחמשה עינים והחרב שלופה בידו. הלך ונתקשט ובא ליכנס בדלת. כשראה אותו הזקן נפל על פניו. תפסו מלאך המות א"ל: אל תירא. א"ל: מעולם לא ראיתי אדם כמותך נכנס בבית הכנסת. א"ל: קום לך.[11] א"ל: למה? א"ל: לשלם נפשך. א"ל: תן לי מקום ואתפלל לפני הקב"ה. נתן לו מקום והתפלל.[12] אמר: רבונו של עולם כתבת בתורתך אורך ימים בימינה [משלי ג, טז], וכת' כי מוצאי

---

1. כ"י ירושלים 3182, 132ב–133א (יסיף, מאה סיפורים, 247–248, סיפור פ'): מעשה באדם אחד ששאל בן ואמר: רבש"ע תן לי בן ואלמדיהו תורה כאוות נפשו. ההשוואות להלן הן למקור זה.
2. תוספת בכ"י ירושלים: ששאלוהו מהקב"ה.
3. ואביו לא היה עושה שום דבר אלא יושב בכל יום ויום בפתח בית הספר. ואם אדם עבר שם וביקש לומר לו שלום עליך (עבר) ומשיב, כדי שלא יתבטל בנו.
4. א"ל, ע' שנים שנתתי לו ואני רוצה ליקחם ממנו.
5. חסר בכ"י ירושלים: ויש אדם–בן יומו.
6. א"ל: שלום עליך רבי. וא"ל מלאך המות: בא כי קראך הקב"ה.
7. א"ל המלאך: התורה קרית ואין אתה מבין הדבר? מה שנתן לך הקב"ה מבקש ממך.
8. א"ל: איזה פסוק הוא שכתוב בתוכו?
9. א"ל: זה הפסוק, וישוב העפר אל העפר שהיה והרוח תשוב אל הא-להים אשר נתנה.
10. א"ל: לוקח נפשי אתה, ח"ו היאך אניח היתומים האילו? לך לשלום.
11. א"ל: קום לך לשלום.
12. אמר לו מלאך המות לבן: כמה יש לי ליקח נפשך? א"ל: תן לי מקום ואתפלל לפני המקום. נתן לו מקום. עמד והתפלל.

He said: To pray for your soul. He said: Give me a place, and I will pray to the Almighty. He gave him a place, and he prayed. He said: Lord of the Universe, it says in your Torah: "Long life is in her right hand" [Proverbs 3:16]. And it says "For whoever finds me finds life" [Proverbs 8:35]. And it says "It is a tree of life to them that lay hold upon it" [Proverbs 3:18]. And it is not for myself that I feel sorry, but for these orphans.

D. At that moment, a divine voice said: What shall I do with these two righteous men—one within and one without—praying to me to continue to hold on to my Torah? Today, he is seventy years old. From this time forward, he will live to the age of 125 years. They said: In those 125 years, no one died during the lifetime of his father, and no person needed the help of another [323b], to fulfill the verse "It is a tree of life to them that lay hold upon it" [Proverbs 3:18].

מצא חיים [משלי ח, לה], וכת' עץ חיים היא למחזיקים בה [משלי ג, יח]. וכל כך איני מרחם על עצמי אלא על היתומים הללו.

D. באותה שעה יצתה בת קול ואמרה: מה אעשה לשני צדיקים הללו, אחד מבפנים ואחד מבחוץ מתפללים לפניי להחזיק תורתי. הרי היום בן שבעים שנה, מיכן ואילך יחיה מאה ועשרים וחמש שנה. אמרו: באותן קכ"ה שנה לא מת אדם בחיי אביו,[13] ולא נצרך אדם לחבירו [323ב] לקיים מה שנ' עץ חיים היא למחזיקים בה [משלי ח, יג]"[14]

13. מכאן ואילך יחיה (כ"ה) [קכ"ה] שנים. אמרו באותן (כ"ה) [קכ"ה] שנים לא מת אדם בחיי אביו.

14. ולא נצטער אדם לחבירו לקיים מה שנאמר: עץ חיים היא למחזיקים בה ותומכיה מאושר.

50. The Pious Pretender (323b–324a)

A. [323b] Once there was a man from the Upper Galilee who ascended to Jerusalem to pray. After he finished praying, he had to fulfill a vow to travel to Babylon. He had with him two hundred gold dinars, and he wished to leave them with someone he could trust. He went to the synagogue and saw a humble man who [always sat] in the same place [in the synagogue] and never changed places. When the man finished praying, he followed him outside. He said to him: Rabbi, I have something [with me], and I wish to leave it with you, and I can see that you are humble, and I want to continue on my way. He said: My brother, what is the thing? He said: Money. He said: Go in life and in peace. If God so decrees it, I will not touch them [the coins] until you return in peace and I see you [lit., your face]. He immediately took the money out of his pocket and gave it to him. He traveled to Babylon and was there eight months and then returned to Jerusalem.

B. When he entered the city, the man he trusted went out for merchandise, because he was a shopkeeper. He went to the synagogue and found someone else sitting in the place of his trustee, someone who resembled him in form and humility. When the services ended, the man left and he followed him. And he said: Greetings to you, Rabbi. He said to him: Greetings to you. And he responded hesitantly [lit., with a soft mouth], because he didn't know him. He said: Give me the deposit that you are holding for me. He said: I don't know what you are talking about. I have never seen you before. He said to him: I will not let you go until you give me the money I deposited with you or swear a vow to me. He said to him: Go in peace. You cannot make me swear, and even if you give me all the money in the world, I will not swear to you. What did the owner of the money do? He took a rope and placed it around the neck of that *ḥasid* and led him throughout the city, declaring: Thus shall be done to he who takes a deposit and denies having done so. The shopkeepers who were present and knew that he was a righteous man wept for him and for what had happened to him. After he had so greatly humiliated him, he let him go and removed the rope from his neck. The man went home in great shame.

C. A few days later, the man who held the deposit went, as was his custom, to sit in his place. When the owner of the money saw him, he thought to himself [Heb. *kal vaḥomer*]: Perhaps that is the man with whom I left the money? Nevertheless, I will test him. After the man went out, he followed him. He said to him: Are you ashamed to ask for what is yours? The owner of the money said: Welcome. He said to him: My brother, perhaps you are fearful for your money? It is known to He who spoke and created the world that, from that time, no hand has touched it. Come and

50. מעשה במתחסד (323ב–324א)

A. מעשה באדם אחד מגליל העליון שעלה לירושלים להתפלל, ועשה תפלתו, והיה לו נדר לירד לבבל. והיו עמו מאתים דינרי זהב וביקש להפקידם ביד נאמן. הלך לבית הכנסת וראה שם אדם עניו מאותו מקום,[1] ולעולם לא היה מחליף מקומו. כשגמר תפלתו ויצא, יצא הוא אחריו. א"ל: ר' יש לי דבר, ומבקש אני להפקידו אצלך <~~ואת~~> ואני מכיר בך שאתה עניו,[2] ומבקש אני ליילך לדרכי. א"ל: אחי מהו הדבר. א"ל: ממון. א"ל: לחיים ולשלום, אם גוזר המקום איני נוגע בהם עד שתחזור לשלום ואראה פניך. מיד הוציא כיסו והפקיד בידו. והלך לבבל והיה שם שמונה חדשים וחזר לירושלם.

B. בשעה שנכנס לעיר יצא נאמן שלו לסחורה לפי שהיה חנווני.[3] הלך לבית הכנסת ומצא במקום נאמן שלו אדם אחר יושב במקומו, בדמותו ובתארו ובענוותו. כשגמרה התפלה יצא האיש ויצא גם הוא אחריו. ויאמר לו: שלום עליך רבי. וא"ל: ועליך שלום. והיה עונה בפה רך, לפי שלא היה מכירו. א"ל: תן לי הפקדון שיש לי <~~בד~~> בידך. א"ל: איני יודע בדבר, לא ראיתיך מימי. א"ל: לא אניחך עד שתתן לי מה שהפקדתי אצלך או תשבע לי. א"ל: לך לשלום, אין לך עלי שבועה. שאפילו אתה נותן לי כל ממון שבעולם לא אשבע לך. מה עשה בעל הממון? נטל החבל ונתנה בצווארו של אותו חסיד, והוליכו בכל המדינה, והיה מכריז עליו: כל הלוקח פקדון וכופר בו ראוי לעשות בו כך. אותן החנוונים שהיו שם ומכירין אותו שהוא צדיק[4] היו בוכין עליו, <על> מה שאירע לו. כיון שעשה לו כל אותה החרפה הניחו והעלה החבל מעל צווארו, והלך בביתו בבושה גדולה.

C. לימים בא בעל הפיקדון, והלך כמנהגו[5] וישב במקומו. וראהו בעל הממון ונתן קל וחומר בעצמו ואמר: שמא הוא זה שהפקדתי אצלו הממון? ואעפ"י אבחננו.[6] כיון שיצא האיש, יצא הוא אחריו. א"ל: וכי מתבייש אתה לשאול את שלך? א"ל בעל הממון: ברוך בואך. א"ל: אחי שמא יראתה מן ממונך? גלוי לפני מי שאמר והיה העולם שמאותה שעה לא נגע בו יד. בוא טול אותו.[7] הלך וקבל ממונו, ובא לביתו והתחיל לבכות. ואמר: אוי לי, איך ימחול לי הקב"ה מה שעשיתי לאותו צדיק. מיד הלך בעל הממון אצל האיש שעשה לו בושה. וא"ל: חטאתי לך ר',

1. כ"י ירושלים 3182, דפים 129ב–130א (יסיף, מאה סיפורים, 240–241, סיפור ע"ד): אדם חכם שישב במקומו. ההשוואות להלן הן לכ"י ירושלים.
2. חכם ועניו.
3. כיוון שנכנס לעיר יצא אותו האיש שהיה פיקדון בידו לסחורה.
4. צדיק גמור.
5. והלך לבית הכנסת כמנהגו.
6. ראהו בעל הממון ונתן עיניו בו ואומר זה הוא שהפקדתי הממון אצלו אעפ"כ אדבר עמו.
7. א"ל אחי שמא יראת מממונך? גלוי לפני מי שאמר והיה העולם שעה שנתת הפקדון בידי לא נגעתי בו ולא שום אדם. בא טול את שלך.

take it. He went and took his money and came home and began to cry. He said: Woe is me! How can God forgive me for what I did to that righteous man? The owner of the money immediately went to the man whom he had humiliated and said: I have sinned toward you, Rabbi. Now please [324a] take the money that I suspected you of taking for no sin of yours, and forgive me for what I did to you. He said: I will not take the money from you, and nor will I do you any harm. May God judge between me and you. The owner of the money went and hired three young men, who placed a rope around his neck, and they did to him as he had done to that man.

D. And the friends of that man who had been suspected came to him to console him for what had happened to him. They said: Each of us will bring something to eat. And each brought from what God provided. And one of them brought a fish wrapped in a napkin and gave it to his [the righteous man's] wife. And she found six hundred golden dinars tied up in the napkin, and she told her husband of it. And the *ḥasid* said: Perhaps the man who brought the fish wishes to test me. Guard it well until they come to eat. When his friends came, that *ḥasid* stood up and said: Gentlemen, one of you brought a fish. The one who brought the fish was embarrassed and said: Perhaps he wishes to shame me because my gift is too small, and he did not confess that it was he who had brought it. The *ḥasid* said: I will not eat anything until the one who sent the fish admits it and says "I sent it." The owner of the fish said: My brother, I am the one who sent it. Please do not shame me. The *ḥasid* said: This is what I found, and I do not know what is inside it. The owner of the fish said: I sent it to you as a gift, and even if there were precious stones and pearls inside it, I would take nothing from you, because this money is not from me, it's from the Almighty. They also answered and said: This gift is from heaven and it is your reward for upholding what it says: "He repays everyone for what they have done" [Job 34:11]. Don't read "repay"; read pays him triple.

עכשיו בבקשה ממך טול [324א] ממני הממון שחשדתיך עליו ויהיה לך בלא עון, ומחול לי מה עשיתי לך. א"ל: לא ממון אקח ממך ולא אעשה לך דבר רע, י"י ישפוט ביני ובינך.[8] הלך בעל הממון והשכיר שלשה בחורים שנתנו החבל בצוארו, ועשו לו כמו שעשה לאותו האיש.

D. וחביריו של אותו הנחשד באו אצלו לנחמו ממה שאירע לו. אמרו: כל אחד ממנו יביא ~~כלום~~ מה שנאכל עמו. והביא כל אחד ממה שהספיק לו המקום. והביא אחד מהן דג במטפחת ונתן לאשתו, ומצאה במטפחת קשורין שש מאות דינרי זהב, וספרה לבעלה. אמר אותו חסיד: שמא אותו שהביא הדג מבקש לנסות אותי, שמרי אותו יפה עד שיבואו לאכול. כשבאו חביריו עמד החסיד ואמר להם: רבותי אחד מכם שיגר דג. ואותו ששיגר דג שמע ונתבייש ואמר: שמא הוא מבקש לביישני לפי שמתנתי קטנה ולא היה מודה לו.[9] ואמר החסיד: לא אוכל כלום עד שיודה מי ששלחו ויאמר: אני שגרתיו. אמר בעל הדג: אחי אני שגרתיו, בבקשה ממך נא אל תבזיני. א"ל החסיד: מה היה בתוך המטפחת? אמר: איני יודע. הוציא החסיד המטפחת כמו שהיה קשורה, ואמר להם: זה מצאתי, ואיני יודע מה בתוכו. ענה בעל הדג ואמר: אני שגרתיו לך במתנה, ואלמלא היה בתוכו אבנים טובות ומרגליות לא הייתי לוקח {עִמ}מך [ממך] כלום, שהממון הזה אינו ממני אלא מן הקב"ה. ענו כולם ואמרו: מתנה זו אֵינה אלא מן השמים, וזו היא שכרך לקיים מה שנ' כי פועל אדם ישלם [איוב לד, יא]. אל תיקרי ישלם אלא ישלש לו"

8. חטאתי אצלך אדוני. בבקשה ממך טול החבל וקשור אותו על צווארי ועשה לי כאשר עשיתי לך. א"ל: ח"ו איני עושה לך כלום. א"ל: אחזור ואפייס אותך ואומר לך טול ממני הממון שחשדתיך ויהיה לך בלא עוון ומחול לי מה שעשיתי לך. א"ל: לא ממון אקח ממך ולא אעשה בך שום דבר כלום. ישפוט ה' ביני ובינך.

9. רבותינו מה הטורח הזה שעשיתי שאחד מכם שיגר דג ושש מאות דינרי זהב עמו קשורים בו? ואותו ששיגר הדג שמע ונתבייש ושתק.

51. The Power of a Single Act of Charity (324a–325a)

A. [324a] Once there was a man, among the great men of his generation, who was very rich but childless. After ten years, God gave him a son, and he named him Saul [lit., borrowed], whom his father and mother borrowed from God. When he was five years old, they put him in school, and he studied there. When he grew up, he would hit all his friends and humiliate people. And the people were afraid to tell his father and mother, because they were rich and great people of the generation and were compassionate toward the poor. And those who were humiliated by the son borrowed money from the father and, consequently, were afraid to tell him.

B. In time, a man who had four daughters became extremely poor. He said to himself: I will go to an inn in case God summons something to me to receive something, and let us not die here. He went there for three years, and God summoned him twenty-one dinars. He said: I will return home so that, hopefully, I will find my wife and daughters still alive and waiting for my return. He came [324b] to set out on his way home. Robbers attacked [met] him and took everything he had, leaving him naked. He began to weep and grieve. He said: If I return home empty-handed, my wife and daughters will beseech me, and what can I give them? Instead, I will go, and perhaps God will still have pity on me. He went, and God summoned him eighteen gold dinars. He said: It is enough for me, lest my wife and daughters have starved to death. I will return to see if they are still alive. He immediately bought himself a donkey and used the rest of the money to buy merchandise, which he loaded onto the donkey, and set out on his way home. He encountered a river, and the donkey entered the river with its load and sank. When the poor man saw that, he rent his clothes. From now on, I would be better off dead near to my town, and I will choke myself so that the people of my town find me and bury me. When he was close to his town, he removed his belt from his waist and tied it around his neck and hanged himself.

51. שכרה של מצווה אחת (324א–325א)

A. מעשה באדם אחד מגדולי הדור, שהיה עשיר הרבה ולא היה לו בן. לעשר שנים נתן לו הקב"ה בן וקרא שמו שאול, ששאלהו אביו ואמו מן הקב"ה. כשהיה בן חמש שנים הכניסוהו לבית הספר והיה לומד. וכשגדל היה מכה כל חביריו ומבזה בני אדם.[1] והיו יריאים להגיד לאביו ולאמו, לפי שהיו עשירים וגדולי הדור והיו מרחמין העניים.[2] והמתבזים מן הנער היו מלוין מאביו,[3] לכך היו מתיראין להגיד לו.[4]

B. לימים העני אדם אחד[5] ביותר, והיו לו ארבעה בנות.[6] אמר אותו עני בלבו:[7] אלך באכסניא שמא יזמין לי הקב"ה כלום,[8] ואל נמות בכאן.[9] הלך והיה {שם} שלש שנים,[10] וזימן לו הקב"ה[11] עשרים ואחד דינרים. אמר: אחזור לביתי, שמא אמצא אשתי ובנותי[12] בחיים והן מחכות לביאתי.[13] בא [324ב] לחזור לביתו. פגעו בו ליסטים ולקחו כל מה שהיה לו, והניחוהו ערום. התחיל בוכה ומצטער. אמר: אם אחזור לביתי ריקם, אשתי ובנותי[14] תלוין עיניהם עלי<~~הן~~> ומה אתן להם? אלא אלך, עוד אולי ירחם עלי הקב"ה.[15] הלך, וזימן לו[16] הקב"ה י"ח דינרים זהב. אמר: דיי לי שמא מתו אשתי ובנותיי ברעב, אחזור ואראה אם הם בחיים.[17] מיד קנה לו חמור, ושאר הממון[18] נתן לסחורה וטען על החמור,[19] והיה חוזר לביתו. פגע בנהר אחד, ונכנס החמור עם המשאוי בנהר ונשקע. כשראה אותו עני כך קרע בגדיו.[20] מכאן ואילך מוטב לי למות

1. בכ"י ירושלים 3182, דף 131א–131ב (יסיף, מאה סיפורים, 243–245, סיפור ע"ז): וכשנתגדל הכה כל חביריו וביזה הרבה בני אדם. ההשוואות להלן הן לכתב יד זה.
2. בכ"י ירושלים חסר: לפי שהיו עשירים–העניים.
3. שם חסר: והמתבזים–מאביו.
4. והיו מתייראין לומר לאביו.
5. לימים היה אדם לשם עני ביותר.
6. והיו לו ד' בנים.
7. תוספת: מה אני עושה בכאן?
8. כמה דינרי זהב.
9. ואפרנס את ביתי.
10. בלי: הלך והיה שם שלש שנים.
11. ומצא נ"א דינרי זהב.
12. אשתי ובני.
13. שהם מצפים אותי מתי אחזור לביתי.
14. אשתי ובני.
15. אלא אחזור עוד אולי ירחם עלי המקום.
16. חזר ושלח לו הקב"ה.
17. אמר: יש לי די סיפוקי ואיני יודע אם אשתי ובני מתו או אם הם בחיים אחזור ואראה אותם.
18. ושאר דינרים.
19. ונתן כל הסחורה על החמור.
20. תוספת: אמר.

C. That young man [Saul] passed by with the students with whom he would congregate as a band. He turned off the path to wet his feet [urinate] and saw a man choking and ran to him. He said: Who are you, and what is your name? The man gave no answer, because he had choked himself. He [the young man, Saul] then caught and released him, and questioned him, and he [the man] told him everything that had happened to him. He [the man] sat and wept. At that moment, he [Saul] took thirty-nine golden dinars out of his pocket and gave them to him. He said: Go home, and I will give you a dinar each month to support you, as God is my witness. At that moment, each went on his way, the poor man went home and he [the young man] went to his friends. They said to him: Why were you delayed? He said: Something happened to me. And that poor man went home, and his family saw him and were exceedingly joyous.

D. That night, the head of the yeshiva saw an angel in his dream, and it took the crown from his head and placed it on the head of that young man. When he awoke, he was frightened and shocked. He sent for the father of that young man and asked him: What deeds has your son done? And he [the father] was fearful and he said: Sir, I know that my son is a fool, and he has not a single [good] deed, except that he learns here all day, and I do not know what to answer you, sir. He said: Tell me his deeds, and if you do not, your life is in danger. He said to him: Sir, let me go and I will ask my wife, in case there is something my son did that I do not know about. He went home weeping and said to his wife: You should know that our only [son] will die. She said to him: Why? He said: I do not know, but I heard that he struck so-and-so in the yeshiva. The wife went and said: Sir, no one has ever come and said: Your son has humiliated me, and was sent away empty-handed. Instead, I would have made him happy. And now bring the boy from school, and let us ask him.

סמוך לעירי ואחנק <<~~לעיר~~>> עצמי,[21] שמא ימצאו אותי בני עירי ויקברוני. כשבא קרוב[22] לעירו התיר איזורו ממותניו,[23] וקשר בצוארו[24] ותלה עצמו.

C. אותו הבחור[25] היה עובר עם התלמידים שהיו הולכין בחבורה. נפנה לדרך להסיך רגליו,[26] וראה אותו החנוק ורץ אצלו. א"ל: מה טיבך ומי אתה? ולא השיב לו כלום שנתן עצמו בחניקה. עד שתפשו בעצמו והתירו,[27] ושאל לו וסיפר לו כל המעשה שאירע לו. ישב ובכה. באותה שעה הוציא[28] מכיסו שלשים ותשעה[29] דינרים זהב, ונתן לו. א"ל: לך לביתך, ועלי ליתן לך דינר בכל חדש לצורך כלכלתיך,[30] ומעיד בי בוראי. באותה שעה באו זה מכאן וזה מכאן,[31] העני לביתו והוא לחביריו. אמרו לו: למה איחרת?[32] אמר להם: דבר[33] היה לי.[34] ואותו עני הלך לביתו, וראוהו בני ביתו ושמחו שמחה גדולה.

D. באותה הלילה ראה ראש ישיבה בחלומו שבא מלאך,[35] ולקח הכתר מראשו ונתנו בראש אותו בחור. עמד בבקר מתפחד ומתבהל.[36] ושלח והביא אביו של אותו בחור, ושאל לו: מה מעשים יש לו לבנך?[37] והיה מתיירא ואמר: אדוני, יודע אני שבני שוטה הוא ומעשה אחד אין לו, אלא שהוא למד כאן בכל שעה,[38] ואיני יודע מה אשיב לאדוני. א"ל: הגד לי מה מעשיו,[39] ואם לא תגיד בן מות אתה.[40] אמר[41] לו: אדוני, שלחני ואשאל לאשתי, שמא עשה בני שאיני יודע.[42] הלך לביתו בוכה ואמר לאשתו: תהי יודעת כי היחיד ימות.[43] אמרה לו: למה? אמר לה:

---

21. כנראה חסרה המלה: אלך, על פי נוסח כ"י ירושלים: אלך סמוך לעיר ואחנק את עצמי.
22. כשבא סמוך לעירו.
23. התיר חגורתו ממתניו.
24. ואסרו בצוארו.
25. ואותו בן החסיד.
26. להטיל מים.
27. ותפשו בן החסיד והתירו והחיה[אותו].
28. הוציא בן החסיד מכיסו.
29. ל"ו דינרי זהב.
30. חסר: לצורך כלכלתיך.
31. הלכו זה לכאן וזה לכאן.
32. מפני מה נתאחרת כל כך?
33. דבר אחד היה לי.
34. שם, תוספת: עם עני אחד.
35. מלאך אחד.
36. והראש ישיבה עמד בבוקר מפוחד ומובהל.
37. מה מעשים יש לך ולבנך?
38. אדוני, איני יודע אלא שבני (עושים) [עושה] מעשים שוטים ואין לי שום מעשים אחרים. והוא עבדך ואיני יודע להגיד לאדוני.
39. אמר לו: הגד לי הן או לאו.
40. בן מות הוא.
41. תוספת: החסיד.
42. שמא היא יודעת אם שום דבר עשה בני.
43. תהא יודעת בנינו יחיד ימות.

E. His mother went and brought him from school. And his father was prostrated on the ground, weeping. He said to him: My son, tell me what you have done, and I will give you all my money. Perhaps I can redeem you, and you will not die. He said: And who told the head of the yeshiva about me? He said: I do not know. He said: My father, bring me to him, and let the Almighty testify for me. His father told him: Confess to the Almighty if you do not wish to tell me. He said to him: Do not [325a] fear this thing, my father. His father and mother immediately took him and led him to the head of the yeshiva. When they came, the head of the yeshiva said to the father: Do you know what your son did? He said: Sir, here is my son before you, and I do not know what he will tell you. The head of the yeshiva said to him: My son, tell me what you have done. He said: I have neither killed nor stolen nor committed adultery. He said to him: That is not what I asked you, rather, what good deed have you done in your life? He said to him: Sir, I was walking with the band, and I found a man choking, and I saved him. I have not told my father or mother until now. The head of the yeshiva immediately bowed down before the Almighty and said: Blessed is the Lord, the God of Israel, that he [the young man] has earned both this world and the next in one moment. He took the crown from upon his head and placed it on the head of the young man and seated him on his chair and called out: "He repays everyone for what they have done" [Job 34:11].

איני יודע,[44] אלא היינו שומעים שהיה מכה זה וזה בישיבה.[45] הלכה האשה ואמרה: אדוני, לא בא אדם מעולם ואמר הנער ביזני שהחזרתיו ריקם, אלא שהייתי משמחו.[46] ועתה נביא הנער מבית הספר ונשאל לו.

E. הלכה אמו והביאתו מבית הספר. ואביו היה מוטל בארץ ובוכה. וא"ל: בני אמור לי מה עשית ואתן לך כל ממוני, אולי אפדה אותך ולא תמות.[47] א"ל: ומי הוא שהודיע עלי לראש ישיבה. א"ל: איני יודע. א"ל: אבי, הביאני אצלו והקב"ה ~~אצלו~~ מעיד בי.[48] א"ל אביו: הודה לו להקב"ה, אם לא רצית לומר לי. אמר לו: לא [325א] תירא אבי מדבר זה.[49] מיד לקחו אותו אביו ואמו, והוליכוהו לראש ישיבה. כשבאו אמר ראש ישיבה לאב: ידעת המעשה שעשה בנך?[50] א"ל: אדוני, הרי בני לפניך ואני איני יודע מה אומר[51] לך. א"ל ראש ישיבה:[52] בני,[53] אמור לי מה מעשיך. א"ל: לא רצחתי ולא גנבתי ולא ניאפתי. אמר לו: לא כך שאלתיך, אלא מה טובה עשית מימיך?[54] א"ל: איני יודע. אמר לו: בשבועה גדולה אני משביעך שתאמר לי מה עשית.[55] א"ל: אדוני הייתי מהלך בחבורה,[56] ומצאתי אדם אחד נתחנק[57] והצלתיו, ולא הודעתיו לאבי ולא לאמי[58] עד עכשיו.[59] מיד השתחוה ראש ישיבה לפני הקב"ה ואמר: ברוך י"י א-להי ישראל שבשעה אחת קנה לו העולם הזה והעולם הבא. ולקח הכתר מעל ראשו ונתנו על ראש הבחור. והושיבו בכסאו וקרא עליו: כי פועל אדם ישלם לו [איוב לד, יא]"

---

44. סיפר לה כל המעשה.
45. חסר: אלא היינו שומעים שהיה מכה זה וזה בישיבה.
46. אמרה לו: [לא] שמעתי על זה, לא בא אדם בעולם ואמר: בנך ביזני והכני והחזירני ריקם.
47. ושאל לו: בני, אמור לי מה עשית ונתן לך כל הממון, אולי נפדה אותך ולא תהיה בן מות.
48. אמר לאביו: הביאני עמך אל ראש ישיבה והקב"ה יעיד בי [מה] עשיתי.
49. א"ל אביו: הודה לי כאן ואל תירא.
50. אמר: אני רוצה לדבר אל ראש ישיבה. אז לקחו אביו והוליכו והוליכו אצלו.
51. מה יאמר לך.
52. חסר התואר: ראש הישיבה.
53. חסרה מלת הפנייה: בני.
54. א"ל ראש ישיבה: לא שאלתי כך, אלא מה עשית מימיך?
55. מה טוב עשית מימיך?
56. הלכתי עם חבורתי.
57. ומצאתי אדם אחד מתחנק.
58. ולא הודעתי לא לאבי ולא לאמי.
59. עד זאת השעה.

52. A Slave for Seven Years (325a–325b)

A. [325a] Once there was a man who used to ask God for a son. And God gave him a son, and he taught him much Torah. Afterward the father died. After some time his mother told him: My son, take your father's money and go engage in commerce. The son took the money and went out to trade. When he saw these and those [people] stealing and robbing, he did not buy anything. He came home, and his mother asked him: My son, why didn't you engage in trade? He said: Mother, this craft is not proper. While they were talking, they saw a man about to be buried. He said to his mother: I shall go and pay my respects with those burying [him]. He went. As he returned, he saw a man plowing with a pair of oxen, and a book lying on his plow, and he was reading as he plowed. The young man saw him and said: Greetings, Rabbi. And that man was Elijah the Prophet, of blessed memory. The young man said to him: What craft is it that you are engaged in? He said: My son, I am plowing so that I and my wife and sons and daughters [together with] the poor and destitute and the birds of heaven, may eat. The young man said: That is the craft I seek. Elijah asked him: What would you wish for? The young man said: God gave me the Torah, and now I seek to marry a God-fearing woman. Elijah said: My son, only two women in the world are called a woman of valor: Sarah in the East and Hannah in the West, and the third is reserved for you. And it was a three days' distance to her city.

B. Elijah took him on his wings and led him to the gate of the woman's home. He placed him there, and Elijah approached her. He asked her: What do you say about marrying this man? She said: If this is from God, it will be done. At once he brought in the young man and matched him [with the maiden] and crowned him, and he [Elijah] would come and go. On the seventh day of the wedding, Elijah, of blessed memory, came and found him sporting with his wife. You have abandoned your Torah and forgotten it, said Elijah. On your life, against the seven days of nuptial festivities, you will be sold as a slave for seven years. Elijah went away, and left him. The young man began weeping and lamenting. His bride said: My lord, why [325b] are you crying? Is there something wrong with me, or perhaps you lack money or garments? Indeed, they are all at your hand. Or perhaps you cry for your parents whom you miss? Let us go to them. They saddled the donkeys, and left with their slaves and maidservants. On the way they encountered a big river. Let us sit down and eat, said the woman. They sat down to eat, and the young man rose to bathe in the river.

52. עבד לשבע שנים (325א–325ב)

A. מעשה[1] באדם אחד ששאל בן מהקב"ה,[2] ונתן לו.[3] ולימדו תורה ביותר. ואחר כך מת האב.[4] לימים אמר[ה] לו האם: בני קח ממון של אביך וצא בסחורה. לקח הבן <~~בסחורה~~> הממון, והלך בסחורה. ראה אילו גוזלין ואילו חומסין,[5] כשראה כך לא קנה כלום.[6] בא לביתו אמר[ה] לו אמו: בני למה לא סחרתה? אמר לה: אמי אינה כשירה זו האומנות.[7] כשהיו שניהם מדברים כן, היו מוציאין אדם לקוברו.[8] אמר הבן לאמו: אצא ואגמול חסד עם היוצאין לקבור. יצא. בחזירתו ראה אדם אחד שהיה חורש בצמדו,[9] והיה נתון הספר במחרישה והיה חורש וקורא. ראהו הנער א"ל: שלום עליך רבי. והוא היה אליהו ז"ל. א"ל הנער:[10] ר' מה האומנות שאתה עושה?[11] א"ל: בני אני חורש, שנאכל ונשתה אני ואשתי ובני ובנותיי, ועניים ואביונים[12] ועופות השמים. א"ל הבחור: הרי האומנות שאני מבקש. א"ל: מה תבקש שאתן ~~ש~~ לך? א"ל הבחור: התורה נתן לי הקב"ה, ועכשיו אני מבקש לישא לי אשה יראת שמים.[13] א"ל: בני לא נקראת אשה בעולם אשת חיל אלא שתים: שרה במזרח וחנה במערב, ושלישית שמורה לך.[14] ומאותו מקום היה מהלך שלשת ימים למקומה.[15]

B. לקחו בכנפיו והוליכו לשער שהאשה בבית.[16] העמידו והלך אליהו אצלה. אמר לה: מה אתה [!] אומרת נשא לך איש?[17] אמרה לו אם מי"י יצא הדבר, יעשה.[18] מיד הביא את הבחור וזיווגו ועיטרו, והיה יוצא ובא <ונכנס>.[19] ביום השביעי לחופה בא אליהו ז"ל, ומצא אותו שהיה שוחק עם אשתו.[20] א"ל אליהו: הנחתה תורתך ושכחת אותה. בחייך, תחת שבעת ימי חופה תימכר שבע

---

1. תוספת פתיחה במעשה"ד, שפירא 207–209, על פי כתבי יד מאוחרים לספר המעשים: אשתו של ר' שאול מאי היא? ההשוואות להלן הן לנוסח זה.
2. ששאל לפני הקב"ה. אמר לפניו: רבונו של עולם, תן לי בן ואלמדנו תורה בתאות לבי.
3. שמע הקב"ה את תפילתו ונתן לו בן, וקרא שמו שאול כי שאלוהו אביו ואמו לפני הקב"ה.
4. ונתגדל ונעשה בן עשרים וחמש שנים ולמד תורה ונתחכם ביותר. אחר כן מת אביו.
5. תוספת: ואלו נשבעים לשקר.
6. וחזר לביתו ריקם.
7. הסחורה קשה בעיני ואינה כשרה אלי.
8. תוך שהיו מדברין האם והבן ראה בני אדם שהיו מוציאין אדם לקברות.
9. חורש בעצמו.
10. אמר לו הבחור.
11. מה זאת האומנות שאתה עמל?
12. תוספת: ובהמות השדה.
13. אמר לו: עושר נתן לי הקב"ה ועכשו אני מבקש אשה בעלת חן ויראת ה'!
14. בחייך לא נקראו אשת חייל אלא שתי נשים, אחת שמה שרה והיא במזרח, ואחת במערב ושמה חנה והיא שמורה לך.
15. מאותו מקום עד לשמה היה מהלך שלש שנים.
16. לקחו אליהו בכנפו והוליכו לשם בשעה קלה.
17. אמר לה: בתי, מה את אומרת – תנשא לזה האיש שבא עמי?
18. מיי' יצא הדבר, אלא אוכל דבר מאומה?
19. במעשה"ד: ואליהו היה יוצא ובא כאב.
20. ושוחק עם הכלה.

C. Elijah came and carried him on his wings to a far-off place and sold him as a slave. The woman waited, and when she saw that he hadn't arrived she realized, and gave thanks to the Almighty. She said to her servants/slaves: I see here a wheat field. Build me here a city and houses, and we will sow and amass wheat here, because I know that there will be a famine in the land, and the whole world will come here to trade. They immediately did so, and everyone came to trade.

D. Five years later, the young man came with his master. And the young man was carrying sacks. And she would ask every one of the people their names. When she saw the young man, she said to his master: Give me the young man so that he can dine with me in my home. She took him home and asked him: What is your name? He said: My name is such and such. She recognized him and said: I am your maidservant, and you are my husband. She stood and embraced and kissed him and said: My lord, tell me what happened to you. He told her all that had happened. He told her: My daughter, I have been a slave for five years only, and I still have two years left. She fed him and gave him to drink and kissed him. Go, my lord, in peace, she said. He went to his master. And she neither shouted nor screamed, but only gave thanks to the Almighty.

שנים לעבד.[21] יצא אליהו והניחו. התחיל הבחור בוכה וסופד.[22] אמרה לו הכלה: אדוני, מה [325ב] אתה בוכה,[23] שמא איני כשרה לפניך או אם חסר ממון או כלים?[24] הרי כולם לפניך,[25] או שמא על אבותיך אתה בוכה ומצטער?[26] נלך אצלם. חבשו החמורים,[27] והלכו להם עם העבדים והשפחות[28] שלהם. כשהיו בדרך פגעו בנהר גדול. אמרה האשה נשב ונאכל. ישבו לאכול, עמד הבחור והלך בנהר לרחוץ.[29]

C. בא אליהו ולקחו בכנפיו והוליכו למקום רחוק, ומכרו לעבד. המתינה האשה כשראתה שלא בא[30] היכירה[31] ונתנה הוד{~~א~~}ה [הודאה] להקב"ה. אמרה <~~להקב"ה~~> לעבדיה: הריני רואה השדה זו עושה חיטים, בנו לי כרך ובתים בכאן ונזרע[32] ונצבור חטים. שאני יודעת שעתיד ליהיות רעב בארץ,[33] וכאן עתידים לבא ולסחור כל העולם.[34] מיד עשו כן, והיו באין הכל בסחורה.[35]

D. לאחר חמש שנים בא הבחור, ואדונו עמו. והבחור היה סובל שקים, והיא היתה שואלת לכל אדם[36] שמותם.[37] כיון שראתה הבחור[38] אמרה לאדונו: תן לי הנער,[39] שיאכל עמי בביתי.[40] לקחתו בביתה ושאלה אותו:[41] מה שמך? אמר לה: כך וכך שמי.[42] הכירה אותו[43] ואמרה: אני שפחתך ואתה בעלי. עמדה וחיבקתו ונשקתו,[44] ואמרה לו: אדוני, ספר לי מה אירע לך. סיפר לה כל המעשה.[45] ואמר לה: בתי,[46] לא הייתי עבד עדיין אלא חמש שנים, ועדיין אני חסר ב' שנים.

---

21. חייך שבע שנים תמכר לעבד תחת שבעת ימי חופה.
22. התחיל הבחור בוכה ומצטער.
23. מה טיב זה?
24. "כלים" בהוראה של "בגדים" ראו דברים כב, ה; שבת קיד, ע"א.
25. חסר: שמא איני כשרה לפניך או אם חסר ממון או כלים הרי כולם לפניך. תוספת: או איני נאה והגונה לפניך?
26. או בשביל אבותיך אתה מצטער? לך אצלם.
27. גמליהם וחמוריהם. תוספת: וקנו עגלות לשאת ממונם.
28. ולקחו עבדים והלכו להם.
29. לרחוץ רגליו.
30. המתינה האשה שנה אחת ולא בא.
31. הבינה הדבר.
32. ונזרע השדה.
33. שעתיד רעב גדול לבא בכאן.
34. לבא ולסחור כל בני אדם.
35. והיו כלם באים אצלה.
36. בני אדם הבאים לקנות חטה.
37. את שמותיהן.
38. כשראתה אותו הכירתהו.
39. הבחור הזה.
40. שיאכל לחם בביתי.
41. מי אתה ומה שמך?
42. אני פלוני.
43. חסר: הכירה אותו.
44. מיד עמדה וחבקתו ונשקתו, הוציאה לו מזון, והאכלתהו והשקתהו וכסתהו וחבקתהו ונשקתו.
45. ספר לה כל מה שאירע לו.
46. חסרה מלת הפנייה: בתי.

E. He went and served two additional years. [Then] Elijah, of blessed memory, came and carried the young man on his wings and led him to his wife. And the young man took his wife and slaves, and he went to his mother and found her alive. And of her [his wife], it is said: "Who can find a woman of valor?" [Proverbs 31:10].

האכילתו והשקתו ונשקתו[47] ואמר לו: לך אדוני לשלום.[48] הלך לאדונו.[49] והיא[50] לא צעקה ולא צרחה אלא נתנה הודיה להקב"ה.[51]

E. הלך[52] ועשה עוד שתי שנים.[53] ואחר כך[54] בא אליהו ז"ל ולקח הבחור[55] בכנפיו והוליכו לאשתו. ולקח הבחור את אשתו ועבדיו,[56] והלך לאמו ומצאה בחיים. ועליה נאמר אשת חיל מי ימצא [משלי לא, י].[57]

---

47. חסר: האכילתו והשקתו ונשקתו.
48. לך לשלום.
49. הלך הבחור עם אדוניו.
50. לא צוֹחה, ולא בכתה ולא צעקה.
51. נתנה עיניה למרום ונתנה שבח והודאה לקב"ה.
52. הלך הבחור עם אדוניו.
53. ועמד עמו עוד שתי שנים בעבדות.
54. ולאחר שתי שנים.
55. נטלו בכנפו.
56. מיד לקח הבחור את אשתו ועבדיה ושפחותיה.
57. במעשה"ד האפילוג הוא: וראה מה היתה אשה זו חשובה ואשת חיל, שלא כחשה בבעלה ולבוראה כל אלו השנים, ועליה הכתוב אומר: אשה יראת ה' היא תתהלל. ומכאן שאשה שחטאת בגופה מעלה עליו הכתוב כאילו מכחשה לפני הקב"ה העוזבת אלוף נעוריה ואת ברית א-להיה שכחה, ומי שהוא חכם ונבון ירחק ממנה.

53. One Man in a Thousand Have I Found (325b–326b)

A. [325b] Once in the days of [King] Solomon, he [the king] would sit in his palace, and the Sanhedrin would sit before him. He said to them: "One man in a thousand have I found, but a woman among all these I did not find" [Ecclesiastes 7:28], and if you like, I will test it now. Solomon immediately said: Bring me a young man who has a wife. They told him of a certain man. They sent for him and brought him to Solomon. He came before the king. Solomon asked him: Where are you from, and who are you? Tell me because I wish to show you honor and give you my daughter and make you the minister in charge of my palace. The man responded and said: I am your servant, and you will find me as befits one of your servants. He said: If so, then go and kill your wife and bring me her head tonight, and I will give you my daughter and make you wealthy and appoint you to be the official in charge of the greater part of Israel. The man said: Fine. The king gave him his sword.

B. He went home and saw that his wife was exceedingly beautiful. And he had small children from her. [326a] He entered home grumbling, and his wife received him and said: Sir, what is the matter, because I see that you are troubled? He said: Let me be, for I am worried at heart. She immediately laid a table before him with food and wine, but he neither ate nor drank. He thought to himself: What shall I do? My wife is beautiful, and I have small sons from her, and he grieved in his heart. He said: How can I kill my wife?! He immediately said to her: Get up and lie down with your sons. She got up and lay down and fell asleep. He stood and unsheathed his sword to kill her. He saw his younger son sleeping between her breasts, and the head of the other on her shoulder. He then thought to himself and said: If I kill her, my little children will die. And he returned his sword to its sheath and said: "The Lord rebuke you, O Satan" [Zechariah 3:2], lest King Solomon had Satan in his heart when he told me: Kill your wife, and I will give you my daughter and wealth. He stood a second time and unsheathed his sword, and his wife's beautiful hair was spread out over the babes. And his heart was filled with compassion, and he said: The Lord rebuke you, O Satan, and he broke the sword into twelve pieces. He said: I ask for neither his house nor his wealth, and even if he gives me his entire house filled with silver and gold, I will not do such a thing. He went to bed forthwith.

53. אדם אחד מאלף מצאתי (325ב-326ב)

A. מעשה היה בימי שלמה יום אחד היה יושב בפלטין שלו והיו סנהדרין יושבין לפניו. אמר להם: אדם מאלף מצאתי ואשה בכל אלה לא מצאתי [קהלת ז, כח],[1] ואם תרצו אני אבדוק עכשיו. מיד אמר שלמה: הביאו לי בחור אחד שיש לו אשה.[2] אמרו לו איש פלוני. שלח אחריו, והביאו אותו. בא לפני המלך. א"ל: מאיזה מקום אתה ומי אתה? אמור לי שאני מבקש לעשות לך כבוד, ואני רוצה ליתן לך בתי ולעשות אותך שר בפלטין שלי.[3] השיב האיש ואמר: אני עבדך ותמצא אותי כעבדך.[4] א"ל: אם כן לך והרוג את אשתך והבא לי את ראשה בלילה,[5] ואני נותן לך בתי ואעשירך ואעשה אותך פקיד על רוב ישראל.[6] א"ל: הן. נתן לו ~~הקב"ה~~ המלך חרבו.[7]

B. הלך לביתו וראה אשתו יפה ביותר,[8] והיו לו ממנה בנים קטנים.[9] [326א] נכנס לביתו והיה מתאונן. פגעה לו אשתו אמרה לו: אדוני, מה לך שאני רואה את נפשך מתאוננת עליך? א"ל: הניחני שדאגה בלבי. מיד הביאה שלחן לפניו ומאכל ויין ולא אכל ולא שתה. הרהר בלבו: מה אעשה אשתי הרי היא יפת תואר ויש לי ממנה בנים קטנים, והיה מתאבל בלבו.[10] אמר איך אהרוג את אשתי?! מיד אמר לה: עמדי שכבי עם בניך. עמדה ושכבה[11] ושקעה בשינה. עמד ושלף חרבו להרגה. מצא בנה הקטן ישן בין שני דדיה,[12] ואחר ראשו על כתפה.[13] מיד הרהר בלבו ואמר: אם אהרוג את זאת, ימותו בני הקטנים. והשיב חרבו אל נדנה ואמר: יגער י"י בך השטן [זכריה ב, ב] שמא שטן בלבו של שלמה המלך,[14] שאמר לי הרוג אשתך ואתן לך בתי ואעשירך.[15] עמד פעם שנייה ושלף חרבו, וראה שערות האשה יפות פרוסות על גבי תינוקות.[16] ונכנס בלבו רחמים ואמר: יגער י"י בך השטן ושבר החרב לשנים עשר חלקים.[17] אמר: איני מבקש לא בתו ולא עושרו, ואפילו אם יתן לי כל ביתו מלא כסף וזהב איני עושה דבר זה. מיד שכב על מיטתו.

---

1. כ"י ירושלים 3182, 124ב–125א (יסיף, מאה סיפורים, 228–229, סיפור ס"ה): אמר להם המלך שמעתם דבר אחד שפשפשתי בכל העולם ולא מצאתי אלא אדם אחד מאלף מצאתי ואשה בכל אלה לא מצאתי. משלים של שלמה, סימן ב: מעשה בשלמה המלך עליו השלום שאמר ברוח הקדש: אדם אחד מאלף מצאתי ואשה בכל אלה לא מצאתי.
2. כ"י ניו-יורק, בהמ"ל, 2374 דף 112א–113ב: אשה נאה. כ"י ירושלים: אשה יפה. במשלים של שלמה: אשה אחת מטובי העיר.
3. כ"י ירושלים: שמעתי עליך שאדם טוב אתה ורצוני ליתן לך בתי ולתתך שר על כל אשר לי. משלים של שלמה: תדע שאני מבקש לך כבוד ולעשות לך שר פלטרין שלי (ללא הצעת נישואים).
4. משלים של שלמה: אני עבדך ואהיה לך כאחד מעבדיך.
5. כ"י בהמ"ל חסר: בלילה.
6. כ"י ירושלים: ועתה לך ותהרוג את אשתך ואני אתן לך בתי.
7. בכ"י ירושלים ובמשלים של שלמה: חסר.
8. בכ"י בהמ"ל: פגעה בו אשתו. בלי: והיו לו ממנה בנים קטנים.
9. תוספת בכ"י ירושלים: כשראה שיצתה לקראתו היה מצטער עצמו עליה.
10. כ"י ירושלים: היה מהרהר בליבו ואמר מה אעשה אהרוג אותה או לאו. משלים של שלמה: הרהר בלבו ואמר מה אעשה אהרוג את אשתי ויש לי בנים קטנים ממנה.
11. תוספת בכ"י בהמ"ל: עם בניה.
12. בכ"י בהמ"ל: בין שדיה.
13. משלים של שלמה: והאחר היה (עומד) [טומן] ראשו בין כתפי(ו)[ה].
14. כ"י בהמ"ל: שמא נכנס שטן; משלים של שלמה: אותה שעה אמר שלמה המלך שטן נכנס בלבו.
15. כ"י ירושלים: שאמר לי הורג את אשתך, ואומר אני איני מבקש לא בתו ולא עושרו.
16. בכ"י ירושלים אין ניסיון שני לביצוע המשימה משלים של שלמה: חזר פעם שנית ואמר להרגה ומחר יתן לי המלך את בתו ומעושרו. מיד שלף חרבו עליה וראה שערה פרוס על פני התינוקות.
17. כ"י בהמ"ל: לשני חלקים.

C. In the morning, he awoke, and the emissaries of the king came for him and brought him to the king. He [the king] said: Did you carry out my order? He said: Your majesty, this is what I did: I wished to preform your decree once and again, but my heart would not allow it. And he departed. Thirty days later the king sent secretly for his [the man's] wife and said: Have you a good husband? She said: Yes. He said: I have heard of your beauty, and I desire to marry you, and you will rule over all the princesses, and I will attire you in golden jewelry from head to toe. She said: I am your servant for whatever you tell me to do. He said: I cannot touch you as long as you have a husband, unless you kill him and then I will take you. She said: Fine. Solomon said to himself: She will certainly kill him. What did he do? He gave her a tin sword. He said: Kill him with this sword. Because she saw that it was shiny, she believed that it was a good sword made of iron. The woman went home and hid the sword.

D. When her husband came home, she stood and embraced and kissed him and said: Sir, crown of my head, be seated. The man sat, amazed, and said: What is this all about, and why is this day different from others? She said: I wish to rejoice with you and watch you be joyous. He drank and became intoxicated, until he fell into a slumber. When she saw this, she rose and girded her loins, and stretched out her arm, and drew the sword that King Solomon gave her, and began to cut off his head. And he awoke from his sleep and saw that she was standing over him and cutting his throat. The man jumped up and stood and saw the sword in her hand. He stretched out his hand to his throat and saw blood gushing from the wound she had cut into his skin. The woman was immediately ashamed [326b] and shaken. He said: Tell me why you did this, and if you don't, I will cut off your head. She said to him: Such and such happened. He took the sword and noticed that it was made of tin. He kept quiet until morning.

C. בבקר השכים ובאו שלוחי המלך בשבילו, והביאוהו למלך. א"ל: קיימת גזירתי? א"ל: אדוני, כך וכך עשיתי, בקשתי לקיים גזירתך פעם ושתים ולא מלאני לבי. יצא מעליו.[18] לסוף שלושים יום שלח המלך אצל אשתו בסתר. א"ל: יש לך בעל טוב? אמרה לו: הן. אמר לה: שמעתי על יופיך ואהבתי אותך[19] לקחתך לי לאשה, ותמליכי על כל השרות ואלבישך[20] עדי זהב מראשך ועד רגלך. אמרה לו:[21] אני אמתך כל אשר תאמר אלי אעשה.[22] אמר: איני יכול ליגע בך שיש לך בעל אלא הרגי אותו, ואחר כך אקח אותך. אמרה לו: הן.[23] אמר שלמה בלבו: ודאי היא הורגת אותו.[24] מה עשה, נתן לה סייף של בדיל. אמר לה: בסייף זה הרגי אותו. כיון שראת שהוא מבריק, סברה החרב טוב הוא של ברזל.[25] הלכה האשה לביתה והסתירה את הסייף.[26]

D. כשבא בעלה עמדה וחבקתו ונשקתו ואמרה לו: אדוני עטרת ראשי, שב.[27] ישב האיש תמה ואמר לה: מה עסקך ומה היום מימים?[28] אמרה לו: רוצה אני לשמוח עמך, כדי שאראה אותך שמח.[29] שתה ונשתכר עד שנשקע בשינה.[30] כיון שראת כך עמדה ואזרה חלציה ועשתה זרועה[31] ושלפה החרב שנתן לה שלמה המלך, והתחילה לחתוך ראשו.[32] והקיץ משנתו, והנה היא עומדת עליו וחותכת גרונו.[33] קפץ האיש ועמד ומצא בידה הסייף, והושיט ידו על גרונו והנה הדם מבצבץ שחתכה מן העור. מיד נתביישה[34] [326ב] האשה ונזדעזעה. אמר לה: הגידי לי מה ראית שעשית כך, ואם לאו אחתוך ראשך. אמרה לו: כך וכך היה המעשה.[35] נטל הסייף והשגיח בה והיתה מן בדיל. שתק עד הבקר.

18. כ"י ירושלים: אם יתן לי המלך מלא ביתו זהב וכסף לא אהרוג את אשתי ולא עשיתי דבר זה כלל. במשלים של שלמה הרחבה של התנצלות האיש: אם טוב בעיני המלך אל יכעס אותי בדבר הזה, ובתוספת מסקנת שלמה: הרי אדם אחד מאלף מצאתי.

19. כ"י בהמ"ל חסר: אותך.

20. כ"י בהמ"ל: ותעדך.

21. בכ"י בהמ"ל יש מלת פנייה: אדוני המלך.

22. תוספת בכ"י ירושלים ובמשלים של שלמה: כל אשר תחפוץ אעשה.

23. הרחבה נוספת במשלים של שלמה: דבר אחד יזיק לנו שאיני יכול לעשות שום דבר שיש ל(י)ך בעל. אמר[ה] לו: והיאך נעשה?

24. משלים של שלמה: נעשה לי זה דבר תקנה שלא ימות.

25. כ"י בהמ"ל: סברה חרב הוא של ברזל.

26. משלים של שלמה: כשראתה אותו שהוא מבריק. אמר: בסייף זה הרגי אותו כי מיד שנגע אותו בצוארו הוא נחתך.

27. משלים של שלמה: כששמע כך שמח שמחה גדולה. וישב בעלה ואין בלבו שום מחשבה רעה. מיד הביאה השלחן ואכלו ושתו.

28. משלים של שלמה: אמר לה בעלה: אשתי מה עסקיך זה הלילה?

29. כ"י ירושלים: רוצה אני לשמוח ולשכר עמך. משלים של שלמה: נבקש לשמוח עמך ולראותך שיכור זה הלילה.

30. כ"י ירושלים: וכך עשה אותו האיש ושתה מאוד והלך וישן על מטתו. משלים של שלמה: שחק לפניה בטוב לב ושתה ונשתכר עד שנשתקע בשינה.

31. כ"י בהמ"ל חסר: ואזרה חלציה. במשלים של שלמה חסר: ועשתה זרועה.

32. במשלים של שלמה האישה חותכת את העור.

33. משלים של שלמה: מיד בעלה הקיץ משנתו וראה הנה עומדת עליו אשתו להרגו.

34. כ"י בהמ"ל: נתפשה.

35. כ"י ירושלים: ואם לא תגידי לי אחתוך את ראשך. אמרה לו כך וכך היה המעשה. משלים על שלמה: אם לא תגידי לי אעשה בשריך אברים אברים. אמרה לו: כך וכך הדבר אמר לי שלמה המלך. אמר לה: אל תראי.

E. In the morning, the messengers of Solomon came for them and brought them before the king. And the Sanhedrin was sitting before him. When the king saw them, he began to laugh and said: What is the matter? He said: Your majesty, did you do this? The king asked: What happened? He said: I awoke and found my wife standing over me about to kill me, and had it been an iron sword, I would already be dead. I took pity on her, and she did not take pity on me. Solomon said: I knew indeed that there is no pity in a woman, and therefore I did not give her an iron sword. He then turned to the Sanhedrin and said: That is what I said: "One man in a thousand have I found, but a woman among all these I did not find" [Ecclesiastes 7:28].

E. ובבקר באו שלוחי שלמה בשבילם, והביאו אותם לפני המלך. והיו סנהדרין יושבין לפניו. כיון שראה אותם המלך התחיל לשחוק ואמר להם: מה עיסקיכם? א"ל: אדוני, אתה עשית את הדבר הזה? אמר לו: היאך היה הדבר?[36] א"ל: הקיצותי ומצאתי אשה[37] עלי להרגיני, ואילו היה הסייף של ברזל[38] כבר הייתי אבוד מן העולם.[39] אני ריחמתי עליה והיא לא ריחמה עלי. א"ל שלמה: אף אני יודע שאין לאשה רחמים, ולכך לא נתתי לה סייף של ברזל.[40] באותה שעה פתח לפני סנהדרין ואמר: זה הוא שאמרתי, אדם אחד מאלף מצאתי ואשה בכל אלה לא מצאתי [קהלת ז, כח]"

36. כ"י בהמ"ל חסר: היה הדבר.
37. כ"י בהמ"ל ומשלים של שלמה: אשתי.
38. כ"י בהמ"ל: ואלו לא היה הסיף מבדיל. משלים של שלמה: אילולי שהיה הבדיל.
39. משלים של שלמה: כבר הייתי מת מן העולם.
40. כ"י בהמ"ל: ולכך נתתי לה סייף של בדיל. משלים של שלמה: אני הייתי יודע רחמנות בנשים לפיכך נתתי לה סייף של בדיל.

54. The Hard-Boiled Egg (326b–327a)

A. [326b] Once the workers of King David were seated at a meal eating eggs. One was especially hungry and ate the portion given to him before the others. And he was ashamed because he [now] had nothing before him. He said to his friends sitting with him: Lend me one egg. He said to him: I will not lend it to you unless you swear to me before witnesses that you will give it [an egg] back to me, and any profit that could be made from one egg for the time that I lend it to you. He said: Fine. He gave it to him before witnesses. After a long period, he came to ask it back from him. He said to him: I owe you only one egg.

B. They went before King David, and they found Solomon seated at the gate, for that was the custom of Solomon, who would sit at the king's gate, and all those who came to be judged before the king, he would ask: What is your business with the king? He said [would say] to him: This and this happened between me and so-and-so. And when the man who had borrowed the egg from his friend came, Solomon said to him: What is your business with the king? He said to him: This and this happened. He said to him: Go before the king, and when you return, tell me what the king says to you. They went before King David. The plaintiff brought witnesses to prove that this was indeed the condition between them, to pay him the profit that a person could make from one egg from that time up to the present. King David said to him: Go and pay him. He said: I don't know how much. They presented their reckoning to the king. In one year, one chick. In the second year, that chick could beget eighteen chicks. In the third year, those eighteen chicks could each beget yet another eighteen chicks. And thus in the fourth year, until the reckoning added up to a great deal of money. The man was greatly dismayed.

C. Solomon met him and said to him: What did the king say to you? He said: This is what the king charged me, and it amounts to a large sum of money. [327a] He [Solomon] said: Listen to me, and I will give you good advice. He said to him: Go ahead [lit., to life]. He [Solomon] said to him: Go and buy beans and cook them. And on such and such a day, the king plans to go to a certain place. So stand you there on the way, and as the king's battalions pass before you, sow the beans in a plowed field that is by the way. And anyone who asks you what you are sowing, say: I am sowing cooked beans. And if they say to you: Who has ever seen cooked beans being sown? Say to him: And who has ever seen a chick emerge from a hard-boiled egg? He went right away and did this. And he would stand on the road and sow his cooked [beans], and when the king's battalions came, they would say to him: What are you sowing? He would say to them: Cooked beans. They would say to him: And

54. ביצה בהלוואה (326ב–327א)

A. מעשה שהיה מעבדי דוד המלך שהיו יושבין בסעודה,[1] והיו אוכלין שם בצים.[2] והיה אחד רעב ביותר ואכל חלקו הניתן לו, קודם חביריו.[3] והיה מתבייש מפני שאין לפניו כלום.[4] אמר לחבירו היושב אצלו: הלויני ביצה אחת. א"ל: לא אלוה לך עד שתדור לי בפני עדים שתתן לי אותו וכל ריוח שיכול אדם להרויח מביצה אחת עד אותו זמן שאשאליהו לך.[5] א"ל: הן. ונתן לו בפני עדים.[6] לאחר זמן מרובה בא ושאלו ממנו. אמר לו: אין לך עלי אלא ביצה אחת.

B. הלכו לפני דוד המלך.[7] ומצאו שלמה יושב פתח שער, שכך היה מנהגו של שלמה שהיה יושב פתח שער המלך, וכל מי שבא לידון לפני המלך היה שואלו: מה טיבך אצל המלך? אמר לו: כך וכך היה מעשה ~~כל~~ ביני ובין פלוני.[8] וכשבא זה שלוה הביצה מחברו א"ל שלמה: מה טיבך אצל המלך?[9] א"ל: כך וכך היה מעשה.[10] א"ל: לך לפני המלך, וכשתחזור ספר לי מה שיאמר לך המלך.[11] נכנסו לפני המלך דוד. הביא התובע עדים שכך היה התנאי ביניהם, לשלם לו הריוח שיכול אדם לעשות מביצה אחת מאותו זמן ועד עכשיו.[12] א"ל המלך דוד: לך ושלם לו. א"ל: איני יודע כמה.[13] נתנו החשבון לפני המלך.[14] בשנה אחת אפרוח אחד. בשנה שנייה אותו אפרוח יכול להוליד עד שמונה עשר אפרוחים. בשנה שלישית אילו שמונה עשרה אפרוחים מביא כל אחד ואחד י"ח אפרוחים. וכן בשנה רביעית עד שעלה החשבון לממון גדול. מיד[15] יצא זה בפחי נפש.

C. פגע בו שלמה וא"ל: מה אמר לך המלך? א"ל: כך חייבני המלך, ועולה לחשבון גדול.[16] [327א] א"ל: שמע בקולי, ואני איעצך עצה טובה. א"ל: לחיים. א"ל: לך וקנה לך פולין, ותבשלם. וביום פלוני רוצה המלך לילך למקום פלוני ותעמוד לו על הדרך, ובכל שעה גדודי המלך עובר לפניך תזרע הפולין על שדה חרושה שעל הדרך. וכל מי שישאל אותך מה אתה זורע, אמור לו פולין מבושלין אני זורע. ואם יאמרו לך: מי ראה מעולם פולין מבושלין נזרעין? אמור

---

1. כ"י ירושלים 3182 דף 117ב (יסיף, מאה סיפורים, 211–212, סיפור נ'): מעשה שהיו יושבים עבדי דוד פעם אחת בסעודה. ההשוואות להלן הן למקור זה.
2. אכלו ביצים.
3. והיה אחד רעב מאוד ואכל חלקו (של חבירו וחבירו) של חברו.
4. היה מתבייש מפני שלא היה כלום לפניו לאכול.
5. שתפרע לי אותה וכל הריוח שלה שיוכל לבא הימנה עד אותו זמן שאטלהו ממך לאחר זמן.
6. כ"י ירושלים חסר: אמר לו–בפני עדים.
7. המלך (לאורך כל הגרסה שמו של דוד אינו מוזכר).
8. כ"י ירושלים חסר: וכל מי שבא–פלוני.
9. וכשבאו אליו השנים אמר להם, מה המעשה?
10. כך וכך היה המעשה בינינו.
11. וכשתחזור אמור לי מה אמר לך.
12. שיוכל לעשות ממנו מאותו זמן עד זמן ששאלו.
13. א[י]ני יודע כמה.
14. חסר בכ"י ירושלים.
15. אז יצא.
16. אמר לו כך וכך.

who has ever seen a cooked egg from which a chick has hatched? And so he would say to each and every battalion, until the king heard about it.

D. When the king heard about it, he asked him: Who taught you this thing? He said: I know it from myself. David said to him: The hand of Solomon was with you in this thing. He said to him: On your life, your majesty, he commanded me to do this thing from beginning to end. The king sent for Solomon. The king said to him: What have you to say about this? Solomon said to him: How can he owe something that never existed? That egg was cooked and could not produce a chick. He said to him: Let him go, and repay him one egg. And in this regard it is said: "For Solomon: Give the king your judgments, O God, and your righteousness to the king's son" [Psalms 72:1].

לו: ומי ראה מעולם ביצה מבושלת שיצא ממנה אפרוח? מיד הלך ועשה כן והיה עומד על הדרך וזורע מבושלין וכשבאו גדודי המלך אמרו לו: מה אתה זורע? אמר להם: פולין מבושלין <נזרעין>. אמרו לו: ומי ראה מעולם ביצה מבושלת שיצא ממנה אפרוח? וכן היה אומר לכל גדוד וגדוד, עד שבא הדבר לפני המלך.

D. כיון ששמע המלך כך, א"ל: מי לימדך דבר זה? א"ל: אני מעצמי. א"ל דוד: יד שלמה היתה עמך בדבר זה. א"ל: בחייך אדוני המלך, הוא ציוני לעשות הדבר הזה מראש ועד סוף.[17] שלח המלך אחרי שלמה. א"ל המלך: מה תאמר בדבר זה?[18] א"ל שלמה: היאך הוא חייב בדבר שלא בא לעולם? אותה ביצה מבושלת היתה, ולא היה ראויה לאפרוח. א"ל: ילך ויפרע לו ביצה אחת.[19] ועל זאת נאמר: לשלמה א-להים משפטיך למלך וצדקתך לבן מלך [תהלים עב, א]"

17. אמר: אדוני המלך שלמה בנך אמר לי לעשות דבר זה.

18. בכ"י ירושלים תוספת של מלת פנייה: בני.

19. א"כ ילך ולא יפרע כי אם את ביצה אחת.

55. The Poor Bachelor and His Maiden Cousin (327a–329a)

A. [327a] Once there were two brothers, one rich and the other poor. The poor brother had many sons and daughters, and the rich one had but a single daughter. And the rich one was very mean to his brother and would refuse him even the slightest favor. And the poor brother had a son named Isaac. And he was a good and handsome young man, who studied well, and the rich brother loved him very much, more than any of his brother's other children.

B. It was Passover eve, and the poor man had nothing with which to buy wheat for Passover to make *maẓot* [unleavened bread eaten on the Jewish festival of Passover] for himself and his children. He approached his wealthy brother and said: Sir, in your kindness, please do me a great favor, and for the love of God our Lord, lend me a measure of wheat to feed myself and my family on this holiday. If you give me a guarantee, I will give you the loan, said the rich brother. He said: What guarantee can I bring you, for I have nothing? He said: Let me have your son Isaac, for you love him more than all your other children, and he will be a guarantee that you will pay me back what I lend you. The poor man went home and brought back his son Isaac, and the rich man lent him a measure of wheat.

C. And every day, Isaac would go to the house of study and learn with his rabbi, day and night. And every night, the daughter of his rich uncle would wait up late for him to come home. And so she did [327b], night after night. One day, the rabbi summoned Isaac and told him: Listen, my son, to my instructions, and God will be with you tonight. As soon as you arrive at your uncle's house and find your cousin there, take her in your arms and embrace and kiss her. Rabbi, said Isaac, how can I commit such a terrible sin, to encourage my evil inclination while I can yet escape it? But the rabbi said: I swear that I will not let you be until you take an oath to do this. So the young man took an oath before him.

D. When Isaac came home, he found her waiting for him, to let him in. She opened the door for him, and they went to sit by the fire. And she prepared food for him, as she was accustomed to do. But he said to her: I will neither eat nor drink. And he sat and wept. My beloved, my cousin, what is the matter with you? she asked. Tell me what is wrong, if you are in need of something, and why you are weeping. But he didn't want to tell her, because he felt ashamed. But she insisted to know all about it. So he told her about his oath to his rabbi and his instructions. She said: My love, man of my heart, this is no reason to weep. And she embraced and kissed him several times on his mouth and said: Don't be ashamed before me, my cousin,

55. בן העני ובת דודו (327א–329א)

A. מעשה היה בשני אחין, אחד עשיר ואחד עני.[1] והיה לעני בנים ובנות הרבה, ולעשיר לא היה לו כי אם בת אחת. והיה העשיר צר עין כנגד אחד [אחיו], כי הוא לא רוצה לעשות לו שום טובה הנאה שבעולם. והיה לעני בן אחד ששמו יצחק. והוא היה בחור, וטוב, יפה תואר מאוד ולומד בטוב. והיה העשיר אוהבו מאוד, יותר מאחיו ומכל בניו.

B. ויהי היום שהיה ערב פסח, ולא היה לעני שום דבר ממה לקנות חטים לפסח לעשות לו מצות ולבניו. בא אל אחיו העשיר וא"ל: אדוני, בחסדך תגמול לי חסד גדול ועשה באהבת השם א-להינו, ולוה לי כור של חטים לפרנס אני וביתי בזה היום טוב. א"ל העשיר: אם תתן לי ערבון, אלוה אותו לך. א"ל: מה הערבון אשר אתן לך, כי אין בידי כלום. א"ל: הבא לי יצחק בנך כי אתה אוהבו יותר מכל בניך,[2] ויהיה לי למשמרת עד שתפרע לי מה שאלוה לך. הלך העני והביא לו יצחק בנו, ולוה לו עליו כור של חטים.

C. ובכל יום ויום אותו יצחק הולך לבית המדרש, ולומד בפני הרב יומם ולילה. ובכל לילה בתו של אותו עשיר דודו מתאחרת, וממתנת אותו עד שבא. וכן היה [327ב] מנהגה תמיד בכל הלילות. יום אחד קרא הרב לאותו יצחק וא"ל: לך בני שמע בקולי לאשר אני מצוה אותך, ויהי א-להים עמך בלילה הזה. ת מיד כשתבא לבית דודך ותמצא שם קרובתך, קחנה ותחבקנה ונשוק אותה. א"ל: ר' איך אעשה הרעה הזאת להשיא יצר הרע עלי כל זמן שיכולתי להמלט ממנו? א"ל: בשבועה לא אניחנך [אניחך] עד שתישבע לי שתעשה זאת. עמד הבחור ו{הי}שבע [וישבע] לו.

D. כשבא לביתו מצאה מוכנת כנגדו לפתוח לו הפתח. ופתחה לו, והלכו וישבו סביב האש. והיא הכינה לו לאכול כמנהגה. והוא אמר לה: לא אוכל ולא אשתה. וישב ובכה. ואמרה לו: אהובי קרובי, מה יש לך? הגד לי מה יש לך, ואם תצטרך לשום דבר, ומה שאלתך ובקשתך, ועל מה אתה בוכה? והוא לא רצה לומר לה, כי נתבייש ממנה לומר לה. ויהי היא מתאמצת לדעת מה זה ועל מה זה והגיד לה הכל כאשר נשבע בפני רבו, וכאשר ציוהו. אמרה לו: אהובי איש כלבבי, אל תבכה בשביל זה. והלכה וחבקה אותו ונשקה לו בפיו כמה פעמים, ואמרה לו: אל תתבייש קרובי ממני, כי אני אוהבת אותך מאד (מ)אהבה עזה.[3] כי אחי ובשרי אתה, ואבי אוהב אותך כבבת עינו ו{ית}דברה [ותדבר] על לבו. ופייסה אותו בדבריה. והאכילתו והשקתו. והלך ושכב במטתו עד למחר.

1. אין בידינו עדי נוסח לגרסה זו.
2. השוו בראשית כב, ב.
3. השוו שיר השירים ח, ו.

because I love you very much indeed [lit., a mighty love; cf. Song of Songs 8:6]. And you are my flesh and blood, and my father loves you, and you are the apple of his eye. And she spoke to his heart and consoled him with her words. And she gave him to eat and drink, and he went to bed until morning.

E. And the next day he came to his rabbi, and he [the rabbi] asked him: Did you do as I ordered you? Yes, he said, and told him all about what had happened. The rabbi said: Make sure to do the same [lit., this] for the nine following nights. And he did. And after nine nights, his rabbi said: Go now and sleep in her bed. He said: How can I do that? If my uncle hears this, he will kill me. Do what I command you, said the rabbi, and don't desist. The boy went home, slept with her in her bed, and took a sword and placed it between them. And they lay side by side and slept until morning. And in the morning, the uncle arose and crossed the courtyard to relieve himself, and he found them lying side by side [lit., together], sleeping with the sword between them. He took his robe and covered them and said: May it be the will of the God of Israel that your bed be whole and that no fault be found with you. He went to the courtyard and returned to his room and told his wife. And she resented Isaac, and did not like him. And she said: Will he make a harlot of our daughter? He said: If he intended to spoil her, he would not have placed a sword between them. But he acted solely out of their love. His wife, however, had intended to give their daughter to her brother, who was ignorant and not a scholar.

F. When they awoke, Isaac saw his uncle's robe spread out over them and he cried, saying: What shall I do, now that my uncle was here and saw us? Woe is me, woe is me, where shall I flee from him, for he will kill me? Better to drown myself in the river and no one will find out [what I have done], than wait for my uncle to come. He must have gone to bring a sword to kill me, for he must have overlooked the sword [between us].

G. What [328a] did he do? He got dressed and got out of bed, and as he was dressed, he planned to drown himself in the river. And while he was running to the river, he encountered his mother. My son, she said, where are you hurrying to? Mother, please let me be, he said. I will not let you be before you tell me where you are going. He told her all about what had happened, and she said: Be neither sad nor troubled, my son, because with God's help I will save you. So come with me, and I will hide you until I know your uncle's state of mind and his plans, and until his anger is spent and he has forgotten what you did to him. He went with his mother and did exactly as she told him, and she hid him. She then went to his uncle's house,

E. ולמחר בא לו לפני רבו. א"ל רבו: עשית כאשר ציויתיך? א"ל: כן. וסיפר לו כל העניין. א"ל: הזהר, שתעשה עד תשעה לילות. וכן עשה. ולאחר תשעה לילות א"ל רבו: לך שכוב הלילה במטתה. א"ל: איך אעשה זאת ושמע דודי והרגני? א"ל רבו: עשה כאשר אני מצוה אותך, ואל תניח. הלך הבחור ושכב עמה במיטתה, ונטל חרב ושם ביניהם וישכבו יחד וישנו עד הבקר.[4] ויקם דודו וילך דרך החצר לעשות צרכיו, וימצאם שוכבים יחד והחרב ביניהם והם ישינים. ונטל טליתו ופרס עליהם ואמר: יהי רצון מלפני א-להי ישראל שתהא מיטתכם שלימה, שלא ימצא בכם פסול. הלך לחצר ושב לחדרו וספר לאשתו. והיא היתה צרת עין על אותו יצחק, כי אינה אוהבת אותו. ותאמר: הכזונה יעשה את בתינו? אמר לה: אם היה בדעתו לפגום אותה, לא היה שם החרב ביניהם. אלא לא עשה כי אם באהבתם זה את זה. והיה בדעת אשתו ליתן בתה לאחיה. והוא עם הארץ ואינו יודע ללמוד.

F. כשנִנערו משנתם וראה יצחק טלית דודו פרוס עליהם, בכה ואמר: ואני אנה אני בא כי דודי היה כאן וראה אותנו. ואמר: אוי לי אוי לי אנה מפניו אברח, כי הוא יהרוג אותי, מוטב לי לילך לטבוע עצמי בנהר ולא יודע לשום אדם, מלהמתין ביאת דודי, כי לא הלך כי אם להביא עמו שום חרב להורגיני, וזה החרב לא ראה אותו.

G. מה [328א] עשה, הלבישו וקם ממטתו. וכשהיה לבוש רצה לטבוע עצמו בנהר. וכשהיה רץ אל הנהר פגעה בו אמו ואמרה לו: בני לאיזה מקום אתה הולך כל כך במהירות? אמר לה: אמי בבקשה ממך הניחני. אמרה לו: לא אניחך עד שתאמר לי להיכן תלך. עמד וסיפר לה כל המעשה. אמרה לו: בני אל תתעצב בלבך ואל תתן דאגה ללבך כי בעזרת הצור אצילך, ולך עמי ואטמין אותך עד שאדע דעת דודך מה חשב לעשות, ועד שוב חמתו ושכח את אשר עשית לו. הלך עם

4. השוו לסנהדרין יט ע"ב על פרשת פלטי ומיכל בשמואל א, כה, מד.

where she found him sitting. Sir, she said, where is my son Isaac? He said: May he who cares for him [lit., knows him; cf. Ruth 2:19] be blessed and safeguard him from all evil. I don't know where he is. He asked her: Why have you come today of all days to ask after him? If you know anything about him, tell me. No, she said. By then it was clear to the woman that he was not plotting against her son. She returned home and told her son all about the events of the day and that his uncle was not planning to harm him, and that he loved him. She took him out [of his hiding place], and he went to his uncle's home, and he heard no anger in his voice, rather he spoke to him gently. What did his mother do? She went to the rabbi and told him what had happened. And the rabbi said: Daughter, I know all about it, because it was I who initiated the whole thing, and my intentions were for the sake of God. Wait and I will speak to his uncle, and perhaps he will give Isaac his daughter's hand. She returned home.

H. He sent for the uncle, and he came, and the rabbi told him: Why don't you marry off your daughter? She is old enough and has reached the age of marriage. The uncle then said: I know that it is time for her to marry, but I would not know to whom to give her. The rabbi said: Whom would you give her to if not to your nephew Isaac, who is handsome and pleasant looking and a Torah scholar and humble and modest and clever, and there is none wiser than him, and better you should give her to him than to any other. He said: I know that all this is true and correct, and he has all those qualities, and he is pleasant and agreeable to my eyes and I love him dearly. But my wife does not want to give our daughter to him, but rather only to her brother. Her brother is ignorant, said the rabbi, and doesn't know how to learn, while Isaac is a Torah scholar, and there is none in the entire yeshiva who knows how to interpret the scriptures as well as he does. He said: If you so wish, send for my wife, and we will see what she plans to do about the matter.

I. He sent for her, and she came to the rabbi and greeted him. And the rabbi said: May God bless you, my daughter. And he told her what he had to say, and she said that she was determined to give her daughter only to her brother. The rabbi said: Your brother is an ignoramus and knows nothing of learning, while that one [Isaac] is a great Torah scholar, and better you should give her to Isaac your nephew, than to any other. There is none wiser than him in the whole yeshiva. She said: If so, let Isaac and my brother go do business. I will give each of them one hundred dinars, and I will give my daughter to the one who earns more in a year's time. Your idea is reasonable, said the rabbi and her husband. [328b] They departed from the rabbi and went home, and each was given hundred dinars and set out on his own way.

אמו ועשה כל אשר צותה עליו. והטמינה אותו. ואחר כך הלכה אל בית דודו, ומצאה שם דודו יושב. אמרה לו: אדוני, היכן יצחק בני? אמר לה: יהי מכירו ברוך וישמרהו מכל רע,[5] לא ידעתי היכן הוא. אמר לה: מה היום מימים שבאתה אלי לשואלו. ידעת ממנו שום דבר? הגידי לי. אמרה לו: לאו. מיד הבינה האשה שאין בדעתו עליו. חזרה לביתה ואמרה לבנו כל המוצאות אותה, וכי אין בדעתו עליו, וכי הוא אוהב אותו בלבו. הוציאה אותו והלך לבית דודו, ולא שמע קול נוגש, ומדבר אליו כי אם טוב. מה עשתה אמו, הלכה לבית הרב וסיפרה לו כל המאורע. ואמר לה: בתי ידעתי כי ממני היתה הדבר, ולכבוד שמים נתכוונתי. והמתיני ואדבר אל דודו, אולי יתן לו בתו. חזרה לביתה.

H. והוא שלח אחרי דודו, ובא אליו ואמר לו: מפני מה אין אתה משיא את בתך, כי היא גדולה מאד ועומדת על פרקה? א"ל: ידעתי כי היא ראויה לינשא, אבל לא ידעתי למי אתן אותה. א"ל הרב: למי אתה רוצה ליתן אותה כי אם ליצחק נכדך, כי הוא טוב תואר, ויפה מראה, ותלמיד חכם, ועניו ושפל רוח ובייישן, וחכם ונבון אין כמוהו, וטוב תתן אותה לו מתתן אותה לאיש אחר. א"ל: ידעתי כי כל זה הדברים אמיתים ונכוחים, וכל המעלות האילו נתקיימו בו, כי הוא נחמד ונעים ואהוב מאד בעיני. אבל אשתי אינה רוצה ליתננה לו, כי אם לאחיה. א"ל הרב: אחיה עם הארץ ואינו יודע כלום ללמוד, וזה תלמיד חכם אין בכל הישיבה סבר כמוהו.[6] א"ל: אם רצונך, תשגר אחר אשתי ונדעה מה יש בלבה לעשות מזה העניין.

I. שיגר אחריה, ובאה לפני הרב ושאלה לו לשלום. ואמר לה הרב: ברוכה את בתי ליי'. ויאמר לה הדברים האילו. ואמרה כי אין בדעתה ליתן לבתי כי אם אחי.[7] א"ל הרב: אחיך עם הארץ הוא ואינו יודע כלום ללמוד, וזה חכם מחוכם בתורה, וטוב תתן אותה אל יצחק נכדך מתתן אותה לאיש אחר. אמרה לו: אם כן הוא ילך, יצחק ואחי, לסחורה ואתן לכל אחד מהם מאה דינרים, ואיזה מהם שירויח יותר בזה השנה לסוף שנה זו, אתן לו בתי. וענה הרב ובעלה: טוב הדבר אשר [328ב] דברת. נפרדו מאת פני הרב והלכו לביתם. ונתנו לכל אחד ואחד מאה דינרים, והלך כל אחד לדרכו.

5. "מכירו" כאן במובן של הכרה בו ולא במובן של מכר ומודע. השוו פרשנות רש"י לרות ב, יט: שנשא ונתן לך פנים ללקוט בשדהו.

6. השוו לפתיחת הסיפור על עוקבא (330ב): עמדו אביה ואמה ונמלכו במשפחתם ואמרו למי נשיא את חנה. או למר עוקבא העשיר רשע או ליוסף שהוא תלמיד?

7. במשפט זה מעבר מדיבור עקיף לישיר ללא השינויים הדקדוקיים המתבקשים מכך.

J. Isaac traveled abroad, and boarded a ship to cross the sea. And while he was at sea, a great storm struck, with a wind powerful enough to tear mountains apart and shatter rocks [cf. 1 Kings 19:11], and the ship broke into pieces, and all the people on the ship drowned, and a miracle was performed for Isaac. He found a plank of wood from the ship and floated on it until he came to an island, one of the sea islands, where he settled. And he was exceedingly hungry, for three days had passed and he had neither eaten nor drunk anything, and there was nothing to eat. What did he do? He gathered herbs and ate them. As he was eating, his stomach swelled, along with his arms and legs and head and all his body, and his fingernails and toenails and hair fell out. He wept bitterly, and when he raised his eyes, he saw an herb growing nearby. And the Almighty guided him to eat from that plant, and he stretched out his hand to eat from it, and as soon as he ate it, his flesh was restored like that of a young child, and he was healed [cf. 2 Kings 5:13]. And he was nourished by these herbs as long as he stayed there. Two weeks later, he saw a ship arriving, and he called the captain and said: Allow me to board your ship, and I shall go wherever you go. And I shall pay you, because I am a professional healer and can heal every wound and disease. He said: Blessed be you to God. What are you doing here, and how did you get here? He told the captain what had happened to him and took with him much of the two kinds of herbs, a load of two donkeys, and boarded the ship.

K. They traveled all together, and the wind took them to a city where most of the inhabitants were lepers, and the king was also a leper. He came to the king and bowed down to the ground. And the king asked: Who are you? Your majesty, he said, I am a healer, and I can cure you of your leprosy. The king said: If you cure me, I will give you half my kingdom. He gave the king to eat of the first kind of herb, the one that swells the stomach, and his stomach and body swelled up. He then gave him the second kind of herbs, and his flesh was all healed, and he had not even one wound or lesion on his body nor any blemish at all, and his flesh was restored and became clean like that of a young boy [cf. 2 Kings 5:13], and he felt healthy, agile, and very strong. The king rose and then prostrated himself before Isaac's feet and said: You have brought me back to life. Here is my kingdom before you. Take half as a gift, go and take whatever you like from all my treasures, because all is yours, and you shall be in charge of my palace, and my people will submit to your orders, and only regarding my throne will I be greater than you [cf. Genesis 41:40]. And Isaac answered: I want nothing of your kingdom except for a certain city that is located in your brother's territory. And [I suggest that] you exchange that city in

J. יצחק הלך למדינת הים, ונכנס בספינה אחת לעבור הימה. וכשהיה בתוך הים באה רוח סערה גדולה בים מפרק הרים <~~וש~~> ומשבר סלעים,[8] וישבר האניה ויטבעו כל האנשים אשר בתוך הספינה, ונעשה לו נס. ומצא קרש אחד מן הספינה ורכב עליו, עד שבא לאי אחד, אחת מאיי הים, וישב שם. וירעב מאד לאכול כי כבר עברו שלשה ימים שלא אכל ולא שתה, ולא היה לו שום דבר לאכול. מה עשה, הלך ולקט עשבים ואכלם. כיון שאכל אותם, צבה בטנו ונפחו זרועיו ויריכיו וראשו, וכל גופו היה נפוח מאד, ונפלו ציפורני ידיו ורגליו ושערות ראשו. בכה בכיה גדולה ומרה. וישא עיניו, וירא עשב אחד גדל בצדו.[9] שם הקב"ה בלבו לאכול ממנו, והושיט ידו ולקח מאותו עשב ואכל, מיד שבה בשרו כבשר נער קטן ונתרפא.[10] ומאותו עשב היה ניזון כל זמן שם. לאחר שתי שבועות ראה ספינה אחת באה וקרא אל רב החובל וא"ל: הניחני ואכנס בתוך ספינתך ואלך עמכם לאיזה מקום שתלכו, ואני אתן שכרך כי אני רופא טוב ומומחה לרפא כל נגע ומחלה. א"ל: בוא ברוך י"י, מה טיבך בכאן והיאך באתה הנה? סיפר לו כל המעשה. ולקח מן השני מיני עשבים הרבה מאוד ~~ב~~ משאוי לשני חמורים ונכנס בספינה.

K. הלכו יחד, והוליכם הרוח אל עיר אחת שהיו רוב ~~ה~~אנשי העיר מצורעים, וגם המלך היה מצורע. בא אל המלך וישתחו לאפיו ארצה. ויאמר לו: מי אתה? א"ל: אדוני, רופא אחד אני, ויודע אני לרפא אותך מצרעתך. א"ל המלך: אם תוכל לרפא אותי, אתן לך חצי מלכותי. נתן לו לאכול מן אותו עשב לצבות בטנו, ואכל ממנו וצבה בטנו ונפח כל גופו. ואחר כך נתן לו מן העשב האחרת, ונתרפא כל בשרו ולא היה בו בכל גופו לא פצע וחבורה ולא כל מום רע, ושבה בשר[ו] כבשר נער קטן[11] והיה בריא וקל וגיבור מאד. עמד המלך ונפל לפני רגליו. וא"ל: אתה החייתני, הנה מלכותי לפניך, קח החצי ממנו ויהיה לך במתנה, ובכל אוצרותיי תלך ותקח כל מה שתרצה, כי הכל שלך ואתה תהיה על ביתי ועל פיך ישק כל עמי רק הכסא אגדל ממך.[12] ויען יצחק ויאמר: איני רוצה מכל מלכותך מאומה, כי אם עיר אחת שיש באותה מדינת פלוני אחיך. ותתן לו בחילוף אותה עיר, עיר אחרת במלכותך, ואני אהיה שליט ומושל מאותה עיר, והאנשים אשר בתוכה יהיו לי למס ויעבדוני. א"ל המלך: כן יעשה כאשר דברת [329א]. ויצו המלך ויכתב ספרים אל אחיו לעשות כל רצון זה האיש אשר יבקש ממנו, ויבחר במלכותו איזה עיר שירצה בחילוף אותה עיר, ויכתב ויחתום בטבעת המלך,[13] וירפא כל החולים וכל המצורעים אשר היו באותה עיר, ויתן לו המלך כסף וזהב לרוב, ואבנים טובות ומרגליות ועבדים ושפחות ואתונות וגמלים טעונים ממון כבד, וישלח אותו אל אחיו לעשות חפצו. ויבא אליו ויאמר לו: אדוני, כדברים האלה שלח אליך

8. השוו מלכים א, יט, יא.

9. המעבר לרובד לשוני מקראי משווה לאירוע מעמד נשגב של נס.

10. השוו למלכים ב, ה יד.

11. השוו מלכים ב, ה, יד.

12. ראו בראשית מא, מ.

13. השוו לאסתר ח, י.

return for another one in your kingdom, and I shall be the ruler and governor of that city, and its citizens will pay me taxes and serve me. The king said: So be it, as you say. [329a] And the king commanded and wrote letters to his brother to do whatever the man wished for, and to let him choose any city he likes in his kingdom, in exchange for another city. And he wrote and sealed it with the king's signet ring [cf. Esther 8:10], and Isaac healed all the lepers in the city. And the king gave him silver and gold and precious stones and pearls and slaves and handmaidens and mules and camels laden heavily with money, and he sent him to his brother to do his bidding. And Isaac came to the king's brother and said: Sir, this is what your brother the king sent you, and here are the letters sealed with his ring. And when the king heard that his brother had been healed of his leprosy, he was overjoyed and made a great feast and gave Isaac much silver and gold and made him ruler over the city where his mother and father and uncle lived. And he was made the ruler of that city, and he arrived in the city in a great litter, with much cattle and silver and gold. And he went and entered a tower, along with all his treasures and slaves and cavalry and soldiers.

L. And that day, the year [appointed to decide who the young maiden's groom would be] was coming to its end. And they [the maiden's family] prepared all that was needed for the wedding of the maiden to her mother's brother. When they saw that Isaac had not returned while the other did, they intended to give him [the mother's brother] to the girl, and prepared everything for the wedding ceremony to take her in marriage. And because the Jews saw that they had a new ruler, they were afraid and trembled greatly before him and did not want to allow her [the maiden] to marry without first receiving permission from the ruler. The girl's mother went to the ruler, and Isaac recognized her, but she did not recognize him. And she spoke to him and prostrated herself before him and said: Your majesty, welcome. May God give you peace, and may you rule for many years. Behold, I have a grown-up single daughter, and the time has come for her to marry, and everything is ready for the marriage feast. Give us permission to marry her off. And she did all this to hasten the wedding ceremony, because she feared lest Isaac might come home. The ruler answered and said: I wish to be there when the man marries your daughter and watch the manner of your wedding ceremonies [lit., how you—i.e., the Jews—marry off your daughters]. As you wish. She went home, and beautified and made up her daughter, and brought her to the marriage house. And all the Jews came to pay honor to the bride and groom. And they sent for the ruler, and he came there. And as the man was about to sanctify the marriage to the girl, the ruler rebuked him and said: You have no right to marry the girl because it is my right by law. I am Isaac. And

המלך לאמר, והנה הספרים חתומים מטבעתו. כיון ששמע כך שנתרפא המלך אחיו, שמח שמחה גדולה ועשה לו משתה גדול ונתן לו כסף וזהב לרוב, והשליטו באותה עיר שהיה אביו ואמו ודודו בה, ונעשה שר ושליט מאותה עיר, ובא בתוך העיר ברכב, גדול מאד במקנה בכסף ובזהב. והלך ופנה בתוך המגדל, הוא וכל אוצרותיו ועבדיו ופרשיו וכל חילו.

L. ואותו היום נשלמה השנה. והכינו כל צרכי החופה ליתן הנערה אל אחי אמה. כיון שראו שלא בא יצחק וזה בא רצו ליתן לו הנערה והכינו הכל לבא ולקדש אותה. וכיון שראו היהודים שהיה להם שלטון חדש עליהם פחדו ורעדו ממנו מאד, ולא רצו להכניסה לחופה בלא רשות השלטון. עמדה אמה ~~כי הי~~ והלכה אל השלטון. ויכירה יצחק והיא לא הכירה אותו, ותדבר לפניו ותשתחו לאפיה ארצה ותאמר לפניו: אדוני, ברוך בואך, ויגדל המקום שלותך ויאריך ימיך במלכותך. הנה יש לי בת אחת גדולה, והגיע זמנה ליכנס לחופה, וכל צרכי הסעודה מוכנים. תן לנו רשות להכניסה לחופה. וכל זה עשתה כדי למהר הקידושין, כי היה לה פחד שמא יבא יצחק. ענה לה השלטון ואמר: אני רוצה להיות שם כשיקדש האיש בתך, ואראה היאך אתם מקדשין נשותיכם. אמרה לו: לחייך ולשלוותך. הלכה לביתה וקשטה ופירכסה בתה, והכניסה לבית הנישואין. ובאו כל היהודים שם לנהוג כבוד לחתן ולכלה. ושלחו אחר השלטון, ובא שם. וכשרצה האיש לקדש הנערה גער בו השלטון ואמר: אין לך דין לקדש אותה כי לי משפט הקידושין. כי אני יצחק, וזה

these are my mother and my father. And this is my uncle, and this was the agreement between us. And he recounted before them all the details of the contract they had made between them, and they all said: Indeed, it is all true and correct. You have the right to marry her, so go marry her. You have won the wager. And he married her under the wedding canopy. And all rejoiced, his mother and father and the whole community, with great joy, and he told his mother and father and uncle all about what had happened to him. And he was exceedingly rich and ruled over the whole country. And he lived many more years, and was righteous and pious the rest of his life, and had sons and daughters. May we too share all these [blessings], amen.

אבי וזאת אמי וזה דודי, וכן היה התנאי בינינו. וסיפר להם ובפניהם כל התנאים שהיו ביניהם, ואמרו כולם מ̇ אמת ונכון הדבר כי לך המשפט לקדש, ולך וקדש אותה וזכה במקחך. והלך וקדש אותה, והכניסה לחופה. וישמחו כולם אביו ואמו וכל הקהל שמחה גדולה, ויספר לאביו ולאמו ולדודו כל הקורות אותו לאמר. והוא היה עשיר גדול ושר ושליט בכל הארץ, ויחי האיש ימים רבים וצדיק וחסיד היה כל ימיו ויולד בנים ובנות וכאשר היה לו יהיה לנו אמן:

56–59. R. Pinḥas b. Yair (329b)

56. There is a tale about R. Pinḥas b. Yair, who lived in the south in a certain city. And people went to earn their livelihood there, and they carried two measures of barley and left them with him and forgot about them and went away. And R. Pinḥas would sow them year after year and put them in a granary and gather them together. And after seven years, those people came there. R. Pinḥas recognized them. He said to them: Come and take your treasures. Come and see human faithfulness. From their faithfulness you will know the faithfulness of the Almighty.

57. And there is another tale about R. Pinḥas, who went to a certain city, and the mice there would eat the grain within the boundaries of that city. They came and asked him to pray for them. R. Pinḥas said to them: Why do you not set aside your tithes as you should? Do you wish me to guarantee that, if you set aside your tithes as you should, the mice will eat no more? They said: Yes. He gave the guarantee, and the mice left, never to be seen again.

58. And there is yet another tale about a man who would dig cisterns for the public. And his daughter walked along the way, and when she was about to cross the river, the river washed her away. When people saw this, they came to tell R. Pinḥas b. Yair: Such and such happened to so-and-so's daughter. He said to them: It cannot be; since it was with water that he used to do God's will, the Almighty would not kill his daughter in water. A cry immediately went through the city: So-and-so's daughter has come [is saved]. Our rabbis said: As soon as R. Pinḥas b. Yair said what he said, an angel came and drew her up.

56–59. רבי פנחס בן יאיר (329ב)

56. [329ב] **מעשה** ברבי פנחס בן יאיר שהיה דר בדרום בעיר אחת.[1] והלכו אנשים[2] להתפרנס שם, והיו בידם שתי סאין של ~~עשע~~ שעורין, והפקידום אצלו ושכחום, והלכו להם. והיה ר' פנחס בן יאיר זורע אותם בכל שנה ושנה,[3] ועשה אותם גורן וכונסן. לאחר שבע {שנים ~~שבע~~}[4] באו אותם אנשים לשם.[5] הכיר אותם ר' פנחס.[6] אמר להם: בואו טולו אוצרותיכם.[7] בואו וראו אמונה של בשר ודם, מאמונתם אתה יודע מה אמונתו של הקב"ה[8]

57. ושוב מעשה ברבי פנחס בן יאיר שהלך לעיר אחת והיו העכברים אוכלים תבואה בתחומה של אותה עיר.[9] באו ובקשו הימנו להתפלל בעדם.[10] אמר להם[11] ר' פנחס כן: למה אין אתם מפרישין מעשרותיכם כראוי? מבקשים אתם שאערוב לכם שאם אתם מפרישין מעשרותיכם כראוי אין עכברים אוכלים עוד? אמרו לו: הן.[12] ערב אותם, וילכו העכברים ולא נראו עוד "

58. ושוב מעשה[13] באדם[14] אחד שהיה חופר שיחין לרבים. ובתו היתה הולכת בדרך.[15] ובאתה לעבור בנהר ושטפה {הנהר}.[16] כיון שראו כך, באו והגידו לר' פנחס בן יאיר: כך אירע לבת פלוני.[17] אמר להם: אי אפשר, כיון שהיה עושה רצונו של הקב"ה במים, אין הקב"ה מאבד בתו במים. מיד יצאה צווחה בעיר: באתה בתו של פלוני. אמרו רבותינו: כיון שאמר ר' פנחס בן יאיר כך, בא מלאך והעלה אותה.[18]

---

1. הטקסט כמעט זהה לדברים רבה, עקב, ג, ג. ההשוואות להלן הן בעיקר לדב"ר, וכן לתלמוד הירושלמי דמאי א, ג כב, א], ולתלמוד הבבלי חולין ז, ע"א].
2. בתלמוד הירושלמי מדובר בשני עניים.
3. דב"ר: בכל שנה.
4. בתלמוד הירושלמי, בלי תיאור זמן.
5. דב"ר: הלכו אותן החברים לשם לתבע אותן לתן להן.
6. שם: מיד הכיר אותם ר' פינחס בן יאיר.
7. בתלמוד הירושלמי אומר להם רפב"י [רבי פנחס בן יאיר] להביא גמלים וחמורים להעמיס עליהם את התבואה.
8. דב"ר: הרי מאומנתו של בשר ודם אתה יודע אמונתו של הקדוש ברוך הוא.
9. שם חסר: בתבואה.
10. שם חסר: להתפלל בעדם.
11. שם: מה עשה ר' פינחס בן יאיר, אמר להן; בתלמוד הירושלמי רפב"י קורא לכל העכברים, שומע אותם מצפצפים, ואומר לבני המקום שהסיבה לכך היא שאין הם מקפידים במעשרות.
12. דב"ר: אין.
13. שם: דבר אחר, מעשה; השוו בבלי, בבא קמא נ, לסיפור דומה על רבי חנינה בן דוסא.
14. בתלמוד הירושלמי: חסיד.
15. בתלמוד הירושלמי: הולכת לינשא.
16. תוספת תלויה מעל לשורה, מסומנת על ידי סימן ^. בירושלמי מסופר שהכול באו לנחמו אך הוא לא קיבל את תנחומיהם, וגם לא את תנחומיו של רפב"י.
17. דב"ר: כיון שראו כך, באו והגידו לר' פנחס בן יאיר: כך אירע לבת פלוני.
18. דב"ר: ירד מלאך והעלה אותה. שתי דעות בתלמוד הירושלמי: שנאחזה בקוץ ויצאה מהמים, או שמלאך בדמות רפב"י הצילה.

59. And yet another tale about R. Pinḥas b. Yair, who was on his way to fulfill a commandment to circumcise someone, and came to the river of Ginnai. And walking with him was a group of people. R. Pinḥas b. Yair said: Divide your waters, for I am going to do the will of my Father in the Heavens, just as you do. It [the river] said to him: You may or may not be doing so, but I certainly am doing so [God's will]. He said: Nevertheless, divide your water for me. It divided them for him, and he passed through. After he passed through, the waters returned to their previous state, and he saw his friends, those who had come with him, across the river. He said to the river: Is that how one should behave to fellow travelers? Divide for them. It divided for them, and they passed through. The rabbis said: What R. Pinḥas b. Yair did was greater than what Moses did, for Moses divided the water only once, and R. Pinḥas b. Yair divided it twice.

59. ושוב מעשה ברבי פנחס בן יאיר שהלך לדבר מצוה למול בן אדם אחד,[19] ופגע בו גינאי נהרא. והיו הולכין עמו סיעת בני אדם.[20] אמר ר' פנחס בן יאיר: חלוק לי מימיך, כי אני הולך לעשות רצון אבי שבשמים כאשר אתה עושה. אמר לו: ספק אתה עושה ספק אין אתה עושה, אבל אני ודאי עושה.[21] א"ל: אע"פ כן חלוק לי מימך.[22] חלק לו ועבר.[23] כיון שעבר שבו המים כבתחילה,[24] וראה חביריו[25] שבאו עמו מעבר לנהר. א"ל לנהר: וכי כך עושין לבני <~~לד~~> לויה, חלוק להם. חלק להם, ועברו. ואמרו חכמים:[26] גדול היה מעשה מר' פנחס בן יאיר ממשה רבינו. שמשה לא חלק המים אלא פעם אחת, ולר' פנחס בן יאיר שני פעמים:[27]

19. בדב"ר מובא כאן סיפור אחר: מעשה בר' שמעון בן שטח שלקח חמר אחד מישמעלי אחד. בתלמוד הירושלמי: הלך לבית הוועד (בית מדרש). בתלמוד הבבלי, חולין ז, ע"א: הלך לפדיון שבויים. במסכת חולין עירוב של עברית וארמית.

20. בתלמוד הירושלמי: לבית וועד. בתלמוד הבבלי בלי איזכור של מלווים, אף שבהמשך משתמע כך.

21. בתלמוד הירושלמי אין חילופי דברים בין נהר גינאי לרפב"י. רפב"י מבקש: גיניי גיניי מה את מנע לי מבית וועדה, וגינאי נבקע מיד.

22. בתלמוד הבבלי רפב"י מאיים עליו, שאם לא יחלוק יגזור עליו שלא יעברו בו עוד מים לעולם.

23. בתלמוד הבבלי רפב"י מבקש מן הנהר לבקוע פעם נוספת עבור מלווהו, משום שהוא שליח מצווה בדרכו לאפיית מצות לפסח. הנהר נעתר לבקשתו.

24. בתלמוד הירושלמי המים אינם שבים למקומם, אך חבריו של רפב"י חוששים לעבור בנהר. לשאלתם רפב"י מציין שרק מי שיודע בנפשו שלא פגע באדם מישראל מימיו, יכול לעבור.

25. בתלמוד הבבלי: "ההוא טייעה" שפירושו ערבי, בדואי.

26. בתלמוד הבבבלי המימרה מובאת בשם רב יוסף.

27. בתלמוד הבבלי: שלוש פעמים. כמו כן נוסף דיון קצר אם רפב"י אכן גדול ממשה רבינו.

60. The *Ḥasid* and the Tax Collector's Son (329b–330b)

A. [329b] A tale of Baya the tax collector, who was the king's deputy and guest. And he was a very harsh man, and wicked. The very day that Baya the tax collector died, a Torah scholar and a perfectly righteous man passed away as well. The entire community came that day and carried the two bodies to the cemetery. And when they arrived at the cemetery, enemies attacked them, striking and wounding them, and they all fled hither and thither and left the corpses there. The only one who remained there [330a] was one of the Torah scholar's disciples, who refused to leave his rabbi, neither for the sake of pleasure nor because [for fear] of any harm the enemies might do to him. Finally, the enemies left and went away. And the Jews returned to the cemetery and showed Baya the tax collector great honor, such as was never seen before. And the disciple who had stayed there cried out and said: That is not my rabbi; it is Baya the tax collector whom you are treating with such great honor. And they were frightened and would not listen to him, and he kept crying and weeping bitterly, for his rabbi was being treated disrespectfully. And they buried Baya the tax collector with much honor and left. And only ten people remained to bury the righteous man, and they buried him and went away. And the student of that scholar remained behind, weeping and crying, because his rabbi had not been honored. And a deep slumber fell upon him, and he slept.

B. And his rabbi appeared to him and said: My son, do not feel upset anymore, and do not wonder at what you saw, because they behaved justly. Do you know why that man, Baya the tax-collector, was worthy of all this honor? Because once the king sent a message to Baya the tax collector, saying: Prepare your house and buy everything needed for me and my soldiers, because I intend to come to you there in your city. Baya did as the king commanded and prepared everything needed for the feast, and the king didn't come and went instead to a different town. What did Baya the tax collector do? He took all that he had prepared and divided it up among the poor. And it was for this merit that he earned all that honor, and this was his portion, due to the good deed that he performed. And as for my part, let me tell you why I did not merit honor: Because once I heard condemnation of a Torah scholar, and I did not protest. That is why I did not merit honor. Now come with me and I will show you my place and his. He went with him, and he saw that his rabbi was sitting in the Garden of Eden on golden chairs, with the clouds of glory covering him, and he was there alongside the greatest righteous men in the Garden of Eden. And he saw Baya the tax collector with an iron bolt inserted in his head from ear to ear. The young man was much perplexed and said to his rabbi: Rabbi, will this

60. החסיד ובן המוכס (329ב–330ב)

A. מעשה היה מבעיא מוכסא, שהיה משנה למלך ואכסנאי שלו. והיה אדם קשה מאוד,[1] ור~~ו~~ע מעללים.[2] אותו יום שמת אותו בעיא מוכסא, מת גם תלמיד חכם וצדיק גמור.[3] באותו יום באו כל הקהל, והביאו ונשאו השני מתים בבית הקברות.[4] וכשבאו בבית הקברות, באו אויבים עליהם והכום ופצעום. וברחו כולם אנה ואנה, והניחו המתים שם. ולא נשתייר שם [330א] כי אם תלמיד אחד מתלמידי החכם, שלא רצה לעזוב רבו לא בשביל הנאה, ולא בשביל שום דבר רע שהיו עושים לו האויבים.[5] עד ש{ה}ניחום האויבים והלכו להם. וחזרו היהודים[6] לבית הקברות, ונהגו כבוד גדול לבעיא מוכסא לא נראה ככבוד הזה שעשו לו.[7] והתלמיד שנשאר שם היה צועק ואומר להם: אין זה רבי, כי הוא בעיא מוכסא שאתם עושים כל הכבוד הזה. והם היו מפוחדים ולא האזינו לו, והוא היה צועק ובוכה במר נפש על שלא נהגו כבוד לרבו.[8] וקברו לבעיא מוכסא בכל הכבוד הזה, והלכו להם. ולא נשאר שם כי אם עשרה אנשים לקבור הצדיק, וקברו אותו והלכו להם.[9] ונשאר עוד שם תלמידו של אותו חכם בוכה וצועק[10] על שלא נהגו לרבו כבוד,[11] ונפל תרדמה עליו ויישן.[12]

B. ויבוא רבו אליו ויאמר לו: בני אל תצטער[13] יותר ואל תתמה על אשר ראית, כי בדין עשו. ידעת מפני מה זכה אותו בעיא מוכסא לכל הכבוד הזה, בשביל שפעם אחת שלח המלך לבעיא מוכסא לאמר: תכין לי הבית וקנה כל מה שצריך לי ולחיילותיי, כי אני רוצה לבוא אליך שם בעירך. ויעש כן בעיא מוכסא כאשר ציוה המלך והכין כל צרכי הסעודה, ולא בא המלך והלך לעיר אחרת. מה עשה בעיא מוכסא, נטל כל מה שהכין וחלק לעניים. ובשביל אותו זכות זכה לכל הכבוד הזה, וזה היה חלקו שנטל בשביל המצוה שעשה.[14] וממני אומר לך מפני מה לא זכיתי לכבוד, בשביל שפעם אחת שמעתי גנות של תלמיד חכם ולא מחיתי, ובשביל זה לא זכיתי ~~כי~~ לכבוד.[15] ולך עמי <~~וארא~~> ואראך מקומי ומקומו. הלך עמו וראה שרבו היה יושב בגן עדן בקתדראות של זהב וענני כבוד סוככין אותו, והוא עם צדיקי עולם בגן עדן.[16] וראה אותו בעיא מוכסא שהיה מנעול אחד מברזל יוצא ובא בתוך ראשו מאוזן לאוזן.[17] תמה מאד הבחור ואמר לרבו: רבי, ~~עד~~ וכי לעולם יהיה זה לו למוקש, או לשנים עשר חדש כפושעי ישראל שדינם שנים

---

1. ברש"י למסכת סנהדרין מד ע"ב, חסר: שהיה משנה למלך ואכסנאי שלו. ההשוואות להלן הן לגרסת רש"י.
2. תוספת ברש"י: ישראל רשע אחד.
3. אדם גדול בעיר.
4. ובאו כל בני העיר ונתעסקו במטתו וקרובי אותו מוכס הוציאו גם את מטת המוכס אחריו.
5. חסר: שלא רצה לעזוב רבו לא בשביל הנאה ולא בשביל שום דבר רע שהיו עושים לו האויבים.
6. גדולי העיר.
7. חסר: לא נראה ככבוד הזה שעשו לו.
8. חסר: התיאור המפורט של צעקות התלמיד.
9. קרובי המוכס קוברים את התלמיד חכם.
10. ונצטער בה.
11. תוספת: מה חטא גרם ליקבר זה בבזיון ומה זכה אותו רשע ליקבר בכבוד גדול כזה?
12. חסר: ונפל תרדמה עליו ויישן.
13. תוספת: בא ואראך בכבודי בגן עדן בכבוד גדול ובא ואראך אותו האיש בגיהנם וציר של פתח גיהנם סובב באזניו.
14. פעם אחת הכין סעודה לשר העיר ולא בא שר העיר וחילקה לעניים וזה היה שכרו.
15. תיאורי גן העדן מובאים לפני תיאור המעשים שזיכו אותם לגן עדן.
16. בלי תיאור מפורט של שכר החכם בגן עדן.
17. מראה עיניו של התלמיד בגיהנום מתואר לפני הסברו של התלמיד חכם לכך.

punishment be there forever, or only for twelve months, like the wicked among the Israelites who are sentenced to twelve months? His rabbi said: No, only until the death of R. Shimon b. Shetaḥ, who will take his place, and then he will be released. The student was amazed and said: Can this be the reward of one who is the head of a yeshiva [R. Shimon b. Shetaḥ], a scholar of the Mishnah and president of the court, close to Yannai the king, and a perfectly righteous man and a perfect *ḥasid*, the likes of which there is none in all the land? His rabbi said: All this is because of the eighty witches that live in Ashkelon, which is [only] three miles from him, and he neither protested nor judged them. The young man awoke from his sleep, and he was very amazed and frightened by the vision he had seen. He was overjoyed at the honor he saw done to his rabbi and saddened for the loss of R. Shimon b. Shetaḥ's honor. What did he do? He went to R. Shimon b. Shetaḥ and told him the whole story and everything he had seen, and he told him what he had heard and seen of himself. And he [R. Shimon] was greatly vexed, and he wept and cried out loudly, because he was saddened that he had not [330b] known about them [the witches].

C. What did R. Shimon b. Shetaḥ do? He took eighty strong young men, and gave each and every one a clay jar, and each placed his robe in the jar. And this is what he told them: Go to Ashkelon, and go to the house of the women witches, and wait in the city until the rains fall in the world, and then go to their home. And if they ask you what you do, say: We are sorcerers. And enter their home, and each of you take one of them and hang them on the trees. And as soon as each of you takes one of them, carry them to the trees and be careful that their feet do not touch the ground, because when the person is in the air, they cannot perform magic. And that is what they did. And when they came to the entrance of the house, they found the door locked. And they called to open the door, and the rains fell on them. And the witches said: Who are you? And they said: We are sorcerers. And the witches said: What sort of magic do you know? They said: Have we not come here untouched by the rain? And they took their robes and wrapped themselves in them and opened the door. Then they hurled their jars to the ground and entered the house, and their robes were dry. Each of them took one witch, and they carried them to the trees and hanged them. And although it is not the law to hang them, it was an emergency order, and they were fearful of their magic; that is why they were hanged immediately. In time, two of their relatives came and testified about the son of R. Shimon b. Shetaḥ, that he had killed a man, before his father. And his father sentenced him

עשר חודש?[18] א"ל רבו: לא, אלא עד מות ר' שמעון בן שטח שיהיה במקומו,[19] והוא יפטר.[20] תמה התלמיד ואמר: וכי זו שכרו שהוא ראש ישיבה, ותנא ואב בית דין, וקרוב לינאי מלכא, וצדיק גמור הוא, וחסיד אין כמוהו בכל הארץ.[21] א"ל רבו: כל זה בשביל שמונים[22] מכשפניות[23] שיש באשקלון קרוב לו שלשה מילין ולא מיחה בהן,[24] ולא עשה דין בהן. וייקץ הבחור משנתו, ויתמה מאוד, ויבהל על החיזיון אשר ראה. וישמח על הכבוד שראה מרבו. ויתעצב אל לבו מפני כבוד ר' שמעון בן שטח.[25] מה עשה, הלך אצל ר' שמעון בן שטח וסיפר לו כל המעשה, וכל המראה אשר ראה, וממנו סיפר לו כל מה ששמע וראה.[26] ויחר לו מאוד ויבך בכי גדול, כי נתעצב אל לבו כי לא [330ב] היה יודע מהם.

C. מה עשה ר' שמעון בן שטח? לקח שמונים בחורים גבורי חיל,[27] ונתן לכל אחד ואחד כד אחת של חרש, ובתוך הכד ~~נתן~~ כל אחד טליתו. וכך אמר להם: לכו אל אשקלון ובואו אל בית הנשים המכשפניות, והמתינו בעיר עד שיהיה מי גשמים יורדים בעולם,[28] ואז תלכו לביתם. ואם הן שואלין לכם מה מעשיכם תאמרו: מכשפנים אנחנו. ותכנסו לביתם, ותקחו כל אחד מכם אחת מהנה, ותלו את כולן על העצים. ומיד כשתקחו כל אחד אחת מהן תשאינה עד העיצים, והזהרו שלא יגעון רגליהן לארץ, לפי כשיהיה אדם באויר אינו יכול לעשות מכשפות.[29] ועשו כן. וכשבאו אל פתח ביתן מצאו הפתח סגור,[30] וקראו לפתוח והיו הגשמים יורדים עליהם.[31] ותאמרנה להם: מה מעשיכם?[32] ויאמרו: אנשים מכשפנים אנחנו.[33] ותאמרנה להם: במה אתם יודעים לכשף? אמרו להן: הרי באנו ולא ירדו הגשמים עלינו.[34] ולקחו הטליתות שלהם ונתעטפו ופתחו הפתח.[35] והם השליכו כדיהם לארץ,[36] ונכנסו לבית, והיו טליתות ~~ל~~שלהם יבישים. ולקחו כל אחד מהם אחת מהן, ונשאו אותן עד העצים ותלו אותן. ואעפ"י שאין דינן להיות נתלות

18. עד מתי יהא אותו האיש נידון בדין קשה.
19. ויכנס תחתיו.
20. חסר: והוא יפטר.
21. בלי תיאורי השבח של רבי שמעון בן שטח, אלא: למה.
22. חסר: שמונים.
23. תוספת: ישראליות.
24. חסר: קרוב לו–בהן.
25. חסר: וייקץ הבחור משנתו–מפני כבוד ר' שמעון בן שטח.
26. וממנו, כלומר עליו - על ר' שמעון בן שטח.
27. בעלי קומה; תוספת: והיה אותו היום יום גשמים.
28. חסר: והמתינו בעיר–מי גשמים יורדים בעולם.
29. בלי הוראות פעולה מפורטות: ובשעה שתכנסו יגביה איש אחת מהן מן הארץ ושוב אין מכשפות שולטות בכם ואם לאו לא נוכל להם.
30. הלך לו שמעון בן שטח לטרקלין שלהם והניח הבחורים מבחוץ.
31. חסר: והיו הגשמים יורדים עליהם.
32. אמרו לו מי אתה.
33. תוספת: ולנסותכם בכשפים באתי.
34. יכולני להביא לכם שמונים בחורים עטופי טליתות נגובות ואע"פ שהוא יום גשמים.
35. ורמז להם הוציאו הטליתות מן הכדים ונתעטפו בהן.
36. חסר: והם השליכו כדיהם לארץ.

[to death]. Before he was taken to be executed, the witnesses said: We said it out of hate. R. Shimon b. Shetaḥ said: It doesn't matter, because after he [a witness] has testified once, he cannot go back on his testimony [according to the law], and they executed him.

הוראה [הוראת] שעה היתה,[37] כי היו יראים ממכַשפות שלהן. לכך תלו אותן מיד.[38] לימים באו שני בני אדם מקרובותיהן[39] והעידו על בנו של ר' שמעון בן שטח שהרג איש אחד, בפני אביו.[40] ודן אותו אביו[41] וקודם שהוליכוהו ליהרג[42] אמרו העדים שבשביל שנאה אמרו.[43] אמר ר' שמעון בן שטח: איני חושש, כיון שהגיד שוב אינו חוזר ומגיד.[44] והרגוהו"[45]

37. להלכה, דינן של מכשפות לסקילה ולא לתלייה. ראו סנהדרין סז, ע"ב.

38. חסר: ואעפ"י–תלו אותן מיד; תוספת: ונתקנאו קרוביהם בדבר.

39. תוספת: וכוונו דבריהם.

40. כלומר, העידו בפני האב, ר' שמעון בן שטח, שבנו הרג אדם, ומכאן שחייב מיתה.

41. ונגמר דינו.

42. כשהיה יוצא ליסקל; תוספת: אמר אם יש בי עון זה לא תהא מיתתי כפרה לי ואם אינו כן תהא מיתתי כפרה על כל עונותי וקולר תלוי בצואר עדים ושמעו אלו.

43. מחמת שנאת הנשים.

44. בלי אמירתו של שמעון בן שטח.

45. ואעפ"כ נפטר.

61. Ukva (version 2; 330b–331b)

A. [330b] Once there was a man named Mar Ukva, whose father and mother died, leaving him a great deal of money. He grew in wicked deeds and became a merchant. He would buy maidservants and lie with them. There was a young girl who lived nearby who was very beautiful, whose name was Hannah, and he loved her very much. And there was a student whose name was Joseph, and he too loved her. Her mother and father consulted with their family and said: To whom should we marry Hannah, to Ukva who is rich and wicked or to Joseph who is a student? They all said: Heaven forbid, heaven forbid; she should marry none other than the student named Joseph, for Mar Ukva only loves her for her beauty, like the other handmaidens. They decided to marry her to Joseph. When Ukva saw that she was to be married to another, he fell so ill with grief that he almost died. They sent for a doctor. He said to him: You have fallen ill because of your passion for a woman. If you lie with [another] woman, you will immediately be cured. He asked the sages to permit it, but they refused, saying: Better he should die than be cured of his illness. It says in the Torah: "He does not leave the guilty unpunished" [Numbers 14:18], and he wishes to lie with her! [331a] He sent for another doctor. He said the same as the first: If you touch her, you will be cured. He sent for the scholars, but they did not allow him to touch her. He sent for yet another doctor, and he said the same as the first: If you even hear her voice, you will be cured. He sent for the scholars, but they refused to allow it. He fell exceedingly ill.

B. Some time later, the student Joseph fell into great poverty, and he borrowed a hundred dinars from a gentile. They used it up. The owner of the money came to demand his money. Her mother and father tried to placate the gentile but were unsuccessful. The money owner put them in jail. They said to Hannah: Go to Ukva. Maybe he will give you [the money]. She said to them: I will not go there lest he sin with me. I am not going there. They spoke to her repeatedly, but she refused. Her husband said: Go, and let us not perish here. She went to him to ask him to give her a hundred dinars, for her husband was in prison because of the money. He said to her: If I give you the money, will you lie with me? She said: Heaven forbid that you do that. You must remember your Maker and overcome your desire and not do such wickedness. What did he do? He listened to her and restrained his desire. He said to one of his handmaidens: Take out and give her what she is asking for. And he, why did he not give it to her himself? In order not to touch her. She took it and left. When her husband Joseph saw her, he sighed. He said to her: Hannah, on your life, did he

61. עוקבא [נוסח שני] (330ב–331ב)

A. מעשה במר עוקבא[1] שמתו אביו ואמו והניחו לו ממון הרבה. ונתגדל במעשים רעים. ונעשה סוחר. והיה קונה שפחות ושוכב עמהם. היתה נערה אחת בשכינותו יפת תואר וחנה שמה[2] והיה אוהב אותה ביותר. והיה שם תלמיד ושמו יוסף. ואף היה אוהב אותה. עמדו אביה ואמה ונמלכו במשפחתם ואמרו: למי נשיא את חנה, או למר עוקבא העשיר רשע או ליוסף שהוא תלמיד? אמרו כולם: חס ושלום חס ושלום, לא תינשא אלא לתלמיד שמו יוסף, כי מר עוקבא אינו אוהבה כי אם עבור יופיה כמו אחת מן השפחות. עמדו והשיאוה ליוסף. כשראה עוקבא שנשאת לאחר, מרוב צער נפל בחולי גדול עד שהגיע למות. שלחו וקראו לרופא. א"ל: לא חלית(י) אלא מתאות אשה, אם תשכב עם אשה מיד תתרפא. שלח לחכמים להתירו ולא קבלו, ואמרו: ימיתוהו ואל יעמוד מחליו. כתיב בתורה לא ינקה [במדבר יד, יח] והוא אומר לשכב עמה. [331א] שלח וקרא לרופא אחר. אמר לו כראשון: אבל אם אתה נוגע בה תתרפא. שלח לחכמים, ולא הניחו לנגוע אליה. שלח לרופא אחר א"ל כראשון: ואם אתה שומע אפילו דיבורה תתרפא. שלח לחכמים ולא קיבלו.[3] נפל בחולי גדול.[4]

B. לימים נפל בעניות גדול אותו יוסף תלמיד.[5] ולוה מאה דינרים מגוי אחד. אכלום. בא בעל הממון לתבוע ממונו. עמדו אביה ואמה לפייס הגוי ולא יכלו. נתנם בעל הממון בבית האיסורין.[6] אמרו לחנה: לכי אצל עוקבא, שמא יתן לך. אמרה להם: לא אלך שמא יחטיא עמי. איני הולכת לשם. אמרו לו כמה פעמים, ולא קבלה.[7] {עֹאֹ}מד [אמר][8] בעלה: לכי ואל נמות כאן. הלכה ובקשה אותו שתתן לה מאה דינרים, כי בעלה בבית האיסורין בשבילם. אמר לה: אם אתן אותם לך, תשכבי עמי. אמרה לו: חלילה לך מעשות זאת, אלא זכור נא בוראך וכבוש יצרך ואל תעשה הנבלה הזאת.[9] מה עשה, שמע לקולה וכבש יצרו.[10] ואמר לאחת מן השפחות: הוציאי ותני לה מה שהיא שואלת. והוא, למה לא נתן לה מידו לידה, כדי שלא יגע בה.[11] לקחה והלכה. כיון שראת יוסף בעלה, נאנח. א"ל: חנה, בחייך שמא נגע בך? אמרה לו: בחיי עולם ובחיי, לא נגע בי אפילו ביד.[12]

1. כ"י בהמ"ל 2374, דף 114ב–116ב: ושמו עוקבא. בכ"י פרמא 2295 (בתוך: קושלבסקי, סיגופים ופיתויים, 142–145) שמו עקיבא. ההשוואות להלן הן לכ"י פרמא 2295 כ"י בהמ"ל וכ"י ירושלים 3184 (106ב–107א), בדרך כלל בפרפרזה.
2. בכ"י פרמא אין איזכור של שמה, חנה.
3. השוו לסנהדרין עה, ע"א.
4. בכ"י פרמא הרחבה בתיאור מחלתו, נסיונות הפיתוי שלו ודחייתם.
5. אין איזכור של שמו.
6. איזכור של מאסר הבעל בלבד.
7. אין תיאור של ניסיונות שכנוע מצד ההורים.
8. נראה שיד מאוחרת זיהתה את האות ד של המילה "עמד" כאות ר ושינתה בהתאם ל: "אמר", בהתאם להקשר.
9. בכ"י פרמא יש הרחבה בחילופי הדברים בינה ובין עוקבא.
10. שם, גם תיאור תפילתו ותשובתו.
11. חסר: והוא למה נתן–כדי שלא יגע בה.
12. חסר: כיון שראת יוסף בעלה–אפילו ביד.

touch you? She said to him: In God's name and on my life, he did not touch even my hand.

C. Some time later, Ukva was traveling on the road, and it appeared as if there was a candle lit at his head. A great yeshiva head and Torah scholar saw him and asked his students: Who is that? They said to him: Ukva the wicked. He said to them: Call him to me. The yeshiva head said to him: My son, tell me of a good deed that you have done. He said: Sir, I have not done any good deed, and being a great sinner, wicked people joined up with me and taught me every bad thing in the world. He said to him: My son, if you have done any good deed, confess it to me. He told him what had happened. The yeshiva head said to him: My daughter is eighteen years old, and I have a lot of money. You too have a lot of money. I will give you my daughter, and together we will study Torah all the days of our lives. He listened to him and took his daughter. And they studied Torah all the days of their lives.

D. They agreed between them that whoever died first would come and tell the other where he was and where the other would sit. The yeshiva head died before Mar Ukva. The Angel of Death came to the yeshiva head. He said to him: I offer you three things. Choose one of them, for no righteous man can be saved from it, even the perfectly righteous. If you wish, I will strike you three times with the scepter [of fire] in my hand, or I will tie it up your loins, or I will place it on the ground and you will pass over it three times. The yeshiva head said: I cannot touch it. The angel said to him: Choose one of the three. He immediately began to pass over it, and he cried out. He passed over it a second and third time, and he cried out very loudly. Mar Ukva heard and realized it was his voice and scream. At that very time, Mar Ukva was ill, because he had fallen ill on the very same day his friend [331b] the yeshiva head died. When they were about to bury him, Mar Ukva stretched out his hand and found fiery boils on his feet. He rent his clothes and said: That must be the voice I heard. They buried him and went home. Mar Ukva fell on his face and wept. The yeshiva head came to him and said: It is not nice that you put your hand under my legs to see my shame. He said to him: Heaven forbid, but I heard your voice and I was frightened, and now I demand that you fulfill your vow and tell me where you sit and where my place is. He said to him: On your life, your place is three steps above mine. Please, will you pray to go down one step and I will go up one step, and then we will be equals? Come and see how great is the power of repentance.

C. לימים היה עוקבא עובר בדרך. והיה כמו נר דלוק על ראשו, וראה אותו ראש ישיבה גדול תלמיד חכם.[13] אמר לתלמידיו: מי הוא זה? אמרו לו: עוקבא הרשע. אמר להם: קראו אותו לי. א"ל ראש ישיבה: בני, אמור לי טובה שעשית. א"ל: אדוני, לא עשיתי כלום טובה, כי בעוונותיי אנשים רעים נתחברו אלי ולמדוני כל רעות שבעולם. א"ל: בני, אם שום טובה עשית תודה לי. הודה לו הדבר.[14] א"ל ראש ישיבה: הרי בתי בת שמונה עשר שנה, ויש לי ממון הרבה, וכמו כן יש לך ממון הרבה. אתן לך בתי, ונשב יחד ונעסוק בתורה כל ימינו. ושמע לו ולקח בתו.[15] ועסקו בתורה כל ימיהם.

D. התנו ביניהם, שכל מי שימות מהם ראשון יבא ויגיד לחבירו היכן הוא והיאך הוא יושב. הקדים ראש ישיבה למר עוקבא.[16] בא מלאך המות לראש ישיבה.[17] א"ל: שלש אני נוטל עליך, בחר לך אחת מהן. שאין כל צדיק יכול להנצל ממנו, ואפילו צדיקים גמורים. אם תרצה אכה אותך שלשה פעמים מן השרביט שבידי, או {א}אזור אותה במותניך, או אני אשימנה בארץ ועבור עליו <גּפּ> שלשה פעמים. אמר ראש ישיבה: איני יכול ליגע בו. א"ל המלאך: בחר לך אחת משלשה. מיד התחיל לעבור עליו והיה בוכה. עבר פעם שנייה ושלישית וצעק צעקה גדולה. שמע מור עוקבא, והבין קולו וצעקתו. ובאותה שעה היה מור עוקבא חולה, כי נפל למשכב באותו יום עצמו שמת אותו [331ב] (אותו) ראש ישיבה חבירו. כשרצו לקוברו בא מר עוקבא ופשט ידו, ומצא ברגליו אבעבועות מן האש. קרע בגדיו. אמר: ודאי זהו הקול ששמעתי. הלכו וקברו אותו. חזרו לביתם. נפל מר עוקבא על פניו, והיה בוכה. בא ראש ישיבה וא"ל: לא יפה עשית שהכנסת ידך תחת רגלי לראות בושתי.[18] א"ל חס ושלום, אבל הייתי שומע קולך ונתבהלתי, ועכשיו אני משביעך שתאמר לי היאך אתה יושב והיכן מקומי. א"ל: חייך שלש מעלות מקומך למעלה ממקומי. בבקשה ממך שתתפלל שתרד אתה מעלה אחת, ואני אעלה מעלה אחת ואז נהיה שוין.[19] בא וראה כמה גדול {כח} התשובה.

---

13. שם, בלי תוארו כתלמיד חכם.
14. פירוט של חילופי הדברים ביניהם.
15. בכ"י פרמא אין אירוע של נישואי עוקבא לבתו של ראש הישיבה.
16. נוסף תיאור אבלו של עוקבא.
17. הדמות אינה מזוהה כמלאך המות.
18. ראש הישיבה אינו מזהה את עקיבא או עוקבא כתלמידו, ומבקש לסקול אותו.
19. מקומו של עקיבא או עוקבא בגן-עדן, גבוה מזה של ראש הישיבה.

62. A Meal of Herbs (331b)

A. A tale is told about Solomon when he lost his kingdom and went begging in the homes of Israel for a living. Once, two men who recognized him came to see him. One came and bowed down before him and said: Your majesty, would it please you to eat at my home? He said: Yes. He went with him to an attic and slaughtered an ox and served him many delicacies. He began to talk with him about matters related to his kingdom, and said: I recall from such and such a date, when you were in your kingdom and were king, and you did this and that. And your servants did this and that. When the man reminded him of the days of his royalty, he began to weep, and this went on throughout that feast, until he was sated with his tears.

B. The next day, he met his friend, who prostrated himself before him and said: Your majesty, would you eat with me today? He said: Do you intend to treat me as your friend did yesterday? He said: Your majesty, I am a poor man, but if you wish to eat with me today, I have some herbs that I would serve you. If you wish, come with me to my home.

62. ארוחת ירק (331ב)

A. מעשה בשעה[1] שירד שלמה ממלכותו, היה מחזיר ובא על פתחי ישראל בשביל פרנסתו.[2] פעם אחת נכנסו אצלו[3] שני בני אדם שהיו מכירין אותו. בא אחד מהם, נשתטח לפניו ואמר לו: אדוני המלך רצונך שתסעוד אצלי?[4] א"ל: הן.[5] הלך עמו לעלייה וזבח לו שור,[6] והביא לפניו הרבה מטעמים. התחיל להשמיע לו דברי[7] מלכותו. ואמר: זוכר אני מיום פלוני כשהייתה במלכותך והייתה מלך, ועשית כך וכך.[8] וכך וכך עשו משרתיך.[9] כיון שהזכיר לו[10] ימי מלכותו, התחיל להיות[11] בוכה. וכן כל אותה סעודה, עד ששבע עצמו מבכייתו.[12]

B. למחר פגע בו חבירו, התחיל להשתטח לפניו.[13] וא"ל: אדוני המלך תאכל עמי היום?[14] א"ל: אתה מבקש לעשות עמי כמו שעשה חברך אתמול?[15] א"ל: אדוני המלך, איש עני אני, אבל אם רצונך תשגיח עלי היום, מעט ירק יש לי שאניח לפניך.[16] אם רצונך, בא עמי לביתי.[17]

1. תוספת במדרש משלי, ויסוצקי, 122–123: טוב ארוחת ירק ואהבה שם משור אבוס ושנאה בו [משלי טו, יז]. א"ר לוי: כנגד מי אמרו שלמה למקרא הזה כנגד שני בני אדם שבשעה [. . .]. ההשוואות להלן הן למדרש משלי.
2. בגוף המהדורה של מדרש משלי: על הפרוסה; בעדי נוסח אחרים: על הפרנסה.
3. פגעו בו.
4. אם רצונך השגיח עלי היום.
5. במדרש משלי אין איזכור של תשובת שלמה.
6. בגוף המהדורה בלי איזכור "וזבח לו שור", אך בעדי נוסח אחרים שבמהדורת ויסוצקי הביטוי נמצא.
7. דברי שלמה ומלכותו.
8. זוכר אתה שעשית כך וכך ביום פלוני כשהייתה מלך.
9. במדרש משלי חסר: כך וכך עשו משרתיך.
10. שהיה מזכיר לו.
11. היה גועה ובוכה.
12. עד שעמד משם שבע מבכיתו.
13. התחיל משתטח לו.
14. רצונך שתשגיח עלי היום.
15. מה אתה לעשות לי כשם שעשה לי חברך אתמול.
16. אלא אם תשגיח על מעט ירק שיש לי.
17. בו עמי לבית.

C. He then went with him to his home. The man washed his hands and feet and served him bread and some herbs. Then the man began consoling him. He said: Your majesty, be consoled, the Almighty swore an oath to your father that He would not deprive his seed of royalty, as it says: "God swore to David in truth" [cf. Psalms 132:11[1]], but this is the way of the Lord, to reprove and then reconcile, as it says: "For whom the Lord loves He rebukes, as a father his son for whom he cares" [Proverbs 3:12], and the Lord will restore you to your kingdom. When Solomon heard this, he was gratified with him and was satisfied with that meal of herbs. And he left there satisfied, and when he returned to his kingdom, he said: "Better a meal of herbs where love is than a fatted ox and hatred with it" [Proverbs 15:17]. Better is the meal of herbs at the home of the poor than the fatted ox I was fed at the home of the rich, because he [the poor man] did not remind me of my grief.

1. "The Lord has sworn in truth to David; he will not turn from it; Of the fruit of your body will I set on your throne."

C. באותה שעה בא עמו לביתו.[18] רחץ ידיו ורגליו, הביא לפניו פת[19] ומעט ירק. התחיל אותו האיש לנחמו. א"ל: אדוני המלך, תתנחם,[20] שבועה נשבע הקב"ה לאביך[21] שאינו פוסק מלוכה מזרעו, שנ' נשבע י"י לדוד (ב)אמת [תהילים קלב, יא],[22] אלא כך הוא[23] דרכו של הקב"ה מוכיח וחוזר ומתרצה,[24] שנ' את אשר יאהב י"י יוכיח וכאב את בן ירצה, [משלי ג, יב] והקב"ה עתיד[25] להחזירך במלכותך.[26] כיון ששמע שלמה כך נתקררה דעתו עליו, והיה שבע[27] מאותה הסעודה של ירק.[28] ועמד משם שבע.[29] כיון שחזר למלכותו[30] אמר: טוב ארוחת ירק ואהבה שם, משור אבוס ושנאה בו [משלי טו, יז].[31] טוב ארוחת ירק שאכלתי בבית העני,[32] משור אבוס שהאכילני העשיר.[33] שלא הזכיר לי[34] צערי"

18. כיוון שהגיע לתוך ביתו.
19. אין איזכור של פת: הביא לפניו מעט ירק.
20. חסר: תתנחם.
21. שבועה נשבע הקב"ה לדוד אביך.
22. תוספת על פי המשך הפסוק בתהלים: לא ישוב ממנה מפרי בטנך אשית לכסא לך.
23. אלא כך היה.
24. מוכיח וחוזר ומרצה.
25. אבל עתיד הקב"ה.
26. להחזירך למלכותך.
27. ושבע.
28. מאותה ירק.
29. תוספת במדרש משלי בשמו של האמורא ר' חייא בר אבא ור' אבוי בן בנימין משום ר' יוסי בן זמרא: כיון שחזר שלמה למלכותו נתנבא במלכותו [. . .].
30. במדרש משלי, סיום הסיפור מובא כציטוט מפי אמוראים המוזכרים בשמותיהם: כיון שחזר שלמה למלכותו נתנבא במלכותו [. . .].
31. במדרש משלי: "טוב ארוחות ירק ואהבה שם", בלי הסיומת של הפסוק: "משור אבוס ושנאה בו".
32. שאכלתי אצל העני.
33. שלא אכלתי אצל העשיר.
34. אלא הזכיר עלי.

63. The Tribulations of Naḥum Ish Gamzo (331b–332a)

A. A tale is told of Naḥum of Gamzo, who was blind in both eyes and had lost both hands and [332a] both feet, and whose body was covered with boils. His bed was placed on four cups of water so that ants would not crawl up on him.

B. Once, he was lying in a dilapidated house, and his students wished to remove his bed. He told them: Remove the household and then take out my bed, because as long as my bed is in the house, I am assured that it will not fall. They removed the household and then turned to [take] his bed. The house immediately collapsed. His students said: Since you are perfectly righteous, why did this come upon you? He said: I myself did it [caused it], because once I was on the way to my father-in-law's house, and I had with me the loads of three donkeys, one of food, one of drink, and the one of all kinds of delicacies. I happened to meet a man, and he said: Rabbi, feed me. I said: Wait until I unload the donkey. I turned around after I had unloaded the donkey and found him dead. I fell upon him and said: My eyes that took no pity on your eyes, may such and such occur to them. My hands and feet that did not hasten to unload the donkey, may such and such occur to them. I could not feel calm until I said: May my whole body be covered with boils. Akiva said: Woe is me that I have seen you thus. He said to Akiva: Happy are you for seeing me thus.

63. נחום איש גמזו בעל הייסורים (331ב–332א)

A. מעשה אמרו על נחום איש גם זו, שהיה סומא בשתי עיניו וגידם בשתי ידיו וקיטע [332א] בשתי רגליו והיה כל גופו מלא שחין. והיה מטתו מונחת בארבע ספלים מלאים מים כדי שלא יעלו עליו הנמלים.[1]

B. פעם אחת היה מיטתו בבית רעוע,[2] ובקשו תלמידיו לפנותו. א"ל: פנו כלים ואחר כך פנו את מטתי, שכל זמן שמטתי בבית מובטח אני שלא תפול.[3] פינו הכלים, ואחר כך פינו מיטתו. מיד נפל הבית.[4] אמרו לו תלמידיו: וכי מאחר שצדיק גמור אתה, מפני מה אירע לך כך?[5] אמר להם: אני בעצמי עשיתי.[6] שפעם אחת הייתי לבית חמי, והיה עמי משאוי שלשה חמורים, אחד של מאכל ואחד של משתה ואחת של כל מיני מגדים. נזדמן לי אדם אחד,[7] א"ל: רבי פרנסני. אמרתי לו: המתן עד שאפרוק מן החמור. חזרתי לאח[ו]רי לאחר שפירקתי את החמור, מצאתיו מת.[8] נפלתי עליו ואמרתי: עיני של{א} חסו על עיניך, כך וכך תעלה עליהם. ידיי ורגלי שלא מהרו לפרק מן החמור, כך וכך תעלה עליהם.[9] ולא נתקררה דעתי עד שאמרתי: יהא כל גופי מלא שחין. א"ל ר' עקיבא: אוי לי שראיתיך בכך. א"ל: אשריך שראיתני בכך.

1. על פי תענית כא, ע"א, נוסח כ"י מינכן 140. ההשוואות להלן הן למקור זה.
2. מתבקש להשלים: והיה נתון בסכנה.
3. שכל זמן שמטתי בתוך הבית מובטח לכם שאינו נופל.
4. מיד נפל הבית.
5. וכי מאחר שצדיק גמור אתה, למה עלתה לך כך?
6. אני עשיתי בעצמי.
7. בירושלמי, פאה ח טז, [לז כא ע"ב] האיש מוכה שחין במסכת תענית האיש עני.
8. לאחר שפרקתי מן החמור חזרתי לאחורי, מצאתיו שמת.
9. בתענית רק איזכור "רגלי".

64. Naḥum Ish Gamzo and His Mission to the Emperor (332a)

A. And why was Naḥum of Gamzo known by that name? Because no matter what befell him he would always say: *Gam zo letovah* [This too is for the best].

B. Once the Israelites sent a gift to the emperor. They said: Who shall we send it with? With Naḥum Ish Gamzo, who is experienced in miracles. They sent him there. He went to a certain house, and its tenants took what he had in his sack and replaced it with earth. When he arrived there, he presented his sack to the king. They saw that it was filled with earth. The king said: The Jews are mocking me. He ordered that they all be killed. Naḥum Ish Gamzo said: This too is for the best.

C. Elijah of blessed memory came, appearing to the king to be one of them. He said: Perhaps this earth is the earth of Abraham, who when he would throw straw, it would be turned into arrows, as it says: "He turns them to dust with his sword, to windblown chaff with his bow" [Isaiah 41:2]. There was a certain country that they were unable to conquer. They threw the earth at it and vanquished it. They entered the treasury and filled the sack with precious stones and pearls.

64. נחום איש גמזו ושליחותו לקיסר (332א)

A. ואמאי קרו ליה [ועל מה קראו לו] נחום איש גם זו?[1] שכל מה שבא עליו היה אומר: גם זו לטובה.[2]

B. פעם אחת שלחו ליה ישראל דורון לבי [לבית] קיסר.[3] אמרו: ביד מי נשלחנו?[4] ביד נחום איש גם זו,[5] דמלומד בניכסי [בנסים].[6] שלחו בהדיה [לשם]. אזל בההוא דיורא,[7] קמו הנהו דיוראי ולקחו מאי דהוה בשקו ומלאוהו עפרא [הלך לאותה דירה, קמו דייריה ולקחו מה שהיה בשקו ומלאוהו עפר].[8] כי מטא התם, שדריה לשקו [כשבא לשם, שלח שקו][9] ראוהו דהוה עפרא [ראוהו שהיה עפר].[10] אמר: אחוכי קמחייכי עלי יהודאי [צוחקים בי היהודים]. צוה עליהם להורגם.[11] אמר: גם זו לטובה.[12]

C. אתא [בא] אליהו זכור לטוב,[13] אידמי ליה כחד מינייהו [נדמה לו (למלך) כאחד מהם]. אמר: ודילמא האי עפרא מעפרא דאברהם הוה [שמא עפר זה מעפרו של אברהם הוא],[14] דכי הוו שדנהו מיניה הוו גירי [כשהיה זורק קש נעשו חצים],[15] דכת': יתן כעפר חרבו כקש נדף קשתו [ישעיהו מא, ב].[16] הוה חדא מדינתא,[17] דלא הוה יכול למיכבשיה. זרקו מינה עלה וכבשוה [היתה מדינה אחת, שלא יכלו לכבשה. זרקו עליה וכבשוה].[18] עיילו ליה לבית גנזיה [נכנסו לבית גנזיו]. ומלא[ו] שקו אבנים טובות ומרגליות.[19]

---

1. בכתב היד, שני הסיפורים על נחום איש גמזו מובאים ברצף אחד.
2. תענית כא, ע"א וסנהדרין קח ע"ב [בתרגום מארמית]: שכל דבר שהיה מגיע <מזדמן> לו אמר גם זו לטובה ההשוואות להלן הן למקורות אלה, בתרגום מארמית.
3. רצו לשלוח.
4. תענית: מי ילך? סנהדרין: בידי מי נשלח?
5. תענית: ילך נחום איש גם זו. סנהדרין: נשלח בידי נחום איש גם זו.
6. שמלומד בנסים הוא.
7. תענית: הלך לן בדירה אחת. סנהדרין: כשבא לבית אחד רצה ללון. כשבא לשם אמרו לו: מה יש אתך? אמר להם אני מוביל את המס לקיסר.
8. תענית: בלילה קמו אותם הדיירים שגרו שם לקחו את התיבה ומלאוה עפר. סנהדרין: עמדו בלילה פתחו את ארגזו והוציאו את כל מה שהיה בתוכו ומלאו אותו בעפר.
9. סנהדרין: נמצא עפר.
10. תענית: כשבא לשם פתחו את התיבה וראו אותה שמלאה עפר. סנהדרין: בדקו ממנו מן העפר הזה וכבשו אותה.
11. תענית: רצה המלך להרוג את כולם. סנהדרין: הוציאוהו ליהרג.
12. מקצת מכתבי היד של מסכת תענית מקדימים מימרא זו לפני גילוי העפר בבית הקיסר.
13. בתענית ובסנהדרין ללא התואר: זכור לטוב.
14. תענית: אברהם אביהם. סנהדרין: אבינו.
15. בתענית מובא גם: כשהיה זורק עפר נעשה חרבות. וכן בסנהדרין: בדקו ומצאו.
16. תענית: דכתיב "יתן כעפר חרבו כקש נדף קשתו". במסכת סנהדרין, ללא ציטוט.
17. סנהדרין: היה מחוז.
18. תענית: בדקו ממנו (מן העפר הזה) וכבשו אותה.
19. בתענית מובא גם: ושלחוהו בכבוד גדול. סנהדרין: אמרו קח מה שנוח לך. מלא את התבה זהב.

D. He [Naḥum] came [back] to that certain house. They said: What did you bring along [for the king] that you deserved all this? He said: What I took from here. They too got up to bring the king of the same earth. They [the king and his ministers] tested the earth, and it did not pass the test. They killed all the tenants.

D. אתא בבית ההוא דיורא [בא באותו בית מגורים].[20] אמר[ו] לו: מאי אמטית בהדך, דעבדו כולי האי בך [מה הבאת אתך, שעשו כל זה לך?][21] אמר להו: מאי {ד}שקליה̄ [דשקלי] מהכא [מה שלקחתי מכאן].[22] קמו אינהו נמי אמטו לבי מלכא מההוא עפרא [קמו גם הם הביאו למלך מאותו עפר].[23] בדקו ולא אשכחו [בדקו ולא מצאו][24] קטלינהו להנך כולהו דיוראי [הרגו את כל הדיירים]"[25]

20. תענית: כשבאו לנו באותו בית.
21. תענית: מה הבאת איתך שעשו לך כבוד גדול כזה? סנהדרין: מה הבאת לבית המלך?
22. מה שלקחתי מכאן הבאתי לשם.
23. תענית: הרסו הבית והביאו לבית המלך. סנהדרין: לקחו הם והביאו לשם.
24. חסר במסכת סנהדרין.
25. תענית: אמרו לו, עפר זה שבא לכאן – משלנו הוא. בדקוהו ולא מצאו אותו, והרגו את הדיירים ההם.

65. The Grateful Dead (332a–333b)

A. [332a] Once there was a *ḥasid* who had but one son. The *ḥasid* was very rich and very old. At the time of his death, he commanded his son to engage in the fulfillment of good deeds and to always give charity to the poor, and to be beloved of and pleasant to people, and that he should never postpone any good deed that came his way [332b]. The man died, and the young man was left with his mother. The young man went to engage in doing good deeds. His mother said to him: My son, listen to me and take our money and divide it into three parts. Take one part to do business with and go to a place near or far and buy and sell from the money that you have, so that we may grow rich from trade. He went and did so, and divided his property and traveled to a distant country, and there he encountered a large group who were arguing and fighting among themselves. He said to one of them: What is this gathering? He said to him: There is a groom to whom the father of the bride promised one thousand gold coins more than he could afford, and the groom does not want to marry the bride, and he says that he is going back to his land the same way he came, and will not marry her. And this whole crowd are all poor and cannot help him. The young man answered and said: Since this good deed has come my way, I will do it. What did that young man do? He took a thousand coins and gave them to the groom, who immediately proceeded to marry his wife, and he [the young man] arranged the wedding ceremony and feasting and singing and musical instruments and all kinds of music, and there was a great celebration. And the young man had nothing left. And he returned home to his mother. She said to him: Tell me, my son, what did you do with all the money you had with you? He told her: Mother, do not take it badly, and don't be angry with me, and don't take it to heart, because I lent it to a certain great lord whose name is known all over the world, and he will pay me double, and I trust that he will pay me my wages for my work. She said to him: My son, to your life and peace [*le'haim u'leshalom*]; and if you wish, take another part and engage in trade, and for the love of our Creator, be careful to act wisely in all your affairs.

B. He took another thousand gold coins and traveled far from his land, until he saw he came to a place where all the inhabitants of the city were weeping and grieving. He said to one of them: What is the reason for all this grief and sorrow? The man said: It has been three days since the rabbi and head of the yeshiva in this town has died, and he was great in Torah and in good deeds and commandments, and also a perfectly righteous and very virtuous man. There is none like him, because he had the spirit of God within him. And the king did not allow this congregation

65. מת מכיר תודה (332א–333ב)

A. מעשה בחסיד אחד שלא היה לו כי אם בן אחד.[1] והיה החסיד עשיר גדול וזקן מאד. בשעה פטירתו צוה לבנו להתעסק במצות, וליתן תמיד צדקה לעניים, ולהיות אהוב ונחמד בעיני הבריות. וכל מצוה שיבא לידו [332ב] שלא תניחנה. נפטר האיש, ונשאר הבחור עם אמו. הלך הבחור ונתעסק במצות. אמרה לו אמו: בני שמע בקולי וקח הממון שלנו, וחלק אותו לשלשה חלקים. וקח חלק אחד ועשה סחורה ממנו, ולך לך לשום מקום קרוב או רחוק, וקנה ומכור מן הממון שיהיה לך למען נתעשר בסחורה. הלך וכן עשה וחלק נכסיו, והלך למדינת הים ופגע סיעה גדולה אחת שהיו מתקוטטים יחד ומריבים. אמר לאחד מהם: מה זה האסיפה הזאת? א"ל: זה חתן אחד שהתנה אבי הכלה לתת לו אלף זהובים יותר מהשגת ידו, ולא רצה החתן לקדש אשתו, ואמר כאשר בא כן ילך לארצו, ולא יקדש אותה לעולם. וכל הקהל הזה כולם עניים, ואינם יכולים לסייעו. ענה בחור ואמר: הואיל ובא לידי זאת המצוה, אעשנה. מה עשה אותו בחור, נטל אלף זוזים ונתן לחתן ומיד קדש את אשתו. ועשה החופה והמשתה בשירים ובכינורות ובכל מיני זמר ועשו שמחה גדולה, ולא נשאר לבחור מאומה. וחזר לביתו לאמו. אמרה לו (אמר~~ה~~): בני, {מה} עשית מן הממון שנשאת עמך? אמר לה: אמי, אל יקשה בעינייך ואל יחר לך ואל תחשבי ממנו, כי לויתי אותו לאדון אחד גדול ושמו נודע בכל העולם, והוא ישלם לי כפליים, ונאמן הוא לשלם לי שכרי ועמלי. אמרה לו: בני, לחיים ולשלום, ואם תרצה קח עוד חלק אחר ולך לסחורה, ובשביל אהבת בוראינו הזהר שתעשה בחכמה כל עניינך.

B. לקח עוד אלף זהובים והלך לו ונתרחק מאד ממדינתו, עד שראה כל בני העיר אשר בא שמה בוכים ומצטערים. ואמר לאחד מהם: מה הצער והבכיה הזאת לכם? א"ל האיש: כבר עבר שלשה ימים שמת הרב ראש ישיבה שבעיר הזאת, והוא היה גדול בתורה ובמעשים טובים ובמצות, וצדיק גמור וחסיד היה מאד, לא קם כמוהו כי רוח א-להים היה בקרבו. ולא הניח המלך את הקהל הזה לקבור הרב ולנהוג בו כבוד. ולכן אנו בוכים ומצטערים. א"ל הבחור: ומפני מה הוא אינו רוצה שיקברוהו הקהל? א"ל: כי שואל אלף זהובים בשוחד לקהל, וכולם עניים מאד ואינם יכולים לתתם לו. אמר הבחור: הרי עלי אלף זהובים, אתנם לו בשביל אהבת בוראינו, ובשביל כבודו של אותו צדיק. הלך הבחור ונתן אלף זהובים למלך, וצוה לקוברו. והלכו כולם לקבור הצדיק ונהגו בו כבוד גדול כראוי לו, והבחור הלך עמהם לנהוג לו כבוד גדול. אחר אשר קברו אותו, חזר הבחור לביתו לאמו. אמרה לו בני מה עשית מן הממון <~~שעשית~~> שנשאת עמך? אמר לה: אמי, אל תחשבי מהם כי בטוב לויתי אותם לנאמן אחד, אין בכל העולם כולו כמוהו שישלם לי גם קרן גם פרי, ומובטח אני בו שלא [333א] יעכב ממני שום דבר. אמרה לו לחייך בני. אמר לה: אם תרצי תני לי עוד האלף זהובים שנשארו, ואני אלך עוד לסחורה וארויח מה שאוכל. אמרה לו: בני, אין לנו עוד אלא אותם אלף זהובים, ואם תפסידם לא נדע מה נעשה כי נשאר~~ו~~ אני

1. אין לסיפור מקבילות קודמות, ככל שידוע לי.

to bury him and show him proper respect. That is why we are weeping and are sorrowful. The young man said [asked]: Why doesn't the king want to allow this congregation to bury him? He said: Because he is demanding a thousand gold coins as a bribe from the congregation, all of whom are very poor and cannot give it to him. The young man said: I have a thousand gold coins on me. I will give them to you for the love of our Creator and to honor that righteous man. The young man went and gave the thousand coins to the king, and he [the king] ordered that he [the righteous man] be buried. And they all went to bury the righteous man and accord him the great respect he deserved, and the young man went with him to pay his respects. After they buried him, the young man went home to his mother. She said to him: My son, what did you do with the money you took with you? He said to her: Mother, do not worry about it, because I did well and lent it to someone who is trustworthy. There is no one like him in the world who will pay me back both the capital and the profit, and I trust that he will not [333a] hold back anything from me. She said: To your life, my son. He said to her: If you like, give me the thousand gold coins that remain, and I will go to trade and profit what I can. She said to him: My son, we have nothing beyond those thousand gold coins, and if you lose them, we will not know what to do for you, and I will remain impoverished, and one who is poor is comparable to one who is dead. Therefore, my son, remain here with me, and we will spend them [the coins] together until the time comes for the lord you spoke of to repay you what you lent him. He said to her: Mother, know that the time is growing closer, to the day that he will pay me well what he owes me, and do not delay me because I must go to my creditor. And it would be better for me to bring money with me, for perhaps God will appear to me, and I will earn much more than I ever had, than to go emptyhanded. His mother said to him: If that is the case, take the coins, and God will send his angel before you to protect you on the way and bring you to that place.

C. He took the money and arrived in a city where he found all the people weeping and crying and mourning unlike anything seen before in the world. The young man said: Why are you all so sorrowful? One of them said to him: Our king is as wicked as can be, and he decreed that the entire congregation be destroyed, and he took everything we have and left nothing in our hands other than our bodies. And he has also decreed that we must not circumcise our sons and that our wives may not immerse [in the ritual bath] and not to conduct marriage ceremonies, and tomorrow we must circumcise three boys because tomorrow is the eighth day after they were born. And it has been four months since any woman has immersed, and

ואתה עניים, ועני חשוב כמות [כמת]. לכן בני, תשאר הנה עמי ונאכלם יחד עד שיגיע זמן שישלם לך האדון שאמרת מה שלויתה לו. אמר לה: אמי, דעי כי הזמן הולך ומקרב (כל) היום שישלם לי בטוב מה שהוא חייב לי, ואל תאחרי אותי הואיל וצריך אני לילך לבעל חובי. וטוב לי להביא עמי הממון, אולי יקרה הא-להים לפני וארויח הרבה יותר ממה שהיה לי מעולם מ{ל}ילך בידים ריקניות. אמרה לו אמו: אם כן קח אותם, והקב"ה ישלח מלאכו לפניך לשמרך בדרך ולהביאך אל המקום הזה.

C. לקח הממון והלך לו ובא אל עיר אחת, ומצא שם כל הקהל בוכים ומתאנחים ועושים הספד, לא נראה כמוהו מעולם. אמר הבחור: מפני מה אתם עושים כל הצער הזה? א"ל איש אחד מהם: המלך שלנו רשע הוא אין כמוהו, וגזר שמד על כל הקהל, ולקח כל אשר לנו ולא נשאר בידינו מאומה בלתי גוייתינו,[2] וגם גזר עלינו שלא למול את בנינו, ועל נשותינו שלא לטבול ושלא להכניס כלה לחופה, ויש למול למחר שלשה בנים, כי למחר יהיה יום שמיני שנולדו. וכבר עברו ארבעה חדשים שלא טבלה שום אשה ונפרדנו מנשותינו, וכלה לא הכניסה לחופה כבר עבר ד' חודשים כמו כן ~~א"ל~~, וטוב מות מחיים אמרנו. א"ל הבחור: וכל כך למה? א"ל: בשביל אלף זהובים שהוא שואל עוד ממנו ואין בידינו כלום, כי לקח כל אשר לנו. אמר הבחור: יהי שם י"י מבורך אשר נחני בדרך אמת להתבטל גזירה רעה כזאת מעל ישראל. הנה נא לי אלף זהובים, אלך ואתנם לו ויבטל הגזירה מעליכם. מה עשה הבחור, הלך אל המלך וא"ל: אדוני המלך, מה לך לגזור גזירה רעה כזאת על ישראל? א"ל המלך: בשביל שהם חייבים לי אלף זהובים. א"ל

2. השוו לבראשית מז, יט.

we have separated from our wives, and no weddings have been held, and four such months have already passed and we would be better off dead. And how did all this come about? He said: Because of a thousand gold coins he demands of us. But we have nothing left, because he has already taken everything we had. The young man said: Blessed be in the name of God, who took me on the path of truth to put an end to this evil decree upon the Jews. Here are a thousand gold coins. I will go and give them to him so that he cancels the decree upon you. What did the young man do? He went to the king and said to him, Your majesty: Why have you issued this terrible decree over the Jews? The king said to him: Because they owe me a thousand gold coins. The young man said to him: If I pay you, will you cancel the decree? He said to him: Yes. He said to him: Here are a thousand gold coins. He took them and ordered that it be proclaimed throughout the kingdom that the decree was canceled and that the Jews may do as they wish. They went and circumcised their sons and held joyous festivities. The young man departed from them and set out on his way. They all blessed him and said: May the Lord repay you for all you have done, and may you be richly rewarded by the Lord, the God of Israel [Ruth 2:12].

D. He arose and set out on his way and said to himself: Where will I go? If I return to my mother emptyhanded, what will I do with all the sorrow and grief that will befall my mother, for being poor and old and having nothing left? And she is anticipating my arrival all day, and that I bring back with me something of what I took from her. And thus [333b] he would ponder to himself. He was sitting on the earth, weeping and praying to the Almighty, saying: Lord of the Universe, it is well known to You that everything I did, I did in Your honor. Guide me in your truth and teach me and give me and my mother livelihood so that we do not become dependent on the generosity of people, because their gifts are meager and their shame is great, but your gifts are plentiful and your shame meager. While he was praying, Elijah the Prophet, of blessed memory, came and said to him: Greetings to you. And the young man answered: Greetings to you, my teacher and rabbi. Elijah said to him: God has heard your prayer and seen your suffering and everything that you have done in his honor. Take these ten gold coins that I will give you, and from them you will become exceedingly wealthy, and you will have large amounts of silver and gold and precious stones and pearls all the days of your life, because you spoke well about lending money to a trustee who will repay you. And he will pay you double and quadruple what he owes you, a thousand times over. The young man said to him: Sir, on your life and the eternal life [of God], I do not wish to take my reward in this world but rather in the world to come. And I will not take it until you show me my

הבחור: אם אפרעם לך תבטל הגזירה? א"ל הן. א"ל: הרי לך אלף זהובים. לקח אותם, ויצו בכל מלכותו להעביר קול ולבטל הגזירה, ויעשו ישראל כל רצונם. הלכו ומלו בניהם, ועשו שמחה ומשתה ויום טוב. והבחור נטל רשות מהם, והלך לדרכו. ויברכו אותו ויאמרו לו: ישלם י"י לך פעלך ותהי משכורתך שלימה מעם י"י א-להי ישראל [רות ב, יב].

D. ויקם וילך לדרכו ויאמר אל לבו: אנה אלך, אם אחזור לאמי בידים ריקניות אנה אני בא מן הצרה והצער אשר ימצא את אמי, כי היא ענייה וזקינה ולא נשאר לה כלום. והיא מצפה כל היום אחרי, שאביא עמי לה מה שלקחתי ממנה. וככה [333ב] היה מדבר אל עצמו. ישב לארץ ובכה והתפלל אל הקב"ה ואמר לפניו: רבונו של עולם גלוי וידוע לפני כסא כבודך, שלכבודך עשיתי כל מה שעשיתי. הדריכני באמיתך ולמדני ופרנסני אני ואמי ואל תצריכני למתנות בשר ודם, כי מתנתם מועטת וחרפתם מרובה, אבל מתנתך מרובה וחרפתך מועטת. בין כך ובין כך שהיה מתפלל, בא אליו אליהו הנביא זכור לטוב וא"ל: שלום עליך. והבחור ענה לו: שלום עליך מורי ורבי. א"ל אליהו: הנה שמע א-להים לקול תפלתך, וראה את ענייך ואת כל אשר עשית לכבודו. הנה נא קח לך עשרה זהובים שאתן לך, ומאותן תעשיר עושר גדול ויהיה לך כסף וזהב ואבנים טובות ומרגליות לרוב מאד כל ימיך, כי יפה דברת שלויתה ממונך לנאמן לשלם לך. והוא ישלם לך כפלי כפליים, אלף פעמים. א"ל הבחור: אדוני, חייך וחיי עולם לא אני רוצה ליקח משכורתי בעולם הזה, כי אם לעולם הבא. ולא אקחם עד שתראה לי מקומי, ומה יהיה מתן שכרי לעולם הבא. א"ל אליהו: בעולם הזה יהיה לך עושר גדול וכבוד כזה, ולעולם הבא בוא ואראך את מקומך ומתן שכרך.

place and what will be my reward in the world to come. Elijah said to him: In this world, you shall have great riches and honor, and in the world to come—let me show you your place and the reward that you will be given.

E. He went with him and he showed him the Garden of Eden. And in the garden, he showed him a throne made of gold, covered with precious stones and pearls, with clouds of glory covering it. And over that throne were ten canopies made of splendor and radiance and glory and honor and majesty and resplendence, and it stood at the center of the righteous. When he saw that, he said to him: Please, allow me to go there immediately. Why should I be in this world at all to see labor and sorrow? Elijah said to him: On your life that your time has not come to be there. Now let me bring you to your mother. He gave him ten gold coins and spread his wings and took him to his mother's home. And Elijah the Prophet left and went on his way. When his mother saw him, she was very happy to see him and asked him: My son, what did you do? He said to her: Mother, with God's help, we have a great deal. What did he do? He went and bought and sold and became very wealthy within a short time, and gathered treasures of silver and gold and [precious] stones and pearls until there was none richer than him in all the land. Come and see how great is the power of charity, that because of his generosity, he gained both this world and the world to come.

E. הלך עמו והראהו גן עדן. ובתוך גן עדן הראה לו קתדרא אחת מזהב מלאה מאבנים טובות ומרגליות, ועֲנני כבוד סוככין אותה, ועליה עשר חופות, מזיו וזוהר ויקר ונוגה וכבוד והוד והדר סוככין אותה קתדרא, והיא עומדת באמצע הצדיקים. כשראה כך א"ל: בבקשה ממך הניחני ואלך שם מיד, למה אהיה עוד בעולם הזה לראות עמל ואון. א"ל אליהו: חייך שאין יומך בא עדיין <להיות> שם, אלא בוא ואביאך אל אמך. ויתן לו העשרה זהובים, ויפרוש כנפיו וישאהו לבית אמו, ואליהו הנביא הלך לדרכו. וכשראתה אותו אמו שמחה מאד ממנו, ושאלה לו: בני מה עשית? אמר לה: אמי, בעזרת הבורא יהיה לנו הרבה. מה עשה, הלך וקנה ומכר ונתעשר מעושר גדול בזמן מועט, וקיבץ אוצרות של כסף ושל זהב ושל אבנים ומרגליות עד שלא היה עשיר כמוהו בכל הארץ. ובוא וראה כמה גדול כח של צדקה, שבשביל צדקותיו קנה העולם הזה והעולם הבא.

66. The Prophecy of the Ravens (333b–336b)

A. [333b] Once there was a man who had a son who was eighteen years old. And that man had but this one son. And the man was exceedingly wealthy. One day the son came before his father and said: Sir, listen—behold you have raised me up and elevated me, and I have much wealth and many assets, yet I do not learn anything from you, neither Torah nor wisdom nor the ways of the world [334a] nor knowledge nor insight. If you wish, I will go and learn in far-away lands, because I have heard that there is a city there filled with very wise men who are most knowledgeable in all the wisdom of the world. I would like to go there and spend three years there, and after three years I will come back to you. The father said to him: Son, why should you go here and there? I have great riches and copious assets, and I have no other son but you. And see that I have grown old, and I know not the day of my death, and your mother is very old, and if we should die, to whom will we leave all this wealth? His son said: I am not worried about all your assets [lit., all that you have], because at the hour of death one has neither silver nor gold nor precious stones nor pearls, but only the Torah and good deeds. When the father heard this, he said: Son, stay with us, and I will hire a rabbi, a scholar of Torah and Talmud, so that you will study here with us, and every day, I will provide livelihood for six poor people on the condition that you remain here. He said: Father, do not be angry with me, but I will not allow any matter in the world to keep me from going there, because I will learn a great deal more there in three years than I can here in ten. And the father saw that he could not prevent him from going and said: If so, then take a thousand gold coins with you and dress yourself in fine and respectable clothes and go in peace, and don't forget to come back in three years' time.

B. The young man went to the distant land and arrived in that city where they were all scholars, and went to the head of all the scholars and studied there before him. Within three years, he had learned a very great deal. When his time came, his father sent for him, and he received permission from his rabbi and went to his father. When his father and mother saw him, they were overjoyed and asked him: Son, what did you learn? He said to them: I learned Torah, and I still want to go there to be there another three years. His father said to him: You have been there a long time. He said: That is the condition I made—to return to him [to his teacher] and sit before [learn from] him three more years, and I will not give it up for anything. His father said: In that case, take another thousand gold coins and nice, new clothing, and go in peace, but when I send for you, come and do not forget. He took what he gave him and returned to his rabbi and studied before him for another three years.

66. נבואת הערבים (333ב–336ב)

A. מעשה באדם אחד שהיה לו בן והיה בן שמונה עשר שנים, ולא היה לאותו אדם כי אם אותו בן.[1] והיה האיש עשיר גדול. יום אחד בא אותו בן לפני אביו וא"ל: אדוני, שמעני הנה גדלתני ורוממתני ויש לי הרבה עושר ונכסים לרוב, ואינני לומד עמך שום דבר, לא תורה ולא חכמה ולא דרך ארץ ולא [334א] בינה ולא תבונה. אם רצונך אלך ואלמוד למדינת הים, כי שמעתי שיש שם עיר אחת מלאה חכמים מאד, מחוכמים ביותר מכל חכמה שבעולם. ויש בדעתי לילך שם ולשהות שם שלש שנים, ואחר שלש שנים אבא אליך. א"ל אביו: בני, מה לך לילך אנה ואנה, יש לי עושר הרבה ונכסים לרוב, ואין לנו בן כי אם אתה. והנה נא זקנתי ולא ידעתי יום מותי, ואמך זקנה מאד, ואם נמות למי נשאר את כל העושר הזה? א"ל בנו: איני חושש מכל מה שיש לך, לפי שבשעה פטירתו של אדם אין מלוין לו לא כסף וזהב ולא אבנים טובות ומרגליות, אלא תורה ומעשים טובים.[2] כיון ששמע אביו כך א"ל: בני, תשאר עמנו ואשכיר לך הנה רב אחד תלמיד חכם ותלמוד כאן עמנו, ובכל יום ויום אפרנס ששה עניים בתנאי שתשאר עמנו. א"ל: אבי, אל יחר בעיניך כי בשום עניין שבעולם לא אניח מלילך שם. כי הרבה יותר אני לומד שם בשלשה שנים, ממה שאעשה הנה בעשר שנים. וירא אביו כי לא יכול לעכבו ויאמר לו: אם כן קח עמך אלף זהובים ובגדים נאים והגונים ולך לשלום, ואל תניח מלחזור לסוף שלש שנים.

B. הלך הנער למדינת הים ובא אל אותה עיר שהיו כולם תלמידים חכמים, והלך אל ראש שבכולם ולמד שם בפניו. בתוך שלש שנים למד הרבה מאד. כשהגיע זמנו שלח אביו אחריו, ונטל רשות מרבו והלך אל אביו. כשראוהו אביו ואמו שמחו שמחה גדולה ושאלו לו: בני מה למדת? אמר להם: למדתי תורה, ועדיין אני רוצה לילך שם ולהיות שם עוד שלש שנים. א"ל אביו: הרבה הייתה שם. א"ל: כך התניתי לבא עוד אליו ולהיות בפניו ללמוד עוד ג' שנים, ולא אניח בשום עניין. א"ל: אם כן הוא, קח עמך עוד אלף זהובים ובגדים חדשים וטובים ותלך לשלום, וכשאשלח אחריך תבא ואל תניח. לקח מה שנתן לו והלך לו ובא אל רבו, ולמד עוד בפניו ג' שנים. באותן שש שנים שהיה שם, למד תורה ונביאים וכתובים ותלמוד ואגדות וסיפרא וספרי ותוספתא ומתניתין[3] וכלליה תלמודא.[4] כיון שהגיע זמנו שלח אביו אחריו, ונטל רשות מרבו והלך לו ובא אל אביו. ושמחו מאד כשראוהו אביו ואמו. ושאל לו אביו: בני, מה למדת? א"ל: הרבה למדתי. א"ל אביו: אמור לנו שום דבר ממה שלמדתה. א"ל: עדיין לא ידעתי תמצית החכמה, ואיני יכול לומר מאומה עד שאהיה עוד שם שלש שנים. א"ל: הרבה הייתה שם ולא תשוב עוד שם, כי אנחנו זקנים מאד ורוצים אנו שתהיה כאן עמנו לשמור אותנו. א"ל [334ב]: אני אפסיד כל מה שעשיתי אם לא אהיה שם עוד שלש שנים. א"ל: אם כן הוא <אם> אין טוב לך להפסיד מה שעשית, לך לשלום.

1. אין בידינו עדי נוסח דומים לסיפור.
2. השוו: "טוב לי תורת פיך מאלפי זהב וכסף" (תהילים קיט, עב).
3. משנה.
4. וכללי התלמוד.

During the six years when he was there, he learned Torah and Prophets and Writings and Talmud and Aggadah and Sifra and the books of the Tosefta, Mishnah, and the methods of the Talmud. When the time came, his father sent for him and he asked permission from his rabbi and returned to his father. His father and mother were overjoyed to see him, and his father asked him: Son, what did you learn? He said: I have learned a great deal. His father said to him: Tell me something of what you learned. He said: I still do not know the essence of wisdom, and I cannot say anything until I have studied there for another three years. He said to him: You have been there a long time, and you will not return there anymore, because we are very old, and we want you here to look after us. He said to him: [334b] I will lose everything that I have done if I do not go back for another three years. He said: If that is the case, you must not lose everything you have done. Go in peace.

C. He went and took with him a thousand gold coins, and he remained there for another three years. It was said of him that, during those three years, he learned the language of the palms, demons, the fables of the foxes, and the language of every animal, beast, and bird, and that there was no wisdom in the world that he did not learn.

D. When the three years were completed, his father himself came after him and gave his rabbi great gifts. His rabbi said to him: Take your son, your only son, and bring him home in peace, for he is exceedingly wise and has mastered every [type] of wisdom in the world, and there is none like him. They asked permission from his rabbi and left. When they came to the ocean, they rented a ship and boarded it. When they were in the middle of the sea, a raven came and landed on the ship's mast and shouted, saying as he shouted: The father of this young man is very rich, and before he dies he will be a poor man, greatly impoverished, unlike anything seen in the world, and finally he will be exceedingly rich, and there will be none like him anywhere in the land. The son heard and was greatly amused. His father said to him: My son, why were you laughing so much? He said to him: Don't pay attention to anything; I was just recalling some amusing thing I did in my youth. That's why I was laughing. He said to him: That is not why you were laughing. There was another reason. But he did not want to tell him, because he did not want to frighten him or make him angry. And his father became angry with him and he incurred his wrath, and he said: Is this why I scattered all my money so that he laughs without knowing why?! He is nothing but a fool, as Solomon in his wisdom said: Laughter rests in the mouth of a fool. What did he do? He took his son and cast him into the ocean.

C. הלך ולקח עמו עוד אלף זהובים, וישב שם שלש שנים אחרות. אמרו עליו שלמד באותן שלש שנים שיחת דקלים, שיחת שדים, ממשלות שועלים ולשון כל בהמה וחיה ועוף, ולא הניח חכמה שבעולם <~~שלא~~> שלא למד.[5]

D. כשנגמרו השלש שנים בא אביו עצמו אחריו. ונתן לרבו מתנות גדולות מאד. ואמר לו רבו: קח בנך יחידך[6] והוליכהו לשלום לביתך, והוא חכם מחוכם מכל חכמת שבעולם, לא נראה כמוהו. נטלו רשות מרבו, והלכו להם. כשבאו אל הים שכרו ספינה אחת, ונכנסו בה. כשהיו באמצע הים בא עורב וישב לו על התורן וצעק, ואמר כצעקתו: אביו של זה הבחור עכשיו הוא עשיר גדול, וקודם שימות יהיה עני מדולדל בעניותו לא נראה מעולם, ולבסוף יהיה עשיר משופע מעושר גדול, ולא יהיה כמוהו בכל הארץ. שמע בנו ושחק מאד. א"ל אביו: בני, מפני מה שחקת כל כך? א"ל: אל תשים ללבך שום דבר, כי זכורני ממעשים שהייתי עושה בנערותי, ובשביל כך שחקתי. א"ל: לא מפני זה שחקת, כי אם בשביל דבר אחר. והוא לא רצה לספר לו, שלא רצה לפחדו ולכעסו. וכעס עליו אביו ויחר לו, ויאמר: וכי בשביל זה פזרתי כל ממוני שהוא שוחק ולא ידע למה, אין זה כי אם שוטה כמו שאמר שלמה בחכמתו: שחוק בפי כסיל ינוח.[7] מה עשה, לקח בנו והשליכו לים.

5. שיחת דקלים השוו סוכה כח, ע"א ודברי רש"י שם: "לא ידענא מאי היא." ממשלות שועלים פירושו: משלי שועלים.

6. השוו בראשית כב, ב: "ויאמר קח נא את בנך את יחידך אשר אהבת".

7. השוו משלי י, כג. קהלת ז, ט.

E. God caused a big fish to come there, and it swallowed him, and took him to a distant place. It took him to a certain kingdom. He sat there on the beach, and a shepherd, who was one of the king's shepherds, saw him and saw that he was naked and had no clothes. He [the shepherd] went to him and said: My son, what are you doing, and where are you from, and what place do you come from? He said: I am a Hebrew, and I fear the God of the heavens who made the sea and the land. And I was on a ship, and a very great wind came and broke the ship, and God caused a fish to come, and it was God who brought me here. He said: Do you know any craft in the world? He said to him: Yes. He said to him: What craft do you know? He said: Your servant has been a shepherd since he was young up to the present. He said to him: If so, stay with me and guard my sheep, and I will pay your wages. He stayed with him, and he dressed and fed and loved him very much, and God blessed him [the shepherd] because of him [the young man], and he placed everything he had in his hands [Gen. 33:4].

F. Once the king was sitting in his palace with his ministers and servants, when a very, very large flock of ravens gathered over the palace, until the entire building was covered with ravens that divided up into two flocks on either side of the house. And between the two groups were three ravens, two males and one female, among them [335a]. And those three ravens were sitting there and did not move from where they sat. And two other ravens would go from flock to flock [lit., from force to force] like emissaries, and no person could force them away, either by firing arrows or throwing stones, or anything else. The king and the ministers were very puzzled, as were all, because they had never heard of or seen anything like it. The king sent envoys to all the provinces of his kingdom to gather all the wise and knowledgeable men, counselors, and sorcerers, and wizards, to journey and come to the king on the appointed day. And they all convened and came to the king. According to the king's command, a message passed through the camp from the king, saying that if anyone could tell the king what this thing was and what it symbolized, the king would give him his daughter in marriage and half the kingdom in his lifetime, and the second half after his death. They came from afar and said to the king: Your majesty, this symbolizes famine and drought. And others said that he would beget sons and bury them, and yet another said this, and that one said that. And none of their words convinced the king. The king said: Neither this one nor that [convinces me], for they do not have the spirit of life in their midst to say things, because they speak lies. And the king sat on the ground, bitter and angry and much saddened,

E. וימן י"י דג גדול ויבלע אותו,[8] ויוליכו למקום רחוק, ויקח אותו שם במלכות אחד. וישב שם על שפת הים, וראה אותו רועה אחד שהיה רועה למלך, וראה אותו ערום בלי לבוש. והלך אליו ואמר לו: בני, <מה> מעשיך ומאין באתה ומאיזה מקום אתה? א"ל: עברי אנכי ואת א-להי השמים אני ירא, אשר עשה את הים ואת היבשה. והייתי בספינה בים, ויבא י"י רוח חזק מאד וישבר את האנייה אשר הייתי בה, וימן י"י לי דג אחד ויוליכני י"י הנה. א"ל: יודע אתה שום מלאכה בעולם? א"ל: הן. א"ל: מה מלאכה ידעת? א"ל: רועה צאן עבדך <~~מע~~> מנעורי ועד עתה. א"ל: אם כן שב עמי ושמור צאני, ואני אתן את שכרך. וישב עמו וילבשהו ויאכילהו ויאהבהו מאד, וי"י ברך אותו בגללו. וישם כל אשר לו בידו.[9]

F. פעם אחת ישב המלך בביתו עם שריו ועבדיו. ויאספו על ביתו עורבים לרוב (ה) חיל גדול מאד מאד, עד שהיה כל מכסה הבית מכוסה מעורבים. ונחלקו לשתי כיתות בשני צידי הבית. ובין שתי הכיתות היו שלשה עורבים, שני זכרים ונקבה אחת ביניהם. [335א] ואותן השלשה יושבין שם, ואינם מזיזין ממקומן. והיו שני עורבים אחרים הולכים מחיל אל חיל כמו שלוחים, ואין אדם יכול להבריח אותם לא בשביל יריית חצים, ולא בשביל <~~זקית~~> זריקת אבנים, ולא בשביל דבר אחר. תמהו המלך והשרים מאד וכל רואיהם יתמהו, כי לא שמעו כזאת ולא ראו כאלה. שלח המלך בכל מדינות מלכותו לקבוץ ולאסוף כל חכם ונבון יועץ וחרטום ואשף לנוד ולבוא אל המלך ליום נועד.[10] ויועדו כולם ויבואו אל המלך, ויצו המלך ויעבר קול במחנה מאת המלך לאמר, כל איש אשר יודע להגיד אל המלך דבר זה ומה המשל הזה, יתן לו המלך בתו לאשה, וחצי מלכותו בחייו וכולו לאחר מיתתו.[11] ויבאו מקצתם ויאמרו למלך: אדוני המלך, זה משל של רעב ושל בצורת. ומקצתם אמרו שהוא מוליד בנים וקובר, וזה אומר ככה וזה אומר ככה. ולא נכנסו דבריהם לתוך לב המלך. ויאמר המלך: לא זה וזה, שאין רוח חיים בקרבו לומר דברים שיכנסו לאוזני, כי כולם דוברי כזב הם. וישב המלך לארץ מר וזעף ויתעצב אל לבו, ולא רצה לאכול ולשתות. ויבואו כולם לנחמו וימאן להתנחם.

---

8. השוו יונה ב, א: "וימן ה' דג גדול לבלע את יונה".

9. השוו בראשית לג, ד.

10. השוו מגילת אסתר, ב, ג: "ויפקד המלך פקידים בכל מדינות מלכותו ויקבצו את כל נערה בתולה טובת מראה". בראשית מא, ח: "וישלח [פרעה] ויקרא את כל חרטמי מצרים ואת כל חכמיה [. . .] ואין פותר אותם לפרעה."

11. השוו שם, ה, ג: "מה לך אסתר המלכה ומה בקשתך עד חצי המלכות וינתן לך".

and wished neither to eat nor drink. And all came to console him, and he refused to be consoled.

G. When the young man saw all the sorrow that the king was suffering, and when he heard about the vow to give such honor to whomever would tell what this meant, he arose in his capacity as a wise and cautious man and went to the king's garden, to the opening of his bedroom, and wished to enter there to speak to the king. The guards saw that his clothes were ragged and his hair unkempt, as he had been in the field with his sheep, but he was very handsome and lovely to behold. The king's guards said to him: What is your business with the king? He said: If you will, I wish to speak with the king and tell him that which is in his heart, and I will tell him everything he wants [to know]. The guards ran to the king and told him, saying: Your majesty, may all who know you be blessed. There is a young man at the door who wishes to speak to you and says that he will tell you that which is in your heart. The king said: Let him enter. The young man came before him and bowed down. He said: Long live the king. I am a young man, and all your wise men are old, and God has given me knowledge and wisdom to tell the king that which is in your heart. It is not from me but rather from the Almighty, who has revealed His secret to His servant. And you, your majesty, have vowed to give your daughter and half your kingdom to whomever will tell you, and your entire kingdom after your soul is bound up in the bundle of life. He said to him: Well spoken. I thus vowed, and I will keep it. [The young man said:] I will tell you what this is and why all the ravens have gathered, and I will tell you the truth of what I say in front of everyone, and may my words be good and right [2 Samuel 15:3]. And they all came to hear the words of the young man.

H. He said: Your majesty, listen to the words of my mouth and hear [335b] the sound of my words [Deuteronomy 32:1]. Once there was a great famine all over the land, and the birds could not find enough to eat in the fields. And understand, your majesty, my words and know that the three ravens that you see—two are male and one in the middle is female. She is the wife of the raven sitting at her right. And in the year of the famine, he drove out his wife and said to her: Go on your way to any place you wish, because it is enough for me to find food for myself to eat, and I cannot help you. The female went on her way and found the raven who sits at her left. He said to her: Who are you, my daughter, and why are you all alone? The female answered and said: Sir, know that my husband drove me out because of the famine, and he said, It is enough for me to find food for myself to eat. He said to her: My wife has just died, and I have no partner. If you wish to be with me, I will feed you

G. כיון שראה הנער כל הצער הזה שהמלך עושה, והנדר שנדר לעשות כל הכבוד הזה למי שיגיד לו מה אלה לו, קם במעמדו כחכם וזהיר ועלה אל גינת ביתן המלך אל פתח חדר משכבו, ורצה ליכנס שם לדבר אל המלך. ויראוהו השוערים, בגדיו פרומים וראשו פרוע כאשר היה בשדה עם צאנו, אבל היה מאד יפה תואר ויפה מראה. ויאמרו לו שוערי המלך: מה טיבך אצל המלך? ויאמר להם: אם רצונכם אני רוצה לדבר אל המלך ואגיד לו את אשר עם לבבו, וכל אשר ירצה אגיד לו. וירוצו השוערים ויגידו למלך ויאמרו לו: אדונינו המלך יהי מכירך ברוך, יש נער אחד עומד בפתח החדר ורוצה לדבר אליך, ואומר שיגיד לך כל אשר עם לבבך. ויאמר המלך יבא. ויבא הנער לפניו, וישתחו לאפיו ארצה. ויאמר: יחי המלך לעולם, הנה צעיר אנכי לימים וכל חכמיך ישישים, ונתן הא-להים בי דעת ותבונה להגיד למלך את אשר עם לבבו, ולא מאתי כי אם מאת הקב"ה אשר גלה סודו לעבדו.[12] ואתה אדוני המלך נדרת ליתן בתך וחצי מלכותך לאשר יגיד לך וכל מלכותך, לאחר אשר תנוח נפשך בצרור החיים. א"ל: כן דברת, כך נשבעתי ואקימה. אומר לך מה זה ועל מה זה נקבצו שם כל העורבים, ואמיתת הדבר אומר לך לעין כל, ותהיו דברי אמיתיים ונכוחים.[13] ויבואו כולם לשמוע דברי הנער.

H. ויען ויאמר: אדוני המלך, הט אזנך לאמרי פי ושמע [335ב] לקול מילתי.[14] פעם אחת היה רעב גדול בכל הארץ, ולא היו העופות יכולים למצוא די סיפוקם בשדות. ובין תבין אדוני המלך לדברי, דע כי השלשה עורבים שאתה רואה השנים זכרים והאחת באמצע נקבה היא. והיא אשתו של אותו עורב היושב לימינה. ובשנת הרעב גירש אשתו ואמר לה: לכי לדרכך לאיזה מקום שתרצי, כי די לי למצוא די סיפוקי ולא יכולתי לעזור לך. הלכה הנקבה לדרכה, ומצאה זה העורב היושב לשמאלה. ויאמר לה: מי את בתי ואנה תלכי יחידה? ענתה הנקבה ואמרה לו: אדוני, דע כי גרשני בעלי מפני הרעב, ואמר די לו למצוא ספוקו. אמר לה: הנה מתה אשתי ואין לי זוג. אם תרצי להיות עמי אזון ואפרנס אותך כפי יכולתי, ובלבד שתהיה אשתי ולא תניחי אותי בשביל אחר לעולם. אמרה לו טובים השנים מן האחד (קהלת ד, ט), כן אעשה כאשר דברת. ויבא זה העורב, ויקחה לו לאשה. ויהיו שניהם יחד, ופירנס אותה כל שני הרעבון. ועתה באו שני השבע, ורוצה בעלה הראשון ליקחיה כבתחילה. ועתה זה אומר: כלכלתיה בשני רעבון ולקחתי אותה לי לאשה כי גרשתה אותה, ועתה באתה לגזול אותה ממני כשהשבע בא לעולם. זה אומר ככה וזה אומר ככה, ובאו לדין. ולכן נקבצו כל העורבים האילו כי הם אינם יודעים הדין, ולשמוע ממך הדבר והדין באו כולם. וזה לך האות, אחר אשר תאמר מה שנראה לך מזה הדין, ילכו כולם על המחוייב ויהרגוהו וישליכו אותו בפני רגליך. ועתה אמור הדין כאשר נראה בעיניך, למי יהיה משפט הנקבה להיות לו לאשה. עמד המלך וכל שריו ועבדיו, ותמהו ורהו[15] על השמועה שהם שומעים.

12. השוו, בראשית מא, טז.
13. השוו שמואל ב, טו, ג.
14. השוו דברים, לב, א.
15. רהו – פחדו.

and support you as best I can, if you become my wife and never leave me for another. She said: Two are better than one [Ecclesiastes 4:9], and I will do as you said. And the raven took her as his wife. They two lived together, and he supported her during the time of the famine. And now the time of plenty has come, and the first husband wants to take her back as they were in the beginning. And the other one said: I supported her in the days of the famine, because you drove her out. And now that the time of plenty has come to the world, you have come to steal her from me. This says one thing, and the other says something else, and they have come to be judged. That is why all these ravens have gathered, because they do not know the law, and they have all come to hear you pronounce the judgment. And this shall be a sign to you, after you have spoken the judgment as you see fit, all will go to the one against whom you have decided and kill him, and cast him at your feet. And now pronounce the judgment as you see fit, to whom is entitled to have the female as his wife. The king and all his ministers and servants stood up and were amazed and fearful at what they had heard.

I. The king went to consult with all his ministers and servants, and they all said that the raven that had driven her out had no right to take her back as his wife, because he had driven her out during the years of famine. And the one who took her in and supported her should have her as his wife. When the decision emerged from the king's mouth, they [the ravens] all arose against the one against whom the king had decided, and struck him with their wings and wounded and killed him and cast him at the king's feet. And they all went on their way. When the king saw this, he said: Since God has informed you of all this, there is no one so discerning and wise as you are. You will be my deputy, and I will give you my daughter. Only in my throne will I be greater than you.

J. And meanwhile, the young man's father grew poor, becoming completely impoverished unlike any poverty ever seen, for nothing was left to him and his wife, not even to cover them, and they were naked and barefoot. The young man said to the king: Your majesty, if I have found favor in your eyes to grant the wish that I will request of you, then I will know you want me [cf. Esther 5:8]. He said: I will fulfill whatever you wish. He said: Let the king send out a message to his entire kingdom that there should not remain [336a] a single old man or woman, poor or rich, who does not attend the wedding of his daughter, and I wish to wash their hands with water when they all come to eat. And letters were sent by couriers to all the king's provinces to come to the wedding ceremony of the king's daughter [cf. Esther 8:10]. And people came from every side and every corner. And his father

I. הלך המלך ויועץ לכל שריו ועבדיו, ויאמרו כולם אותו שגירש אותה אין לו משפט לשוב אותה לו לאשה כי גרשה אותה בשני רעבון. והואיל שזכה זה בה ופירנס אותה, לו תהיה האשה. הדבר יצא מפי המלך וקמו כולם על המחוייב והכוהו בכנפיהם ופצעוהו והרגוהו, והשליכו אותו לפני רגלי המלך. והלכו כולם לדרכיהם. כיון שראה המלך כך אמר: אחרי אשר הודיע א-להים אותך את כל זאת, אין נבון וחכם כמוך. אתה תהיה משנה ואתן לך בתי, רק הכסא אגדל ממך.[16]

J. ובין כך ובין כך העני אבי הבחור, ונעשה עני גמור לא נראה כעניותו מעולם. כי לא נשאר לו ולאשתו מאומה אפילו כדי לכסות אותם כי הם ערומים, ויחיפים הם. אמר הבחור למלך: אדוני המלך, אם מצאתי חן בעיניך לתת את שאלתי אשר אשאל מעמך,[17] בזאת אדע כי חפצת בי. אמר לו: כל שאלתך אמלא. א"ל: תשלח המלך להודיע בכל מלכותו שלא ישאר [336א] זקן וזקנה עני ועשיר שלא יבואו לחופת בתו, וגם אני רוצה ליתן מים לרחוץ ידיהם כשיבואו כולם לאכול. ונשלוח ספרים אל כל מדינות מלכותו ביד הרצים לבא לחופת בת המלך. ויבואו כולם מכל צד ומכל פנה. וגם אביו ואמו באו כמו כן, כי כן מצות המלך. ובאו אביו ואמו וישבו להם אחורי הדלת, כי ערומים ויתבוששו.[18]

16. השוו בראשית מא, לט-מ: "אין נבון וחכם כמוך. אתה תהיה על ביתי [. . .] רק הכסא אגדל ממך". וראו להלן רמיזות נוספות לפרשת יוסף ואחיו.
17. השוו אסתר, ז, ג: "ותאמר אסתר המלכה ותאמר, אם מצאתי חן בעינים המלך [. . .] תינתן לי נפשי בשאלתי ועמי בבקשתי". וכן אסתר ה, ח: "אם מצאתי חן בעיני המלך ואם על המלך טוב לתת את שאלתי ולעשות את בקשתי".
18. השוו בראשית ב, כה: "ויהיו שניהם ערומים [. . .] ולא יתבוששו".

and mother also came, because that is what the king commanded. And his father and mother came and sat behind the door, for they were naked and were ashamed.

K. The young man went to every side and every corner to search for them, until he found them behind the door. He said to them: Come, blessed of God, why do you stand? Here, come inside the house with the others and do not sit here. They said: Sir, do not be angry with us, and if you don't mind, leave us here, for we are naked and barefoot, and we are ashamed to go in with the others. The young man went and ordered his chief steward: Bring this man and woman into the house, wash them and oil them and give them food and drink of all the good things that you can find, and dress them in clothes of silk and embroidery. Do everything that gives them pleasure, and be careful to do whatever they tell you and say nothing to anyone. Do this for three days as much as you can. And that is what he did.

L. On the fourth day, the young man came to see his father and mother, and he saw that they were happy and satisfied. He said to them: Who are you, and where do you live? Do you have any children, and what do they do? They said: We are Hebrews, and we live in such and such a place. We have never had but one son. I was a rich merchant up to the present, and now in my old age, I have fallen into poverty as you have seen, and now God has allowed us to find favor in your eyes. May God reward you for all these good things, because we have found favor in your eyes, and you have given us support and sustenance this day. He said to them: That son that you spoke of—where is he? Please tell me if he is dead or alive and where he is. And they were unable to restrain themselves any longer, because they felt sorry and began to weep [cf. Genesis 45:1]. He said: Why are you crying? Do you lack anything or desire anything to eat or drink? They said: No, sir, we shall leave nothing out about that son that we had. And they told him everything that had happened to them and all that had occurred, leaving nothing out. They raised their voices in great weeping, and he too felt pity and wept, and he wept together with them intensely. He called out: Remove everyone from my presence, and there was no one with him when he made himself known to them. He said: I am your son who you cast into the sea, and this is my mother. And because I did not want to tell you why I was laughing, you threw me into the sea. And God caused a great fish to come and swallow me. And he told them the whole matter. Now do not be grieved or angry with yourselves, for God sent me before you to preserve life. And now I will be the son-in-law of the king and deal benevolently with you, and you will be at my head. And they were unable to respond, because they were frightened of him.

K. הלך הבחור ובקש בכל צד ובכל פנה אחריהם, עד שמצאם אחורי הדלת. ויאמר להם: בואו ברוכי י"י למה תעמדו, הנה בואו אל תוך הבית עם האחרים ואל תשבו פה. אמרו לו: אדוני אל יחר בעיניך ואם רצונך הניחנו הנה. כי אנחנו ערומים ויחיפים ויש לנו בשת ליכנס עם האחרים. הלך הבחור ויצו לאשר על ביתו: הבא אותו האיש ואת אשתו הביתה, ורחצם וסכם והאכילם והשקם מכל טוב שתוכל למצוא, והלבישם בגדי שש ורקמה. ועשה להם כל הנאותם, והוי זהיר למצותן לכל אשר יצוו אליך, ואל תאמר דבר זה לשום אדם. וכה תעשה שלשה ימים להם, כל מה שתוכל. וכן עשה.

L. ויהי ביום הרביעי, ויבא הבחור לראות אביו ואמו. וירא אותם והנם שמחים וטובי לב. אמר להם: מי אתם ובאיזה מקום אתם דרים, היש לכם שום בנים ומה מעשיכם? אמרו לו: עברים אנחנו, ובמקום פלוני אנחנו דרים, ולא היה לנו מעולם כי אם בן אחד. ועשיר וסוחר הייתי מעודי ועד היום הזה. ועתה נפלתי בזקנה ובעניות כאשר ראית, ועתה נתננו א-להים למצוא חן וחסד לפניך. ויהי מכירך ברוך אשר גמלתנו כל הטובות האילו, כי מצאנו חן בעיניך לתת אותנו למחיה ולחיותינו כיום הזה. אמר להם: אותו בן שאמרתם היכן הוא? הגידו נא לי אם הוא מת או חי, ובאיזה מקום הוא.[19] ולא יכלו עוד להתאפק, כי נכמרו רחמיהם לבכות.[20] ויאמר להם: למה אתם בוכים, <~~וה~~> וכי חסירים אתם שום דבר או תאבים אתם לאכול ולשתות? ויאמרו: לא אדוני, לא נכחד מאדוני דבר מה היה המעשה מאותו בן שהיה לנו. ויספרו לו את כל המוצאות אותם ואת כל קורותם, ולא כחדו. וישאו את קולם בבכי גדול וגם נכמרו רחמיו לבכות, ויבך עמהם עד כי הגדיל. ויקרא הוציאו כל איש מעלי,[21] ולא עמד איש אתו בהתודע אותו להם. ויאמר: אני הוא בנך אשר השלכתני אל הים, וזאת אמי. ובשביל שלא רציתי לומר לך מפני מה שחקתי, השלכת אותי אל הים. וימן ה' א-להים דג גדול ובלעני. וסיפר להם כל העניין. ועתה אל תעצבו ואל יחר בעיניכם, כי למחיה שלחני א-להים לפניכם.[22] ועתה אהיה חתן למלך ואטיב לכם, ואתם תהיו לי לראש. והם לא יכלו לענות אותו, כי נבהלו מפניו.

19. השוו בראשית מג, כח: "השלום אביכם הזקן [. . .] העודנו חי"?
20. השוו שם, מה, א: "ולא יכל יוסף להתאפק לכל הנצבים עליו".
21. השוו שם: "הוציאו כל איש מעלי".
22. השוו שם, פסוק ה: "ועתה אל תעצבו ואל יחר בעיניכם [. . .] כי למחיה שלחני א-להים לפניכם".

M. And it became known that [336b] his father and mother had come, and this found favor in the eyes of the king and ministers. And the king said to him: Your father and mother have come to you, settle them in the best part of the land. The young man arose, and they bowed down and prostrated themselves before him. He said: Long live his majesty the king forever. And they held a great feast and wedding, and finally he was crowned king, to fulfill the verse: "The stone that the builders rejected has now become the cornerstone" [Psalms 118:22].

M. ויודע הדבר כי [336ב] באו אמו ואביו, וייטב הדבר בעיני המלך והשרים. ויאמר לו המלך: אביך ואמך באו אליך, במיטב הארץ הושב אותם.[23] ויקם הבחור וישתחו לו אפים ארצה.[24] ויאמר: יחי אדוני המלך לעולם. ועשו המשתה והחופה ולסוף נעשה מלך. לקיים מה שנאמר: אבן מאסו הבונים היתה לראש פינה [תהלים קיח, כב]"

23. השוו שם, פסוק י: "וישבת בארץ גשן", וכן בראשית מז, ו: "ארץ מצרים לפניך היא במיטב הארץ הושב את אביך ואת אחיך ישבו בארץ גשן".

24. השוו שם, מח, יב: "ויוצא יוסף [. . .] וישתחו לאפיו ארצה".

67. The Maiden in the Tower (336b–337a)

A. Once King Solomon provoked King Ḥiram of Tyre, and they attacked one another and waged a war. And there was a river between them, and across the river was the army of the king of Tyre in a certain forest, and they set up their tents there. And Solomon and his army were on the other side of the river. And it was summer, and the sun was shining, and the day was very hot, and they could not bear the great heat. What did Solomon do? He sent for birds to flock and come to him, to spread their wings, hovering over the soldiers to shade him and his army with their wings. And many birds came and spread their wings above them, covering them to shade all his soldiers, for in his wisdom Solomon was the king of all the animals and beasts and birds, as it says: "For he was wiser than all men" [1 Kings 5:11]. All the birds raised their voices, and each sang in its own way.

B. The sound of their voices reached the camp of Ḥiram, king of Tyre. Ḥiram said: And what is that sound I hear? His servants said: Your majesty, we do not know. He said: Go and see what that clamor is. They emerged from their tents and saw the birds spreading their wings over all of Solomon's soldiers. They said: This is what we have seen. He said: Who has heard or seen such a thing?! I will not be satisfied until I have seen it for myself. What did he do? He took two horsemen with him, and they went to Solomon's camp and arrived there unarmed. And when Solomon saw Ḥiram approaching him, he was very surprised and said: Why have you come to me? Ḥiram said: To see the great wonders that God does for you. Solomon took him in his arms and embraced him and showed him great honor, and sat at his side as they spoke with one another. And as they were talking, an eagle came and withdrew one of his wings, and the sun shone on Solomon's head. Solomon said to the eagle: Why have you done this, and why have you disobeyed my commandment? The eagle said: Your majesty, do not be angry because I drew toward my female to speak to her, and she told me, Did you know that Joshua, the high priest, will die, and his daughter will marry a bastard? And I was very upset at this, and that is why I drew myself toward her. He said: In that case, I will guard the girl carefully, and you did well to reveal this to me. Ḥiram said to King Solomon: What did you tell the eagle, and what did it respond? He said: Such and such and told [337a] him everything. He said: If so, if you rule over the high and the low, who can withstand you? [Indeed] you are worthy of dominion. Blessed are you and blessed are all your servants who serve you. They made peace between them, as it says: "And there was peace between Ḥiram and Solomon; and they made a peace pact" [1 Kings 5:26].

67. הנערה הכלואה במגדל (336ב–337א)

A. מעשה בשלמה המלך שהיה מתגרה עם חירם מלך צׄר. ויבואו זה על זה. ויערכו אתם מלחמה. והיה ביניהם נהר אחד, ובעבר הנהר היה חיל מלך צׄר ביער אחד, ויטעו שם אהליהם. ושלמה וחילו היו מצד אחר לנהר. ובימי הקיץ היה, ויזרח להם השמש. והיה היום חם מאד, ולא יכלו לסבול החמימות הגדול. מה עשה שלמה, שלח אחרי עופות להקבץ ולבא אליו ולפרוש כנפיהם להיות סוככים עליו ועל חיילותיו, להיות להם לצל. ובאו עופות לרוב מאוד ויפרשו כנפיהם למעלה מהם, סוככים בכנפיהם עליהם, ויעשו להם צל על כל חיילותיו, כי שלמה היה מלך על כל החיות והבהמות והעופות בחכמתו, שנ' בו: ויחכם מכל האדם [מלכים א, ה, יא]. וישאו כל העופות את קולם וירונו כל אחד לפי עניינו.

B. וילך קולם עד מחנה חירם מלך צר. ויאמר חירם: ומה קול הזה באזני? ויאמרו עבדיו: אדוני, לא ידענו. אמר להם: צאו וראו מה קול ההמון הזה. יצאו מאהליהם, וראו העופות פרושות בכנפיהם על כל חיל שלמה. אמרו לו: כך ראינו. אמר להם: מי שמע כזאת מי ראה כאלה, לא יתקרר דעתי עד שאלך אני בעצמי. מה עשה, לקח שני פרשים עמו והלכו אל מחנה שלמה, ובאו שם בלא שום כלי זין. וכשראה שלמה את חירם בא אליו תמה ואמר לו: מה זה כי באתה אלי? א"ל: לראות נפלאות גדולות א-להים שהוא עושה עבורך. לקחו שלמה בין זרועותיו ויחבקהו ויעש לו כבוד גדול, וישב אותו בצדו וידברו יחד. וכאשר היו מדברים יחד בא נשר אחד ומשך אליו אחת מכנפיו, וזרח השמש על ראש שלמה. אמר שלמה לנשר: מדוע עשית את הדבר הזה ועברתה מצותי? א"ל הנשר: אדוני, אל יחר בעיניך כי משכתי אותי אל נקיבתי לדבר <עמה> ואמר{ה} אליה֗, ידעת כי יהושע כהן גדול ימות ובתו תינשא לממזר אחד? ומזה חרה לי מאוד, ועל זה נמשכתי אצלה. א"ל: מזה אשמור הנערה בטוב, ויפה עשית לגלות לי את הדבר הזה. א"ל חירם למלך שלמה: מה דברת אל הנשר ומה השיב לך? א"ל כך וכך, וסיפר [337א] לו הכל. א"ל: אם כך, שמלכת על העליונים ועל התחתונים, מי יוכל להיות כנגדך? לך יאתה מלוכה. אשריך ואשרי עבדיך המשרתים אותך. הלכו ועשו שלום ביניהם. וזהו שכתוב: ויהי שלום בין חירם ובין שלמה ויכרתו ברית שניהם [מלכים א, ה, כו].

C. What did Solomon do? He sent for the daughter of Joshua, the high priest, and placed her under guard in a tower. He appointed a woman to guard over her and locked all the doors to the tower, and no one in the world could approach them. They obtained their food by pulling on a rope. Once an eagle flew over them and dropped a baby into the tower from between its feet. And the baby was a bastard that had been cast away by its mother, and the eagle came and took it and brought it there. And the women fed and washed and anointed him, and he grew up with them there. And they fell in love, the young man and the daughter of Joshua, until he came upon her and she conceived from him.

D. One day, Solomon arrived there and opened the door and found that man there and was greatly amazed. He said: Who are you, and how did you get here? And they told him the whole story. Solomon said: May the name of the Almighty who fulfilled his good word be blessed. And of me it is said: "For he was wiser than all men," but my wisdom did not reach this far, for I wished to cancel the decree but was unable to do so.

C. מה עשה שלמה, שלח אחר בתו של יהושע כהן גדול, וישם אותה למשמרת בתוך מגדל אחד. וישם עמה אשה לשומרה. ויסגור כל דלתות המגדל. ולא היה יכול שום אדם בעולם לבא אליהן. והן מביאין מאכלן בחבל שהן מושכין אליהן. פעם אחת בא נשר פורח עליהן, ונפל לתוך המגדל מבין רגליו תינוק אחד ביניהן. והוא היה ממזר. כי השליכו אמו ובא הנשר ולקחו והביאו שם. והן האכילוהו ורחצוהו וסכוהו, ונתגדל עמהן שם מאד. והיו אוהבים זה את זה הנער (ואת) [את] בתו של יהושע עד שבא עליה, ותהר האשה ממנו.

D. יום אחד בא שלמה לשם ויפתח את הדלת וימצא שם אותו האיש, ויתמה מאד. ויאמר לו: מי אתה והיאך באתה הנה? וסיפרו לו כל העניין. אמר שלמה: יהי שם י"י מבורך אשר קיים דברו הטוב. ועלי נאמר ויחכם מכל האדם אך לא חכמתי הנה שרציתי לבטל הגזירה ולא יכולתי.

68. The War of Jacob and His Sons with Nineveh (337a–338b)

A. [337b] A tale of Jacob and his sons, how they took the city of Shekhem. It says: "And they journeyed: and the terror of God was on the cities that were round about them" [Genesis 35:5].

B. Our rabbis said: When Shimon and Levi killed Shekhem, fear and trembling fell on all the nations around them. They said: Two of Jacob's sons killed the great city of Shekhem. If they all gather together, it will be all the more so. What did Jacob do? He collected all his property to go to Isaac, his father. And when he had traveled for eight days, he encountered a very great army like sand on the seashore. And that army had set out from Nineveh to collect tax from the whole world and conquer the entire world to subjugate it. And when that army arrived near Shekhem, they heard the news of what Jacob's sons had done. At once, the people of Nineveh became very angry and rose up against Jacob to fight him. And when Jacob saw that army, he said to his sons: Fear not, my sons, for the Almighty will fight for you against your enemies. Just remove any foreign gods from in your midst and purify yourselves and change your robes [Genesis 35:2]. And Jacob fastened his sword on his right hand and his bow on his left and strode, facing that army. And he began by killing ten thousand and [then] eighty thousand of their weakest.

68. מלחמות בני יעקב: מלחמת נינוה (337א–338ב[1])

A. מעשה היאך לקחו יעקב ובניו את עיר שכם.[2] כתיב ויסעו ויהי חתת א-להים [בראשית לה, ה].[3]

B. אמרו רבותינו:[4] כשהרגו שמעון ולוי את שכם, נפלה פחד ורעדה על כל האומות שסביבותם.[5] אמרו: שני בני יעקב הרגו כרך גדול של שכם,[6] אם יתקבצו כולם על אחת כמה וכמה. מה עשה יעקב, אסף כל רכושו[7] ללכת אל יצחק אביו.[8] וכיון שהלך מהלך שמונה ימים, פגע בחיל כבד מאוד כחול אשר על שפת הים.[9] ואותו חיל יצא מנינוה לקחת מס מכל העולם, ולכבש את כל העולם תחתיו.[10] וכיון שבא אותו חיל בארץ[11] קרוב לשכם שמעו השמועה[12] מה שעשו בני יעקב,[13] מיד חרה אפם של אנשי נינוה, ובאו כנגד יעקב להלחם עמו.[14] וכיון שהרגיש יעקב באותו חיל[15] אמר יעקב לבניו: אל תיראו בני, הקב"ה ילחם לכם כנגד אויביכם רק הסירו אלהי הנכר אשר בתוככם, והטהרו והחליפו שמלותיכם.[16] וחגר יעקב חרבו בימינו וקשתו בשמאלו,[17] והלך כנגד אותו חיל, והתחיל להרוג בהם, כנגד עשרה ושמונים אלפים מן החלשים שבהם.[18]

---

1. הדרה זו של "מלחמות בני יעקב בנינווה", אשר נודע גם כ"מדרש ויסעו", מתבססת על שלושה כתבי יד מן המאות הי"ג–ט"ו, שחשיבותם למחקר הנוכחי היא בזיקותיהם לאשכנז ובשיוכם לימי הביניים החל מן המאה השלוש עשרה: (א) כ"י וטיקן 323 (113א–113ב, מקוטע; 171א–171ב, כתיבה אשכנזית מרובעת, מאות י"ג–י"ד); (ב) כ"י ירושלים, מוזיאון ישראל, 180/51/16 (341–342ב, כתיבה איטלקית, מרובעת וכתיבה אשכנזית, מאה ארבע עשרה). במהדורות קודמות, כתב יד זה עדיין לא נבדק כעד נוסח ל"מדרש ויסעו"; (ג) כ"י לונדון-מונטיפיורי 431 (38א–39א, כתיבה איטלקית-אשכנזית, מאה ט"ו). סימניהם להלן: (א) כ"י וטיקן = ט1 (113א–113ב); ט2 (171א–171ב); (ב) כ"י ירושלים, מוזיאון ישראל = ז. (ג) כ"י לונדון-מוטניפיורי = מ. שני כתבי יד אחרים שלא התבססתי עליהם משיקולים שונים הם: כ"י פרנקפורט 35 מן המאה הי"ג–י"ד, הכולל רק את תחילת הסיפור על מלחמת בני יעקב בנינווה; וכ"י ורשה 281 מן המאה הט"ז באיטליה, הכולל נוסח קטוע של הסיפור. ההדרות קודמות התבססו על כתבי יד אחרים: מהדורה אקלקטית של לאוטרבך, שהתבססה בין השאר על כ"י לונדון, הספרייה הבריטית Add. 27089 (Catalogue Margaliyot, 1076); תמר אלכסנדר ויוסף דן, "מדרש ויסעו", על פי כ"י המבורג 150, מתימן, המאה הי"ח.
2. ז, ט2, מ ללא פתיחה זו, ובכותרת: "מדרש ויסעו".
3. ז ויסעו, ויהי חתת אלה' על הערי' וגו'; ט2 ויהי חיתת אל'הים על ההרים אשר סביבותיהם.
4. ל: אמרו חכמים.
5. ט2 נפלה על בני יעקב פחד ורעדה ונתקבצו מכל העולם אומות עליהם להלחם בהם; ל שסביבותם.
6. ט2 חסר: אמרו שני בני יעקב–עמו.
7. מ אסף את כל רכושו.
8. ז ללכת ארצה כנען אל יצחק אביו.
9. ז בהשמטה של "אשר" ושל "על שפת"; ל פגע בו חיל גדול מאוד. והשוו יהושע יא, ד על מלחמת יהושע במלכיהם של שבעת העמים: "ויצאו הם וכל מחניהם עמם עם רב כחול אשר על שפת הים".
10. מ ולכבש כל העולם כולו תחתיו.
11. מ בלי: בארץ.
12. מ שמעו את השמועה.
13. ז, מ בתוספת: לשכם.
14. ט עד כאן מקוטע וחסר.
15. ט חסר; מ מיד אמר יעקב לבניו.
16. השוו בראשית לה, ב: "הסירו את אלהי הנכר אשר בתכֻכם והטהרו והחליפו שמלתיכם".
17. מ ואת קשתו.
18. מ צ' אלפים מן החלשים.

C. His son Judah said to him: My father, you are already tired and fatigued. Allow me to fight them. Jacob said to him: My son, Judah, I know [337b] that your strength and valor are great, and there is none as courageous as you. Your father's fear [i.e., God; cf. Genesis 31:42: "The Fear of Isaac"] will come to your aid. Go and fight them.[1] Judah set out against them with great fury, and his face was like the face of a lion. He fought them and killed a hundred and twenty thousand of the army, all skilled and distinguished warriors. Levi, his brother, came to help him, and the war was won before and behind by Judah and Levi and their brothers. Judah prevailed in the war, and he killed another five thousand of the army, all of them with their swords unsheathed. And Levi came and struck on the right and left, and the army fell before him like the wheat falls before the harvesters.

D. The people of Nineveh said to one another: How much longer will we fight against these destroyers? Let us return to our land lest they kill us and leave not a remnant alive. But the king said to them: Where are the heroes? Where are the great? Where are the mighty? How dare you entertain the thought of returning to your land. Is this the courage [with which] you conquered so many lands and kings and nations, and now you are unable to fight against twelve people? And when the nations and kings that we have conquered and subjugated to give us tax hear, they will unite against us as one and will torment us and do as they will with us. Be strong, the people of Nineveh, the great city, so that your honor and name will grow great, and you will not become prey before your enemies. When they heard the words of their king, they agreed to continue fighting. They sent messengers to all the lands they had conquered to come to their aid, and fought a war against Jacob's sons.

E. Jacob said to his sons: My sons, be strong and valiant [lit. men], and fight your enemies. And Jacob's sons divided into twelve distant from one another, and Jacob, their father, marching before them with his sword fastened on his right and his bow on his left. That day, Jacob fought before and behind, striking them very mightily. And two thousand people were gathered against Jacob alone to strike him, but Jacob sprang and leapt two thousand cubits in one leap, so that they did not know where he was. Jacob prevailed over the army, killing some two hundred and twenty thousand that day, all warriors. When evening came, and Jacob thought he might rest from them, ninety thousand suddenly rose up. Jacob stood in the breach, and he began to kill them as before. [Then] the sword in Jacob's hand broke. When Jacob saw that his sword had broken, he took large stones and ground them like lime

1. From this point on the linguistic stratum becomes biblical, typified by the "waw conversive." This is obvious in the Hebrew version of the tale.

C. א"ל יהודה בנו: אבי, כבר יגעת ויעפת הניחני[19] להלחם כנגדם. א"ל יעקב: יהודה בני ידעתי [337ב] את כחך ואת גבורתך כי רב הוא ואין כמוך בעולם בגבורה, פחד אביך יהיה בעזרך,[20] לך והלחם כנגדם. וילך[21] יהודה כנגדם בחימה עזה ופניו כפני אריה. וילחם בהם ויהרוג בהם מן החיל[22] שנים עשר ריבוא, כולם אנשי מלחמה ואנשי שם. ויבא לוי אחיו לעזור לו,[23] ותהי המלחמה פנים ואחור ליהודה וללוי אחיו.[24] ותגבר יד המלחמה על יהודה, ויהרוג מן החיל עוד חמשת אלפים כולם שולף חרב.[25] ויבא לוי ויך בימינו ובשמאלו, ויפלו החיל לפניו[26] כאשר יפול התבואה לפני הקוצרים.[27]

D. ויאמרו אנשי נינוה איש אל רעהו:[28] עד מתי נלחם עם המשחיתים האילו,[29] נחזור ~~לדברינו~~ לארצינו פן ישחיתו בנו עד בלתי[30] השאיר לנו שריד. ויאמר להם המלך: אי גבורים אי אדירים אי חזקים,[31] מה עלתה בדעתכם שאמרתם לשוב לארצכם, וכי זו היא גבורתכם שכבשתם כמה ארצות וכמה מלכים[32] וכמה אומות, ועתה אינכם יכולים להלחם כנגד שנים עשר איש? וכאשר ישמעו האומות והמלכים שכבשנו תחת ידינו לתת לנו מס ויתאספו עלינו כולם כאיש אחד, ויתעוללו בנו ויעשו בנו כרצונם. ויתחזקו [התחזקו] אנשי נינוה העיר הגדולה ויגדל כבודכם ושמכם, ולא תהיו לכם לבז לפני אויביכם.[33] ויהי כאשר שמעו את דברי מלכם ויאותו להלחם עוד, וישלחו שלוחים בכל הארצות שכבשו לבא להם לעזרה.[34] ויערכו מלחמה עם בני יעקב.

E. ויאמר יעקב לבניו: בניי התחזקו והיו לאנשים,[35] והלחמו בשונאיכם. ויתחלקו בני יעקב לשנים עשר זה רחוק מזה, ויעקב אביהם הולך לפניהם, וחרבו בימינו וקשתו בשמאלו. וילחם יעקב ביום ההוא ותהי המלחמה פנים ואחור, ויך בהם מכה רבה מאוד[36] ונקבצו אלפים איש על יעקב לבדו להכותו,[37] ויקפוץ יעקב וידלג באלפים אמה בדילוג אחד עד שלא ידעו היכן הוא.[38] ותגבר יד יעקב על החיל, וישחת ארצה ביום ההוא כעשרים ושתים ריבוא כולם אנשי

19. מ כבר עייפתה ויגעתה, הנח לי להלחם כנגדם; ז כבר יעפת ויגעת הניחני להלחם כנגדם.
20. מ ידעתי שאתה בכוחך ובגבורתך ואין גבור בעל כוח כמותך בעולם, א-להי אביך יהיה בעזרך.
21. מכאן ואילך צורת הפעלים היא מקראית, ומתאפיינת בו"ו ההיפוך.
22. מ וילחם בם ויהרג מן החיל.
23. מ בלי: לעזור לו.
24. מ ותהי המלחמה ללוי ויהודה. בלי: אחיו.
25. מ שלופי חרב.
26. מ ויפלו לפניו החיל.
27. מ התבואה בשדה לפני הקוצרים.
28. מ איש אל אחיו.
29. ז בלי: האילו.
30. מ בלתי
31. מ אי גבורים, אי תקיפים, אי אדירים, אי חזקים.
32. מ מלכיות.
33. מ אויבנו.
34. מ לבוא להלחם לעזרה לאנשי נינוה.
35. מ חסר: לבניו.
36. ז מכה גדולה. מכאן ועד "וישחקם" מחוק או מטושטש.
37. מ וכאשר באו אלפיים איש על יעקב.
38. מ וידלג יעקב כאלפיים אמה בדלוג אחד עד אשר לא ידעו אנא הוא.

and cast them on the faces of the army, and they could not see because of the lime. And when the night came and the sun set, Jacob rested that night.

F. The next day, Judah said to Jacob: You fought yesterday, my father, and you are exhausted and fatigued, and I will fight today. Jacob said to him: Judah, my son Judah, go on and do well. Judah went to fight that day, and when the army saw Judah's face that was like the face of a lion and his teeth that were like the teeth of a lion, they were greatly afraid of him. They fortified themselves to fight against him defiantly, and intensified [338a] the war against Judah very, very greatly. Judah sprang and leapt among the army on this side and that, and struck them repeatedly, like a flea. He struck from the morning, for nine hours, 8,496 men, all with swords unsheathed and bows drawn. He was very fatigued, and Zebulon his brother came on his left and helped him. He fought and killed thirty thousand of them. And when Judah had rested, he arose in rage and fury, gritting his teeth firmly as the skies thunder in the period of Tammuz. The army heard this and fled eighteen miles, and that night Judah rested.

G. The next day, on the third day, the army came to fight and avenge and blew trumpets. Jacob said to his sons: My sons, go and fight your enemies. Issachar and Gad said: Today, we will fight our enemies. Their father said to them: Go and fight, and the rest of your brothers will stand guard until you are tired and fatigued and will help you. Issachar and Gad set out and fought and killed forty-eight thousand of the army that day. The army fled from them in caves, one hundred and twenty thousand. Issachar and Gad came and took [branches] from the trees in the forest and made a big fire at the entrance to the cave. When the fire grew great, the [soldiers of the] army said to one another: Why are we sitting in this cave where we will die from the smoke and fire? Let us go out and fight them, and perhaps we will be saved. They emerged from the cave to the north and prepared to fight against Issachar and Gad, and the war was before and behind. Dan and Naphtali saw and ran swiftly up to the army, and struck on the right and left until they reached their brothers. The four of them fought, Issachar and Gad, Dan and Naphtali.

מלחמה.[39] ויהי לעת ערב כאשר סבר יעקב לנוח מפניהם, ויבאו פתאום תשעים אלף[40] ויקם יעקב[41] ויעמד בפרץ, ויחל להרוג בהם כפעם בפעם, ותשבור החרב אשר ביד יעקב. ויהי כאשר ראה יעקב כי נשברה החרב בידו, לקח[42] מן האבנים הגדולות וישחקם בידו כמו סיד,[43] וישלך על פני החיל[44] ולא יכלו לראות מפני הסיד. ואף כי הגיע הלילה כי בא השמש,[45] וינח יעקב בלילה ההוא.

F. ויהי ממחרת ויאמר יהודה ליעקב: הנה נלחמת אבי אתמול,[46] ואתה עיף ויגע, ואני אלחם היום. ויאמר לו יעקב: יהודה בני, לך והצלח.[47] וילך יהודה וילחם ביום ההוא.[48] וכאשר ראו החיל את פני יהודה שהיו פניו כפני אריה ושיניו כשיני אריה,[49] וייראו ממנו מאד.[50] ויתחזקו להלחם כנגדו ביד רמה,[51] ותגבר [338א] המלחמה על יהודה מאד מאד.[52] וידלג יהודה[53] ויקפוץ בתוך החיל מזה לזה ומזה על זה הלוך והכות, כאשר יעשה הפרעוש.[54] ויך יהודה מן הבק{ר} עד תשעה שעות ביום שמונים אלף וארבע מאות ותשעים ושש, כולם שולף ודורכי קשתות.[55] וייעף יהודה מאד. ויבא זבולון אחיו משמאלו ויעזור לו, וילחם וישחת מהם ארצה שלשים אלף איש. וכאשר נח יהודה עמד בזעפו ובקצפו,[56] ויחרוק שיניו בחזקה כאשר מרעים השמים בתקופת תמוז.[57] וישמעו החיל ~~וינס~~ וינוסו שמונה עשר מיל. וינח יהודה בלילה ההוא.

G. ויהי ממחרת ביום השלישי, ויבאו החיל עוד להלחם ולהנקם,[58] ויתקעו בשופרות. ויאמר יעקב אל בניו: בניי, לכו והלחמו בשונאיכם.[59] ויאמרו יששכר וגד: אנו נלחם היום בשונאינו. ויאמר להם אביהם: לכו והלחמו,[60] ושאר אחיכם יעמדו על המשמר עד אשר תיעפו ותיגעו, ויעזרו לכם. ויצאו יששכר וגד, וילחמו ביום ההוא וישחיתו מן החיל כארבעים ושמונה אלף,

39. מ חסר: כולם.
40. מ צ' אלף איש.
41. מ וירגז יעקב.
42. ז ויקח.
43. מ וישליכם דק כסיד בידו.
44. מ אל החיל.
45. מ כי הגיע וקרבה השמש וקרבה הלילה ויבא השמש.
46. מ אבי הנה אתה נלחמת אתמול.
47. מ יהודה בני: לך והלחם עמהם.
48. מ וילחם עם החיל ביום ההוא.
49. מ תוספת: וקולו כקול אריה.
50. מ חסר: ממנו.
51. מ ויתחזקו להלחם בכלי מלחמתם כנגדו.
52. ט חסר: וידלג יהודה–יצחק אביו.
53. מ ויקפוץ יהודה.
54. מ הלוך והכה כאשר יעשה הפרעוש.
55. מ שולף חרב.
56. מ חסר: עמד.
57. מ השמש.
58. מ ויבא יום ג' החיל עוד להלם והתנקם.
59. מ חסר: לכו.
60. מ לכו והלחמו בשונאיכם היום.

H. On that day, there came a huge multitude like the sand on the seashore to help the people of Nineveh. Jacob's sons saw the immense army and gathered together like one, and stood to strike and kill a countless number of the army. Judah's hand prevailed over the army, and he struck them very mightily, and the entire army fled before him. When Jacob's sons saw the flight of the army, they arose in great fury and pursued them. The army said: Why should we flee from them? Let us fight them. Perhaps we will overcome them, for they are tired. They came and fought against them, and the war was very great. When Jacob saw that his sons were being overcome in the fighting, he arose and leapt up and struck with his right and left, and they fell before him like the grass falls before the beast. And the army began to prevail and separated Judah from his brothers. Jacob saw that Judah gritted his teeth too, and his brothers heard and came to help him. He was exhausted and thirsty and had no water. He inserted his finger in the earth mightily, and water arose up at him. The army saw the rising of the water toward Judah, and they said to one another: I will flee from these destroyers, for God is fighting for them. The entire army fled through the forest. Jacob's sons pursued them and struck a countless number of them mightily [338b], and some of them fled for their lives. And Jacob's sons could not pursue them. They blew their trumpets and returned to their tents and Joseph was not there. And Jacob's brothers were very sorrowful about their brother Joseph and they said: Perhaps they have killed him or taken him captive.

וינוסו מן החיל במערות כנגד שנים עשר ריבוא.[61] ויבאו[62] יששכר וגד, ויקחו מן האילנות אשר ביערים, ויעשו אש גדול לפני פתח המערה.[63] וכאשר רבתה האש[64] אמרו החיל זה לזה: על מה אנחנו יושבים במערה הזאת ונמות מן העשן ומחום האש, נלךם ונלחם כנגדם אולי נינצל. ויצאו מן המערה לצדדין דרך צפוני, ויערכו מלחמה כנגד יששכר וגד. ותהי המלחמה[65] פנים ואחור. ויראו דן נפתלי וירוצו בחוזקה עד החיל,[66] ויכו מימינם ומשמאלם, עד אשר באו אצל אחיהם. וילחמו ארבעתן, יששכר וגד דן ונפתלי.[67]

H. ויבאו ביום ההוא משאר ארצות לעזור לאנשי נינוה, עם רב כחול אשר על שפת הים,[68] ויראו בני יעקב את החיל הגדול הזה, ויקבצו כולם כאיש אחד, ויעמדו להכות ולהרוג[69] בחיל מכה רבה מאד בלי מספר. ותגבר יד יהודה על החיל, ויך בהם מכה רבה מאד.[70] וינוסו כל החיל מפניו.[71] וכראות בני יעקב את מנוסת החיל ויקומו בחימה עזה וירדפו אחריהם ויאמרו החיל: למה ננוס מפניהם, נלחם כנגדם.[72] אולי נגביר עליהם, כי עייפים המה. ויבאו וילחמו כנגדם ותהי המלחמה גדולה מאד. וירא יעקב כי גברה המלחמה על בניו,[73] ויקם ויקפוץ ויך בימינו ובשמאלו ויפלו לפניו[74] כאשר יפול העשב לפני הבהמה. ותגבר יד החיל ויפרידו בין יהודה ובין אחיו, וירא יעקב ויחרוק {יהודה} בשניו גם הוא,[75] וישמעו אחיו ויבואו אליו לעזור לו, וייעף מאוד[76] ויצמא למים ולא היה לו מים.[77] ויתקע אצבעו בארץ בחזקה ויעלו המים כנגדו.[78] ויראו החיל את עליית המים כנגד יהודה[79] ויאמרו איש אל אחיו:[80] אנוסה לי מן המשחיתים האילו, כי א-להים נלחם להם.[81] וינוסו כל החיל דרך היער.[82] וירדפו בני יעקב אחריהם[83]

---

61. מ חסר: ויצאו יישׂשכר וגד–שנים עשר ריבוא.
62. מ ויבואו.
63. מ אש גדולה לפני הפתח במערה.
64. מ שיבוש: אשר רבתה הקול על האש ואש על החיל.
65. מ ורבה המלחמה.
66. מ בתוך החיל.
67. מ דן ונפתלי, גד ואשר.
68. ז עם רב כחול הים.
69. מ להרוג ולהכות.
70. מ חסר: ותגבר יד יהודה–מכה רבה מאד.
71. מ מפניהם.
72. מ חסר: מפניהם.
73. מ שיבוש: על כפו.
74. מ בתוספת: חללים חללים.
75. ה מלים "גם הוא" מעידות על השמטה. השלמה על פי ז: וירא יעקב ויחרוק בשניו וישמע יהודה ויחרוק גם בשניו. מ ויחרוק גם הוא בשיניו.
76. ז וייעפו הם מאד. מ ויחלוש יהודה מאד.
77. ז ויצמא יהודה למים ולא היו לו.
78. ז חסר: בחזקה.
79. ז חסר: כנגד יהודה.
80. מ איש אל רעהו ואיש אל אחיו.
81. ז ויאמרו נברחה מפניהם כי השם נלחם להם; מ ננוסה מפני המשחיתים האילו כי א-להים נלחם בעבורם;
82. מ וינוסו החיל דרך היערים.
83. מ וירוצו.

I. They blew the trumpet, and Naphtali his brother ran to search after him and found him fighting with the army. Naphtali called out: Are you Joseph my brother? He said: I am. And Naphtali helped him, and they killed a countless number of people. They pursued those that remained and drowned them in the river. The army fled before them, and they ceased to pursue them. And it is of them Solomon said: "Two are better than one" [Ecclesiastes 4:9]. They came to Jacob, their father, and he was joyous. And the other sons of kings did not pursue them. And he went in confidence to his father, Isaac.

וירדפום ויכום מכה גדולה [338ב] בלי מספר, וקצת מהם נסו אל נפשם. ולא יכלו בני יעקב לרדוף אחריהם.[84] ויתקעו בשופרות ויחזרו אל אהליהם.[85] ויוסף לא היה שם, ויצר לבני יעקב מאד מאד על יוסף <~~על~~> אחיהם,[86] ויאמרו שמא הרגוהו או הוליכוהו בשבי.[87]

I. ויתקעו בשופר, וירץ נפתלי אחיו לחפש אחריו[88] וימצא{י}הו נלחם עם החיל. ויקרא נפתלי: האתה זה יוסף אחי, ויאמר: אני. ויעזור לו נפתלי, וישחיתו מן העם[89] בלי מספר. וירדפו הנשארים ויטב(י)עו[90] במי היאור. וינוסו החיל לפניהם, ויחדלו לרדוף אחריהם. ועליהם אמר שלמה טובים השנים מן האחד [קוהלת ד, ט]. ויבאו אל יעקב אביהם, וישמח.[91] ולא רדפו אחריהם שאר[92] בני המלכות. וילך בטח אל יצחק אביו.[93]

84. מ כי עייפים הם ויחדלו לצאת אחריהם.
85. מ וישובו.
86. ז וייצר לבני יעקב מאד על אחיהם; מ וייצר לבני יעקב על יוסף.
87. מ לאמור שמא יהרגוהו או יוליכוהו בשבי.
88. ז לחפש אחריו; לונדון-מונטיפיורי: ויתקעו עוד בשופרות וירץ נפתלי אחריו לחפש.
89. מ מן החיל.
90. ז ויטבעו; מ ויטביעום.
91. ז וישמחו שמחה גדולה, היינו דכת' ויסעו ויהי חתת אלהי' על הערים אשר סביבותיה'; מ וישמח עמהם.
92. מ שהם בני המלכים.
93. ז וילך אל יצחק אביו ארצה כנען; מ וילך יעקב אל יצחק אביו בטח. סליק מדרש ויסעו.

69. The Portal to Gehenna (338b–339b)

A. [338b] Once there was a very rich man. And he had a very beautiful wife, and he loved her very much. And in his courtyard were four high and mightily fortified walls. And it had an opening into his courtyard. And within those walls, there was a custom [i.e., rule]: Anyone who entered would neither exit nor return home. And goats danced there. Some say that the portal to Gehenna was there. And the man was very wicked and villainous, and his wife was wicked, and they had no children. And she desired very much to approach that opening to see what was inside it, and her husband always prevented her from doing so and guarded her, because he knew that she wanted to go there.

B. Once the king needed that man and sent for him. And the man commanded his chief servant to guard over his wife and to be with her always and follow her wherever she went. The man went to the king when he sent for him and lingered there. Meanwhile, the woman came and said to the chief servant: Listen and do my bidding and let me go to the opening, and I will give you whatever you wish. For I know well that if you do what I ask of you, I will benefit you highly. He said: Please, mistress, do not do this, and do not cause yourself to be lost for nothing, for my lord has commanded me to watch over you like the apple of his eye, because his love for you is wondrous, and you are very pleasant to him. And do not commit this terrible wickedness, and do not bring down his gray hairs with sorrow to the grave. She said: I swear that I will not approach the opening closer than the span of an arrow. And he did not want to allow her, and she tried mightily to go, until she went to the courtyard against his will and permission, and there was no one else at home with them. The man cried out loudly and clapped his hands [in sorrow] and was extremely upset, and ran after her, and she walked up to the opening. And as she came there, someone from within stretched out his hand and pulled her toward him inside, and the door closed behind her. The man said: As for me, where am I to go now that this calamity has befallen my master? [339a]

C. The man went and hid in a room and remained there until his master returned home. And when he came, he saw neither his wife nor his servant, and he fell on his face and prostrated himself, and his spirit was greatly agitated, and he fainted. And all his neighbors came to console him, but he refused to be consoled. He said: I shall go down to Sheol to my wife, mourning. And he wept greatly. He went and searched through all his house and found nothing, until he reached his bedroom, where he heard someone groaning and sighing. He said: Who are you? Are you my slave so-and-so whom I hear groaning? He said: I am your slave who is devoted to

69. פיתחו של גיהנום (338ב–339ב)

A. מעשה באדם אחד שהיה עשיר גדול. והיה לו אשה יפה מאד והיה אוהב אותה ביותר.[1] והיה בחצירו ארבע חומות גבוהות ובצורות מאד. והיה בו פתח פתוח לחצירו. ובתוך ובאותן החומות יש מנהג, כל הנכנס לא יצא ולא יחזור לביתו. ושעירים ירקדו שם.[2] ויש אומרים ששם פתחו של גיהנם.[3] והיה האיש רע ובליעל מאד ואשתו רשעה, ובנים לא היו להם. והיא היתה מתאוה תמיד לבא עד אותו פתח ולראות מה שבתוכו, ובעלה ממאן אותה תמיד ושומר, לפי שיודע שדעתה לשם.

B. פעם אחת היה צריך המלך לאותו איש, ושלח אחריו. וציוה האיש לאשר על ביתו לשמור אשתו ולהיות תמיד <עמה> ולילך אחריה בכל מקום שתלך. הלך האיש אל המלך כאשר שלח אחריו ושהא [!] שם. ובין כך בא האשה ואמרה לאשר על ביתה: שמעני ועשה רצוני והניחני לילך בפני הפתח, ואני אתן לך כל מה שתרצה. כי ידעתי, אם תעשה לי מה שאני מבקשת ממך כי הטיב אטיב עמך. אמר לה: אל נא אדונתי, אל נא תעשי זאת ואל תפסידי ותאבדי עצמך בחנם, ואדוני צוה אותי לאמר לשמורך כבבת עינו, כי נפלאת אהבתך עליו ומאד נעמת לו.[4] ואל תעשי הרעה הגדולה הזאת, ולא תורד שיבתו ברעה שאולה.[5] אמרה לו: חייך, שלא אלך אלא כנגד הפתח מרחוק כמטחוי קשת. והוא לא רצה לתת לה רשות. ויהי היא מתאמצת ללכת מאד, עד שהלכה לחצר בעל כורחו ושלא בטובו, ואין איש אתם בבית. צעק האיש בקול גדול ויספוק כפיו ויצטער האיש מאד וירץ אחריה, והיא הלכה עד לפני הפתח. וכיון שבאתם[6] שמה הושיט אחד מבפנים את ידו ומשכה אליו לפנים, והדלת סגר אחריה. אמר האיש: ואני אנה אני בא מן הצרה אשר ימצא את אדוני.[7] [339א]

C. הלך האיש והטמינו בחדר, והיה שם עד בא אדוניו אל ביתו. וכיון שבא ולא ראה את אשתו ואת עבדו, נפל לאפיו ארצה ויתפעם רוחו ויתעלף. ובאו כל שכיניו לנחמו וימאן להתנחם. ויאמר: כי ארד אל אשתי אבל שאולה, ויבך אותה בכי גדול.[8] הלך ופשפש בכל ביתו ולא מצא עד שבא לחדר משכבו. ושמע שם גונה ומתאנח. ויאמר: מי אתה, האתה זה פלוני עבדי אשר שמעתי

1. אין בידינו עדי נוסח לסיפור.
2. השוו ישעיהו יג, כא: "ושכנו שם בנות יענה ושעירים ירקדו שם". וראו רש"י לויקרא יז, ז, המפרש ש"שעירים" הם שדים.
3. על פתח הגיהנום ראו רש"י לסנהדרין מד, ע"ב.
4. השוו לשמואל ב, א, כו: "צר לי עליך אחי יהונתן נעמת לי מאד נפלאתה אהבתך לי מאהבת נשים".
5. השוו בראשית מב, לח: "ויאמר לא ירד בני עמכם [. . .] וקראהו אסון בדרך והורדתם את שיבתי ביגון שאולה".
6. מחיקה של האות הסופית ם בקו אלכסוני.
7. השוו בראשית לז, לא: "הילד איננו ואני אנא אני בא".
8. השוו בראשית לז, לה: "ויקומו כל בניו וכל בנותיו לנחמו, וימאן להתנחם, ויאמר כי ארד אל בני אבל שאולה".

you. He came to him and fell on his face and wept and pleaded with him. He said to him: Where is my wife? He stood and told him the whole story. He said to him: I swear, I will not sit or be silent or rest until I find out where she is and what place she is in and what she is doing, and if I can be with her.

D. What did he do? He gave everything he had to his relatives and went out to [save her from] captivity, until he entered a very great forest. He walked in it for six days and met a very tall, black man who was exceedingly ugly. He greeted him, and he responded in kind. The man [the husband] was very fearful and frightened of him, because he had never seen anyone like him. The tall man said to him: I know what you seek. You wish to see your wife. If you will come with me, I will show you where she is, and you can speak to her. He said to him: For all the king's treasures, if he desired to give them to me, I would not go with you. The tall man said to him: Is there anyone in your house whom you trust? He said to him: Yes. Bring him to me [in] eight days from today, and you will find me here.

E. He departed from him and went home, and all his friends gathered round and asked him if he had found or heard anything about his wife. He said to them: Yes. Is there among you anyone who wishes to do what I ask? If I have ever done a favor for anyone of you in the world, now is the time, and the time has come to pay me back for what I have done for him all my life. One of his servants came and said: My lord, you reared me and brought me up from youth to this day [Isaiah 1:2]. Command me what you wish, and I will fulfill your every command. And I will be cautious and careful about whatever you order me to do. He said to him: I want you, because I have found you to be very faithful and pleasant, and I trust you. Come with me and do whatever I tell you to do. And the two of them went on together [Genesis 22:6]. They arrived in the forest in the place where they had been before, and he found the tall man there. The servant saw him and was very frightened of him. His master said to him: My son, you must go with this man, and he will take you to the place where my wife is, and you will speak to her, and if you bring her back with you, I will give you a great deal of money, and you will inherit everything I own. He said: This I will do.

F. He went with him and took him to Gehenna and showed him many people he knew who were suffering their judgment in Gehenna. And his master returned home. The servant said to him: Show me my master's wife. [339b] He took him to a room, and it appeared to him that the entire room, its walls, and ceiling were covered in the finest gold and the floor with precious red and flaming stones. Then he

גונח? א"ל: אני עבדך המחוייב לך. ויבא אליו, ויפל לפניו ויבך ויתחנן לו. א"ל: היכן אשתי? עמד וספר לו כל המעשה. א"ל: בשבועה, לא אשב ולא אשקוט ולא אנוח עד שאדע היכן היא ובאיזה מקום היא, ומה היא עושה ואם אוכל להיות עמה.

D. מה עשה, נתן כל אשר לו לקרוביו, והלך לו בשבי[9] עד שנכנס בתוך יער גדול אחד. והלך בתוכו מהלך ששה ימים, ופגע באיש אחד גדול מאד בקומה ושחור ומכוער ביותר.[10] נתן לו שלום, והחזיר לו שלום.[11] ויחרד האיש ויפחד מאד ממנו, כי לא רא{ה} מעולם כמוהו. א"ל האיש הגדול: ידעתי מה אתה מבקש, את אשתך אתה מבקש לראות. אם תרצה לבא עמי אראך את מקומה, ואתה תדבר אליה. א"ל: בשביל כל אוצרות המלך אם הוא רוצה ליתנם לי, לא הייתי רוצה לילך עמך. א"ל האיש הגדול: יש בביתך ~~בבית~~ שום אדם שאתה בוטח בו? א"ל: הן. א"ל: הוליכהו אלי היום שמונה ימים ותמצא אותי הנה.

E. נפטר ממנו והלך לו ובא לביתו, ונתקבצו כל אוהביו אליו ושאלו לו אם <~~רצה~~> מצא או שמע שום דבר מאשתו. אמר להם: הן. מי יש בכם אדם שרוצה לעשות מה שאצונו? אם עשיתי שום טובה שבעולם לשום אדם מכם, עתה בא העת והגיע הזמן שיכול לגמול לי כל מה שעשיתי לו כל ימיי. בא אחד מנעריו ואמר: אדוני אתה גדלתני ורוממתני מנעורי ועד עתה. תגזור עלי כל רצונך ואקיים כל מצותך, ואהיה זהיר ונזהר לכל אשר תצוני. א"ל: בך חפצתי כי מצאתיך נאמן ונעים מאד, ובך אני בוטח. בא עמי ועשה כל אשר אצוך. וילכו שניהם יחדיו [בראשית כב, ו]. ויבאו ביער עד מקום אשר היה שם בתחילה, וימצא שם <~~האיש~~> האיש הגדול. וירא אותו הנער, ויפחד ממנו מאד. א"ל רבו: בני צריך אתה לילך עם זה האיש והוא יוליכך למקום אשתי ואתה תדבר אליה, ואם תוכל להביאה עמך אתן לך ממון כבד ותהיה יורש מכל אשר לי. א"ל: כן אעשה כאשר דברת.

9. נראה: הלך למקום השבי (מעבר לפתח הדלת האסורה?) כדי להציל את אשתו.
10. טופוס דמוני המקובל בימי הביניים. השוו למעשה ירושלמי בכתב יד זה (552ב–652ב): ויפגע בו אדם אחד שחור מאוד ומכוער מאוד, ול'תנא והמת הנודד' בכתב היד (דף 552א–552ב).
11. השוו ל'תנא והמת הנודד' כנ"ל.

saw the master's wife sitting on a golden throne wearing golden robes, and it appeared to him that everything around her was gold. And in front of her was a golden table set with all sorts of red foods, and she had many servants, and some would cut her food for her in front of her, and others would pour her white wine into a golden chalice. When he saw her, he fell on his face and prostrated himself and said to her: Blessed is He who has given part of his glory to flesh and blood, for I have never ever seen a queen so honored as I see you are being honored. And my master is sorrowful because of you and does not eat and fasts all the days. And he sent me after you so that you should come to him if you can. She said to him: Sir, listen: Everything that you see here all around me is burning fire. This room and table and everything I am wearing and the throne upon which I am seated and everything that I eat is fire—until destruction it will consume my body and flesh. And the white wine that you see them pouring for me in a golden chalice—the chalice is made of fire, and the wine is molten lead that I drink every hour. And if the entire world was mine, I would give it willingly to go outside to cool myself off for one moment because my body and soul are burning.

G. And say this to my master and tell him that this is how those of Israel who sin with the body are in Gehenna, and tell him to repent for all his wicked deeds, because immense is the power of repentance. He said to her: For what sin have you been judged so harshly? She said to him: Because of the wicked deeds and sins that I committed, because I committed adultery with another man and desecrated the Sabbath, and when I was impure, I lay with my husband, and I had no pity on the poor and orphans, and I did this and that. He said to her: Can anyone redeem you from this judgment? She said to him: No, because I never had any children. If I had had one son from my husband who could say in public, God is blessed, with the congregation answering after: The name of God be blessed for ever and ever,[1] and the entire *Kaddish* prayer, I would be redeemed at the end of my year. She [he] said to her: I will go and tell him all this. And she gave him a ring that was still on her finger, which he had given to her, and she said to him: Tell him that this will be a sign that you are telling the truth in everything you tell him.

1. *Sifrei*, ed. Finkelstein, *ha'azinu*, 306, 342.

F. הלך עמו והוליכו לתוך גהינם, וראה שם הרבה בני אדם שהיה מכיר סובלים דינם בגהינם. ואדונו חזר לביתו. א"ל הנער: הראיני את אשת אדוני. [339ב] הוליכו לחדר אחד וכמדומה לו שהיה כל החדר הקירות והגג מצפה זהב מופז, והרצפה מאבנים טובות אדומות ומתלהבות. וראה אשת אדונו יושבת בקתדרא של זהב ומלובשת בגדי זהב, וכל סביבותיה זהב כמדומה לו.[12] והיה בפניה שולחן של זהב ערוך וכל מיני מאכלה אדומים, ויש לה שמשים הרבה יש מהם חותכין בפניה מאכלה, ויש מהם מוזגין לה מיין לבן בתוך כוס של זהב. כיון שראה אותה נפל לאפיו ארצה ואמר לה: ברוך שחלק מכבודו לבריות בשר ודם, שלא ראיתי מעולם שום מלכה מכובדת כל כך כאשר אני רואה שמכבדין אותך. ואדוני מצטער עבורך ואינו אוכל, כל הימים הוא מתענה. והוא שלחני אחרייך, שתבואי אליו אם תוכלי. אמרה לו: אדוני, שמעוני כל מה שאתה רואה סביבותיי אש בוערה, החדר הזה והשולחן וכל מה שאני מלובשת וקתדרא שאני יושבת בה, וכל מה שאני אוכלת אש הוא. עד אבדון תאכל גופי ובשרי. והיין לבן שאתה רואה שהן מוזגין לי בכוס של זהב, הכוס של אש והיין הוא אבר מהותך שאני שותה כל שעה ושעה. ואילו היה כל העולם כולו שלי הייתי נותן אותו ברצון לצאת שעה אחת לחוץ לקרר אותי, שאני שורפת נשמתי וגופי.

G. וכך תאמר אל אדוני, ותאמר לו שכל פושעי ישראל בגופן כך הם בגהינם, ותאמר לו שיעשה תשובה מן מעשיו הרעים. כי גדול כח התשובה. אמר לה: ובאיזה עון יש לך כל הדין הקשה הזה? אמרה לו: מפני הרבה רעות ועונות שעשיתי, כי ניאפתי לאיש אחר, וחיללתי שבת, ונדה הייתי שוכבת עם בעלי, ועל עניים ויתומים לא ריחמתי וכזאת וכזאת עשיתי. אמר לה: היש יכולת לשום אדם לפדותך מן הדין הזה? אמרה לו: לא, הואיל שלא היה לי בנים מעולם. ואם היה לי בן אחד מבעלי שיוכל לומר ברבים ברכו את י"י המבורך והציבור עונין ברוך י"י המבורך לעולם ועד,[13] וקדיש כולו, הייתי נפדת בסוף שנתי.[14] (אמרה לו) [אמר לה]: אלך ואספר לו כל זאת. ונתנה לו טבע{ת} אחד שעדיין היה באצבעה שהוא נתן לה, ואמרה לו: אמור שיהא זה לו לאות שאתה אומר אמת מכל אשר תאמר אליו.

12. השוו למעשה ירושלמי בכ"י ורשה (42ב–48א): "שהיתה יושבת בקתדרא של זהב ועמה בתולות רבות מרקדות ושמחות לפניה". הדימוי של גיהנם משותף.

13. ראו ספרי לדברים, האזינו, פיסקה ש"ו, מהדורת פינקלשטיין, 342.

14. השוו ל'תנא והמת הנודד' כנ"ל.

H. He left her and went with the man who had brought him there, and he led him to the place from where he had taken him and left, and he went home. When his master saw him, he was overjoyed. He told him everything he had seen and gave him the sign, and he believed what he had said. What did the man do? He went to the synagogue and asked God for mercy, crying loudly with a broken heart, and he totally repented and did not move from there, until his soul left him. A voice from heaven said: That man is ready for life in the world to come, to fulfill the verse: "To endow those who love me with wealth, that I may fill their treasuries" [Proverbs 8:21].

All is Done
with No Fault or Disgrace

H. נפטר ממנה והלך לו עם האיש שהביאו שמה והוליכו עד המקום שלקחו ונפטר ממנו, והלך לביתו. כיון שראהו אדונו שמח שמחה גדולה. וסיפר לו כל מה שראה, ונתן לו האות והאמין לדבריו. מה עשה אותו האיש, הלך לבית הכנסת ובקש רחמים לפני הקב"ה בבכי גדול ובשברון לב, ועשה תשובה גמורה ולא זז משם עד שפרחה נשמתו. יצתה בת קול ואמרה אותו: האיש מזומן לחיי העולם הבא. לקיים מה שנ' להנחיל אוהבי יש ואוצרותיהם אמלא [משלי ח, כא]"

סליק כל הנמצא
בלי דופי ושמצה

An Analytical and Comparative Overview

Sefer ha-ma'asim, Its Tales, and Its Parallels

1. The Bizarre Deeds of Elijah the Prophet (300a–300b)

The story is a theodicy legend that preaches the justification of divine judgment, in the vein of "the righteous suffer and the wicked thrive."[1] Events that seem clearly unjust are explained in a broad context known only to Elijah, as God's messenger. Words that sound like a curse are actually a blessing, slight damage is an opportunity for much benefit, and the suffering of the righteous in this world is offset by the promise of a reward in the world to come. This rationale is embodied in the episodic structure of the tale, typical of travel narratives, and derived from the journey taken by Elijah and R. Joshua b. Levi to various sites. It represents the demand for a judgment based on a series of events, not on a single event taken out of context. Furthermore, the full context of Elijah's odd actions is constructed not only through the accumulation of events in the different episodes on their journey but mainly from those details known to Elijah but concealed from R. Joshua b. Levi.[2]

The theodicy motif is combined with "the revelation of Elijah," which drives the development of the plot. R. Joshua b. Levi greatly desires to see Elijah's revelation and, in the words of *Sefer ha-ma'asim*, "yearn[s]" to join him. For that there is both a price and a condition. He is forbidden to ask or comment on what he sees. He must observe Elijah's actions silently and endure the metaphysical as a painful and esoteric (although not mystical, in this story) experience. Elijah says: "You will not be able to endure what I do." R. Joshua answers: "I will." During the shared journey, and in view of Elijah's odd behavior, the theodicy question arises. When R. Joshua b. Levi can no longer endure the things he sees, he questions them, and Elijah reveals to him the reasoning that motivates the human drama. Elijah's explanations put R. Joshua b. Levi's mind to rest, but the breach between the two, because R. Joshua b. Levi violated the prohibition, expresses the expectation that divine judgment should be incontrovertibly accepted, and is a result of his inability to endure what he saw. A story about a desire for revelation develops into a theological discourse about the vindication of divine judgment.

Scholars who have studied the tale have pointed out its affinity with a parallel in the Koran (Sura 18:59–81), especially according to a different, somewhat expanded

1. Cf. *Berakhot* 7a.
2. The link between the two figures, Elijah and R. Joshua b. Levi, already exists in the Talmud (*Ketubot* 77b; *Sanhedrin* 98a) in different contexts. R. Joshua b. Levi is depicted as a man who deals with broad issues that deviate from the everyday, such as eschatological questions. On his figure in the Talmud, see Fraenkel, "R. Joshua b. Levi in the Talmud Bavli."

version in *Ḥibbur yafeh mehayeshu'a.*[3] In any event, the immediate source for *Sefer ha-ma'asim* is *Midrash aseret hadibrot.*[4] Several factors suggest this: (1) the scribe's reference in *Midrash aseret hadibrot* to "what I wrote above," namely to the story in *Sefer ha-ma'asim* (349b)—the scribe himself created an affinity between the two collections he copied in the same manuscript; (2) the epilogue, which is partially identical in the two versions; (3) the original form of the root *samekh/bet/lamed* [ס.ב.ל.] ("You cannot endure") is common to *Midrash aseret hadibrot* and *Sefer ha-ma'asim*. In *Midrash aseret hadibrot*, Elijah forbids R. Joshua b. Levi to accompany him, "Because you will see many things that you will not be able to endure."[5] In *Sefer ha-ma'asim*, Elijah warns: "You will not be able to endure what I do." And Joshua replies: "I will." In contrast, in the medieval adaptations to Hebrew of *Ḥibbur yafeh mehayeshu'a*, the Hebrew root *tzadi/bet/resh* [צ.ב.ר.], which means "patience," is translated to "*laset*" (endure; "You will not be able to endure").[6] Obviously, *Sefer ha-ma'asim* did not rely on *Ḥibbur yafeh mehayeshu'a.*

Although *Midrash aseret hadibrot* is the source of our tale in *Sefer ha-ma'asim*, it did not influence the editing and embedding trends in the compilation. The story was not copied in proximity with the other tales from *Midrash aseret hadibrot*, nor is there any reference to the commandment "Thou shalt not covet," as would be expected. Rather, it opens the entire compilation. Possibly the figure of Elijah, who appears in this tale and the following one, "The Loan," is the motif that links them. Elijah functions in many popular stories as a figure heralding redemption and as a miracle-worker in times of distress, and that is the case in *Sefer ha-ma'asim* itself.[7] In our story Elijah walks from place to place, performing deeds that turn out later to be correct and beneficial, although they do not seem so at first sight.

3. See the story in *Ḥibbur yafeh mehayeshu'a*, ed. and trans. Hirschberg, no. 2, 7–8; Brinner, ed., *An Elegant Composition Concerning Relief after Adversity*, no. 2, 13–16. Schwarzbaum compares Koranic and post-Koranic versions to the one in *Ḥibbur yafeh mehayeshu'a*, and concludes that the source of the latter is in Muslim writings, which differs from the opinion of Obermann and others. See Schwarzbaum, "Elijah the Prophet and R. Joshua b. Levi," 33–39; idem, "The Jewish and Moslem Versions of Some Theodicy Legends," 87–122. For references to other studies, see Ben-Amos, *Mimekor yisrael*, no. 103, 188.

4. *Midrash aseret hadibrot*, ed. Shapira, 89–92.

5. Ibid., 90. The original phrase in *Ḥibbur yafeh mehayeshu'a* (note 3, above) is: "*Lā tastaṭī' al-ṣabr 'alā ma tanẓurhu min a'mālī*" (lit., in Judeo-Arabic: "You do not have the ability for patience when you will see my actions").

6. Ms. Paris 716 f. 169a and Rome-Casantense 3097, 73a, of *Ḥibbur yafeh mehayeshu'a*, in Hebrew, from the fourteenth and the early fifteenth century, respectively.

7. Of the vast material collected and studied on the prophet Elijah, I will cite *Yeda-'am* 7 (1960), devoted in its entirety to Elijah.

Nonetheless, this does not explain the editorial choice to place the story at the opening of the compilation, nor does it seem to set a trend for the entire compilation—for example, a focus on Elijah as a legendary figure.

The story has contemporary parallels in the exempla of Jacques de Vitry, Étienne de Bourbon, and, later, the *Gesta Romanorum*.[8] In these sources, it is a theodicy narrative par excellence. A monk has some heretical thoughts and questions divine justice. An angel is sent to him to demonstrate the justice of divine judgment on earth and to restore his faith. He suggests to the monk a shared journey, and during it he behaves very strangely in the homes of their various hosts, and his deeds seem iniquitous. He steals a very precious chalice from a generous host, and the following day gives it to a bad, miserly host; he throws into the river the young servant of a host who had treated them very cordially, and drowns him; and he chokes the young child of another host while the boy cries in his sleep. These actions arouse the monk's opposition and make his initial position even more extreme. He grows more and more puzzled and upset, becoming convinced that his companion is Satan and not an angel. Finally he receives an explanation that shows him how little he knows of God, and how those who were harmed by the angel in this world would be rewarded in the next. For example, the young servant who was drowned had been planning to murder his master the following day; by throwing him into the river, the angel had saved their host and had also saved the servant from a more severe punishment in hell. Following the explanation and after he constantly hesitates and wavers, the monk's faith is restored at once.

In the Jewish story, R. Joshua b. Levi is required to restrain his feelings, doubts, and puzzlement, and to observe what he sees in silence,[9] but the Christian parallels do not impose this requirement. On the contrary, the role of the angel is to induce the monk to experience his doubts intensely and to openly express them, so he can then instruct him on how to cope with them. The monk's recognition of the justice of God's judgment is a conclusion he arrives at after he has undergone a change, not in reaction to a prohibition laid down in advance. Accordingly, the Christian tale does not open with a prohibition against questioning divine justice.

---

8. Jacques de Vitry, *Exempla*, no. 109, 50–51 (English, 179–180); Étienne de Bourbon, *Anecdotes historiques*, no. 396, 346–349; *Gesta Romanorum* (Swan) no. 53, 194–196; ibid., (I) no. 220, 234–237; ibid., (Ö) no. 80, 396–399. See references in Tubach 2558: "Hermit and Angel I"; ATU 759: "Hermit and Angel"; Th. J225.0.1: "Angel and Hermit."

9. In *Midrash aseret hadibrot* Elijah warns: "If you ask me anything, I will leave you at once." A similar warning appears in *Sefer ha-ma'asim*, toward the end of the story.

The two parallels differ in yet another way: the motif of R. Joshua's strong desire for Elijah's revelation (he "yearned to accompany Elijah") is absent from the Christian parallel. This reflects disparate trends in the Jewish and Christian sources, in keeping with their different sources in the non-Jewish literature.[10] The Jewish tale focuses on the experience of Elijah's revelation, although it does imply a theodicy question as well,[11] while the Christian parallels deal mainly with divine justice and the process that leads to conversion.

Despite differences in trends and emphasis, there is a certain coordination between *Sefer ha-ma'asim* and the Christian versions that does not exist in *Midrash aseret hadibrot*. The motif of the taboo, which distinguishes between the Jewish and the Christian sources, is deferred in *Sefer ha-ma'asim* to the end of the story, and is mentioned only once, unlike its strategic location at its opening in *Midrash aseret hadibrot*, where it occurs twice. Also, the description of R. Joshua b. Levi's yearning for Elijah's revelation is summarized in *Sefer ha-ma'asim*, while it is dramatized in *Midrash aseret hadibrot*.[12] Although this is a stylistic attribute in *Sefer ha-ma'asim* in general, its specific effect here is to gloss over the distinction between the themes of "the revelation of Elijah" and "divine justice," and the gap between them closes somewhat. A more emphatic affinity in *Sefer ha-ma'asim* with the Christian parallels is implied. The movement of the story in *Sefer ha-ma'asim* is, then, bidirectional. Its source is in *Midrash aseret hadibrot*, as discussed in the first part of this essay, and indirectly also in the Koran; and from this standpoint it was transferred from East to West, from *Midrash aseret hadibrot* to *Sefer ha-ma'asim*. In parallel, its versions in Europe left their imprints on *Sefer ha-ma'asim*, as deduced from the comparative analysis of the various parallels.

A special affinity is created between *Sefer ha-ma'asim* and Jacques de Vitry's exempla. In both sources there is a preference for a succinct summary of the events, in contrast to other exempla compilations. In Jacques de Vitry's collection of sermons, the background for the monk's doubts is not explained but simply reported as a given fact: "Unde cum quidam heremita, spiritu blasphemie temptatus,

10. See Crane's comment in his edition of Jacques de Vitry's exemplum (181) about the development of the Christian and Muslim versions from different, independent sources; however he does not discuss the various differences and trends.

11. The prohibition against questioning the reason for Elijah's behavior bridges the two themes—that of Elijah's revelation and that of divine justice—and makes possible the transition between them.

12. *Sefer ha-ma'asim*: "He prayed, and Elijah appeared before him"; *Midrash aseret hadibrot*: "He sat for several days praying and pleading until his prayer was accepted by the Almighty" (ed. Shapira, 90).

cogitaret quod non essent justa Dei judicia, qui bonos affligit et mali prosperati sunt" ("A hermit, tempted by the spirit of blasphemy, thought the judgements of God were not just, for he afflicted the good and prospered the wicked").[13] The same holds true later for the monk's reactions to the angel's deeds, as reported by the narrator: "valde cepit heremita dolere credens quod ille non esset a Deo" ("Thereupon the hermit grieved, believing the angel was not from God"). For a comparison, in the later source, *Gesta Romanorum*, the underlying cause of the monk's doubts, as well as his later reactions, are described in detail. A clearly unjust incident causes him to lose faith. He witnesses the theft of a flock of sheep while the shepherd responsible for them was asleep. As a result, the owner of the flock kills the innocent shepherd, which arouses heretical thoughts in the monk's mind.[14] In parallel to Jacques de Vitry's exempla, versus the *Gesta Romanorum*, the description in *Sefer ha-ma'asim* is condensed, as compared to the expanded narrative in *Midrash aseret hadibrot*. This does not suggest there is a genealogical link between the Jewish and the Christian exempla but rather a similar aesthetic taste and a common set of expectations.

After the Middle Ages, the story was included in various anthologies and collections usually based on the *Midrash aseret hadibrot* version, as well as in story compilations from the nineteenth and twentieth centuries.[15] However, a few versions follow *Ḥibbur yafeh mehayeshua*, which was largely adapted by R. Nissim of Kairouan.[16] Others are abridged or combine story materials from *Midrash aseret hadibrot* and *Ḥibbur yafeh mehayeshu'a*.[17] The story also exists in oral traditions archives in IFA, after having been adapted to modern life.[18]

13. See Jacques de Vitry, *Exempla*, no. 109, 50 (Latin); 179 (English translation), as well as the following quotation.

14. *Gesta Romanorum* (Swan), no. 80, 194.

15. *Ḥibbur hama'asiyot vehamidrashot vehahagadot*, no. 12; Ms. JTS, mic 1480, 28a–38a; Elijah Hacohen, *Me'il ẓedakah*, no. 439, ed. Hillel Kuperman, A, 77; *Yalkut me'am lo'ez*, Numbers, *shelakh*, 141–143; Dayan, *Zikharon lanefesh*, 66–67; Araki, *Sefer hama'asiyot*, no. 12, 12a–13b, and ed. Ḥuẓin, no. 12, 11b–12b; Farḥi, *Oseh pele*, 61–62; Jellinek, *Bet hamidrasch* 2:6, 131–133.

16. Heilperin, *Seder hadorot* (Karlsruhe, 1769), "*Seder tana'im ve'amoraim*," the letter *yod*: Joshua b. Levi, 11a–b; Dayan, *Zikharon lanefesh* (n. 15 above); Jellinek, *Bet hamidrasch*, 2:5, 133–135; Grünwald, *Yalkut sippurim* 1, Leviticus, 18:7, 36b–37a, 72–73; Eisenstein, *Oẓar midrashim*, 211–212, Bin Gorion, *Mimekor yisrael*, no. 325, 219; Ben-Amos, *Mimekor yisrael*, no. 103, 188–190.

17. London Ms. Or. 9965, 2b–6b (Byzantine script, 15th century); Fekhman, *Ma'asei hashem*, 29b–30a (1881); Joseph Ḥaim b. Eliahu, *Nifla'im ma'asekha*, 140, 129b–130a.

18. ATU 759 (IFA); Ben-Amos, *Mimekor yisrael*, no. 103.

2. The Loan (300b; 318b–319a)

The tale has two versions in *Sefer ha-ma'asim* (nos. 2, 34). One is inserted at the beginning of *Sefer ha-ma'asim*, immediately after the opening story in which the figure of Elijah also appears. The second is adjacent to two tales that have a similar substructure: a conflict between matter and spirit, and more concretely, a comparison between a material gift from heaven and a spiritual experience.[1]

The tale appears first in midrash *Ruth zuta*, in relation to Naomi's words to her daughters-in-law when she returns from the field in Moab: "Call me not Naomi, call me Mara; for the Almighty has dealt very bitterly with me. I went out full, and the Lord has brought me back empty" (Ruth 1:20–21).[2] *Ruth zuta* says, "All suffering, but the suffering of poverty is greater than all others." Moreover, "All suffering is fleeting and leaves no permanent mark. But the suffering of poverty darkens one's eyes." It is a story of the tribulations of poverty and of redemption and rescue from this suffering. Its versions split into three branches, represented in *Ruth zuta* and in the two versions in *Sefer ha-ma'asim*.[3]

There is a gap in *Ruth zuta* regarding the circumstances of the loan and its motive. It is not clear whether Elijah initiated the loan or was acting as a divine messenger, and whether it was given out of compassion or as a trial for the recipient of the loan. The two possibilities are implied in the midrash and create tension between material prosperity and piety. Wealth is a blessing that may turn out to be a burden, and it may impair the spiritual, intimate relationship between man and God during prayer. It is also not clear whether, later on, the man persevered in his piety and prayer after he was impoverished and later regained his wealth, or whether he once again neglected his duties. His oath was meant to promise that he would indeed keep the commitment he had undertaken, but the story ends without stating whether that was indeed the case after he grew wealthy again.[4] The type of gift is also not defined—whether it was a loan or a deposit—since when the time came he was asked to return the same coins as if it were a deposit, the use of which is forbidden.[5] A third

1. The sequence of the stories is "The Loan" (no. 34), "A Valley Filled with Gold" (no. 35), and "A Precious Stone from Heaven" (no. 36).
2. *Ruth zuta*, ed. Buber, 1:20, 22a. See Ben-Amos, *Mimekor yisrael*, no. 220, 429; Assis, "The Loan." For a study of the midrashic tale and its affinities with "The Seven Good Years" and the *Sefer ha-ma'asim* version, see Shoshany, "A Study of Two Tales in *Midrash Ruth Zuta*."
3. On this classification, see Assis, "The Loan," 130.
4. Cf. the motif "Punishment for neglecting prayer" (Th. Q223.1).
5. From this standpoint, the story belongs to the type of deposit tales, such as ATU 1617.

possibility is also suggested: that it may be a gift, based on the tale's exposition, which introduces him as a *ḥasid*, a righteous man who resolved never to receive a gift from anyone.[6] The blurring of the boundaries among "gift," "loan," and "deposit" represents an equivalence among them, to express the transitory nature of wealth and man's dependence on God.

The gaps in *Ruth zuta* are filled in various ways in *Sefer ha-ma'asim*. In the first version (300b), God in his compassion commanded Elijah to give the *ḥasid* seven zuzim, but as soon as he accepted them, he suffered one disaster after another, like the tribulations suffered by Job. The good and the bad—both come from God.[7] The deposit motif, which is only alluded to in *Ruth zuta*, is emphasized in *Sefer ha-ma'asim* by means of an episode from "The Pious Pretender," which is also included in *Sefer ha-ma'asim* (323b), and where the *ḥasid*, who sits in the synagogue, denies that he received any deposit.

In the second version of the tale (no. 34), Elijah initiates the loan to the poor man to test him, although he does pity him: "[He] wished to show him compassion." As in the Book of Job (1:8–12), Elijah asks permission to give him a sum of money, and God agrees on condition that he does not "drive him away from me."[8] The man becomes rich, neglects his religious duties, and then falls back into poverty. He then realizes the reason for his poverty and swears to mend his ways. That he keeps to his oath is demonstrated in the episodic closure of the tale. Some merchants plot to "test his riches," namely to trade with him in exchange for a large sum of money. When they approach him, he agrees to any expense, as long as he can maintain his piety and his practice of prayer, thus resisting the temptations inherent in commerce.

This episode is based on a homiletic tale in *Genesis rabbah* about Abraham and Sarah going down to Egypt to escape the famine in the land of Canaan, and the apprehension of Abraham (or as he was then called, "Abram") about how Sarah (then "Sarai") would fare among the Egyptians (Genesis 20:1–2). When they come to the

6. An asterisk in the IFA tales denotes a Jewish oikotype, namely a type adapted to the Jewish culture. In general, an oikotype is a tale type adapted to a particular culture. In the AT index, oikotypes are denoted by an asterisk following the tale type number. Cf. oikotype (IFA) AT *776, which involves gifts from Elijah to human beings. See also Th. Q223.1: "Punishment for neglecting prayer."

7. Job 1:13–22. And see Shoshany ("A Study of Two Tales," 85–86), who points to the infrastructure from Job that already exists in *Ruth zuta*. That, as I noted, is further expanded in *Sefer ha-ma'asim*.

8. Job 1:8–13. The motif of a test already exists in *Ruth zuta*, as Shoshany shows ("A Study of Two Tales," 87), and is expanded in *Sefer ha-ma'asim*.

gates of Egypt, *Genesis rabbah* relates, Abram hides Sarai in a case and tries to smuggle her in secretly, so that the Egyptians would not harass her because of her beauty. But the customs inspectors become suspicious and accuse him of smuggling goods into the country. They insist that he pay the custom dues, which Abram was prepared to do without arguing. When they see that he would pay whatever they asked, even though they steadily increased the fees and fines, they understand that he is trying to prevent them from opening his case. When he is forced to open it, Sarai is revealed, and "the land of Egypt was irradiated with her luster."[9] In this way the episode of the merchants, which seems detached from any context, closes the gap in *Sefer ha-ma'asim* (the first version, no. 2), where there is no information as to whether the man succeeded in keeping his oath and persevering in his prayers after he recovered his wealth. A clear hierarchy is created between material and spiritual possessions, expressing the change in the figure of the *ḥasid.*

A special emphasis is placed in *Sefer ha-ma'asim* on intention in prayer within the day-to-day routine of life, in particular in the second version about Abraham of Ashkelon (318b–319b). The venue of the synagogue and the length of time spent there before and after prayer ("[H]e would always close and open the synagogue") are motifs that represent an intention toward the sacred during prayer, in the liminal situation of transition from the problems of practical life to the realm of the synagogue. The worshipper in the synagogue must cope with the sharp transition between the opposing worlds of the secular and the sacred. In this liminal situation, prayer is an attempt to do so, and its success depends on man's awareness of his dependence on God.

Sefer ḥasidim and the exegetic literature of the Tosafists often offer guidance to the *ḥasid* in praying with intention and emphasize the sanctity of the synagogue as a place of an intimate relationship with God.[10] Sources in Ashkenaz advise the worshipper to spend much time in the synagogue ("The early *ḥasidim* would sit one hour before prayer and one hour after prayer"[11]) for a prayer spoken with concentration and not hastily, and to maintain the sacred sphere of the synagogue. It is also written in *Sefer ḥasidim* that "it is a great mitzvah to close the doors of the synagogue," namely to stay there until the last of the worshippers leaves (no. 466).

9. *Genesis rabbah* 40:5, ed. Albeck, 384–385.

10. See an elaborate exposition of this issue, including reference to *Sefer ha-ma'asim*, in Baumgarten, *Practicing Piety*, 195–202.

11. *Sefer ḥasidim*, no. 466, based on the *Mishnah Berakhot* 30b: "The pious men of old used to wait an hour before praying in order that they might concentrate their thoughts upon their father in heaven."

Another example is "the case of a man who hired the beadle to close the door of the synagogue, and he would say supplicatory prayers before the Almighty and would say '*aleinu leshabe'ach*' while standing" (no. 467, 133).[12]

The value of a test is an additional aspect in the story. In Ashkenaz the test is a theological principle not only in one-time situations of death in sanctification of the Holy Name but also, first and foremost, in day-to-day life and the trials it presents, as a means of sanctifying God.[13] Of the two versions in *Sefer ha-ma'asim*, it seems the second (more expanded and more complex) one is anchored in the world of the Ashkenazi Pietists, in contrast to the first, which is more similar to the basic version in *Ruth zuta*. That is most likely why it, more so than the first version, particularly influenced later story compilations.[14]

12. See Tosafot on *Berakhot* 6a, the custom of Ri-haZaken (R. Isaac of Dampierre [1189]) to extend his prayer "until all the others left" (see Baumgarten, *Practicing Piety*, 200). On praying customs, see also *Sefer ḥasidim*, nos. 418, 124; 451, 131; 465, 133 and 470, 133–134. Other tales in *Sefer ha-ma'asim* that emphasize the value of the *ḥasidic* customs of prayer are "Do Not Fail to Attend Public Prayers" (no. 41) and "The Seven Good Years" (no. 29)

13. Dan, "The Sanctification of God in the Philosophy of the Ashkenazi Pietists," 214–215.

14. Medieval versions include Ms. Cambridge-Harvard 39, 117b–118b; Ms. Jerusalem 3182; Yassif, ed., *Ninety-nine Tales*, no. 70, 234–235; *Ma'asim shel ḥasidim* (*Tales of ḥasidim*) in Ms. New York in JTS 2374, 118a–118b; *Midrash aseret hadibrot* in Ms. Vatican 107, 181b–182a; and Ms. Paris, Bibliothèque Nationale Heb. 719, 188b–189b. And see references to additional literature and research on tales in Ben-Amos, *Mimekor yisrael*, no. 229, 429.

3. The Heir's Test (301a)

The tale has its source in *Lamentations rabbah*, in the framework of a cycle of tales about the wisdom of the people of Jerusalem in contrast to the people of Athens, the city that was the center of Greek-Hellenist culture in ancient times.[1] The cycle of tales, one of the most coherent in rabbinic literature, was imparted in the form of sermons on the names of Jerusalem in Lamentations (1:1)—"She that was great among the nations"—to denote the importance of her previous status. The stories reflect, with stark contrast, the lowly status of Jerusalem in the present, following the destruction of the Temple, but at the same time the superior wisdom of the Jerusalemites compared to their enemies. The opposition here is between Jerusalem and Athens rather than Rome, which in fact conquered Jerusalem and destroyed the Temple. That is because Athens was perceived as the ancient Greek-Hellenist center of culture. In these stories, Athens and Jerusalem represent opposing cultures. In the very midst of destruction, these tales relate an experience of victory in the struggle over the crown of wisdom.[2] "The Heir's Test" (no. 3) opens the cycle. A son who is being tested as a potential heir to his father's fortune proves his keen intelligence time after time, manages to overcome a poor start, and is found worthy.

The tale, which is of the riddle genre, expresses a pain of loss in keeping with a key theme in *Lamentations rabbah* and in Lamentations. As Galit Hasan-Rokem observes, the riddle genre "presents categories, mixes them, reconstructs them and disintegrates them from within. Riddles thus truly express the chaotic and despairing vacillation between the stable collective self-confidence . . . and the threat of the annihilation of the individual and the group."[3] The playful element in the riddle, along with its chaotic potential, are vehicles that can provide an appropriate expression for the experience of destruction. The riddle and its solution are both in the story itself, but the identity of the person who is riddling is ambiguous: is he the host, the trustee of the father who is testing the son's wisdom as an explicit condition for his receiving the inheritance, or the son who is carrying out enigmatic deeds that puzzle his host? As a riddle, the tale contributes to the variety of genres in

1. The story is told in Aramaic, in the two editions of *Lamentations rabbah*: *Midrash rabbah*, vol. 2, 1, 4: *Rabbati bagoyim*; and the Buber edition, 1, 46–47.
2. Hasan-Rokem, *The Web of Life*, 62. On story cycles in the *Aggadah*, see Yassif, *Kemargalit bemishbeẓet*, 31–75, 209.
3. Hasan-Rokem, *The Web of Life*, 63.

Sefer ha-ma'asim. It is inserted between tales from two other genres typical of the Middle Ages: "The Loan," of the religious exemplum, and "Joab's Valor," a kind of medieval epic poem about battles and victories.

In *Sefer ha-ma'asim* the story is taken out of the homiletic context of Lamentations, and of the cycle of stories about the competition between the Jerusalemites and the Athenians over the crown of wisdom. It lacks the nationalistic aspect of *Lamentations rabbah*, since the event occurs in an anonymous city by the sea, not in Athens, with its cultural significance. The exposition of the tale presents the son as his father's only child, a detail not mentioned in *Lamentations rabbah*: "If my son comes for it, test and examine him in three ways. Should he prove that he is wise, give him my money, and if not, let it be sanctified to heaven." In this story, did the son know about his father's will in relation to him? Did he seek his father's inheritance at his own initiative, or did he know in advance about the condition his father had stipulated? That is not clear. In any case, the requirement for wisdom as a condition for receiving the inheritance was meant to ensure that the father's great wealth would be preserved. Indirectly, it is a command to properly and wisely manage the inherited fortune. From this standpoint, the heir's test is a rite of passage from childhood to adulthood, which involves taking responsibility and possessing commercial skills. Father-son relations on the family level are at the center of this tale in *Sefer ha-ma'asim* and the father's indirect command to his son through his trustee. The motif of a father's last command to his son appears frequently in *Sefer ha-ma'asim*.

Father-son relations are linked in this tale with broader types of relations within the family, and these are coded in the riddle scene. The guest is asked to divide the meat among the members of the family, which he does in an enigmatic manner. Instead of dividing it equally, he gives the father, who was also his host, the head of the chicken, signifying his status as the head of the family; the tail to the wife, indicating her base at home; the wings to the daughters, who are due to marry and leave home; and the legs to the sons, who are intended to take over in due time as the heads of the family, and are therefore the "pillars of the home." His explanation for his decisions sound logical to the host, and fit into his preconceptions and ideas of family structures: hierarchies, stability, and lineage. The tale fits into a larger discourse in *Sefer ha-ma'asim* on the institution of the family and its values.

Another context is the motif of the deposit, which is also often found in *Sefer ha-ma'asim*. The money is given to the trustee as a deposit until the son gains his inheritance.[4] In *Sefer ha-ma'asim*, the father's words to the trustee are a direct quotation: "He called his host and said to him: I hereby leave all my money in your hands." In *Lamentations rabbah*, the event is related indirectly by the narrator: "(and he deposited his money with that same man with whom he was staying)." The deposit motif is particularly emphasized in *Sefer ha-ma'asim* by its modus of direct speech. Two key transformations occur, therefore, in *Sefer ha-ma'asim* in contrast to its source in *Lamentations rabbah*: from a national narrative to a tale about father-son relations, and from a test of wisdom to a deposit story.

The story is cited in other sources in Ashkenaz later than *Sefer ha-ma'asim*: in a fourteenth-century Jewish chronicle edited by Yassif (*The Book of Memory*), and in the 1602 *Mayse bukh.*[5] It also influenced current international and Israeli folklore.[6]

4. Nonetheless, it is not a typical deposit tale, since the trustee does not misuse the deposit but rather faithfully carries out his duties.

5. Yassif, ed., *The Book of Memory*, 336–338; 551, n. 2; *Mayse bukh* (Basel), no. 186; *Ma'aseh Book*, trans. Gaster, vol. 2, no. 187, 404–410.

6. ATU 1533 (IFA); cf. ATU 1663: "Dividing Eggs Equally between Two Men and One Woman."

4. Joab's Valor (301a–302a)

No earlier versions of this tale are extant, whether in the Talmud, Midrash, or medieval story compilations in the East, such as *Ḥibbur yafeh mehayeshu'a* and *Midrash aseret hadibrot.* It is mentioned, however, in one of the text witnesses of *Maḥzor Vitry,*[1] which quotes *Midrash Tehilim*, also entitled "*shoḥer tov*," in a commentary on a *piyyut* (liturgical poem) recited on the festival of Shavuoth:[2] "*Shoḥer tov* elaborates on his [Joab's] valor among the Ammonites."[3] Two additional versions of the tale in Ashkenaz and one in Provence are from the fourteenth century.[4] The story was also transmitted in Ashkenaz after the Middle Ages, in *Mayse bukh.*[5]

In a sense, "Joab's Valor" resembles the medieval heroic epics (*les chansons de geste*) about the knights' battles against pagans and Muslims (Saracens), the "enemies of Christianity." These epic poems were at their height in the mid-twelfth century and still very popular in the thirteenth century, when they were circulated in many manuscripts. *Chanson de Roland*, the earliest of the French vernacular epic poems still extant, was presumably written in the twelfth century, when the church and the king were united in their war against heretics.[6]

Roland was the finest among the knights who commanded the Frankish armies of King Charlemagne of France, fighting against the Saracens in northern Spain. After long years of inconclusive fighting, his enemy, Marsilion, king of Saragossa, decided to pretend to surrender and to convert to Christianity on condition that Charlemagne desist and return to France. Roland and his knights agreed, but when one of his warriors betrayed him, he and the knights with him were caught and ambushed in the narrow Rencesvals passage in the Pyrenees. They fought courageously but had no chance of winning. Roland died of his wounds, but not before he succeeded in forcing Marsilion to withdraw from the battlefield.[7] The religious and

1. This text witness, which indicates a terminus ad quem of the story, is from the end of the twelfth century. See *Maḥzor Vitry*, ed. Horowitz, 332, and the Goldschmidt edition (2: 555).
2. The *piyyut* is cited in connection with the commandment "Thou shalt not kill."
3. This version of *Midrash Tehilim* is lost.
4. In Ashkenaz: Ms. Cambridge-Harvard, Heb. 39, 119a–121a, and Ms. Darmstadt, Cod. Or. 25, 67b–68a; in Provence: *Yalkut hamakhiri*, Psalms, ed. Buber, psalm 61, 115–116. For a chronological list of the story's versions, see Kushelevsky, *Penalty and Temptation*, 305–306.
5. *Mayse bukh*, no. 145, trans. Gaster, as *Ma'aseh Book*, vol. 1, no. 145, 280–286.
6. An earlier, unrhymed version of *Chanson de Roland* is dated to 1098, while the rhymed version is dated after 1180 (Gilbert, "The Chanson de Roland," 23).
7. *La Chanson de Roland*; *The Song of Roland.*

nationalistic fanaticism interwoven in *Chanson de Roland* is typical of the First Crusade discourse.[8]

Joab is depicted, like Roland and other heroes of epic poems, as an arrogant, brave hero, fanatically devoted to his religion and his king, prepared to fight relentlessly to the bitter end. Joab remains alive, whereas Roland dies in battle, but their loyalty to their king, either King David or Charlemagne, is an ethos common to both works. Other shared motifs are the warrior's special sword, the lengthy siege, and the decisive outcome of the battle while fighting goes on in the rear. As Eli Yassif has claimed, "Joab's Valor" might be regarded as a sort of Jewish epic poem, which shares a similar discourse with the medieval hero epics prevalent in Western Europe.[9] In the reality of the Crusades, Ashkenazi Jews were victims, but in the story they take on the image of the hero-knight, attributing it to the brave commander of King David's army.

Nonetheless the plot deviates from the conventions of epic poems in several major details, and Joab's portrait is not totally consistent with the topoi of the courageous, noble warrior-knight. He cuts open the stomach of a pregnant woman who treated his wounds and gave him shelter in her home, and strikes a local blacksmith who is not a soldier. In these details, the story is resonant of another topoi, that of the war against Amalek in Jewish sources, from the Bible and thereafter (Exodus 15:14–15; Deuteronomy 25:17–19). In Jewish sources, Amalekites—in the ethnic sense as the descendants of Eliphas b. Esau—are the essence of evil who should be annihilated, their name and memory erased forever, without mercy even for women and children: "you shall blot out the remembrance of Amalek from under heaven; you shall not forget it" (Deuteronomy 25:19).[10]

"Joab's Valor" is in fact set in the land of Amalek, and the backdrop is the biblical account of Joab's war against the Edomites (1 Kings [11:16]): "For six months Joab remained there with all Israel, until he had cut off every male in Edom." The Talmud (*Baba Batra* 21a–b) depicts this episode as a war against the Amalekites in the land of Edom, in which Joab failed to execute the biblical command. Instead of destroying the very memory of Amalek, he killed the males only, the result of an

8. Newth, *French Epic*, vii–xiv. The context of the Crusades is particularly marked in the cycle of epic poems about the First Crusade.

9. See Yassif, "The Story of Joab's Deeds of Valour," 22–23, which compares the story to the Alexander Romance.

10. In the postbiblical sources, the war is postdated to the end of days, when the ethnic identification of Amalek will be possible.

error in reading the biblical word *zekher* (remember) as *zakhar* (masculine).[11] Joab's victory over Amalek in "Joab's Valor" is depicted as a rectification of this failure. When he strikes the blacksmith with his sword and particularly when he slays the pregnant woman, he is demonstrating that he is able this time to overcome his natural feelings of compassion and act according to the commandment in the Bible, blotting out even the remembrance of Amalek, and never forgetting.

"Joab's Valor" is patterned, then, on two models of religious wars: the chivalric wars against enemies of Christianity in the epic poems and the war against Amalek from Jewish sources. These models conflict with each other in the story, and are presented in a contrasting analogy, while they also complement each other as a Jewish replacement for the Christian epic poems in France. The story reflects an interest in French epic poems among Jews, but it is adapted according to the distinct archetype of a religious war in Jewish sources: the war against Amalek.

In the modern era, beginning with *Ḥibbur hama'asiyot vehamidrashot vehahagadot* of the sixteenth century (no. 9), there is a trend to rationalize Joab's deeds and to render them less horrific. The scene of his encounter with the girl in which he kills her does remain in the story—folktales tend to recur in set formulas—but her pregnancy, which makes Joab's action more brutal, is not mentioned. That is also true of a version in Ms. Krup from the eighteenth century;[12] in Shabbtai Farḥi's *Oseh pele*;[13] in *Sefer hama'asiyot* by El'azar Araki in the nineteenth century;[14] and in several rabbinical and literary collections: Adolf (Aaron) Jellinek's *Bet hamidrasch*, Jehudah Eisenstein's *Oẓar midrashim*, Micha Joseph Bin Gorion's (Berdyczewski's) *Mimekor yisrael*, and Louis Ginzberg's *Legends of the Jews.*[15] The historical context of the Crusades was no longer relevant, and the war against Amalek, which in *Sefer ha-ma'asim* is told against the backdrop of the Crusades, takes on the aura of a medieval epic poem only on the rhetorical level, not as a lived experience.

11. "Thou shalt blot out the remembrance [*zekher*] of Amalek from under heaven; thou shalt not forget it" (Deuteronomy 25:19). *Zekher* and *zakhar* share the same consonants but differ in their vowels.

12. Krupp, "Joab's Acts," 141–145.

13. Farḥi, *Oseh pele* 1, 49–50.

14. Araki, *Sefer hama'asiyot*, no. 9, 8a–10a, and in Ḥuẓin's edition of *Sefer hama'asiyot*, no. 9, 8b–10a.

15. Jellinek, *Bet hamidrasch* 2:5, 146–148; Eisenstein, *Oẓar midrashim* 2, 327–328; Bin Gorion, *Mimekor yisrael*, no. 54, 55–56; Ginzberg, *The Legends of the Jews*, 5, 97–101.

5. The Two-Headed Man (302a–302b)

The tale is mentioned in a commentary on the Tosafot to *Menaḥot* 37a with no further elaboration, which probably indicates its circulation in Ashkenaz in the twelfth and thirteenth centuries and its reception as a well-known story. Only its first part, in which Asmodeus takes the two-headed man out from under the earth, is cited in the Tosafot in relation to a talmudic discussion of the rules of tefillin.[1] Pelemo asks R. Judah HaNasi: "If a man has two heads, on which one must he put the tefillin?" Rabbi, regarding the question as either provocative or jocular, reacts sharply: "You must either leave or regard yourself under the ban." In Rashi's words: "Leave and go out into exile, or accept the ban." The Tosafists mention the story under the name *midrash*[2] and explain that, in the reality known to Rabbi, there was no such creature, but he indeed existed under the earth. The tale was also mentioned by Mordechai (Mordekhai b. Hillel, 1250–1298) in relation to the same halakhic discussion of the rules of tefillin, but there too it is not cited in full.[3]

Sefer ha-ma'asim detached the tale from its halakhic context to illustrate the marvelous and the bizarre, as inferred from Asmodeus's daring promise to Solomon to show him "something the likes of which you have never seen before." The marvelous is a key theme in the medieval Hebrew and Christian tale in Europe.[4] The antipodal figure of the two-headed man is pulled up by Asmodeus from a land called Tuval in *Sefer ha-ma'asim* and Tevel in other versions. It is the land of the offspring of Cain, which is run both similarly and differently from the ways of ordinary

1. R. Beẓalel b. Abraham Ashkenazi, in the sixteenth century, cites the second part of the story in his commentary "*Shitah mekubetzet*" (tractate *Menachot*, no. 18). His version differs in one detail from *Sefer ha-ma'asim*, in that Solomon covers one head and pours boiling water on the other. On the tale, its contexts, and versions, see Avida (Zlotnik), "*Anashim benei shnei rashim*" ("People with Two Heads"), 17–25; Daniel Sperber, *Magic and Folklore in Rabbinic Literature*, 13–24.

2. The expression *midrash* is apt to be an *aggadah* that was preserved only in Ashkenaz and lost thereafter, thus remaining unknown to us today. It might also indicate an interpolation in one of the manuscripts of a certain midrashic work, in keeping with the trend among Torah scholars in Ashkenaz to proofread the Talmud and other works according to traditions prevailing in Ashkenaz.

3. See his commentary on tractate *Menachot*, 37a, in the Romm editions of Talmud, *Hilkhot tefillin*, starting with the words: "*ba'ai minai pelemo*" ("He asked Pelemo").

4. See Rotman, *Dragons*, and the definition of "marvelous" in the medieval context on pp. 62–65. It seems that the category of the "outsiders," which Rotman ascribes to demons as a trait of the marvelous, can also be applied to the man with two heads, a descendant of Cain. For the Christian allegorical significance of the creature with two heads, see *Gesta* (Swan), no. 176, 367.

people.[5] From many standpoints, the offspring of Cain resemble demons, which in turn resemble humans in several of their traits and differ from them in others. Some of them study Torah and pray like Jews.[6] The theme of the marvelous is particularly prevalent in medieval travel literature, which acquaints its readers with new sights and territories that are unfamiliar and challenging.[7] In the present tale, the two-headed "tourist" is brought by Asmodeus to Solomon's palace, which is five hundred travel years away. The marvelous here is depicted from the vantage point of Solomon and his men, who are amazed at the sight of the creature from the land of Asmodeus, king of the demons.

In the presence of the two-headed man in Solomon's palace, a clash ensues between Solomon and Asmodeus that is intended to prove Solomon's limitations and challenge his authority. Asmodeus's provocative words to Solomon—"Are you the one of whom it is written that he is wiser than all men?"—call for a comparison to another tale of a conflict between the two (*Gittin* 68b), in which Solomon provokes Asmodeus and asks: "What is your superiority over us?"; namely, how do the demons have greater power than humans? In the talmudic story, Asmodeus overthrows Solomon and ousts him from his throne, while in *Sefer ha-ma'asim* Solomon overcomes Asmodeus and proves he is indeed the wisest of all men.

In the second part of the story, the conflict deviates from the encounter between Solomon and the two-headed man and moves to the latter's offspring. Years later, a struggle over the inheritance ensues between the two-headed man's sons, six of whom, like ordinary men, resemble his wife, and one of whom has two heads, thus resembling his father. Solomon's prestige and his status as the king and the wisest of judges are put to a test, similar to the conflict between Asmodeus and Solomon in the talmudic story. From this aspect, the story also belongs to the "clever judge" tale type in *Sefer ha-ma'asim* (ATU 926A), like others of this type, such as "Who Is the Thief? (no. 16), "One of Ten" (no. 17), and "The Hard-Boiled Egg" (no. 54). The story is not placed adjacent to them, however, but rather between "Joab's Valor" (no. 4) and "The Drunkard and His Sons" (no. 6), and there does not seem to be an

5. See Ginzberg's references to sources, mainly from the *Zohar*, about the residence of the offspring of Cain under that of human beings, in *The Legends of the Jews*, 5, esp. "The Ten Generations," 143, n. 34. In these sources "Tevel" is the country of human beings, the uppermost of the seven lands, one below the other. See also Avida (Zlotnik), "*Anashim benei shnei rashim*," 23–24.

6. On the traits of demons in affinity with humans, see *Ḥagigah* 17a; and on the orders of the country of the demons who learn and pray there, marry, and bear children, see *Ma'aseh yerushalayim*, copied in Ms. Bdl. Or. 135 (255b–256b).

7. See Dan, ed., *Alilot Alexander Mocedon*.

editing principle that determined this location. Its style is succinct, in keeping with the scribe's tendency to forego details that are clear from the context, such as epithets and repeated words that do not change the content but only create a certain compression, in contrast to later versions such as *Midrash aseret hadibrot* in Ms. Vatican 285 from the fifteenth century.[8]

After *Sefer ha-ma'asim*, the tale was mainly transmitted according to a printed version in *Meshalim shel Shelomo hamelekh*[9] and in *Ḥibbur hama'asiyot vehamidrashot vehahagadot* (no. 11).[10] A somewhat different version is copied in Ms. Manchester-Gaster 82, from the sixteenth century;[11] according to this version, Solomon spilled boiling water on one head and wine on the other. Both heads screamed with pain, and both became intoxicated. That proved the two were as one and were not entitled to a double inheritance. The transmission of the tale continued into the nineteenth and twentieth centuries, when it was included in rabbinical and literary collections such as *Oẓar midrashim, Mimekor yisrael* and *The Legends of the Jews*.[12] In international folklore the "two-headed man" was classified as motif J1176.4.

8. See 83a–84a.

9. The story was not included in the 1517 Constantinople edition of *Meshalim shel Shelomo hamelekh* but rather beginning with the Jellinek edition only (*Bet hamidrasch* 2:4, 151–152). Regarding the time of its inclusion in in *Meshalim shel Shelomo hamelekh*, see Yassif, *Kemargalit bemishbeẓet*, 240, nn. 8–9.

10. For a selection of versions in Hebrew after the Middle Ages, see Ms. Munich 222, 46b–47b, and copies in manuscript form based on printed editions: Ms. New York JTS mic. 1480, 25a–28b; Ms. Cincinnati 61a, 21a–25a; Ms. British Library 27186, 16b–17b. In later story compilations, see Araki, *Sefer hama'asiyot*, no. 11, 11a–12a, and in Ḥuẓin's edition, no. 11, 10b–11b; Farḥi, *Oseh pele* 1, 40–42.

11. See an abridgment in Gaster, *Exempla*, no. 392, 150.

12. Levner, *Kol agadot yisrael* (*The Legends of Israel*), vol. 1, part 3, no. 331, 375–379; Grünwald, *Yalkut sippurim*, part 2, 114b–115b; Joseph Ḥaim b. Eliahu, *Nifla'im ma'asekha*, 28, 21a–21b; Eisenstein, *Oẓar midrashim* 2, 533–534; Bin Gorion, *Mimekor yisrael*, no. 73, versions a–b, 66–67; Ben-Amos, *Mimekor yisrael*, no. 30, 52–53; Ginzberg, *The Legends of the Jews*, vol. 4, 131–132.

6. The Drunkard and His Sons (302b–303a)

The first written version of the tale appears in *Leviticus rabbah*, in the framework of a series of homilies on the verse: "Do not drink wine nor strong drink" (Leviticus 10:9).[1] While the homilies in general denounce drunkenness, the story supposedly legitimizes it, since it concludes on a positive note. The drunkard's sons are forced to provide their father with his daily portion of wine and let him be. However, the outcome of the story is not clear-cut. The sons leave their drunken father in the burial chamber and almost cause his death in their attempt to wean him from his drunkenness, which is eating up all of their money. Despite the ending, which seems to praise drunkenness, and in contrast to the entire chapter in *Leviticus rabbah*, the story's moral is that one should cope with the damage inflicted by intoxication instead of humiliating and abandoning one's father. The value of honoring parents prevails over the disapproval of drunkenness.[2]

There are two textual traditions of the story, one more expanded than the other, each represented by a number of manuscripts of *Leviticus rabbah*,[3] as well as *Esther rabbah* (5:1) and *Yalkut shimoni* on Proverbs (no. 960), both of which quote the shorter version.[4]

The tale's wittiness and its comic tone when the sons conclude that they should provide their father with his daily portion of wine—which are in marked contrast to the shocking effect of their plot to kill him and the putative incongruity between the tale and its context in *Leviticus rabbah*—have given rise to a variety of studies.[5] The affinity of the tale to an ancient parallel in *Aesop's Fables* has been noted as well.[6]

---

1. See *Leviticus rabbah*, 12, 1, ed. Margulieus, 245–247.
2. This is the conclusion reached by both Shinan and Shoshany: Shinan, "*Kiso, Koso vekaso: Al haYay'in beSifrut Ḥazal*" ("His Pocket, Cup and Anger"), 47–49; Shoshany, "The Story of the Drunk and His Sons," 315–338.
3. For some examples of the expanded narrative, see Ms. Münich 117, which was determined as the main body of chapter 12 in Margulies's edition; and Ms. T—S C2.162 (cited in Margulies's edition., vol. 2, "Seridei vayikra rabbah," 26–27).
4. See Margulies's apparatus to the tale, 245–247
5. Other than Shinan and Shoshany (n. 2), see, in chronological order: Bin Gorion, *The Paths of Legend*; Heinemann, "The Art of the Sermon"; Elbaum, "Tales of a Drunkard and of an Ugly Man," 122–129; Yassif, *The Hebrew Folktale*, 175–177; Levinson, "Upside-down World"; Mali, "The Drunkard and His Sons"; and Ben-Amos, *Mimekor yisrael*, no. 95, 179. See also comments to a parallel in *Mishlei shu'alim* by R. Berakhiah Hanakdan: Schwarzbaum, *Mishle shu'alim*, no. 115, 538–540. Cf. ATU 1706D: "How the drunken man was cured"; Th. J1321: "The unrepentant drunkard."
6. Elbaum, "Tales of a Drunkard and an Ugly Man."

In the expanded version in *Leviticus rabbah*, the sons' intention to kill their father is obvious, although it is not explicitly stated, as Ronit Shoshany has pointed out. Their plot is inferred from their intention to publicize his death in advance and stage a funeral, first getting him drunk and then carrying him to the cemetery while spreading the word that he had died. That intention is also underscored by the long lapse of the three days during which they left their father in the burial chamber, until they returned to check on him. In contrast, the shorter version sounds apologetic in its tendency to gloss over the sons' intention. The conversation during which they conspire is condensed, and there is no mention of their intention to see if he was actually dead.

Sefer ha-ma'asim has the expanded version. Although it is quite similar to its source in *Leviticus rabbah*, it has some unique features: (1) The description of the burial chamber is realistic, depicting a "rock [cave] that resembled [a building]," in contrast to the general term given in *Leviticus rabbah*—*bet olam* (lit., house of eternity). The explanation added to *Sefer ha-ma'asim* was apparently meant to bridge a historical gap and clarify the real-life circumstances in the time of the Amoraim, when goods could be hidden in a burial chamber.[7] Similarly, the reason given in *Sefer ha-ma'asim* for the Ishmaelites' flight is that "pursuers had come to the city," in contrast to *Leviticus rabbah*, where they fear they may be forced to pay with their labor for a tax imposed on the goods by the authorities (*angariah*). The change probably reflects a reality of persecutions in Ashkenaz. (2) The sons are not as negatively depicted as in *Leviticus rabbah*, although their intention to murder their father is not glossed over. So impoverished are they because of their father's habit of wasting all their earnings on wine that they cannot even buy themselves shoes. Yet they support their old father and look after him. This would imply that it is not greed that drives them to take such a desperate step but rather poverty. (3) Paradoxically, they are harshly and explicitly denounced by the father, a detail not mentioned in *Leviticus rabbah*. He calls them wicked and rejects their help. (4) The "neighbors" who are informed by the sons of their father's "death" are not mentioned in *Leviticus rabbah*. (5) The affinity with the story of Joseph and his brothers (Genesis 37:12–36), which is already alluded to in *Leviticus rabbah*, is particularly emphasized here in *Sefer ha-ma'asim* by means of an allusion to the biblical story of Joseph: "you intended to do me harm, and God turned it into something good, and kept me alive on this day."[8] The depiction of the merchants as "Ishmaelites" also alludes to the biblical story in

7. Shoshany, "The Story of the Drunk and His Sons," 320, n. 24, where she refers to Elbaum, "Tales of a Drunkard and an Ugly Man."

8. Cf. Genesis 3:20: "You thought evil against me, but God meant it for good."

which Joseph is sold to Ishmaelites (Genesis 37:27–28), and implies criticism of the sons' plot.

The motif of the shoes is especially striking in *Sefer ha-ma'asim*, because of its intertextual affinity with *Midrash aseret harugei malkhut* (*The Ten Martyrs*), as it was known in Ashkenaz.[9] The Roman emperor placed ten Jewish sages in a room full of shoes and demanded that they decide on the appropriate punishment for someone who steals a human being and sells him. When they agree on a death verdict, the emperor applies this to them, because their ancestors, Joseph's brothers, had sold Joseph in exchange for shoes. They were given a three-day postponement, during which they heard from behind the partition in heaven that they were indeed sentenced to death for the sin of Joseph's brothers; and then they exposed themselves to a cruel death. Particularly relevant to the present context is a quotation of a verse from Amos (2:6), specifically in the Ashkenazi tradition of *Aseret harugei malkhut*: "For three transgressions of Israel I will turn away his punishment, but for the fourth I will not turn away its punishment; because they sold the righteous for silver, and the poor for a pair of shoes." The verse was applied to the sale of Joseph in a late midrash and in biblical commentary in Ashkenaz.[10] *Midrash aseret harugei malkhut* presents a dialectic position in relation to the death of the ten sages who are killed for the sake of Joseph's brothers: expressing a profound identification with them as sanctifiers of the Almighty while also making them, the representatives of the Jewish collective, responsible for selling Joseph to the Ishmaelites.

Alongside the Jewish narrative of *Aseret harugei malkhut*, a Christian narrative was prevalent in Europe according to which the sale of Joseph prefigured the betrayal of Jesus by Judas Iscariot, for which the Jews and their leaders were being punished.[11] In this Christian narrative, the sale of Joseph and the motif of the shoes linked to it represent a topoi of base treachery.[12] Turning back to our tale of the drunkard and his sons in *Sefer ha-ma'asim*, these resonances regarding the motif of the shoes in

9. On its version in Ashkenaz, also known as *Midrash Eleh Ezkerah*, see Yassif, *The Book of Memory*, 383–389; a different version is in Jellinek, *Bet hamidrasch*, 2, 64–72.

10. *Tanḥuma, Vayeshev*, 2; *Pirkei d'rabbi eliezer*, 36:5: "*Uba el habayit*" ("And he came to the house"); *Da'at zekenim*, Genesis 37:28. See also *Midrash mishle*, ed. Visotzky, 1, 13, 18, but this version is not in affinity with the verse in Amos and the motif of the shoes.

11. See Marcus, "Sanctity in Ashkenaz and the Story of R. Amnon of Mainz," 137–138.

12. The ten martyrs are also mentioned in the chronicles of the Jews' persecutions in Ashkenaz during the Crusades, where the ancient sin of the Jews is that of worshipping the golden calf (idolatry as an act of treachery). In this manner sanctification of the Holy Name is represented as a rectification of the sin of worshipping the golden calf. See Habermann, *Sefer gezerot Ashkenaz veẓorfat*, 73; Haverkamp, ed., *Hebräische Berichte . . . Kreuzzugs*, 68 [558]; and a discussion in Marcus, "Sanctity in Ashkenaz and the Story of R. Amnon of Mainz," n. 33, 138–139.

Jewish and Christian culture intensify the criticism of the sons' betrayal of their father, but also promote some empathy toward them due to their distressing poverty, which is concretized by the motif of the shoes. The tale has an affinity in Ashkenaz with *Midrash aseret harugei malkhut* which does not exist in *Leviticus rabbah*, and it is created by the motif of the shoes.

Following *Sefer ha-ma'asim*, the sons are somewhat more sympathetically depicted in Ms. Jerusalem 3182 (108a), probably in reaction to the moral and emotional difficulties of describing sons plotting to kill their father: "And thus they were honoring him as well as they could for many years until they could no longer bear the life of their father who troubled them more and more in his old age."[13] This probably indicates an indirect influence of *Sefer ha-ma'asim* on the later compilation of stories in Ashkenaz.[14]

13. Yassif, *Ninety-nine Tales*, 189, no. 20, and notes on p. 270.

14. For additional late sources and research, see Ben-Amos, *Mimekor yisrael*, no. 95, 179.

7. The Three Treasures (303a)

This story, of the tale type ATU 834,[1] is not known from Jewish sources that predate *Sefer ha-ma'asim*. It was adapted to Jewish culture in *Sefer ha-ma'asim* through the motif of "charity saves from death," which often recurs in Jewish sources, specifically in medieval tales.[2] The international tale type is summarized as follows: A couple dreams about a pot full of gold hidden somewhere (or the man finds a treasure and leaves it in place). Robbers who learn about this dig and find the pot, only to discover that it is full of scorpions or snakes. In revenge, they throw the pot at the man's house, and the scorpions turn into gold. The story presents opposing values, manifested in the protagonist's decision not to take what is not his, while his antagonists, the robbers, do not hesitate to steal. The tale ends with the edifying message that, whatever happens, things turn out as they should. The treasure is restored to the one for whom it was intended.

Sefer ha-ma'asim's version is not quite the same, but it does have the basic opposition between the different attitudes toward the treasure: namely a protagonist who has the ability and the generosity either to leave the treasure untouched for the sake of others (in the international tale type) or to share it with them (in the Jewish parallel), and an antagonist who is ruled by greed and envy. In all versions, Jewish and non-Jewish, the treasure actually ends up with the person for whom it was intended, while in the hands of the others it turns into scorpions. The epilogue, which values charity, is analogous to the exposition about the charitable protagonist in the opening of the tale: "He that has a bountiful eye shall be blessed; for he gives of his bread to the poor" (Proverbs 22:9).

The ethos of charity is linked with hospitality in the tale: "Eat not the bread of he who is stingy. . . . Eat and drink, he says to you; but his heart is not with you" (Proverbs 23:6–7). In Proverbs this is an instruction not to dine in the home of a

1. ATU 834a: "The Poor Brother's Treasure." See references to the tale type by Ḥaim Schwarzbaum and Dan Ben-Amos and their comments: Schwarzbaum, *Studies in Jewish and World Folklore*, 74–77; Ben-Amos, *Mimekor yisrael*, no. 212, 415, no. 246, 456–457. I did not find any versions of the type in medieval Europe, but its many oral parallels in the East and West, which are prevalent today, may indicate their dissemination in the Middle Ages. Cf. Tubach 5054, "Treasure of Usurer Turns to Serpents."

2. See, for example, the legend about R. Akiva's daughter and the snake (*Shabbat* 156b), which is also included in *Sefer ha-ma'asim*. On the oikotype as a universal tale type adapted to a specific culture, see Von Sydow, "Geography and Folk-Tale Oicotypes," 44–59. Tales of charity in *Sefer ha-ma'asim* include, among others, "R. Meir and Judah of Anatot" (no. 25), "Ben Sever and Shefifon Ben Layish" (no. 27), "The Seven Good Years" (no. 29), and "Saved from Drowning by Charity" (no. 31).

stingy host who receives his guest due to social pressure rather than because he sincerely cares about him: Eventually the guest will vomit because of the miserly eye that is watching him.[3] In *Sefer ha-ma'asim*, in a misogynistic tone, the transformation of the gold into scorpions (and into ants and fleas) is a concretization of the woman's stinginess, in contrast to her husband's generosity. And because she is miserly, she suspects her husband of having deliberately left her with pots full of scorpions, ants, and fleas, in contradiction of his words: "But all my treasures are in your hands."[4] In her husband's absence, she apparently intended to give his guests the same amount of charity as he would have given, but for her own selfish reasons (as indicated in her embarrassment about receiving them with empty hands). Hospitality is interpreted here as a modus of charity, through the quotation from Proverbs and its implied criticism of the wife in contrast to appreciation for the man.

This idea of hospitality as a modus of charity given either willingly or only because of social pressure is amplified in *Sefer ḥasidim*, in relation to a talmudic tractate in *Ḥullin* (7b). The Talmud tells about R. Pinḥas b. Yair, one of the early *ḥasidim*, who was careful never to dine in a place where he was not truly welcome, or where the meal was not sufficient for his hosts.[5] *Sefer ḥasidim* further expands on the issue:

> There are things that are not strictly robbery, but may be worse than robbery, for example, a guest who avails himself of a person's hospitality may be guilty of robbery, because the host may be either righteous or rich but [in any case] he is a miser who is ashamed to send the guest away. Or if a guest comes to a poor man who does not have enough food for himself but is ashamed to say so, morally this is plain robbery, and so we read: "Do not eat of a stingy man's food."

This statement in *Sefer ḥasidim* is an extract from a larger discourse about the behavior of hosts toward their guests, whether hospitable or miserly, found in the chapter on Torah learners.[6] The verse quoted in *Sefer ha-ma'asim* is cited in *Sefer*

3. "The morsel which you have eaten shall you vomit up" (23:8).

4. This may be an allusion to *Avoth de-Rabbi Nathan*, ed. Schechter (prolegomenon by Kister), version 2, chap. I, 7. It resembles the case of the king whose wife gained control over his money, gold, and all he possessed; he said, "Everything I have is in your hands except this barrel full of scorpions." Cf. a similar use of this topos in "Slander Kills Three" (no. 30).

5. Cf. *Baba Meṣia* 22a and *Sotah* 38b.

6. Although hospitality is apt to interrupt the study of Torah, in contradiction of the commandment to "meditate on it day and night" (Joshua 1:8), *Sefer ḥasidim* advises its readers to honor their guests (ed. Wistinetzke, no. 850. For the quotation above see no. 848, 214).

ḥasidim too: "He that has a bountiful eye shall be blessed; for he gives of his bread to the poor" (Proverbs 22:9). *Sefer ḥasidim* deduces from this verse that he who has a bountiful eye will be blessed, rather than the one who under duress grudgingly serves as a host (no. 851, 214). Elsewhere *Sefer ḥasidim* relates to a situation in which the wife, not the husband, is the one with a bountiful eye (no. 844, 213). The very distinction drawn between the different approaches of the spouses is interesting, in view of the reverse in *Sefer ha-ma'asim.*

The special amplification in *Sefer ḥasidim*, the degree of gravity ascribed to the subject, the motif of shame, the context of "Torah learners," and the implications of stinginess toward guests for husband-wife relations are probably in the background of our tale in *Sefer ha-ma'asim*.

The hierarchy among talmudic scholars and other guests, and its implications for the amount of charity to be given to them compared to that for widows and orphans who are not students, also reflect norms set in *Sefer ḥasidim*, which instructs the community to give preference to those who study Torah for its own sake and not for personal interests (*Torah lishma*) over the donor's poor relatives.[7] Orders of priority for giving charity, in the broad sense of helping the other, already exist in previous sources,[8] but they are applied in *Sefer ḥasidim* as detailed and concrete guidelines for giving charity especially in situations of conflict between different principles. It seems that the distinction between Torah scholars and other poor people in "The Three Treasures" in *Sefer ha-ma'asim* draws its inspiration from *Sefer ḥasidim*, thus anchoring the tale in Ashkenaz.

After *Sefer ha-ma'asim*, the tale was included in the story compilation in Ms. Jerusalem 3182 (105a),[9] and in the *Mayse bukh* (Basel, no. 196).[10] This indicates that *Sefer ha-ma'asim* influenced later story compilations. In the modern age, the story was adapted by Micha Joseph Bin Gorion in his collection *Ẓefunot ve'agadot* and in *Mimekor yisrael.*[11]

7. R. Judah b. Samuel, *Sefer ḥasidim*, ed. Wistinetzke, no. 919, 227.
8. See M. *Horayot* 3, 6–8; *Baba meṣia* 71a; M. *Terumot* 4c; *Berakhot* 10b.
9. Yassif, *Ninety-nine Tales*, no. 11, 182.
10. See also *Ma'aseh Book*, trans. Gaster, vol. 2, no. 196, 441–443.
11. Bin Gorion, *Ẓefunot ve'agadot*, 182–183; idem, *Mimekor yisrael*, no. 644, 395; Ben-Amos, *Mimekor yisrael*, no. 212, 415, n. 1. And see the *Sefer ha-ma'asim* version in Gaster, *Exempla*, no. 302, 193–194; Eisenstein, *Oẓar midrashim*, 2, 242–343.

8. The Demon in the Carob Tree (303a–303b)

"The Demon in the Carob Tree" is the first in a series of tales in *Sefer ha-ma'asim* that illustrate the Ten Commandments.[1] It relates to the second commandment ("Thou shalt have no other gods") and was apparently already included in an early version of *Midrash aseret hadibrot*,[2] and thereafter copied time after time, in various story and homiletic compilations, during the Middle Ages and thereafter.[3] The story was still being transmitted even when a warning about the prohibition of idolatry supposedly became superfluous. The high status of the Ten Commandments in Jewish culture; the scarcity of tales about the First and particularly the Second Commandment ("thou shalt have no other gods"); and the popularity of *Midrash aseret hadibrot*—all of these created suitable conditions for the recurrent reception of "The Demon in the Carob Tree" in Jewish works throughout the centuries.

The story, of the tale type AT 1168b, has many parallels in the Far and Near East.[4] It roots are apparently in Manichean myths in the Mani Codex (CMC) from the third century,[5] and in medieval story collections in Persian and Arabic from the thirteenth and fifteenth centuries. One of these latter texts is *Marzbān-nāma* (in Persian), from the thirteenth century, a collection of tales embedded in a frame story;[6] the other (in Arabic) is *Fākihat al-khulafā' wa-mufākahat al-ẓurafā'*, from the fifteenth century.[7]

The anthropomorphism of a tree that screams at the owner of the field not to dare cut it down is linked to the doctrine of Manicheanism, which was prevalent in the East in general and in Persia in particular, and polemicizes with it. According to this doctrine, the organic material in the world has a soul. Vegetables bleed when they are gathered, cutting down a tree is tantamount to murder, and the punishment

1. See references to parallels in Gaster, *Exempla*, no. 307, 236; no. 395, 258.
2. This is suggested by its consistent inclusion in many versions of *Midrash aseret hadibrot*, for example, in Ms. Paris 716 (212b--213a); Vatican 285, 67b–68b; Vatican 107, 162b; Moscow-Ginzburg 111, 103a–103b; Warsaw 374, 187a–187b; Vatican 249, 326a–326; Ms. Zurich 192, 61b–62a.
3. See R. David Hanagid, *Midrash david hanagid*, Exodus, Jethro; 89–90; Ms. Jerusalem 3182, 133b–134a (Yassif, *Ninety-nine Tales*, 249–250, no. 82); Ms. JTS 2374, 111a–111b; *Ḥibbur hama'asiyot vehamidrashot vehahagadot*, no. 15; Ms. Cincinnati 61a, 37a–39b; *Mayse bukh*, no. 189; *Ma'aseh Book*, trans. Gaster, 2, no. 190, 421–424; Araki, *Sefer hama'asiyot*, no. 15, 16a–16b, and Ḥuẓin's edition, no. 15, 14a–14b; Bin Gorion, *Mimekor yisrael*, no. 653, 402–403; and oral folklore in Israel, including Nana, *Oẓar hama'asiyot*, 255–256.
4. *Midrash aseret hadibrot*, ed. Shapira, 46, n. 73. Motifs relevant to the story include F402.6.1, N699.5.
5. For further elaboration, see Kushelevsky, "Medieval and Oral Variants of 'The Tree Demon'" 200–213, and her reference to Henrichs, "Thou Shalt Not Kill a Tree."
6. *Marzbān-nāma*, ed. Khalīl Khaṭīb Rahbar, 397–402.
7. Freytag, *Fākihat al-khulafā' wa-mufākahat al-ẓurafā'*, vol. 1, 130–131.

for this act is metamorphosis into a tree of the same kind. Such stories were included in the Mani Codex (CMC).[8]

At the center of the story is a tree as the site of an idolatrous ritual.[9] The narrator's focus on a single tree underscores the vertical structure against the backdrop of the horizontal field as a kind of "center of the world," the point of contact between heaven and earth. In mythic thought, the tree represents vitality, rejuvenation, and fertility. As a metonym of nature, it is perceived as a cosmic symbol.[10] The potential for vitality and rejuvenation is represented by means of the motifs of "field," "seeds," and the productivity of a "thousand measures," but also, conversely, to express the antimythical trend of the narrator. Accordingly, the ritual of the tree leads to a loss of the seeds; only after the tree is cut down, in keeping with the Sanhedrin's instruction, do the crops grow. The potential for fertility is also embodied in the erotic act that accompanies the tree ritual, which is denounced by the narrator as debauchery: "*Vehayou mesaḥakim sham*" ([people] indulging in revelry there").[11] The man's daily visits to the tree to collect the dinars is another signifier of a ritual. From the narrator's point of view, the mythical ritual's power of seduction lies in the antithetical opposition between the forces of nature and Judaism as a monotheistic religion.

The epilogue, which ends with a verse from Psalms (145:19)—"He will fulfill the desire of those who fear him"—expresses an intimacy between God and those who turn to him for help, in contrast to the "wicked," whom he will destroy (Psalms 145:20). The mythical tree and its idolatrous ritual are countered by the oneness of God and his power to benefit whoever fears him, and even to double their reward. The promise of productivity and rejuvenation in the tale turns out to be dangerously misleading, for it could have cost the *ḥasid* his life if the tree had succeeded in killing him.

The motif of deception and temptation is particularly marked in *Sefer ha-ma'asim* as compared to other versions. It is manifested by the limited vantage point of the man, who does not know what the Sanhedrin later tells him—that he was under the spell of the vain charm of idolatry. Accordingly it does not include the narrator's comment in other versions of *Midrash aseret hadibrot*, which explicates the nature of the tree as a ritual site. What the people visiting the tree are actually doing to worship it also becomes clear only gradually. The temptation of the coins and the

8. Henrichs, "Thou Shalt Not Kill a Tree," 16, 1–2, 92–108; Schier, "Ánimismus," 551–558.

9. On the tree ritual, see Deuteronomy 12:2; 1 Kings 14:23. On the carob as a sacred site in folklore, see Spanier, "The Distribution of the Carob Tree in Ancient Times," 175.

10. See, at length, Eliade, *Patterns in Comparative Religion*, 265–326.

11. For a similar, negative connotation of *mesaḥakim* (revelry), see *Sefer ḥasidim*, ed. Wistinetzke, no. 63, 48.

man's addiction to the tree and the power embodied in it grow constantly. Even when he comes to the tree, determined to cut it down following the deaths of his sons, he is seduced into amusing himself in front of it (*mesaḥakim sham*), namely worshipping it.[12] In other versions he refuses to join in the ritual of the tree, even when the demon threatens to kill him.

The emphasis in *Sefer ha-ma'asim* on the act of seduction and the transgression also stands out in light of the discrepancy between the *ḥasid* at the start of the story, when he "observed all the commandments," and the later part, when he was seduced by the "being" inside the tree. His characterization as a man who observed all the commandments, which is unique to *Sefer ha-ma'asim*, underscores the motif of seduction and may be a reaction to the temptations of Christianity. Although Christianity was not perceived as idolatry, its rituals do contain such concrete components.[13]

A tale that is similar in several aspects is cited in the Palestinian Talmud, tractate *Shabbat* 1c (3b):[14] "There was the story of a pious man, who was sitting and repeating the tradition as follows: 'Do not trust yourself until the days of your old age.' " Being old, he thought himself exempt from this rule, but was proven wrong when he was seduced by a spirit in the form of a beautiful woman. In both stories the protagonist, who is called a "*ḥasid*," is seduced by a demon or a spirit, despite his piety.

Various manuscripts of *Midrash aseret hadibrot*, although not *Sefer ha-ma'asim*, contain a follow-up story to "The Demon in the Carob Tree," in which the protagonist is seduced into worshipping a demon living in a marble stone. At first the stone demands that he wash it and place it in his home, and in return it bestows on him a large fortune. Then he is seduced into placing it in his room and beautifying it with attractive dishes, and in return the man gains another large fortune. Finally the stone demands that he light a candle before it, and the man realizes that there is a demon inside the stone, who tries to seduce him into idolatry. When he takes up a hammer to shatter the stone, the demon comes out and promises him a greater fortune if he leaves it alone. This time the *ḥasid* withstands the temptation. He shatters the stone and is much rewarded.[15] In this story, as in "The Demon in the Carob Tree," the motif of seduction is underscored. The tree, the stone, and the tombstone as a variant of the stone create the cosmic site that they symbolize in mythic thought.[16]

12. Although it is possible that "indulging in revelry there" may refer to the people who came to the tree, as mentioned at the beginning of the story.
13. Yassif, *The Hebrew Folktale*, 357.
14. Academy of the Hebrew Language edition, 370.
15. *Midrash aseret hadibrot*, ed. Shapira, 195; Gaster, *Exempla*, no. 396, 152–153.
16. Eliade, *Patterns in Comparative Religion*, 266.

9. Abraham in the Furnace (303b–305a)

Various episodes in the legend of Abraham in the furnace already exist in the rabbinic literature, but *Sefer ha-ma'asim* is the first evidence in writing of the expanded narrative that was prevalent in the Middle Ages.[1] It is also mentioned in *Midrash aseret hadibrot* in the same Bodl. Or. 135 manuscript (348b), with a reference to its version in *Sefer ha-ma'asim*. Its source is probably in *Midrash aseret hadibrot*, which circulated in the Middle Ages in many manuscripts, and from there it was copied into *Sefer ha-ma'asim*.[2] The consistent appearances of the story in *Midrash aseret hadibrot* in its various versions suggest that it is meant to illustrate the Second Commandment ("Thou shalt have no other . . ."). This conclusion is reinforced by the epilogue in *Sefer ha-ma'asim*, which also relates to that commandment, as well as from the adjacent location of "Abraham in the Furnace" and "The Mother and Her Sons" in both compilations. The tendency to summarize in *Sefer ha-ma'asim* in contrast to the extensive versions in *Midrash aseret hadibrot* (Ms. Paris 716) may also indicate that it was copied from an earlier known source. For example, the repeated description, in *Midrash aseret hadibrot*, of Abraham's attempt to test the reliability of each and every idol (by feeding it)[3] is omitted in *Sefer ha-ma'asim*, which summarizes the scene instead in a few words only, probably because the story was familiar and its details could easily be filled in.[4]

The story has developed in a number of versions, beginning with *Genesis rabbah* up to the expanded print versions, *Ma'aseh Avraham* and *Ma'aseh Avraham avinu mimah she'ira lo im nimrod*.[5] For centuries, the story was expanded, as narrative

1. On the story and its versions in Jewish literature, see Tohar, *Abraham in the Furnace of Fire*, 21–26.
2. The reference in the manuscript to *Sefer ha-ma'asim* may also indicate the opposite, as Tohar (p. 49) concluded: i.e., that the source of the story was *Sefer ha-ma'asim*, and the scribe linked it to *Midrash aseret hadibrot* by referring to its aforementioned version. The story may also have been copied into *Sefer ha-ma'asim* from a third source and then reworked, but it seems more likely to me that its source was *Midrash aseret hadibrot*, for the reasons that follow in the discussion.
3. Cf. ATU 1572*: "The saints ate the cream." See also ATU 2031: "Abraham learns to worship God."
4. "And he did the same to all of them." A similar rhetoric is also in the story of "The Mother and Her Sons" (no. 12). The eldest son's sanctification of the Holy Name is described in detail, while that of the other sons is summed up in a few words: "and each and every one."
5. For the classification of the versions into eight prominent groups, see Tohar, *Abraham in the Furnace*, 152–156. A selection of early rabbinical versions includes *Genesis Rabba*, 38, 25, 361–364, ed. Theodor and Albeck; b*Pesaḥim* 118a; *Pseudo-Jonathan*, Genesis 11:28, ed. Ginsburg, 19; *Tanḥuma, Teẓaveh*, no. 12; *Pirke R. Eliezer*, 26, 185–186; *Seder Eliahu Rabba*, ed. Ish Shalom, 6, 27; *Midrash aggadah on the Torah*, ed. Buber, 25; *Midrash Psalms* (*Shoḥer*

materials from earlier sources were added and then reworked into one comprehensive plot.[6] At the same time, unique narrative traditions that distinguish among the various versions are evident. For example, the vision of the star that heralds the birth of Abraham, which opens the version in *Midrash aseret hadibrot* and in *Sefer ha-ma'asim*, is not included in *Midrash hagadol* from Yemen or in the fourteenth-century compilation of tales *Sefer hama'asiyot*, edited by Gaster in the *Exempla of the Rabbis*. On the other hand, the ritual of Nimrod's chair is described in Gaster's *Exempla*[7] but not in *Midrash aseret hadibrot* or in *Sefer ha-ma'asim*.

The story was received in Ashkenaz as a martyrological narrative influenced by the persecutions of the Jews, as is evident from the epilogue in *Sefer ha-ma'asim* and from the message it conveys to the doubters and the converts: "God uproots anyone who worships idols both from this world and the next, and he will see all the good that God will do for the righteous ones, and they will be ashamed and say: Woe unto us that we did not merit this honor, because we abandoned a living God to worship a dead one. And then fire will emerge and consume all the apostates who abandoned God and did not repent." There is a similar epilogue in "The Mother and Her Sons," which is adjacent to it in *Sefer ha-ma'asim*. It contains a warning that the apostates will be uprooted from this world and the next, the repentance of the idolaters for having neglected a living God for a dead one, and an admonition that a fire will consume them. In *Midrash aseret hadibrot* the message of the epilogue is more general: "And every idolater will be uprooted by God from this

tovi), ed. Buber, psalm 117, 118. For Pseudepigraphical and Hellenistic parallels, see "The Book of Jubilees," 12: 1–20, in *The Apocrypha and Pseudepigrapha of the Old Testament*, ed. Charles, vol. 2, 30–31; *Philo*, vol. 6, ed. T. E. Page et al., trans. F. H. Colson, "On Abraham," 17: 78, 45 (an allusion only).

A selection of versions in the medieval and early modern ages in Ashkenaz includes Rashi on Genesis 11, 28, quoting *Genesis rabbah*, 38, 25 (361–364, ed. Theodor and Albeck); R. Judah he-Ḥasid, *Sefer gimatriot*, 145–146; *Yalkut Shimoni*, Genesis, vol. 1, no. 62, ed. Shiloni, 236–237, and no. 76, 301–304; R. Jacob Isaac Ashkenazi, *Ẓena ure'ena, Bereshit*, 95–96. For a reference to the story in commentary on liturgy in Ashkenaz, in particular in the context of the furnace of fire, see Hollender, *Clavis Commentariorum of Hebrew Liturgical Poetry*, 498–499.

6. Aside from *Sefer ha-ma'asim*, additional expanded medieval versions in manuscripts, including *Midrash aseret hadibrot*, are Ms. Paris 716, *Midrash aseret hadibrot*, ed. Shapira, 40–45; Ms. Cambridge Add. 663, 305a–307b; Ms. Vatican 249, 324b–326a; Ms. Vatican 107, 163b–164a; Ms. Moscow-Ginzburg 111, 105a–107a; and specifically in Ashkenaz: Yassif, ed., *The Book of Memory*, 131–135; Ms. London, Beth-Din, 28, 66a; Ms. Parma 2269 (De Rossi 443), 54a–55a. For the expanded print versions, see *Ma'aseh Avraham* (Constantinople, 1519); *Agadat agadot* (collection of *midrashim ketanim*), ed. Horowitz, 43–46, and Jellinek, *Bet hamidrasch*, 2, no. 2, 119–188; *Ma'aseh Avraham avinu mimah she'ira lo im nimrod* (Salonica, 1593); Jellinek, *Bet hamidrasch*, 1, no. 1, 25–34.

7. R. David ha-Adani, *Midrash hagadol*, Genesis, ed. Margulies, 202–207; Gaster, *Exempla*, no. 2b, 3–5.

world and the next, and will not behold the majesty of the Lord."[8] The martyrological moral in *Sefer ha-ma'asim* is emphasized in comparison to other morals and emphases in earlier sources and in sources in the East, such as *Midrash hagadol* from Yemen, which deals primarily with a legendary-hagiographic aspect.[9]

The martyrological aspect is also expressed in the centrality of the motif of fire in the *Sefer ha-ma'asim* version. As Baumgarten shows, the motif of fire is repeated in the *Sefer ha-ma'asim* version three times: when Abraham burns the idols after realizing they are worthless; in the motif of the furnace of fire; and in the epilogue, in the fire of hell that awaits apostates who fail to repent.[10] A reverse analogy between the fire of hell that will burn all the apostates and the fire of the furnace in the story, from which Abraham will emerge unharmed, is implied.

The narrative of "Abraham in the Furnace" was also known in Christian sources from late antiquity, both as a text and as visual art in manuscript illustrations.[11] Hieronymus cited it in his commentary on Genesis, and following him, others did as well. Moreover, it was included in various editions of *Glossa Ordinaria*, which was received and widely disseminated in the twelfth century as part of biblical commentary. It was also inserted into the historiographic work by Petrus Comestor, *Historia scholastica*, which was translated from Latin into many vernacular languages, and thus resonated even more widely. In the early fourteenth century, the story was included, and illustrated as well, in a theological work that was very popular in the Middle Ages, *Speculum humanae salvationis*, as a prefiguration of Jesus' vision of the future liberation of the souls from Hades. The story of Ḥananiah, Mishael, and Azaria,[12] added in *Sefer ha-ma'asim* to the story about Abraham in the furnace of fire, was also widespread among Christians as part of the canon, even to a somewhat greater extent than "Abraham in the Furnace," as Baumgarten demonstrates. Thus similar narrative traditions were prevalent in both Jewish and Christian societies, and functioned as a means of bolstering monotheistic faith and sharpening distinct definitions of religious identities.

8. *Midrash aseret hadibrot*, ed. Shapira, 45.
9. Tohar, *Abraham in the Furnace of Fire*, 72–75; 144.
10. Baumgarten, "Seeking Signs?" 220.
11. The following discussion about the reception of the story in Jewish and Christian society is based on Baumgarten, "Seeking Signs?" The story was also prevalent among Muslims, beginning with the Koran, sura 2, "The Cow," verse 258, but we are concerned here with the Jewish-Christian audiences in Ashkenaz and northern France.
12. Tale no. 10, which is followed by tale no. 11 ("Generation of Dispersion and the Tower of Babel"), was also added to "Abraham in the Furnace."

12. The Mother and her Sons (305a)

This story is known in two main textual traditions:[1] (1) in 2 Maccabees and 4 Maccabees in the Apocrypha;[2] and (2) in two representative versions in rabbinical literature, an expanded one in the Palestinian midrash *Lamentations rabbah* (1:50)[3] and the other abridged, in the Babylonian Talmud, *Gittin* 57b.[4]

In Ashkenaz, the story was known in the two versions, the one from the Apocrypha via the popular work *Book of Josippon*, from the tenth century in Italy,[5] and the other from the rabbinical literature. The story takes place against the backdrop of the edicts of Antiochus Epiphanes, a historical figure from the second century BC, and includes detailed, horrific descriptions of the torture of the sons after they refused to obey the king's command to eat pork. The version in *Josippon* was copied by Jerahme'el in the early twelfth century in a historiographic work later reworked by Eliezer b. Asher Halevi in the thirteenth century.[6]

The other version, whose plot is set in the time of the Hadrian edicts, about two hundred years after Antiochus, was known in Ashkenaz through the Palestinian Midrash and the Babylonian Talmud, as well as through *Midrash aseret hadibrot*.[7] In chronicles about sanctifiers of the Holy Name in Ashkenaz, the story is presented

1. Two classic studies on the story are Gutmann, "The Story of the Mother and Her Seven Sons," 25–37; and Cohen, "The Tale of Chana and Her Seven Sons," 109–123. See Yassif's references in *The Hebrew Folktale*, 475, n. 18. To his references add Haber, "The Woman and Her Seven Sons"; Hasan-Rokem, *The Web of Life*, 128–135; Doran, "The Martyr," 67–81; Young, "The Woman with the Soul of Abraham," 189–221. The following discussion, which focuses solely on individual examples, is based on a lengthier article by Baumgarten and Kushelevsky, "From 'The Mother and Her Sons' to 'The Mother of the Sons,'" 301–342.
2. 2 Maccabees 7:42, *The Apocrypha and Pseudepigrapha of the Old Testament*, ed. Charles, vol. 1, 140–142; 4 Maccabees 5–18, *The Apocrypha and Pseudepigrapha of the Old Testament*, vol. 2, 671–685.
3. *Lamentations rabbah*, ed. Buber, no. 420, 84–86; *Lamentations rabbah, Midrash rabbah*, vol. 2. Additional versions of this branch are *Seder eliahu rabbah*, 30, 151–153; *Ḥibbur yafeh mehayeshu'a*, ed. Hirschberg, 15–17; *Ḥibbur yafeh mehayeshu'a*, ed. Brinner, 6, 29–32; *Yalkut shimoni*, Deuteronomy, no. 938, ed. Shiloni, Deut. 571–573; Yassif, *The Book of Memory*, 351–353; Rabbenu Baḥya, "*Kad hakemaḥ*," in *Kitvei rabbenu Baḥya*, ed. Chavel, 67–68.
4. A selection of other versions in this textual tradition include *Midrash aseret hadibrot*, ed. Shapira, 48–50; R. David ha-Adani, *Midrash hagadol* on Deuteronomy, ed. Fish, 621; *Hagadot hatalmud, Hanizakin*, 65a.
5. *The Josippon*, ed. Flusser, 1, 70–75, no. 15. This reflects the renewed use of sources from the Apocrypha during the Middle Ages, after their exclusion from earlier rabbinic literature.
6. Yassif, *The Book of Memory*, 289–292.
7. *Midrash aseret hadibrot*, ed. Shapira, 48–50; Ms. Bodl. Or. 135, 349a–349b.

as an archetype of tales of martyrdom during the persecutions of the Crusades.[8] In addition to prose adaptations, the story was also found in commentary on liturgical poetry in Ashkenaz.[9]

Sefer ha-ma'asim follows the talmudic version and that in *Midrash aseret hadibrot*, which, as I noted, are shorter than those in *Lamentations rabbah*. A lengthy argument in the latter between the emperor and the young son, who insists that the idols are worthless, is not included in *Sefer ha-ma'asim*. Moreover, the mother is not mentioned by her names, which appear in *Lamentations rabbah* and in one version of *The Book of Josippon*—Miriam, daughter of Tanḥum, and Ḥannah, respectively.[10] The story is copied twice in Ms. Bodl. Or. 135: in *Midrash aseret hadibrot*, and in *Sefer ha-ma'asim* on the basis of the version in *Midrash aseret hadibrot*, with certain changes. In *Sefer ha-ma'asim*, the story opens by introducing the mother and her sons, the emperor's demand that they bow down to the idol, the older sons' martyrdom, which is briefly reported, and the incidents with the younger son, which are described in greater detail. The son consults with his mother, she encourages him to sanctify the Holy Name, he rejects the temptation to merely give the impression of bowing to the idol, and finally he is executed by the emperor. The mother sends a message to the patriarch Abraham, telling him how much greater her sacrifice is than his, and the story ends when she commits suicide by jumping off the roof, with a voice from heaven announcing that her sons have earned a portion in the next world, followed by a didactic epilogue.

Sefer ha-ma'asim deviates from its basic models in the Talmud and in *Midrash aseret hadibrot* by assigning a more central role to the mother than to her sons. In these sources (and certainly in *Lamentations rabbah*), the sons' arguments with the emperor are related in detail, and in each of the son's words, different verses are intertwined. In a repeated ritual, the emperor tries to tempt each of the sons in turn, and each rejects him on the basis of biblical verses. More words are devoted to the sons' martyrdom in their confrontation with the emperor than to the mother. Although her emotional responses are described in detail, the emphasis, as indicated by the amount of space devoted to it, is on the sons' sanctification of the Holy Name

8. See R. Shlomo bar Shimshon, "*gezerot tatnu*" ("Decrees of 1096"), Habermann, *Sefer gezerot ashkenaz vetzorfat*, 34; Haverkamp, *Hebräische Berichte . . . Kreuzzugs*, 32 [594]. Goldin dealt with this story in *The Ways of Jewish Martyrdom*, 81–84; see also Cohen, *Sanctifying the Name of God*, 106–129.

9. For a list of commentaries on liturgical poetry, see Hollender, *Clavis Commentariorum of Hebrew Liturgical Poetry*, 128–129.

10. *Josiphon*, ed. Hominer, 73–78, chap. 19.

and the ideological explanation each of them gives for his action.[11] *Sefer ha-ma'asim* does not describe the mother in less detail than its sources do, but the internal ratio in the story changes. The scene of the sons' martyrdom is summed up in only a few words: "He [the emperor] summoned each one separately and said the same, and each and every one quoted a verse from the Torah to him" (305a).[12] The succinct rhetoric underscores, by way of contrast, the mother's emotional actions, her parting kisses to her sons, and her words of encouragement to her youngest son.[13] The martyrdom in the story does not belie the emotional ordeal or maternal love but rather is parallel to them. In the story, "sanctification of the Holy Name" is the ultimate fulfillment of a mother's love for her children, in her efforts to prevent their spiritual death even if it means sacrificing their lives.

The intimate, very human character of the mother, along with her determination to sanctify God's name as the sole choice available to her, is particularly salient when compared to parallels of the story in the books of the Maccabees in antiquity. Those play down the conflict between maternal feelings and values of sanctification of the name of God, and depict the mother as a woman who fulfills the masculine ideal with restraint:

> The mother was the most remarkable of all, and she deserves to be remembered with special honor. She watched her seven sons perish within the space of a single day, yet she bore it bravely, for she trusted in the Lord. She encouraged each in turn in her native language; filled with noble resolution, her woman's thoughts fired by a manly spirit, she said to them.[14]

In addition, the mother comes on stage at a later point in the story. Her character does not stand out as much as it does in Ashkenaz. Her image changed when the story moved from the ancient era to medieval Ashkenaz.

The image of the mother as a martyr underwent a similar process among Christians, as part of the cult of the Virgin Mary, which reached its peak in the twelfth and thirteenth centuries, and which introduced into the Christian martyrological

11. In *Midrash aseret hadibrot* (ed. Shapira), the proportion of text devoted to the sons is approximately twice as much as that devoted to the mother, while in *Sefer ha-ma'asim* the proportion devoted to the mother is about two-thirds of the story.

12. The eldest and the youngest are the exceptions, and their words to the emperor are cited.

13. The trend toward brevity and succinctness is characteristic of *Sefer ha-ma'asim*, and it also exists in *Midrash aseret hadibrot* in the same manuscript (349a): "Commanded the first son and executed him. And thus them all." The effect in the present story is to emphasize the character of the mother.

14. 2 Maccabees 7:20–22, *The Apocrypha and Pseudepigrapha*, ed. Charles, vol. 1, 141.

discourse metaphors of motherhood and birth.[15] A parallel very similar to "The Mother and Her Sons" is included in *The Golden Legend* by Jacob of Voragine in the thirteenth century.[16] It is a legend about Saint Felicity (ATU 920C, Tubach 1272) and her seven sons, who were killed by Publius, the Roman prefect, during the reign of the emperor Antoninus. She persuades her sons to die and joins them. The author of *The Golden Legend* emphasizes Felicity's femininity and motherhood, rather than the masculine traits ascribed to her in the 2 Maccabees version quoted earlier.[17]

Similar images of the mother-martyr figure in both societies serve to highlight a common background for a discourse of martyrology in Western Europe at the time, in narratives that were accepted by Jews and Christians as models for defining distinctive religious identities. The language for doing so existed in Ashkenazi society in the Jewish sources, in descriptions of the mother's reaction in the Talmud, in *Lamentations rabbah*, and in *Midrash aseret hadibrot*, but the emphases change.

The historical context of sanctification of the name of God in Ashkenaz is particularly explicated in the scribe's epilogue in the thirteenth century. It directly addresses the listeners and readers, calling on them to adhere to their faith, while Christianity is a cult of the dead: "You may not exchange me for idols, because God is a jealous and eternal God. Bow not to the dead but to He who puts to death and revives the dead." Similarly, in *Midrash aseret hadibrot* in the same manuscript, the epilogue touches on current matters:

> Then a fire will come forth and consume the apostates who have left the Almighty and failed to repent. Hence every son of Israel, take care to be in fear of the Almighty until the day of your death, so you may sit alongside the righteous in the garden of Eden . . . and do not bow to the dead but to He who slays and revives, and He lives forever.[18]

Moreover, the narrator explains that the Jews must suffer the tribulations of exile because they are destined to recount throughout the world the wondrous deeds of the Almighty. This is a reversal of the Christian doctrine, according to which the role of the Jews is to serve as witnesses, to attest to the truth of Christianity.

15. For this and the following discussion, see Baumgarten, *Mothers and Children*, 178–183; Baumgarten and Kushelevsky, "From 'The Mother and Her Sons' to 'The Mother of the Sons,'" 316–318.

16. Jacobi a Voragine, *Legenda aurea*, no. 91, 396; Jacobus de Voragine, *The Golden Legend*, vol. 1, no. 91, 364–365.

17. For a more elaborated discussion, see Baumgarten and Kushelevsky, "From 'The Mother and Her Sons' to 'The Mother of the Sons,'" 318.

18. Ms. Bodl. Or. 135, 149b.

13. The Man Who Never Took an Oath (305a–306b)

This tale in *Midrash aseret hadibrot*, which was the model for the *Sefer ha-ma'asim* version,[1] illustrates the Third Commandment ("Thou shalt not take the name of the Lord in vain").[2] Aside from the versions in *Midrash aseret hadibrot* and *Sefer ha-ma'asim*, medieval and postmedieval versions were included in Hebrew and Yiddish story compilations,[3] and in twentieth-century anthologies.[4]

International parallels are of the tale type ATU 938 and Tubach 1920 (titled "Placidus" or "Eustacius"). These do not include the motif of the oath, which was added to the Jewish tale already in *Midrash aseret hadibrot* as a means of adaptation to the Jewish context, and there are some substantial differences in plot between the non-Jewish traditions in the East and the West,[5] as well as between them and their Jewish parallels in *Midrash aseret hadibrot* and *Sefer ha-ma'asim*. Nonetheless, the main plot line was preserved in all variants, Jewish and non-Jewish, Eastern and Western: A captain of a boat kidnaps a woman; there is a compulsory separation of the woman's two sons from their father; finally, a happy ending reunites the father, mother, and two sons.

Rather than comparing the *Sefer ha-ma'asim* version to its source in *Midrash aseret hadibrot* by depicting differences of plot, I prefer to demonstrate a change of discourse in the former, which I attribute to the tale's transference from Eastern to Western Europe. I claim that, while its model in terms of plot was *Midrash aseret hadibrot*, its discourse—that is, the implied significance of the tale against the background of nuanced changes of style and content—was influenced by its parallels in Europe and modified for its Jewish audience. A comparison of our *Sefer ha-ma'asim* version to its parallel in *The Golden Legend* by Jacob of Voragine will demonstrate this point.[6]

1. *Midrash aseret hadibrot*, ed. Shapira, 54–59. See Yassif's monograph on the tale's adaptation, in *Midrash aseret hadibrot*, from non-Jewish sources, as well as its transmission in current Israeli folklore: "From Jewish Oicotype to Israeli Oicotype," 216–235.
2. The tale restricts even a true oath, a norm that exceeds the Third Commandment but is recommended in various Jewish sources. See Lerner, "The Homilies on the Ten Commandments," 219–221, and his references.
3. Ms. Jerusalem 3182, 137a–138b (in Yassif, *Ninety-nine Tales*, no. 68, 257–260); *Mayse bukh*, no. 221; *Ma'aseh Book*, ed. Gaster, vol. 2, no. 222, 542–546.
4. Grünwald, *Yalkut sippurim*, I, part 2, 136–139; Bin Gorion, *Mimekor yisrael*, no. 615, 344; Gaster, *Exempla*, no. 378, 143–144.
5. The tale type and its different traditions were studied by Gerould, "Forerunners, Congeners and Derivatives of the Eustace Legend."
6. Jacobi a Voragine, *Legenda aurea*, no. 161, 712–718; Jacobus de Voragine, *The Golden Legend*, vol. 2, no. 161, 266–271. See also later parallels in editions of *Gesta Romanorum*, *Gesta* (M), no. 69, 311–322; *Gesta* (I), no. 150, 111–118; *Gesta* (Ö), no. 110, 444–451; *Gesta* (Swan),

Eustace—or Placidus, as he was known before converting to Christianity—is a general in the army of the Roman emperor Trianus and a charitable man. He experiences a revelation that leads to his conversion. During a hunt Jesus appears before him between the antlers of a deer, and he instructs Placidus to be baptized along with his family. After he does so, Jesus reveals himself again and informs Eustace that he is going to rise to the peak of spiritual joy, but not before he is tested, like Job, in extremely difficult trials. From here his ordeals become progressively more difficult: An epidemic kills his slaves, servants, goats, and cattle; then criminals exploit his ruin and rob him. Eustace and his family go down to Egypt, and on their way by ship, the sea captain abducts his beautiful wife and forces Eustace to get off the ship with his two sons. In their wanderings, the boys are carried off, in front of Eustace, by wild animals. Local people save the boys and raise them. The father, certain that his sons are dead, finds his way to a village, where he works tilling the land. He sinks into despair but then has another revelation. From then on his fortune changes completely. The emperor's soldiers find him and ask him to return to his previous position as a general in the army, and his sons join him as soldiers, not knowing in the meantime that they are related. By coincidence, they arrive at the dwelling of their mother, who has remained faithful to her husband, and they learn her identity. The story ends with Eustace's death as a martyr, after suffering horrific torture, and he is declared a saint. In *The Golden Legend* the story was adapted as a martyrological exemplum.

Both in *The Golden Legend* and in *Sefer ha-ma'asim*, the narrative is consistent with the topoi of the Book of Job. In *The Golden Legend* Eustace complains to the Lord:

> Memini, domine, te mihi dixisse, quia oportet te tentari sicut Job, sed ecce plus aliquid in me fieri video, ille enim, etsi possessionibus nudatus fuerit, tamen stercus habuit, super quod sedere potuit, mihi autem nil horum remansit; ille amicos sibi compatientes habuit, ego immites feras habui, quae meos filios rapuerunt; illi uxor est relieta, a me vero ablata; da requiem, domine, tribulationibus meis et pone custodiam ori meo, ne declinet cor meum in verba malitiae et ejiciar a facie tua.
>
> (I remember, Lord, that you told me it was my lot to be tried as Job was tried, but it seems to me that even more ills have come to me than to him.

no. 110, 239–247. See also references by Gerould, "Forerunners, Congeners and Derivatives of the Eustace Legend," 356–369.

Even if he was stripped of his possessions, he could at least have dung to sit on, but I have not even that! He had his friends to share his misery, but I have only the fierce beasts that stole my sons. Job's wife was left to him, I am bereft of mine. Give pause, O Lord, to my tribulations, and set a guard over my mouth, lest my heart incline to evil words, and I be cast out of thy sight!)[7]

In *Sefer ha-ma'asim*, the protagonist's ordeals come one after the other, as demonstrated by the use of adverbs denoting time: first, the swindler's demand; "afterward" the demand of other swindlers, until he is left penniless; "then" a cruel man comes and demands his last dinar; and finally the protagonist is arrested and imprisoned.[8] Three times the swindlers assail him with their demands for his money. This narrative syntax is not evident in *Midrash aseret hadibrot*, where only one temporal adverb indicates the frequency of the events,[9] and the pace of the events is slower in comparison to those in the Book of Job or *Sefer ha-ma'asim*. Additionally, the swindlers in *Midrash aseret hadibrot* demand the man's money only twice, and the frequency of their visits is not emphasized.[10]

The affinity with the tale's parallels in Europe is implied in *Sefer ha-ma'asim* in two additional ways. First, the beauty of the protagonist's wife is emphasized more in *Sefer ha-ma'asim* than in *Midrash aseret hadibrot*, in line with a similar trend in their non-Jewish parallels in the West and East. Her beauty is mentioned in *Sefer ha-ma'asim* when she first appears in the story, as an expositional detail conveyed by the omniscient narrator: "And his righteous wife was very beautiful." The woman stands out as an exceptional personality, combining morality and beauty. In *Midrash aseret hadibrot*, she is first introduced only as a righteous wife ("What did his righteous wife do?"), and her beauty comes up only later, in an erotic context, as an explanation for her abduction, and from the relative viewpoint of the coveting

7. Jacobi a Voragine, *Legenda aurea*, 715; Jacobus de Voragine, *The Golden Legend*, 269. This affinity with Job is especially emphasized in the Western parallels in contrast to the Eastern. See Yassif, "From Jewish Oicotype to Israeli Oicotype: The Tale of 'The Man Who Never Swore an Oath,' " 11–12.

8. Cf. Job 1:14–20, and the repeated expression, "While he was still speaking, another came and said," which indicates the frequency of the troubles that befall Job.

9. "Finally, a swindler came and said you still have one more dinar" (*Midrash aseret hadibrot*, ed. Shapira, 54 [Hebrew]).

10. On the stylistic level, there is, however, an allusion to the Book of Job in *Midrash aseret hadibrot* as well ("Naked came I out of my mother's womb, and naked shall I return there" [ed. Shapira, 55]) but not on the level of narrative syntax. Consequently this allusion does not necessarily attest to the fact that the topoi of the Book of Job was already assimilated into the tale in the East.

captain: "When the captain of the ship saw she was beautiful, he secretly coveted her."[11] The postponement of the "beauty" motif to a later stage in the story and the change of context reduce its effect.[12] This change in emphasis is even more explicit in the non-Jewish parallels. The beauty motif appears only in the Western versions, and not in the Indian, Persian, or Arab ones.[13] In *The Golden Legend* the narrator states:

> Videns autem dominus navis uxorem Eustachii, quae pulchra esset nimis, ipsam plurimum habere desideravit.[14]
>
> (Eustace's wife was a beautiful woman, and the ship's captain lusted after her.[15]

Later she is also described as a beautiful woman when the young son speaks to his friend, before he realizes they are related:

> ego, dum infans essem, nihil aliud recolo, nisi quod pater meus magister militum erat et mater mea speciosa valde.[16]
>
> (I can't remember anything about my childhood, except that my father was the commander of the armies, and my mother was a very beautiful woman.)[17]

The second aspect of the tale's affinity with its Western parallels relates to the wife's social status: *Sefer ha-ma'asim* does not mention that the wife came from a royal family, nor does *The Golden Legend* (or the later *Gesta Romanorum*). In the Indian parallel, the hero and his family are from the royal family, a detail that was retained in *Midrash aseret hadibrot*: "When the captain of the ship saw she was beautiful, he secretly coveted her, and said: she must surely be from a royal family."[18]

11. *Midrash aseret hadibrot*, ed. Shapira, 55.
12. The wife's beauty is also mentioned in some other versions of *Midrash aseret hadibrot* in Provence and in other areas in Europe, apparently under an influence of *Sefer ha-ma'asim*. However the theme does not appear in all such versions, and they lack the emphasis that exists in *Sefer ha-ma'asim*.
13. I am relying on a paraphrase, in Gerould's detailed research, of the parallels from the East ("Forerunners, Congeners and Derivatives of the Eustace Legend," 343–353) and from the West (ibid., 354–369).
14. Jacobi a Voragine, *Legenda aurea*, no. 161, 714.
15. Jacobus de Voragine, *The Golden Legend*, vol. 2, 268.
16. Jacobi a Voragine, *Legenda aurea*, no. 161, 716.
17. Jacobus de Voragine, *The Golden Legend*, vol. 2, 270.
18. *Midrash aseret hadibrot*, ed. Shapira, 55.

This detail is of no importance in *Sefer ha-ma'asim* or in Christian traditions of the tale in Europe, and it was thus omitted.

On the whole, the tale's plot was in keeping with the textual tradition of *Midrash aseret hadibrot* even when it was transferred to *Sefer ha-ma'asim*, but its literary and didactic discourses are anchored in the European religious exemplum that echoes the narrative of Job, where beauty is both a source of moral strength and a dangerous cause of temptation and immorality. In view of the story's dual affinities with its source in *Midrash aseret hadibrot* and its parallels in Christian Europe, *Sefer ha-ma'asim* can be regarded as a link mediating between East and West and, at the same time, as a means of mediation between the Christian legendary literature and the Jewish literature of the time.

14. The Sabbath Observer and the Bear (306b–307a)

This is the first written record of the tale. The versions that followed are also from Ashkenaz.[1] Based on the tradition of the story, its details, and the setting of the plot, "The Sabbath Observer and the Bear" probably was created in Ashkenaz, where it was introduced into *Midrash aseret hadibrot*, with the addition of an epilogue lauding the Sabbath.[2] Versions from around the nineteenth century on, frequently found in hagiographies and anthologies, follow the version of Ms. Jerusalem 3182, in which the bear is replaced by a lion (along with other changes).[3] One example is from the hagiographies about R. Masoud Alfasi of Fez (1700?–1774).[4] A number of versions of the tale are stored in the Israel Folktale Archives (IFA).[5]

In human thought, the bear exemplifies an ambiguous combination as both a dangerous predator and a friend of man. Its hibernation, its fur, its passion for honey, and its devotion to its cubs, as well as its ability to be trained, create an image of loyalty, laziness, and simplicity combined with the instincts of a wild animal.[6] Especially in medieval bestiaries, the bear was depicted as the king of the animals before the lion arrived in Europe. It is strong and dangerous, but can be tamed for the sake of man's pleasure. Therefore the bear was considered a prestigious diplomatic gift. When it stands on its hind feet, the bear seems human, but it also symbolizes the sins of gluttony and sloth because of its lust for honey and its long winter slumber. At the same time the bear's "disappearance" during his winter sleep is compared to Jesus' disappearance after his crucifixion, an analogy that attributes a religious significance to the animal's existence.[7]

In "The Sabbath Observer and the Bear," the bear, grateful to the man for sharing his meal, defends the Sabbath observer against the robbers, and then savagely kills the merchants who abandoned him. The creature is thus both "human" and very

1. Ms. London, Bet-Din 28, 70a; Ms. Parma 2295, De Rossi 473, 62a (15th century); Ms. Jerusalem 3182, 123a (Yassif, *Ninety-nine Stories*, 225, no. 63, where the bear is replaced by a lion); *Mayse buch* (Basel), no. 138; *Ma'aseh Book*, trans. Gaster, vol. 1, no. 138, 252–254.
2. For a different opinion, cf. Yassif, *Kemargalit bemishbeẓet*, 140, n. 20.
3. For a list of versions, although with no reference to "The Sabbath Observer and the Bear," see Lipsker-Albeck, "Ariel: The Recluse and the Lion," 300–301, under the entry "Ariel."
4. Shushan, *Sefer pilei haẓadikim*, no. 6, 17–19.
5. See E.D.N.A.: AT*776 B–C (IFA). See also Lipsker, "A Study of 'R. Ephraim Al-Nakawa and the Lion," 112–116.
6. On the symbolism of the bear in its two aspects, as reflected in myth and folklore, see Rowland, *Animals with Human Faces* ("Bear"), 31–35.
7. Heck and Cordonnier, *The Grand Medieval Bestiary* ("The Bear" [Ursus]), 571; Pastoureau, *L'ours: Histoire d'un roi déchu.*

dangerous. The motif of the "grateful animal" recurs frequently in folklore and expresses relations of friendship and trust between man and animal. Here it is adapted to the figure of the bear and its medieval ambiguous significance.

The symbolism of the Sabbath as a covenant of trust between man and God is elucidated in "The Sabbath Observer and the Bear" against the background of the other relationships. In contrast, the covenant of trust between humans is fragile, based as it is on a mutual agreement that can be violated at any given moment. The relationships in the story extend between two extremes, of trust and treachery. Furthermore, relations of trust between God and man are linked in the story to holiness, manifested in time (the Sabbath) and space (the saintlike figure of the *ḥasid* and his delimited territory during the Sabbath).

As I noted, no sources for the story are found in rabbinical literature, nor are parallels found in the medieval non-Jewish literature. Nonetheless, there are some affinities with several tale types that have common motifs. These relate to the character of the bear as a dangerous wild animal, to the road as a chaotic extraterritory, and to symbols of sanctity, such as the Sabbath, in the present story. In some of the parallels, a common substructure can be perceived. Thus a talmudic tale in the tractate *Berakhot* (60b–61a) may be a source of inspiration for "The Sabbath Observer and the Bear." According to the Talmudic tale, R. Akiva, who was on his way, was forced to stop in a field, because there was nowhere to spend the night in the city. At night the wind put out his candle, a cat killed his rooster, and finally a lion killed his donkey. It later turned out that everything was for the best, since that same night soldiers broke into the city and took all its inhabitants prisoner. If the rooster and the donkey had remained with him and the candle had not been extinguished, R. Avika would have been caught. Motifs common to the talmudic tale and its parallel in *Sefer ha-ma'asim* include the road full of dangers, the night spent outside a town, and the appearance of wild animals—a lion in one case and a bear in the other. In both tales the protagonist finds a spot in the chaotic territory of the road and performs a series of ritual actions, thus creating a delimited enclave. In the Talmud, the spot is delimited through the act of lighting a candle, and in "The Sabbath Observer and the Bear," through the observance of a series of ritual commandments connected to the sanctity of the Sabbath—the *Kiddush*, the meal, the blessing over the food, and *Havdallah*—which calm the protagonist emotionally. Despite these analogies, the main motif of a wild animal submitting to a man, accompanying him, and protecting him is lacking.

Other analogous tale types include those regarding a lion's submission to a man—whether an ordinary man or one who possesses special qualities or magic powers (a saint or a knight)—in a gesture of gratitude.[8] The fifth-century legend about St. Hieronymus was widely circulated in the Middle Ages by means of Voragine's *The Golden Legend.* Hieronymus cured a limping lion that had a thorn in its paw, thus winning its trust. The lion lived with him in his monastery in Bethlehem and supervised the donkey in his role as the bearer of burdens. But the lion neglected his duties, and as a result the donkey was stolen. The lion then did the donkey's work himself, dragging the cut-down trees from the woods to the monastery. Later the lion found the merchants who had stolen the donkey, and returned it to the monastery.[9]

The motif of the lion's submission, either through magic or following its rescue and gratitude, is found in various Jewish tales of the Middle Ages and thereafter—for example, in the Book of Ahima'atz and in hagiographies on the founders of Ḥasidism in Ashkenaz.[10] The motif of a wild animal's loyalty as a mark of gratitude, and the protection the creature provides thereafter, also exists in romance literature, in Chrétien de Troyes' well-known romance *Yvain, The Knight of the Lion.*[11] While Yvain, the knight and protagonist, is walking inside a thick forest, he hears a loud, pain-filled cry and discovers a tormented lion whose tail is caught by a snake or dragon that is attempting to burn the lion's legs. Ivan decides to help the lion. He draws his sword, protects himself against the fire with his shield, and slashes the snake to bits. Then the lion submits to Yvain: He stretches forth his front legs, lowers his face to the ground, and bows to him. Yvain understands that the lion is thanking him for having saved his life. From then on the lion accompanies Yvain constantly, serving him and protecting him against all evil. The two experience various adventures, during which the lion proves his loyalty and saves his master from his enemies. Two episodes of this tale are particularly relevant to the present comparative discussion. First, in the scene in which Yvain and the lion spend the night on their way, Yvain shares his food with the lion; he later lies down to sleep while the lion watches over him and his horse for the entire night.[12]

8. See ATU 156 ("Androcles and the Lion"), 156A: "The Faith of a Lion"; Tubach 3057, on a lion faithful to a knight who saved him from a dragon; Tubach 2771, on St. Hieronymus and the lion.
9. Jacobi a Voragine, *Legenda aurea*, no. 146, 655–656; Jacobus de Voragine, *The Golden Legend*, vol. 2, no. 146, 213–214.
10. Bonfil, "Myth, Rhetoric, History?" 99–135; Lipsker-Albeck, "Ariel: The Recluse and the Lion."
11. Chrétien de Troyes, *Yvain, The Knight of the Lion*. See Rotman, *Dragons*, 337, n. 34.
12. Verses 3456–3484, 104–105. See in particular: "Que qu'il menja, devant lui jut / Ses lions, c'onques ne s'en mut, / Ains l'a tout adés regardé / Tant qu'il ot pris tant du lardé" (v. 3469–3472, 264). "Du chevroil trestout le sorplus / Menga li leons juqu'ad os" (v. 3473–3474, 264).

Second, the knight later battles two fighters, called "sons of the devil" (v. 5512), in order to free a group of virgins being held prisoner in the master's castle. The lion wrests itself free and saves his master, who is on the verge of death; in a fit of rage, the animal rips apart the two fighters. The mission is accomplished, and the virgins are released.[13]

The analogous features in "The Sabbath Observer and the Bear" in *Sefer ha-ma'asim* include the bear's actions and enraged mood; its accompanying the *ḥasid* as a mark of gratitude for having shared his meat and bread; and its attack on the merchants who left the *ḥasid* on his own: "When the bear saw the two men who had desecrated the Sabbath, it attacked them furiously and ferociously and killed them." The forest as the setting of the story and the figure of the king and his palace imbue the tale with a medieval ambience; they parallel the castle and the figure of the master in Chrétien's courtly romance. Some of the episodes in Chrétien's work, either in its oral performances or in written form, may have been a source of inspiration for the present story.

Another partial parallel is included in the German collection of tales *Schimpf und Ernst*, by Johannes Pauli.[14] In this work, a man hires an escort to protect him on his way through a forest. Suddenly, a bear appears; the escort abandons the man and climbs a tree. The man lies sprawled out on the ground, holds his breath, and pretends to be dead. His life is saved when the bear concludes the man is no longer alive and goes on its way. When the escort asks what the bear whispered in the man's ear, the man "quotes" the animal as purportedly saying that a man is a fool to place his trust in someone he doesn't know. This popular anecdote is still in circulation in numerous versions (ATU 179). Oral versions underlying Pauli's collection may have influenced the Jewish tale.[15]

A motif common to both stories is that of the bear protecting the man or at least not harming him, and by implication the bear protecting the man from the

---

"Et li leons ot tant de sens / Qu'il veilla et fu en espens / Du cheval garder, qui paissoit / L'erbe qui petit l'encrassoit" (v. 3479–3482, 266).

("As he ate, the lion lay / motionless beside him, watching him / the whole time, until / he'd eaten as much as he wanted of his steak [. . .] and whatever was left of the deer / the lion ate to the bone" [v. 3471–3477, 105].)

After the meal the knight lay down to sleep, "and the lion showed such good sense / that he stayed awake, carefully / guarding the horse, who grazed / in the grass" [v. 3478–3484, 105].)

13. Chrétien de Troyes, *Le chevalier au lion ou le roman d'Yvain*; idem, *Yvain, The Knight of the Lion*. See in particular: "Qu'en son venir si le navra / Li leons, qui si vint iriés, / Que laidement fu enpiriés" (v. 5660–5662, ed. Hult, 400). ("The lion / had charged so furiously, so wildly, / that his [the rival's] wounds were terrible" [v. 5563–5665, 169].)

14. Pauli, *Schimpf und Ernst*, no. 422. And see Tubach, no. 522.

15. On the tale type, its sources in *Aesop's Fables*, and in its popular versions, see Moser-Rath, "Baer," 1207–1209.

treachery of his own kind. In Pauli's collection it is the escort who flees from the bear and abandons the man; in "The Sabbath Observer and the Bear," the merchants accompanying the Sabbath observer leave him alone and go on their way, lest they lose their money. If "The Sabbath Observer and the Bear" can in fact be viewed as a Jewish oikotype of this tale type—namely, as a tale type adapted to a specific culture—the means of adaptation include the setting of the tale on a Sabbath, the motif of the blessing of the meal, and, centrally, the substructure of the talmudic *aggadah* from tractate *Berakhot*. Nonetheless, the parallel is not a complete one. The bear's submission is not a consummate one and is limited to the viewpoint of the treacherous escort. Instead, the motif of deception is central to Pauli's story—by pretending to be dead, the man is saved from the bear.

None of the tales mentioned is a true parallel. The suggestions raised here merit further study, and the points of contact among the different tales that share narrative materials and functions are the starting points for a study of this sort.[16]

16. For "Ukva" (no. 15), see discussion of its parallel (no. 61).

16. Who Is the Thief? (307b–308b)

"Who Is the Thief?" is known in Indian, Persian, and Turkish folklore in the East as "Which Was the Noblest Act?" (ATU 976). In the Turkish *Tuti Nameh,* the daughter of a rich merchant gets into trouble because of a whim. She desires a beautiful rose surrounded by thistles and promises to fulfill the wish of anyone who obtains it for her. The family's gardener picks it for her, and she is forced to promise to visit him on her wedding night. On that night she confesses to her husband; being a man of truth, he permits her to fulfill her promise. On her way she is attacked by a wolf and a robber, but they release her when they learn of her husband's noble response. The gardener also foregoes her visit and sends her back to her husband.[1] The story found its way into *Midrash aseret hadibrot* in the East as an illustration of the commandment "Thou shalt not steal."[2]

The tale arrived in Ashkenaz through the mediation of *Midrash aseret hadibrot.* We may infer this from its mention in *Midrash aseret hadibrot* in the same manuscript (Ms. Bodl. Or. 135, 352b), which references the *Sefer ha-ma'asim* version.[3] The tale was prevalent in Ashkenaz in additional story compilations that are contemporary with or postdate *Sefer ha-ma'asim.*[4] It existed in Provence, too, in translations into Hebrew of *Ḥibbur yafeh mehayeshu'a* in the Middle Ages.[5] In the modern era it was included in story compilations from the nineteenth century, such as *Sefer hama'asiyot* by El'azar Araki and *Oseh pele* by Joseph Shabbtai Farḥi;[6] in literary anthologies from the twentieth century, such as *The Book of Legends* by Ḥayyim Nahman Bialik and Yehoshua Hana Ravitzky;[7] and *The Legends of the Jews* by Louis Ginzberg;[8] as well as in rabbinical collections,

1. *Tuti Nameh,* 173–185.
2. *Midrash aseret hadibrot,* ed. Shapira, 81–84.
3. See also, in Ashkenaz, *Midrash aseret hadibrot* in Ms. Wolfenbuettel 36.25 (14th century), and *Midrash aseret hadibrot* in Ms. Parma 2269, 77a–78a (15th century).
4. Ms. Parma 2295, 135b–136a (in Kushelevsky, *Penalty and Temptation,* 181–182 [Hebrew]); Ms. Jerusalem 3182, 105b–106b (in Yassif, *Ninety-nine Stories,* 184–185, no. 13); *Mayse bukh* (Basel), no. 223; *Ma'aseh Book,* trans. Gaster, vol. 2, no. 223, 547–555. For a list of the tale's versions, see Kushelevsky and Tohar, "The Thief Who Has Given Himself Away," 123–124.
5. Hirschberg regarded it as an addition, in the Hebrew translations from the Middle Ages, to the body of the original work by R. Nissim in Judeo-Arabic. See the introduction to his edition (55), and the tale as an appendix on pages 105–106.
6. Araki, *Sefer hama'asiyot,* no. 46, 40a–41b, and in Ḥuẓin's edition, no. 46, 30–31; Farḥi, *Oseh pele,* 1, 38–39.
7. Bialik and Ravntizky, *The Book of Legends,* no. 233, 745–746; reworked in Bialik, *And It Came to Pass,* 128–133
8. Ginzberg, *The Legends of the Jews,* vol. 4, 132–134.

such as *Oẓar midrashim* by Jehudah Eisenstein.[9] These are in addition to its circulation in manuscripts and printed versions of *Midrash aseret hadibrot*. "Who Is the Thief?" is also widely circulated in Israeli ethnic folklore, as demonstrated in the IFA documentation.[10]

The frame story of "Who Is the Thief?" is of the "wise judge" tale type, and it relates to a trial by Solomon in particularly obscure circumstances. One of three merchants secretly steals his friends' money. Since there were no witnesses to prove his guilt, Solomon has to solve the mystery in a different way, so that his authority as a king and the wisest of judges will not be undermined. He succeeds in identifying the thief by means of a ruse. He tells them the story, asks for their advice, and observes their reactions in order to trap the thief with his own words. Which of the characters is the most worthy of praise—the girl who was faithful to her husband? Her husband, who enabled her to fulfill her commitment to the boyfriend of her youth? The robber, who suppressed his desire and did not carry out his evil intention? Or perhaps the boyfriend, who relinquished his right and released the girl from her promise? In his reply, the thief reveals his greed and his theft. Thus Solomon mustered all of his wisdom to distract the thief from the fact that a trial was going on, and indirectly forced him to implicate himself.

The tale ends with an epilogue that is unique to *Sefer ha-ma'asim*, one that creates an affinity between the frame story, which relates the trial of the thief, and the embedded story, which praises the girl for her loyalty to her husband and the husband for suppressing his desire. The moral of the epilogue is "The sin of stealing causes ugly acts," namely promiscuity and adultery; it is based on current exegesis on the verse it quotes from Job 24:15: "And he will disguise his face."[11] The epilogue also alludes to talmudic exegesis in tractate *Sanhedrin* (38b) on Psalms 139:5: "You have beset me behind and before, and laid your hand upon me." The verse is quoted in the Talmud to illustrate the complexity of human nature. Man has the potential to resemble God but is also prone to moral degradation. That is the background, in the Talmud, to a fierce debate between God and the angels about the justification for creating Adam. At first Adam could reach from earth to heaven, but after he sinned God "laid His hand" on Adam and diminished him. This is the context for the narrator's phrase in the epilogue: "They were as high as the angels, and the Almighty placed His hand on them and they were lowered down." The

9. Eisenstein, *Oẓar midrashim*, vol. 2, 459.

10. See E.D.N.A.-AT 976; AT 976A.

11. See Rashi to this verse, where he refers to the "diluvial generation" who sinned both by stealing and committing adultery; *Yalkut Shimoni*, Job, no. 510, ed. Shiloni, 456.

citations and allusions in the epilogue indicate a scribe well-versed in the sources of the Talmud, the Midrash, and Rashi's commentaries on the Bible; in particular they demonstrate his skill in combining them into a homily in its own right in the epilogue. They are, however, worded as a paraphrase and in a lower linguistic register than that in the sources.[12]

The tale's tradition in Ashkenaz differs from that in the East mainly in the characterization of the girl in the embedded story. In *Midrash aseret hadibrot*, in keeping with its non-Jewish parallel in *Tuti Nameh*, the tone is misogynous: "I praise the young girl, for women are known to be unfaithful even to their husband when they lie together, and women are frivolous. And this one did remain loyal, and she is praiseworthy in my view."[13] The girl is found praiseworthy for her loyalty to her husband, but she is exceptional in comparison to women in general, who are known to be frivolous. In the praise of the girl there is an implied criticism of her oath as taken out of a childish whim. In Ashkenaz the misogynous comment is omitted. It is not the frivolity of the girl that is the focus of the tale but rather the conflict she experiences as a result of her two commitments: the oath she took in her youth, which amounts to an engagement, and the marriage she entered into as an adult. She manages to save her marriage without disregarding her childhood vow. Her initiative and courage evoke her childhood friend's empathy, and he foregoes his right over her in favor of her husband. Another typical trait in Ashkenaz is the vow-taking scene, when the two enter into a mutual covenant, in contrast to the one-sided vow of the girl in *Midrash aseret hadibrot*. Consequently, only in Ashkenaz are there linguistic affinities with the tale "The Weasel and the Pit," which was accepted as an explanation for the custom of handshaking at the betrothal ceremony. In Ashkenaz the handshake was often perceived as a gesture of avowal, and its violation would lead to a ban by virtue of the community's regulations.[14]

An affinity between *Sefer ha-ma'asim* and its non-Jewish parallels in the West is also evident. Oral folklore traditions were embedded in later works by Boccaccio in *The Filocolo* and *The Decameron* and by Chaucer in *The Canterbury Tales*, from the fourteenth and fifteenth centuries, respectively.[15] In *The Decameron* (tenth day,

12. See, for example, the wording in *Sefer ha-ma'asim*—"They were as high as the angels, and the Almighty placed His hand on them and they were lowered down"—compared to that in the Talmud, *Sanhedrin* 38b.

13. *Midrash aseret hadibrot*, ed. Shapira, 197.

14. Grossman, *Pious and Rebellious*, 52.

15. See the claim regarding the influence of Celtic oral traditions on these works, mediated by the *lais* of Marie de France: Schofield, "Chaucer's Franklin's Tale," 405–449, esp. 418. And see parallels: Boccaccio, *Decameron*, ed. Segre, 613–617, trans. McWilliam, 757–761. (An

fifth tale), a married woman attempts to reject the persistent suit of a knight who is in love with her. She instructs him to give her a garden with fragrant flowers in midwinter, assuming he would be unable to perform that task. He succeeds nonetheless, with the help of a sorcerer, and she is forced to fulfill her part of the bargain and give in to his importunities. She tells her husband, and he permits her to fulfill her promise, even at the cost of lending the knight her body, but not her soul. Amazed at the husband's respect for his wife's vow, the knight and the magician relinquish their claim on her, and she returns to her husband.

In this context of the different parallels, mutuality is a norm unique to Europe and Ashkenaz, and it is shared by *The Decameron* and *Sefer ha-ma'asim*. In *The Decameron* the story relates to the ethos of courtly love and the principle of mutuality that underlies it: on the one hand, the knight's total love for and devotion to his lady, and on the other, the lady's commitment to him after he has proved his *virtus* and performed his tasks. In parallel, the ecclesiastical ethos of the Christian sacrament of marriage is also embedded in *The Decameron*, conforming to the principles of mutuality in the vows of the bride and groom. The ethos of courtly love that entails adultery is, of course, absent from *Sefer ha-ma'asim*, but the principle of mutuality in the betrothal ceremonies is preserved. The versions of the story in the East and the West establish different cultural concepts of marriage and betrothal—in Ashkenaz, as a profound, mutual commitment between the spouses and their families, in contrast to the one-sided commitment of the woman to the man in the Jewish-Muslim countries in the East.

---

earlier parallel to *Decameron* is Boccaccio, *Filocolo*, 2 [Florence: Motiers 1829], IV.4. 48, and a translated edition by D. Cheney and T. G. Bergin, book IV, question 4, neither of which I was able to consult.) Chaucer, "The Franklin's Prologue and Tale," in *The Canterbury Tales*, ed. Kolve and Olson, 169–191; Chaucer, "The Franklin's Tale," in *The Canterbury Tales*, trans. Nevill Coghill (modern English), 426–451.

17. One of Ten (308b)

This story, of the tale type "Shooting the Father's Corpse as a Test of Paternity" (ATU 920C, Tubach 1272),[1] developed in Jewish culture in two textual traditions. One is in *Sefer ha-ma'asim*, which is based on an earlier source that is found in the Talmud (*Baba Batra* 58a).[2] A father discovers that only one of his ten sons is really his, and he leaves an obscure will insofar as his estate is concerned. Only one of the sons is entitled to it. The paternity test is meant to determine which of the ten is the legal heir entitled to the inheritance. The assumption is that the legal son would have a hard time showing disrespect to his father, and that his feelings of respect and love would overcome any greed on his part. In the Middle Ages this tale appeared mainly in books of *responsa*, Halakhah, and commentary on the Talmud,[3] often as a legal precedent in cases where the authority of the *dayan* to rule in a trial is questioned because of the absence of any witnesses. In such situations, he can decide based on his opinion, namely by employing logic and reason.[4] Against this background of legal aspects linked to the tale, the *Sefer ha-ma'asim* version stands out as a narrative on its own, lacking any halakhic implications, and fit for a story compilation as such. A second branch of the tale developed from the twelfth century in *Sefer ḥasidim* in Ashkenaz, and in *Sefer sha'ashu'im* (*Book of Delight*) by Joseph b. Meir Ibn Zabara (b. about 1140) in Spain.[5] The characters are a man, his slave, and a son who lived in distant lands for many years. When the father dies, the slave takes over the inheritance, claiming he is the son, while the son is rejected as a foreigner. The truth is revealed in a paternity test ordered by the judge. This narrative circulated widely after it was printed in *Meshalim shel Shelomo hamelekh*[6] and in the popular

1. Stein, "Schuss auf den Toten Konig."
2. See references of Ben-Amos, *Mimekor yisrael*, no. 110, 200.
3. Abulafia, *Yad ramah*, Baba Batra 58a, 400; *Piskei hari'az*, ed. Wertheimer, ch. 3, *halakhah* 12, no. 9, 128–129; Hameiri, *Bet habeḥira* (*The Chosen House*), on *Baba Batra*, ed. Menat, 230. R. Asher b. Yeḥiel (Rosh), *Responsa of R. Asher b. Yeḥiel*, rule 34, no. 6, 152; rule 68, no. 23, 265; rule 78, no. 3, 328; rule 107, no. 6, 444 (Ashkenaz-France-Spain, 13th–14th century). R. Jacob b. Asher, *Arba'ah turim* (Four Pillars), *Ḥoshen mishpat*, no. 65; Duran, *Sefer hatashbeẓ*, part 1, no. 60, 173 (Spain-Algeria, prior to 1444).
4. The legal term for this is *umdena*. See *Encyclopedia Talmudit* 1, 295–302.
5. *Sefer ḥasidim*, no. 291, 91; Zabara, *The Book of Delight*, trans. Hadas, 85–88. On these versions, see Alexander, "The Formation of Ḥasidic-Ashkenazic Stories," 7–8; Dishon, *The Book of Delight*, 96–97, in the broader context of its "wise judge" tales. See comments and references for this text tradition in Ben-Amos, *Mimekor yisrael*, no. 22, 35.
6. *Meshalim shel Shelomo hamelekh* (*Solomon's Fables* [Constantinople, 1519], unpaginated).

collection *Ḥibbur hama'asiyot vehamidrashot vehahagadot*,[7] and it consequently was included in rabbinical and literary collections.[8] There are clear affinities between the two traditions of the tale. First, there is the motif of treachery—a slave who is like a son betrays his master, an adulteress betrays her husband, and her sons betray their father. Second, the paternity test varies—a demand to beat and disgrace the father's grave, the requirement to burn the father's bones, and the "tissue test," conducted by soaking one of the father's bones in the blood of the slave and the son. Only the blood of the authentic son will be absorbed.[9]

After the Middle Ages, the tale was embedded in a variety of frameworks, such as compilations of Talmudic legends,[10] rabbinical-exegetic and popular literature in Hebrew and Yiddish,[11] literary collections,[12] and oral folktales preserved in the IFA archives.[13] In parallel, it is still being mentioned and cited in *responsa* and halakhic literature, often to illustrate inheritance cases without witnesses.[14]

"One in Ten" can also be depicted as a trial tale (ATU 926 and 926C), based on the biblical model of the "wise judge" in the judgment of Solomon (1 Kings 3:16–28). In an insurmountable situation in which there are no witnesses and the father's will has left no room for any compromise, the judge succeeds in resolving the predicament and issues a just verdict. In the well-known case of an infant in dispute between two women, each of whom claimed to be the mother, Solomon ordered that the child be split in two, assuming that the true mother would object. "One in Ten" represents a similar legal strategy, on the assumption that the true son would not betray his father even if that meant relinquishing his

7. Venice, 1599, no. 10. Following *Ḥibbur hama'asiyot vehamidrashot vehahagadot*, the story was also printed in Araki's *Sefer hama'asiyot*, no. 10, 10a–11a, and in Ḥuẓin's edition, no. 10, 10a–10b.

8. Ben Abraham, *Mateh moshe (The Staff of Moses)*, part 5, no. 764, 244; Aaron Berekhiah b. Moses of Modena, *Ma'avar yabok*, 286, *Ma'amar siftei renanot*, no. 24; Grünwald, *Yalkut sippurim*, vol. 1, part 2, 227–228; Levner, *Kol agadot yisrael* (*The Legends of Israel*), vol. 1, part 3, 298–302; Eisenstein, *Oẓar midrashim*, vol. 2, 531; Bialik, "The Inheritance," in *And It Came to Pass*, 69–74; Bin Gorion, *Ẓefunot ve'agadot* (*Secrets and Legends*), 113; Gaster, *Exempla*, no. 391, 150; Ginzberg, *Legends of the Jews*, vol. 4, 131.

9. Cf. Thompson's motif of the paternity test: H486.2.

10. *Hagadot hatalmud*, Baba Batra, *Ḥezkat habatim*, 93a; Ibn Ḥabib, *En Jacob*, Baba Batra, 58a.

11. *Mayse bukh* (Basel), no. 128; *Ma'aseh Book*, trans. Gaster, vol. 1, no. 128, 229–231; Figo, *Bina le'itim*, part 2, Elul, *Niẓavim*, 249–250 (Italy, prior to 1647); Margolis, *Sippurei yeshurun* (1877), 165–166, Ḥuẓin, *Ma'asim mefo'arim* (*Marvelous Deeds*), no. 22, 19–20; Eisenstein, *Oẓar midrashim*, part 2, Hebrew letter *mem* entry, no. 6, 343.

12. Bialik and Ravitzky, *The Book of Legends*, no. 263, 637–638; *Mimekor yisrael*, no. 339, 227; Ben-Amos, *Mimekor yisrael*, no. 110, 200.

13. See E.D.N.A: AT920C, and Kurt, *Folktales of Afghanistan Jews*, 114–115.

14. Moses b. Isaac Elshakar, *She'elot u'teshuvot maharam elshakar*, 116, 379 (prior to 1542).

inheritance. The psychological and bidirectional link between father and son is not contingent on rational considerations but rather on blood ties, and hence the son's emotional reaction is indeed a criterion for determining his right to the inheritance.

Although *Sefer ha-ma'asim* follows the talmudic source in tractate *Baba Batra*, it omits its closing episode. In the talmudic tale the other sons, wanting to gain revenge, slander R. Bana'ah; representatives of Roman rule arrest him; and his wife cleverly manages to obtain his release. An argument develops between him and the Romans, after which they acknowledge his wisdom and appoint him as a *dayan.* Thus an additional aspect—that of a national conflict manifested in the character of the "wise judge"—is added to the paternity test in the Talmud. In *Sefer ha-ma'asim* the story ends with the verdict about the identity of the legal son and with a didactic epilogue preaching "cleanliness," namely the purity of the family, with no mention of R. Bana'ah's arrest. It would seem that the character of the judge, R. Bana'ah, is secondary, while the story focuses mainly on the values of honor, loyalty, and brotherhood within the family. This aspect, which is implicit in the story, is explicit and even stressed in the epilogue, in light of its appearance only in *Sefer ha-ma'asim* and not in the Talmud. The epilogue is based on a commentary in *Tanḥuma* on the verse in Job "And he disguises his face," according to which the Almighty, who "dwells in the shelter of the Most High" (Psalms 91:1), thwarts the adulterer's plan to hide his deeds, and makes the face of the transgressor look like the face of the adulterer in order to publicize what he has done.[15] The explicit moral in the epilogue is presented in a counter analogy to the opening of the story, with the mother's advice to her daughter to be promiscuous in secret so her husband will not know. It also differs from the talmudic tale by describing in detail the son's emotional response to the judge's decision, beyond the fact that he refuses to carry it out.[16] The emotional facet is more prominent in *Sefer ha-ma'asim.*

The story was known in Europe in a number of non-Jewish parallels and variations. The first, from the twelfth century, is in *Le jugement de Salemon* (*The Judgment of Solomon*), in Old French.[17] The judge here is a wise prince whose identity is unclear, although there is some suggestion that he is Solomon. He has to judge between the two sons of one of his barons, deciding whether they are entitled to

15. *Tanḥuma, naso,* no. 4, and in Buber's edition of the *Tanḥuma,* no. 6.

16. In the Talmud it is in Aramaic: "So they all went to do so [to knock on the father's grave]. The one who was really his son, however, did not go."

17. See Barbazan, *Fabliaux*, 440–442. I thank Ilana Klutstein and Elisheva Baumgarten for their translation of the tale.

their father's inheritance after his death. The elder son demands an immediate decision before the deceased is buried, while the younger son refuses to discuss the matter until after the funeral and the mourning period. The paternity test becomes a test of courage: The one who can best hurl his spear at his father's corpse will prove he is entitled to the inheritance. The younger son refuses to perform that act, not even for all the gold in the world, and swears to take revenge on his brother if he dares harm his father's body. In this way, he proves his right to the inheritance. The conflict between the two sons and the test of courage are reminiscent of a duel, according to the knightly conventions of the Middle Ages. It has been suggested that this parallel was the model on which Joseph b. Meir Ibn Zabara based his *Book of Delight* in the twelfth century.[18]

There is a parallel more similar to the tale in *Book of Delight*; it is in a twelfth-century work by Alexander Neckam (1157–1217), *De naturis rerum*, a commentary on Ecclesiastes written while the author was in Paris.[19] The feudal setting also exists in this parallel, as it does in *Le jugement de Salemon*. A very virtuous soldier married to a woman of noble birth discovers she is betraying him. He reacts with profound pain and asks his friend, the master of the estate, to determine his rightful heir. After the soldier's death, the friend orders that the soldier's corpse be hanged, and he tells the sons to compete to see who is the most proficient and accurate in spearing it. Two of them pierce the corpse in an "atrocious manner," while the young man throws down his spear in a "flood of tears" and declares he would "never carry out such a great crime." He threatens the master and his brothers "fearlessly" and, offended, leaves. He is then called back to receive the inheritance.

The thirteenth-century collection of sermons, historical anecdotes, and legends of the French preacher Étienne de Bourbon contains a tale about an adulteress who tells her husband that only one of her sons is his.[20] She does not reveal which one because she fears he might love him more than the others. Therefore in his will he leaves his property to the true son, without specifying his name. The matter is brought before a judge, and he recommends that the sons hold a contest to determine which of them is entitled to the inheritance. They have to shoot arrows at their father's corpse. One son bursts into sobs and refuses, and he is determined to be the legitimate heir.

18. See comment by Hadas (20) in his English translation of Zabara, *The Book of Delight.*

19. Neckar, *De naturis rerum*, chap. 176, 313.

20. Étienne de Bourbon, *Anecdotes historiques*, no. 160, 136–137.

In the fourteenth century, the story was included in *Speculum Morale*, attributed to Vincent of Beauvais,[21] and in various editions of *Gesta Romanorum*.[22] In *Speculum Morale*, three sons are required to shoot arrows at their father's corpse. The third son bursts into tears, refuses to participate in the contest for the inheritance, and declares he will oppose anyone who tries to shoot at his father. In *Gesta Romanorum* one son hits the right arm of the corpse; another, the mouth; and the third strikes straight at the heart and supposedly wins the contest. The fourth son groans and declares he will not hurt his father, dead or alive. The ministers of the kingdom and the people name him as the heir to the kingdom, and the other three are banished. The element that all these parallels have in common with *Sefer ha-ma'asim* is the dominant emotional, subliminal aspect to the relationship between father and son.

Nonetheless, there are two consistent disparities between the Jewish versions and all of their European parallels. In the former, there are ten sons, in contrast to three (or a combination of three and one) in the Christian parallels. In addition, the paternity test is very brutal in the non-Jewish parallels—usually a competition of shooting arrows into the father's corpse and aiming at his heart. These differences have symbolic meanings that are deeply rooted in Judaism and Christianity. The number of sons in the ancient and medieval Jewish tale is ten. In Jewish culture ten men constitute a *minyan* and create a "public," a collective to which the individual is committed vis-à-vis certain religious rituals. In the context of the story, the emphasis in *Sefer ha-ma'asim* is on relations in the family as a collective, which is more than the sum total of its members. In the Christian parallels, the number 3 refers to the symbolism of the Holy Trinity. In the didactic epilogue in *Gesta Romanorum*, the number relates to the chosenness of Jesus over the other sons, who represent the pagans, the Jews, and the heretics. The paternity test is also anchored in Christian symbolism, which does not exist in *Sefer ha-ma'asim*. The harshness of the test, and the arrows shot at the corpse and aimed at his heart, situate the story in the Christian discourse about Jesus' suffering in the passion scene and its imitations; these fit with the ethos of suffering that reached its peak in the mid-medieval period. A story about father-son relations becomes an allegory about the relations between the

21. Vincentius Bellovacensis, *Speculum Morale*, libri III, distinctio X, pars. V, 1188. For a similar version, see also libri III, distinctio XXV, par. X, 1490–1491. The *Speculum Morale* was added to the *Speculum Maius* in the fourteenth century and is not integral to the original work of Vincent of Beauvais.

22. *Gesta* (Ö), no. 45, 162; *Gesta* (I), no. 103, 59–60; *Gesta* (M), no. 42, 167–170; *Gesta* (Swan), no. 45, 143–144. In other parallels the paternity test determines that one of the sons is the heir of a tree capable of curing leprosy (*Gesta* [Ö], no. 196C, no. 262).

Christian believer and Jesus, and an ascetic dimension is added to it that does not exist in the Jewish source. In this way the tension in Christianity between family life and asceticism is given expression. The differences between the *Sefer ha-ma'asim* version and its Christian parallels, as well as their common aspects, have implications for the image of the family and for religious and family identities in Ashkenaz.[23]

23. For a detailed discussion, see Kushelevsky, "Family Images and Identities in a Medieval Jewish Version of 'Shooting at Father's Corpse.' "

18. The Commandment of *Ẓiẓit* (Fringes) (308b–309a)

While the earliest version of this tale appears in the tannaitic midrash the *Sifrei* on Numbers (115),[1] the direct source of *Sefer ha-ma'asim* is the Babylonian Talmud in *Menaḥot* (54a), where it follows a saying by R. Nathan: "There is not a single precept in the Torah, even the lightest, whose reward is not enjoyed in this world; and as to its reward in the future world I know not how great it is." Even a precept as minor as the one on fringes earns a man a reward in this world and in the next. The theological issue of reward and punishment is illustrated in the tale by its closure, with the marriage of R. Meir's disciple and the repentant harlot, and the reward awaiting them in the next world. The tale belongs to a talmudic topos of "visits to a harlot" that ends with a suppression of desire and a change of heart, such as the tale of R. Dordia in tractate *Avodah Zarah* (17a). It counterposes two antithetical cultures: On the one hand is the whore who swears "On my word" (lit., "by the Roman capital")—the gentile woman of the alien culture—and on the other is R. Ḥiyya's disciple, who is meticulous in observing the commandment of fringes. Following the encounter with the man with the fringes, the harlot repents.[2]

After the Talmudic era, the story was cited in halakhic contexts linked to the Jewish law of fringes, and more often in exegetic, moral, and literary contexts. The tension already existing in the *Sifre* and the Talmud—between the halakhic aspect of the commandment of fringes and the moral aspect manifested in the requirement to restrain one's drives and to resist temptation—was retained in all the versions, but the emphases varied according to the context of the story and the purpose of the compilation in which it was included.[3]

1. *Sifre d'be rab*, ed. Horovitz, 128–129. For a selection of studies on the talmudic source, see Balberg, "Between Heterotophas and Utopias"; Berkovits, *Crisis and Faith*, 64–73; Goshen-Gottstein, "The Commandment of the Fringes"; Ḥevroni, *An Arrow in Satan's Eye*, 235–240; Kosman, "New Interpretation of the Story on the Pupil, the Harlot and the Fringes"; Harvey, "The Pupil, the Harlot and the Fringe Benefits."
2. Cf. Tubach 2443: "Harlot and Repentant Priest."
3. See a selection of versions: *Ḥibbur yafeh mehayeshu'a*, ed. Hirschberg, 22–23; Brinner, ed., *An Elegant Composition Concerning Relief after Adversity*, 9, 41–43; *Pesikta zutarta* on Numbers, "*Shelah lekha*," ed. Buber, 103a; Mordekhai b. Hillel, *Halakhot ketanot*, tractate Menaḥot, Hatekhelet, no. 951; R. Ḥaim b. Moses, *Piskei halakhah* (*Derashot MHR"H*), Toledot, 17–18; Ms. Oxford, Bodleian Library, 28/2680 (Cowley 21297), 212a; *Yalkut shimoni*, Numbers, no. 750, ed. Shiloni, 311–312; Gaster, *Exempla*, no. 35, 25–26; R. David ha-Adani, *Midrash hagadol*, Numbers, ed. Rabinowitz, 259–260; Aboab, *Menorat hama'or*, 3, 3, no.123, 270–271; Ms. Jerusalem 3182, 131a (Yassif, *Ninety-nine Tales*, no. 75, 242). Some versions after the Middle Ages and in the modern era include Elijah Hacohen, *Me'il ẓedakah*, no. 602, ed. Kuperman, 163. Versions in the twentieth-century literary collections include Bin Gorion,

In *Sefer ha-ma'asim* the tale was embedded between other tales that allude to the Ten Commandments, as an illustration of "Thou shalt not commit adultery," although *Midrash aseret hadibrot* is not its direct source (instead the Talmud is), and the commandment is not explicitly mentioned in the epilogue but only implied. The story is located between "One in Ten," which preaches "cleanliness"—namely purity in family life (prohibition of adultery)—and "The Book of Genesis," which is about honoring one's parents. Three unique aspects in *Sefer ha-ma'asim* which can be viewed in their contexts in medieval northern France are:

(1) The images of the Garden of Eden. The general statement in the Talmud—"This is the reward [of the precept] in this world; and as for its reward in the future world I know not how great it is"—becomes concrete in *Sefer ha-ma'asim* by means of a more detailed description of the reward awaiting the man and the woman in the next world: "they will bask in the radiant light of the Divine presence," and "I am He who will give reward to the righteous who do my will in the future."[4] The motif of the "next world" is also underscored in *Sefer ha-ma'asim* by the omission of details that originate in the Talmud. Thus the Talmud's plastic description of the harlot's bed of steps, which the man had to climb to get to her, is absent from *Sefer ha-ma'asim*: "and between one bed and the other there were steps of silver, but the last were of gold. She then went up to the top bed and lay down upon it naked. He too went up after her in his desire to sit naked with her."[5] The quote demonstrates the man's fervent desire for her, and consequently his achievement in repressing it. In *Sefer ha-ma'asim* this is condensed: "and he too climbed up and sat at her side."

(2) The fact that the man and the woman are assigned equal representation in *Sefer ha-ma'asim*, apparently due to the relative high status women enjoyed in Ashkenaz compared to women in Jewish communities in the East. The words of R. Ḥiyyah—"This was their reward in this world, and in the next, they will bask in the radiant light of the Divine presence"—were meant for both of them, in contrast to the Talmud passage, which relates only to the woman (in reference to the bedclothes, which she would now spread out lawfully) or only to the man (his reward in the next world).

(3) The emphasis on the value of loyalty between spouses in the epilogue, which is unique to *Sefer ha-ma'asim*: "And always make sure that your sons are born in purity. And marry a pure [honest] woman who will not betray you. For this you will

---

Mimekor yisrael, no. 311, 214–215, and *Ẓefunot ve'agadot*, 174–175, no. 5. See comments and references by Ben-Amos, *Mimekor yisrael*, no. 98, 181–182.

4. In the Talmud: "I am He who will give reward in the future."

5. *Menahot* 45a.

be rewarded with righteous sons, who will respect and honor you." The emphasis on purity and faithfulness between the spouses is also found in the preceding story, "One in Ten," and in others, as well as in other sources in Ashkenaz, such as *Sefer ḥasidim*.[6] The tale may have been written in reaction to the prevalent courtly literature and in an attempt to grapple with the ethos of courtly love, which in the Jewish and Christian cultures is perceived as adultery. In any case, faithfulness between spouses as a constitutive value of the marriage institution is an aspect in *Sefer ha-ma'asim* that is added to the moral of repentance and repression of desire, which is more dominant in versions of the tale outside Ashkenaz.

6. This is a key distinction in a dissertation by Ayala Friedman, "The Man Who Was Meticulous about the Commandment of Fringes," written under my guidance. The source of the word *neki'ut* (cleanliness) is in a *baraita* in the name of R. Pinḥas b. Yair, in tractate *Avodah Zarah* 21a, which describes a series of traits that gradually lead to piety, one of which is cleanliness.

19. The Book of Genesis (309a–309b)

The tale is first extant in the Geonic literature.[1] It praises Torah study and constitutes a reminder of the father's duty to teach his son Torah. It also reflects a controversy during the Geonic period about the book with which small children should begin their Torah study.[2] It was written against the background of the alternative of teaching the child Leviticus first, the idea being, "Let the pure come and engage in the pure."[3] Often the reason implied in the tale for beginning with the more accessible Book of Genesis rather than Leviticus is the son's learning difficulties. Accordingly, the epilogue in these sources praises the father's devotion to his son and his efforts to teach him at least this one book.[4] It informs him of the reward owing to anyone who teaches his son "Torah, Mishnah, and *hagadot*."[5]

Throughout the Middle Ages, the story developed along two lines.[6] The shorter of the two is cited in "*Pirkei derekh ereṭz*," annexed to *Seder eliahu zuta*, in the fourteenth-century *Midrash hagadol* and in the story compilation edited by Gaster in the *Exempla of the Rabbis*.[7] The reason put forth for beginning with the Book of Genesis was not only its status as the first book of the Torah but also its narrativity, which was considered suitable for young children, especially those with learning difficulties. The other tale tradition, more extensive and developed, is in Geonic *she'iltot* on the portion *Lekh lekha*; *Midrash aseret hadibrot*; *Ḥibbur yafeh mehayeshu'a*, of R. Nissim of Kairouan;[8] and Ms. Jerusalem 3182 (126a–126b).[9] In

1. See the *she'iltot* (halakhic questions) on *Lekh lekha*, Ms. Dropsie College 118, in Abramson, *R. Nissim Gaon Libelli Quinque*, 400; "*Pirkei derekh ereṭz*," 2 (in *Seder Eliahu zuta*, chap. 17), 21–22; *Ḥibbur yafeh mehayeshu'a*, ed. Hirschberg, no. 16, 51–52; Brinner, ed., *An Elegant Composition Concerning Relief after Adversity*, no. 16, 86–87. For versions of the tale up to Bialik's adaptation in *Va'yehi hayom* (*And It Came to Pass*), 255–266, see Dina Levin, "The Tale of the Book of Genesis," *Encyclopedia of the Jewish Story*, vol. 1, 342–343 (and 333–349, a survey on the development of the tale [Hebrew]). See also references by Ben-Amos, *Mimekor yisrael*, no. 82, 162.
2. Yassif, "Hebrew Prose in the East," 58–59.
3. See *Leviticus rabbah* 7:3, ed. Margulies, 156.
4. See, for instance, in Gaster, *Exempla*, no. 38, 27.
5. R. David ha-Adani, *Midrash hagadol*, Deuteronomy, ed. Fish, 153.
6. For this distinction, see Levin, "The Tale of the Book of Genesis" (n. 1, above), 340–341.
7. "*Pirkei derekh ereṭz*" (see *Eliahu zuta*, n. 1 above); R. David ha-Adani, *Midrash hagadol*, Deuteronomy, ed. Fish, 153; Gaster, *Exempla* (n. 4 above); Kohut, *Notes on . . . Al Damari*.
8. Hirschberg edition (see n. 1). In terms of narrative, this version belongs to the expanded and more developed tradition of the tale, although the span of its pages is not very long. For a selection of the *Midrash aseret hadibrot* versions, see Shapira's edition (567–569), as well as in Ms. Vatican 285, 73a–73b, and Ms. Moscow-Ginzberg 111, 116a–117 (different versions, both from the 14th century).
9. Yassif, *Ninety-nine Tales*, 31–233, no. 77.

the more developed tradition of the tale, the boy studies Genesis because of the decision of his father, who preferred to begin with praises of the Almighty. The book is chosen on the basis of its content, not due to didactic considerations regarding the accessibility of the book to the child or its placement as the first book of the Bible. *Sefer ha-ma'asim* represents the expanded tradition in *Midrash aseret hadibrot*, despite its more usual tendency to omit words and phrases that are understood from their contexts.

The tale is composed of two analogical plot lines: one about the boy and his family, relating to his abduction, and the other about the king. The motif of the Book of Genesis connects the two. On the human level, the abducted boy is saved thanks to his study of Genesis with his father, and he is restored to his family. The yearning for a son, the joy of his birth, and the son's rearing and education are especially underscored in the expanded version.[10] In parallel, the king is cured and the orders of the kingdom are restored by virtue of the new insights the king gains from the boy's commentary on the Book of Genesis.[11] On the cosmic level, the transition from chaos to order is embodied in the narrative of the creation of the world from "*tohu wabohu*," which functions as a constitutive model.[12] While studying the Book of Genesis, the parent and the king become participants of a sort in the ongoing Creation. The transition from chaos to order on the human and the cosmic level is made possible by means of the Book of Genesis.

The tale came into *Sefer ha-ma'asim* through the mediation of *Midrash aseret hadibrot*, where it illustrates the Fifth Commandment about honoring parents. The boy insists on going to school on his own, without troubling his father to carry him on his shoulders.[13] An affinity is created between two values that are two sides of the same coin: the father's duty to teach his son Torah and the son's duty to honor his parents. However, in *Sefer ha-ma'asim* the context of the Fifth Commandment is less emphasized compared to that of *Midrash aseret hadibrot*, since the act that illustrates it—namely the boy's concern for his father—is specified only in the

10. Cf. T548.1: "Child born in answer to prayer."

11. Cf. ATU 551: "The sons on a quest for a wonderful remedy for their father/the water of life." The present tale can be regarded as a Jewish oikotype in which the Book of Genesis replaces other marvelous remedies that can cure the hero.

12. Cf. Levin, "The Tale of the Book of Genesis" (see n. 1), 335.

13. "He who honors his father only in saying to him, 'do not carry me on your shoulders,' the Almighty gave him this property; he who honors him all the days of his life, all the more so [deserving is he]" (*Midrash aseret hadibrot*, ed. Shapira, 69). As Dina Levin noted, the image of the Greek pedagogue, a slave who carries his master's child to school on his shoulders, is in the background.

sequence of the plot, not in the epilogue.[14] On the other hand, in *Sefer ha-ma'asim* there is an added emphasis on the value of Torah study, manifested in the inclusion of a detailed explanation—which does not exist in *Midrash aseret hadibrot*—of the father's considerations in transferring his property to Torah scholars: "so that they do not have to engage in trade and can study Torah."[15] The sequence of events also underscores this special emphasis, since the Torah scholars are mentioned first, and only then, the young boys: "He would go every day and ask boys their verses." In *Midrash aseret hadibrot*, the Torah scholars and the young boys are mentioned in the opposite order.[16] In this way, the story is linked to others in *Sefer ha-ma'asim* that highlight the value of Torah study in Ashkenaz.

14. In *Sefer ha-ma'asim*: "He who honored his father but one moment in this world received a reward; he who honors him all his life, all the more so that the Almighty will pay him a great reward." Cf. the phrasing of this idea in *Midrash aseret hadibrot*, ed. Shapira, n. 69, as in note 13.
15. In *Midrash aseret hadibrot*, ed. Shapira, 68: "He stood and distributed his property to the Torah scholars and said: So that I might share with them their portion in the world to come."
16. In *Midrash aseret hadibrot*, ed. Shapira, 67: "and when the children came out, he would embrace and kiss them"; only later is his support of the Torah scholars mentioned.

20. The Cow That Observed the Sabbath (309b–310a)

This story, of the animal tale type, is first known from *Pesikta rabbati*.[1] The story centers on an animal: a cow that is sold to a gentile and refuses to plow on the Sabbath. The anthropomorphism of the cow as a creature possessed of free will draws its inspiration from the biblical command: "You shall not do any work, you, nor your son, nor your daughter, nor your manservant, nor your maidservant, nor your ox, nor your ass, nor any of your cattle, nor your stranger who is inside your gates; that your manservant and your maidservant may rest as well as you" (Deuteronomy 5:15).[2] If the cow, an animal inferior to humans, acknowledges the sanctity of the Sabbath, the gentile concludes, he certainly ought to behave in the same manner, and he decides to convert to Judaism.

The tale developed along three trends: (1) In *Pesikta rabbati* the focus is on the cow, in the context of *para adumah*—the issue of the "red heifer" (Numbers 19:20)—which is also a special cow, but in a different way, since its purpose is to purify the defiled. (2) In *Midrash aseret hadibrot* the story illustrates the value of the Sabbath, which is also the dominant message in *Sefer ha-ma'asim*, as is obvious from the epilogue, "So come and see how much good is brought about by observing the Sabbath."[3] (3) In traditional historiographic books the context is biographical, to tell about the conversion of the Tanna R. Joḥanan b. Torta, and to explain his name—both literally "son of the bull" and "great in the Torah."[4] These trends are evident in the way the stories are shaped and reworked, particularly in the epilogue.

In *Sefer ha-ma'asim*, more than in other sources, the tale is linked to the halakhic issue of the prohibition against selling big cattle to a gentile (*Avodah Zarah* 15a).[5]

---

1. 56b–57a. On the story, its sources, and analysis, see Ben-Amos, *Mimekor yisrael*, no. 91, 175; Yassif, *Kemargalit bemishbeẓet*, 141–142; Drori, "The Sabbath-Observing Cow"; cf. ATU 200–219 ("Domestic animals") and with a more specific affinity with the Jewish tale, motif Th. B259.2 ("Sabbath-keeping cow").
2. Cf. Exodus 20:10.
3. See *Midrash aseret hadibrot*, ed. Shapira, 62–63.
4. See Judah b. Kalonymus of Speyer, *Erkhei tanna'im ve'amora'im*, 1, 296; Heilperin, *Seder hadorot*, "*Seder tan'aim ve'amoraim*," no. het, "Ḥaninah b. Torta," 101a. The word *torta* has two meanings: *tor*, which is Aramaic, means both "ox" as well as "Torah," thus conveying that the convert grows into a great Torah scholar. And see at length Drori, "The Sabbath-Observing Cow," on the development of the tale, and its trends in *Encyclopedia of the Jewish Story*, vol. 2, 252–257.
5. *Behema gasa* ("big cattle") is the term for a large animal, such as a horse or cow, in contrast to *behema daka* ("small cattle"), such as goats and sheep. For a summary of the issue, see *behema gasa*, *Encyklopedia Talmudit* 2, 368–369.

The reasoning here is that the sale may cause the Jewish seller to desecrate the Sabbath during the interim period between the time the cow is given to the buyer for a trial and the final sale. The fear is that the gentile may work the cow on the Sabbath, find a flaw in it, and return it to its Jewish owner. The Jew is commanded to allow the animal to rest on the Sabbath, thus even if the animal is worked by a gentile, the Jewish owner would be desecrating the Sabbath during the trial period, when the cow is still his property.[6] This scenario does seem to take place in the tale, because the gentile regrets his purchase and insists on returning the cow to its Jewish owner. But the outcome is the opposite—the Jew did not desecrate the Sabbath, since the cow refused to work, and moreover the gentile decides to convert and accept the sanctity of the Sabbath. This context is given expression in *Sefer ha-ma'asim* in the emphasis on the conditions of the sale of the cow: "I am buying the cow on the condition that you know not of any blemish with it." And later: "[the gentile] called out to the man who had sold him the cow and said: Why did you cheat me? Well do you know that you guaranteed that the cow you sold me had no blemish. He said: Yes. [The gentile said:] But, she does have a blemish."[7]

This may indicate that *Sefer ha-ma'asim* was created in a scholarly environment. The environment where the manuscript originated, the Champagne region where the Tosafists lived and wrote, may support this hypothesis. The issue of selling large cattle to a gentile was discussed by the Tosafists (*Avodah Zarah*, 15a). While in the talmudic period such a sale to a gentile was absolutely forbidden due to the fear that it might lead to desecration of the Sabbath during the trial period, the prohibition later was limited because of the changed circumstances of Jewish life (in an urban rather than an agricultural society) and economic necessity (a lack of Jewish buyers of cattle). The Jews were no longer able to abide by this prohibition. The Geonim, therefore, and the Tosafists of the high Middle Ages who followed them, ruled that the prohibition against selling cattle to gentiles would be restricted to purposes of commerce and profit, but not in cases of a probable financial loss. Against this backdrop it is possible that the tale "The Cow That Observed the Sabbath" was transmitted from *Midrash aseret hadibrot* to the school of the Tosafists, and from there into *Sefer ha-ma'asim*. This is supported by a mention of the story in *Tosafot Yeshanim* (Early Tosafot) on tractate *Yoma* 9a. In connection with R. Joḥanan

6. The Jew is commanded to give his animal rest on the Sabbath, even if it is worked by a gentile.

7. The "flaw" mentioned in the *Midrash aseret hadibrot* version appears only once and thus is less emphasized: "Take back your cow that you sold me for she has a flaw; she does not want to plow today."

b. Torta, it states: "The *Pesikta* [*rabbati* no. 14] explains that he was converted by a cow but it is stated there R. Judah b. Torta [not R. Joḥanan]."[8] It seems, then, that the story was known to the Tosafists. On the other hand, the scribe may have been familiar with the halakhic issue of the prohibition against the sale of large cattle to a gentile, and he introduced it into *Sefer ha-ma'asim* without any connection to the tale itself within the Tosafists' circles.

The sanctification of the holy name in Ashkenaz is an additional context in *Sefer ha-ma'asim*.[9] In this rendition, the process of the gentile's conversion is given in greater detail than in other versions. As Itamar Drori claims, the epilogue about his share in the next world and the overall conversion of his entire household might allude to descriptions of the mass martyrdom of entire families in Ashkenaz: "What did the gentile do? He converted to Judaism, he and his wife and all the members of his household, and he studied in school and became a Torah scholar, and was appointed to a high position over the public and carried out many acts of charity among the Jews of Israel. And a divine voice proclaimed that he was entitled to life in the world to come."

In the substructure of the tale, there is a binary paradigm of "profane versus sacred." The sacred paradigm includes the Sabbath, the Jew, the commandment represented in the Jew's whisper into the cow's ear, the study of the convert who becomes a Torah scholar and is commanded to keep the Sabbath, the area of the synagogue, the next world, and by implication, as I noted, also the sanctifiers of the Holy Name, whom the divine voice invites to receive their share of the next world. In contrast, the paradigm of the profane in the substructure of the tale includes the weekdays, the gentile, the physical violence in the form of the blows the gentile wanted to give the cow because of her refusal to plow on the Sabbath, the act of plowing (which represents the profane), and this world in contrast to the next one. The transition from the profane to the sacred—namely the act of conversion—entails a transition from physical violence to speech, from the open space to the delimited space, which the cow signals by collapsing on the Sabbath; it is also implied by the motif of the "synagogue" which, more often than in its sources, is frequently mentioned in *Sefer ha-ma'asim*. The biblical commandment to give a beast a day of rest on the Sabbath is the point of departure for a story that reflects the tendency of the sacred to spread out and influence the broad environment: man and beast.

8. I am grateful to Lior Yakobi for drawing my attention to this source.

9. See Drori, "The Sabbath-Observing Cow," 254.

Versions from Ashkenaz that postdate *Sefer ha-ma'asim* are in Ms. Cambridge-Harvard 39, from the early fourteenth century (118b–119a); *Midrash aseret hadibrot* in Ms. Wolfenbüttel 36.25, from the fourteenth century (13–14, unpaginated); Ms. Jerusalem, 3182 (127b–128a);[10] *Midrash aseret hadibrot* in Ms. Parma 2269, from the mid-fifteenth century (60b); and *Mayse bukh* no. 208.[11]

10. Yassif, *Ninety-nine Tales*, no. 70a, 235–236.

11. *Mayse bukh*, no. 208; *Ma'aseh book*, trans. Gaster, 2, no. 209, 503–505.

21. Joseph-Who-Reveres-the-Sabbath (310a)

This story, whose source is in the Babylonian Talmud, tractate *Shabbat* (119a), was widely circulated, and it resonated greatly throughout the centuries up to the present day.[1] As an exemplum it is brief and catchy, and its message is sharp and clear.[2] The anonymous character of Joseph is an example for every Jew, anywhere in the world, and the Sabbath is also a key value in Jewish society at large. The contrast between poor Joseph and the rich gentile is marked and unequivocal, and the reward Joseph earns is concrete and given to him in this world. The tale's inclusion in *Midrash aseret hadibrot*, in the context of the Fourth Commandment ("Remember the Sabbath day"), also contributed to its dissemination, since *Midrash aseret hadibrot* was copied in various versions and in numerous manuscripts.[3] The sources of the tale represent all sections of Hebrew literature throughout the generations: Amoraic literature (*Shabbat* 119); Geonic literature (*she'iltot* [*responsa*] of R. Aḥai Gaon and *Ḥibbur yafeh mehayeshu'a* of R. Nissim of Kairouan)[4]; midrashic literature (*Yalkut shimoni*, Genesis, no. 16,[5] and Isaiah, no. 496[6]); literature of Halakhah and *minhag* (customs; Aboab, *Menorat hama'or*)[7]; story collections and *aggadah* compilations (*Midrash aseret hadibrot*, *Sefer ha-ma'asim*, *Hagadot hatalmud*, and *Mayse bukh*)[8]; folktale and literary collections from the nineteenth and twentieth centuries, such as Araki's *Sefer hama'asiyot*, Bialik and Ravnitzky's *The Book of Legends*, and Bin Gorion's *Mimekor yisrael*;[9] and oral folk literature in several versions in IFA.[10]

1. For the story and its versions and parallels, see Elstein and Lipsker, "Joseph Who Honors the Sabbath," 87–112.
2. On the story as an exemplum, see Yassif, *Kemargalit bemishbeẓet*, 141.
3. Versions of the story in manuscripts of *Midrash aseret hadibrot* are Paris 716, ed. Shapira, 61; Vatican 285, 71a–71b; London, Beth-Din 28, 69b–70a; Ms. Cincinnati 61a, 76b–78a; Vatican 107, 167b; Moscow-Ginzberg 111, 113a; New York in JTS 3847, 36a; Parma 2269 (De Rossi 473), 61a–61b; Zurich 8, 181, 69a; Gaster 2, 354 33a–33b; Sasson 1195, 156–157; Oxford-Bodleian 46d. Heb. (2643), 50a–51b.
4. *She'iltot of Rav Aḥai Gaon*, Genesis, 1, 15; *Ḥibbur yafeh mehayeshu'a*, ed. Hirschberg no. 8, 21–22; Brinner, ed, *An Elegant Composition Concerning Relief after Adversity*, no. 8, 39–40.
5. Shiloni's edition., vol. 1, 52.
6. Ibid., *Latter Prophets*, 306.
7. Ḥorev and Katzenelenbogen edition, 3, 4, no. 146, 338.
8. *Hagadot hatalmud, kol kitvei*, 17a; *En Jacob*, ed. Glick, vol. 1, 191; *Mayse bukh*, no. 6, *Ma'aseh Book*, trans. Gaster, vol. 1, no. 6, 9–11.
9. Araki, *Sefer hama'asiyot*, no. 33, 31a–31b (in *Ma'aim al aseret hadibrot*), and in Ḥuẓin's edition, no. 33, 24a; Bialik and Ravnitzky, *Book of Legends*, no. 61, 363; Bin Gorion, *Mimekor yisrael*, no. 300, 211; Ben-Amos, *Mimekor yisrael*, no. 91, 175.
10. See AT*776 A–C (IFA): "He who Respects the Sabbath or a Holiday Is Rewarded." The story is also very popular in didactic children's literature.

The *Sefer ha-ma'asim* version principally follows *Midrash aseret hadibrot.* Like the latter, it is in Hebrew, and expanded compared to the talmudic version in Aramaic. Nonetheless, the influence of the Babylonian Talmud is palpable. For example, the rhythm and syntactic structure of the sentence "All your property will Joseph inherit" in *Sefer ha-ma'asim* is more compatible with the rhythm of the parallel phrase in the Talmud ("All your property Joseph-who-reveres the Sabbath will consume"[11]) than its parallel in *Midrash aseret hadibrot* ("All of your property Joseph-who-reveres-the Sabbath is consuming"). The inverted syntax of the phrase is common to all three sources, but only the Talmud and *Sefer ha-ma'asim* use the future tense, while the sentence in *Midrash aseret hadibrot* is in the present ("is consuming"), which influences the rhythm.

The story is located in *Sefer ha-ma'asim* between two additional tales about the value of the Sabbath whose sources are in *Midrash aseret hadibrot* but not in the same order: "The Cow That Observed the Sabbath" and "The Butcher from Ludkiya." "Joseph-Who-Reveres-the-Sabbath" and "The Butcher from Ludkiya" come one after the other, as they do in the Talmud.

Despite the story's affinity with its sources in the Talmud and *Midrash aseret hadibrot*, the emphasis in *Sefer ha-ma'asim* is on Joseph's designation as the one who "reveres the Sabbath." He is at the center, and his image in the minds of his friends and neighbors also implies a collective image in the mind of contemporary readers and audiences. This is unlike its sources in the Talmud and *Midrash aseret hadibrot*, which focus on honoring the Sabbath as a halakhic value in itself—namely *kevod ha-Shabbat* (honoring the Sabbath)—and on the reward earned by those who attain it.[12] Three features unique to *Sefer ha-ma'asim* indicate this nuance, which becomes significant in its broader literary and cultural context.

The first feature is that parts of the epilogue in the Talmud and *Midrash aseret hadibrot* which make Joseph's reward contingent on his custom of honoring the Sabbath, and which focus the story on the halakhic value of *kevod ha-Shabbat*, are omitted. In the Talmud the epilogue is embedded in the moral imparted to Joseph: "A certain old man met him [and] said, 'He who lends to the Sabbath, the Sabbath repays him.' "[13] Similarly, in *Midrash aseret hadibrot* (for example, in Ms. Vatican 285), the epilogue reads: "And all this happened to him because he used to honor the Sabbath." In *Sefer ha-ma'asim* the tale ends with the description of Joseph's reward—"thirteen

11. "*Coolhoo Nikhsei, Yosef Mokir Shavi Akhil lehoo*" (Aramaic) This is the wording in Ms. Vatican Bibliotheca Apostolica-Ebr. 108 on Tractate *Shabbat*, as well as in the Vilna Romm edition.

12. For *kevod ha-Shabbat*, see *Encyklopedia Talmudit*, s.v. *kevod ha-Shabbat.*

13. Shabbat, 119a.

roomfuls of gold dinars"—without the didactic messages or summarizing epilogue. The narrator's comment in *Midrash aseret hadibrot,* that Joseph "bought [the large fish] and hastened to prepare it in honor of the Sabbath," was omitted, and was replaced by "and he [Joseph] bought it," without further explanation. The reason for this purchase is of course implied but not explicit, and it is therefore less emphasized.

The second feature is the omission of the precise time when Joseph bought the fish on the Sabbath eve, at late afternoon before dark in the talmudic version and at "twilight" in *Midrash aseret hadibrot.*[14] Instead, *Sefer ha-ma'asim* notes only that it was "on the eve of the Sabbath." Accordingly, in the Talmud and Midrash, the value of honoring the Sabbath is expressed in Joseph's willingness to buy the expensive fish as late as just before dark on the eve of the Sabbath, while he has probably prepared his Sabbath in advance.[15] The specific time marker in the Talmud and *Midrash aseret hadibrot* that implies the halakhic norms of *kevod ha-Shabbat* was apparently not required in *Sefer ha-ma'asim* in order to designate Joseph, whom everyone knew, as "Joseph-Who-Reveres-the-Sabbath." The omission of the words *apania* or "twilight" in *Sefer ha-ma'asim* shifts the center of gravity from "honoring the Sabbath" as a norm in itself to the image of Joseph in everyone's eyes, Jews and gentiles alike.

The third feature of the *Sefer ha-ma'asim* version relates to the antithesis between fate and human choice, which is stressed in the talmudic version, where it is represented by the soothsayers and Joseph,[16] but which is tempered in *Sefer ha-ma'asim.* Instead of the soothsayers who predict that the rich gentile will lose all of his property to Joseph, *Sefer ha-ma'asim* presents the people of his neighborhood as a collective: "All those who saw him would say." This accentuates Joseph's image as someone who greatly reveres the Sabbath in his surrounding society, among Jews and gentiles alike, an image that is also implied by the familiar use in *Sefer ha-ma'asim* of only his first name, even by the acquaintances of the rich gentile who sought to give him good advice.[17] The strong affinity in the sources between the act of revering the Sabbath and the person who is known to revere the Sabbath enabled a certain nuance in *Sefer ha-ma'asim,* which focuses more on Joseph's social image and designation than on the value of honoring the Sabbath itself.

14. In the Talmud, "*apania,*" or just before dark; in *Midrash aseret hadibrot* (ed. Shapira, 61), "*ben ha'shemashot*" or twilight—apparently just enough time to allow Joseph to prepare his fish before the Sabbath. The following discussion was inspired by Spiegel, "Why Did Joseph-Who-Honors-the-Sabbath Buy the Fish?"

15. For the norm of replacing products that were prepared for the Sabbath with others of better quality, see tractate *Beiẓah* 16a.

16. On this antithesis, see Fraenkel, *Iyyunim be'olamo haruḥani shel sipur ha'aggada,* 16–18.

17. "And all those who saw him would say: All your property will Joseph inherit."

Possibly, the broader context of this shift is the motif of a pearl or some other precious stone in the belly of a fish, which was widespread in medieval Europe. In these prevalent narratives, the precious stone in the fish's belly designates the finder as a saint, or the stone may be seen as a sign of forgiveness of sin.[18] In the narrative poem "Gregorius on the Rock," by the poet Hartmann von Aue, Gregorius is born from an incestuous union between a brother and sister, and in later years unknowingly marries his mother. When he learns of his sin, he undertakes severe acts of repentance, asks a fisherman to bind him to a rock in the middle of the sea, and throws away the key to his chains. A long time later, he finds the key in the belly of a fish. A group of cardinals on their way to seek an heir to the papacy see a sign that Gregorious is destined to become the next pope.[19]

Another legend tells that St. Arnulf relinquished all his wealth and left his family to live as a monk in the desert. On one occasion, he threw his ring into the Moselle River and said: "If the ring returns to me, I will know that my sins have been absolved." Later, after he was appointed bishop of Metz, the ring was restored to him; he was served a fish whose belly contained the ring, thus confirming the absolution of his sins.[20] A story cited by Caesarius of Heisterbach in *Dialogus Miraculorum* relates that once, when he was in Xanten, his ring fell into the Rhine. It was restored to him (retrieved from the belly of a fish) only after he returned to the same spot a year later, and hence he was designated the commander of Xanten. In this manner, the ring also singled out Conrad, provost of the St. Severin church in Cologne, as commander of Xanten, although he did not reside there permanently.[21] In another legend about St. Kentigern, the patron of Glasgow, the ring in the fish's belly signifies the absolution of the sin of betrayal committed by the king's wife after she profoundly repented, and it designates Kentigern as a saint and miracle-worker.[22] These legends containing the motif of a ring in the belly of a fish which is restored to its owner all designate a certain character as a saint and leader. "Joseph-Who-Reveres-the-Sabbath," with a certain nuance peculiar to *Sefer ha-ma'asim*, thus fits into a broader discourse in medieval Europe.

18. See Tubach 4102, ATU 736A; Th N211.1: "Lost ring found in fish" (Polycrates). And see Loomis, "Ring of Polycrates," 44–47.

19. Elstein, "The Gregorius Legend," 196–200.

20. See Loomis, "Ring of Polycrates," 44–45.

21. Caesarii Heisterbacensis, *Dialogus Miraculorum*, vol. 2, 10.61, 258–259; Caesarius of Heisterbach, *The Dialogue on Miracles*, book 10, no. 61, 221. Apparently the dual function of Conrad in different places at the same time rendered it necessary to designate him as commander of the place he visited only occasionally.

22. See Clouston, *Popular Tales*, vol. 1, 400, and the more extensive discussion of other parallels on 398–403. See also in Loomis, "Ring of Polycrates," 45.

22. The Butcher from Ludkiya (310a)

This story is introduced with the opening "and once I was the guest of . . . ," instead of the usual opening in *Sefer ha-ma'asim* of "*Ma'aseh*," or its English formulaic equivalent "Once." This suggests a continuation of the previous story about Joseph-Who-Reveres-the-Sabbath, but at the same time a new story that requires an opening of its own, with the usual expression "Once." Thus *Sefer ha-ma'asim* follows the editing trend of *Midrash aseret hadibrot*, where this story comes right after "Joseph-Who-Reveres-the-Sabbath" and opens with, "And R. Ḥiyya bar Abba also said, once . . ."[1] However, the sequence of the other tales about the Sabbath is not identical in the two sources. In *Midrash aseret hadibrot*, "The Cow That Observed the Sabbath" comes after the story about the butcher of Ludkiya, and in *Sefer ha-ma'asim* it precedes it.[2] Thus *Sefer ha-ma'asim* was inspired by *Midrash aseret ha-dibrot* as one of its sources, but it is not an exact copy.

The tale is cited in the Amoraic literature in two different versions: one in *Genesis rabbah* and the other in the Babylonian Talmud, tractate *Shabbat*.[3] *Sefer ha-ma'asim* follows the talmudic version. A butcher gains great wealth for having honored the Sabbath and putting aside the best cuts of meat he had for it. The versions differ in a motif that exists only in *Genesis rabbah*, of an infant placed in the center of the table laden with delicacies.[4] The infant calls forth from the table top in a loud voice: "The earth is the Lord's, and all that fills it," so that the butcher will remember to bless the food and thank the Lord as the source of all plenty.[5] The butcher, who has a lowly image in the sources, because he engages in slaughtering beasts and works with blood, becomes in this story a model for emulation, since he sets aside his best merchandise for the Sabbath.[6] The moral is interpreted

1. *Midrash aseret hadibrot*, ed. Shapira, 61.
2. In *Sefer ha-ma'asim* the sequence is: "The Cow That Observed the Sabbath (no. 20); "Joseph-Who-Reveres-the-Sabbath" (no. 21); and "The Butcher from Ludkiya" (no. 22). In *Midrash aseret hadibrot*, ed. Shapira, it is "Joseph-Who-Reveres-the-Sabbath," "The Butcher from Ludkiya," and "The Cow That Observed the Sabbath."
3. In *Genesis rabbah*, 11:4, ed. Albeck and Albeck, 91; *Shabbat* 119a.
4. Occasionally two infants appear, citing also a verse from Haggai: "The silver is mine, and the gold is mine, says the Lord of hosts" (Haggai 2:8). See R. David ha-Adani *Midrash hagadol*, Exodus, ed. Margulies, 413; Gaster, *Exempla*, no. 119, 81.
5. Compare to the figure of the Messiah as an infant in *Lamentations rabbah* (ed. Buber, 89–90).
6. Cf. *Beiẓah* 16a on Shamai, whose custom was to reserve the best meat for the Sabbath ("if he found a well-favoured animal he said, Let this be for the Sabbath"), to Hillel, who was certain that all he needed for the Sabbath would become available to him, in the sense of "blessed is the Lord, who daily bears our burden."

accordingly: "Blessed is the Almighty for giving you the reward you deserve." The story illustrates the meaning of *kevod ha-Shabbat* (the honor of the Sabbath), a Jewish legal term that requires a person to distinguish between the weekdays and the Sabbath and to celebrate the latter in a special way, albeit in keeping with his financial means.[7] Thus in its substructure the tale contrasts the sacred and the profane. The anonymous character of the butcher, the Sabbath as a collective value, and the concrete reward of great wealth mark the story as an exemplum par excellence.

The tale, anecdotal and appealing to both the layman and the scholar, was very popular throughout the generations in the talmudic version.[8] In its various contexts it was inserted within homilies on the Sabbath and in *Midrash aseret hadibrot* as an illustration of the Fourth Commandment.

The figure of the butcher also appears in the tale "R. Joshua b. Elem and Ninus the Butcher" (no. 47 in *Sefer ha-ma'asim*), of the "Companion in Paradise" tale type (809*-*A [IFA]). In tales of this type, a simple man, often a sinner, gains an honorable place in the Garden of Eden alongside a sage and righteous man, as a reward for a single good deed that he performed in his lifetime. In both "The Butcher of Ludkiya" and "R. Joshua b. Elem and Ninus the Butcher," a butcher is given a big reward, despite his lowly social image. In "R. Joshua b. Elem and Ninus the Butcher," a butcher is rewarded because of the exceptional way he treated his parents, and in "The Butcher from Ludkiya" because of the great honor he had for the Sabbath. In the "The Butcher from Ludkiya," no mention is made of the butcher's reward in the

7. See *Pesaḥim* 112a: Though R. Akiva said, "Treat your Sabbath like a weekday rather than be dependent on men, yet one must prepare something trifling at home." In other words, he must do something differently in his home in honor of the Sabbath.

8. For medieval versions of the tale based on the tractate *Sabbath*, see: *Midrash aseret hadibrot*, ed. Shapira, 61; *Ḥibbur yafeh mehayeshu'a*, ed. Hirschberg; and Brinner, ed., *An Elegant Composition Concerning Relief after Adversity*, no. 8, 39–40; *Midrash hagadol*, Exodus, ed. Margulies, 413; Judah b. Barzilai, *Sefer ha'itim*, no. 166; *Yalkut shimoni* on Isaiah, no. 496, ed. Shiloni, *Latter Prophets*, 307; Ms. Moscow-Ginzburg 111, 162a, as part of the homilies on the Sabbath (and not within the framework of *Midrash aseret hadibrot* [15th century]); Ms. Moscow-Ginzburg, 275, 251a (also as part of the homilies on the Sabbath [15th century]). Sources based on *Genesis rabbah* are *Pesikta rabbati*, ed. Ish Shalom, ch. 23, the Ten Commandments, 119b; *Midrash aseret hadibrot*, ed. Shapira, 61; Gaster, *Exempla*, no. 119, 81; *Yalkut shimoni* on Genesis 16, ed. Shiloni, vol. 1, 52; Ms. London, British Library Or. 1389, 51a (Ashkenaz, 14th c.). A selection of later versions based on the Talmud include Ms. Munich 100, 74b (in archaic Yiddish); Ms. Jerusalem 3182, 123a (Yassif, *Ninety-nine Tales*, no. 62, 224–225); Ms. JTS, ENA 727, mic 1480, 77b; Ms. Moscow-Ginsberg 275, 251a; Ms. Cincinnati 61a, 78a–78b; Ms. London, Sasson collection 256, 42b. For versions in printed collections of tales, see *Hagadot hatalmud*, ch. *kol kitvei*, 17b; *En Jacob*, ed. Glick, vol. 1, 191–192; *Mayse bukh*, no. 7; *Ma'aseh book*, trans. Gaster, 1, no. 7, 11–12; Jellinek, *Bet hamidrasch*, 1, 75; Bialik and Ravnitzky, *The Book of Legends*, no. 62, 49; Bin Gorion, *Mimekor yisrael*, no. 302, 211–212.

Garden of Eden, and therefore it does not belong to the "Companion in Paradise" tale type; yet both tales share a motif of a reward for a single good deed, given to a despicable character or a simple man.[9]

In addition to this thematic affinity, there is a stylistic affinity as well between the "Butcher from Ludkiya" (no. 22) and "R. Joshua b. Elem and Ninus the Butcher" (no. 47), which is expressed in an identical linguistic and syntactic structure. In the "Butcher from Ludkiya," the butcher is asked, "*Ma ma'asekha shezakhita le'khakh*?" (lit., "What are your deeds that you earned all this?"; i.e., "What have you done to earn all this?"), and in "R. Joshua b. Elem and Ninus the Butcher," he is asked, "*Ma melakhtekha*?" ("What is your occupation?"). In both tales, the sentence consists of an interrogatory word, "what" (*ma*), and a noun, "deeds" or "occupation" (*ma'asekha* and *melakhtekha*, respectively). In *Midrash aseret hadibrot*, which is the source for the "Butcher from Ludkiya" in *Sefer ha-ma'asim*, the syntax is different: "*Me asita shezakhita le'khakh?*" ("What have you done to earn all this?)." It combines the interrogatory word *Me* ("what") and the verb *asita* (have you done), rather than the noun *ma'asekha* ("deeds"). Thus in *Midrash aseret hadibrot* a nominal sentence turns into a verbal sentence. This linguistic deviation from the model of *Midrash aseret hadibrot* in *Sefer ha-ma'asim* indicates an associative affinity in the latter, in its tales' common motifs.

"The Butcher from Ludkiya" is followed by a story about an argument between Turnus Rufus and R. Akiva (no. 23). It is marked as a new story by the larger amount of white space between the two, but it does not begin with the usual opening "*Ma'aseh*," or "Once."

9. See in this edition: "The Power of a Single Act of Charity" (no. 51).

23. Turnus Rufus and R. Akiva (310a–310b)

This is one of three polemic tales in the Talmud concerning an argument between Turnus Rufus and R. Akiva. One of them centers on the commandment of the *brit milah* (circumcision), which the Romans forbade at the beginning of the second century, and another is about charity: "If your God loves the poor, why does he not support them?"[1] The present tale about the Sabbath is cited in tractate *Sanhedrin* 65b in the context of the prohibition against consulting a sorcerer.[2] Although these would seem to be philosophical debates about the nature and purpose of the world, in which Turnus Rufus and R. Akiva present opposing cultural positions, the images of the two men charge the stories with the tension that exists between the foreigner and the Jew, the occupier and the occupied, who is fighting for the right to observe his religion. Turnus Rufus, who in the Jewish sources is "an evil man" (*rasha*),[3] was the Roman governor of the province of Judea during the time of the Bar Kokhba revolt, and the founder of Aelia Capitolina.[4] In marked contrast, R. Akiva's place in the collective Jewish memory is that of the greatest of the Tana'im, the leader who supported Bar Kokhba during the revolt, and one of the ten great martyrs who died in consecration of God's name.

The present tale about the Sabbath is included in *Sefer ha-ma'asim* as a direct continuation of "The Butcher from Ludkiya," and it lacks the usual opening, "Once." It is therefore not treated in *Sefer ha-ma'asim* as a tale in itself but rather as an anecdote that is attached to the previous story about the Sabbath and its uniqueness. This hierarchy is probably the result of editorial considerations in *Midrash aseret hadibrot*, although evidence for this is in manuscripts from the fourteenth and fifteenth centuries—later than the manuscript of *Sefer ha-ma'asim*. In them, "Turnus Rufus and R. Akiva," as well as an anecdote that is not included in *Sefer ha-ma'asim*, "The Seasoning of the Sabbath," appear as a continuation of a previous tale and not as one that stands on its own.[5] "The Seasoning of the Sabbath," about Hadrian and

1. See *Baba Batra* 10a on charity. On the *brit milah*, see *Tanḥuma, tazri'a*, no. 5; *Tanḥuma*, ed. Buber, no. 7; Hevroni, "Circumcision as Revolt," 61–73.
2. See additional sources: *Genesis rabbah*, ed. Theodor and Albeck, 11, 5, 92–94; *Tanḥuma, ki tisa*, no. 33 (at greater length); *Pesikta rabbati*, ed. Ish Shalom, ch. 23, the Ten Commandments, 119b.
3. See *Tanḥuma*, ed. Buber, *tazri'a*, no. 7.
4. His name, Tieius Rufus (Quintus), was changed to Turnus Rufus in the Talmud.
5. In Ms. Wolfenbüttel 36.25 from the fourteenth century, the sequence is "Joseph-Who-Reveres-the-Sabbath," followed by "The Seasoning of the Sabbath" (without the opening "Once—"), and "Turnus Rufus and R. Akiva." (For the same version and the same sequence, see Jellinek, *Bet hamidrasch*, v. 1, 1, 75.) In Ms. Parma 2269 (de Rossi 473) from the fifteenth century, the

R. Joshua b. Ḥananiah, is analogous to the Turnus Rufus tale in that it shares the motif of the Sabbath, the genre of polemic tales concerning a representative of the Roman government and a Jewish sage, and the question-and-answer format.[6] The emperor asks why the Sabbath dishes of the Jews have such a fragrant aroma, and R. Ḥananiah replies that it is a seasoning called "Sabbath," which gives them that special taste but is of no use to anyone who does not observe the Sabbath.[7] In *Sefer ha-ma'asim*, however, there is no mention of the "seasoning of the Sabbath."

In "Turnus Rufus and R. Akiva," the hallmarks of the uniqueness of the Sabbath, in contrast to the weekdays, involve the smoke that rises from Turnus Rufus's father's grave all week because he is burning in hell, the flowing of the River Sambatyon, and the manna that fell on the Children of Israel in the desert. The smoke from the grave of Turnus Rufus's father does not appear on the Sabbath, when the fire burning the sinners in hell is extinguished;[8] the River Sambatyon flows during the week, carrying stones in its wake, but rests on the Sabbath; and the manna that fed the Israelites in the desert did not fall on the Sabbath—on Friday they had to collect enough for the Sabbath as well (Exodus 16:23–31). The sequence of tales about the Sabbath in *Midrash aseret hadibrot* and in *Sefer ha-ma'asim*—"The Butcher from Ludkiya," "Joseph-Who-Reveres-the-Sabbath," "The Seasoning of the Sabbath" (in *Midrash aseret hadibrot* only), and "Turnus Rufus and R. Akiva"—stems from a shared substructure, even though the relative hierarchy among them varies. The tales represent a binary paradigm of sacred and profane, Jewish and gentile, spirit and matter.

Following "Turnus Rufus and R. Akiva," and in the same sequence, there are several epigrams praising the Sabbath from the tractate *Sabbath* 119 a–b. The one about two angels who escort a man to his home from the synagogue is also included in *Midrash aseret hadibrot*, after "The Cow That Observed the Sabbath," and just before concluding the tales and homilies on the Fourth Commandment regarding the Sabbath.[9] The others relate to the power of three Sabbath meals to save one from the tribulations of the Messiah, the law of hell, and Gog and Magog, and the reward of he who delights in the Sabbath.

---

sequence is "The Butcher from Ludkiya," "The Sabbath Observer and the Bear," and next "The Seasoning of Sabbath" (without the formula "Once—"), and "Turnus Rufus and R. Akiva." In Ms. London, British Library Or. 1389, which is not a manuscript of *Midrash aseret hadibrot*, the sequence is "Joseph-Who-Reveres-the-Sabbath" (50b), "The Butcher from Ludkiya" (51a), and "Turnus Rufus" (53a).

6. See *Shabbat* 119a, where the tale comes immediately after the "The Butcher from Ludkiya."
7. This is one of several tales about these characters in the same genre.
8. See Avida (Zlotnik), "Legends of the Sabbath and Its Customs."
9. *Midrash aseret hadibrot*, ed. Shapira, 63.

24. The Defamed Woman (310b–311b)

The story is of the "Crescentia" tale type (ATU 712; Tubach 1898), which circulated in the East and the West as part of a broader cycle of tale types about persecuted innocent women.[1] The basic plot of the Crescentia tale type begins with an exposition about a highly placed man (emperor, cadi, merchant, and the like) who goes on a voyage for his business affairs and leaves his wife in the care of his brother. In the man's absence, the brother tries unsuccessfully to seduce the woman. When she rejects him, he falsely accuses her of committing adultery, and she is sentenced to death (by stoning or being hanged by her hair). She is saved but defamed, time after time, in various situations and occasions. Later on she becomes a well-known healer (by virtue of her mystic personality and prayers, in the East; by means of healing herbs given her by the Virgin Mary, in the West), and her brother-in-law and others who slandered her come to her to obtain a cure for their illness (leprosy and other diseases). They are forced to confess to their deeds, and her husband learns the truth. In the end she is reunited with her husband (or becomes a nun). The story presents misogynistic stereotypes about faithful women and treacherous, cunning women, as well as prejudiced views about lepers, who in the Middle Ages were associated with moral sin.[2]

The various versions of the tale represent three major textual traditions,[3] one from the East and two from the West: (1) in Persian-Muslim sources, the *Tuti Na'meh* (*Tales of a Parrot*), which is a Turkish-Persian adaptation of *Sukasaptati*; the fourteenth-century mystic work *Ocean of the Soul*; and several editions of *A Thousand and One Nights*;[4] (2) in medieval collections of legends of miracles about the

1. See Yassif, *Kemargalit bemishbeẓet*, 148–150; Ben-Amos, *Mimekor yisrael*, no. 202, 386. For parallels to the tale type and a research bibliography, see ATU 712 ("Crescentia"), as well as the site http://gahom.ehess.fr/index.php?434 (last accessed July 25, 2016), for *Thesaurus Exemplorum* M.A., Tubach 1898. (On the Gahom site, click on "ThEMA" to search for the tale type Tubach 1898.) And see the motif Th. K2112: "Woman slandered as adulteress." For further studies from the gender perspective, see Frauke, "Die unschuldig verfolgte." And from the philological and comparative perspectives, see Marzolph, *The Tale of the Pious Man and His Chaste Wife*. For a broader context of the tale, see Jones, "The Innocent Persecuted Heroine Genre," which is a structural, symbolic, and psychoanalytic study of various tale types of this same theme.
2. On the image of lepers in the context of the slandered woman, see Brody, *The Disease of the Soul*, 45–146. The discussion there centers on the *Gesta Romanorum* version.
3. The suggested typology for them is based on Uther, "Crescentia."
4. See Nakhshabi, *Tales of a Parrot*, 201–208; Ritter, *The Ocean of the Soul*, 341–381. For parallels in different editions of *A Thousand and One Nights*, see Marzolph, "Crescentia's Oriental Relatives."

Virgin Mary, against the background of her cult at the time;[5] and (3) in renditions of *Gesta Romanorum* in fourteenth-century Europe with no reference to the Virgin Mary, thus implying a secular nuance.[6] The parallels in the East and the West differ in their details (the motif of the healing herbs, for example, which exists only in the Western versions), and in the number of episodes they contain about the woman's tribulations until her innocence is proven. Scholars who studied this tale type have searched for its primary sources and its modes of development, but for our purposes here the comparison between the tale's traditions in the East and the West is relevant for an understanding of the *Sefer ha-ma'asim* version in its European context.

As far as we know, the *Sefer ha-ma'asim* version is the earliest written source of the Crescentia tale type in Jewish sources.[7] Yassif attributed it to the Eastern branch of the tale type based on two salient features:[8] (1) The figure of the merchant, who generally leaves his wife in his brother's keeping, is found in the Eastern versions, versus the emperor in the Western parallels. In *Sefer ha-ma'asim* the husband is a merchant.[9] (2) An episode found in the Western versions is absent from the Eastern ones; in it, the wife locks up her brother-in-law to put a stop to his attempts to seduce her in her husband's absence. This episode is missing from *Sefer ha-ma'asim* as well.

The stoning motif in *Sefer ha-ma'asim*, in parallel to the Eastern versions of the tale, also provides support for Yassif's hypothesis. In Europe the woman is banned to the forest to be killed there, or her brother-in-law hangs her by her hair, on their way to greet her husband, the emperor. The story's ending, with the wife's reconciliation with her husband, is consistent with a trend more prevalent in the Eastern

5. See references in the Oxford Library site: csm.mml.ox.ac.uk/index.php?p=poemdata_view&rec=5 (last accessed July 25, 2016). I am grateful to Elisheva Baumgarten for referring me to this site and for providing me with Latin parallels that were collected by Na'ama Cohen HaNegbi for her research on Virgin Mary legends. For the motif of the Virgin Mary and her revelation to the defamed woman, see Étienne de Bourbon, *Anecdotes historiques*, no. 136, 115–117; *Viaticum*, no. 37, 57–59.

6. See various renditions of *Gesta Romanorum*: *Gesta* (I), no. 150, 111–118; *Gesta* (M), no. 69, 311–322; *Gesta* (Ö), no. 249, 648–654. These versions also differ from the Virgin Mary legends in that they end with the woman's return to the palace with her husband and their reunion.

7. See further: *Midrash aseret hadibrot* in Ms. Vatican 107, 180a–181b; Ms. Moscow-Ginzberg 111, 129b–131b, and Ms. Zurich 192, 75b–77a; Dayan, *Holekh tamim upoel ẓedek* ("He that walketh uprightly, and worketh righteousness"), no. 30, 40–41; and the discussion of Chana Hendler on this version ("The Characteristics of the 'Pious' Literature Genre," 39–40). The story also exists in the IFA archives; see E.D.N.A.: AT 712.

8. Yassif, *Kemargalit bemishbeẓet*, 149.

9. Sometimes the tale includes the figure of a cadi in Eastern versions, along with the merchant.

versions, while in the West she usually becomes a nun.[10] Based on the points of contact with the Eastern versions, the story may have come into *Sefer ha-ma'asim* through the mediation of *Midrash aseret hadibrot* as an illustration of the Ninth Commandment, "Thou shalt not bear false witness." The tale does exhibit the harsh implications of slander and perjury. This is also supported by the reference in *Midrash aseret hadibrot*, in the Ninth Commandment, to "what I wrote above,"[11] as well as by the inclusion of the story in manuscripts of *Midrash aseret hadibrot* in Europe in the fifteenth century.[12]

The attribution of the *Sefer ha-ma'asim* version to the Eastern tradition of the Crescentia tale type may suggest an additional adaptation in Ashkenaz, which stands out when compared to the Virgin Mary legends prevalent in Europe against the backdrop of her cult. In the legendary parallels in Europe, the Virgin Mary is revealed to the persecuted and slandered woman and gives her healing herbs, with which she cures the ill, in particular lepers. By devoting herself to Mary, the woman in a certain sense becomes, like her, a saint. In *Sefer ha-ma'asim* and in the spirit of the Jewish audiences, the figure of the Virgin Mary does not appear, and it is the Almighty who gives the woman curative herbs to heal lepers, but the legendary discourse on miraculous acts is retained: "God provided her with all kinds of herbs, and she healed lepers and every [kind of] disease"; and "What did God do? He caused those people who had testified falsely against her, along with the husband's brother, to fall ill with leprosy." In *Midrash aseret hadibrot* (Ms. Vatican 107), the emphasis is on the rational aspect: "And God gave her understanding and intelligence and she knew all manner of cures in the world and sold all manner of balms and herbs, which were capable of healing all bodily diseases."[13] The description of what happened to her on the ship and the end of the story are also characterized as miracles: "And God performed a miracle for her, and none of those pirates touched her"; or "[And they] gave praise to their Creator for all these miracles." The motif of miraculous acts also exists in *Midrash aseret hadibrot*, but as I noted, it is accompanied by a rational explanation. Intertextual affinities to the Book of Jonah

10. There are often exceptions to this classification; for example, in *Gesta Romanorum* the wife is reunited with her husband, and in Nakhshabi, *Tales of a Parrot*, the end is left open, with no mention of the reunification of husband and wife.

11. Marzolph's hypothesis as to the Jewish source of the tale may support my conclusion that the *Sefer ha-ma'asim* version originated in *Midrash aseret hadibrot*.

12. See n. 7, above.

13. Ms. Vatican 107, 181a.

establish the tale's legendary character in *Sefer ha-ma'asim*, and the special biblical style of these allusions imbues them with a lofty nature:

> And God cast a storm wind on the sea, and there was a great storm at sea, and the ship almost sank. And the sailors saw, and each cried out to his gods and said to one another: Let us cast lots and see why this calamity has happened to us. And they cast lots, and the lot fell on the woman. They said to her: Tell us what work you do? And she told them: I am a Hebrew woman, and I fear the God of the heaven who made the seas and the land.[14]

Sefer ha-ma'asim takes part in the discourse that exists in the Western versions of Crescentia, but the Christian motif of the Virgin Mary is neutralized.[15]

The affinity with these parallels in Europe is manifested in other ways as well: (1) The structure of the *Sefer ha-ma'asim* version is consistent with the abridged versions of the tale in Europe, in the exempla of Étienne of Bourbon, Vincent of Beauvais, and the *Viaticum*. These do not include an episode, typical of parallels from the East, about an ungrateful thief who betrays the defamed woman after she saves him from hanging or a beating with the last of her money and jewels. Instead, the thief sells her to the captain of a ship anchored in port, claiming he is her master.[16] (2) The motif of rape is characteristic of European parallels, in contrast to attempts at seduction and persuasion in the East. In *Sefer ha-ma'asim* the woman's brother-in-law sends away his servant on some pretext, plotting to rape her, and in non-Jewish legendary versions, the king's slaves take her to the forest to kill her and plan to rape her first. (3) The woman is supposed to serve as the governess of the son of her rescuer and to educate him, similar to her role in the *Speculum morale*. This is in accordance with versions in the West, in which her role is more that of a nursemaid than a governess-teacher. One could conclude that the scribe or the narrator adapted the *Midrash aseret hadibrot* version that he had before him but reworked it based on legendary traditions of the tale that were widespread in his locale.

14. Cf. Jonah 1:4–15.

15. A further adaptation to Jewish norms is manifested in the different endings of the tale: a reconciliation between the woman and the men who defamed her in the non-Jewish versions, both in the East and the West, in contrast to *Sefer ha-ma'asim*, in which they are not forgiven.

16. This episode is in *Tales of a Parrot* and in parallels from *A Thousand and One Nights* (n. 4 above); in Europe, it is in renditions of *Gesta Romanorum*. In Jewish sources, see *Midrash aseret hadibrot*, ed. Shapira, 218–219.

The gendered aspects of the story are generalizable to other relationships as well. The few manifestations of brotherly love in *Sefer ha-ma'asim*, along with the more frequent displays of infidelity and betrayal (between brothers, between employer and servant, between a rescued person and his benefactor, between a minor and an adult), as well as the legendary character of the woman, all serve to clarify the nature of relations between humans vis-à-vis the relations between humans and God.

25. R. Meir and Judah of Anatot (311b–312a)

The medieval tale of "R. Meir and Judah of Anatot" is based on the tale type "charity saves from death" in rabbinical literature, although it deviates from it in some respects and has no source in the Talmud or in Midrash.[1] A snake threatens Judah of Anatot, but R. Meir manages to rescue him. He induces Judah of Anatot to give him charity, almost against his will, and so Judah is saved from death. The motifs of the Angel of Death, in the form of a snake, sent as an emissary of God to take a man's life and that of postponing death by an act of charity both exist in the Talmud: for example, in the well-known story of R. Akiva's daughter, who was saved from a snake's bite on her wedding day because she gave her own portion of food to a poor man (*Shabbat* 156b).[2] The story also fits in with tales in the Talmud about R. Meir, such as the one in *Avodah Zarah* (18a–b), which describes how he saved his wife's sister from a brothel. The formula mentioned in the talmudic tale—"O God of Meir, answer me!"[3]—probably inspired Judah of Anatot's cry of distress in *Sefer ha-ma'asim*: "R. Meir, save me from this snake that seeks to kill me." Additional motifs are characteristic of the way R. Meir is depicted in the Talmud and the *midrashim*: his radiant expression and the glow of his skin as a concretization of his name ("he was called R. Meir because he enlightened the Sages in the Halakhah"),[4] and his custom of spending much time in the synagogue and delivering exceedingly lengthy sermons at the synagogue in Ḥamat, which is written about in *Leviticus rabbah*.[5]

1. For parallels of this tale type, cf. ATU 934, "Tales of the Predestined Death"; IFA 934*F, "Charity Rescues from Death"; Schwarzbaum, *Studies in Jewish and World Folklore*, 278–280, and the tale of "R. Meir and Judah of Anatot" on 280; Schwarzbaum, *The Mishle shu'alim (Fox Fables)*, 121–122; and Ben-Amos, *Mimekor yisrael*, no. 115, 205.
2. Two other examples include the case of Ablet, the astronomer, and the Amorai Samuel (*Shabbat* 156b), and the case of the two disciples of R. Ḥanina (p*Shabbat* 6: 9 [8:4]). On the snake as Satan, the Angel of Death, and the evil inclination, see *Baba Batra* 16a. On its role as an emissary of God sent to take the lives of men, see *Leviticus rabbah*, 22,4, ed. Margulies, 505.
3. After the Middle Ages the expression "O God of Meir, answer me!" was taken to be a magical formula, and R. Meir became known as a miracle-worker.
4. *Eruvin* 13b.
5. *Leviticus rabbah*, 9, 9, ed. Margulies, 191–193.

Nonetheless, the story is a product of the Middle Ages,[6] particularly in light of intertextual affinities with the seduction episodes in two contemporary works: *Mishlei R. Berakhiah Hanakdan* and the vernacular fables of Marie de France.[7] They tell about a goat that leaves her home to graze in the field so that she can produce abundant milk for her kid. At first she intends to leave the kid at home with the billy goat, and warns him gravely not to open the door to anyone. But the billy goat joins her; the kid remains at home and, following its mother's instructions, locks the house very well.[8] Then the wolf arrives, imitating the mother's voice, and it tries unsuccessfully to persuade the kid to let it into the house. The moral is that one should beware the hypocritical advice of evil people.[9] The tale in *Sefer ha-ma'asim* is about a snake rather than a wolf, but the situation is similar. The snake comes to take the life of Judah of Anatot and knocks on the locked door of his house. When Judah does not answer, he imitates time after time the voices of members of Judah's family, pleading to be taken into the house and saved from cold and hunger. The seduction scene behind a locked door, the warning not to open the door, the imitation of the voices of the family members, and the failure of the attempted seduction are all common motifs in both narratives. In Berakhiah's fable the goat tries to entice the kid in its mother's voice: "Open for me, for the milk that I bring thee in my udders is abundant. I am weary of grazing, and they cannot carry more food."[10] In *Sefer ha-ma'asim* the snake, while imitating the voices of all the family members, repeatedly asks Judah to open the door:

6. This is not the only medieval tale about R. Meir. There is also "R. Meir and the Wife of His Friend," which first appears in *Midrash aseret hadibrot* and has no sources in rabbinical literature. See in *Midrash aseret hadibrot*, ed. Shapira, 76–79.

7. *The Mishle shualim (Fox Fables) of Rabbi Berekhiah Hanakdan*, no. 21, ed. Habermann, 30–31; *Fables of a Jewish Aesop*, trans. Hadas, no. 21, 44. See also in the thirteenth-century manuscripts: Ms. Bodl. Or. 135, 265b; Munich 207, 21b–22a; Darmstadt, Cod. Or. 26, 75b. See Schwarzbaum's comments on the fable (*Mishle shu'alim*, 119–122). Cf. Marie de France, *Fables*, no. 90, 229–231. (In most editions of this work, the number of this fable is 89.) Cf. also the *Exempla* of Jacques de Vitry, no. 283, 119, and in English translation, 257–258. On parallels of the fable in earlier sources, including *Aesop's Fables*, see ATU 123, "The Wolf and the Kids." I am grateful to Revital Refael-Vivante and to Tovi Bibring for having shared with me the findings of the their joint Israel Science Foundation (ISF) research on fox fables, specifically the "wolf and kid" fable in medieval manuscripts and in Marie de France's fables.

8. In Ms. Bodl. Or. 135: "Close your door after me and do not open it until I return"; and then: "And the two of them went and told the little kid to lock the door. And she closes and locks the house."

9. And see ATU 123: "The Wolf and the Kids"; cf. Tubach 2309: "Goat Enticed by Wolf." See also Th J144: "Well-trained kid does not open door to wolf."

10. Ms. Bodl. Or. 135, f.265b; Hadas, trans., *Fables of a Jewish Aesop*, no. 21, 44.

> After waiting awhile, the snake came and took on the voice of his [Judah's] wife, saying: My husband, open the door, for I am cold. And he [Judah] intended to open [the door]. R. Meir told him: Beware not to open the door, because it is not your wife. He [the snake] waited awhile, and came and took on the voice of his eldest son. And he said: Father, open the door for me, for I am dying of thirst. R. Meir said: Beware not to open, because it is not your son. And similarly, he took on the guise of his sons and daughters-in-law.

The parallels are important because of the use *Sefer ha-ma'asim* made of a fable that was widespread at the time in Provence and in northern France. The scribe was familiar with the work by R. Berakhiah Hanakdan, which was copied in the same manuscript (Ms. Bodl. Or. 135, 256b–290a). He probably also knew of the French fable, perhaps in the form of oral performances,[11] although the influence of R. Berakhiah Hanakdan is more evident. The detailed seduction scene and the stylistic choice of the root *peh/taf/ ḥet* (.פ. ת. ח) create a closer affinity with the fables of R. Berakhiah Hanakdan, since Marie de France's fable only mentions the situation, without going into such great detail.[12] The setting of the seduction scene—the cold weather the snake complains about in the voice of Judah's wife—also implies that the tale was produced in Europe. I would suggest that the *Sefer ha-ma'asim* version relies on the Hebrew text of R. Berakhiah Hanakdan, with the mediation of Marie de France, and it is remodeled on the prevalent tale type of "charity saves from death" in the Jewish sources. The broader cultural context of the tale is the popular genre of fable literature in France.

The story was also adapted to the format of *Sefer ha-ma'asim* through the addition of an exposition based on a model frequently found in this compilation. A fictional character remains longer in the synagogue or is commanded to do so in order to honor it and to achieve a state of intention (*kavanah*) in his prayers. For instance, the story "Do Not Fail to Attend Public Prayers" (no. 41) opens with the

11. No conclusion has been reached yet regarding Marie de France's influence on R. Berakhiah Hanakdan, and there is some controversy regarding their dates, the relationship among their fables, the extent to which R. Berakhiah Hanakdan was familiar with Marie de France's fables and other works by her, as well as the affinity of their fables with a third, earlier source. See recent conjecture about Marie de France as a source of influence on R. Berakhiah Hanakdan: Bibring, "'Would That My Words Were Inscribed,'" 316–323.

12. "Od tele voiz de sa mere oï" ("He tried to sound like mama goat"): Marie de France, *Fables*, 230–231.

father instructing his son not to hurry to leave the synagogue, and as a result, he is saved. "The Loan" (no. 34) opens by introducing Abraham of Ashkelon, who came to the synagogue early and was among the last of the worshippers to leave. And in "The Pious Pretender" (50), which tells about a pious man who never changed his seat in the synagogue, the motif is apparent, with a certain variation. In the present story, R. Meir leaves the synagogue early, unlike his usual custom, and that is a sign that an unusual event awaits him. It later turns out that his hasty departure from the synagogue was meant to create the conditions and circumstances for saving Judah of Anatot from death.

The tale comes after "The Defamed Wife," which illustrates the Ninth Commandment, "Thou shalt not bear false witness." It is not entirely clear whether it was intended to illustrate the Tenth Commandment, "Thou shalt not covet," as a continuation of the series of tales in *Sefer ha-ma'asim* that relate to the commandments, or whether it stands on its own. On the one hand, the following tale is "R. Meir and Kiddor," which opens a new sequence about R. Meir. On the other hand, the motif of charity and the epilogue, which quotes a verse from Proverbs 11:4 ("Riches will not help on the day of wrath; but charity saves from death"), create an indirect affinity with the commandment "Thou shalt not covet."[13] Charity is presented as a more reliable asset in time of death than material wealth, and as an antithesis to greed. The greedy man envies his friend's wealth, while the charitable man is generous in his relations to others. The tale is indeed included in several later manuscripts of *Midrash aseret hadibrot*, in the context of the Tenth Commandment.[14]

During and after the Middle Ages, the influence of *Sefer ha-ma'asim* is evident in a nearly identical version in the story compilation in Ms. Jerusalem 3182,[15] and in an archaic Yiddish version in *Mayse bukh*, probably with the mediation of *Ḥibbur hama'asiyot vehamidrashot vehahadagot.*[16] In the nineteenth and twentieth centuries, it was printed in story collections such as Elijah Hacohen's *Me'il*

13. This addition is copied in small letters, following the beginning of the verse.

14. In Ms. Vatican 285 (78b), the epilogue is expanded and relates explicitly to the commandment "Thou shalt not covet." In Ms. Moscow-Ginzberg 111 (136b), the verse from Proverbs is cited, without a homily linked to the commandment. In Ms. Paris 716 (226a–227a), the story (92–94 in the Shapira edition) is copied in the framework of a section of tales and sermons that opens and closes with "Thou shalt not covet."

15. Yassif, *Ninety-nine Tales*, no. 57, 221–223.

16. *Ḥibbur hama'asiyot vehamidrashot vehahagadot*, no. 13. And see *Mayse bukh*, no. 215; *Ma'aseh Book*, trans. Gaster, vol. 2, no. 216, 525–528.

ẓedakah, Joseph Shabbtai Farḥi's *Oseh pele*, and Micha Joseph Bin Gorion's literary compilation *Mimekor yisrael.*[17] Y. L. Pereṭẓ, in his story "*Mesirut nefesh*" ("Self-Sacrifice"), borrowed the motif of the conversation between two snakes that takes place at the beginning of the tale.[18]

17. Elijah Hacohen, *Me'il ẓedakah*, 60–61, no. 442, ed. Kuperman; Araki, *Sefer hama'asiyot*, no. 13, 13b–15a, and in Ḥuẓin's edition, no. 13, 12b–13b; Farḥi, *Oseh pele*, part 1, 62–64; Bin Gorion, *Mimekor yisrael*, no. 354, 232–233; Ben-Amos, *Mimekor yisrael*, n.1, 205–207. Additional versions are Heilperin, *Seder hadorot*, no.10 ("Judah Ha'anatoti"), 105b; Manish Hacohen, *Todat yitzḥak*, no. 25, 12–13; Zis, *Ma'asiyot mehagedolim vehaẓadikim* (*Tales from the Great and Righteous*), 69–70; Sathon, *Tokpo shel nes* (*The Power of a Miracle*), 10. For summaries of versions of *Sefer ha-ma'asim* and *Ḥibbur hama'asiyot vehamidrashot vehahagadot* in English, see Gaster, *Exempla*, no. 314, 115; no. 394, 151.

18. "He saw two snakes saying to one another: 'Where are you going?' One said: The Almighty has sent me to kill Judah of Anatot and his children and his wife and his entire household." And cf. Y. L. Pereṭẓ, "*Mesirut nefesh*," in *Mepi ha'am*, 176–177.

26. R. Meir and Kiddor (312a–312b)

The name "Kiddor" was first mentioned in the PalestinianTalmud, in the tractate *Rosh Hashanah* 3:9.[1] There it is presented as a combination of the words "*ki dor*" from Deuteronomy 32:20, which reads in Hebrew "*ki dor tahapukhot hema, banim lo emun bam*" ("for they are a very perverse generation, children in whom there is no faith"). This verse is recited in *Shirat ha'azinu*, which refers to the sinners among the Israelites. On the basis of this homily, R. Meir concluded that Kiddor was a "wicked man" he couldn't trust.[2] The complete tale about Kiddor, which is the major source of the tale in *Sefer ha-ma'asim*, is in *Yoma* 83b.

In the main *Sefer ha-ma'asim* and *Yoma* follow the same plot: The story opens with an exposition about R. Meir's custom of being meticulous about names, unlike R. Judah and R. Yossi, his travelling companions. The three stay as guests in Kiddor's home; two of the men deposit their money with Kiddor on Sabbath eve, while R. Meir refrains from doing so because of Kiddor's name, and instead hides his money in the cemetery. Kiddor's dead father appears to his son in a dream and reveals to him where R. Meir's money is, but R. Meir thwarts his scheme, and his friends use a ploy to get their money back from Kiddor's wife.

In the Talmud the tale is told in tandem with other narratives about R. Meir, to illustrate his caution in relation to people's names and to underscore the importance of washing one's hands after a meal, a custom known as *mayim aḥaronim*.[3] Because Kiddor failed to wash his hands after the meal, the remains of lentils on his hands gave him away, and he ended up killing his own wife. However *Sefer ha-ma'asim* deviates from the talmudic version in its omission of the motif of *mayim aḥaronim* (unlike other versions in Ashkenaz which follow the Talmud)[4] and in its epilogue, which succinctly sums up the inevitable descent from greed to bloodshed.[5]

1. Academy of the Hebrew Language edition, 59a, 676.
2. Cf. also p*Berakhot* 8:2 [12:1], Academy of the Hebrew Language edition, 61, where the tale is alluded to.
3. *Mayim aḥaronim*: meaning water for washing hands without a blessing after the meal, in contrast to washing hands with a blessing before the meal.
4. Other versions that contain a warning about washing hands after the meal are R. Isaac b. Moses of Vienna, *Or zaru'a*, 1, Rules about washing hands, no. 72, 31–32; *Yalkut shimoni* on Isaiah, no. 459, ed. Shiloni, *The Latter Prophets*, 190; Ẓedekiah harofe (b. Abraham Anav), *Shibbolei haleket*, "*Seder Berakhot*," no. 149, 59.
5. Cf. *Midrash aseret hadibrot*, ed. Shapira, 94–95, where a similar epilogue relates to a different tale: "Come and see that in coveting another man's wife he was transgressing the Ten Commandments."

However, the main difference between the talmudic source and its parallel in *Sefer ha-ma'asim* is the motif of the deposit. While the motif of *mayim aḥaronim* is left out, the motif of the deposit is emphasized, thus making it more central to the story. In addition, the negotiations between R. Meir's friends and Kiddor's wife, which in the Talmud are reported only after the fact ("*azlu veyahavu simana le'devitu, veshekaluhu lekhisaihu ve'aitu*" ("They went and gave his wife the sign and took their wallets and brought them [back home]"), are described in detail in *Sefer ha-ma'asim*. The inspiration for this elaboration is the midrash *Tanḥuma* on the portion of Balak in Numbers.[6] The story there is quite different, but the remnants of the lentils (in *Tanḥuma*, the general term is "pulses") by which the thief is exposed is a shared motif, and it enabled the scribe to adapt its elaborate ending to his tale of "R. Meir and Kiddor."

The broad context of this trend of expansion involves tales of deposits in *Sefer ha-ma'asim*. "R. Meir and Kiddor" is one of five tales in the compilation that can be categorized as tales of deposit, which are also very popular tale types.[7] The four others are "Who Is the Thief?" (no. 16), "The Loan" (nos. 2, 34), "That Which Was Stolen Is Returned by Guile" (no. 48), and "The Pious Pretender" (no. 50). The tales differ in certain aspects and are similar in others, but for our purposes they share, explicitly or implicitly, the motif of reclaiming stolen property, a deposit, or a loan by means of a ruse. *Sefer ha-ma'asim*, in comparison to other story compilations in the Middle Ages and thereafter, contains a relatively large number of tales about a deposit. This reflects a special interest in the subject.[8]

The transition from the Talmud's emphasis on being particular about a person's name to the motif of the deposit in *Sefer ha-ma'asim* was made possible by a substructure common to "R. Meir and Kiddor" and other tales of deposits and ruses—the gap between an external appearance that inspires confidence and the true state of affairs. The plot develops in *Sefer ha-ma'asim* (as well as in tractate *Yoma*) toward a breakdown of trust. In the first part nothing about Kiddor's appearance or actions suggests he is not trustworthy, except for his suggestive name, Kiddor. In the

6. *Tanḥuma*, Balak, no. 15: "The case of a man who ate lentils"; *Tanḥuma*, ed. Buber, Balak, no. 24, 146; *Numbers rabbah*, ch. 20, no. 21.

7. See ATU 1617: "Unjust banker deceived into delivering deposits"; Tubach 4969: "Chest Full of Stones"; Tubach 696: "Blind Man Regains Twenty Pounds"; Tubach 3355: "Man Tricked into Returning Money"; motif Th. K1667: "Unjust banker deceived into delivering deposits by making him expect even larger treasure"; and Schwarzbaum's references to Jewish parallels (Schwarzbaum, *Studies in Jewish and World Folklore*, 239–241).

8. For example, in *Midrash aseret hadibrot*, ed. Shapira, two of the four are included: "Who Is the Thief?" and "That Which Was Stolen Is Returned by Guile."

second half details crop up that confirm R. Meir's judgment. In parallel, in the deposit tales, a man betrays the trust of those who leave their property in his hands, denies he has received such a deposit, or abandons his usual good behavior and changes for the worse ("The Loan"). This substructure also exists in another tale about R. Meir and Kiddor, in *Tanḥuma* (ed. Buber) on Genesis (no. 30). Kiddor was known among his friends as a "Torah scholar," but R. Meir doubts his reliability because of his inauspicious name and warns his pupils against him. That warning turns out to be well-founded, for later Kiddor steals his friends' clothing in the bath house.[9]

The emphasis on the motif of the deposit in *Sefer ha-ma'asim* in general, and in the story about R. Meir and Kiddor in particular, may indicate an intertextual link to Petrus Alfonsi's *Disciplina Clericalis*, which in Europe served as a mediating link between East and West. According to tale 15, called "The Ten Boxes," a pilgrim on his way to Mecca from Spain deposits his money with a man known to be reliable. When the time comes to return the deposit, that man denies having received it and threatens its owner, who leaves in despair. Then the pilgrim meets an old woman who helps him with a wise bit of advice. He must locate a trustworthy man to appear before the man who is holding the deposit; the man should bring with him ten colorful boxes, silver-plated and covered with locks (to suggest they contain money), to leave in his trust. At first he should carry only one box, with a convoy of porters carrying the other boxes visible on the horizon. The pilgrim is told to arrive there in the midst of the transaction and to demand the return of his property. When he does so, the swindler hastens to give it to him to avoid missing out on a bigger deal, which of course comes to naught because the first box was full of gravel, and none of the others actually arrive.[10]

Disciplina Clericalis, which was written in Arabic and Latin, was translated into rhymed French and rewritten in prose in the twelfth century. It had a strong impact on popular and didactic literature, appearing in more than sixty extant manuscripts and in parallels in later compilations, such as *Gesta Romanorum*.[11] Its tales also were used by Jacques de Vitry and Odo of Cheriton (for example, in their sermons), as well as by storytellers and troubadours, who disseminated them and were instrumental

9. *Tanḥuma*, ed. Buber, 22; *Yalkut shimoni*, Isaiah, no. 449, ed. Shiloni, *Latter Prophets*, 190.

10. *Die Disciplina Clericalis*, ed. Hilka and Werner Söderhjelm, no.15: "De deceme cofris," 22–23; *The Disciplina Clericalis of Petrus Alfonsi*, trans. and ed. Hermes, no. 15, 128–130. And see Tubach 3355. Cf. Ibn Sahula, *Meshal haqadmoni*, vol. 2, part 4, 520–534. This tale type also has parallels in IFA; see E.D.N.A: AT 1617.

11. *Gesta Romanorum* (Swan), no. 118, 256–257.

in their incorporation into written literature, such as fabliaux and Marie de France's works.[12]

In *Sefer ha-ma'asim* only, and not in the Talmud and *Tanḥuma*, the word *teiva* (box) was used to describe the place where R. Meir's friends' money was cached, perhaps under the influence of Alfonsi's tale "The Ten Boxes."[13] Kiddor's wife goes over to the box, the secret hiding place of the deposit, and returns their purses to them. The ornate appearance of the box in "The Ten Boxes," and the expectation that others would follow later, stirred the imagination of the man holding the deposit in Alfonsi's story and led him to return the stolen money, fearing he might lose the new transaction. In both parallels, the box is a metonym of the treasure it contains. The sources for the tale in *Sefer ha-ma'asim* are Jewish—the Talmud and the *midrashim*—but the expansion of the motif of the deposit, as well as the relatively large number of tales of this tale type in the compilation, may stem from a familiarity with the tale and its parallels in the surrounding society.

After *Sefer ha-ma'asim*, the story appears in halakhic literature, in relation to a circumcision ceremony attended by R. Jacob b. Moses Moelin ("Maharil"; 1360–1427, Ashkenaz). Because the baby was a bastard, Maharil ruled that he should be given the suggestive name "Kiddor," based on the verse "*ki dor tahapukhot hema.*" Moreover, according to his instruction, the customary request at the ceremony "to safeguard the child for his father and mother" was omitted. The child died at the age of ten.[14] In later *responsa* some objected to this ruling, which stigmatized the baby in advance (e.g., R Ḥaim Palachi, 1788–1869, Izmir). In keeping with the rule "Do not place a stumbling block before the blind," they claimed that stigmas as such are apt to affect one's future choices.[15] In any event, it is obvious that the concerns in these sources about the halakhic implications of the tale of Kiddor are not the focus in *Sefer ha-ma'asim*, which is concerned mainly with the deposit motif.

12. On the distribution of *Disciplina Clericalis* and its influence, see comments by Hermes (n. 10 above), in the introduction to his edition (5). See also Ramon and Keller, *The Scholar's Guide: A Translation of the Twelfth-Century Disciplina Clericalis of Pedro Alfonso*, 27; *Gesta* (Swan), n. 1.

13. Or perhaps the use of the word *teiva* (box) in *Sefer ha-ma'asim* was influenced by material circumstances in the Middle Ages, so it does not necessarily point to intertextual affinities.

14. See [Maharil], *The Book of Maharil*, ed. Spitzer, no. 20, 485–486.

15. Israel, *Responsa Ben yamin*, no. 15; Palachi, *Responsa ḥaim be'yad*, no. 70.

Late medieval and later versions of the story in Ashkenaz exist in manuscripts of *Mayse bukh*[16] and in the printed edition (Basel, 1602).[17] *Sefer ha-ma'asim* obviously influenced *Mayse bukh*, particularly in relation to the expanded description of the ruse and its circumstances in both sources. However, *Mayse bukh* does not contain the motif of the box (*teiva*) that is in *Sefer ha-ma'asim*.

In the Jewish-Muslim space in the Middle Ages, the story is in an expanded version of *Ḥibbur yafeh mehayeshu'a* by R. Nissim of Kairouan,[18] and in the twelfth century in *Sefer sha'ashu'im* (*Book of Delight*) by Joseph b. Meir Ibn Zabara. In the latter work, details of the plot were changed, but the narrative functions were retained. The story takes place in Cordoba, the deposit is a precious necklace given on loan to a minister of the city, and the sign that convinces his wife to return the deposit is his shoe.[19] These emphasized differences between Zabara's tale in the *Book of Delight* and the *Sefer ha-ma'asim* tale throw further light on the latter's affinity with Alfonsi's narrative in Western Europe.

16. See Tsfatman's references ("The Mayse-Bukh," 150) to Ms. Jerusalem 5245, no. 45 (Innsbruck), and Kotlerman's reference ("The Complete Index of Stories in the 'Mayse-bukh,'" 303) also to Ms. Munich 495, no. 53 (Robera).

17. *Mayse bukh* (Basel, 1602), no. 86, and in Gaster's trans., *Ma'aseh Book*, vol. 1, no. 85, 141–143.

18. *Ḥibbur yafeh mehayeshu'a*, ed. Hirschberg, no. 23, 63; Brinner ed., *An Elegant Composition Concerning Relief after Adversity*, 108–110.

19. Zabara, *Book of Delight*, trans. Hadas, 83–85. And see comments by Judith Dishon on this book: *The Book of Delight*, 94–96 and n. 16.

27. Ben Sever and Shefifon Ben Layish (312b–313a)

This story first appears in Ashkenaz, beginning with story collections in the thirteenth century (*Sefer ha-ma'asim* and Parma 2295), and then with manuscripts and printed editions of *Mayse bukh* in the sixteenth and seventeenth centuries.[1] In the East the story was included in *Sefer hama'asiyot*, from Persia, in the fourteenth century,[2] and further expanded in a commentary on tractate *Avoth* (6:12) attributed to R. David Hanagid, apparently from the same period.[3] With the invention of printing in the sixteenth century, an abbreviated version of it was included in *Ḥibbur hama'asiyot vehamidrashot vehahagadot*[4] and printed in story compilations from the eighteenth and nineteenth centuries: *Me'il ẓedakah* by Elijah Hacohen from Izmir and *Sefer hama'asiyot* by El'azar Araki.[5] In the twentieth century it was included in Micha Joseph Bin Gorion's (Berdyczewski's) literary collection *Mimekor yisrael* and reworked by him in *Ẓefunot ve'agadot*; it is also found in Asher Barash's *Menorat hazahav*.[6]

Even though the tale is a product of the Middle Ages, probably in Ashkenaz, it belongs to a tale type found in rabbinical literature about delaying the time of death through charity, the study of Torah, and other means, such as repentance and prayer.[7] One clear example is the legend about King David's death in the tractate *Shabbat* (30a). As long as David was studying the Torah, the Angel of Death could not take him. To distract him from his studies, the Angel of Death rustled the branches of trees in his garden, and when David went to find out what was causing the noise, his soul was taken.[8] In "Ben Sever and Shefifon Ben

1. See the list of versions in Kushelevsky, *Penalty and Temptation*, 318–319, and discussion of the story on 216–232. Versions in Ashkenaz from *Sefer ha-ma'asim* and thereafter are Ms. Cambridge-Harvard 39, 115a–116b; Ms. Jerusalem 3182, 125b–126a; Yassif, *Ninety-nine Tales*, 229–231, no. 66; *Mayse bukh*, Ms. Jerusalem 5245, no. 63; *Mayse bukh*, Ms. Munich 495, no. 115 (references by Kotlerman, "The Complete Index of Stories," 319); *Mayse bukh*, no. 199; *Ma'aseh book*, trans. Gaster, no. 200, 456–461.
2. Gaster, *Exempla*, no. 137, 94–97.
3. *Sefer midrash david*, 134–136.
4. *Ḥibbur hama'asiyot vehamidrashot vehahagadot*, no.18; Venice 365, 16b–17b.
5. Elijah Hacohen, *Me'il ẓedakah*, no. 434, ed. Kuperman, I, 73; Araki, *Sefer hama'asiyot*, no. 18, 17b–19b, and in Ḥuẓin's edition, no. 18, 15a–15b.
6. Bin Gorion (Berdyczewski), *Ẓefunot ve'agadot*, 169–170; *Mimekor yisrael*, no. 361, 235; Ben-Amos, *Mimekor yisrael*, no. 117, 210–211; Barash, *Menorat hazahav*, 26–29.
7. Cf. Th. K551: "Respite from death granted until particular act is performed"; ATU 1191: "Prayer without end." On the postponement of death in Jewish and world folklore, see Schwarzbaum, *Studies in Jewish and World Folklore*, 144–145, 277.
8. See also other stories about the postponement of death: *Baba meṣiah* 66a, *Moed katan* 28a, *Ketubot* 77b.

Layish," an additional motif was added to the delay of death through Torah learning: that of *arevut hadadit* (mutual responsibility), in the sense of "*Kol Yisrael arevim ze l'ze*" ("all Jews are responsible for one another").[9] Shefifon Ben Layish was prepared to take personal responsibility for Ben Sever, even at the cost of his own life.

The uniqueness of "Ben Sever and Shefifon Ben Layish" stands out when compared to talmudic tales of the same type (postponing death through charity and Torah study). In certain aspects these were reworked in the tale of Ben Sever in the format of medieval Christian legends of saints fighting the dragon. There is a marked affinity with the legend of Gregorius, which was very widely circulated in the thirteenth century by means of *The Golden Legend*.[10] Gregorius, a native of Cappadocia and a soldier in the Roman army, arrives at the city of Silena, in Libya, where he hears about a dragon living near the city that constantly threatens its inhabitants. Terrified, the people are forced to appease the creature on a daily basis, at first sacrificing sheep and later their own children. At a certain stage, it is the turn of the king's only daughter to be sacrificed. When the time comes, she is sent, ornamented like a bride, to the dragon's residence. Seeing her, Gregorius fights the dragon and saves her life. He crosses himself and strikes a blow with his lance, felling the dragon. The girl then leads the dragon back to the city,[11] where the amazed inhabitants convert to Christianity. Gregorius kills the dragon and throws its body outside the city. The legend continues with Gregorius's martyrdom when the Christians were being persecuted by the Roman emperors. By surviving a long series of dreadful tortures, he induces his tormentors to become Christians, and he is finally beheaded. He was canonized as a saint of the Christian warrior knights. More than any other source, the thirteenth-century *Golden Legend* established the unequivocal affinity between Gregorius's narrative and the figure of the dragon.[12] Several characteristics are common to this legend and the story of Ben Sever; these are unique features not found in rabbinical parallels:

(1) There are two protagonists—Ben Sever and Shefifon Ben Layish—in contrast to only one in rabbinical parallels. The name "Shefifon Ben Layish" is

9. *Seder eliahu rabbah* and *Seder eliahu zuta*, 12: "Why are all Jews similar," ed. Ish Shalom, 56.

10. See Tubach 2375: "Romance of St. Gregory." Cf. B. 11.11 "Fight with dragon."

11. In the Jewish story, the dragon's submission to the saint takes place with the help of a crocodile-dragon that turns itself into a bridge. Cf. the motifs Th. B549.2: "Dragon makes bridge over a stream for a holy person"; Th. B498.1: "Helpful dragon."

12. Jacobi a Voragine, *Legenda aurea*, no. 58; Jacobus de Voragine, *The Golden Legend*, 1, no. 58, 238–242; and Kleinberg's comments, "Beauty and the Beast: St. George," in *Fra Ginepro's Leg of Pork*, 357–362.

figurative: It embodies the icon of a dragon—the combination of a serpent and a lion—like the one that threatens Ben Sever. The conflict between equal antagonistic forces is mythological in nature.

(2) The bright light reflected from Ben Sever's face imbues the tale with a Christian-mythic dimension. Ben Sever is depicted as a saint struggling with a dragon and overcoming it. The identification of the "*tanin*" as a dragon rather than a serpent, in accordance with its biblical meaning, is implied by the etymological meaning of the word[13] and by its mythical description. It is enormous and dwells on a huge mountain, like monsters in ancient myths that block the path to hidden treasures.[14] This is particularly implied by the fire the creature spat from his mouth: "And there was a great dragon [*tanin*] there that used to bite and burn all who passed by."

(3) The city to which Ben Sever flees is called Luz (Genesis 28:19), the place over which, in Jewish sources, the Angel of Death does not rule. Those of its inhabitants who wish to die must go outside its gates.[15] The name of the city is not explicitly mentioned in *Sefer ha-ma'asim*, but it is implied by the motif of the city gates: "until he reached a big city, and he met a certain man at one of the gates." Luz is mentioned expressly in Ms. Cambridge-Harvard 39 and in Ms. Jerusalem 3182: "And he went and wept until he came to a city called Luz, where he met a man at the city gate and greeted him."[16] These themes are linked to the myths of monsters and dragons guarding the path to immortality, to the Tree of Life, and are absent from the print version of *Ḥibbur hama'asiyot vehamidrashot vehahagadot.*

(4) The structure of the tale is episodic and circuitous: a three-stage conflict between the protagonist and the Angel of Death in its various manifestations, unlike the one-time, decisive victory in the talmudic legends. This aspect also exists in medieval courtly romances that develop as a series of repeated clashes, in which the knight faces great danger to prove his loyalty to the lady he adores, as well as in the Gregorius legend in *The Golden Legend*, which combines martyrological tests and an episode of a fight with a dragon. The rejection of death in "Ben Sever and Shefifon Ben Layish" depends on the characters' ability to withstand ever-more difficult clashes. The Christian legendary substructure is evident in the tale, alongside the substructure of rabbinical legends about a man's clash with the Angel of Death and

13. *Tanin* in the Bible is a snake and also a collective noun for all large sea animals. *Drakōn* in Greek and *draco* in Latin is a snake and a dragon, respectively.

14. Eliade, *Patterns in Comparative Religion*, 291.

15. *Sotah* 46b.

16. See n. 1, above.

the postponement of his dying through charity and the study of Torah. The tale of "Ben Sever and Shefifon Ben Layish" is somewhat mythic in nature, and is well anchored in the space in which it was created in Ashkenaz.

The story undergoes a certain sublimation in comparison to the Christian legend about the saint's fight with the dragon, because the Angel of Death in the form of a dragon is merely an emissary of God and dependent on him. In the final analysis, the conflict is decided by the postponement of death. Additional means of adaptation are biblical allusions, such as the name "Shefifon Ben Layish," based on Jacob's blessing to Dan (Genesis 49:17) and in Moses's blessing to the tribe of Israel on the eve of his death (Deuteronomy 33:22), and the name of the city of Luz, the biblical Beth-El (Genesis 28:19). After the Middle Ages, in the print version of *Ḥibbur hama'asiyot vehamidrashot vehahagadot*, the story underwent an additional sublimation, and the mythical dimension was almost entirely obscured.

28. Joḥanan and the Scorpion (313b–317b)

"Joḥanan and the Scorpion" is the longest, most convoluted story in *Sefer ha-ma'asim*, replete with twists and mythical, fantastic motifs. It is not known from earlier Jewish sources, nor is there any complete parallel tale type. Only three hundred years later, in 1602, was it recorded in a Yiddish version in the story collection *Mayse bukh.*[1] In it, the frog replaces the scorpion. There were probably other, mediating versions that were lost, since it is unlikely that the lengthy, convoluted version in *Sefer ha-ma'asim* could have been transmitted orally for hundreds of years.

Parts of the story were assigned to two tale types in folklore research: that of the rise to greatness of a hero and his marriage after he has fulfilled extremely difficult tasks (ATU 531; "The clever horse"), and that of grateful animals (ATU 554; "The grateful animals").[2] Its formulaic opening, with the motif of a father's last will, is typical of several other tales in *Sefer ha-ma'asim*. The epilogue, with the verse "Cast your bread upon the waters for after many days you may find it" (Ecclesiastes 11:1), is also familiar in Jewish folklore from a similar episode in a homily on this verse from Ecclesiastes.[3] Another partial parallel is an anecdote related by Walter Map in his book *De nugis curialium*, about a compassionate monk who had the custom of feeding a small snake that begged for the leftovers of his meal. Over time the snake grew so large that it displaced the monk from his home.[4]

The story combines Christian and Celtic-Welsh myths, adapted to the receiving society: the scorpion that eats enormous amounts of food and grows so large that it no longer fits into the chalice; the motif of the fish and the fisherman; the figure of the queen who has the power to join Joḥanan's limbs together and bring him back to life. In the substructure this is a story of a quest meant to fill a void—either through motifs of inexhaustible abundance (food, the scorpion) or through recurring adventures with the aim of achieving impossible objectives. The tale depicts the challenge and risk in every quest for a greatly desired imaginary, unachievable goal, as well

1. *Mayse bukh*, no. 143; *Ma'aseh book*, trans. Gaster, vol. 1, no. 143, 265–276; Gaster, *Exempla*, no. 316, 238–239, and citation of the story from *Sefer ha-ma'asim* (Ms. Bodl. Or. 135), no. 305, 197–206.
2. Yassif, *Kemargalit bemishbeẓet*, 150, n. 52, and previously, Gaster, who ascribes the second half of "Joḥanan and the Scorpion" to the tale type "The grateful animals": Gaster, "Fairy Tales," v. 2, 918. For an English translation of the tale, see p. 923 and thereafter. For pagan elements in the tale and their adaptation, see Yassif, *The Hebrew Folktale*, 270–272.
3. Cf. *Mimekor yisrael*, no. 738; Ben-Amos, *Mimekor yisrael*, no. 242, 451; Gaster, *Exempla*, no. 381, 145–146.
4. Map, *De nugis curialium*, 2.6, 141–142. For this reference to it as a parallel, see Rotman, *Dragons*, 122–123.

as the tempting, threatening abundance on its wide-open boundaries. From this aspect of the quest motif, "Joḥanan and the Scorpion" was suggested as a romance-like narrative.[5]

By classifying the story as a romance centered around the motif of the quest—for the chalice and the queen-fairy-lady—it becomes possible to place it in the context of the Vulgate cycle in the twelfth and thirteenth centuries, where the quest for the Holy Grail is a dominant motif.[6] In "Joḥanan and the Scorpion," the chalice is described as "a very beautiful chalice," extraordinary and valuable, which contains a mysterious creature: a scorpion that lives forever. Joḥanan pays a large sum of money for it and is prepared to sacrifice himself and his family to maintain and nurture the scorpion, which is growing ever larger inside the chalice and taking over the whole house. The container is described as a vessel that has a cover: apparently a serving dish (Joḥanan has a hard time opening it) wide and deep enough to contain another chalice and a scorpion. It has a religious aspect, because it embodies the father's will, and as such it is brought to the seder table "in honor of the holiday." Because of Joḥanan's strict obedience to his father's will, the chalice becomes a metonym of the father and from this standpoint is an antithesis to the Holy Grail, which contains the blood of Jesus, the son.

The scorpion is presented in the tale as a variation of the phoenix that destroys itself and is regenerated in an unending cycle. Like the phoenix, it symbolizes the potential of transformative states: destruction and rejuvenation, death and rebirth. Joḥanan and his wife are saved from their intolerable situation by the scorpion. The wife is given great wealth in keeping with her wish, and Joḥanan attains the height of success in the royal palace. In Christianity the tensions between destruction and regeneration, death and life, are linked to the doctrine of Jesus' incarnation and resurrection. As a matter of fact, the Christian phoenix, parallel to the *milḥam ha'of* in the Jewish sources, symbolizes Jesus and his resurrection.[7] In the Jewish story, the

5. Tohar, "The Story of Johanan and the Scorpion," 1–12. The tale also has been identified as a folk novella that combines adventure and realism (Yassif, *Kemargalit bemishbeẓet*, 144–145). Anat Shapira ("To Make a Short Story Long," 313–315) ascribes the story as a folktale, based on Northrop Frye's distinction between the "naïve romance" identified with the folktale and the "sentimental romance" identified with *belles lettres*. And see Rotman (*Dragons*, 104–118), for a psychoanalytic perspective.

6. See a lengthier discussion of the story in Part I, pages 68–69.

7. See Rotman on the phoenix and references to earlier studies (*Dragons*, 125–127), as well as his reservations about identifying the motifs of death and rebirth with the figure of the scorpion in the tale. On the figurative level, however, the cyclicity of shrinkage and growth is also descriptive of the processes of death and rejuvenation. And see Tubach 3755: "Phoenix arises out of flames"; Th. B32: "Phoenix."

structure of extinction and rejuvenation, death and rebirth, is manifested in Joḥanan's death at the hands of his enemies in the royal palace and his revival at the hands of the queen-fairy with water from the Garden of Eden;[8] in transformative states in the plot (from poverty to wealth and greatness); and, on the national level, in the symbolism of Passover as a holiday of redemption from slavery and exile. On the seder eve, for the first time, Joḥanan opens the chalice left to him in his father's will, and in it he finds the scorpion that will make his life a misery but will also bring personal and national redemption. In this respect the tale also follows the model of the Book of Esther. The Jews are facing the danger of annihilation, and Joḥanan's success in bringing the king the queen he desires abolishes that threat and moreover gives him the throne.

The motif of the seder meal and, at its center, the opening of the chalice, is also linked to the Christian symbolism of the Last Supper. According to the New Testament, that meal was held on the eve of Passover, and during it Jesus informed his disciples that one of them would betray him and turn him over to the Romans. He gives them wine, which embodies his blood, to drink, and bread, which is his flesh, to eat, to imbue them with his presence. In medieval Christian art the scorpion symbolizes the betrayal of Jesus at the Last Supper by Judas Iscariot as a Jewish archetype.[9] In the tale the scorpion is the authority that represents the word of the God of the Jews and his protection of them: "The Lord has heard your prayer and given me permission to speak to you." Thus distinctly Christian symbols are implicit in the story—the Last Supper, the chalice that contains the blood and body of Jesus, and the scorpion that represents the image of the Jew among the Christians. "All's well that ends well": Joḥanan, the Jewish courtier, who has the same name as one of the Apostles, becomes king, overcomes all those who wish him evil, and opens an era of peace and tranquility for himself and his people.

The epilogue provides one of the means of adapting the story, by linking it to the verse from Ecclesiastes—"Cast your bread upon the waters for after many days you may find it"—and it fits in with additional structural and stylistic means of adaptation, which Yassif has discussed at length.[10]

8. See ATU 551: "Water of life."

9. Cirlot, "Scorpio," in *Dictionary of Symbols*, 280, and additional references by Rotman, *Dragons*, 118.

10. Yassif, *Kemargalit bemishbeẓet*, 151–152. One of these means is the oikotype AT *730A (IFA): "Miraculous rescue of a Jewish community threatened by an evil ruler."

29. The Seven Good Years (317b–318a)

This story has its source in an abbreviated version in midrash *Ruth zuta*,[1] which was expanded in later sources, such as *Ḥibbur yafeh mehayeshu'a* by R. Nissim of Kairouan in Tunis and *Sefer ha-ma'asim* in Ashkenaz.[2] Some of its motifs are common to the expanded versions in Ashkenaz and to *Ḥibbur yafeh mehayeshu'a*, but are absent from *Ruth zuta*. For example, the woman's practice of deciding how much charity a person would receive depending on his habits and way of life before he became poor is one of the details common to both expanded versions in *Sefer ha-ma'asim* and in *Ḥibbur yafeh mehayeshu'a*, but it is not found in *Ruth zuta*. This leads to a conclusion that the expanded version was created in Palestine before being transmitted to Ashkenaz and arrived through two separate channels—to North Africa via *Ḥibbur yafeh mehayeshu'a* and to Ashkenaz via *Sefer ha-ma'asim*. *Sefer ha-ma'asim* is important in this context because it preserved an expanded textual tradition in Ashkenaz whose primary source is lost.

Nonetheless, there are of course features common to *Ruth zuta* and the expanded versions in *Ḥibbur yafeh mehayeshu'a* and *Sefer ha-ma'asim*. The woman, compared to her husband, is more striking in her initiative, wisdom, and faith. In *Ruth zuta* she is depicted as the ideal woman, "a woman of valor" resembling Ruth in the biblical story. The character of the husband is also quite similar in both the abbreviated and expanded versions, particularly regarding his distrust of what seemed to him to be vain promises, magic charms, and temptations; his uncertainty, in contrast to his wife's decisiveness, about accepting the offer made to them; his concern about the fate of his family even after the decision was made; his reproach that after seven years they would be unable to accustom themselves to a life of poverty in their old age.[3] In all versions the story highlights a tension between a person's responsibility to support himself and his family and the demand to place one's trust in God as a steady source of income rather than relying on temporary material

1. Ed. Buber, no. 4, 11, 48–49. For a study of the tale, see Shoshany, "A Study of Two Tales in *Midrash Ruth Zuta*." For references to sources and research, see Ben-Amos, *Mimekor yisrael*, no. 219, 427. For an IFA oikotype, see AT 938*C IFA: "The Seven Good Years," and for a list and survey of versions and a discussion of their development, see Berlovitz, "Seven Good Years." R. David Hanagid, *Sefer Midrash david*, 80, should be added to the list.
2. Text witnesses in Ashkenaz for the *Sefer ha-ma'asim* version can be found in Ms. Jerusalem 3182, 132a–132b (Yassif, *Ninety-nine Tales*, no. 79, 245–247); Warsaw 281, 26a–26b. Expanded versions are also in *Mayse bukh*, Ms. Munich 495, no.148; *Mayse bukh* (Basel), no. 148; *Ma'aseh book*, trans. Gaster, vol. 1, no. 148, 292–294.
3. Cf. the literary analysis of Shoshany and Berlovitz (n. 1 above), and in Naḥam, "A Decent Woman."

assets. The woman, in the charity she gives, represents the aspect of trust in God far more clearly than the man does. In *Sefer ha-ma'asim* this is expressed in her decision to "lend" money to the Almighty in an investment that appears to be dubious but which, in her view, will produce a return in the future.

In *Sefer ha-ma'asim* the characters' actions, considerations, and feelings are delineated, the figure of R. Ḥiyya from Tiberias is added, and a verse from Proverbs 19:17) is cited: "He that has pity on the poor lends to the Almighty."[4] The dialogue between the characters is also more detailed than those in the abbreviated version in *Ruth zuta*. The *Sefer ha-ma'asim* version is unique especially in two stylistic and thematic aspects: The first is its tendency to omit words whose meaning is clear from the context, a trend that is particularly marked in comparison to the later version in Ms. Jerusalem 3182. For example, consider the wife's instructions to her husband, "Any poor man who comes here . . . ," while Ms. Jerusalem 3182 has, "Anyone who comes to you *to ask for something*." The italic words are absent from *Sefer ha-ma'asim*, being too obvious. She then instructs her husband to support the poor man at his door according to his previous standard of living, and to supply him even with very expensive clothes and a horse on which to ride. The second is its affinity with values of piety in Ashkenaz. This is especially evident in the exposition unique to *Sefer ha-ma'asim*: "Once there was a man who was exceedingly poor. He would sit in the synagogue for many long hours and pray." The character of the protagonist is based on the model of the pious Jew in Ashkenaz, the *ḥasid* who prays at length to reach a state of *kavanah* (intense concentration) and who is among the last to leave.[5] The motif of prayer is also in the epilogue: "Now come and see the power of charity and prayer." In *Ruth zuta*, only the value of charity is stressed through the woman's charitable acts during the seven prosperous years, acts which are to her and her husband's credit in bad times. Similar motifs of much time spent in the synagogue, a permanent seat there, and lengthy prayers are found in other tales in *Sefer ha-ma'asim*, particularly in "The Loan" (no. 34). The affinity between the two stories—"The Seven Good Years" and "The Loan"—already exists in *Ruth*

4. For commentary on this verse from Proverbs, see *Tanḥuma*, *Mishpatim*, no. 15: "Whoever lends to the poor is, as it were, as if he were lending to the Holy One and he will repay him his due. . . . The Holy One said: When a poor person's soul [*nefesh*] was seeking to leave, you revived him. By your life I am returning to you life [*nefesh*] for life. Tomorrow, when your son or daughter comes into the hands of guilt or into the hands of death, [this deed] will be remembered on their behalf, and I will give them a life for a life" (*Midrash Tanḥuma*, trans. Townsend, vol. 2, Exodus and Leviticus, 118). See also in *Tanḥuma*, ed. Buber, no. 8, 85; Rashi, Proverbs 19:17 and *Baba Batra* 10a; *Yalkut Shimoni*, Proverbs, no. 959, Salonika edition, vol. 2, 156b.

5. Cf. *Sefer ḥasidim*, no. 466, 467. For further elaboration, see the earlier discussion regarding "The Loan" (no. 2).

zuta, and it is enhanced in *Sefer ha-ma'asim* in the context of the value of prayer.[6] This affinity has a further implication: The grant in "The Seven Good Years" is presented as only a temporary loan, which must be returned to its owner when the time comes. This is a key element in "The Loan," and it is brought into "The Seven Good Years" by means of the similar openings in the two stories.[7]

Despite the accentuated thematic similarity in *Sefer ha-ma'asim*, and although the two stories are adjacent in *Ruth zuta*, they are separated in *Sefer ha-ma'asim*. "The Seven Good Years" is quite a few pages removed from "The Loan," and next to "Joḥanan and the Scorpion." This is one expression out of many of the eclectic nature of the tales in the compilation, from the standpoint of the criteria for their choice and inclusion.

6. For a comparison of the two tales in *Ruth zuta*, see Shoshany, "A Study of Two Tales," 92–94.
7. The comparison also suggests itself because the two stories exist in *Ruth zuta*.

30. Slander Kills Three (318a)

Apparently, the source of the story is *Midrash aseret hadibrot*.[1] This is suggested by two versions that indirectly point to an independent tradition of the tale in the Jewish-Muslim cultural context: *Midrash hagadol* from Yemen in the thirteenth century and *Sefer hama'asiyot* from the fourteenth century at the latest in Ms. Jerusalem 1970, both of which were based on a third, earlier source.[2] With the mediation of *Midrash aseret hadibrot*, the story was imported into northern France, included in *Sefer ha-ma'asim*, and, after further adaptation, was once again inserted into various versions of *Midrash aseret hadibrot*.[3] *Sefer ha-ma'asim* was, then, a mediating link as *Midrash aseret hadibrot* passed from East to West. In the late Middle Ages, the story was included in *Mayse bukh*.[4]

The tale's versions represent two medieval textual traditions. In the Muslim countries—in *Midrash hagadol* from Yemen;[5] *Midrash aseret hadibrot* (Ms. Paris 716 and other manuscripts);[6] *Sefer hama'asiyot*, edited by Gaster in the *Exempla of the Rabbis*;[7] and *Menorat hama'or* by Al-Nakawa of Spain[8]—the approach is misogynistic. The character of the woman is depicted in a totally negative light, in contrast to her irreproachable father and father-in-law, who are the victims of her schemes. Her father-in-law is in the habit of "rising each morning and asking after her health,"[9] a rather innocuous description, which leaves a favorable impression

1. See *Midrash aseret hadibrot* in several manuscripts: Ms. Paris 716 (ed. Shapira, 86–87); Ms. Vatican 285, 76a–b; Ms. Vatican 107, 178a–b; Ms. Moscow-Günzburg 111, 127b. The story is meant to illustrate the Ninth Commandment, "Thou shalt not bear false witness." See the comprehensive entries and list of 46 versions of the story up to the modern era and in oral IFA versions: Rubin, "Slander Kills Three." Also see comments by Ben-Amos, *Mimekor yisrael*, no. 89, 173; Yassif, *The Hebrew Folktale*, 451–452.
2. R. David ha-Adani, *Midrash hagadol*, Leviticus, ed. Steinsaltz, 550–551; Ms. Jerusalem 1970, 14b–15b, recopied in Ms. Manchester-Gaster 82 (Gaster, *Exempla*, no. 142, 103–104). For a hypothesis about an earlier source common to both *Midrash hagadol* and *Sefer ha-ma'asim*, see Kushelevsky, "Some Remarks on the Date and Sources of 'Sefer ha-Ma'asiyyot,'" 157; Kiperwasser, "Midrash haGadol," 436.
3. For versions of *Midrash aseret hadibrot*, see n. 1 above, and for additional references to later versions of *Midrash aseret hadibrot* in the print edition, see Rubin, "Slander Kills Three," 254.
4. *Mayse bukh*, no, 220; *Ma'aseh book*, trans. Gaster, vol. 2, no. 220, 537–540.
5. As in note 2, above.
6. Vatican 107; Moscow-Günsburg 111, Zurich 192.
7. As in note 2, above.
8. Ed. Enelow, v.4, 341–432. In *Menorat hama'or*, the woman is indirectly blamed for her father-in-law's loss of control due to her sexual intimations: "And he would embrace her and kiss her out of his love for her."
9. In R. David ha-Adani, *Midrash hagadol*, as in note 2, above.

that is not dissipated later when he kisses her on her head in a paternal gesture.[10] When he visits her, he tries to give her the opportunity to tell him about her problems and her expectations of her husband, and by doing so to deflect any inclination to slander into a more constructive channel. With the information he gleans from her, he tries to mediate between her and husband, and to persuade his son to meet all her needs. It would appear that he really does succeed: "And she would say nothing to him."[11] But later her schemes are revealed. The main point of the story concerns the serious implications of slander when it spreads throughout the social environment and no one has any control over its consequences: "Oh, you have learned that slander kills three. He who speaks it, he who hears it, and he about whom it is said" (*Midrash hagadol*).[12] The woman as a typological figure is the agent responsible for these immoral social processes.

Sefer ha-ma'asim in northern France represents a different version of the tale. The father and the father-in-law are as guilty as the girl herself, which undercuts the gender-based stereotype of the Muslim space. The narrator appears to be as critical of the father as he is of the girl, because in a moment of anger he puts aside all of his piety (he is called "a pious man," or "*ḥasid*," in *Sefer ha-ma'asim*), loses all self-control, and ends up killing his daughter's father-in-law. Criticism of the father-in-law is also implied. Although his intention was to create a peaceful atmosphere at home, he created a situation of shared secrets, which culminated in slander: "And he would tempt her with words." The stylistic choice of the verb "tempt" introduces negative connotations into the story.[13] The gender-based discourse differed in the East and the West.

The epilogue concludes with a comparison between slander, on the one hand, and incest, bloodshed, and idolatry, on the other, and the Jew who violates those prohibitions is condemned to death.[14] In this manner the severity of slander is emphasized. The elements common to these four grievous sins are unfaithfulness, treachery, and prostitution, and slander is consequently conceived of as

10. On a kiss on the head as a paternal gesture, see, for example, in the Mishnah, tractate *Rosh HaShanah* 2:9.

11. *Midrash aseret hadibrot*, Ms. Paris 716.

12. PT *Pe'ah* 1:1(15:4), phrased slightly different; b*Arakhin* 15b. Slander is speaking ill of another person, which may be true or have a core of truth but is not necessarily a falsehood. See Maimonides, *Mishneh torah, Hilkhot de'ot*, 7: 2.

13. In light of *Sefer ha-ma'asim*, there is in *Midrash hagadol* some criticism of the father-in-law kissing his daughter-in-law on the head, but it is not explicit, and the stereotypical image of the man falling victim to the woman's schemes is retained.

14. See *Arakhin* 15b.

treachery. The source for this comparison between slander and the other three prohibitions, about which it is said "be killed rather than transgress," is in the Talmud (*Arakhin* 15b), but it is incorporated in the story only in *Sefer ha-ma'asim*. In the above-mentioned versions in the Muslim space, the emphasis, based on the Talmud, is rather on the nature of slander when it is out of control and has disastrous consequences. The epilogue in *Midrash aseret hadibrot* reads: "Slander kills three. He who speaks it, he who hears it and he about whom it is said." The father, the father-in-law, and the husband are all killed as a result of the woman's slander.[15] The particular stress on the severity of slander in *Sefer ha-ma'asim*, compared to other versions that relate only to its unavoidable consequences, may have been influenced by the focus placed in the Middle Ages on the Seven Cardinal Sins, which are the vices that impose themselves as a type of evil in the world.[16]

A hapax legomenon homily is added to the epilogue. It relates to Joseph's slander of his brothers:

> And so it was with Joseph, the Righteous: "And Joseph slandered them to their father," telling him: My brothers call the sons of the maidservants slaves. And that is why he was sold into slavery. And he said: They look at the girls of the land, and that is why "His master's wife cast her eyes at Joseph." And he said: They eat the flesh of a living animal, and for this "They slaughtered a male goat and dipped the tunic in the blood." Slander is worse than idolatry and incest and murder.[17]

The sources of this homily are in the rabbinical literature, but without the concluding line that compares slander to the three grievous acts of incest, idolatry, and bloodshed. Possibly the epilogue represents a version of *Midrash aseret hadibrot* that is not extant, but since no interim documentation exists, it is reasonable to assume that the link was made in *Sefer ha-ma'asim* itself. If so, then the identification of the homily on Joseph's sin, its inclusion in *Sefer ha-ma'asim*, and its connection to the aforementioned rabbinical aphorism indicate that the scribe and the narrating

15. Ed. Shapira, 87. This moral is also implied in *Sefer ha-ma'asim*, alongside the epilogue that explicitly states that slander is as grievous as incest, bloodshed, and idolatry.

16. Sloth and greed are included among this list of sins, but not gossip or slander. See Rubin, n. 1, above, 251–252 (quote from p. 252), and her references; also Bejczy and Newhauser, *Virtue and Ethics*.

17. Cf. PT *Pe'ah* 1a (15, 4–16, 4); *Genesis rabbah*, 64, 7, ed. Albeck, 1009; and a different version in *Tanḥuma, Vayeshev*, no. 7; *Tanḥuma*, ed. Buber, no. 5, 90b (180).

society he represents were quite literate, and that he made creative contributions to the compilation.

The meaning of the tale was retained in its transition to the West despite the changes introduced in it. The story ranges from the idea of faith as a constructive force in human relations, expressed in the father-in-law's attitude toward his lazy daughter-in-law (and by implication, also toward the one who is a thief), to the opposite extreme of treachery as a destructive force, represented by the slanderous daughter-in-law (and by implication, in the figure of the father-in-law). The conflict stems from the tension between these two extremes.

31. Saved from Drowning by Charity (318a–318b)

The tale's earliest versions are in the rabbinic literature, originating between the third to sixth centuries.[1] In these sources it appears as a legal precedent, in the framework of a discussion of the conditions that make it possible to determine the death of the husband of an "*agunah*" (lit., "chained"), in order to permit her to remarry.[2] The testimony of R. Akiva, who saw the ship sink, ought to have sufficed to release her from her condition of *aginut*, but when her husband, who had survived, suddenly appeared, her remarriage was thwarted. An epilogue, which is omitted from *Sefer ha-ma'asim*, presents R. Akiva's amazement at the reach of the Halakhah, which relates even to unforeseen circumstances.

In the post-Amoraic works, *Avoth de-Rabbi Nathan* and *Ecclesiastes rabbah* (11a),[3] the halakhic trend is weakened, and the focus changes. From then on, the emphasis is on praise for charity and its power to save from death,[4] while referring to the verse in Ecclesiastes 11:1: "Cast your bread upon the waters, for you shall find it after many days." The act of charity, which has far-reaching, unforeseen results, resembles the casting of bread into a stormy sea, a futile investment from which no one expects to profit. In *Ecclesiastes rabbah* the tale appears in a broad cycle of tales centered on the epigrammatic verse.[5] It contains a play on words based on the two meanings of the Hebrew homonym *yamim*—meaning both "seas" and "days"—so the encounter between them creates a unit of time-space in which the tale takes place and reflects the dilemma that underlies the condition of *aginut* (the disappearance of the husband to an unknown place for an undefined period of time). Charity as a humanitarian act, without any expectation of reward, has the power to save the *agunah* and to bring her husband back from the unknown. The

1. *The Tosefta*, ed. Liebermann, *Yebamot* 14:5, 52; and Liebermann, *Tosefta ki-fshutah, Yebamot* 14:5, 52–53; p*Yebamot* 16:4 (15, 4), Academy of the Hebrew Language edition, 902; b*Yebamot* 121a. For a discussion of the story based on a version from Ashkenaz and a chronological list of versions, see Kushelevsky, *Penalty and Temptation*, 199–215.
2. *Agunah* is a halakhic term for a deserted wife who lacks an official divorce or proof of death of her husband.
3. *Avoth de-Rabbi Nathan*, Schechter-Kister edition, version 1, ch. 3, 9. On the dating of the work in its two versions and the modes of editing, see Kister, 8–14.
4. On the tale in the context of the tale type of "Charity saves from death" in Jewish sources, see Schwarzbaum, *Studies in Jewish and World Folklore*, 279. Cf. ATU 1199, on the postponement of death through prayer.
5. See Yassif, *The Hebrew Folktale*, 249, on the affinity between the cycle of tales in *Ecclesiastes rabbah* and the above epigrammatic verse. And see Noy, "The Jewish Versions of the 'Animal Languages' Folktale," 171–208; Hasan-Rokem, *Proverbs in Israeli Folk Narratives*, 52–58.

terms *yam* and *yom* (the singular forms for "sea" and "day," respectively), and in particular the interaction between them, again take on their concrete meanings as units of space and time that can be delimited and identified. Thus the epigrammatic verse expresses the affinity in the tale between an act of charity and the woman's release from the state of *aginut.*[6]

In the coming centuries throughout the Middle Ages, as well as in the modern era, the tale was transmitted with its two orientations: one halakhic, in the context of *aginut* in the *responsa* literature;[7] the other in story compilations and literary anthologies as an illustration of the ethos of charity.[8]

In northern France, the tale was included in two story compilations in very similar versions: in *Sefer ha-ma'asim*, which is our focus here, and in Ms. Parma 2295 (136a). The tale probably came into these compilations from the houses of study of the Tosafists, who dealt with it in connection with the law of *agunah*, and it was then reworked as a moral tale about charity based on *Avoth de-Rabbi Nathan* and *Ecclesiastes Rabbah.* That appears to be the case in light of the *Tosafot Rosh* (R. Asher b. Yehiel) on the tractate *Yebamot* 16, no. 4 (previously 1327). The tale is cited there as part of the discussion about a woman who is an *agunah.*

Sefer ha-ma'asim follows the version of *Avoth de-Rabbi Nathan* with certain stylistic changes, thus enhancing didactic messages in praise of charity. Accordingly, it is placed next to the tale about R. Akiva's daughter, who was saved from death on the day of her wedding owing to her charitable deed. The motif of the *agunah* is omitted from *Sefer ha-ma'asim*, and the implied link to the verse in Ecclesiastes[9] emphasizes a moral message rather than the halakhic issue of *agunah.* As a result of these omissions, the tale became very short—shorter than its model in *Avoth de-Rabbi Nathan*—and from this formalistic aspect, it resembles the talmudic version, in which the tale is brief and succinct.

6. On the centrality of tales as part of the context that creates the meaning of the proverb, see Hasan-Rokem, *Proverbs in Israeli Folk Narratives*, 69–95.

7. See R. Isaac Alfasi (Rif), *Hilkhot rav alfasi*, *Yebamot* 45b, version 1 and version 2; Commentary on the *Talmud* of R. Asher b. Yeḥiel, *Yebamot*, 16:4. The talmudic version, with a halakhic orientation, is also found in *Yalkut shimoni*, Ecclesiastes, no. 969, ed. Salonika, 234a; and in Gaster, *Exempla*, no. 262, 173.

8. See, as an example, R. David ha-Adani, *Midrash hagadol* on Deuteronomy, ed. Fish, 313; Gaster, *Exempla*, no. 99, 69; *Hagadot hatalmud*, *Perek ha'isha*, 60a; *En Jacob*, ed. Glick, vol. 1, 217; Elijah Hacohen, *Me'il ẓedakah*, no. 430, ed. Kuperman, 72; Bialik and Ravnitzky, *The Book of Legends*, 667, no. 268.

9. "I heard a noise at sea, and they were saying to one another: Run and save that man because he is worthy and accustomed to giving charity."

32. R. Akiva's Daughter and the Snake (318b)

This story is inserted in tractate *Shabbat* 156b, as part of a discussion as to whether the planets have any influence on Jews. It was intended to support the view that "Israel is free of planetary influence" (*Shabbat* 156a); namely that a Jew, unlike a gentile, can change the influence of the planets through an act of charity and be saved from death.[1] The astrologers' prophecy about the expected death of R. Akiva's daughter on her wedding day was foiled because she gave food to a poor man. Based on that incident R. Akiva commented, "Charity delivereth from death: and not [merely] from an unnatural death, but from death itself" (*Shabbat* 156b). In *Sefer ha-ma'asim*, the story was removed from the context of the talmudic discussion about planetary influence, and in the plot itself the Chaldeans are not mentioned as the source of the information about the death of R. Akiva's daughter. Instead, "everyone would say" that would be her fate. These editorial decisions point to a more emphasized literary orientation in *Sefer ha-ma'asim* than in the Talmud, whose purpose is rather ideological or philosophical.

The version differs greatly from its source in the Talmud in several other aspects: In regard to the relations between R. Akiva and is daughter, R. Akiva's daughter knows what awaits her, while in the Talmud that information is given to her father, who (implicitly) conceals it from her. Consequently, in *Sefer ha-ma'asim* the story does not relate to the father's feelings about his daughter's imminent death on her wedding day or the conflict it entails. The decision is left entirely in the hands of the bride. Also, the conversation between her and R. Akiva, her father, is more explicit than in the Talmud: "I thought you would not live until morning." In the Talmud he asks a more general question: "What did you do?"

The sequence of events is related in the order of their occurrence: first the charity given to the poor man and then the incident with the snake. In the Talmud the events are related back to the incident with the snake in order to express a process of reflection and learning on the part of R. Akiva.[2] Apparently it was not R. Akiva's

1. See references to parallels and other tales about charity saving from death: Schwarzbaum, *Studies in Jewish and World Folklore*, 280, and Gaster, *Exempla*, no. 318, 239. And see the oikotype AT 934F* (IFA): "Charity rescues from Death." For a selection of studies of the Talmudic version, see Fraenkel, *Studies of the Spiritual World of the Aggadah*, 13–16; Raveh, *Fragments of Being*, 48–50.
2. Cf. a manuscript of tractate *Shabbat*: Bodl. Heb. d. 21 (2676), f. 4–5, in which the story is related according to the chronological order of the events. See this comparison in Friedman, "A New Branch of the Textual Tradition of Bavli Shabbat," 162–167.

learning process that was the focus in *Sefer ha-ma'asim* but rather the plot itself, the dramatic and romantic potential in the character of the bride.

The bride's relations with her newlywed husband is yet a third aspect in the *Sefer ha-ma'asim* version. On the night of the wedding, it is not entirely clear whether she moves away from her husband in order to stick her hairpin into the snake's eye and thus save herself or whether the events involving the snake and the hairpin became unwittingly entwined, as is implied in the Talmud. The latter hypothesis might be deducted from her discovery of the dead snake in the morning: "When she awoke and took her hairpin, she found the dead snake entwined in the hairpin." Nonetheless, the alternative hypothesis of her intention to kill the snake to save herself still remains in the background, hovering over the text as a potential plot line. In any case, there is an erotic aspect to the occasion of the marriage and the wedding night that is associated with the symbolism of the snake in the sources as the archetypal temptress and as evil inclination.[3] In *Sefer ha-ma'asim* the groom is described as a very handsome young man, and the situation of the wedding night is explicitly mentioned ("When she got into bed with her husband"), while it is merely alluded to in the Talmud.[4] One connotation may be that this was a marriage of love that overcame the fear of an anticipated disaster, which is implied also because it was she who decided to go ahead with the marriage despite the prophecy of her death on her wedding day. Against the background of social norms of arranged marriages on the one hand, and the literary norms of the ethos of love in court romances in northern France on the other, this may suggest a broad context in *Sefer ha-ma'asim*, which should be taken into consideration in further discussions of the affinities in the tale among "charity," "marriage," "love," and "heavenly decree."[5]

The epilogue is yet another unique aspect in *Sefer ha-ma'asim*, when compared to the Talmudic version. It does not contain the homily that is in the Talmud: "Charity saves from death." Instead, the message is worded as a general moral: "and R. Akiva went and told it to all his disciples. He said: See how great is the power of charity." On the other hand, the epilogue contains a different homily. It is R. Eliezer who says: " 'The Lord safeguards your going and coming' and 'The Lord is your shade on your right hand.' " The emphasis is on the observance of the commandment, "Have faith in and fear of the Almighty"—namely, act in good faith without any thought of profit or personal gain: "When a person observes numerous commandments faithfully and out of fear of the Almighty, God preserves him and preserves

3. See identification of the snake with the evil inclination, *Baba Batra* 16a.
4. *Sabbath* 152b: "on the night of her marriage."
5. Cf. my comments on "The Poor Bachelor and His Maiden Cousin" (no. 55) and "Ukva" (no. 61), as well as Kushelevsky, "Chastity Versus Courtly Love."

his body." The verses from Psalms that follow enhance this moral: "The Lord safeguards your going and coming" (Psalms 121:8); and "The Lord is your shade on your right hand" (Psalms 121:5). The scribe's creativity thus is evident in the epilogue as well, in keeping with the characterization of the girl throughout the story—a blend of assertiveness (in her decision to go ahead with the marriage even though she has been advised that she will die) and good faith (in her charitable gift of food to the poor man). He may have designed a tale meant for a broad audience yet quite oriented to Jewish sources, as is obvious from the unique epilogue.

The tale appears in additional medieval sources, which represent the talmudic version. These are *Yalkut shimoni*, *Midrash hagadol* on Deuteronomy, and *Menorat hama'or* by Isaac Aboab.[6] In light of the epigonic nature of these versions, the unique adaptation in *Sefer ha-ma'asim* is striking. The tale was included in the printed editions of *Hagadot hatalmud* (20b) and *En Jacob*. In the modern era a special note should be made of its inclusion in Bialik's literary collection *The Book of Legends*,[7] and of its popularity in didactic children's literature.

6. *Yalkut shimoni*, on Proverbs no, 945, Salonika edition, 149a; David ha-Adani, *Midrash hagadol*, on Deuteronomy, ed. Fish, 322–323; Aboab, *Menorat hama'or*, 3, 7, no. 174, 409.

7. Bialik and Ravnitzky, *The Book of Legends*, no. 269, 667.

33. Mattiah b. Ḥarash (318b)

The sources of the story about Mattiah b. Ḥarash, a Tanna of the third generation, are in the *Midrash yelamdenu*; the *Midrash abkir* (one of the *midrashim* that was lost and is extant only in Ashkenaz); and the *Midrash aseret hadibrot* (which served as an immediate source for *Sefer ha-ma'asim*).[1]

The tale may have a certain affinity with the Book of Job, since it depicts Satan as being envious of Mattiah b. Ḥarash and asking God's permission to tempt him to prove that he is not "a perfectly righteous man."[2] In the Book of Job, the disasters follow one after the other, from the loss of Job's property to the death of his children. In *Sefer ha-ma'asim* the severity and intensity of the temptation are expressed in Mattiah b. Ḥarash's extreme reaction: He puts out his eyes with red-hot nails. This act shocks even Satan himself, and diverges from any halakhic norm.[3]

The story illustrates asceticism and abstinence as an overall way of life, as a means of coping with sexual temptation. This is implied in the opening lines that introduce Mattiah b. Ḥarash as a man who "had never raised his eyes to look at a woman in his life." This is a more generalized characterization compared to that in *Midrash aseret hadibrot*, in which the tale illustrates the prohibition "Thou shalt not commit adultery," relating it specifically to adultery with a married woman ("who had never raised his eyes to look at another man's wife").[4] In *Sefer ha-ma'asim* the scribe used *Midrash aseret hadibrot* as a source but left out the context of "Thou shalt not commit adultery," which shifts the focus from the prohibition against adultery to asceticism and abstinence. In this regard *Sefer ha-ma'asim* may also have been relying on *Midrash Abkir*, which states, "[A]nyone who does not look at

1. For a selection of sources, see *Midrash yelamdenu, vayehi*, no. 77, in Wertheimer, *Batei Midrashot*, 161 (a note only); Buber, *Likkutim memidrash Abkir*, no. 30, 11–12; *Midrash aseret hadibrot*, ed. Shapira, 74–78. See further in *Tanḥuma*, ed. Buber (130), an addendum to the portion *hukat* (supplement A), which Buber attributes to *Tanḥuma yelamdenu*. See references by Ben-Amos, *Mimekor yisrael*, no. 69, 139–140. For a list of versions and a survey, see Lipsker, "Mattiah b. Heresh." To be added to the list of versions: Al-Nakawa, *Menorat hama'or*, v. 3, chapter on *teshuvah*, 125–126. A selection of versions in Ashkenaz in the Middle Ages and thereafter include *Yalkut shimoni, vayehi*, 161, ed. Shiloni, Genesis, 848; Ms. Frankfort on Main 35, 49b–50b; Ms. Oxford, Bodleian Library 404, 8a–8b; Ms. Wolfenbüttel 36.25 (17), *Midrash aseret hadibrot* (14th century); Ms. Parma 2269 (De Rossi 473), 74b–75a, *Midrash aseret hadibrot* (15th century.); Ms. Bodl., Opp. 27, 240b, *Midrash aseret hadibrot* (16th–17th century); *Mayse bukh* (Basel), no. 247; Gaster, trans., *Ma'aseh Book*, vol. 2, no. 246, 646–647.

2. Cf. particularly Job 2:3–7, and 42:12–17.

3. See, on self-mutilation, *Baba Kama* 91b; Maimonides, *Mishne Torah, hilkhot ḥobel* and *mezik*, 5,1.

4. *Midrash aseret hadibrot*, ed. Shapira, 75.

women, all the more so at the wife of another, is not ruled by the evil inclination."[5] What appears in *Midrash Abkir* as a general recommendation is presented in *Sefer ha-ma'asim* as a distinct characteristic of Mattiah b. Ḥarash.

A possible context for the version in *Sefer ha-ma'asim* is the significance, in Ashkenazi pietism, of overcoming the evil inclination and standing up to trials and temptations, an experience that reached its peak in Ashkenaz with the incidence of martyrdom, but which was also manifested in norms of asceticism connected with penance. In *Sefer haroke'aḥ* the *gader*-penance for a sin related to a woman (making safeguards or preventive fences around the forbidden) is "that he should not see the face of a woman nor her clothes other than his own wife."[6] Mattiah b. Ḥarash's act of self-mortification by blinding himself is also consistent in its spirit with the doctrine of penance in Ashkenazi pietism, which embraces many harsh acts of mortification, in particular as a penance for adultery.[7]

Christian parallels to the story also introduce to it the martyrological and ascetic context. These include the legend of St. Anthony, who is tormented by Satan through recurrent sexual fantasies, which he counters with abstinence and severe self-mortification; and the legend of St. Andrea, to whom Satan appears in the guise of a woman in order to test him.[8] In *Sefer ha-ma'asim*, the treatment of "Mattiah b. Ḥarash" as a story about a test of temptation rather than as a warning against adultery is well established in the norms of Ashkenazi pietism, and in the Jewish and Christian exempla that shaped the medieval martyrological consciousness.[9]

5. Buber, *Likkutim memidrash Abkir*, 12.
6. R. Eleazar b. Judah, *Sefer haroke'aḥ*, no. 206, 98.
7. On an affinity in Ashkenazi pietism between a demand to stand up to temptations and the sanctification of God, see Dan, "The Sanctification of God in the Philosophy of the Ashkenazi Pietists," 214–215. On the problematic of self-mortification by Ashkenazic Pietists, which violates the halakhic prohibition against self-mutilation, see Ta-Shma, "Suicide and Murder for the Sanctity of God," 390–394.
8. On the asceticism of St. Anthony and on the significance of "asceticism" in Christianity as a criterion for the high status of the martyr in Christianity, see Kleinberg, *Fra Ginepro's Leg of Pork*, 124–139. On the legend of St. Andrea, see Jacobi a Voragine, *Legenda aurea*, no. 2, 12–22, esp. no. 2.9, 19–20; Jacobus de Voragine, *The Golden Legend*, vol. 1, no. 2, 19–20. See also references in Tubach 214; motif Th. T333.3.1.
9. For comments on "The Loan" (no. 34), see "The Loan" (no. 2).

35. A Valley Filled with Gold (319a)

This brief anecdote—set, in certain versions, in a valley near Meron, the city of the Tanna R. Shimon bar Yoḥai (=Rashbi)[1]—is an exemplum par excellence that illustrates the concept of the next world in the rabbinic doctrine of reward. It preaches the importance of devotion to Torah study and the willingness to forego the pleasures of this world. The reward of the Torah is not given in this world but rather in the next. Thus the principle of the next world is consistent with the value of Torah study represented by Rashbi.[2]

The tale was already mentioned in p*Berakhot* 9:2 (13d), 71, and in *Genesis rabbah* (35, 2),[3] as a well-known narrative that does not call for any elucidation and which was told in praise of the Rashbi, a great Torah scholar who was also "learned in miracles."[4]

In later sources, it was transmitted in two textual traditions or branches. They differ mainly in the closing verses of the epilogue and also in some other stylistic variations. *Sefer ha-ma'asim* generally follows certain versions of the *Tanḥuma* on Exodus and *Midrash hashkem*, which is one of the small *midrashim* that were preserved in Ashkenaz but lost in later years.[5] It closes with a verse from Proverbs 31:25: "And she [the worthy woman] shall rejoice in time to come," which refers in our tale to the day of death and the next world. The other textual tradition is represented in *Midrash Psalms* (*Shoḥer tov*) and in *Yalkut shimoni* on Psalms, and it closes with the verse: "For You, Lord, have made me glad through your work; I will triumph in the works of your hands" (Psalms 92:6).[6]

Other stylistic differences between these branches relate to the step taken by Rashbi's disciple when he left his Torah studies and turned to a life of commerce, as well as the envy of his fellow students when he grew rich abroad. These are

1. That is what is stated in *Tanḥuma*, ed. Buber, *Pekudei* no. 7, 66, and in Gaster, *Exempla*, no. 151, 110. Other expressions are "*pagi medon*," which Buber reads as "Meron" (*pagi*—an unripe fig); "outside the country"; and "in the city." In *Sefer ha-ma'asim*, the location is not specified and remains obscure: "outside the city, into a valley."
2. On the value of Torah study in Rashbi's view, see b*Berakhot* 35b; p*Berakhot* 9:5 (14:4); *Sifrei*, ed. Finkelstein, *ekev* 48, 113; *Leviticus rabbah*, 35, 6, ed. Margulies, 824.
3. *Genesis Rabbah*, ed., Albeck, 329.
4. On these qualities of Rashbi, see b. *Shabbat* 11a; b. *Me'ilah* 17b.
5. *Tanḥuma*, ed. Buber (as in n. 1); *Exodus rabbah* 52, 3. In midrashic collections from the Middle Ages, see *Pesikta zutarta*, *Pekudei*, no. 38, 111; Grünhut, *Midrash hashkem*, 11a, *Sefer halikkutim*; Ḥefets Aluf, *Sefer vehizhir*, ed. Friemann, 130; Gaster, *Exempla*, no. 151, 110.
6. The other textual tradition of the tale includes Buber, *Midrash Psalms* (*Tehilim*), hymn 92, no. 8, 204a; *Yalkut shimoni*, Psalms, no. 843, Salonika edition, 49b.

emphasized more in the second textual tradition, for example in *Midrash Psalms*—and surprisingly also in *Sefer ha-ma'asim*, as we shall see below, although it belongs to the first branch (that of the *Tanḥuma* version), according to its epilogue.[7]

In most of the sources, as well as in *Sefer ha-ma'asim*, the tale precedes "A Precious Stone from Heaven" (no. 36).[8] Both tales close with the aforementioned epilogue, "[S]he shall rejoice in time to come." In both tales the instruction is to reject material benefit in this world to avoid losing the anticipated reward in the next world. In "A Precious Stone from Heaven," rejection of material benefit is demanded for the sake of Torah study. Thus the principle of the next world in rabbinic thought is consistent with the value of Torah study represented by Rashbi.[9] At the same time, the reward in the next world, which is spiritual in its essence, is described in concrete terms: golden coins in this story and a precious stone in "A Precious Stone from Heaven." Whoever takes golden coins in this world will be subtracting from his portion in the next world. The concept of "joy" is transposed in this tale from the material sphere of worldly pleasures to the spiritual, heavenly sphere.

In *Sefer ha-ma'asim*, in contrast to its model in the *Tanḥuma* of the first branch, the disparity between material and spiritual assets is greatly emphasized. Against the background of a demand to engage in Torah study without expecting material benefit in this world, Rashbi's students' envy of their friend's wealth is underscored. The reference to material wealth is repeated three times in this brief anecdote: the student "became rich," a phrase that reflects the process of his accumulation of wealth abroad; the students "saw he had become rich," and the valley filled up with golden coins ("the entire valley"). The student who went abroad, apparently to engage in commerce, and came back rich becomes an object of envy. The others wish to go abroad "like him," which emphasizes their envy of his wealth. The image of the valley filling up with gold coins demonstrates, through the hyperbolic nature

7. Thus, for example, *Tanḥuma, Pekudei* and *Exodus rabbah*, which belong to the first branch of the tale, tell about a student who returned from abroad: "and he came back rich." In *Yalkut shimoni* on Psalms and in *Midrash Psalms*, which belong to a second branch of sources, this same event is recited differently: "and he profited and grew rich" (*Yalkut shimoni*); "and he returned loaded" (*Midrash Psalms*). The envious reaction of the students is also particularly emphasized in *Yalkut shimoni* on Psalms and *Midrash Psalms* (second branch): "And the students saw the profits he earned and wanted to go abroad." *Exodus rabbah* 52, 3, of the first branch, has: "the students saw him and envied him." While the students' envy of their friend is mentioned in versions of the first branch of the tale, it is more emphasized in those of the second branch.

8. The version in *Lekaḥ tov* is an exception. It includes "A Valley Full of Gold" but not the adjacent tale, "A Precious Stone from Heaven."

9. On the paramount value of Torah study in Rashbi's view, see *Berakhot* 35b; p*Berakhot* 9:5 (14:4); *Sifrei*, ed. Finkelstein, *ekev* 48, 113; *Leviticus rabbah*, 35, 6, ed. Margulies, 824.

of the description and the iconic effect of the gold coins, the opportunities available to the students for a life of wealth and comfort abroad.[10] It is a kind of fulfillment of the students' aspirations.

In the *Tanḥuma*, on which *Sefer ha-ma'asim* is based and from which it deviates, the aspects of wealth and envy are more subdued. The students' reactions express a legitimate, understandable desire for some degree of prosperity, and not necessarily for wealth, in a situation of economic distress, as well as the hardship of coping with the poverty that goes hand in hand with a life devoted to Torah study: "Once R. Shimon Bar Yoḥai had a student who went abroad and became rich. The other students saw he had become rich, and they too desired to go abroad like him."[11] The word "rich" appears only once, and it does not express a process of growing rich abroad but rather only the final outcome: "and became rich." The words "like him" in *Sefer ha-ma'asim* are absent from the *Tanḥuma*. Consequently, the effect of the abundance of gold in the description of the valley filling up with coins is more subdued in *Tanḥuma* in comparison to *Sefer ha-ma'asim*: "and the valley filled up with gold coins," without the addition of the word "entire," which reflects the abundance of gold and underscores the hyperbole of the description. Thus *Sefer ha-ma'asim*'s version is based on the *Tanḥuma* (first branch), but the students' attitude toward their friend and his economic prosperity resembles rather *Midrash Psalms* of the second branch.

Rashbi's reaction in *Sefer ha-ma'asim* as well as in *Tanḥuma* makes clear to his students the price they might have to pay for their desire: Their reward in the next world would be reduced. In his eyes the students' aspirations to improve their economic lot (in the *Tanḥuma*) and to gain wealth (in *Sefer ha-ma'asim*), as well as to leave the Land of Israel to go abroad, attest to their preference for worldly pleasures over Torah study and spiritual joy in the next world.[12] Delight in wealth in this tale is the very antithesis of delight in the Torah, and they cannot coexist. Engaging in commerce or any other occupation, such as farming (*Berakhot* 35b), requires total

10. For Rashbi's attitude toward leaving the country and traveling abroad, even in times of severe economic distress, see *Baba Batra* 91a.

11. Cf. *Ethics of the Fathers*, ch. 6: "Such is the way of Torah: Bread with salt you shall eat, water in small measure you shall drink, and upon the ground you shall sleep; live a life of deprivation and toil in Torah." Later the Mishnah speaks about the reward of the student in the next world, and warns him against the honor and property of others.

12. There is a similar attitude in his saying: "Do you welcome your suffering? For three good gifts that the nations of the world yearn for. And they were not given to them but rather by suffering, and these are: the Torah, the Land of Israel, and the next world" (*Sifre*, ed. Finkelstein, *va'etḥanan* 32, 57).

devotion, which implies the need to forego Torah study. Whether the students envied their fellow student and wanted to be rich like him (as in *Sefer ha-ma'asim*) or saw he was rich and wanted some improvement in their situation (as in the *Tanḥuma*), Rashbi reacts in the same manner. His attitude, expressed in his harsh criticism of his students, also represents the view of the narrator in *Sefer ha-ma'asim*, as is evident from his trends of adaptation. In its substructure the tale presents two paradigms that embody the antithesis between matter and spirit: wealth (money), travel abroad, and this world, in contrast to the Torah, the Land of Israel, and the next world. In the story the meanings of the different signifiers within each paradigm are equivalent and exchangeable: abroad is viewed as a material experience, a source of wealth and pleasures in this world, as opposed to the Land of Israel, which is an experience of holiness and spiritual pleasure, a kind of next world, and an environment of Torah study.

The motif of wealth is further underscored in light of a stylistic affinity with the preceding tale in *Sefer ha-ma'asim*: "The Loan" (no. 34). The expression "became rich" appears there as well,[13] and denotes the negative influence of money on Abraham, the protagonist: "Then, Abraham became very rich and a great merchant, and all the other merchants would come to him." Abraham's new wealth caused him to neglect his prayers, and the intimacy of his relationship with the Almighty was adversely affected. The affinity between the two tales lies mainly in the fact that the expression "and he became rich" appears only in the *Sefer ha-ma'asim* version of "A Valley Filled with Gold." In the other versions of this tale, such as in the *Tanḥuma*, the student who went abroad "came back rich"; that is, he returned to his home rich. A stylistic affinity is created between "The Loan" and "The Valley Filled with Gold" by replacing "returned rich," which is the common phrase in the latter's sources and parallels, with "became rich," which is unique to the *Sefer ha-ma'asim* version of the tale and resembles in its linguistic structure the parallel phrase in "The Loan." In the two tales the possibilities for accumulating a fortune, by engaging in commerce rather than devoting oneself to prayer and Torah study, are likely to undermine an intimate relationship with God. This is apparent also in a third story in *Sefer ha-ma'asim* that uses the same linguistic structure and vocabulary in a similar context. The phrases "became rich" or rather "has become rich," and "filled with gold" appear in "Hadrian and the Old Man" (no. 38), a tale about a greedy woman who envies her rich neighbor and wants her husband to be "like so-and-so." These analogies support the characterization of Rashbi's students as

13. In "The Loan" (no. 34): ". . . became very rich."

greedy in their envy of their fellow student's wealth and their eagerness to be "like him."

I would suggest that the emphasis placed on the motif of wealth in "A Valley Filled with Gold" in *Sefer ha-ma'asim* and its implication as desire for money signify a discourse on the Seven Cardinal Sins, which underwent intense development in the Middle Ages—in particular the sin of greed, the pursuit of money, and the obsessive devotion to its preservation. While this discourse existed in Christian theology from the early Middle Ages, it became more pronounced at the end of the tenth century, in particular from the eleventh century and thereafter. With the development of commerce after the conquests of Charlemagne, the method of payment for goods was changed: Cash money and currency took the place of property and barter. Even the lower social classes, who were not landowners or aristocrats, now had the opportunity to become rich. The aspiration to make money by engaging in commerce then began to gain a certain legitimation that it did not have in previous periods, and instead of being entirely disallowed, it was restricted. From then on criticism was not leveled at the motivation to earn money but rather at the manipulation of money for its own sake, the crude passion to accumulate money, to own it. The value of charity became a means of maintaining a correct balance between the prohibition against greed and the permission to engage in commerce, as well as a criterion by which to judge the motives of the merchant. Greed became a prevalent, pronounced topos in the religious discourse about the Seven Cardinal Sins and was likened to "a queen who governs the entire world."[14] Economic and social processes in Western Europe therefore changed the discourse conducted in it, centered on the Seven Cardinal Sins.[15]

Obviously, there cannot be a precise correlation between the story and the prevailing discourse in the Middle Ages about the sin of greed, since tales do not reflect the reality but merely respond to it. However, it does seem that the tale played a part in the medieval discourse about the Seven Cardinal Sins, and fitted into the semantic field that this discourse created. The tale does not speak about greed or manipulations to accumulate wealth as aims in themselves, but motifs of envy and a desire for wealth, as well as the image of the valley filled with gold coins as an invitation to the students to take some for themselves, mark the tale as one that exists at the margins of the Seven Cardinal Sins discourse in Europe.

14. Newhauser, *The Early History of Greed*, 127.

15. Ibid., 125–128, and quote on 127; Newhauser, "Towards Modus in Habendo: Transformations in the Idea of Avarice," 17–20.

The context of the discourse on the Seven Cardinal Sins is implied not only in the trends of adaptation of earlier sources but, first of all, in the very choice of this tale, rather than others, from *Tanḥuma* or perhaps the ninth-century *Midrash hashkem*. The choice of this brief anecdote in *Sefer ha-ma'asim* and its function as an exemplum signify an existing discourse in its place and time. The source of the story in the rabbinical literature and the values it represents are Jewish and intracultural (reward in the next world and the value of Torah study), but the trends of adaptation and editing in *Sefer ha-ma'asim*, which place the story in the context of the Seven Cardinal Sins, sharpen the opposition between this world and the next world, the pleasures of the body and joys of the soul, and imbue it with an emphatic medieval tone.

36. A Precious Stone from Heaven (319a–319b)

This story, like "A Valley Filled with Gold," which precedes it, illustrates the theodicy principle of reward. A person's reward is not necessarily a concrete object in this world but rather a spiritual benefit that awaits him in the next world.[1] In the two tales, "A Valley Filled with Gold" and "A Precious Stone from Heaven," this principle is applied to Torah study, the reward for which is given in the next world. Accordingly, the two tales end with an epilogue that refers to the verse from Proverbs (31:25), "And she shall rejoice in time to come." Since the reward of Torah is given in the next world, the Torah scholar should not fear the day of his death.[2] Torah study was a greatly esteemed value in Ashkenaz, and the two adjacent tales in *Sefer ha-ma'asim* enhance its discourse.

There are two textual traditions to the story, one long and detailed in *Ruth rabbah* (3, 4),[3] and the other brief and succinct in *Tanḥuma.*[4] *Sefer ha-ma'asim* represents the brief version, where an episode about R. Simon b. Ḥalafta and R. Ḥiyya is excluded. In the *Ruth rabbah*, unlike in *Sefer ha-ma'asim*, the two were studying Torah together one day when they heard the sound of the crowd outside—the voices of the workers coming to their master to receive their wages. When they realized this was the source of the noise, R. Simon b. Ḥalafta decided to ask his master for his share as well, and went out to pray to the Almighty for his family's needs. At once a hand holding a precious stone was extended from heaven. His wife, however, refused to accept it, even when the great scholar and leader R. Judah HaNasi promised he would fill her table in the next world from his own. She insisted that her husband should return the stone, since in the next world each

---

1. Two other tales of this rabbinical topoi were not included in *Sefer ha-ma'asim*: one on R. Ḥanina and the golden table leg that came down from heaven (*Ta'anit* 25a), and the other on R. Abbahu, who at the moment of his death was shown his reward—thirteen rivers of persimmon (oil) (*Tanḥuma*, Genesis, no. 1). For the stone as a concrete object from heaven, see Th. motif F1037.
2. See *Genesis rabbah*, 59, 2, ed. Albeck, 631: " 'Strength and dignity are her clothing, and she laugheth at the time to come' (Prov. xxxi, 25). This means: Strength and dignity are the clothing of the Torah. When reward? In the Hereafter."
3. See Lerner's comment on *Ruth rabbah*, part 3, 109. Cf. *Exodus rabbah*, 52, 3.
4. See brief versions of the tale in *Tanḥuma*, *Pekudei*, 7, Buber edition, 132, and comparative comments there; *Yalkut shimoni*, Psalms, no. 843, Salonika edition, 49b; *Yalkut hamakhiri* on Proverbs, ed. Grünhut, 101; Ms. Jerusalem 1970, 19b; Ms. Manchester-Gaster 82, 113b (published in Gaster, *Exempla,* 110, no. 52); Ms. London, British Library Or. 1389, 54a. With the addition of the hand extended from heaven to receive the stone, see Ḥefets Aluf, *Sefer vehizhir*, Exodus, ed. Friemann, vol. 1, 130; *Midrash hashkem*, *Sefer halikkutim*, ed. Grünhut, 11b; Aboab, *Menorat hama'or*, 1, 407.

one is on his own with his own share, and R. HaNasi's promise would be of no advantage.

The *Sefer ha-ma'asim* version lacks another episode as well, which appears in *Midrash Psalms*. On the eve of Passover, so the story goes, R. Simon b. Ḥalafta's wife is so ashamed of her poverty that, while her neighbors are busy cooking for the festive meal, she places a pot of water on the fire, as if she too was preparing food for the Passover. When her husband sees that her pot is empty, he goes out of the city to pray for help, and his prayer is answered. A precious stone is handed down to him from heaven. The rest of the story resembles the other versions, including the one in *Sefer ha-ma'asim*: R. Simon b. Ḥalafta mortgages the stone; with the money he buys food for the holiday and brings it to his wife. But she refuses to enjoy any part of their share in the next world, and he gives back the stone to a hand that descends from heaven to accept it.[5] This additional episode about R. Simon b. Ḥalafta's wife and her neighbors was probably inspired by the story of the miracle wrought for the wife of R. Ḥanina b. Dosa, in *Ta'anit* 25a–25b.

Sefer ha-ma'asim follows the brief *Tanḥuma* version of the first branch rather than the elaborated versions of the second branch, as in *Ruth Rabbah* and *Midrash Psalms*, but condenses it. The exchanges between R. Simon b. Ḥalafta and his wife are concise. Repetitions are omitted, such as his wife's words, "I will taste nothing," which appear in *Tanḥuma* twice and in *Sefer ha-ma'asim* only once.[6] Another distinct stylistic feature is the expression "in paradise," which replaces the phrase "the next world" in the parallels, thus depicting a concrete image of paradise in Ashkenaz.[7]

Rabbinical and literary compilations that contain this tale from the eighteenth century and thereafter include Elijah Hacohen's *Me'il ẓedakah*,[8] Ḥayyim Nahman Bialik and Yehoshua Hana Ravnitzky's *The Book of Legends*,[9] Judah David Eisenstein's *Oẓar midrashim*,[10] and Micha Bin Gorion's *Secrets and Legends*, as well as his *Mimekor yisrael*.[11]

---

5. Buber, *Midrash Psalms*, psalm 92, no. 8, 204a–204b.

6. The phrase "I will taste nothing," which is repeated in *Tanḥuma*, appears only once in the *Sefer ha-ma'asim* version.

7. On the image of paradise (and hell) in Ashkenaz, see Kushelevsky, *Penalty and Temptation*, 33–35.

8. Elijah Hacohen, *Me'il ẓedakah*, no. 560, ed. Kuperman, 134–135; no. 541, 506.

9. No. 348, 209.

10. V. 1, 141 (quotation from *Midrash hashkem*); and see references in Ben-Amos, *Mimekor yisrael*, no. 67, 138.

11. *Ẓefunot ve'agadot*, 157; *Mimekor yisrael*, no. 258, 195.

37. From Rejoicing to Mourning (319b)

The source of this story is in *Leviticus rabbah* (20, 3), in a *petihah* homily on *Aharei mot*, and in *Pesikta de-Rav Kahanah*, ch. 26, which is also devoted to *Aharei mot.*[1] Later versions are in two editions of *Tanḥuma* on the portion *Shemini.*[2] The broad context in *Leviticus rabbah* is the death of Aaron's two sons, Nadav and Avihu, when they were in the midst of offering sacrifices in the tabernacle (Leviticus 10:1). The story illustrates the situation of joy tempered by sorrow, as stated in the opening verse of the *petihah*: "I said of laughter, It is madness" (Ecclesiastes 2:2). The joyful wedding turns into a period of mourning. In the very midst of preparing for the ceremony, the father sends his son, the groom, to bring wine from the attic to serve to the guests, and when he fails to return, it turns out he was bitten by a snake and died.

The reversal from rejoicing to mourning occurs during the wedding ceremony, a liminal state and hazardous time in the groom's transition from bachelorhood to couplehood.[3] From this standpoint the story belongs to ATU 934 type, "Tales of Predestinated Death." The story about R. Akiva's daughter who was saved from death by a snake bite on her wedding day (*Shabbat* 156a) is a good example of this tale type.[4] In the present story, the groom, unlike R. Akiva's daughter, is not saved, although he was bitten while carrying out a task for his father. The commandment to honor one's parent was of no avail to him in this case. The father's reaction is one of resignation and acceptance of divine justice: "You came here to bless the groom, bless the mourners. You have come to place him under the bridal canopy, place him in his grave."

Sefer ha-ma'asim relies on a number of sources that predate it, particularly on the more popular version in *Tanḥuma*. It is unique in its style. As often in *Sefer ha-ma'asim*, it is succinct and devoid of any narrative excess. Thus, for example, the dramatic description in previous sources—of the son lying lifeless among the wine barrels—is neutralized in *Sefer ha-ma'asim*. Here the style is matter-of-fact and focused: "He went and found him dead."[5] In addition, the father's description as a "pious man" is omitted. Another typical characteristic in *Sefer ha-ma'asim* is the

1. *Leviticus rabbah*, ed. Margulies, 451–452; *Pesikta de rav kahana*, ed. Mandelbaum, *Aharei mot*: "I said of laughter, It is madness," 387.
2. *Tanḥuma*, ed. Buber, *shemini* no. 3, 12a–12b, and comparative comments in the appendix; *Tanḥuma*, *shemini* no. 2.
3. On the liminal characteristics of a wedding ceremony in rabbinical literature, see Rubin, *The Joy of Life*, 216–308.
4. See Schwarzbaum, "The Hero Predestined," 223–252.
5. In *Tanḥuma*, "His father went up and found him lying there among the barrels, lifeless."

omission of homiletic features. The commentary on the verse in *Tanḥuma* (ed. Buber) is omitted: R. Zakai of Kabul arose and said: "I said of laughter, It is madness" (Ecclesiastes 2:2).[6]

Tale versions contemporary with *Sefer ha-ma'asim* and later include *Ecclesiastes Rabbah*, last edited in the thirteenth century;[7] *Yalkut shimoni* on Ecclesiastes no. 967 (which refers to *Pesikta de rav kahana* as its source);[8] and *Exempla*.[9] These are based on earlier sources without including any far-reaching changes. In the twentieth century special mention should be made of the story's inclusion in Bialik and Ravnitzky's *Book of Legends*.[10]

6. There is a similar commentary in the print edition of *Tanḥuma*.
7. *Ecclesiastes rabbah*, Vilna, 2:4: "I said laughter is madness."
8. Salonika edition, 225a.
9. Gaster, *Exempla*, no. 238, 157.
10. No. 427, 536.

38. Hadrian and the Old Man (319b)

This tale appears first in *Leviticus rabbah*, in the context of the biblical verses about the Israelites' entrance into the Land of Israel after years of wandering in the desert: "You shall come into the land, and shall have planted all kinds of trees for food" (Leviticus 19:23).[1] The Israelites were in the desert for forty years, where they subsisted on the miracles of manna, the well, the quails, and the pillar of the cloud that went before them. When they came into the land, Moses told them to each take up a hoe and plant trees. The story about the old planter illustrates this scene of farming and planting.

The tale developed in three textual traditions that differed in their style, motifs, and degree of expansion. The first, which was published by Jonah Fraenkel,[2] is preserved in a number of manuscripts of *Leviticus rabbah*, *Midrash hagadol* on Genesis,[3] and Gaster's *Exempla*.[4] This tradition of the tale was apparently known also to R. Nathan b. Yeḥiel haRomi, author of the *Arukh*.[5] The second is represented by a number of manuscripts and print editions of *Leviticus rabbah*,[6] as well as in *Ecclesiastes rabbah*.[7] The third is represented by the *Tanḥuma* (the Mantua, 1563 edition, reprinted, and the Buber edition), which has a shorter opening compared to *Leviticus rabbah* but includes a longer dialogue between the neighbor and her husband.[8] Another version appears in *Yalkut shimoni*, *Kedoshim* (no. 615),[9] composed of the *Leviticus rabbah* and *Ecclesiastes rabbah* versions, and that of the *Tanḥuma*. In addition to the story's written versions, it was also transmitted orally, as documented in IFA.[10]

1. *Leviticus rabbah* 25, 5, ed. Margulies, 576–579.
2. *Harmony of Form and Content*, 163–165 (Hebrew). Fraenkel's text is based on Ms. Munich 117.
3. See Margulies's references (as in n. 1, above), in n. 5, to mss. Oxford (147), Oxford (2335), Münich 117, Jerusalem, 245, and additional versions, and his notation of the differences among them.
4. Gaster, *Exempla*, no. 26, 19–20.
5. See the *Arukh*'s notation of the tale in the entry "*keraẓ*" (got up early): Nathan b. Jeḥiel, *Arukh*, ed. Kohut, vol. 3, 212–213
6. See *Leviticus rabbah*, ed. Margulies. Based mainly on Ms. London, British Museum 340, and the first print edition of *Leviticus rabbah*.
7. *Ecclesiastes rabbah* 2, 5: "I went about." See also *Yalkut shimoni*, Salonika edition, Ecclesiastes, no. 568, 226b.
8. *Tanḥuma*, *kedoshim*, no. 8; *Tanḥuma*, ed. Buber, *kedoshim*, no. 8, 76–77.
9. Ed. Shiloni, Leviticus, 606–607.
10. E.D.N.A.: AT 1689; Noy, *The Beautiful Maiden*, 54, and his references on 245.

Sefer ha-ma'asim is based on the *Tanḥuma* version. This becomes clear in view of a number of common features: the opening formula "Once . . ."; the time and place of the events; Hadrian's march with his troops to a war against a rebellious state; the three-year time lapse between the first meeting between the old man and Hadrian and their second meeting; the neighbor's sobs when he is beaten and humiliated after he offers a basket of fruit to Hadrian with the clear purpose of receiving a suitable reward for it; the omission of the neighboring woman's names, which appear in other versions (such as *Barat paḥim*); a stereotypical epilogue about the nature of wicked women who cause their husbands to fall; and finally the use of Hebrew rather than Aramaic.

The *Sefer ha-ma'asim* version, however, differs from the *Tanḥuma* in its brevity and its emphasized grotesque-comic tone, particularly in the words of the woman to her husband: "You sit all day at home and never do anything like so-and-so, and see how he has become rich." While her husband sits at home, their neighbor is cultivating his land and even arranges a visit by the emperor. The difference between the two men is striking: The neighbor is successful despite his age, while her husband is indolent. In *Tanḥuma* (ed. Buber), the contrast is tempered: "[A]ll men work and the Almighty gives them some benefit, but you sit in your house in the darkness." Her words are not as harshly critical as they are in *Sefer ha-ma'asim*: "and never do anything like so-and-so." Later, when he returns home, beaten and weeping, she reacts with disappointment rather than sympathy, as the narrator notes: "his wife thought that he was bringing a basket filled with gold." The misogynistic message is underscored more in *Sefer ha-ma'asim* than in *Tanḥuma*, and in the epilogue it is formulated with the sweeping generalization that "all" women are wicked. Added to this is a warning to men that is not included in *Tanḥuma*: "woe is he who listens to them." In *Tanḥuma* the statement is qualified, although the tone is still misogynistic. It refers to wicked women without claiming that wickedness is an essential trait of the entire female gender. There is a certain affinity, albeit one that is only implied, to the fabliau genre, which was popular in northern France in the twelfth and thirteenth centuries,[11] and is characterized by misogynistic messages and the stereotype of the foolish, deceived husband.

The story also corresponds to international tale types. It is divided into two parts, and each stands on its own from the standpoint of its structure, genre, and the tale type to which it belongs.[12] One part is the episode about the man who plants, despite

11. Rubin and Sells, "Fabliau."

12. For a discussion of the structure of the story, see Fraenkel, *Harmony of Form and Content*, 165–173; for a comparative discussion of the tale, see Hasan-Rokem, *Tales of the Neighborhood*, 86–137.

his age, on the assumption that if he does not live to enjoy the fruit, his children will.[13] The other, which was widespread in Europe at the time of *Sefer ha-ma'asim*, is the episode about the neighbor who was beaten and humiliated after he, in a deceitful gesture, presents a basket of fruit to the emperor and his wife.[14] One of the parallels of this tale type is in the Italian collection *Le Cento Novelle Antiche*, which was first printed in 1525 and is based on an earlier and anonymous edition called *Novellion*, from 1281–1300.[15] The tale relates how the king desires a ripe fig that was at the top of a tree on one of the plots of his estate. He reaches up and picks it. The vassal sees this, and he fences the fig trees so that he can later pick the fruit and present it to his master to gain his gratitude. But he is too late—by then, at the end of the season, the figs are so cheap they are being fed to the pigs. Angry and offended by this worthless gift, the king orders that the figs be thrown at his vassal. When one nearly hits his eye, the vassal speaks words of praise for his master. He is then asked to explain his strange reaction, and he replies: "Messere perkè io fu incorato di recare pesche kess'io l'avessi recate io sare' ora cieco" ("Sire, because had I been encouraged to pick peaches instead; and if I had picked them, I'd be blind by now").[16] There is also a humoristic saying in this vein in two of the Jewish parallels: "It's a good thing they weren't peaches," or "etrogs" (in the *Midrash hagadol* and in Gaster's *Exempla*, respectively).[17]

13. Cf. ATU 928: "Planting for the next generation."

14. Cf. ATU 1689: "Thank God they weren't peaches."

15. See *The Novellino or One Hundred Ancient Tales*, novella no. LXXIIII, 98 and 100 (Italian), 99 and 101 (English). On its earlier version and other details about the collection of novellas and its different versions, see ibid., introduction, xi–xxi.

16. Ibid., 100, and in English translation, 101.

17. See nn. 3–4, above. On the story's affinity to this saying, see Clouston, *Popular Tales*, v. 2, 467–472.

39. The *Ḥasid* and the Ruler (319b–320a)

In general, the editing principle in *Sefer ha-ma'asim* is eclectic. In this case, however, three tales were gathered into one thematic unit on the issue of prayer. "The *Ḥasid* and the Ruler" is one of three adjacent tales in *Sefer ha-ma'asim* about the importance and significance of prayer. The other two that follow are "R. Ḥanina b. Dosa and the Snake" (no. 40) and the medieval tale (tale type Tubach 1282) known as "Do Not Fail to Attend Public Prayers" (no. 41).

"The *Ḥasid* and the Ruler" and "R. Ḥanina b. Dosa and the Snake" already appear in sequence in the *baraita* quoted in b*Berakhot* 32b–33a, which addresses the question of prayer: its frameworks, force, value, and the proper attitude it requires. The Talmud notes in particular the prayers of the "early *ḥasidim*" (*ḥasidim rishonim*): the preparations for achieving intention in prayer, and time spent at the end of the prayer before returning to the daily routine.[1] The Talmud also discusses situations in which the worshipper may interrupt his prayers in case of *piku'ah nefesh*, to save someone's life, and others in which he may shorten his prayer but not stop it. *Sefer ha-ma'asim* represents the talmudic version but in condensed form. Words and expressions that are made clear by the context are omitted.

Prayer—its intentions and meanings—is a distinct and key sphere among the *ḥasidim* of Ashkenaz; this is given expression not only in *Sefer ḥasidim* but also in their esoteric literature and liturgical commentary, as well as among talmudic scholars in France in general, such as the Tosafists. The significance and importance of intent in prayer, and in the present context the prohibition against interrupting prayer even when a snake is wound around one's heel, are discussed in Ashkenaz in various sources: in *Sefer ḥasidim*, in the *Maḥzor Vitry* of Rashi's school, in *Or zaru'a* by R. Isaac b. Moshe of Vienna (first half of the thirteenth century), and in a commentary on the Tosafot on the tractate *Yoma* 19b.[2] The tale "The *Ḥasid* and the Ruler" is mentioned in *Sefer ḥasidim* in a chapter devoted largely to the subject of prayer (no. 391 and thereafter), and it is cited as an appropriate illustration of the need

1. See the tale about R. Ḥanina b. Dosa and the *arod* (snake) in *Tosefta, Berakhot* 3, and Liebermann's comments on "*arod*" as a striped black snake that results from the mating of a snake and a turtle (Liebermann, *Tosefta ki-fshuta, Berakhot*, 46). For a discussion of "The *Ḥasid* and the Ruler" in the Talmud and the model of *ḥasidim rishonim*, see Feintuch, " 'Anonymous *Ḥasid*' Stories."

2. On intent in prayer, not necessarily when the story itself is cited, see R. Issac b. Moses, *Or zaru'a*, I, *hilkhot tefilah*, no. 103, 38, in the context of "even if a snake is coiled about his heel he will not stop"; Tosafot 19b: "*velo betefila*" (and not in prayer). Cf. Tosafot, tractate *Menakhot*, 44a: "*kol kohen*"; *Maḥzor Vitry*, ed. Goldschmidt, v. 1, no. 18, 24; *Maḥzor Vitry*, ed. Horowitz, 13 (without mentioning "even with a snake around his heel").

for rigorous observance of prayer even in time of danger: "Once a *ḥasid* was praying and did not stop even for the ruler. For if a man is strict in his prayer even if his life is in danger, that is a good deed . . . so they said even if a snake is wound around . . . and so forth."[3] Although the stories "The *Ḥasid* and the Ruler" and "R. Ḥanina b. Dosa and the Snake" are not included in the aforementioned sources, they are alluded to in the quotation in *Berakhot* 33a: "Even if a snake is wound round his foot he should not break off." After the fourteenth century, the tale's tradition in Ashkenaz continued into the *Mayse bukh* (1602).[4]

"Do Not Fail to Attend Public Prayers," the third in the series of adjacent tales about prayer in *Sefer ha-ma'asim*, is also linked to the norms of prayer within Ashkenazi pietism. It relates the tale of a man who was in the custom of staying in the synagogue after the prayers were over and the last of the worshippers had left, in keeping with his father's will. It describes all the trials and adventures the hero underwent as a result of this strict approach, and the reward he received for it. Thanks to his pious customs of prayer, he was saved from a murder plot against him. In *Sefer ḥasidim* there is a tale of an old woman in the opposite situation. After her death she was refused a place among the righteous men and women in the Garden of Eden; although she had always come early to prayer, she was also among the first to leave the synagogue before the worship had ended.[5]

The propensity to become so engrossed in one's prayer as to forget oneself is also illustrated in a story whose source is unknown, but its traces are left in later versions from the fourteenth century: Ms. Cambridge-Harvard 39 (116b–117a) from Ashkenaz, as well as in *Menorat ha-ma'or* from Provence. It tells of a pious Jew who did not interrupt his prayers even when a wolf came and carried off his son. The end is optimistic, since the infant is saved thanks to his father's piety. The author's recommendation in *Menorat hama'or* is: "Although these miracles were wrought for the early *ḥasidim*, the ordinary man should not depend on the miracle, but when he is in great danger he should stop [his prayer]."[6] The tale was included also in the fifteenth-century Ms. Jerusalem 3280,[7] and in the sixteenth-century early print editions of talumdic *aggadah* collections.[8]

3. *Sefer ḥasidim*, no. 485, 137; *Sefer ḥasidim*, ed. Margulies, no. 767, 467.
4. *Mayse bukh* (Basel), no. 130; *Ma'aseh Book*, Gaster, vol. 1, no. 130, 233–234.
5. *Sefer ḥasidim*, ed. Wistinetzke, no. 464, 132. For further references, see my comments to the tale (no. 41).
6. Aboab, *Menorat hama'or*, ed. Ḥorev and Katzenelenbogen, no. 3, 3, no. 108, 241.
7. See Yassif, *Ninety-nine Tales*, no. 15, 187.
8. *Hagadot hatalmud*, 6a; *En Jacob*, ed. Glick, vol. 1, 70–71.

Oral and popular versions of "The *Ḥasid* and the Ruler" were recorded: in the twentieth century by IFA (no. 3262, from Tunisia)[9] and by Ansky. The latter version is about R. Lieber of Berdichev, who aroused the ire of the *paritz* (landowner) by ignoring him while he was praying. But when the nobleman heard the explanation for his behavior, he was impressed, and he built a large synagogue for the Berdichev community. Thus the talmudic tale became a local etiological legend.[10] Three literary versions were included in Bin Gorion's compilation, *Mimekor yisrael* (no. 321), on the basis of *Menorat hama'or* and other sources.

9. Published by Noy as *Seventy Tales of the Jews of Tunisia*, no. 53, 149.

10. Schwarzbaum, *Roots and Landscapes*, 144–146.

40. R. Ḥanina b. Dosa and the Snake (320a)

The tale is copied in *Sefer ha-ma'asim* along with "The *Ḥasid* and the Ruler" and "Do Not Fail to Attend Public Prayers," both of which are on the topic of prayer. While the motif of prayer is not explicitly mentioned in "R. Ḥanina b. Dosa and the Snake," it is implied from its textual context within the compilation. "The *Ḥasid* and the Ruler," which precedes it, illustrates the value of intent in prayer and the prohibition against interrupting it. R. Ḥanina, who was known as a *ḥasid* (a pious man), ignores the ruler's greeting even at the risk of his life, because he would not interrupt his prayer. "Do Not Fail to Attend Public Prayers," which follows the present tale, illustrates the importance of public prayer as a means of sanctifying the Holy Name. Thus a cluster of stories was created to underscore the value of intent in prayer and its importance in general.

Sefer ha-ma'asim's direct source is a *baraita* quoted in the Babylonian Talmud (*Berakhot* 33a) regarding the issue of "intent in prayer." The *baraita* is preceded by a discussion in the Mishnah (*Berakhot* 5a): "[E]ven if a snake is coiled around his foot, he should not break off." On this point, a discussion develops in the Talmud: Is the snake the individual case that casts light on the general rule that a man is obliged to take all risks to avoid discontinuing his prayer? Or is the snake a concrete illustration that in certain dangerous conditions he can stop—for example, when a scorpion is drawing close to him?[1] Here, the tale of R. Ḥanina b. Dosa is cited to illustrate that indeed one should not interrupt his prayer because, "[I]t is not the snake that kills, but rather the sin that kills."[2] The story does not directly address the subject of prayer, but it does develop out of the previous halakhic discussion. The *baraita* ends with the maxim: "Woe to the man who encounters a snake, and woe to the snake that encounters R. Ḥanina b. Dosa."[3]

The snake in this tale represents the archaic serpent, the archetypal tempter that shattered the intimacy between God and Adam and Eve that existed in the Garden of Eden—an intimacy the worshipper must try to achieve through intent in prayer. In *Sefer ha-ma'asim* this is expressed in the stylistic choice of the biblical word for "snake" (*naḥash*) rather than its Talmudic equivalent (*arod*). The word *naḥash*

1. This refers to a particular standing prayer, the *Shemoneh esre* ("The Eighteen"), and not to prayer in general. Cf. the following discussion with the earlier introduction to "The *Ḥasid* and the Ruler."
2. See Rashi's explanation for "*arod*," in *Berakhot* 33a, according to *Ḥullin* 127a, and Liebermann's comment that *arod* is a black snake or a striped reptile created from the crossbreeding of a snake and a turtle (Liebermann, *Tosefta ki-fshutah, Berakhot*, 46).
3. For some variations of the tale, cf. *Tosefta Berakhot* 3:20, and a later midrashic version in *Tanḥuma, va'era*, no. 4; it is merely mentioned in *Exodus rabbah*, ed. Shinan, 135 (and n. 15).

appears three times in a tale of only a few lines, which underscores this stylistic choice of diction. (Of course this may also indicate a preference in *Sefer ha-ma'asim* for using a lower linguistic register.) Not only is R. Ḥanina b. Dosa unharmed, but it is the snake that is harmed: It dies when it bites R. Ḥanina b. Dosa. Through his trust in God and the intimacy of their relationship, R. Ḥanina b. Dosa is privileged as a *ḥasid* who is "learned in miracles" (*melumad benisim*).[4]

The Palestinian Talmud (*pBerakhot* 5:1) adds to the *baraita* a dialogue between R. Dosa and his disciples that is not included in the Babylonian Talmud (and accordingly not in *Sefer ha-ma'asim* either): "His disciples said to him, 'Master, didn't you feel anything [when the snake (*arod*) bit you]?' He said, 'I swear! I was concentrating on my prayer and felt nothing.' "[5] He was so engrossed in his prayer that he did not feel the bite of the snake, which in the Talmud is called a *ḥavarbar* (a striped, poisonous snake; a cat-snake). The Palestinian Talmud also expands on the manner in which R. Ḥanina b. Dosa was saved: God created a spring under his feet, which prevented his death.[6] The story, which is a typical exemplum, posits an extreme norm of behavior that is expected both from the great R. Ḥanina b. Dosa and the ordinary man when engaged in prayer.

In the Middle Ages, in addition to its inclusion in *Sefer ha-ma'asim*, the tale appears in Aboab's *Menorat hama'or* (fourteenth century) in a chapter of tales about intent in prayer[7]: "The *Ḥasid* and the Ruler" and "The Man Whose Son Was Carried off by a Wolf" (mentioned earlier in relation to the previous tale of "The *Ḥasid* and the Ruler"). In *Menorat hama'or*, unlike the other versions of the tale, an anonymous figure replaces R. Ḥanina b. Dosa as the hero of the tale, perhaps to appeal to its audience, the ordinary man: It begins, "Once there was a man."[8]

From the fourteenth to the early seventeenth century, the story appeared in *Sefer hama'asiyot* from Persia;[9] in the early printed compilations of talmudic tales in

4. For the expression: "*Melumad benisim*," see tractate *Sanhedrin* 109a, there referring to Naḥum Ish Gamzo.

5. *Talmud Yerushalmi*, ed. Academy of the Hebrew Language Library, 44.

6. According to the Palestinian Talmud, if a man manages to get to a source of water, he will be saved, but if the snake gets there first, he will not be saved. On this, and in comparison to the Babylonian Talmud, see also Zilkah, *In the Eyes of the Aggadah*, 142–150.

7. *Menorat hama'or*, ed. Ḥorev and Katzenelenbogen, no. 3, 3, no. 108, 241. Cf. Kaltz, *Sefer hamusar*, ch. 4, 64.

8. See Yassif's differentiation between the identified or anonymous heroes of the exempla in *The Hebrew Folktale*, 128–130.

9. Gaster, *Exempla*, no. 164, 117. See its manuscripts: Ms. Jerusalem 1970, 26a–26b (14th century); and again in the Ms. Manchester-Gaster 82, 120b–121a (16th century). Cf. Gaster, *Exempla*, no. 165, based on the Talmud (p*Berakhot* 5:1).

Hagadot hatalmud and *En Jacob*;[10] and in the *Mayseh bukh*, in archaic Yiddish.[11] In the nineteenth and twentieth centuries, the story was included in story compilations: *Sefer hama'asiyot*;[12] Grünwald's *Yalkut sippurim*;[13] Levner's *Kol agadot yisrael*;[14] Bialik and Ravnitzky's *Book of Legends*;[15] Bin Gorion's *Mimekor yisrael*;[16] and *Ẓefunot ve'agadot*.[17] In modern times, then, the story was circulated not only through the Talmud but also through tale collections.

10. *Hagadot hatalmud*, 6a; *En Jacob*, *Berakhot* 33b, ed. Glick, vol. 1, 71.
11. See also in *Ma'aseh book*, ed. Gaster, 1, no. 195, 191.
12. Araki, *Sefer hama'asiyot*, no. 56, 48a, and in Ḥuẓin's edition, no. 56, 35a–35b.
13. Grünwald, *Yalkut sippurim*, "*va'ethanen*," 111, nos. 9, 29.
14. Levner, *Kol agadot yisrael*, vol. 2, part 5, 76–78.
15. Bialik and Ravnitzky, *The Book of Legends*, no. 179, 610.
16. Bin Gorion, *Mimekor yisrael*, no. 321, 217.
17. Bin Gorion, *Ẓefunot ve'agadot*, no. 4, 155.

41. Do Not Fail to Attend Public Prayers (320a–320b)

This story is of the tale type Tubach 1282 ("Three counsels given to son"), which was widespread in medieval Europe and in the East.[1] It is based on a version from Europe, cited by Joseph Klapper in a medieval collection of tales,[2] that begins with a father on his deathbed instructing his son to observe certain precepts: to always honor God; to serve his lady faithfully; to attend mass each and every day and "respect the body of the Lord" (i.e., to eat of the holy wafer which, in Christianity, embodies the flesh of Jesus). The tale develops as follows: The father gives his son to the king to serve him as an advisor, and then the father dies. The king places the son in charge of the queen's chambers, where he serves her faithfully, in keeping with his father's instruction, and also regularly attends mass. Because he is so devoted, the queen prefers him to all her other servants. The others become jealous and accuse him of committing adultery with the queen. The traitor who slanders the son advises the king to send him to a lime-burning furnace in the morning, and the king does so. On the way, the young man stops to attend mass, and so is delayed. In the meantime, the slanderer is sent to see if the king's order was carried out, and he is thrown into the furnace. The son then arrives, and the truth is revealed. The king understands that it is the traitor who was burned, and that the queen's young servant is innocent. The young man tells the king about his father's instructions, and the king marries him to a relative of his. The title of the tale is "It Is Good to Attend Mass."[3]

The prevalent motifs in this tale type (both in the East and the West) which also exist in *Sefer ha-ma'asim* include clever advice;[4] an accusation of adultery with the queen; the Uriah letter (based on 2 Samuel 11:14–16, 9);[5] thwarting a plot by

1. See parallels in medieval Europe: Jacobi a Voragine, *Legenda aurea*, no. 181, 839–841; Jacobus de Voragine, *The Golden Legend*, vol. 2, no. 181, 380–381; *Gesta* (Ö), no. 283, 688–691; *Gesta* (Swan), no. 20, 118–120. For a survey of this tale type, see Klapper, *Erzählungen des Mittelalters*, no. 182, 377–379. For a number of paraphrases of parallels in the East and the West, see Clouston, *Popular Tales*, vol. 2, 448–457.
2. Klapper, *Erzählungen des Mittelalters*, no. 182. Cf. a similar version: Klapper, no. 139.
3. Cf. motif T1282 in the Thompson index. Additional relevant motifs in the Thompson index are K1612 and J.21.17.
4. The nature of the advice varies—in the main it is religious in the exempla of the Middle Ages and marked by common wisdom in later parallels. Nonetheless, the distinction between the trends is not clear-cut. In *Gesta Romanorum*, e.g., the advice is love God, obey your lady, and attend mass (regularly), in parallel to the kind of advice in later versions, according to ATU 910K: Stay away from the envious and slanderers; always identity with your master's feelings; always enter the church when you pass by it (never miss attending mass).
5. Cf. "Uriah's Letter" to Uriah in 2 Samuel 11:14–16, 9.

postponing the fulfillment of a task, as a result of the designated victim's decision to follow the advice given to him; and the hero's marriage to the king's daughter. These motifs also appear on their own, in other tale types, and are not necessarily combined. The "clever advice" motif does not necessarily appear with the "letter to Uriah,"[6] and vice versa.[7] In certain parallels the adultery motif is substituted with another slander.[8] Insofar as our discussion of the *Sefer ha-ma'asim* version is concerned, Uriah's letter is a key motif.

Although the *Sefer ha-ma'asim* version also has Indian and Muslim parallels, as Yassif has pointed out, its affinity to the Christian tale type is striking.[9] The queen is depicted as a pious woman who is as much a victim of the slander as her servant is, in contrast to her portrayal in Eastern versions where she is an adulteress who invited the aspersion.[10] The *Sefer ha-ma'asim* version is then anchored in Europe against the background of its time and place, like other tales in the compilation that conduct a dialogue with their parallels in the same cultural surrounding.

The Christian narrative was adapted in *Sefer hama'asim* by replacing the motif of the "mass" with the Jewish *Kaddish* and *Barkhu*, which are recited during public prayers. The son is commanded never to leave the synagogue from the moment the prayer leader begins reciting the *Kaddish* prayer.[11] Nor should he leave until the introductory *Barkhu* prayer is recited for those who came late and missed it the first time.[12] The *Barkhu* prayer has two meanings in Jewish sources: (1) It represents the Torah and is perceived as its metonym, because it is spoken in the synagogue when a member of the congregation is called up to the reading of the Torah (the *aliyah*). (2) It is also perceived as a means of sanctifying the Holy Name, because it is recited only in the presence of a *minyan* (i.e., at least ten men). Hence the name of the Almighty is proclaimed and sanctified. In the story the *Kaddish* and *Barkhu* prayers fulfill similar functions of proclaiming and sanctifying the name of God as a substitute for his sanctification in the martyrological sense, which is alluded to in the

6. See *Gesta* (Swan), no. 103, 227–229; no. 167, 347–348.
7. *Legenda aurea* (*The Golden Legend*) and *Gesta Romanorum*, in n. 1, above.
8. Tubach 2205: "Fridolin."
9. Yassif, *Kemargalit bemishbeẓet*, 152. Yassif, however, refrains from assigning the *Sefer ha-ma'asim* version exclusively to either the Eastern or the Western tradition of the tale type.
10. On this distinction between East and West, see Kawan, "Gang zum Eisenhammer," 666.
11. This probably refers to the Ashkenazic *Kaddish*, which is recited before the verses that open with the prayer "*Mizmor shir*" (that is, before *Pesukei dezimra*).
12. In the Ashkenazic tradition this introductory *Barkhu* is recited after the prayer *Aleinu*; in the Sephardic tradition it is recited before *Aleinu*.

rescue of the hero from being burned in the furnace of fire.[13] The distinction drawn between the *Barkhu* and *Kaddish*, on the one hand, and the Christian mass, on the other, underscores, however, the strong thematic similarity between the Jewish and Christian parallels.

An additional aspect in the story, against the background of its time and place, is its affinity with a prominent issue in Ashkenaz: the importance of remaining in the synagogue until the completion of the prayers. In northern France, it was said that R. Isaac of Dampierre (Ri) would stay in the synagogue until everyone had finished their prayers, including those who came late.[14] In Germany *Sefer ḥasidim* stresses the importance of reciting prayers with intent and in public.[15] The story opens with the father's deathbed commandment to his son, a format similar to those in the Christian parallels of tale type Tubach 1282; but it also fits in with other tales in *Sefer ha-ma'asim* that open with a similar episode of a father's last wish at his deathbed, thus underscoring the Jewish values of prayer and Torah study. The epilogue also affirms the value of prayer—in this case with an emphasis on public prayer, as discussed in *Sefer ḥasidim*.[16]

The *Sefer ha-ma'asim* version is the first written appearance of the tale in Hebrew, as far as we know. From the Middle Ages until the present, it has appeared in contemporary epigones of the *Sefer ha-ma'asim* version;[17] in adaptations that relate to Maimonides;[18] and in a sixteenth-century version adapted by R. Zakhariah Aldhahiri.[19] Apparently the tale was mainly transmitted orally, with close affinity with its vast circulation in non-Jewish folklore in the East and the West.[20]

13. See Kushelevsky, *Penalty and Temptation*, 257–261.

14. See Baumgarten's elaboration on this and other characterizations of piety in the synagogue in *Practicing Piety*, 200–202, and her reference to the case of Ri in Tosafot, *Berakhot*, 6a, s.v. "*hamitpallel.*"

15. See Baumgarten, *Practicing Piety*, and also nos., 132–133, in the Wistinetzke edition of *Sefer ḥasidim*. Cf. my comments on the "The *Ḥasid* and the Ruler" (no. 39) in this volume.

16. The motif of a father, before dying, commanding his son to adhere to Jewish law often appears also in Hebrew compilations of tales in the East, as Yassif has pointed out and which he has related to its relevant historical and cultural contexts (*The Hebrew Folktale*, 307).

17. See Gaster, *Exempla*, no. 308, 207–208, and no. 320, 116–117 (English); Eisenstein, *Oẓar midrashim*, 2, no. 12, 351–352; *Mimekor yisrael*, no. 663, 406. For additional references, see Gaster, *Exempla*, no. 320, 239–240; Ben-Amos, *Mimekor yisrael*, no. 218, 424–425.

18. See a paraphrase of this version in Gaster, *Exempla*, no. 345, 126, based on Ms. Gaster 66.

19. Based on Schwarzbaum's reference to the book *Sefer hamusar* and a paraphrase in *Roots and Landscapes*, 184.

20. Cf. ATU 910K: "Walk to the Ironworks."

42. Solomon's Scribes (320b)

This brief anecdote about Solomon—who tried to fool the Angel of Death and to keep his scribes away from him, but unwittingly led them straight into his arms—appears in the Talmud in two versions. They differ mainly in the trick employed against the Angel of Death, as well as in their opening phrases.[1] According to the Palestinian Talmud, in tractates *Kela'im* and *Ketubot*, Solomon sends them skyward, but the Angel of Death takes them from there.[2] In the Babylonian Talmud, tractate *Sukkah* (53a), Solomon sends the scribes to Luz, the city where no one dies, but they die at the gate before they manage to enter the city.

The *Sefer ha-ma'asim* version is based on the Babylonian Talmud, but it is not an exact quotation. Rather, the scribe is quite creative in copying the talmudic tale. The Aramaic is translated into Hebrew, apart from one saying that is left in the original language: "*raglohi devar enish inun arvin bei, le'atar demitba'ei taman movilin yatei*" ("A person's legs are responsible for him. They take him to the place where he is wanted"). Furthermore, Rashi's commentary on *Sukkah* is integrated into the tale. Filling gaps in the Talmud where Luz is mentioned without any further elaboration, Rashi explains in his commentary: "Their time has come to die, and he [the Angel of Death] could not take hold of their soul, because they were not doomed to die anywhere but at the gate to the city of Luz"; and further on: "Luz was a city in which the Angel of Death held no sway." Accordingly it says in *Sefer ha-ma'asim*: "And anyone who was within the city of Lod, the Angel of Death had no control over."[3]

The scribe's creativity is also evident from the description of Solomon's affection for his scribes, the motivation for his attempt to keep them from the Angel of Death: "And because Solomon was fond of them, he made Asmodeus swear that he would take them there." His emotional attitude toward his scribes is not mentioned in other sources, although it can be inferred. The idea that it was Asmodeus who carried them to Luz is also an invention of the scribe, since in the Talmud the devils are denoted by their general name: *se'irim*.[4] These manifestations of creativity in

---

1. In the Palestinian Talmud the story is told in the names of R. Jonah and R. Ḥama bar Ḥanina, while in the Babylonian Talmud it is told in the name of R. Johanan.
2. *Kila'im*, 9:32 (3:3); *Ketubot*, 12:35 (2:3).
3. It reads "*Lud*" in the Hebrew, but it should be "*Luz*."
4. See also in manuscripts of tractate *Sukkah*, where neither Solomon's great affection for his scribes nor Asmodeus is mentioned (British Library, London, Harley 5508; Biblioteca Apostolica Vaticana, EBR, 134).

Sefer ha-ma'asim imply a cultural image of scribes in Ashkenaz who were inspired writers, not merely copiers.

Sefer hama'asim influenced later sources, specifically the *Mayse bukh* in its sixteenth-century manuscripts and in the 1602 printed version.[5] Shared motifs with *Sefer hama'asim*, such as Solomon's affection for his scribes and the mention of Luz "where the people do not die,"[6] indicate an unbroken continuity of the tale's tradition in Ashkenaz, despite a loss of text witnesses in manuscripts later than the thirteenth century. Other sources from the sixteenth century, such as *Hagadot hatalmud* and *En Jacob*, quote the talmudic version instead.[7] Literary collections in the modern era that include the tale are *The Book of Legends* and *The Legends of the Jews*.[8]

5. See *Mayse bukh* no. 82; *Ma'aseh book*, trans. Gaster, no. 81, 135–136, and the earlier manuscripts in Yiddish on which the printed *Mayse bukh* relied: Ms. Innsbruck, no. 41; Ms. Robera, no. 47.
6. *Ma'aseh Book*, trans. Gaster, 136.
7. *Hagadot hatalmud, Succa, haḥalil*, 49a; *En Jacob, Succa*, 53a, ed. Glick, 2, 129–130.
8. Bialik and Ravnitzky, *The Book of Legends*, no. 78, 583; Ginzberg, *The Legends of the Jews*, vol. 4, 175. And see references in Gaster, *Exempla*, no. 139a, 215–216.

43. The Weasel and the Pit (320b–321a)

This story apparently has its source in the Amoraic period, based on its mention in the tractate *Ta'anit* 8a: "R. Ammi said: Come and see how great the Men of Faithfulness are as is evidenced from the episode of the Weasel and the Well. If this is the case with one who trusts in the Weasel and the Well, how much more so if one trusts in the Holy One blessed be He!"[1] The incident is not written about in any detail in the Talmud, but it is mentioned as an example of the superiority of the men of faithfulness, namely those who always keep their promises. Nor do we have any versions that are documented in the Gaonic literature. It was first cited in Ashkenaz, in a commentary attributed to Rashi (R. Shelomo Yitzchaki, 1041 [?]–1105), and in the Tosafot on the tractate *Ta'anit* 8a,[2] but its mention in the Talmud suggests that it was known before the Middle Ages. In the commentary attributed to Rashi in *Ta'anit*, the story is very condensed:

> Once there was a young man who promised a young woman he would marry her. She said: Who will be the witness, and there was a pit there and a weasel. The young man said: The pit and the weasel will be our witnesses. Later he broke his promise and married another, and fathered two sons. One fell into a pit and died, and one was bitten by a weasel and died. His wife said to him: What is it that caused our sons' strange deaths? And he said: This and this happened.[3]

In the Tosafot commentary on *Ta'anit*, more details are added which indicate a different source, probably the *Arukh* dictionary by Nathan b. Jeḥiel of Rome, from the end of the eleventh century.[4]

1. For a hypothesis that the story originated among the Amoraim, although no written version is extant, and on versions of the story in Ashkenaz as I've summarized here, see Malchi, "On Deeds Alluded to in the Talmud," 243. See also references to versions and existing research in Ben-Amos, *Mimekor yisrael*, no. 87, 170–171, to which I should also add Levner, *Kol agadot yisrael*, vol. 2, part 4, 308–317. See also Alexander-Frizer, *The Beloved Friend-and-a-Half*, 60–76; Zohar, "The Story of the Weasel and the Well in the Literature of the Enlightenment," 121–155; Kosman, *Man's Tractate*, 37–52; Har Shefi, "The Rat and the Pit," list of versions (201–204) and discussion (237–261).
2. For references to research on the commentary attributed to Rashi on tractate *Ta'anit*, see Grossman, *The Early Sages of France*, 216, n. 275.
3. See the commentary attributed to Rashi in *Ta'anit* 8a: *meḥulda ubor* (=from the weasel and the pit).
4. Nathan b. Jeḥiel of Rome, *Arukh hashalem*, "*ḥoled*" (a mole), 395–396, and Urbach's view of the *Arukh* as the Tosafot's source; see Malchi, "On Deeds Alluded to in the Talmud," 144, n.

In the East, the story was included in the *Midrash hagadol* on Genesis, which was edited in Yemen in the fourteenth century, and in *Sefer hama'asiyot* in Persia, during the same period.[5] These sources, which present the story in the expanded versions of *Arukh* and *Sefer ha-ma'asim*, make it possible to reconstruct its path from the East, presumably from the time of the Talmud, through Gaonic literature, and then up to the fourteenth century and its transfer to Italy and Ashkenaz in the *Arukh* and Talmudic commentaries of the Tosafists.[6]

Sefer ha-ma'asim follows the *Arukh* version almost verbatim, but the girl here is affiliated with the maternal home rather than the paternal home: "Once there was a girl who was walking to her mother's home." This may have been altered to make it consistent with what the girl says later: "Follow me to my father and mother, and I will become engaged to you."[7] This may also indicate a version of *Arukh* that is no longer extant but preserved in *Sefer ha-ma'asim*.[8] In any event, the girl's exclusive affiliation, in *Sefer ha-ma'asim*, with her mother's home and her exposure to the road's dangers while traveling alone express a highly positive image of women in Ashkenaz, as well as norms—not accepted in the East—that affirm their presence in the public sphere.[9]

The tension between the instinctual, chaotic, and dangerous aspects of nature and the institutionalized, civilized aspects that underlie sociohistorical processes does exist in the substructure of the story, and is evident from its binary paradigms. On the one hand we have the extraterritorial and demonic path, the symbols and dangers of the weasel and the pit, and madness and death; on the other we see stability, family, social hierarchy, norms of religious rituals, and marriage, birth, and fertility.

The impression made by the story in Ashkenaz is not necessarily reflected in textual changes introduced into it—since earlier versions do not exist—but rather in

---

25, and his reference to Urbach, n. 24. The *Arukh* version was also cited by Levin, *Oẓar hage'onim*, as a story rooted already in a Gaonic tradition (vol. 5, 57–58).

5. See R. David ha-Adani, *Midrash hagadol*, on Genesis 16:6, ed. Margulies, 250–252; *Sefer hama'asiyot* (Gaster, *Exempla*, no. 89, 59.)

6. On the development of the story after the Middle Ages, from the *Mayse bukh*, no. 101 (*Ma'aseh book*, trans. Gaster, vol. 1, no. 100, 173–270), up to modern versions, see Zohar and Har Shefi, n. 1, above.

7. This is the same as in the *Arukh hashalem*, 396.

8. See the version cited by Levin, n. 4, above, about "a girl who was going to her mother's home," in which there is no mention of her beauty. And see Malchi, "On Deeds Alluded to in the Talmud," 144, n. 27.

9. On the status of women in Ashkenaz and their involvement in earning the family's livelihood, see Grossman, *Pious and Rebellious*, 117–121.

its social function. It was received as an explanation for the custom of shaking hands at engagement ceremonies to indicate the gravity of the event as a binding agreement between the couple and their families. In light of the mutual oath between the boy and the girl and the serious implications of its violation, as well as the authority of the Babylonian Talmud, which was regarded as the source of the story, it was received in Ashkenaz as a discourse of engagement ceremonies. The commitment between the parties is, in "The Weasel and the Pit," a "covenant," and that is indeed how engagement ceremonies were viewed in Ashkenaz.

Engagement ceremonies were given formal validity and were nearly as binding as the marriage ceremony, and so their violation culminated in bans and heavy penalties. In the engagement ceremony, which was also an occasion at which formal conditions were agreed upon, the parents of the young couple committed themselves never to marry off their children to anyone else. Financial guarantees were given to ensure the agreement, and the bill of conditions was signed. In Jewish communities in Islamic countries, however, the nullification of an engagement was not thought to be very serious. It would seem that the Ashkenazic norm was in many respects parallel to the institutionalization of marriage by the church in the Christian society, where it gradually became a sacrament.[10]

10. Grossman, *Pious and Rebellious*, 49–55, 60–64, 88–98, 206–211.

44. The Spies and the Giants in Canaan (321a–321b)

The tale about the spies in Canaan who hid from the native giants in a pomegranate peel is based on the biblical description in the Book of Numbers (13: 22–23). Aḥiman, Sheshai, and Talmai are introduced as giants, the "descendants of Anak,"[1] and fruits in Canaan are so big and heavy that it took two men to carry one bunch of grapes. The suggestive figures of the giants and the subjective reactions of the spies—"and we were in our own sight as grasshoppers, and so were we in their sight"—were the inspiration for the *Sefer ha-ma'asim* anecdote.

An early version of the tale appears in *Pitron torah*, which is a collection of *midrashim* and commentaries on the Torah from as early as the eighth century in Babylonia.[2] It is embedded in a homily on the biblical phrase "descendants of Anak" (*yelidai ha'anak*; lit., "the sons of Anak"),[3] preceding "The Soft-Shelled Walnuts," a sequence retained also in *Sefer ha-ma'asim*. In the four hundred years after the eighth century in Babylonia, there is no documentation of the tale, as far as we know. It reappeared in the twelfth and thirteenth centuries in northern France in several sources of the Tosafists: a commentary on the Torah compiled by R. Nethanel, the disciple of R. Jeḥiel of Paris;[4] *Tosafot Shanz* (R. Samson b. Abraham of Sens) on *Sotah* 35a; *Tosafot Rosh* (R. Asher b. Yeḥiel) in the exegetical work "*Hadar zekenim*";[5] and *Sefer ha-ma'asim*.[6] The fact that the versions were concentrated in sources of the Tosafists in northern France is interesting. Urbach's assumption is that the Tosafists relied on a no longer extant Palestinian Midrash on Numbers that served *Pitron torah* and was preserved in Ashkenaz.[7] The story may have come into Ashkenaz from there.

The parable about the precious stones in the epilogue of the tale is unique to *Sefer ha-ma'asim*; it does not exist in any other version known to us. Its source in

1. In the Bible, "Anak" is the name of a very large man, and in Hebrew the word has taken on the meaning of a giant.
2. *Pitron torah*, ed. Urbach, 155.
3. See in Even Shoshan, *The New Dictionary*, vol. 1, s.v. "*yelid*."
4. The work was copied in Ms. Parma 2342, 1a–107b. On its nature and its author, see Shechter, "Notes on a Hebrew Commentary to the Pentateuch in a Parma Manuscript," 485–494, and citation of the tale, 492.
5. *Hadar zekenim, shelakh lekha*, 13, 2, 66.
6. Also see the tale in Habermann, *Texts: Old and New*, 203, based on Ms. Adler.
7. Urbach, introduction to *Pitron torah*, n. 2, 24. On earlier Palestinian works in the "libraries" of the Ashkenazic scholars, see Ta-Shma, "The Library of the Sages of Ashkenaz and Ẓorfat," 34–38. On lost *midrashim* that were preserved in Ashkenaz only, see Geula, "Lost Aggadic Works," esp. 291–336.

the Palestinian Midrash may also have been lost. The parable relates to Caleb's behavior in the eyes of his fellow spies: At first he joined them in denigrating the land of Canaan, but when he praised the land to the Israelites, they saw him as a traitor. When they first came into Canaan, Caleb was apprehensive about the reaction of the spies, even if he disagreed with them about their slander of Canaan. Only when they returned to the Israelites in the desert did he find the courage to describe the land as one of milk and honey. The spies reacted by saying: "Were you not together with us as part of the same plan?" The parable compares Caleb's behavior to that of the merchant, who told the robbers his precious stones were merely glass but, once the danger had passed, presented them as precious gems.[8]

The story contraposes two opposing vantage points—that of the spies and that of Caleb—and sharpens the opposition by means of the parable, in which there is an explicit distinction between the different positions. The spies become increasingly fearful because of what they encounter: the pomegranate peel the size of a cave, their concealment in it from the giant inhabitants of Canaan, the giant's daughter even taller than they are (they are about three meters in height), and the way they are thrown out of the orchard, along with the peel, without even being noticed. They grapple with their fright and rationalize it: "See the strength of the women. The men must be even stronger." Caleb, on the other hand, does not deny what he sees but interprets it in a positive sense. At the time, he says nothing, but when they return to the Israelites, he assures them: "Let us go up at once, and possess it; for we are well able to overcome it."

As is his wont, the scribe of *Sefer ha-ma'asim* omitted the homiletic function of the tale in Numbers—where it is brought as an explanation for the biblical expression "the children of Anak"—and inserted it in the synchronic sequence of the compilation. The unusual choice of a story unknown from other medieval story collections probably reflects an attraction to the marvelous: the sights of the new, foreign land whose inhabitants are giants and whose fruits are enormous. This "defamiliarization" arouses a mixture of wonder and fear. The marvelous as a representation of the other and the foreign is threatening; it deviates from the human and yet belongs to it.[9]

The story may have been received in *Sefer ha-ma'asim* due to the popularity of the Alexander Romance and the perception of the marvels underlying it, namely

8. Cf. to *Sotah* 35a.

9. On this function of figures of giants and other motifs of the marvelous in medieval narratives, see Huot, "Others and Alterity." On the figure of the giant in the Middle Ages as "the intimate other," see Cohen, *Of Giants*, xi–xx.

wonders of the universe in India and other places in the East, where Alexander the Great came and conquered. This romance was widespread in the Middle Ages in Latin, in various vernacular languages, and in a number of versions in Hebrew translated from Greek, Latin, Arabic, and French.[10] Like the spies in Canaan, Alexander the Great, on his campaigns to foreign lands, saw huge fruits, giants, dwarfs, and other marvels that create an accentuated effect of defamilarization.[11] In the Hebrew version of the Alexander Romance, there are also affinities with the narrative of the spies in Numbers and to other events that occur to the Israelites on their way from Egypt to Canaan. For example, the opposition of Alexander's warriors and their complaints about the order to go to war against India—"And now let us choose a leader and return to our homes"[12]—evokes the Israelites' reaction in the desert to the disparaging words of the spies in Numbers 14:4: "Let us choose a leader, and return to Egypt." Alexander replies to his soldiers: 'I will show you compassion and risk my own life, and I shall go to the city on foot to learn all its entrances and exits, and will send none of you."[13] The biblical narrative of the spies functions as a model for both the Alexander Romance and the *Sefer ha-ma'asim* anecdote. They both satisfy curiosity about and attraction to the marvelous in the Middle Ages.

The tale has further affinities with traditions about Alexander the Great in the scroll of *Ta'anit*,[14] in *Genesis rabbah* (61, 6),[15] and in the Talmud (*Sanhedrin* 91a). There is an argument in these sources between Jews and members of other nations—Canaanites called Africans and Ishmaelites—regarding their right to own the land of Canaan. The dispute is brought before Alexander the Great, who was known not only for his strength but for his wisdom as well. This occasion of the dispute is described, in the commentary of the Gaonim and Rashi, as an "*eiẓa*" (plan or counsel), whose connotation in *Sefer ha-ma'asim* is negative (as a plot). The Jews' right to the Land of Israel was challenged: "Were you not together with us as part of the same plan [*eiẓa*]?"[16] The disparate positions taken by Caleb and the other spies

10. Yassif, "The Hebrew Traditions about Alexander the Great," 359–407.
11. Cf. Dan, "*Alilot Alexander Mocedon*" ("The Deeds of Alexander Mocdon"), 78–79, 86, 92, 107. Later, in the modern era, Jonathan Swift would use defamilarization in his satire *Gulliver's Travels.*
12. Dan, "*Alilot Alexander Mocedon,*" 78.
13. Ibid., 79, in the context of Alexander's plans of conquest in India, his men's opposition, and his reaction.
14. *Megillat Ta'anit*, ed. Noam, 70–75, to the twenty-fifth of the month of *Sivan.*
15. Ed. Theodor Albeck, 666–668.
16. For "*eiẓa*" in the negative sense of a plot, see, for example, "Happy is the one who does not take the counsel of the wicked for a guide" (Psalms 1:1), and the expression "the counsel of

represent a dispute about the right of ownership of Canaan. Is the land acquired merely by force of occupation, as the spies believe—a position implied by their doubts about the chances of gaining the land and the spies' willingness to forego ownership—or is it acquired by force of the divine promise to the patriarchs of the people, as Caleb believes, regardless of any realistic facts on the ground?[17] In *Sefer ha-ma'asim* the tacit dispute between Caleb and the spies about the right of the Israelites to the land—which in the narratives about Alexander the Great is explicit—as well as the spies' use of the word *eiẓa*, signify a discourse about the right of ownership of the land that is maintained through the mediation of cultural images in medieval Ashkenaz.

Aḥithophel" (from 2 Samuel 16:20); and in the context of the debate over the right to the Land of Israel, cf. *Ta'anit* to the twenty-fifth of *Sivan*, a date connected with the tradition about a dispute between "the Africans" or the Canaanites and the Jews in the time of Alexander the Great (*Ta'anit*, ed. Noam, 198): "On the 25th they took *dimosnai min yarosh*." In the time of the Gaonim, "*dimosnai*" was interpreted as a counsel or a challenge (see discussion by Noam in her edition of *Ta'anit*, 205).

17. See the discussion about the opposing positions of the spies and of Moses (who is represented by Caleb and Joshua), in the context of modern concepts of nationalism and exile: Ilana Pardes, "Imagining the Promised Land: The Spies in the Land of the Giants."

45. Soft-Shelled Walnuts (321b)

This anecdote has its source in the Amoraic midrash *Pesikta de rav kahana*, as part of a sermon for Shabbat Rosh Ḥodesh (when the first day of the month falls on the Sabbath) on the verse from Proverbs 13:25 ("The righteous eats to his heart's content; but the belly of the wicked shall want").[1] Similar versions in the later *midrash* include *Midrash Proverbs* and *Pesikta rabbati*,[2] as well as a version in *Yalkut hamakhiri* from the fourteenth century in Provence.[3] The antithesis between the righteous man who eats his fill and the wicked man who is never satisfied is presented as a contrast between "spirit" (*nefesh*) and "belly" (*beten*), between this world and the next, between the material and the spiritual. The story takes this antithesis to the level of the absurd. All the delicacies in the meal served to the gentile failed to satisfy him because there were no soft-shelled walnuts on his table. The dichotomy, nonetheless, is not clear-cut, since eating in company creates a sense of intimacy.

There is an intertextual affinity with another story of a meal—a kind of mirror image of "Soft-Shelled Walnuts"—in "The Butcher from Ludkiya," whose primary source is the Talmud and other midrashic compilations,[4] and which was also copied into *Sefer ha-ma'asim* (310a). A butcher gains much wealth and a golden table laden with "all kinds of food and delicacies" as a reward for having greatly honored the Sabbath and put aside the best cuts of meat for it. Motifs common to the two stories are the ornate, large table, laden with the finest delicacies, the golden table, and the expression: "all kinds of food," which denotes the quantity and variety of foodstuffs on the table.[5] In "The Butcher from Ludkiya," however, the host is a Jew, a butcher who is in the habit of setting aside all the best he possessed for the Almighty, in

1. *Pesikta de rav kahana*, 6, ("My offering, and my bread for my sacrifices"), ed. Mandelbaum, 115–116.
2. *Midrash Proverbs*, ed. Buber, ch. 13, no. 14, 37b, 74; *Midrash Proverbs*, ed. Visotzky, 108 (in the apparatus), opening phrase: "*u'beten resha'im tehsar*"; *Pesikta rabbati*, ch. 16, ed. Ish Shalom, 82b; *Pesikta rabbati*, ed. Ulmer, vol. 1, 342–343. This version is quoted also in Makhir b. Aba Mari, *Yalkut hamakhiri*, Proverbs, ed. Grünhut, *Sefer halikkutim*, vol. 4, part 6, ch. 13, no. 25, 7b; *Yalkut hamakhiri*, ed. Greenup, on Proverbs, 17.
3. *Yalkut hamakhiri*, ed. Greenup, on Proverbs, supplement on Hosea and Proverbs, 17–18.
4. For a selection of sources, see *Shabbat* 119a; *Pesikta rabbati*, ch. 22, ed. Ish Shalom, 111b; *Yalkut shimoni* on Genesis, no. 16, ed. Shiloni, 52–53; and on Isaiah, no. 496, ed. Shiloni, *Latter Prophets*, 307.
5. In a few of the versions there is also a linguistic affinity created by use of the expression "the six days of the creation of the world" to describe the abundance and variety of the food that was served.

marked contrast to the gentile in "Soft-Shelled Walnuts," whose main desire is to enjoy the pleasures of this world and whose gluttony was regarded by Christianity in ancient times and in the Middle Ages as one of the gravest of the Seven Cardinal Sins.[6] The figure of the gentile does not appear in "The Butcher from Ludkiya," but in the comparison of the two tales, the contrast between the spiritual and the material in "Soft-Shelled Walnuts" is intensified, since even a simple butcher who engages in a lowly occupation and is rewarded by material plenitude is conscious of the uniqueness of the Sabbath and the source of the abundance awarded him.

"Soft-Shelled Walnuts" is exceptional when compared to its sources. First, the story is cut off from its homiletic framework in the Midrash and stands on its own between "The Spies and the Giants in Canaan" and the story about R. Joshua b. Levi and the Angel of Death. Second, the genre changes: In earlier sources, such as *Pesikta de rav kahana* and *Pesikta rabbati*, the story is denoted as a "memorate," namely as an eyewitness report of an event as told to Rav Dostai, a Tanna from Kokhba, by someone who took part in it: "a gentile prepared a meal for all the elders of the city and invited me along with them."[7] *Sefer ha-ma'asim* presents a coherent story that "once" took place, instead of the memorate in earlier sources. The narrating situation, which is a dialogue between a concrete addresser and addressee, is not given. Third, for the first time in the versions of the story, the guest invited to the meal is Rabban Gamliel (the elder), a Tanna and head of the Sanhedrin in the first century A.D., while it was R. Meir in the earlier sources. Fourth, the homonyms *min* or *minin*, which appear in the sense of "species," or "kind," also imply a "heretic," a Christian. The root *mem/yod/nun* appears three times in the version in its different forms but not even once in earlier versions; this repetition is particularly striking in light of the tale's brevity. The gentile in the story most likely represents the Christian. Finally, the dialogue between the diners varies. The expressions "My heart and yours know" and "That is why I pleasure my spirit with all my strength" do not exist in earlier sources, in which the gentile cites the position of the Jews from an external vantage point: "You say that this world is ours, and the next world is yours."[8] The negative image of the gentile is internalized as a self-image in *Sefer ha-ma'asim* through the stylistic choice of emotional diction ("My heart and yours know") and the syntax that ascribes to the two of them, the Jew and the gentile, the shared knowledge that the gentile belongs to this world and is excluded from the next. The use of the word *nefesh* (spirit) to denote the gentile's

6. On the sin of gluttony in medieval theology, see, e.g., Hill, "The Ooze of Gluttony," 57–70.

7. *Pesikta de rav kahana*, 6, 2, ed. Mandelbaum, 115.

8. E.g., in *Pesikta de rav kahana*.

fixation on the pleasures of this world instead of the expected word *guf* (body) further stresses his addiction to the material, even in his spirit.[9]

The context of "*min*" as a heretic is also implied by the appearance of Rabban Gamliel in only *Sefer ha-ma'asim*'s version. He debated with the first Christians who were known as *minim*, and who, on the other hand, regarded Rabban Gamliel as Paul's teacher.[10] In the Middle Ages, Christians called the Jewish books of *aggadah* "the books of Gamliel," and they linked his name to the Talmud in general, "quoted" statements in his name in polemical literature, and attributed various works to him.[11] In the clash mentioned in the Talmud between him and one of the *minim*, the latter raises the Christian claim that God has forsaken the Jewish people, an assertion that became dominant in the Jewish-Christian polemic in the Middle Ages.[12] The polemical context is also inferred from the gentile's words, "I have no portion in the world to come," an expression that does not exist in other versions of the tale.[13] This is the language employed in the Mishnah in *Sanhedrin*, about the skeptic (a *min*) who has no part in the next world.[14] In *Pesikta de rav kahana*, for example, the wording is more temperate, and it is attributed to a Jew: "Rabbi, you say this world is ours and the next one is yours."[15]

Sefer ha-ma'asim places the story in the context of the relations between Jews and gentiles: Though Christians are portrayed as heretics, Jews, as a minority living within a dominant Christian majority, also had reciprocal relations with them. The antithesis between this world and the next, between the material and the spiritual, is expressed in the antithesis between the Jew and the gentile. Definitions of identity in this tale are based on attitudes and approaches to "food."

9. I am grateful to Richard Newhauser and Esther Cohen for calling my attention to the unusual use of the word *nefesh* in this tale (at the International Conference on Medieval Studies at Leeds, 2013).

10. Acts 22:3.

11. Merchavia, *The Church versus Talmudic and Midrashic Literature*, 121; 208–212.

12. *Yebamot* 102b: "You are a people with whom its God has performed *halitzah*" (a people whose God has abandoned it).

13. In other versions: "You say this world is ours and the next is yours."

14. Mishnah, *Sanhedrin* 10a, has a list of those "who have no part in the next world," in contrast to the Jews "who have a part in the next world."

15. *Pesikta de rav kahana*, 6, 2, ed. Mandelbaum, 116.

46. R. Joshua b. Levi and the Angel of Death (321b–322a)

The earliest written source of this tale is in tractate b*Ketubot* 77b.[1] In it, R. Joshua b. Levi tricks the Angel of Death and asks him to show him his place in the Garden of Eden.[2] He enters there alive, carrying the knife of the Angel of Death, and swears he will never leave. His oath is considered valid, because throughout his life he never swore, and the Torah was the very essence of his life. Indeed, he was protected from death even when he was sitting among gravely ill people suffering from *ra'athan*; he taught them Torah despite the contagiousness of the disease and the danger of infection.[3] In the Garden of Eden he meets R. Shimon b. Yoḥai (Rashbi), who questions his right to be there. R. Joshua b. Levi admits that he has seen a rainbow during his lifetime, and hence does not have the right to atone for the sins of his generation and is not a completely righteous man. Therefore he is not entitled to remain in the Garden of Eden during his lifetime. The narrator questions Rashbi's conclusion, because in his view R. Joshua b. Levi replied with humility, taking no credit for himself.

In the Middle Ages the story developed in two textual traditions: one in the East, based mainly on the talmudic version and sometimes with a mention of inhabitants of the Garden of Eden, such as Bithiah, the daughter of Pharaoh, who converts to Judaism, and the Patriarchs;[4] the other in Ashkenaz, from the thirteenth century, with the addition of lengthy descriptions of the Garden of Eden and Gehenna—their topography and inhabitants, their sins and their virtues, and, accordingly, their rewards and punishments. These descriptions are based on a store of medieval sources about the sights of the world to come, some of them written in the name of R. Joshua b. Levi.[5] In Western Europe the focus shifts from the talmudic narrative to the sights of the world to come, and the genre changes from a legend about R. Joshua b. Levi to a vision

1. For the sources of the story, a survey of its development, and existing research, see Kushelevsky, *Encyclopedia of the Jewish Story*, vol. 1, 261–279; and for a discussion of the broader context of Jewish and Christian traditions about heaven and hell, see Perry, *Tradition and Transformation*, 197–252. Also see references to literature and research about the story in Ben-Amos, *Mimekor yisrael*, no. 118, 211–212.
2. Cf. the AT 330*: "Heaven entered by trick"; ATU 330: "The Smith and the Devil."
3. *Ra'athan* is a skin disease similar to leprosy; it is contagious through bodily secretions. See Jastrow, *A Dictionary of the Targumim, the Talmud Babli and Yerushalmi, and the Midrashic Literature*, 1438; and for additional information, Steinsaltz, in tractate *Ketubot*.
4. Versions of this textual tradition are *Midrash aseret hadibrot*, ed. Shapira, 51–53; Hadassi, *Eshkol hakofer*, no. 64, 36b; *Sefer hama'asiyot*, trans. Gaster (Gaster, *Exempla*, no. 138, 96–97); Al-Nakawa, *Menorat hama'or*, v. 4, 388–389; *Ḥibbur yafeh mehayeshu'a*, ed. Hirschberg, appendix, 106–107. The tale is not included in Brinner's edition, *An Elegant Composition Concerning Relief after Adversity*.
5. See the lengthier discussion in Part I, Chapter 2, pp. 57–59.

narrative, in the form of visions of the next world. In those visions a person about to die is transported to the next world, sees its sights, and returns to earth to tell its inhabitants about it. Similarly, in *Sefer ha-ma'asim*, R. Joshua b. Levi, on the verge of death, tours the next world to report to the people on earth about the sights he sees there.

The story in *Sefer ha-ma'asim* is based primarily on the talmudic version, particularly since it has none of the lengthy descriptions of the Garden of Eden and Gehenna that appear in the other manuscripts in Ashkenaz, and it contains words in Aramaic diction taken from the Talmud. Nonetheless, the affinity with the Ashkenazic tradition of the tale is implied. R. Joshua b. Levi asks to see "Gehenna and the Garden of Eden," and later "[h]e showed him Gehenna and the Garden of Eden," while in the Talmud only the Garden of Eden is mentioned. The suggestive force of the word coinage "*Gehenom ve-gan eden*" (Gehenna and the Garden of Eden) introduces medieval images of the next world and the topoi of tours after death in paradise and hell. Thus the medieval trend to incorporate sights of the next world in the tale is preserved in *Sefer ha-ma'asim*, albeit only through an allusion.

The epilogue is also unique to *Sefer ha-ma'asim* and does not appear in the other sources. The scribe's conclusion is that one should avoid "even a [casual] conversation [of lies] that contains neither good nor bad," since "He who tells lies shall not remain in my presence" (Psalms 101:7). A conversation based on a lie is undesirable, even if it is harmless in the sense of being "neither good nor bad." This is an expansion of the demand, in earlier versions, to refrain from vain oaths in the name of God, even if they are true oaths. The verse from Psalms may suggest that the epilogue should be read in the context of the school of the Tosafists in Ashkenaz and northern France. In the Babylonian Talmud, tractates *Sotah* and *Sanhedrin*, four classes are mentioned that will not appear before the presence of the *Shekhinah,* and one of them is the "class of liars."[6] The proof given in the Talmud that the *Shekhinah* will shun the class of liars is the verse from Psalms cited in the epilogue. R. Jonah of Gerona (1210–1263) refers to this talmudic issue in his book *Sha'arei teshuvah*; he interprets "class of liars" to mean those who tell a fabrication that is partly or wholly a lie, and who thus will not be allowed to appear in the presence of the *Shekhinah* regardless of whether their lies are beneficial or harmful.[7] This interpretation is implied in the epilogue of the *Sefer ha-ma'asim* version, which warns against

6. *Sotah* 52a; *Sanhedrin* 103a.

7. R. Jonah, *Sha'arei teshuvah*, third part (*sha'ar*), no. 161, 286: "[The fourth category consists of] those who lie in recounting things they have heard, deliberately distorting some of them. Such as these derive no benefit from their lies nor injure others thereby, but pursue this pattern

"a [casual] conversation [of lies] that contains neither good nor bad," on the basis of that same verse from Psalms. It is quite likely that R. Jonah's commentary on the verse from Psalms and that of the scribe in the epilogue are anchored in the study hall of the Tosafists, although there is no mention of such a commentary in tractates *Sotah* and *Sanhedrin*. R. Jonah's approach strongly draws on the commentaries of the Rabbinical scholars of France in the thirteenth century and of the Pietists of Ashkenaz; the epilogue in *Sefer ha-ma'asim* may also be another example of that influence.

Midrash aseret hadibrot was an additional influence on *Sefer ha-ma'asim*, as is evident from R. Joshua b. Levi's request for the Angel of Death to wait thirty days until he completes his studies. The source of this episode is in the subsequent story in the Talmud about R. Ḥanina Papa, who was also visited by the Angel of Death, who asked to let him take his soul. R. Papa asks for a postponement of thirty days so he can complete his studies, and the angel agrees. The story about R. Papa was already combined with that of R. Joshua b. Levi in *Midrash aseret hadibrot*, and consequently also in *Sefer ha-ma'asim*. The influence of *Midrash aseret hadibrot* is also evident from certain omissions of material that appeared in the Talmud, such as the description of R. Joshua b. Levi sitting among those ill with *ra'athan*, which is an exposition to the story of his trickery of the Angel of Death, and the clash between him and Rashbi in the Garden of Eden. These were left out of *Midrash aseret hadibrot*, and consequently also *Sefer ha-ma'asim*.

Nonetheless, the versions of *Midrash aseret hadibrot* and *Sefer ha-ma'asim* are not identical. Certain details in *Midrash aseret hadibrot* are omitted from *Sefer ha-ma'asim*, which changes the emphases. Here R. Joshua b. Levi explains why he is asking for a thirty-day postponement so he can complete his studies: "Happy is he who comes here with his studies in hand"—and that is also what R. Papa contended in the Talmud, in the story that follows the one about R. Joshua b. Levi. The scribe of *Sefer ha-ma'asim* borrowed this expression from the Talmud and inserted it into this story. In *Midrash aseret hadibrot*, however, R. Papa's words are not quoted, and only his request for a postponement is stated in detail: "R. Joshua said to him: wait for me thirty days so I may revise my studies, and so he did."[8] Apparently, in *Midrash aseret hadibrot* the emphasis is on the motif of R. Joshua's trick and his success at escaping death, while in *Sefer ha-ma'asim*, in which the expression "Happy is he who comes

because they love falsehood rather than speaking righteousness." R. Jonah, *Sha'arei teshuvah* (*The Gates of Repentance*), trans. Silverstein, 287.

8. *Midrash aseret hadibrot*, ed. Shapira, 52.

here with his studies in hand" is added, the import is shifted to the judgment expected in the next world. In *Sefer ha-ma'asim*, Torah study is presented as the major element in the Day of Judgment after death, and not only as a means of delaying death in this world. The emphasis on the value of Torah study in this world, combined with images of the next world and the judgment in it, is a nuance that is unique to *Sefer ha-ma'asim*, and it does not exist in the talmudic version.

The story also circulated via non-Jewish sources in both the East and the West. A Muslim parallel from the eleventh century exists in a work in the genre of tales of prophets, where a figure named Idris corresponds to R. Joshua b. Levi.[9] Two medieval Christian parallels exist in the polemical literature. Petrus Alfonsi (1062–1110), a convert whose previous name was Moses Sephardi, cited them in his work *Dialogi Petri et Moysi Iudaei* (*Dialogues between Peter and Moses the Jew*)—or under another title, *Ex Judaeo Christiani Dialogi*—written around 1106.[10] In a parallel work by Peter the Venerable (1094–1156), the abbot of Cluny, R. Joshua b. Levi is depicted as a liar and ingrate who duped Pharaoh's daughter Bithiah, and took her place; and the Jews in general, Peter's contemporaries, are the enemies of Christianity and believers in the Talmud, their Satanic book.[11] The attitudes of Petrus Alfonsi and Peter the Venerable are consistent with an overall trend, pointed out by Jeremy Cohen, of a change in the Christians' approach to Jews in the twelfth century. This was a new rationalist trend in the anti-Jewish polemic, and in the final analysis, in the thirteenth century, it undermined the Jews' status as witnesses in the Augustinian doctrine, which centered on the command: "Do not kill them."[12]

9. For a summary of the story and a reference to the tale type (AT 330), see Schwarzbaum, *Biblical and Extra-Biblical Legends*, 146–147. For the complete version, see Al-Thalabi, *Ara'is Al-Majalis*, 83–85. On the author and the genre of stories about prophets, see the introduction to Thalabi's book (xi–xxxii). On the prophet Idris, the source of his name, and his identification with Enoch or Elijah, see Vajda, "Idris."

10. Merchavia, *The Church versus Talmudic and Midrashic Literature*, 93–108. For English translation, see Petrus Alfonsi, *Dialogue Against the Jews*, trans. I. M. Resnick, 94–96.

11. See the Latin version by Peter the Venerable in Perry, *Tradition and Transformation*, 284–286; for the translation into Hebrew, see Liebermann, *Shki'in*, 38–42.

12. For a summary of this claim presented at length throughout the book, see Cohen, *Living Letters*, 217–218, 270 (on Petrus Alfonsi and Peter the Venerable).

47. R. Joshua b. Elem and Ninus the Butcher (322a–322b)

The tale of "R. Joshua b. Elem and Ninus the Butcher" belongs to the oikotype known as "A Companion in Paradise" (AT 809*-*A [IFA])[1] which circulated in various Jewish parallels in the Middle Ages.[2] The plot line is consistent in all its parallels: An ordinary man, often a sinner, earns an honorable place in the Garden of Eden next to a distinguished Torah scholar, thanks to a single special deed. There are, however, differences in motifs. The occupation of the "companion" in paradise varies among tax collector, pimp, and butcher, and the unique act that gains them an honorable place in paradise may be charity, the ransom of prisoners, or the restraint of lust.

The sources for the *Sefer ha-ma'asim* version about R. Joshua b. Elem and Ninus the butcher are in *Midrash aseret hadibrot* (as an illustration of the Fifth Commandment);[3] and mainly in *Genesis rabbati*, from the school of R. Moses ha-Darshan of Narbonne in the eleventh century,[4] with which *Sefer ha-ma'asim* shares certain motifs in the epilogue and some stylistic attributes. As in *Genesis rabbati*, Esau is depicted as having great respect for his father (a motif absent from *Midrash aseret hadibrot*). As in *Genesis rabbati*, the punishment for anyone belittling his own father is depicted on the basis of the verse in Proverbs (30:17): "The eye that mocks at his father and scorns to obey his mother, will be picked out by the ravens of the valley and the young vultures shall eat it."[5] Because Esau was so meticulous in honoring his parents, and because "honoring one's father and mother is as

1. Cf. ATU 809*: "Rich man allowed to stay in heaven for a single deed of charity."
2. For a selection of Jewish parallels of the "Companion in Paradise" tale type from antiquity up to the Middle Ages, see: p*Ta'anit* 1:4 (64: 2); b*Ta'anit* 22a; *Tanḥuma*, ed. Buber, Introduction, no. 51, 68; *Sefer ḥasidim*, no. 80, 53; R. David ha-Adani, *Midrash hagadol* on Deuteronomy, ed. Fish, 314–315; and additional references in *Midrash aseret hadibrot*, ed. Shapira, 69, n. 136. See also comments and references by Ben-Amos, *Mimekor yisrael*, no. 94, 177–178. For a discussion of Ashkenazic parallels, see Alexander, "The Formation of Ḥasidic-Ashkenazic Stories"; Kushelevsky, *Penalty and Temptation*, 161–163. For the figure of a butcher as the companion in paradise in a different version of this tale type, cf. *Ḥibbur yafeh mehayeshu'a*, ed. Hirschberg, no. 15, 48; Brinner, ed., *An Elegant Composition Concerning Relief after Adversity*, no. 15, 81–85.
3. *Midrash aseret hadibrot*, ed. Shapira, 69–72.
4. *Genesis rabbati*, *Vayishlaḥ*, ed. Albeck, 146–147.
5. Cf. p*Pe'ah*, 1:15 (1:5), which expands the biblical analogy in Proverbs (30:17): The raven, who is cruel to his children, will pick out the eyes of the corpse but will not eat from it, while the vulture, who is compassionate toward his fledglings, will have a meal from it.

powerful as [Jacob's] study of Torah,"[6] Jacob feared him and entreated his favor with an offering, on his way with his family to Sukkot (Genesis 33:1–17)

The influence of *Midrash aseret hadibrot* on *Sefer ha-ma'asim* is manifested in an excerpt of the epilogue that does not appear in *Genesis rabbati*, about the three who partake in the creation of a child: the Almighty, the father, and the mother. Owing to this partnership, "He who honors his father and mother is as if he had honored the Almighty."[7] Nonetheless, only parts of the *Midrash aseret hadibrot* epilogue were included in *Sefer ha-ma'asim*. The description of the extinction of the body after death is omitted from *Sefer ha-ma'asim*.[8] The homily on the Fifth Commandment is also shorter in *Sefer ha-ma'asim* than in *Midrash aseret hadibrot*, and a balance is created between the commitment of children to honor their parents and the motif of "A Companion in Paradise." The scribe's creativity is manifested in the combination and integration of the various sources: *Genesis rabbati*, *Midrash aseret hadibrot*, and *Pesikta rabbati*.

Contextualized in the doctrine of reward and punishment, the tale underscores the relativity of the *mitẓvot* within their overall system and the way they balance each other: Torah study and the *mitẓvot* of fringes and phylacteries attributed to R. Joshua b. Elem, compared with Ninus's care and honor for his parents. The butcher's honoring of his parents is contraposed with the Torah learning and deeds of the scholar.[9] The butcher, an ordinary and unlearned man, gains an important place in the Garden of Eden alongside a great Torah scholar. This implies an indirect criticism of the scholar, who assumes that his reward in paradise will be greater than that of the butcher, who engages in such a lowly pursuit,[10] as well as a social criticism of human nature—people's tendency to relate to others based on external features.[11] The Mishnah, tractate *Pe'ah* (1:1), singles out the honoring of parents as one of the commandments that entitles a person to a reward not only in this

6. *Genesis rabbati, Vayishlaḥ*, ed. Albeck, 146.
7. *Midrash aseret hadibrot*, ed., Shapira, 71.
8. Thus, e.g., in *Midrash aseret hadibrot*, ed. Shapira, 71: "After seven days, his abdomen splits open, after twenty the flesh rots, after thirty, his tendons fall apart," etc.
9. Cf. the hierarchy of Torah study and observing the *mitzvot* (ritual and moral deeds, such as wearing the phylacteries and doing charity) in tractate *Baba Kama* 17a and in *Kiddushin* 40b, as well as *Sefer ḥasidim*, no. 767, 193–194. In the present story the scholar studies, teaches, and also observes the commandment of fringes and phylacteries, so the comparison relates to the weight of certain deeds—such as honoring parents—in contrast to other deeds, not to learning versus performing.
10. On the lowly image of the occupation of a butcher, also called a "*tabaḥ*," see *Shabbat* 156a, where the occupation is presented as the sublimation of the inclination to shed blood.
11. See Yassif, *The Hebrew Folktale*, 288–289.

world—as noted explicitly in the Bible, in the Ten Commandments ("Honor your father and mother, that your days may be long" [Exodus 20:12])—but also in the next world. In addition to being promised an honorable place in the next world, the butcher gains much honor in this world when he is visited by the Torah scholar and his entourage.

The sequence of the tale, with "R. Joshua b. Levi and the Angel of Death" (no. 46) preceding it, may be due to the common motif of one's place in paradise or the shared name of the protagonist, "Joshua" (albeit not the same person). In the first, R. Joshua b. Levi wishes to view his place in paradise, and in the latter, R. Joshua b. Elem is told about his companion in paradise, an anonymous butcher who will be seated right next to him. In any case, the concreteness of the other world in medieval cultural consciousness is reflected not only in the narratives of these two tales but also in the way they were inserted into the compilation.

The tradition of the tale in Ashkenaz also continued after the Middle Ages. The influence of *Sefer ha-ma'asim* on the *Mayse bukh* is evident not only from the overall plot of the tale but also from the title given to R. Joshua b. Elem by the elders of the city: "a great and important man" in *Sefer ha-ma'asim* and a "king" in *Mayse bukh.*[12] Story compilations of the nineteenth and twentieth centuries preferred the *Midrash aseret hadibrot* version in general and the title *ḥasid* in particular.[13] The "Companion in Paradise" tale type is also widespread in the oral tradition, as documented in the IFA archives in Haifa and partially published in the IFA series "*Midei hodesh be-ḥodesho*" ("Each and Every Month").

12. *Mayse bukh*, no. 139; *Ma'aseh book*, trans. Gaster, no. 139, 256.

13. Araki, *Sefer hama'asiyot*, no. 39; Elijah Hacohen, *Me'il ẓedakah*, no. 441, ed. Kuperman, part 2, 79; *Mimekor yisrael*, no. 306, 212–213 (without an epilogue).

48. That Which Was Stolen Is Returned by Guile (322b)

"That Which Was Stolen Is Returned by Guile" originated in *Midrash aseret hadibrot*,[1] as is obvious not only from the story itself but also from the epilogue, which explicitly relates to the commandment "Thou shalt not steal." It is one of five tales in *Sefer ha-ma'asim* about regaining stolen or deposited money by means of a trick.[2] Here the trick is in a staged situation that the victim of the theft initiates to get his money back, assuming that the thief's greed will induce him to return the money to its place in hopes of procuring a larger sum instead.[3]

In *Midrash aseret hadibrot* the story is contiguous with "Who Is the Thief?," with which it shares a similar frame story—namely, a judge's dilemma in a complex legal situation and his solution for apprehending the thief. In *Midrash aseret hadibrot*, since there were no witnesses to the theft, the judge decides to elicit the thief's reaction to a fictive juridical dilemma, thereby trapping him with his own words.[4] Similarly, in the present story, the thief falls into the very trap he himself set, and he returns the stolen money to its original hiding place. As in *Midrash aseret hadibrot*, the thief unknowingly gives himself away due to his greed.

In *Sefer ha-ma'asim*, unlike *Midrash aseret hadibrot*, the stories are not contiguous. "Who Is the Thief?" appears in the sequence of the Ten Commandments, while "That Which Was Stolen Is Returned by Guile" is copied separately. The editorial principle underlying the sequence of the tales is not thematic but rather eclectic. Interestingly, after the Middle Ages the two tales were integrated into one narrative in the *Mayse bukh*.[5]

The story is of the tale type Tubach 696, which originated in the East:[6] A monk steals a sum of money that a blind man hid under a chair in the church. The blind man asks his young attendant to lead him to the monk, reveals his hiding place, and says he intends to add more money, doubling the sum, and then donate it for the

1. Ed. Shapira, 84. The story was consistently copied in manuscripts of *Midrash aseret hadibrot* between the fourteenth and seventeenth centuries in Ashkenaz, in Italy and Provence, but not in the Ms. Bodl. Or. 135 version of *Midrash aseret hadibrot*.
2. The four other tales are "Who Is the Thief?" (no. 16), "R. Meir and Kiddor" (no. 26), and "The Pious Pretender" (no. 50), and in a way also "The Loan" (nos. 2, 34).
3. See further discussion in notes to "R. Meir and Kiddor," in this volume.
4. See the Shapira edition, 81–85.
5. *Mayse bukh*, 159b, no. 215; *Ma'aseh book*, trans. Gaster, vol. 2, no. 215, 523–525.
6. See Clouston's references to *A Thousand and One Nights* and to other sources: Clouston, *A Group of Eastern Romances*, 560–561.

redemption of his soul. The monk is afraid he will lose the money and hastens to put it back in place. That is how the blind man gets his money back.[7]

A closely related tale type is Tubach 3355,[8] which was widespread in the East and the West in the Middle Ages: A man refuses to return a deposit, but when he believes he is going to receive an additional, larger deposit, he hastens to return the first one to gain the man's trust.[9]

7. Tubach refers to a fifteenth-century work (see Dunn, ed., *The Facetiae of the Mensa Philosophica*, no. 20.82, 33), and to motif Th. J1141.6. *Sefer ha-ma'asim* documents an earlier appearance of the story in Europe.

8. Cf. ATU 1617; Th. K1667.

9. See the description of the sources and a more detailed discussion of the story "R. Meir and Kiddor" (no. 26) in this volume.

49. Torah Saves from Death (322b–323b)

The motif of postponing death by various means, such as through charity or Torah study, perceived to be the source of life and vitality, is frequently found in the repertoire of Jewish sources and world folklore.[1] Although this particular tale is unknown from earlier sources, it does make use of narrative materials familiar from sources prior to the Middle Ages: "*Reuven halavlar*" ("Reuven the Scribe")[2] and "Matanya"[3] in the *Midrash Tanḥuma*,[4] and "Ben Sever and Shefifon Ben Layish."[5] In the first two, a bride saves her husband from death on their wedding day through her wisdom and devotion.[6] The third is about two Torah scholars, Ben Sever and Shefifon Ben Layish, who both struggle against a death sentence pronounced on one of them. Through their Torah study, they succeed in having it revoked.

"Torah Saves from Death" employs other ready-to-use models as well: the parents' prayers for their son; the poor man who turns up on their son's doorstep when he is in danger, just in time to save him from death, or to the contrary, to cause his death; the Angel of Death and the terror he inflicts on the parents; the negotiations between the Angel of Death and the son, intended to prepare him for his death; and, finally, the quoting of biblical verses as a means of persuading the angel to rescind the order of the son's death. These familiar materials were reworked in new ways that created a particular medieval discourse.

Saul, the son and the protagonist of our tale, is depicted as an ascetic—a sort of saint. From the day of his birth, he has been destined to study Torah. While his father guards the door to protect him from intruders who would interrupt his study, he sits among orphans or beggars and devotes himself to the Torah. At the age of seventy, when he is summoned to surrender his soul to the Angel of Death, he is still unmarried.

1. Cf. ATU 1199: "Prayer without end." This tale type has many parallels in IFA, particularly in the context of prayer and reciting the *Shema* as a means of postponing death.
2. See discussion and list of versions for this tale, as well as "Matanya": Lipsker-Albeck, "Predestined to Die on His Wedding Day," 211–235; references by Ben-Amos, *Mimekor yisrael*, no. 116, 207.
3. *Midrash aseret hadibrot*, ed. Shapira, 206; Gaster, *Exempla*, no. 139, 215.
4. *Tanḥuma, ha'azinu*, no. 8, and see additional references in Ben-Amos, *Mimekor yisrael*, no. 521.
5. Ben-Amos, *Mimekor yisrael*, no. 117, 210; Kushelevsky, *Penalty and Temptation*, 318–319.
6. Cf. ATU 899: "Alcestis"; ATU 934: "Predestined Death."

The son's depiction as an ascetic is evident also in comparison with two other tales in *Sefer ha-ma'asim* that are introduced in a similar fashion but develop differently. The first, "The Power of a Single Act of Charity," is about "a man, among the great men of his generation, who was very rich but childless. After ten years, God gave him a son, and he named him Saul [lit., borrowed]" (324a).[7] Saul grew up as an idler, wild and disobedient, unlike the Saul in the present story, who devotes himself to the Torah and to caring for orphans and the poor. "A Slave for Seven Years," which is the second tale of the two, also commends the ideal of asceticism, albeit from a different aspect. Like the other tale, it opens with an exposition of a father yearning for a son: "Once there was a man who used to ask God for a son. And God gave him a son" (325a–325b).

The story was apparently influenced by saint legends in Europe in the twelfth and thirteenth centuries, as well as by Jewish and intracultural models. During this period popular saints' legends flourished—a tendency the Church preferred to domesticate rather than oppose.[8] Exempla of this sort were told, for example, about Francis of Assisi (1181–1226), who founded the first Mendicant order and helped, in Aviad Kleinberg's words, "to turn popular preaching into a key part of the Church's program of activity, and served as a catalyst for the great awakening of hagiography in the late Middle Ages."[9] Asceticism, the idealization of poverty, and sensitivity to the pauperism and suffering of others characterize him in these exempla. Even if there may not have been any direct influence of a particular story, and although our Jewish tale in *Sefer ha-ma'asim* does not address asceticism as an ideal value, saints' stories probably were a source of inspiration.

7. Cf. 1 Samuel 1:20: "and [Ḥannah] called his name Samuel, saying, Because I have asked him from the Lord."

8. Kleinberg, *Fra Ginepro's Leg of Pork*, 228–254.

9. Ibid., 255. The texts that he cites (268–281) are narratives sent to the monastery authorities about twenty years after St. Francis' death, for the purpose of writing his autobiography.

50. The Pious Pretender (323b–324a)

This is a unique adaptation in Ashkenaz of a tale first mentioned in p*Berachot* 2:3 (4:3), which follows this plot line: A man once deposited something with a friend who later denied he had it. The man said to his friend: I did not believe you but rather that which was on your head. The phylacteries on the head of that man made him appear to be a pious and trustful person, with whom he could safely leave his deposit, but it turned out he was a scoundrel. The tale is told very briefly in the PalestinianTalmud in the context of a *halakhah* that "a clean body is necessary for phylacteries," and as an explanation for wearing them for morning prayers only, rather than throughout the day. This is because "swindlers" may have the appearance of pious men but are secretly sinners.[1]

The story is based on the Talmud, but it was expanded in a number of sources in the rabbinical literature during the Middle Ages.[2] Details of background and setting were added, and the Talmudic plot was expanded: A man wishes to deposit his money with someone he trusts before going on a long voyage. He goes to the synagogue and there finds a man wrapped in a prayer shawl and wearing phylacteries. The man seems reliable, and the traveler deposits his money with him. When he returns from his trip, he asks for his deposit, but the man denies he ever received it. He then prays to God, whose name is engraved on phylacteries, which is what had led him to trust the man with whom he left the deposit. In the man's dream, Elijah instructs him to go to the swindler's wife while he is absent and recover his money. If he mentions certain secret signs known only to her and her husband—namely that at Passover they ate *ḥametz* and on Yom Kippur they did not fast—she will be trapped and return his deposit to him. He does as he was instructed, and indeed convinces her. After she and her husband are exposed, they openly abandon their Jewish religion. In this expanded version, which appears in the twelfth-century work of Ibn Sahula, *Fables*

1. See p*Berakhot* 2:3 (4:3) and cf. "Elisha, Man of Wings," in *Shabbat* 49a and 130a, for a similar context. In times of danger, his phylacteries miraculously turn into the wings of a dove.
2. See sources quoting the Palestinian Talmud and others that expand the plot: *Pesikta rabbati*, ed. Ish Shalom, ch. 22, 111b, on the commandment "Thou shall not steal"; *Midrash aggadah*, ed. Buber, *Yitro*, no. 20, 152–153; *Ḥibbur yafeh mehayeshu'a*, ed. Hirschberg, no. 22, 60–81; *Ḥibbur yafeh mehayeshu'a*, ed. Brinner, no. 22, 103–107; Tosafot on *Shabbat* 49a (in the context of "Elisha, Man of Wings"); R. Isaac ben Aba Mari, *Sefer ha'itur, hilkhot tefillin*, 60; Ibn Sahula, *Fables from the Distant Past*, part 4, "On Humility," vol. 2, 520–532; Refael-Vivante, "*Ma'aseh beḥenef* (A Tale of a Hypocrite)," 338–341; R. Isaac b. Moses, *Or zaru'a*, 1, *hilkhot tefillin*, no. 531, 149 (copied also in *Sefer halekutim*, ed. Grünhut, 120); R. Shimshon b. Ẓadok, *Tashbeẓ*, no. 371, 30, 59; Hameiri, *Bet habeḥira al masekhet Shabbat*, ch. 4, 180–181; R. David ha-Adni, *Midrash hagadol* on Exodus, ed. Margulies, 410; Gaster, *Exempla*, no. 123, 83.

from the Distant Past, the deposit in the hands of the man who turns out to be a pious pretender and the trick employed to get the money are at the center of the story, and the motif of phylacteries, which is the reason the tale was included in the Palestinian Talmud, is missing. This expanded tale is one more of the frequent deposit tales in medieval Jewish and non-Jewish folklore (ATU 1617 and Tubach 4969).[3]

In *Sefer ha-ma'asim* this narrative changes greatly and in fact is turned completely on its head. A *ḥasid* denies that he received a deposit, not because he is a cheat and a pious pretender but because the owner of the money misidentified him. Instead of a pious pretender wrapped in a prayer shawl and wearing phylacteries, the story depicts an authentic *ḥasid*, "who [always sat] in the same place [in the synagogue] and never changed places." This greatly changes the story, and it is based, as Elisheva Baumgarten has shown, on pietistic norms at the time of *Sefer ha-ma'asim* and on attitudes toward pretenders of piety as a symptom of religious devoutness.[4] A recommendation to retain a permanent seat in the synagogue already exists in the Babylonian Talmud (*Berakhot* 6b), and in *Sefer ha-ma'asim* it is linked to other pietistic norms relating to prayer, which are also mentioned and recommended in *Sefer ḥasidim*: praying at length, coming early to the synagogue, and leaving late. At the same time, *Sefer ḥasidim* warns against religious hypocrisy, which may go hand in hand with the strict practice of piety that goes beyond the normative *halakhah*.[5]

Norms of Ashkenazic piety are also expressed in the *ḥasid*'s readiness to overlook the insult and not be offended. The narrative attests to his outstanding virtue: "I can see that you are humble." Among the local people he is also known as a righteous man in the self-restraint he displays when he is publicly humiliated and led through the city streets with a rope around his neck. This allusion to the Book of Esther intensifies the impression made by his humiliation and his heroic self-restraint. The owner of the deposit calls out: "Thus shall be done to he who takes a deposit and denies having done so," in an analogy to "Thus shall it be done to the man whom the king delights to honor" (Esther 7:9). The relatively frequent use of words from the semantic field of "shame" and "embarrassment" creates a similar discourse on self-restraint in the face of an offense. The demand to show forbearance in the face

3. On the deposit motif, see Marzolph, "Kredit erschwindelt," *EM* 8 (1996): 375–380.

4. Baumgarten, *Practicing Piety*, 195–202. (See also, "Pious Pretenders," 74–76, and the story in the appendix, 89–90 [Hebrew].)

5. See in *Sefer ḥasidim* the typological figure of the hypocrite, "who sits at a podium in the synagogue . . . and behaves as if he is a *ḥasid*, while he is totally evil and impious" (ed. Wistinetzke, no. 404, 121, and in *Sefer ḥasidim*, ed. Margulies, no. 771).

of an insult is one of the marked traits of the Pietist, and this is underscored in *Sefer ḥasidim* by reference to the pietistic practice of wearing *ẓiẓit* (fringes) and phylacteries all day long rather than only at set times.[6] *Sefer ḥasidim* calls on the pietist to show restraint when he is insulted and mocked by society because of this practice, which emphasizes his otherness. The words "*bushah*" (shame) and "*ḥerpah*" (disgrace) appear frequently in *Sefer ḥasidim* in this ideological context.

In the second part of the tale, the *ḥasid*'s friends give him gifts to compensate him for the offense he suffered, and one of them, when asked to identify his gift in public, is ashamed because it is so meager: a fish wrapped in a napkin. "The one who brought the fish was embarrassed and said: Perhaps he wishes to shame me because my gift is too small." Later it turns out that the gift is far more valuable, because the napkin contains golden dinars. The *ḥasid*, who practices self-restraint when he is mocked or insulted and has the ability to cope with shame, meets a test, which is of paramount importance in Ashkenazic pietism. It is manifested in all walks of daily life and is perceived as analogous to the unique test of death in sanctification of the Holy Name. In "The Pious Pretender" the *ḥasid* proves that he is capable of enduring an insult with self-restraint and accepting his humiliation with love. In contrast to the hypocrite who exposes his (false) piety, the *ḥasid* in *Sefer ha-ma'asim* is self-effacing. The antithesis, in earlier versions of the story, between an external image and an inner identity is turned upside-down in *Sefer ha-ma'asim*.

After "The Pious Pretender" first appeared in the thirteenth century, it was included in additional later compilations in Ashkenaz. The time gap between its appearances in the thirteenth century and in later manuscripts is significant, but since the story is unknown from sources predating *Sefer ha-ma'asim*, it is reasonable to assume that it was transmitted in a consecutive manner, and that *Sefer ha-ma'asim* continued to exert influence even after its time. It appears again in a fifteenth-century collection of Hebrew tales apparently from Italy, written in Sephardic script and titled in the manuscript (JTS 2374), "Tales of *Ḥasidim*."[7] It is also documented in the tale collection partially published by Brüll in 1889,[8] and recently by Yassif (Ms. Jerusalem 3182, 129b–130a).[9] In these versions the hero is depicted not only as a *ḥasid* but also as a *hakham* (a scholar), an addition that somewhat glosses over the focus on

6. See *Sefer ḥasidim*, ed. Wistinetzke, nos. 976, 986, and 1589.

7. 121b–122a and 111a–124b.

8. N. Brüll, "Beiträge zur jüdischen Sagen- und Spruchkunde im Mittelalter," *Jahrbücher für jüdische Geschichte und litteratur* 9 (1889): 1–71.

9. Yassif, *Ninety-nine Tales*, no. 74, 240–241, and discussion on 60–61.

his piety in *Sefer ha-ma'asim*. The story was not included in *Mayse bukh*, although Ms. Jerusalem 3182 was one of its sources.

A later adaptation of the tale appears in a book by Ẓvi Hirsch Kaidanover, *Kav hayeshar*, about a person named Alexander in a "Jewish community in a city of the Ishmaelites";[10] and it is quoted in nineteenth-century story collections: Araki's *Sefer hama'asiyot*,[11] and *Oseh pele* (Joseph Shabbtai Farḥi).[12] Twentieth-century versions in literary story collections return to the talmudic version: *Mimekor yisrael*, no. 338 (in three versions); *Sefer eliyahu hanavi* by Judah Rosenberg;[13] and *Sefer hama'asiyot* by Mordekhai ben Yeḥezkel.[14] The exceptional adaptation of the tale in *Sefer ha-ma'asim* was apparently received in Ashkenaz only.

10. *Kav hayashar*, ch. 52, 160–162.

11. Araki, no. 105, 112a–112b, and in Ḥuẓin's edition, no. 105, 74b–75a.

12. Farḥi, *Oseh pele*, part 3, 36–37.

13. Rosenberg, *Sefer eliyahu hanavi*, 33–34.

14. Ben Yeḥezkel, *Sefer hama'asiyot*, vol. 6, 69–71.

51. The Power of a Single Act of Charity (324a–325a)

In several Jewish sources, the tale type ATU 809* ("Rich Man Allowed to Stay in Heaven for a Single Act of Charity") takes the plot line of an ordinary man or even a sinner who earns his place in the next world thanks to a single deed of devotion, weighed against an entire lifetime.[1] The story also relates to the tale type "A Companion in Paradise," according to which an ordinary person gains a worthy place in paradise next to a highly esteemed righteous man thanks to a single remarkable act.[2] It opens with a familiar format in *Sefer ha-ma'asim* about a childless father who is finally blessed with a son; it particularly resembles "Torah Saves from Death" (no. 49), which is also about a "Shaul" (Saul; lit., "borrowed," in Hebrew), who was "borrowed" from God. Its biblical model is the scene of Ḥannah's prayer in 1 Samuel (1:20): "and called his name Samuel, saying, because I have asked him from the Lord."

Unlike the use of familiar materials in the exposition, the motif of "saved from the gallows," which comes up further on, is atypical of Jewish narratives up to the Middle Ages[3] and may have been borrowed from Christian exempla. While I have not found a concrete parallel to the tale, the many references in Tubach to the "gallows" motif in Christian exempla seem to support this hypothesis.[4]

The story was recopied with certain stylistic variations in Ms. Jerusalem 3182 (131a–131b),[5] which demonstrates the influence of *Sefer ha-ma'asim*. A late Ḥasidic tale, which may be an adaptation of the *Sefer ha-ma'asim* narrative or an independent parallel, is in *Sippurei ẓadikim heḥadash* by Abraham Isaac Sobelman.[6] In it a

1. Three talmudic stories of this type appear in tractate *Avodah Zara*: 10b, 17a, 18a. For a discussion and parallels in *ḥasidic* literature, see Elstein, "Morphology and Symbolism in Ḥasidic Tales Based on the Theme 'A single act can save one's soul.'"
2. ATU 809*-*A (IFA): "A Companion in Paradise." Cf. *Sefer ha-ma'asim*, "R. Joshua b. Elem and Ninus the Butcher" (no. 47).
3 The motif does appear in Farḥi, *Oseh pele*, from the nineteenth century: "A Tale about the Man Saved from Death by Hanging" (part 2, 128–133).
4 See "gallows" entry in the Tubach index, on a doomed man's rescue from hanging by a saint, but not in the context of an attempted suicide. Cf. a tale of a son who offered to be hanged in place of his father to save his father's life; St. James interceded and saved the man instead (Caesarii Heisterbacensis, *Dialogus Miraculorum*, vol. 2, 8.58, 130–131; Caesarius of Heisterbach, *The Dialogue on Miracles*, vol. 2, book 8, chap. 58, 60–61). See also Yassif's reference to a partial Jewish parallel in *Sefer ma'aseh nisim* by Josepha ha-shamash, no. 5 (*Ninety-nine Tales*, 285).
5. Yassif, *Ninety-nine Tales*, 243–245, no. 77.
6. Sobelman, *Sippurei ẓaddikim heḥadash*, no. 20, 37–38. I am grateful to Chana Hendler for drawing my attention to this reference.

carter, who represents the simple man, tells R. Aaron of Karlin that he has earned a room for himself in the Garden of Eden by saving a man from hanging. As a consequence R. Aaron of Karlin now understands the talmudic saying that he had struggled with, that "one can earn his world in a single moment."[7] Although these two parallels appear in Ms. Jerusalem and in Sobelman's Ḥasidic compilation, the tale, which is quite idiosyncratic, was not received within the Jewish narrative tradition, and the talmudic models were preferred.

7. *Avodah Zara*, 10b.

52. A Slave for Seven Years (325a–325b)

As far as we know, the first written version of the tale is this one in *Sefer ha-ma'asim*, in northern France. Throughout the Middle Ages, up to the printed edition of the *Mayse bukh* in the early seventeenth century,[1] it was copied in a number of manuscripts of *Midrash aseret hadibrot*, particularly in Ashkenaz, with hardly any changes.[2] In these manuscripts the story illustrates the Seventh Commandment, "Thou shalt not commit adultery," and consequently an expanded epilogue was added to praise the wife's loyalty to her husband. Besides *Midrash aseret hadibrot*, the story appears in two other tale collections from the fourteenth and fifteenth centuries: in *Ma'asim shel ḥasidim* in Ms. JTS 2374 (120a–121a) and in Ms. Jerusalem 3182.[3] In the modern era, the nineteenth and twentieth centuries, it was included in rabbinical anthologies and in literary collections.[4]

"A Slave for Seven Years" employs well-known models, Jewish and Christian. The young man is abducted by Elijah and sold as a slave because he has neglected his Torah studies and was "sporting with his wife," an expression that refers to love games and courting. Five years later, he happens to meet her while traveling to her town with his master, and she introduces herself to him as his wife. Though they are anxious to unite, he asks for her permission to complete his term of slavery for an additional two years, after which Elijah carries him on his wings to his wife. The implied model he should emulate is that of Elijah, who plowed to support himself and his family while perusing the book that lay on his plow.

The most distinctive source relating to the conflict in this story—between love of a woman and love of God—is in tractate *Ketubot* (61b–63a),[5] which illustrates how difficult it is for a man to observe the commandment, "Meditate on it [Torah] day and night" (Joshua 1:8), while at the same time fulfilling his duties toward his

1. *Mayse bukh*, no. 216; *Ma'aseh Book*, trans. Gaster, 2, 528–533.
2. *Midrash aseret hadibrot* in the following manuscripts: Ms. Wolfenbuttel 36.25, 19–20; Ms. Vatican 107, 175a–176a; Ms. Parma 2269 (De Rossi 473), 76a–77a; Ms. Moscow Günsburg 111, 123a–124a; Ms. Bodl. 268 Opp. 27, 242a–242b.
3. Yassif, *Ninety-nine Tales*, no. 73, 238–240, and notes, 284.
4. See, in chronological order: Jellinek, *Bet hamidrasch*, vol. 1, section 1, 84–86; Grünwald, *Yalkut sippurim*, 1, 23–24; Rosenberg, *Sefer eliyahu hanavi*, 41–44; Eisenstein, *Oẓar midrashim*, 2, 458–459; Gaster, *Exempla*, no. 327, 118; Gaster, *Ma'aseh Book*, vol. 2, 528–533; *Mimekor yisrael*, no. 714, 341–344. See also Ben-Amos's references in *Mimekor yisrael*, no. 196, 357. Ben-Amos views this story as a parallel to "The Seven Good Years" (no. 29 in *Sefer ha-ma'asim*), and accordingly assigns it to tale type AT938B: "Better in Youth." See my suggestion for a different typology in the discussion that follows.
5. Cf. another version in tractate *Nedarim* 50a.

wife (satisfying her physical and emotional needs: "her food, her garment, and her duty of marriage" [Exodus 21:10]).[6] The well-known story of R. Akiva's initiation as a Torah scholar, cited in tractate *Ketubot* (62b–63a), introduces him as an unschooled shepherd whom his master's wealthy daughter (or granddaughter) wishes to marry, realizing that he is most "modest and noble." She marries him in spite of her father's objection and sends him far away to the house of study. He is absent from home for twenty-four years, first returning after twelve years to obtain his wife's permission to part for another period of learning. Even before entering the house, he hears his wife from behind the door expressing her wish that he further devote himself to Torah study, even for another twelve years. He then leaves home, returning to her after twelve additional years as a great Torah scholar. Upon his return he dedicates his Torah to his wife, declaring to his twenty-five thousand disciples that "mine and yours are hers."[7]

The following aspects are common to the talmudic story and the medieval tale of "A Slave for Seven Years": the husband's return home at an interim stage and consequently two separation periods; the wife's permission as a precondition for her husband's absence from home; and, finally, the ideal of love of God, which in the Talmud is manifested in Torah study and realized.

However, the points of departure in both narratives are very different, even conflicting. In the Talmud men are called on to keep in touch with their wives during their absence;[8] R. Akiva's achievements in learning are attributed to his wife; and his identity as a Torah scholar is realized on his return home with his disciples—aspects that imply the narrator's esteem for the institution of marriage despite long but temporary periods of abstinence. In contrast, "A Slave for Seven Years" implies an objection to marriage as a cause of temptation and distraction, an objection that is tempered only at the end of the story, when the young man returns to his wife. It would seem that the talmudic story is not the only model for "A Slave for Seven Years." The Christian legend of St. Alexis, which was extremely widespread in Western Europe in the Middle Ages in Latin and in various vernaculars, apparently functioned as an additional and salient model for "A Slave for Seven Years."[9] An

6. On the conflict underpinning the story and the entire issue in *Ketubot*, see Boyarin, *Carnal Israel*, 134–166; Valler, *Women and Womanhood*, 56–80. Valler emphasizes the emotional aspect in the talmudic stories, beyond the gratification of the woman's physical needs.

7. *Ketubot* 63a.

8. This is deduced from the story's context in the Talmud.

9. I elaborate this idea in Kushelevsky, "Abstinence in Medieval Northern France."

anonymous Latin version in the *Acta Sanctorum*[10] is as follows: Alexis is born to rich, until then childless, parents, in answer to their prayers for an heir, and as a reward for their piety and charitable deeds toward the poor and the needy. After his birth, his parents decide to embark on a life of abstinence and purity. They appoint the best teachers to instruct him in the sacraments of the church and other intellectual and spiritual studies. When he has reached the appropriate age, they choose a worthy wife for him from the emperor's family, and marry them in a splendid church ceremony. When night falls, the father encourages his son to approach his wife, who is waiting on an ornately decorated marriage bed. When the couple is alone, Alexis lectures his bride on the principles of religion, gives her the buckle of his belt, and leaves her for a life of abstinence. He goes to the port, boards a ship, and travels to Laodicea, and from there to Edessa in Syria, where he visits the church of St. Mary. He distributes his belongings to the poor and, dressed in rags, settles among them in the churchyard. In Rome, when his father learns that he has left, he sends his servants to search for him, but when they arrive in Edessa, they do not recognize him.

Throughout those years of his absence, his wife remains in his mother's home, and they both mourn him, the son and the husband. For seventeen years Alexis huddles with the poverty-stricken and beggars in the courtyard of the church, until the Virgin Mary recognizes him as a saint and orders him brought into the church. But Alexis spurns all expressions of admiration and embarks on a sea journey for another destination. Due to a storm he ends up in Rome, the city of his parents. Assuming that his parents would not recognize him, and to avoid becoming a burden to strangers, he returns home, where he lives, unrecognized, for another seventeen years under his parents' staircase, wretched and humiliated. After his death his memoirs, written in his handwriting on a parchment, are found. His parents are racked by grief, shock, and frustration. Alexis is declared a saint and buried in the Boniface church.

Several motifs are common to "A Slave for Seven Years" and "The Life of St. Alexis": a childless father given a son thanks to his piety, based on a well-known topos in *Sefer ha-ma'asim* and in contemporary Christian literature;[11] the son's devotion to spiritual studies; the wedding ceremony as a juncture that leads to a life of abstinence (whether by coercion and later willingly, as in *Sefer ha-ma'asim*, or

10. *Acta Sanctorum*, Julii, v. IV, 251–253, cited by Carl J. Odenkirchen (*The Life of St. Alexius*, 34–51), along with an English translation.

11. "Torah Saves from Death" (no. 49) in *Sefer ha-ma'asim*, and in *The Life of St. Alexis*, (Odenkirchen, *The Life of St. Alexius*, 65).

by choice, as in *The Life of St. Alexis*); two periods of the husband's absence from home; charitable deeds; and, centrally, abstinence. There are obvious differences between the perceptions of abstinence in the two stories. In "A Slave for Seven Years," abstinence is a means of achieving a balance between married life and Torah study, while in *The Life of St. Alexis* it is a preferred ideal. In the former it is only an interim stage, while in the Christian legend Alexis dies in his home as an ascetic saint and is united with his wife only in paradise, after their deaths (according to certain parallels). Only after his death does his identity become known to his wife and parents. Despite the disparate trends, in both stories a life of abstinence is assigned a positive value, unlike the case in the talmudic story about R. Akiva and his wife.[12]

The Life of St. Alexis appears in Old French versions from the twelfth and thirteenth centuries that share a trend to describe the emotional aspects in the parting scene between Alexis and his bride, the erotic implications and intensification of the conflict in Alexis between sexual passion and love of God, alongside the Latin versions. "A Slave for Seven Years" in *Sefer ha-ma'asim* was probably modeled mainly after the French versions, which are at times more emotional. Alexis's separation from his bride is charged with emotional and erotic tension, which intensifies his conflict, in marked contrast to the matter-of-fact report about his departure in the Latin versions.[13] In the parallel scene in *Sefer ha-ma'asim*, "the young man began weeping and lamenting" over this anticipated separation from his wife for seven years of slavery. And when they meet five years later, "she stood and embraced and kissed him," and so it was when they parted for another two years. The affinity with French versions of *The Life of St. Alexis*, in contrast to the Latin source, is also expressed in the motif of the bride's agreement to her husband's life of abstinence, which does not exist in *The Golden Legend*[14] but does in "A Slave for Seven Years": "She neither shouted nor screamed, but only gave thanks to the Almighty."[15] "A Slave

12. A similar version appears in Jacobus de Voragine, *The Golden Legend* (v. 1, no. 94, 371–374).

13. Odenkirchen, *The Life of St. Alexius*, 31, 68, 96, L. 56–60, and his translation on 97; Stebbins, *A Critical Edition of the 13th and 14th Centuries Old French Poem Versions of the "Vie de Saint Alexis,"* 72–80; Stebbins, 28–31, stanzas VIII, IX, X, in the Ms. Paris version, in contrast to the Latin version quoted in Stebbins, 37; Campbell, "Clerks and Laity," 215–219. I am grateful to Tovi Bibring for translating lengthy sections of the parallels in Old French for me.

14. See Kleinberg's reference to the vernacular textual tradition, *Li roumans de saint Alessin*, in *Fra Ginepro's Leg of Pork*, 419.

15. The wife's consent to her husband's departure is a key motif in the aforementioned talmudic story, in *Ketubot*; it is common to all the stories discussed here: "R. Akiva and His Wife," "A Slave for Seven Years," and *The Life of St. Alexis*.

for Seven Years" seems to be firmly rooted in medieval northern France, where it was created, despite its affinities with the talmudic source and its support of marriage, in contrast to the Alexis legend. The scribe or narrator created a narrative analogical to the Christian legend, while using the talmudic model of "R. Akiva and His Wife," which was accessible to him.

"A Slave for Seven Years" also contains an episode that is analogous to "The Defamed Woman" (no. 24). In both narratives the unification of the couple is made possible by means of a ruse perpetrated by the wife. Over time she becomes well known as a healer or a trader, which causes her husband to seek her assistance, among all the others who turn to her for advice. In "A Slave for Seven Years," based on the biblical story of Joseph and his brothers in Egypt (Genesis 41:46, 41:7), she foresees a time of famine in the world and plants a field of wheat in preparation for that time; among those who come to her to trade money for wheat are her husband and his master. She reveals herself to her husband, but they separate once again for two more years of slavery, before finally reuniting for good. A similar reunion occurs in "The Defamed Woman," in which the female figure becomes famous as a healer, which sets the circumstances for her reunion with her husband. Motifs and narrative functions that were ready at hand were reworked.

53. One Man in a Thousand Have I Found (325b–326b)

This is one of two contiguous stories in *Sefer ha-ma'asim* about Solomon as a king and a judge, and it comes immediately before "The Hard-Boiled Egg."[1] In a misogynistic tone, the tale intends to "prove" to the Sanhedrin the treacherous nature of all women. In Ecclesiastes, a book attributed to Solomon, he states: "One man in a thousand have I found, but a woman among all these I did not find" (7:28). He then puts his claim to the test. Thus an epigrammatic verse is expanded into a story, on the basis of the opposition between the genders that it contains.[2]

The tale first appears in writing in *Ḥibbur yafeh mehayeshu'a* by Nissim of Kairouan, in the eleventh century.[3] Another version, from a different tradition of the tale, is cited in *The Book of Delight* by Joseph b. Meir Ibn Zabara in Spain, in the twelfth century.[4] There, the king is "one of the kings of Arabia" and not Solomon. In a way, it may be assigned to tale type ATU 612, which originated in Indian literature, although the plot differs.[5] In both parallels, the Jewish and the Indian, the test of loyalty is administered in identical conditions, but only the male passes it successfully, unlike his treacherous wife.[6]

It is not clear how the story came into Ashkenaz. *Sefer ha-ma'asim* represents a third branch of the tale's tradition, besides *Ḥibbur yafeh mehayeshu'a* and *The Book of Delight*. It is similar in its details to *Ḥibbur yafeh mehayeshu'a* (for example, the king there is Solomon), but very different in style.[7] Apparently it was

1. There are additional tales in the compilation about King Solomon. These are "Who Is the Thief?" (no. 16), "Solomon's Scribes" (no. 42), "A Meal of Herbs" (no. 62), "The War of Jacob and His Sons with Nineveh" (no. 68).
2. On the affinity between proverbs and tales that embody them, see Hasan-Rokem, *Proverbs in Israeli Folk Narratives*. For other tales based on this proverbial verse, see Noy, *The Beautiful Maiden and the Three Princes*, 217, and comparative notes; Schwarzbaum, *Studies in Jewish and World Folklore*, 112–113, no. 33; Ben-Amos, *Mimekor yisrael*, no. 34, 59–60. For a discussion of the misogynistic nature of the story, see Yassif, *Ninety-nine Tales*, 282.
3. *Ḥibbur yafeh mehayeshu'a*, ed. Hirschberg, no. 12, 30–33; Brinner ed., *An Elegant Composition Concerning Relief after Adversity*, no. 12, 54–57.
4. Zabara, *The Book of Delight*, trans. Hadas, 61–66. Another difference is that in *The Book of Delight* the man does not wake up when the woman tries to murder him, and she informs King Solomon that the dagger was defective. See a comparison of the two versions in Yassif, *Kemargalit bemishbeẓet*, 245.
5. "The Three Snake-Leaves," reference in Yassif, *Kemargalit bemishbeẓet*, 244, n. 19.
6. See assignment of the story to the tale type ATU 1384: "The husband hunts three persons as stupid as his wife."
7. See in *Ḥibbur yafeh mehayeshu'a*, Ms. Vatican 107, 183b–184b; *Ḥibbur yafeh mehayeshu'a*, ed. Hirschberg, no. 12, 30–33; Brinner, ed. *An Elegant Composition Concerning Relief after*

not *Ḥibbur yafeh mehayeshu'a* that mediated the transmission of the tale to the West.

Additional versions of the *Sefer ha-ma'asim* type are from the fifteenth and sixteenth centuries in Ashkenaz and Italy.[8] In the late fifteenth century, it was received into *Meshalim shel Shelomo hamelekh*, with slight changes.[9] *Meshalim shel Shelomo hamelekh* had a decisive influence on the reception of the story from the late Middle Ages and thereafter.[10]

Adversity, 54–57; Ms. Warsaw, 281, 36a–37a; Ms. London, British Museum Or. 10851 (Gaster 942), 5b, as well as in Araki, *Sefer hama'asiyot*, no. 61, 51b–53a; and Ḥuzin's edition, no. 61, 37a–38a.

8. See in Ms. JTS 2374, 112a–113b; Ms. Jerusalem 3182, 124b–125a; Yassif, *Ninety-nine Tales*, no. 65, 228–229, and 146–149; Ben-Amos, *Mimekor yisrael*, no. 33, 57–60.

9. See *Meshalim shel Shelomo hamelekh* (11–12) and in Jellinek, *Bet hamidrasch*, 2, section 4, 146–148; for the dating of *Meshalim shel Shelomo hamelekh* to the late fifteenth century, see Yassif, *Kemargalit bemishbeẓet*, 237–240.

10. See the *Meshalim shel Shelomo hamelekh* version in manuscripts and print: Ms. Paris Heb. 675, 16b–21b; London Jews' College 35, 66b–69a; Farḥi, *Oseh pele*, 1, 42–44; Jellinek, *Bet hamidrasch*, n. 9, above; Grünwald, *Yalkut sippurim*, vol. 1, part 2, 51–52; Eisenstein, *Oẓar midrashim*, 2, 531–532; *Mimekor yisrael*, no. 76, 68–69. Adaptations relying on the *Meshalim shel Shelomo hamelekh* version are Jacob ben Isaac, *Ẓe'enah ur'enah*, Ruth, 11a–b; Levner, *Kol agadot yisrael*, vol. 1, part 3, no. 344, 335–339; Ginzberg, *Legends of the Jews*, vol. 4, 135–136; literary adaptations by Bin Gorion (Berdyczewski) in *Ẓefunot ve'agadot*, 113; Bialik, "Uzziel and Hannah," in *And It Came to Pass*, 134–141.

54. The Hard-Boiled Egg (326b–327a)

This story was inserted into *Sefer ha-ma'asim* immediately after "One Man in a Thousand Have I Found," probably because King Solomon appears in both of them. The source and place of the story are not clear. It first appeared in writing in *Sefer ha-ma'asim*, and since no parallel exists in known Jewish sources, it is reasonable to assume that it has a European source, no later than the thirteenth century. Folklorists tend to regard the Jewish story as a source of non-Jewish parallels, without citing a specific reference.[1] However, by the same token it is possible that the tale type preserves a non-Jewish source in Europe that also served as a basis for the story in *Sefer ha-ma'asim.*

The attribution of "The Hard-Boiled Egg" to the Middle Ages is also supported by certain narrative details, besides its inclusion in *Sefer ha-ma'asim* of the thirteenth century. Michal Tadjar points out that Solomon's judgment in the story is consistent with the trial system in the Middle Ages at that time: The contract between the lender and the borrower was worded as a commercial agreement in every detail, in contrast to religious trials. The economic activity of lending against interest, which is the background for the conflict in the story, was widespread then among Jews in Europe. From the legal and social aspects, King Solomon was protecting the hungry worker employed by King David, his father, against exploitation by those of a higher economic position.[2] From this perspective, the story is of tale type "The Clever Judge" (ATU 926A), and it is affiliated in particular with a cluster of tales about a young judge who succeeds where his elders failed, thanks to his ability to come up with creative solutions. Solomon takes to an extreme the claim of the plaintiff that he should receive imaginary profits from the loan of a hard-boiled egg. Another tale of this type is "The Jars of Honey," about the young David, who succeeds where King Saul failed.[3]

1. See this attribution to the Jewish story in ATU 821B: "Chickens from Boiled Eggs"; 920A: "The Case of the Boiled Eggs." I would like to note that the reference in these entries to a parallel in Pauli's fifteenth-century work, *Schimpf und Ernst*, vol. 2, no. 807, is mistaken (based on a clarification with Uther).
2. Tadjar, "'And One of Them was Extremely Hungry,'" 164, n. 3.
3. Hendler, "The Jars of Honey," 301.

After *Sefer ha-ma'asim*, and probably under its indirect influence, the story was documented in additional story collections.[4] There is a twentieth-century literary adaptation in Bialik's *And It Came to Pass.*[5] Among Jewish ethnic communities, the story was transmitted orally, and this is documented in IFA.[6]

4. Ms. JTS 2374, 113b–114a. In this compilation, too, as in *Sefer ha-ma'asim*, the story is adjacent to "One Man in a Thousand Have I Found"; Ms. Jerusalem 3182, 117b (Yassif, *Ninety-nine Tales*, no. 3, 211–212, and his notes on 278).

5. See Bialik, "The Egg," in *And It Came to Pass*, 65–68. For additional reference, see Ben-Amos, *Mimekor yisrael*, no. 21, 33, and the tale on 33–34.

6. See IFA 32, 7649, 10572, 13417, 23484. See references and discussion by Alexander-Frizer, *The Beloved Friend-and-a-Half*, 342.

55. The Poor Bachelor and His Maiden Cousin (327a–329a)

The story is not known from previous sources; it first appeared in *Sefer ha-ma'asim.*[1] In part it fits the tale type "Suitors' Contest Over the Hand of the Young Girl," which was extant in Western Europe both among Jewish[2] and Christian audiences or readerships.[3] According to this type, the parents deliberate over two prospective husbands for their daughter and prefer the poor man, who has a higher status (in the Jewish context in Ashkenaz, a Torah scholar) than the rich man does. To win the girl the suitors must prove why each is preferable to the other. In the present story Isaac, the poor nephew of the girl's father, is the father's choice because he is a Torah scholar and a man of virtue, while the mother's nephew, an ignorant but apparently practical and rich man, is the mother's preference. The parents agree to a competition between the two young men. Whoever succeeds in his commercial activities and returns with a bountiful profit will win their daughter. After various adventures and experiences, Isaac returns to his city as the ruler and arrives at the marriage ceremony moments before the girl was about to marry his rival.

The plot line of the suitors' competition for the girl's hand is combined with a love story between the poor young man and his rich cousin, as well as with the motif of a quest, which is typical of the romance and entails a process of the development of self-awareness and the overcoming of obstacles. The young Isaac experiences the torments of forbidden love and passion, grapples with the hardships on his way, and gradually wrests free from his dependence on his rabbi and his mother until he gains the girl he loves and marries her.[4] The story has a distinct affinity with *Tristan and Iseult*, one of the most popular romances in the Middle Ages, and

1. The opening of the story with the marriage of a poor nephew to his rich cousin is in the print edition of *Tanḥuma* but not the story as a whole. See *Tanḥuma, ha'azinu*, no. 8 (a later addition by scribes), where the marriage is the result of economic distress.
2. See an exposition of this tale type in "Ukva" (no. 15) and the discussion therein: Kushelevsky, *Penalty and Temptation*, 148–149. See also the discussion of Sara Tsfatman in *Megilat Ahimatz* and in a parallel tale in *Mayse bukh*: *The Jewish Tale in the Middle Ages*: *Between Ashkenaz and Sefarad*, 7–80.
3. See *La Tabula Exemplorum Secundum*, no. 161, 45, based on the reference in Tubach 1444 ("Daughter married to poor man"). Cf. also tale type ATU 1688A ("The envious suitors"), about a poor suitor who wins out over his rich competitor and gets the woman. The tale type of a competition between prospective grooms is also anchored in courtly literature; on this matter see my comments on "Ukva" (no. 61).
4. The process of the protagonist's maturing, which epitomizes the motif of the quest, is particularly emphasized by the structure of the story—i.e., the precedence of the love story to the suitors' contest. After the young man experiences passions and emotions that he had not previously known, he is ready to struggle in the competition over his right to marry the girl.

in particular to Béroul's twelfth-century version in Old French: *The Romance of Tristan*.[5]

According to Béroul's version, King Mark discovers his wife, Iseult, with his nephew Tristan inside the forest, sleeping side by side with a sword between them. He had been suspicious of them for some time, but since they are fully dressed and separated by Tristan's sword, he decides that Iseult is faithful to him. He removes her ring, his gift to her, from her hand and places his own ring on her finger. He places his gloves over her face to protect her from the glaring sunlight, and goes on his way. When they awake and discover that the king had been there, Tristan expresses his distrust of the king's intentions. He is sure the king will return and kill them, so they flee.[6]

As discussed in Part I (chapter 3, pp. 73–74), there are clear parallels between this scene in Béroul's *The Romance of Tristan* and the Jewish tale in *Sefer ha-ma'asim*. The most striking is the sword between the sleeping lovers as a sign of their innocence.[7] The reaction of the uncle, who in the *Tristan and Iseult* narrative is also Iseult's husband, is analogous to that of the uncle in this story. He leaves an item of his clothing with the sleeping couple—a robe in the Jewish story and gloves in Béroul's French parallel—as a sign that he had visited them while they slept. In the Jewish story the uncle was in favor of the marriage between the two from the start. In the French romance, King Mark concludes that Tristan and Iseult are innocent. Additional parallel motifs are: (1) the cast of characters (the uncle, his beloved nephew, and the desired maiden);[8] (2) the disparities in status between the lovers (the son of a poor man and the daughter of a wealthy man in *Sefer ha-ma'asim*; a knight and a lady married to the lord in *Tristan and Iseult*); (3) forbidden passion and the intervention of authority figures (the figure of the rabbi in "The Poor Bachelor and His Maiden Cousin" and, in the French romance, Iseult's mother, who prepares a love potion for her daughter and unwittingly impairs the relations between the king and his wife); (4) the city of lepers in the Jewish story and the

5. At more length, see Kushelevsky, "Chastity versus Courtly Love." The earliest extant versions of *Tristan and Iseult* are from the twelfth century in Old French: one of Béroul (*The Romance of Tristan*), and the other of Thomas, "Le Roman de Tristan." For the time of the Béroul's work, see *The Romance of Tristan*, ix.

6. See, in Béroul's version, *The Romance of Tristan*, v. 1995–2000, 94, ed. and trans. Lacy (English trans., 95). On the motif of the sword in Jewish sources, see *Sanhedrin* 19b: Palti placed a sword between him and Michal because he believed she was not his wife but rather David's wife, although her father, Saul, had taken her from David and given her to Palti (1 Samuel 25:44).

7. See motif Th.T351: "Sword of Chastity."

8. The relationship between King Mark and his nephew is one of love-hate.

camp of lepers that gains control of Iseult in one of the scenes in *Tristan and Iseult*;[9] and (5) a magical cure by means of healing herbs. Some of these motifs, such as the lepers or the healing herbs, were very prevalent in the Middle Ages, but in their entirety, and in particular with the motif of the sword between the lovers, they create intertextual affinities between the two narratives, "The Poor Bachelor and His Maiden Cousin" and Béroul's *The Romance of Tristan*.

In addition to the thematic similarity, a stylistic-syntactic analogy is also evident, expressed in the use of the conditional tense. When the uncle, in *Sefer ha-ma'asim*, discovers the couple sleeping with the sword between them, he concludes that they are innocent and reports that to his wife: "If he intended to spoil her, he would not have placed a sword between them. But he acted solely out of their love" (327b). In *Tristan and Iseult*, King Mark reacts in a similar manner: "Bien puis croire, se je ai sens / Se il s'amasent folement / Ja n'i eüsent vestement / entr<è> eus deus n'eüst espee / Autrement fust cest' asenblee."[10] The ethos of courtly love was neutralized in the Jewish story and accordingly also the conflict between it and the sacrament of marriage. This story does not relate to a love triangle—the love of the knight for his lady, the lord's wife. The conflict in medieval romances in Europe—between forbidden courtly love and the sanctity of marriage—is replaced in the Jewish story by the conflict between love matches and arranged marriages.[11] Allusions to biblical verses and transitions to a biblical linguistic register are an additional means of adapting the story to a Jewish one.

The rabbi's instructions to his student to kiss the girl, hug her, and sleep beside her in bed are scarcely within the boundary lines of the Halakhah. They have an effect of transgression, since, according to Jewish law, physical contact between an unmarried couple is forbidden.[12] Nonetheless, they still are in keeping with Jewish law in the specific context of Isaac's frame of mind. The rabbi expects Isaac to treat the situation as if it were a mission to be successfully completed, excluding any erotic

9. On the motif of leprosy in *Tristan and Iseult*, in the context of the image of the leper in the Middle Ages, see Brody, *The Disease of the Soul*, 179–186, based on references by Ẓfatman, *The Jewish Tale in the Middle Ages: Between Ashkenaz and Sefarad*, n. 1, 67.

10. Béroul, *The Romance of Tristan*, v. 2001–2006, 94, and the translation that follows on 95: "It is reasonable to conclude that / if they loved each other sinfully / they would not be dressed / and there would not be a sword between them / they would be together in quite a different way!"

11. See Part I, chapter 3, pp. 73–74 of this book.

12. See Leviticus 18:19: "Also thou shalt not approach a woman in the impurity of her menstrual flow to uncover her nakedness." The verse is applied in Jewish law to forbid kissing and embracing as well (Maimonides, *Mishne Torah*, "*hilkhot isurei bi'ah*," ch. 21). Cf. *Tanḥuma*, ed. Buber, *meẓora*, no. 11, 51.

connotations, and to inform his rabbi that it has been performed.[13] He is expected to carry out his instructions, reinforced as a vow, out of a single motive: obedience to his rabbi out of trust in his wisdom. The rabbi, the head of the yeshiva, probably believed that he could take the risk and rely on his student—which turns out to be true. The boy fears he will bring the evil inclination on himself, something he has managed to avoid up to then, but his rabbi trusts him. To quote Isaac: "[H]ow can I commit such a terrible sin, to encourage my evil inclination while I can yet escape it?" In comparison to the similar expression, which is often used in Ashkenaz but has a very different meaning—namely "to overcome one's evil inclination" ("*likhbosh et ha-yetzer*" or "*lehitgaber al ha-yetzer*")—Isaac's words relate to his success, throughout his stay at his uncle's home, in totally engaging in the study of the Torah, in a state of mind that excludes any other notions.[14] Hearing his rabbi's instructions, he is terrified that the barriers he built around him will collapse, enabling the evil inclination to intrude into his world.[15]

The narrator seems to be supporting the rabbi's strategy. Like the narrator of *Tristan and Iseult*, who identifies with the lovers' overpowering love due to the love potion they unwittingly drank,[16] the Jewish narrator identifies with the head of the yeshiva, even though he takes Jewish law to its extreme. By choosing the irregular and unexpected—albeit permitted—strategy, by exploiting a *rhetoric* of transgression rather than active transgression, the tale caters both to the appeal the romance has for its Jewish audience and to Jewish notions of proper relations between sexes only within marriage. At this point the happy ending, with the couple's marriage and its implied polemic against the romance, becomes compatible with the preceding descriptions of the rabbi's instructions and their performance. Romance-like

13. Cf. *Ketuvoth* 17a, where it is written that R. Aha, a prestigious sage, used to go out of his way to amuse brides on their wedding day and make them happy (which is a specific percept in Jewish law); he would dance at their weddings and carry them on his shoulders. When his students ask whether they should act similarly when dancing at weddings, his instruction is that it depends on the context of the situation. If the bride in this specific situation is nothing more than a "plank of wood for them"—namely their frame of mind while dancing is absolutely the performance of the *mitzvah* (commandment, percept), excluding any erotic connotations—they may do the same.

14. Cf. *Sefer ḥasidim*, ed. Wistinetzke, no. 53, 45, where a person makes a conscious effort to place himself in a situation of temptation in order to resist it and overcome his evil inclination. This is criticized in *Sefer ḥasidim.*

15. The demand in *Sefer ḥasidim* to resist temptation in the context of repentance relates to an effort to overcome the evil inclination that is already within the repentant, which is a different situation.

16. This stance of the narrator is particularly evident in the Thomas version, as in n. 5, in contrast to Béroul's anti-courtly version.

attributes—especially the rhetoric of transgression—on the one hand, and the value of marriage as the central motive of the tale on the other, place it between the romance and the exemplum, implying the existence of a unique horizon of expectation of a Jewish audience in medieval France.

We have no knowledge of the history of the story's transmission, either in lost manuscripts or orally, after its appearance in *Sefer ha-ma'asim* in the thirteenth century, until versions of it were included in *Mayse bukh* in archaic Yiddish.[17] The affinity with *Tristan and Iseult*, which imbued the *Sefer ha-ma'asim* version with its romantic character, is no longer evident in the adaptations in *Mayse bukh.* It is no longer a love story that involves passion and the breach of a taboo. Instead it is a tale of a competition based on the social class and finances of the prospective suitors. In the twentieth century the story was adapted by Bin Gorion in various versions, based on the *Sefer ha-ma'asim* version. In *Ẓefunot ve'agadot* it is a love story between a poor young man and a rich girl, without any of the religious attributes of the rabbi and the sword between the lovers. The motif of the suitors' competition and the plot line derived from it are also omitted.[18] In *Mimekor yisrael* Bin Gorion split the story into two independent versions.[19] One, "The "Poor Bachelor and His Maiden Cousin," places the love story between the two young people at its center, as does the one in *Ẓefunot ve'agadot* (although it contains the religious attributes); and the other focuses on the suitors' competition.[20]

17. Versions of *Mayse bukh* are Ms. Paris Heb. 589, 118a–124b; *Mayse bukh,* no. 223; Gaster, trans., *Ma'aseh book,* 2, no. 224, 556–568; see references and texts in Ẓfatman, *The Jewish Tale in the Middle Ages: Between Ashkenaz and Sefarad,* 179–205, and her lengthy discussion in chapters 1–6. Yassif suggests the story under discussion here is a source of the *Mayse bukh* versions: Yassif, *Kemargalit bemishbeẓet,* 153, n. 62. And see references by Ben-Amos, *Mimekor yisrael,* no. 203, 389.

18. Bin Gorion, *Ẓefunot ve'agadot,* 269: "The Father's Blessing."

19. By doing so he simplified the story, with the intuition of a creative writer, in contrast to the hybridic version in the Middle Ages, which is comprised of two different tale types adapted into two plot lines that intersect.

20. *Mimekor yisrael,* no. 728, 363–364; and no. 729, 364–729. See version based on *Sefer ha-ma'asim* in Eisenstein, *Oẓar midrashim,* I, 348–350.

56–59. R. Pinḥas b. Yair (329b)

The four anecdotes about R. Pinḥas b. Yair, a Tanna of the fifth and last generation of Tana'im, depict a *ḥasid* who practices strict norms of behavior beyond the requirements of the normative law, a man who is mindful of the public needs and is "learned in miracles" ("*melumad benisim*").[1]

As a *ḥasid*, R. Pinḥas b. Yair goes to greater trouble than the Halakhah requires to look after the measures of barley left with him.[2] He takes steps to remedy the laxness of the city dwellers in paying their tithes, has unshakable faith in the ways of the Almighty and divine reward, and crosses the river on his way to carry out the commandment of circumcision. As a man and leader concerned about the public welfare, he is prepared to help passersby and fellow travelers and to increase the worth of a deposit left with him, without any charge. He does not hesitate to give his guarantee to a community greatly distressed by a plague of mice and acknowledges the importance of the cistern digger's work for the public good. As a man learned in miracles, R. Pinḥas b. Yair commands the mice to leave the city; with the help of an angel, he saves the cistern digger's daughter; and he is compared to Moses, who split the sea only once, while R. Pinḥas b. Yair split the river twice.

The four tales about R. Pinḥas b. Yair have their sources in the rabbinical literature, where they are placed either in one cycle or separately. The editing contexts also vary, depending on the collection and the specific issue to which they relate.[3] The direct source for *Sefer ha-ma'asim* is primarily *Deuteronomy rabbah* (Ekev 3, 3), which is obvious from the identical style and the consecutive arrangement of three of the tales: the deposit of barley, the saving of the city from the plague of mice, and the rescue of the cistern digger's daughter. The fourth tale, about the division of the Ginnai River, is from tractate *Ḥullin* 7a, not from *Deuteronomy rabbah*.

The choice of the tales and their adaptation indicate a deliberate purpose in their editing. In *Deuteronomy rabbah* they are condensed, written in Hebrew rather than Aramaic, and focused on R. Pinḥas b. Yair's activities for the sake of the public welfare as a *ḥasid*. The fourth tale, which originates in *Ḥullin*, is a typical miracle legend about the division of the Ginnai River, and hence was apparently preferred

1. See this phrase, for example, in *Me'ila* 17b, about Shimon b. Yoḥai.
2. On laws regarding "the unpaid bailee," see Maimonides, *Mishne Torah*, *sefer mishpatim*, 1:1.
3. See in p*Demai*, I, 3 (4, 1)—the deposit of barley, saving the city from the damage caused by mice, the splitting of the Ginnai River, and the cistern digger's daughter; in *Shekalim*, 5, 1 (22, 1)—the cistern digger's daughter; in b*Ḥullin*, 7a—the division of the water of the Ginnai River; and *Deuteronomy rabbah*, *Ekev* (3, 3).

over another tale in that tractate, "R. Pinḥas b. Yair's Donkey."[4] The tale's conclusion in *Ḥullin*, which compares the miracle of the Ginnai River to the division of the Red Sea, glorifies R. Pinḥas b. Yair as a person learned in miracles, since the Ginnai River was divided twice in his honor while the Red Sea divided only once for Moses. This, then, is an apt chord with which to end the entire cycle of stories in *Sefer ha-ma'asim*. Another aspect in the story about the Ginnai River is stylistic. The *Sefer ha-ma'asim* version is shorter than the one in the Talmud, and consequently the epilogue also differs. Apparently the focus is not on the development of the plot into a dramatic and redundant narrative but rather on the core event itself and the overall impression of R. Pinḥas b. Yair as a pious *ḥasid*, a doer of good deeds and a man learned in miracles. This impression is created by the melding of the separate stories into one cycle, the choice of the stories, the way they are shaped compared to their sources, and the editing strategy employed in *Sefer ha-ma'asim*. This also seems to be the case in light of the editing and adaptation of the R. Pinḥas b. Yair tales in other story compilations, such as *Ḥibbur yafeh mehayeshu'a* in Tunis in the eleventh century and the *Mayse bukh* in Ashkenaz several centuries later. These two compilations have a different selection of tales from those in the *Sefer ha-ma'asim* cycle.[5]

The tales about R. Pinḥas b. Yair may be part of a broader phenomenon in medieval Europe—the reception and wide circulation of Virgil's legends. In the words of Domenico Comparetti, the author of the monumental monograph about Virgil's image in the Middle Ages: "There is no book in that period in which one cannot expect to find Virgil's legends."[6] Stories about him were also known in the Jewish society in the Middle Ages, such as the well-known tale "Basilius in the Basket,"

4. R. Pinḥas b. Yair's donkey supposedly refused to eat barley from which the tithe was not set aside, and it nearly starved to death. The story is also included in *Genesis rabbah* (60, 32), ed. Albeck, 648–649. R. Pinḥas b. Yair's piety is expressed in it only metonymically, by means of his donkey, and he is not depicted in the story as a man "learned in miracles" and a benefactor of the public.

5. *Ḥibbur yafeh mehayeshu'a*, ed. Hirschberg, 67, contains the tale about the deposit of barley, which is also widely cited in commentary on the Talmud and in the *responsa* literature as well as in *musar* literature (Elijah Hacohen, *Me'il ẓedakah*, no. 500, 154–155). *Mayse bukh* (*Ma'aseh Book*, trans. Gaster, vol. 1, no. 55, 97–98) includes the tale about R. Pinḥas b. Yair and his donkey, alongside that about the Ginnai River (no. 55, trans. Gaster, *Mayse bukh*, vol. 1, no. 54, 93–94). For the references to the appearance of the story in manuscripts of *Mayse bukh* (Ms. Munich 495, no. 26, and Jerusalem 5245, no. 25), see Kotlerman, "The Complete Index of Stories in the 'Mayse-bukh,'" 299.

6. Comparetti, *Vergil in the Middle Ages*, 254; see pp. 239–308 for a discussion of the images of Virgil in medieval popular literature, and on reciprocal affinities between this literature and canonical literature. See also the survey of Virgil's legends in the Middle Ages in Spargo, *Virgil the Necromancer*, 3–68.

which was included in the historiographic work *The Book of Memory*.[7] Virgil, the poet of ancient Rome, was perceived in the Middle Ages as the patron and protector of the inhabitants of Naples, and as a magician who used white magic to control the forces of nature.

In one of the legends about a plague of flies, Virgil attaches to the city gate of Naples a bronze talisman in the form of an artificial fly, which destroys the flies, drives them away, or prevents their entry into the city. Thus he protected the citizens of Naples and by force of his magic kept them safe from the plagues of flies that threatened the city.[8] According to another tale, he saved the people of Naples from a plague of poisonous leeches by throwing a leech made of gold into a well.[9] The rescue of the inhabitants of the city from a plague of vermin is a motif that is common to these tales and to the story about R. Pinḥas b. Yair, who saved the inhabitants of an unnamed city from a plague of mice. In the Christian tale Virgil succeeds by virtue of his magical powers. In *Sefer ha-ma'asim* the rabbi succeeds by getting the people of the city to promise to strictly pay their tithes and by giving them his guarantee as a *ḥasid* learned in working miracles.

In the background of the Jewish story, a distinction is drawn between sorcery and white magic, particularly in light of R. Pinḥas b. Yair's words in a talmudic tale that is not included in *Sefer ha-ma'asim*, where he says, "What am I, a sorcerer?!"[10] The disparate narrative materials represent different societies and perhaps also polemical trends. However, in light of certain common motifs and their editing in the tale cycles, the reception of the R. Pinḥas b. Yair tales in *Sefer ha-ma'asim* marks the compilation as a product of its own time and place in Western Europe during the Middle Ages.

7. See Yassif, *The Book of Memory*, 313–315, discussion and references, 46–47, 506.

8. On the fly amulet and its legendary context, see Comparetti, *Vergil in the Middle Ages*, 266–267; Spargo, *Virgil the Necromancer*, 70–79.

9. Neckam, *De naturis rerum*, no. 174, 310. For references to citations of this story and the tale about the flies in Christian medieval literature, see the table in Spargo, *Virgil the Necromancer*, 60–68.

10. p *Demai*, 1:3 (4:1), and n. 2, above.

60. The *Ḥasid* and the Tax Collector's Son (329b–330b)

The story already appears in the the Palestinian Talmud in two similar versions, in the tractates *Hagigah* 2:2 (77d)[1] and *Sanhedrin* 6:4 (23c).[2] Two major traditions are discernible: one in the versions of the Gaonim, according to the talmudic version,[3] and the other—one that developed independently in Ashkenaz—appearing in Rashi's commentary on *Sanhedrin* 44b; here in *Sefer ha-ma'asim*; in *Darkhei teshuvah*, which is attributed to R. Eleazar of Worms;[4] and in Ms. Parma 2295, 92a–93a. In Ashkenaz the reference is usually to the sin of listening to gossip about a Torah scholar rather than to the improper laying of phylacteries, which appears in earlier sources. And the flight of those accompanying the deceased is explained by their alarm at being suddenly attacked rather than by their fear of the authorities or rainfall, as in the versions of the Gaonim. Another disparate version in Ashkenaz is included in *Sefer haroke'aḥ* by Eleazar of Worms, which focuses on the laws relating to menstruating women (*nidah*).[5]

In *Sefer ha-ma'asim* the tale is expanded, particularly in comparison to earlier versions. It contains three consecutive episodes that make up one cohesive story, about the *ḥasid* and the tax collector, the witches from Ashkelon, and the son of R. Simon b. Shetaḥ, who was wrongly sentenced to death because of a false testimony. The figure of R. Simon b. Shetaḥ connects the three episodes. The one about the *ḥasid* and the tax collector ends with a description of R. Simon b. Shetaḥ's failure, after his appointment as the head of the Sanhedrin, to act against the witches and his consequent future punishment in hell. The one about the witches from Ashkelon describes the action taken by him, after he was appointed head of the Sanhedrin, to drive out sorcery and the consequent annulment of his punishment. The third episode is about R. Simon b. Shetaḥ's son. A second linking motif is the city of Ashkelon, where the rabbi, his disciples, and the witches live. These three episodes are not usually told sequentially. "The *Ḥasid* and the Tax Collector's Son" frequently stands alone; sometimes the "Witches from Ashkelon" is added to it,

1. Academy of the Hebrew Language edition, 787–788.
2. In the Academy of the Hebrew Language edition, 1293–1294. For a list of versions, see Kushelevsky and Tohar, "The Pious Man and the Tax-Collector's Son," 244–246. See also references by Ben-Amos, *Mimekor yisrael*, no. 101, 185. For an early Christian parallel, see Tubach 815, which refers to the *Vitae Patrum*.
3. Roth, "*Responsa* of Paltoi Gaon," 146–148; *Ḥibbur yafeh mehayeshu'a*.
4. *Sefer Shut maharam* (*Responsa of Maharam*), ed. Blokh, 162–163.
5. R. Eleazar b. Judah, *Sefer haroke'aḥ*, no. 318, 206; the version is based on a post-Amoraic version in *Baraita de-masekhet Niddah*, 2:4, ed. Horowitz, *Tosefta atikta*, part 5, 15–16.

while the third tale, about b. Shetaḥ's son, is cited for the first time in Rashi's commentary on *Sanhedrin* 44b.[6] From this standpoint, the influence of Rashi's version on *Sefer ha-ma'asim* is salient.

The theme of theodicy—justification of God—unites the three episodes. In the first it is represented in the student's amazement at the dishonor shown to his rabbi in contrast to the preferential treatment given to the tax collector. The supposed injustice is exacerbated in view of the punishment that awaits R. Simon b. Shetaḥ, the head of the Sanhedrin, after his death. The second episode is intended to explain this seeming injustice; and the third raises the question of theodicy again in view of the death sentence pronounced on b. Shetaḥ's son because two people gave false witness. The halakhic explanation, intended to preserve the status of the court and the judicial system, is that, once a witness's testimony has been accepted by the court, it cannot be rejected. In the final analysis, the answer is on the metaphysical plane, in the gap between the limitations of human knowledge and the omniscient God; human beings, however, find it psychologically difficult to come to terms with this discrepancy. The narrative materials are dramatic and emotive: the fright and turmoil when the attackers suddenly appear at the cemetery; the dedication of the student to his rabbi and his willingness to endanger his own life; the intensity of his sorrow at the dishonor shown to his rabbi; his amazement at the expected punishment of R. Simon b. Shetaḥ; and finally R. Simon's vexation when the student tells him what he has seen in his vision. By means of a narrative comprised of three episodes, the story presents an attempt to cope with a human reality perceived as meaningless—particularly relating to life-and-death situations—and to provide answers on a different plane.

The metaphysical sphere is actualized in *Sefer ha-ma'asim* by the motif of Torah study, which was highly esteemed in Ashkenaz, and the exalted image of the Torah scholar.[7] Several motifs are unique to the tale tradition in Ashkenaz, including *Sefer ha-ma'asim*. These motifs are (1) the figures of the two friends, the rabbi and his student, in contrast to the two *ḥasidim* or students in the Palestinian Talmud; (2) the sin of accepting the defamation of Torah scholars; and (3) the characterization of R. Simon b. Shetaḥ and his son in the third tale, and their readiness to accept the death sentence given the absolute authority of the Halakhah in their world. In *Sefer ha-ma'asim* the study of Torah is the accepted means of coping with the question of divine justice; nonetheless even the Torah scholar who has spent his entire life

6. For a reference to sources that separate "The *Ḥasid* and the Tax Collector's Son" from "Witches from Ashkelon," see Kushelevsky and Tohar, "The Pious Man and the Tax-Collector's Son."

7. Grossman, *The Early Sages of Ashkenaz*, 400–411.

studying the Torah cannot totally fathom its meaning. The gap between human limitations and divine knowledge widens in this version, since even the Torah scholar cannot bridge it, and he learns to reconcile himself to questions for which he has no answers.

The metaphysical plane is also represented by the motif of the Garden of Eden and hell as real spheres, which are described in more detail than in the Talmud. The Garden of Eden is the place of righteous men who sit on golden chairs, with clouds of glory covering them, a description similar to that in the chronicles about the sanctifiers of God's name in Ashkenaz.[8] In hell the sinners are punished by hanging. Baya, the tax collector, is hung on an iron bolt that passes between his ears. The topos of hanging in hell has its roots in a long tradition (Jewish and Christian) also given expression in versions of "The *Ḥasid* and the Tax Collector's Son," beginning with the Talmud.[9] The image of hell differs, however, in *Sefer ha-ma'asim*. For the first time in the history of the story, hell is depicted as a dynamic space of purification, in which there is a possibility of change even in the next world, by means of a transfer from there to the Garden of Eden. Although this motif of purification does appear in the Talmud—for example in tractate *Rosh Hashanah* 17a—it is given more emphasis in medieval texts such as *Masekhet gehenom*.[10] In this story it qualifies the finality of death and suggests an optimistic outlook. The images of hell in *Sefer ha-ma'asim* thus influence the way the concept of death is formulated, with its particular nuance. The emphasis on the doctrine of purgatory, in thirteenth-century Christian society, as a space of purification that separated hell from paradise may explain the inclusion of the motif of purification in *Sefer ha-ma'asim*.[11] The story deals with the concept by amplifying the motif, on the one hand, and by relating to hell and the Garden of Eden as a binary rather than tertiary space, on the other.

8. Habermann, ed., *Sefer gezerot ashkenaz vetzorfat*, 31; Haverkamp, *Hebräische Berichte . . . Kreuzzugs*, 24 (603), 26 (601). On the medieval nature of descriptions of paradise in chronicles, and on their sources in the Talmud and the *midrashim*, see Goldin, *The Ways of Jewish Martyrdom*, 111–118. See also the treatises on the Garden of Eden in various sources in Ashkenaz, e.g., "*Seder gan eden*," in Yassif, *Book of Memories*, 103–109, and "*Seder gehenom*" in ibid., 99–103. For a comprehensive discussion of the reservoir of these texts and the history of their transmission, their penetration into Europe from the East and through Spain, and their further development in Ashkenaz, see Perry, *Tradition and Transformation*, 197–252.

9. See Liebermann, *Al Ḥata'im veonsham* (*On Sins and Their Punishments*); Himmelfarb, *Tours of Hell* (127–134, 169–173); and their different approaches. Liebermann presents a linear development of traditions of hanging in hell whose primary source is the Palestinian Talmud; in contrast, Himmelfarb points to an unknown metatext as a common source for ancient Jewish and Christian sources.

10. See, e.g., "*Seder gehenom*" from the Middle Ages in Yassif, *Book of Memory*, 100–101.

11. Le Goff, *The Birth of Purgatory*, 155–157, 289–333.

In summary, three aspects mark this version as a medieval work in Ashkenaz, and as a narrative with a literary rather than a halakhic purpose. These include an emotive description that reflects the psychological difficulty of coping with theodicy; the value of Torah study in Ashkenaz and the role of the Torah scholar in it; and intensified images of paradise and hell, in particular the depiction of hell as a place of purification. The story's affinity with Rashi's version in contrast to other versions in Ashkenaz is striking, and this choice may be an indication that *Sefer ha-ma'asim* did in fact originate in northern France.

61. Ukva (307a–307b; 330b–331b)

This story first appeared in writing in the Gaonic period, in the early eleventh century, in *Ḥibbur yafeh mehayeshu'a* by R. Nissim Kairouan.[1] Although it is not certain that its source is in the Talmud, this appears to be a likely possibility. A similar tale is included in *Sanhedrin* 75a, about a man who fell ill due to a forbidden, unrequited passion. In addition, in the Talmud there is a mention of a repentant man known as Natan de-Ẓuẓita (Nathan of the Radiance), which is his name in the Gaonic tradition of the tale.[2] The story was probably known in the time of the Talmud but was not written down.[3] In the Middle Ages it developed along the lines of two textual traditions: one according to the tale tradition in the Gaonic literature (e.g., in *Menorat hama'or* from the fourteenth century in Spain),[4] and the other in Ashkenaz, which first appeared, as far as we know, in Rashi's commentary on *Sanhedrin* 31b. In the twelfth century the tale appeared in Ashkenaz in a number of additional versions: a penitential poem for the ten days of repentance by R. Barukh b. Samuel of Mainz;[5] two versions in *Sefer ha-ma'asim* in the thirteenth century (one expanded [330b–331b] and the other different and shortened [307a–b]); and one in Ms. Parma 2295 from northern France, also in the thirteenth century.[6] The major differences between the narrative traditions in the East and the West involve the name of the repentant man (Natan de-Ẓuẓita in the East, and Ukva or Akiva in Ashkenaz); the status of the woman (who in the Gaonic tradition is married and in Ashkenaz is not); and the additional expansion of the story in versions from Ashkenaz. An episode about Ukva in the next world, which does not exist in *Ḥibbur yafeh mehayeshu'a,* was added.

In comparison to the story in other manuscripts in Ashkenaz, the expanded version (330b–331b) in *Sefer ha-ma'asim* represents two folkloric tale types: "Suitors

1. *Ḥibbur yafeh mehayeshu'a*, ed. Hirschberg, no. 27, 73–76; Brinner, ed., *An Elegant Composition Concerning Relief after Adversity*, no. 27, 127–131.
2. See b*Shabbat* 56b; b*Sanhedrin* 31b.
3. Another possibility is that the story was created in the Gaonic period, on the basis of fragmented mentions in the Talmud.
4. Al-Nakawa, *Menorat hama'or*, v. 3, 127–129.
5. Habermann, "The Piyyutim of R. Baruch Bar Shemuel of Mainz," 128. For a list of versions of the story, see Kushelevsky, *Penalty and Temptation*, 311–313. See also references by Ben-Amos, *Mimekor yisrael*, no. 70, 141; and an entry on the story (Lipsker, "Nathan of the Radiance," *Encyclopedia of the Jewish Story*, vol. 2, 215–232).
6. See Kushelevsky, *Penalty and Temptation*, 142–145.

Compete for the Hand of a Girl"[7] and "A Companion in Paradise."[8] In the first, the decision as to the appropriate groom is made following his success in the competition. At the beginning of this story, the parents are undecided about the choice of a husband for their daughter: "Her mother and father consulted with their family and said: To whom should we marry Hannah, to Ukva who is rich and wicked or to Joseph who is a student? They all said: Heaven forbid, heaven forbid; she should marry none other than the student named Joseph." However, Ukva proved himself to be a more worthy groom, worthy even for the daughter of the yeshiva head, and the judgment of the girl's parents turned out to be shortsighted:

> and it appeared as if there was a candle lit at his head. A great yeshiva head and Torah scholar saw him. . . . The yeshiva head said to him: My daughter is eighteen years old, and I have a lot of money. You too have a lot of money. I will give you my daughter, and together we will study Torah all the days of our lives. He listened to him and took his daughter.

The girl's parents appear one more time in the story, when they insist that she go to that same Ukva whom they had previously rejected to ask him for a loan to gain her husband's release from prison. She adamantly refuses, and the narrator appears to be critical of the parents, who are ignoring the price their daughter may be forced to pay. There may also be implied criticism of the parents' indifference to their daughter's wishes when they married her to Joseph and not to Ukva. Some hints in the story can lead to this conclusion: not only her husband's jealousy of his wife's former suitor, while he himself is in prison, but also the familiarity in the conversation between her and Ukva, in the course of which she leads him to thoughts of repentance. The parents are responsible for their choice of a husband for their daughter and their other errors, which have long-term implications. A similar criticism is also

7. On the "Suitors Compete for the Hand of a Girl" in Ashkenaz, beginning with *Sefer ha-ma'asim* and up to a story collection in archaic Yiddish from the sixteenth century, see Ẓfatman, *The Jewish Tale in the Middle Ages*, 15–17. She refers to a different story in *Sefer ha-ma'asim* ("The Poor Bachelor and His Maiden Cousin" [no. 55]).

8. ATU 809*. Several of the parallels to "A Companion in Paradise" are p*Ta'anit* I, 4 (64b); *Tanḥuma*, ed. Buber, Introduction, no. 41, 68; *Sefer ḥasidim*, no. 80, 53. For a selection of parallels of this tale type, see Schwarzbaum, *Studies in Jewish and World Folklore*, 129; Yassif, *The Hebrew Folktale*, 316–317; Alexander-Frizer, *The Pious Sinner*, 87–120. For "A Companion in Paradise" in IFA, see AT 809*-*A1.

implied in *Sefer ḥasidim*, which cautions against imposing a marriage on a girl against her will, in particular marriage to an old man.[9]

The story, as it is adapted in *Sefer ha-ma'asim*, can also be viewed in the context of the courtly romances in Europe. Jousts between knights for the sake of winning a lady, impossible tasks that the lady imposes on the knight courting her to prove that he is worthy of her, a conflict between imposed political marriage and a love affair between the knight and the seigneur's wife—all these are motifs frequently found in this literature. In "Chaitivel," a poem by Marie de France, four men court an adored lady and are required to prove their excellence and superiority to gain her love. They do not know they are competing with one another, nor do they know that the lady is uncertain about which of them to choose, but from the standpoint of the narrator and the reader, they are competing for her heart. In the end, in attempting to accomplish the tasks assigned them, three of the men are killed, and the fourth, "the unhappy one,"[10] is severely injured. Similarly, the tension between political marriages and love marriages is given expression in the well-known work *Tristan and Iseult*. Iseult is given to King Mark, who has donkey ears, but her heart belongs to Tristan.[11] The special emphases in *Sefer ha-ma'asim* and the implied criticism of the parents' decision regarding the worthy husband for their daughter are consistent with existing trends in the French literature of the time, and they reflect them. Nonetheless, the story is in keeping with the norms of Jewish society (e.g., the supreme value of faithfulness in marriage), and does not develop in the direction of the solutions of courtly love. The preference of a love marriage over an arranged marriage is not explicit but is only implied.

Another context to the story is the tale type "A Companion in Paradise," which is evident in *Sefer ha-ma'asim* from the ending:

> and now I demand that you fulfill your vow and tell me where you sit and where my place is. He said to him: On your life, your place is three steps above mine. Please, will you pray to go down one step and I will go up one step, and then we will be equals? Come and see how great is the power of repentance.

In tales of this type, a scholar studies Torah diligently throughout his life and asks to know who his neighbor in paradise will be. In a dream he is told that his

9. See Grossman, *Pious and Rebellious*, 55–60, and his references to *Sefer ḥasidim*.
10. Marie de France, "Chaitivel," in *Lais*, 248–261.
11. Béroul, *The Romance of Tristan*, verses 12332–1334, 64 (French); 65 (English).

companion will be a simple, even despicable man—a tax collector, a butcher, or a pimp. He is amazed, and goes forth to seek out the man and to find the reason why he will be his neighbor. He learns that a single deed the man has done—he has ransomed prisoners, given charity, restrained his evil inclinations, or the like—has gained him an honorable place in paradise. Then the pious man informs his future companion, the simple man, of the reward that awaits him in the next world.

The present story about Ukva is not totally consistent with this plot sequence, but it does fit the type of "A Companion in Paradise." Ukva, who was a great sinner, gained an honorable place in the Garden of Eden, near the head of the yeshiva where he studied, thanks to one deserving act—he restrained himself and overcame his desire for the woman who was in his presence. The transition from a story about repentance to a story about a "Companion in Paradise" occurs when the yeshiva head and his son-in-law arrive at an agreement. According to the agreement, one would go up one step and the other would go down one step, so their places in paradise are equal. While it is said about the repentant that "in the place where penitents stand even the wholly righteous cannot stand" (*Berakhot* 34b), the tale type of "A Companion in Paradise" attempts to equate the places of the simple man and the scholar in paradise, like neighbors of the same rank. The end of the story was intended to make it conform to this tale type.

The character of the woman, Hannah, and the way she changes when the story moves from East to West, is an additional feature in *Sefer ha-ma'asim*. Her loyalty to her husband is a consistent element in all versions of the story, as well as in *Ḥibbur yafeh mehayeshu'a* in the Jewish-Muslim territory; but in Ashkenaz, in *Sefer ha-ma'asim* as well as in other versions, the woman is also opinionated and resourceful, which conforms to the image of women in Ashkenaz. In Ms. Parma 2295, which is also from northern France, her assertiveness is obvious in her exchanges with her husband. In an attempt to find a way out of the unfortunate situation, she offers a practical solution. She suggests that her husband give her a divorce: "Release me, free me, so that he will have no sin upon him."[12] In *Ḥibbur yafeh mehayeshu'a*, she is equally strong and moral, but also submissive toward her husband. Her request for a divorce, for example, is depicted as a desperate plea, and as a way out that is preferable to a sin, not as a pragmatic suggestion: "Husband, divorce me and send me away, so that I may not be obliged to him."[13] In *Sefer ha-ma'asim* her dominant personality is manifested when she disagrees with her parents, who want her to go

12. Ms. Parma 2295 (de-Rossi 563), 130b, in Kushelevsky, *Penalty and Temptation*, 143.
13. See, at length, Kushelevsky, *Penalty and Temptation*, 151–154.

to Ukva to ask for a loan so they can be released from prison, and in doing so to surrender herself to her former suitor, thus sacrificing herself for their sake. She adamantly refuses: "They said to Hannah: Go to Ukva. Maybe he will give you [the money]. She said to them: I will not go there lest he sin with me. I am not going there. They spoke to her repeatedly, but she refused."

Another context that is relevant to the story is the doctrine of *teshuvah* (repentance) of Ashkenazi *ḥasidism*, in particular "*teshuvat haba'ah*": literally, the *teshuvah* of "what comes before him." Its source is in the b*Yoma* 86b: "How is one proved a repentant sinner?—Rab Judah said: If the object which caused his original transgression comes before him on two occasions, and he keeps away from it. Rab Judah indicated: With the same woman, at the same time, in the same place." The sinner's repentance is proven by his ability to refrain from repeating a transgression when he finds himself in the same circumstances. In Ashkenazi pietism this is one stage in the all-embracing process of repentance. It includes two additional stages that contain an element of self-mortification,[14] which is intended as a substitute for the torments of hell. This aspect is very salient in the Ms. Parma 2295 version, but it is also implied in *Sefer ha-ma'asim* in its use of the term "to restrain one's desire" ("He listened to her and restrained his desire"), which in Ashkenaz is closely linked to the doctrine of repentance in *Sefer ḥasidim* and *Sefer ha-Rokeaḥ*. It is also implied by the episode added to the story only in Ashkenaz, about the suffering of the yeshiva head before he is transferred to paradise—fiery burns administered by the Angel of Death. This doctrine of repentance exerted its influence on everyone in Ashkenaz and also left its imprint for hundreds of years after the thirteenth century, when the Ashkenazi Pietists were active.

This story about Ukva (no. 61) in *Sefer ha-ma'asim* (330b–331b) has a variety of historical-cultural contexts: the matchmaking norms in Ashkenaz and the conflict between love marriages and arranged marriages; the courtly romances of the period; the image of paradise; and the doctrine of repentance of Ashkenazi Pietists.

The tale about Ukva was also copied in *Sefer ha-ma'asim* in a brief version lacking any mention of his name (no. 15). The protagonist is an anonymous "*ḥasid*." The couple's economic distress is explained by the husband's illness, and there is no mention of his being imprisoned ("My husband is very ill, and I have nothing to support him with"). Despite the crisis between the couple, they try to resolve it jointly. First they fast for three days (with an allusion to the three-day fast in the Book of Esther

14. These stages are *teshuvat hamishkal* (lit., "of the measure") and *teshuvat hakatuv* (lit., "of what is written"). See *Sefer ḥasidim*, no. 37, 39; Marcus, *Piety and Society*, 44–50.

4:17); and later the husband gives his wife a divorce for one day (at his wife's suggestion, which he immediately accepts, without questioning). Accordingly, the reconciliation between them at the end of the story alleviates the situation: "At once the *ḥasid* rejoiced, believing his righteous wife." This is in contrast to the husband's suspicion in the expanded version. The conflict between an arranged marriage and a love marriage is muted in this version, since the relationship that was built over the couple's years of shared married life is strong and able to overcome passing crises. This version is, therefore, particularly interesting in the way it depicts the relations between husband and wife.

This tale tradition in Ashkenaz endured even after *Sefer ha-ma'asim* in the thirteenth century. The influence of Ms. Jerusalem 3182 (106b–107a), a large tale collection compiled in Ashkenaz, is especially palpable. The story is cited in Ms. Jerusalem 3182 in a version very similar to that in the aforementioned Ms. Parma,[15] and in Ms. JTS 2374 (214b–216b) from the fifteenth century.[16] From the sixteenth century up to the nineteenth century, in story anthologies such as Elijah Hacohen's *Me'il ẓedakah*, Araki's *Sefer hama'asiyot*, and Farḥi's *Oseh pele*, the distinction between the tale tradition in Ashkenaz and the Muslim region was blurred, and the story was also transmitted in Ashkenaz according to the *Ḥibbur yafeh mehayeshu'a* version.[17] There is an example in *Ẓe'enah ur'enah*, a collection of commentaries and tales in Yiddish based on the weekly portion of the Torah (intended also for women),[18] which follows all the details of the plot as they appear in *Ḥibbur yafeh mehayeshu'a*. Twentieth-century literary versions include those of Bin Gorion (Berdyczewski), in *Ẓefunot ve'agadot* and *Mimekor yisrael*.[19]

15. Yassif, *Ninety-nine Tales*, no. 14, 186–187; see Yassif's comment, ibid., 145.

16. For a description and discussion of the manuscript, see Kushelevsky, "What Is a 'Story Collection' in the Middle Ages? A Study of Ms. JTS 2374."

17. Elijah Hacohen, *Me'il ẓedakah*, no. 501, 161–163; Araki, *Sefer hama'asiyot*, no. 108, 115a–117a, and Ḥuẓin, no. 108, 75b–77a; Farḥi, *Oseh pele*, part 3, 367–371.

18. Jacob ben Isaac, *Ẓe'enah ur'enah*, Ruth, 8a–b.

19. *Ẓefunot ve'agadot*, 169–170; *Mimekor yisrael*, no. 366b, 197–198.

62. A Meal of Herbs (331b)

This is one of several tales about Solomon in *Sefer ha-ma'asim*, including "One Man in a Thousand Have I Found" (no. 53), "The Hard-Boiled Egg" (no. 54), "Solomon's Scribes" (no. 42), and "The War of Jacob and His Sons with Nineveh" (no. 68). As we have seen, this compilation does not adhere to a central thematic principle. In this case the stories are dispersed sporadically throughout the compilation and are not joined together into a consecutive cycle about Solomon. The source of this story is the *Midrash Proverbs* from the ninth century, as a homily on the verse, "Better is a dinner of herbs where love is, than a fatted ox and hatred with it" (Proverbs 15:17).[1] In *Sefer ha-ma'asim* the story does not begin with the quotation but rather with the usual opening, "Once . . ." The story is brief and anecdotal, and it is written in a standard style instead of the lofty style of the source.[2] Medieval versions other than those in *Sefer ha-ma'asim* and in *Yalkut shimoni* include a commentary by R. Baḥya (1255–1340) on Exodus,[3] and *Sefer hama'asiyot*, from the fourteenth century, edited by Gaster in the *Exempla* of the rabbis.[4] In the nineteenth and twentieth centuries, the story appeared frequently in rabbinical and literary anthologies.[5] The story was given an extensive literary adaptation in Bialik's *And It Came to Pass*.[6]

The story could have been received as an episode in another longer and more developed narrative about Solomon's expulsion from his kingdom by Asmodeus, the king of the demons; his wanderings in his exile; and finally his return to his kingdom.[7] The story of Solomon's ouster has a long tradition, beginning with the Palestinian and Babylonian Talmuds, up to this very day,[8] and it includes various

1. *Midrash mishle* (Proverbs), ed. Visotzky, 15, 17; 122–123, and in the Buber edition of *Midrash Proverbs*, 39b–40a. For its date, see Visotzky's comment in the introduction to his edition, 7.
2. The expression in *Midrash Proverbs*—"*tashgiah alai hayom*" ("attend with me")—is replaced by a more commonplace expression: "Would you eat with me today?"
3. R. Baḥya, *Commentary on the Torah*, Exodus, *pekudai*, 376–377; *Mikra'ot gedolot, me'orei haḥasidut, Exodus*, ed. Halperin, 737b–738b.
4. No. 246, 163–164.
5. Farḥi, *Oseh pele*, part 3, 315–317; Levner, *The Legends of Israel*, vol. 1, part 3, no. 334, 383–385; Grünwald, *Yalkut sippurim*, vol. 2, part 3, 109; Bialik and Ravnitzky, *The Book of Legends*, no. 123, 130; *Mimekor yisrael*, no. 72, 66; Ginzberg, *Legends of the Jews*, 5, 108–110; Magriso, *Yalkut me'am lo'ez*, Proverbs, 254–255. For references to versions of the story and research on it, see Ben-Amos, *Mimekor yisrael*, no. 29, 51.
6. Bialik, "A Fatted Ox and a Dinner of Herbs," in *And It Came to Pass*, 199–220.
7. On the development of the story and its versions and reception throughout the generations, see Kushelevsky, "King Solomon and Asmodeus."
8. See p*Sanhedrin* 2:6 (20c); b*Gittin* 68b.

episodes about what happens to him during his wanderings as well as descriptions of the insults and mockery he suffered when he repeatedly claimed he was the king. One would have expected "A Meal of Herbs" to be inserted into this expulsion story, but that is not the case. Instead it developed along an independent track, beginning with the *midrash* on Proverbs. It is likely that the main point of the story is not the account of Solomon's life in exile but rather the moral at its end, in the wake of Solomon's experiences in the homes of his hosts. The story was received as a parable, and as such it was granted a status of its own. Perhaps a dissonance between the story and the talmudic source led to this independent development. In "A Meal of Herbs," Solomon is recognized as a king, while in the talmudic expulsion story, no one believes he is King Solomon.

The choice of "A Meal of Herbs" in *Sefer ha-ma'asim* instead of "Solomon and Asmodeus," a far more popular and widespread story, may have been influenced by another tale about Solomon—"Solomon and Marcolf"—that was very popular throughout Europe, particularly in France, in the Middle Ages. In it Solomon, the learned, wise king, and Marcolf, a simple, shrewd peasant, compete with riddles, sayings, and various witticisms. Solomon wins with parables taken from the Bible, and Marcolf, like the popular figure of the village fool, contends with witty, salacious parables. There is an ancient tale tradition in Latin from twelfth-century France and in later manuscripts, with roots in oral folk literature.[9] Solomon is defeated in this context, and the story is received as a subversive one, a parody on Solomon's learned erudition and a recognition of vulgar, witty folk wisdom.

Several motifs in "A Meal of Herbs" create an implied affinity with "Solomon and Marcolf." These motifs are (1) the common wisdom that Solomon acquires in the homes of his two hosts as a king in exile; (2) the contrast between the authoritative characters of Solomon in "Solomon and Marcolf" and the rich host in "A Meal of Herbs," and the character of the poor, simple man in both tales; (3) the carnival-like grotesqueness of the meal of the fatted ox—a potential motif in "A Meal of Herbs" that was later fulfilled in Bialik's adaptation of the story[10]—in parallel to the carnivalesque atmosphere of "Solomon and Marcolf," as Mikhail Bakhtin described it on the basis of Rabelais' adaptation;[11] and (4) the pathetic character of

9. See Ziolkowski's introduction to the translated edition, *Solomon and Marcolf*, 6–12. And see references by Tubach to tale type 4462.

10. See n. 6, above.

11. See Ziolkowski's comment in the introduction to his edition, 15.

Solomon, offended and weeping after the feast of the ox, which is similar to his defeated character in "Solomon and Marcolf."

Beyond all these, the major element the two narratives have in common is the *modus* of the parable. In "A Meal of Herbs," the coda is the proverb, "Better a meal of herbs where love is than a fatted ox and hatred with it," and in "Solomon and Marcolf" the first part is a contest of proverbs and parables. The affinity with "Solomon and Marcolf" is mainly cultural, rather than thematic. Both tales may express an aesthetic taste of the period as well as an interest in the literature of proverbs.[12] While the stories greatly differ, despite the parallels in some motifs, the reception of "A Meal of Herbs" in *Sefer ha-ma'asim*—in preference to the more popular story about Solomon's expulsion, which is richer in narrative materials—may suggest that it was part of the literary-cultural discourse represented in "Solomon and Marcolf" and in the folk literature of northern France.

12. Ibid., 28–44, about the popularity of the genre and its wide reception in the Middle Ages. One may also consider the popular parable of Berakhiah Hanakdan in his *Fox Fables*, "The City Mouse and the Country Mouse" (no. 10, ed. Hadas, 25–27), as a possible motivation for the choice of "A Meal of Herbs" in *Sefer ha-ma'asim*, and as an indication of the fondness for parables at the time. Berakhiah's parable ends with a moral similar to that of "A Meal of Herbs," thus alluding to the aforementioned verse cited from Proverbs 15:17. However this idea should be further investigated.

63. The Tribulations of Naḥum Ish Gamzo (331b–332a)

The story has two textual traditions, a brief one in the Palestinian Talmud (*Pe'ah* 8:9 [21:2];[1] *Shekalim* 5:6 [49:2][2]), and the other an expanded one in the Babylonian Talmud (*Ta'anit* 21a). The contexts in the Talmuds differ, and consequently their literary form differs as well,[3] but the main plot lines are the same. A poor man begs for charity from Naḥum Ish Gamzo, who puts off helping the man; as a result, the man dies of hunger. Naḥum asks for a punishment commensurate with his misdeed—to be blinded and to have his limbs cut off. His student, Akiva, is shocked by the sight of his rabbi's tribulations, but Naḥum Ish Gamzo's mind is at ease, and he feels the punishment is justified. When Naḥum met the poor man, he was on his way to his father-in-law's home, bringing gifts and delicacies.[4]

Sefer ha-ma'asim represents the expanded version in the Babylonian Talmud.[5] It is adjacent to the story "Naḥum Ish Gamzo and His Mission to the Emperor," which is in tractate *Ta'anit*.[6] In that tale, Naḥum Ish Gamzo is sent to the emperor as a representative of the community, bearing gifts of precious stones and pearls. On his way he spends the night at an inn, where the treasure is stolen and his bag is filled with earth. This incident might have ended badly, but miraculously the bag of earth turns out to be an effective weapon in the emperor's war against his enemies. Naḥum Ish Gamzo is sent home with great honor and precious gifts. The two tales about Naḥum and his tribulations and his mission to the emperor create a unit that explains why he is called "Naḥum Ish Gamzo" (from the Hebrew idiom "*gam zo letovah*"; lit., "this too is for the best"), since he was unfalteringly prepared to

1. Academy of Hebrew Language edition, 113.
2. Ibid., 622.
3. For a summary and comparison of the versions, see Ḥaikin, "The Nachum Ish Gamzo Midrashim," and references by Hendler, "Naḥum of Gamzo and His Errand to King Caesar," 244–256; Ben-Amos, *Mimekor yisrael*, no. 74, 148. See a selection of medieval versions, other than the one in *Sefer ha-ma'asim*: *Ḥibbur yafeh mehayeshu'a*, ed. Hirschberg, no. 4, 12–13; Brinner, ed, *An Elegant Composition Concerning Relief after Adversity*, no. 4; Aboab, *Menorat hama'or*, 3:7, no. 191, 402–403; Ms. Paris, Heb. 589, 95a–97a (15–16th century), as well as early print versions in *Hagadot hatalmud*, *Ta'anit*, 52b; *En Jacob Ta'anit* 21a, ed. Glick, vol. 2, 199–200. See also, in Ashkenaz: Ms. Jerusalem 5245, 46a–46b (1596); *Mayse bukh*, no. 94; *Ma'aseh Book*, v. 1, no. 94, 159–160.
4. This is stated explicitly in the Palestinian Talmud and implied in the Babylonian Talmud.
5. According to Ms. Munich 140 on *Ta'anit* (which differs from the textual tradition of the Vilna Press).
6. On the various editing trends of the story, see Hendler, "Naḥum of Gamzo and His Errand to King Caesar," 248.

accept the good and the bad. The Palestinian Talmud contains only the story of his tribulations, without the one about his mission to the emperor.

The *Sefer ha-ma'asim* version centers on the tormented figure of Naḥum Ish Gamzo, already described in tangible detail at the beginning of the story: "A tale is told of Naḥum of Gamzo, who was blind in both eyes and had lost both hands and [332a] both feet, and whose body was covered with boils. His bed was placed on four cups of water so that ants would not crawl up on him." This opening is consistent with its source in tractate *Ta'anit*. In the Palestinian Talmud, in contrast, the story begins with a description of Naḥum Ish Gamzo on his way to his father-in-law's home, and the motif of self-punishment and torments appears later. The motif of torment and self-mortification in *Sefer ha-ma'asim* is further emphasized by the severity of the punishment Naḥum Ish Gamzo has imposed on himself in relation to his sin. Whereas in the Palestinian Talmud Naḥum Ish Gamzo keeps the poor man waiting until he returns from his father-in-law's home, in *Sefer ha-ma'asim* he asks the poor man to wait until he unloads his merchandise from the donkey. Thus in the Palestinian Talmud he is more responsible for the poor man's death, since he makes him wait so long, but the motif of torment is given greater emphasis in the Babylonian Talmud and consequently also in *Sefer ha-ma'asim.*

The preference in this story for the Babylonian version over the one in the Palestinian Talmud is interesting. It is likely that this reflects general trends of reception in Ashkenaz regarding the Talmud, namely the dominant authority of the Babylonian Talmud over the Palestinian. Nonetheless, in this particular story it may also be a preference due to thematic trends. If so the choice of the Babylonian Talmud's version, which contains a more emphasized motif of self-mortification and a more tangible description of the limbless Naḥum Ish Gamzo, reflects an aesthetic taste of the period. The tale, in its version from the Babylonian Talmud, may also be a polemic response to the images of saints and martyrs that were widespread in Western Europe, and more specifically to the St. Francis (1181–1226) legends in the Middle Ages. According to contemporary sources, the crucified Jesus revealed himself to Francis in 1224. When he disappeared, Francis discovered bleeding wounds and bits of flesh on his palms, on the soles of his feet, and on his side—the signs of Jesus' stigmata. To hide the miracles, Francis covered his hands with bandages and concealed his bare feet with shoes, but the bloodstains gave away his condition. After Francis's death, his successor described the stigmata in a letter to all the members of the Franciscan order. In doing so, he immortalized the image of Francis as the man who reconstructed the suffering of Jesus for the sake of humanity in the most authentic way.

Francis preached the ethos of extreme poverty and the imitation of Jesus (*imitatio Christi*) without the need for the mediation of the Church hierarchical establishment. This ethos was expressed in his last will and testament, and in the collection of biographical narratives about him related by his friends and written down five hundred years after his death.[7] The inclusion in *Sefer ha-ma'asim* of the story about Naḥum Ish Gamzo—in particular the version found in the Babylonian Talmud—may, then, express an associative response to similar narrative materials in a shared cultural context, with the purpose of determining the limits of self-mortification in view of its Christian manifestations. In contrast to Franciscan asceticism as a permanent way of life and as a collective demand of members of the order, the asceticism of Naḥum Ish Gamzo is a deviant, one-time expression of profound repentance.

7. See Kleinberg's introduction to the chapter in his book about Francis of Assisi (*Fra Ginepro's Leg of Pork*, 255–268), and a selection from the hagiographical bibliography, 268–281, as it is represented in a collection of stories sent by the saint's friends (Leo, Rufino, and Angelo) to the authorities of the Franciscan order in 1246.

64. Naḥum Ish Gamzo and His Mission to the Emperor (332a)

This story, which follows the one about the tribulations of Naḥum Ish Gamzo, is based on the talmudic model in *Ta'anit* 21a, and it provides an explanation for his sobriquet.[1] On every occasion, in times of distress and trouble, he was in the habit of saying "*gam zo letovah*" ("this too is for the best").[2] Another version appears in *Sanhedrin* 108b, where the story stands on its own. Sometimes his name is explained on the basis of his place of origin—the settlement of Gimzu on the plain of Lydda—and he is then identified as Naḥum haMadi.[3]

Sefer ha-ma'asim alternately combines the two versions that appear in tractates *Ta'anit* and *Sanhedrin*. The style is elliptical and relies on the reader's acquaintance with the fuller versions in the Talmud.[4] The scribe's prior knowledge of the talmudic sources is also implied by the use of talmudic Aramaic. The story was obviously addressed to readers who were familiar with the Babylonian Talmud to some extent. On the other hand, the partial translation into Hebrew suggests that Aramaic was no longer their spoken language. This is also evident from the dominance of Aramaic throughout the story in the *Midrash hagadol* and in *Sefer hama'asiyot*, edited by Gaster in the Middle Ages, according to the talmudic source.

The reference to Elijah "of blessed memory," which does not appear in the talmudic versions, also indicates the existence of a broad readership. This appellation also exists in *Midrash hagadol* and in *Sefer hama'asiyot*, so that it may reflect the image of Elijah in popular thought as a herald of redemption at the End of Days and as a wondrous redeemer of Jewish communities and individuals in times of crisis

1. See Hendler, "Naḥum of Gamzo and His Errand to King Caesar," for a list of 39 versions of the story (252–254 and n. 1 on 255) and a survey of the story (248–259); Ben-Amos, *Mimekor yisrael*, no. 111, 200–201. For a selection of medieval versions, see *Ḥibbur yafeh mehayeshu'a*, ed. Hirschberg, no. 4, 12–13; Brinner, ed., *An Elegant Composition Concerning Relief after Adversity*, no. 4, 24–25; Makhir ben Abba Mari, *Yalkut hamakhiri*, ed. Buber, 117–118; R. David ha-Adani, *Midrash hagadol*, Genesis, ed. Margulies, 238; Aboab, *Menorat hama'or*, 3:7, no. 191, 403. From the sixteenth and early seventeenth centuries, see *Hagadot hatalmud*, *Ta'anit*, 52b; Ibn Ḥabib, *En Jacob*, *Ta'anit* 21a, ed. Glick, vol. 2, 200–201; *Ma'aseh Book*, trans. Gaster, vol. 1, no. 94, 160–163; Ms. Jerusalem 5245, no. 57.
2. The motto of "this is also for the best" is also known from the talmudic tale about the student of Naḥum Ish Gamzo, R. Akiva, in tractate *Berakhot* 60b. The student, like his teacher, would say about every event: "*kol ma'an de'avid rahmana letab avid*"—that is, everything the Almighty does is for the best.
3. For his identification with Naḥum Hamadi, see *Midrash hagadol* (*Genesis*, ed. Margulies, 238), and Gaster, ed., *Sefer hama'asiyot* (*Exempla*, no. 25, 18). For his identification with his origins in Gimzu, see R. Nathan of Rome, *Arukh hashalem*, vol. 2, ed. Kohut, "Gamzo," 307.
4. E.g., "Who shall we send it with? With Naḥum Ish Gamzo," in contrast to the wording in *Sanhedrin*: "By Naḥum of Gimzo we will send it."

(oikotype 730*A). In the story about Naḥum Ish Gamzo, Elijah's sudden appearance as one of the emperor's ministers and the solution to the dilemma that he suggests, as well as the miracle in the emperor's war against his enemies, saved Naḥum and the entire community from death.

The story has two anonymous parallels in Latin from southern Germany, the earliest of the two probably from the early thirteenth century. In the research they are assigned to the tale type known as Raparius or "Two Gifts to the King" (ATU 1689A).[5] According to medieval versions, a poor peasant brings the king a huge turnip and is given a great reward. His brother, a wealthy knight, is jealous, and he presents the king with a larger gift in the hope of receiving a larger reward than his brother did. The king ponders over an appropriate reward, since the knight has enough money and gold, and finally he gives him the huge turnip he received from his poor brother. The motif of "two gifts" and their comparison, as well as the motif of envy, also exist in the Jewish story about Naḥum Ish Gamzo. The owners of the house where Naḥum sleeps envy him because of the great reward he has received, and they too bring a sack of earth to the emperor. The earth is found to be worthless. This angers the emperor, and he sentences them to death. There are more differences than similarities between the parallels: in particular the hyperbolic modus in the motif of the huge turnip and the aspect of relations within the family between two brothers, which do not exist in "Naḥum Ish Gamzo and His Mission to the Emperor." However, the common motifs create a certain affinity between the stories. "Two Gifts to the King," which was a very prevalent story in the Middle Ages in Western Europe, and which relates to the medieval feudal hierarchy and the crumbling social orders, may have exerted a certain influence on the inclusion of "Naḥum of Gamzo and His Mission to the Emperor" in *Sefer ha-ma'asim*. The talmudic infrastructure in *Ta'anit* is, however, more central to the considerations that affected the editing of the story and its inclusion in *Sefer ha-ma'asim* as one unit along with "The Tribulations of Naḥum Ish Gamzo."

5. On the medieval versions of the tale type 1689A in comparison to the adaptation of the story by the Grimm brothers, see Ziolkowski, "The Wonder of the Turnip Tale," 190–199, and the tales, 322–331, 331–339. See also the entry on this tale type in *EM* 11:1 (2003), 219–224. Cf. "Hadrian and the Old Man" (no. 38) in *Sefer ha-ma'asim*, also of type 1689A.

65. The Grateful Dead (332a–333b)

The infrastructure of the story is apparently in the apocryphal Book of Tobit, of the "The Grateful Dead" tale type (ATU 505),[1] as well as in medieval versions of this type, some of them exempla and some expanded and episodic narratives that were widespread in Western Europe between the thirteenth and fifteenth centuries. A distinct example of an expanded narrative of "The Grateful Dead," which postdates *Sefer ha-ma'asim*, is the fourteenth-century courtly romance *Rittertreue*.[2]

In *Sefer ha-ma'asim* the story is divided into three episodes that take place between the departure of the protagonist from his mother and his return home, with the exception of the opening prologue and the concluding epilogue.[3] These episodes, influenced by the Book of Tobit and medieval versions of "The Grateful Dead," were adapted in *Sefer ha-ma'asim* according to familiar models in Jewish sources. These include "The *Ḥasid* and the Tax Collector's Son" in the Palestinian Talmud,[4] "The Annulment of the Three Decrees" in the Babylonian Talmud,[5] and the tale type "A Companion in Paradise," as in *Tanḥuma* (ed. Buber).[6] The combination of independent episodes of divergent sources and tale types created an eclectic narrative that is consistent with the aesthetic taste of its audience in the Middle Ages.

The Book of Tobit takes place in the time of Sennaḥerib, king of Assyria, and his decrees, after the Ten Tribes had been exiled to Nineveh by Shalmaneser.[7] Tobit, the father of Tobias, is a man who provides proper burials[8] for the Jews slain by Sennaḥerib; like Job, he is tested by many difficult tribulations but remains faithful to God. The book contains a detailed description of his treatment of a man whose corpse is cast into the marketplace in the midst of the Pentecost. Tobit leaves the

1. "The Book of Tobit," in *The Apocrypha and Pseudepigrapha of the Old Testament*, ed. Charles, vol. 1, 1:1–14:15, 202–241.
2. Meier-Branecke, *Die Rittertreue*.
3. On the tale's structure, see Yassif, *Kemargalit bemishbeẓet*, 161, and his references to relevant tale types.
4. See *Ḥagigah* 2:2 (77d), 787–788, and *Sanhedrin* 6:4 (23c), 1293–1294. For discussion and sources, see Kushelevsky, *Penalty and Temptation*, 50–77; 302–306.
5. For the story of the annulment of the three decrees, see *Me'ilah* 17a–b; for discussion and additional sources, see Kushelevsky, *Penalty and Temptation*, 233–252, 319–320.
6. *Tanḥuma*, ed. Buber, Introduction, no. 41, 135–136. There are different versions of "A Companion in Paradise"; here the one most relevant to a discussion of the present story was chosen.
7. See references to sources and research of the Book of Tobit: Ben-Amos, *Mimekor yisrael*, no. 40, 74–75.
8. The Hebrew term for an act of burial with no intention of profit and benefit is "*ḥesed shel emet*" (lit. "the truest act of charity").

festive meal, goes into the market, and brings the corpse into his home until nightfall, when he can bury him secretly in the dark (2:1–8).

Tobit commands his son to observe the commandments throughout his life and to do many charitable deeds. He sends him to Gabael, in the land of Media, to collect the repayment of a loan he had given him in the days when he still owned much property. Then an angel appears before Tobias in the form of a handsome young man and offers to escort and protect him from the dangers of the road. After investigating a few details about the man, Tobias agrees, sets his wages, and promises to pay him more when they return safely. The angel saves him from a fish that tries to swallow him and guides Tobias to the home of Raguel, a relative, so that he may marry his daughter Sarah and become his heir. Tobias does so, although he knows about her previous seven husbands, all of whom were killed by Asmodeus. On the wedding night, Tobias follows the instructions of his escort and succeeds in driving off the demon. His wife's father hastens to give Tobias half of his fortune and chooses him as his heir after his death. In the meantime Raphael, Tobias's escort, continues on his way to Gabael to collect the debt, while Tobias and his new wife remain with his father-in-law. The mission is accomplished, and now they all travel together to Tobias's parents, in particular to his mother, who is greatly concerned about the fate of her son. When they arrive, Tobias wishes to pay his escort half of his fortune, but the latter reveals himself to him and his father to be the angel Raphael, who was sent to Tobit as a reward for his good deeds in burying the dead at great risk to his own life.

Several incidents in the Book of Tobit are parallel to events in the story in *Sefer ha-ma'asim*: a father's command to his son to strictly observe the commandments and especially to give charity; the burial of the dead (in *Sefer ha-ma'asim*, by paying a bribe); the arranging of a delayed marriage of a bride (by paying the dowry); a crisis in the life of the protagonist, followed by prayer; an angel (Elijah/Raphael) who escorts the hero on his way and protects him, as a reward for his or his father's good deeds in burying the dead. In *Sefer ha-ma'asim*, the mother anxiously wishes for the safe return of her son from his dangerous travels; in her words: "God will send his angel before you to protect you on the way and bring you to that place." Toward the end of the story, her words are given dramatic form in the figure of a real, concrete escort: Elijah, who accompanies the young man on his way and also returns him, now a wealthy man, safely home to his mother.

In both narratives the hero is so strongly and absolutely committed to the value of charity that he risks his own life and clashes with his surroundings. Accordingly, they share a number of motifs:

1. "The Grateful Dead" motif.[9]
2. The motif of charity as a loan to God or a deposit that will be returned in the future, based on the verse in Proverbs: "He who gives kindly to the poor lends to the Lord; and that which he has given will he pay him back" (19:17). In the Book of Tobit the verse is implied,[10] and here it is embodied in the recurrent motto in the hero's words to his mother: "I lent it to a certain great lord whose name is known all over the world, and he will pay me double, and I trust that he will pay me my wages for my work."
3. The motif of the evil decrees visited upon the Jews, which is in the background of Tobias's good deeds and are an episode in *Sefer ha-ma'asim.*
4. The motif of the experience of passing a test,[11] and the relinquishment of a material reward for the sake of a spiritual reward. Tobit allots a certain payment for his son's escort and also promises him an additional sum upon their return (5:16–17). The escort, Raphael, forgoes his payment, since he is an angel. Similarly, in *Sefer ha-ma'asim* the hero is prepared to forgo his reward in this world to gain one in the world to come, because he prefers a spiritual reward to a material one. In both cases there is a hierarchy between the material and the spiritual reality, although in *Sefer ha-ma'asim* the hero gains both great wealth and an honorable place in the Garden of Eden.

While all of these similarities do not suffice to clearly determine that the Book of Tobit is the direct source of the story—in particular since the order of the events differs—this does seem to be a likely possibility.[12]

The tale has a clearer affinity with the medieval versions of "The Grateful Dead," which were widespread in brief, didactic exempla intended to encourage people to carry out charitable deeds for the dead and to point to the benefit of such acts for the living, as well as in courtly romances such as *Rittertreue* of the fourteenth century.[13]

9. See Kahana's reference to this tale type in his introduction to the Book of Tobit (*Sefarim hiẓonim*, vol. 2, 306–307).
10. Ed. Charles, vol. 1, 4: 11, 212: "Alms is a good offering in the sight of the Most High for all that give it."
11. In *Sefer ha-ma'asim* Elijah says: "God has heard your prayer and seen your suffering and everything that you have done in his honor" and in the Book of Tobit: "I was sent unto thee to try thee" (12:14, ed. Charles, 234).
12. For an another affinity with the Book of Tobit in *Sefer ha-ma'asim*, cf. Baumgarten and Kushelevsky, "From 'The Mother and Her Sons,'" 323–324.
13. The following discussion is based on Bohler, "Béances de la Terre et du Temps: . . . Le Motif du Mort Reconnaisant."

Their basic shared plot delineates the adventures of a knight who goes to an inn owned by a usurer (implied to be a Jew), where he sees an unburied corpse. When he asks why, he is told that the man was ostracized and not buried because he did not pay his debt to the owner of the inn. The knight, who was on his way to joust, sells his horse and pays the man's debts so he can be buried. Without his horse, he can no longer joust—a problem that is, however, immediately solved. The deceased, in the form of a stranger, "happens" to pass by, and he awards the knight a special horse. In return the knight promises that, after he wins the duel, he will equally share his prize with him. On the knight's wedding night, the stranger appears to demand his share. The knight is prepared to honor his commitment, but the stranger declares that all he wanted to do was to test the knight. He disappears, and the knight and his princess live happily ever after.

This basic plot, often expanded and appended to additional tale types, epitomizes a chivalry ethos of mutual loyalty among knights, self-sacrifice for an ideal (the knight gives up all of his property for the man's burial), commitment to one's word, tests of heroism, and jousting for the sake of a beloved lady. Along with secular characteristics of the romance genre centered on the quest motif, "The Grateful Dead" also preaches Christian religious values, such as a covenant between the living and the dead and redemption of the dead from the sufferings of purgatory, as Daniel Bohler has shown. The story developed into its various versions between the thirteenth and fifteenth centuries, parallel to the process in which the doctrine of purgatory was officially accepted in Christian society. There is also a political aspect in the story that Bohler does not relate. The figure who is putatively responsible for the failure to bury the corpse is the moneylender: a Jewish occupation in the Middle Ages, since it was forbidden to Christians, which led the poor to resent the Jews. The negative image of the Jewish moneylender is embedded in the story[14] and makes it part of the anti-Semitic discourse that is also known from medieval blood-libel tales, although it is not as blatant and explicit as they are.[15]

In *Sefer ha-ma'asim* the young man devotes all of his money to pay a bribe in order to enable the man's burial, which is similar to "The Grateful Dead" narrative in Europe. In the same way the bride-to-be, who is rejected because of her poverty, is married thanks to the young man's payment of her father's debt to the groom, parallel to the knight's success in winning the princess thanks to the intervention of the grateful dead. The debt motif is more central and emphasized here, and in the

14. The term given to the moneylender in the story—"jouteur"—has a negative connotation.

15. See Rubin, *Gentile Tales.*

non-Jewish parallels of "The Grateful Dead" in Europe, than in the Book of Tobit. It is also found in the third episode in this story, in which the young man pays the required bribe so that the government's decrees against the Jewish community will be annulled. This may be a further development of some background details in the Book of Tobit about the anti-Jewish decrees of Sennaḥerib, or a Jewish reaction to hostile attitudes in medieval versions of "The Grateful Dead." The combination of the different episodes—the marriage of the bride-to-be, the burial of the deceased by virtue of the payment of his debts, and the evil decrees against the background of a religious conflict—into one story indicates that the Book of Tobit and medieval versions of "The Grateful Dead" constitute the infrastructure of the story.

The narrative materials of the Book of Tobit, and especially of the medieval versions of "The Grateful Dead," were reshaped in *Sefer ha-ma'asim*. They were inserted into models available in Jewish sources, which are evident in parallel motifs and occasionally recurring idiomatic phrases. The first episode after the prologue, which centers on the payment of a dowry that enables the marriage of the bride and groom, seems to draw its inspiration from a story cited by Buber in his introduction to *Tanḥuma*.[16] A butcher pays a large sum of money to ransom two hundred Jewish prisoners being held by a captain on his ship. He then arranges a marriage between one of the prisoners and his son, but in the midst of the wedding feast he discovers that the girl was betrothed to another, also a prisoner. He tells this to his son, who immediately divorces her so that she can marry her intended fiancé. The butcher then marries them and gives them a large sum of money, which awards him an honorable place in paradise. The affinity between this tale of the "Companion in Paradise" type and the first episode of "The Grateful Dead" in *Sefer ha-ma'asim* is created by the combination of the payment of a ransom (to free prisoners or pay a dowry) and the marriage of an intended bride. The ending, with the promise of the hero's reward among the righteous in the Garden of Eden, supports this hypothesis, in light of a similar promise in the *Tanḥuma* version: "Blessed is the Almighty who has granted me a place with you in the Garden of Eden."[17] The disparities between the tales are obvious, but apparently the parallel between the major motifs provided a sufficient basis for refashioning "The Grateful Dead" according to the available Jewish model in the *Tanḥuma*.

16. Vol. 1, 135–136, no. 41. The tale appears in one of Buber's text witnesses, which are described in his introduction, vol. 1, 124.

17. *Tanḥuma*, ed. Buber, vol. 1, 136.

The second episode, which centers on the payment of a bribe to enable the burial of the dead, is inspired by the "The *Ḥasid* and the Tax Collector's Son," which was also copied into *Sefer ha-ma'asim* (329b–330b). A greatly honored rabbi does not receive a proper burial and funeral because his corpse is switched with that of another man, who was known for his wickedness. The rabbi is presented in a similar manner as "a Torah scholar and a perfectly righteous man."[18] The rabbi's student and the rest of the community are shocked and bereaved. The words "honor" and "respect" recur in both stories—sorrow and shock at the way the rabbi is humiliated and deprived of the respect he merits. As in "The Grateful Dead," "The *Ḥasid* and the Tax Collector's Son" has a description of the great reward of the *ḥasid* in paradise: "he saw that his rabbi was sitting in the Garden of Eden on golden chairs, with the clouds of glory covering him, and he was there alongside the greatest righteous men in the Garden of Eden."

The third episode is parallel to the "Annulment of Evil Decrees," in tractate *Me'ilah*. A Jew, an advisor to the king, succeeds in convincing the emperor of Rome to annul the king's decrees against observance of the Sabbath, circumcision, and the law against intercourse with menstruating women.[19] The story ends with an epilogue about the great reward of the protagonist in this world and in the next.

The main difference between the Book of Tobit from the Apocrypha and the tale in *Sefer ha-ma'asim*, as well as in the expanded non-Jewish versions of "The Grateful Dead" in the Middle Ages, is the episodic composition in the medieval narratives, which contrasts with the causal logic in the Book of Tobit. In the latter, each event is the consequence of a prior event, until the climax of Tobias's return—now with his wife and much wealth—to his parents. In *Sefer ha-ma'asim*, the episodes are loosely linked, and if they had been separated, the story would still be intact. What we have here is a poetic that strives for variety, disparity, multiplicity, and heterogeneity, all of which are assembled into a new disintegrated whole. And since the building blocks of the story existed in the narrative and folklore repertoire of the narrating community, it was received as familiar, even though, as far as we know, in the entire history of Hebrew literature it appears only once, in *Sefer ha-ma'asim*.

18. Cf. in the present tale of "The Grateful Dead": "great in Torah and in good deeds and commandments, and also a perfectly righteous and very virtuous man."

19. Cf. the oikotype 730*A ("Miraculous rescue of a Jewish community") and Yassif's reference to it in *Kemargalit bemishbeẓet*, 161.

66. The Prophecy of the Ravens (333b–336b)

As far as we know, the first written version of "The Prophecy of the Ravens" appears in *Sefer ha-ma'asim*. Its non-Hebrew source is a parallel in *The Seven Sages of Rome*, which resonated greatly in the Middle Ages—in Latin and in nearly every vernacular language in Europe; it is the European rendition of *Tales of Sendebar* (or "Sendebad") from the East. Both *Tales of Sendebar* in the East and *The Seven Sages of Rome* in the West are frame stories within which internal tales are embedded (thus resembling the structure of *A Thousand and One Nights*). They share a similar frame story but differ in the scope and content of the embedded tales.[1]

In the frame story of *The Seven Sages of Rome*, the sultan sends his son far away to learn wisdom from seven wise masters. Upon his return to the palace, the prince sees in the stars that a grave danger awaits him; to avoid this fate he undertakes to remain silent for seven days. The queen, his stepmother, tries unsuccessfully to seduce him. To get her revenge she reverses the facts, tells the sultan that his son tried to seduce her, and incites him against his son with various tales about treacherous sons. The father intends to kill his son, but the seven sages manage to put off his death by telling the sultan tales about treacherous women. At the end of the seven days, the prince begins to talk again, the truth is revealed, and the treacherous queen is executed.

The story entitled *Vaticinium* ("Prophecy"),[2] which is the source for "The Prophecy of the Ravens" in *Sefer ha-ma'asim*, is the last among the embedded tales in *The Seven Sages of Rome*, and it is unique to the European rendition of the work.[3] It is not found in the Eastern *Tales of Sendebar*. This may provide a clue as to the date of *Sefer ha-ma'asim*. Since the earliest version of *The Seven Sages of Rome* is in Old French in the second half of the twelfth century (1155–1190), and text witnesses are found from the thirteenth century on,[4] *Sefer ha-ma'asim* can probably be dated to sometime in the thirteenth century, when *The Seven Sages of Rome* was popular and accessible to broad readerships.

1. See a research review in Speer, *Le Roman des Sept*, 14–17, and earlier studies by Epstein, *Tales of Sendebar*, 31–37; Campbell, ed., *The Seven Sages of Rome*, xi–xvi; an annotated bibliography, Runte, Wikeley, and Farrell, *The Seven Sages and The Book of Sindbad.*
2. The story is of tale type ATU 517: "The Boy Who Understands the Language of Birds." Cf. also AT 725: "Prophecy of Future Sovereignty" (reference by Thompson, *The Folktale*, 138).
3. See references to the tale's European versions in Runte, Wikeley, and Farrell, *The Seven Sages*, 170.
4. See Campbell, ed., *The Seven Sages of Rome*, xxi–xxvii, and Speer, *Le Roman des Sept Sages de Rome*, 67–71, about the dating of the compilation. The comparative discussion that follows is based on the Speer edition (284–289, as summarized in English, 84–85) and on the frame story in this edition (114–137, and the summary in English, 74–76).

The narrator of *Vaticinium* is the prince himself, after the seven days of silence he imposed on himself, and its characters are a father and his son. The son, who masters the language of animals, hears from ravens that one day his parents will lose all their property and end up as his servants.[5] He is forced to tell this to his father, who angrily casts him into the sea. In due time the prophecy is indeed fulfilled. The son becomes the king, and his father, who has lost everything, must serve his son, whom he does not recognize.[6] The story deals with father-son relations and is intended to show, from the prince's point of view, how unjust his father was in planning to kill him and how loyal he was to his father nonetheless.

"The Prophecy of the Ravens," unlike *Vaticinium*, appears on its own in *Sefer ha-ma'asim* and not as an embedded tale within a frame story. The plot of *Vaticinium* is adapted to Jewish values, to render it appropriate for *Sefer ha-ma'asim*. The conflict between the son and his parents is tempered, and the deterministic message is replaced by one of Divine providence. In the Jewish story, as in the European parallel, the parents lose all of their possessions and arrive before their son totally impoverished and unaware of his identity, but unlike in *Vaticinium*, they are not required to serve him, nor are they humiliated. On the contrary, the son shows them respect and care. Attributing to God the accumulation of the events up to his parents' appearance before him, he says: "Now do not be grieved or angry with yourselves, for God sent me before you to preserve life."[7] This is resonant of the biblical narrative of Joseph, the son who was rejected and lost, and who then achieved dignity as deputy to the king of Egypt, and yet honored his father. A tale in *The Seven Sages of Rome*, whose theme is one of predeterminism, is interpreted in *Sefer ha-ma'asim* as a narrative of providence.

The Eastern tradition of the work in *Tales of Sendebar* and its Hebrew rendition in *Mishlei Sendebar* also influenced "The Prophecy of the Ravens," particularly in the first half of the story. *Mishlei Sendebar* was copied in the same manuscript of *Sefer ha-ma'asim* (Ms. Bodl. Or. 135), and was obviously familiar to its narrator. Motifs from the frame story of *Mishlei Sendebar* were integrated into "The

5. On the image of the raven in the Middle Ages as a bird that knows the future, see Cirlot, "Crow," in *Dictionary of Symbols* 71.
6. According to the ceremonial rules in the king's palace, the father holds his son's sleeves when he washes his hands, and the mother prepares a towel for him to dry them. See also Speer's reference to research on this ceremony in her comments on L 4517–19 in her edition (*Le Roman des Sept Sages de Rome*, 331).
7. And cf. Genesis 45:5. For more references to the biblical narrative of Joseph, **see part 2, tale no. 66.** See Thompson's reference to the affinity of the tale type (AT 517) to the Joseph narrative (Thompson, *The Folktale*, 138).

Prophecy of the Ravens": the figure of a father of an only son; his anxiety for the fate of the kingdom, or for his legacy, after his death; the son's initiation away from home for the purpose of learning wisdom; the figure of a sage; the motif of "Understanding Animal Languages"; the silence the son imposed on himself (for seven days or as a reaction to the prophecy of the ravens); and the conflict between the father and his son due to a pretext that later turns out to be baseless (the father's disappointment at his son's ignorance and the queen's libel about him).[8] The long period of study, which the protagonists of "The Prophecy of the Ravens" and *Mishlei Sendebar* spent away from home, and the difficulties they had to cope with, reflect an existential tension between the challenge of attaining the essence of wisdom and the transitory nature of time.[9] There is also a stylistic affinity with *Mishlei Sendebar*. Both texts, the frame story of *Mishlei Sendebar* and "The Prophecy of the Ravens," allude to the Book of Esther.[10]

Two motifs from the frame story of *Mishlei Sendebar* are conspicuous in their absence from "The Prophecy of the Ravens." These are the queen's attempted seduction of the prince and her defamation of him, which in *Sefer ha-ma'asim* is replaced by the hero's marriage to the king's daughter and the deterministic motif of reading signs in the stars. While some of the narrative material from *Mishlei Sendebar* is left out of "The Prophecy of the Ravens," the emphasis there is on the son's quest for wisdom and his defining his self-identity against the background of his flawed relationship with his father.[11] In *Sefer ha-ma'asim* wisdom is equated with Torah, and the sage is equated with the Torah scholar, who had an exalted status in Ashkenaz and was the object of special esteem: "because at the hour of death one has neither silver nor gold nor precious stones nor pearls, but only the Torah and good deeds."[12] During the nine years of his study, the son acquired the essence of

8. The context of the frame story may, then, explain the father's extreme reaction to his son's stupidity, albeit without justifying it.
9. Although most of the motifs common to the "The Prophecy of the Ravens" and *Mishlei Sendebar* are in the first part of "The Prophecy of the Ravens," some of them also appear in the second half, which is parallel to *Vaticinium*.
10. See Epstein's comment on thematic and stylistic affinities in *Mishlei Sendebar* to the Book of Esther in his introduction to *Tales of Sendebar*, and his references to notes in various places in the edition.
11. The quest and its combination with the motif of marriage to the king's daughter imbue the story with a somewhat romance-like character, and from this standpoint, too, it is parallel to *The Seven Sages of Rome*.
12. See quote in *The Ethics of the Fathers*, 6:9, as a homily on the verse from Psalms (119:72)—"The Torah of your mouth is better to me than thousands of gold and silver"—and in the framework of a story about R. Yossi ben Kisma, as well as in the *Maḥzor Vitry* (no. 429) in northern France.

wisdom, embodied in knowledge of all branches of the Torah, and learned "the language of the palms, demons, the fables of the foxes, and the language of every animal, beast, and bird."[13] The story contraposes wisdom to wealth and transitory goods, and shows that choice is made possible by the wisdom acquired through Torah study, although the future is known in advance. The combination of the first part of the story, based on the frame story of the non-Jewish parallels, and the second half, about the prophecy of the ravens, produces a romance-like narrative about an initiation journey and a quest for the essence of wisdom that entails the son's struggle with his father for his own life and self-identity, his success in proving his loyalty to his father, and finally his marriage to the king's daughter.

After the Middle Ages only one version of the story is extant, in a sixteenth-century manuscript from Persia published by Gaster.[14] Gaps in *Sefer ha-ma'asim* are filled in this version: for example, the reason the young man's father threw him into the sea. In *Sefer ha-ma'asim* the implied reason is the father's disappointment at his son's stupidity, after he had sent him to learn wisdom from the finest sages. In the Persian manuscript, and according to *The Seven Sages of Rome*, the son dreamt that his parents would in the future wash his feet (i.e., serve him).[15] Given that the source of *The Seven Sages of Rome* is European, this suggests that the tale tradition may have existed in channels other than *Sefer ha-ma'asim*, that it continued to exist afterward, and that it then moved to the East.[16]

13. Cf. the description of the wisdom of R. Johanan ben Zakkai, one of Hillel's disciples, in tractate *Succa* 28a: "They said of R. Johanan b. Zakkai that he did not leave [unstudied] Scripture, Mishnah, Gemara, Halakhah, Aggada, details of the Torah, details of the Scribes, inferences a minori ad majus, analogies, calendrical computations, gematrias, the speech of the Ministering Angels, the speech of spirits, and the speech of palm-trees, fullers' parables and fox fables."
14. Gaster, *Studies and Texts*, vol. 2, 938–941.
15. The father reacts angrily to his son's dream, according to which he and his wife would wash his son's feet (i.e., serve him).
16. For a different conclusion regarding the dating of the version in the manuscript from Persia, see Yassif, *Kemargalit bemishbeẓet*, 155–156.

67. The Maiden in the Tower (336b–337a)

This story is composed of two episodes: one concerning the pact between Solomon and Ḥiram, and the other about the girl locked in the tower. The first takes place against the backdrop of the war between King Solomon and Ḥiram, king of Tyre. In the midst of the summer heat, the sun blazes over Solomon's camp, and the king orders the birds to gather there and spread their wings over him and his troops to give them shade. The clamor of the birds reaches the Tyre camp across the river and arouses the king's curiosity. When Ḥiram learns about the flocks of birds providing shade to Solomon and his soldiers, he travels, escorted by two unarmed horsemen, to see the sight for himself and to learn the great wonders God does for Solomon. After another development of the plot, this part ends with a pact between Solomon and Ḥiram: "And there was peace between Ḥiram and Solomon; and they made a peace pact." The second half centers on the daughter of Joshua, the high priest. An eagle reveals to Solomon that Joshua's daughter is predestinated to marry a bastard,[1] and this leads Solomon to lock her up in a high tower, with absolutely no access from the outside. Nonetheless, an eagle drops a bastard infant into the tower; when the child grows up, the two fall in love, and she conceives from him. Thus the prophecy is fulfilled. Solomon discovers this and realizes he is unable to cancel the decree. A causal connection joins the two parts into one story. Solomon tells Ḥiram about the prophecy he heard from the eagle; Ḥiram is amazed at Solomon's control over the birds and enters into a pact with him; and Solomon attempts unsuccessfully to cancel the decree over the daughter of Joshua, the high priest. Despite this causal connection, the story is episodic, like others in *Sefer ha-ma'asim*, since it could have ended with the pact between Solomon and Ḥiram.

These episodes were probably received in the Middle Ages as independent stories. In another, not entirely identical, tale from the twelfth century, published by Habermann, the episodes are in an opposite order and are combined.[2] Solomon dreams that his daughter will marry a poor man; to prevent this he locks her in a tower where no strangers are allowed to visit. Despite these precautions, her designated groom arrives, wrapped inside the carcass of a horse and carried to the roof of the tower by a large bird. The girl conceives from him. Solomon is reconciled to the match and holds a splendid wedding feast, at which he hosts important kings, including one who was previously his enemy. Solomon orders the birds to shelter

1. A bastard, in the halakhic terminology, is someone born out of an incestuous relationship.
2. Ms. Taylor-Schecter K27/19 at Cambridge, in Habermann, *Texts: Old and New*, 193–196.

the guests under their wings. However, the bird that covered Solomon disappears, and the eagle reveals the reason to Solomon. It turns out that the bird was in heaven, attending the wedding of Solomon's daughter that was being held there at the same time as the one on earth. Then the kings, who see how great Solomon is, accept his authority over them.

The reception of the story in the Middle Ages, at least insofar as the pact between Solomon and Ḥiram is concerned, may also be inferred from the commentary of the Tosafists on the Talmud.[3] In their commentary on the tractate *Yebamot* (23a), the Tosafists question the pact between Solomon and Ḥiram, which is related in 1 Kings (5:26), because of the words in Deuteronomy (7:2): "You shall make no covenant with them, nor show mercy to them."[4] The conclusion in *Yebamot* is that the prohibition against showing "mercy to them" applies to the gentiles in general, and not only to the Canaanites. One of the pretexts allowing for the resolution of the problem of Solomon's pact with Ḥiram is that Ḥiram is a "*ger toshav*" (lit., an "alien resident"), so the prohibition does not apply to him.[5] The present story about Ḥiram does explain the background for the pact—Ḥiram's amazement at Solomon's wisdom and the wonders God does for him.[6] It is possible, therefore, that the story preserves an unknown tradition of the Tosafists, irrespective of whether it emerged from their discussion of the matter or formed the background to that discussion.

The episode of the pact in its present form is not documented in earlier sources, but the motif of the eagle covering Solomon is familiar in a certain variation from the description of the death of his father, King David, in *Ruth rabbah*.[7] David stumbles on the stairs of his home and dies on the Sabbath in his garden. The Halakhah does not permit his body to be carried on the Sabbath. To protect him from the sun and to preserve his corpse until the closing of the Sabbath, Solomon invites the eagles to provide shade by covering him with their wings.

3. Tosafot, *Yebamot* 23a; *Tosafot Rosh, Kiddushin* 68b.
4. The discussion in the Talmud relates to the status of the offspring of a slave and a Jewish woman and the prohibition against such relations; the Tosafot expands the discussion to the issue of Solomon and Ḥiram's pact, since the two prohibitions are cited in the same portion on seven nations in Deuteronomy 7:1.
5. A *ger toshav* is someone who undertakes, in a religious court, to observe the Noahide commandments and to accept Jewish rule in the Land of Israel. (See *Avodah Zara* 64b, which includes various opinions as to the definition of a *ger toshav*.)
6. A totally different image of Ḥiram as a proud king who rebels against God emphasizes a change of personality in the present story. See Ms. Jerusalem Museum 180/051 JER 264b (from the 14th century), in Ashkenazi and square Italian script (cited from other sources by Jellinek, *Bet hamidrasch*, 5, 111–112).
7. *Ruth rabbah* 3,2, ed. Lerner, 84–86.

The second episode in this story is better documented, although its parallels relate to Solomon's daughter rather than to Joshua's.[8] According to Ms. Bodl. Opp. 187, Solomon sees in the stars that his beautiful daughter is destined to marry a poverty-stricken man. To cancel the decree, he builds a high tower in the sea, completely sealed, and assigns seventy elders of the Sanhedrin to be in charge of it. At the same time, the story relates what happens to the very poor man, her intended spouse. In his wanderings at night, hungry, thirsty, and exhausted, he finds shelter inside the carcass of a bull cast into the field, and falls asleep. A bird carries him, still wrapped inside the carcass, onto the roof of the tower. When he awakens in the morning and the girl sees him, he tells her he is a Jew from Acre, and describes all that has happened to him. She looks after him, they fall in love, and the young man, who is sharp and quick-witted, marries her according to her request. He writes the *ketubah*, the Jewish marriage contract, with his blood, and their witnesses are the angels Michael and Gabriel. She conceives from him, and when their keepers discover this, they call on Solomon to come to the tower. His daughter tells him how things came about: "The Almighty brought me a young man, lovely and good, learned and holy, and he married me." Solomon understands that he is the young man he saw in the stars, and blesses the Almighty for having arranged this match for his daughter.[9] Although there are some narrative changes, all three versions mentioned here basically share the same plot. However in *Sefer ha-ma'asim*, Ms. Bodl. Or. 135, it is the fear of his daughter's marriage to a bastard that motivates Solomon to lock the maiden in an isolated tower, while in the other two versions—Ms. Bodl., Opp. 187 and Ms. Cambridge—Solomon disapproves of the marriage because of the intended groom's financial and social inferiority.

About Joshua, the high priest, introduced in *Sefer ha-ma'asim*, it is written in Zechariah 3:3:"And Joshua was clothed with filthy garments"; that Satan stands on his right to thwart him (ibid., 3:1); and that he is "a brand plucked out of the fire" (ibid., 3:2). On the basis of these verses, it is stated in *Sanhedrin* 93a that his filthy

8. For a list of parallels, see Elstein, "The Theme of 'The King's Daughter Locked-up in a Tower,'" 80–82. Also see references to sources and research in Ben-Amos, *Mimekor yisrael*, no. 38, 70–71.

9. Oxford, Ms. Bodl., Opp. 187, in Buber's introduction to the *Tanḥuma* (68b, no. 42). The tale is not integral to the Buber edition of *Tanḥuma*, and it should be dated according to the manuscript, in keeping with the nature of *Tanḥuma* as an open "book" given to additions and changes while being disseminated. I am grateful to Mark Bregman, whom I consulted on the subject, for referring me to the precise manuscript of this addition to *Tanḥuma*. The manuscript, in Ashkenazi script, dates to the fourteenth century, and was apparently also known in Ashkenaz earlier, in the Middle Ages.

garments symbolize the errors of his ways: "Because his sons married wives unfit for the priesthood; and he did not protest."[10] Because of this criticism, when he was thrown into the furnace by Nebuchadnezzar, king of Babylon (for reasons that I will not go into here), his clothing was singed (even though his life was saved). The Talmud compares this situation to the case of Hananiah, Mishael, and Azariah, who were not affected by the fire at all, not even their clothes.[11]

The shift in *Sefer ha-ma'asim* from Solomon's daughter to the daughter of Joshua the high priest, and from marriage to a man of a lower class to a marriage lacking in "cleanliness" (a term used elsewhere in *Sefer ha-ma'asim*), apparently reflects a marked tendency in *Sefer ha-ma'asim* to uphold family purity, in contrast to the ethos of courtly love in medieval romances in the West. At the same time the story emphasizes the value of love as a decisive element in the relations between men and women, in the framework of marriage. Solomon was incapable of doing anything to prevent the love between the young man and the maiden, about which he was told even before it came into being.

The motif of the girl locked up in a tower to prevent an undesirable marriage does in fact appear in medieval romances. The most prominent example is the anonymous romance *Aucassin and Nicolette*,[12] a work of prose with excerpts in rhymed poetry, intended for an oral performance (according to staging instructions). It has survived in only one manuscript from the thirteenth century. It relates the fierce love of Aucassin, the son of a high-ranking duke, and Nicolette, a prisoner, the daughter of the Muslim king of Carthage. Their love survives all the travails and obstacles placed in its way by Aucassin's father, who is obstinately opposed to his son's marriage to a Muslim prisoner. And yet the two are finally united, as their love triumphs over political considerations and the prevailing social norms. A striking scene in the romance represents Nicolette's imprisonment in the tower for the purpose of supposedly saving her from the long reach of her lover's father. It is an unreserved paean to love.

10. And cf. Ezra 10:18: "And among the sons of the priests who had taken foreign wives were found: of the sons of Joshua, the son of Jozadak." The sons of Joshua the high priest married alien women (and perhaps women who converted), and therefore they were found unfit for the priesthood.

11. Cf. the story about the false prophets Ahab ben Kulia and Zedekiah ben Ma'aseiah in *Midrash aseret hadibrot*, and to the incident in which Joshua the high priest was cast into the furnace owing to their lustful actions: *Midrash aseret hadibrot*, ed. Shapira, 209–210, and her references to Jeremiah 29:21–23, and to sources in the rabbinical literature, as well as in the *Book of Memory* edited by Yassif (246–247 in his edition).

12. Mason, ed., *Aucassin and Nicolette*, 4–5, 13.

From this comparative standpoint, "The Maiden in the Tower" responds to the aesthetic taste of its medieval readers. It meets the expectations of its audience and is anchored in the Jewish and non-Jewish literature of the period.

The story, which in folklore belongs to the tale type "Rapunzel" or "The Maiden in the Tower" (ATU 310),[13] is based on classical sources of ancient Greece and earlier medieval sources in the Muslim territories, and it developed in the modern era in Italy and France in the seventeenth and eighteenth centuries.[14] In Jewish sources it developed in mystical literature in the Middle Ages and thereafter, in a different manner from the present version in *Sefer ha-ma'asim* and in the other manuscripts mentioned earlier. In the twentieth century it was shaped in literary works, the best known of which is Bialik's "The Legend of Three and Four" (in two versions), in *And It Came to Pass*.[15]

13. For references to parallels and research on the tale type, see Schwarzbaum, *Studies in Jewish and World Folklore*, 273–275; Gaster, *Exempla*, no. 335, 244 (English side); Ben-Amos, *Mimekor yisrael*, no. 38: "Solomon's Daughter," 70–71, and the tale, 71–72. AT 930*K III (IFA): "King's daughter marries a bastard." Cf. the more general type, 930A: "The predestined wife."

14. For the following discussion, see Elstein, "The Theme of 'The King's Daughter Locked-up in the Tower,'" 88–104.

15. Bialik, *And It Came to Pass*, 221–281.

68. The War of Jacob and His Sons with Nineveh (337a–338b)

This is one of three narratives about the wars waged by Jacob and his sons against their enemies, known also as *Midrash vayissa'u.*[1] The two other narratives are about their war against the kings of the Amorites and against Esau and his sons. According to the first, Jacob returned to Shekhem—seven years after its destruction by Simon and Levi, to avenge the rape of their sister, Dina—and intended to settle there. When the kings of the Amorites heard this, they joined together to wage war against Jacob and his sons for fear that they, too, would be injured and killed by Jacob and his sons, as the previous inhabitants of Shekhem were. There are detailed, tangible descriptions of the battles—each one waged by Jacob's sons in turn against the enemy—the names of the kings, the weaponry, the number of defeats, and the surrender. The second narrative, about the war against Esau, who attacked Jacob in the midst of their mourning over the death of their mother, Leah, is similarly described.

There are primarily two sources that inspired these war narratives: the Apocrypha—namely *The Book of Jubilees* and, even more so, *The Testament of Judah*[2]—and medieval epic poems.[3] There may also have been a mediating source

1. The title is based on the opening words of the verse: "And they journeyed [*vayissa'u*] and the terror of God was upon the cities around them" (Genesis 35:5). For an eclectic edition of *Midrash vayissa'u,* inter alia according to London-British Library Add. 27089 (1076 in Margoliouth catalog), see Lauterbach, "Midrash vayissa'u or the Wars of the Sons of Jacob." See also Tamar Alexander and Joseph Dan, "The Complete Midrash vayissa'u," 69–76 (according to Ms. Hamburg 150, from Yemen, 18th century, compared to other text witnesses but not to the *Sefer ha-ma'asim* version in Ms. Bodl. Or. 135). My edition here, of the *Sefer ha-ma'asim* version, is based on three manuscripts: Ms. Jerusalem, Israel Museum 16/51/180, 341b–342b (square Italian script and Ashkenazic, 14th century); Ms. Vatican 323, 113a–113b (fragmented) and 171a–171b (square Ashkenazic script, 13–14th century); Ms. London-Montefiore 431, 38a–39a (Italian-Ashkenazic script, 15th century). These are early text witnesses of *Midrash vayissa'u,* and the first among them, Ms. Jerusalem, Israel Museum, was not examined by previous editors. The other two narratives, about the wars against the Amorites and Esau, were left out of these manuscripts. Two other text witnesses were not included in the critical apparatus to this edition: Ms. Frankfurt 35 (Frankfurt a.M. Hebr. Oct 5/35), from the thirteenth and fourteenth centuries, which contains only the beginning of the story about the war against Nineveh (41b); and a fragmented and late text in Ms. Warsaw 281, 147a (Italian script, 17th century).
2. *Book of Jubilees* 34: 1–10, *Apocrypha and Pseudepigrapha,* ed. Charles, vol. 2, 64–65 (The war against the kings of the Amorites); ibid., 38: 1–14, 69 (the war against Esau and his sons); ibid., vol. 2, *The Testament of Judah,* chs. 3–7, 316–318 (the war against the kings of Canaan and others), and 9: 1–8, 318 (the war against the sons of Esau); Safrai ("*Midrash vayissa'u*") points to a systematic parallel between sources in the Apocrypha, in particular "The Testament of Judah," and *Midrash vayissa'u,* expressed mainly in the stages of the war, the names of the fighting kings, and the battle zones in Samaria. This example is one of several about the reception of the Apocrypha in the Middle Ages, after it was rejected for inclusion in the Talmud and the *midrashim.*
3. Alexander and Dan commented on this in "The Complete Midrash vayissa'u," 68.

between *The Testament of Judah* and the expanded narratives in the Middle Ages.[4] While the influence of the apocryphal literature is manifested in parallel details of the plot, the influence of medieval epic poems is manifested in hyperbolic rhetoric, which is achieved through the use of various literary devices and supports the abundance of actions in the story. In "The War of Jacob and His Sons with Nineveh," the hyperbole is particularly evident in the descriptions of the numerical ratio between the forces of Jacob and his sons and their enemies, the men of Nineveh. Jacob, and later Judah, as well as members of the other tribes, fight alone against tens of thousands of soldiers and defeat them. The superlatives "very" and "greatly" are sprinkled throughout the text, and the additional superlatives that emphasize them are meant to intensify the description: the storm and difficulties of the battle, the impression of the victory, and the strength of the warriors.[5] This stylistic device is very evident in comparison to descriptions of Judah's battles in the Apocrypha, which lack any superlative adjectives and merely contain a narrative sequence of facts and actions.[6] The hyperbolic rhetoric is also expressed in the narrator's use of topoi, of standard repeated images that appear in the literature and the culture: The Nineveh army is as numerous as the grains of "sand on the seashore," and it is defeated by the sons of Jacob "like the wheat falls before the harvesters"; Judah grinds his teeth strenuously "as the skies thunder in the period of Tammuz." And his resemblance to a lion is very concrete: his face is "like the face of a lion."

Epic poetry in France is often characterized by rhetoric that is not necessarily hyperbolic but is intended to heighten the semantic effect in another way, and to depict the object by doing more than simply providing information about him.[7] One such device is the use of syntactical structures of noun+adjective ("Li estur fut fier

4. Safrai ("*Midrash vayissa'u*," 714–716) puts forth a hypothesis about an additional version from the early Middle Ages, translated from Latin or Greek on the basis of an expanded version of *The Testament of Judah*.

5. A selection of examples: "My son, Judah, I know that your strength and valor are great, and there is none as courageous as you"; "That day, Jacob fought before and behind, striking them very mightily"; "They fortified themselves to fight against him defiantly, and intensified the war against Judah very, very greatly"; "On that day, there came a huge multitude like the sand on the seashore to help the people of Nineveh"; "When Jacob's sons saw the flight of the army, they arose in great fury and pursued them"; "and the war was very great."

6. For example: "And fear fell upon them, and they ceased warring against us" ("The Testament of Judah," in *The Apocrypha and Pseudepigrapha*, ed. Charles, vol. 2, 3: 8, 316); "And the next day it was told us that the king of the city of Ga'ash with a mighty host was coming against us" (1:42, 235).

7. See these distinctions in *Gormont and Isembart*, in *Heroes of the French Epic: A Selection of Chansons de Geste*, trans. Michael Newth, 5–6.

e pesant" [11.9], "the fight was hard")[8] or verb+verb ("le hauberc desmaele e dement" [II.21], "he ripped and wrecked," 111). An especially prominent device doubles this syntactic structure and repeats it: "Li estur fut fier e pesant, /e la bataille fut mut grant" (II. 9–10, 1; "The fight was hard / the fray was fierce," 11). Apparently the different rhetoric in the story in *Sefer ha-ma'asim,* in comparison to its parallel in *The Testament of Judah,* is the result of a difference in genre. On the one hand, in the Apocrypha, there is the father's testament to his son prior to his death, intended to illustrate Judah's success in all his endeavors in keeping with the divine blessing. His purpose is to encourage his sons to act like him and, at the same time, to avoid his errors. On the other hand, there is a heroic plot typical of the Middle Ages, in keeping with its poetic rules and trends.[9] There is no way of knowing for certain where and when in the Middle Ages the war narratives of Jacob and his sons were created on the basis of earlier versions, but the inclusion of descriptions of their war against Nineveh in *Sefer ha-ma'asim* and the hyperbolic rhetoric suggest that this story represents a trend of reception and aesthetic taste typical of the period.

Along with the main sources of influence on "The War of Jacob and His Sons with Nineveh"—namely the apocryphal literature and medieval epics—there are also affinities with the rabbinical literature. The image of the tribes, in particular of Judah, as men of physical strength, also appears in *Genesis rabbah,* although not in the context of events related in these stories. In *Genesis rabbah* Judah's reaction when Benjamin, his youngest brother, is held as a hostage in Joseph's house in Egypt (Genesis 44:17) was: "At once Judah grew angry and roared in a loud voice, and his voice carried for four hundred parasangs until Ḥushim b. Dan heard him and leaped and came to Judah and they both roared and tried to overturn the land of Egypt."[10] Later in the quotation, Judah is explicitly likened to a lion, as he is in *Sefer ha-ma'asim*: "Judah set out against them with great fury, and his face

8. The quotations in English are from Newth's translated edition in *Heroes of the French Epic,* 11. The quotations in French are from *Gormont et Isembart: Fragment de Chanson de Geste Du XII Siècle,* ed. Bayot. Variations in the quoted lines exist throughout the work, and they maintain the same syntactic structures.

9. In *Sefer ha-ma'asim* a religious-Jewish vein was added to the Jewish heroic plot: "And when Jacob saw that army, he said to his sons: Fear not, my sons, for the Almighty will fight for you against your enemies. Just remove any foreign gods from in your midst and purify yourselves and change your robes."

10. *Genesis rabbah,* (93, 14), ed. Albeck, 1162, and there too about Joseph's brothers: "When they saw Judah so angry they too were filled with wrath, and kicked at the land and turned it into furrows."

was like the face of a lion."[11] About Jacob, "a quiet man, living in tents" (Genesis 25:27), *Genesis rabbah* recounts that, in reaction to the deeds of his sons Simon and Levi in Shekhem, despite his criticism, he "took his sword and his bow and stood at the entrance to Shekhem. He said if the gentiles come here to have sexual intercourse, I will fight them."[12] This homily contains a narrative potential that was realized in the Apocrypha (and rejected in *Genesis rabbah*?) and in expanded medieval tales.

A follow-up of the reception of these stories in the Middle Ages yields interesting conclusions: (1) The stories are copied both jointly and separately, and in particular "The War of Jacob and His Sons with Nineveh" is copied on its own, as in *Sefer ha-ma'asim*, unlike the other two about the wars against the Amorites and Esau that appear jointly. They were probably not perceived as an integral unit.[13] (2) The context of the copying and the editing varies. They were copied alongside homiletic, liturgical, and midrashic writings, exegeses of *midrashim*, and tales (as in *Sefer ha-ma'asim*). This is also implied from citations and quotations, in certain variations, found in a number of medieval works:[14] *Genesis rabbati* 36:6, which quotes scenes from the war against Esau;[15] Maimonides' commentary on Genesis 34:7;[16] commentaries by the Tosafists cited in *Hadar zekenim* on Genesis 48:22 and in *Moshav zekenim al hatorah* on Genesis 48:22;[17] *Yalkut shimoni* on

11. See Part II, tale no. 68, page 356.

12. *Genesis rabbah* (60, 28), ed. Albeck, 966.

13. Also see this conclusion in Safrai, "*Midrash vayissa'u*," 714, and cf. Alexander and Dan in the introduction to their edition, "The Complete Midrash vayissa'u," 67–68.

14. See references and comments by Lauterbach, "Midrash vayissa'u or the Wars of the Sons of Jacob"; Ginzberg, *The Legends of the Jews*, vol. 5, 315–316, n. 292, and the stories themselves: in vol. 1, "The War with the Amorites," 408–411; "The War with the Ninevites," 404–408. See also Yassif, *The Book of Memory*, 478.

15. Albeck edition, 162–163.

16. And these are Maimonides' words: "And if we are to believe in the book, 'The Wars of the Sons of Jacob,' their father's fear was due to the fact that the neighbors of Shechem gathered together and waged three major wars against them, and were it not for their father who also donned his weapons and warred against them, they would have been in danger, as is related in that book" (*Commentary on the Torah*, ed. Chavel, 193).

17. See Lauterbach's comment in his edition ("Midrash vayissa'u or the Wars of the Sons of Jacob," 306, n. 1), and see *Hadar zekenim*, *Vayehi*, 22, 48: "with my sword and my bow"; "After Simon and Levi killed the men of Shekhem, everyone gathered around to kill them. Jacob came and girded his sword and bow, and with him all the tribes. And Naphtali carried Judah on his shoulders and they slew all of their enemies. Jacob asked his sons after their war: who did more in the war, you or I? They said: Father, you are old, what could you have done? He said to them: Now you will see who possesses strength. Jacob led them to a gate and locked it. They all pushed against it but could not open it. They immediately admitted that the war was won owing to him. And here it is written: With my sword and my

Genesis, no. 133, which notes *Midrash vayissa'u* as its source and leaves out the story about the war with Nineveh;[18] the historiographic work *The Book of Memory*, on the war against the kings of Amorites and Esau;[19] and the commentary by R. Abraham Saba in the fifteenth-century *Ẓror hamor* (on *Vayishlaḥ* 35:6).[20] The contexts of the copying and the embedding of *Midrash vayissa'u* or "The War of Jacob and His Sons with Nineveh" may be a sign of the tale's changing status in different time periods: as an exegesis on relevant verses in the Bible, as a kind of rabbinical *midrash*, as "history," as an epic, and even as liturgy, based on its insertion into the prayer book in the Österreich custom and under the influence of the French custom, from the thirteenth and fourteenth centuries in Ms. Vatican 323.[21] In any case, based on the manuscripts of the stories and the works in which they are included, there seems to have been, during the Middle Ages, a growing interest in these stories about the wars of Jacob's sons. They also suggest that there was a cluster of sources in Ashkenaz in the thirteenth and fourteenth centuries, probably against the background of the non-Jewish epic poetry and in response to the widespread aesthetic taste of the time. The war narratives of Jacob and his sons were also quoted and cited in later sources, such as *Sefer hayashar* in the sixteenth century,[22] and Jacob Kuli's *Yalkut me'am lo'ez* in the early eighteenth century.[23]

---

bow"; and the same in *Moshav zekenim*, 99, without any mention of Judah carried on the shoulders of Naphtali.

18. Shiloni edition, vol. 2, 691–694.
19. Yassif, *The Book of Memory*, 136–143.
20. R. Abraham Saba, *Ẓror hamor*, I, 252: "And perhaps there is a hint here as to what was said in the midrash that although now he did not fight with them [with Esau and his camp], after some time they went out to meet him and engaged in a war with Jacob, as mentioned in the 'Book of Wars.' "
21. On the other hand, the text may have been copied without any affinity whatsoever to the works copied in its surroundings, based on different considerations, such as the place where the manuscript was at the scribe's disposal. The editing contexts are more marked when the stories are inserted into a known work: for example, Maimonides' commentary, the prayer book, and *The Book of Memory*.
22. *Sefer hayashar*, ed. Dan, ch. 13, 149–186 (without the war against Nineveh). On the dating of *Sefer hayashar* in the sixteenth century, see the introduction to Dan's edition, 7–17.
23. Jacob Kuli, *Yalkut me'am lo'ez*, Genesis, *vayishlah*, ch. 9, no. 32, 657–762 (on the wars against the kings of Canaan and the Amorites, without the story of the war against Esau or Nineveh).

69. The Portal to Gehenna (338b–339b)

This story first appears in *Sefer ha-ma'asim* and has no earlier versions.[1] Nonetheless, it does have some affinities with *Ma'aseh yerushalmi*, a medieval narrative that was copied into the Ms. Bodl. Or. 135 (255b–256b), along with *Sefer ha-ma'asim.* In the former, a man who has a wife and children is abducted and taken to a city of demons and married against his will to the daughter of their king, Asmodeus. He sorely misses his wife and home and obtains the demon's permission to visit there for one night only. But then he refuses to return, and the demon gets her revenge by causing his death.[2] The stories—*Ma'aseh yerushalmi*, as summarized here, and "The Portal to Gehenna" in *Sefer ha-ma'asim*—share several motifs: the opening into the demons' land, the prohibition against entering it, and the severe implications of its violation;[3] the abduction of a human being by the demons; the stereotypical image of the demons as "black" and "ugly";[4] the man's yearning for his wife, who is left behind in the human sphere or is held captive in the land of the demons. Although they are certainly not absolute parallels—the main motif of marriage between a man and a demon in *Ma'aseh yerushalmi* is absent from "The Portal to Gehenna," while the "hell" motif does not have a major function in *Ma'aseh yerushalmi*—the point of contact between the two narratives lies in the affinity between the demonic and hell, which is typical of the medieval culture.[5]

Joseph Dan and Eli Yassif have pointed to a Christian parallel in the *exempla* of Caesarius of Heisterbach, *Dialogus Miraculorum*. There, a young man is abducted by a demon disguised as a beautiful maiden, after he is tempted and extends his

1. The story was published by Yassif, *The Hebrew Folktale*, 387–389.
2. See Yassif's references to research on *Ma'aseh yerushalmi*, including one to Joseph Dan, who published widely on this subject: *The Hebrew Folktale*, 661, n. 112.
3. In *Ma'aseh yerushalmi* the motif is embodied in the prohibition against entering the room of Asmodeus's daughter or in the father's prohibition forbidding his son to exit the city. The archetype of the motif is in Genesis 2:16–17: "Of every tree of the garden you may freely eat; But of the tree of the knowledge of good and evil, you shall not eat of it; for in the day that you eat of it you shall surely die." And cf. the tale type ATU 312: "Maiden Killer (Bluebeard)." In *Sefer ha-ma'asim* the motif is only alluded to (and this point calls for expansion elsewhere).
4. At the opening to hell: "and met a very tall, black man who was exceedingly ugly." And in *Ma'aseh yerushalmi* (Ms. Bodl. Or. 135): "and he was met by a man who was very black and very ugly."
5. See numerous references to the entries "demon/devil/hell" in Tubach's index of legends, 437–441; 456.

finger outside a magic circle to receive her ring. He is taken to hell, returned to his friends after numerous efforts, and becomes a devout monk.[6]

"The Portal to Gehenna" also has recourse to a topos, widespread in medieval Christian and Jewish vision literature, of tours in hell. A high-ranking figure in the world of the living arrives in hell, observes the punishments of those doomed to dwell in it, returns to earth, and warns others about the dangers of sin so they will repent: "and tell him that this is how those of Israel who sin with the body are in Gehenna, and tell him to repent for all his wicked deeds, because immense is the power of repentance." It does appear that the woman's suffering is weighed against her sins, based on the principle "a measure for measure": the punishment should fit the crime. The gold as an indication of external splendor is nothing other than a burning fire, chastising the woman for having pretended to be a decent woman in her lifetime, while she was actually a sinning hypocrite.[7] As Louis Landau has shown, the story also has an affinity with "The Wandering Dead," which relates how a sinner is saved from hell when his son recites *Kaddish* and "bless the Blessed Name."[8] This, then, is a contemporary heterogeneous work that joins episodes and materials from various tales and sources: *Ma'aseh yerushalmi*, vision literature, and "The Wandering Dead."

After the Middle Ages, the motif of a woman abducted by a demon and taken to hell exists in "The Proud Prince," in the various renditions of *Ma'aseh Book*, as does the motif of repentance under the influence of the sights of hell. This may indicate the existence of the tale traditions in channels unknown to us even after the thirteenth century, in a manner that enabled the assimilation of its motifs into the *Mayse Bukh*.[9] In the modern era the story was copied into Bin Gorion's literary collection *Mimekor yisrael*,[10] but in general it did not pass through the barrier of the society's reception, at least according to written documentation.

6. See Caesarius of Heisterbach, *Dialogus Miraculorum*, vol. 1, 5.4; *The Dialogue on Miracles*, vol. 2, book V, ch. 4, 318–320. And see Yassif's references in *The Hebrew Folktale*, 358. Joseph Dan states that this story is a parallel to *Ma'aseh yerushalmi*: Dan, "Five Versions of the Story of the Jerusalemite," 107–108. And see Yassif's interesting comparison of the Jewish tale to the medieval Orpheus myth, in *Ninety-nine Tales*, 132–140.

7. Cf. Tubach 2505: "Seneca's vision of the punishment awaiting Nero, the Emperor, as well as greedy advocates, who sits in a bathtub of gold, into which his servants pour molten gold"; Tubach 5039: "Usurer eats [molten] gold in hell."

8. Landau, "The Wandering and Threatened Dead," 152–157.

9. Ms. Jerusalem 5245, no. 89 (1596, known as Ms. Innsbruck); *Mayse bukh*, vol. 2, no. 179, 383–390; *Ma'aseh Book*, trans. Gaster, no. 180, 391–392.

10. Bin Gorion, *Mimekor yisrael*, no. 652, 401–402; Ben-Amos, *Mimekor yisrael*, no. 200, 373–384.

Appendix A

Facsimile Pages

חסרתי דבר · אלא שאילתי ובקשתי ממך דעלך סניו לחברך לא תעביד ·
ואהבת לרעך כמוך · ויעש המלך כעצתו · ויחי המלך מאה ושלשים שנה
וימת וימלוך בנו תחתיו ויחכם מכל חכמי הודו ״ נשלם הספר
בעזרת הא״ל עושה נסי״ם · אחל לכתוב מעשי״ם ״
מעשה ברבי יהושע בן לוי שהיה מתאוה
לילך עם אליהו · ועשה תפלה ונעה
ואין אלין · א״ל רבי יהושע רצונך
שאלך עמך ולראות מעשיך בעולם · א״ל אליהו אין אתה יכול לסבול
מעשיי · א״ל אני אוכל לסבול · הלכו שניהם כיחד · בלילה אחד לן
עם אדם עני · כיון שראה אותם כבדם מתוך ענותו · בחצי הלילה
עמד אליהו והרג פרתו שהייתה שווה אלף זוזים ״ לילה שנייה לנו
אצל אדם עשיר כיון שראה שלא כבדם עמד אליהו לבקר ולקח מל
בידו חבל · ור׳ יהושע כראש החבל ומדדן כחצירו שמונים ומאה
בתים · ובנה אותם כולם · לילה שלישית לנו למקום שכולם עניים
ומתוך ענותם כבדו אותם · לבקר א״ל אליהו המקום יתן לכם ראש
אחד · למחר באו למקום שכולם עשירים · והיו יושבים בקתדראות
של זהב העשיר לפי עשרו והעני לפי ענותו · ולא כבדו אותם
א״ל אליהו המקום יעשה כולכם ראשים · והיה תמיה ר׳ יהושע ·
א״ל ר׳ יהושע אתמהא הרגת פרתו של עני שכבדנו · וכי אליהו הורג
פרתן של עניים · והלא אליהו דרכו לפרנס עניים · אין אתה אליהו ·
אלא פרוש לי מעשיך · א״ל אם אפרוש לך אפרוש ממך · אומר לו
אף על פי כן פרוש לי · ומפני מה הרגת פרתו של עני · א״ל לפי
שהיתה אשתו נטויה למות · לכך הקדמתי והרגתי פרתו · כדי
שתעמוד נפש תחת נפש · ואותו עשיר שלא כבדנו למה בנית
חצירו · אומר מפני שהיה ממונו באותו חצר ובאותו מקום ושם
חקוק עליו שאם היה חופר שתי אמות בקרקע היה מוציא שם
ממון שאין לו הפסק לעולם לכך הקדמתי ובניתי חצירו · ואחר
יפול הבנין · ולאותן עניים שכבדו אותנו מפני מה אמרת להם
המקום יתן לכם ראש אחד · א״ל ברכתי אותם כך מקום שאין
ביניהם אלא ראש אחד הכל שומעין לו · וזו היא ברכה · ולעשירים
שהיו יושבין בקתדראות של זהב · מפני מה אמרת להם המקום
יעשה כולכם ראשים · א״ל זו קללה היא · שקללתם שהם מנ
משולים לספינה שמלחים מרובים כלומר שסופן ליטבע · א״ל
רצונך שאלך עמך · א״ל כבר נפסק דבר שלא תלך עמי · ואם

תראה רשע שהשעה משחקת לו אל תתמה כי כשבא רעתו בא לו יו׳
ואם תראה אדם שבא לידי חסרון כיס כשבא רעתו בא לו אחו ל׳
בשביל כפרת נפשו: אחר״

מעשה

בחסיד אחד שהיה מתפלל בכל
יום שלשה תפלות והיתה
תפלתו עולה לפני כסא הכבוד כתמיד שהיה קרב על גבי המזבח
וקבל עליו אותו חסיד שלא יקבל מתנה משום אדם והיה מהלך
בכל יום באשפות ומלקט סמרטוטין ונותן לפניו ולאחרים לכסות
ערותן וכך היה מנהגו וכשראה הקב״ה עלבונו וענותו אומר
לאליהו לך ותן לו ד׳ זוזים הלך אליהו ומצאו מתפלל כמנהגו המת׳
המתין עד שנתפלל א״ל שלום עליך רבי והחזיר לו שלום ורצה
אליהו ליתן לו ד׳ זוזים כמו שצוהו הקב״ה ולא רצה לקבלם עד שפייס
אותו וקבל הלך לשוק וקנה מהם כבר לצרכו ובא לו אדם אחד וחן
וחמד אותו טלית שעליו א״ל מכור לי טלית זה א״ל בכמה א״ל בכ
בעשרים וארבעה זהובים א״ל קחהו ומן אותן כד׳ זהובים נתעשר
וקנה מהם עבדים ושפחות עיירות וספינות היו לו פרושות בים
כיון שנתעשר נמנע מהתפלה ושכח מנהגו הראשון אומר הקב״ה
לאליהו ראה מאותו צדיק שהרבתי לו עושר ונכסים וכבוד ומנע
תפלתו לך וקח ממנו מה שנתתי לו הלך אליהו ומצאו שהיה יושב
בקטידרין של זהב בבית הכנסת א״ל שלום עליך רבי והחזיר לו
שלום א״ל אליהו עשה לי טובה החזר לי מה שהפקדתי אצלך
א״ל מה המעשה שהפקדת אצלי א״ל ד׳ זוזים שנתתי בידך א״ל
איני מכירך מיד א״ל אליהו כך שמי ונתתי לך כשהיית מתפלל בב
בבית הכנסת א״ל יפה הזכרתני מיד רצה ליתן לו א״ל אליהו אותן
עינוק תן לי ולא אחרים א״ל ומי מכירן ומי יכול לפשפש אחר
אחריהן תביא ארנקי שלך ואכיר אותן מיד נעשה לו נס ולקח
אותן עינמן והלך לו מיד נתמעט אותו חסיד ומתו כל בניו וכל
בנותיו ועבדיו ושפחותיו וספינותיו טבעו בים וחזר אותו חסיד
למנהגו הראשון ומלקט סמרטוטין באשפות ומתפלל ג׳ תפלות
בכל יום כבש הקב״ה רחמיו ואמר אותו חסיד חביב עלי ביותר
ואיני יכול לראות צערו לך והלוה לו עשרה זוזים והשביעהו בש
בשמי שלא יבטל תפלתו לעולם כמנהגו מיד בא אליהו אצלו ומצ׳
ומצאו מתפלל והמתין עד שנתפלל ונתן לו שלום וא״ל על מה
שאני נותן לך ואשביעך בה׳ שלא תבטל תפלתך לעולם:

נט·

מעשה באדם אחד שהלך למדינת הים
והיה לו ממון גדול · ולא היה לו אלא
בן אחד · חלה אותו האיש ונטה למות
קרא לאושפיזו ואמר לו הרי ממוני מופקד בידך · אם יבא בני
בשבילו בחנהו ונסהו בשלשה דברים · אם תראה שהוא חכם תן לו
ממוני · ואם לאו יהיו הקדש לשמים · והלך האיש לבית עולמו · לי
ימים שמע הבן שמת אביו · והלך לאותה מדינה · וכך היה מנה
מנהגם לא היו מראים מקום לאורח להכנס שם ללון · מה עשה
אותו הבן הלך למקום שהיו מוכרים עצים וקנה מהם · ואמר הבן
לאיש אחד לך והבא העצים האילו שקניתי לבית האושפיזכן ואני
אתן שכרך · והלך האיש והביא העצים לבית האושפיזכן והבן הלך
אחריו · עמד וקרא לפתח הבית יצא אליו בעל הבית · וא״ל מי אתה
א״ל אני בן פלוני שהפקיד אצלך · א״ל ומי הראך מקומי · א״ל כך וכך עשיתי ·
חשב אותו האיש בלבו · הנה אחד משלשה דברים שצוה לי אביו ·
הלינו בבית הלילה · ישבו לאכול הביאו לפניו תרנגולת מבושלת · א״ל
האושפיזכן חלוק אותה תרנגולת בינינו · והיה לבעל שני בנים
ושתי בנות · נתן הראש לבעל הבית ואת האליה נתן לאשתו
והכנפים נתן לבנותיו · והיריכים לבניו · והחזה לקח לעצמו · א״ל
מפני מה חלקת כך · א״ל אתה הראש ונתתי לך ראשה · ואשתך
יושבת בבית על כן נתתי לה האליה · בנותיך למחר ינשאו ובעליהן
ויפרחו מביתך לכך נתתי להן הכנפים · בניך שהם עמודי ביתך
נתתי להם היריכים · ואני על ספינה באתי · ועליה אני חוזר · על
כן לקחתי את החזה שהוא דומה לספינה · א״ל יפה חילקת ·
למחר הביאו לפניו חמשה תרנגולות · א״ל חלוק אותן בינינו · נתן
תרנגולת אחת בינו ובין אשתו · ואחת בין שתי בנותיו ואחרת
לשני בניו · ושנים נטל לעצמו · א״ל למה עשית כך · א״ל יפה חי
חילקתי · אתה ואשתך ותרנגולת הרי ג׳ · שתי בנותיך ותרנגולת
הרי ג׳ בניך ותרנגולת הרי ג׳ · ואני ושתי תרנגולות ג׳ · אמר
הבעל ודאי זה ראוי לירש ממון אביו · ונתן לו הכל ׃

מעשה היה בימי דוד ששלח יואב בן צרויה
לקיסרי מדינת עמלק להלחם עליה וסבבו
וסבבו העמלקיים דלתות המדינה · והיו
בני ישראל מקיפין את החומה ששה חדשים · והיו מגבורי ישראל
עם יואב שנים עשר אלפים · לאחר ששה חדשים נתקבצו הגב

הגבורים׳ ועמדו כלם על יואב׳ ואמרו פה אחד לא נוכל לסבול זאת להדיף
החומה׳ הרי כמה זמן עבר שהנחנו עיירות וכפרים שלנו ובנינו׳ אומר
להם יואב ומה אתם רוצים לעשות׳ אמרו כלם נרצה לחזור בבתינו׳ אומר
להם לא נחזור בפחי נפש׳ ונשוב למלך פנינו ריקם׳ וישמעו כל העמים ויב
וילחמו עמנו׳ עשו קלע וקלעו אותי בעיר׳ מיד לקח יואב אוף כסף והסייף
שלו׳ ואומר להם יואב המתינו לי ארבעים יום׳ אם תראו הדם יוצא מתחת
דלתי המדינה׳ דעו שאני חי׳ ואם לאו דעו שאני מת׳ ולכו לבתיכם׳ וקלע
וקלעוהו ונפל יואב בחצר המדינה על גג אלמנה אחת׳ והיה לה בת אחת
נשואה לבעל ויצאה הנערה ומצאה יואב מושלך כחצב לא חי ולא מת
ויראו שלשתן וישאו אותו והכניסוהו לבית ורחצוהו במים וסכוהו
בשמן׳ ותשב רוחו ושאלו אותו מי אתה׳ אומר להם עמלקי אני והייתי
בגדוד ישראל ותפשוני והביאוני למלך וגזר עלי וקלעוני במדינה׳ ואתם
עשו טוב עמי והחיוני׳ לקח עשרה כספים ונתנם לבעל הנערה׳ ואמ׳ לו
לך קנה מהם לנו מה שתרצה׳ והיה עמהם עשרה ימים׳ ובקש לילך
בעיר׳ ולעיין׳ ואמרו לו לא תלך בזה הלבוש׳ והלבישוהו משלהם׳ ויצא
לשוק׳ והיו במדינה מאה וארבעים שווקים׳ וכל שוק ושוק גדול מחבירו׳
ראיה מוצאיו ומובאיו׳ והלך אצל נפח אחד׳ ואמ׳ עשה לי סייף כמו זה
שמור בידי׳ כשראה הנפח הסייף נזדעזע׳ אמ׳ למה נזדעזעת׳ אמ׳
שלא ראיתי כמוהו מימיי׳ אמ׳ עשה לי כזה ואני אתן לך שכרך׳ עשה
לו ותפשו בידו ונענע ונשבר׳ וכן השנייה וכן השלישית׳ עשה לו סייף
אחד ונענע ולא נשברה׳ אמ׳ לנפח מה נכה עם זה הסייף׳ אמ׳ מלך
יואב׳ אמ׳ אני טוחן׳ הלא יואב אני׳ הבט לאחריך׳ חזר הנפח ראשו
והכהו בבטנו׳ אמ׳ יואב מה יש בבטנך׳ אמ׳ שלג׳ דחפו ונפל ומת׳ חצינו
לכאן וחצינו לכאן׳ ויצא לחוץ ונכנס לחצר׳ ומצא שם שמונה מ
מאות גבורי מלחמה והרגם ולא מלט מהם איש׳ ושם חרבו לתערה׳
וחזר לבית שהיה שוכן שם׳ ונשמע קול על ההרוגים׳ והיו אומרים שבני
אנשי העיר אשמדאי מלכא דשידי הרגם׳ ושאלו אנשי הבית ליואב
כלום אתה יודע משמועה זו׳ אומר להם לא׳ והוציא עוד עשרה כספים׳
ונתן להם׳ המתין עמהם ימים׳ ואחר כך יצא לשער ואחרנו שלופה
בידו׳ והרג אלף וחמש מאות איש׳ ותדבק ידו על החרב׳ ויצא ידו על
זרועו׳ ובא לאותו הבית׳ ומצא שם הנערה׳ עשי לי מי חמין אולי
יפטר החרב מידי׳ עשתה ואמרה עמנו תוכל ותהרוג אנשי עירינו
והיא מעוברת תקע החרב בבטנה ונתפרק ידו׳ וחזר לשוק׳ שמע
כרוז שמכריזין כל מי שיש לו אורח יביאנו למלך׳ פגעו בו יואב והרגו

556

302

69

וכל מי שהיה פוגע בו היה הורגו עד שהרג ב' אלפים חוץ מן הראשונים
עד שבא לשערי המדינה והכה שם על העיר ופתח שערי העיר והיה
הדם מתגלגל ויוצא חוץ למדינה וישראל בוכים על יואב ורואים לחזור
לבתיהם וכשראו הדם יוצא מן העיר שמחו ואמרו שמע ישראל ה' אלהינו
ה' אחד כשראה יואב כך עלה לגג המגדל שיראוהו ישראל והרים קולו
ואמר כי לא יטוש ה' את עמו ה' ילחם לכם ואתם תחרישון שבו למלך
ונכנסו כולם למדינה ולבשו כלי זיין ושלפו חרבותם מתערה וחזר יואב
ראשו וראה על רגלו הימין פסוקים כתובים יענך ה' ביום צרה ה' הושי׳
הושיעה המלך וכשבא דוד אל יואב א"ל מה עשית הרגת העמלקיים
שבעיר כמו שכתב תמחה את זכר עמלק א"ל כך עשיתי ולא נשתייר
מהם כי אם המלך לבדו והלך יואב והביאו המלך לפני דוד והרגו דוד
בידו ולקח יואב הכתר ונתן על ראש דוד והיה הכתר מככרים זהב מזוקק
והיה בה אבן יקרה והוציא כל הרכוש כל אוצר בעיר ושרפו עבודה זרה
שלהם לקיים מה שכתב את מזבחותם תתוצון ובאו כל ישראל לירושלם
בשמחה גדולה ומהללים לאל חי שוכן שמים ונפל פחדם על כל העמים מאימת
ואימתו של דוד שנ' ויהי דוד בכל דרכיו משכיל: אחר

Cat. N. 3870, 11

מעשה

היה בימי שלמה יום אחד נכנס
עליו אשמדאי א"ל אתה הוא שכת'
עליו ויחכם מכל האדם א"ל כך הבטיחו
הקב"ה א"ל אשמדאי אם תרצה אראה לך דבר שלא ראית מעולם מיד
הושיט ידו בארץ והוציא משם איש בעל שני ראשים וד' עינים מיד
נבעת שלמה ונבהל ואמר הכניסהו לחדר שלח לקרוא לבניהו
בן יהוידע א"ל ידעת אם יש תחתינו בני אדם א"ל חי נפשך אדוני לא
ידעתי אבל שמעתי מאחיתופל אלופי אביך שיש בני אדם תחתינו
א"ל אראה לך אחד מהם א"ל והיאך אתה יכול להראותו והלא
עומקה של ארץ זו חמש מאות שנה מהלך וכן ארץ לארץ מהלך ה'
מאות שנה מיד הביאו אליו וכיון שראהו נפל על פניו ואמר ברוך
אתה ה' אלהינו מלך העולם שהחיינו וקיימנו והגיענו לזמן הזה א"ל בן
מי אתה א"ל מבן אדם מתולדות קין א"ל ובאיזה מושבכם א"ל בארץ תבל
יש לכם שמש וירח א"ל כן ואנו חורשים וזורעים ובעלי צאן ובאיזה
מקום תזרח שמש א"ל ממערב ותשקע במזרח ואנו מתפללים ומה
היא תפלתכם א"ל מה רבו מעשיך ה' כולם בחכמה עשית א"ל תרצה
שנחזור אותך במקומך מיד קרא לאשמדאי וא"ל חזור אותו למקומו א"ל
א"ל אינו יכול להחזירו לעולם כיון שראה כך נשא אשה והוליד ממנה

שבעה בנים ששה מהם כדמות האם ואחד כדמות האב והיה
חורש וזורע ונעשה עשיר גדול ולאחר זמן מת האיש ונעשו די
והניח ירושה גדולה לבנו ששה בנים היו אומרים את שבעה והאיש
לשני ראשים אומר אנחנו שמונה הלכו לפני שלמה לדין כיון שראה
שלמה כך נתעלם ממנו הדבר מיד קרא לסנהדרין שאל להם ושתקו
אמר להם המתינו לי עד הבקר כחצי הלילה נכנס בהיכל ועמד
בתפלה לפני הקב"ה ואמר לפניו רבונו של עולם כשנגלית לי בגבעון
ואמרת לי שאל מה אתן לך לא שאלתי לא כסף ולא זהב אלא חכמה
כדי לשפוט עמך ישראל א"ל הקב"ה לבקר אני נותן לך ותדע כי החכמה
מה' שנ' לאדם מערכי לב ומה' מענה לשון לאחר שלח וקבץ כל סנ
סנהדרין ואמר הביאו לפני אותו האיש בעל שני ראשים אמר להם
ראו אם זה הראש יודע מה שהשני עושה בידוע שהוא אחד ואם לאו
הרי שנים אמר הביאו לי מים חמים ויין ישן ובגד של שש והניח
הבגד על פניו וזרק בו מים חמין ויין ישן וצעקו השני ראשים
ואמרו אנו מתים שאנו אחד ולא שנים א"ל והלא אומרת ליתן לך
פי שנים כיון שראו ישראל כך משפט המלך תמהו ורעדו ופחדו
ממנו

מעשה

בזקן אחד שהיו לו שני בנים והיה משוך אחר היין
מאד ואוהב לשתות ובכל מה שמרויחים
בנו בכל יום שותה אביהם בערב אמר האחד לחבירו מה נעשה
מאבינו ששותה הכל ואין אנו יכולים מנעלים לרגלינו אם תשמע לקנות
לעצתי נערב שכירותינו או מ' ימים או מ"ג ונתן לו לשתות עד
שיהא שכור מה עשו השקו את אביהם יין עד שחטפתו שינה
עזה קראו לשכינין ואמרו בואו ראו אבינו שנפטר עשו לו תכריכים
והוליכוהו לבית הקברות והנקברים מקברים [illegible]ם בסלעים נקוקים
שהיו שם בית ומניחין אותם על הארץ ומתוך השינה עזה
שחטפתו ומתוך היין ששתה לא קם ולא ידע במית וקברוהו ובני
ונפטרו לבתיהם ולאחר כאן ישמעאלים טוענים יין ומבשר
עליה ולחם וכל מיני מאכל להביא אותו העיר שהיה במערה
ופגעו בהם הרודפים וכשהבינו הסוחרים שרודפים באו לעיר
החביאו כל המאכל והמשתה במערה וברחו להם והלכו על גמלי
גמליהם ליום שלישי ניעור הזקן ותמה על עצמו ולא ידע
היכן הוא ומשש אצלו וקרא אליו ולא מצא שום אדם הולך
בתוך הסלע ומשש בידו ומצא גדי יין ובשר ולחם וגבינה

303

סט

אומר כמו שכתוב כיון · ובירך בוראו שעזרו · מה עשה ישב לאכול ול
ולשתות עד שנשתכר ועמד לשחק · והיה מונח בידו · לאחר ג׳ ימים הלכו
בניו לבקרו · אם מת יום לאו · הלכו על הסלע · ומצאו שהיה מונח אביהם
אמרו עדיין חי · הלכו אצלו ושאלו לו מה לך אבינו · אומר להם רשעים
אתם חשבתם עלי רעה · והקב״ה חשבה לטובה · למען החיותני כיום
הזה · לכו וכבדו ועזרוני כל ימי חיי ומינו דברי יין ולחם ובשר וגבינה
לרוב · אמרו לאביהם בא נא לביתנו ונשבע לך שנפרנס אותך כל ימי
חייך · ועשו המאכל והיין לבתיהם וזנו אותו כל ימיהם :

מעשה

בחסיד אחד שהיה רגיל ליתן צדקה
והיה עושה טובות הרבה וגמילות
חסדים · עם בעלי תורה וכל אדם והייתה
אשתו יפת עין · והיו לו שלשה אוצרות אחד של דינרי זהב · ואחד
של כספים ואחד של פרוטות · וכשבאין אצלו תלמידין היה נותן
להם מדינרי זהב וליתומים ולאלמנות משל כספים · וליתומים שא
שאינם הולכים ללמוד היה מתפרנס בפרוטות · ואיך היה מפרנס
כל אחד שהיה לו חמש נפשות בתוך ביתו היה נותן לו ה׳ דינרי זהב
לכל אחד ואחד מהם · וכן היה רגיל לעשות בכל יום · פעם אחד
הלך למקום אחד ובאו אלמנות ויתומים וחכמים ולא מצאוהו שם ·
מה עשתה אשתו נכנסה לבית האוצרות כדי ליתן לחכמים דינרי
זהב · ומצאה שם עקרבים · הלכה לאוצרות של כסף ומצאה שם
נמלים · לאוצר של פרוטות ומצאה שם פרעושים · כיון שראתה כך
הייתה מתביישת לצאת · והם יושבים בחוץ ומצפין עד שבא ר
בעלה · ומצאן כשהן עומדין · אומר להם רבותיי מה אתם עושים
כאן ומפני מה לא נכנסתם לבית · אמרו לו לא כך דרך ארץ שיכנסו
בני אדם בבית שאין בעל הבית בתוכו · נכנס הוא לביתו · ומצא
אשתו בוכה ואומרה לו למה הנחתני בלא כסף · אומר לה והלא
כל אוצרותי בידיך · אומרה לו לא מסרת לי אלא אוצרות של נמלים
עקרבים ופרעושים · נכנס הוא ומילא חפניו דינרי זהב ונתן לחכמים
ומילא חפניו כסף ונתן ליתומים ולאלמנות והפרוטות · לפיכך כתיב
אל תלחום לחם רע עין · אומר הקב״ה טוב עין הוא יבורך כי נתן
מלחמו לדל ·

מעשה

3870, 15 בחסיד
אחד שהיה מקיים
כל המצות
כולם והיה לו שדה
אחד · והיה
שם חרוב אחד · והיו שם עוברים ושבים · והיה מפסיד כל

הזרעי״ם שהי׳ה זורע אותו חסיד באותו שדה׳ לפי שהיו עוברים
ושבים יושבים בצילו של אותו חרוב׳ ואמר לאשתו לך ונקצץ את
החרוב שלא נפסיד הזרעי״ם הלך לקוצצו ולקח הקורדום ובא לקוצצו
ענה לו האילן ואמר לו אל תקצצני ואני אתן לך דינר זהב בכל יום׳ א״ל
ואו׳ א״ל אתן לך ג׳ בכל יום מיד הניחו והלך לו לביתו׳ ביום השני חזר
אצל האילן ומצא שם ג׳ דינרים של זהב׳ וכן עשה בכל יום עד שנתעשר
ובנה אוצרות וקנה עבדים ושפחות׳ והוא לא היה יודע מהיכן היו
באים׳ אותם ג׳ דינרים זהב׳ והתחילו בנו ובנותיו ועבדיו למות׳ מן
טריחה כך אומר וכי בעל עבירות אני שמתים בניי ועבדיי מה עשה הלך
הוא ואשתו לאותו אילן והיו משחקים שם׳ ולא מצאו שם כמנהגם׳ ובק
ובקש לקוצצו יצא שעיר אחד מתחת האילן׳ וא״ל אין לך על שמר
ובקש לקוצצו׳ ענה לו האילן אם תקצצני אהרוגך׳ והיה מתיירא א
אותו צדיק׳ מה עשה נכנס אצל סנהדרין וספר להם כל המעשה אמרו
לו לך ומכור כל מה שקנית מאותם דנרי זהב וחזור אותם לו וקוצצהו׳
מיד׳ הלך ועשה כן ~~וקראו לעבדיו~~ ורצה לקוצצו וקרא לעבדיו ובקש
לקוצצו יצא אותו שעיר כנגדו׳ וא״ל טול עשרים זהובים בכל יום ואל
תקצצני׳ א״ל אפילו אתה נתן לי אלף דינרים של זהב איני מניחך עד
שיקוץ אותך מיד הלך אותו שעיר וקצץ אותו חסיד את האילן וחזר
לביתו׳ וזרע איפה באותו שדה׳ ומצא באותה שנה אלף איפות ומכר
אותן כח מאות דינרי זהב׳ ועוד כשהיה חורש מצא מטמון של זהב
תחת האילן והביאו לביתו להודיעך שכל העושה מצוה הקב״ה מכי
מכפיל לו שכרו של׳ והיה שדי בעזרך׳ כיון ששמעו חכמים כך קראו עליו
רצון יראיו יעשה:

מעשה

כשנולד אברהם אבינו בשעה היי־ך
אבריהם קם כוכב אחד שעלה
ובלע ד׳
כוכבים מד׳ רוחות שבעולם׳ כשראו אצטגנינים של נמרוד כך
הלכו לפניו ואמרו לו נולד היום בן אחד לך והרגנו ותן לאביו ולא
ולאמו כל מה שירצה׳ אומר להם נמרוד מה זו הכן שאתם רואים
להמיתו׳ אמרו לו אותו יום שנולד קם כוכב ובלע ד׳ כוכבים מד׳
רוחות השמים ועתיד לירש העולם הזה והעולם הבא׳ אמר להם
תרח שוטים אמשול לכם משל למה הדבר דומה לפרד שאמרו לו
ניתן לך כור שעורים ונחתוך ראשך׳ אומר להם הפרד שוטים
שבעולם אם תחתכו את ראשי מי יאכל השעורים שתתנו לי׳ וכך
אם תהרגו את הבן׳ הנכסים שתתנו לאביו ולאמו מי ירשם׳ אמרו

304

לו לדבריך רואים אנו שבן נולד לך · אומר להם כן נולד לי · והוא מרב׳
אמרו לו על כן חי אנו ולא על בן מת · אחר כן כששמע את הדברים · בא
תרח והחביא את אברהם במערה ג׳ שנים · לאחר כן הוציאו משם ·
וכשראה אברהם את השמש שזורח במזרח · אומר בלבו זה השולט אך
אדון לכל העולם · ולו אתפלל אליו לאותו שמש שבראני · וברא כל העולם
כולו · מיד התפלל אליו כל היום · וכששקע השמש במערב ופסק אור
השמש · וזרחה הלבנה · אומר בלבו ודאי זה אדון לכל העולם שלאחר
שפסק זה זרחה זאת · ולא אתפלל אלא לזה כי הוא אדון לכל העולם כי
הוא בראני וברא כל העולם · ויתפלל לה כל הלילה עד הבקר · וכששקעה
הלבנה וזרחה השמש · אומר ודאי עתה ידעתי כי לא זה ולא זה אדון
לכל העולם · אלא שניהם עבדים לאדון אחד · ואותו אדון ברא שמים
וארץ וכל העולם · מיד שאל אברהם את תרח אביו · מי ברא שמים וארץ ·
א״ל בני האלהים שלנו · א״ל אברהם אם כן הוא אני מקריב קרבן לפניהם ·
ויראוני כולן שרוצין בני אדם · מיד הלך אל אמו · ואומר לה עשי לי ע׳
עוגה אחת של סולת · ואקריב אותו לאלהי אבי · מיד עשתה לו עוגה
אחת של סולת · מה עשה אברהם לקח העוגה וישם אותה לפני הגדול
שבצלמים כי תרח אביו היה עושה הצלמים · ואומר אברהם לגדול שבהם
קבל ממני זה הקרבן לא לקח ממנו · ונתן אברהם העוגה לתוך פיו ·
אמר לו אכל ממנו ולא אכל ולא שתה · הלך לפני הקטן שבכולם · וכ׳
והקריב לפניו ולא אכל ולא שתה · וכן עשה לכולם · מה עשה אברהם
נתן בהם אש ושרפם · מיד שרתה עליו רוח הקודש ואומר עינים להם
ולא יראו אזנים להם ולא ישמעו וגו׳ · וכשבא תרח אל אלהיו ומצאם
שרופים · אמר לבנו מי שרף אלהי · א״ל אברהם אבא הגדול כעס על
האחרים ושרפם · א״ל שוטה אינו רואה ואינו הולך ואינו שומע ואינו
מדבר · ואיך תאמר שהוא שרפם · א״ל אברהם אבא השמיע לאזניך
מה שאתה מוציא מפיך · ולמה תעזוב אלהים שברא שמים וארץ וכ׳
ותעבוד זה שאינו שומע ואינו מדבר · הלך תרח אצל נמרוד עם
אברהם · אומר לנמרוד מי ששרף את אלהי מה יעשה לו · א״ל נמרוד
מי הוא ששרף אלהיך · א״ל בני · א״ל נמרוד לאברהם למה שרפת
אותם · א״ל לא שרפתים · א״ל ומי שרפם · א״ל הגדול שבהם שרפם
לפי שכעס בהם · א״ל נמרוד שוטה אינו שומע ואינו מדבר היאך
שרפם · א״ל אברהם ולמה תעזוב אלהים חיים שברא שמים וארץ וכל
העולם ותעבוד למי שאינו שומע ואינו מדבר · א״ל נמרוד מי ברא
שמים וארץ אם לא אני לבד · א״ל אברהם בזאת אדע שבראתה

הכל יום השמש שזורח במזרח ושוקע במערב · אם תעשה כן שיזרח
במערב ותשקע במזרח בזאת אדע שבראת הכל · מיד תלה עמוד
מדברין · והשאיס ידו בזקנו · כשראו אותו אסטגנינ׳ הכירוהו ואמרו
אל נמרוד אי אדונינו המלך · זה התינוק שאמרנו לך ונביאו עליו
ונשרפנו ונתן לאביו ולאמו ממון גדול · ועתה אדונינו המלך הואיל בא
לידינו נשרפנו בראש · אומר להם נמרוד עשו חפציכם ממנו · ולה עשו
הסיקו כבשן שבעה ימים ושבעה לילות · והשליכו אותו לתוך אותו
כבשן · מיד אמרו המלאכים לפני הקב״ה עך ונצל צדיק זה מן ה
הכבשן · והיה קטטה ביניהם · זה אומר אני ארד להצילו וזה אומר
אני ארד להצילו · אומר מיכאל אני ארד · אומר גבריאל אני ארד · אומר
הקב״ה אני ארד שהוא יחיד שאחד שמי בעולם ראשון · ואני יחיד
ודין הוא שארד · מיד ירד הקב״ה בכבודו ובעצמו · והצילו מכבשן ה
מכבשן האש · ואח״כ גבריאל הציל חנניה מישאל ועזריה כשהפילם
נבוכד נצר לכבשן · וגם היו מתקוטטין המלאכים לירד להצילם · ואומר
מיכאל אני ארד ואצילם · אל גבריאל לא גבורתו של הקב״ה צריכין כל
כך · לפי שאתה ממים ומנהגו של עולם שהמים מכבין את האש ·
אבל אני מאש ואצנן את הכבשן מבפנים ואחמם אותו מבחוץ ·
ובכך נראין נפלאותיו של הקב״ה · והפילן שלשה ונמצאו ארבעה ד
והרביעי היה גבריאל · ובאותה שעה נתקבצו כל מלכי האומות הו
הפחות והסגנים לראות אם שלטה בהם האש אם לאו וראו שלא
חרך שער ראשם ומלבושיהם לא נשתנו וריח אש לא שלט בהם · ו
מיד שבחו כל האומות לפני הקב״ה · והיו מכין וחובטין את ישראל
ומרקדין לפניהם ואומרים להם היה לכם אלהים כזה והשתחויתם
לצלם · מיד נפלו פניהם של ישראל ופתחו פיהם ואמרו לך
ה׳ הצדקה ולנו בשת הפנים כהיום הזה · וכל העובד ע״ז הקב״ה
עוקרו מן העולם הזה והעולם הבא · ויראה הטובות שעשה הקב״ה
לצדיקים ויבושו ויאמרו אוי לנו שלא זכינו לכבוד זה · על כי
שהנחנו אל חי ועבדנו לאל מת · ואז תיצא אש ותאכל כל המשתחוים
שעזבו הקב״ה ולא חזרו בתשובה · וכן מצינו באנשי דור הפלגה
שעזבו הקב״ה שאמרו הבה נבנה לנו עיר ומגדל ונעלה לש
לשמים ונכנו בקרדומות ונבקע את הרקיע וידובו המים שלמעלן
כדון עלמן למטה שלא יעשה לנו כאשר עשה לדור המבול · ונ
ונעשה מן השמים חתיכות ונעשה מלחמה עם אותן שבשמים ·
ונעמיד שם ע״ז · והיאך היו יכולין לבנות את העיר שלא היה להם

אבנים לשם. ואלו מה היו עושים לבינים ובנו העיר והמגדל גד
גבוהים מאד ושבעים מעלות היו לו וכשעולין עולין ממזרח
וכשיורדין יורדין במערב. וכשנופל אדם מהם לא היו שמים על
לב. ורואה אברהם מעשיהם מקולקלים וקילל בשם י"י. ולא היו
חוששין לדבריו. וירד הקב"ה עם שבעים מלאכין הסובבים את
כסא הכבוד. ובילבל את לשונם לשבעים לשון:

מעשה באשה אחת שהיו לה שבעה בנים
והביאו לפני קיסר. ואמר הקיסר
לגדול עבוד ע"ז. א"ל לא אני כופר
באלהים שכך כתוב לנו אנכי י"י אלהיך. והרגוהו. קרא לכל אחד ואחד.
ואומר להם כך. וכל אחד ואחד אומרו לו פסוקו. והרג כולם. ולשביעי
אמר עבוד ע"ז. א"ל אלך ואתייעץ ואמי. א"ל לך. הלך אצל אמו אומר
לה אמי מה אעשה. אומרה לה וכי תדעה שכל אחיך ישבו במ'
מחיצת הקב"ה שבריום ואתה תשב מחוץ. אל תשמע אל זה הר'
הרשע. חזר אצל קיסר ואומר לו איני כופר באלהים. שכתוב לנו
את י"י האמרת היום וי"י האמירך ונשבענו לאלהינו שאין אנו מ'
ממירין אותו באל אחר. והוא נשבע לנו שלא ימיר אותנו באומה
אחרת. א"ל קיסר אשליך טבעתי לארץ בפני העם וכרע ולקח
אותו. לפי שיאמרו ריצוני עשית. א"ל אוי לך קיסר שלכבודך עשית
כך. ולכבוד הקב"ה על אחת כמה וכמה. הוציאוהו והרגוהו. אומרה
להם אמם בבקשה מכם תנו אותם לי ואנשקם. נתנו אותם לה.
ואומרה להם בני אמרו לאברהם אבינו שלא יגבה לבו אם עקד
הוא בן אחד. אני עקדתי שבעה. ואף היא עלתה לגג ונפלה ומתה.
ויצתה בת קול ואומרה אם הבנים שמחה. ויש להם חלק לעולם הבא
עם הצדיקים. על כן אומרו חכמים שבחו את הקב"ה בפני הגוים
כי על כן פיזרתי אתכם בין הגוים אשר לא ידעוני למען תספרו
נפלאותי. ראו נא אל תמירוני באלילים. כי אל קנא אני. חי עולמים
ואל תשתחוו לאחרים. אולי לאמית ומחייה. וכן אומר להם כשאומר
להם הדיבור לא יהיה לך. מיד חדרו ישראל ואמרו בפה אחד
שמע ישראל י"י אלהינו י"י אחד. אומר להם הקב"ה אתם מייחדים
שמי בעולם הזה ואני אייחד אתכם לעולם הבא. שנאמר ומי
כעמך ישראל גוי אחד בארץ:

מעשה בחסיד אחד שהיה עשיר
מאד. ולא נשבע מימיו ובשעה

פטירתו קרין לבנו לפני זקני העיר' ראו בני הזהר שלא תשבעו לי
אפילו באמת' ואני אותן לך כל נכסיי' שכל העושר שיש לי בשביל
ששמרתי את פי משבועה' ועונה לו מקיים צווייך ולא ישבע אפילו
באמת' וכשנפטר החסיד' היה הבן מקיים מצות אביו' כששמעו ה
ראמאים שלא נשבע אפילו באמת' באו לו ואמרו לו שמענו שכל ה
נכסי אביך יש לך' והוא היה מחוייב לנו ממון רב' ולפי שנאמן היה
לא חששנו' וכיון שמת תשלם לנו עבורו' אומר להם לא שמעתי מ
מעולם שאבי היה מחוייב לשום אדם שבעולם' אמרו לו השבע לנו
שלא ידעת ותפטר' אמר החסיד בלבו' אם אשבע אחלל שם שמים
ואבטל מצות אבי' ועוד שאיני יודע אם אמת אמרו אם לאו' ושמא
כנים דבריהם' מוטב שאפרע אליהם ולא אשבע' ופרע להם כל מה
שאמרו' ואחרי כן באו רמאים אחרים עד שלא נשאר לו מאומה וכל
כך לפי שלא רצה לבטל מצות אביו' ואחר כך בא אדם אכזר
אחד ואמר לו תן לי דינר זהב אחד שהיה מחוייב לי אביך' א"ל אין לי
כלום לפרוע' א"ל השבע לי שאין לך כלום לפרוע ותפטר' א"ל לא אשבע'
הוליכהו לפני הדיין ולא רצה לישבע' מיד חבשו אותו בבית האיס
האיסורין' ואשתו היקרת הייתה יפה מאד' והייתה מתביישת לבקש
כלום' והיתה עושת בגדים לכבס לפרנס את בעלה ואת בניה' יום אחד
הלכה לנהר לכבס בגדים' ובאותה ספינה אחת' וכשראתה בעל הספי
הספינה חמדה בלבו' ואמר לה כבס לי בגדי ואתן לך דינר זהב נטלה
את הדינר ונתנה אותו לבעל הגבול והלך ופדה את אבין מן הסוהר' וכן
וכבסה את הבגדים' וכשהלכה להחזירם' חטפה בעל הספינה והוליכה
לה' ובניה היו רואין אותה מרחוק' ובוכין ואומרין אמינו אמה עשה'
הלכו לאביהם וסיפרו לו המעשה' היאך נשבית אמם' מיד נתן עיניו
לשמים ונתן קולו בבכייה גדולה' ואמר ישתבח שמו של הקב"ה מרוב
נכסים שנשאר לי מאבי' ועתה נשארתי בלא מינוח ובלא שום
ממון ובלא שום מחייה שבעולם' ובלא אשתי' וכל כך לפי שקיימתי
מצות אבי' והלך יחיד עד שהגיע לחוף הנהר' וזימן לו הקב"ה דף
אחד וישב על אותו דף והלך לו' עד שהוליכו רחוק' ונפל למדינה
אחרת' והנערים בוכים עד שבאתה ספינה אחת ולקחם והוליכם
בשבי' אמרו לו אנשי העיר לאותו חסיד' מאין באתה ומאיזה מק
מקום אתה' מיד סיפר להם כל המעשה' אמרו לו יודע אתה לעשות
כלום' אמר להם יודע אני ללמוד תורה ולכתוב ספרים' אמרו לו אין
אנו רוצים בכך' אלא רעה צאן לנו את צאננו' וניתן לך מיטב הי

היאון וכגויטב הנזה· הלך ורעה את מקניהם· יום אחד היה יושב על
הנהר שהיה מלא נחשים ועקרבים· וזכר מן העושר שנשתייר לו מן
אביו· והרים קולו בבכי גדול מאד· ואומר רבונו של עולם מרוב עבדים
ושפחות ומכל טוב שנשארו לי מאבי זכור לטוב· לא נשתייר לי מאומה·
ורצה להשליך עצמו בנחל· וכשראוה ההרוגים שהרגו הנחשים והעקר
והעקרבים· ורצה לשוב· וראה איש אחד עומד כנגד אחד על שפת
הנהר· ואומר לו פלוני אל תלך אנה ואנה כי כבר עברו כמה שנים שאני
שומר לך ממון גדול· שהקבה מעלה אותך גדולה על ששוררת מעלת
אביך· ואין חילות שם שמים· וטול את הממון הזה וקח לך עבדים
ושפחות וקרקעות וספינות· וקנה הכל· אזל האיש· ואותו האיש היה
מלאך· לך וקנה הנחל הזה מבני העיר· הלך אצל בני העיר· ואמר להם
מכרו לי את הנחל הזה· אמרו לו שוטה אתה ומה תעשה ממנו· ית
אומר להם מכל מקום מכרו אותו לי· ואני אתן לכם את הדמים· מכ
מכרוהו לו בשטר· הלך אצל המלאך ואזל עשיתי כאשר צויתני· ועת
ונתעשר האיש עד שנעשה מלך· ונשמע שמועתו בכל העולם· והיה
והכריז שכל מי שרוצה לקרות עמו· יבוא ויטול עשרה זהובים בכל
יום· כששמע נתקבצו מכל האוניות ובאות עמו· עד שבאות ספינה
ששם היו בנו· וכשראתה אותם החסיד הכירם וקנה אותם מבעל
הספינה· בממון גדול· ועשה להם טובה מכל עבדיו· יום אחד באתה
ספינה ששם אשתו· והיה מנהגו של אותו חסיד שכל ספינה של
שבאת לשם מזמן אנשי הספינה לסעודתו· מה עשה זימן בעל הי
הספינה· ואזל אדוני יש לך לי לשמור ספינתי· ואין אבחנה באחיך· אזל
החסיד הרי שני בני שישמרוה· הלכו בנו ושמרו הספינה וגם אשתו
כשראו הנערים את הספינה הכירוה ובכו בכייה גדולה· ואומרים אוי
לנו שהספינה הזאת דומה לאותה ספינה שנשבית אמינו· אומר להם
האשה בני מה לכם שתבכו· מיד סיפרו לה כל המעשה היאך נשבית
אמם· מיד הכירה האשה כל המעשה· וידעה שהם בניה בכתה כל
הלילה עמהם ולא הודיעם כלום עד הבקר כשראוה אותה בעל הספינה
ראותה עצבת רוח· אומר לה מה לך· ואמרה לו שלחת אלי הנערים של
ששחקו בי כל הלילה· כששמע בעל הספינה כך· הלך אצל החסיד·
ואזל שלחת לספינתי אנשים לענות והתעללו באשתי מיד שלח
אחרי בנו· ואומר להם זאת הדבר שזה אומר· אמרו לו חלילה לנו מן
מעשות כדבר הזה· תבוא האשה אם היא אומרת כך תמיתנו· מיד
שלח לקרוא לאשה· אומר לה בתי אל תפחדי ומוע ואל תכחדי ממני

ואמר לו היאך היה המעשה׳ ויגד השתחוה לפניו ונפלה ואמרה
אדוני המלך בחייך בניי הם׳ וסיפרה לו כל המעשה היאך נתנה לבנו
הדינר לפדות את אביהם׳ וכשהלכה להחזיר שחטפה בעל הספינה הַדְּבָרִים
ויגד הדבר החסיד כל המעשה וידע שהיתה אשתו׳ אמר לבעל הספינה
איפה מצאת את הילדה הזאת׳ אם לא תגיד אחתוך ראשך׳ ויגד אל בעל
הספינה בחייך אדוני המלך אני שביתיה מהנהר שמכבסת בגדים
ובחייך מיום ששביתיה לא יכולתי לנגוע אליה׳ והרי אני בידך עשה
ממני מה שתרצה ויגד נתן לו לבעל הספינה ממון גדול ושלחו ועתה
נחזרו לו בניו ואשתו׳ ברוך המקום שאינו מקפח שכר לצדיקים של
ששומרים את עצמם משבועה׳

מעשה

בשלשה אנשים שבאו מן
הסחורה וקדש עליהם שבת
אמרו זה לזה׳ מה נעשה כי זה הדרך דרך ליסטים וחיות רעות׳ אז
אמרו השנים מוטב שנחלל את השבת׳ ואל נפסיד ממוננו׳ אמר
השלישי לא אזוז מכאן׳ ולא אחלל את השבת׳ הקב״ה שנתן לנו שבת
נוח ושומר׳ הוא יכול לשומרינו ולהצילנו מן החיות רעות ומן הל׳
הליסטים׳ ומה עשו השנים הלכו לדרכם וחללו את השבת׳ והאחד
שלא רצה לחללו תקע אהלו וערך שולחנו והדליק את נרו וקדש השבת׳
וכשאוכל בא דוב אחד שלא היה כמוהו ועמד נגדו׳ כשראה החסיד
הדוב אצלו נתן לו מפתו ומבשרו ואוכל׳ ומעולם לא עלה פחד בלבו׳
ואחר אכילתו בירך ברכת המזון׳ ושכב וישן׳ והדוב שכב אצלו׳ ואחר
שהוא שבת ראה את הדוב שהוא שוכב אצלו׳ נתן עיניו למרום׳ ונתן
שבח והודיה למקום שלא הזיקו את הדוב מה עשה החסיד הלך
וסידר תפלתו׳ וישב ואכל ולקח מפתו ומבשרו ונתן לדוב׳ ועמד אצ׳
אצל הדוב כל היום׳ לערב התפלל תפלת ערבית ועשה הבדלה והלך לו
לדרכו׳ והלך הדוב עמו כל אותו הלילה׳ ימצאו ליסטים מעבדי המלך מן
היער׳ ומצאו שני האנשים שחיללו את השבת׳ ושללו אותם וגזלו
מהם כל ממונם׳ בין כך ובין כך בא זה החסיד עם הדוב כשראה
הדוב את שני האנשים שחיללו שבת׳ בא בחימה וקרעם בזו והרג
אותם׳ כשראה זה האיש שהרגם היה מינטער כעיניו׳ בין כך
פגע את הליסטים׳ אמרו לו מי אתה׳ אמר להם יהודי אני׳ אמרו לו
מאין אתה אמר להם מבית המלך׳ אמרו לו מי נתן לך את הדוב׳ אמר
להם המלך ויצוה לו המלך ששומרני מן הליסטים׳ אמרו הליסטין
זה לזה כמה אוהב המלך אותו האיש׳ אמרו שמא ילשין אותנו למלך

307

-85-

ויתלה אותו׳ אומרו לו נתן לך ממון רב ואל תאמר למלך מאומן ומאומה׳
מה עשו נתנו לו ממון רב׳ והוליכוהו עד ביתו לשלום׳ כשבא לביתו ח
חזר הרוב לדרכו׳ ועתה בא וראה כמה שכרן של צדיקים׳ עושי מצ
מצות ושומרי שבת׳ ומה זה ששמר שבת עשה לו הקב״ה נס׳ השו
השומר שבת כל ימיו על אחת כמה וכמה׳

מעשה בחסיד אחד שהייתה אשתו יפה
ביותר׳ והיה החסיד עני גמור׳ והיה
שם בחור אחד בעירו שהיה עשיר
ביותר׳ וחמד אשתו של אותו חסיד מאד׳ יום אחד חלה החסיד׳
שלח לה הבחור שלוחיו לומר עשי רצוני ואני אתן לך כל מה
שתרצה׳ אומרה להם הצדקת לא אכחש בבעלי׳ שכל אשה ש
שמכחשת בבעלה מכחשת לבוראה׳ הלכו לאדוניהם ואמרו לו כך
וכך דברה לנו האשה׳ שלא תעשה רצונך׳ הלכו פעם אחרת וכ
ואומרה להם כך׳ מיד הלך הבחור הוא עצמו׳ ואומר לה פלונית
השמעי לי׳ ואני אתן לך כל מה שתרצי׳ ועד שבעלך עני ואני
עשיר׳ והוא מכוער ביותר׳ ואני יפה ועשיר׳ אומרה לו הצדקת
אם אתה יפה כחוה ובעלי מכוער ביותר לא אכחש בו׳ שכל
המכחשת לבעלה מכחשת לבוראה׳ אומר לה עשי רצוני׳ שאם
לא תעשי רצוני אמות כאהבתך׳ אומרה לו מוטב שתמות
ולא נאבד אני ואתה׳ בעולם הזה ובעולם הבא׳ כשראה הבחור
שלא רצתה לעשות רצונו׳ הלך הבחור לביתו ונפל למטה בשי
כשכיבה׳ מה עשתה הצדקת׳ הולכה לראות בעלה׳ מה היה
עושה׳ ומצאו לא חי ולא מת׳ אומר לה החסיד אוי אשה רעה׳
ידעתי מה את מבקשת לעשות נתת עיניך באותו בחור׳ וחשבת
להמיתני׳ ויקח אותו לבעלי׳ הקב״ה יבקש דמי נפשי ממך׳ וכ
והיא היתה מפרנסת בעלה בכל יום׳ יום אחד היו גשמים ולא
היה לה מלאכה לעשות׳ אל בעלה לכי לאותו בחור שהוא ע
עשיר מאד וילוה לך מנכסיו׳ אומרה לו אוי לה היום כמה ימים
ביקש ליתן לי כל נכסיו דום אעשה רצונו׳ ואתה חשדתני ממנו׳
בשבועה לא אלך׳ עמדו ביום שלשה ימים שלא אכלו ולא שתו׳
לאחר ג׳ ימים אומרה הצדקת לבעלה תן לי גט ליום אחד
שאם אעשה חטא עם אותו בחור לא יהא חטא גדול כל כך׳
וכן עשה החסיד׳ הולכה לבחור׳ ואומרה בהליכתה אלהי אברהם
יצחק ויעקב שומריני היום שלא אחטא עם אותו בחור

הלכה לשער ואומר הבחור ראו מי קורא לשער ' יצאו וראו שאשתו של
אותו חסיד הייתה ' אמרו פלונית היא ' ואומר הבח' אם אמת הדבר
תהיו כולכם משוחררים ' והלכו אחריה ופתחו לה ' וכשראה אותה הבחור
נפל על מחולין ' ואומר לה ברוכה את בתי לה' שבאתה לכאן ' אמרה לו דבר
אחד שיגרני אליך ' א"ל דבר ' א"ל בעלי חולה מאוד ולא היה לי לפרנסו '
למען חסדך לוה לי לפרנסו ' אומר לה עשי רצוני ואני אתן לך כל מה
שתרצה ' אמרה לו ידוע בך שתינך כאלהים שתעשה חסד בשביל
בוראך ' וכבוש את יצרך ואל תעשה עמי נבלה היום ' ותדע שאם
תכבוש יצרך עתיד אתה להיות לך חלק עם הצדיקים לעולם הבא '
מיד נתגלגלו רחמיו של אותו בחור ' ושמע אליה ' ואומר לה' אלהי א
אברהם תזכור לי שעה זו שבאתי לידי מעשה כזו וכבשתי את יצרי '
מה עשה הבחור נתן לאותה הצדקת כסף וזהב לרוב והלכה לבעלה '
וספרה לו כל המעשה ' ולא האמין לה ' לימים נתרפא החסיד מחוליו '
והלך לשוק ופגע הבחור שנתן לאשתו הממון ' והיה נר דולק על ר
ראשו ' א"ל החסיד בני מה מעשיך שנר דולק על ראשך ' א"ל עשיתי
צדקות ' א"ל הרבה ישראל עושין צדקות ולא היה להם כך ' משביעך
אני שתאמר לי האמת ' א"ל הואיל והשבעתני אומר לך ' כך וכך מעשה
לידי וכבשתי את יצרי ' מיד שמח החסיד והאמין לדברי אשתו ה בא
הצדקת ' אומר אשה טובה עטרת בעלה ' וכל אשה רעה אוכלת
בעלה בתולעת העץ ' שכל המנופת מכחשת לאותה ' שנאמר
העוזבת אלוף נעוריה ' את ברית אלהיה שכחה ' וכל חכם ונבון יש
ירחק ממנה '

מעשה

היה בימי שלמה
בשלשה בני אדם שהיו סוחרים
והלכו בדרך וקדש עליהם השבת
ולקחו כל צרורותם והטמינם במקום אחד ' והיו יודעים כולם
אותו מקום ' ובמוצאי שבת הלך אחד מהם ולקח הכל ' וכשבאו
שלשתם אל המקום ליקח כיסם לא מצאו כלום ' והיה קטטה בין
ביניהם ' זה אומר אתה לקחתם ' וזה אומר לא כי אתה לקחתם ' וכן
השלישי ' הלכו לדין לפני המלך שלמה ' וספרו לו כל המעשה ' מיד
שמע שלמה דבריהם ' וחישב על הדבר ואומר בלבו ' אם לא אודיע
באותה עתה יאמרו נסתלקה חכמתו ממני ' ואומר בלבו אחקור
בחכמתי בדבריהם ' ויאמר להם שמעו שאשאלכם את הדבר הזה '
מלך כיבר שאל דבר אחד לי להודיעו מה טוב ' שהיה מעשה בב'
בתינוק ובתינוקת שהיו דרים בחצר אחת ויקחו ברית ביניהם וע

308

·פא·

ויאמר האיש לאשה שהוא יקח אותה לאשה· והיא אותו לבעל· ועשו שני
שניהם שבועה מזה תנאים· אם יזמין להם הקב״ה· ואם לא יזמין להם שלא
יהיה רשות לזה ליקח אשה בלא רשותה· והיא לא תהיה נשואת לאיש אחר
בלא רשותו· לימים קדש אותה אביה לאיש אחר ונשאה· וכשרצה בעלה
לשכב אצלה אומרה הנערה כי אדוני אל תגע בי ואדברה אליך דבר אחד·
כשנערותי התניתי עם נער שלא ישכב אדם לעולם עמי עד שאטול רשות
ממנו· וישמע הנער הבחור לדברי הנערה וכבש יצרו ולא נגע אליה ולאחר
השכימו והלכו אצל הנער ואמרה הנערה אדון אדוני חביבי ידעתי כי
באמת עשינו תנאי בינינו כאשר אתה יודע· ועתה לא הזמין הקב״ה לעשות
ונשאתי הבחור הזה· ובחסד קבל ממני מזון ותן לי רשות לשכוב עמו·
ויען הנער חביבתי יהי לך אשר לך שלא אקח כלום ממך· הואיל שלא בא
הדבר מאת ה׳ הרי את לכל אדם· ויצאו ממנו בשלום· ופגעו בהם זקן אחד
ולקח כל מה שלהם ופשטם ערומים· ורצה להרוג בעלה· והנערה הניח הז׳
הזקן לשכב עמה· ואמרה האשה לזקן אדוני כבוש את יצרך כי אתה
זקן וזה איש בחור וכבש יצרו בשבילי· ויאמר לה הזקן איך היה המעשה·
וספרה לו הכל ואמרה לו ומה בעלי שהוא בחור ויכול לעשות
חפצו בלא חטא כבש יצרו· ואתה זקן לא כל שכן· מה עשה הזקן השיב
להם כל מה שלקח מהם ונתן להם ממון רב·· ועתה שאל אני לך כבר
איזה מהם מכל אלה יפה עשה· ועתה הבינו אתם בדבר ואם שמע המעשה
מכם· ענה האחד ואמר משבח אני את הנערה שלא עזבה הברית שהתנתה
עם הנער· והשני אמר משבח אני את החתן שהוא יכול חפצו לעשות
חפצו בלא חטא· וכבש יצרו·· ענה השלישי שגנב את הממון משבח
אני את הזקן שהשיב להם כל מה שגזל· ומנע עצמו מלהרוג את החתן·
ולשכב עם הכלה·· אבל תמיה אני על זאת לא די שלא הרגו והניחו ללכת
אלא שחזר להם הממון· ועוד שהוסיף להם משלו ממון רב· ודאי שוטה
היה·· ויען שלמה ויאמר לו רשע ומה ממון שלא ראית ולא בא לידך
לא ידעת כי אם לשמוע האזן אתה מתחרט וחושב רעות על זה· ממון
שראית וידעת ולקחת על אחת כמה וכמה שלא תחזור אותו כי אם בכח·
מיד תפשוהו והלקוהו מכות גדולות עד שהודה·· ועתה בא וראה גדולתו
של הקב״ה שהוציא את הסתר לגלוי· לפיכך יהא אדם זהיר
שלא יחמוד ממון חבירו ושלא יגנב אותו לפי שהקב״ה לא יכנס במחיצתו
והוא יוציא הכל לאור· ש״נ וסתר פנים ישים· שבעון גנבה באים מעשים
מכוערים לבושים נעשו ערומים· בא וראה שהרי אדם הראשון וחוה עשה להם הקב״ה
עשר חופות בגן עדן ממרגליות וכשפשטו ידיהם בגזל בפירות האילן

ונרעשים ונגן עדן׳ והיו גבורים כמלאכים׳ והניח הקב״ה ידו עליהם ולא עשם
ונעשו שפלים הם היו לבושים מענני כבוד׳ והיה עורם כציפורן׳ ונעשו
ערומים׳ וכל כך למה׳ שלא התגברו ושלא תגלה על דעתך לפשוט ידך
בגניבה׳ **מעשה** באשה אחת שהייתה מיי
מייסרת בתה זונה׳ והיית אומרת לה בת
בתי אם את עשה זנות אל תעשי כי
אם בצנעא׳ כדי שלא ידבר בך בעולם כדרך שעשיתי אני שעשרה
בנים יש לי ואינם מאביך אלא אחד מהם שמע הבעל דברי הרע שהיה
שהייתה מדברת עם בתה ושמר את הדבר בלבו׳ ועת כשעת פטירתו
שלא יתן מן הנחלה כי אם לאחד׳ ולא אומר לאיזה מהן׳ כי לא היה
יודע איזה מהן היה בנו׳ לאחר שמת התגרו זה בזה כולם עשרה
זה אומר שלי הנחלה׳ וזה אומר שלי׳ באו לדין לפני רבי בנאה׳ אמר
להם עשו הדבר שאומר לכם כי הדבר סתום׳ ואין יכול לדעת אדם׳
ועתה לכו חיטטו קבר אביכם וחבטו עליו כדורכם עד שיגלה לכם
לאיזה מכם עלה בדעתו ליתן המתנה׳ שמעו הדבר והלכו התחילו
וחבטו את הקבר באלות׳ ואותו האיש שהיה בנו בודאי אומר חלילה
לי להכות על אבי מוטב לי לאבד כל הירושה ולא יבזה את אבי כי
כשראה ר׳ בנאה הדיין כך נתן לו כל הירושה לזה׳ ובזו ראה איך
נתקיים זה הפסוק ועין נאף שמרה נשף לאמר לא תשורני עין ו׳
וסתר פנים ישים׳ מי שיושב בסתר פנים ישים לדבר לסוף עתידה
להגלות׳ לכך יהיו בניך נקיות׳ **מעשה** בבחור
אחד שהיה זהיר במצות ציצית ושומע
שהיתה זונה בכרכי הים שנוטלת ארבע
מאות זהובים וקבע לה זמן בא וישב לה על פתח ביתה נכנסה
נכנסה שפחתה ואמרה לה אותו ששיגר לך ארבע מאות זהובים
בא וישב לו על הפתח אמרה לו יכנס׳ נכנס׳ והיא היציעה שבע מ׳
מטות׳ שש של כסף ואחד של זהב׳ ועלתה וישבה לה על העליונה
ערומה ואף הוא עלה וישב לה כנגדה׳ באו ארבע ציציות וטפחו לו
על פניו נשמט וישב לו על גבי קרקע׳ ואף היא נשמטה על גבי
קרקע׳ אמרה לו גפה של רומי שלא אניח עד שתאמר לי מה
מום ראית בי׳ אמר לה העבודה לא ראיתי אשה יפה כמותך׳ אלא
מצוה אחת ציונו אלהינו וציצית שמה וכתוב בה שני פעמים אני
ה׳ אלהיכם׳ האחד לומר אני הוא העתיד ליפרע׳ והאחד לומר
אני הוא שעתיד ליתן שכר טוב לצדיקים עושי רצונו׳ ועכשיו נ׳

309

·כא·

שדומה לי כמרכבה עלים׳ אמרה לו העטרה שלי אניחך עד שתאמר
לי מה שמך ושם עירך ושם רבך ושם מדרשך שאתה לומד בו׳ וא״ל״
כתב לה בכתב כל זה׳ מה עשתה האשה חילקה כל נכסיה שליש למלך
ומלכות שליש לעניים ושליש נטלה בידה חוץ מאותן מלבושות שהיו לה׳
ובאתה לפני מדרשו של ר׳ חייא׳ אמרה לו ר׳ צוה עלי ועשוני עבריה׳
אמר לה שמא עיניך נתת בתלמיד מן התלמידים׳ הוציאה כתב מידה ונתנה
לו׳ א״ל לך זכי במקחך׳ ואותן מלבושות שהציען באיסור׳ עתה הציעם
בהיתר׳ וזה היה מתן שכרן בעולם הזה׳ ולעולם הבא איני יודע כמה׳
ולעולם שהיה בנך עורים בנקיות ושא אשה נקייה שלא יבגד בך
כדי שיהו בניך ורידים כמשנתך כדרך:

מעשה בחסיד אחד שהיה בן שבעים שנה
ולא היה לו בן וחשב בלבו ואומר למה
לי נכסים אלא אתן אותן לתלמידי ח
חכמים שלא יעשו סחורה ויעסקו בתורה כדי שאזכה עמהם לעולם
הבא והיה הולך בכל יום ויום ושואל הנערים מפסוקיהם׳ ואומר לו כל
אחד ואחד פסוקו׳ והשיב ואומר אשרי יולדתכם שזכו לבנים שעוסקים
בתורה׳ מיד נתגלגלו רחמיו של הקב״ה ונתן לו בן לשבעים שנה׳ וכש׳
וכשהגדיל השים אותו אפי׳ לבית הספר הלך לרבו ואומר לו רבי באיזה
ספר נתחיל לנער יא״ל בספר ויקרא׳ א״ל ר׳ מוטב שיתחיל בספר בראשית
שהן גבורותיו של הקב״ה׳ ועשה כן׳ ובכל יום מוליכו אומן על כתפו
ומוליך לבית המדרש יום אחד אומר לו הנער אבא למה תטרח עלי בכל
יום אני ידעתי הדרך ואני בעצמי אלך׳ הלך הנער יחיד לבית רבו׳ ג׳
וכשהיה הולך בדרך מצאו אותו אחד מעבדיו של קיסר וכשראה אותו
יפה ומלובש הרכיבו עמו על הסוס והוליכו לאדוניו׳ כשבא לערב שהנערים
נפטרים מבית רבן׳ ראה אותו חסיד שלא בא בנו הלך אצל רבו׳ וא״ל איה
הנער ששלחתי אצלך׳ א״ל לא ראיתי היום׳ מיד בכה בכייה גדולה ומרה׳
והתיל פניו באפר והלך בפרשת דרכים ושאל לעוברי דרכים׳ ראיתם נער
אחד כך וכך פנים סימנים היו בו׳ אמרו לו לא ראינו אותו׳ מיד זעקו ג׳
ובכו הוא ואשתו בכייה גדולה ומרה מיד נתגלגלו רחמיו של הקב״ה׳
ושלח חולי גדול למלך קיסר׳ והביאו לפניו ספר רפואות׳ נעשה נס והחזר
ונחזר אותו ספר בראשית׳ פתחו הספר ולא היו יודעים לקרות בו׳
אמרו לו אדונינו המלך הספר הזה של יהודים הוא׳ ושלח בכל מדינה
לבקש שם יהודי ולא מצאו׳ מיד ענה אחד מהם וא״ל אדוני המלך פעם
אחת הלכתי לעיר אחת של יהודים וראיתי נער יהודי אחד ולקחתיו

שאינו הוא יודע לקרוא בספר הזה׳ א״ל המלך הוליכו אצלי׳ מיד הביא
הביאוהו׳ א״ל המלך בני יודע אתה לקרוא בספר זה׳ כיון שראה הנער
הספר נפל ואין קולו ארעה על הספר ונשקו ובכה׳ א״ל קיסר בני
אל תירא ומה וקרין בספר הזה׳ א״ל אדוני המלך אין אני ירא ממך
יותר כחייך אדוני המלך בזה הספר התחיל לי רבי ומורי׳ א״ל יודע
אתה לקרות בו׳ א״ל כן׳ א״ל המלך בני קרא בו׳ מיד קרא הנער מבראשית
מבראשית עד ויכלו׳ א״ל המלך יודע אתה לפרש׳ נתן לו הקב״ה דיעה
ובינה ופירש לו מבראשית עד ויכלו׳ כששמע המלך גבורותיו של
הקב״ה קם מכסאו וישב לו בארץ כעבדו׳ וא״ל בני רפואה גדולה באה לי
על ידך בקש ממני כל מה שאתה רוצה׳ א״ל הנער איני מבקש ממך
כלום׳ אלא שתחזירני לאבי ולאמי׳ מיד הלך המלך לבית גנזיו ונתן
לו כסף וזהב אין מספר והחזירו לאביו ולאמו׳ וכשראו אותו נתנו ש׳
שבח להקב״ה׳ ואמרו חכמים ומה זה שלא כיבד אביו אלא שעה א׳
אחת בעולם׳ שלם לו הקב״ה שכר המכבד כל ימיו על אחת כמה וכמה׳
שישלם לו הקב״ה שכר גדול׳׳

מעשה

באדם
אחד שהיה לו פרה אחת והיה חורש
בה כל השבוע ובשבת אינו חורש׳ שעוני
ולען יעוח׳ לימים נצטרך בעל הפרה׳ ומכרה לגוי אחד׳ א״ל על מנת כן
אני קונה את הפרה שאינך יודע בה מום׳ ולקח הגוי וחרש בה כל ה
השבוע׳ וכן דיעה ועשית ביום השבת׳ ונתן עליה עול לחרוש׳ ולא
עשתה הפרה הפילה עצמה לארץ שהיה מתנהג לעת בשבתך׳
והכה הגוי כמה פעמים׳ ולא רצתה לקום ולחרוש׳ והלך הגוי לבית
הכנסת׳ וקרא לאותו שמכרה לו׳ וא״ל למה רמיתני׳ הלא ידעת כי
ערכת לי הפרה שמכרת לי שאין מום בה׳ א״ל הן׳ והנה היא בעלת
מום׳ כל זה שמכרתני שחרשתי עמה׳ והיום רציתי לחרוש ולא
רצתה שהיא נפלת בשדה׳ הבין האיש והלך עם הגוי בשדה
ומצאה שהיא נפלת׳ וראה הגוי להכותה׳ א״ל אל תכה אותה׳ ואמר
האיש לאוזן הפרה׳ פרה פרה אין אתה יודעת שכל זמן שהיית
עמי הייתה נחה ביום השבת׳ ועתה בעונותי מכרתיך לגוי׳ שלא
נתח אותו ולא נהוגה׳ ובחסדך קומי ועשי מלאכתך ואל תגרומי
לי להתקוטט עם הגוי׳ כששמעה הפרה עמדה על רגליה ועל
ועשתה מלאכתה׳ כשראתה אותה הגוי׳ א״ל מה דברת לאוזן י
הפרה׳ וכי כל זמן שאני רוצה לחרוש אלך כשכילך לומר לחש
באזנה׳ הורע הלחש ואם לאו חזור לי מעותי ותקח פרתך ת

Nasim

כפליים׳ ואמרו חכמים לעולם יסדר אדם שולחנו בהכנסת שבת׳ ואפי׳
ואפילו לא יש לו לאכול אלא כזית ששני מלאכים מלוין לו לאדם לביתו
מבית הכנסת׳ אחד טוב ואחד רע׳ כשבאו לביתו ומוצאו נר דלוק
ושולחן ערוך ומיטה מוצעת מלאך טוב אומר יהי רצון מלפני הקב״ה
שיהא לשבת האחרת הבאה כך׳ ומלאך רע עונה בעל כרחו אמן׳
ואמר ר׳ שמעון בן פזי כל המקיים ג׳ סעודות בשבת ניצול משלש
פורעניות מחבלו של משיח ומדינה של גהינם ומגוג ומגוג׳ ואמ׳
ר׳ יוחנן כל המענג את השבת נותנין לו משאלות לבו שנ׳ והתענג
על ה׳ ויתן לך משאלות לבך׳׳

מעשה

באדם אחד שהלך לסחורה והניח את אשתו לאחיו׳ וצוה לו ואמר שים עינך על
אשתי ולך לעבדה ולשמרה עד שאשוב לשלום׳ וענה לו אחיו
אעשה כדבריך׳ הלך האיש לסחורתו בדרך רחוקה ותשאר הא׳
האשה לבדה מיד אחי בעלה׳ מה עשה היה אוכל ונכנס והולך
אצלה יום אחר יום ואומר לה השמיעני ואעשה כל חפצך ואתן לך
כל מה שתרצה׳ והיא אומרת לו חלילה לי מעשות זאת שכל הא׳
המכחשת לבעלה מכחשת להקב״ה לבוראה׳ ועוד כי נפשה נדונת
בדינה של גהינם׳ ועוד כי בעלי אחיך הוא׳ והפקידני בידך לשמור
אותי ולא לחלל נפשי ונפשך׳ ואיך תעלה בדעתך לשלוח יד בפקדון
אחיך׳ כי כתיב פקדון שנתנו בידך כלי ליכנס ברשות שאינה שלו׳
וכל שכן שאשת אחיך אני ואסורה אני עליך מחיים׳ וכל החומד
אשת חבירו יתרחק ממנו ממונו׳ ולסוף בא לידי עריות׳ ועתיד
להיות נידון בגהינם ארוך ואין עולה׳ מה עשה אותו האיש יום
אחד בא ונכנס אצלה בביתו׳ ויאמר אל העבד׳ קח את הבקבוק
ולך לשאוב מים׳ וכיון שהלך למים קפץ האיש עליה ורצה לאונסה׳
ואומר לה עשי רצוני ונצעקה האשה צעקה גדולה ומרה ואין מ׳
מושיע לה׳ עד שהניחה מפני שצעקה׳ ויצא לשוק ושכר עליה
עדים שקרים׳ ואמר להם בואו והעידו שאותה ראיתם שזנה ואיך
מעשיה עם עבד בביתה׳ מה עשו הרשעים הלכו לפני סנהדרין׳
והוציאה לפניהם והעידו כן וכך ראינו שעשתה פלונית זאת עם
עבדה׳ ודנוה סנהדרין לסקילה׳ מיד לקחוה ונתנו על צואריה חבל
המעידי׳ והוציאוה לבית הסקילה והניחו לידו שלום וסקלוה׳ עד
שנעשה בה גל של אבנים כדין הנסקל׳ ויהי ביום השלישי בא אדם
אחד מעיר אחרת שמולך את רבו ללמוד תורה בירושלים וכשה׳

311

וכשהגיעו לבית הסקילה חשך עליהם היום ולא יכלו להגיע לירושלים
ולנו הלילה באותו מקום ושמו ראשיהם על הגל׳ וישכבו במקום ההוא׳
וישמעו קול מדבר בתוך האבנים שהיתה מתאנחת ומנוחת ואומרת
אוי לי כי נסקלתי בלשון הרע׳ וישמע האיש את הקול מדבר בתוך ה
האבנים׳ ויהפוך את האבנים כל הלילה לגל אחד וירא כי אשה היא׳
ויאמר לה מי את בתי׳ ותאמר לו אשת פלוני הייתי׳ ויאמר אליה מה
לך פה׳ אומרה לו כך היה מעשה וסקלוני בלא פשע ובלא חמס בכפי׳
אומרה לו מדוע לאן אתה הולך׳ אל׳ לירושלם ללמוד תורה לבני׳ אומרה
לו אם תוליכני לאורינך אני אלמדנו תורה נביאים וכתובים׳ אומר לה
וכי יודעת את ללמוד׳ אומרה לו הן׳ מיד הוליכה לאורינן עמו ולימדה
תורה לבנו׳ יום אחד נתן עבד הבית עיניו בה׳ ויאמר לה השמיעי לי
ועשי רצוני ואני אתן לך כל מה שתרצי׳ ולא אבתה לשכב עמו׳ מה
עשה העבד לקח סכין אחד ויצא להורגה׳ והכה את הנער והרגו׳
ויברח והקול נשמע בית אבי הנער כי מת העלם׳ ויאמר לאשה מאחר
שכן הוא לך מביתי ועמי לדרכך׳ כי בכל עת שאני רואה אותך לבי
סוער והומה על בני׳ מה עשתה האשה הלכה לדרכה ובשהגיעה
על שפת הים באה ספינה מליסטים ולקחוה ושבאוה בשבי׳ ויהי
העלו רוח סערה אל הים׳ ויהי סער גדול בים והאניה חשבה להשבר׳
וייראו המלחים ויזעקו איש אל אלהיו ויאמרו איש אל רעהו לכו ונ
ונפילה גורלות ונדעה בשלמי הרעה הזאת לנו׳ ויפילו גורלות ויפול
הגורל על האשה ויאמרו לה הגידה לנו מה מלאכתך׳ ותאמר להם
עבריה אנכי ואת ה׳ אלהי השמים אני יריאה אשר עשה הים ואת
היבשה וסיפרה להם כל הקורות אותה׳ מה עשו האנשים נתגלגלו
רחמים על האשה׳ ועשה הקב״ה לה נס׳ ולא נגעו כל הליסטים אליה
וישליכוה אל היבשה ועשו לה דירה קטנה׳ וישתוק הים מזעפו׳ ו
ודיתה ותלך האניה לדרכה והאשה הזאת נשארה במחוז רופאות מעט
מעונה ובחונה׳ והזמין לה הקב״ה כל מיני עשבים שבעולם והיתה
מתרפאות כל זב ומצורע׳ וכל חולי ועשתה האשה מעט מעט׳ ות
ותקבץ זהב וכסף לרוב עד שיצא שמעה בכל העולם׳ ויהיה אחר מעלה
לירושלים לסחורתו אותו האיש ובא שם׳ ושמע קול בעיר שאשתו נ
נסקלת׳ מה עשה הקב״ה הביא צרעת גדול על אותן אנשים שהעידו
שקר עליה ועל אחי בעלה׳ שמעו שמטרוניתא אחת רופאת י
היתה בכרכי הים׳ אומרו האיש אל אחיו נתנה ראש ונלך אל הרופאת
ויאמר האיש אל אחיו לך עמנו הלכו כולם ארבעה עד שהגיעו למד

לאיקומיה· נכנסו אצלה· ומיד הכירם· והם לא הכירוה· אמרו לה אדוננו
אדונתינו מארץ רחוקה באנו ושמענו שמעך שאת רופאת מעולה
ורפאי אותנו מצרעתנו· ותקח ממנו כסף וזהב לרוב· אמרה להם לא
אוכל לעשות רפואה לשום אדם אם לא יגיד לי עונו הגדול כי לא יועיל
לו· אמרו לו כזאת וכזאת עשינו· אמרה להם ראיה אני פניכם שחטא
שחטאים גדולים אתם ולא גליתם לי כל עונותיכם· וכל זמן שתכסו
על פשעיכם· לא יועיל רפואה לכם· מה עשו ספרו והודו ולא כחשו· וכל
וספרו כל המעשה לפני בעל האשה· אמרה להם הרעותם ופניכם עמה
לכם· בשבועה לא אעשה לכם רפואה· כי כל רפואות שבעולם לא יועילו
לכם· כי לא איש אל ויכזב· מאשר דבר מיד משה עבדו נאמנו וביד כל
עבדיו הנביאים· דכת' לא תלך רכיל בעמך ולא תעמוד על דם רעך·
עמדו שהרכילות מביא לידי רע· ואתם רשעים· אני היא האשה הי
הנעלבת עמכם אשר עשיתם כל הרעות האלה· והוצאתם אותי לסק
לסקילה בשבל לשונכם שקר· והקב"ה הצילני מעל רחמיו וחסדיו
הרבים· וזהו מעשי אשר הולכתם לפניכם אלו· והקב"ה יודע רזי עולם
ותעלומות סתרי כל חי· וכל סתר מביא לגלוי· שנ' וסתר פנים ישים·
ואותם שלשה אנשים לקו בצרעת ומתו כו'· מיד הכיר האיש כל הי
המעשה וידע שהיא אשתו· והיו שמחים וטובי לב· ונתנו שבח לה
לבוראם על כל הנסים האילו· וכאן וראה כמה גדול ענש לשון הרע
ומעידי שקר ומוציאי דבה סופו ללקות בצרעת· וכל יראי השם ינצ
ישמרו לשונם מדבר רע· שנ' שומר פיו ולשונו שומר מצרה נפשו:

מעשה

ברבי מאיר שלא היה רגיל לצאת
מבית המדרש עד ארבע שעות
ביום· יום אחד התפלל תפלת שחרית
והקדים לצאת לאחר שיצא תמה בעצמו· ותאמר ומפני מה יצ
יצאתי היום מהרה· שמא הקב"ה יעשה היום נס על ידי· כיון
שעמד קימעה ראה שני נחשים שהיו אומרים אחד לחבירו
לאן אתה הולך· אל הקב"ה שיגרני להרוג יהודה הענתותי וכל בניו
ואשתו וכל ביתו· אל למה· אל מפני שלא עשה צדקה מימיו· ?
אומר ר' מאיר אלך שמא אוכל להצילן· מיד גזר עליו ר' מאיר
שלא לעבור והלך ר' מאיר לביתו של יהודה· וכסה פניו שלא יכירנו
כיון שראה אותו ואמר זה בודאי גנב הוא שרוצה לגנוב נכסינו
כיון ששמע כך הלך ונתחבא בין הגמלים· וכשישב יהודה לסעוד
בא ר' מאיר וישב ביניהם התחילו בניו מריבין זה עם זה לגרשו

משם· אומר להם אם אתם הורגים זה עם זה לא אזוז מכאן עד שאוכל
ואשבע· לאחר שאכל ושתה· נטל חלת לחם בידו· ואומר ליהודה טול
חלת לחם בידך ותנה לי ואומר זו יהיה לך לצדקה· א"ל יהודה לא דייך
שאכלת ושבעת אלא שתריצה שאתן לך חלת לחם מה עשה ר' מאיר
כבה את הנר· והסיר הצעיף שעל ראשו· והבהיק הבית לאורו של רבי
מאיר· כיון שהכירוהו שהיה ר' מאיר מיד עמדו על רגליהם לפייסו
וכשנתפייס נטל יהודה החלה ואמר זו יהיה לך לצדקה· א"ל ר' מאיר שמע
לעצתי ושגר אשתך במקום אחר ובנך וכלותיך ובנותיך כמו כן וי'
ואמור להם שלא ישובו הנה עד שיעברו ג' שעות ביום· וכן עשה· ו'
ונשתיירו בבית ר' מאיר ויהודה לבדיהן· כיון שעברו ג' שעות בלילה
התיר ר' מאיר לנחש ועבר הנהר ובא לבית יהודה· ויצו ר' מאיר ליצרכו'
ונכנס הבית אותו נחש· ובקש להרוג· והיה צועק ואומר ר' מאיר הוש'
הושיעני מן הנחש שמבקש להורגני· מיד נכנס ר' מאיר לבית ומצא
הנחש· וא"ל מה טיבך· א"ל המקום שיגרני להרוג יהודה וביתו· א"ל ולמה·
א"ל מפני שלא עשה צדקה מנכסיו מעולם· א"ל ר' מאיר והלא אמש ר'
האכילני והשקני ואחר כך נתן לי חלת לחם לצדקה מיד גזר ר' מאיר
והוציאו מן הבית בעל כרחו· וסגר הדלת· ואומר ליהודה שלא יפתח
הדלת עד למחר· כיון שהאמין שעה באו אותו נחש ונראה כקול אשתו·
והיה אומרת בעלי פתח לי הדלת שהרי אני בצינה ודינה לפתוח· א"ל
ר' מאיר הזהר שלא תפתח שאינה אשתך· המתין מעט ובאו ונדמה
בקול בנו הגדול· וא"ל אבי פתח לי שאני מת בצינה· א"ל ר' מאיר הזהר
שלא תפתח שאינו בנך· ובאותו דמות דמה לבנו ולכלותיו· מכל מקום
לא הניחו ר' מאיר לפתוח ובטריזה הנחש שלא היה יכול להרוג יהודה
עמד על כוחו וצעק ובכה ואמר אוי שהעליונים גוזרין והתחתונים
מבטלים· אוי שהקב"ה גוזר ור' מאיר מבטל מיד נפל לארץ ובקע
כריסו ומת. ולמחר כיון שעברו ג' שעות ביום באתה אשתו ובנו ו'
וכלותיו ואומר להם בואו וראו מי היה קורא אמש מיד עמדו עם רבי
מאיר ומצאו הנחש שנפל ומת· א"ל זה שקרא כל הלילה מיד קרא עליו
זה הפסוק· לא יועיל הון ביום עברה ·· וצדקה תציל ממות ו

מעשה ברבי מאיר ור' יוסי ור' יהודה שהיו
הולכין בדרך· והיה ר' מאיר מדקדק
בשם שלא רצה ליכנס בבית אם לא
היה שם טוב לאדם· הגיע לבית אותו אדם ששמו כידור· אומר
להם ר' מאיר רשע הוא· שנ' כי דור תהפוכות המה· מה עשו רבי

יהודה ור׳ יוסי הפקידו לו את כיסיהם ור׳ מאיר לא הפקיד לו את כיסו
והלך ושם כיסו בכדור וקברה בקבר דאבי כידור׳ בא לו אביו של כידור
בחלום׳ א״ל בני בא וקח כיס אחד שהיא מונחת בראש קברי ולאחר בא
כידור לפני ר׳ מאיר׳ א״ל כך וכך ראיתי הלילה א״ל חלום דשבת בין הך
השמשות כתב הוא׳ מה עשה ר׳ מאיר שמר כיסו כל אותו היום ולי
ולמוצאי שבת נטל כיסו לאחר ביאו ר׳ יהודה ור׳ יוסי ושאלו כיסם ויל
ואמרו לכידור תנה כיסינו שהפקדנו אצלך ערב שבת׳ א״ל לא היו ד
דברים מעולם׳ א״ל ולמה לא דקדקתם בשם׳ אמרו לו מפני מה לא אמ
אמרת לנו׳ מה עשו משכוהו והכניסוהו לחנות אחת להשקותו יין
והוציא מפיו שישלם להם כיסם ראו בזקנו שאוכל עדשים בביתו׳
הלכו ואמרו הסימן לאשתו׳ ואמרו לה תני לנו הכיסין שהפקדנו לו
לבעלך ערב שבת׳ וזה לך האות שאכלו עדשים היום׳ ואמרה בלבה
באמונת אמרו הלכה הביאה ומסרה להם כיסיהם׳ כשבא כידור לביתו
א״ל איה הכיסין אמרה לו והלא שלחת אלי אות ושלם הכיסין לבעליהן
מה עשה הלך והרג את אשתו ובא ורוח כי ומפני חיאור ממון ביוין
לידי הרג נפש:

מעשה באדם אחד שהיו
קורין לו בן סבר לפי שהיה גדול בתורה
ובעל צדקה פעם אחת שמע שיש
יתום אחד בארץ ישראל שארס אשה והיה בן ז׳ שנים שלא היה
יכול לכונסה מה עשה בן סבר נטל כלי כסף וזהב וכל מיני מאכל
משאוי חמשה חמורים והלך והלך ט״ו יום עד שבא לעיר של י׳
אותו יתום והכניסו עם אשתו ועשה לו שבעה ימי המשתה ושושן
ושושבינין ואחר כן הלך לביתו הלך להר גבוה שהיה אורכו שמונה
עשר מילין׳ והיה בו תנין גדול אחד שהיה עשן ושורף כל עבר
ושב׳ וכשהגיע לאותו מקום עשה התנין עצמו כנשר׳ ועבר
עלין לכשירד מן ההר׳ פגע בו אדם מכוער ביותר והיה מלאך
המות׳ וא״ל מי אתה׳ א״ל אני פלוני בן פלוני והולכתי אני אותנו
יתום והכנסתיו עם אשתו׳ א״ל אני מלאך המות כבר נתנו פתקיך
מן השמים ולאחר אני נטל נשמתך בזאת שעה נשא בן סבר
עיניו לשמים וכפיו והתפלל ויצעק ובכה לפני הקב״ה ואמר רבש״ע
עולם הלא כתוב בתורתך שומר מצוה לא ידע כל דבר רע אני הולכתי
לדבר מצוה דאמות בדרך ולא אעשה את בני׳ יצתה בת קול ואמרה
לו כבר המתינו לך חמש עשרה ימים עד שתלך לביתך ותצוה את
בניך והיה הולך ובוכה עד שבא לעיר אחד גדול ופגע בשער אחד

313

.אמ

אדם אחד · וא״ל כלום יש תלמיד חכם בעיר · א״ל הרבה תלמידים יש
בעיר · ויש כאן תלמיד חכם גדול ושמו שפיפון בן לייש · ויש שנים
עשר אלף תלמידים כמותו · א״ל הוליכני אצלו והיו פניו של בן סבר
מבהיקות כזיו חמה · כיון שראה אותו שפיפון הכיר בו שהוא חכם
גדול · עמד לפניו וכל תלמידיו · כיון שעמד מעט נשתנו פניו · א״ל ומה
נשתנו פניך שמא צריך אתה לאכול או שמא דבר יש לך · א״ל לאו · ?
הודיעני מה ליבך · מיד הודיעו · וא״ל אל תתיירא מדבר זה · שב עמי
ולמדני קהלת ואיוב ואני ערב לך שלא תמות בפעם הזאת · א״ל היאך
אתה יכול לערב בי · והלא כתיב אח לא פדה יפדה איש ולא יתן לאלהים
כפרו · א״ל שב עמי ואני פודה אותך מיד ישב עמו והיה מלמד לו · כיון
שבא יום שישי בא מלאך המות וחשך כנגד שפיפון בן לייש · ואמרו
לו רבינו חשך העולם עלינו וראו יום כל העולם כולו חשך · ואם סביב
חצירנו חשך בטוחים אנו ברחמי שמים שתפלתינו נשמעת · בא
מלאך המות ורבץ כנגד שפיפון בן לייש · א״ל תן לי הפקדון שהפקדתי
אצלך · א״ל איזה פקדון · א״ל בן סבר תנהו לי שכבר הגיע זמנו ל
ליפטר באותה שעה השביע שפיפון למלאך המות בשם ע״ב אותיות
וסילקו · חזר מלאך המות ובא ועמד לפני הקב״ה · וא״ל רבונו של עולם
אחן בן לייש לתת לו רשות להעלות נפש אחד מידי · א״ל הקב״ה חביב ?
הוא עלי מאוד · לך ואמור לו אם נפש בן סבר חביב עליך ימשלך תמורת
תחתיו · ואם לאו ימות הוא · הלך ואמר לשפיפון בן לייש · א״ל לא נפשי
חביב עלי מנפשו ולא נפשו חביב עלי מנפשי · ואני לך אומר אל
הקב״ה אם יחיינו יחיינו יחד ואם ימיתנו יחד · ואל ימות לפנינו
צדיק זה ונחיה אחריו · חזר המלאך ואמר להקב״ה · באותה שעה
עומד שפיפון בתפלה ובתחנונים · לפני הקב״ה עד שיצתה בת קול
ואמרה מה אעשה לצדיקים הללו שאני גוזר והם מבטלין אותה
בצדקתם לכו והוסיפו על חייהם מאתים שנה לכל אחד מהם · ואת
ואמרו אותם מאתים שנה לא היה רעב בעולם · ולא מת אדם פחות
מן משבעים שנה ולא מת הבן בפני האב ולא הקטן לפני הגדול ·
ולא הפילה אשה פרי בטנה · ולאחר מיתתן היה רעב גדול בעולם ·
עשו ארבע תעניות וקבלו עליהם ליתן צדקה משלהם ולא יחמדו
ממון חביריהם · ועמדו בתפלה ובתחנונים לפני המקום · ואמרו
לפניו רבונו של עולם אנו בני אברהם אוהביך וזרע יצחק בחיריך
שב עלינו במדת רחמים · מיד ירדו גשמים ונתרווח והתיר שער
היוקר לקיים מה שנ׳ אז יבקע כשחר אורך ·

מעשה בחסיד אחד שהיה עשיר מאד
וזקן ולא היה לו כי אם בן אחד
ושמו ר׳ יוחנן והיה לאותו ר׳ יוחנן
אשה יפה וצדקת מאד׳ לימים חלה אותו זקן למות׳ וקרא לבנו
וציוהו להתעסק במצות הבורא ולעשות צדקה תמיד ונתן לו כל
אשר לו׳ וגם ציוהו וכן אמר לו בני כשיתמו ימי בכי אבלך לך בשוק
ושב שם עד שתראה שום אדם מביא שום סחורה למכור בשוק׳
ואותה סחורה שתראה ראשונה קנה אותה ואל תניח ותביא אותה
לביתך ותהיה לך למשמרת׳ נפטר הזקן והלך לבית עולמו׳ ויבך אותו
בנו שלשים יום ויתמו ימי בכיתו׳ ויקם ר׳ יוחנן ויזכור מה שציוהו
אביו הלך לשוק וישב שם וראה איש אחד נושא בידו גביע אחד
יפה מאד׳ א״ל ר׳ יוחנן רוצה אתה למכור לי זה הגביע שאתה
נושא׳ א״ל הן׳ א״ל בכמה׳ א״ל במאה זהובים׳ א״ל תן אותה לי בנ׳
בששים זהובים׳ ולא רצה והלך לו׳ אמר ר׳ יוחנן עלבון זה מעשה
מצות אבי אם לא יקנה אותו׳ קרא אחריו ואמר לו תן אותה לי
וקח מאה זהובים כאשר דברת׳ א״ל אם תרצה ליתן לי ב׳ מאות
זהובים אתן אותה לך׳ ואם לאו הניחני לילך לדרכי׳ א״ל לא אתן לך
כי אם ק׳ כאשר אמרת׳ הלך לו׳ וחזר ר׳ יוחנן ואמר בעל כרחי צריך
אני לקנותו בשביל מצות אבי׳ קרא אחריו ואמר לו קח הב׳ מאות
כאשר דברת׳ א״ל האיש אם רצונך ליתן לי אלף זהובים בעבורו
אתן לך׳ ואם לאו הניחני׳ חשב ר׳ יוחנן בלבו כי הוא הולך ומייקר
אותו תמיד׳ וצריך הוא לקנותו בעל כרחו משום מצות אביו׳ מה
עשה הביאו לביתו ונתן לו אלף זהובים בעבורו ויהי לו למשמרת
ופעמים הרבה נסה לפתוח אותו ולא יכול לפותחו׳ והיה בפני חג
הפסח׳ וכשישבו לאכול בליל ראשון של פסח׳ אומר לאשתו הביאי
לי הגביע שקניתי במצות אבי ויהיה על השלחן לכבוד יום טוב׳
הלכה הצדקת והביאה לאותו׳ לקחו ר׳ יוחנן לנסות לפותחו ויפתח
אותו מיד וימצא בתוכו גביע קטן בתוך הגדול ויפתח הקטן וי׳
וימצא בתוכו עקרב אחד קטן ויתמהו מאוד ולקחו ר׳ יוחנן ונתן לו
לאכול ואכל וירץ סביב שלחנו ויחבק לו וינשק לו וכשהיה שבע
הלך לו ונכנס בתוך הגביע קטן וסגר אותו ר׳ יוחנן וישם הקטן תוך
הגדול כאשר בתחילה׳ ויאמר ר׳ יוחנן אל אשתו לא בחנם צוני
אבי דבר זה שקנינו ונגדלנו ונדע מה יהיה בסופו׳ האכילוהו ומגדלו
בכל יום וגדל העקרב ולא היה יכול עוד ליכנס בגביע קטן והיה בתוך

314

הגדול וגדל לרוב מאוד עד שעשה לו בית לחיות בה׳ ונפל ר׳ יוחנן מאוד
מנכסיו כי זה העקרב אוכל כל מה שיש להם עד שגדל שלא היה יכול
ליכנס בשום בית והיה בחצר וגדל מאוד עד שהיה כהר גדול ואחר
ולא היה לר׳ יוחנן עוד מה ליתן לו לאכול בכה ר׳ יוחנן ואמר לאשתו
מה נעשה עוד לתת לו לאכול כי אין בידינו מאומה כי הוא אכל כל
אשר היה לנו׳ אמרה לו הצדקת מכור עליתך היום וקנה לו לאכול
ואני אמכור סרבלי למחר ואתן לו׳ וכן עשו׳ ולא היה להם יותר
מאומה ויבא ר׳ יוחנן בפני העקרב ויפול לפניו ויבך ויתפלל אל ה׳
ויאמר רבונו של עולם גלוי וידוע לפניך כי נתתי כל מה שהיה לי
בשביל לקיים מצות אבי ולא נשאר לי מאומה ולא ידעתי מה יש
לי לעשות מעתה כי אין לי עוד כלום ואני ואשתי ובני ערומים
ויחיפים ורעבים וצמאים מכל טוב׳ פרנסנו אלהי כי אתה רחמן
וחסיד על כל מעשיך׳ והודיעני אלהי ישעי מה טיבו של זה הר
העקרב שגדלתי ורוממתי ומה יהיה בסופו׳ ויפתח העקרב את
פיו ויאמר שמע אלהים תפלתך ונתן לי רשות לדבר אליך׳ ידעתי
כי עשית לי כל מה שתוכל ולא מנעת אותך מלהנות לי בכל כחך
ועתה שאל נא לי כל דבר אחד מה שתרצה ואתן לך׳ ענה ר׳ יוחנן
אם כן הוא למדני שם׳ כל לשונות שבעולם אמר לו׳ והיה יודע
בטוב להבין לשון בהמות ועופות וחיות. וכל לשונות שבעולם׳
ואשתך הצדקת אשר היתה תדיר מטרחת בעבורי וזריזה לי.
לשמשני תשאל ממני דבר אחד ממה שתרצי ואני אתן לה׳
ותבא האשה ותאמר לו אדוני עושר לי גדול כדי שאוכל לפרנס
בעלי ובני ביתי בכבוד׳ אמר לה בואו אחרי והביאו עגלות וסוסים
וחמורים וכל מה שתוכלו מבהמות עמכם׳ ואעמיס אותם מכסף
וזהב ומאבנים טובות ומרגליות׳ וכן עשו׳ וילכו אחריו עד
שהוליכם אל יער אחד ששמו יער רבי עולאי ונכנסו בעבי
היער׳ והתחיל העקרב לשרוק בפיו ובאו אליו כל החיות מכל
שבעולם נחשים ועקרבים וכל מיני חיות וכל אחד ואחד היה
מביא לו דורון כסף וזהב ואבנים טובות ומרגליות וישליכו ל
בפניו כשם שמביאין דורון למלך׳ ויאמר העקרב אל ר׳ יוחנן ר׳
ולאשתו קחו לכם ומלאו אמתחותיכם והעגלות וכל מה שיש
לכם מלאו הכל כדי שיהיה לכם הרבה שלא תצטרכו לשום אדם
ויעשו כן׳ ויאמר ר׳ יוחנן אל העקרב אל נא יחר לאדוני ואדברה
אליו הודיעני מי אתה ומאין באתה׳ אל בן אדם הראשון אנכי

שקרא אדם הראשון על כל בהמה וחיה ועוף· וכשבא על אותו הז׳
הוליד אותו· וכן אני הולך ומתמעט מכל אלף שנה עד סוף האלף·
ולאחר האלף אני גדל עד סוף האלף שנה אחרות· ולא הייתי בכלל
כי ביום אכלך ממנו מות תמות· אמר ר׳ יוחנן כי בן אדם הראשון ר׳
אתה בדרכיני· אומר לו המקום יצילך מן הרעות העתידות לבא עליך·
תמה ר׳ יוחנן ואמר לו מה הן הרעות העתידות לבא עלי ולא רצה
לומר לו כלום· נפטר ממנו בשלום והלך לו ור׳ יוחנן שבלבותו והיה
עשיר גדול וחכם אין כמוהו· שמע המלך מן חכמתו ושלח אחריו ו׳
ושאל לו חכמות וענינים הרבה ומצא אותו חכם מחוכם ונבון לכל
דבר והיה המלך אוהב אותו מכל חכמיו ואותו המלך לא היה לו אשה·
גם יום אחד באו לפניו חכמיו ואמרו לו אדונינו המלך לא נאה לך
להיות תמיד בלא אשה ואין לך בן לישב על כסא מלכותך אחריך ו׳
וכשתנוח נפשך תשאר המלכות לא יורש וישאר המלכות ביד איש
נכרי ולא יהיה לך זכר בעולם הזה· לכן יבקשו לאדונינו נערה יפה
בכל מדינת מלכותו וישאנה ותהיה לו לאשה· ולא רצה המלך לשמוע
אליהם ליקח אשה· עד שבאו לפניו פעם שניה ושלישית ורביעית
וכמה פעמים עד שהכריחו אותו מאוד· אמר להם אם כן הוא שאתם
רוצים שאקח אשה תנו לי זמן שלשה ימים ואשיבלכם דבר אם
דין הוא שאקח אותה אם לאו· נתנו לו זמן שלשה ימים· יום שני ו׳
הלך וישב לו בחצירו נתפס מאוד ממחשבות בתוך המחשבות שהיה
פרח עורב אחד עליו והביא בין רגליו שער אחד יפה מאוד ודומה לזהב
ונפל על המלך אותו שער לקחו והביאו אל חכמיו ביום השלישי·
אמר להם אתם רוצים שאקח אשה אם תלכו להביא לי אותה
אשה שזה השער היה מראשה מוטב ואם שאינה· ואם לא תלכו
אחתוך ראשיכם· ואמרו לו תנה לנו זמן שלשה ימים לידע מה
נעשה· נתן להם· ונתייעצו יחד ואמרו אין איש בעולם יכול לעשות
דבר זה אלא ר׳ יוחנן כי הוא יודע כל הלשונות ואין חכם כמוהו בכל
הארץ· באו ביום השלישי אל המלך ואמרו לו כך חכם אחד יש ב׳
במלכותך ושמו ר׳ יוחנן והוא יודע כל לשונות שבעולם ואין אדם
יכול לעשות דבר זה שאתה שואל כי אם אותו· שלח המלך אחריו
ובין כך ובין כך עבר עורב אחד פורח על בית מדרשו של ר׳ יוחנן
וצועק ואומר המקום יצילך ר׳ יוחנן מן כל הרעות העתידות
לבא עליך· שמע ר׳ יוחנן ותמה מאוד כי בלשון הזה ברכו העורב·
ואז באו עבדי המלך אליו ואמרו קום בא אל המלך כי הוא שלח

315

·פט·

אחריך׳ ויחרד ר׳ יוחנן חרדה גדולה ויקם אל המלך וישתחו לפני
לפני המלך ויאמר לו המלך שמעתי עליך שאתה חכם ונבון ת׳
ויודע כל הלשונות שבעולם ורוצה אני ליקח אשה שאין דין מלכות
להיות בלא אשה ובלא כנס׳ לכן לך והביא לי אותה אשה שזה
השער יש מראשה כי עורב אחד הביא אותו והשליך אותו לפני׳
וידעתי כי שער ראש אשה הוא וחפץ אני בה׳ ענה ר׳ יוחנן ואמר
לו כל מלך שר ונגיד ושלטון לא שאל כדבר הזה שאתה שואל
לבקש אשה אחת אחרי שער אחד שיש בידך׳ א״ל המלך אם
לא תביאנה לי אחתוך ראשך וכל אנשי דתך׳ א״ל ר׳ יוחנן אם כן
הוא תנה לי זמן שלש שנים לבקש אותה ולהביאה אליך׳ נתן לו
זמן׳ והלך ר׳ יוחנן לביתו וצוה את אשתו ואת בנו וסיפר להם
כל המעשה׳ ויבכו אותו בנו ובתו ואשתו על דאגתו׳ לכן נטל ר׳
רשות מהם והלך לו דרך אותו יער דבי עילאי כי אמר אולי יקרה
לפני העקרב שגדלתי ורוממתי׳ ונשא עמו שלשה חלות לחם ור׳
ועשרה זהובים׳ נכנס בתוך עובי היער ופגע כלב אחד גדול מאוד
כי לא ראה כמוהו מימיו׳ כי הבהמות שבאותו יער היו משונות
וגדולות מאד׳ והיה הכלב צועק ומתאונן ואומר רבונו של עולם
יצרתני כלב גדול ומשונה כי לא יכולתי למצוא לאכול די סיפוקי
כי אין הקומץ משביע את הארי׳ ואילו הייתי קטן כמו כלבים
אחרים הייתי מתפרנס בדבר מועט׳ ואתה רחום וחנון על כל
מעשיך וכי בראתני למות ברעב׳ ענה ר׳ יוחנן וא״ל לא בראך
הקב״ה למות ברעב כי רחמיו על כל מעשיו׳ טול חלת לחם שיש לי
ואכול׳ לקח הכלב אותה ואכלה׳ ויאמר האלהים יצילך מכל מיני
פורענות העתידות לבוא עליך׳ ויתן לי מקום שאוכל לגמול לך זה
החסד שעשית עמדי׳ הלך לו ר׳ יוחנן ופגע בעורב אחד גדול
ואין מזונו צועק וגונח ואומר כאשר אמר הכלב ונתן לו ר׳ יוחנן
החלה האחרת שהיה לו׳ וברכו העורב כאשר עשה הכלב בשוה
הלך ר׳ יוחנן לדרכו ויצא מן היער וראה לפניו נהר אחד הלך וישב
על שפת הנהר ואכל שם החלה שנשאר לו ושתה מן המים׳ ור׳
וראה כנגדו דייג אחד במים׳ וא״ל הדייג רוצה אתה לקנות מה
שתעלה מצודתי׳ א״ל הן׳ א״ל בכמה תתן אותו לי׳ א״ל בממון ר׳
עשרה זהובים שיש בכיסך׳ תמה ר׳ יוחנן ואמר מי סיפר לזה
שהיו עשרה זהובים בכיסי׳ אין זה כי אם מאת האלהים׳ לקחם
ונתנם לו׳ עלה מצודתו והיה בה דג גדול ויפה מאד והיה שוה

מאה זהובים׳ כשראה הדייג הדג גדול חיה לו עד מות׳ על הסחורה
טובה שעשה לו׳ בא הדייג והשליך הדג בספון׳ בא הדג ונשתטח לפני
ר׳ יוחנן ואמר לו ידוע אתה ידעת כי אני גדול ואין יכולת בידך להביאני
אנה ואנה ואם תרצה לאכול ממני מאחתיכה קטנה יש לך הרבה׳ עשה
הישר והטוב והשליכני אל הנהר אשר יצאתי משם ובעזרת השם אני
אשלם לך משכורתך׳ ויהיה אלהים עמך ויצילך מכל הרעות העתידות
לבא עליך ויתן לי מקום לגמול החסד שעשית עמדי׳ בא ר׳ יוחנן והשליך
אותו אל תוך הנהר׳ והדייג ראה והטיב חרה לו׳ וא״ל מדוע עשית כן
להשליכו אל הנהר עתה הסכלות עשה׳ כי הוא היה שוה מאה זהובים׳ א״ל
ר׳ יוחנן כך עלה בדעתי לעשות׳ משום דכתיב ורחמיו על כל מעשיו׳ קם ר׳
יוחנן והלך לו על שפת הנהר וראה מעבר הנהר כרך גדול ויפה ויושב
על הנהר׳ ובפני הכרך היו שם שתי נשים האחת היתה מלכה מן אותו
כרך וצדקת מאד והיא בתולה ואיש לא ידעה והיא היתה אשה יפה אין
כמוה בכל הארץ׳ והאחרת היתה שפחתה׳ אמרה המלכה אל שפחתה
ראי זה הצדיק שבעבר הנהר הוא בא אחרי׳ ורוצה הוא להוליכני עמו
ולתתן לי מלך אחר רשע אין כמוהו׳ ואומנם לא ראה אותי מימין ולא שומע
ממני אך עורב אחד לקח אחד משערות ראשי והביאו אליו׳ והוא שולח
זה הצדיק אחרי׳ וידעתי כי אלך עמו אם יוכל לעשות לי שלשה דברים
שאשאל ממנו׳ לכי ותאמר אל הספן להביאו אלי׳ הלך הספן אחריו והב׳
והביאו לפני המלכה׳ עמד ר׳ יוחנן לפניה וישתחו לה׳ וישאלה לשלום׳
ותאמר לה ברוך אתה בבואך׳ מאין באתה׳ ולאן אתה הולך׳ אומר לה מארץ
רחוקה באתי׳ ולבקש אשה אחת אשר שער ראשה דומות לשער זהב
שאני עשה׳ והבאתי הנה׳ אמרה לו שב עמנו חדש ימים ונשיב לך
דבר מה שתבקש׳ וישב עמה׳ ותצו המלכה לאשר על ביתה לשים עיניו
ר׳ יוחנן׳ ויקחהו וירחצהו ויסכהו׳ ויתן לו לאכול ולשתות מכל טוב׳ ויהי
מקץ חדש ימים׳ ויבא ר׳ יוחנן אל המלכה ויאמר אליה גברתי הגידי
לי אם תוכל למצוא מה שאני מבקש במלכותך׳ ואמרה לו הן׳ אני היא
האשה הנמצאת לקראתך שאתה מבקש וזה לך האות ששערותי דומות
לשער שאתה עשה׳ ותדע כי אלך עמך אך צריך אתה לעשות לי של
שלשה דברים אם תרצה שאלך עמך׳ אומר לה ר׳ יוחנן אל תאמרי אותי
ואל תצליח דרכי בעיני עמי והציל כל ישראל כי עיני כל ישראל עלי׳ אם ורבע
לא אביאך אל המלך בתוך חדשים דע כי הוא יאבד שארית שונאיהם
של ישראל׳ אמרה לו שני דברים יש לי רוצה אני שתביא לי האחד
מלא מים של גהינם והאחר של מים מגן עדן׳ בכה ר׳ יוחנן ואמר

316

פט

מי יוכל לעשות זאת. אומרה לו אם לא תעשה כן לא אלך עמך. אומר לה
אם כן הואיל הביאי לי אותן שני דרדורים ואעשה יכולתי. הביאו לו ועבר
הנהר והלך עד שבא אל יער דבי עלאי וישב שם ובכה במר נפש והתח
והתפלל לפני הקב"ה ואומר לפניו רבונו של עולם יהי רצון מלפניך שתשלח
לי העורב אשר נתתי מלחמי אליו ונדר לי לשלם גמולי כזה כך ובזה כך
בא העורב פורח עליו ואומר לו הנני אדוני הנני מוכן למשלחתך גזור עלי
ואקיימה כי שמע י"י את קולך וראה את עניך. א"ל ר' יוחנן ברוך י"י אשר
לא עזב חסדו ואמתו מעם עבדו אנכי בדרך נחני בית האשה אשר אמ
בקשתי. לקח הדרדורים ותלה אותם על צואר העורב. וא"ל תביא לי אחד
מלא ממים של גן עדן והאחר של מים מגהינם. א"ל כן אעשה כאשר
דברת. וישלח העורב את מאתו וילך לדרכו ויבא ויטבול מתוך נהר גהינם
וימלא האחד ממימי הנהר והיו המים רותחין מאוד וחמים ביותר כי לא
יוכל אדם לשים אצבעו מתוך המים מפני חמימותן ואילולא רחמי שדי
עליו בזכות הצדיק היה נשרף. ומשם הלך אל נהר ההולך מתוך גן עדן
וימלא האחר מן אותם מים. ויטבול במים וירחץ כל גופו וישב בשרו וירפאו
מן החבורות והפצעים אשר היו לו ממי גהינם. נטל דרדורין והליך לו ובא
אל ר' יוחנן. וא"ל הנני אדוני הנני. עשיתי כאשר צויתני. ולך לשלום ואלהי
ישראל ישמרך מכל רע. לקח ר' יוחנן הדרדורים והלך לו ובא אל המלכה.
ואומר לה אדונתי הנה הדרדורים מלאים ממי גן עדן וממי גהינם כאשר
שאלת. לקחם המלכה מידו ויראו המים ויכירם כי אותן מים של גהינם
היו חמים ביותר ומסריחים מאוד. ואותן של גן עדן קרים מאוד וריחם
כריח של בשמים. שמחה המלכה שמחה גדולה. ואומרה לו יהי מבורך בזה.
ו' עוד דבר אחד יש לי שצריך אתה לעשות. הנה כבר עבר עשרים וחמש
שנים שמת אבי ונתן טבעתו מעל ידו והיה בו אבן טובה אחת לא היה
כמותה בכל העולם. יום אחד הלכתי לשוט על פני הנהר ונפל הטבע' מידי
אל תוך הנהר ובקשוהו עבדיי ויעשו שכר במים ויוליכו המים דרך אחר
ולא מצאוהו. ואם תוכל להביאו אלי אלך עמך בלא איחור. אומר לה ר' יוחנן
מי יוכל לעשות זאת דבר הנאבד בנהר כבר עברו עשרים וחמש שנים
היאך יוכל אדם למצוא אותו. אומרה לו אם לא תביאנו אלי לא אלך
עמך. הלך ר' יוחנן על שפת הנהר עד מקום אשר השליך הדג שקנה
מתוך הנהר. וישב שם ובכה והתפלל לפני הקב"ה ואומר יהי רצון מלפ
מלפניך י"י אלהי ישראל שתשלח לי הדג שנדר לי לגמול לי מה שעשיתי
לו בארץ מדבר. ומתפלל והדג בא. וא"ל אדוני שמע אלהים תפלתך והנני
מוכן לעשות רצונך. וידעתי את אשר אתה מבקש. ומדע הענ' כי אין

ואתה ברשותי אבל אני יודע ומכיר אותו דג שלקחו ועכשיו ברשותו
וצריך אני להזמינו לדין לפני הלויתן כי יספר לו כל המעשה ושכל ישראל
תלוין באותו טבע ובעזרת הבורא הוא ישלם לי אותו׳ הלך לו אותו דג ובא
לפני הלויתן ואמר לו אדוני שמעני יש צדיק אחד עומד על שפת הנהר
וספר לו כל המעשה אל הלויתן לך אחריו אותו דג ונשאוה את פיו אם
הוא יודע היכן הוא אותו טבע ואבקש פניו לשלם אותו לך הלך אחריו
והביאו לפני הלויתן ואמר יש לך טבע אחד שלקחת ומציאת באותו זמן
שלם אותו אל זה הדג והוא ישלמנו אל צדיק אחד העומד על שפת הנהר
וכל ישראל ערבים בעבור כשבילו אותו טבע הלך אותו דג ונתנו לדג אחר
ואותו דג הביאו אל ר׳ יוחנן וכשהקיא אותו ומפיו בא חזיר אחד גדול
ולקח אותו טבע ובלעו והלך לו בכה ר׳ יוחנן במר נפש ויצעק ויאמר אוי לי
אוי לי גם הדג היה כעס ממך דעניינו ויאמר אל ר׳ יוחנן לא יכולתי עוד
לעשות לך שום דבר מזה העניין אך המקום יתן לך משאלות לבך ומיד
ויצעק מצרה לרווחה ונפטר הדג והלך לדרכו ור׳ יוחנן היה מתפלל [illegible]
ואומר רבונו של עולם גמלתי חסד עם כלב אחד והוא נדר לי לשלם לי מה
שעשיתי עמו יהי רצון מלפניך שתביאנו אלי ועד אני והוא לבקש אותו
חזיר אם על ומציאו אותו׳ בין כך ובין כך שהוא מדבר בו אותו כלב
עבה ויצעק ויאמר אדוני שמע אלהים את קולי ואת תפלתי׳ וישלחני
אלהים לפניך והנה עשיתי מצותך ובקשתך פגעתי אותו חזיר אשר
לקח הטבע בפניך והרגתיו והרעתי את קרבו ובני מעיו ועצמותי חוץ מן
מגופו והנם שוכבים לארץ והטבע בתוך הבני מעים ולך עמי ואוליכך
שם ותפתח הבני מעים ותמצאנו בתוכן׳ הלך ר׳ יוחנן אחריו ומצאו את
כאשר אמר ויפתח את בני מעין וימצא את הטבע בתוכם נטל אות
הטבע והלך לדרכו ושמח שמחה גדולה׳ וגם הכלב הלך לדרכו׳ ובא רבי
יוחנן אל המלכה ונתן לה הטבע׳ וכשראתה אותו לקחה אותו ונשקה
אותו ועשתה ממנו שמחה גדולה׳ אמר לה ר׳ יוחנן המלך והצליח ה׳ את
דרכי שלחני מלכה יחד אל מקומי ואמרי כי עשיתי לך כל מה שבקשת
ממני לא כחדתי ממך׳ לכן עשי הישר והטוב ואל תאחר אותנו׳ אמרה
לו המלך ומה יצא הדבר לא אוכל לדבר אליך רע או טוב׳ אלא עמך
אלך לאיזה מקום שתרצה להוליכני׳ ויקומו וילכו שניהם יחדיו ויבואו [illegible]
עד מקום המלך אשר שלח אחריה׳ וישמע המלך כי הם באים ויצא לך
לקראתם הוא ופרשיו עמו ויביאו אותם אל בית מלכותו׳ וכשבאו אל
בית המלכות שמע ר׳ יוחנן שאשתו מתה ובניו הלכו בשבי ואבדו כל מה
שנשאר להם ולא נשאר להם מאומה כי לקחו וגזלו אותם חכמים שהיו

317

80

מתקוממים באביהם כל ימיהם ונשכו אותם. וכששמע ר' יוחנן כך היה
כועס מאד מאשתו ומבניו ובכה ויצעק עליהם ויבואו כולם לנחמו וגם
המלכה דברה על לבו וינחמו וישלחו אחרי בניו אשר היו מחזרים על
הפתחים. וכששמעו שבא אביהם שמחו שמחה גדולה. ובאו אליו ודברו
אותם וספרו לו את כל התלאה אשר מצאתם וילבישם ויאכילם ויהיו
עמו. והיה ר' יוחנן אהוב ונחמד בעיני המלך כי הביא לו אשה יפה ועוברת
מראה לא היתה כמוה בכל מלכותו. ויצו המלך לכונסה מיד ולהכניסה
לו לחופה. ועתה ואמרה אותה צדקת. לא כן יעשה במקומינו לדבר
אל אשה ולהכניסה מיד לחופה. אלא תן לי זמן שנים עשר חודש כי
כן ימלאו ימי מרוקי הבתולות להיות ששה חדשים בשמן המור וששה
חדשים בבשמים ובתמרוקי הנשים. ובזה ראויה הבתולה לבוא אל
המלך. ויאמר לה המלך כל שאלתך ובקשתך ימלא עשי הטוב בעיניך.
המלך
ותעש כן. ויהי ר' יוחנן אהוב ונחמד מאד בעיני המלכה. ויסר המלך
את טבעתו מעל ידו ויתנהו לו וישימהו אדון לכל ביתו ומושל בכל אשר
לו. ויקנאו בו החכמים ויאמרו איש אל אחיו אם לא נשים עצה להרוג
את ר' יוחנן עתה ימלוך ובן את כל הרעה אשר גמלנו לו ולבניו. ויקומו ר'
ויארבו לו ויכוהו ויחתכו אותו אבר אבר. וישמע הדבר בית המלך כי
נהרג ר' יוחנן ומי חתכו אותו אבר אבר. ויתעצבו מאד המלך והמלכה
ולקחה
ותאמר המלכה הוליכוני אל מקום שהאיברים שם. הוליכו אותה כל אבר
ואבר ותחברה אותם יחד כאשר היו בתחלה ולקחה הטבעת שלה
ונטלה מן האבן הפנינים ונתחברו העצמות והגידים משמו בכח האבן
שהיה בתוך הטבע וגם לקחה מן המים של גן עדן ורחצה כל בשרו ר'
ונתרפא וישב בשרו כבשר נער קטן. ואז שכבה עליו ותשם פיה תוך
פיו ונשקה אותו. ונתפללה אל הקב"ה וישמע אליה אלהים והחזיר לו את
נשמתו ויחי ויקם וילך על רגליו. וכשראו כך שהיא מחייה מתים במ'
תמהו ופחדו ורהו ממנה. ויאמר המלך אם כן הוא עד ונלחם אל כל ר'
סביבותינו אם יהרג במלחמה היא תחייה אותי. וכן עשה המלך
הלך הוא וכל שריו ועבדיו וחכמיו לעזר מלך אחד ויערכו אתם מלחמה
גדולה ויהרג המלך וכל שריו ועבדיו. ויבואו אחר המלכה ויאמרו לה
בואי ותחיי את המלך ושריו ועבדיו כי הם נפלו בחרב הלכה ושם עם
ר' יוחנן ועשתה להם כאשר עשתה אל ר' יוחנן ולקחה המים של גהינם
והשליכה עליהם ונשרפו כולם. ואמרה להם ראו את נפלאות אלהים. כי
לא ממני החכמה והדעה להמית ולהחיות. כי האלהים הוא ממית ומחיה
Deut. 32
ומוחץ ומרפא ומשפיל ומרומם. ולא נאה לפני להחיות אלו הרשעים

כשם שהחיה זה הצדיק׳ ולא ידעתי לעשות שום מזימה׳ הלכו ל
לביתם ונשאר המלכות בלא מלך׳ נתנו עיניהם על ר׳ יוחנן והמליכו ר׳
אותו עליהם כי מתו כל האנשים המבקשים את נפשו׳ ונתנו לו את
הצדקת לאשה׳ וחיו יחד ימים רבים בשלום ובהשקט ובהנחה
והולידו בנים ובנות׃ ועל זה נאמר שלח לחמך על פני המים כי ברוב
הימים תמצאנו׃ **מעשה** באדם
אחד שהיה עני ביותר והיה
יושב בבית הכנסת ומאריך בתפלתו׳
ובכל יום ויום היה משכים עצמו לתפלה׳ פגע בו אליהו זכור לטוב׳
א״ל שבע שנים גזר לך הקב״ה לטובה ותאמר אם אתה רוצה בזק
בזקנותיך או בבחרותיך׳ א״ל שמא אתה אדם קוסם קסמים ואין לי
בידי ליתן לך כלום׳ הניח אותו והלך׳ בא אליו פעם שנייה ואחריכן
בא אליו פעם שלישית׳ וא״ל אם אתה מקבלם מוטב ואם לאו לא ל
אשוב אליך׳ א״ל המתן לי עד שאדבר לאשתי ולבני ביתי׳ הלך וספר
להם כל הדברים׳ אומרה לו אשתו קבל מעכשיו׳ אומר לה עכשיו אני
בחור׳ ויכול אני לטרוח׳ טוב לקבל לעת זקנה׳ אמרה לו ברוך ה׳ יום
יום׳ חזר לו אליהו אומר לו אני מקבל עכשיו׳ א״ל לך׳ היה מהלך
ברגלו אחת׳ ואומר לו כאיזה צד אעשה להם אם אלך לביתי נתך
עתכלותי ממלאכתי ואפילו עשבים לא ליקטתי׳ א״ל לך וסמוך על
בוראך׳ יצאו בניו לקראתו׳ והיו מבקשים ממנו עשבים׳ והיה
מתבייש מהם שלא היה בידו ליתן להם כלום׳ נשמט מהם ונכנס
לבית׃ מצאו הבית מליאה כל טוב׳ בא הוא ואשתו ונתנו הודאה
להקב״ה׳ אומרה לו אשתו לא תהנה כלום עד שתביא לי סופר שיכתוב
לי כל מה שאותן לעניים׳ הלך והביא הסופר אצלה׳ באה והושיבו
אצל פתח הבית׳ אמרה כל עני שיבא אצלך אם דרכו לרכוב על
הסוס תרכיבהו׳ ואם דרכו ללבוש כלי מילת תלבישהו׳ כל אחד לפי
דרכו׳ וכתוב הכל כמו שכתוב׳ מלוה ה׳ חונן דל׳ לאחר שבע שנים
הלכה כל הטובה׳ ונשאר ערומים מכל טוב כאשר בתחלה׳ התחיל ו
הוא בוכה׳ אומר לה כבעלה הלא זה שאמרתי׳ עתה העולם סבורים שא
שאנו עשירים ונואות יוחנן ובנינו בר עב׳ מיד הלכה לבית המדרש
של ר׳ חנינא בעכבריא׳ והוא כתיב מלוה ה׳ חונן דל׳ והרבה צדקות ויאמרה
עשיתי והלויתי להקב״ה׳ ועכשיו אני וביתי מתים ברעב׳ אומר לו
ר׳ חייא כמה הלויתה׳ אמרה לו שלש עשרה גמלים טעונים כתבים
ובכולם כתוב מלוה ה׳ חונן דל׳ אומר לה לכי ותביאי הכתבים ופשטי

318

·יט·

אותם על הגג מבית המדרש ובעת קרות הגבר עומדי על ימין לפני הקב"ה ואומרי לפניו רבונו של עולם כתבת מלוה ה' חונן דל ולך והרבה עשיתי צדקות ונשארתי עבודה מכל טוב יהי רצון מלפניך ה' אלהי שתביאם לי ואז אומר אני וכו' באותה שעה אומר הקב"ה לאליהו לך ופרנסם כל ימיהם בעולם הזה ועתה בא וראה כחה של צדקה ושל תפלה"

מעשה בחסיד אחד שהיו לו שלשה בנות אחת עצלה ואחת גנבת ואחת מספרת לשון הרע והיו בני אדם ירואים ליקח אותם אותם וגם הוא בעצמו לא רצה להטעות בני אדם בא עשיר אחד וטוב היה א"ל הנה בנותיך זקינות תשיאן אותם א"ל הרבה יש בהן מומין א"ל אל תחוש יש לי שלשה בנים לאותן בנותיך לאותה עצלה נתן לה עבדים ושפחות הרבה אמר להם השמרו לכם שתעבדו אותה בכל מה שתאמר לאותה גנבתה נתן כל מפתחות שלו מן הממון ואמרה למה אהיה גונבת הכל שלי לאותה שהיתה מספרת לשון הרע כל יום ויום היה משכים ואומר לה בתי אם את צריכה לשום דבר תודיעני והייך את נוהגת עם בעלך והיה מפתה אותה בדברים לך לימים בא החסיד לראות בנותיו בתחלה נכנס אצל העצלה אמרה לו אבי תבא עליך ברכה כי נתתני לאדם טוב ואחר כן נכנס אצל המספרת לשון הרע מיד שראתה אותו התחילה לבכות אמרה לו אוי אתה נתת לי שני בעלים הבן והאב ואם אין תאמינו לי תבוא בחדר ותראה הלך בחדר בא אותו חמיה כמנהגו בשחרית ונשקה על ראשה אמרה לו אל תגע בי כשראה אביה כך אמר זה שבא על כלתו חייב מיתה עמד עליו והרגו בא חתנו וראה אביו הרוג והרג את חמיו בא אחי הנערה וראו אביהם הרוג הרגו את בעל אחותו ראיתם כמה פורענות גדול באה בשביל לשון הרע וכן מיוסף הצדיק ויבא יוסף את דבתם רעה אל אביהם שאמר לראובן ואחיו קורין לבני השפחות עבדים לפיכך נמכר לעבד ואומר הם שתולין עיניהם בבנות הארץ לפי כך ותשא אשת אדוניו ואומר הם אוכלים אבר מן החי לפיכך וישחטו שעיר עזים וטבלו את הכתנת בדם ולשון הרע קשה מעז וכלוי עבירות ושפיכות דמים לפיכך אמר שלמה שומר פיו ולשונו שומר מצרה נפשו"

מעשה באדם אחד שהיה רגיל ליתן צדקה פעם אחת נכנס בספינה בא הרוח וטבעה ורבי

עקיבא ראה אותו שנכנס בספינה בא והעיד על אשתו שמותרת
לינשא עד שלא חזר ר' עקיבא לביתו בא אותו האיש כנגדו א"ל רבי
עקיבא וכי לא ראיתי אותך שטבעת בים א"ל הן ומי העלך אומר
הקב"ה העלני בשביל הצדקות שעשיתי שמעתי קול רעש בים ואומר
זה לזה רוצו והעלו את האיש כי הוא ראוי ורגיל בצדקה.

מעשה

בבתו של ר' עקיבא שהיו אומרים
לה כל העולם ראוי ביום שתכנס לחופה
תמות. קדשה בחור אחד נאה ביותר.
באותה לילה נכן החופה בא עני אחד וביקש לחם. ובשראות אותו הולכה
והאכילתו והשקתו. אותו עני הלך לו. והיא הולכה לחופתה עד הערב
כשנכנסה עם בעלה במיטה. בא נחש אחד בחור הכותל לנשכה והיא
והרחיקה מבעלה ולקחה מכבנתה ונתנה אותה בחור. ונתקשר הוא
המכבנת בראש הנחש ונחנק ומת. השכימה ולקחה המכבנת ומצאה
הנחש מת במכבנת. אומר לה ר' עקיבא הייתי סבור שלא תחיי עד
הבקר. וסיפרה לו כל הענין מן העני והלך ר' עקיבא וספר לכל התלמ
התלמידים. אומר ראו כמה כחה גבולה של צדקה. תניא רבי אליעזר
אומר כשאדם נדבה במעות באמונה וביראת הקב"ה הוא משמרן
ושומר גופו. כדכתיב ה' ישמור צאתך וביאך. וכת' ה' שומרך ה' צלך
על יד ימינך"

מעשה

ברבי מתיא בן חרש
שהיה יושב ועוסק
בתורה והיו פניו
דומין למלאכי חמה
ולא נשא עיניו לאשה
מעולם. עבר שטן וראה אותו ונתקנא בו. הלך לפני הקב"ה אומר לו מתיא
בן חרש מהו לפניך. א"ל צדיק גמור. א"ל תן לי רשות ואפתה אותו. אומר
לו לך. הלך השטן ומצאו שהיה יושב ועוסק בתורה. ונדמה לו כאשה
יפה. שלא הייתה כמותה. כיון שראה אותה הפך פניו לצד ימין. והיא
הלכה לצד ימין. אומר ומתירא אני מיצר הרע. הלך והביא אש ומסמ
ומסמרין בידו ונתנן בעיניו ועיור עיניו. כיון שראה כך שטן נזדעזע
הלך לפני הקב"ה א"ל כך וכך היה. א"ל וכי לא ראיתי אומרתי לך כך. בא
באותה שעה קרא הקב"ה לרפאל א"ל לך רפא את מתיא בן חרש. הלך
אצלו אומר לו אני רופא שמא היום או למחר כמו כן יעשה לי יצר
הרע. הלך אצל הקב"ה. א"ל כך וכך אומר לי. אומר לו לך ותאמר לו כי אני
ערב שלא יהיה לו עדיין יצר הרע. חזר אצלו א"ל כך אומר הקב"ה א"ל
אם כן עשה רצונו"

מעשה

ברבי אברהם
שהיה שרוי
באשקלון והיה

319

· בט ·

עני מאד והיה סובב בית הכנסת ופותח · כי היה ראשון ואחרון ראה
אותו אליהו הנביא ובקש לרחמו · אומר לפני הקב"ה תן לי רשות ואתן לו
כדי לפרנסו · אומר לו הקב"ה עשה כרצונך ואל תרחיקהו מעלי · הלך אליו
אליהו נתן לו סלע הלך בשוק לקנות פלים נזדמן לו אליהו בדמות בחור
אחד · והיה עשוי בידו בגד שוה זהב · אמ' לו קח זה הבגד · אמ' לו אין לי כי אם
הסלע · לקח הסלע ונתן לו · אחר כך בא אליהו בדמות זקן · אמ' מכור לי את
הבגד · אומר לו מה תתן לי · אמ' עשרה זהובים והסלע · ואמ' ברצון עד ש'
שנעשה עשיר גדול ונעשה סוחר גדול · והיו כל הסוחרים באים אצלו ·
ולא הלך לבית התפלה · אמ' הקב"ה היה לי אהוב אחד והרחיקתו מעלי · מיד
והלך אליהו אצל האיש · אומר לו תן לי הסלע שנתתי לך · אומר לו קח מה
ממוני מאה דנרי זהב · כי לא מצאתי הסלע · הלך ופשפש עד שמצאו
והחזיר לו מיד הלך כל ממונו ותהו ובהו · ונעשה עני יותר ממה שהיה
בתחילה · התחיל לילך לבית הכנסת כבתחילה והתחיל לינעל ולבכות
אומר אליהו לפני הקב"ה איני יכול לסבול צעקתו הנח לי ואתן לו כדי
לפרנסו · אמ' הקב"ה עשה כרצונך ואל תרחיקהו מעלי · אמר אליהו אני
ערב בדבר · אמ' הקב"ה עשה רצונך · הלך אליהו אליו אמ' לו אני הוא ·
שנתתי לך הסלע וחזרתי ולקחתי ממך בשביל שהייתה מפסיד תפלה ·
ואם תבינה תשבע לי שלא תפסיד תפלה ואני אשים לך · אמ' ברצון ·
ובירכו יותר מבתחילה · פעם אחת שמע סוחרים את שמועתו הלכו
אליו חמשה סוחרים לנסות את עשרו · אמרו לו קח כל סחורתינו ותן
לנו פלפלין מן הכל · אמר להם ברצון · אחרי כן אמרו לו · אין אנו רוצים
כי אם שמן ותקח כל סחורתינו · אמר להם ברצון · אחרי כן אמרו לו אין
אנו רוצים כי אם כסף וזהב · הביאום לאוצרותיו ונתן להם כרצונם
והלכו להם ·

מעשה בתלמיד אחד של רבי שמעון בן יוחי שיצא לחוצה לארץ · ונעשה עשיר והיו התלמידים
רואים אותו עשיר · והיו הם מבקשים לצאת לחוצה לארץ כמותו · כיון
שהרגיש ר' שמעון בדבר הוציאם כולם מחוץ לעיר בבקעה ונתפלל
נתמלאו כל הבקעה דנרי זהב · אמר להם מי שרוצה לי טול יטול · אבל
היו יודעין · שכל הנוטל הוא נוטל מחלקו של העולם הבא כי מתן שכרה
של תורה אינה לעולם הזה אלא לעולם הבא · שנ' ותשחק ליום אחרון ·

מעשה ברבי שמעון בן חלפתא שלא היה לו
מה לאכול לשבת ונתנה לשולחני יצא
חוץ לעיר ונתפלל נתן לו הקב"ה אבן

טובה מן השמים ונכנס ונתנה לשולחנו ופירנס את השבת והיה
אוכל ויושב בלילי שבת אומרה לו אשתו והיכן אילו אמר לה ר׳
ממה שפירנס הקב״ה בריותיו אומרה לו אם אין אתה אומר לי אין
אני עושה טוב׳ אומר לה כל הענין אומרה לו החזר הכל אומר לה
למה אומרה לו למחר אתה בא בגן עדן עם חביריך והם יטלו את
מחך לפי שאין מתן שכרה של תורה אלא לעתיד לבוא שנ׳ ותשחק
ליום אחרון לאחר שבת החזירה הכל״

מעשה באחד מגדולי בבל שהיה משיא בנו
להכניסו לחופה ועשה סעודה
גדולה לחכמים אומר לבנו הבא לי מן
יין פלוני מן חבית שבעלייה הלך בנו כיון נחש ונשכו ומת המתין אביו
עם המסובין אומר אלך ואראה מה עשה בני הלך ומצאו מת מה
עשה אביו המתין עד שאכלו ושתו כיון שגמרו סעודתם אומר להם
באותם לברך ברכת חתנים ברכו ברכת אבילים באותם להכניס בני
לחופה הכניסו אותו לקבורה״

מעשה באדריינוס המלך שהיה יוצא
למלחמה וגייסות עמו מצא זקן א׳
אחד נוטע תאינים אמר לו המלך אתה זקן ואתה נוטע אומר לו
שמא אוכל מהם ואם לאו בני יאכלו מהם חזר לאחר שלש שנים
מצא הזקן באותו מקום הלך הזקן ומלא סלו מן התאינים אומר
לו אני הוא הזקן שראיתני נוטע והילך מן הפירות שנטעתי מן
היפות שבהן כששמע המלך נבהל מאד אומר לו מלאו הסל הזה
מדינרי זהב תחת התאינים והיתה שכינתו עומדת ואומרה
לבעלה לעולם אתה יושב בביתך ואין אתה עושה כמו פלוני כי הי׳
עתה נעשה עשיר הלך ולקח סל אחד א״ל שמעתי עליך כי אותו
זהב הפירות הבאתי לך מן היפות של׳ מן התאינים והפירות
הלך סרדיוט אחד והכה אותו ותלאו כולו חבורות עד שחזר
והיה בוכה ואשתו היתה סבורה שהיה מביא הסל מלא זהב אמר
אוי לי ששמעתי לדבריך ללמדך שכל הנשים רעות ומפילות
את בעליהן ואוי לו למי ששומע להם׳

מעשה בחסיד אחד שהיה מהלך בדרך
פגע בו הגמון אחד נתן לו שלום
ולא החזיר לו המתין לו עד שסיים
תפלתו א״ל והלא כתיב בתורתכם רק השמר לך ושמור את נפשך

329

·83·

מיד וכת ונשמרתם מאד לנפשותיכם · אילו הייתי מתיר ראשי כסייף
מה היה · אול תמתין לי עד שאומר לך דבר · אילו הייתי עומד לפני המ'
המלך להתכן לו ואדם אחד היה נותן לך שלום הייתה משיבו אומר לו לאו
ומה לפני מלך בשר ודם שהיום כאן ולמחר בקבר כך · לפני מלך מלכי
המלכים הקב"ה שהייתי עומד ומתפלל לפניו על אחת כמה וכמה · נתפייס
ההגמון · ואחרי כן נפטר החסיד ממנו ·

מעשה

בנחש אחד שהיה מזיק את הבריות
באו והודיעו לר' חנינא בן דוסא · אמר
להם טאו והודיעו לי את חורו בדקו ומצאו אותו הלך והניח עקיבו
על פתח חורו · יצא ונשכו ומת הנחש נטלו ר' חנינא על כתיפו והביאו
לבית המדרש · אמר להם ראו בני שאין נחש ממית · אלא החטא
ממית · אמרו אוי לו לאדם שפגע בו נחש ואוי לו לנחש שפגע בר'
חנינא בן דוסא ·

מעשה

בחסיד אחד שהיה
עשיר וקרוב למלכות
והיה לו בן אחד יפה
תואר ויפה מראה ·
וחכם · ובעת פטירתו
צוה אותו חסיד יצוה לבנו שלא יצא מבית הכנסת משעה שיקום
החזן להתפלל ויתחיל קדיש עד שיגמור כל תפלתו וגם אם יקום אחד
לומר ברכו · שלא שמע תפלה ממתין אותו עד שיגמור תפלתו · וכן
עשיתי כל ימי · והצלחתי במעשי · וגם אם תעבור בעיר שיש בו בית
הכנסת ותשמע החזן תכנס ולא תצא עד שיגמור החזן תפלתו ·
והלך אותו חסיד לבית עולמו · והבן היה מאד נחמד לכל רואיו והיה
משרת לפני המלך ומוזג יין בכוס המלך והמלכה וחותך להם ובשר
לפניהם · והיו אוהבים אותו ביותר זולתו לשמים · וירא אותו משנה המ'
המלך ויקנא בו ויבא אל המלך · ויאמר לו אדוני המלך עינים לך ואין
אתה רואה · כי זה הבחור אוהב את המלכה ומנאפים יחד · ויגער בו
המלך ולא האמין לו עד כי אומר לו היום ומחר עד שהכניס קנאה
בלבו · ויהי היום וילך המלך לראות פועלים שהיו עושין לו מדורות עצים
ואבנים לעשות סיד · ויאמר לרב הפועלים אותו האיש אשר יבא הנה
למחר ראשון קח אותו והשליכהו לתוך כבשן האש · בלא יאחר · ואם אדו
לא תעשה זאת נפשך תחת נפשו · ויען לו המלך אעשה כמצותך ·
וישב לו המלך לביתו · ויהי הלילה וישרת הבחור לפני המלך ויקרא הבחור
ויתן לו השכם בבקר למחר ולך למקום שעושין הסיד ואמור לרב
הפועלים שידליק האש היטב · ויען הבחור אני אעשה כמצותך · ויהי
בבקר ויקם הבחור וירכב על הסוס ויעבר לפני בית הכנסת ושמע

החזן וירד מעל הסוס ונכנס לבית הכנסת ויתפלל. אחר שסיים החזן
עמד אחר שלא שמע תפלה ואמר ברכו והמתין עד שגמר ואיחר עד
שהיה היום גדול. ויקרא המלך אל המשנה ויאמר לו לך למקום שעושין
הסיד ושאל לרב הפועלים אם עשו מצותי. ויאמר המשנה וירכב
על סוסו ויאמר לרב הפועלים עשית מצות המלך. ויקחו המשנה ויאסרו
אותו וישליכו אותו בכבשן ויבא הבחור לשם וירא כי השליכו המשנה
בכבשן ויאמר לרב הפועלים המלך יהרוג אתכם אם ידע זה ויען רב
הפועלים ויאמר לו המלך צוני אתמול האיש אשר אשלח לך למחר
בבקר ראשון השליכהו בכבשן האש. והנה הוא בא ראשון. וישב הבחור
אל ~~הבחור~~ המלך ויאמר לו אדוני המלך ודרוש צוית לשרוף המשנה ויחרד
המלך חרדה גדולה ויתמה מאד ויאמר אל הבחור עתה ידעתי כי
ירא אלהים אתה וכדרך אוהב אותך כי כך וכך הלשין המשנה אותך
אל המלך. ויצויתי להשליך אותך כאשר האיש אשר אשלח ראשון אל
רב הפועלים אשר עושה הסיד. ואותך צויתי לילך ראשון. ואחר כך
אמרתי למשנה לך וראה אם עשו מצותי ואתה איחרת והשליכו אותו
במקומך. עתה ידעתי שאתה נקי היינו הכי דכתיב צדיק מצרה נחלץ
ויבא רשע תחתיו. ולכך יש להמתין בבית הכנסת עד שיגמור החזן
התפלה. ואפילו קם אחד שלא שמע עם הציבור.

מעשה

באליחורף ואחיה שני סופרי שלמה
המלך שהיה עליהם גזירה מן המקום
שלא ימותו כי אם בשער לוז. והיה מל'
מלאך המות ממתין עליהם שלא היה יכול להם. וכל מי שהיה בתוך
העיר של לוז. לא היה שולט בהם מלאך המות. ומתוך שהיה שלמה
מחכים השכיל אשמדאי לנשאם לשם. כשהיו בשער לוז בא מלאך
המות והרגם. אמר שלמה רגלוהי דבר נש אינון ערבין ביה לאתר
דמתבעי תמן מובלין יתיה.

מעשה

בנערה
אחת שהיתה הולכת לבית
אמה
והיתה מקושטת בכסף וזהב
ותעה
בדרך והולכה [illegible] כיון שהגיע חצי היום צמאה ולא היה לה
מים. ראתה באר וחבל דלי תלוי עליו. אחזה בחבל וירדה בתוך הבאר
ושתתה. בקשה לעלות ולא יכלה והיתה צועקת ובוכה עד שעבר
עליה אדם אחד ושמע קולה והכיר בה ולא היה יכול להבחין. אמר לה
מבני אדם את. או מן המזיקין. אומרה לו מבני אדם אני. אומר לה
שמא מן הרוחות את ומתגברת עלי. אומרה לו לאו מבני אדם אני.

הסכימו׳ ונשבעה לו׳ אומר לה אם אני יודע תנשאי לי׳ אומרה לו הן׳
העלה אותה׳ כיון שהעלה אותה ביקש להיזקק עליה מיד׳ אומרה לו
מאיזה עם אתה׳ אומר לה מישראל אני׳ ממקום פלוני וכהן׳ אף אני
ממקום פלוני ומבני אדם ידועים ונקובי שם׳ אומרה לו עם קדוש כמותך
שבחר בך הקב״ה מכל ישראל וקידש אותך׳ ואתה מבקש לעשות כבהמה
בלא קידושין ובלא כתובה׳ בוא אחרי אצל אבי ואמי ואני מתארסת
לך׳ נתנו ברית זה לזה׳ אומר לה מי יהיה עד ביני ובינך׳ והיתה חולדה
אחת עוברת לפניהם׳ אומר לה השמים וחולדה ובור יהיו עדים׳ הלכו
כל אחד לדרכו׳ אותה נערה עמדה באמונתה וכל מי שהיה תובעה
היתה ממאנת עליו כיון שהחזיקו בה התחילה לנהג עצמה כשוטה
ומכפת ומקרעת בגדיה׳ ובגדי כל מי שהיה נוגע בה עד שמנעו כל
ממנה בני אדם׳ והוא כיון שעבר מנגד פניה תקפו יצרו ושכחה
והלך לעירו׳ ונשא אשה אחרת ונתעברה׳ וילדה בן׳ כשהגיע שלשה
חדשים חנקתו חולדה׳ ועוד נתעברה וילדה בן ונפל לבור׳ אומרה לו
אשתו אם כדרך בני אדם מתים בנינו הייתי מצדקת הדין׳ עכשיו
שמתו מיתה משונה אין זה בלא שום דבר׳ ספר לי מה מעשיך׳ גילה
לה כל המעשה ונתגרשה ממנו׳ ואומרה לו לך אצל חלקך שנתן לך
הקב״ה׳ הלך ושאל אותה הנערה׳ אמרו לו נכפית היא׳ וכל מי שתבעה
שתובעה כך וכך עושה לו׳ הלך אצל אביה סיפר לו כל המעשה׳ אומר
לו אני מקבל כל המומין שבה עלי׳ העמיד עליו עדים. כיון שעלה אצלה
התחילה לעשות כמנהגה ספר לה כל המעשה דחולדה ובור׳ אומרה
לו אף אני בבריתי עמדתי׳ מיד נתיישבה דעתה׳ ופרו ורבו בבנים
ובנכסים׳ ועליה אומר הכתוב עיני י״י בנאמני ארץ׳׳

מעשה בבתו של ענק שנכנסה לפרדס׳
ואכלה רמון אחד׳ והשליכה קליפתו
כיון שראו המרגלים אותה קליפה היו
סבורים שמערה היתה הלכו השנים עשר מרגלים ונכנסו בתוכה
ונטמנו שם׳ לאחר שעה נזכרה בת הענק שאכלה רמון ואמרה
אלך ואשליך הקליפה שלא יראה אותה אבי הלכה והשליכה הקלי׳
הקליפה עם השנים עשר איש אשר בתוכה חוץ לפרדס ולא הר
הרגישה בהם כשיצאו אמרו ראו הגבורה שיש בנשים כאנשים
על אחת כמה וכמה׳ אומר ר׳ יוחנן כל אחד מן המרגלים גומהן
שיש אמה׳ וכיון שסיפר כלב שבחה של הארץ נתביישו ואמרו
לכלב ולא עוד הייתה באותה עינינה׳ ומשל למרגליטוס הוא סוחר

עשרה אבנים טובות ומרגליות שהיה הולך בדרך ונושא סחורתו
פגעו בו ליסטים אמרו לו תן לנו כל מה אשר בידך אמר להם אין
עמי רק כלי זכוכית הניחוהו ונכנס למדינה ושם שלחן לפניו וערכן
עליו האבנים ומרגליות וכל אחת ואחת אין שיעור לדמיה בא אחד
מן הליסטים לפניו ובקש ליגע באחת מהן אמר הנח שאין לאדם
כמוך ליגע בהן נכהו אותו ליסטים אומר וכי אין איש מאותן כלי
שאומרת לנו של זכוכית הן אף כלב כשהיה עם המרגלים השלים
עליהם שהיה מתירא מהם וכיון שבא אל ישראל אמר להם אר'
ארץ זבת חלב ודבש עלה נעלה וירשנו אותה

מעשה היה בגוי אחד שדומן את רבן גמליאל ועשה שלחן אחד משלשים
ככרי זהב ועלה למשתה והביא
להביא ומכל מיני מאכל שבעולם והביאו לו לבד מאגוזי פרך כיון
כשבאו לאכול ראה שאין שם אגוזי פרך נטל השלחן ושברה
בכעס אמר רבן גמליאל למה שברת את השולחן ששוה ממון גדול
מפני מין קטן שחיסרו עבדיך השיב לו לפי ולכך יודעני שאין לי
חלק לעולם הבא לכן אתענג נפשי בכל כחי ולכן אני עושה כך שאין
לפני כל מינין שבעולם לבד ממין אחד ועל זה אומר שלמה בחכמתו
צדיק אוכל לשובע נפשו ובטן רשעים תחסר

מעשה היה ברבי יהושע בן לוי שלא נשבע
ממימין אפילו באמת וכשהגיע
זמנו ליפטר מן העולם אמר הקב"ה
למלאך המות לך לר' יהושע בן לוי ועשה לו כל רצונו ואחר כך טול
נשמתו הלך מלאך המות אצל ר' יהושע ומצאו שהיה עוסק בת'
בתורה אמר מלאך המות אני שלוחו של הקב"ה והוא שלחני ליטול
נשמתך אמר הבא זמן עד שלשים יום עד שאחזור תלמודי שכך
אומרים לשם אשרי מי שבא לכאן ותלמודו בידו הבא ליה לסוף
תלתין יומין הדר לו אמר הקב"ה שלחני אליך שאעשה כל מה שתי'
שתשאל ואחר כך אטול נשמתך אמר הראיני גיהנם וגן עדן אמר
הן כד הוו קאזלי באורחא אמר ר' יהושע למלאך המות הבא סכינך
דקא מעבבת לבני אינשי הבא ליה הראה לו גיהנם וגן עדן אמר
הראה מקומי הראהו לו ומקומו קפץ ממנו וברח למקומו ומלאך
המות נטלו בכנפו ומעלו והניח ר' יהושע טליתו בידו אמר לו עדו ושם
ואטול נשמתך אמר חי ה' לא אצא הלך המלאך אצל הקב"ה אמר לו כך

322

85

וכך עשה לו ר' יהושע. א"ל לך בכל מקומות שהיה שם ר' יהושע אם
נשבע מימיו שום שבועה אפילו באמת. הלך ומצא שלא נשבע מי'
מימיו. חזר מלאך המות אל ר' יהושע. א"ל מאחר שכך עשית החזר
לי סכיני. א"ל לא אעשה. אלא עד שתחזור להקב"ה. הלך ומצא בת
קול ואמרה הב ליה מטום דעביד לכ"ייתו הדר ליה. ועדיין ר' יהושע
חי בגן עדן על ששמר פיו משבועה. ואפילו סיחה שאין בה לא
טוב ולא רע אין אדם רשאי לאומרה משום שנ' דובר שקרים לא
יכון לנגד עיני.

מעשה

היה ברבי יהושע בן אלם שראה בחלום אהים וא"ל שמח בלבך שאתה ונגס בן כפר קיצור
קעב ראה מושבך ומושבו בגן עדן שוין. כשנעור משנתו חשב
בלבו ואמר ווי לאותו איש שמיום שנולד תמיד היה בריאת קוע ולא
היה עמל אלא בתורה ולא הלך ד' אמות בלא ציצית ובלא תפילין
והיו לו ש"ע תלמידים. ועכשיו שקולים מעשי ותורתי עם קעב אחד
באומנה לא אשב עד שאראה חבירי. מה עשה הלך מעיר לעיר
וממדינה למדינה עד שבא לעירו. אמר להם היכן ננס. אמרו לו
אדונינו אותו האיש אתה מבקש שאתה גדול ושר והוא הדיוט.
ומה אתה צריך לו. אמר להם העבודה שאין אוכל עד שאראה
אותו האיש מיד שגבו בשבילו הלכו ואמרו לו ר' יהושע משגר
בשבילך. אמר להם ומה אני ומה אבותי של ר' יהושע ושגב בשבילי
אמרו לו עמוד ולך עמנו. אמר להם לא אלך עמכם. חזרו ואמרו לר'
יהושע אדונינו אינו רוצה לבוא. אמר להם העבודה שלא אשב
עד שאראנו. מיד עמד הוא וכל תלמידיו והזקנים אחריו יוצאים
אצלו והיו טלים הולכים עמו. מיד נפל לפני ר' יהושע. א"ל אדוני מה
היה זה שיאור ישראל כמו אצל עבדו. א"ל דבר לי. א"ל אדוני אמור
א"ל מה מלאכתך. א"ל אני קעב ויש לי אב ואם זקנים ואינם יכולים
לעמוד ולא לישב. ואני מלבישן ומאכילן ומרחיצן. מיד עמד ר' יהו'
יהושע ונשקו על ראשו. וא"ל אשריך ואשריני שזכיתי להיות חב'
חבירך בגן עדן. הרי למדת כמה גדול כבוד אב ואם. ואף יעקב
לא היה ירא מאחיו אלא בשביל שהיה זריז בכבוד אביו. וכל האו'
המכבד אב ואם כאילו מכבד הקב"ה. ששה שותפין יש באדם.
ביצירת הולד הקב"ה ואב ואם. מן האב עצים מוח וצינוורד
וגידים וצפורנים ולובן שבעינים. ומן האם עורים שער ובשר
ושחור שבעינים. והקב"ה נתן בו רוח ונשמה חכמה ובינה וכשנ'

וכשנפטר מן העולם הקב"ה עלו חלקו וחלק אביו ואמו מניח לפניהם·
וכל המבזה אביו ואמו ולועג מהם אינו זוכה לקבורה ואוכלים בשרו
עוף השמים· שנ' עין תלעג לאב יקרוה עורבי נחל ויאכלוה בני נשר
וכל המכבד אביו ואמו הקב"ה נותן לו שכר טוב בעולם הזה ולעולם
הבא·

מעשה

שהיה בסוחר אחד והלך
לסחורה במקום אחד והיו עמו ד'
חמש מאות זהובים· אמר אותו סוחר
בלבו· היאך אעשה· אם אני מוליכם עמי· אולי רמאים יגנבו אותם
לי· אלא אטמינם עד שיבא יום שיזמן לי סחורה· מה עשה הלך
למקום צנוע ויפן כה וכה וירא כי אין איש ועשה חפירה וגנזו שם
הממון· והחפירה היתה אצל קיר ובאותו מקום היה חור בקיר
והוא לא ידע. וראהו בעל הבית לאחר שהלך הסוחר משם והלך
בא אותו האיש וגנב הממון· לימים בא הסוחר ליטול ממונו ולא
התחיל לצעוק עצמו· אמר מה אעשה למי אבקש הממון והלא כל
כשגנזתי הממון לא היה שם שום אדם נשא עיניו ויחפש בחדר
וראה אותו חור· חשב בלבו ואמר שמא בעל הבית הזה ראני· ושאל
עליו מי הוא והראוהו לו· בא אצלו ואמר לו אדוני הנה באתי ושמ'
ושמעתי עליך שאתה יועץ טוב· מבקש אני ממך עצה· א"ל אמור
א"ל אדוני בכאן לסחורה והבאתי עמי שני ארנקות האחד של חמש
מאות זהובים· והאחד של אלף זהובים· ואני כשבאתי לכאן לא
הייתי מכיר שום אדם בזאת העיר להפקיד ממוני מה עשיתי ?
הלכתי למקום צנוע ושמתי שם הארנקי של חמש מאות זהובים
והיא עדיין שם שמורה· ואותה של אלף אני נושא עמי ולכן אני
שואל ממך מה אעשה אם אטמינה באותו מקום· או אפקידנה
באותו מקום לאדם נאמן· א"ל אם אתה שומע לעצתי אל תפקידנה
לפי שאין אתה מכירם וכפרו בך· לך טמון אותה עם האחרת· א"ל
אעשה כדבריך מיד חשב אותו גנב כשילך לטמון האחרת ולא ימצא
זו לא ישים שם כלום הלך והחזירה· אמר הסוחר בלבו אולי החזיר
הממון שהוא סבור ליטול את שתיהן הלך לשם ומצאה· אמר ברוך
המחזיר אבידה לבעלים· ולכך לא יפשוט אדם את ידו בגניבה"

מעשה

באדם אחד ששאל בן מהקב"ה ואמר
רבונו של עולם תן לי בן על מנת
שילמדנו תורה שמע הקב"ה תפלתו
ונתן לו בן וקרא שמו שאול· ונתגדל ונעשה בן חמש שנים ולמד

323

·פט·

תורה הרבה ונתחכם ביותר והיה אביו זקן כל יום וכל ענ׳ ויתומדר
שהיה רואה חכם והבינו לבנו ואמר לו בני נאור את אילו והיה יושב
ומלמדן וכך היה מנהגו של אביו בכל יום היה יושב בדלת של בית הס
הספר ואם היה אדם עובר ושב ומבקש לומר שלום לבנו עונה ומשיב
לו כדי שלא יענה הוא ויבטל מן התורה כך היה עושה עד שנעשה בן
שבעים שנה ואז שלח הקב״ה מלאך המות ליטול את נפשו ועשה לו
עצמו כבשר ודם ובא ליכנס בדלת פגע בו אביו כמנהגו א״ל היכן
אתה רוצה לילך א״ל יש לי דבר בבנך והיכן בנך א״ל מה הוא ואני משיב
לך א״ל בחיי סוד הוא ביני ובין בנך ואיני אומרו לך תפש בו ואומר
בחיי לא תיכנס לשם עד שתאמר לי הסוד א״ל יש לו שבעים שנה
שנתתי לו דבר ואני רוצה ליטול אותו היום אמר הזקן בחיי כל שנותיו
של בני אינן אלא שבעים שנה ויש אדם שנואמין דבר לתפעק בן
ימיו א״ל מלאך המות איני יודע אם הוא בן שבעים או בן שמונים
אבל ביום הזה יש שבעים שנה שהוא חייב לי אמר הזקן ולאת
הודיעני בני הכנס נכנס ואמר שלום עליך רבי השיב לו שלום בוא
שקראך הקב״ה א״ל ברוך בואך לאיזה מקום נעלה ענה איני רואה
שלום איני רואה א״ל מלאך המות רי התורה קריתה ואין אתה
מבין בדבר שניתן לך ממנו אותו הוא מבקש א״ל איזה דבר א״ל
קריתה וישוב העפר אל הארץ כשהיה והרוח תשוב למעלה אל
המקום אשר נתנה כך כי את נפשך הוא מבקש א״ל חס ושלום
היאך אעזוב את התנאים הללו לך לשלום הלך מלאך המות ואמר
רבונו של עולם אינו רוצה א״ל לך קשט עצמך סימני מיתה אמרו
עליו על מלאך על המות שיש לו שלש מאות ראשים וששים וחמשה
פיות ושלש מאות וחמשה עינים והחרב שלופה בידו הלך ונתקשט
ובא ליכנס בדלת כשראה אותו הזקן נפל על פניו תפסו מלאך המות
א״ל אל תירא א״ל מעולם לא ראיתי אדם כמותך נכנס בבית הכנסת
א״ל קום לך א״ל למה א״ל לשום נפשך א״ל תן לי מקום ואתפלל לפני
הקב״ה נתן לו מקום והתפלל אמר רבונו של עולם כתבת בתורתך אורך
ימים בימינה וכת׳ כי מוצאי מצאי חיים וכת׳ עץ חיים היא למחזיקים
בה וכל כך איני מרחם על עינויי אלא על התנאים הללו כיוון אותה
שעה יצתה בת קול ואמרה מה אעשה לשני צדיקים הללו אחד
מבפנים ואחד מבחוץ מתפללים לפני להחזיק תורתי הרי היום
בן שבעים שנה מיכן ואילך יחיה מאה ועשרים וחמש שנה אמרו
באותו קב״ה שנה לא מת אדם בחיי אביו ולא נערך אדם לחבירו

לקיים מה שנ׳ עץ חיים היא למחזיקים בה״

באדם אחד מגליל העליון שעלה
לירושלים להתפלל ועשה תפלתו
והיה לו נדר לירד לבבל והיו עמו
מאתים דינרי זהב וביקש להפקידם ביד נאמן הלך לבית הכנסת
וראה שם אדם עומד מאותו מקום ולעולם לא היה מחליף מקומו כן
כשגמר תפלתו ויצאו יצא הוא אחריו׳ א״ל ר׳ יש לי דבר ומבקש אני
להפקידו אצלך׳ אמת ואני מכיר בך שאתה נאמן׳ ומבקש אני לילך
לדרכי׳ א״ל אחי מהו הדבר׳ א״ל ממון׳ א״ל לחיים ולשלום׳ אם עזר
המקום אני נוגע בהם עד שתחזור לשלום ואראה פניך׳ מיד הוציא
הוציא כיסו והפקיד בידו׳ והלך לבבל והיה שם שלשה חדשים
וחזר לירושלים בשעה שנכנס לעיר׳ יצא נאמן שלו לסחורה לפי
שהיה חנווני הלך לבית הכנסת וראה במקום נאמן שלו אדם
אחר יושב במקומו בדמותו ובתארו ובעמדתו כשגמרו התפלה
יצא האיש ויצא גם הוא אחריו׳ ויאמר לו שלום עליך רבי׳ וא״ל
ועליך שלום והיה עונה כפה רך לפי שלא היה מכירו׳ א״ל תן לי
הפקדון שיש לי מה בידך׳ א״ל איני יודע בדבר׳ לא ראיתיך מימי׳
א״ל לא אניחך עד שתתן לי מה שהפקדתי אצלך או תשבע לי׳
א״ל לך לשלום אין לך עלי שבועה׳ שאפילו אתה נתן לי כל ממון
שבעולם לא אשבע לך׳ מה עשה בעל הממון נטל החבל ונתנה
בצוארו של אותו חסיד׳ והוליכו בכל המדינה׳ והיה מכריז עליו
כל הלוקח פקדון וכופר כן ראוי לעשות לו כך׳ ואותן החנוונים
על שהיו שם ומכירין אותו שהוא צדיק היו בוכין עליו׳ מה שאין
שאירע לו׳ כיון שעשה לו כל אותה החרפה הניחו והעלה החבל
מעל צוארו והלך בביתו בבושה גדולה׳ לימים בא בעל הפקדון
והלך כמנהגו וישב במקומו וראהו בעל הממון ונתן קול וחזר
בעיניו ואמר שמא הוא זה שהפקדתי אצלו הממון׳ ואם עפי ?
ואבחנגו כיון שיצא האיש יצא הוא אחריו׳ א״ל רבי מתבייש אני
אתה לשאול את שלך׳ א״ל בעל הממון ברוך בואך׳ א״ל אחי שמא
יראתה מן ממונך גלוי לפני מי שאמר והיה העולם שמאותה
שעה לא נגעתי בו יד׳ בוא עמי ואותו הלך וקבל את ממונו ובא
לביתו והתחיל לבכות׳ ואמר אוי לי איך ימחול לי הקב״ה מה
שעשיתי לאותו צדיק׳ מיד הלך בעל הממון אצל האיש של
שעשה לו בושה׳ וא״ל חטאתי לך ר׳ ועכשיו בבקשה ממך מחול

324

-98-

וממון הממון שחשדתיך עליו ויהיה לך כאן עון ומחול לי מה
עשיתי לך · א"ל לא ממון אקח ממך · ולא אעשה לך דבר רע ׃
ישפוט בינו ובינך · הלך בעל הממון והשכיר שלשה בחורים שנג
שנתנו החבל בצוארו ועשו לו כמו שעשה לאותו האיש וחביריו
של אותו הנחשד כדי אעלו ונחמו ומה שחיר עלנו · אומרו כל
אחד ממנו יביא כוס מה שנפל עמו והביאו כל אחד ומה שהיה
שהספיק לו המקום · והביאו אחד מהן דג במטפחת ונתן לאשתו
ומצאה במטפחת קשורין שש מאות דינרי זהב וספרה לבעלה ·
אמר אותו חסיד שמרו אותו שהביא הדג ומבקש לנסות אותי
שמרו אותו יפה עד שיבואו לאכול כשבאו חביריו אמר החסיד
ואמר להם רבותי אחד מכם שיגו דג · ואותו ששיגו דג שמע
ונתבייש · ואמר שמא הוא מבקש לביישני לפי שמתנתי קטנה ·
ולא היה מודה לו · ואמר החסיד לא אוכל כוס עד שיודה מי
ששלחו · ויאמר אני שגרתיו · ואמר בעל הדג אחי אני שגרתיו כי
בבקשה ממך נא אל תבזיני · א"ל החסיד מה היה בתוך המטפחת ·
אמר איני יודע · הוציא החסיד המטפחת כמו שהיה קשורה ואמר
להם זה מצאתי · ואיני יודע מה בתוכו · ענה בעל הדג ויאמר
אני שגרתיו לך במתנה ואלמלא היה בתוכו אבנים טובות ומר
ומרגליות לא הייתי לוקח ממך כלום שהממון הזה אינו ממני
אלא מן הקב"ה · ענו כולם ואמרו נתנה זו אינה אלא מן השמים
וזו היא שכרך לקיים מה שנ' כי פעל אדם ישלם · אל תיקרי כי
ישלם אלא ישלש לו ׃

מעשה

באדם אחד מגדולי הדור שהיה עשיר הרבה ולא היה לו בן לעשר שנים נתן
לו הקב"ה בן וקראו שמו שאול ששאלו להו אביו ואמו מן הקב"ה
כשהיה בן חמש שנים הכניסוהו לבית הספר והיה לומד ·
וכשגדל היה מכה כל חביריו ומבזה כל אדם · והיו יראים
להגיד לאביו ולאמו לפי שהיו עשירים וגדולי הדור · והיו מרחמין
ומרחמין העניים · והמתבזים מן הנער היו מלין מאוחין לכך
היו מתיראין להגיד לו · לימים העני אדם אחד ביותר והיו לו
ארבעה בנות · אמר אותו עני בלבו אלך ברוכסניא שמא כי
יזמין לי הקב"ה כלום ואל מות בביון הלך והיה שם שש שנים
וזימן לו הקב"ה עשרים ואחד דינרים אמר אחזור לביתי
שמא אמצא אשתי ובנותי בחיים והן מחכות לביאתי כי

לחזור לביתו׳ פגעו בו ליסטים ולקחו כל מה שהיה לו והניחוהו ערום
התחיל בוכה ומיצטער׳ אמר אם אחזור לביתי ריקם אשתי ובנותי
תלוין עיניהם עליהם ומה אתן להם׳ אלא אלך עוד אולי ירחם
עלי הקב״ה הלך וזימן לו הקב״ה י״ח דינרים זהב׳ אמר דיי לי שאוכל
ואתן אשתי ובנותי ברעב אחזור׳ ואראה אם הם בחיים׳ מיד קנה
לו חמור׳ ושאר הממון נתן לסחורה וטען על החמור והיה חוזר
לביתו פגע בנהר אחד ונכנס החמור עם המשאוי בנהר ונשקע כי
כשראה אותו על כך קרע בגדיו מסון ואילך ומוטב לי למות סמוך
לעירי ואחנק לעיר עינוי שולין ימינו אותי בני עירי ויקברוני
כשבאו קרוב לעירו התיר איזורו מאותנו וקשר בצוארו ותלה על
עצמו אותו הבחור היה עובר עם התלמידים שהיו הולכין בחוץ
בחטירה׳ נפנה לדרך להסיך רגליו וראה אותו החונק ורץ ואילנו׳
א״ל מה טיבך ומי אתה ולא השיב לו כלום׳ שנתן עיניו בחנקה׳
עד שתפשו בעיניו והתירו ושאלו לו וסיפר לו כל המעשה שאירע
לו׳ ישב ובכה׳ באותה שעה הוציא מכיסו שלשים ותשעה דינרים זהב
ונתן לו׳ א״ל לך לביתך׳ ועלי ליתן לך דינר בכל חדש לצורך כלכלתיך וכ׳
ומעיד לי בוראי׳ באותה שעה באו זה מכאן וזה מכאן׳ הענו לביתו׳
והוא לחביריו׳ אמרו לו למה איחרת׳ אומר להם דבר היה לי ואותו עני
הלך לביתו ומצאוהו בני ביתו ושמחו שמחה גדולה׳ באותה הלילה ראה
ראש ישיבה בחלומו שבא מלאך ולקח הכתר מראשו ונתנו בראש
אותו בחור׳ עמד בבקר ונתפחד ונתבהל ושלח והביא אבין של אותו
בחור׳ ושאלו לו מה מעשים יש לך לבנך והיה מתיירא ואומר אדוני יודע
אני שבני שוטה הוא ומעשה אחר אין לו׳ אלא שהוא לומד כיון בכל
שעה׳ ואיני יודע מה אשיב לאדוני׳ א״ל הגד לי מעשיו׳ ואם לאו תגד
בן מות אתה׳ אמר לו אדוני שלחני ואשאל לאשתי שמא עשה בני
שאיני יודע׳ הלך לביתו בוכה ואומר לאשתו׳ תהי יודעת כי היום ירד
אותי׳ אומרת לו למה׳ אמר לה איני יודע׳ אלא היינו שומעים שהיה
מכה זה וזה בישיבה׳ הלכה האשה ואומרה אדוני לא כיון אדם
מעולם ואומר הנער ביזוי שהחזרתיו ריקם׳ אלא שהייתי משמחו׳
ועתה נביא הנער מבית הספר ונשאלו לו׳ הלכה אמו והביאתו מבית
הספר׳ ואביו היה מוטל בארץ ובוכה׳ וא״ל בני אמור לי מה עשית וכ׳
ואתן כל ממוני אולי יסדה אותך ולא תמות׳ א״ל ומי הוא שהודיע׳
עלי לראש ישיבה׳ א״ל איני יודע׳ א״ל אבי הביאני אצלו׳ והקב״ה ישלח
ומעיד בי׳ א״ל אבין הודה לו להקב״ה אם לא ריניית למור לי׳ אמר לו לאו

תירין אבי מדבר זה׳ מיד לקחו אותו אביו ואמו והוליכוהו לראש
ישיבה׳ כשבאו אמר ראש ישיבה לאב ידעת המעשה שעשה בנך׳
א״ל אדוני הרי בני לפניך ואני איני יודע מה אומר לך׳ א״ל ראש ישיבה
בני אמור לי מה מעשיך׳ א״ל לא רצחתי ולא גנבתי ולא ניאפתי אמר
לו לא כך שאלתיך אלא מה טובה עשית מימיך׳ א״ל איני יודע אמר
לו בשעה גדולה אני משביעך שתאמר לי מה עשית׳ א״ל אדוני
הייתי מהלך בחבורה ומצאתי אדם אחד נתחנק והצלתיו ולא הי׳
הודעתי לאבי ולא לאמי עד עכשיו מיד השתחוה ראש ישיבה
לפני הקב״ה ואמר ברוך אלהי ישראל שבשעה אחת קנה לו העולם
הזה והעולם הבא׳ ולקח הכתר מעל ראשו ונתנו על ראש הבחור׳
והושיבו בכסאו וקרא עליו כי פועל אדם ישלם לו״

מעשה באדם אחד ששאל בן מהקב״ה ונתן
לו ולימדו תורה ביותר׳ ואחר כך
מת האב לאיים אמר לו האם בני קח
ממון של אביך וצא בסחורה לקח הבן בסחורה הממון והלך בסך
בסחורה ראה אלו גודלין ואלו חוסין כשראה כך לא קנה כלום
בא לביתו אמר לו אמו בני ומה לא סחרתה אמר לה אמי ראיתה
כשירה זו האומנות׳ כשהיו שנים מדברים כן׳ היו מניחין אדם
לקוברו׳ אמר הבן לאמו אילך ואגמול חסד עם המניחין לקבור׳ יצא
בחזירתו ראה אדם אחד שהיה חורש ביגרו והיה נתון הספר
במחרישה והיה חורש וקורא׳ ראהו הנער א״ל שלום עליך רבי והוא
היה אליהו ז״ל׳ א״ל הנער ר׳ מה האומנות שאתה עושה׳ א״ל בני אני ד׳
חורש שניזכו ונשתה אני ואשתי ובני ובנותי׳ ועניים ואביונים ועופות
השמים׳ א״ל הבחור הרי האומנות שאני מבקש׳ א״ל מה תבקש שאתן
לך א״ל הבחור התורה נתן לי הקב״ה ועכשיו אני מבקש לישא לי אשה
יראת שמים׳ א״ל בני לא נקראת אשה בעולם אשת חיל אלא שתים׳
שרה במזרח וחנה במערב ושלישית שמורה לך ומאותו מקום היה
מהלך שלשה ימים למקומה׳ לקחו בכנפיו והוליכו לשער שהאשה
בבית העירו והלך אליהו אצלה אמר לה מה אתה אומרת נשין
לך איש׳ אמרה לו אם מה׳ יצא הדבר יעשה׳ מיד הביא את הבחור
וזינו ועיטרו והיה יוצא ובא׳ ביום השביעי לחופה בא אליהו ז״ל׳ א׳ ונכנס
ומצא אותו שהיה שוחק עם אשתו׳ א״ל אליהו הנחתה תורתך ושכחת
אותה בחייך תחת שבעת ימי חופה׳ תיזכר שבע שנים לעבד׳ יצא
אליהו והניחו׳ התחיל הבחור בוכה וסופד׳ אמרה לו הכלה אדוני מה

אתה רוצה שמא אינ כשרה לפניך או אם חסר וממון או כלים
הרי כולם לפניך · אז שמע על אבותיך אתה רוצה ומעט עד
אילים חבשו החמורים והלכו להם עם העבדים והשפחות שלהם
כשהיו בדרך פגעו בנהר גדול אמרה האשה נשב ונאכל ישבו
לאכול · עמד הבחור והלך בנהר לרחוץ · בא אליהו ולקחו בכנפיו וכ'
והוליכו למקום רחוק ומכרו לעבד המתינה האשה כשראתה שלא
בא היכירה ונתנה הודאה להקב"ה · אומרת להקב"ה לעבדיה הריני
רואה השדה זו עשה חיטים כעלי כרך ובתים כבאן ונזרעו וכ'
ונגמר חטים שאני יודעת שעתיד להיות רעב בארץ וכאן עד
עתידים לבא ולסחור כל העולם מיד עשו כן והיו באין הכל בסחר
בסחורה · לאחר חמש שנים בא הבחור ואדונו עמו והבחור היה
סובל שקים והיין היתה שוות לכל אדם שמותם · כיון שראתה
הבחור אומרה לאדונו תן לי הנער שיאכל עמי בביתי לקחתו בביתה ·
ושאלה אותו מה שמך · אמר לה כך וכך שמי · הכירה אותו ואומרה
אני שפחתך ואתה בעלי · עמדה וחיבקתו ונשקתו · ואומרה לו אדוני
ספר לי מה אירע לך סיפר לה כל המעשה · ואמר לה בתי לא הייתי
עבד עדיין אלא חמש שנים · ועדיין אני חסר ב' שנים · האכילתו
והשקתו ונשקתו ואמר לו לך אדוני לשלום הלך לאדונו · והיין לא
צעקה ולא צרחה אלא נתנה הודיה להקב"ה · הלך ועשה עוד שתי
שנים · ואחר כך בא אליהו ז"ל ולקח הבחור בכנפיו והוליכו לאשתו
ולקח הבחור את אשתו ועבדיו · והלך לאמו ומעשה בחיים ועליה
נאמר אשת חיל מי ימצא׃

מעשה

היה בימי שלמה יום אחד
היה יושב בפלטין שלו והיו
סנהדרין יושבין לפניו אמר להם אדם מחלף ודעתי ואעשה
בכל אלה לא ודעותי · ויום תרינו אני אבדוק עכשיו · מיד אמר
שלמה · הביאו לי בחור אחד שיש לו אשה ואמרו לו איש פלוני
שלח אחרין והביאו אותו · בא לפני המלך · א"ל מאיזה מקום אתה
ומי אתה אומר לי שאני מבקש לעשות לך כבוד · ואני רוצה ליתן
לך בתי ולעשות אותך שר בפלטין שלי · השיב האיש ואמר אני
עבדך · ותמצא אותי כעבדך · א"ל אם כן לך והרוג את אשתך
והבא לי את ראשה בלילה ואני אתן לך בתי ואעשירך ואעשה
אותך פקיד על כל ישראל · א"ל הן נתן לו הקמ"ה המלך חרבו ל
הלך לביתו וראה אשתו יפה ביותר והיו לו מנה בנים קטנים ·

326

·89·

נכנס לביתו והיה מתאונן פגעה לו אשתו אומרה לו אדוני מה
לך שאני רואה את נפשך מתאוננת עליך אל העלני שדאגה
בלבי · מייד הביאה שלחן לפניו ומאכל ויין ולא אכל ולא שתה
הרהר בלבו מה אעשה אשתי הרי היא יפת תואר ויש לי ממנה
בנים קטנים והיה מתאכל בלבו · אמר איך אהרוג את אשתי · מייד
אמרו לה עמדי שכבי עם בניך · עמדה ושכבה ושקעה בשינה ·
עמד ושלף חרבו להרגה · ומצא בנה הקטן ישן בין שני דדיה · ואחד
ראשו על כתפה · מייד הרהר בלבו ואמר אם אהרוג את זאת ·
אמות בני הקטנים והשיב חרבו אל נדנה ואמר יגער יי' בך השטן ·
שמא שטן בלבו של שלמה המלך שאמר לי הרוג אשתך ואתן
לך בתי ואעשירך · עמד פעם שניה ושלף חרבו וראה שערות
האשה יפות פרוסות על גבי תינוקות · ונכנס בלבו רחמים · ואמר
יגער יי' בך השטן · ושבר החרב לשנים עשר חלקים · ואמר אני לא
מבקש לא בתו ולא עושרו ואפילו אם יתן לי כל ביתו מלא כסף
וזהב איני עושה דבר זה · מייד שכב על מיטתו · בבקר השכים
ובאו שלוחי המלך בשבילו והביאוהו למלך · אל קיימת גזירתי ·
אמ' אדוני כך וכך עשיתי בקשתי לקיים גזירתך פעם ושתים
ולא מלאני לבי · יצאו מעליו · לסוף שלשים יום שלח המלך ואצל
אשתו בסתר · אל יש לך בעל טוב · אומרה לו הן · אומר לה שמע
שמעתי על יופיך ואהבתי אותך לקחתך לי לאשה ותמליכי על כל
השרות ואלבישך עדי זהב מראשך ועד רגלך · אומרה לו מה אומרך
כל אשר תאמר אני אעשה · אומר איני יכול ליגע בך שיש לך בעל
אלא הרגי אותו ואחר כך אקח אותך · אומרה לו הן · אומר שלמה
בלבו ודאי היא הורגת אותו · מה עשה נתן לה סייף של בדיל ואמר
לה בסייף זה הרגי אותו · כיון שראת שהוא מבריק סברה החרב
טוב הוא של ברזל · הלכה האשה לביתה והסתירה את הסייף · ל
כשבא בעלה עמדה וחבקתו ונשקתו · ואומרה לו אדוני עטרת
ראשי שב · ישב האיש תמה ואומר לה מה עסקך ומה היום
מימים · אמרה לו רוצה אני לשמוח עמך כדי שאראה אותך שמח
שתה ונשתכר עד שנשקע בשינה · כיון שראת כך עמדה ויצ
ואזרה חלציה ועשתה זרועה ושלפה החרב שנתן לה שלמה
המלך והתחילה לחתך ראשו והקיץ משנתו והנה היא עומדת
עליו וחותכת גרונו קפץ האיש ועמד ומצא בידה הסייף והושיט
ידו על גרונו והנה הדם מבעבע שחתכה ומן הצער מייד נתביישה

האשה ונידעזעה · אומר לה הגידי לי מה ראית שעשית כך ·
ואם לאו אחתוך ראשך · אומרה לו כך וכך היה מעשה · נטל הסייף
והשגיח בה והיתה מן ברזל · שתק עד הבקר ובבקר באו שלוחי ש
שלמה בשבלם והביאו אותם לפני המלך והיו סנהדרין יושבין
לפניו · כיון שראה אותם המלך התחיל לשחוק ואמר להם מה עסק
עסקיכם · אל אדוני אתה עשית את הדבר הזה · אומר לו היאך היה
הדבר · אל הקיניתי ומעיותי אשה עלי להרגני · ואילו היה הסייף
של ברזל כבר הייתי אבוד מן העולם · אני ראיתי עליה והייא לא
ריחמה עלי · אל שלמה אף אני יודע שאין לאשה רחמים · ולכך
לא נתתי לה סייף של ברזל · באותה שעה פתח לפני סנהדרין ואומר
זה הוא שאמרתי אדם אחד מאלף מצאתי ואשה בכל אלה לא מצ
מצאתי ·

מעשה

בעים שהיה מעבדי דוד המלך שהיו יושבין בסעודה והיו אוכלין שם והיה אחד רעב ביותר
ואוכל חלקו הניתן לו קודם חביריו והיה מתבייש מפני שאין לפניו
לפניו כלום · אומר לחבירו היושב אצלו הלויני ביצה אחת · אל אם
אלוה לך עד שתדור לי בפני עדים שתתן לי אותה וכל ריוח שיכול
אדם להרויח מביצה אחת עד אותו זמן שאשאלהו לך · אל הן ונתן
לו בפני עדים לאחר זמן מרובה בא ושאלו ממנו · אומר לו אין לך
עלי אלא ביצה אחת הלכו לפני דוד המלך · ומצאו שלמה יושב
פתח שער שכך היה מנהגו של שלמה שהיה יושב פתח שער
המלך · וכל מי שבא לידון לפני המלך היה שואלו מה טיבך אצל
המלך · אומר לו כך וכך היה מעשה של ביני ובין פלוני · וכשבא זה
שלוה הביצה מחבירו · אל שלמה מה טיבך אצל המלך · אל כך וכך
היה מעשה · אל לך לפני המלך וכשתחזור ספר לי מה שיאמר לך
המלך · נכנסו לפני המלך דוד הביא התובע עדים שכך היה הת
התנאי ביניהם לשלם לו הריוח שיכול אדם לעשות מביצה אחת
מאותו זמן ועד עכשיו · אל המלך דוד לך ושלם לו · אל איני יודע
כמה נתנו החשבון לפני המלך בשנה אחת אפרוח אחד · בשנה
שנייה אותו אפרוח יכול להוליד עד שמונה עשר אפרוחים ·
בשנה שלישית אילו שמונה עשרה אפרוחים מביאין כל אחד
ואחד יח אפרוחים · וכן בשנה רביעית עד שעלה החשבון
לממון גדול מיד יצא זה בפחי נפש · פגע בו שלמה ואל מה
אומר לך המלך · אל כך חייבני המלך ועלה לחשבון גדול · אל

327

·יסף·

א"ל שמע בקולי ואתה איעצך עצה טובה· א"ל לחיים· א"ל לך וקנה
לך פולין ותבשלם וביום פלוני רוצה המלך לילך למקום פלוני ותה
ותעמוד לו על הדרך ובכל שעה שגדולי המלך עוברים לפניך תזרע
הפולין על שדה חרושה שעל הדרך וכל מי שישאל אותך מה אתה
זורע אמור לו פולין מבושלין אני זורע· ואם יאמרו לך מי ראה
מעולם פולין מבושלין זורעין אמור לו ומי ראה מעולם ביצה מן
מבושלות שיצא ממנה אפרוח· מיד הלך ועשה כן והיה עומד על
הדרך וזורע מבושלין וכשבאו גדולי המלך אומרו לו מה אתה זורע
אמר להם פולין מבושלין· אמרו לו ומי ראה מעולם ביצה מן — זרעין
מבושלות שיצא ממנה אפרוח· וכן היה אומר לכל וגדול וק
ונגיד עד שבא הדבר לפני המלך· כיון ששמע המלך כן· א"ל
ומי לימדך דבר זה· א"ל אני מעצמי· א"ל דוד יד שלמה היתה
עמך בדבר זה· א"ל בחייך אדוני המלך הואיל עיני לעשות דבר
הזה· ודריוש ועדסופו· שלח המלך אחרי שלמה· א"ל המלך מה
תאמר בדבר זה· א"ל שלמה היאך הוא חייב בדבר שלא בא לעולם·
אותה ביצה מבושלת היתה ולא היה ראויה לאפרוח· א"ל ילך
ויפרע לו ביצה אחת· ועל זאת נאמר לשלמה אלהים משפטיך
למלך תן וצדקתך לבן מלך·

מעשה

היה בשני אחין אחד עשיר
ואחד עני והיה לעני בנים ובנות
הרבה ולעשיר לא היה לו כי אם בת אחת והיה העשיר צר עין
כנגד אחיו כי הוא לא רוצה לעשות לו שום טובה הנאה שמעולם
והיה לעני בן אחד ששמו יצחק והוא היה בחור וטוב יפה תואר
מאד ולומד בטוב והיה העשיר אוהבו מאד יותר מאחיו ומגדל
בנו· ויהי היום שהיה ערב פסח ולא היה לעני שום דבר מאודה
לקנות חטים לפסח לעשות לו מצות ולכנין· בא אל אחיו העשיר
א"ל אדוני בחסדך תגמול לי חסד גדול ועשה באהבת השם והלוה
ואת לי כור של חטים לפרנס אני וביתי בזה היום טוב· א"ל העשיר
אם תתן לי ערבון אלוה אותו לך· א"ל מה הערבון אשר אתן לך
כי אין בידי כלום· א"ל הבא לי יצחק בנך כי אתה אוהבו יותר מכל
בניך ויהיה לי למשכורת עד שתפרע לי מה שאלוה לך· הלך העני
והביא לו יצחק בנו ולוה לו על כור של חטים ובכל יום ויום אותו
יצחק הולך לבית המדרש ולומד לפני הרב· יומם ולילה· ובכל לילה
בתו של אותו עשיר דודו מתאחרת וממתנת אותו עד שבא· וכן היה

ומנהגה תמיד בכל הלילות׳ יום אחד קרא הרב לאותו יצחק ואמ׳ לך
בני שמע בקולי לאשר אני מצוה אותך ויהי אלהים עמך. בלילה הזה
מייד כשתבא לבית דודך ותמצא שם קרובתך קחנה ותחבקנה ונשוק
אותה׳ אמ׳ ר׳ איך אעשה הרעה הזאת להשיאני יצר הרע עלי כל זמן
שיכולתי להמלט ממנו׳ אמ׳ בשבועה ש לא אניחך עד שתשבע לי כי
שתעשה זאת׳ עמד הבחור והשבע לו׳ כשבא לביתו מצאה מוכנת
כנגדו לפתוח לו הפתח ופתחה לו והלך וישב סביב הראש והיא הכינה
לו לאכול כמנהגה׳ והוא אמר לה לא אוכל ולא אשתה וישב ובכה׳ ויל
ואמרה לו אהובי קרובי מה יש לך הגד לי מה יש לך ואם תצטרך
לשום דבר ומה שאלתך ובקשתך ועל מה אתה בוכה׳ והוא לא רצה
לומר לה כי נתבייש ממנה לומר לה׳ ויהי היא מתאוונת לדעת מה זה
ועל מה זה׳ והגיד לה הכל כאשר נשבע בפני רבו וכאשר צוהו׳ אמרה
לו אהובי איש כלבבי אל תבכה בשביל זה׳ והלכה וחבקה אותו ונשקה
לו בפיו כמה פעמים ואמרה לו אל תתבייש קרובי ממני כי אני א׳
אוהבת אותך מאד ואהבה עזה׳ כי אחי ובשרי אתה ואני אוהבך אל
אותך כבבת עינו ודברה על לבו ופייסה אותו בדבריה׳ והאכילתו ו
והשקתו׳ והלך ושכב במטתו עד למחר׳ ולמחר בא לפני רבו׳ אמ׳ רבו
עשית כאשר צויתיך׳ אמ׳ כן׳ וסיפר לו כל הענין׳ אמ׳ הזהר שתעשה
עד תשעה לילות׳ וכן עשה׳ ולאחר תשעה לילות׳ אמ׳ רבו לך שכוב
הלילה במטתה׳ אמ׳ איך אעשה זאת ושמעו דודי והרגני׳ אמ׳ רבו עשה
כאשר אני מצוה אותך ואל תניח׳ הלך הבחור ושכב עמה במטתה
ונטל חרב ושם ביניהם וישכבו יחד וישנו עד הבקר׳ ויקם דודו וילך
דרך החצר לעשות צרכיו וימצאם שוכבים יחד והחרב ביניהם והם
ישנים ונטל טליתו ופרש עליהם ואומר יהי רצון מלפני אלהי ישראל
שתהיו ומטתכם שלימה שלא ימצא מכם פסול׳ הלך לחצר ושב לחדרו
וספר לאשתו והיא היתה צרת עין על אותו יצחק כי אינה אוהבת
אותו׳ ותאמר הכוונה יעשה את בתינו׳ אמר לה אם היה בדעתו לפגוס
אותה לא היה שם החרב ביניהם׳ ולא עשה כי אם כאוהבת זה
את זה׳ והיה כדעת אשתו ליתן בתה לאחיה והוא עם הארץ ואינו
יודע ומאוד׳ כשנתעוררו משנתם וראה יצחק טלית דודו פרוש עליהם
בכה ואמר ואוי אנה אני בא כי דודי היה כאן וראה אותנו ואמר אוי
לי אוי לי אנה מפניו אברח כי הוא יהרוג אותי מוטב לי לילך ולטבוע
עצמי בנהר ולא יודע לשום אדם׳ מלהמתין ביאת דודי כי לא הלך
כי אם להביא עמו שום חרב להורגני וזה החרב לא ראה אותנו׳ מה

328

יט

עשה הלבישו וקם ממטתו וכשהיה לבוש רצה לטבוע עצמו בנהר
וכשהיה רץ אל הנהר פגעה בו אמו ואמרה לו בני לאיזה מקום אתה
הולך כל כך במהירות· אמר לה אמי בבקשה ממך הניחני· אמרה לו לא
אניחך עד שתאמר לי להיכן תלך· עמד וסיפר לה כל המעשה· אמרה
לו בני אל תתעצב לבך ואל תתן דאגה ללבך כי בעזרת השם אלך
ולך עמי ואמתין אותך עד שאדע דעת דודך מה חשב לעשות ועד
שוב חמתו ושכח את אשר עשית לו· הלך עם אמו ועשה כל אשר צותה
עליו· והטמינה אותו· ואחר כך הלכה אמו אל בית דודו ומצאה שם
דודו יושב· אמרה לו אדוני היכן יצחק בני· אמר לה יהי מכירו ברוך
וישמרהו מכל רע. לא ידעתי היכן הוא· אמר לה מה היום מימים
שביאתה אלי לשואלו· ידעת ממנו שום דבר הגידי לי· ואמרה לו לאו·
ומיד הבינה האשה שאין בדעתו עליו· חזרה לביתה ואמרה לבנו כל
המאורעות אותה וכי אין בדעתו עליו וכי הוא אוהב אותו כבנו· הוציאה
אותו והלך לבית דודו ולא שמע קול נגש ומדבר און כי אם טוב· מה
עשתה אמו הלכה לבית הרב וסיפרה לו כל המאורע· ואמר לה בתי
ידעתי כי ממני היתה הדבר ולכבוד שמים נתכוונתי· והמתיני ואדבר
אל דודו אולי יתן לו בתו· חזרה לביתה והוא שלח אחרי דודו ובא אליו
ואמר לו מפני מה אין אתה משיא את בתך כי היא גדולה מאד ועו
עומדת על פרקה· א"ל ידעתי כי היא ראויה לינשא אבל לא ידעתי למי
אתן אותה· א"ל הרב למי אתה רוצה ליתן אותה כי אם ליצחק נכדך
כי הוא טוב תואר ויפה מראה ותלמיד חכם וענו ושפל רוח וביישן
וחכם ונבון אין כמוהו ועוב תתן אותה לו מתתן אותה לאיש אחר· א"ל
ידעתי כי כל זה הדברים אמיתים ונכוחים וכל המעלות האילו נתקיימו
בו· כי הוא נחמד ונעים ואהוב מאד בעיני· אבל אשתי אינה רוצה
ליתנה לו· כי אם לאחיה· א"ל הרב אחיה עם הארץ ואינו יודע כלום
ללמוד וזה תלמיד חכם אין בכל הישיבה סבר כמוהו· א"ל אם רצונך
תשוב אחר אשתי ונדעה מה יש לבה לעשות מזה הענין· שיגר אל
אחריה ובאה לפני הרב ושאלה לו לשלום· ואמר לה הרב ברוצה את
בתי לו· ואמר לה הדברים האילו· ואמרה כי אין בדעתה ליתן לבתי
כי אם אחי· א"ל הרב אחיך עם הארץ הוא והוא אינו יודע כלום ללמוד
וזה חכם מחוכם בתורה· ועוב תתן אותה אל יצחק נכדך מתתן
אותה לאיש אחר· אמרה לו אם כן הוא ילך יצחק ואחי לסחורה
ואתן לכל אחד מהם מאה דינרים· ואיזה מהם ירויח יותר כמה
השנה לסוף שנה זו אותן לו בתי· וענה הרב ובעצה טוב הדבר אשר

דברית׳ נפרדו מאת פני הרב והלכו לביתם ונתנו לכל אחד ואחד
מאה דינרים והלך כל אחד לדרכו׳ יצחק הלך למדינת הים ונכנס
בספינה אחת לעבור הימה׳ וכשהיה בתוך הים׳ באה רוח סערה
גדולה כים מפרק הרים גש ומשבר סלעים וישבר האניה ויע
ויטבעו כל האנשים אשר בתוך הספינה ונעשה לו נס׳ ומצא
קרש אחד מן הספינה ורכב עליו עד שבא לאי אחד׳ אחת מאיי
הים וישב שם׳ וירעב מאד לאכול כי כבר עברו שלשה ימים שלא
אכל ולא שתה ולא היה לו שום דבר לאכול׳ מה עשה הלך ולקט
עשבים ויאכלם׳ כיון שאכל אותם עלה בטנו ונפחו דרועיו וירכיו
וראשו וכל גופו היה נפוח מאוד ונפלו צפורני ידיו ורגליו ושערות
ראשו׳ בכה בכיה גדולה ומרה׳ וישא עיניו וירא עשב אחר גדל
בעדן שם הקב״ה בלבו לאכול ממנו והושיט ידו ולקח מאותו עשב
ואכל ומיד שבה בשרו כבשר נער קטן ונתרפא׳ ומאותו עשב היה
ניזון כל זמן שם׳ לאחר שתי שבועות ראה ספינה אחת באה׳ וקרא
אל רב החובל וא״ל הניחני ואכנס בתוך ספינתך ואלך עמכם לאיזה
מקום שתלכו׳ ואני אתן שכרך כי אני רופא טוב ומומחה לרפאות כל
נגע ומחלה׳ א״ל בוא ברוך ה׳ מה טיבך בכיון והיאך באת הנה׳
סיפר לו כל המעשה׳ ולקח מן השני מיני עשבים הרבה מאוד
מ משאוי לשני חמורים ונכנס בספינה׳ והלכו יחד והוליכם הרוח
אל עיר אחת שהיו רוב אנשי העיר מצורעים וגם המלך היה
מצורע׳ בא אל המלך וישתחו לו ואפיו ארצה׳ ויאמר לו מי אתה׳
א״ל אדוני רופא אחד אני׳ ויודע אני לרפאות אותך מצרעתך׳ א״ל
המלך אם תוכל לרפאות אותי אתן לך חצי מלכותי׳ נתן לו לאכול מן
אותו עשב ליעבות בטנו ואכל ממנו ועבה בטנו ונפח כל גופו׳ ואח
ואחר כך נתן לו מן העשב האחרת ונתרפא כל בשרו ולא היה כן
בכל גופו לא פגע וחבורה ולא כל מום רע׳ ושבה בשרו כבשר נער
קטן והיה בריא וקל וגבור מאוד׳ עמד המלך ונפל לפני רגליו׳ וא״ל
אתה החייתני הנה מלכותי לפניך קח חציה ממנו ויהיה לך במתנה
ובכל אוצרותי תלך ותקח כל מה שתרצה כי הכל שלך ואתה תהיה
על ביתי ועל פיך ישק כל עמי רק הכסא אגדל ממך׳ ויען יצחק
ויאמר איני רוצה מכל מלכותך מאומה כי אם עיר אחת שיש לך
באותה מדינת פלוני אחיך׳ ותתן לו בחילוף אותה עיר׳ עיר אחת
במלכותך ואני אהיה שליט ומושל מאותה עיר והאנשים אשר
בתוכה יהיו לי למס ויעבדוני׳ א״ל המלך כן יעשה טושר דברית

329

-יב-

ויען המלך ויכתב ספרים אל אחיו לעשות כל רצון זה האיש אשר
יבקש ממנו ויבחר במלכותו איזה עיר שירצה כחפצו אותה עיר
ויכתב ויחתום בטבעת המלך וירפא כל החולים וכל המצורעים אשר
היו באותה עיר ויתן לו המלך כסף וזהב לרוב ואבנים טובות ומרגליות
ועבדים ושפחות ואתונות וגמלים טעונים מזון כבד וישלח אותו
אל אחיו לעשות חפצו ויבא אליו ויאמר לו ידוע כדברים האלה שלח
אליך המלך לאמר והנה הספרים חתומים מטבעתו · כיון ששמע כך
שנתרפא המלך אחיו שמח שמחה גדולה ועשה לו משתה גדול ונתן לו
כסף וזהב לרוב והשליטו באותה עיר שהיה אביו ואמו ודודו בה
ונעשה שר ושליט מאותה עיר ובנו בתוך העיר ברכב גדול מאד
מקנה בכסף ובזהב · והלך ופנה בתוך המגדל הזה וכל אוצרותיו ועבדיו
ופרשיו וכל חילו · ואותו היום נשלמה השנה · והכינו כל צרכי החופה
ליתן הנערה אל אחי אמה · כיון שלא בא יצחק וזה בא רצו
ליתן לו הנערה והכינו הכל לבא ולקדש אותה · וכיון שראו היהודים
שהיה להם שלטון חדש עליהם פחדו ורעדו ממנו מאד ולא רצו
להכניסה לחופה בלא רשות השלטון · עמדה אמה [illegible] והלכה אל
השלטון והכירה יצחק והוא לא הכירה אותו ותבא לפניו ותשתחו
לאפיה ארצה ותאמר לפניו ידוע כבודך מאוד ויגדל המקום שאותך
ויאריך ימיך במלכותך הנה יש לי בת אחת גדולה והגיע זמנה ליכנס
לחופה וכל צרכי הסעודה מוכנים ואין לנו רשות להכניסה לחופה
וכל זה עשתה כדי למהר הקידושין כי היה לה פחד שמא יבא יצחק ·
ענה לה השלטון ואמר אני רוצה להיות שם כשיקדש האיש בתך
ואראה היאך אתם מקדשין נשותיכם · אמרה לו לחייך ושאתך
הלכה לביתה וקשטה ופירכסה בתה והכניסה לבית הנשואין ול
ובאו כל היהודים שם לנהוג כבוד לחתן ולכלה · ושלחו אחר השלטון
ובא שם · וכשרצה האיש לקדש הנערה גער בו השלטון ואמר אין
לך דין לקדש אותה כי לי משפט הקידושין כי אני יצחק · וזה אבי
וזאת אמי · וזה דודי וכן היה התנאי בינינו וסיפר להם ובפניהם
כל התנאים שהיו ביניהם ואמרו כלם אמת ונכון הדבר כי לך
המשפט לקדש ולך לקדש אותה וזכי במקחך · והלך וקדש אותה
והכניסה לחופה · וישמחו כלם אביו ואמו וכל הקהל שמחה גדולה
ויספר לאביו ולאמו ולקרוביו כל הקורות אותו לאמר · והוא היה עם
עשיר גדול ושר ושליט בכל הארץ ויחי האיש ימים רבים וצדיק
וחסיד היה כל ימיו ויולד בנים ובנות וכאשר היה ה' יהיה לנו אמן :

מעשה ברבי פנחס בן יאיר שהיה דר בדרום
בעיר אחת והלכו אנשים להתפרנס
שם. והיו בידם שתי סאין של שעו
שעורין והפקידום אצלו ושכחום והלכו להם. והיה ר' פנחס בן יאיר
זורע אותם בכל שנה ושנה. ועשה אותם גורן וכונסן לאוצר שבע שנים
שבע כיון שבאו אנשים לשם הכיר אותם ר' פנחס אומר להם בואו
טלו אוצרותיכם. בואו וראו אמונה של בשר ודם מאמונתם אתה יודע
מה אמונתו של הקב"ה. ושוב מעשה ברבי פנחס בן יאיר שהלך
לעיר אחת והיו העכברים אוכלים תבואה בתחומה של אותה עיר באו
ובקשו הימנו להתפלל בעדם. אומר להם ר' פנחס בן' למה אין אתם
מפרישין מעשרותיכם כראוי. מבקשים אתם שאעבור לכם שאם
אתם מפרישין מעשרותיכם כראוי אין עכברים אוכלים עוד. אמרו
לו הן. ערב אותם. וילכו העכברים ולא נראו עוד. ושוב מעשה
באדם אחד שהיה חופר שיחין לרבים. ובתו היתה הולכת בדרך ובאתה
לעבור בנהר ושטפה הנהר כיון שראו כך באו והגידו לר' פנחס בן יאיר. כך
אירע לבת פלוני. אמר להם אי אפשר כמו שהיה עושה רצונו של
הקב"ה במים אין הקב"ה מאבד בתו במים. מיד יצאה צווחה בעיר
באתה בתו של פלוני. אמרו רבותינו כיון שאומר ר' פנחס בן יאיר כך
בא מלאך והעלה אותה: ושוב מעשה ברבי פנחס בן יאיר שהלך
לדבר מצוה לגמול בן אדם אחד ופגע בו גנאי נהר והיו הולכין עמו
סיעת בני אדם. אומר ר' פנחס בן יאיר חלוק לי מימיך כי אני הולך
לעשות רצון אבי שבשמים כאשר אתה עושה. אומר לו ספק אתה
עושה ספק אין אתה עושה אבל אני ודאי עושה. אמ"ל אם אין אתה חולק
לי מימך חלק לו ועבר כיון שעבר שבו הולכים בתחילה וראה חביריו
שבאו עמו מעבר לנהר. אמ"ל לנהר וכי כך עושין לבני אדם והיה חולק
להם חלק להם ועברו. ואמרו חכמים גדול היה ומעשה של ר' פנחס בן
יאיר ממשה רבינו שמשה לא חלק המים אלא פעם אחת ולר' פנחס
בן יאיר שני פעמים:

מעשה היה
מבעיר מוכסא שהיה משנה ומלך
ואכסנאי שלו והיה אדם קשה מאד
ורע מעללים. אותו יום שמת אותו בעיר מוכסין מת גם תלמיד חכם
וצדיק גמור באותו יום באו כל הקהל והביאו ונשאו השני מתים
בבית הקברות וכשבאו בבית הקברות באו אויבים עליהם והכום
ופגעם וברחו כולם אנה ואנה והניחו המתים שם ולא נשתייר שם

330

·צג·

כי יום תלמיד אחד מתלמידי החכם שלא רצה לעזוב רבו לא בשביל
הביזה ולא בשביל שום דבר רע שהיו עושים לו האויבים · עד שנחום
האויבים והלכו להם · וחזרו היהודים לבית הקברות ונהגו כבוד גדול
לבעיא מוכסא לא נראה ככבוד הזה שעשו לו · והתלמיד שנשאר שם
היה צועק ואומר להם אין זה רבי כי הוא בעיא מוכסא שאתם עושים
לו הכבוד הזה והם היו מפוחדים ולא האזינו לו והוא היה צועק ומכה
במר נפש על שלא נהגו כבוד לרבו וקברו לבעיא מוכסא בכל הכבוד
הזה והלכו להם ולא נשאר שם כי אם עשרה אנשים לקבור הצדיק
וקברו אותו והלכו להם · ונשאר עד שם תלמידו של אותו חכם טוכה
וצועק על שלא נהגו לרבו כבוד ונפל תרדמה עליו ויישן ויבא רבו אלין
ויאמר לו בני אל תצטער יותר ואל תתמה על אשר ראית כי כבר עשו
ידעת מפני מה זכה אותו בעיא מוכסא לכל הכבוד הזה בשביל שפעם
אחת שלח המלך לבעיא מוכסא לאמר תכין לי הבית ותקנה כל מה שצריך
לי ולחיילותיי כי אני רוצה לבא אליך שם בעירך · ויעש כן בעיא מוכסא
כאשר צוה המלך והכין כל צרכי הסעודה ולא בא המלך והלך לעיר
אחרת מה עשה בעיא מוכסא נטל כל מה שהכין וחלק לעניים · ובשביל
אותו זכות זכה לכל הכבוד הזה · וזה היה חלקו שנטל בשביל המעשה
שעשה · וממני אומר לך מפני מה לא זכיתי לכבוד בשביל שפעם
אחת שמעתי גנות של תלמיד חכם ולא מחיתי ובשביל זה לא זכיתי מן
לכבוד · ולך עמי ואראך ואראך מקומי ומקומו הלך עמו וראה שרבו היה
יושב בגן עדן בקתדראות של זהב ועושים כבוד סובבין אותו והוא עם
צדיקי עולם בגן עדן · וראה אותו בעיא מוכסא שהיה מנעל אחד
מברזל יוצא ובא בתוך ראשו מאוזן לאוזן · תמה מאד הבחור ואמר
לרבו · רבי עד כי לעולם יהיה זה לו ומוקש · אז ושנים עשר חדש · כפי
כפושעי ישראל שדינם שנים עשר חדש · אמר רבו לא · אלא עד מות
ר' שמעון בן שטח שיהיה במקומו · והוא יפטר · תמה התלמיד ואמר
וכי זו שכרו שהוא ראש ישיבה ותנא ואב בית דין וקרוב לינאי מלכא ·
וצדיק גמור הוא וחסיד אין כמוהו בכל הארץ · אמר רבו כל זה בשביל
שמונים מכשפות שיש באשקלון קרוב לו שלשה מילין · ולא מיחה
בהן ולא עשה דין בהן · וייקץ הבחור משנתו ויתמה מאד ויבהל על
החיזיון אשר ראה · וישמח על הכבוד שראה מרבו · ויתעכב או לכן
מלפני כבוד ר' שמעון בן שטח · מה עשה הלך אצל ר' שמעון בן שטח
וסיפר לו כל המעשה וכל המראה אשר ראה · וממנו סיפר לו כל הד'
מה ששמע וראה · ויחר לו מאד ויבך בכי גדול כי נתעכב או לכן כי לא

היה יודע מהם׳ מה עשה ר׳ שמעון בן שטח לקח שמונים בחורים גבורי חיל ונתן לכל אחד ואחד כד אחת של חרש ובתוך הכד נתן כל אחד טליתו׳ וכך אמר להם לכו אל אשקלון ובאו אל בית הנשים המכ המכשפות והמתינו בעיר עד שיהיה מי גשמים יורדים בעולם ואז תלכו לביתם׳ ויום הן שואלין לכם מה מעשיכם׳ תאמרו מכשפים אנחנו ותכנסו לביתם ותקחו כל אחד מכם אחת מהנה ותלו את כולן על העצים׳ ומיד כשתקחו כל אחד אחת מהן תשאינה על העצים והזהרו שלא יגעו רגליהן לארץ לפי כשיהיה אדם באויר אינו יכול לעשות מכשפות׳ ועשו כן ונכנסו אל פתח ביתן ומצאו הפתח סגור וקראו לפתוח והיו הגשמים יורדים עליהם ותאמרנה להם מה מעשיכם ויאמרו אנשים מכשפים אנחנו׳ ותאמרנה להם במה אתם יודעים לכשף אמרו להן הרי כאן ולא ירדו הגשמים עלינו ולקחו הטליתות שלהם ונתעטפו ופתחו הפתח והם השליכו כדיהם לארץ ונכנסו לבית והיו עליהם טליתות שלהם יבישים׳ ולקחו כל אחד מהם אחת מהן ונשאו אותן על העצים ותלו אותן ואעפי שאין דינן להיות נתלות הוראה שעה היתה כי היו יראים ממכשפות שלהן לכך תלו אותן מיד׳ לימים באו שני בני אדם מקרובותיהן והעידו על בנו של ר׳ שמעון בן שטח שהרג איש אחד בפני אביו ודן אותו אביו וקודם שהוליכוהו ליהרג אמרו העדים שבשביל שנאה אמרו׳ אמר ר׳ שמעון בן שטח אינו חושש כיון שהגיד שוב אינו חוזר ומגיד׳ והרגוהו׳׳

מעשה במר עקבא׳ שמתו אביו ואמו וה והניחו לו ממון הרבה׳ ונתגדל בין במעשים רעים׳ ונעשה סוחר׳ והיה קונה שפחות ושוכב עמהם׳ היתה נערה אחת בשכונתו׳ יפת תואר ונאה שמה והיה אוהב אותה ביותר׳ והיה שם תלמיד ושמו יוסף׳ ואף היה אוהב אותה עמדו אביה ואמה ונמלכו במשפחתם ואמרו למי נשיאה ותחנה או למר עקבא העשיר רשע׳ או ליוסף שהוא תלמיד׳ אמרו כולם חס ושלום לא תנשא אלא לה התלמיד שמו יוסף׳ כי מר עקבא אינו אוהבה כי אם עבור יופיה׳ כמו אחת מן השפחות׳ עמדו והשיאוה ליוסף׳ כשראה עקבא שנשאת לאחר מרוב צער נפל בחולי גדול עד שהגיע למות׳ שלחו וקראו לרופא׳ אמר לו אין לו חליה אלא מתאות אשה׳ אם תשכב עם אשה מיד תתרפא׳ שלח לחכמים להתירו ולא קבלו׳ ואמרו ימות ואל יעמוד מחליו׳ כתיב בתורה לא ינקה׳ והוא אומר לשכב עמה׳

331

שלח וקרא לרופא אחר· אומר לו כראשון· אבל אם אתה עושה צדקה
תתרפאי· שלח לחכמים ולא הניחו לעשות אותה· שלח לרופא אחר אמר לו
כראשון· ואם אתה שומע אפילו דיבורה תתרפאי· שלח לחכמים ולא
קיבלו· נפל בחולי גדול לימים נפל בעניות גדול אותו יוסף תלמיד· ולוה
מ' זה דינרים מגוי אחד· אכלום· כי כלו הממון לתשע מאות· עמדו
אביה ואמה לפייס הגוי ולא יכלו· נתפס כלו הממון בבית האיסורין
ואמרו לחנה· לכי אצל עקיבא שמא יתן לך· אומרת להם לא אלך שמא
יתעייר עלי אני הולכת לשם· אמרו לו כמה פעמים ולא קבלה· עמד
בעלה לכי ואל עוות· כיון הלכה ובקשה אותו שיתן לה מאה דינרים
כי בעלה בבית האיסורין כשכלם· אומר לה אם אתן אותם לך תשכבי
עמי· אמרה לו חלילה לך מעשות זאת אלא זכור נא בוראך וכבוש
יצרך ואל תעשה הנבלה הזאת· מה עשה שמע לקולה וכבש יצרו·
ואמר לאחת מן השפחות הוציאי ותני לה מה שהיא שואלת· והיא
ומה לא נתן לה מידו לידה· כדי שלא יגע בה· לקחת והלכה· כיון
שראת יוסף בעלה נאנח· אמר לה חנה בחייך שמא נגע בך· אומרת לו
בחיי עולם ובחיי לא נגע בי אפילו ביד· לימים היה עקיבא עובר
בדרך· והיה כמו נר דלוק על ראשו· וראה אותו ראש ישיבה גדול ר'
תלמיד חכם· אמר לתלמידיו מי הוא זה· אמרו לו עקיבא הרשע·
אמר להם קראו אותו לי· אמר לו ראש ישיבה בני אמור לי טובה שעשית·
אמר לו אדוני לא עשיתי שום טובה כי בעונותי אנשים רעים נתחברו
אלי ולמדוני כל רעות שבעולם· אמר לו בני אם שום טובה עשית תודה
לי· הודה לו הדבר· אמר לו ראש ישיבה· הרי בתי בת שמונה עשר שנה
ויש לי ממון הרבה· וכמו כן יש לך ממון הרבה· אתן לך בתי· ונשב יחד
ונעסוק בתורה כל ימינו· ושמע לו ולקח בתו ועסקו בתורה כל ימיהם
התנו ביניהם שכל מי שימות מהם ראשון יבא ויגיד לחבירו היכן הוא
והיאך הוא יושב· הקדים ראש ישיבה למר עקיבא· בא מלאך המות
לראש ישיבה· אמר לו שלש אני עושה עליך· בחר לך אחת מהן· שאין
כל צדיק יכול להנצל מהן· ואפילו צדיקים גמורים· אם תרצה אכה
אותך שלשה פעמים מן השרביט שבידי· או אחזור אותה במתניך
או אני אשימנה בארץ ועבור עליו גם שלשה פעמים· אמר ראש
ישיבה איני יכול ליגע בו· אמר המלאך בחר לך אחת משלשה· מיד
התחיל לעבור עליו והיה בוכה· עבר פעם שנייה ושלישית· וצעק
צעקה גדולה· שמע מר עקיבא והכין קולו וצעקתו· וכאותה שעה
היה מר עקיבא חולה כי נפל למשכב באותו יום עצמו שמת אותו

אותו ראש ישיבה חבירו׳ כשראו לקוברו בא מר עוקבא ופשט ידו
ומצא ברגליו אבעבועות מן האש קרע בגדיו׳ ואמר ודאי זהו הקול
ששמעתי׳ הלכו וקברו אותו׳ חזרו לביתם נפל מר עוקבא על פניו׳
והיה בוכה׳ בא ראש ישיבה ואמ׳ לו יפה עשית שהכנסת ידך תחת
רגלי לראות בושתי׳ אמ׳ לו חס ושלום׳ אבל הייתי שומע קולך ונתבהלתי׳
ועכשיו אני מבקש שתאמר לי היאך אתה יושב והיכן מקומך׳ אמ׳ ל
חייך שלש מעלות מקומך למעלה ממקומי׳ בבקשה ממך שתתפלל ל
שתרד אתה מעלה אחת׳ ואני אעלה מעלה אחת׳ ואז נהיה שוין׳ בא
וראה כמה גדול כח התשובה׳ **מעשה** בשעה
שירד שלמה ממלכותו׳ היה מחזיר
ובא על פתחי ישראל בשביל פרנסתו׳
פעם אחת נכנס אצלו שני בני אדם שהיו מכירין אותו בא אחד
מהם נשתטח לפניו ואמר לו אדוני המלך רצונך שתסעוד אצלי׳
אמ׳ לו הן׳ הלך עמו לעלייה וזבח לו שור והביא לפניו הרבה מטעמים׳
התחיל להשמיע לו דברי מלכותו׳ ואמר זוכר אני מיום פלוני
כשהיית במלכותך׳ והיית מלך ועשית כך וכך׳ וכן וכך עשו
משרתיך׳ כיון שהזכיר לו ימי מלכותו התחיל להיות בוכה ובוכה
אותה סעודה עד שטבע עיניו מבכייתו׳ למחר פגעו חבירו
התחיל להשתטח לפניו׳ ואמ׳ לו אדוני המלך תאכל עמי היום׳ אמ׳ ל
אתה מבקש לעשות עמי כמו שעשה חברך אתמול׳ אמ׳ לו אדוני
המלך איש עני אני׳ אבל אם רצונך תשגיח עמי היום מעט ירק
יש לי שאניח לפניך׳ אם רצונך בא עמי לביתי׳ באותה שעה
בא עמו לביתו׳ רחץ ידיו ורגליו הביא לפניו פת ומעט ירק׳ התחיל
אותו האיש לנחמו׳ אמ׳ לו אדוני המלך תתנחם שבועה נשבע הקב״ה
ואמן שאינו פוסק מלוכה מזרעו׳ שנ׳ נשבע י״י לדוד באמת׳
ועוד כך הוא דרכו של הקב״ה מוכיח וחוזר ומתרצה׳ שנ׳ כי את
אשר יאהב י״י יוכיח וכאב את בן ירצה׳ והקב״ה עתיד להחזירך
במלכותך׳ כיון ששמע שלמה כך נתקררה דעתו עליו והיה שב
שבע מאותה הסעודה של ירק׳ ועמד משם שבע׳ כיון שחזר
למלכותו׳ אומר טוב ארוחת ירק ואהבה שם משור אבוס ושנאה
בו׳ טוב ארוחת ירק שאכלתי בבית העני׳ משור אבוס שאכלתי
העשיר׳ שלא הזכיר לי צערי׳ **מעשה** אומרין
על נחום איש גם זו׳ שהיה סומא
בשתי עיניו׳ וגידם בשתי ידיו וקיטע

332

·קפ·

בשתי רגליו והיה כל גופו מלא שחין׳ והיה מטתו מונחת בארבע
ספלים מלאים מים כדי שלא יעלו עליו הנמלים׳ פעם אחת היה
מיטתו בבית רעוע׳ ובקשו תלמידיו לפנותו׳ א״ל פנו כלים׳ ואחר
כך פנו את מטתי׳ שכל זמן שמטתי בבית מובטח אני שלא תי
תפול׳ פינו הכלים ואחר כך פינו מיטתו׳ מיד נפל הבית׳ אמרו לו
תלמידיו׳ רבי מאחר שצדיק גמור אתה מפני מה אירע לך כך׳
אמר להם אני בעצמי עשיתי׳ שפעם אחת הייתי לבית חמי׳
והיה עמי משאוי שלשה חמורים אחד של מאכל ואחת של מי
משתה׳ ואחת של כל מיני מגדים׳ נזדמן לי אדם אחד׳ א״ל רבי
פרנסני׳ אמרתי לו המתן עד שאפרוק מן החמור׳ חזרתי לאחרי
לאחר שפרקתי את החמור׳ מצאתיו מת׳ נפלתי עליו ואמרתי
עיני שלא חסו על עיניך׳ כך וכך תעלה עליהם׳ ידיי ורגליי שלא
מהרו לפרק מן החמור כך וכך תעלה עליהם׳ ולא נתקררה דעתי
עד שאמרתי יהיה כל גופי מלא שחין׳ א״ל ר׳ עקיבא אוי לי
שראיתיך בכך׳ א״ל אשריך שראיתני בכך׳ ואמאי קרו ליה
נחום איש גם זו׳ שכל מה שבא עליו היה אומר גם זו לטובה׳
פעם אחת שלחו ליה ישראל דורון לבי קיסר׳ אמרו ביד מי
נשלחנו׳ ביד נחום איש גם זו׳ דמלומד בניסי׳ שלחו בי
בהדיה אזל בההוא דירא׳ קמו הנהו דיוראי׳ ולקחו מאי דהוה
בשקו ומלאוהו עפרא׳ כי מטא התם שדריה לשקו ראוהו דה
דהוה עפרא׳ אמר דאחוכי קמחייכי עלי יהודאי׳ עמדו עליהם
להורגם׳ אמר גם זו לטובה׳ אתא אליהו זכור לטוב׳ אידמי ליה
כחד מינייהו׳ אמר ודילמא הא׳ עפרא מעפרא דאברהם הוא׳
דכי הוו שדו מיניה הוו גירי׳ דכת׳ יתן כעפר חרבו כקש נדף
קשתו׳ הוה חדא מדינתא דלא הוה יכול למיכבשיה׳ זרקו מינה
עלה וכבשוה׳ עיילו ליה לבית גנזיה׳ ומלאו שקו אבנים טובות
ומרגליות׳ אתא בבית ההוא דיורא׳ אמר לו מאי אמטית בהדך
דעבדו כולי האי בך׳ אמר להו מאי דשקלית מהכא׳ קמו אינהו
נמי אמטו לבי מלכא מההוא עפרא בדקו ולא אשכחו קטלינהו
להנך כולהו דיוראי׳׳

מעשה בחסיד
אחד שלא היה לו בן כי אם בן אחד
והיה החסיד עשיר גדול וזקן מאד
בשעת פטירתו צוה לבנו להתעסק במצות וליתן תמיד צדקה
לעניים ולהיות אוהב ונחמד בעיני הבריות׳ וכל מעה שיבא לידו

שלא תניחנה׳ נפטר האיש ונשאר הבחור עם אמו׳ הלך הבחור ונתן
ונתעסק במצות׳ אמרה לו אמו בני שמע בקולי וקח הממון שלנו
וחלק אותו לשלשה חלקים׳ וקח חלק אחד ועשה סחורה ממנו ולך לך
לשום מקום קרוב או רחוק וקנה ומכור מן הממון שיהיה לך׳ למען
נתעשר בסחורה׳ הלך וכן עשה׳ וחלק נכסיו והלך למדינת הים׳ ופגע
סיעה גדולה אחת שהיו מתקוטטים יחד ומריבים אומר לאחד מהם
מה זה היוסיפה הזאת׳ א״ל זה חתן אחד שהתנה אבי הכלה לתת
לו אלף זהובים יותר מהשגת ידו׳ ולא רצה החתן לקדש אשתו ואומר
כאשר בא כן ילך לארצו ולא יקדש אותה לעולם׳ וכל הקהל הזה כולם
עניים ואינם יכולים לסייע׳ ענה הבחור ואמר הואיל ובאו לידי זאת
המצוה אעשנה׳ מה עשה אותו בחור נטל אלף זוזים ונתן לחתן ומייד
קדש את אשתו ועשה החופה והמשתה בשירים ובכינורות ובכל מיני
זמר ועשו שמחה גדולה׳ ולא נשאר לבחור מאומה וחזר לביתו לאמו׳
אמרה לו אמו בני מה עשית מן הממון שנשאת עמך׳ אמר לה אמי אל
אל יקשה בעיניך ואל יחר לך ואל תחשבי ממנו כי לויתי אותו לאדון
אחד גדול ושמו נודע בכל העולם והוא ישלם לי כפלים ונאמן הוא ושלם
לי שכרי ועמלי׳ אמרה לו בני לחיים ולשלום׳ ואם תרצה קח עוד חלק
אחר ולך לסחורה׳ ובשביל אהבת בוראינו הזהר שתעשה בחכמה
כל ענינך׳ לקח עוד אלף זהובים והלך לו ונתרחק מאוד ממדינתו׳ עד
שראה כל בני העיר אוסרים שמה כנוסים ומצטערים׳ ואומר לאחד
מהם מה זה הצער והבכיה הזאת לכם׳ א״ל האיש כבר עבר שלשה
ימים שמת הרב ראש ישיבה שבעיר הזאת והוא היה גדול בתורה
ובמעשים טובים ובמצות וצדיק גמור וחסיד היה מאוד לא קם כמוהו
כי רוח אלהים היה בקרבו׳ ולא הניח המלך את הקהל הזה לקבור הרב
ולהוגן בכבוד׳ ולכן אנו בוכים ומצטערים׳ א״ל הבחור ומפני מה
הוא אינו רוצה שיקברוהו הקהל׳ א״ל כי שואל אלף זהובים בשוחד
לקהל וכולם עניים ואחד ואינם יכולים לתתם לו׳ אמר הבחור הרי
עלי אלף זהובים אתנם לו בשביל אהבת בוראינו ובשביל כבודו של
אותו צדיק׳ הלך הבחור ונתן אלף זהובים למלך וצוה לקוברו והלכו
כולם לקבור הצדיק ונהגו בו כבוד גדול כראוי לו והבחור הלך עמהם
ונהגו בו כבוד גדול׳ אחר אשר קברו אותו חזר הבחור לביתו לאמו
אמרה לו בני מה עשית מן הממון שעשית שנשאת עמך׳ אמר לה
אמי אל תחשבי מהם כי בטוב לויתי אותם לנאמן אחד אין בכל
העולם כמוהו שישלם לי גם קרן גם פרי ומובטח אני בו שלא י

333

קפ

יעכב ממני שום דבר · אמרה לו לחייך בני · אמר לה אם תרצי תני לי
עוד האלף זהובים שנשארו ואני אלך עוד לסחורה וארויח מה שאוכל ·
אמרה לו בני אין לנו עוד אלא אותם אלף זהובים ואם תפסידם לא
נדע מה נעשה כי נשארנו אני ואתה עניים ועני חשוב כמת · לכן בני
תשאר הנה עמי ונאכלם יחד עד שיגיע הזמן שישלם לך האדון שאמרת
מה שלויתה לו · אומר לה אמי רעי כי הזמן הולך ומקרב עד היום שיש
שישלם לי בטוב מה שהוא חייב לי · ואל תאחרי אותי הואיל וצריך אני
ללך לבעל חובי · ועוד לי להכין עמי הממון · אולי יקרה האלהים לפני
וארויח הרבה יותר ממה שהיה לי מעולם מאלף בידים ריקנות · אמרה
לו אמן אם כן קח אותם והקב"ה ישלח מלאכו לפניך וישמרך בדרך
והפליאך אל המקום הזה · לקח הממון והלך לו ובא אל עיר אחרת
ומצא שם כל הקהל בוכים ומתאננים ועושים הספד לא נראה כמוהו
מעולם · אמר הבחור מפני מה אתם עושים כל הענין הזה · אמר איש
אחד מהם המלך שלנו רשע הוא אין כמוהו וגזר שמד על כל הקהל
ולקח כל עושר לנו ולא נשאר בידינו מאומה כי אם גויתנו וגם גזר
עלינו שלא למול את בנינו ועל נשותינו שלא לטבול ושלא להכניס
כלה לחופה · ויש למול למחר שלשה בנים · כי למחר יהיה יום שמיני
שנולדו · וכבר עברו ארבעה חדשים שלא טבלה שום אשה ונפרדנו
מנשותינו · וכלה לא הכנסה לחופה כבר עבר ד׳ חדשים כמו כן ·
וטוב מות מחיים אמרנו · אמר הבחור וכל כך למה · אמר בשביל אלף
זהובים שהוא שואל עוד ממנו ואין בידינו כלום · כי לקח כל אשר
לנו · אמר הבחור יהי שם ה׳ מבורך אשר נחני בדרך אמת · להתבטל
גזירה רעה כזאת מעל ישראל הנה נא לי אלף זהובים אלך ואתנם
לו ויבטל הגזירה מעליכם · מה עשה הבחור הלך אל המלך · ואמר אדוני
המלך מה לך לגזור גזירה רעה כזאת על ישראל · אמר המלך בשביל
שהם חייבים לי אלף זהובים · אמר הבחור אם אפרעם לך תבטל הגזירה
אמר הן · אמר הרי לך אלף זהובים לקח אותם · ויצו בכל מלכותו להעביר
קול ולבטל הגזירה ויעשו ישראל כל רצונם · הלכו ומלו בניהם ועשו
שמחה ומשתה ויום טוב · והבחור נטל רשות מהם והלך לדרכו ·
ויברכו אותו ויאמרו לו ישלם ה׳ לך פעלך ותהי משכורתך שלמה
מעם ה׳ אלהי ישראל · ויקם וילך לדרכו ויאמר אל לבו אנה אלך אם
אחזור לאמי בידים ריקנות אנה אני בא מן העיר והנער אשר
יזונו את אמי כי היא עניה וזקינה ולא נשאר לה כלום · והיא מן
מענה כל היום אחרי שאכלנו עמי לה מה שלקחתי ממנה ובכה

היה מדבר אל עצמו ישב לארץ ובכה והתפלל אל הקב"ה ואמר לפני
רבונו של עולם גלוי וידוע לפני כסא כבודך שלכבודך עשיתי כל מה
שעשיתי הדריכני באמיתך ולמדני ופרנסני אני ואמי ואל תצריכני
למתנת בשר ודם כי מתנתם מועטת וחרפתם מרובה אבל מתנתך
מרובה וחרפתך מועטת בין כך ובין כך שהיה מתפלל בא אליו
אליהו הנביא זכור לטוב וא"ל שלום עליך והבחור ענה לו שלום עליך
מורי ורבי א"ל אליהו הנה שמע אלהים לקול תפלתך וראה את עניך
ואת כל אשר עשית לכבודו הנה נא קח לך עשרה זהובים שאתן לך
ומאותן תעשיר עושר גדול ויהיה לך כסף וזהב ואבנים טובות ומר
ומרגליות לרוב מאד כל ימיך כי יפה דברת שלויתה ממונך לאומן
לשלם לך והוא ישלם לך כפלי כפליים אלף פעמים א"ל הבחור אדוני
חייך וחיי עולם לא אני רוצה ליקח משכרתי בעולם הזה כי אם
לעולם הבא ולא אקחם עד שתראה לי מקומי ומה יהיה מתן ש
שכרי לעולם הבא א"ל אליהו בעולם הזה יהיה לך עושר גדול וכבוד
כזה ולעולם הבא בא ואראך את מקומך ומתן שכרך הלך עמו
והראהו גן עדן ובתוך גן עדן הראה לו קתדרא אחת מזהב מלאה
מאבנים טובות ומרגליות ועגני כתר סובבין אותה ועליה עשר חופות
מזיו וזוהר ויקר ונוגה וכבוד והוד והדר סובבין אותה קתדרא
והיא עומדת באמצע הצדיקים כשראה כך א"ל בבקשה ממך
הניחני ואלך שם מיד למה אהיה עוד בעולם הזה לראות עמל ואון
א"ל אליהו חייך שאין יומך בא עדיין שם אלא בא ואוליכך אל אמך
ויתן לו העשרה זהובים ויפרוש כנפיו וישאהו לבית אמו ואליהו
הנביא הלך לדרכו וכשראתה אותו אמו שמחה מאד ממנו ושאלה
לו בני מה עשית אמר לה אמי בעזרת הבורא יהיה לנו הרבה מה
עשה הלך וקנה ומכר ונתעשר מעושר גדול כמאן מוצא ויקבץ אוצ
אוצרות של כסף ושל זהב ושל אבנים ומרגליות עד שלא היה עשיר
כמוהו בכל הארץ ובוא וראה כמה גדול כח של צדקה שבשביל
צדקותיו קנה העולם הזה והעולם הבא:

מעשה בעשיר אחד שהיה לו בן והיה
בן שמונה עשר שנים ולא היה
לאותו עשיר כי אם אותו בן והיה
האיש עשיר גדול יום אחד בא אותו בן לפני אביו וא"ל אדוני אבי
שמעני הנה גדלתני ורוממתני ויש לי הרבה עושר ונכסים לרוב
ואינני לומד עמך שום דבר לא תורה ולא חכמה ולא דרך ארץ ולא

334

·צח·

בינה ולא תבונה׳ אם רצונך אלך ואלמוד למדינת הים כי שמעתי
שיש שם עיר אחת מלאה חכמים מאד מחוכמים ביותר מכל חכמה
שבעולם׳ ויש בדעתי לילך שם ולשהות שם שלש שנים׳ ואחר שלש
שנים אבא אליך׳ א״ל אביו בני מה לך לילך אנה ואנה יש לי עושר
הרבה ונכסים לרוב ואין לנו בן כי אם אתה והנה נא זקנתי ולא
ידעתי יום מותי ואמך זקנה מאד׳ ואם נמות למי נשאר את כל
העושר הזה׳ א״ל בנו איני חושש מכל מה שיש לך לפי שבשעת
פטירתו של אדם אין מלוין לו לא כסף וזהב ולא אבנים טובות
ומרגליות׳ אלא תורה ומעשים טובים׳ כיון ששמע אביו כך א״ל
בני תשאר עמנו ואשכיר לך הנה רב אחד תלמיד חכם ותלמוד
כאן עמנו ובכל יום ויום אפרנס ששה עניים בתנאי שתשאר
עמנו׳ א״ל אבי אל יחר בעיניך כי בשום ענין שבעולם לא אניח
מלילך שם׳ כי הרבה יותר אני לומד שם בשלשה שנים ממה
שאעשה הנה בעשר שנים׳ וירא אביו כי לא יכול לעכבו ויאמר לו
אם כן קח עמך אלף זהובים ובגדים נאים והנעסולך לשלום
ואל תניח מלחזור לסוף שלש שנים׳ הלך הנער למדינת הים ובא
אל אותה עיר שהיו בוס תלמידים חכמים׳ והלך אל ראש שבכולם
ולמד שם בפנו׳ בתוך שלש שנים למד הרבה מאד׳ כשהגיע
זמנו שלח אביו אחריו ונטל רשות מרבו והלך אל אביו׳ כשראוהו
אביו ואמו שמחו שמחה גדולה׳ ושאלו לו בני מה למדת׳ אמר להם
למדתי תורה ועדיין אני רוצה לילך שם ולהיות שם עוד שלש שנים׳
א״ל אביו הרבה הייתה שם׳ א״ל כך התניתי לבא עוד אליו ולהיות
בפנו ללמוד עוד ג׳ שנים ולא אניח בשום ענין׳ א״ל אם כן הוא
קח עמך עוד אלף זהובים ובגדים חדשים וטובים ותלך לשלום
ובשמשלח אחריך תבא ואל תניח׳ לקח מה שנתן לו והלך לו ובא
אל רבו ולמד עוד בפנו ג׳ שנים׳ בסוף שש שנים שהיה שם
למד תורה נביאים וכתובים ס׳ ותלמוד ואגדות וסיפרין וספרי
ותוספתא ומתניתין ובליה תלמודין׳ כיון שהגיע זמנו שלח
אביו אחריו ונטל רשות מרבו והלך לו ובא אל אביו ושמחו מאד
כשראוהו אביו ואמו׳ ושאל לו אביו בני מה למדת׳ א״ל הרבה למדתי
א״ל אביו אמור לנו שום דבר ממה שלמדתה׳ א״ל עדיין לא ידעתי
תמצית החכמה ואיני יכול לומר מאומה עד שאהיה עוד שם
שלש שנים׳ א״ל הרבה הייתה שם ולא תשוב עוד שם כי אנחנו
זקנים מאד ורוצים אנו שתהיה כאן עמנו לשמור אותנו׳ א״ל

אני אפסיד כל מה שעשיתי אם לא יהיה עם עד שלש שנים א"ל
אם כן היא אם אין טוב לך להפסיד מה שעשית לך לשלום הלך
ולקח עמו עד אלף זהובים וישב שם שלש שנים אחרות אמרו
עליו שלמד באותן שלש שנים שיחת דקלים שיחת שדים מושלות
שועלים ולשון כל בהמה וחיה ועוף ולא הניח חכמה שבעולם שלא
שלא למד כשגמרו השלש שנים בא אביו עמו אחריו ונתן לרבו
מתנות גדולות מאד ויאמר לו רבו קח בנך יחידך והוליכהו לשלום
לביתך והוא חכם מחוכם ומכל חכמות שבעולם לא נראה כמוהו נטלו
רשות מרבו והלכו להם כשבאו אל הים שכרו ספינה אחת ונכנסו
בה כשהיו באמצע הים בא עורב וישב לו על התורן וינעק ויאמר
בנעקתו אבינו של זה הבחור עכשיו הוא עשיר גדול וקודם שימות
יהיה עני ודלדל בעניותו לא נראה מעולם ולבסוף יהיה עשיר
משופע מעושר גדול ולא יהיה כמוהו בכל הארץ שמע בנו ושחק
מאד א"ל אביו בני מפני מה שחקת כל כך א"ל אל תשים לבך שום
דבר כי זכרתי ממעשים שהייתי עושה בנערותי ובשבל כך ש
שחקתי א"ל לא מפני זה שחקת כי אם בשביל דבר אחר והוא לא
רצה לספר לו שלא רצה לפחדו ולכעסו וכעס עליו אביו ויחר לו
ויאמר וכי בשביל זה פזרתי כל ממוני שהוא שוחק ולא ידע למה
אין זה כי אם שוטה כמו שאמר שלמה כחכמתו שחוק כפי כסיל
עתה מה עשה לקח בנו והשליכו לים וימן ה' דג גדול ויבלע אותו
ויוליכו למקום רחוק ויקיא אותו שם במלכות אחרי וישב שם על
שפת הים וראה אותו רועה אחד שהיה רועה למלך וראה אותו
ערום בלי לבוש והלך אליו ויאמר לו בני מעשיך ומאין באתה ומאיזה מח
מקום אתה א"ל עברי אנכי ואת אלהי השמים אני ירא אשר עשה
את הים ואת היבשה והייתי בספינה בים ויבוא ה' רוח חזק מאד
וישבר את האניה אשר הייתי בה וימן ה' לי דג אחד ויולכני ה'
הנה א"ל יודע אתה שום מלאכה בעולם א"ל הן א"ל מה מלאכה ידעת
א"ל רועה יהיה עבדך מנעורי ועד עתה א"ל אם כן שב עמי
ושמור צאני ואני אתן את שכרך וישב עמו וילבשהו ויאכילהו
ויאהבהו מאד וה' ברך אותו בגללו וישם כל אשר לו בידו פעם
אחת ישב המלך בביתו עם שריו ועבדיו ויאספו על ביתו עורבים
ב׳ לרוב חיל גדול ואיד מאד עד שהיה על מכסה הבית מכוסה
מעורבים ונחלקו לשתי כיתות כשני צדדי הבית ובין שתי הכי
הכיתות היו שלשה עורבים שני זכרים ונקבה אחת ביניהם

335

·פט·

ואותן השלשה יושבין שם ואינם מוציאין ממקומן· והיו שני ערבים
אחרים הולכים מחיל אל חיל כמו שלוחים· ואין אדם יכול להבריח
אותם לא בשכל ידיעת חיים ולא בשכל גדית זריקת אבנים ולא בכל
בשכל דבר אחר· תמהו המלך והשרים מאד· וכל רואיהם יתמהו· כי
לא שמעו כזאת ולא ראו כמוה· שלח המלך בכל מדינות מלכותו וקבץ
ואסף כל חכם ונבון יועץ וחרטום ואשף לבא ולבוא אל המלך
ליום מועד· ויועדו כולם ויבואו אל המלך· ויען המלך ויעבר קול במחנה
מאת המלך לאמר כל איש אשר ידע להגיד אל המלך דבר זה ומה
המשל הזה יתן לו המלך בתו לאשה וחצי מלכותו בחייו וכולו לאחר
מיתתו· ויבואו מקצתם ויאמרו למלך אדוני המלך זה משל של רעב
ושל כיעור· ומקצתם אמרו שהוא מוליד כעס וקוצר וזה אומר
ככה וזה אומר ככה· ולא נכנסו דבריהם לתוך לב המלך· ויאמר המ
המלך לא זה וזה שאין רוח חיים בקרבן לומר דברים שיכנסו לי
לאזני· כי כולם דוברי כזבים· וישב המלך לארץ מר וזעף ויתעצב
אל לבו ולא רצה לאכול ולשתות· ויבואו כולם ונחמו וימאן להתנחם·
כיון שראה הנער כל הצער הזה שהמלך עושה והנדר שנדר
לעשות כל הכבוד הזה למי שיגיד לו· וזה אחד לו· קם כמו עמדו כל
כחכם וזהיר ועלה אל גנת ביתן המלך אל פתח חדר משכבו ורצ
ורצה ליכנס שם לדבר אל המלך· ויראוהו השוערים בגדיו פרועים
וראשו פרוע כאשר היה בשדה עם צאנו· אבל היה מאד יפה
תואר ויפה מראה· ויאמרו לו שוערי המלך מה טיבך אצל המלך·
ויאמר להם אם רצונכם אני רוצה לדבר אל המלך ולהגיד לו את
אשר עם לבבו וכל אשר ידיעה אגיד לו· וירוצו השוערים ויגידו
למלך· ויאמרו לו אדונינו המלך יחי מלכך ברוך· יש נער אחד
עומד בפתח החדר ורוצה לדבר אליך ואומר שיגיד לך כל אשר
עם לבבך· ויאמר המלך יבא· ויבא הנער לפניו וישתחו ואפיו אר
ארצה· ויאמר יחי המלך לעולם הנה צעיר אנכי לימים וכל חכמיך
ישישים ונתן האלהים בי דעת ותבונה להגיד למלך את אשר עם לבבו
ולא מאתי כי אם מאת הקב״ה אשר גלה סודו לעבדו· ואתה אדוני
המלך נדרת ליתן בתך וחצי מלכותך לאשר יגיד לך וכל מלכותך לאחר
אשר תצא נפשך בעבור החיים· אל כן דברת· כך נשבעת ואקיימה·
אומר לך מה זה ועל מה זה נקבצו שם כל העורבים ואמיתת הדבר
אומר לך לעין כל ותהיו דברי אמיתים ונכוחים· ויבואו כולם לשמוע
דברי הנער· ויען ויאמר אדוני המלך הט אזנך לאמרי פי ושמע

יכול מילתי׳ פעם אחת היה רעב גדול בכל הארץ׳ ולא היו העופות
יכולים למצוא די ספוקם בשדות׳ ובין תבין אדוני המלך לדברי דע
כי השלשה עופות שאתה רואה השנים זכרים והאחת באמצע
נקבה היא׳ והיא אשתו של אותו עורב היושב לימינה׳ ובשנת הרעב
גירש אשתו ואומר לה לכי לדרכך לאיזה מקום שתרצי׳ כי דיי לי
למצוא די ספוקי ולא יכולתי לעזור לך׳ הלכה הנקבה לדרכה ומצאה
זה העורב היושב לשמאלה׳ ואומר לה מי זאת בתי ואנה תלכי יחידה׳
ענתה הנקבה ואמרה לו אדוני דע כי גרשני בעלי מפני הרעב ואמר
די לו למצוא ספוקו׳ אומר לה הנה אתה אשתי ואין לי זוג׳ אם
תרצי להיות עמי אזון ואפרנס אותך כפי יכולתי ובלבד שתהיה
אשתי ולא תעזבי אותי בשביל אחר לעולם׳ אומרה לו טובים השנים
מן האחד׳ כן אעשה כאשר דברת׳ ויבא זה העורב ויקחה לו לאשה׳
ויהיו שניהם יחד׳ ופירנס אותה כל שני הרעבון ועתה כאשר שני
השבע ובא עתה בעלה הראשון ליקחיה כבתחילה׳ ועתה זה אומר
לכלכלתיה בשני רעבון ולקחתי אותה לי לאשה כי גרשתה אותה׳
ועתה באתה לגזול אותה ממני כשהשבע בא לעולם׳ זה אומר
ככה וזה אומר ככה׳ ובאו לדין׳ ולכן נקבצו כל העורבים האילו׳ כי הם
אינם יודעים הדין׳ ולשמוע מתוך הדבר והדין באו כולם׳ וזה לך האות
אחר אשר תאמר מה שנראה לך׳ מזה הדין ילכו כולם על המחוייב
ויהרגוהו וישליכו אותו כפני רגליך׳ ועתה אמור הדין כאשר יראה
בעיניך למי יהיה משפט הנקבה להיותלו לאשה׳ עמד המלך וכל
שריו ועבדיו ותמהו ודהו על השמועה שהם שומעים׳ הלך המלך
ויועץ לכל שריו ועבדיו ויאמרו כולם אותו שגרש אותה אין לו משפט
לשוב אותה לו לאשה כי גירשה אותה בשני רעבון׳ והואיל שזכה זה
בה ופירנס אותה לו תהיה האשה׳ הדבר יצא מפי המלך׳ וקמו כולם
על המחוייב והכוהו בכנפיהם ופצעוהו והרגוהו והשליכו אותו לפני
רגלי המלך והלכו כולם לדרכיהם׳ כיון שראה המלך כך׳ אומר אחרי
אשר הודיע אלהים אותך את כל זאת אין נבון וחכם כמוך׳ אתה
תהיה משנה ואתן לך כתי רק הכסא אגדל ממך׳ ובין כך ובין כך
העני אבי הבחור׳ ונעשה עני גמור לא נראה כעניותו מעולם כי לא
נשאר לו ולאשתו מאומה אפילו כדי לכסות אותם כי הם ערומים
ויחיפים הם׳ אמר הבחור למלך אדוני המלך אם מצאתי חן בעיניך
לתת את שאלתי אשר אשאל מעמך בזאת אדע כי חפצת בי׳ אומר
לו כל שאלתך דומלא׳ אז תשלח המלך להודיע בכל מלכותו שלא ישאר

333

99

זקן וזקנה עני ועשיר שלא יבואו לחופת בתו וגם אני רוצה ליתן
מים לרחוץ ידיהם כשיבואו כולם לאכול ונשלח ספרים אל כל מדינת
מלכותו ביד הרצים לבא לחופת בת המלך ויבואו כולם מכל עיר ומכל
פנה וגם אביו ואמו באו כמו כן כי כן מצות המלך ובאו אביו ואמו ו
שכבו להם אחורי הדלת כי ערומים ויתבוששו הלך הבחור ובקש בכל
עיר ובכל פנה אחריהם עד שמצאם אחורי הדלת ויאמר להם בואו
ברוכי ה' למה תעמדו הנה בואו אל תוך הבית עם האחרים ואל תשכבו
פה אמרו לו אדוני אל יחר בעיניך ואם רצונך הניחנו הנה כי אנחנו
ערומים ויחיפים ואין לנו בשת ליכנס עם האחרים הלך הבחור ויצו ל
אשר על ביתו הבא אותו האיש ואת אשתו הביתה ורחצם וסכם
והאכילם והשקם מכל טוב שהכן למענו והלבישם בגדי שש ורקמה
ועשה להם כל צרכם הוד והדר ולמענך לכל אשר יצוו אליך ואל
תאמר דבר זה לשום אדם וכה תעשה שלשה ימים להם כל מה שי
שתוכל וכן עשה ויהי ביום הרביעי ויבא הבחור לראות אביו ואמו
וירא אותם והנם שמחים וטובי לב אומר להם מי אתם ובאיזה
מקום אתם דרים היש לכם שום בנים ומה מעשיכם ויאמרו לו
עברים אנחנו ובמקום פלוני אנחנו דרים ולא היה לנו מעולם כי אם
בן אחד ועשיר סוחר הייתי מנעורי ועד היום הזה ועתה נפלתי
בזקנה ובעניות כאשר ראית ועתה נתנו אלהים למענו חן וחסד
לפניך ויהי מבורך ברוך אשר גמלתנו כל הטובות האלו כי מצאנו
חן בעיניך לתת אותנו למחיה ולחיותינו כיום הזה אומר להם ואותו
בן שאמרתם היכן הוא השיבו לו אם הוא מת או חי ובאיזה מקום
הוא ולא יכלו עוד להתאפק כי נכמרו רחמיהם לבכות ויאמר להם
למה אתם בוכים ואולי חסרים אתם שום דבר או תאבים אתם
לאכול ולשתות ויאמרו לא אדוני לא נכחד מאדוני דבר מה היה
המעשה מאותו בן שהיה לנו ויספרו לו את כל המעשיות אותם
ואת כל קורותם ולא כחדו וישאו את קולם בבכי גדול וגם נכמרו רחמיו
לבכות ויבך עמהם עד כי הגדיל ויקרא הוציאו כל איש מעלי ולא
עמד איש אתו בהתודע אותו להם ויאמר אני הוא בנך אשר השל
השלכתני אל הים וזאת אומר ובשביל שלא רציתי לומר לך מפני מה
שחקתי השלכת אותי אל הים וימן ה' אלהים דג גדול ובלעני ויספר
להם כל הענין ועתה אל תעצבו ואל יחר בעיניכם כי למחיה שלחני
אלהים לפניכם ועתה אהיה אחיך למלך ואטיב לכם ואתם תהיו לי
לראש והם לא יכלו לענות אותו כי נבהלו מפניו ויודע הדבר כי

כאו אותו ואביו׳ וייטב הדבר בעיני המלך והשרים׳ ויאמר לו המלך
אבין ואמר כאן אליך׳ כמיטב הארץ הושב אותם׳ ויקם הבחור וישתחו
לו אפיו ארצה ויאמר יחי אדוני המלך לעולם׳ ועשו המשתה והחופה
ולסוף נעשה מלך׳ לקיים מה שנאמר אכן מאסו הבונים היתה לראש
פינה׃

מעשה

בשלמה המלך שהיה מתגרה עם חירם מלך צר׳ ויבואו זה על זה׳ ויערכו אותם מלחמה׳
והיה ביניהם נהר אחד׳ ובעבר הנהר היה חיל מלך צר בעבר אחד
ויטעו שם אהליהם׳ ושלמה וחילו היו מעבר אחר לנהר׳ ובימי הק
הקיץ היה׳ ויזרח להם השמש׳ והיה היום חם מאד׳ ולא יכלו ל
לסבול החמימות הגדול׳ מה עשה שלמה שלח אחרי עופות
הקיץ ולבא אליו ולפרוש כנפיהם להיות סוככים עליו ועל
חייליותיו להיות להם לצל׳ ובאו עופות לרוב מאוד ויפרשו כנפיהם
ומעלה מהם סוככים בכנפיהם עליהם ויעשו להם צל על כל חיי
חיילותיו׳ כי שלמה היה מלך על כל החיות והבהמות והעופות
בחכמתו שנ׳ כן ויחכם מכל האדם׳ וישאו כל העופות את קולם
וירננו כל אחד לפי ענינו׳ וילך קולם עד מחנה חירם מלך צר׳
ויאמר חירם מה קול החזה באזני׳ ויאמרו עבדיו אדוני לא ידענו
אמר להם צאו וראו מה קול ההמון הזה׳ יצאו ויאהלו הם וראו
העופות פרושות בכנפיהם על כל חיל שלמה׳ ואמרו לו כך ראינו
אמר להם מי שמע כזאת ומי ראה כאלה׳ לא יתקרר דעתי עד
שאלך אני בעיני׳ מה עשה לקח שני פרשים עמו והלכו אל
מחנה שלמה ובאו שם בלא שום כלי זין׳ וכשראה שלמה את
חירם בא אליו תמה ואמר לו מה זה כי באתה אלי׳ אל ראות נ
נפלאות גדולות אלהים שהוא עושה עבורך׳ לקחו שלמה בין זר
זרועותיו ויחבקהו ויעש לו כבוד גדול וישב אותו בינו וידברו
יחד וכאשר היו מדברים יחד׳ בא נשר אחד ומשך אליו אחת
מכנפיו׳ וזרח השמש על ראש שלמה׳ אמר שלמה לנשר מדוע
עשית את הדבר הזה ועברתה מצותי׳ אל הנשר אדוני אל
יחר בעיניך כי משכתי אותי אל נקבתי לדבר ואומר אליה על
ידעת כי יהושע כהן גדול יאות׳ ובתו תינשין וממזר אחד
ומזה חרה לי מאוד׳ ועל זה משכתי אליה׳ אל מזה אשמור
הנערה בטוב׳ ויפה עשית לגלות לי את הדבר הזה׳ אל חירם
למלך שלמה מה דברת אל הנשר ומה השיב לך׳ אל כך וכך׳ וסיפר

337

לו הכל· א״ל אם כן שמלכת על העליונים ועל התחתונים מי יוכל
להיות כנגדך לך אתה מלכה אשריך ואשרי עבדיך המשרתים
אותך· הלכו ועשו שלום ביניהם· וזהו שכתוב ויהי שלום בין חירם
ובין שלמה ויכרתו ברית שניהם· מה עשה שלמה שלח אחר בתו
של יהושע כהן גדול· וישם אותה למשמרת בתוך מגדל אחד· וישם
עמה אשה לשומרה· ויסגר כל דלתות המגדל· ולא היה יכול שום
אדם בעולם לבא אליהן· והן מביאין מאכלן בחבל שהן מושכין אליהן·
פעם אחת בא נשר פורח עליהן ונפל לתוך המגדל מבין רגליו תינוק
אחד ביניהן· והוא היה ממזר· כי השליכו אמו ובא הנשר ולקחו ·ל
והביאו שם· והן האכילוהו ורחצוהו וסכוהו ונתגדל עליהן שם
מאד· והיו אוהבים זה את זה הנער ואת בתו של יהושע עד
שבא עליה· ותהר האשה ממנו· יום אחד בא שלמה לשם ויפתח
את הדלת ומצאו שם אותו האיש· ויתמה מאד· ויאמר לו מי ל
אתה והיאך באתה הנה וסיפרו לו כל הענין· אמר שלמה יהי שם
ה׳ מבורך אשר קיים דברו הטוב· ועלי נאמר ויחכם מכל האדם און
לא חכמתי הנה טרחתי לבטל הגזירה ולא יכולתי·

affert a Jalkut et Catal. l. N. 3740

מעשה היאך לקחו יעקב ובניו את עיר
שכם· כתיב ויסעו ויהי חתת
אלהים· ואמרו רבותינו כשהרגו
שמעון ולוי את שכם נפלה פחד ורעדה על כל האומות שסמ
שסביבותם· ואמרו שני בני יעקב הרגו כרך גדול של שכם· אם
יתקבצו כולם על אחת כמה וכמה· מה עשה יעקב אסף כל
רכושו ללכת אל יצחק אביו· וכיון שהלך מהלך שמונה ימים
פגע בחיל כבד מאד כחול אשר על שפת הים· ואותו חיל
יצא מנינוה לקחת מס מכל העולם· ולכבש את כל העולם תח
תחתיו· וכיון שבא אותו חיל בארץ קרוב לשכם· שמעו השמועה
זה שעשו בני יעקב· מיד חרה אפם של אנשי נינוה· ובאו
כנגד יעקב· להלחם עמו· וכיון שהרגיש יעקב בבואת חיל· אמר
יעקב לבניו אל תיראו בני הקב״ה ילחם לכם כנגד אויביכם
רק הסירו אלהי הנכר אשר בתוככם והטהרו והחליפו שמל
שמלותיכם· ויחגר יעקב חרבו בימינו וקשתו בשמאלו· והלך
כנגד אותו חיל· והתחיל להרוג בהם· כנגד עשרה ושמונים
אלפים מן החשובים שבהם· אז יהודה בנו אבי כבר יגעת
ויעפת הניחני להלחם כנגדם· א״ל יעקב יהודה בני ידעתי

את כחך ואת גבורתך כי רב הוא ואין כמוך בעולם בגבורה׳ פחד אביך
יהיה בעזרך׳ לך והלחם בעדם׳ וילך יהודה כנגדם כחיה עזה ופניו כ
כפני אריה׳ וילחם בהם ויהרוג בהם מן החיל שנים עשר ריבוא׳ כולם
אנשי מלחמה׳ ואנשי שם׳ ויבא לוי אחיו לעזור לו׳ ותהי המלחמה פנים
ואחור ליהודה וללוי אחיו׳ ותגבר יד המלחמה על יהודה׳ ויהרוג מן ה
החיל עוד חמשת אלפים כולם שולפי חרב׳ ויבא לוי ויך בימינו ובש
ובשמאלו׳ ויפלו החיל לפניו כאשר יפול התבואה לפני הקוצרים׳ ויאמ
ויאמרו אנשי נינוה׳ איש אל רעהו עד מתי נלחם עם המשחיתים הא
האלו׳ נחזור לדרכינו לארצינו׳ פן ישחיתו בנו עד בלתי השאיר לנו ש
שריד׳ ויאמר להם המלך אי גבורים אי אדירים אי חזקים׳ מה עלתה
בדעתכם שאמרתם לשוב לארצכם׳ וכי זו היא גבורתכם שכבשתם
כמה ארצות וכמה מלכים וכמה אומות׳ ועתה אינכם יכולים להלחם
כנגד שנים עשר איש׳ וכאשר ישמעו האומות והמלכים שכבשנו תחת
ידינו לתת לנו מס ויתאספו עלינו כולם כאיש אחד׳ ויתעוללו בנו ויעשו
בנו כרצונם׳ ויתחזקו אנשי נינוה העיר הגדולה ויגדל כבודכם ושמכם׳
אל תתנו לכם לבוא לפני אויביכם׳ ויהי כאשר שמעו את דברי מלכם
ויאותו להלחם עוד וישלחו שלוחים בכל הארצות שכבשו לבא להם
לעזרה׳ ויערכו מלחמה עם בני יעקב׳ ויאמר יעקב לבנו בני התחזקו
והיו לאנשים׳ והלחמו בשונאיכם׳ ויתחזקו בני יעקב ושנים עשר וה
רחוק מזה ויעקב אביהם הולך לפניהם׳ וחרבו בימינו וקשתו בשמאלו׳
וילחם יעקב ביום ההוא ותהי המלחמה פנים ואחור׳ ויך בהם מכה
רבה מאד׳ ונקבצו אלפים איש על יעקב לבדו והכותו ויתפשו יעקב
וידלג באלפים אלה כדילוג אחד׳ עד שלא ידעו היכן הוא׳ ותגבר
יד יעקב על החיל וישחת ארינה ביום ההוא כעשרים ושתים ריבוא
כולם אנשי מלחמה׳ ויהי לעת ערב כאשר סבר יעקב לעת מפעהרי׳
וימצא פתאום תשעים אלף׳ ויקם יעקב ויעמד בפרץ׳ ויחל להרוג בהם
כפעם בפעם׳ ותשבור החרב אשר ביד יעקב׳ ויהי כאשר ראה יעקב
כי נשברה החרב בידו׳ לקח מן האבנים הגדולות וישחקם בידו כמו
סיד׳ וישלך על פני החיל ולא יכלו לראות מפני הסיד׳ ואף כי הגיע הע
הלילה כי בא השמש׳ וינח יעקב בלילה ההוא׳ ויהי ממחרת ויאמר
יהודה ליעקב הנה נלחמת אבי אתמול׳ ואתה עיף ויגע׳ ואני אלחם
היום׳ ויאמר לו יעקב יהודה בני לך והנצח׳ וילך יהודה וילחם ביום
ההוא׳ וכאשר ראו החיל את פני יהודה שהיו פניו כפני אריה׳ ושיניו
כשיני אריה׳ וייראו ממנו מאד׳ ויתחזקו להלחם כנגדו ביד רמה ותגבר

338

·ט·

המלחמה על יהודה מאד מאד וידלג יהודה ויקפוץ בתוך החיל מזה
לזה ומזה על זה הלוך והכות כאשר יעשה הפרעש ויך יהודה מן
הבקר עד תשעה שעות ביום שמונים אלף וארבע מאות ותשעים וששה
איש שולף חרב ודורכי קשתות ויעף יהודה מאד ויבו זבולון אחיו מ׳
משמאלו ויעזור לו וילחם וישחת מהם ארבעה שלשים אלף איש וכאשר
נח יהודה מעט בנעשו ובקינתו ויחרוק שיניו בחזקה כאשר מרעים
השורים בתקופת תמוז וישמעו החיל וינוסו שמונה עשר מילי
וינח יהודה בלילה ההוא ויהי ממחרת ביום השלישי ויבאו החיל עוד
להלחם ולהנקם ויתקעו בשופרות ויאמר יעקב אל בניו בני לכו והלחמו
בשונאיכם ויאמרו יששכר וגד אנו נלחם היום בשונאינו ויאמר להם
אביהם לכו והלחמו ושאר אחיכם יעמדו על המשמר עד אשר תיעפו
ותיגעו ויעזרו לכם ויגשו יששכר וגד וילחמו ביום ההוא וישחיתו מן
החיל בארבעים ושמונה אלף וינוסו מן החיל במערות כנגד שנים עשר
ריבוא ויבואו יששכר וגד ויקחו מן האילנות אשר ביערים ויעשו אש
גדול לפני פתח המערה וכאשר רבתה האש אמרו החיל זה לזה על מה
אנחנו יושבים במערה הזאת ונמות מן העשן ומחום האש טרם נלחם
כנגדם אולי ניגע ויצאו מן המערה לעדרין דרך צפוני ויערכו מלחמה
כנגד יששכר וגד ותהי המלחמה פנים ואחור ויראו דן ונפתלי וירוצו
בחוזקה עד החיל ויכו מימינם ומשמאלם עד אשר באו אל אחיהם
וילחמו ארבעתם יששכר וגד דן ונפתלי ויבאו ביום ההוא משאר
ארצות לעזור לאנשי ניגה עם רב כחול אשר על שפת הים ויראו בני
יעקב את החיל הגדול הזה ויקבצו כולם בראש אחד ויעמדו להכות
ולהרוג בחיל מכה רבה מאד בלי מספר ותגבר יד יהודה על החיל
ויך בהם מכה רבה מאד וינוסו כל החיל מפניו ובראות בני יעקב יורד
מעסת החיל ויקומו בחומה עזה וירדפו אחריהם ויאמרו החיל למה
נגוס מפניהם נלחם כנגדם אולי נגביר עליהם כי עייפים המה ויבאו
וילחמו כנגדם ותהי המלחמה גדולה מאד וירא יעקב כי גברה המלחמה
על בניו ויקם ויקפוץ ויך בימינו ובשמאלו ויפלו לפניו כאשר יפלו העשב
לפני הבהמה ותגבר יד החיל ויפרידו בין יהודה ובין אחיו וירא יעקב
ויחרוק [יהודה] בשיניו גם הוא וישמע אחיו ויבאו אליו לעזור לו וייעף מאד
ויצמא למים ולא היה לו מים ויתקע אצבעו בארץ בחוזקה ויצאו המים
כנגדו ויראו החיל את עליית המים כנגד יהודה ויאמרו איש אל אחיו [illegible]
אעסה [illegible] מן המשחיתים האלו כי אלהים נלחם להם וינוסו כל החיל
דרך היער וירדפו בני יעקב אחריהם וירדפום ויכום מכה גדולה

כלי מספר· וקיעת מהם נסו אל נפשם· ולא יכלו בני יעקב לרדוף אחר
אחריהם· ויתקעו בשופרות ויחזרו אל אהליהם· ויוסף לא היה שם
וייער לבני יעקב מאד מאד על יוסף על אחיהם· ויאמרו שמא הרגוהו
או הוליכוהו בשבי· ויתקעו בשופר וירץ נפתלי אחיו לחפש אחריו וימצ
וימצאהו נלחם עם החיל· ויקרא נפתלי הראתה זה יוסף אחי· ויאמר
אני· ויעזור לו נפתלי· וישחיתו מן העם כלי מספר· וירדפו הנשארים
ויטביעו במי היאור· ויעסבו החיל לפניהם ויחזרו לרדוף אחריהם· ול
ועליהם אמר שלמה טובים השנים מן האחד· ויבאו אל יעקב אביהם
וישמח ולא רדפו אחריהם שאר בני המלכות· וילך בטח אל יצחק

מעשה

אביו: באדם אחד שהיה עשיר
גדול והיה לו אשה יפה מאד והיה
אוהב אותה ביותר· והיה בחצירו ד
ארבע חומות גבוהות ובצורות מאד· והיה בו פתח פתוח לחצירו· ובתוך
גבאותן החומות יש מנהג כל הנכנס לא יצא ולא יחזור לביתו וטע
ושעירים יקרו שם· ויש אומרים ששם פתחו של גהינם· והיה האיש
רע ובליעל מאד ואשתו רשעה· ובנים לא היו להם· והיו היתה
מתאוה תמיד לבא על אותו פתח ולראות מה שבתוכן· ובעלה
ממאן אותה תמיד ושומר לפי שיודע שדעתה לשם· פעם אחת
היה צריך המלך לאותו איש ושלח אחריו· וצוה האיש לאשר על עמיה
ביתו לשמור אשתו ולהיות תמיד· וילך אחריה בכל מקום שתלך· הל
הלך האיש אל המלך כאשר שלח אחריו ושהא שם· ובין כך באו ל
האשה ואמרה לאשר על ביתה· שמעני ועשה רצוני והניחני לילך
לפני הפתח ואני אתן לך כל מה שתרצה· כי ידעתי אם תעשה לי ד
מה שאני מבקשת ממך כי הטיב איטיב עמך· אמר לה אל נא אדונתי
אל נא תעשי זאת ואל תפסידי ותאבדי עצמך בחנם ואודיע עלה
אותי ויאמר לשומרך כבבת עינו· כי נפלאת אהבתך עליו ומאד
נעימת לו· ואל תעשי הרעה הגדולה הזאת· ולא תורד שיבתו ברעה
שאולה· אמרה לו חייך שלא אלך אלא כנגד הפתח מרחוק כמטחוי
קשת· והוא לא רצה לתת לה רשות· ויהי היא מתאוית ללכת
מאד עד שהלכה לחצר בעל כרחו ושלא בעובן· ואין איש אתםד
בבית· צעק האיש קול גדול ויספק כפיו וינער האיש מאד
וירץ אחריה והיא הלכה על לפני הפתח· וכיון שבאת שם שמה
השטן אחד מכפים את ידו ומשכה אלין לפנים והדלת סגר אחריה·
אמר האיש ואני אנה אני בא מן העיר אשר ימינו את אדוני:

339

הלך האיש והטמינו בחדר והיה שם עד בוא אדוניו אל ביתו וכיון
שבא ולא ראה את אשתו ואת עבדו נפל לאפיו ארצה ויתעצב
רוחו ויתעלף ובאו כל שכיניו לנחמו וימאן להתנחם ויאמר כי ארד
אל אשתי אבל שאולה ויבך אותה בכי גדול הלך ופשפש בכל ביתו
ולא מצאו עד שבא לחדר משכבו ושמע שם גנח ומתאונח ויאמר
מי אתה האתה זה פלוני עבדי אשר שמעתי גונח א״ל אני עבדך
המחויב לך ויבא אליו ויפל לפניו ויבך ויתחנן לו א״ל היכן אשתי
עמד וסיפר לו כל המעשה א״ל בשבועה לא אשב ולא אשקוט ולא
אנוח עד שאדע היכן היא ובאיזה מקום היא ומה היא עושה ואם
אוכל להיות עמה מה עשה נתן כל אשר לו לקרוביו והלך לו בשבי
עד שנכנס בתוך יער גדול אחד והלך בתוכו מהלך ששה ימים
ופגע באיש אחד גדול מאד בקומה ושחור ומכוער ביותר נתן
לו שלום והחזיר לו שלום ויחרד האיש ויפחד מאד ממנו כי לא
ראה מעולם כמוהו א״ל האיש הגדול ידעתי מה אתה מבקש את
אשתך אתה מבקש לראות אם תרצה לבא עמי אראך אותה
מקומה ואתה תדבר אליה א״ל בשביל כל אוצרות המלך אם היא
רוצה ליתנם לי לא הייתי רוצה לילך עמך א״ל האיש הגדול יש בביתך
בביתך שום אדם שאתה בוטח בו א״ל הן א״ל הוליכהו אלי היום
שלשה ימים ותמצא אותי הנה נפטר ממנו והלך לו ובא לביתו
ונתקבצו כל אוהביו אליו ושאלו לו אם מצא עצה או שמע שום דבר
מאשתו אמר להם הן מי יש בכם שום אדם שרוצה לעשות מה
שאני אומר אם עשיתי שום טובה שבעולם לשום אדם מכם עתה
בא העת והגיע הזמן שיכול לגמול לי כל מה שעשיתי לו כל ימיו
קם אחד מנעריו ואמר אדוני אתה גדלתני ורוממתני מנעורי ועד
עתה תגזור עלי כל רצונך ואקיים כל מצותך ואהיה זהיר ושמר
לכל אשר תצוני א״ל בך חפצתי כי מצאתיך נאמן ונעים מאד
וכך אני בוטח בך בא עמי ועשה כל אשר איעצך וילכו שניהם יחדיו
ויבאו ביער עד מקום אשר היה שם בתחילה וימצאו שם האיש
האיש הגדול זירזו הנער אותו ויפחד ממנו מאד א״ל דבר כבר
צריך אתה לילך עם זה האיש והוא יוליכך למקום אשתי ואתה
תדבר אליה ואם תוכל להביאה עמך אתן לך ממון כבד ותהיה
יורש מכל אשר לי א״ל כן אעשה כאשר דברת הלך עמו והוליכו
לתוך גהינם וראה שם הרבה בני אדם שהיה מכיר סובלים דינם
בגהינם ואדונו חזר לביתו א״ל הנער הראיני את אשת אדוני

הוליכו לחדר אחד וכדומה לו שהיה כל החדר הקירות והגג מינעה
זהב אופיר והריצפה מאבנים טובות ואדומות ומתלהבות וראה אשת
אדוני יושבת בקתדרא של זהב ומלובשת בגדי זהב וכל סביבותיה
זהב כמדומה לו והיה בפניה שולחן של זהב ערוך וכל מיני מאכלה
אדומים ויש לה שמשים הרבה ויש מהם חותכין בפניה מאכלה ויש
מהם מוזגין לה יין לבן בתוך כוס של זהב כיון שראה אותה נפל לארץ
ליופיה וזיוה ואומר לה ברוך שחלק מכבודו לבריות בשר ודם שלא
ראיתי מעולם שום מלכה מכובדת כל כך כאשר אני רואה שמכבדין
אותך ואדוני מתענה עבורך ואינו אוכל כל הימים הללו ומתענה ואנ
והוא שלחני אחריך שתבואי אליו אם תוכלי אומרה לו אדוני שמעני
כל מה שאתה רואה סביבותיי אש בוערה החדר הזה והשולחן וכל
מה שאני מלובשת וקתדרא שאני יושבת בה וכל זה שאני אוכלת אש
הוא עד אבדון תאכל גופי ובשרי והיין לבן שאתה רואה שהן מוזגין
לי בכוס של זהב הכוס של אש והיין הוא אבר מהותך שאני שותה
כל שעה ושעה ואילו היה כל העולם כולו שלי הייתי נותן אותו כדי עון
לעת שעה אחת לחוץ לקרר אותי שאני שורפת נשמתי וגופי וכך
תאמר אל אדוני ותאומר לו שכל פושעי ישראל בגופן כך הם נדונים
ותאומר לו שיעשה תשובה מן מעשיו הרעים כי גדול כח התשובה
אומר לה ובאיזה עון יש לך כל הדין הקשה הזה אומרה לו מפני הרבה
רעות ועונות שעשיתי כי נאפתי לאיש אחר וחיללתי שבת ונדה
הייתי שוכבת עם בעלי ועם עניים ויתומים לא ריחמתי וכזבות וטמאות
עשיתי אומר לה היש יכולת לשום אדם לפדותך מן הדין הזה אומרה
לו לא הואיל שלא היה לי בנים מעולם ואם היה לי בן אחד מבעלי
שיוכל לומר ברכו את ה' המבורך והציבור עונין ברוך ה' המ
המבורך לעולם ועד וקדיש כמו הייתי נפטרת בסוף שנתי אומרה לו
אלך ואספר לו כל זאת ונתנה לו טבעת אחד שעדיין היה באצבעה שהוא
נתן לה ואמרה לו אמור שיהיה זה לו לאות שראתה אומר אות מכל
אשר תאמר אליו נפטר ממנה והלך לו עם האיש שהביאו שמה
והוליכו עד הדוקוס שלקחו ונפטר ממנו והלך לביתו כיון שראוהו אד
אדונו שמח שמחה גדולה וסיפר לו כל מה שראה ונתן לו האות והאמין
לדבריו מה עשה אותו האיש הלך לבית הכנסת ובקש רחמים לפני
הקב"ה בבכי גדול ובשברון לב ועשה תשובה גמורה ולא זז משם עד
שפרחה נשמתו ויצתה בת קול ואמרה אותו האיש מזומן לחיי העולם
הבא ולקיים מה שנאמר להנחיל אוהבי יש ואוצרותיהם אמלא

סליק ע' המעשה
בלי שום דופי ושטינה

Appendix B

List of Tales in *Sefer ha-Ma'asim*

1. The Bizarre Deeds of Elijah the Prophet
2. The Loan
3. The Heir's Test
4. Joab's Valor
5. The Two-Headed Man
6. The Drunkard and His Sons
7. The Three Treasures
8. The Demon in the Carob Tree
9. Abraham in the Furnace
10. Ḥananiah, Mishael, and Azaria
11. Generation of Dispersion and the Tower of Babel
12. The Mother and Her Sons
13. The Man Who Never Took an Oath
14. The Sabbath Observer and the Bear
15. Ukva
16. Who Is the Thief?
17. One of Ten
18. The Commandment of *Ẓiẓit* (Fringes)
19. The Book of Genesis
20. The Cow That Observed the Sabbath
21. Joseph-Who-Reveres-the Sabbath
22. The Butcher from Ludkiya
23. Turnus Rufus and R. Akiva
24. The Defamed Woman
25. R. Meir and Judah of Anatot
26. R. Meir and Kiddor

27. Ben Sever and Shefifon Ben Layish
28. Joḥanan and the Scorpion
29. The Seven Good Years
30. Slander Kills Three
31. Saved from Drowning by Charity
32. R. Akiva's Daughter and the Snake
33. Mattiah b. Ḥarash
34. The Loan
35. A Valley Filled with Gold
36. A Precious Stone from Heaven
37. From Rejoicing to Mourning
38. Hadrian and the Old Man
39. The *Ḥasid* and the Ruler
40. R. Ḥanina b. Dosa and the Snake
41. Do Not Fail to Attend Public Prayers
42. Solomon's Scribes
43. The Weasel and the Pit
44. The Spies and the Giants in Canaan
45. Soft-Shelled Walnuts
46. R. Joshua b. Levi and the Angel of Death
47. R. Joshua b. Elem and Ninus the Butcher
48. That Which Was Stolen Is Returned by Guile
49. Torah Saves from Death
50. The Pious Pretender
51. The Power of a Single Act of Charity
52. A Slave for Seven Years
53. One Man in a Thousand Have I Found
54. The Hard-Boiled Egg
55. The Poor Bachelor and His Maiden Cousin
56–59. R. Pinḥas b. Yair
60. The *Ḥasid* and the Tax Collector's Son
61. Ukva
62. A Meal of Herbs
63. The Tribulations of Naḥum Ish Gamzo
64. Naḥum Ish Gamzo and His Mission to the Emperor
65. The Grateful Dead
66. The Prophecy of the Ravens
67. The Maiden in the Tower
68. The War of Jacob and His Sons with Nineveh
69. The Portal to Gehenna

Appendix C

List of Texts in Ms. Bodl. Or. 135 (1466)

1. Abraham Habavli, *Sefer hashorashim* (a grammatical treatise), 1a–6a
2. A list of homonyms, 6a–10b
3. Solomon Pirḥon, *Maḥberet ha'arukh* (on grammar issues and a dictionary), 11a–230b
4. Blank pages, 231a–231b
5. A list of homonyms with a French translation, transcribed, 232a–237b
6. Alphabet of Ben-Sira, 237b–255a
7. The tale of "The Tannah and the Restless Dead," 255a–255b
8. "*Ma'aseh Yerushalmi*" ("The Tale of a Jerusalemite"), 255b–256b
9. *Mishlei shu'alim shel R. Berakhiah Hanakdan* (*Fox Fables of R. Berakhiah Hanakdan*), 256b–290a
10. The tale of "The Deposit," 290b–291b
11. *Mishlei Sendebar* (*Tales of Sendebar*), 292a–300a
12. *Sefer ha-ma'asim* (*The Book of Tales*), 300a–339b
13. *Divre hayamim shel Moshe Rabbenu* (*The Chronicles of Moshe Rabbenu*), 340a–346b
14. *Midrash aseret hadibrot* (*Midrash of the Ten Commandments*), 346b–352a
15. *Midrash vayosha*, 352a–356a
16. *Agadot shel dibrot* (*Tales of the [Ten] Commandments*), 356a–358b
17. *Otot hamashiaḥ* (*Signs of the Messiah*), 358b–361a
18. R. Menaḥem b. Perez of Hebron, "*Masa be'eretẓ yisra'el*" ("A Trip in the Land of Israel"), 361a–363b

Appendix D

Indexes of Tale Types and Motifs

Note: Left column refers to the tale type or motif, and right column to tale no. in *Sefer ha-ma'asim.*

Tubach

214	Three Questions Asked of St. Andrew—A bishop, devoted to St. Andrew, is tempted by the devil in the shape of a young woman	33
223	Angel Explains God's Justice	60
255	Hermit and Angel I	1
281	St. Anthony Puts Foot in Fire	33
506	King's Daughter as Bath-woman. A hermit wishes to know his rewards and learns that they are inferior to those of a bath-woman	47
522	Bear Whispers to Man	14
636	Bird-language as Reward	66
696	Blind Man Regains Twenty Pounds	26, 48
815	Honorable Burial for Rich Man	60
1025	Christ-child in Star	9
1071	Scholar Vanishes from Magic Circle—A scholar vanishes from the magic circle when he takes a gold ring offered him by a demon in the form of a beautiful woman. He is carried to hell.	69
1272	Shooting at Father's Corpse	17
1282	Three Counsels Given to Son	41
1444	Daughter Married to Poor Man	61
1651	Devils as Women Tempt Man in Vain	33
1898	Chaste Empress	24

1920	Legend of St. Eustace	13
2205	Fridolin	41
2309	Goat Enticed by Wolf	25
2375	Romance of St. Gregory (Legend of St. Gregory)	27
2443	Harlot and Repentant Priest	18
2500	Heaven and Hell shown in Vision	60
2832	Love for St. John the Baptist	61
3057	Lion Faithful to Knight	14
3355	Man Tricked into Returning Money	26, 48
3755	Phoenix Arises Out of Flames	28
4102	Ring in Fish	21
4741	Temptation Resisted by Fire	33
4964	Treasure Stolen by Youngest Son	16
4969	Treasure-chest Full of Stones	26, 50
5039	Usurer Eats Gold in Hell	69
5054	Treasure of Usurer Turns to Serpents	7

ATU

123	The Wolf and the Kids	25
156	Androcles and the Lion	14
156A	The Faith of a Lion	14
179	What the Bear Whispered in His Ear	14
310	The Maiden in the Tower (Rapunzel)	67
312	Bluebeard	69
330	The Smith Outwits the Devil	46
505	The Grateful Dead	65
507	The Monster's Bride	65
517	The Boy Who Learned Many Things/The Boy Who Understands the Language of Birds	66
531	The Clever Horse	28
551	The Sons on a Quest for a Wonderful Remedy for Their Father/Water of Life	28
554	The Grateful Animals	28
612	The Three Snake-Leaves	53
653	The Four Skillful Brothers	55

Th.

B11.11	Fight with Dragon	27
B32	Phoenix	28
B143.0.8	Crow as Prophetic Bird	66
B211.6.1	Speaking Snake	25
B216	Knowledge of Animal Language	66
B259.2	Sabbath-keeping Cow	20
B391	Transformation of Serpent to Person	25
B498.1	Helpful Dragon	27
B549.2	Dragon Makes Bridge over a Stream for a Holy Person	27
B613.1	Snake Paramour	25
D452.3	[Transformation of] Sand to another Object	64
D1080	Magic Weapon	64
D1856	Death Evaded: Person Enters the Next Life without Dying	46
D2003	Forgotten Fiancée	43
E341	The Grateful Dead	65
F402.6.1	Demon Lives in Tree	8
G303.3.1.12	Devil in Form of Woman	33
H1556	Test of Fidelity	53
H486.2	Test of Paternity: Shooting at Father's Corpse	17
H492	Test of Faithfulness of Husband and Wife	53
H492.1	Husband Refuses to Murder His Wife for High Honor	53
J123	Wisdom of Child Decides Lawsuit	54
J214	Suffering in Youth or Old Age	29
J225.0.1	Angel and Hermit	1
J225.0.1.1	Angel Explains to Hermit Why God Lets a Sinner Die in Peace and Have Big Funeral While Holy Hermit Is Slain by a Wild Beast	60
J1176.4	A Two-Headed Man Is Only One Man	5
J1191.2	Suit over Chickens Produced from Boiled Eggs	54
J1321	The Unrepentant Drunkard	6
J1321.1	Where Did He Get the Wine?	6
J144	Well-trained Kid Does Not Open Door to Wolf	25
J2411	Foolish Imitation of a Miracle (magic)	64
K523.0.1	Illness Feigned to Escape Unwelcome Marriage	43

IFA

Glossary

aggadah Lit. "narrative"; rabbinic teaching that is not Halakha (i.e., Jewish law). The *aggadah* encompasses those portions of the Bible that include narrative, history, ethical maxims, and prophecies. Like Halakha, it is part of the literature of the Oral Law. It is mainly the work redacted in the Land of Israel from the time of the Second Temple to the end of the Talmudic period.

arod A mythological black snake or a striped reptile mentioned in the Talmud, created from the crossbreeding of a snake and a turtle.

bekerasim ubelula'ot Lit., "with clips and loops" (cf. Exodus 26:11): a technical term in Ashkenazi pietism that designates a mystical system of numerical links between Jewish prayers and scriptures based on analogical structures of word counts and letters.

ger toshav A legal term for the status of gentiles who undertake certain defined Jewish precepts.

Halakha Jewish law as prescribed in the Bible and rabbinic literature.

ḥasid (sing.); *ḥasidim* (pl.) A pious man; at times indicates a social status, such as that of the Pietists in medieval Ashkenaz.

Ḥasidei Ashkenaz An ideological and social circle of Ashkenazic Pietists founded in the second half of the twelfth and early thirteenth century by R. Samuel he-Ḥasid, and his son, R. Judah (1150–1217). The first centers of this movement were in Germany, in the communities of Mainz, Speyer, and Worms, later spreading also to northern France. *Sefer ḥasidim*, mainly written by R. Judah he-Ḥasid and influential throughout the centuries, teaches the ethics of piety and the theology of *Ḥasidut Ashkenaz*. The repentance doctrine of *Ḥasidei Ashkenaz* is prominent in *Sefer ḥasidim* and in *Sefer haroke'aḥ*, by

R. Eleazar b. Judah of Worms, in its layered and severe atonement system. Another literary trend of *Ḥasidei Ashkenaz* is manifested in a body of esoteric works, some including mystical elements.

ḥesed shel emet An act of true kindness without expectation of reward, usually relating to acts done on behalf of the dead, such as attending a funeral and burial.

Ḥibbur yafeh mehayeshu'a An eleventh-century collection of homilies and stories by R. Nissim of Kairouan intended to hearten his audience in times of distress.

Kaddish A hymn of sanctification of God's name that is part of the daily liturgy. During the Middle Ages a custom emerged in which orphans would recite the *Kaddish* to benefit their deceased parents in the afterlife.

Ma'aseh be- "A Tale of . . ."; an opening formula for tales, equivalent to "Once upon a time." In the Talmud, it designates a tale that is believed to be true.

melumad benisim Lit., "learned in miracles"; the phrase usually relates to a righteous person who often experiences miracles through intentional prayer.

Midrash (sing.); *midrashim* (pl.) A body of interpretations to the biblical verses as taught by the rabbis of the post-Temple era, including stories based on biblical scenes and characters.

Midrash aseret hadibrot A tenth-century compilation of homilies and tales on the Ten Commandments; originating from Persia or Babylonia, it was copied and redacted throughout the Middle Ages in many different versions from the East and from Europe.

Mishnah Earliest authoritative work of rabbinic law, redacted c. 200 CE in the Land of Israel.

miẓva (sing.); *miẓvot* (pl.) A deed that follows Jewish precepts or commandments.

petiḥah A midrashic proem used to introduce the weekly Torah reading.

Rashi R. Shlomo Yitzhaki (France, 1040–1105): One of the most important rabbinic scholars of the Middle Ages. His commentaries on the Bible and the Talmud provide basic explanations of the texts that are the basis for virtually all further rabbinic study of the works.

reẓon habore Lit., "the will of the Creator"; a theological term in Ashkenazi pietism. It signifies a norm of behavior that seeks to reflect the internal will of the Creator by way of intensive study of scripture and rabbinic texts.

Shekhinah The Divine Presence; in rabbinical literature the term refers to the immanence of God in the world.

sodot hatefila Lit., "The secrets of the liturgy"; a term used by the *Ḥasidei Ashkenaz* to designate the mysticism of the prayers. Cf. *bekerasim ubelula'ot.*

Talmud bavli The Babylonian Talmud; the foundational work of Jewish law, theology, and interpretation completed in Sasanian Iraq around the sixth century CE.

Talmud yerushalmi The Palestinian Talmud or Jerusalem Talmud; a parallel work to the Babylonian Talmud, redacted in the Land of Israel around the fifth century CE. It never achieved the same importance or authority as the Babylonian Talmud.

Tanḥuma A later Midrashic compilation containing homilies on the Pentateuch. The work exists in multiple recensions, which reached their final forms sometime between the seventh and ninth centuries CE.

teshuvat haba'ah Lit., "the penance that involuntarily confronts the sinner." In this stage of repentance, if the sinner is involuntarily confronted with the cause of his past sin, he is expected to withstand temptation (cf. b*Yomah* 86b).

teshuvat hagader Lit., "the penance of [making] a safeguard." The sinner is instructed to surround himself with safeguards, beyond the normative percepts of Jewish law, to avoid committing the same sin he committed in the past. *Teshuvat hagader* and *Teshuvat haba'ah* cannot be practiced simultaneously.

teshuvat hakatuv Lit., "the penance equivalent to Scripture." The sinner commits himself (through his rabbi's instructions) to a penance that is equivalent to that designated for an identical sin according to scripture. Thus, for example, a death decree in scripture would be equivalent, in the Ashkenazi penalty system, to severe mortifications that are experienced as death.

teshuvat hamishkal Lit., "the penance of weighed suffering"; a penance that is weighed against the pleasure derived from the sin.

(The four stages of *teshuvah* form a coherent and systematic repentance doctrine of *Ḥasidei Ashkenaz*, which combines objective and objective-spiritual parameters.)

Torah The Pentateuch.

Tosafot A genre of commentaries on the Talmud composed in France and Germany during the High Middle Ages. The Tosafist school was founded by students and descendants of Rashi, but in contrast to Rashi's focus on the simple meaning of the text, the Tosafists emphasized dialectical argument and debate. Tosafot commentaries are found on the pages of all printed editions of Talmud, opposite Rashi's commentary.

ẓadeket A righteous woman.

ẓadik (sing.); *ẓadikim* (pl.) A righteous man; righteous people.

ẓidduk hadin Vindication of divine judgment.

ẓiẓit Lit. "fringes"; ritual knotted tassels worn by Jewish men on the *tallit* or *tallit katan* (cf. Numbers 15:38–39).

Epilogue

Tales in Context
A Historical Perspective

By Elisheva Baumgarten

With the help of God who works miracles
I shall embark on writing these tales.

With these words, the copyist/editor of *Sefer ha-ma'asim* set out to create the collection of sixty-nine tales that comprise the compilation.[1] The rhymed formula used here connects between the tales (*ma'asim*) and the miracles (*nissim*). These stories are just that—tales—and at the same time they communicate explicit messages to their audience: the miracles of God, along with pointers on how to encourage oneself and one's offspring to be better Jews. The reference to the miracles of God suggests, at least partially, the appeal of the stories.[2] Alongside the entertainment derived from them, they were expected

The research for this essay began as part of the author's joint work with Rella Kushelevsky (ISF grant 693/08) and was completed as part of her current European Research Council Project, Beyond the Elite: Jewish Daily Life in Medieval Europe (GA No. 681507).

1. Bodleian Library, University of Oxford, Ms. Bodl. Or. 135, fol. 300a.
2. The appeal of miracles to medieval audiences is evident in many collections, Jewish and non-Jewish. See Rachel Koopmans, *Wonderful to Relate: Miracle Stories and Miracle Collecting in High Medieval England* (Philadelphia: University of Pennsylvania Press, 2010), 6–8. See Jody Enders, *Death by Drama and Other Medieval Urban Legends* (Chicago: University of Chicago Press, 2002), 156–165, for her differentiation between belief in miracles in medieval and early modern culture.

to reveal the ways of God and to help their audience make sense of the world around them and set it in order.[3]

Stories and Historians

Collections of stories were once traditionally squarely within the purview of literary scholars, and historians interested in the communities that produced them were hesitant to address this rich repository. Methods for utilizing narrative collections historically have expanded remarkably over the past decades as disciplinary boundaries have become more blurred.[4] Following Robert Darnton's *Great Cat Massacre* and Natalie Davis's *Fiction in the Archives*, to mention two of the early forerunners of this genre of research from the 1980s,[5] the "literary turn" in historical studies has become more pronounced over the past years, and narrative texts have become accepted sources for historical research alongside the "classical" historical genres, such as legal texts, theological treatises, charters, and chronicles. Moreover, recent studies have demonstrated the extent to which stories and collections of stories serve as useful points of entry to oral traditions that were not recorded.[6] These traditions serve as a window to the authors and copyists and also to those who did not write and could not write, and they thus potentially allow glimpses of a broader segment of society, providing new ways to extricate social relations from texts and elaborating frameworks for communal memory.[7]

Among historians of medieval Jewish society, this development has recently gained momentum as well, with some distinctions that underline the characteristics of the Hebrew sources and the medieval Jewish communities.[8] Considerable

3. Michel de Certeau, *The Practice of Everyday Life*, trans. Steven Rendall (Berkeley: University of California Press, 1984), 22–24.

4. I list many such studies in the notes that follow. For examples of the earlier works in this vein, see Jean-Claude Schmitt, *Le saint lévrier: Guinefort, guérisseur d'enfants depuis le XIIIe siècle* (Paris: Flammarion, 1979), as well as Claude Brémond, Jacques Le Goff, and Jean-Claude Schmitt, eds., *L'exemplum* (Turnhout: Brepols, 1982); Alain Boureau, *The Lord's First Night: The Myth of the Droit de Cuissage*, trans. Lydia Cochrane (Chicago: University of Chicago Press, 1988).

5. Robert Darnton, *The Great Cat Massacre and Other Episodes in French Cultural History* (New York, 1984); Natalie Zemon Davis, *Fiction in the Archives: Pardon Tales and Their Tellers in Sixteenth-Century France* (Stanford: Stanford University Press, 1987).

6. Koopmans, *Wonderful to Relate*, 9–27.

7. Ibid. See also Joel T. Rosenthal, *Telling Tales: Sources and Narration in Late Medieval England* (University Park: Penn State University Press, 2003), xii–xiv, 149–150; de Certeau, *Practice*, 89–90.

8. For a recent survey of the field, see Eli Yassif, "The Hebrew Story in the Middle Ages: An Introduction," *Jewish Studies Quarterly* 20 (2013): 3–8, as well as Kushelevsky's introduction to this book, *Tales in Context*, 8–18.

attention has been paid to individual stories that appear within halakhic compositions, liturgy, and chronicles,[9] as opposed to those within collections of tales that are by genre literary.[10] Thus although collections of stories have been studied and analyzed by literary scholars,[11] historians have tended to keep their distance.[12] Scholarly debates and discussions among historians and literary scholars

9. See, for example, the extensive work on the story of Amnon of Mainz, a story that first appeared in connection to the liturgy: Ivan G. Marcus, "*Kiddush hashem be-ashkenaz ve-sippur Rabbi Amnon mi-Magentza*," in *Sanctity of Life and Martyrdom: Studies in Memory of Amir Yekutiel*, ed. Isaiah M. Gafni and Aviezer Ravitsky (Jerusalem: Merkaz Zalman Shazar, 1992), 131–48 [Hebrew]; Lucia Raspe, *Jüdische Hagiographie im mittelalterliche Aschkenas* (Tübingen: Mohr Siebeck, 2006), 130–198; Rella Kushelevsky, *Penalty and Temptation: Hebrew Tales in Ashkenaz—Ms. Parma 2295 (de Rossi 563)* (Jerusalem: Magnes Press, 2010), 100–118 [Hebrew]. For other studies of individual figures, see Avraham Grossman, "A Typological Legend about the Conversion of the Son of R. Gershom Me'or ha-Golah," in *Ma'aseh Sippur: Studies in Jewish Narrative*, ed. Avidov Lipsker and Rella Kushelevsky (Ramat Gan: Bar Ilan University Press, 2006), 65–76 [Hebrew]; Jeremy Cohen has explored this path in different studies, and see multiple examples in his *Sanctifying the Name of God: Jewish Martyrs and Jewish Memories of the First Crusade* (Philadelphia: University of Pennsylvania Press, 2004), as well as the work of Susan E. Einbinder, "Pulcellina of Blois: Romantic Myths and Narrative Conventions," *Jewish History* 12 (1998): 29–46; Ora Limor and Israel J. Yuval, "Judas Ischariot und die Juden," in *Christliches und jüdisches Europa im Mittelalter*, ed. Lukas Clemens and Sigrid Hirbodian (Trier: Kliomedia, 2011), 197–205.

10. See, for example, Robert Bonfil, "Cultural and Religious Traditions in Ninth-Century French Jewry," *Binah* 3 (1994): 1–17; Elchanan Reiner, "From Joshua to Jesus—The Transformation of a Biblical Story to a Local Myth: A Chapter in the Religious Life of the Galilean Jew," in *Sharing the Sacred: Religious Contacts and Conflicts in the Holy Land, First–Fifteenth Centuries CE*, ed. Arieh Kofsky and Guy G. Strousma (Jerusalem: Yad Yizhak Ben Zvi, 1998), 223–271 [Hebrew]; Ephraim Shoham-Steiner, "Jews and Healing at Medieval Saints' Shrines: Participation, Polemics and Shared Culture," *Harvard Theological Review* 103 (2010): 111–129. An exception to some extent is the work by Lucia Raspe that focuses primarily on stories, but in this case the stories come from a variety of manuscripts rather than one central compilation, and Raspe's work is driven, among other motivations, by the search for central medieval historical contexts. See Raspe, *Jüdische Hagiographie*, as well as other works by her, including "When King Dagobert Came to Halle: Place and Displacement in Medieval Jewish Legend," *Jewish Studies Quarterly* 20 (2013): 146–158.

11. Eli Yassif, *The Book of Memory That Is the Chronicles of Jerahme'el*, a critical edition by Eli Yassif (Tel Aviv: Tel Aviv University Press, 2001) [Hebrew]; idem, *Ninety-nine Tales: The Jerusalem Manuscript Cycle of Legends in Medieval Jewish Folklore* (Tel Aviv: Tel Aviv University Press, 2013); Kushelevsky, *Penalty and Temptation*. For a treatment of stories within a slightly different genre, see Robert Bonfil, *History and Folklore in a Medieval Jewish Chronicle: The Family Chronicle of Ahima'az ben Paltiel* (Leiden: Brill, 2009).

12. This is rapidly changing. See above, notes 8 and 9. Also see Micha Perry, *Tradition and Transformation: Knowledge Transmission among European Jews in the Middle Ages* (Tel Aviv: Ha-kibbutz ha-meuhad, 2010), 195–215; Elisheva Baumgarten, "Shared Stories and Religious Rhetoric: R. Judah the Pious, Peter the Chanter and a Drought," *Medieval Encounters* 18 (2012): 36–54; eadem, "A Tale of a Christian Matron and Sabbath Candles: Religious Difference, Material Culture and Gender in Thirteenth Century Germany," *Jewish Studies Quarterly* 20 (2013): 83–99; and most recently David Shyovitz, "'You Have Saved Me from the Judgment of Gehenna': The Origins of the Mourner's Kaddish in Medieval Ashkenaz," *AJS Review* 39 (2015): 49–73

and folklorists have served to underscore both the growing use of writings in this genre by historians as well as some disciplinary differences.[13]

The stories in *Sefer ha-ma'asim*, like the majority of texts that have reached us from the medieval European Jewish communities, are set on the whole within a religious framework and relate to canonic literature such as the Bible, the Talmud, Midrash, liturgy, and legal rulings. Discussions of these canonic texts and their medieval commentators in much of current scholarship have been devoted to their authors and their intellectual underpinnings.[14] *Sefer ha-ma'asim*, with its anonymous copyist and its wide range of stories, allows for a broader reflection on some of the assumptions that have accompanied the study of individual scholars or groups of them, and the relationship between known and named individuals and the community at large.

The movement from the author/editor/copyist to the audience of the tales is complicated and has presented a challenge for scholars of Jewish and non-Jewish collections of tales. A first obstacle is language. Much like the case of Latin in medieval Christian compilations, Hebrew was a language of which many members of the Jewish communities did not have full command. Much like Christian laity in medieval Europe, who spoke and understood the vernacular rather than Latin, most medieval Jews did not speak Hebrew, although many of the men had a basic literacy.[15] In the case of *Sefer ha-ma'asim*, this raises the question of audience. While certainly some readers could have handled the Hebrew—as indicated in

13. This conversation was spurred most recently by Eli Yassif, "Legends and History: Historians Read Hebrew Legends of the Middle Ages," *Ẓion* 64 (1999): 187–220 [Hebrew], and the exchanges that followed this piece: Moshe Rosman, "The Art of Historiography and the Methods of Folklore," *Ẓion* 65 (2000): 209–218, and Eli Yassif, "Legend and History: Second Thoughts," *Ẓion* 65 (2000): 219–227.

14. For a recent summary of the field, see Ephraim Kanarfogel, *The Intellectual History and Rabbinic Culture of Medieval Ashkenaz* (Detroit, MI: Wayne State University Press, 2012), 1–36.

15. For recent work on the Jewish laity, see Ephraim Kanarfogel, "Prayer, Literacy, and Literary Memory in the Jewish Communities of Medieval Europe," in *Jewish Studies at the Crossroads of Anthropology and History: Authority, Diaspora, Tradition*, ed. Ra'anan S. Boustan, Oren Kosansky, and Marina Rustow (Philadelphia: University of Pennsylvania Press, 2010), 250–270. For distinctions between levels of literacy, see Paul Saenger, "Books of Hours and Reading Habits of the Later Middle Ages," in *The Culture of Print: Power and the Uses of Print in Early Modern Europe*, ed. Roger Chartier (Princeton, NJ: Princeton University Press, 1989), 142; Michael T. Clanchy, "Did Mothers Teach Their Children to Read?" in *Motherhood, Religion, and Society in Medieval Europe, 400–1400: Essays Presented to Henrietta Leyser*, ed. Lesley Smith, Conrad Leyser, and Henrietta Leyser (Burlington, VT: Routledge, 2011), 129–153, esp. 152–153. See also Elisheva Baumgarten, "Conceptions of Childhood: Education of Young Children in Medieval Jewish Communities," in *Medieval Children and Childhood*, ed. Joel Rosenthal (Sheffield: Shaun Tyas, 2007), 56–74.

Kushelevsky's introduction to this book and in other recent work on story collections—many could not. As a result, I suggest we view this compilation as an example of a repository of stories that were used by preachers and teachers and retold as part of everyday medieval culture. It not only exposes the ideals and ideas of those who copied and edited but also provides insight into the people who then transmitted these stories orally, most probably in the vernacular.[16] Taking into consideration what Richard Southern has called "the chatting atmosphere" of medieval culture, we can assume these stories were transmitted orally and changed shape and form as part of this process.[17]

This essay will focus on *Sefer ha-ma'asim* and explore some of the ways in which the tales can be used for further historical inquiry. The main intent of this essay is to point to potential directions rather than provide an exhaustive survey of the stories and their historical import. As such, this epilogue will highlight some of the aspects mentioned briefly in Kushelevsky's introduction and indicate other areas in which *Sefer ha-ma'asim* and the details it conveys can broaden or complicate existing areas of research.[18] Analyzing a story collection offers unique opportunities for discovering features that may not be remarkable in the analysis of a single particular story but which can gain additional significance when paired with details and other texts, allowing a glimpse into cultural conventions that would have been pertinent to the copyist/editor and his audience.

At the same time, when one reads these stories it is evident that they are just that: tales meant to entertain and educate. Thus I do not contend that the stories in *Sefer ha-ma'asim* present actual events, but rather that they can be seen as conveying norms, anxieties, tensions, and popular concepts of the time.[19] The stories in the compilation tell of everyday occurrences within the home and on the road, of

16. The adaptation and reiteration of many of the stories in this collection and in other contemporary story compilations, as well as in the *Mayse Bukh*, attest to its popular appeal. See Kushelevsky, *Tales in Context*, 30–31.

17. Koopmans, *Wonderful to Relate*, 11–18. She builds on the insights of Southern, *Saint Anselm: A Portrait in a Landscape* (Cambridge: Cambridge University Press, 1992), 278.

18. Throughout this epilogue I refer to the stories alongside their number in the edition, as in Kushelevsky, *Tales in Context*.

19. I am paraphrasing Darnton, *Great Cat Massacre*, 3–4. For a more recent description of the same idea, see James R. Simpson, "Feudalism and Kingship," in *The Cambridge Companion to Medieval French Literature*, ed. Simon Gaunt and Sarah Kay (Cambridge: Cambridge University Press, 2008), 197: "A society's sense of its preoccupations does not invariably offer a secure guide to actual practices. . . . Texts do not merely advance claims or accounts of events, they also question the ways in which such claims are made and legitimized."

parent-child relationships, of individual fortunes and misfortunes alongside divine occurrences and interventions.

The entertainment value of the tales does not outweigh the pitfalls that face scholars trying to learn from them about medieval life. The stories in *Sefer ha-ma'asim* are often fantastic and do not pretend to stick to reality.[20] As this edition shows, the tales have long trajectories, originating in other geographic locations and textual traditions; authors often mixed stories together, leaving readers of later compilations at a loss as to what was added by each layer or storyteller. The possible manipulations of any tale are numerous.[21] Reading a story as a tale of what actually happened is not the point: The stories were meant to entertain and educate, not to present historical truths or facts.

How then can *Sefer ha-ma'asim*, copied in thirteenth-century Champagne, enrich the work of historians of the Jewish communities of that place and period (and beyond)? In the pages that follow, I argue that the stories not only augment known facets of medieval Jewish life but also help develop questions with which one can return to the texts that have traditionally been studied by historians and to examine and reassess long-held ideas. I will begin with the area in which I believe *Sefer ha-ma'asim* has the most to contribute and for which it has been least utilized: insight into the everyday lives of medieval Jews. From there I will examine the questions that traditionally have been investigated, such as Jewish-Christian relations and specific legal and political circumstances.[22]

Jewish Communal Life and *Sefer ha-ma'asim*

As Kushelevsky outlines in her introduction, the Jewish communities of Champagne where the copyist/editor of the manuscript lived included some of the most eminent Torah scholars and prominent leaders of the Tosafist school. The Tosafists were scholars who glossed and explained the canonic texts in a complex manner that

20. This is characteristic of medieval literature. For specific examples, see Koopmans, *Wonderful to Relate*, 9–28. See also Karina Marie Ash, *Conflicting Femininities in Medieval German Literature* (Burlington, VT: Ashgate, 2012), 3–4. For a broad overview, see part IV of Simon Gaunt and Sarah Kay, eds., *The Cambridge Companion to Medieval French Literature*, which includes articles on feudalism and kingship, clergy and laity, others and alterity, and marriage, and how they are reflected historically in medieval literature. The challenge is identifying what elements struck a rhetoric of truth. See Elliott Oring, "Legendry and the Rhetoric of Truth," *Journal of American Folklore* 121 (2008): 27–66.

21. Kushelevsky, *Tales in Context*, 28031.

22. Like Kushelevsky, I have striven to balance between the immediate surroundings, namely Champagne and northern France, or northern Europe/Ashkenaz as a broader cultural unit. See Kushelevsky, *Tales in Context*, 13–20.

required command of large parts of this literature. They were known for their breadth of knowledge and for their in-depth study of texts. Scholars of Jewish texts have long sought to understand this form of analysis as well as the motivations and knowledge of those who undertook textual interpretation in this mode.[23] Defining the Tosafists and the texts they wrote has inevitably led to differentiating between them and those who did not have the same textual skill set these rabbinic scholars possessed.[24] Differences between the Tosafists and other groups of scholars, such as *Ḥasidei Ashkenaz*, have also been central in the research.[25] It is within this framework that the copying of *Sefer ha-ma'asim*—and indeed of the entire manuscript, which consists of different compilations of stories—is both intriguing and revealing. Scholarship about the Tosafists has demonstrated their wide-ranging halakhic and exegetical interests.[26] *Sefer ha-ma'asim* exposes an additional genre that has not figured centrally in studies of medieval Jewish learning. As Kushelevsky demonstrates, *Sefer ha-ma'asim* was copied by a learned Jewish man in Champagne during the thirteenth century, and the copyist/editor was well versed in the Bible and other talmudic and midrashic traditions as well as vernacular literature. He also was knowledgeable of Tosafist traditions and commentaries, although it is impossible to determine the range of his scholarship beyond this compilation.[27]

23. For a survey of the Tosafists as a group, see the by now classic Ephraim Elimelech Urbach, *The Tosaphists: Their History, Writings and Methods* (Jerusalem: Mossad Bialik, 1980) [Hebrew], and also see Israel Moses Ta-Shma, "Tosafot," in *Encyclopaedia Judaica*, 2d ed., vol. 20, ed. Michael Berenbaum and Fred Skolnik (Detroit, MI: Macmillan Reference USA, 2007), 67–70. For a recent survey, see Kanarfogel, *Intellectual History*.

24. Ephraim Kanarfogel ("Prayer, Literacy") has recently underscored the extent to which many members of the Jewish community were far from well versed in the materials in which the Tosafists were immersed. See also Kirsten Fudeman, *Vernacular Voices: Language and Identity in Medieval French Jewish Communities* (Philadelphia: University of Pennsylvania Press, 2010), 23–25.

25. See Kushelevsky, who raises the question of the relationship between the tales in *Sefer ha-ma'asim* and the literature of *Ḥasidei Ashkenaz*. For some of the distinctions between Tosafists and *Ḥasidei Ashkenaz*, see Haym Soloveitchik, "Piety, Pietism and German Pietism: 'Sefer Hasidim I' and the Influence of 'Hasidei Ashkenaz,'" *Jewish Quarterly Review* 92 (2002): 480–483; Israel M. Ta-Shma, "*Mitzvat talmud torah keba'aya hevratit-datit be-sefer Hasidim: Le-bikoret shitat ha-tosafot be-ashkenaz ba-me'ah ha-yud-gimel*," in *Ritual, Custom and Reality in Franco-Germany 1000–1350*, ed. Ta-Shma (Jerusalem: Magnes Press, 1996), 112–29.

26. The Tosafists discuss and critique Jews who read troubadour romances: see, s.v., "*Ve-kol sheken be-shitrei hedyotot*," BT *Shabbat* 116b, where R. Judah of Paris is said to have forbidden reading them on Sabbath and on weekdays. See Fudeman, *Vernacular Voices*, 120–121.

27. Kanarfogel has suggested different tiers of learning; see his *Intellectual History*, 359–361; idem, "Midrashic Texts and Methods in Tosafist Commentaries," in *Midrash Unbound: Transformations and Innovations*, ed. Michael Fishbane and Joanna Weinberg (Oxford: Littman Library of Jewish Civilization, 2013), 318–319.

Sefer ha-ma'asim presents a thirteenth-century version of tales that circulated in northern France and more broadly in northern Europe and, in some cases, throughout the medieval Jewish world. Kushelevsky has pointed to the linguistic features that suggest French as the copyist's language, and to the textual connections between additions to texts that originate in the Talmud and Midrash as well as to connections between stories in *Sefer ha-ma'asim* and medieval French literature from the twelfth and thirteenth centuries. Oral elements embellished these as well. Whereas considerations of authorship or copyists focus on individual knowledge, the tales in *Sefer ha-ma'asim* allow a rare view of the members of society who did not leave written testimony of their lives and who often are not present in the documents—religious, economic, or legal—that have survived.[28] The text turns to the audience and conveys messages to it throughout. I thus will treat the text as a product of oral and written traditions from within France and its environs during the High Middle Ages.

Who were the Jews who read, heard, and retold the stories in *Sefer ha-ma'asim*? By the thirteenth century, the period when this collection was copied and edited, the heart of the Tosafist endeavor was no longer in Champagne but in Paris.[29] Thus the immediate audience was wider than a highly erudite one. Based on the writings of other scholars from northern France during the mid- and late thirteenth century (such as R. Moses of Coucy and R. Isaac of Corbeil, the authors of the handbooks *Sefer miẓvot gadol* and *Sefer miẓvot katan*, respectively), it would seem that many French Jews, in Paris and Champagne, were not capable of studying on a high level.[30] Whether the copyist/editor was very erudite or only somewhat learned, I suggest that perhaps one need not draw such distinct differences among the Tosafists, their audiences, and the concerns of their communities. Following the insights of historians and folklorists, who have argued convincingly that the elite figures who wrote the surviving texts were part of the cultural world of their times and shared the current popular beliefs, one can see that the stories

28. See Eli Yassif, "Storytelling as Midrashic Discourse in the Middle Ages," in *Midrash Unbound: Transformations and Innovations*, ed. Fishbane and Weinberg, 172–172; idem, *The Hebrew Folktale: History, Genre, Meaning*, trans. Jacqueline S. Teitelbaum (Bloomington: Indiana University Press, 1999), 2–7.

29. See the discussion that follows, where I outline the history of the Jews in Champagne.

30. See Judah D. Galinsky, "The Significance of Form: R. Moses of Coucy's Reading Audience and His *Sefer ha-Mizvot*," *AJS Review* 35 (2011): 293–321; and more recently, idem, "Between Ashkenaz (Germany) and *Tsarfat* (France): Two Approaches toward Popularizing Jewish Law," in *Jews and Christians in Thirteenth-Century France*, ed. Elisheva Baumgarten and Judah D. Galinsky (New York: Palgrave, 2015), 77–92.

reveal important facets of the everyday lives of both erudite scholars and less learned members of the community, and serve to mediate among different members of Jewish society.[31] Since stories were heard and told by men, women, and children alike, they also serve as a background for a more inclusive consideration of the community at large.

In the pages that follow I will explore the contours of the society that emerges from this collection. What kind of Jews are featured in these stories? What do the tales teach us about medieval Jewish concerns and anxieties? How do the protagonists allow for reflection on the educational and moral lessons that listeners/readers were meant to learn from this compilation? My responses to these queries will focus primarily on the stories in *Sefer ha-ma'asim* that tell of anonymous protagonists rather than known biblical or Tannaitic/Amoraic figures, although they will be addressed in some cases.

Pious, Righteous, and Beautiful?

Let us begin by looking at the protagonists in the stories. Aside from traditional figures, such as Elijah the prophet, Solomon, and Talmudic heroes such as R. Meir, R. Akiva, and others, the protagonists in approximately half of the stories are anonymous men and women. One of the most common adjectives describing the men is the designation of *ḥasid* (pious), whereas women are described as "beautiful" and "righteous" (*yafah, ẓadeket*). These men and women are most often featured within their family frameworks, at times with a single son and occasionally with sons and daughters. In the cases in which they have single sons, these sons often become central to the plot. Thus families are at the heart of this collection, and family concerns are foremost.[32] This focus is all the more evident when one seeks references to communal authorities or institutions within the stories. Featured within their families, these *ḥasidim* consult rabbis surprisingly infrequently.[33] The main communal institutions mentioned are primarily the synagogue and to a lesser extent the study house. (In some communities the same building

---

31. One of the forerunners of this approach was Peter Brown. See his "The Saint as Exemplar in Late Antiquity," *Representations* 2 (1982): 1–25. Compare Yassif, *Ninety-nine Tales*, 101–172.

32. This is also one of Kushelevsky's main conclusions: *Tales in Context*, 54–57.

33. This stands out in comparison, for example, to the stories in *Sefer hasidim*, where consulting a Sage is the norm. See Ivan Marcus, *Piety and Society: The Jewish Pietists of Medieval Germany* (Leiden: Brill, 1981), 71–86; Eli Yassif, "The Exemplary Story in Sefer Hasidim," *Tarbiẓ* 57 (1988): 217–255 (reprinted in *The Hebrew Collection of Tales in the Middle Ages* [Tel Aviv: Ha-kibbutz ha-meuhad, 2004], esp. 190–202).

was simultaneously the synagogue and the study house.) In cases of strife or vows, one rarely hears of the courts;[34] in cases of poverty there is almost no communal charity, although charity is a most important deed. It is the nuclear family, the house, and the synagogue, along with voyages to far places, that provide a blueprint for this collection. Moreover, unlike most of the other Hebrew sources that have reached us that center on text and interpretation, liturgy, halakhah, or communal affairs, these stories tell us about everyday dramas intentionally rather than coincidentally.

Within this framework, in which most of the people and places mentioned are abstract and nameless,[35] what are the characteristics of the *ḥasid*-hero? Interestingly, the traits of piety that illustrate the unique features of the *ḥasid* are not the study of Torah[36] or even the observance of commandments, characteristics of the Tosafists of the time.[37] While Torah study is underlined in some of the stories, and is certainly presented as positive,[38] most of the featured *ḥasidim* are noted as pious for other reasons. Although I do not wish to exaggerate the dichotomy between Tosafist and *ḥasid*, something that has been characteristic of studies concerning individual scholars, I do want to underline that, in the context of *Sefer ha-ma'asim*, the appellation *ḥasid* was not specifically connected to Torah study, nor was it consistently evidence of a connection between mundane and divine worlds.[39] In the story "The Loan" (no. 2), the *ḥasid* is characterized by his prayer habits and his self-denial, but no knowledge or study of Torah is mentioned:

34. "The Man Who Never Took an Oath" (no. 13). Here the elders of the city hear the pledge made by the son never to take an oath. This is somewhat ironic, as it is a pledge not to take an oath.

35. This is not a unique feature of *Sefer ha-ma'asim*; rather it is a feature of the genre.

36. In the case of "The *Ḥasid* and the Tax Collector's Son" (no. 60), the *ḥasid* is specifically a Torah scholar. Thus the story recounts: "A tale of Baya the tax collector, who was the king's deputy and guest. And he was a very harsh man, and wicked. The very day that Baya the tax collector died, a Torah scholar and a perfectly righteous man passed away as well. The entire community came that day and carried the two bodies to the cemetery."

37. In the story "The Demon in the Carob Tree" (no. 8), we hear of a pious man who observed all the commandments.

38. See below, n. 98.

39. Talya Fishman suggests this definition in her discussion of the history of this concept. Fishman, *Becoming the People of the Talmud: Oral Torah as Written Tradition in Medieval Jewish Cultures* (Philadelphia: University of Pennsylvania Press, 2011), 185–186. See also Marcus, *Piety and Society*, 59; Judith R. Baskin, "From Separation to Displacement: The Problem of Women in 'Sefer Hasidim,'" *AJS Review* 19 (1994): 1–18, explores the boundaries of these definitions. See also Elisheva Baumgarten, *Practicing Piety in Medieval Ashkenaz: Men, Women, and Everyday Religious Observance* (Philadelphia: University of Pennsylvania Press, 2014), 1, 13–17, 70, 212, 224.

> Once there was a *ḥasid* [a pious man] who used to recite the three prayers every day, and his prayers would rise before the Divine throne like a daily sacrifice placed upon the altar. And the *ḥasid* resolved never to accept a gift from anyone. And every day, he would go to the garbage heap and gather rags, and he put them on his front and back to cover his nakedness.

Poverty and prayer are characteristic of other *ḥasidim* in the collection, such as Ukva ("Ukva," no. 15), who is both a *ḥasid* and poor. However poverty is not a requirement for qualifying as a *ḥasid.* Joḥanan ("Joḥanan and the Scorpion," no. 28) is rich, as is the *ḥasid* in the story about the man who did not miss public prayers ("Do Not Fail to Attend Public Prayers," no. 41). In the latter case, the *ḥasid*'s piety was manifested by his long hours in synagogue and his constant pursuit of opportunities to pray with the community. He does not manifest connections to divine worlds or erudition. Similarly, in "The Man Who Never Took an Oath" (no. 13), the protagonist's father is described as a "very rich *ḥasid*," and his piety led him to his successful business rather than to spiritual or Torah-related pursuits.[40] In some of the epilogues, the hero, who is described as a *ḥasid* or who becomes a *ḥasid*, transforms into a very rich man.[41] In general these epilogues—which in some cases even end with the explicit explanation that one should hope to merit the good fortune that befell the hero—emphasize the man's wealth rather than his knowledge of Torah.

In other cases the pious man is just designated as a *ḥasid*, without an explanation for what made him into a *ḥasid* ("The Book of Genesis," no. 19; "Slander Kills Three," no. 30). The narrator expected his listeners to know what he meant when he said "*ḥasid*," as in the case of "The Pious Pretender" (no. 50), where the pious man is described simply as looking pious. His *ḥasidut* is expressed not only by the fact that he never left his place in synagogue but is also discernable from his form and humility.[42] It is noteworthy that, in previous versions of this tale from other diasporas, the detail that identifies the piety of the man is the fact that he wears tefillin constantly, a feature that is substituted here by his remaining in the synagogue.[43]

---

40. Compare between *Sefer ha-ma'asim* and the version that appears in Yassif, *Ninety-nine Tales*, 98, 257–260; *Sefer ha-ma'asim* is less focused on Torah study. In addition and in distinction to the collection Yassif analyzed, there are no named medieval figures in *Sefer ha-ma'asim*, whereas Yassif's collection focuses on R. Judah and Samuel specifically.

41. See, for example, the stories "The Man Who Never Took an Oath (no. 13), "Joḥanan and the Scorpion" (no. 28), "The Poor Bachelor and His Maiden Cousin" (no. 55), and "The Grateful Dead" (no. 65).

42. See "The Pious Pretender" (no. 50), p. 266–269, 530–533, in this edition.

43. Baumgarten, *Practicing Piety*, 201.

This is not to say that Torah study is not an admired quality or noble pursuit; rather, it is not the most prominent feature of the *ḥasid*, and if the collection is viewed as a window on to the concerns and values of the narrating society, this is an important qualification.[44] In some stories there is even a distinction made between the *ḥasid* and the Torah scholars. For example, in "The Three Treasures" (no. 7), charity and gifts to Torah scholars are emphasized, but Torah study itself does not make a pious man: "Once there was a *ḥasid* [a pious man] who used to give charity and perform numerous favors and benevolent acts for Torah scholars and ordinary people."

In "The Poor Bachelor and His Maiden Cousin" (no. 55), Isaac, who was a Torah scholar before leaving on a quest and returning to marry his cousin, is described as marrying and living a pious life: "And he lived many more years, and was righteous and pious the rest of his life, and had sons and daughters." There is no mention made of the excellence in studying that characterized him before he left on his quest and became a ruler of a city. It is possible that the scholarly attributes of these *ḥasidim* were so obvious they needed no mention, but it is striking that the acts of piety described could all characterize men who were less learned and in fact incapable of complicated biblical and Talmudic study. It is telling that only in a story that includes the conversion of a gentile ("The Cow That Observed the Sabbath," no. 20) is knowledge of Torah emphasized, to define the qualities of this convert as a good Jew.[45]

Close to a quarter of the stories in *Sefer ha-ma'asim* feature *ḥasidim* whose piety is either unspecified or related to specific traits that are not those associated with erudition, and no rabbinic authority is mentioned in them. One could argue that this is perhaps a question of genre. *Ma'asiyot* (tales/exempla) are on the whole short, anonymous, and popular.[46] Yet when one compares *Sefer ha-ma'asim* to other compilations from its close surroundings, this feature stands out. For example, in the fourteenth- (or perhaps fifteenth-) century collection edited recently by Eli Yassif, Yassif emphasizes that the stories in Ms. Heb. 3182 speak to a broad, non-halakhic audience, yet many of the protagonists in that collection are known rabbinic figures who often determine what the law is.[47] Even if we dismiss the stories that belong to a hagiographic cycle in Yassif's edition, one can see more rabbis in the stories, even

44. My argument is not that Torah study was not admired but that, within this narrative that helps create and cement communal identity, it is not as central as one might expect. See de Certeau, *Practice*, 77–90. This is an asset of narratives such as these, as they help underscore elements that otherwise could have been taken for granted.

45. See below for further discussion of this story.

46. For detailed consideration of the different genres, see Yassif, *The Hebrew Folktale*, 283–369; Raspe, *Jüdische Hagiographie*, 47–69.

47. Yassif, *Ninety-nine Tales*, 15–22, 101–17.

when they remained unnamed. Another telling comparison to *Sefer ha-ma'asim* is *Sefer ḥasidim*. Although in both collections there are many exempla that relate to family affairs, lovers, promises, and other such quandaries, in the *Sefer ḥasidim* stories the Sage plays a central role.[48] Similarly, the thirteen stories in MS Parma 2295—a comparable, much slighter collection, also copied during the thirteenth century in northern France—feature known rabbis from the Talmud or biblical figures in each and every tale. Even in the story that begins with a protagonist similar to the one in *Sefer ha-ma'asim*, "a man who was used to giving charity every day," this man is not called a *ḥasid*, and he also is not the main character in the story, as R. Akiva takes over the continuation of the narrative.[49]

In sum, a closer look at the different *ḥasid*-heroes and their traits can help us relate back to the question of the copyist/editor and his surroundings. Although the copyist/editor of this collection was surely a learned man, of whatever tier of learning, this story collection does not express ideals that would have resonated only within a learned milieu. Undoubtedly, the more learned the listener/reader, the more he or she would have appreciated the complex literary allusions outlined by Kushelevsky in the introduction to the present book. But it is likely that many listeners enjoyed the stories despite lacking this knowledge, and it is evident that the compilation was geared toward them and expressed their cultural world as well.[50]

This direction can be further developed when we turn to the women in the stories. Here one finds a mix of righteous and wicked or lazy, as befits any work of fiction. The "positive" women are described as beautiful, with the addition of the word *ẓadeket* (righteous).[51] Interestingly, there is no use of the word *ḥasidah*, the female parallel to the male *ḥasid*, and although the word *ẓadik* is used throughout the collection, it is never used in the presentation of the story but only in later comments, and far less frequently.[52] While there are some women who are described only as beautiful, those who are described as righteous are also always beautiful. The wife of the man who never took an oath ("The Man Who Never Took an Oath," no. 13) was righteous, very beautiful, and also shy. As a result she never asked for

48. See n. 33.

49. Kushelevsky, *Tales in Context*, story no. 31, 216–217, 478–479.

50. See n. 25, above.

51. See the stories: "The Man Who Never Took an Oath" (no. 13); "Ukva" (no. 15); and "Joḥanan and the Scorpion" (no. 28). In all three, the term replaces the woman's name.

52. On different titles and their use in medieval Jewish culture, see Avraham (Rami) Reiner, "'A Tombstone Inscribed': Titles Used to Describe the Deceased on Tombstones from Würzburg Between 1147–1148 and 1346," *Tarbiẓ* 78 (2008): 142–144.

anything. She worked as a washerwoman (a laundress) to support her family. She is taken captive on a ship, along with her sons, until her husband gains her release. Her beauty causes the ship's captain to accost her time and again, but her righteousness allows her to preserve her chastity. This story, which is told in even greater detail than in versions of *Midrash aseret hadibrot*, depicts the woman as being active and influential, and attributes deeds and words to her.[53] As feminist scholars have demonstrated, the agency of women in medieval texts can be read cautiously as a reflection of their place in society.[54]

Another example of this theme of righteous and beautiful women can be seen in the story of Ukva ("Ukva," no. 15), whose wife is described as both a *ẓadeket* and beautiful. (Both attributes are central to the story: Because she is beautiful, she is put to the test; because she is righteous, she survives it.) In this case, her husband wrongly accused her of adultery and calls her an evil woman ("*isha ra'ah*"), but she manages to prove her virtue.[55] In the case of Ukva's wife, we can see the tremendous agency attributed to the wife, in comparison to the wife's role in Eastern versions, such as that of Nissim of Kairouan.[56] Joḥanan's wife is also both beautiful and very righteous ("*ẓadeket me'od*"). Her virtue is not tested; rather, she provides counsel and solutions at a crucial juncture in the story, and is a central player in the first part of the story. When the scorpion agrees to help R. Joḥanan on his quest, he grants both him and his wife a wish, explaining:

> And your righteous wife who would take such trouble for me and served me skillfully may also ask for one thing from me, and I will give it to her. And the woman came and said to him: Sir, give me great riches so that I may support my husband and family decently. It said to her: Follow me and bring wagons and horses and donkeys and any beasts you can bring with you, and I will load them with silver and gold and precious stones and pearls.

53. This story does not appear in the version of *Midrash aseret ha-dibrot* in Ms. Oxford Bodl. Or. 135. Compare to *Midrash aseret ha-dibrot*, ed. Anat Shapira (Jerusalem: Mossad Bialik, 2005), 54–59.

54. See Ash, *Conflicting Femininities*, 211–113.

55. An important topic for future study is the portrayal of rape and chastity in these stories. See Kathryn Gravdal, *Ravishing Maidens: Writing Rape in Medieval French Literature and Law* (Philadelphia: University of Pennsylvania Press, 1991), 21–25; Sarah Salih, "Performing Virginity: Sex and Violence in the Katherine Group," in *Constructions of Widowhood and Virginity in the Middle Ages*, ed. Cindy L. Carlson and Angela J. Weisl (New York: Palgrave MacMillan, 1999), 245–264; Corrine J. Saunders, *Rape and Ravishment in the Literature of Medieval England* (Cambridge: Boydell and Brewer, 2001), 187–233.

56. Kushelevsky, *Penalty*, 151–154; eadem, *Tales in Context*, 314–317.

Similarly, the woman who becomes queen in the continuation of this story is righteous and beautiful and portrayed as having a mind of her own.[57] She refuses to have sexual relations with the king upon her arrival and demands sufficient time before her marriage. At the end of this story, when Joḥanan rather surprisingly marries the queen, the narrative explains: "And they gave him the righteous woman to be his wife, and they lived for many years together in peace and tranquility and had many sons and daughters."[58]

This same portrayal of women's agency and power stands out in "The Weasel and the Pit" (no. 43) and in "The Seven Good Years" (no. 29). Although neither story classifies the women as beautiful or righteous, they both underline her central role. In "The Weasel and the Pit," two women direct the plot. The first is the young woman who, on the way to her mother's house, is rescued from the pit. She promises to marry her rescuer but refuses to have sex with him, and insists they become betrothed according to local custom.[59] She then later shows her steadfastness and loyalty by refusing to marry anyone else. The second woman in this story is the woman who marries the man who forgets his vow. She insists on getting to the bottom of the deaths of her children and initiates divorce proceedings, sending her (ex-) husband back to the woman to whom he had pledged himself.[60] In "The Seven Good Years" (no. 29), the woman is the figure who both decides to accept the treasure that leads to seven good years and bargains with God at the end of the seven years, requesting that the treasure remain with her family. She is depicted as a businesswoman who has all the charitable transactions she performs recorded, and she also brings the written evidence of her practice to prove her point.[61]

These positive portrayals of women are coupled with misogynistic ones.[62] The wife in "One Man in a Thousand Have I Found" (no. 53) is willing to kill her husband and abandon her children. The mother in "One of Ten" (no. 17) repeatedly deceives and betrays her husband. "The Defamed Woman" (no. 24), too, contains an

57. It is not clear whether she is Jewish; and see Kushelevsky, *Tales in Context*, 194–209.

58. Kushelevsky, *Tales in Context*, 208.

59. Kushelevsky interprets this as evidence of local engagement customs; and see *Penalty*, 187–192.

60. See my analysis of these stories: Elisheva Baumgarten, "Mothers and *Ma'asim*: Maternal Roles in Medieval Hebrew Tales," in *Motherhood in the Jewish Cultural Imagination*, ed. Jane L. Kanarek, Marjorie Lehman, and Simon J. Bronner (Oxford: Littman Library of Jewish Civilization, 2017), 345–358.

61. See tale no. 29.

62. For a discussion of this dichotomy in medieval European culture, see Alcuin Blamires, ed., *Woman Defamed and Woman Defended: An Anthology of Medieval Texts* (Oxford: Clarendon Press, 1992), 1–17.

admonition against evil women. Yet the stories that portray women favorably are far more plentiful than those that do not; and beyond the question of positive or negative depiction, it is striking that, in all the stories, even those where women are not in the spotlight, the women are all involved in family affairs and much more visible than in collections of tales from the East.[63] Kushelevsky and Yassif have both pointed to the similar agency of women in other story collections from Ashkenaz as well.[64] This activity complements the conclusions historians of medieval Ashkenaz have come to, based on other genres of rabbinic writing, first and foremost *responsa* literature, along with halakhic and exegetical commentaries and moral writings. Thus Avraham Grossman has concluded that Jewish women in medieval Ashkenaz enjoyed a relatively high status and played a central role in Jewish society. He uses mainly legal texts to demonstrate women's rights and agency within medieval society.[65]

This conclusion can be reaffirmed but also seen as nuanced when one examines the stories in *Sefer ha-ma'asim*. While *responsa* literature and other halakhic texts can tell us about actual women and what they did, and exegesis conveys expectations and prescriptions, the stories in *Sefer ha-ma'asim* add an additional dimension to the popular imagination. They provide both a fictive description of a wide variety of women's actions—oftentimes confirming stereotypes—and a framing that sets the social stage in a more general way, allowing insight into the norms of society and the way they were scripted.[66]

To understand the contribution provided by *Sefer ha-ma'asim*, let us look at two stories in which women are active figures, as well as the way their activities are framed. In the story "The Poor Bachelor and His Maiden Cousin" (no. 55), the rich cousin is the daughter of the rich uncle. She falls in love with Isaac, her poor cousin, and displays tremendous agency. The story continues:

> And every day, Isaac would go to the house of study and learn with his rabbi, day and night. And every night, the daughter of his rich uncle would wait up late for him to come home. And so she did [327b], night after night. One day,

63. See "Seven Good Years" (no. 29). Compare to the version in *Midrash zuta*, ed. Solomon Buber (Vilna: Romm, 1925), Ruth 4:11, 48–49, and see Kushelevsky, 210–213.
64. Yassif, *Ninety-nine Tales*, 143–162; Kushelevsky, *Penalty*, 195–198.
65. Avraham Grossman, *Pious and Rebellious: Jewish Women in the Middle Ages* (Waltham, MA: University Press of New England, 2004), 273–277.
66. Ash, *Conflicting Femininities*; Campbell, "Clerks and Laity," in *The Cambridge Companion to Medieval French Literature*, ed. Simon Gaunt and Sarah Kay (Cambridge: Cambridge University Press, 2008), 219–223.

> the rabbi summoned Isaac and told him: Listen, my son, to my instructions, and God will be with you tonight. As soon as you arrive at your uncle's house and find your cousin there, take her in your arms and embrace and kiss her. Rabbi, said Isaac, how can I commit such a terrible sin, to encourage my evil inclination while I can yet escape it? But the rabbi said: I swear that I will not let you be until you take an oath to do this. So the young man took an oath before him.
>
> When Isaac came home, he found her waiting for him, to let him in [lit., to open the door]. She opened the door for him, and they went to sit by the fire. And she prepared food for him, as she was accustomed to do. But he said to her: I will neither eat nor drink. And he sat and wept. My beloved, my cousin, what is the matter with you? she asked. Tell me what is wrong, if you are in need of something, and why you are weeping. But he didn't want to tell her, because he felt ashamed. But she insisted to know all about it. So he told her about his oath to his rabbi and his instructions. She said: My love, man of my heart, this is no reason to weep. And she embraced and kissed him several times on his mouth and said: Don't be ashamed before me, my cousin, because I love you very much indeed [lit., a mighty love; cf. Song of Songs 8:6]. And you are my flesh and blood, and my father loves you, and you are the apple of his eye. And she spoke to his heart and consoled him with her words. And she gave him to eat and drink, and he went to bed until morning.

These passages contain many details of interest and describe a situation in which the two young people are amorously pursuing each other under the supervision of a rabbi.[67] Of greatest importance for my argument is the active role the young woman plays. She actively encourages Isaac to follow his desires with her. She also waits for him, prepares food for him, and convinces him of their course of action. I am not arguing that these events took place, although one can assume that in the Middle Ages many a couple engaged in such activities, with or without rabbinic encouragement, and that the depiction of these everyday encounters and activities resonated with the audience and lent a rhetoric of truth to the story.[68]

67. This point is worthy of further attention, as this is an odd role for a rabbi to play and very different from similar stories in late antiquity where slaves often play this role (see Dina Stein, "A Maidservant and Her Master's Voice: Discourse, Identity, and Eros in Rabbinic Texts," *Journal of the History of Sexuality* 10 [2001]: 376–379), or from medieval parallels where there are jesters (see Yassif, *Ninety-nine Tales*, 70–76).

68. Oring, "Rhetoric," 127–130.

At the same time the young cousin's actions also depict conventions. She is active mainly inside the house. She also outlines patriarchal norms in her words. For example, this (nameless) young woman reassures Isaac that her father will approve their marriage and argues: "You are my flesh and blood, and my father loves you, and you are the apple of his eye. And she spoke to his heart and consoled him with her words."[69] Here we can see how this woman serves the patriarchal norm in her speech, underlining the preference medieval Jews had to create marriage within the extended family.[70]

I will return to the themes of patriarchal norms and their expression, but now let us look at the other roles allotted to women in this plot. As the story progresses a number of other women become involved, including Isaac's mother and the girl's mother. The latter wants her daughter to marry her brother, whereas the former is called to action when Isaac decides he is doomed and contemplates suicide, after his uncle finds him and his cousin sleeping alongside each other. As Kushelevsky points out, the entire plot resembles medieval French romances more than traditional Jewish tales.[71] Together these women spur the continuation of the story. Isaac's mother persuades him not to commit suicide and gets the local rabbi involved in a compromise, sending Isaac on a quest according to the request of the girl's mother that the suitors contest each other. This part of the plot in and of itself is significant, as it stands in contrast to halakhic literature that presents the choice of marriage partners first and foremost as a paternal prerogative.[72]

Skipping to the end of this story, we see a much more formulaic expression of how this marriage was created, once again underlining male agency and power. After Isaac and his beloved are reunited we are told:

> And he married her under the wedding canopy. And all rejoiced, his mother and father and the whole community, with great joy, and he told his mother and father and uncle all about what had happened to him. And he was exceedingly rich and ruled over the whole country. And he lived many more years, and was righteous and pious the rest of his life, and had sons and daughters. May we too share all these [blessings], amen.

69. "The Poor Bachelor and His Maiden Cousin" (no. 55).

70. For marriage patterns, see Jacob Katz, *Tradition and Crisis: Jewish Society at the End of the Middle Ages* (New York: Free Press, 1961), 137–138; Grossman, *Pious and Rebellious*, 55.

71. Kushelevsky, *Tales in Context*, 11–12.

72. See n. 70.

In this case, the bride vanishes in the narrative, while the parents and especially her husband remain center stage. After such a complicated plot in which far more than the patriarchal hierarchy reigned, the end of the story allows an understanding of how life should be ideally organized. The text leaves no doubts about this intention, as the story ends with the hope: "May we too share all these [blessings], amen." Put differently, the story combines female agency and patriarchal norms; the balance of the two is particularly interesting and allows for a nuanced message to those hearing or reading the story.

This same process and balance are evident in "The Weasel and the Pit" (no. 43). In this case the young man and woman betroth themselves to each other without any parental agreement. The young woman also has the wherewithal to convince the man not to rape her and to pledge his loyalty. At the same time, she outlines current social norms when she asks:

> Of which people are you? He said: I am from Israel, from such and such a place, and I am from a priestly family. [She said]: I am from such and such a place, descended from well-known and respected people. She said to him: You who are from such a holy people, whom the Almighty chose and sanctified from among all the nations, yet you wish to act like a beast without a marriage ceremony or marriage contract? Follow me to my father and mother, and I will become engaged to you.

The end of this story further emphasizes paternal authority, as her marriage is presented as a negotiation between her future husband and her father. Thus while one can note her tremendous involvement and steadfastness—she refuses to marry and even pretends to suffer from epileptic seizures—the official social norms take over at the end of the story.

These stories allow us to glimpse lived experience and the official social norms, as well as the spectrum between them. Future scholars should be encouraged to search for this variety in other genres and to revise our understandings of medieval society and culture. *Sefer ha-ma'asim* portrays social settings in which both men and women were active; where the patriarchal norm bookends the stories rather than serving as a main theme. In contrast, halakhic and custom literature, which is of a prescriptive nature, focuses more on the norm than on the variations. The inclusion of the perspective provided by *Sefer ha-ma'asim* can perhaps help revise our understandings of everyday life and dynamics within the patriarchal frameworks provided at the beginnings and ends of the stories, with the knowledge that in all cases these fictive narratives, like reports of actual occurrences, are scripted according to the prevailing customs.[73]

Returning to the contours of the society presented in the tales and to the audience for the compilation, one can conclude that the picture that emerges is one emphasizing *ba'ale batim*: members of the community who pray and give charity but who are not unusually learned. Even the study hall does not feature primarily within the story. The people's goal, as presented in the various stories, is to become successful merchants and rich men while remaining pious and God-fearing. They may support Torah scholars but are not necessarily themselves part of this class. Like the patriarchal beginnings and endings to the stories, these characterizations portray the Torah scholars as important authority figures but also provide a glimpse of alternative social layers that have hardly been explored to date in medieval communities. Of necessity we rely on the authors whose texts have survived; these men, themselves scholars, presented themselves as exemplars of medieval Jewish society and thus have received the most attention. These scholars indeed represented a part of the contemporaneous society, but *Sefer ha-ma'asim*—even as it allows for future study of these men's writings—also casts attention to the other community members who did not leave a written record.

The women featured in the stories also reflect the society that heard these stories. They are most often depicted within their homes, on the road, or doing business. There is hardly a mention of a woman in the synagogue or study house, except when a woman must expressly seek out rabbinic guidance (a rare occurrence).[74] The gendered division of space is noteworthy, but with a caveat, which continues the point made earlier: The men, while often presented at synagogue, are doing no more than attending and participating in services. They are not leading them or commenting on them. Moreover, the moral endings appended to the different stories further reinforce this point. The epilogues focus on ordering society and creating a morally sound community: honoring one's parent or raising respectful children, giving charity, not stealing, and honoring the Sabbath. None of these messages is complex or especially learned, even if some of the means by which the messages are conveyed are sophisticated. Some rely on familiarity with biblical verses; others state

73. I hope to develop this perspective in future work.

74. Here we have a contrast to existing studies concerning women and synagogue in halakhic sources, as the latter give the impression that women frequented the synagogues. See Ivan G. Marcus, "Mothers, Martyrs, and Moneymakers: Some Jewish Women in Medieval Europe," *Conservative Judaism* 38 (1986): 34–45; Grossman, *Pious and Rebellious*, 180–185.

the message more explicitly. Those that pertain to marriage are the most explicit, wishing on the listeners the blessing bestowed on the heroes of the stories.[75]

It would not be an exaggeration to say that these stories provide a representation of a broader segment of society than does any other source available to those studying medieval Jewish culture, as the rabbinic sources focus on their authors more than on society at large, and even *responsa* literature that describes actual occurrences is constrained to those who turned to the rabbis. In this way attention to *Sefer ha-ma'asim* and other collections of tales has the potential to expand our view of the medieval Jewish communities and their members.[76]

Within the Jewish Community and Beyond

I have focused up until this point on the portraits of men and women as featured in the stories in the collection. In this section I wish to connect these men and women to their communities at large, by looking at how the stories in *Sefer ha-ma'asim* can be contextualized in their surroundings. Few details are provided in the stories to allow one to identify the settings in which they take place.[77] Kings and rulers are unidentifiable; so too the geographical descriptions are fairly sparse.[78] Jerusalem remains a place of pilgrimage in some stories ("The Pious Pretender" [no. 50] and "The Defamed Woman" [no. 24]), but it is not a place where one lives. Solomon's scribes are from Lod (no. 42), but there is no significance to the sacred geography. Nor is a new geography substituted for earlier locations, as one can see in some cases in other retellings of ancient stories.[79] This characteristic fits with the more general ones Yassif has outlined in his discussion of Hebrew tales and even more generally with international ones regarding these types of stories.[80] In addition there are no

75. See, for example, the end of "The Poor Bachelor and His Maiden Cousin" (no. 55) and "The Weasel and the Pit" (no. 43).

76. David Shyovitz has recently underlined the need for such an effort. See his review of *Practicing Piety*: thetalmudblog.wordpress.com/tag/david-shyovitz/ (last accessed August 18, 2016).

77. Kushelevsky, *Tales in Context*, 11–13.

78. In contrast to Yassif, *Ninety-nine Tales*, where the cities of Germany are central; Joseph Bamberger, "The King-Maker: Jewish Adaptations of Christian Legends," *Jewish Studies Quarterly* 20 (2013): 129–145; Raspe, *Jüdische Hagiographie*, where geography plays a central role. See, for example, in her analysis of the story about Amram of Regensburg (119–129).

79. See, for example, Nissim b. Jacob of Kairouan, *Ḥibbur yafeh mehayeshu'a*, ed. Ḥaim Z. Hirschberg (Jerusalem: Mossad ha-rav Kook, 1954), 60, where Iraq is substituted for Jerusalem.

80. Yassif, *The Hebrew Folktale*, 283–369. For an in-depth discussion of genre in *Sefer ha-ma'asim*, see his "Sepher ha-Ma'asim," *Tarbiẓ* 53 (1984): 409–430 (reprinted in his *Hebrew Collection of Tales*, 142–156); see Kushelevsky, *Tales in Context*, 49–54.

cases in which the storyteller tries to connect the geography of the stories to that of his audience, as can be found in other medieval and especially early modern compilations of tales.[81] With the exception of local rivers and sea travel, there are few markers of local or general geography, and these too are vague. There is, however, an explicit flavor of European geography (depicting, for example, a washerwoman working or a person attempting suicide in a river), although one cannot pinpoint a specific river using these details. Significantly, particulars such as rivers feature more frequently in stories that appear for the first time in *Sefer ha-ma'asim*. So too does the forest—a constant feature of northern European life but less typical of the world of late antiquity—feature in stories that appear in *Sefer ha-ma'asim* for the first time, such as "The Sabbath Observer and the Bear" (no. 14) or "Joḥanan and the Scorpion" (no. 28). These geograpical details are to a large extent a feature of the genre, but when one compares *Sefer ha-ma'asim* and other collections of stories, it is still remarkable.[82]

Many of the stories, including those which Kushelevsky has demonstrated to be dependent on Christian tales, include details that "Judaize" the plots. As Yassif and others have noted, this "Judaizing" is a common feature of medieval Jewish storytelling.[83] Yet, as in the case of the community members and geographical spaces, the events used to Judaize the stories demand further scrutiny. A basic method of Judaizing a story is to append a biblical verse to it. This method is so common that it does not require further comment here, although it offers a possibility for future exploration: One could envision a project that examined parallel uses of verses in Jewish and Christian collections of stories.[84]

Another central method of emphasizing the Jewish character of the stories is the insertion of Jewish annual cycle events. The Sabbath features centrally, as does Passover. In some stories the observance of the Sabbath is the point of the tale, whereas in others the Sabbath serves simply as an identifying marker.[85] Both "Joḥanan and the Scorpion" (no. 28) and "The Poor Bachelor and His Maiden Cousin" (no. 55),

81. Raspe, *Jüdische Hagiographie*, throughout the stories, focuses on the importance of specific locations and the audiences' familiarity with them.

82. Compare to Kushelevsky, *Penalty*, where a collection of thirteen stories in a Parma manuscript are discussed.

83. Yassif, *Ninety-nine Tales*, 118–124, and see Kushelevsky, *Tales in Context*, 67, 69.

84. Dov Noy, "The Jewish Versions of the 'Animal Languages' Folktale (AT 670): A Typological-Structural Study," *Scripta Hierosolymitana* 12 (1971): 186–194. For the important place of the biblical text within medieval French narratives, see Xavier-Laurent Salvador, *Vérité et écriture(s)* (Paris: Champion, 2007), 54–78.

85. Noy discusses this tactic as well: "The Jewish Versions of the 'Animal Languages' Folktale," 173.

which, as Kushelevsky has shown, have their origins in medieval Christian tales, stress Passover. I readily concur with this emphasis on the Judaizing effect (including the Sabbath or Passover in a narrative, turning a festive meal into the Passover seder, or depicting the needs of a poor family as their lack of money for buying Passover food); however it is also important to notice the mechanisms through which this effect is produced. Significantly absent are the High Holidays.[86] Passover and Sabbath are not elements that require a deep knowledge of or extensive familiarity with Jewish culture, and they would have resonated with all members of the Jewish community. Once again, this collection is not aimed at a highbrow audience. Undoubtedly those who were erudite would have easily recognized some of the complex adjustments Kushelevsky outlined in chapters 2 and 3 of this volume; but even for those who could not follow these plays on words, the Jewish characteristics of the stories would have been obvious.

Turning to the life-cycle rituals, one discerns a similar phenomenon. Death and marriage feature prominently, but there is only one general mention of circumcisions.[87] The discussion of death is not elaborated with any specific customs except for the carrying of the body outside the city.[88] Marriage receives the most emphasis, and its Jewish character is underlined by statements concerning the holiness of Jews in general and, in one case, a mention of priestly descent.[89] In addition, stories about marriage end with a declaration of the desirability of marriage and an emphasis on procreation. This may be seen as an assertion of Jewish ideals of marriage and procreation along with a simultaneous veiled comment on Christian ideas of celibacy,[90] although the stories on which the Hebrew tales are modeled are not clerical, and they too promote the ideals of married life. William Burgwinkle concludes his discussion of northern European laity by stating that happy marriages

86. I do not mean to argue that Rosh Hashanah was not an important holiday for medieval Jews; however it is telling that the High Holidays are not mentioned at all.

87. The only mention of circumcision is in the story about Pinḥas b. Yair (nos. 56–59), in which it is mentioned in passing.

88. Kushelevsky points out that the expansion in the story about the drunkard has to do with the burial customs in Amoraic literature that would not have been understood by medieval listeners; see *Tales in Context*, 393–396.

89. Ibid., 244–245.

90. For a discussion of this tension, see David Berger, *The Jewish-Christian Debate in the Middle Ages: Sefer Nizzahon Vetus* (Philadelphia: Jewish Publication Society, 1979), 69–70, 205; Esther Cohen and Elliott Horowitz, “In Search of the Sacred: Jews, Christians and Rituals of Marriage in the Later Middle Ages,” *Journal of Medieval and Renaissance Studies* 20 (1990): 237–238; Kenneth R. Stow, *Alienated Minority: The Jews of Medieval Latin Europe* (Cambridge, MA: Harvard University Press, 1992), 207–208.

"remain the rock on which medieval society defined itself," and this idea seems to be shared by both religions.[91]

Whether weaving the Sabbath, Passover, or marriage into the stories, these references provide the rhetoric needed to make them integrally Jewish. As Yassif has recently explained, this appropriation of elements from contemporary cultures and then their Judaization allow for a deep integration of these stories in Jewish culture.[92] Without dismissing the depth of this process and the identification of listeners/readers with these stories as authentically Jewish, one also may find it worth contemplating how little was needed for the story to travel this route. A holiday, a life cycle event, or in other cases a Jewish institution such as a synagogue or prayer within it would suffice. So too can a Jewish protagonist lend credence to the narrative. At the same time, the integration of the story, from whatever source, within the traditional Jewish context does not dismiss our need to assess the significance of the complex relationship between the Christian and Jewish traditions. Of particular interest and potential, in my opinion, are stories that not only contain a tension between shared and different practice but also reflect on topics that were undergoing change during the twelfth and thirteenth centuries.

Returning once again to "The Weasel and the Pit" (no. 43), one can see such an example. This story features a man and a woman who vow to marry each other, with a weasel and a pit as witnesses to their vow. This vow is considered binding, although the woman seeks to further the promise by becoming betrothed before her parents. This discussion reflects an awareness of one of the issues that was current in northern European Christianity at the time, when consent for marriage between two people was seen as binding, regardless of parental acquiescence.[93] Indeed marriage became a Christian sacrament at the same time *Sefer ha-ma'asim* was copied and the stories within it were retold; thus the question of parental agreement and the tension between it and vows made between men and women were at their apex. As this story is already found in Nathan b. Jeḥiel's *Sefer ha'Arukh*, and it is mentioned briefly by Rashi as well as the Tosafists, it can be seen as reflecting an ongoing conversation taking place in medieval northern Europe.[94]

---

91. William Burgwinkle, "The Marital and the Sexual," in *The Cambridge Companion to Medieval French Literature*, ed. Gaunt and Kay, 236.

92. Yassif, *Ninety-nine Tales*, 137–140. See also his discussion, "Sepher ha-Ma'asim," 157–162.

93. On the importance of vows, see Ruth Mazo Karras, *Unmarriages: Women, Men, and Sexual Unions in the Middle Ages* (Philadelphia: University of Pennsylvania Press, 2012), 56–59.

94. Jeḥiel b. Nathan, *Sefer ha-arukh ha-shalem*, ed. Alexander Kohut (Vienna: Menora, 1926), 3: 395–396; Rashi, BT *Ta'anit* 8a, s.v. "*ba'alei emunah*" and Tosafot *ad locum*.

As I noted earlier, the young woman's statement when she urges the man to return home with her and receive parental approval can be read as a comment on Christian practice and the difference between Christian and Jewish practices. The couple's conversation can also be read as an indication of values and tensions shared by Jews and Christians of the time. He states: "I am from Israel . . . from a priestly family. [She says:] I am . . . from well-known and respected people." She specifies: "You who are from such a holy people, whom the Almighty chose and sanctified from among all the nations, yet you wish to act like a beast without a marriage ceremony or marriage contract?" This statement underlines a difference between Jews and others, but it also fleshes out the issue at stake. Christians and Jews alike were contemplating the significance of such promises. So too the feigned possession of the girl when she refuses all marriage offers recalls a common theme in saints' lives where women were reported as possessed when they refused to marry.[95] Despite the story's emphasis on Jewish holiness, its encouragement of parental approval for marital agreements was not unique to Jews, "holy nation" or otherwise. The Church recognized marriages contracted with private vows between individuals but much preferred those with which the parents were involved.[96] Thus the moral suggested in the tale confirmed more than differed from that of contemporary Christians.

The place of charity, penance, and oaths are further examples I will briefly explore. These themes feature in multiple stories. Charity is a fascinating example, as it is the trait of the *ḥasid*, as we saw earlier. At the same time charity was the hallmark of Christian urban piety in medieval Europe.[97] At times it is specified in the exposition as being given by a *ḥasid* who was in synagogue or as given to supporting Torah scholars, as in "The Three Treasures" (no. 7), where the charity of the pious man is described in this way:

> [H]e had three treasures: one of gold coins, one of silver, and one of pennies. When he came to his students, he would give them of the gold coins; to

95. Caroline W. Bynum, *Holy Feast and Holy Fast: The Religious Significance of Food to Medieval Women* (Berkeley: University of California Press, 1987), 245–251; Elizabeth Alvina Petroff, *Medieval Women's Visionary Literature* (Oxford: Oxford University Press, 1986), 41–45.

96. Karras, *Unmarriages*, 57.

97. Michel Mollat, *The Poor in the Middle Ages: An Essay in Social History*, trans. A. Goldhammer (New Haven, CT: Yale University Press, 1986); James Brodman, *Charity and Religion in Medieval Europe* (Washington, DC: Catholic University of America Press, 2009); Adam J. Davis, "The Social and Religious Meanings of Charity in Medieval Europe," *History Compass* 12/12 (2014): 935–950.

> orphans and widows, he would give of the silver coins; and he would support orphans who did not study with the pennies. And how would he support them? He would give five gold coins to whomever had five souls in his home. And that was his practice every day.

This description is the exception, as most often charity is given as part of the plot, in keeping with a father's instructions or when en route.[98] Interestingly, the travels of the different protagonists contain little emphasis on their encounters with other Jews or contact with other Jewish communities.[99] Moreover, charity in these tales is not usually given to a community but rather to an individual, an attribute that differentiates these stories from communal documents that have reached us.[100] So how was charity depicted as a characteristic of Jewish piety or of Jewish behavior? The narrator underlines charity as a central Jewish trait, but aside from the religious identity of the donor, he sees little need to explain how or to whom the charity that was given. This leads me to a series of questions that *Sefer ha-ma'asim* opens up for scholars interested in charity: What were the modes of charity within the community? Did Jews give to non-Jews? What regulations did the community enforce? How should the assumption in the story that a Jewish *ḥasid* giving charity was doing an identifiable Jewish deed be understood, and what are its implications? Scholars have tried to outline the contours of medieval Ashkenazic piety—specifically in northern France but also beyond the French environs—and have repeatedly stressed how little material was at their disposal. *Sefer ha-ma'asim* and other collections of stories provide further material for this avenue of inquiry—if not of actual deeds, then at least of the way these deeds were presented.

The theme of penance also runs through the stories. The protagonists often repent at the ends of the stories and then return to the environments or the blessings

98. See "The Man Who Never Took an Oath" (no. 13). In this case, as Kushelevsky documents, the basis for this version seems to be *Sefer ḥasidim*. This opens up the question of the relationship between the two books, a question that is worthy of further scrutiny; and see Kushelevsky, *Tales in Context*, 410–414, and in parallels.

99. Charity is most often given on the road. See, for example, "Ben Sever and Shefifon Ben Layish" (no. 27); "Saved from Drowning by Charity" (no. 31); "The Power of a Single Act of Charity" (no. 51); "The Grateful Dead" (no. 65). In other cases it is depicted as an act performed within the home; see, for example, "The Three Treasures" (no. 7).

100. For patterns of giving charity among medieval Christians, see Sharon Farmer, *Surviving Poverty in Medieval Paris: Gender, Ideology, and the Daily Lives of the Poor* (Ithaca, NY: Cornell University Press, 2002). Compare Baumgarten, *Practicing Piety*, 116–128; and see Judah D. Galinsky for an overview of the difficulty of locating sources on charity: "Public Charity in Medieval Germany: A Preliminary Investigation," in *Toward a Renewed Ethic of Jewish Philanthropy*, ed. Yossi Prager (New York: Ktav Publishing, 2010), 79–92.

that had been lost along the way.[101] While penance was part of Jewish ritual well before the Middle Ages, these stories contain hints to medieval practices.[102] In "The Pious Pretender" (no. 50), a pious man who is falsely accused is led around the city square in shame:

> What did the owner of the money do? He took a rope and placed it around the neck of that *ḥasid* and led him throughout the city, declaring: Thus shall be done to he who takes a deposit and denies having done so. The shopkeepers who were present and knew that he was a righteous man wept for him and for what had happened to him. After he had so greatly humiliated him, he let him go and removed the rope from his neck. The man went home in great shame.

The words describing his parade echo the Book of Esther, however the practice of leading penitents by a chain around their necks was contemporary.[103] Medieval penitents walked around the city in chains. Examples such as this, alongside the repeated emphasis on repentance, all contribute to a flavor of medieval penance that was current among contemporary Jews and Christians.

Vows and oaths are other examples of an important theme, and they, too, feature in the collection, echoing traditional Jewish narratives from late antiquity alongside medieval innovations. Many stories feature sons making vows to their parents. Others—specifically "R. Joshua b. Levi and the Angel of Death" (no. 46) and "The Man Who Never Took an Oath (no. 13)—showcase protagonists who refuse to take an oath and as a result go on wondrous journeys.[104] Both the latter stories are found in *Midrash aseret hadibrot* as illustrations of the Third Commandment, and are

101. For example, "Do Not Fail to Attend Public Prayers" (no. 41).

102. For literature on medieval penance, see Rob Meens, *Penance in Medieval Europe, 600–1200* (Cambridge: Cambridge University Press, 2014), as well as Abigail Firey, ed., *A New History of Penance* (Leiden: Brill, 2008). Compare Baumgarten, *Practicing Piety*, 85–91.

103. Mary C. Mansfield, *Humiliation of Sinners: Public Penance in Thirteenth-Century France* (Ithaca, NY: Cornell University Press, 1995), 126.

104. One must distinguish between oaths within the Jewish community and those that were related to non-Jewish courts. Jacob Katz, *Exclusiveness and Tolerance* (Oxford: Oxford University Press, 1961), 35; Judah D. Galinsky, "Different Approaches Towards the Miracles of Christian Saints in Medieval Rabbinic Literature," in *Ta Shma: Studies in Judaica in Memory of Israel M. Ta-Shma*, ed. Rami Reiner et al. (Alon Shevut: Tevunot, 2011), 195–196, n. 2; David Berger, "Jacob Katz on Jews and Christians in the Middle Ages," in *The Pride of Jacob: Essays on Jacob Katz and His World*, ed. Jay Harris (Cambridge, MA: Harvard University Press, 2002), 60–61.

copied in *Sefer ha-ma'asim* based on these traditions.[105] These stories expose the centrality of oaths in medieval Jewish society while revealing the tremendous angst surrounding them—not just the result of religious deliberations but also because of local practice. Oaths were used regularly and constantly as part of medieval business interactions. All medieval men had to take oaths of this sort as part of regular interactions, and many women did as well, as they were required as part of legal processes (although we have little evidence of them in *Sefer ha-ma'asim*).[106] Within the medieval Christian world of northern Europe, oaths and their validity and use were also undergoing tremendous revision and debate. Oaths were taken to prove knightly loyalty and were also used in everyday conduct in the courtroom and in business transactions. Documentation by notaries, for example, was on the rise in medieval Europe, and the validity of different sorts of testimony was under deep discussion.[107] Here *Sefer ha-ma'asim*, in its traditional Jewish tales and in its "Judaized" tales, joins this conversation. The ending of "The Man Who Never Took an Oath" underlines these tensions by inserting a blessing unknown in other versions: "Blessed is the Lord who does not deprive the righteous who refrain from swearing their reward." This replaces the biblical quotation that ends this story in *Midrash aseret hadibrot* and spells out the matter at hand, indicating the anxiety around it.

Thus the Judaization of the stories serves to emphasize not only the way Jews made these stories their own—a feature that has been noted repeatedly—but also, to some extent, how little effort this took. Alongside reading the stories as indications of Jewish and Christian difference, as has been common to date, one can also read some of them as mirrors of cultural aspects of medieval Jewish life—aspects that in many cases were shared by their Christian neighbors as well. Literary analysis exposes the dialogue with contemporary French and Latin compositions,[108] and I believe the work in this book is just the tip of the iceberg. Studying the balance between the more general tensions and those specific to Jews has the potential to

105. See *Midrash aseret hadibrot*, 52–59, and see Perry, *Tradition and Transformation*, 82–83. Also see *Sefer ḥasidim*, ed. Judah Wistenetzky (Frankfurt: Mekize Nirdamim, 1924), no. 1285, where Judah the Pious similarly objects to any kind of oath.

106. For a description of these procedures, see Rachel Furst, "Striving for Justice: A History of Women and Litigation in the Jewish Courts of Medieval Ashkenaz," PhD diss., Hebrew University (Jerusalem, 2014), 158–197.

107. Anders Winroth, "The Legal Revolution of the Twelfth Century," in *European Transformations: The Long Twelfth Century*, ed. Thomas X. Noble and John Van Engen (Notre Dame, IN: Notre Dame University Press, 2012), 346–351. See also Susan Alice McDonough, *Witnesses, Neighbors, and Community in Late Medieval Marseille* (New York: Palgrave, 2013); Esther Cohen, *The Crossroads of Justice: Law and Culture in Late Medieval France* (Leiden: Brill, 1993), 54–59.

108. See chapter 3, 65–82.

further nuance our understanding of Jews as a minority within their Christian surroundings. The ease with which stories were Judaized reflects both the intimacy between Jews and Christians as well as the deep rift between the cultures.

Christian Rulers and Christian Culture in *Sefer ha-ma'asim*

I have argued that *Sefer ha-ma'asim* can be mined for information, directions, and evidence of tensions that have to do with daily life and with multiple levels of Jewish society. Yet my emphasis thus far has been on internal Jewish relations and on the ways these stories Judaized elements from their surroundings. What else can be said about the relationship of the Jews to the Christian culture around them besides the appropriation of elements from within it and their use within Jewish culture?

As discussed in the introduction to this edition, *Sefer ha-ma'asim* was copied as part of a larger collection of narrative materials in thirteenth-century Champagne.[109] Champagne was the geographic area where the Tosafists, including (R. Shlomo Yitzchaki) and his grandsons, Rabbenu Tam [R. Jacob b. Meir] and Rashbam [R. Samuel b. Meir] as well as well as many others, were active.[110] It was also the home of numerous famous medieval French authors of courtly literature who hailed from this area, among them Marie de France and, even more important, Chretien de Troyes, as well as others whose names are less known.[111] Thus *Sefer ha-ma'asim* fits both into the Jewish scholarly milieu, in which writing and copying were a constant, as well as into the more general cultural environment, in which the telling and writing of stories were of great import.

Recent research by Rami Reiner has deepened the associations modern scholars have pointed to between Jews and Christians in Champagne in the cultural sphere. Reiner has documented evidence of the actual connections that existed between the Jewish and Christian elites not only concerning matters of taxation or policy but also around cultural topics.[112] Reiner has found evidence of a discussion of biblical

109. Oxford Bodl. Or. 135 contains more than a dozen compilations of collected tales; see Kushelevsky, *Tales in Context*, 3–8.

110. See Avraham Grossman, *The Early Sages of France: Their Lives, Leadership and Works* (Jerusalem: Magnes Press 1995), 121–131 [Hebrew].

111. See Kushelevsky, *Tales in Context*, 65–66, 75–76, 80–81. See also Jean Frappier, *Chrétien de Troyes: The Man and His Work*, trans. Raymond J. Corvier (Athens: Ohio University Press, 1982), 157–182, and more recently Sarah-Jane K. Murray, *From Plato to Lancelot: A Preface to Chrétien de Troyes* (Syracuse, NY: Syracuse University Press, 2008), 253–262, which discusses the rapid spread and influence of Chrétien's work.

112. Avraham (Rami) Reiner, "Bible and Politics: A Correspondence between Rabbenu Tam and the Authorities of Champagne," in *Entangled Histories: Knowledge, Authority, and Transmission in Thirteenth-Century Jewish Cultures*, ed. Elisheva Baumgarten, Ruth Mazo

passages that took place between R. Tam and Henri of Champagne in the late twelfth century. The friendly and familiar character of the conversation stands out in the Hebrew account of it and joins additional evidence of the interchanges among French Jews and Christians.[113]

Jewish studies scholars have often noted the cultural vitality of the northern French environment in the High Middle Ages, with an emphasis on the twelfth century in Champagne and the thirteenth century in Paris.[114] Synthetic summaries tend to combine centuries and the various geographic locales, but the differences between the time periods and the geographies are potentially crucial in the case of *Sefer ha-ma'asim*. The legal and political realities of the Jews of Champagne were distinct from those of the Jews under the French monarchy during the last quarter of the twelfth century and the early thirteenth century. As opposed to the Jews of Paris, who were under the jurisdiction of the French king and experienced multiple expulsions from 1182 onward, the Jews of Champagne, who were under the rule of the counts of Champagne—Henry, Thibaut, and others—were not exiled or financially pressured in the same way during the late twelfth century. Their situation changed markedly during the early thirteenth century, after the death of Thibaut and his wife Blanche's accession to the throne and her dealings with King Philip II Augustus. It is from these years that there is evidence of Jews from Champagne who attempted to leave the region and move to Paris where, although under monarchic control, the situation allowed Jews more prosperity.[115]

Karras, and Katelyn Mesler (Philadelphia: University of Pennsylvania Press, 2017), 59–72. See also Aryeh Grabois, "The *Hebraica veritas* and Jewish-Christian Relations in the Twelfth Century," *Speculum* 50 (1975): 613–634; David Berger, "Mission to the Jews and Jewish-Christian Contacts in the Polemical Literature of the High Middle Ages," *American Historical Review* 91 (1986): 576–591.

113. Fudeman, *Vernacular Voices*, 16.

114. Robert Chazan, *Medieval Jewry in Northern France* (Baltimore, MD: Johns Hopkins University Press, 1973).

115. My main source for this period and its events has been William Chester Jordan, *The French Monarchy and the Jews* (Philadelphia: University of Pennsylvania Press, 1989). See also M. Gerson, "Les Juifs en Champagne," *Mémoires de la Société académique d'agriculture, des sciences, arts et belles-lettres du départment de l'Aube* 63 (1899): 173–261; Emily Taitz, *Jews of Medieval France: The Community of Champagne* (Westport, CT: Greenwood Publishing Group, 1994), 95–118, 119–147. See also Solomon Grayzel, *The Church and the Jews in the Thirteenth Century* (Philadelphia: Jewish Publication Society, 1969), 1: 268–269, 252–253.

Alongside the testimonies concerning the efforts of Champenois Jews to leave Champagne there is also evidence of a considerable Jewish population in Champagne throughout the thirteenth century. William Chester Jordan estimates there were forty towns in which Jews dwelled in 1285, and while a significant number of Jews left Champagne during the thirteenth century, the number of cities they inhabited was still far larger than in other territories outside of the control of the monarchy, and perhaps the community enjoyed a relative prosperity.[116]

In short, the period during which *Sefer ha-ma'asim* was copied was one of great unrest. The challenges facing the Jewish communities were mounting. *Sefer ha-ma'asim* does not express these tensions. One could argue that, since we can date only when *Sefer ha-ma'asim* was copied but do not know whether the stories were collected in an earlier manuscript and copied from it, it is impossible to understand the exact circumstances of its creation. Was the copying of Oxford, Ms. Bodl. Or. 135 an act of preservation? Was it based on a twelfth-century version that didn't survive and, as such, did it reflect a period of greater security? Alternatively, does *Sefer ha-ma'asim* reflect life continuing despite hardship in medieval Champagne? Based on *Sefer ha-ma'asim*, Jewish life in Champagne continued, and the communities seemed to have remained dynamic, despite the gradual departure of community members to other locales.[117] As we lack sufficient evidence, these questions must remain open.

One last aspect related to ruling powers and hierarchies that has been noted by scholars studying other collections of tales is Christianity itself. What about polemic references to Christianity as a religion? In his recent work Eli Yassif has underlined the extent to which medieval Hebrew stories can help us better understand Jewish-Christian relations, especially from an internal Jewish perspective. In contrast, as Kushelevsky notes briefly in her introduction, *Sefer ha-ma'asim* contains what she calls a "subdued tension" with Christianity.[118] Jewish motifs are substituted for Christian ones, and values that are considered Jewish, such as the Sabbath, are emphasized without overt references to Christian culture. What, then, can be deduced from these stories that can further a historical understanding of the narrating society and its relations with Christianity?

116. Jordan, *French Monarchy*, 190, 309 n. 95.

117. Ibid.

118. Kushelevsky, *Tales in Context*, 18.

In the story of the three youths from the Book of Daniel, which follows the story of Abraham breaking his father's idols, a classic story from late antiquity, a pointed epilogue appears:

> God uproots anyone who worships idols both from this world and the next, and he will see all the good that God will do for the righteous ones, and they will be ashamed and say: Woe unto us that we did not merit this honor, because we abandoned a living God to worship a dead one. And then fire will emerge and consume all the apostates who abandoned God and did not repent.

This reference to those who abandon a living God and worship a dead one is pointedly intended against Christians. However it is perhaps more noteworthy that the phrase is even more specifically employed against converts "who abandoned God and did not repent."

The same statement can be found in Oxford, Ms. Bodl. Or. 135 at the end of the story of the mother and her seven sons—not in *Sefer ha-ma'asim* but in *Midrash aseret hadibrot*, another example of the close connections between our collection of stories and the Midrash, as Kushelevsky has demonstrated. This emphasis is fascinating, for it is an objection not against people who converted per se but rather against those who converted but chose not to return to Judaism when they had the opportunity to do so. They "abandoned God and did not repent." While these epilogues clearly contain anti-Christian content, this is not their focus; instead they are more closely related to the Jewish community itself and the converts from within it.

Indeed within the context of northern French Jewry during the thirteenth century, the question of converts and their return to Judaism or lack thereof was a pressing issue. Throughout the thirteenth century it became harder for converts to return to Judaism, and there is evidence of significant numbers of converts, even if, as Susan Einbinder has argued, the conversion project undertaken in France was not a success.[119] The epilogue suggests that critique was directed less at the actual conversion—which perhaps, under dire circumstances, was a common course of action—but rather at those who converted and did not return to Judaism when they had the chance.[120] Moreover, the explicit emphasis on converts in the epilogue is of importance, even if

119. Einbinder, *Beautiful Death: Jewish Poetry and Martyrdom in Medieval France* (Princeton, NJ: Princeton University Press, 2002), 126–130.

120. See the recent study by Paola Tartakoff, "Testing Boundaries: Jewish Conversion and Cultural Fluidity in Medieval Europe, c. 1200–1391," *Speculum* 90 (2015): 733–744, which suggests a new understanding of conversion in which converts came from the margins of society.

it is a feature of only two stories. These stories are both well known from antiquity. Thus the copyist/compiler of *Sefer ha-ma'asim* chose to embellish the traditional narrative. Although the additions are not major, the fact that they are added on to a narrative that was well known and fairly standardized is of significance.

In the broader context of Jewish society in medieval northern Europe, this emphasis on the converts is somewhat discordant with another voice that has been described (perhaps overdescribed) at length in scholarly discussions of Jews in medieval northern Europe and their experience vis-à-vis Christian attempts to convert them. The trope of martyrs who preferred death to conversion is a well-known one throughout medieval Ashkenaz, including northern France, the Rhineland, and other parts of modern Germany, as well as medieval England. The Rhineland suicides during the First Crusade and the chronicles documenting them thereafter set the tone both in medieval texts and in modern scholarship; yet *Sefer ha-ma'asim* contains few references to martyrdom, with the exception of the two stories described here, which, despite the presence of a martyrological tenet, call on repentance from conversion in the epilogue.[121] My argument is not that martyrology was not a common theme among the audience of *Sefer ha-ma'asim*.[122] Rather, if these stories are to be read as reflecting local tensions and conflicts, I suggest that they point us in a different direction, to a social problem that has received far less attention than perhaps it deserves: that of converts and their return or lack of return to Judaism.

In sum, reading *Sefer ha-ma'asim* with an eye to Jewish-Christian relations is not all that fruitful. Based on most of the historical research to date concerning thirteenth-century Jews of northern France at large, one could expect strong Jewish-Christian tensions to stand out in the retellings and embellishments of Jewish stories. Instead, even the stories that are novel to this compilation contain few references to surrounding tensions. Combining this with the strong rhetoric we saw earlier in the story of the mother and her seven sons and that of Ḥananiah, Mishael, and Azaria in the fire, one sees little evidence of the events the Jews of Champagne faced during this period, aside from the expectation that converts return to Judaism

121. For the relationship between Rhineland suicides and processes of conversion in northern France, see Einbinder, *Beautiful Death*.

122. For French cases of martyrology, see the events analyzed by Einbinder, *Beautiful Death*. Blois (1171) and Troyes (1288) have been discussed by Einbinder and others at great length. See, for example, Robert Chazan, "The Blois Incident of 1171: A Study in Jewish Intercommunal Organization," in *Proceedings of the American Academy for Jewish Research* 36 (1968): 13–32; Kirsten Fudeman, "Restoring a Vernacular Jewish Voice: The Old French Elegy of Troyes," *Jewish Studies Quarterly* 15 (2008): 190–221. For a less-known and less-discussed event, see Robert Chazan, "The Bray Incident of 1192: Realpolitik and Folk Slander," *Proceedings of the American Academy for Jewish Research* 37 (1969): 1–18.

when the time was right. If the tension with converts was exemplified by those who converted and returned to Judaism as opposed to those who left the fold more permanently, this story opens a new vista for examining conversion and the return from conversion, and provides an insight into Jewish identity that is worthy of further consideration.[123]

The questions I have raised throughout this essay are meant to point to the potential the stories in *Sefer ha-ma'asim* have for future historical and cultural research, much like the commentaries on the stories in this edition are not meant as definitive and finite but as opening analyses ready for fuller exploration of this material in the future. Pointing to one focus that has emerged throughout this essay, I suggest that *Sefer ha-ma'asim* allows a path toward a social history of the Jewish communities of northern France and beyond that has hardly been explored to date. With its numerous portrayals of Jewish families—even if in some cases these are only the bare bones of a family—it allows for a better understanding of cultural conceptions of familial structures that were at the foundation of the communities as a whole. So too is the place of community qua community worthy of further investigation based on these stories. As the narratives comment on rather than reflect reality, they point to how medieval people construed their world, invested it with meaning, and interpreted it with emotion; they provide avenues for further scrutiny of all the sources we have for studying these communities and perhaps for new emphases and directions of research. Collating the information and anxieties in the story with sources from other genres can help flesh out the nuances of medieval life and enrich the picture to which we have access.

In conclusion, one anonymous Jew from medieval Champagne, during the mid-thirteenth century, saw the need to copy/compile *Sefer ha-ma'asim* as part of an elaborate effort to preserve and transmit narrative collections. One can only surmise what his motives were, but reaching beyond the copyist/editor, to the society for whom this collection was compiled, allows us access to the stories medieval Jews told and made part of their cultural repertoire. The stories told resonated with his audience, and studying them allows us access to the mentality of the community

123. We look forward to Ephraim Kanarfogel's book on converts. See Jessica M. Elliott, "Jews 'Feigning Devotion': Christian Representations of Converted Jews in French Chronicles before and after the Expulsion of 1306," in *Jews and Christians in Thirteenth-Century France*, ed. Baumgarten and Galinsky, 169–182.

and especially their tensions and anxieties. Kushelevsky began her introduction to this volume by underscoring the story about Solomon's scribe and, as befits a literary scholar, noting the important role of the copyist/editor of this text. I conclude by restating the value of these stories to scholars who are interested in medieval Jews, named and unnamed, and their everyday lives.

Bibliography

Manuscripts, Primary Sources, and Studies

Manuscripts

Cambridge (Mass.), Harvard University

Cambridge-Harvard, Heb. 39, tales, 115a–124b

Cambridge Add. 663, tales, 243b–320b

Cincinnati, Hebrew Union College

Cincinnati 61a, tales, 51a–85b

Darmstadt, Hessisches Landes-und Hochschulbibliothek

Darmstadt, Cod. Or. 25, tales, 67b–68b

Darmstadt, Cod. Or. 26, *Fables of R. Berakhiah Hanakdan*, 1a–28b

Jerusalem, Israel Museum

180/051, *Midrash vayissa'u*

Jerusalem, National and University Library

Jerusalem 1970, tales

Jerusalem 3182, tales, 102a–140b (published by Yassif, *Ninety-nine Tales*)

Jerusalem Heb. 5245 (Innsbruck), *Mayse bukh*, 1–117, no. 1–no. 109 (archaic Yiddish)

London, Beth Din and Beth Hamidrash

London, Bet-Din 28, *Midrash aseret hadibrot*, 64–70

London, British Library

Or. 1389, tales scattered among moral and midrashic compositions

BL Harley 5508, tractate b*Succa*

London, Montefiore Library

431, *Midrash vayissa'u*, 38a–39b

Manchester, John Rylands University Library

Manchester-Gaster 82

Moscow, Russian State Library

Günzburg 111, *Midrash aseret hadibrot*, 99a–138a

München-Bayerische Staatsbibliothek

Munich, Cod. Hebr. 207, *Fables of R. Berakhia ha-Nakdan*, 64a–103b

Munich, Cod. Hebr. 222 (aggadic and moral compositions)

Munich, 100, tales in archaic Yiddish, 74b–89b

Munich, 140, tractate b*Ta'anit*

Munich Cod. Hebr. 495 (Robera), *Mayse bukh*, 1b–156 (archaic Yiddish)

Munich, Cod. Hebr. 95, tractate b*Succa*

New York, Jewish Theological Seminary

JTS 2374, tales, 111a–124b

Oxford, Bodleian Library (order of items according to their numbers in Cat. Neubauer)

Bodl. Or. 135 (1466), *Sefer ha-ma'asim*, 300a–339b

Opp. 27, *Midrash aseret hadibrot*, 234b–244a

Paris, Bibliothèque Nationale

Hébreu 716, *Midrash aseret hadibrot*, 206b–228a; *Ḥibbur yafeh mehayeshu'a*, 167b–206b

Parma, Biblioteca Palatina

Cod. Parm. 2269 (De Rossi 473), *Midrash aseret hadibrot*, 49b–89a

Cod. Parm. 2342 (De Rossi 541), Commentary on the Torah of R. Nethanel, 1a–107b

Cod. Parm. 2295 (De Rossi 563), tales, 87a–88b; 92a–93a; 121a;126b–140b (published in Kushelevsky, *Penalty and Temptation*)

Vatican, Biblioteca Apostolica

ebr. 107, *Midrash aseret hadibrot*, 160a–183a

ebr. 249, *Midrash aseret hadibrot*, 319b–331b

ebr. 285, *Midrash aseret hadibrot*, 67a–79b

ebr. 323, *Midrash vayissa'u*, 113a–113b; 171a–171b

ebr. 134, tractate b*Succa*

Warszaw, Zydowski Instytut Historyczny

Warsaw 374, *Midrash aseret hadibrot*, 181a–202b

Wolfenbuettel, Herzog August Bibliothek Cod. Guelf. Aug.

Wolfen Herz. Aug. fol. 36.25, *Midrash aseret hadibrot*, 4a–12b

Zurich, Zentralbibliothek Heid

Heid Zurich 192, *Midrash aseret hadibrot*, 61a–78b

Compilations and Primary Sources

Aboab, Isaac. *Menorat hama'or* (*The Candelabrum of Light*). Ed. Judah Paris Ḥorev and Moses Ḥaim Katzenelenbogen. Jerusalem: Mossad Ha-Rav Kook, 1961. [Hebrew]

Abramson, Shraga. *R. Nissim Gaon Libelli Quinque*. Jerusalem: Mekitze-nirdamim, 1965. [Hebrew]

Abulafia, Meir Halevi Todrus. *Yad ramah* (lit., "The Upraised Hand"; an acronym of the auther's Hebrew name). Tractate *Baba-Batra*. Jerusalem: Sifri'at Bnei Torah Hamerukezet, 1992. [Hebrew]

Aḥai Gaon. *She'iltot* [*Responsa*] *of R. Aḥai gaon*. Ed. Samuel K. Mirsky. Jerusalem: Sura Research and Publication Foundation, Yeshiva University, 1977. [Hebrew]

Alfasi, Isaac (Rif). *Hilkhot rav alfasi* (*Rules of Rav Alfasi*). Tractate *Yebamot*, *Talmud bavli*. Vilna: Romm, 1880–1886. Repr., *The Babylonian Talmud*. [Hebrew]

Alfonsi, Petrus. *Dialogue against the Jews*. Trans. I. M. Resnick. Washington, DC: Catholic University of America, 2006.

———. *Die Disciplina Clericalis des Petrus Alfonsi*. Ed. Alfons Hilka und Werner Söderhjelm. Heidelberg: Carl Winter, 1911.

———. *The Disciplina Clericalis of Petrus Alfonsi*. Trans. and ed. Eberhard Hermes. English trans. P. R. Quarrie. Berkeley: University of California Press, 1977.

[Ibn] Al-Nakawa, Israel. *Menorat hama'or* (*The Candelabrum of Light*), vols. 1–4. Ed. H. G. Enelow. New York: Bloch, 1929–1932. [Hebrew]

Al Thalabi, Ara'is Abu Ishaq Ahmad Ibn Muhammad Ibn Ibrahim. *Ara'is Al-Majalis fi Qisas Al-Anbiya or Lives of the Prophets*. Trans. and annotated William M. Brinner. Leiden: Brill, 2002.

Araki, El'azar, *Sefer hama'asiyot*. Calcutta, 1842. [Hebrew]; Repr., Baghdad: Solomon Bekhor Ḥuẓin, 1852. [Hebrew]

Asher b. Yeḥiel (Rosh). Commentary on the Talmud, tractate Yebamot, *Talmud bavli*. Vilna: Romm, 1880–1886. Reprint. [Hebrew]

———. *Responsa of R. Asher b. Yeḥiel*. Ed. Isaac Solomon Udlov. Jerusalem: Jerusalem Institute, 1994. [Hebrew]

Aucassin and Nicolette and Other Medieval Romances and Legends. Trans. Eugene Mason. London: Dent, 1910.

Avoth de-rabbi Nathan. Ed. Solomon Schechter. With references to parallels in the two versions and to the addenda in the Schechter edition. Prolegomenon by Menaḥem Kister. New York: Jewish Theological Seminary, 1997. [Hebrew]

Baḥya [b. Asher]. *Commentary on the Torah*. Vol. 1. Ed. Ḥaim Dov Chavel. Jerusalem: Mosad ha-Rav Kook, 1982. [Hebrew]

———. *Kad hakemaḥ* (*Receptacle of the Flour*), *Kitvei rabbenu Baḥya*. Ed. Ḥaim Dov Chavel. Jerusalem: Mosad ha-Rav Kook, 1970. [Hebrew]

Bar-Ilan University. The Responsa Project, Global Jewish Database: http://responsa .biu.ac.il

Baraita de-masekhet niddah. Ed. Ch. M. Horowitz. In *Tosefta Atikta*. Frankfurt am. Main: Bet Meshar ha-Sefarim shel Horowitz, 1889. [Hebrew]

Barash, Asher. *Menorat hazahav* (*The Golden Candelabrum*). Tel Aviv: Masada, 1965. [Hebrew]

Barbazan, Étienne. *Fabliaux et Contes Des Poetes Francois Des XI, XII, XIII, XIV et XV Siecles*. Paris: de l'imprimerie de Crapelet, 1808.

Ben Yeḥezkel, Mordekhai. *Sefer hama'asiyot* (*Book of Tales*). Vols. 2, 6. Tel Aviv: Dvir, 1958. [Hebrew]

Berakhiah. *Fables of a Jewish Aesop*. Translated from the *Fox Fables of Berechia Ha-nakdan* by Moses Hadas. New York: Columbia University Press, 1967.

———. *The Mishle shualim (Fox Fables) of Rabbi Berekhiah Hanakdan*. Ed. A. M. Habermann. Jerusalem: Schocken, 1946. [Hebrew]

Berekhiah b. Moses of Modena, Aaron. *Ma'avar yabok* (*The Yabok Passage*). Jerusalem: Ahavat Shalom, 1996. [Hebrew]

Béroul. *The Romance of Tristan*. Ed. and trans. Norris J. Lacy. Garland Library of Medieval Literature, vol. 36, series A. New York: Garland, 1989.

Bialik, Ḥayyim Nahman. *And It Came to Pass: Legends and Stories about King David and King Solomon*. Told by Hayyim Nahman Bialik. Trans. Herbert Denby. New York: Hebrew Pub., 1938. Repr. Whitefish, MT: Kessinger Publising, 2010.

Bialik, Ḥayyim Nahman, and Yehoshua Hana Ravnitzky. *The Book of Legends, Sefer Ha-Aggadah: Legends from the Talmud and Midrash*. Trans. William G. Braude. Intro. David Stern. New York: Schocken, 1992.

Bin Gorion (Berdyczewski), Micha Joseph. *Mimekor yisrael*. Tel Aviv: Dvir, 1965. [Hebrew]

———. *Mimekor yisrael: Classical Jewish Folktales.* Abridged and annotated edition. Collected by Micha Joseph Bin Gorion. Ed. Emanuel Bin Gorion; trans. I. M. Lask. Prepared and with introduction and headnotes by Dan Ben-Amos. Bloomington: Indiana University Press, 1990.

———. *Ẓefunot ve'agadot* (*Secrets and Legends*). Tel Aviv: Am-Oved, 1956. [Hebrew]

Boccaccio, Giovanni. *Decameron.* A cura di Cesare Segre. Commento di Maria Segre Consigli. Milano: Grande Universale Mursia, 1966–1970. (English edition trans. and intro. G. H. Mcwilliam [Harmondsworth: Penguin, 1972].)

"Book of Jubilees, The." In *The Apocrypha and Pseudepigrapha*, vol. 2. Ed. Robert Henry Charles. Oxford: Clarendon Press, 1913, 1–82.

"Book of Tobit, The." In *The Apocrypha and Pseudepigrapha*, vol. 1. Ed. Robert Henry Charles. Oxford: Clarendon Press, 1913, 174–241.

Brinner, William M., trans. *An Elegant Composition Concerning Relief after Adversity by Nissim ben Jacob ibn Shahin.* New Haven, CT: Yale University Press, 1977.

Buber, Solomon. *Likkutim memidrash abkir* (*Extracts from Midrash Abkir*). Vienna, 1883. [Hebrew]

Caesarii Heisterbacensis Monachi ordinis Cisterciensis. *Dialogus Miraculorum.* 2 vols. Ed. Josephus Strange. Cologne: Sumptibus J. M. Heberle (H. Lempertz & comp.), 1851.

Caesarius of Heisterbach. *The Dialogue on Miracles.* Vols. 1–2. Trans. H. Von E. Scott and C. C. Swinton Bland. Intro. G. G. Coulton. London: Routledge & Sons, 1929.

Le Cento Novelle Antiche, secondo l'edizione del MDXXV corrette ed illustrate con note [. . .]. Ed. Carlo Gualteruzzi, Paolo Antonio Tosi, Michele Colombo. Milano: Tip.di F. Rusconi, 1825.

[Ibn] Chabib, Jacob. *En Jacob.* Rev. and trans. into English by S. H. Glick. Vols. 1–5. New York: S. H. Glick, 1916–1921. [Text in English and Hebrew]

La chanson de Roland. Lettres Gothiques. Paris: Livre de Poche, 1990.

Charles, R. H., ed. *The Apocrypha and Pseudepigrapha of the Old Testament.* Vols. 1–2. Oxford: Clarendon Press, 1913.

Chaucer, Geoffrey. *The Canterbury Tales: Nine Tales and the General Prologue.* Selected and edited by V. A. Kolve and Glending Olson. New York: W. W. Norton & Company, 1989.

———. "The Franklin's Tale." In *The Canterbury Tales*. Modern English trans. Nevill Coghill. Baltimore, MD: Penguin Books, 1951, 426–451.

Chrétien de Troyes. *Le chevalier au lion ou le roman d'Yvain.* Ed. David. F. Hult. Collection lettres gothiques. Paris: Le livre de Poche, 1994.

———. *Erec et Enide*. Ed. J. M. Fritz. Collection lettres gothiques. Paris: Le livre de Poche, 1992.

———. *Erec and Enide*. Trans. and intro. Dorothy Gilbert. Berkeley: University of California Press, 1992.

———. *The Story of the Grail* (*Li contes del Graal or Perceval*). Ed. Rupert T. Pickens. Trans. William W. Kibler. Garland Library of Medieval Literature, vol. 62, series A. New York: Garland Publishing, 1990.

———. *Yvain, The Knight of the Lion.* Trans. Burton Raffel. New Haven, CT: Yale University Press, 1987.

Da'at zekenim (*Wisdom of the Elders*). Livorno, 1783. [Hebrew]

Dan, Joseph, ed. *Alilot Alexander Macedon* (*The Deeds of Alexander Mocdon*). Jerusalem: Bialik Institute, 1969. [Hebrew]

David ha-Adani. *Midrash hagadol* (*The Great Midrash*), Deuteronomy. Ed. Solomon Fish. Jerusalem: Mosad ha-Rav Kook, 1997. [Hebrew]

———. *Midrash hagadol*, Exodus. Ed. Mordecai Margulies. Jerusalem: Mosad ha-Rav Kook, 1997. [Hebrew]

———. *Midrash hagadol*, Genesis. Ed. Mordecai Margulies. Jerusalem: Mosad ha-Rav Kook, 1997. [Hebrew]

———. *Midrash hagadol*, Leviticus. Ed. Adin Steinzalts. Jerusalem: Mosad ha-Rav Kook, 1997. [Hebrew]

———. *Midrash hagadol*, Numbers. Ed. Zvi Meir Rabinowitz. Jerusalem: Mosad ha-Rav Kook, 1997. [Hebrew]

David Hanagid. *Midrash david hanagid.* Trans. and ed. Abraham I. Katsh. Jerusalem: Mossad Harav Kook, 1969. [Hebrew]

———. *Sefer midrash david: Commentary on Tractate Avot.* Jerusalem: Ben Ẓion Krinpis, 1944. [Hebrew]

Dayan, Abraham b. Jeshaya. *Holekh tamim upoel ẓedek* (*He That Walketh Uprightly, and Worketh Righteousness*). Livorno, 1850. [Hebrew]

———. *Zikharon lanefesh* (*A Memory for the Soul*). Jerusalem: Mechon haketav, 1985. [Hebrew]

Deuteronomy rabbah (*Devarim rabbah*), *Midrash rabbah.* Vol. 2. [Hebrew]

E.D.N.A. IFA Search Engine. http://ifa.haifa.ac.il (last accessed August 28, 2016). [Hebrew]

Eisenstein, Jehudah David. *Oẓar Midrashim* (*A Treasure of Midrashim*). 2 vols. New York, 1915. Reprint, New York: Grossman, 1956. [Hebrew]

Eleazar b. Judah [of Worms]. "*Darkhei Teshuva.*" In *Shut Maharam* (*Responsa* of Maharam), R. Meir of Rotenberg. Prague, 1608. Reprint ed. M. A. Bloch. Budapest, 1895, 162–163.

———. *Sefer haroke'aḥ hagadol.* Fano, 1505. Reprint ed. Baruch Simon Elazar Shneorson. Jerusalem: Ozar haposkim, 1967. [Hebrew]

Elijah Hacohen. *Me'il zedaka* (*A Coat of Charity*). Izmir, 1731. Reprint ed. Hillel Kuperman. 2 vols. Jerusalem, 1990. [Hebrew]

Elshakar, Moses b. Isaac, *She'elot u'teshuvot maharam elshakar* (*Responsa of Maharam Elshakar*). Jerusalem: Safra, 1959. [Hebrew]

Enzyklopädie des Märchens: *Handwoerterbuch zur historischen und vergleichenden Erzaehlforschung.* Founded by K. Ranke. Ed. R. W. Brednich et al. Berlin: Walter de Gruyter, vol. 1 (1977); vol. 5 (1987); vol. 8 (1996); vol. 12 (2006).

Epstein, Morris, ed. *Tales of Sendebar.* Philadelphia: Jewish Publication Society of America, 1967. [Text in Hebrew, with English trans. and notes]

Étienne de Bourbon. *Anecdotes historiques, Légendes et Apologues, publiés par A. Lecoy de la Marche.* Paris, 1877.

Exodus rabbah, Midrash rabbah. Vol. 1. [Hebrew]

[*Exodus rabbah,*] *Midrash shemot rabbah.* Ed. Avigdor Shinan. Chapters 1–14. Jerusalem: Dvir, 1984. [Hebrew]

Farḥi, Joseph Shabbtai. *Oseh pele* (*Performing Miracles*). Livorno, 1870. [Hebrew]

Fekhman, Zvi Hirsh b. Moses. *Ma'asei hashem* (*The Deeds of God*). Warsaw, 1881. [Hebrew]

Figo, Azariah. *Bina le'itim* (*Wisdom for Occasions*). Vol. 1. Jerusalem: Wagshal, 1989.

Freytag, Gustav. *Fākihat al-khulafā' wa-mufākahat al-ẓurafā'.* Vol. 1. Bonn, 1832.

Gaster, Moses. *Exempla of the Rabbis* (*Sefer hama'asiyot*). New York: Ktav, 1924. Reprint, 1968. [English and Hebrew]

Genesis rabbah (*Bereshit rabba*). Ed. J. Theodor and Ch. Albeck. Vols. 1–3. Jerusalem: Vaharman, 1965. Reprint, Shalem, 1996. [Hebrew]

Genesis rabbati (*Bereshit rabbati*). Ed. Ch. Albek. Jerusalem: Mekize Nirdamim, 1940. Reprint, Jerusalem: Vagshal, 1984. [Hebrew]

Gesta Romanorum. Old English Version. Ed. F. Madden. London, 1838. Reprinted and enlarged in *EETS* (Early English Text Society), vol. 33.

Gesta Romanorum. Ed. H. Österley. Berlin, 1872.

Gesta Romanorum: Entertaining Moral Stories. Trans. Charles Swan. Preface by E. A. Baker. London: Routledge, 1905.

Die Gesta Romanorum, Nach der Innsbrucker Handschrift vom Jahre 1342 und vier Münchener handschriften. Ed. W. Dick. Erlanger Beiträge zur englischen philologie 7 (1890).

Ginzberg, Louis. *The Legends of the Jews.* Vol. 1. Philadelphia: Jewish Publication Society of America, 1968; vol. 4, 1968. [Hebrew]

Gormont and Isembart. In *Heroes of the French Epic: A Selection of Chansons de Geste*. Trans. Michael Newth. Woodbridge: Boydell Press, 2005, 11–28.

Gormont et Isembart: Fragment de Chanson de Geste Du XII Siècle. Ed. Alphonse Bayot. Les Classiques Français du Moyen Age. Paris: Librairie Ancienne Honoré champion, éditeur, 1914.

Grünhut, Elazar haLevi. *Sefer ha-Likkutim Sammlung*. Jerusalem, 1898–1904. Reprint, Jerusalem, 1967. [Hebrew]

Grünwald, Ze'ev Wolf. *Yalkut Sippurim* (*A Collection of Tales*). 2 vols. Jerusalem: Warsaw, 1948. Reprint, Jerusalem: Eshkol, 1982. [Hebrew]

Habermann, A. M., ed. "The Piyyutim of R. Baruch Bar Shemuel of Mainz." In *Studies of the Research Institute for Hebrew Poetry in Jerusalem*, vol. 6. Jerusalem: Schocken, 1945. [Hebrew]

———, ed. *Sefer gezerot ashkenaz vetzorfat* (*The Book of Decrees in Ashkenaz and France*). Jerusalem, 1945. [Hebrew]

———, ed. *Texts: Old and New* (*Ḥadashim gam yeshanim: Ḥiburim shonim metokh kitvei-yad*). Jerusalem: Rubin Mass, 1975. [Hebrew]

[Ibn] Ḥabib, Jacob. *En Jacob*. Saloniki, 1516. [Hebrew]

Hadar zekenim: Tosafists and the Rosh on the Torah. Livorno, 1840. Reprint, Jerusalem: Limudei Kiryat No'ar, 1963. [Hebrew]

Hadassi, Judah. *Eshkol hakofer*. Goslow, 1746. [Hebrew]

Hagadot hatalmud (*Legends of the Talmud*). Constantinople, 1511. Reprint, Jerusalem: Vaharman & Bamberger, 1961. [Hebrew]

Ḥaim b. Moses (*Or zaru'a*). *Piskei halakha* (*Jewish Rulings*). Ed. Isaak Simson Lange. Jerusalem, 1972. [Hebrew]

Hameiri, R. Menahem. *Bet habeḥira* (*The Chosen House* [i.e., the Temple]). Tractate *Baba Batra*. Ed. Baruch Joseph Menat. Tel Aviv, 1971. [Hebrew]

Haverkamp, Eva, ed. *Hebräische Berichte über die Judenverfolgungen waehrend des Ersten Kreuzzugs*. Monumenta Germaniae Historica, Band 1. Hannover: Hahnsche Buchhandlung, 2005.

[Mar] Ḥefets Aluf. *Sefer vehizhir* (*The Book of Vehizer* [lit., "and He Warned"). Exodus. Ed. Yisrael Meir Friemann. Warsaw, n.d. Reprint, Israel, 1964. [Hebrew]

Heilperin, Jeḥiel. *Seder hadorot*. Karlsruhe, 1769. [Hebrew]

Ḥibbur hama'asiyot vehamidrashot vehahagadot (*A Compilation of Tales, Homilies, and Legends*). Venice, 1599. [Hebrew]

Horowitz, Ḥaim Meir Halevi, ed. *Agadat agadot* (*Collection of* Midrashim ketanim). Berlin, 1881. [Hebrew]

Ḥuẓin, Solomon Bekhor. *Ma'asim mefo'arim* (*Marvelous Deeds*). [Baghdad], 1890.

IFA. http://ifa.haifa.ac.il/index.php/he/ (last accessed July 28, 2016).

Isaac b. Moses (of Vienna). *Sefer Or zaru'a* (*The Book of Shining Light*). Vol. 1. Zhitomir, 1862. [Hebrew]

Isaiah di Trani. *Piskei hari'az* (*The Rulings of R. Isaiah Aharon z"l*). Ed. Abraham, Joseph Wertheimer. Jerusalem: Mechon ha-Talmud ha-Yisraeli ha-Shalem, 1988. [Hebrew]

Israel, Raḥamim Ḥaim Jehudah. *Responsa ben yamin*. Kiryat Sefer: Machon Naḥalat Israel, 2000. [Hebrew]

Jacob b. Asher. *Arba'ah turim* (Four Pillars). Hoshen Mishpat. 2 vols., Jerusalem: Me'oroth, 1969. [Hebrew]

Jacob b. Isaac of Janów (Yankev b. Yitskhok). *Ẓe'enah ur'enah* [*Come Out and Look*]*: The Five Books of the Torah in the Language of the Ashkenazi Jews*. Vol. 2, *The Five Scrolls*. Basel, 1622. [Yiddish]

Jacobi a Voragine. *Legenda aurea: Vulgo Historia Lombardica Dicta*. Ed. Theodor Graesse. Dresden, 1846.

Jacobus de Voragine. *The Golden Legend: Readings on the Saints*. Vols. 1–2. Trans. William Granger Ryan. Princeton, NJ: Princeton University Press, 1993–1995.

Japhet, Sara, ed. *The Commentary of Rabbi Samuel b. Meir (Rashbam) on the Song of Songs*. Jerusalem: World Union of Jewish Studies, 2008. [Hebrew]

Jellinek, Adolf. *Bet hamidrasch*, 2 vols. Jerusalem: Wahrmann Books, 1967. [Hebrew]

Jerushalmi, Samuel. *Yalkut me'am lo'ez*. Proverbs. Jerusalem: Vagshal, 1980. [Hebrew]

Jonah Gerondi (of Gerona). *Homilies and Commentaries of R. Jonah Gerondi*. Ed. S. Yerusalmi. Jerusalem: Vagshal, 1988. [Hebrew]

———. *Sha'arei teshuvah: The Gates of Repentance*. Trans. Shraga Silverstein. Jerusalem: Feldheim, 1967.

Joseph Ḥaim b. Eliahu. *Nifla'im ma'asekha* (*Wonderful Are Your Deeds*). Jerusalem, 1911. [Hebrew]

Josiphon. Ed. Hayim Hominer. Jerusalem: Hominer Publications, 1971.

Josippon, The. Vol. 1. Ed. David Flusser. Jerusalem: Bialik Institute, 1978. [Hebrew]

Judah b. Barzilai. *Sefer ha'itim*. Ed. Jacob Shor. Cracow, 1903. [Hebrew]

Judah b. Kalonymus. *Erkhei tanna'im ve'amora'im* (*Entries on the Sages of the Mishnah and the Talmud*). Ed. Moshe Judah ha-Cohen Blau. Brooklyn, NY: M. Y. Blau, 1994. [Hebrew]

Judah b. Samuel. *Sefer Gematriot of R. Judah the Pious*. Los Angeles: Cherub Press, 1998. [Hebrew]

———. *Sefer ḥasidim* (*The Book of the Pious*). Bologna, 1538. Reprint, ed. Reuven Margaliot. Jerusalem: Mosad ha-Rav Kook, 1957. [Hebrew]

———. [*Sefer ḥasidim.*] *Das Buch der Frommen, nach der rezension in Cod. de Rossi No. 1133.* Ed. Jehuda Wistinetzke. Berlin, 1891. Reprint, Jerusalem: Vagshal, 1998. [Hebrew]

Kahana, A. *Sefarim ḥiẓonim* (*The Apocrypha*). Vol. 2. Jerusalem: Makor, 1970. [Hebrew]

Kaidanover, Ẓvi Hirsch. *Kav hayashar* (*The Just Measure*). Warsaw, 1879. [Hebrew]

Kaltz, Judah. *Sefer hamusar* (*The Book of Morals*). Constantinople, 1537. Reprinted, intro. A. J. Wertheimer. Jerusalem: Liberman, 1973. [Hebrew]

Klapper, J. *Erzählungen des Mittelalters.* Wort und Brauch, vol. 12. Breslau: M & H Marcus, 1914.

Kohut, Alexander. *Notes on a Hitherto Unknown Exegetical and Philosophical Commentary of the Pentateuch Composed by Aboo Manzur al Damari.* New York, 1892.

Kuli, Jacob, *Yalkut me'am lo'ez.* Genesis. Jerusalem: Or Ḥadash, 1968. [Hebrew]

Kurt, Zevulun. *Folktales of Afghanistan Jews.* Tel Aviv: Dvir, 1983. [Hebrew]

Lamentations rabbah [*Ekhah rabbah*], *Midrash rabbah.* Vol. 2. Vilna: Romm, 1887, and reprinted editions. [Hebrew]

Lamentations rabbati [*Midrash Ekhah rabbati*]*: Sammlung aggadischer Auslegungen der Klagelieder.* Ed. Solomon Buber. Wilna, 1899. Reprinted, Hildesheim, 1967. [Hebrew]

Lauterbach, Jacob Zallel. "*Midrash vayissa'u* or the Wars of the Sons of Jacob." In *Essays in Memory of R. Tzvi Peretẓ Ḥayut.* Ed. Avigdor Aptowitzer and Zecharia Shwartz. Vienna: Foundation in the Memory of Alexander Kohut, 1932, 212–222. [Hebrew]

Levin, B. M. *Oẓar hage'onim.* Vol. 5. Jerusalem: Hebrew University Press Association, 1932. [Hebrew]

Leviticus rabbah [*Vayyikra rabbah*]. Vols. 1–2. Ed. Mordecai Margulies. New York: JTS, 1993. [Hebrew]

Levner, Israel Benjamin. *Kol agadot yisrael* (*The Legends of Israel*). 2 vols. Jerusalem: Tushia, 1950. [Hebrew]

Ma'aseh Avraham avinu alav hashalom mima she'erah lo im Nimrod (*A Tale of Abraham our Father of Blessed Memory about What Happened to Nimrod*). Salonika, 1593. [Hebrew]

Ma'aseh Book. Trans. Moses Gaster. Vols. 1–2. Philadelphia: Jewish Publication Society of America, 1934.

"Maccabees, 2. " Trans. James Moffatt. In *The Apocrypha and Pseudepigrapha*, vol. 1, ed. R. H. Charles, 125–154.

"Maccabees, 4." Trans. R. B. Townshend. In *The Apocrypha and Pseudepigrapha*, vol. 2, ed. R. H. Charles, 666–685.

Magriso, Isaac. *Yalkut me'am lo'ez,* Numbers. Trans. Samuel Jerusalmi. Jerusalem: Or ḥadash, 1968. [Hebrew]

[Maharil]. *The Book of Maharil: Customs by Rabbi Yaacov Mulin.* Ed. Shlomoh J. Spitzer. Jerusalem: Machon Yerushalayim, 1989. [Hebrew]

Maḥzor Vitry. Ed. Arieh Goldschmidt. 2 vols. Jerusalem: Mekhon oẓar haposkim, 2004. [Hebrew]

Maḥzor Vitry. Ed. S. Halevi Horowitz. Jerusalem: A. Makhon lehoẓat sefarim, 1963. [Hebrew]

Makhir b. Aba Mari. *Yalkut hamakhiri on Proverbs.* In *Sefer halikkutim*, ed. Grünhut, vol. 4, part 1, 1a–17b. Jerusalem, 1898–1904. [Hebrew]

———. *Yalkut hamakhiri on Proverbs and Hosea.* Ed. A. J. Greenup. Jerusalem: Hametar, 1968. [Hebrew]

———. *Yalkut hamakhiri on Psalms.* Ed. S. Buber. Berdichev, 1900. Reprinted, Jerusalem: Monzon, 1964. [Hebrew]

Manish Hacohen, Isaac Menakhem. *Todat yizḥak* (*The Gratitude of Isaac*). Vilna, 1894. [Hebrew]

Margolis, Isaac. *Sippurei yeshurun.* Berlin, 1877. [Hebrew]

Marie de France. "Chaitivel." In *Lais de Marie de France*, ed. Laurence Harf-Lancner. Paris: Livre de poche, collection Lettres Gothiques, 1990, 248–261.

———. "Chaitivel." Trans. Judith P. Shoaf. 1996. http://users.clas.ufl.edu/jshoaf/marie/chaitivel.pdf

———. *Fables.* Ed. and trans. Harriet Spiegel. Toronto: University of Toronto Press, 1987.

Marzbān-Nāma. Ed. Khalīl Khaṭīb Rahbar. Tehran, 1987.

Mayse bukh. Basel, 1602. [Yiddish]

Meir b. R. Barukh [Maharam of Rotenberg]. *Bet habeḥira, tractate Sabbath.* Ed. Isaak S. Lange Jerusalem, 1965. [Hebrew]

———. *Sefer Shut maharam* (*Responsa Book of Maharam*). Ed. Arhieh Blokh. Budapest, 1895. [Hebrew]

Meshalim shel Shelomo hamelekh (*Tales of Solomon*). Kushta, 1517. [Hebrew]

Midrash aggadah. Ed. S. Buber. Vienna, 1894. [Hebrew]

Midrash aseret hadibrot (*A Midrash on the Ten Commandments*)*: Text, Sources and Interpretation.* Ed. and comp. Anat Shapira, with a literary critical commentary. Jerusalem: Bialik Institute, 2005. [Hebrew]

Midrash hashkem. In Elazar Halevi Grünhut, *Sefer halikkutim*, vol. 1, part 1, 2–20. Jerusalem, 1967. [Hebrew]

Midrash mishle [Proverbs]. Ed. Burton L. Visotzky. New York: JTS, 1990. [Hebrew]

Midrash mishle [Proverbs]. Ed. S. Buber. Vilna: Romm, 1893. Reprint, Jerusalem, 1965. [Hebrew]

Midrash rabbah. 2 vols. Vilna: Romm, 1887, and reprinted editions. [Hebrew]

Midrash tehilim [Psalms], *Shoḥer tov.* Ed. S. Buber. Vilna, 1801. Reprint, Jerusalem, 1963. [Hebrew]

Mikra'ot gedolot, me'orei haḥasidut, Exodus. Ed. Shraga Baur and Shraga Eisenbach. Jerusalem: Nezer Shraga, 2008. [Hebrew]

Mordekhai b. Hillel. *Halakhot ketanot, Talmud bavli, tractate Menakhot.* Vilna: Romm, 1880–1886. Reprint. [Hebrew]

Moses b. Abraham. *Mateh moshe.* London: C. Y. L. Henig, 1958. [Hebrew]

Moses b. Jacob of Coucy. *Sefer miẓvot gadol* [*Semag*]. Vol. 1, *Lo-ta'aseh.* Jerusalem: Shelomo Uman Institute, 1993. [Hebrew]

Moses b. Maimon (Maimonides). *Mishneh torah.* Jerusalem: Pardes, 1955. Reprinted. [Hebrew]

Moses b. Naḥman (Naḥmanides). *Commentary on the Torah,* vol. 1. Ed. C. D. Chavel. Jerusalem: Mossad Harav Kook, 1962. [Hebrew]

Moshav zekenim al hatorah, koveẓ perushei rabbotenu ba'alei haTosfot (*A Collection of Exegetics of Our Rabbis, The Tosafists*). Ed. Saliman b. David. Jerusalem: Sifrei rabbanei Bavel, 1982. [Hebrew]

Nana, Reuven. *Oẓar hama'asiyot* (*A Treasury of Tales*). Jerusalem, 1976. [Hebrew]

Nathan of Rome. [*Sefer*] *Arukh hashalem,* vol. 2. Ed. Alexander Kohut. New York: Pardes, 1955. [Hebrew].

Neckam, Alexandri. *De naturis rerum libri duo: With the Poem of the Same Author, De laudibus divinae sapientiae.* Ed. Thomas Wright. Reprint of London, 1863, edition. Liechtenstein: Kraus Reprint, 1967.

Nissim. *Ḥibbur yafeh mehayeshu'a.* Ed. and trans. Ḥaim Ze'ev Hirschberg. Jerusalem: Mossad Harav Kook, 1954. [Hebrew] (For English translation, see Brinner.)

The Novellino or One Hundred Ancient Tales. Ed. and trans. Joseph P. Consoli, based on the 1525 Gualteruzzi edition. New York: Garland, 1997.

Obermann, Julian Joël., ed. *The Arabic Original of Ibn Shahins' Book of Comfort, known as the Ḥibbur Yaphe of R.Nissim B. Ya'akobh.* New Haven, CT: Yale University Press, 1933. [Judeo-Arabic]

Odenkirchen, Carl, J. ed. *The Life of St. Alexius.* Brookline, MA: Classical Folia Editions, 1978.

Palachi, Ḥaim. *Responsa ḥaim be'yad.* Izmir, 1873.

Paltiel, Ḥaim. *Perushei hatorah* (*Commentary on the Torah*). Ed. Samson Lange Isaac. Jerusalem, 1981.

Pauli, Johannes. *Schimpf und Ernst.* Ed. J. Bolte. Berlin: Herbert Stussenrauch, 1924. [Hebrew]

Peretẓ, Isaac Leib. *Mepi ha'am.* Tel Aviv: Dvir, 1971. [Hebrew]

Pesikta de rav kahana. Ed. Bernard Mandelbaum. Vols. 1–2. New York: JTS, 1962. [Hebrew]

Pesikta rabbti. Ed. Meir Friedman [Ish Shalom]. Vienna, 1880. [Hebrew]

Pesikta rabbti: A Synoptic Edition of Pesiqta Rabbati Based upon All Extant Manuscripts and the Editio Princeps. Vol. 1. Ed. Rivka Ulmer. South Florida Studies in the History of Judaism, no. 155. Atlanta, GA: Scholars' Press, 1997. [Hebrew]

Philo. Vol. 6. Ed. T. E. Page et al. Trans. F. H. Colson. Cambridge, MA: Harvard University Press and William Heinemann LTD, 1929.

Pirkei de r. Eliezer. Ed. Michael Higger. *Ḥorev* 8 (1944): 82–119; 9 (1946): 94–166; 10 (1948): 185–294. [Hebrew]

[Sefer] *Pitron torah: A Collection of Midrashim and Interpretations*. Ed. Ephraim E. Urbach. Jerusalem: Magnes and Jewish National and University Library Press, 1978. [Hebrew]

Pseudo-Jonathan (*Targum Jonathan ben Usiel zum Pentateuch*). Ed. Moses Ginsburger. Hildesheim: Georg Olms, 1971. [Aramaic]

PUSHD. https://etc.princeton.edu/sefer_hasidim/ (last accessed August 28, 2016).

Ramon, Joseph, and John Esten Keller. *The Scholar's Guide: A Translation of the Twelfth-Century Disciplina Clericalis of Pedro Alfonso*. Toronto: Pontifical Institute of Mediaeval Studies, 1969.

Rosenberg, Judah. *Sefer eliyahu hanavi* (*The Book of Elijah the Prophet*). Petrikau: A. Sylingald, 1911. [Hebrew]

Roth, Ernst. "*Responsa* of Paltoi Gaon in 'The Kaufmann Genizah.' " *Tarbiẓ* 25 (1956): 140–148. [Hebrew]

Ruth rabbah, Midrash rabbah. Vol. 2. [Hebrew]

Ruth zuta, Midrash zuta. Ed. S. Buber. Berlin: Mekize Nirdamim, 1894. [Hebrew]

Saba, R. Abraham. *Ẓror hamor*. Collected and ed. Jacob Meir Vikhalder. Bnei Brak: Heikhal Hasefer, 1990. [Hebrew]

[Ibn] Sahula, Isaac. *Meshal haqadmoni: Fables from the Distant Past*. Vol. 2. Parallel Hebrew-English text. Ed. and trans. Raphael Loewe. Portland, OR: Littman Library of Jewish Civilization, 2004.

Samson b. Ẓadok. *Tashbaẓ* (*Responsa of R. Samson Ẓadok*). Cremona, 1556. Reprint, Jerusalem: Makhon Torah Shebikhtav, 2005. [Hebrew]

Sathon Ḥaviv, Hayim David. *Tokpo shel nes* (*The Power of a Miracle*). Jerusalem: La'avi, 1899. [Hebrew]

Seder eliahu rabbah und pseudo-seder eliahu zuta. "*Derekh ereẓ*." Ed. Meir Friedmann. Jerusalem: Wahrmann, 1969. Reproduction of Vienna: Achiasaf, 1902. [Hebrew]

Sefer haḥinukh [R. Aaron Halevi of Barcelona]. Ed. Ḥaim Dov Chavel. Jerusalem: Mosad ha-Rav Kook, 1954. [Hebrew]

Sefer hayashar. Ed. Joseph Dan. Jerusalem: Bialik Institute, 1986. [Hebrew]

Shaḥam, David. *Gulliver's Travels to the Land of the B'blonghee*. Ramat-Gan: Reshafim, 1975. [Hebrew]

Shimon Hadarshan of Frankfurt. *Yalkut shimoni*. Ed. Isaac Shiloni. Jerusalem: Mosad ha-Rav Kook, 1973. [Hebrew]

———. *Yalkut shimoni*. Vol. 2. Salonika, 1526. Reprint, Jerusalem, Makor, 1973. [Hebrew]

Shushan b. Moses Hacohen. *Sefer pilei haẓadikim* (*The Wonders of the Righteous*). Jerba, 1935. [Hebrew]

Sifre d'be rab (*Sifre on Numbers*). Ed. H. S. Horovitz. Jerusalem: Shalem, 1992. [Hebrew]

Sifre on Deuteronomy. Ed. Louis Finkelstein. New York: JTS, 1993. [Hebrew]

Simon b. Ẓemaḥ Duran. *Sefer hatashbeẓ* (*Responsa of Simon b. Ẓemah*). Ed. Joel Katan. Sha'albim, 1988. [Hebrew]

Sobelman, Abraham Isaac. *Sippurei Ẓaddikim heḥadash*. Piotrkow, 1884. Reprint, Jerusalem: Israel [1965]. Reproduction of Piotrkow, 1809. [Hebrew]

The Song of Roland. Trans. and intro. Frederick Goldin. New York: W. W. Norton, 1978.

Speer, Mary B., ed. *Le Roman des Sept Sages de Rome: A Critical Edition of the Two Verse Redactions of a Twelfth-Century Romance*. Edward C. Armstrong Monographs on Medieval Literature, 4. Lexington, KY: French Forum Publishers, 1989.

Stebbins, Charles E. *A Critical Edition of the 13th and 14th Centuries Old French Poem Versions of the "Vie de Saint Alexis."* Tübingen: M. Niemeyer, 1974.

La Tabula Exemplorum Secundum Ordinem Alphabeti, Recueil d'exempla compile en France àla du XIIIe siècle. Ed. J. Th. Welter. Paris: E. H. Guitard, 1926.

Talmud bavli. Vilna: Romm, 1880–1886. Reprint, *The Babylonian Talmud*, trans. I. Epstein (with notes, glossary and indexes). London: Soncino Press, 1935–1952.

Talmud bavli. Commentary, trans., and punctuation Adin Even-Yisrael (Steinsaltz), sponsored by Mirkin. Jerusalem: Israeli Institute for Talmudic Publications, 1997. [Hebrew]

Talmud yerushalmi. Published according to Ms. Or. 4720 (Scal. 3) of the Leiden University Library [. . .]. Jerusalem: Academy of the Hebrew Language, 2001.

[*Midrash*] *Tanḥuma*. Mantua, 1563. Reprint, Jerusalem: Levin-Epstein, 1958. [Hebrew]

[*Midrash*] *Tanḥuma*. Ed. Buber. Vilna: Romm, 1880 (and reprinted editions). [Hebrew]

[*Midrash*] *Tanḥuma: Translated into English with Indices and Brief Notes*. Ed. John T. Townsend. S. Buber Recension. Vol. 2, *Exodus and Leviticus*. Hoboken, NJ: Ktav, 1997.

Targum Jerushalmi to the Torah. Ed. M. Ginsburger. Jerusalem, 1969. Reproduction of Berlin, 1899. [Aramaic]

"The Testament of Judah." In *The Apocrypha and Pseudepigrapha*, vol. 2. Ed. Charles, 315–325.

Thomas. "Le Roman de Tristan." In *Tristan et Iseut: Les Poèmes français, la saga norroise, textes originaux et intégraux préséntes, traduits et commentés par Daniel Lacroix et Philippe Walter*. Letters gothiques. Paris: Librairie Générale Française, 1989.

Tobias b. Eliezer. *Midrash Lekah tov* (*Good doctrine*), *Pesikta zutarta*. Ed. S. Buber. Lvov, 1884. [Hebrew]

Tuti Nameh: Das Papageinbuch, nach der Turkischen Fassung, übersetzt von Georg Rosen. Leipzig: Insel-Verlag, 1900.

Viaticum Narrationum des Heumannus Bononiensis, Das. Ed. A. Hilka. Berlin: Weidmann, 1935.

Vincentius Bellovacensis (Vincent of Beauvais). *Speculum Morale*. Graz, 1964.

de Vitry, Jacques. *The Exempla: Illustrative Stories from the Sermons Vulgares*. Ed. Thomas F. Crane. New York: Lenox Hill, 1971. Reprinted.

Wertheimer, Abraham Joseph. *Batei midrashoth*. 2 vols. Jerusalem: Ktab-Yad Vasepher, 1989. [Hebrew]

Yassif, Eli, ed. *The Book of Memory That Is the Chronicles of Jerahme'el*. Tel Aviv: Tel Aviv University, Ḥaim Rosenberg School of Jewish Studies, 2001. [Hebrew].

———. ed. *Ninety-nine Tales: The Jerusalem Manuscript Cycle of Legends in Medieval Jewish Folklore*. Tel Aviv: Ḥaim Rubin University Press, 2013. [Hebrew]

Yonah b. Avraham of Gerona. *Sha'arei teshuvah* (*The Gates of Repentance*). Trans. Shraga Silverstein. Jerusalem: Boys' Town/Feldheim, 1967. [Hebrew]

[Ibn] Zabara, Joseph b. Meir. *The Book of Delight by Joseph b. Meir Zabara*. Trans. Moses Hadas. Intro. Merriam Sherwood. New York: Columbia University Press, 1932. [Hebrew]

Ẓedekiah Harofeh. *Shibbolei haleket*. Ed. S. Buber. Vilna: S. Buber, 1887. Reprint, Jerusalem: Machon lehotsat sefarim, 1962. [Hebrew]

Zis, Israel David. *Ma'asiyot mehagedolim vehaẓadikim* (*Tales from the Great and Righteous*). Warsaw, 1898. Reprint, Berlin: Beith Hillel, 1987. [Hebrew]

Ziya'U'd-Din Nakhshabi. *The Cleveland Museum of Art's Tuti-Nama: Tales of a Parrot.* Trans. and ed. Muhammed A. Simsar. Cleveland, OH: Cleveland Museum of Art, 1978.

[*Sefer ha*] *Zohar.* Genesis. Ed. Reuven Margaliot. Jerusalem: Mosad ha-Rav Kook, 1999. [Hebrew]

Secondary Literature

Aarne, Antti, and Stith Thompson. *The Types of the Folktale: A Classification and Bibliography* (FFC 184). Helsinki: Suomalainen Tiedeakatemia Academia Scientiarum Fennica, 1961.

Alexander, Tamar. "The Formation of Ḥasidic-Ashkenazic Stories: The Folktale in Its Theological Context." In *Studies in 'Aggadah and Jewish Folklore*, ed. Issachar Ben-Ami and Joseph Dan. Jerusalem: Magnes, 1983, 197–225. [Hebrew]

Alexander, Tamar, and Joseph Dan. "The Complete Midrash vayissa'u." In *Studies of the Center for Folklore Research.* Jerusalem: Magnes, 1973.

Alexander-Frizer, Tamar. *The Beloved Friend-and-a-Half: Studies in Sepharadic Folk-Literature*. Jerusalem: Magnes and Ben-Gurion University Press, 1999. [Hebrew]

———. *The Pious Sinner: Ethics and Aesthetics in the Medieval Ḥasidic Narrative.* Texts and Studies in Medieval and Early Modern Judaism, 5, ed. Maurice R. Haoun, Ivan G. Marcus, Peter Schäfer. Tübingen: J. C. B. Mohr, 1991.

Assis. Amit. "The Loan." In *Encyclopedia of the Jewish Story*, vol. 2, 129–144. [Hebrew]

Avida (Zlotnik), Yehuda Leib. "*Anashim benei shnei rashim.*" *Sinai* 19 (1946): 17–25. [Hebrew]

———. "*Me'agadot hashabbat uminhage'ah*" ("Legends of the Sabbath and Its Customs"). *Sinai* 26 (1950): 75–89. [Hebrew]

Balberg, Mira. "Between Heterotophas and Utopias: Two Rabbinic Stories about Journeys to Prostitutes." *Jerusalem Studies in Hebrew Literature* 22 (2008): 191–213. [Hebrew]

Bar-Tikva, Binhyamin. "The Ten Trials of Abraham in the Eyes of Liturgical Poetry." In *Piyyut in Tradition*, 2, ed. Binyamin Bar-Tikva and Ephraim Hazan. Ramat-Gan: Bar-Ilan University Press, 2000, 127–142. [Hebrew]

Barber, Richard. *The Holy Grail: Imagination and Belief.* Cambridge, MA: Harvard University Press, 2004.

Baumgarten, Elisheva. *Mothers and Children: Jewish Family Life in Medieval Europe*. Princeton, NJ: Princeton University Press, 2004.

———. "Pious Pretenders: A Gendered Look at Medieval Jewish European Piety." In *Tov Elem: Memory, Community and Gender in Medieval and Early Modern*

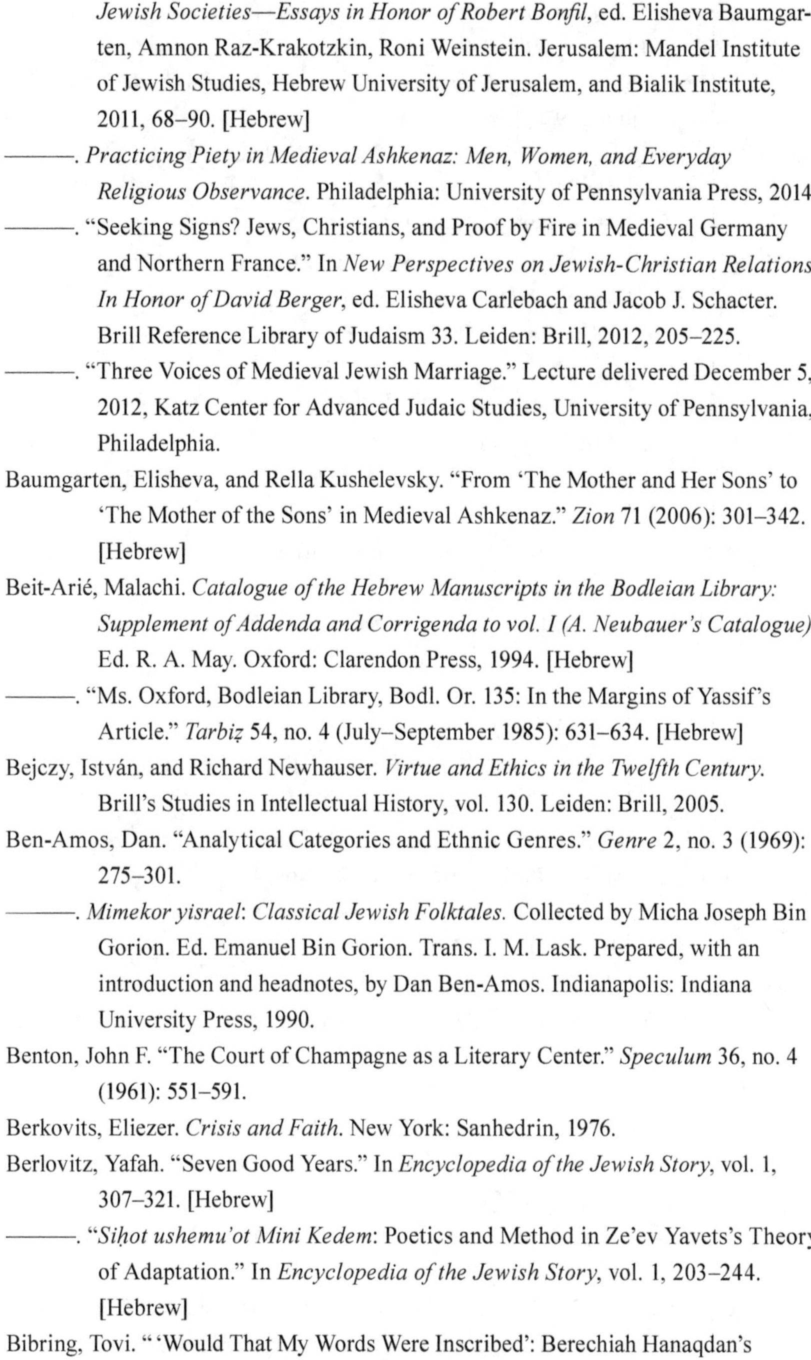

Jewish Societies—Essays in Honor of Robert Bonfil, ed. Elisheva Baumgarten, Amnon Raz-Krakotzkin, Roni Weinstein. Jerusalem: Mandel Institute of Jewish Studies, Hebrew University of Jerusalem, and Bialik Institute, 2011, 68–90. [Hebrew]

———. *Practicing Piety in Medieval Ashkenaz: Men, Women, and Everyday Religious Observance*. Philadelphia: University of Pennsylvania Press, 2014.

———. "Seeking Signs? Jews, Christians, and Proof by Fire in Medieval Germany and Northern France." In *New Perspectives on Jewish-Christian Relations: In Honor of David Berger*, ed. Elisheva Carlebach and Jacob J. Schacter. Brill Reference Library of Judaism 33. Leiden: Brill, 2012, 205–225.

———. "Three Voices of Medieval Jewish Marriage." Lecture delivered December 5, 2012, Katz Center for Advanced Judaic Studies, University of Pennsylvania, Philadelphia.

Baumgarten, Elisheva, and Rella Kushelevsky. "From 'The Mother and Her Sons' to 'The Mother of the Sons' in Medieval Ashkenaz." *Zion* 71 (2006): 301–342. [Hebrew]

Beit-Arié, Malachi. *Catalogue of the Hebrew Manuscripts in the Bodleian Library: Supplement of Addenda and Corrigenda to vol. I (A. Neubauer's Catalogue)*. Ed. R. A. May. Oxford: Clarendon Press, 1994. [Hebrew]

———. "Ms. Oxford, Bodleian Library, Bodl. Or. 135: In the Margins of Yassif's Article." *Tarbiẓ* 54, no. 4 (July–September 1985): 631–634. [Hebrew]

Bejczy, István, and Richard Newhauser. *Virtue and Ethics in the Twelfth Century*. Brill's Studies in Intellectual History, vol. 130. Leiden: Brill, 2005.

Ben-Amos, Dan. "Analytical Categories and Ethnic Genres." *Genre* 2, no. 3 (1969): 275–301.

———. *Mimekor yisrael*: *Classical Jewish Folktales*. Collected by Micha Joseph Bin Gorion. Ed. Emanuel Bin Gorion. Trans. I. M. Lask. Prepared, with an introduction and headnotes, by Dan Ben-Amos. Indianapolis: Indiana University Press, 1990.

Benton, John F. "The Court of Champagne as a Literary Center." *Speculum* 36, no. 4 (1961): 551–591.

Berkovits, Eliezer. *Crisis and Faith*. New York: Sanhedrin, 1976.

Berlovitz, Yafah. "Seven Good Years." In *Encyclopedia of the Jewish Story*, vol. 1, 307–321. [Hebrew]

———. "*Siḥot ushemu'ot Mini Kedem*: Poetics and Method in Ze'ev Yavets's Theory of Adaptation." In *Encyclopedia of the Jewish Story*, vol. 1, 203–244. [Hebrew]

Bibring, Tovi. "'Would That My Words Were Inscribed': Berechiah Hanaqdan's *Mishlei ShuŶalim* and European Fable Traditions." In *Latin-into-Hebrew:*

Texts and Studies, vol. 1, Studies, ed. Resianne Fontaine and Gad Freudenthal. Leiden: Brill, 2014, 309–329.

Bin Gorion, Imanuel. *The Paths of Legend: An Introduction to Folktales*. Jerusalem: Bialik Institute, 1970. [Hebrew]

Bohler, Danielle. "Béances de la Terre et du Temps: La Dette et le Pacte dans le Motif du Mort Reconnaissant au Moyen Age." *L'Homme* 111–112 (July–December 1989), 29 (3–4): 161–178.

Bonfil, Robert. "Myth, Rhetoric, History? A Study in the Chronicle of Aḥima'az." In *Culture and Society in Medieval Jewry*, ed. R. Bonfil, M. Ben-Sasson, and J. Hacker. Jerusalem: Zalman Shazar Center for Jewish History, 1989, 99–135. [Hebrew]

Boyarin, Daniel. *Carnal Israel: Reading Sex in Talmudic Culture*. Berkeley: University of California Press, 1993.

Brody, S. N. *The Disease of the Soul: Leprosy in Medieval Literature*. Ithaca, NY: Cornell University Press, 1974.

Busby, Keith. "Narrative Genres." In *The Cambridge Companion to Medieval French Literature*, ed. Gaunt and Key, 139–152.

Campbell, Emma. "Clerks and Laity." In *The Cambridge Companion to Medieval French Literature*, ed. Gaunt and Key, 210–224.

Campbell, Killis, ed. *The Seven Sages of Rome*. With introduction, notes, and glossary. Boston: Gin, 1907.

Cirlot, J. E. *A Dictionary of Symbols*. Trans. Jack Sage. London: Routledge, 1971.

Clouston, William Alexander. *A Group of Eastern Romances and Stories from the Persian, Tamil and Urdu*. Glasgow: W. Clouston, 1889.

———. *Popular Tales and Fiction: Their Migrations and Transformations*. Vol. 2. Edinburgh: Blackwood, 1887.

Cohen, Gershon D. "The Tale of Chana and Her Seven Sons in Hebrew Literature." In *Jubilee Book in Honor of Mordecai Menaḥem Kaplan*. New York: JTS, 1953, 109–123. [Hebrew]

Cohen, Jeffrey Jerome. *Of Giants, Sex, Monsters, and the Middle Ages*. Medieval Cultures, vol. 17. Minneapolis: University of Minnesota Press, 1999.

Cohen, Jeremy. *Living Letters of the Law: Ideas of the Jews in Medieval Christianity*. Berkeley: University of California Press, 1999.

———. *Sanctifying the Name of God: Jewish Martyrs and Jewish Memories of the First Crusade*. Philadelphia: University of Pennsylvania Press, 2004.

Comparetti, Domenico. "Five Versions of the Story of the Jerusalemite." *Proceedings of the American Academy for Jewish Research* 35 (1967): 451–463.

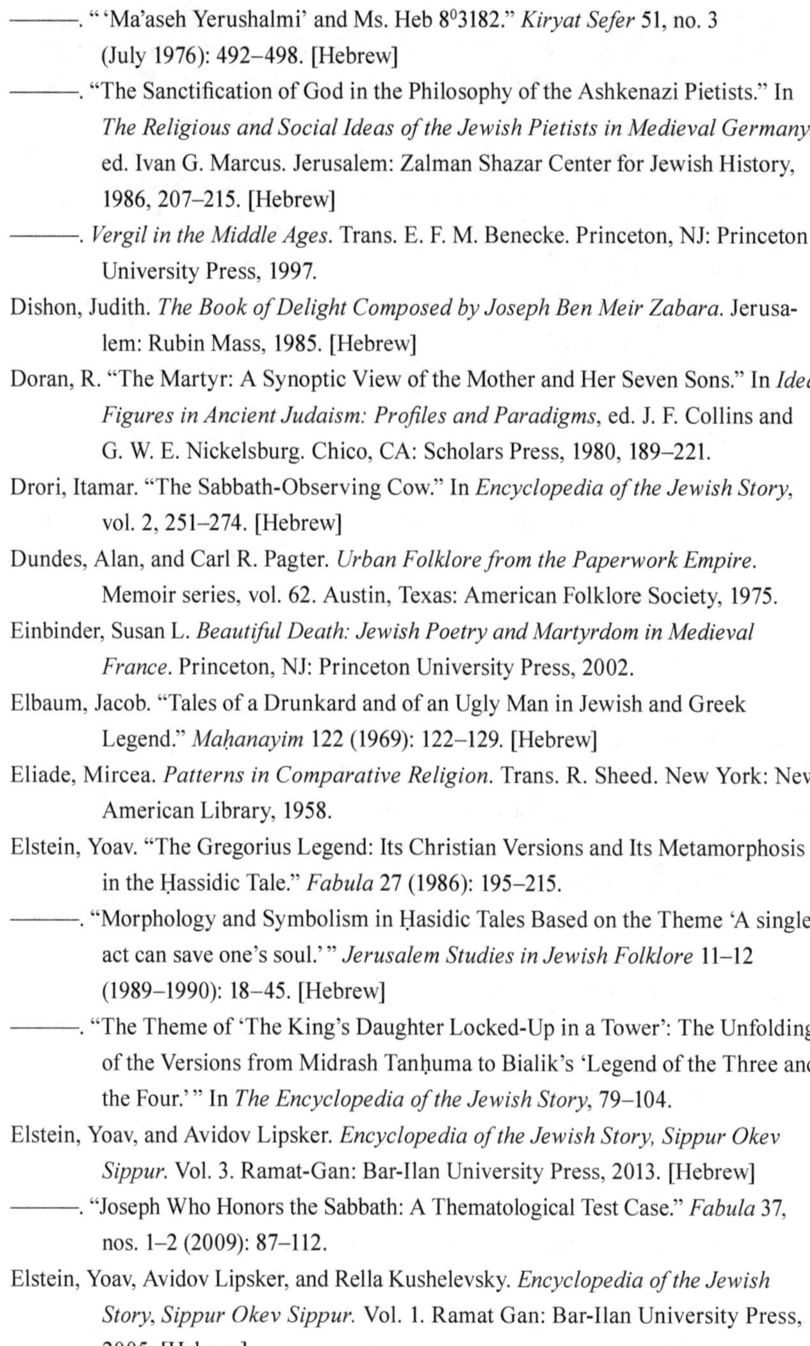

———. " 'Ma'aseh Yerushalmi' and Ms. Heb 8°3182." *Kiryat Sefer* 51, no. 3 (July 1976): 492–498. [Hebrew]

———. "The Sanctification of God in the Philosophy of the Ashkenazi Pietists." In *The Religious and Social Ideas of the Jewish Pietists in Medieval Germany*, ed. Ivan G. Marcus. Jerusalem: Zalman Shazar Center for Jewish History, 1986, 207–215. [Hebrew]

———. *Vergil in the Middle Ages*. Trans. E. F. M. Benecke. Princeton, NJ: Princeton University Press, 1997.

Dishon, Judith. *The Book of Delight Composed by Joseph Ben Meir Zabara*. Jerusalem: Rubin Mass, 1985. [Hebrew]

Doran, R. "The Martyr: A Synoptic View of the Mother and Her Seven Sons." In *Ideal Figures in Ancient Judaism: Profiles and Paradigms*, ed. J. F. Collins and G. W. E. Nickelsburg. Chico, CA: Scholars Press, 1980, 189–221.

Drori, Itamar. "The Sabbath-Observing Cow." In *Encyclopedia of the Jewish Story*, vol. 2, 251–274. [Hebrew]

Dundes, Alan, and Carl R. Pagter. *Urban Folklore from the Paperwork Empire*. Memoir series, vol. 62. Austin, Texas: American Folklore Society, 1975.

Einbinder, Susan L. *Beautiful Death: Jewish Poetry and Martyrdom in Medieval France*. Princeton, NJ: Princeton University Press, 2002.

Elbaum, Jacob. "Tales of a Drunkard and of an Ugly Man in Jewish and Greek Legend." *Maḥanayim* 122 (1969): 122–129. [Hebrew]

Eliade, Mircea. *Patterns in Comparative Religion*. Trans. R. Sheed. New York: New American Library, 1958.

Elstein, Yoav. "The Gregorius Legend: Its Christian Versions and Its Metamorphosis in the Ḥassidic Tale." *Fabula* 27 (1986): 195–215.

———. "Morphology and Symbolism in Ḥasidic Tales Based on the Theme 'A single act can save one's soul.' " *Jerusalem Studies in Jewish Folklore* 11–12 (1989–1990): 18–45. [Hebrew]

———. "The Theme of 'The King's Daughter Locked-Up in a Tower': The Unfolding of the Versions from Midrash Tanḥuma to Bialik's 'Legend of the Three and the Four.' " In *The Encyclopedia of the Jewish Story*, 79–104.

Elstein, Yoav, and Avidov Lipsker. *Encyclopedia of the Jewish Story, Sippur Okev Sippur*. Vol. 3. Ramat-Gan: Bar-Ilan University Press, 2013. [Hebrew]

———. "Joseph Who Honors the Sabbath: A Thematological Test Case." *Fabula* 37, nos. 1–2 (2009): 87–112.

Elstein, Yoav, Avidov Lipsker, and Rella Kushelevsky. *Encyclopedia of the Jewish Story, Sippur Okev Sippur*. Vol. 1. Ramat Gan: Bar-Ilan University Press, 2005. [Hebrew]

Elstein, Yoav, and Rella Kushelevsky. *Encyclopedia of the Jewish Story, Sippur Okev Sippur.* Vol. 2. Ramat Gan: Bar-Ilan University Press, 2009. [Hebrew]

Encyklopedia Talmudit (*Talmudic Encyclopedia*). Jerusalem: Yad Harav Herẓog, vol. 1, 1978; vol. 2, 1979; vol. 9, 1976. [Hebrew]

Even Shoshan, Abraham. *The New Dictionary* (Hebrew–Hebrew). 3 vols., with a supplementary vol. Jerusalem: Kiryat-Sefer, 1987.

Feintuch, Yonatan. "'Anonymous *Ḥasid*' Stories in Halakhic 'Sugyot' in the Babylonian Talmud." *Journal of Jewish Studies* 63, no. 2 (2012): 238–262.

Fraenkel, Jonah. *The Aggadic Narrative Harmony of Form and Content.* Tel Aviv: Hakibbutz Hameuchad, 2001. [Hebrew]

———. "*Hazeman ve'iẓuvo batalmud habavli*" ("The Shaping of Time in the *Talmud bavli*"). In *The Aggadic Narrative Harmony of Form and Content*, 171–239. [Hebrew]

———. *Iyyunim be'olamo haruḥani shel sipur ha'aggada* (*Studies of the Spiritual World of the Aggadah*). Tel Aviv: Hakibbutz Hameuchad, 1982. [Hebrew]

———. "R. Joshua b. Levi in the Talmud Bavli." In *The Aggadic Narrative Harmony of Form and Content*, 273–294. [Hebrew]

Frauke, Stiller, "Die unschuldig verfolgte und später rehabilitierte Eherfrau, Untersuchung zur Frau im 15 jahrhundertam Beispiel der Crescentia-und sibillen-Erzaehlungen." PhD diss., Berlin: Humboldt University, 2001.

Friedman, Ayala. "The Man Who Was Meticulous about the Commandment of Fringes." Master's thesis equivalent, Bar-Ilan University, 2012. [Hebrew]

Friedman, Shamma. "A New Branch of the Textual Tradition of Bavli Shabbat: Three Sage Stories—A Study of the Formation of the Texts and the Textual Tradition." *Oqimta* 1 (2013): 133–193. [Hebrew]

Fudeman, A. Kristen. *Vernacular Voices: Language and Identity in Medieval French Communities.* Philadelphia: University of Pennsylvania Press, 2010.

Gafni, M. Isaiah, and Aviezer Ravitzky. *Sanctity of Life and Martyrdom: Studies in Memory of Amir Yekuktiel.* Jerusalem: Zalman Shazar Center for Jewish History, 1992. [Hebrew]

Galinsky, Judah. "The Significance of Form: R. Moses of Coucy's Reading Audience and His *Sefer ha-Miẓvot.*" *AJS Review* 35, no. 2 (November 2011): 293–321.

Gaster, Moses. "Fairy Tales from Inedited Hebrew Mss. of the Ninth and Twelfth Centuries." In *Studies and Texts in Folklore, Magic, Medieval Romance, Hebrew Apocrypha and Samaritan Archaeology*, vol. 2. New York: Ktav, 1971, 908–941.

Gaunt, Simon, and Sarah Kay, eds. *The Cambridge Companion to Medieval French Literature*. Cambridge: Cambridge University Press, 2008.

Gerould, G. H. “Forerunners, Congeners and Derivatives of the Eustace Legend.” *Publications of the Modern Language Association of America* 19 (1904): 335–448.

Geula, Amos. “Lost Aggadic Works Known Only from Ashkenaz: Midrash Abkir, Midrash Esfa and Devarim Zuta.” PhD diss., Hebrew University, 2006. [Hebrew]

Gilbert, Jane. “The Chanson de Roland.” In *The Cambridge Companion to Medieval French Literature*, ed. Gaunt and Kay, 21–34.

Golb, Norman. *The Jews in Medieval Normandy: A Social and Intellectual History.* Cambridge: Cambridge University Press, 1998.

Goldin, Simha. *The Ways of Jewish Martyrdom.* Ganei Aviv-Lod: Dvir, 2002. [Hebrew]

Goshen-Gottstein, Alon. “The Commandment of the Fringes, the Harlot, and the Exegetical Story.” In *Rabbinic Thought: Prodeedings of the First Conference on “Mahshevet Ḥazal,”* ed. Marc Hirshman and Tsvi Groner. Haifa: Haifa University Press, 1989, 45–58. [Hebrew]

Greimas, A. J. *Le Dictionnaire de l’ancien français.* Paris: Larousse, 2012.

Grossman, Avraham. *The Early Sages of Ashkenaz.* Jerusalem: Magnes, 1988. [Hebrew]

———. *The Early Sages of France: Their Lives, Leadership, and Works.* Jerusalem: Magnes, 1996. [Hebrew]

———. *He Shall Rule Over You? Medieval Jewish Sages on Women.* Jerusalem: Zalman Shazar Center for Jewish History, 2011. [Hebrew]

———. *Pious and Rebellious: Jewish Women in Medieval Europe.* Tauber Institute Series for the Study of European Jewry & HBI Series on Jewish Women. Waltham, MA: Brandeis University Press, 2004.

Gutmann, J. “The Story of the Mother and Her Seven Sons in the Aggadah and the Second and Fourth Books of Maccabees.” In *The Johanan Levi Book*, ed. M. Shuva and J. Gutmann. Jerusalem: Magnes, 1949, 25–37. [Hebrew]

Gutmann, Joseph. “Abraham in the Fire of the Chaldeans: A Jewish Legend in Jewish, Christian and Islamic Art.” *Frühmittelalterliche Studien* 7 (1973): 342–352.

Haber, Zvi. “The Woman and Her Seven Sons.” *Ma’alot* 18 (1997): 137–162. [Hebrew]

Ḥaikin, Itamar. “The Nachum Ish Gamzo Midrashim—A Methodological Analysis.” *Pathways Through Aggadah* 2 (1999): 65–75. [Hebrew]

Halbertal, Moshe. “Menaḥem Ha-Me’iri—Talmudist and Philosopher.” *Tarbiẓ* 63, no. 1 (1993): 63–118. [Hebrew]

Har Shefi, Avishar. “The Rat and the Pit.” In *Encyclopedia of the Jewish Story*, 3, 181–210. [Hebrew]

Harvey, W. Z. “The Pupil, the Harlot and the Fringe Benefits.” *Prooftexts* 6 (1986): 259–271.

Hasan-Rokem, Galit. *Proverbs in Israeli Folk Narratives: A Structural Semantic Analysis. FFC* 232. Helsinki: Suomalainen Tiedeakatemia Academia Scientiarum Fennica, 1982.

———. *Tales of the Neighborhood: Jewish Narrative Dialogues in Late Antiquity.* Berkeley: University of California Press, 2003.

———. *The Web of Life: Folklore in Rabbinic Literature—The Palestinian Aggadic Midrash Eikha Rabba.* Tel Aviv: Am Oved, 1996.

Heck, Christian, and Remy Cordonnier. *The Grand Medieval Bestiary Animals in Illuminated Manuscripts.* New York: Abbeville Press, 2012.

Heinemann, Joseph. "The Art of the Sermon of Palestinian Amora'im: Analysis of Two Proems." *Hasifrut* 25 (1977): 69–79. [Hebrew]

Hendler, Chana. "Characteristics of the 'Pious' Literature Genre." Master's thesis, Bar-Ilan University, 1993. [Hebrew]

———. "The Jars of Honey." In *Encyclopedia of the Jewish Story*, 1, 297–305. [Hebrew]

———. "Naḥum of Gamzo and His Errand to King Caesar." In *Encyclopedia of the Jewish Story* 1, 247–259. [Hebrew]

Henrichs, Albert. " 'Thou Shalt Not Kill a Tree': Greek, Manichaean and Indian Tales." *Bulletin of the American Society of Papryrologists* 16, nos. 1–2 (1979): 92–108.

Ḥevroni, Ido. "An Arrow in Satan's Eye: Symbols and Domains of Significance in a Compilation of Temptation Stories from Babylonian Talmud, Kiddushin 81a–b." PhD diss., Ramat Gan: Bar-Ilan University, 2005. [Hebrew]

———. "Circumcision as Revolt." *Tekhelet* 28 (2007): 61–73. [Hebrew]

Hill, Susan E. " 'The Ooze of Gluttony': Attitudes Towards Food, Eating, and Excess in the Middle Ages." In *The Seven Deadly Sins: From Communities to Individuals*, ed. Richard Newhauser. Leiden: Brill, 2007, 57–70.

Himmelfarb, Martha. *Tours of Hell: An Apocalyptic Form in Jewish and Christian Literature.* Philadelphia: University of Pennsylvania Press, 1983.

Hollender, Elisabeth. *Clavis Commentariorum of Hebrew Liturgical Poetry.* Leiden: Brill, 2005.

Horowitz, Elliott. "From the Generation of Moses to the Generation of the Messiah: The Jews Confront 'Amalek' and His Incarnations." *Zion* 64, no. 4 (1999): 425–454. [Hebrew]

Huot, Sylvia. "Others and Alterity." In *The Cambridge Companion to Medieval French Literature*, ed. Gaunt and Kay, 238–250.

———. *The Romance of the Rose and Its Medieval Readers: Interpretation, Reception, Manuscript Transmission.* Cambridge: Cambridge University Press, 1993.

Jaffé, Dan. "La Wissenschaft des Judentums à la Française: L'étude de la littérature talmudique et de origines du christianisme par les savants Français du XIXe siècle: le cas d'Israël Lévi." In *Tsarfat: Mutations de l' Identité juifs à l'époque moderne et contemporaine*, ed. Erick H. Cohen. Ramat Gan: Bar-Ilan Press, 2014, 59–76.

Jastrow, Marcus. *A Dictionary of the Targumim, the Talmud Babli and Yerushalmi, and the Midrashic Literature*. London: Luzac, 1903. Reprinted.

Jauss, Hans Robert. *Toward an Aesthetic of Reception*. Trans. Timothy Bahti. Intro. Paul de Man. Minneapolis: University of Minnesota Press, 1982.

Jones, Steven Swann. "The Innocent Persecuted Heroine Genre: An Analysis of Its Structure and Themes." *Western Folklore* 52, no. 1 (January 1993): 13–41.

Kanarfogel, Ephraim. *The Intellectual History and Rabbinic Culture of Medieval Ashkenaz*. Detroit, MI: Wayne State University Press, 2013.

———. *Peering Through the Lattices: Mystical, Magical, and Pietistic Dimensions in the Tosafist Period*. Detroit, MI: Wayne State University Press, 2000.

———. "Prayer, Literacy, and Literary Memory in the Jewish Communities of Medieval Europe." *Jewish Studies at the Crossroads of History and Anthropology: Tradition, Authority, Diaspora*, ed. R. S. Boustan, O. Kosansky and M. Rustow. Philadelphia: University of Pennsylvania Press, 2011, 250–404.

———. "R. Judah he-Ḥasid and the Rabbinic Scholars of Regensburg: Interactions, Influences and Implications." *JQR* 96, no. 1 (2006): 17–37.

Kawan, Christine Shojaei. "Gang zum Eisenhammer (Kalkofin)." *EM* 5 (1987): 662–671.

Kay, Sara. "Genre, Parody and Spectacle." In *The Cambridge Companion to Medieval French Literature*, ed. Gaunt and Kay, 167–180.

Kiperwasser, Reuven. "*Midrash haGadol*, the Exempla of the Rabbis (*Sefer Ma'asiyot*), and Midrashic Works on Ecclesiastes: A Comparative Approach." *Tarbiẓ* 75, nos. 3–4 (April–September 2006): 409–436. [Hebrew]

Kleinberg, Aviad. *Fra Ginepro's Leg of Pork: Christian Saints' Stories and Their Cultural Role*. Tel Aviv: Zmora-Bitan, 2000. [Hebrew]

Kogman-Appel, Katrin. *A Maḥzor from Worms: Art and Religion in a Medieval Jewish Community*. Cambridge, MA: Harvard University Press, 2012.

Kohut, Alexander. *Notes on a Hitherto Unknown Exegetical and Philosophical Commentary of the Pentateuch Composed by Aboo Manzur al Damari*. New York: A. Ginsberg, 1892.

Kosman, Admiel. *Man's Tractate: Rav and the Butcher and Other Stories—On Manhood, Love, and Authentic Life in Aggadic and Hasidic Stories*. Jerusalem: Keter, 2002. [Hebrew]

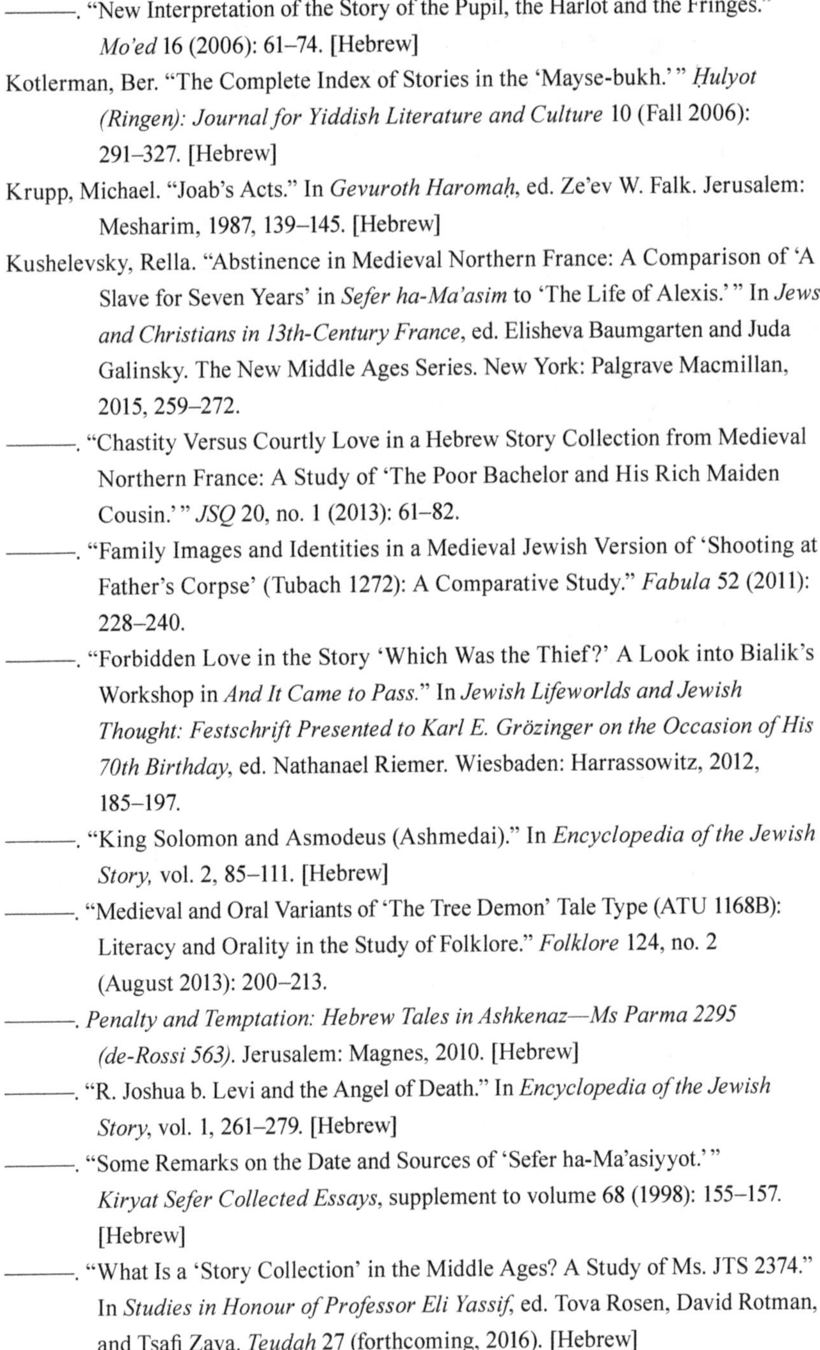

———. "New Interpretation of the Story of the Pupil, the Harlot and the Fringes." *Mo'ed* 16 (2006): 61–74. [Hebrew]

Kotlerman, Ber. "The Complete Index of Stories in the 'Mayse-bukh.'" *Ḥulyot (Ringen): Journal for Yiddish Literature and Culture* 10 (Fall 2006): 291–327. [Hebrew]

Krupp, Michael. "Joab's Acts." In *Gevuroth Haromaḥ*, ed. Ze'ev W. Falk. Jerusalem: Mesharim, 1987, 139–145. [Hebrew]

Kushelevsky, Rella. "Abstinence in Medieval Northern France: A Comparison of 'A Slave for Seven Years' in *Sefer ha-Ma'asim* to 'The Life of Alexis.'" In *Jews and Christians in 13th-Century France*, ed. Elisheva Baumgarten and Juda Galinsky. The New Middle Ages Series. New York: Palgrave Macmillan, 2015, 259–272.

———. "Chastity Versus Courtly Love in a Hebrew Story Collection from Medieval Northern France: A Study of 'The Poor Bachelor and His Rich Maiden Cousin.'" *JSQ* 20, no. 1 (2013): 61–82.

———. "Family Images and Identities in a Medieval Jewish Version of 'Shooting at Father's Corpse' (Tubach 1272): A Comparative Study." *Fabula* 52 (2011): 228–240.

———. "Forbidden Love in the Story 'Which Was the Thief?' A Look into Bialik's Workshop in *And It Came to Pass.*" In *Jewish Lifeworlds and Jewish Thought: Festschrift Presented to Karl E. Grözinger on the Occasion of His 70th Birthday*, ed. Nathanael Riemer. Wiesbaden: Harrassowitz, 2012, 185–197.

———. "King Solomon and Asmodeus (Ashmedai)." In *Encyclopedia of the Jewish Story*, vol. 2, 85–111. [Hebrew]

———. "Medieval and Oral Variants of 'The Tree Demon' Tale Type (ATU 1168B): Literacy and Orality in the Study of Folklore." *Folklore* 124, no. 2 (August 2013): 200–213.

———. *Penalty and Temptation: Hebrew Tales in Ashkenaz—Ms Parma 2295 (de-Rossi 563)*. Jerusalem: Magnes, 2010. [Hebrew]

———. "R. Joshua b. Levi and the Angel of Death." In *Encyclopedia of the Jewish Story*, vol. 1, 261–279. [Hebrew]

———. "Some Remarks on the Date and Sources of 'Sefer ha-Ma'asiyyot.'" *Kiryat Sefer Collected Essays*, supplement to volume 68 (1998): 155–157. [Hebrew]

———. "What Is a 'Story Collection' in the Middle Ages? A Study of Ms. JTS 2374." In *Studies in Honour of Professor Eli Yassif*, ed. Tova Rosen, David Rotman, and Tsafi Zava. *Teudah* 27 (forthcoming, 2016). [Hebrew]

Kushelevsky, Rella, and Vered Tohar. "The Pious Man and the Tax-Collector's Son." In *Encyclopedia of the Jewish Story*, vol. 2, 233–250. [Hebrew]

———. "The Thief Who Has Given Himself Away." In *Encyclopedia of the Jewish Story*, vol. 2, 113–128. [Hebrew]

Landau, Louis. "The Wandering and Threatened Dead." In *Sadan: Studies in Hebrew Literature*, vol. 6, ed. Eli Yassif. Ramat-Aviv: Tel-Aviv University Press, 2007, 157–172. [Hebrew]

Lee, A. Collingwood. *The Decameron: Its Sources and Analogues*. New York: Haskell House, 1972.

Le Goff, Jacques. *The Birth of Purgatory*. Trans. Arthur Goldhammer. Cambridge: Cambridge University Press, 1990.

Lerner, Meron Bialik. "Book of Ruth in Aggadic Literature and Midrash Ruth Rabba." PhD diss., Jerusalem: Hebrew University, 1971. [Hebrew]

———. "The Homilies on the Ten Commandments." In *Mehqerei Talmud*, ed. Yaacov Sussmann and David Rosenthal. Talmudic Studies, 1. Jerusalem: Magnes, 1990, 217–236. [Hebrew]

Levin, Dina. "The Tale of the Book of Genesis." In *Encyclopedia of the Jewish Story*, vol. 1, 333–349. [Hebrew]

Levinson, Joshua. "Upside-down World: The Story of the Drunk and His Sons." *Jerusalem Studies in Hebrew Literature* 14 (1993): 7–29. [Hebrew]

Liebermann, Saul. "*Al Ḥata'im veonsham*" ("On Sins and Their Punishments"). In *Jubilee Book in Honor of Louis Ginzberg*, ed. Saul Liebermann et al. New York: American Academy for Jewish Studies, 1946, 249–266. [Hebrew]

———. *Shkiin, Jewish Legends,Customs, and Literary Sources Found in Karaite and Christian Polemical Writings*. Jerusalem: Shalem Books, 1992. [Hebrew]

———. *The Tosefta*. Parts 6–7, Order *Nashim, Yebamot*. New York: JTS, 1996. [Hebrew]

———. *Tosefta ki-fshutah*. Parts 6–7. New York: JTS, 1995. [Hebrew]

Lipsker, Avidov. "Mattiah b. Heresh." In *Encyclopedia of the Jewish Story*, vol. 2, 275–290. [Hebrew]

———. "Nathan of the Radiance." In *Encyclopedia of the Jewish Story*, vol. 2, 215–232. [Hebrew]

———. "A Study of 'R. Ephraim Al-Nakawa and the Lion.'" In *The Power of a Tale: The Jubilee Book of IFA*, ed. Haya Bar-Itzhak and Idit Pintel-Ginsberg. Haifa: Haifa University Press, 2008, 112–116. [Hebrew].

Lipsker-Albeck, Avidov. "Ariel: The Recluse and the Lion." In *Encyclopedia of the Jewish Story*, vol. 3, 289–301. [Hebrew].

———. "The Exile of the Tzaddik who Subdued a Lion." In *Encyclopedia of the Jewish Story*, vol. 3, 263–277. [Hebrew]

———. "Predestined to Die on His Wedding Day." In *Encyclopedia of the Jewish Story*, vol. 3, 211–235. [Hebrew]

———. "Rabbi Shmuel he-ḥassid Rescues a Lion from a Panther." In *Encyclopedia of the Jewish Story*, vol. 3, 279–288. [Hebrew]

Liss, Hanna. *Creating Fictional Worlds: Peshat-Exegesis and Narrativity in Rashbam's Commentary on the Torah*. Leiden: Brill, 2011.

Loomis, C. Grant. "The Ring of Polycrates in the Legends of the Saints." *JAF* 54, nos. 211/212 (1941): 44–47.

Malchi, Yirmiyahu. "On Deeds Alluded to in the Talmud and Interpreted by Rashi and Other Sources." In *Studies in Jewish Narrative, Ma'aseh Sippur*, vol. 2, ed. Avidov Lipsker and Rella Kushelevsky. Ramat Gan: Bar-Ilan University Press, 2009. [Hebrew]

Mali, Yael. "The Drunkard and His Sons." *Sifrut haaggadah* (*The Literature of the Aggadah*), 2 (2004): 36–45. [Hebrew]

Map, Walter. *De nugis curialium* (*Courtiers' Trifles*). Ed. and trans. Montague Rhodes James. Oxford: Oxford University Press, 1983.

Marcus, G. Ivan. *Piety and Society: The Jewish Pietist of Medieval Germany*. Leiden: Brill, 1981.

———. "Sanctity in Ashkenaz and the Story of R. Amnon of Mainz." In Gafni and Ravitzky, *Sanctity of Life and Martyrdom*, 131–147.

———. "Why Is This Knight Different? A Jewish Self-Representation in Medieval Europe." In *Tov Elem: Memory, Community and Gender in Medieval and Early Modern Jewish Societies—Essays in Honor of Robert Bonfil*, ed. Elisheva Baumgarten, Amnon Raz-Krakotzkin, and Roni Weinstein. Jerusalem: Mandel Institute of Jewish Studies, Hebrew University of Jerusalem, Bialik Institute, 2011, 139–152.

Marzolph, Ulrich. "Crescentia's Oriental Relatives: Four Translations." *Marvels & Tales: Journal of Fairy-Tale Studies* 22, no. 2 (2008): 299–311.

———. "Kredit erschwindelt." *EM* 8 (1996): 375–380.

———. "The Tale of the Pious Man and His Chaste Wife in the Arabian Nights and the Sources of Crescentia in Oriental Narrative Tradition." *Marvels & Tales: Journal of Fairy-Tales Studies* 22, no. 2 (2008): 240–258.

Meier-Branecke, Marlis. *Die Rittertreue: Kritische Ausgabe und Untersuchungen*. Hamburg, 1969.

Merchavia, Chen. *The Church versus Talmudic and Midrashic Literature, 500–1248*. Jerusalem: Bialik Institute, 1970.

Moser-Rath, Elfriede. "Baer: Was der B. dem sich Totstellenden ins Ohr Fluestert (AT 179)." *EM* vol. 1, 1207–1209.

Naḥam, Ilan. "A Decent Woman, Favors, and Charity—Between an Explicit Dialogue and an Implicit Polemic." In *Ayin Tovah: Dialogue and Polemics in Israeli Culture—A Jubilee Volume in Honor of Tova Ilan*, ed. Ilan Naḥam. Tel Aviv: Hakibbutz Hameuchad, 1999, 180–196. [Hebrew]

Neubauer, Adolf, and Arthur Ernest Cowley. *Catalogue of the Hebrew Manuscripts in the Bodleian Library*. Oxford: Clarendon Press, 1886. Reprinted, 1994.

Newhauser, Richard. *The Early History of Greed: The Sin of Avarice in Early Medieval Thought and Literature*. Cambridge: Cambridge University Press, 2000.

———. "Towards Modus in Habendo: Transformations in the Idea of Avarice." In *Sin: Essays on the Moral Tradition in the Western Middle Ages*. Aldershot: Ashgate, 2007, 17–20.

Newth, Michael. *Heroes of the French Epic: A Selection of Chansons de Geste*, trans. Michael A. H. Newth. Woodbridge: Boydell Press, 2005.

Noam, Vered, ed. *Megillat Ta'anit: Versions, Interpretation, History*. Yad Ben-Zvi, 2003. [Hebrew]

Noy, Dov. *The Beautiful Maiden and the Three Princes: 120 Jewish-Iraqi Folktales*. Tel Aviv: Am Oved, 1965. [Hebrew]

———. "The Jewish Versions of the 'Animal Languages' Folktale (AT 670): A Typological-Structural Study." In *Scripta Hierosolymitana* 22, Studies in Aggadah and Folk-Literature, ed. Joseph Heinemann and Dov Noy. Jerusalem: Magnes, 1971, 171–208.

———. *Seventy Tales of the Jews of Tunisia*. Jerusalem: Betefuzot hagola, 1966. [Hebrew]

Pardes, Ilana. "Imagining the Promised Land: The Spies in the Land of the Giants." *Theory and Memory* 6, no. 2 (1994): 5–23.

Pastoureau, Michel. *L'ours: Histoire d'un roi déchu*. Paris: Editions du Seuil, 2007.

Perry, Micha. *Tradition and Transformation: Knowledge Transmission among European Jews in the Middle Ages*. Tel Aviv: Hakibbutz Hameuchad, 2010. [Hebrew]

Petrucci, Armando. *Writers and Readers in Medieval Italy: Studies in the History of Written Culture*. Ed. and trans. Charles M. Radding. New Haven, CT: Yale University Press, 1995.

Putter, Ad. "The Twelfth-Century Arthur." In *The Cambridge Companion to the Arthurian Legend*, ed. Elizabeth Archibald and Ad Putter. Cambridge: Cambridge University Press, 2009, 36–52.

Raveh, Inbar. *Fragments of Being—Stories of the Sages: Literary Structure and World-View*. Or Yehuda: Kinneret, Zmora-Bitan, Dvir, and Heksherim Institute, Ben-Gurion University of the Negev, 2008. [Hebrew]

Refael-Vivante, Revital. "*Ma'aseh Beḥenef* (A Tale of a Hypocrite): Origins, Influences and Paths of a Story from Spain to the Balkans." In *Mahbarot Liyehudit: Studies Presented to Professor Judith Dishon*, ed. Ephraim Hazan and Shmuel Refael. Ramat Gan: Bar-Ilan University Press, 2012. [Hebrew]

Ritter, Hellmut. *The Ocean of the Soul: Men, the World and God in the Stories of Farid al-din 'Attar*. Trans. John O'Kane. Ed. assistance Bernd Radtke. Leiden: Boston: Brill, 2003, 341–381.

Rotman, David. *Dragons, Demons and Wondrous Realms: the Marvelous in Medieval Hebrew Narrative*. Hevel Modi'in and Beer-Sheva, Kinneret Zmora-Bitan Dvir and Heksherim Institute, Ben Gurion University of the Negev, 2016. [Hebrew]

Rowland, Beryl. *Animals with Human Faces: A Guide to Animal Symbolism*. Knoxville: University of Tennessee Press, 1973.

Rubin, David Lee, and A. Lytton Sells. "Fabliau." In *The New Princeton Encyclopedia of Poetry and Poetics*, ed. Alex Preminger and T. V. F. Brogan. Princeton, NJ: Princeton University Press, 1993.

Rubin, Miri. *Gentile Tales: The Narrative Assault on Late Medieval Jews*. New Haven, CT: Yale University Press, 1999.

Rubin, Nissan. *The Joy of Life: Rites of Betrothal and Marriage in the Talmud and Midrash*. Tel Aviv: Hakibbutz Hameuchad, 2004. [Hebrew]

Rubin, Noga. "Slander Kills Three." In *Encyclopedia of the Jewish Story*, vol. 3, 237–261. [Hebrew]

Runte, Hans R., J. Keith Wikeley, and Anthony J. Farrell. *The Seven Sages of Rome and The Book of Sindbad: An Analytical Bibliography*. With the collaboration of the Society of the Seven Sages. New York: Garland, 1984.

Safrai, Zeev. "*Midrash vayissa'u*: The War of the Sons of Jacob in Southern Samaria." *Sinai* (1987): 713–727. [Hebrew]

Schier, Kurt. "Animismus." *EM* 1 (1977): 551–558.

Schimmel, S. *The Seven Deadly Sins: Jewish, Christian and Classical Reflections on Human Nature*. New York: Free Press, 1992.

Schofield, William Henry. "Chaucer's Franklin's Tale." *Modern Language Association Publications* 16, n.s. 9 (1901): 405–449.

Schwarzbaum, Ḥaim. *Biblical and Extra-Biblical Legends in Islamic Folk Literature*. Waldorff-Hessen: Verlag für Orientkunde Dr. H. Vorndran, 1982.

———. *The Chronicles of Jerahmeel*. New York: Ktav, 1971.

———. "Elijah the Prophet and R. Joshua b. Levi." *Yeda-'am* 7, no. 27 (1962): 22–31. [Hebrew]

———. "The Hero Predestined to Die on His Wedding Day." *Folklore Research Center Studies* 4 (1974): 223–252.

———. "The Jewish and Moslem Versions of Some Theodicy Legends." *Jewish Folklore Between East and West*, ed. Eli Yassif. Beer-Sheva: Ben-Gurion University of the Negev Press, 1989, 75–126.

———. *The Mishle shu'alim (Fox Fables) of Rabbi Berechiah ha-Nakdan*. Kiron: Institute for Jewish and Arab Folklore Research, 1979.

———. *Roots and Landscapes: Studies in Folklore*. Ed. Eli Yassif. Beer Sheva: Ben-Gurion University of the Negev Press, 1993. [Hebrew]

———. *Studies in Jewish and World Folklore*. Berlin: Walter de Gruyter, 1968.

Shapira, Anat. "To Make a Short Story Long: A Study of Medieval Hebrew Narrative." PhD diss., Jerusalem: Hebrew University, 2004. [Hebrew]

Shechter, S. Z. "Notes on a Hebrew Commentary to the Pentateuch in a Parma Manuscript." In *Semitic Studies in Memory of Alexander Kohut*, vol. 2. Berlin: Calvary, 1897, 485–494. Reprint, Jerusalem: Makor, 1972.

Shinan, Avigdor. "The Aggadic Literature: Written Tradition and Transmission." *Jerusalem Studies in Jewish Folklore* 1 (1981): 44–60. [Hebrew]

———. "*Kiso, Koso vekaso: Al haYay'in beSifrut Ḥazal*" ("His Pocket, Cup, and Anger: On Wine in the Rabbis' Literature"). *Migvan De'ot veHashkafot beTarbut Ḥazal* (*Various Opinions and World Views in Rabbinic Culture*) 9 (1999): 37–52. [Hebrew]

Shoshany, Ronit. "The Story of the Drunk and His Sons (*Leviticus rabbah* 12:1): Meaning, Context and Later Versions." *Sidra* 27–28 (2013): 315–338. [Hebrew]

———. "A Study of Two Tales in *Midrash Ruth Zuta* and Their Adaptation in *Ḥibbur Yafeh me-ha-Yeshu'a*." *JSIJ* 7 (2008): 81–103. [Hebrew]

Spanier, Yossi. "The Distribution of the Carob Tree in Ancient Times." *Al Atar* 3 (1997): 175–176. [Hebrew]

Spargo, John Webster. *Virgil the Necromancer*. Cambridge, MA: Harvard University Press, 1934.

Sperber, Daniel. *Magic and Folklore in Rabbinic Literature*. Ramat Gan: Bar-Ilan University Press, 1994. [Hebrew]

Spiegel, Boaz. "Why Did Joseph-Who-Honors-the-Sabbath Buy the Fish?" *Sinai* 133 (2004): 44–69. [Hebrew]

Stein, Hans Joachim. "Schuss auf den Toten Konig." *EM* 12 (2006): 255–259.

Stemberger, Günter. *Introduction to the Talmud and Midrash*. Edinburgh: T&T Clark, 1996.

Ta-Shma, Israel. "*Sifriyatam shel ḥakhmei Ashkenaz ve-Ẓorfat bnei hame'ot ha'aḥat esre–shtemesre*" ("The Library of the Sages of Ashkenaz and Ẓorfat [France] of the 11th and 12th Centuries"). In *Studies in Medieval Rabbinic Literature*, vol. 1: *Germany*, ed. J. Ḥovav. Jerusalem: Bialik Institute, 2004, 34–38. [Hebrew]

———. "Suicide and Murder for the Sanctity of God: The Role of Aggadah in Traditions of Halakhic Ruling in Ashkenaz." In *Studies in Medieval Rabbinic Literature*, vol. 1: *Germany*, ed. J. Ḥovav. Jerusalem: Bialik Institute, 2004, 390–394. [Hebrew]

Tadjar, Michal. " 'And One of Them Was Extremely Hungry': Court, Poverty and the Involvement of Lawyers for the Community." *Ma'asei Mishpat* 2 (2009): 151–166. http://www.law.tau.ac.il/Heb/_Uploads/dbsAttachedFiles/tadjer-heb.pdf (last accessed April 11, 2014). [Hebrew]

Taylor, Jane H. M. "The Thirteenth-Century Arthur." In *The Cambridge Companion to the Arthurian Legend*, ed. Elizabeth Archibald and Ad Putter. Cambridge: Cambridge University Press, 2009.

Thompson, Stith. *The Folktale*. New York: Holt, Rinehart and Winston, 1946.

———. *Motif Index of Folk-Literature*. 6 vols. Bloomington: Indiana University Press, 1955–1958.

Tite, Colin G. C. "Lost or Stolen or Strayed: A Survey of Manuscripts Formerly in the Cotton Library." http://www.bl.uk/eblj/1992articles/pdf/article8.pdf (last accessed August 29, 2016).

Tohar, Vered. *Abraham in the Furnace of Fire: A Rebel in a Pagan World*. Ramat Gan: Bar Ilan University Press, 2010. [Hebrew]

———. "The Story of Johanan and the Scorpion: A Thirteenth-Century Hebrew Romance." *Fabula* 50 (2009): 1–12.

Tsfatman, Sara. *The Jewish Tale in the Middle Ages: Between Ashkenaz and Sefarad*. Jerusalem: Magnes, 1992. [Hebrew]

———. "The Mayse-Bukh: An Old Yiddish Literary Genre." *Hasifrut (Literature)*, 28 (1979): 126–152. [Hebrew]

Tubach, Frederic. *Index Exemplorum: A Handbook of Medieval Religious Tales* (FFC 204). Helsinki: Suomalainen Tiedeakatemia/Academia Scientiarum Fennica, 1969.

Uther, Hans-Jörg. "Crescentia." *EM* 3. Berlin: De Gruyter, 2011, 167–171.

———. *The Types of International Folktales: A Classification and Bibliography* (FFC 284–286). Vols. 1–3. Helsinki: Suomalainen Tiedeakatemia/Academia Scientiarum Fennica, 2004.

Vajda, G. "Idris." In *The Encyclopaedia of Islam*. New ed., vol. 3. Leiden: Brill 1971, 1030–1031.

Valler, Shulamit. *Women and Womanhood in the Stories of the Babylonian Talmud*. Tel Aviv: Hakibbutz Hameuchad, 1993. [Hebrew]

Von Sydow, C. W. "Geography and Folk-Tale Oicotypes." In *Selected Papers on Folklore*, ed. Laurits Bodker. Copenhagen: Rosenkilde and Bagger, 1948, 44–59.

Yassif, Eli. "From Jewish Oicotype to Israeli Oicotype: The Tale of 'The Man Who Never Swore an Oath.'" *Fabula* 27 (1986): 3–4, 216–236.

———. *The Hebrew Folktale: History, Genre, Meaning*. Trans. Jacqueline S. Teitelbaum. Bloomington: Indiana University Press, 1999.

———. *The Hebrew Folktale: History, Genre, Meaning*. Jerusalem: Bialik Institute, 1994. [Hebrew]

———. "Hebrew Prose in the East—Its Formation in the Middle Ages and Transition to Modern Times." *Pe'amim* 26 (1986): 53–70. [Hebrew]

———. "The Hebrew Traditions about Alexander the Great: Narrative Models and Their Meaning in the Middle Ages." *Tarbiẓ* 75, nos. 3–4 (April–September 2006): 359–407. [Hebrew]

———. "Intertextuality in Folk-Literature: Pagan Motifs in Jewish Folktales and Their Theological Significance." *Jerusalem Studies in Jewish Folklore* 19–20 (1997–1998): 309–287. [Hebrew]

———. *Kemargalit bemishbeẓet: The Hebrew Collection of Tales in the Middle Ages*. Tel Aviv: Hakibbutz Hameuchad, 2004. [Hebrew]

———. "'Leisure' and 'Generosity': Theory and Practice in the Creation of Hebrew Narratives in the Late Middle Ages." *Kiryat Sefer* 62, nos. 3–4 (1988–1989): 887–905. [Hebrew]

———. "Moses Gaster—Pioneer in Folklore and Jewish Studies." *Pe'amim* 100 (2004): 113–123. [Hebrew]

———. "*Sepher ha-Ma'asim*: Character, Origins and Influence of a Collection of Folktales from the Time of the Tosaphists." In *Kemargalit bemishbeẓet*, 135–136. First published in *Tarbiẓ* 53, no. 3 (April–June 1984): 409–429. [Hebrew]

———. "The Story of Joab's Deeds of Valour: The Literary Aspects of the Medieval Heroic Tale." *Yeda-'am* 19, nos. 45–46 (1979): 17–27. [Hebrew]

———. "Theory and Practice in the Creation of the Hebrew Narratives in the Middle Ages." *Kiryat Sefer* 62, nos. 3–4 (1988–1989): 887–905. [Hebrew]

———. "'Virgil in the Basket': Memory and Authority in the Hebrew Narratives of the Middle Ages." In *Studies in Hebrew Literature of the Middle Ages and Renaissance in honor of Professor Yona David*, ed. Tova Rosen and Avner Holtzman. Te'uda series 19 (2002): 285–308. [Hebrew]

Yeda-'am 7. Special issue. "Elijah in Jewish Tradition" (1961). [Hebrew]

Young, R. D. "The Woman with the Soul of Abraham: Traditions about the Mother of the Maccabean Marytrs." In *"Women Like This": New Perspectives on Jewish Women in the Graeco Roman World,* ed. A. J. Levine. Society for Biblical Literature Early Judaism and Its Literature, 1. Atlanta: Scholars Press, 1991, 67–81.

Zilkah, Yaffa. *In the Eyes of the Aggadah of the Yerushalmi.* Jerusalem: Jewish Agency for Israel–Eliner Library and Beit Morasha of Jerusalem, 2009. [Hebrew]

Ziolkowski, Jan. M. *Solomon and Marcolf.* Harvard Studies in Medieval Latin, vol. 1. Cambridge, MA: Harvard University Department of the Classics, Harvard University Press, 2008.

———. "The Wonder of the Turnip Tale." In *Fairy Tales from before Fairy Tales*: *The Medieval Latin Past of Wonderful Lies*. Ann Arbor: University of Michigan Press, 2006, 190–199.

Zohar, Naomi. "The Story of the Weasel and the Well in the Literature of the Enlightenment." *Criticism and Interpretation* 20 (1994): 121–155. [Hebrew]

Index of Tales

Index

www.ingramcontent.com/pod-product-compliance
Lightning Source LLC
LaVergne TN
LVHW010351080826
844660LV00004B/249

* 9 7 8 0 8 1 4 3 4 2 7 1 8 *